USBORNE WORLD OF KNOWLEDGE ENCYCLOPEDIA

This book contains material published separately as The Usborne Encyclopedia of Science, The Usborne Encyclopedia of The Living World, The Usborne Encyclopedia of Geography.

USBORNE WORLD OF KNOWLEDGE ENCYCLOPEDIA

CONTENTS

SCIENCE

Annabel Craig and Cliff Rosney

Designed by
Steve Page and Russell Punter

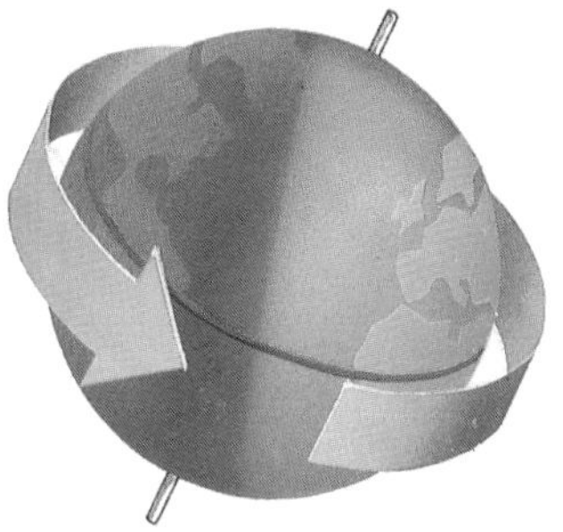

Illustrated by
Chris Lyon, John Shackell
and Ian Jackson

Additional illustrations by
Peter Bull, Russell Punter, Robert Walster,
Steve Page, Martin Newton and Guy Smith.

Contents

The *Science* section

Scientists study the world around us. They look for explanations for everyday things, such as where lightning comes from and why rivers flow downhill. They make new discoveries and inventions, such as electricity, cars and computers, that change the way people live. This part of the book answers questions about the world around you and explains the science in everyday life. It is divided into eight sections, which are shown by shaded bands.

Counting and measuring	**Heat and energy**	**Forces and machines**	**Light and colour**
Sound and hearing	**Atoms and molecules**	**Electricity and technology**	**Lists and tables**

On some pages there are quizzes. You can look up the answers on page 128.

You can tell which section you are reading by looking at the coloured band along the top of the page.

There are simple experiments that can be done using everyday things.

Some things in this part of the book have a red line around them. This is to warn you that they can be dangerous.

Words are written in **bold type** where they are first explained. There is also a list of words with their explanations in the glossary on pages 124-127. There is an index on pages 380-391 to help you find things in this book.

Some words have an asterisk after them, like this: gravity*. This means that you will find them in a footnote at the bottom of the page. The footnote tells you where those words are explained in the book.

**Footnotes are written at the bottom of the page.*

Counting and numbers

People use numbers and counting so often in everyday life that it is difficult to imagine that they both had to be invented.

People had a rough idea of quantity before they invented numbers. They could tell that there were more animals in one herd than in another, but they could not count how many more. They could think in numbers of one, two, and perhaps three. They probably thought of more than three as just 'many'.

Keeping a tally

The first way people found to record an amount was to make a mark, like a scratch on a stick, for each item they were counting.

This is called keeping a **tally**. The Incas of Peru kept tallies of their animals and harvests by tying knots in cords. They called these cords **quipus**.

You probably also use tally marks sometimes. For instance, you may keep the score in a game by making a mark for each point a player makes.

Inventing numbers

After tally marks, people invented symbols, called **numerals**, to stand for various amounts. Different civilizations invented their own numerals.

Greek	A	B	Γ	Δ	E	F	Z	H	Θ	I
Roman	I	II	III	IV	V	VI	VII	VIII	IX	X
Hindu	१	२	३	४	५	६	७	८	९	१०
Medieval Arabic	/	2	3	ℓ	ч	6	∧	8	9	10
Arabic numerals *	1	2	3	4	5	6	7	8	9	10
Binary *	1	10	11	100	101	110	111	1000	1001	1010

 **Arabic numerals, 5; Binary, 5.*

Roman numbers

Ancient Roman numerals are a mixture of tally marks and letters of the alphabet.

If the numeral on the right is smaller than, or equal to, the left one, you add them up.

If the numeral on the left is smaller, you subtract it from the one on the right.

Roman numerals were used in Europe for more than 1,500 years. Where can you see them today? (Answer on page 128.)

DID YOU KNOW?

The earliest known written numbers are about 5,000 years old and were found in the ancient city of Sumer (Iraq). They were scratched on wet clay tablets and then dried.

Changing numbers

The symbols we use to write numbers were invented about 1,500 years ago in India by Hindu mathematicians.

Arabs learnt the numerals from them about 1,200 years ago.

Arab traders, 900 years ago, brought them to Europe. So they are often called **Arabic numerals**.

Arabic numbers are much shorter and simpler to write than Roman ones, because the value of each numeral changes, depending on its position. In Roman numerals, 2987 would be written as MMCMLXXXVII.

MM	CM	LXXX	VII
2	9	8	7

Arabic numerals have a symbol for zero. This makes it possible to show the difference between 2, 20, 200.

Different bases

We count in batches of 10, probably because we have ten fingers. This is called **base 10**, or the **decimal** system.

The Sumerians, 5,000 years ago, used base 60. It is the lowest number that can be divided equally by 2,3,4,5 and 6, so it is good for sharing things out.

Base 60 is still used today for measuring time. A minute has 60 seconds, and an hour has 60 minutes.

The binary system

Computers* and calculators use base 2, called the **binary system**, because they only use two symbols, 1 and 0.

**Computers, 108.*

Measuring things

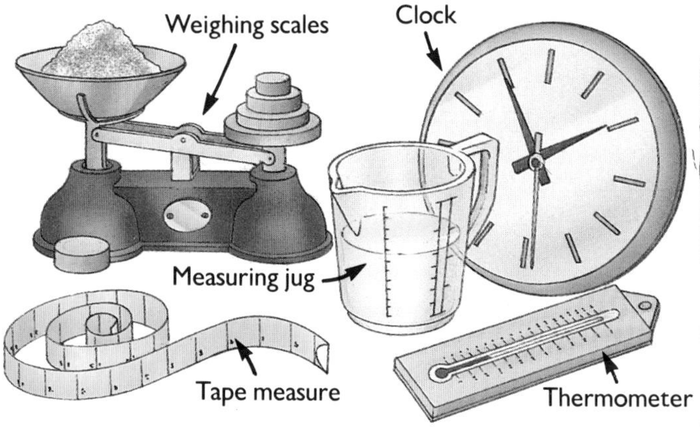
Weighing scales
Clock
Measuring jug
Tape measure
Thermometer

What time is it? How tall are you? How much do you weigh? What temperature is it outside? How far away are your nearest shops? You measure things every day. Measuring instruments help you measure things precisely.

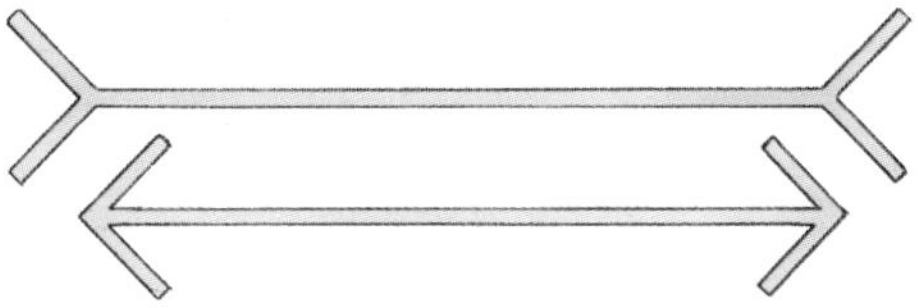

You cannot always believe what you think you see. Look at the two blue lines above: the top one looks longer than the bottom one. But if you measure them with a ruler, you will find that they are both the same length.

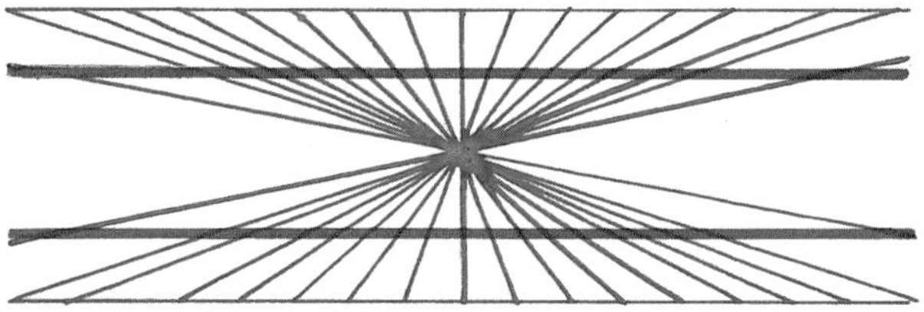

Move the book around and look at the two red lines above from different angles. The lines look as though they bend a bit in the middle. But they are, in fact, straight and parallel.

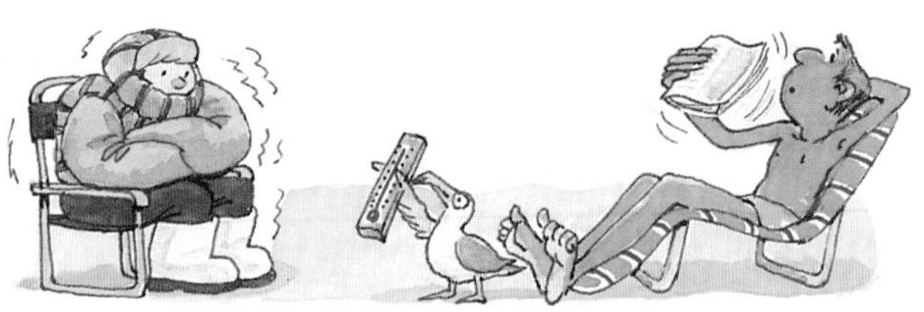

You cannot always rely on what you feel either. You may feel that it is cold outside, but the same air may feel warm to someone else. A thermometer measures the temperature exactly.

Body measurements

When you measure something, you are really comparing it to a fixed quantity, like a metre. This is called a **unit of measurement**. The first units of measurement were based on the body. The Ancient Egyptians used units of measurement called **cubits**, **palms** and **digits**.

Ancient Egyptian measurements

One digit
One cubit
= seven palms
One palm
One cubit
= elbow to
tip of
middle
finger.
One palm
= four digits

Roman measurements

The Romans used the length of a foot to measure distance. To measure smaller lengths, they divided one **foot** into 12 thumb widths. They called each thumb width an **uncia**.

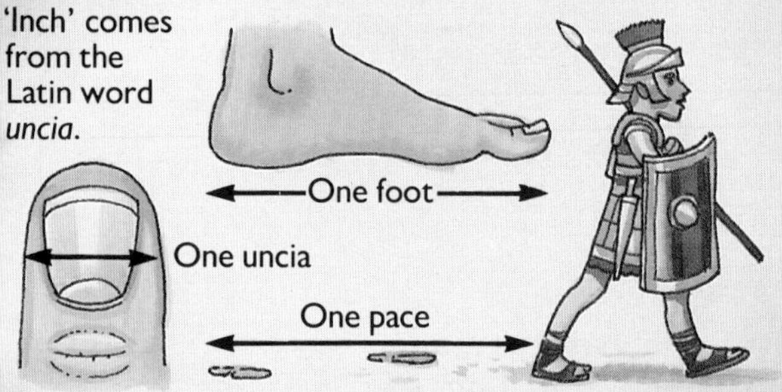
'Inch' comes
from the
Latin word
uncia.
One foot
One uncia
One pace

They measured longer distances in **paces**, counting each pace as two steps. They called 1,000 paces a **mile**. The word 'mile' comes from a Latin word, *mille*, meaning one thousand.

Yards

One yard

Cloth traders invented a unit of measurement called the **yard**. Every yard was a length of fabric stretched between chin and fingertips.

Imperial units

Any unit of measurement can be used to measure things, as long as other people can use the same unit. The problem with measurements based on the body is that they vary, depending on people's sizes. About 900 years ago, King Henry I of England made a law to make all yards the same length, this was the length between *his* chin and fingertips. Later, more laws fixed other measurements. They became known as **Imperial units** and are still used in some countries today.

How heavy you are is measured in stones, pounds and ounces.

Distance is measured in miles, yards, feet and inches.

Volume is measured in gallons, pints and fluid ounces.

The metric system

The first unit of measurement that was not based on the body was a unit of length called the **metre**. The **metric system** of measurement is based on the metre.

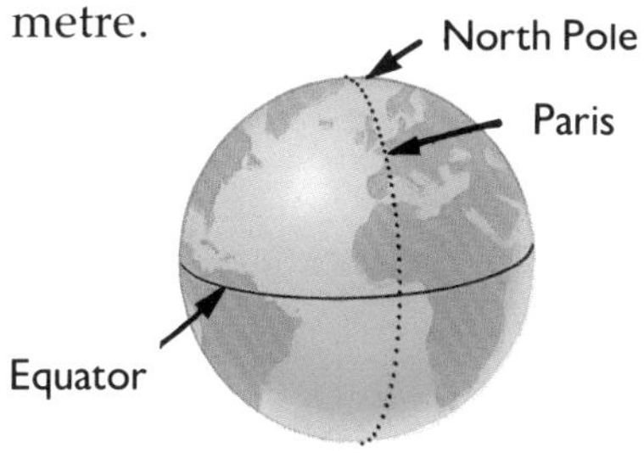

The metre was invented about 200 years ago in France. It was calculated by dividing the distance between the North Pole and the Equator, through Paris, by 10 million.

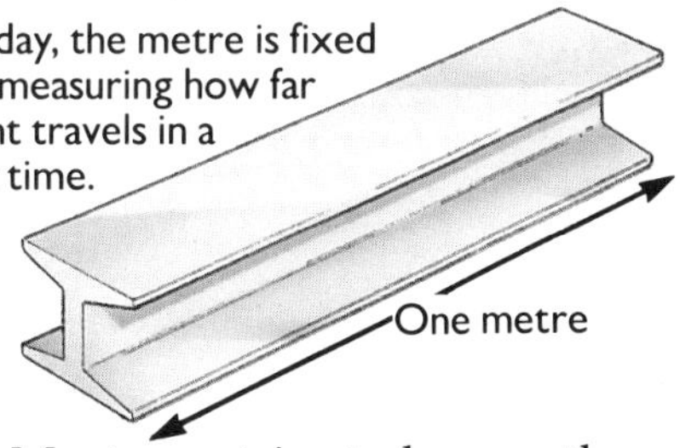

Today, the metre is fixed by measuring how far light travels in a set time.

A platinum bar was made exactly one metre long. Copies were made of it so that a record of a metre could be kept in different places.

Most countries today use the metric system. Buying and selling between countries is much easier if everyone uses the same system.

How tall are you?

Lie on the floor and get a few people of different sizes to measure your height. First ask them to use Egyptian cubits, palms and digits, and then Roman feet and *uncia*. How different are their answers and why? (Answer on page 128.)

DID YOU KNOW?

The amount of space an object fills is called its **volume***. The amount of material in that space is called its **mass***. In the metric system, you measure volume in **cubic metres (m^3)** or in **litres (l)**.

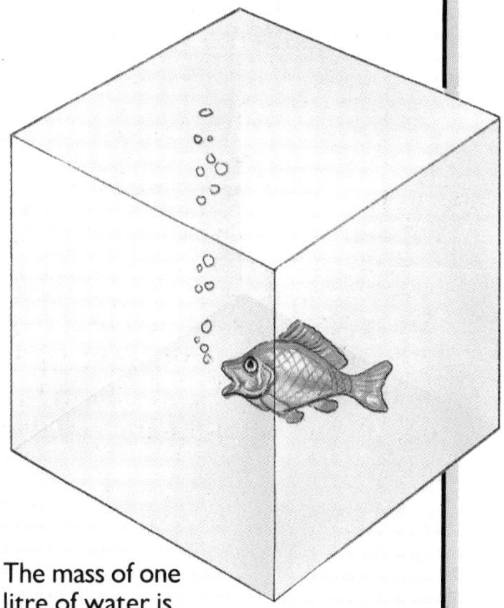

The mass of one litre of water is one kilogram.

Mass is measured in **grams (g)** and **kilograms (kg)**. Mass is different from weight. You can read more about it on page 33.

**Mass, 33; Volume, 38.*

Time

Thousands of years ago, people did not need to measure time in any detail. They only needed to count days and nights and observe the seasons to know when to plant their crops.

Today, time is measured very precisely in units of hours, minutes and seconds. You can see this on train and bus timetables. They show the departure and arrival times to the minute.

The Egyptian year

As long as 5,000 years ago, the Ancient Egyptians divided their calendar into 365 days. They noticed that every 365 days a star called Sirius appeared in the sky just before sunrise.

They knew that, at about the same time the star appeared, the River Nile would flood. After the floods, the farmers were able to plough their fields and plant their crops.

DID YOU KNOW?

The Romans called the hours before noon *ante meridiem*, and the hours after noon, *post meridiem*. Today, these are shortened to *a.m.* and *p.m.* and are still used to mean morning and afternoon.

Measuring time

1. Egyptian shadow clocks are the earliest known clocks and were used 4,000 years ago. The time was read from the shadow on the scale.

2. Water clocks were used by the Egyptians on cloudy days or at night. As water trickled out of a stone pot, the time was shown by the water level.

3. Candle clocks were invented about 1,000 years ago. As the candle burned down, it showed how many hours had passed.

4. Pendulum clocks were the first clocks able to measure seconds. Galileo invented the pendulum, but the first pendulum clock was made by Christiaan Huygens in 1667.

5. Quartz crystal clocks were first made in 1929. The first quartz crystal wristwatches were made in 1969. They keep time very accurately.

6. Atomic clocks are used by scientists to measure time very precisely. They are accurate to about one second every 300,000 years. The first was built in 1948.

Why are there days and nights?

The Earth spins on an imaginary line called the **axis**. The side facing the sun has daylight, while the other side is dark. It takes the Earth 24 hours to complete each spin.

Leap years

The Earth takes 365¼ days to orbit the Sun, but a calendar year has only 365 days. So every four years, an extra day is added to February. These years have 366 days and are called **leap years**.

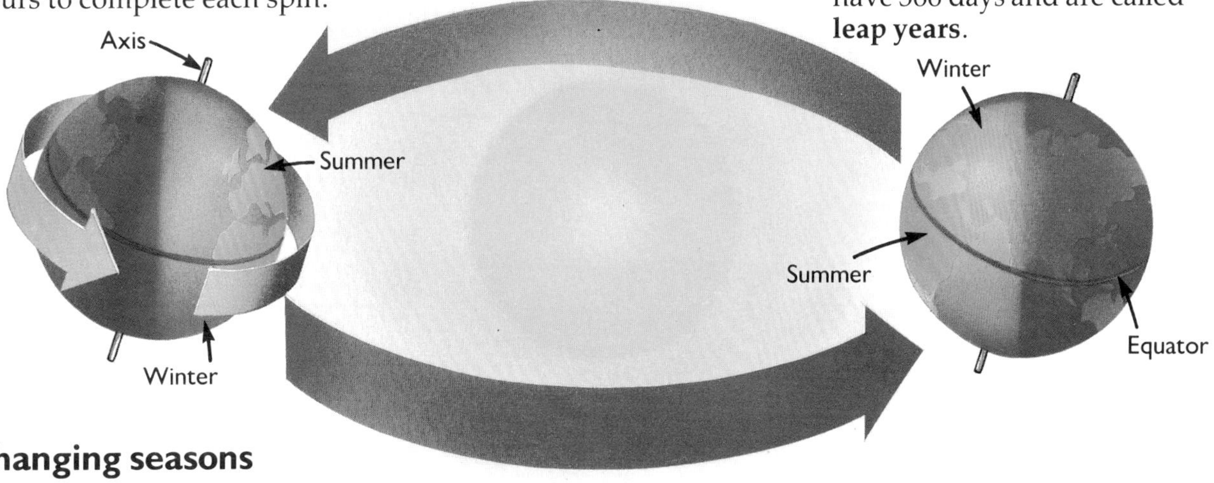

Changing seasons

The Earth leans to one side, so one half is tilted nearer to the Sun. That half has summer while the other half has winter.

As the Earth orbits the Sun, a different part of the Earth is gradually tilted nearer the Sun. This makes the seasons change.

Places on the Equator do not have summers or winters because they always stay the same distance from the Sun.

Time zones

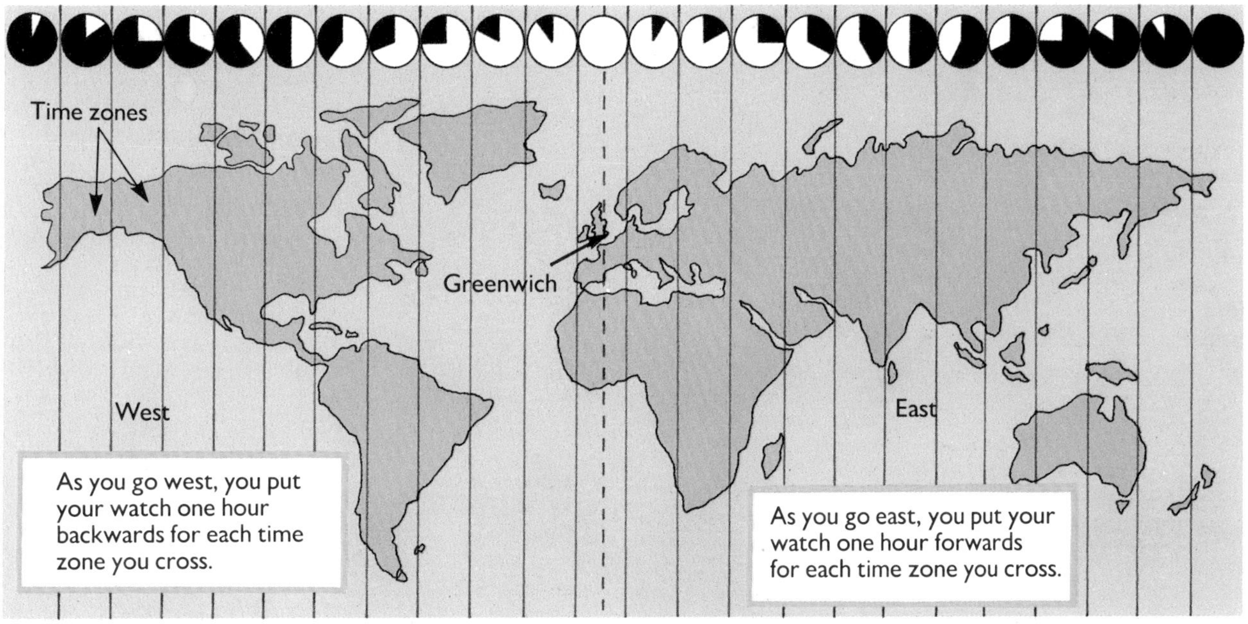
Time zones
Greenwich
West
East
As you go west, you put your watch one hour backwards for each time zone you cross.
As you go east, you put your watch one hour forwards for each time zone you cross.

The world is divided into 24 **time zones**. The time is counted from Greenwich, London. The time zone east of Greenwich is an hour ahead, the one to the west is an hour behind Greenwich.

What is energy?

All around you things are happening. The wind may be blowing, cars may be driving by, and people talking and moving about. As you read this, your eyes are moving and blood is flowing around your body.

In this picture, you can see many different types of energy making lots of different things happen. All these things are happening because of **energy**. Energy is what makes things happen all over the Earth and the Universe.

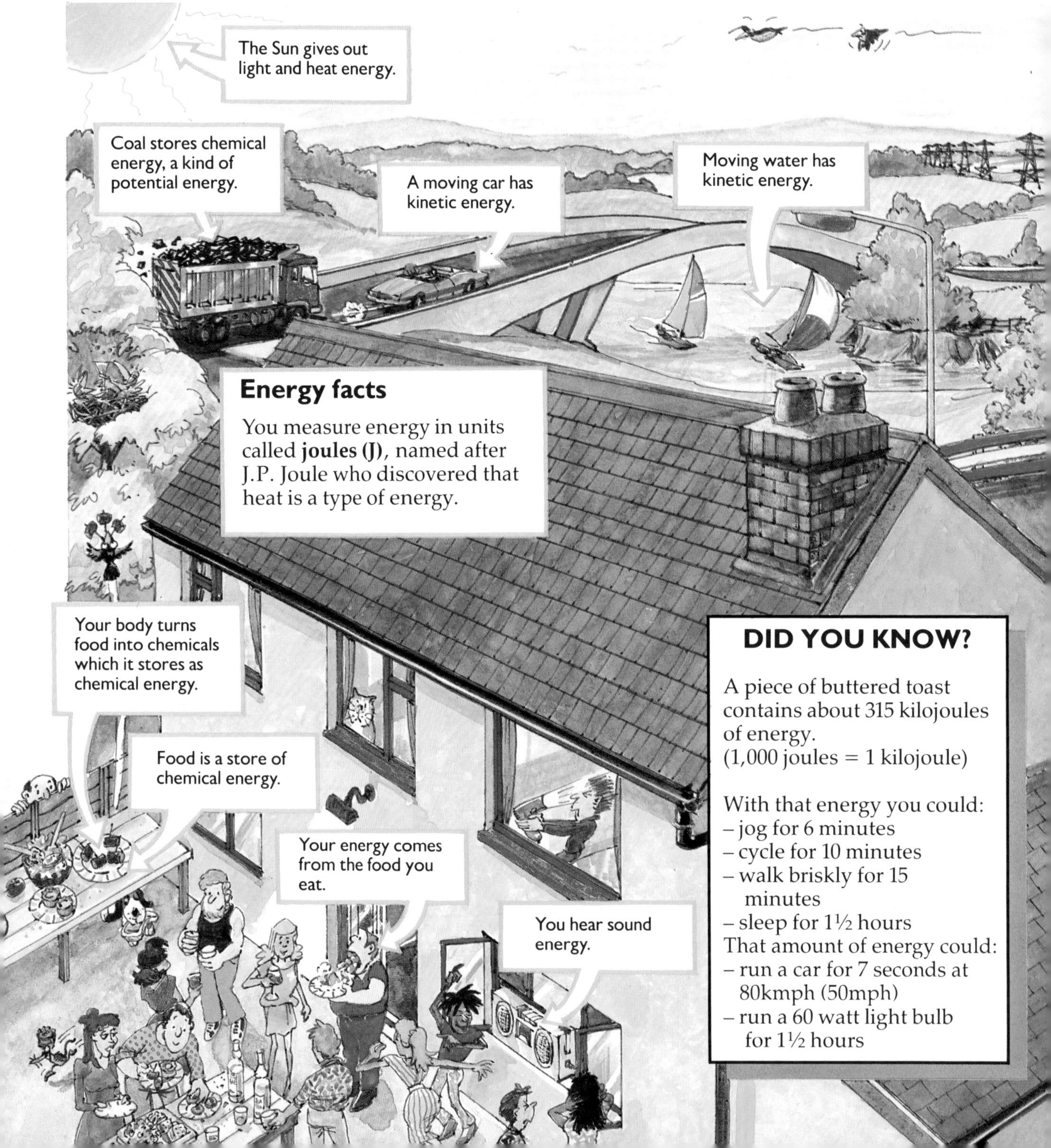

The Sun gives out light and heat energy.
Coal stores chemical energy, a kind of potential energy.
A moving car has kinetic energy.
Moving water has kinetic energy.
Your body turns food into chemicals which it stores as chemical energy.
Food is a store of chemical energy.
Your energy comes from the food you eat.
You hear sound energy.

Energy facts

You measure energy in units called **joules (J)**, named after J.P. Joule who discovered that heat is a type of energy.

DID YOU KNOW?

A piece of buttered toast contains about 315 kilojoules of energy.
(1,000 joules = 1 kilojoule)

With that energy you could:
- jog for 6 minutes
- cycle for 10 minutes
- walk briskly for 15 minutes
- sleep for 1½ hours

That amount of energy could:
- run a car for 7 seconds at 80kmph (50mph)
- run a 60 watt light bulb for 1½ hours

Energy is needed to make cars go, to heat and light your home and to keep your body working. The different types of energy can be divided into two groups, depending on whether the energy is moving or stored.

Energy that is moving is also called **kinetic energy**. Energy that is stored is also called **potential energy**. You can find out more about different types of energy and how they are used in the next few pages.

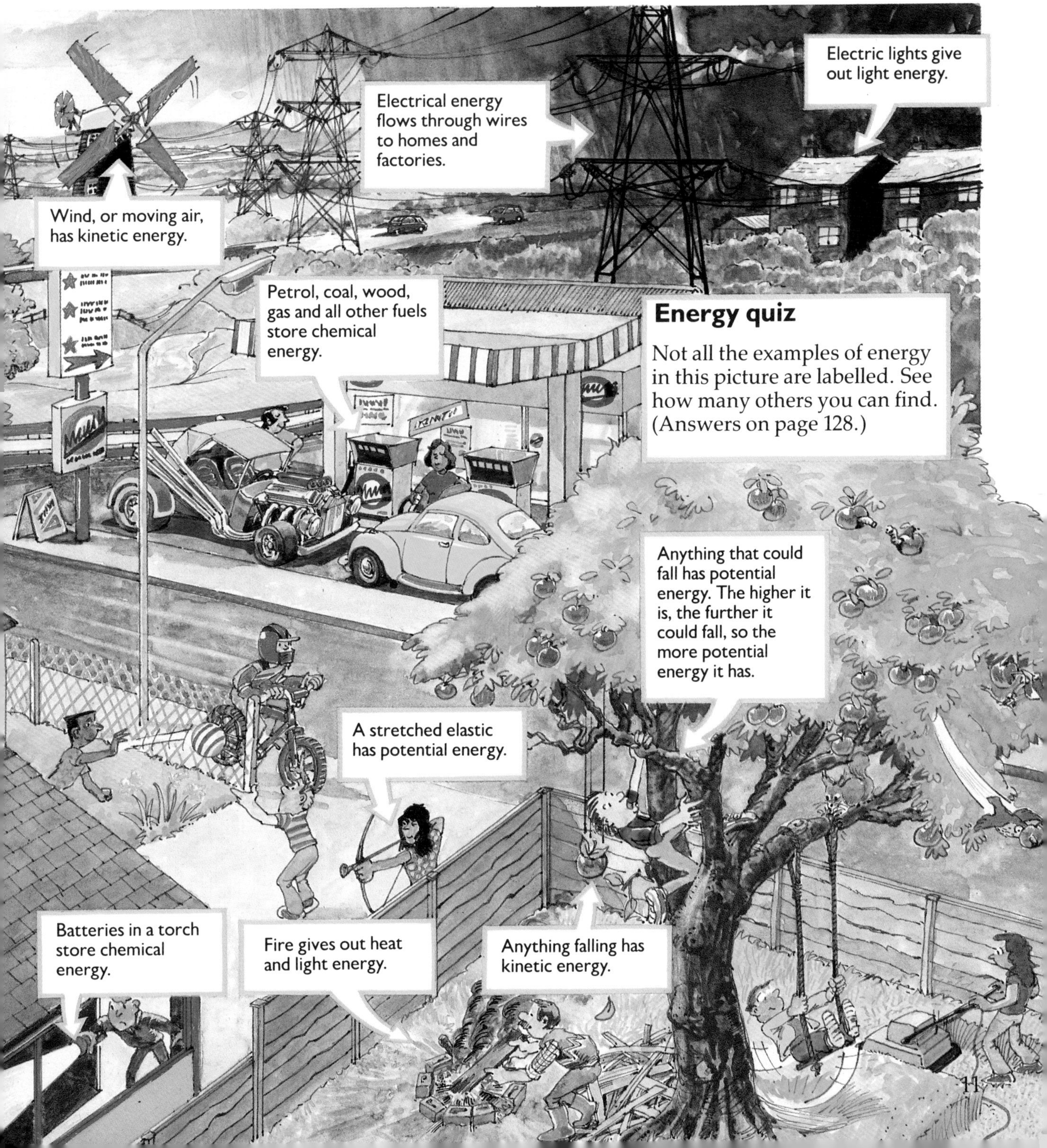

Wind, or moving air, has kinetic energy.
Electrical energy flows through wires to homes and factories.
Electric lights give out light energy.
Petrol, coal, wood, gas and all other fuels store chemical energy.
Anything that could fall has potential energy. The higher it is, the further it could fall, so the more potential energy it has.
A stretched elastic has potential energy.
Batteries in a torch store chemical energy.
Fire gives out heat and light energy.
Anything falling has kinetic energy.

Energy quiz

Not all the examples of energy in this picture are labelled. See how many others you can find. (Answers on page 128.)

Energy changes

All the different sorts of energy around you can be changed into other sorts of energy.

In fact, energy cannot be made or destroyed, it can only be changed into another sort of energy.

An electric clock works because chemical energy inside its batteries* is changed to electrical energy*. When the alarm rings, electrical energy is changed to sound energy*.

If you eat too much, your body stores the extra food as fat.

Your energy comes from the food you eat. Your body changes chemical energy inside food into a different sort of chemical energy, and stores it.

The sound of your voice is changed into electrical energy . . .
. . . and the electrical energy is changed back to sound energy.

Telephones change sound energy into electrical energy, and electrical energy back into sound energy.

When you move, your body changes chemical energy from the food you eat into moving, or **kinetic**, energy*.

Cars need chemical energy stored in fuel to move. The engine* changes chemical energy into kinetic energy.

Power stations change the chemical energy of fuel or the kinetic energy of moving water into electrical energy.

Nuclear energy* can be changed into electrical energy. Solar panels change the Sun's heat energy into electrical energy.

Electrical energy is changed into light energy* by light bulbs, and into heat energy by heaters.

**Batteries, 95; Electricity, 92; Engines, 45; Kinetic energy, 11; Light energy, 50; Nuclear energy, 77; Sound energy, 64.*

Electric ovens, toasters and irons change electrical energy into heat energy*. An electric whisk changes electrical energy into kinetic energy. Televisions* change electrical energy into light and sound energy.

When a firework explodes, its chemical energy changes into light energy, sound energy and heat energy.

The potential, or stored, energy* of anything that could fall changes into kinetic energy as it begins to fall.

Find the energy changes

What sorts of energy are being changed into other sorts of energy in this picture? (Answers on page 128.)

DID YOU KNOW?

When you run, only about 25% of the chemical energy in your muscles changes into kinetic energy. The rest changes into heat energy.

People need to change energy from one sort to another to do many things. But not all of the energy changes into the sort of energy they want. How much energy you get out compared to how much you put in is called **efficiency**. In most cars only about a quarter, or 25%, of the chemical energy of petrol changes into kinetic energy. The rest is lost as heat energy and sound energy. Cars are only about 25% efficient.

**Heat energy, 14; Potential energy, 11; Television, 107.*

Heat and temperature

Heat is a form of energy. You use it for lots of everyday things like keeping warm, heating water and cooking food.

Heat moves

Heat energy does not stay still, it moves. It spreads out from hotter things to cooler things until both are the same temperature.

Leave a hot and cold drink out for a few hours. The hot drink cools down and the cold drink warms up until both reach room temperature.

Heat energy moves in three ways, by **conduction** (see below), by **convection*** and by **radiation***.

Conduction

Stir a hot drink with a metal spoon. The handle gets hot because heat travels through it. This is called **conduction**. Heat moves through solids by conduction. Through some solids, like metals, it moves very quickly. These are called good **conductors**. Other solids, like plastic, are poor conductors. These are called **insulators**.

Saucepans are made of metal so that they conduct heat to the food to cook it.

Pan handles are made of plastic or wood because they are insulators.

Why does metal feel cold?

When you touch metal, it feels cold. Because metal is a good conductor, the heat from your hand flows out into it. It is not the metal that is cold, it is your hand losing heat.

Air can keep you warm

Your clothes keep you warm because they stop you losing your body heat. This is because they trap air. Your body heat cannot get through the trapped air, because air is an insulator.

Snow is a good insulator, because it traps lots of air.
People lost in blizzards dig holes in the snow for warmth.
Walls have a gap filled with air for insulation.
Feather-filled jackets keep you warm because they trap a lot of air.
Thick winter clothes trap lots of air.
Birds fluff up their feathers in winter to trap more air.
Wool feels warm because it traps lots of air in its fibres.

Convection, 16; Radiation, 18.

About one-third of the heat from a house is lost through the roof, unless the roof is insulated.
The air between double-glazing is for insulation.
Mammals that live in cold places have thick fur to trap more air for warmth.

DID YOU KNOW?

You sometimes have goose-pimples when you are cold. Next time, look at your skin. You can see that the goose-pimples make each hair stand on end. This traps air to keep in your body heat.

Air can keep you cool

As well as keeping you warm, air can keep you cool. In hot countries, people wear loose clothes that let air circulate. This stops heat from the Sun being conducted to their bodies.

Heat and temperature

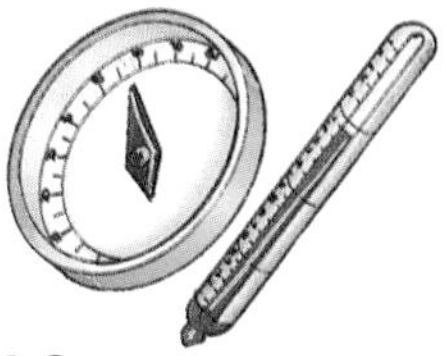

To measure how hot or cold something is, its **temperature**, you use a **thermometer**.

How do thermometers work?

This thermometer is filled with mercury. The more it is warmed, the more the mercury rises up the tube. The height of the mercury shows the temperature. Temperatures below freezing are shown with a minus sign.

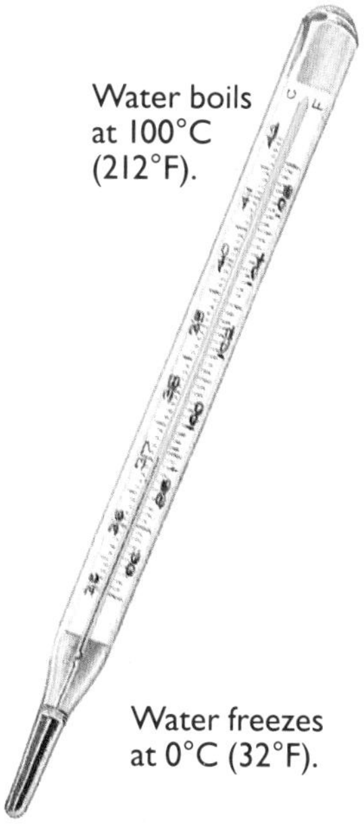
Water boils at 100°C (212°F).
Water freezes at 0°C (32°F).

Temperature facts

Surface of the Sun.	5500°C 9900°F
Steel melts.	1427°C 2600°F
Gas cooker flame.	600°C 1100°F
Surface of hottest planet, Venus.	470°C 880°F
Water boils.	100°C 212°F
Earth's hottest place, Libya.	58°C 136°F
Normal human body temperature.	37°C 98.6°F
Comfortable room temperature.	18°C 64°F
Water freezes.	0°C 32°F
Earth's coldest place, Antarctica.	-88°C -126°F
Surface of coldest planet, Pluto.	-230°C -382°F
The coldest temperature.	-273°C -459°F

Temperature and heat energy are not the same. The coffee and the bath-water in this picture have the same temperature, but the water has more heat energy because there is more of it.

You measure temperature in units called **degrees Celsius (°C)** or **degrees Fahrenheit (°F)**, and heat energy in units called **Joules (J)**.

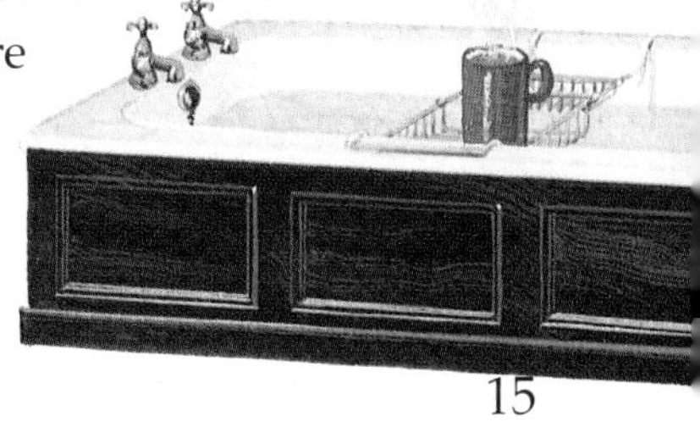

Heating air and water

Gases, like air, and liquids, like water, are usually bad conductors* of heat. This means that if they are trapped so that they cannot move, heat does not pass through them easily. But if a gas or liquid is free to move, it can carry heat energy with it. A heater is able to heat a whole room because the air in the room is free to move. When you turn a heater on, moving air carries heat energy from the heater to all parts of the room.

How does heat move around this room?

The heater warms up the air just around it. This heated air rises, because hot air is lighter than cold air.

As the warm air rises, cold air sinks down to take its place. This cold air is then warmed by the heater, and in turn rises.

Soon, air is moving around the room, carrying heat energy with it, until the temperature of the whole room is higher.

This moving air is called a **convection current**. The air in the room has been heated by **convection**.

How is water heated up?

Heat energy also moves through liquids by convection. When a pan of water is heated, the pan heats up first. This happens by conduction*. The hot pan then heats the water next to it.

The heated water rises, and cold water takes its place. This is because warm water is lighter than cold water. The water starts to move, setting up a convection current. All the water heats up eventually.

Watch heat move

Hold a piece of tissue paper over a heater and watch the convection current make it flutter.

Look at something that is hot. The air above it shimmers. This is the hot, lighter air rising through the colder air.

On very hot days, road surfaces sometimes become so hot that you can see the air shimmering above them.

 Conduction, 14; Conductors, 14.

Why does smoke rise?

Smoke rises from a bonfire by convection. You can often see pieces of ash float up with the smoke.

Volcanic ash

When volcanoes erupt, they set up very strong convection currents which send ash and dust high up in the sky.

In 1980, Mount St Helen's, USA, erupted. It blew ash 9km ($5^1/_2$ miles) above the Earth, blocking out heat and light from the Sun.

Wind* is simply moving air. It is made by convection currents over the surface of the Earth. Land heats up more quickly than sea. On a hot, sunny day, warm air above the land rises and cold air blows in from the sea, taking its place. Land also cools down faster than sea, so at night the opposite happens. Warm air rises above the sea, and cold air blows out from the land.

Keeping up with convection

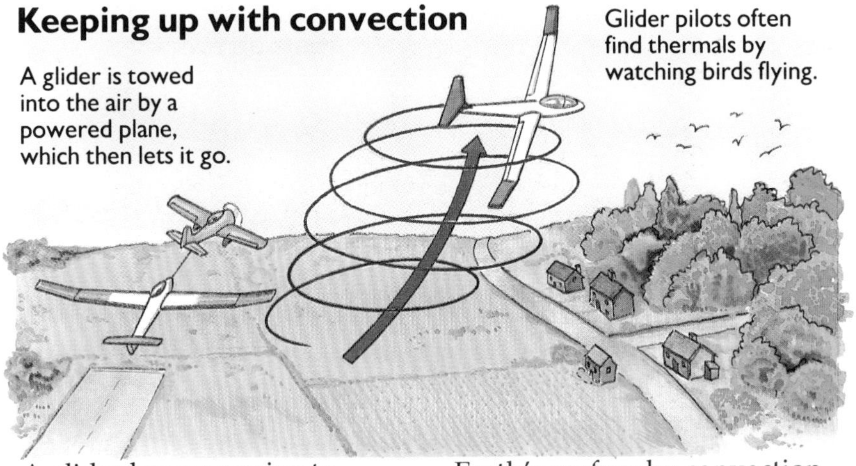
A glider is towed into the air by a powered plane, which then lets it go.
Glider pilots often find thermals by watching birds flying.

A glider has no engine to power it, but it can fly for long distances and even climb higher. This is because of the warm air that rises from the Earth's surface by convection. These convection currents are called **thermals**. A glider is able to fly for as long as the pilot can find thermals.

DID YOU KNOW?

Swifts fly non-stop for their first two or three years, until they are old enough to breed. They eat and drink while flying. At night, they rest on thermals high in the sky. (Not, of course, as shown in the picture, but in a gliding position.)

**Wind, 84.*

Heat rays

When you stand in sunshine, the sunlight feels warm, because you are taking in heat energy from the Sun. This energy passes through vast distances of Space to reach the Earth. Heat energy cannot reach the Earth by conduction* or convection* because Space is empty. The heat travels to Earth in invisible straight lines called heat rays, which spread out, or radiate, from the Sun. Heat moving in this way is called heat radiation.

Heat rays from the Sun

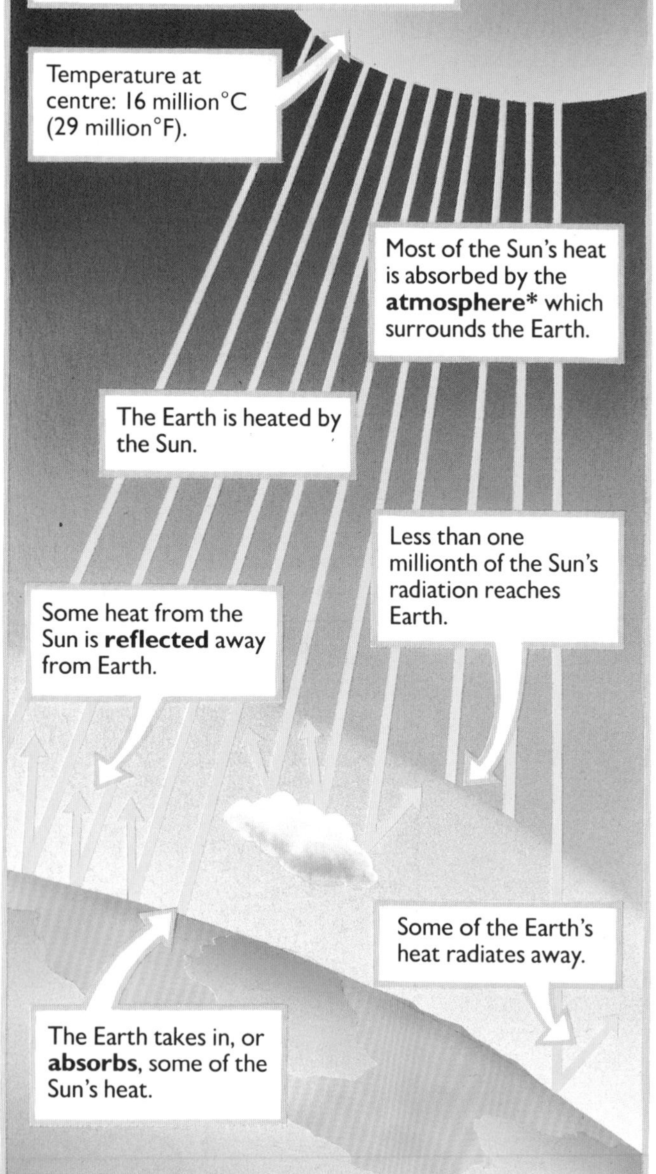

Temperature at centre: 16 million°C (29 million°F).
Most of the Sun's heat is absorbed by the **atmosphere*** which surrounds the Earth.
The Earth is heated by the Sun.
Less than one millionth of the Sun's radiation reaches Earth.
Some heat from the Sun is **reflected** away from Earth.
Some of the Earth's heat radiates away.
The Earth takes in, or **absorbs**, some of the Sun's heat.

If some heat did not radiate away, the Earth would just get hotter and hotter. Clouds help keep the heat in, but they also block out some of the heat radiation from the Sun.

How does a grill work?

A grill cooks food by heat radiation. The food absorbs heat rays from the grill.

The grill stays hot after you have switched it off, until the heat has radiated away.

The heat moves downwards to the food. It cannot be moving by convection because convection carries heat upwards. It cannot be moving by conduction because air is a good insulator and does not conduct heat well.

Heat pictures

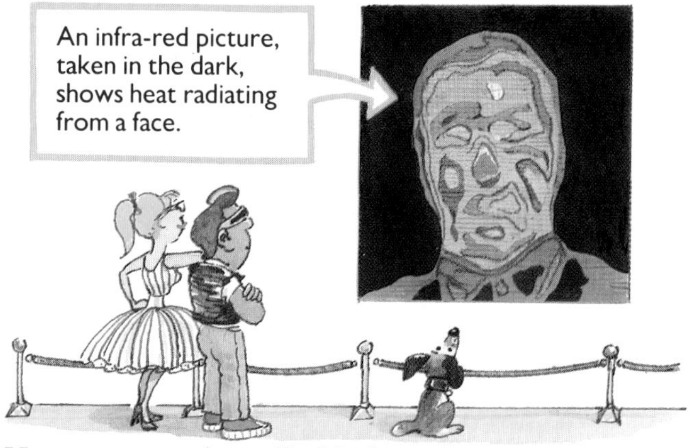

An infra-red picture, taken in the dark, shows heat radiating from a face.

Heat rays are also called **infra-red rays***. A photograph can be taken of heat with a special infra-red camera. Different colours show the amount of heat that radiates from things. Hot things radiate more heat than cold things.

**Atmosphere, 23; Conduction, 14; Convection, 16; Infra-red rays, 105.*

Absorption and reflection

The more heat rays that something absorbs, the hotter it becomes. Things that reflect some of the radiation away will not become as hot. Some surfaces absorb more heat rays than others. Dull and dark surfaces absorb more heat rays than shiny and light surfaces, which reflect them away.

Heat reflected from surface

Heat absorbed by surface

Red tiles

Black things left in the Sun feel hotter than white things.

Shiny metal

White wall

Concrete

In hot countries, people paint their houses white to reflect heat away.

Soil

Shiny spacesuits

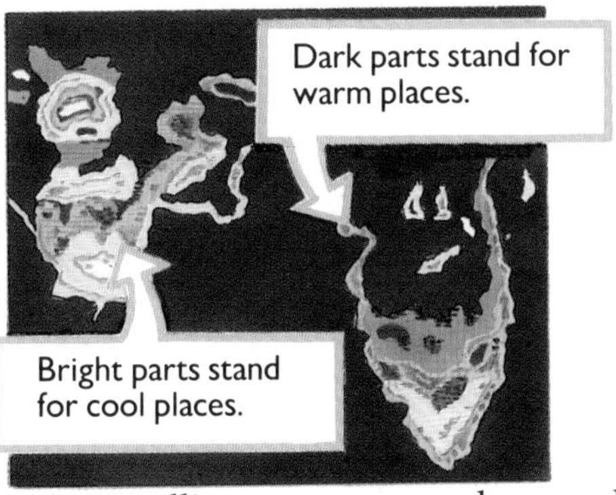

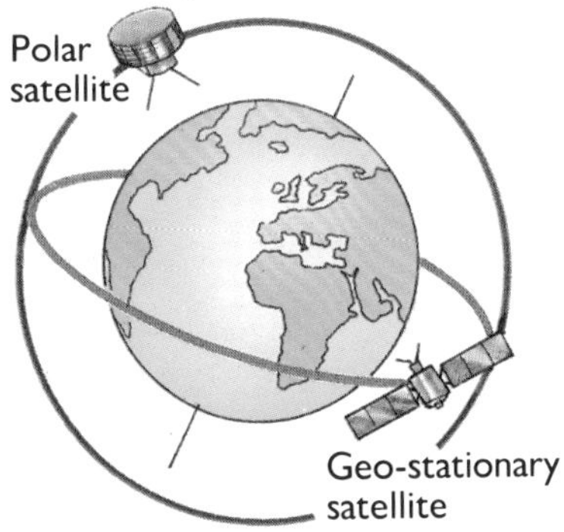

There is no atmosphere around the Moon to absorb the Sun's heat radiation. This means that the Sun feels much hotter there. To help keep them cool, astronauts wear shiny suits that reflect the heat away.

Soot and snow

Black things absorb much more heat radiation than white things. So snow will melt more quickly in sunshine if you put soot on it.

Weather satellites

Scientists who study weather are called **meteorologists**. They use infra-red photographs taken by satellites to help them make weather forecasts. There are two types of weather satellites, **geo-stationary** and **polar satellites**. Geo-stationary satellites stay in one place, high above the Equator.

Dark parts stand for warm places.

Bright parts stand for cool places.

Polar satellite

Geo-stationary satellite

Polar satellites move around, or orbit the Earth, passing over the North and South Poles on each orbit. They are able to photograph the whole of the Earth's surface, because the Earth spins on its axis beneath them.

DID YOU KNOW?

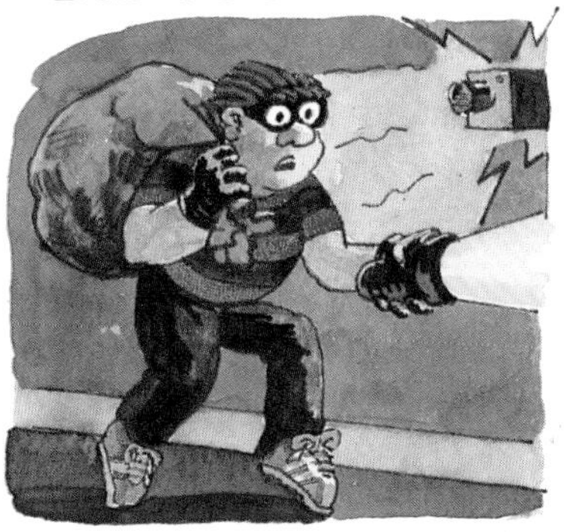

Some burglar alarms work by detecting infra-red rays. The alarm goes off when it detects the heat radiating from a burglar's body.

Energy in living things

The living world of plants and animals stretches from the bottom of the deepest oceans to the top of the highest mountains. Every plant and animal in it needs energy to keep alive. Their energy comes from food. All that food depends on the Sun's energy.

Food chains and food webs

Green plants are able to change the Sun's light energy into chemical energy which they use as food. They are the only living things that can do this.

Some animals eat green plants, and they, in turn, are eaten by other animals. In this way, the Sun's energy passes from one living thing to another. This is called a **food chain**.

This picture shows which animals eat each other to get their food. It is called a **food web**.

DID YOU KNOW?

Nearly three-quarters of the Earth is covered by sea. Tiny plants called plankton live in the sea and make nearly three-quarters of the Earth's oxygen. The biggest is about 1mm (0.04in) across, the smallest is about fifty times smaller.

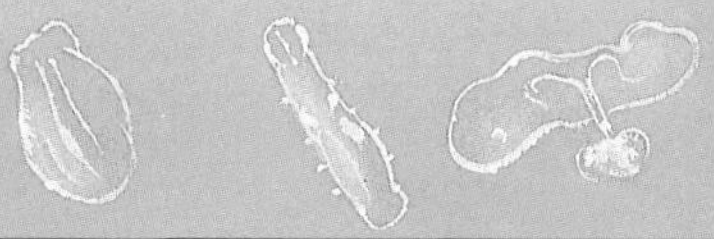

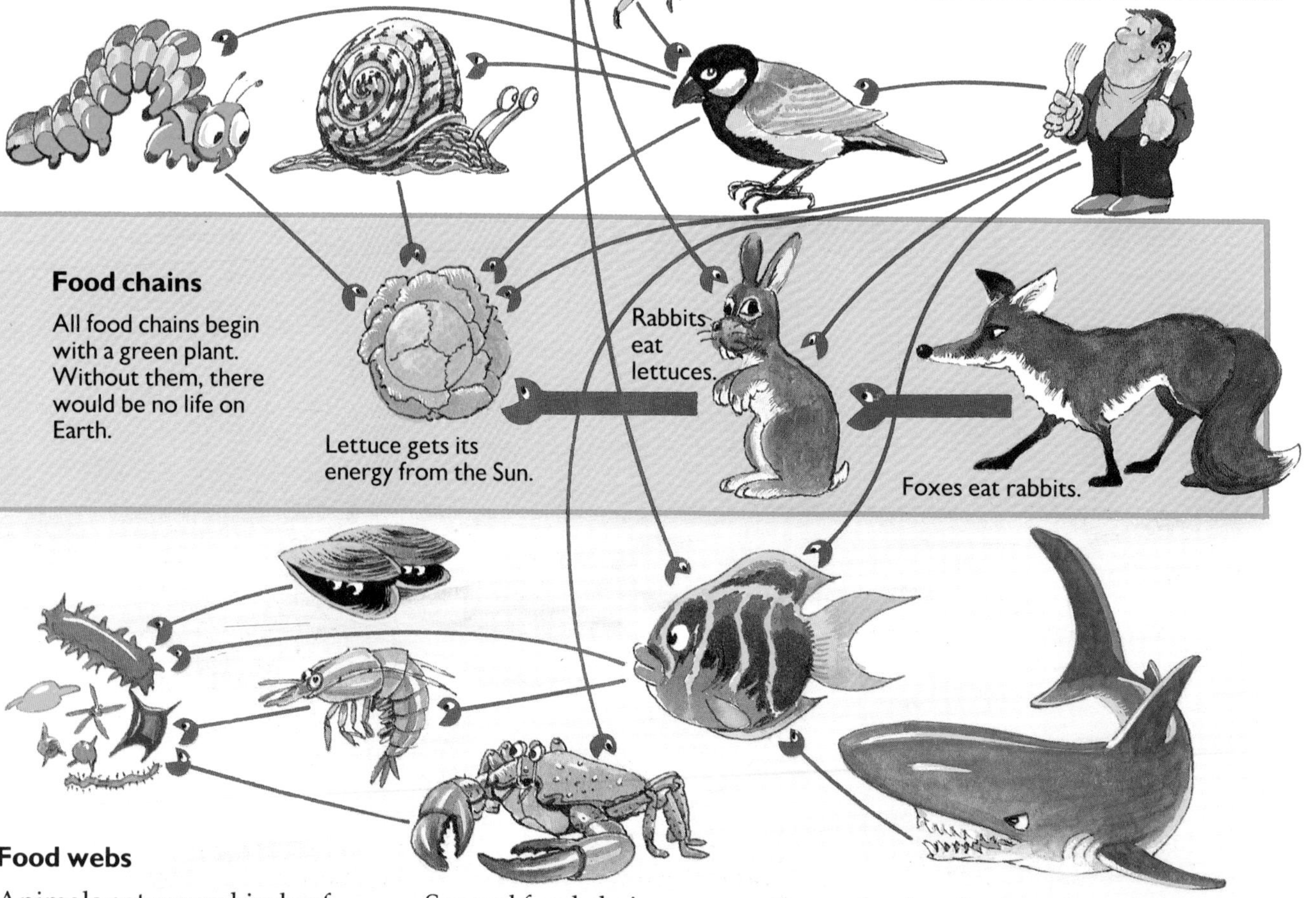
Rabbits eat lettuces.
Lettuce gets its energy from the Sun.
Foxes eat rabbits.

Food chains

All food chains begin with a green plant. Without them, there would be no life on Earth.

Food webs

Animals eat many kinds of food, so each animal belongs to many different food chains. Several food chains, connecting the lives of many different plants and animals, are called a **food web**. Any change to one part of a food web can change the lives of the other things in it.

How do plants make their food?

Green plants make their own food. They take in sunlight and a gas, **carbon dioxide**, from the air. Sunlight and carbon dioxide join up with water and a chemical, **chlorophyll**, inside the leaves. This makes the plant's food, a sugar called **glucose**. At the same time, the plant gives out oxygen through its leaves. This is called **photosynthesis**.

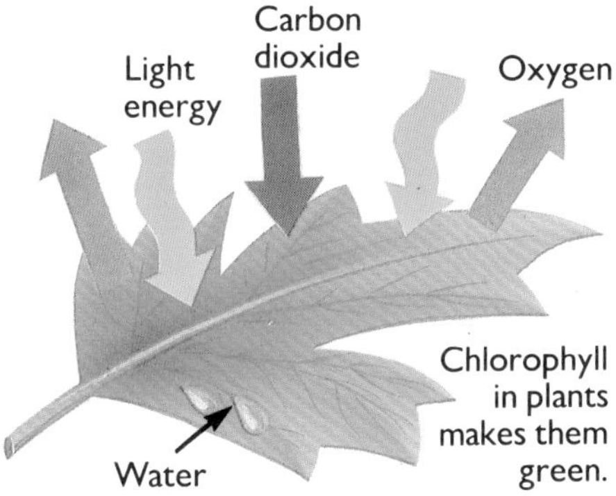
Light energy
Carbon dioxide
Oxygen
Chlorophyll in plants makes them green.
Water

Energy from plants to animals

When animals eat green plants, glucose from the plant joins with oxygen inside their bodies. This is how they get their energy. While this happens, carbon dioxide and water are also formed. This way of changing food back into energy is called **respiration**.

Why do you need food?

You use energy to make your muscles move and to keep your body warm.

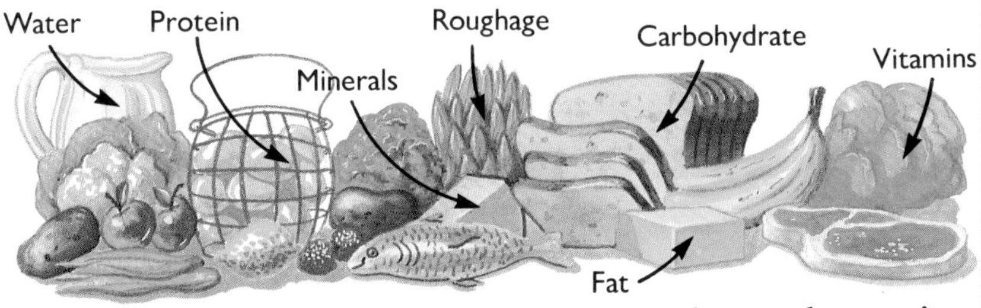
Water
Protein
Minerals
Roughage
Carbohydrate
Vitamins
Fat

You need different foods to keep your body healthy. Your energy comes from foods that contain carbohydrates and fats. Your body also needs **proteins** to grow and to repair itself, as well as **vitamins**, **minerals**, **roughage** and water.

Why do you breathe?

You breathe in because your body needs the oxygen in air for respiration. This is how you get your energy. You breathe out to get rid of the carbon dioxide and water made during respiration. Breathe out on to a mirror. The moisture you see is the water made by respiration.

Plants in the dark

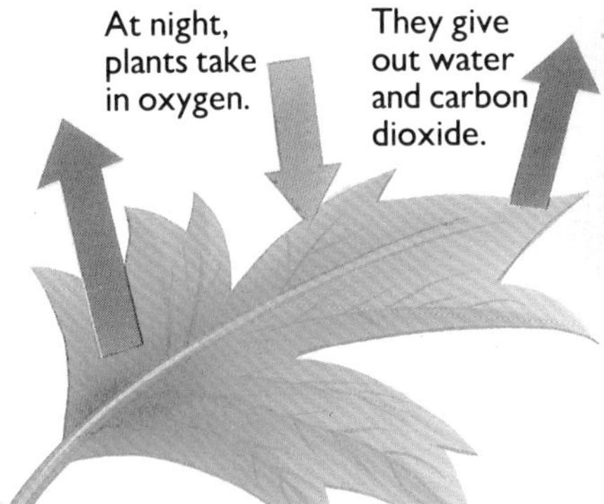
At night, plants take in oxygen.
They give out water and carbon dioxide.

In daylight, plants make their food by photosynthesis. At night, when there is no light, they take in oxygen to get their energy by respiration.

Balancing gases in the air

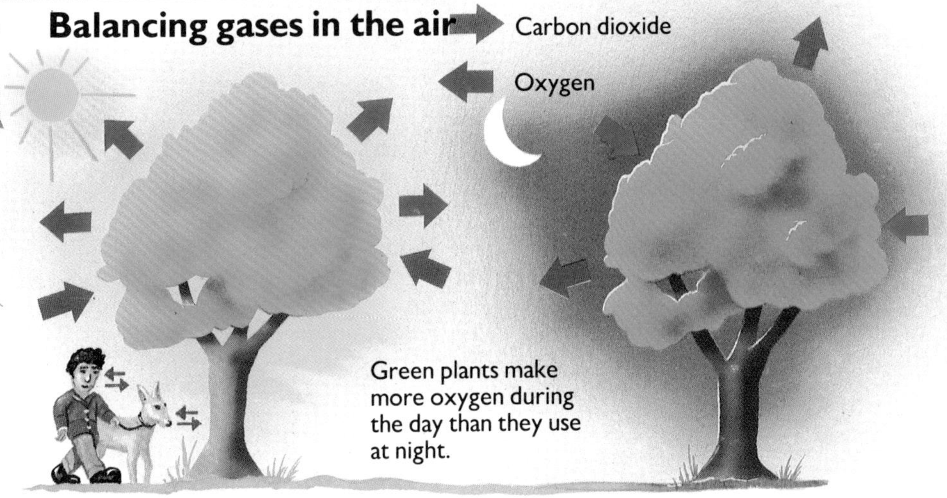
Carbon dioxide
Oxygen
Green plants make more oxygen during the day than they use at night.

Oxygen and carbon dioxide are always being added to the air and taken from it by living things. Green plants make all the Earth's oxygen by photosynthesis during the day. People and animals need to breathe oxygen to stay alive, so without plants there could be no animal life on Earth.

Planet Earth

The story of the Earth

The Earth was formed about 4,500 million years ago. It probably started off as a huge, swirling cloud of dust and gases.

The cloud began to shrink and turned into a ball of hot, liquid rock.

When the surface cooled, it turned to a solid crust of rock that gave off clouds of steam and gases.

Heavy rain poured down from the clouds. It flooded the Earth, forming the first seas.

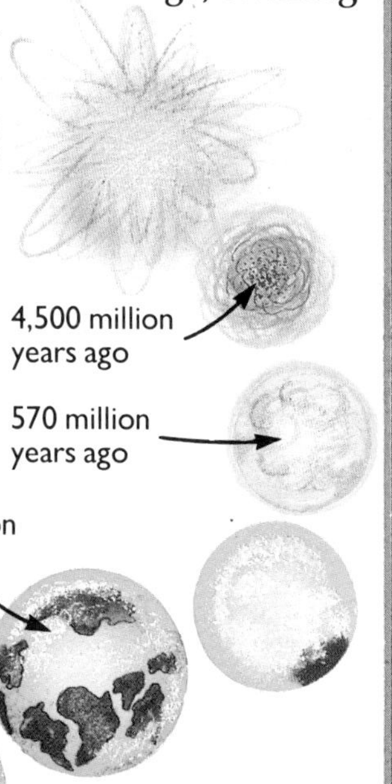
4,500 million years ago
570 million years ago
340 million years ago

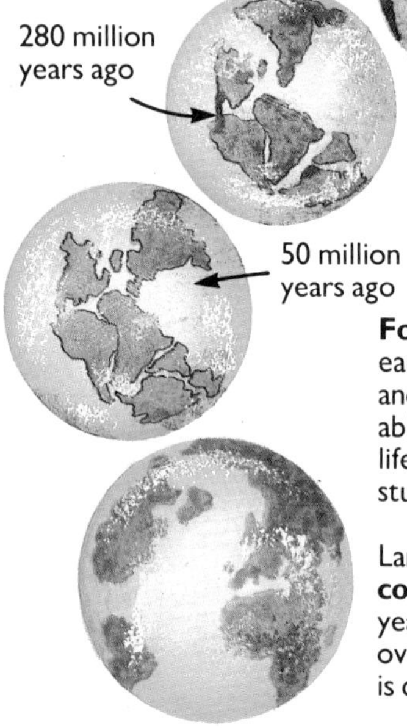
280 million years ago
50 million years ago

The Earth's distance from the Sun makes it just the right temperature for life to exist.

Fossils are the remains of early plants or animals left in ancient rocks. Scientists are able to build up a picture of life millions of years ago by studying fossils.

Land is divided into seven **continents**. Over millions of years, they have slowly moved over the Earth's surface. This is called **continental drift**.

The Earth's surface is still changing today. Every year the Atlantic Ocean gets about 40mm (1½ in) wider. In a million years it will be 40km (25 miles) wider.

DID YOU KNOW?

It has taken millions of years for the seas to become salty. The water from rain and melting snow has gradually dissolved salt from rocks, and the salt has built up in the seas.

The planet Earth

The Earth is one of nine planets that orbit the Sun. This is called our **solar system**.

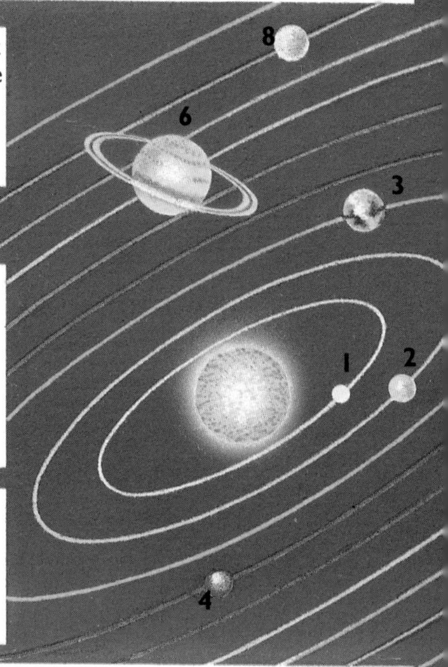

The Sun is a star, just like the stars you see at night. It looks much brighter because it is nearer.

Scientists believe that the Sun was formed about 5,000 million years ago, when a large cloud of gas began to shrink and heat up.

The Sun is about 150 million km (93 million miles) away from the Earth.

Stars are gathered in groups, called **galaxies**. There are millions of stars in each galaxy and millions of galaxies in the Universe. Our solar system is in a galaxy called the **Milky Way**.

The changing Earth

The Earth's crust is made of separate pieces called **plates**, which float on the hot magma. The plates fit together like a giant jigsaw puzzle.

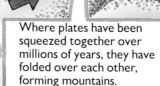

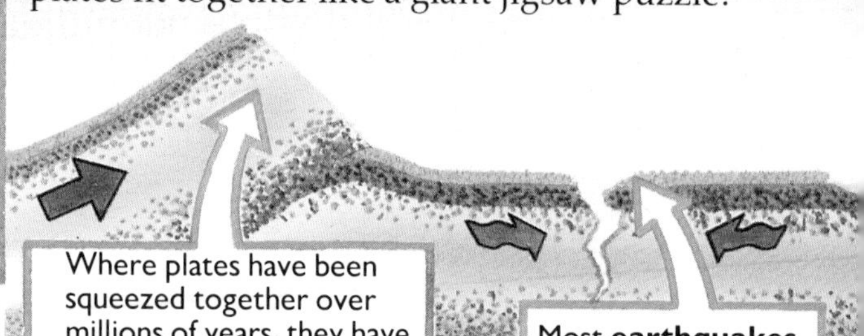

Where plates have been squeezed together over millions of years, they have folded over each other, forming mountains.

Most **earthquakes** happen near the edge of plates where there are cracks called **faults**. Earthquakes are caused when the plates move against each other.

There are a total of 46 moons in our solar system. The Earth has one moon orbiting it, but Jupiter has 14 moons.

What is the Earth made of?

The Earth is a huge ball of rock. There are three parts, the **crust**, **mantle** and **core**.

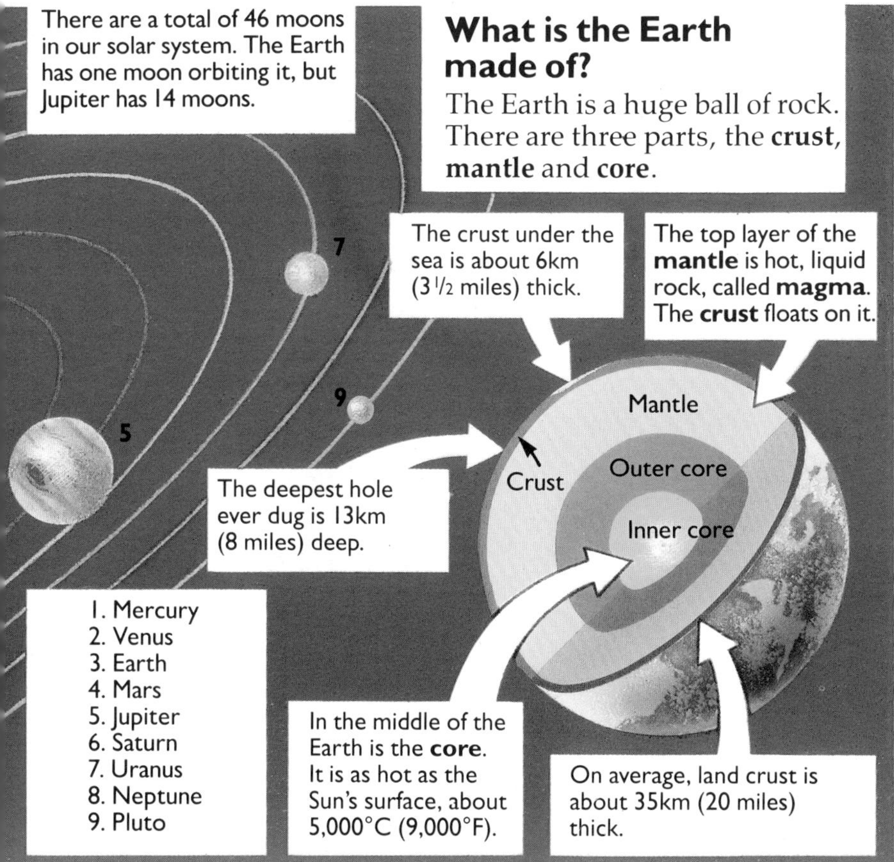
7
9
5
Mantle
Crust
Outer core
Inner core

The crust under the sea is about 6km (3 1/2 miles) thick.

The top layer of the **mantle** is hot, liquid rock, called **magma**. The **crust** floats on it.

The deepest hole ever dug is 13km (8 miles) deep.

1. Mercury
2. Venus
3. Earth
4. Mars
5. Jupiter
6. Saturn
7. Uranus
8. Neptune
9. Pluto

In the middle of the Earth is the **core**. It is as hot as the Sun's surface, about 5,000°C (9,000°F).

On average, land crust is about 35km (20 miles) thick.

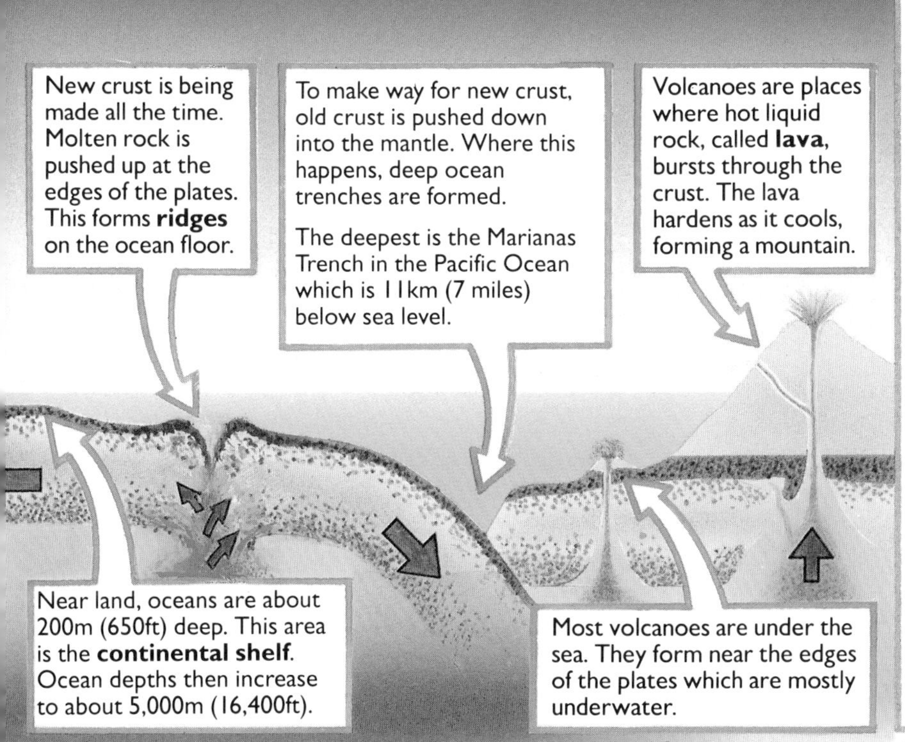

New crust is being made all the time. Molten rock is pushed up at the edges of the plates. This forms **ridges** on the ocean floor.

To make way for new crust, old crust is pushed down into the mantle. Where this happens, deep ocean trenches are formed.

The deepest is the Marianas Trench in the Pacific Ocean which is 11km (7 miles) below sea level.

Volcanoes are places where hot liquid rock, called **lava**, bursts through the crust. The lava hardens as it cools, forming a mountain.

Near land, oceans are about 200m (650ft) deep. This area is the **continental shelf**. Ocean depths then increase to about 5,000m (16,400ft).

Most volcanoes are under the sea. They form near the edges of the plates which are mostly underwater.

The atmosphere

The Earth is surrounded by a layer of air about 10,000km (6,200 miles) thick, called the **atmosphere**. Air is a mixture of **gases**. The main gases are **nitrogen**, **oxygen**, **argon** and **carbon dioxide**.

Ionosphere
Stratosphere
Ozone layer
Troposphere

The atmosphere is held around the Earth by gravity*. There is less air higher up and the atmosphere gradually blends into Space, where there is no air at all.

The **ionosphere** is about 450km (280 miles) thick. Radio waves* travel around the Earth by bouncing off it.

Jets fly in the lower **stratosphere**, which is about 45km (28 miles) thick. This is above the weather.

About 20km (12 miles) above the Earth, there is a thin layer of gas, called **ozone**. It protects the Earth from ultraviolet rays* from the Sun.

The **troposphere** is about 10km (6 miles) thick. The weather* takes place here.

A blanket around the Earth

The atmosphere acts as a layer of insulation between the Earth and the Sun. During the day, it protects the Earth from the burning heat of the Sun. At night, it acts like a blanket, keeping in the heat absorbed from the Sun during the day.

**Gravity, 32; Radio waves, 106; Ultraviolet rays, 104; Weather, 84.*

Fuels of the Earth

A huge amount of energy is needed to run all the world's machines and industries. Most of it comes from three fuels: oil, coal and gas. These fuels are used to heat houses, to drive cars and to make electricity. Oil, coal and gas are called fossil fuels because they were formed from the remains of prehistoric plants and animals.

How old is a piece of coal?

About 300 million years ago, the Earth was covered in swampy forests full of giant plants. As the plants died, they were buried under mud.

The mud gradually hardened into rock. The rotting plants were squashed between heavy layers of rock and heated by the Earth. Over millions of years they changed into coal.

Coal mines

Coal is collected from pits or mines deep underground. Miners use explosives to blast the rock and cut the coal out with machines.

Fossil hunt

If you look carefully at lumps of coal, you may be able to find a fossil of a leaf that lived many millions of years ago.

Oil and gas

Oil and gas were formed over millions of years. They come from the remains of tiny animals that lived in the prehistoric seas. Gas formed as the animals rotted away.

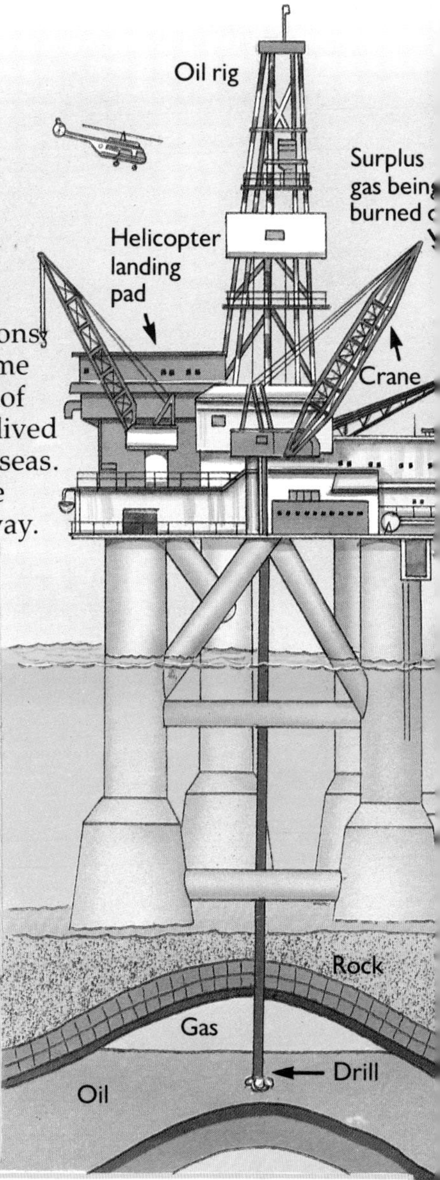

Oil rig
Surplus gas being burned off
Helicopter landing pad
Crane
Rock
Gas
Drill
Oil

Oil is reached by drilling holes in the ground. The oil may gush to the surface or it may have to be pumped up.

Nearly half the world's oil is found under the sea floor. It is reached from enormous oil rigs. They are among the largest structures ever built.

Rigs are also used to drill for gas, in the same way as oil. The gas is then piped to tanks on land.

Finding fossil fuels

Coal, oil and gas are not always found at the same depths under the Earth's surface. This is because the Earth's crust* has changed over millions of years. Places that were land are now sea. Others that were sea are now land.

When the fuels run out

Fossil fuels supply three-quarters of the Earth's energy. They took millions of years to form, so they cannot be replaced when they run out.

The Earth's coal supply has been used for many hundreds of years. There is probably enough left to last for another thousand years.

People only began to use oil as a fuel after car engines* were invented, about 100 years ago. There may only be enough to last for another 60 years.

 **Car engine, 45; Earth's crust, 22*

Using fossil fuels

Soap
Paint
Tar
Coke

Coal is burnt to make heat. But it can also be used to make other useful things. It is used to make soap, dyes, perfumes, paints, tar and many chemicals.

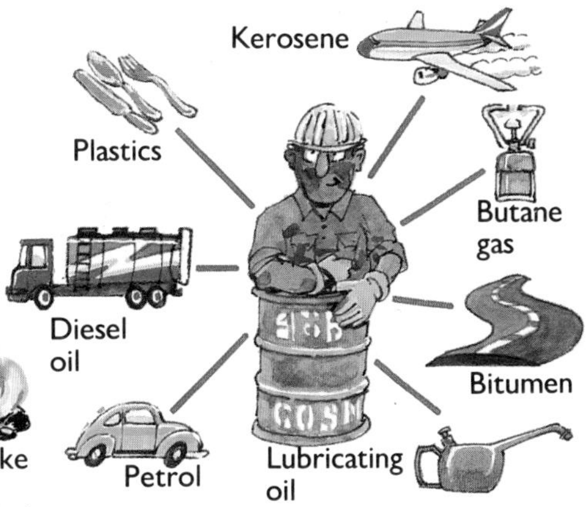
Kerosene
Plastics
Butane gas
Diesel oil
Bitumen
Petrol
Lubricating oil

Oil from the ground is called **petroleum**, or **crude oil**. It is a mixture of useful chemicals. These are separated, or **refined**, in a place called a **refinery**.

DID YOU KNOW?

The longest pipeline is 2,856km (1,775 miles) long. It carries crude oil and runs from Edmonton, Canada to Buffalo, USA.

Pollution

To get energy out of a fossil fuel, it has to be burnt. The heat of the burning fuel can be used for warming something up, or it can be used to make an engine work.

When fossil fuels are burnt, they dirty, or **pollute**, the air. They let off smoke and gases that are very harmful to people, plants and animals. This is called **pollution**.

When petrol is burnt in car engines, it makes a very poisonous gas called **carbon monoxide**. Tiny specks of soot from burning coal dirty the air.

Burning coal also makes a gas, called **sulphur dioxide**. It causes **acid rain**, which poisons trees and plants, and wears away metal and stone.

Nuclear energy

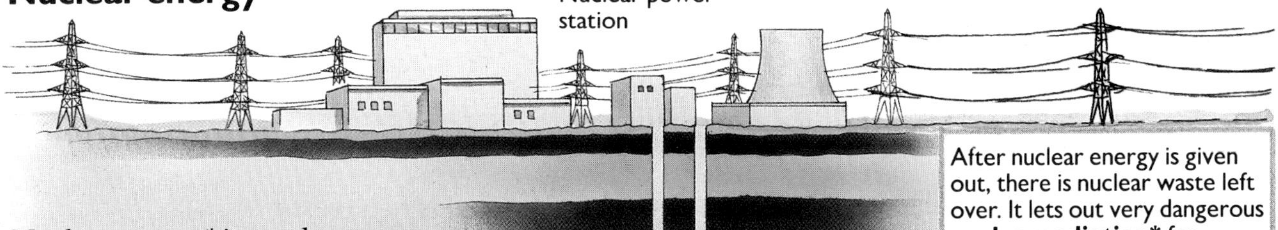
Nuclear power station

Nuclear energy* is used to produce electricity. The energy comes from a fuel called **uranium**, which is a rare metal that is dug out of the ground. The energy is not released by burning. Instead it is given out by splitting the uranium **atoms***.

After nuclear energy is given out, there is nuclear waste left over. It lets out very dangerous **nuclear radiation*** for thousands of years.

Nuclear waste harms living things so it is buried underground. People worry that the waste may leak out and cause pollution.

**Atoms*, 76; *Nuclear energy*, 77; *Nuclear radiation*, 77.

Alternative energy

Fossil fuels cause harmful pollution and are running out. So people are finding new kinds of energy to produce electricity and run machines. Energy that does not come from oil, coal, gas or nuclear power is called alternative energy. It mostly comes from water, sun and wind.

Water power

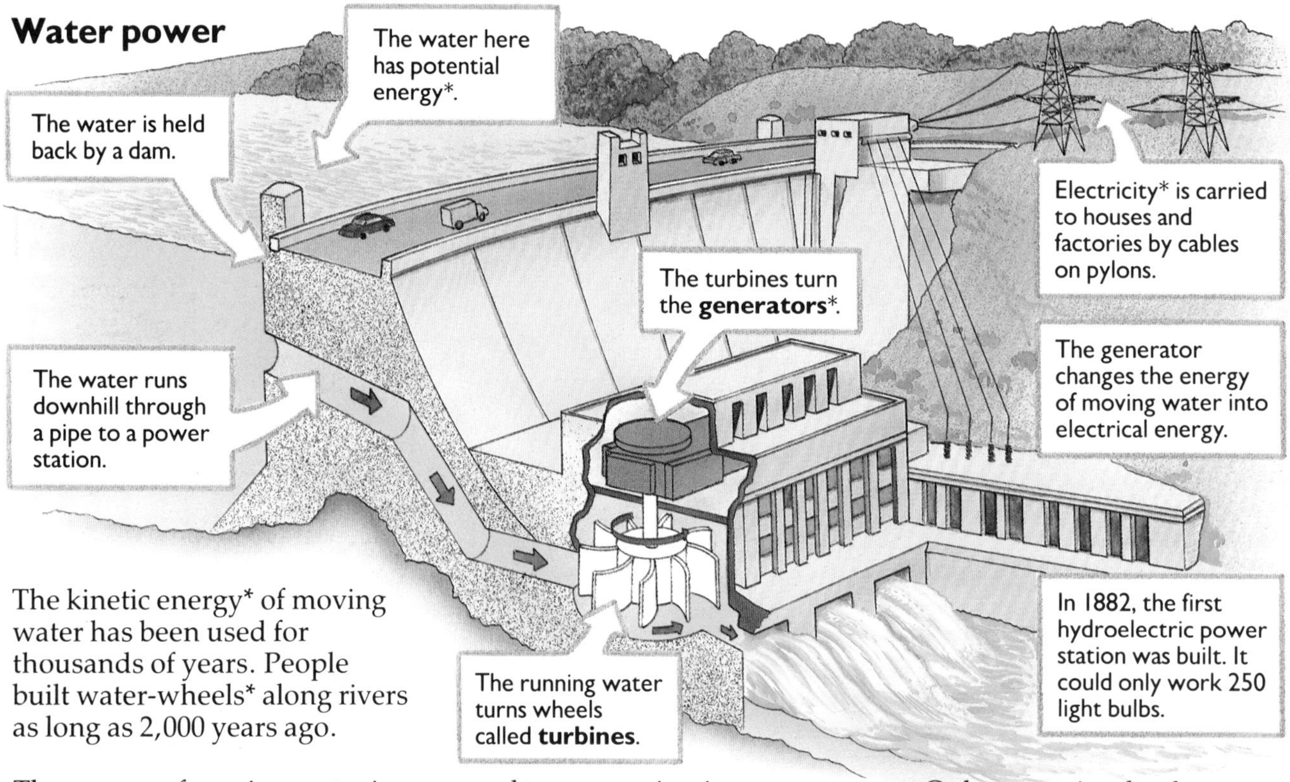

The water here has potential energy*.
The water is held back by a dam.
Electricity* is carried to houses and factories by cables on pylons.
The turbines turn the **generators***.
The water runs downhill through a pipe to a power station.
The generator changes the energy of moving water into electrical energy.
The running water turns wheels called **turbines**.
In 1882, the first hydroelectric power station was built. It could only work 250 light bulbs.

The kinetic energy* of moving water has been used for thousands of years. People built water-wheels* along rivers as long as 2,000 years ago.

The energy of moving water is now used to produce electricity in **hydroelectric power stations**. Hydroelectricity provides over six per cent of the energy used in the world today. Because the water comes from rain or melting ice, it never runs out. Only countries that have lots of water can produce electricity this way. Scandinavia, North America and Russia are able to produce large amounts of their electricity from hydroelectric power.

Tide and wave energy

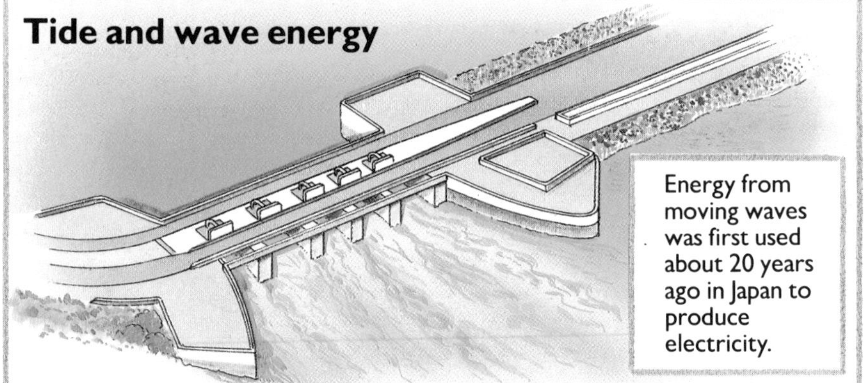

Energy from moving waves was first used about 20 years ago in Japan to produce electricity.

The energy from tides can be used to produce electricity. Tide water coming in is trapped behind a dam and then allowed to flow back through turbines.

The first tidal power station was built on the River Rance, France, in 1966. It provides enough electricity for a town of about 300,000 people.

Wind energy

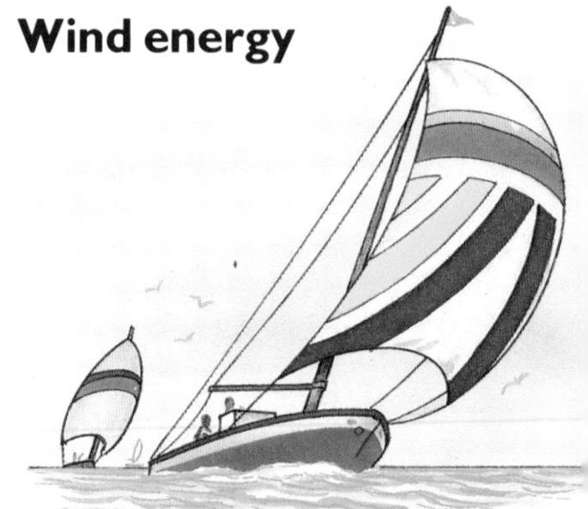

For thousands of years, wind energy has been used to push sailing boats and turn windmills. Today, windmills are used to produce electricity.

**Electricity, 102; Generators, 99; Kinetic energy, 11; Potential energy, 11; Water-wheels, 44.*

Solar energy

The Sun's energy, called **solar energy**, can be changed into electrical energy in **solar cells** or can be used to heat water.

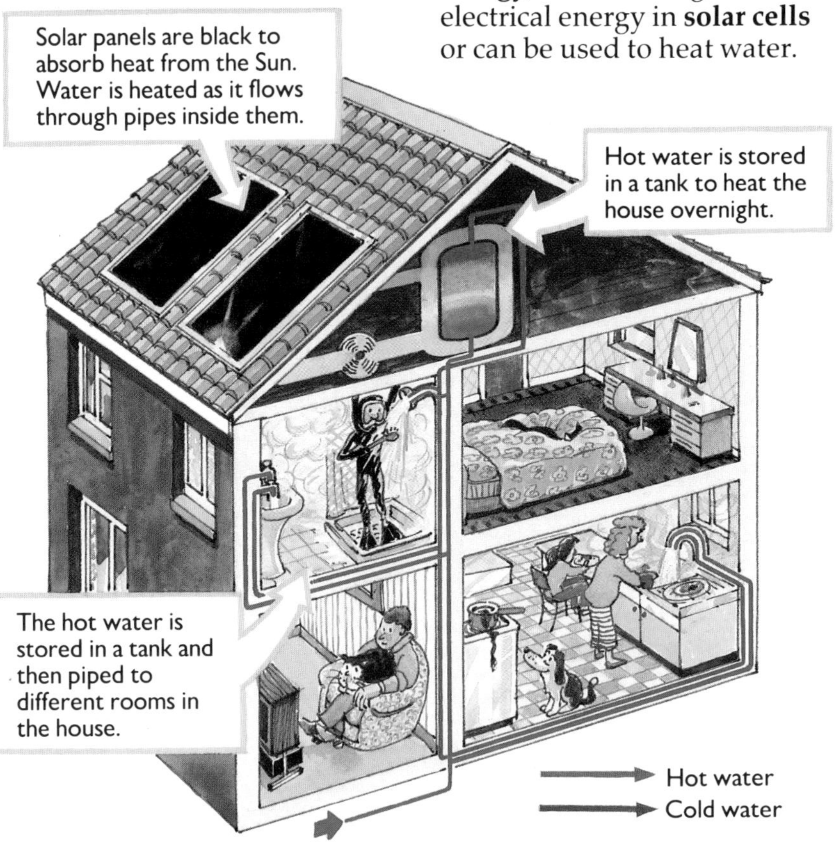
Solar panels are black to absorb heat from the Sun. Water is heated as it flows through pipes inside them.
Hot water is stored in a tank to heat the house overnight.
The hot water is stored in a tank and then piped to different rooms in the house.
Hot water
Cold water

Some houses are heated by the Sun. They have solar panels which absorb the Sun's energy, even on cloudy days.

The amount of energy reaching Earth from the Sun in a year is more than 10,000 times greater than the world's energy needs.

DID YOU KNOW?

In 1981, the Solar Challenger became the first solar-powered aircraft to cross the English Channel. Its 262km (163 mile) journey took about $5^1/_2$ hours.

Where does the world's energy come from?

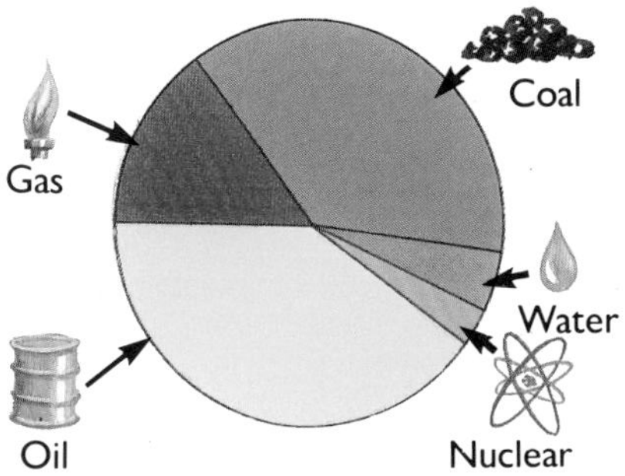
Coal
Gas
Water
Oil
Nuclear

Windmills do not cause pollution, but they are large and noisy. To provide large amounts of energy, they take up huge areas of land.

Geothermal energy

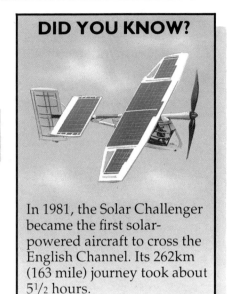

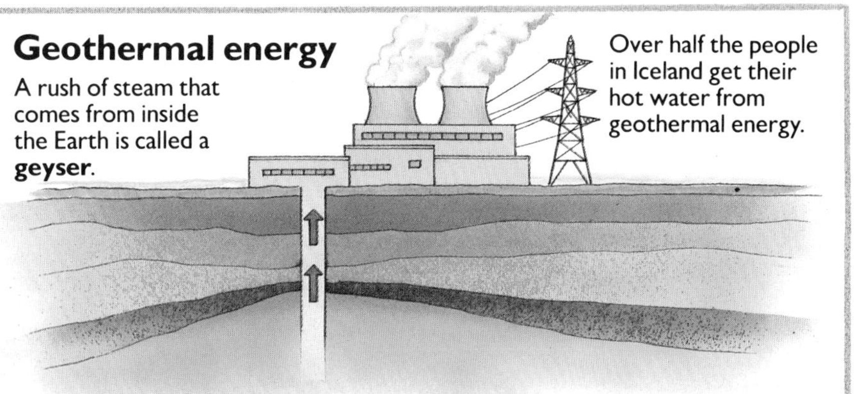
A rush of steam that comes from inside the Earth is called a **geyser**.
Over half the people in Iceland get their hot water from geothermal energy.

The inside of the Earth is very hot. It gets steadily hotter the deeper into the Earth you go. In some places, especially near faults*, boiling water or steam rushes to the surface. This kind of energy, called **geothermal energy**, can be used for heating and to produce electricity.

**Faults*, 22.

Why do things move?

Nothing moves by itself. Things only move when they are pushed or pulled. Something which pushes or pulls is called a force. If there are no forces pushing or pulling, objects stay still or keep on moving at a steady speed in the same direction. There are many types of force.

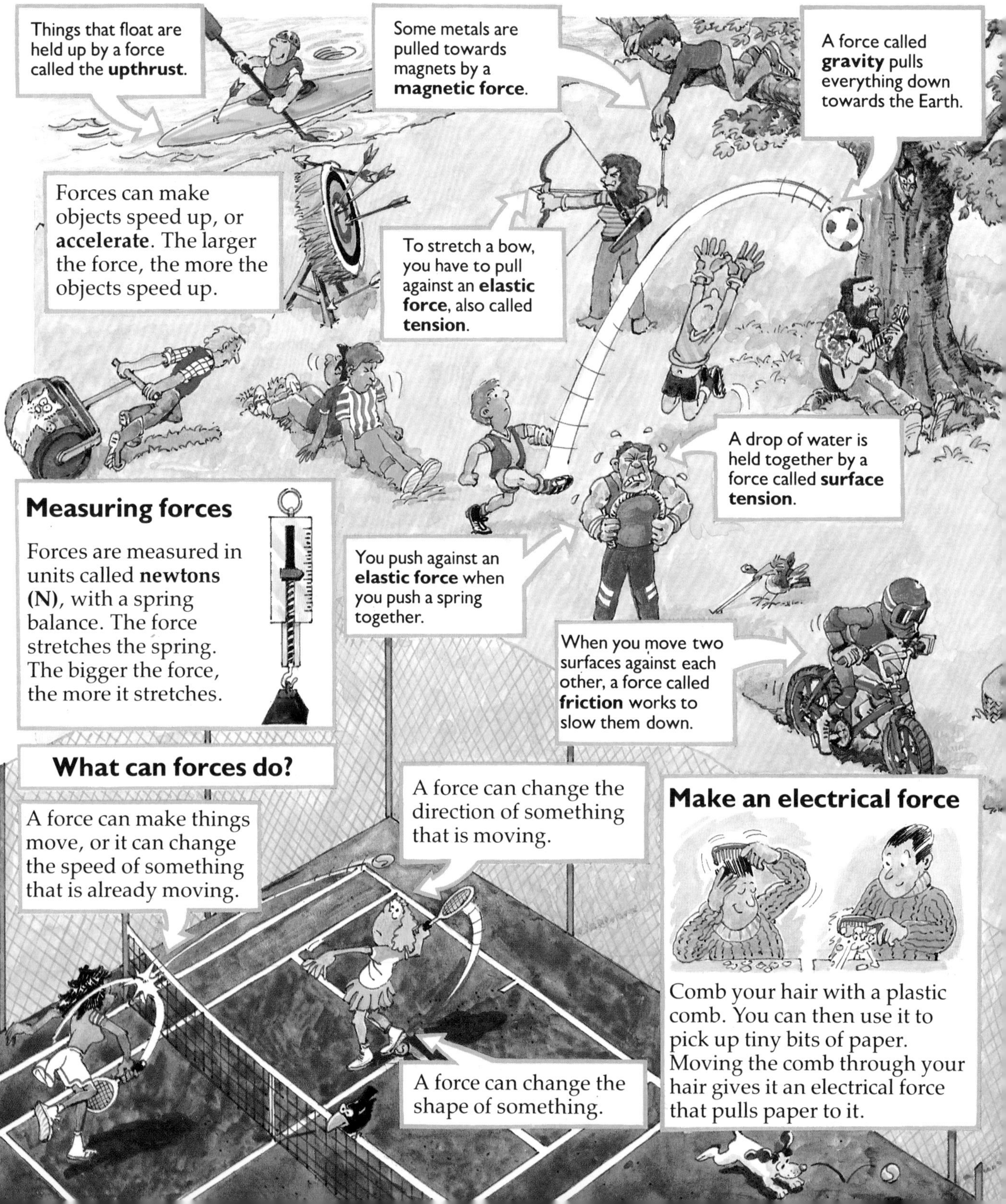

Things that float are held up by a force called the **upthrust**.

Some metals are pulled towards magnets by a **magnetic force**.

A force called **gravity** pulls everything down towards the Earth.

Forces can make objects speed up, or **accelerate**. The larger the force, the more the objects speed up.

To stretch a bow, you have to pull against an **elastic force**, also called **tension**.

A drop of water is held together by a force called **surface tension**.

You push against an **elastic force** when you push a spring together.

When you move two surfaces against each other, a force called **friction** works to slow them down.

Measuring forces

Forces are measured in units called **newtons (N)**, with a spring balance. The force stretches the spring. The bigger the force, the more it stretches.

What can forces do?

A force can make things move, or it can change the speed of something that is already moving.

A force can change the direction of something that is moving.

A force can change the shape of something.

Make an electrical force

Comb your hair with a plastic comb. You can then use it to pick up tiny bits of paper. Moving the comb through your hair gives it an electrical force that pulls paper to it.

Joining and balancing forces

In a tug of war, the force of each person in a team pulling in the same direction adds up to make a bigger force.

When the force of both teams pulling in opposite directions is balanced equally, neither team moves.

When one team pulls harder than the other, the forces are unbalanced. Then both teams move in the direction of the team that pulled hardest.

Unbalanced forces

When a bicycle moves at a steady speed on a flat road, the force moving it forward is balanced equally by the force of friction* pulling it back.

Friction slows the bicycle down.
When the forces are unbalanced, the bicycle changes speed.
The force of the cyclist's legs moves the bicycle forward.

When the cyclist pushes harder, the bicycle goes faster. The force pushing it forward is greater than the force of friction holding it back.

When the cyclist stops pushing as hard, the bicycle slows down. The force of friction slowing it down, is greater than the force of the cyclist pushing it.

Action and reaction

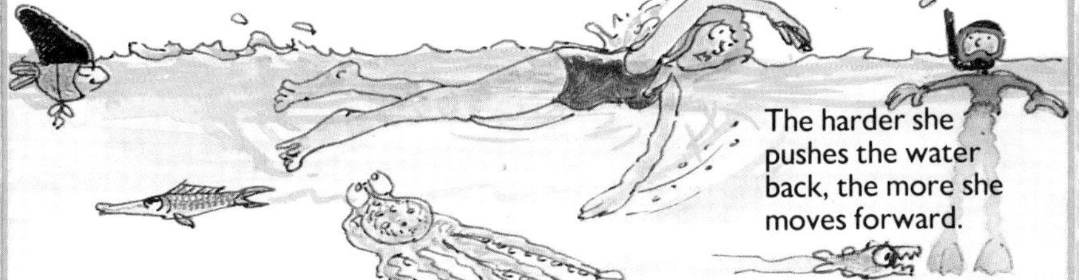
The harder she pushes the water back, the more she moves forward.

Forces always come in pairs. The swimmer pushes the water back, making her move forward. The force pushing backwards is called the **action**. The force pushing forwards is called the **reaction**. Every action has an equal and opposite reaction. This means that whenever one thing puts a force on another, a force of equal size works in the opposite direction.

DID YOU KNOW?

Not all the cannons on one side of a 16th century sailing ship could be fired at once. The action would have caused such a big reaction that the ship would have capsized.

*Friction, 30.

Friction

If you try to push a book gently along a table, at first it will not move. This is because a force called friction holds it back. As you push harder, the book eventually begins to slide. But as the book rubs along the table, the force of friction slows it down. Friction always works to stop things moving, or to slow them down when they are moving.

No surface is ever completely smooth. Even something that looks smooth, like metal, looks bumpy through a microscope. There is more friction on rough surfaces than smooth ones. When you write, friction makes the pencil lead rub off on to the paper. But try writing on glass. Glass is smoother than paper, so there is less friction, and the pencil will not write well.

Friction can be a help

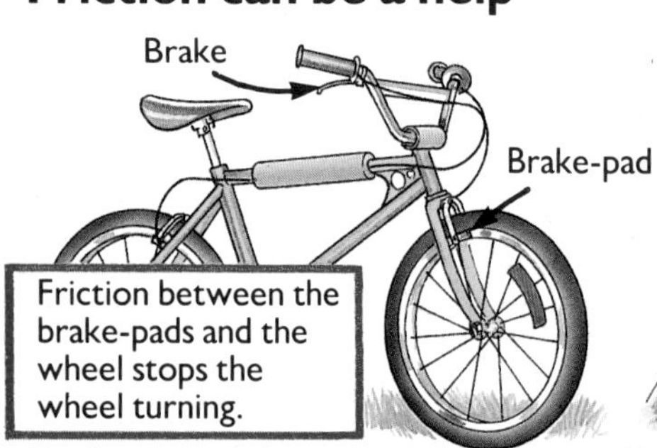
Brake
Brake-pad
Friction between the brake-pads and the wheel stops the wheel turning.

Brakes work because of friction. The harder you squeeze them, the more the brake-pads push against the wheels and the quicker you stop.

Boots that climbers wear have rough, rubber soles. The friction between them and the rock stops the climbers' feet from sliding.

If a road is icy, there is less friction, so car tyres have less grip.

Roads and car tyres are made with rough surfaces so that there is as much friction as possible between them. This is what stops cars skidding.

Friction is a drag

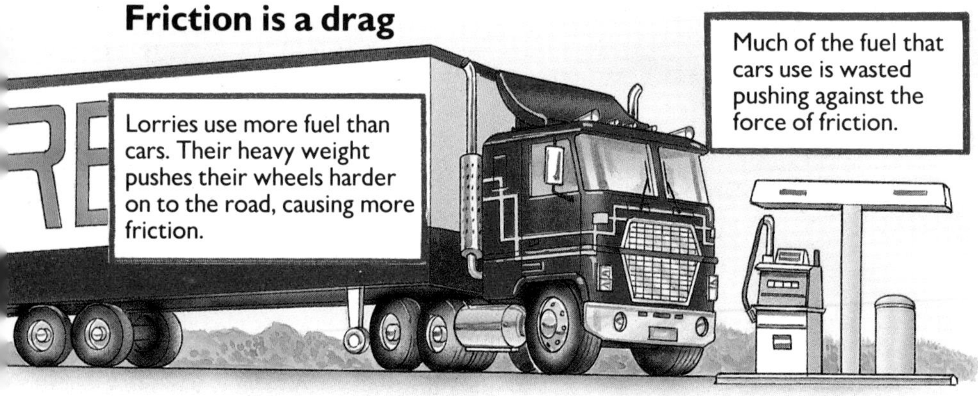
Lorries use more fuel than cars. Their heavy weight pushes their wheels harder on to the road, causing more friction.
Much of the fuel that cars use is wasted pushing against the force of friction.

There is always friction between the moving parts in a machine. Machines need extra energy and use up more fuel as they push against the force of friction. Because the parts of a machine rub against each other, they eventually wear out.

DID YOU KNOW?

When you rub your hands together, the heat you feel comes from friction. The harder you rub, the warmer they get. The energy used to push against friction changes into heat. This is why machines are hot after use.

Getting rid of friction

A **lubricant**, like oil, reduces friction.

Smooth surfaces are easier to dance on than rough surfaces, because there is less friction.

Putting a thick liquid, like oil, on the moving parts in a machine stops them rubbing against each other. This cuts down friction which saves energy and stops the machine wearing out.

Rolling over friction

After wheels had been invented, they were used instead of logs.

Thousands of years ago, people found that it was easier to move heavy loads by rolling them on logs, than by dragging them along the ground. Rolling causes less friction than dragging.

Friction in the air

Things with a smooth shape are called **streamlined**.

The friction between anything moving and the air around it is called **air resistance**. How much air resistance there is on something depends on its shape. Cars are designed so that air moves smoothly over them, to cut down air resistance.

Ball-bearings

Another way of reducing friction inside machines is to use **ball-bearings**. These are small balls that roll over each other, keeping the moving parts of the machine apart.

Red-hot friction

There is no air in Space, so there is no friction to slow things down. Spacecraft only use their engines now and then so that they can change course.

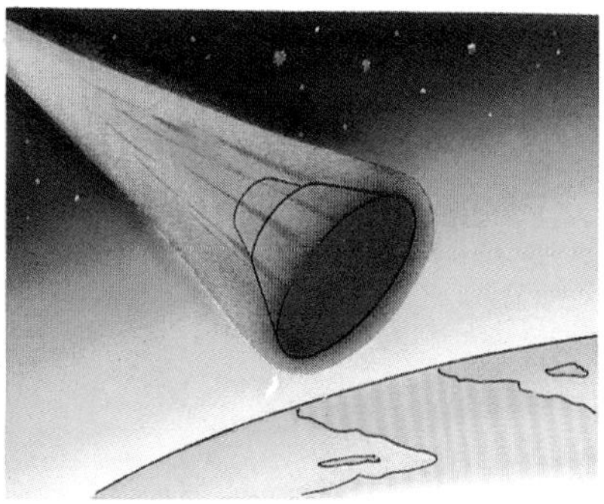

Spacecraft enter the Earth's atmosphere* so fast that they glow red-hot. This is because there is so much friction between them and the air.

A cushion of air

Hovercraft can travel over ground as well as over the water.

The world's largest hovercraft can carry over 400 passengers and 60 cars, and travel at a speed of 120kmph (75mph).

Boats and submarines have to push through water. Friction between them and the water slows them down. **Hovercraft** work by floating on a cushion of air. This keeps them apart from the dragging force of the water. There is so much less friction that they can move much faster than ordinary boats.

Gravity

If you let go of something, it falls downwards. There is an invisible force called gravity pulling everything towards the Earth.

Without gravity, things would not be held on to the Earth's surface. They would fall off the Earth and go into Space.

What does gravity do?

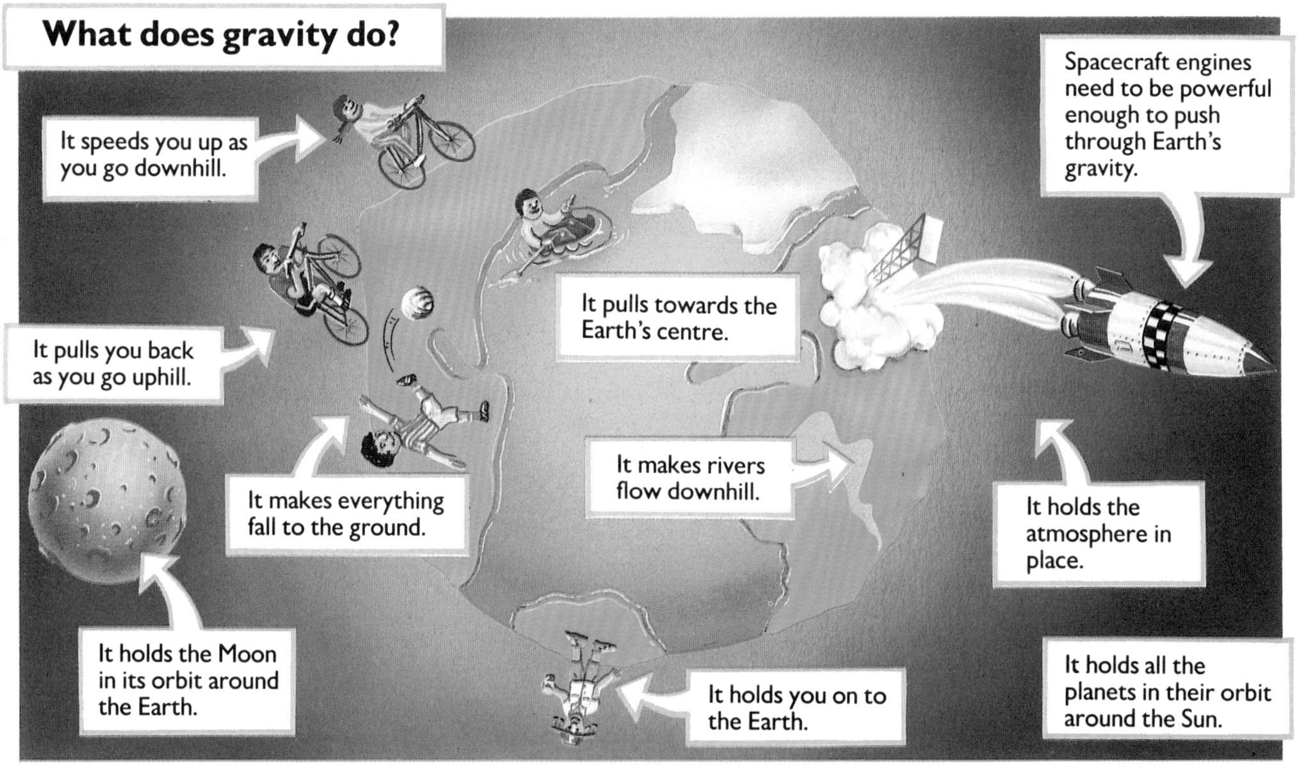
It speeds you up as you go downhill.
Spacecraft engines need to be powerful enough to push through Earth's gravity.
It pulls towards the Earth's centre.
It pulls you back as you go uphill.
It makes rivers flow downhill.
It makes everything fall to the ground.
It holds the atmosphere in place.
It holds the Moon in its orbit around the Earth.
It holds you on to the Earth.
It holds all the planets in their orbit around the Sun.

Gravity was first understood about 300 years ago by Isaac Newton. Gravity is a force that attracts every object to every other object. You only notice the pull of gravity with things that are very large, like the Earth.

When you weigh something, you are measuring the force of gravity pulling it towards Earth. The further from the centre of the Earth you go, the smaller the pull of gravity. So things weigh slightly less on top of high mountains.

Balancing things

Centre of gravity
Centre of gravity
Centre of gravity

All things have a point, called their **centre of gravity**, where their weight balances. A tray will only balance if you hold it under this point. Things that are top-heavy have a high centre of gravity. This makes them fall over more easily.

DID YOU KNOW?

The seas rise and fall at regular intervals called **tides**. They are caused by the Moon's gravity which pulls the seas directly below it.

Changing gravity

The strength of gravity is different on other planets than it is on Earth. So the **weight** of an object changes if you take it to another planet. But the amount there is of the object, its **mass**, stays the same wherever it is.

Like all forces, weight is measured in **newtons (N)**. But when you weigh something, you really want to know how much there is of it, that is, its mass. Weighing scales measure the weight, and then convert the answer into units of mass, such as kilograms*.

On Earth, this astronaut has a weight of about 600N and a mass of 60kg (132lbs).
On the Moon he weighs 100N, because the Moon's gravity is only 1/6 as strong as Earth's. However, his mass is still 60kg (132lbs).
Jupiter's gravity is 264 times stronger than Earth's. There, his weight is 158,400 N. His mass is still 60kg (132lbs).
Quiz
On Earth 1kg (2.2lbs) weighs 10N. What is your weight in N? What would your weight be on the Moon?†

Falling and gravity

About 400 years ago, Galileo noticed that objects speed up, or **accelerate**, as they fall.

He found that heavy and light things, of the same shape and size, take the same time to fall to the ground. Gravity pulls them down equally.

Try this for yourself with different objects, like a slipper and a heavy boot.

Air resistance

Objects of different shapes and sizes fall at different rates. The shape of a parachute makes people fall more slowly.

The air pushing against the parachute causes a lot of air resistance*. A person without a parachute falls faster because less air pushes against them.

The faster something falls, the more air resistance there is on it. Eventually, the air resistance slowing it down becomes as strong as the pull of gravity. Then its speed no longer changes. This is called **terminal speed**.

Free fall

If there were no air, there would be no air resistance. All falling objects would just get faster and faster at the same rate. This is called **free fall**.

†*The answer is on page 128.*

**Air resistance, 31; Kilograms, 7.*

Going straight

Things move because a force pushes or pulls them. Once moving, things only slow down, speed up or change direction if a force makes them. If no forces pushed on a moving object, it would carry on moving forever at the same speed in the same direction.

Speeding up is called **accelerating** and slowing down is called **decelerating**.
The heavier things are, the bigger the force needed to make them accelerate.
The force of the engine pushes the car forwards. The more powerful the engine, the higher the acceleration.
The force of friction* in the brakes makes cars decelerate. Fast cars need strong brakes to decelerate quickly.

How far something moves in a certain time is called its **speed**. To measure speed, count how many metres (or feet) something moves every second, or how many kilometres (or miles) it moves every hour. How fast something goes in a *particular direction* is called its **velocity**. For example, the velocity of a racing car may be 150kmph (93mph) towards North.

Getting things moving . . . and stopping them

Things with a large mass* have more inertia than things with a small mass.

Things that are not moving prefer to stay still, and things that are moving prefer to carry on moving. This is called **inertia**. Everything has inertia, and the bigger its mass, the more inertia it has. When a bus starts moving, you feel yourself being pulled backwards because your body's inertia makes it want to stay still. When the bus stops, you feel yourself being pulled forwards because your body's inertia makes it want to carry on moving at the same velocity.

 **Friction, 30; Mass, 33.*

Inertia tricks

Put a tumbler of water on a sheet of paper on a table. Then pull the paper away, very quickly and firmly.

Use an unbreakable tumbler.
The tumbler and paper must be dry.

The glass stays where it is because of its inertia. This only works if you pull the paper quickly enough.

Liquids have inertia too

You can tell the difference between a raw egg and a hard-boiled egg using inertia. Spin both eggs on saucers. As they spin, catch them and let them go again as quickly as you can. The boiled egg stays still. But the raw egg will start to spin again because of the inertia of the liquid inside it.

Bumps and blows

The force of hitting a ball makes it move. The ball then carries on going by itself. Once any object is moving, it carries on moving with what is called its own **momentum**.

The harder you hit a ball, the more momentum it has and the further it goes. The lighter the ball, the less momentum it has. A ping-pong ball has less momentum than a baseball.

If a moving ball bumps into another ball, the momentum of the first makes the second one move. When you catch a ball, the momentum of the ball makes you move too, but only slightly because you are so much heavier than the ball.

When you jump up and down, your momentum makes the Earth move. But because the Earth is 100,000 million million million times heavier than you are, the movement is very, very tiny and you do not notice it.

DID YOU KNOW?

The fastest land animal in the world is the cheetah, which can run at over 100kmph (60mph). It can accelerate from 0 to 70kmph (45mph) faster than most cars.

Round the bend

Moving in a circle is different from moving in a straight line*. All things move in a straight line unless another force makes them change direction. When something is moving around a corner, it is changing direction the whole time, so there must be a turning force keeping it moving in a circle. That turning force is called a centripetal force.

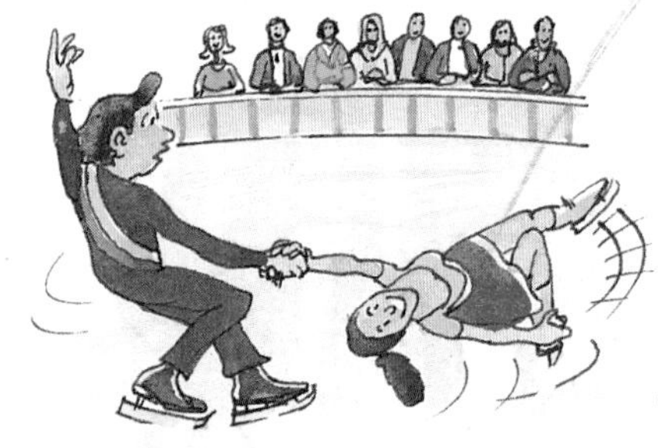

When you swing something around, the centripetal force keeping it in a circle comes from your arm.

When you let go, the pulling force stops. Whatever you are turning will then move off in a straight line.

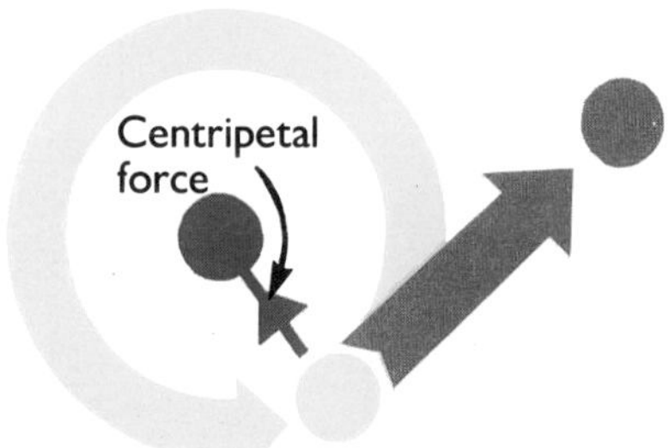

Without a centripetal force to keep her moving in a circle, the skater would move off in a straight line.

Spinning water

If you spin a bucket full of water around fast enough, the water will not fall out. The centripetal force keeps the water moving in a circle.

The centripetal force comes from the bottom of the bucket pushing on the water. If you do not swing it fast enough, the water falls out.

Going round a bend

The force keeping you driving around in a circle comes from friction* between the tyres and the road. Racetracks have bends built on sloping banks.

The sloping bank helps to keep the bicycles going round the corner. They can go round the corner faster because the slope stops them skidding off in a straight line.

Spinning things dry

Washing machines spin wet clothes to get rid of water. The centripetal force comes from the drum pushing on the clothes, keeping them moving in a circle. Water is able to get through the holes, so it flies off in a straight line.

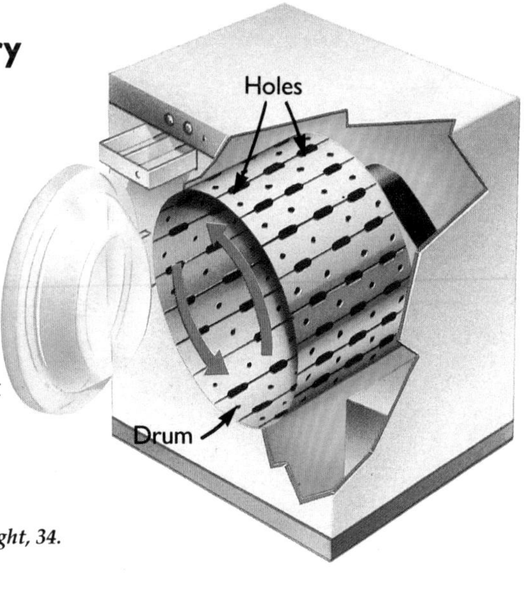

 **Friction, 30; Going straight, 34.*

Keeping moving around a corner

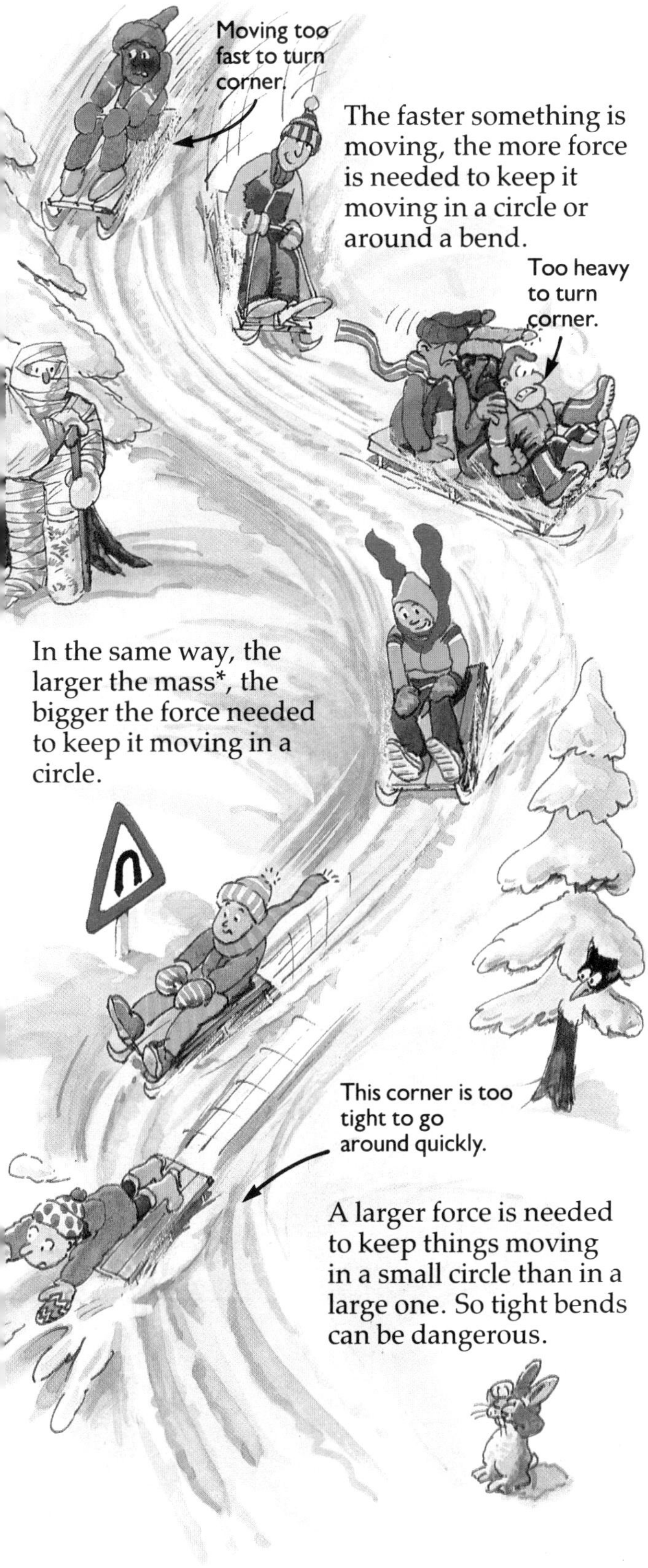
Moving too fast to turn corner.
Too heavy to turn corner.
This corner is too tight to go around quickly.

The faster something is moving, the more force is needed to keep it moving in a circle or around a bend.

In the same way, the larger the mass*, the bigger the force needed to keep it moving in a circle.

A larger force is needed to keep things moving in a small circle than in a large one. So tight bends can be dangerous.

Tight corners

The friction between you and a car seat keeps you moving around a gentle curve. But if you go around a tight corner, you slide across the seat. This is because the force of friction is not strong enough to hold you.

DID YOU KNOW?

When pilots loop-the-loop, the centripetal force turning them can be so strong that they feel about four times heavier than normal.

Momentum

Things that are moving in a circle have momentum* just like things which move in a straight line. Momentum keeps a spinning top standing up. When it stops spinning it has no momentum so it falls over.

Mass, 7, 33; Momentum, 35.

Floating and sinking

Mark the water level on a container full of water. Then add stones to the water and see how the water level rises. The water is pushed out of the way, or displaced, by the stones.

In water, things feel lighter than they really are. The water pushes on them, holding them up. When they are out of the water, they feel heavy again because the water no longer holds them up.

The bigger things are, the more water they displace, and the harder the water pushes back on them. The pushing force of a liquid is called **upthrust** or **buoyancy**.

Why does an iron ship float?

Solid iron is very dense, so even a small piece is very heavy. It sinks because the upthrust of water is not strong enough to hold it up. But ships are not just made of solid iron. They are hollow, full of big spaces filled with air.

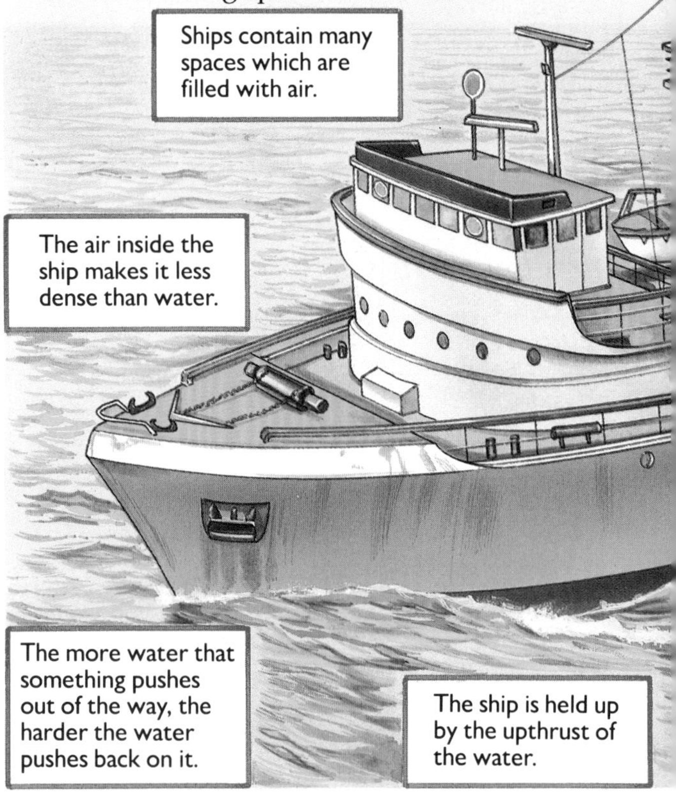
Ships contain many spaces which are filled with air.
The air inside the ship makes it less dense than water.
The more water that something pushes out of the way, the harder the water pushes back on it.
The ship is held up by the upthrust of the water.

Why do some things float?

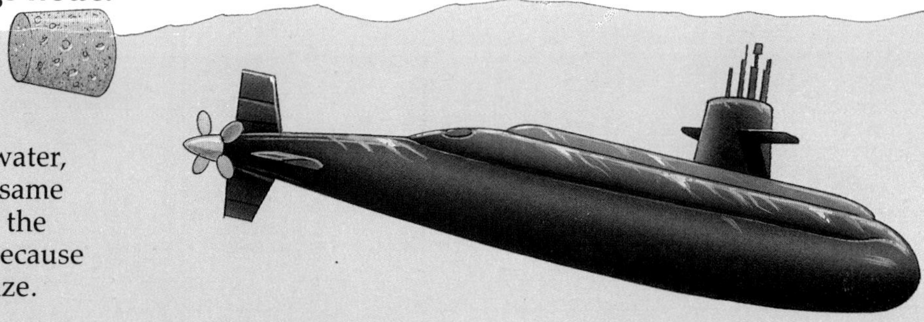

A piece of cork floats in water, but a piece of iron of the same size sinks. They displace the same amount of water, because they are both the same size.

The cork floats because it is much lighter for its size than the iron. How heavy something is for its size is called its **density**.

If something is less dense than water, it will float. This is because the upthrust of the water is strong enough to hold it up.

Submarines are able to change their density. When they fill their tanks with air, they float. When they fill their tanks with water, they sink.

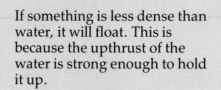

Even though a ship may be very large, the air inside it makes it light for its size. The ship pushes so much water out of the way, that the upthrust of water pushing on it is strong enough to hold it up, making it float.

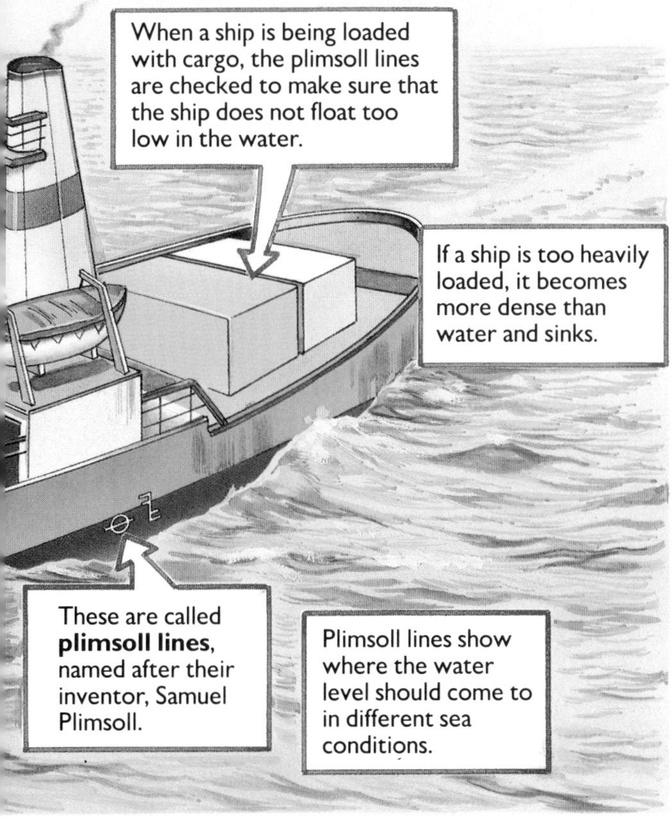
When a ship is being loaded with cargo, the plimsoll lines are checked to make sure that the ship does not float too low in the water.
If a ship is too heavily loaded, it becomes more dense than water and sinks.
These are called **plimsoll lines**, named after their inventor, Samuel Plimsoll.
Plimsoll lines show where the water level should come to in different sea conditions.

Walking on water

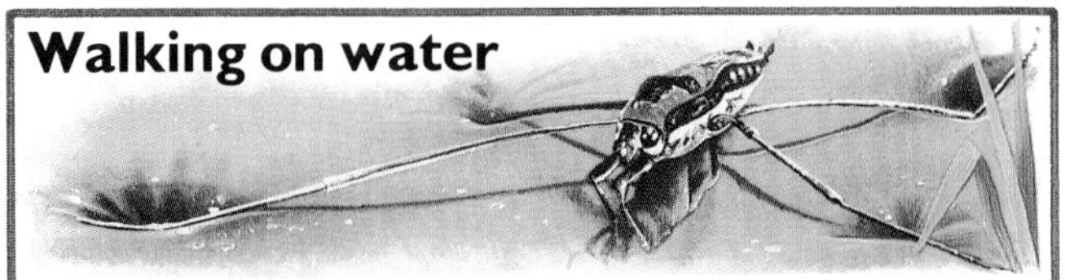

The surface of water has a sort of skin which is strong enough for tiny insects, like pond skaters, to walk on. This skin is called **surface tension**. It is surface tension that holds water together in drops.

Soapy water

When you add soap to water, you reduce its surface tension. This makes the water's skin stretchier. That is why you can make bubbles with soapy water.

Measuring upthrust

About 2,200 years ago, Archimedes noticed that water was pushed out of the way while he was getting into his bath. He found that the weight of water pushed out of the way is equal to the force pushing up on a floating object.

Anything can float

Things can float in any liquid or gas, as they do in water. Balloons float in air because they are less dense than air. Put some drops of cooking oil in water. The oil floats because it is less dense than water.

Salty water

Salt water has a greater density than fresh water, so ships float higher in salty water than in fresh water.

You can see this in the next experiment. Dissolve about 10 teaspoons of salt in a glass of warm water. Pour fresh water in another glass. Put an egg in each glass. The egg in the fresh water sinks, but the egg in the salty water floats.

DID YOU KNOW?

In the Dead Sea, the water is so salty that people can float in it without swimming. They can even sit in the water and read a book.

Pressure

The larger the area, the smaller the pressure.

The smaller the area, the larger the pressure.

Your feet sink into snow, unless you spread your weight over a larger area by wearing skis or snow-shoes. The push of your weight is then less on each point of the snow. The force pushing on a certain area is called pressure.

The girl's heels put more pressure on the ground than the elephant's feet, even though she weighs less. Why do you think sharp knives cut better than blunt ones? Why do nails have sharp points? (Answers on page 128.)

Pushing liquids

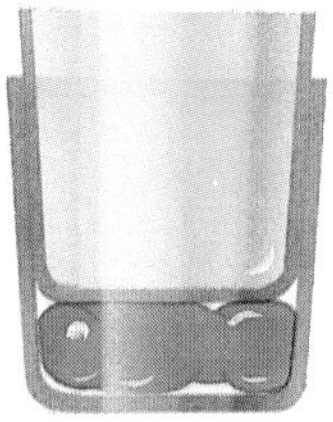

Fill a balloon with a little water and tie the end. Squeeze it between two plastic beakers. You cannot squash the water into a smaller space.

Liquids* cannot be squashed, so when you push on one part of a liquid, pressure is carried to all other parts of it.

In a car, pushing the brake pedal pushes liquid down a tube to the brakes. Because the liquid cannot be squashed, it carries the pressure from the pedal to the brakes.

Car disc brakes

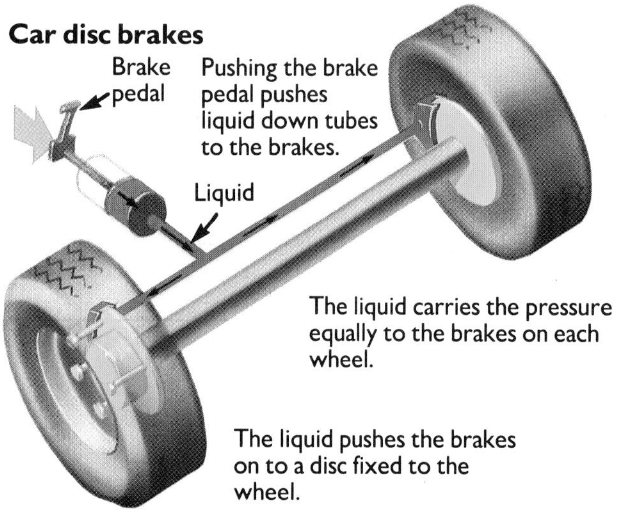

Brake pedal
Pushing the brake pedal pushes liquid down tubes to the brakes.
Liquid
The liquid carries the pressure equally to the brakes on each wheel.
The liquid pushes the brakes on to a disc fixed to the wheel.

Pushing gases

Blow a little air into a balloon and tie up the end. Squeeze it between two beakers. Unlike water, you can squash the air into a slightly smaller space.

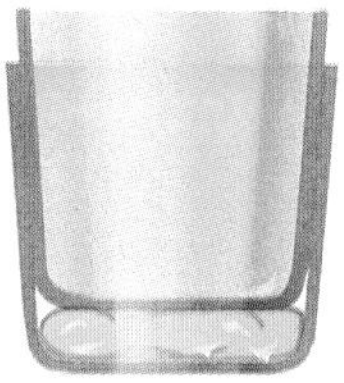

Gases* can be squashed, or **compressed**, into a smaller space. A compressed gas, like air in a balloon, pushes out equally in all directions. The more you compress a gas, the higher the pressure inside it.

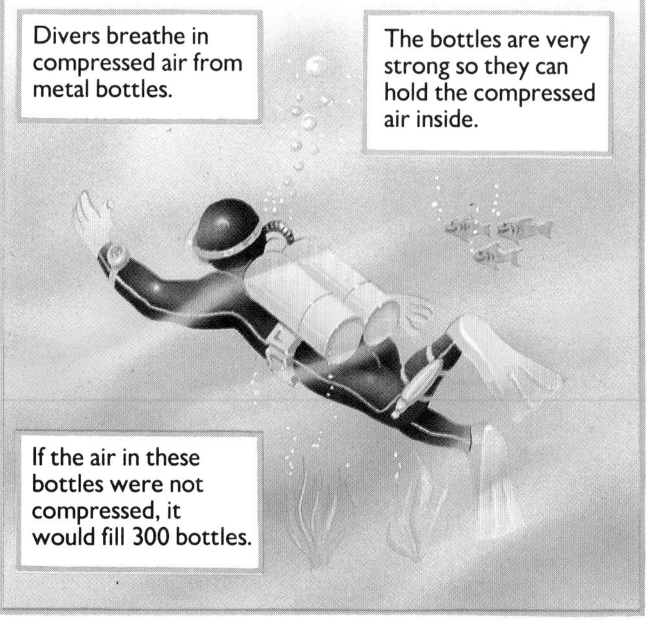

Divers breathe in compressed air from metal bottles.
The bottles are very strong so they can hold the compressed air inside.
If the air in these bottles were not compressed, it would fill 300 bottles.

 **Gases, 78; Liquids, 78.*

Pressure in liquids

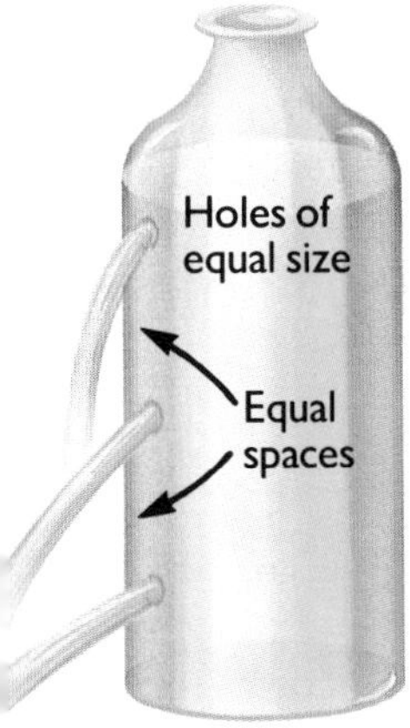

Holes of equal size
Equal spaces

Make three holes in a plastic bottle and cover them in sticky tape. Fill the bottle with water and then take off the tape.

Water from the bottom hole will squirt out furthest, because the weight of the water on top pushes on the water below it. The deeper the water, the greater the pressure.

Submarines are very strong so they are not crushed by the huge pressure deep in the sea.

Pressure in the air

Pressure in the atmosphere* works just like it does in water. The weight of the air above pushes on the air beneath it. This is called **atmospheric pressure**. The closer you get to the ground, the greater the atmospheric pressure.

Air pressure is measured with a **barometer**.

Changes in air pressure affect the weather*.

Pressure balance

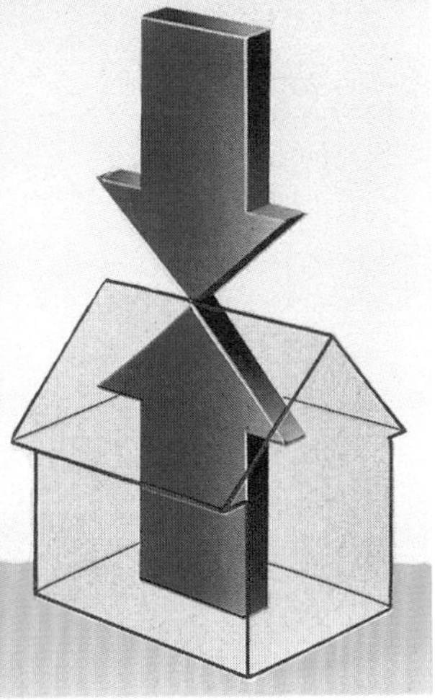

Things do not collapse from the atmospheric pressure pushing down on them. This is because they are full of air which pushes out as hard as the air outside pushes in.

Your body is made so that you do not feel atmospheric pressure.

Liquid levels

Look inside a coffee pot or a teapot. The liquid inside the pot and the spout are always at the same level. This is because atmospheric pressure is pushing down evenly on both sides.

How does suction work?

When you push a suction pad on to something, you push some air out, so the air pressure inside the pad is less than outside. The pad is held in place by the push of atmospheric pressure.

Pumps

Your body has two pumps. Your heart pumps blood and your lungs pump air.

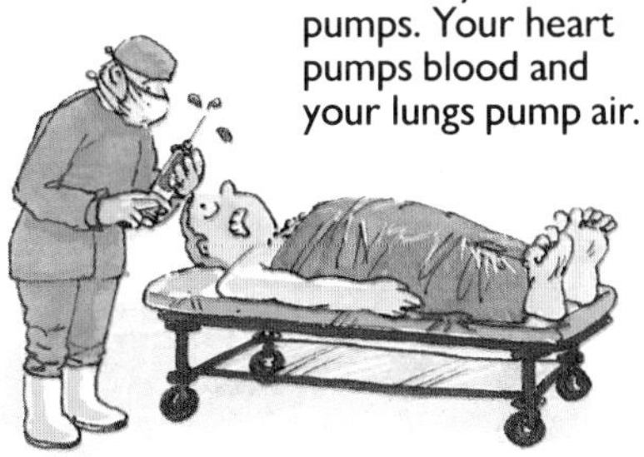

Pumps are used for moving liquids and gases around. A syringe is a simple pump. Pushing the plunger in increases the pressure inside, so the liquid is pushed out.

DID YOU KNOW?

Air pressure changes as you change height. In a plane, this can make your ears feel blocked. Yawning or swallowing lets air in or out of your ears, making the pressure in them the same as outside.

*Atmosphere, 23; Weather, 84.

Simple machines

Thousands of years ago, people did everything using only their own or their animals' muscle power. Over the years, they invented machines to help make work easier. Work can mean many things, but in science, doing work means using a force to move an object.

Long ago, people found that it was easier to drag heavy loads by rolling them along logs. Later, they invented **wheels**.

They found that it was easier to split logs and stones by hammering in a triangular shaped piece of wood. This is called a **wedge**.

Lifting loads

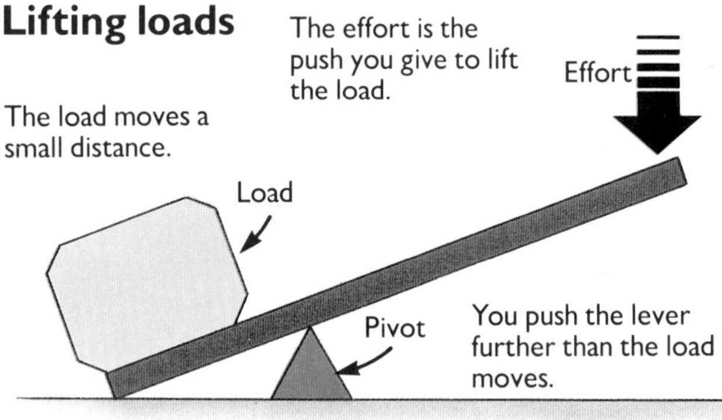
The effort is the push you give to lift the load.
Effort
The load moves a small distance.
Load
Pivot
You push the lever further than the load moves.

It is much easier to move a heavy load using a long stick called a **lever**. The lever is propped up on an object called a **pivot**. You have to push the lever further than you would have to push the load, but this is less effort than moving the load directly. A wheelbarrow is a type of lever. Its wheel works like a pivot. Scissors and shears are levers. The pivot is where the blades cross.

DID YOU KNOW?

The largest machine in the world is a coal digger in Hambach, Germany. It is twice as long as a soccer field and as tall as a building with thirty floors.

Try using a lever

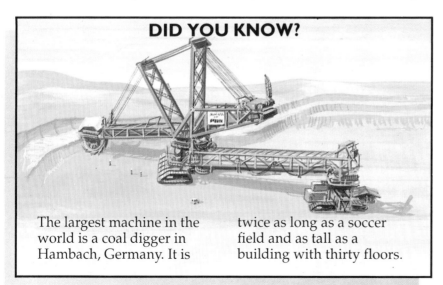

Push down here to lift lid.

Long levers make work easier. Prise the lid off a tin with a coin. Then try with a spoon. It is less effort with the spoon because it is a longer lever.

Slopes and screws

A **slope** makes lifting loads easier. Although you have to go further, it is less effort to carry a load up a gentle slope than to lift it straight up.

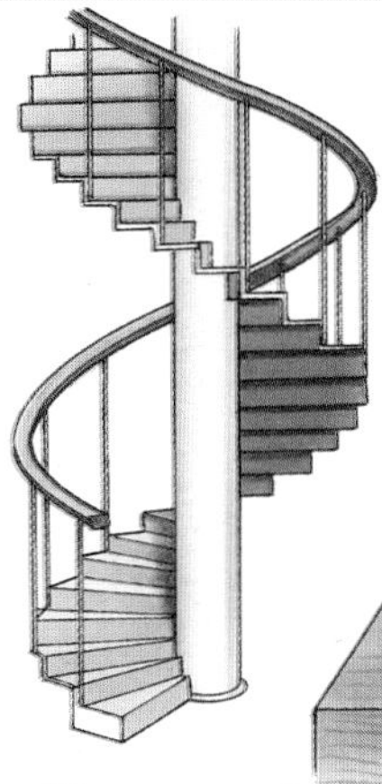

A spiral staircase works like a coiled up slope. It is easier to walk up the stairs than to climb straight up, but you have to walk further.

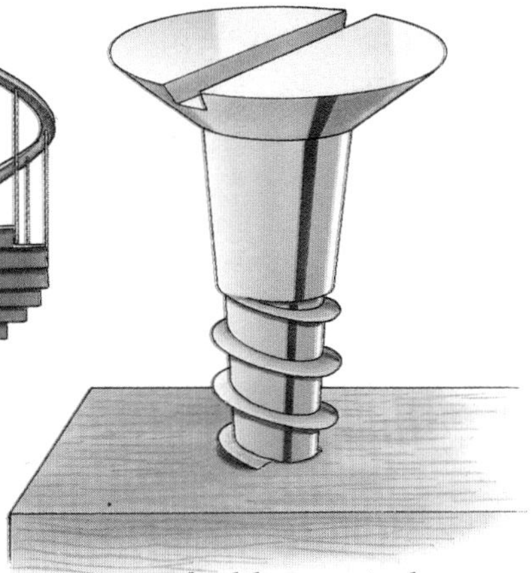

A **screw** works like a spiral staircase. You have to turn a screw round and round to get it in a wall, but this is easier than pushing it straight in.

Pulleys

A **pulley** helps you lift things. Pulling down with a pulley is easier than pulling things up, because your weight helps you.

Pulling here lifts the load.

Using more than one pulley wheel allows you to lift even heavier loads. The weight is then spread out over more rope.

Archimedes' screw

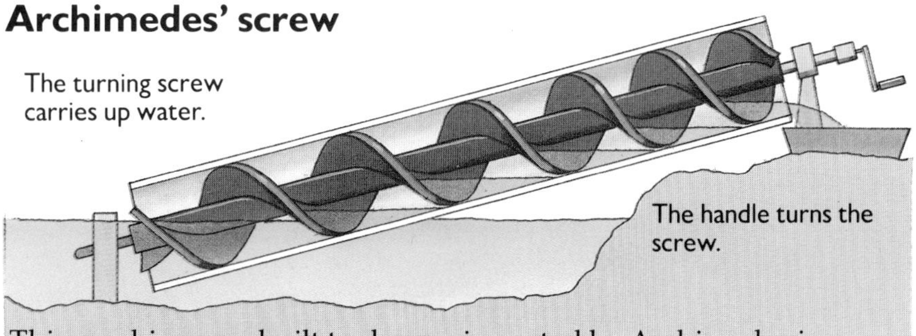

The turning screw carries up water.
The handle turns the screw.

This machine was built to draw up water using a screw. It was invented by Archimedes in Greece, about 2,200 years ago.

Gears

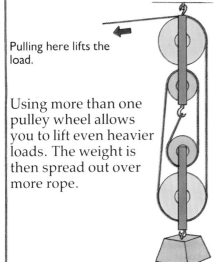

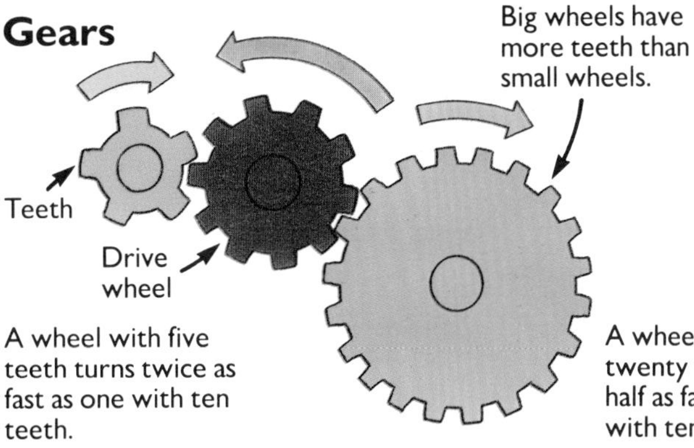

Big wheels have more teeth than small wheels.
Teeth
Drive wheel
A wheel with five teeth turns twice as fast as one with ten teeth.
A wheel with twenty teeth turns half as fast as one with ten teeth.

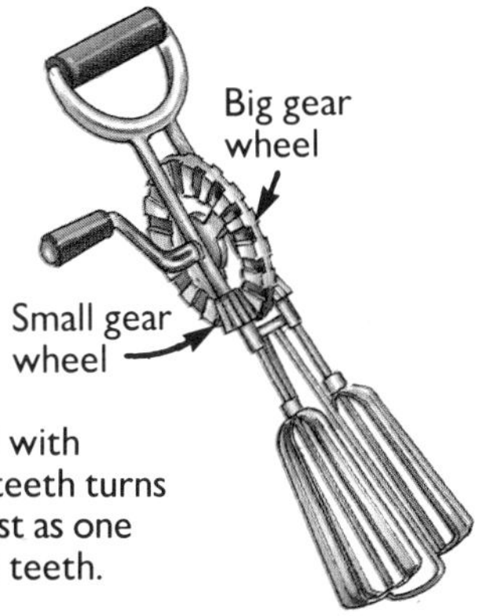

Big gear wheel
Small gear wheel

Gears are toothed wheels. They are used to change speed. When one wheel, the drive wheel, goes round, it turns the one next to it. The drive wheel can make a smaller wheel turn faster, or a larger wheel turn slower.

You can see this with a whisk. The big gear wheel turns when you turn the handle. This makes the small wheel and the whisk connected to it spin much faster than you could turn them by hand.

Engines

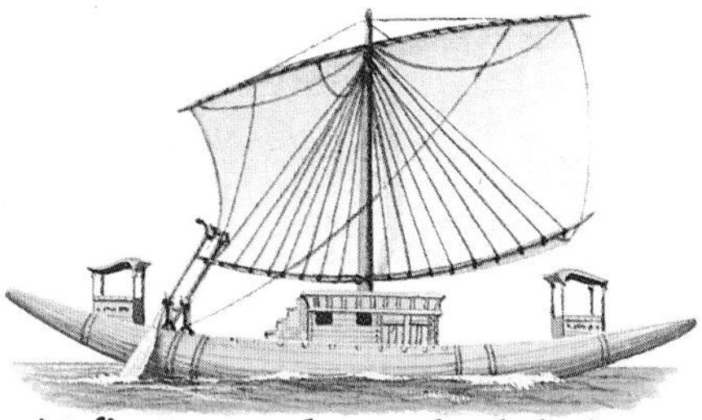

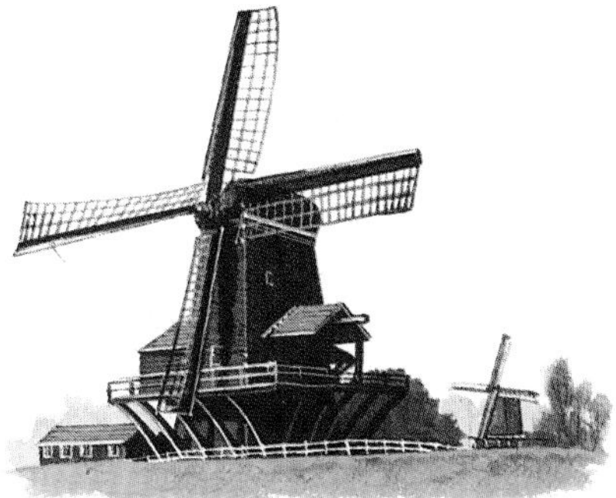

At first, people worked their simple machines by hand or with the help of animals. Then they learned to use the power of wind to push their sailing-boats along. They also used the wind to turn sails to grind grain into flour.

Later, they used the power of moving water in rivers to turn water-wheels. These pumped water or worked machinery.

Steam engines

1. Coal or wood is burned to heat water. The water is boiled and changes into a gas, called **steam**.

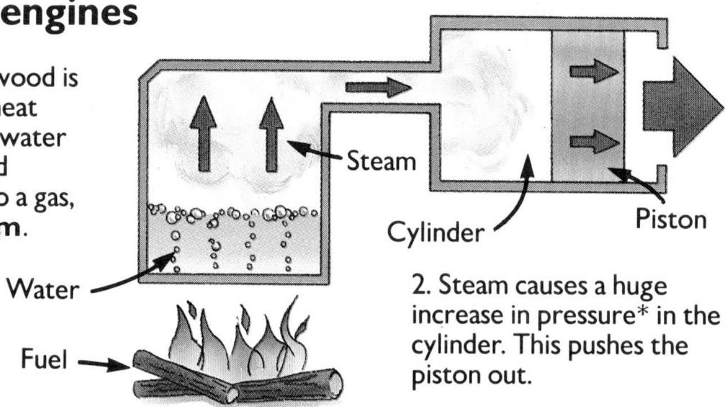

Steam
Cylinder
Piston
Water
Fuel

2. Steam causes a huge increase in pressure* in the cylinder. This pushes the piston out.

3. Steam takes up about 1,700 times more space than the water it comes from.

The first engine invented to work a machine was a **steam engine**. Steam engines change the heat from burning fuel into movement.

The steam age

The steam engine was invented in 1777. Steam power was soon used to work many machines, and people moved into towns to work in new factories. The time when this was happening is called the **Industrial Revolution**.

Steam locomotives

Later, steam engines were fitted on to wheeled carriages that ran on rails. These were called **steam locomotives**.

The first passenger railway opened in 1825 in Britain. Just 100 years later, railways had spread all over the world.

Steam turbines

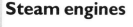

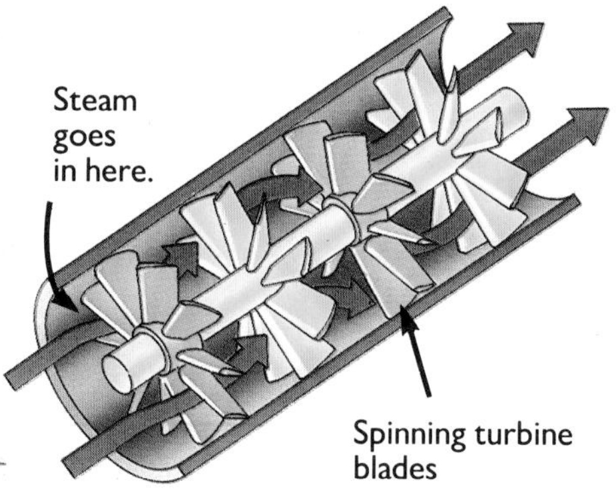

Steam goes in here.
Spinning turbine blades

Today, steam power is used in power stations*. Steam pushes the blades of a turbine around, producing electricity.

 *Power stations, 102; Pressure, 40.

Cars

Until the steam engine was invented, people rarely travelled far. They either rode on horse-back or in a horse-drawn carriage.

The first car, built in 1769, had a steam engine. Steam cars were slow and dirty. Their engines were large and heavy, and they carried a lot of fuel.

The first successful cars were built in Germany by Daimler and Benz in 1885-86. They used a new type of engine, called an **internal combustion engine**.

Internal combustion engines

Nikolaus Otto built the first **internal combustion engine** in 1876. It was smaller than a steam engine. It used a new fuel, **petrol**, which was light and easy to carry.

> **DID YOU KNOW?**
>
> 
>
> There are about 300 million cars in the world today. That is one car for every 15 people. Every year, about 30 million cars are made.

How does a car work?

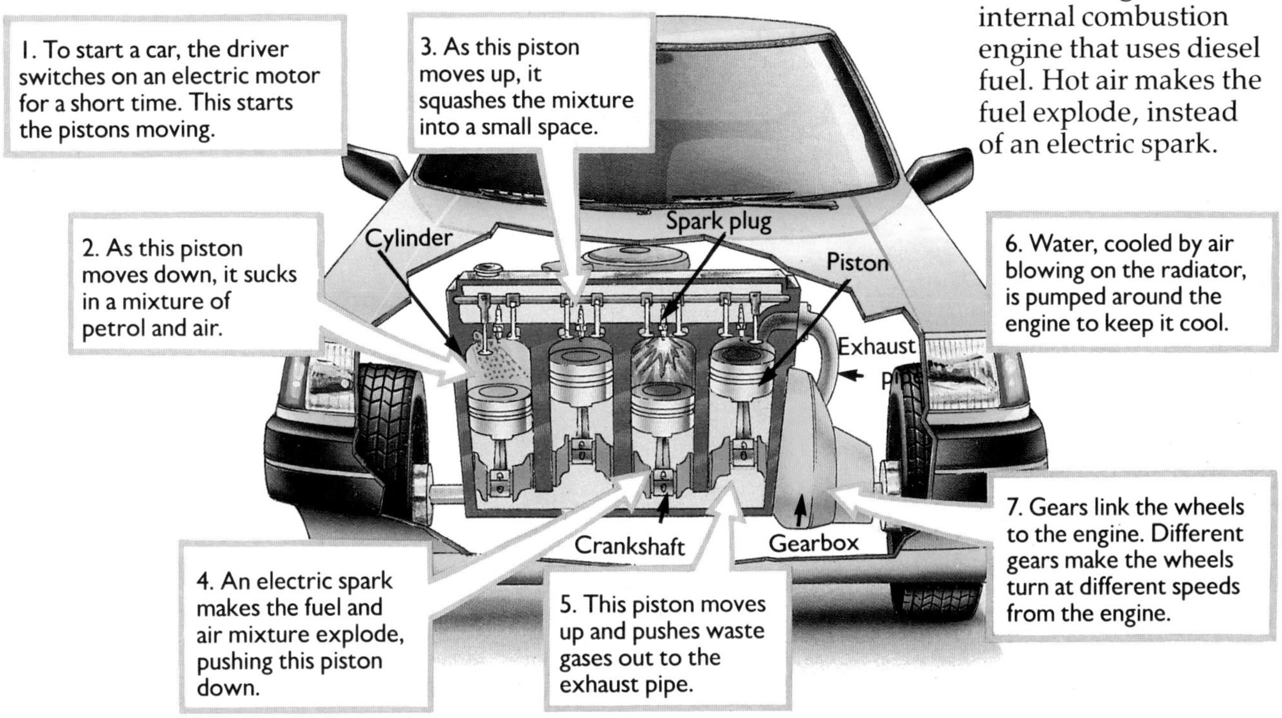
1. To start a car, the driver switches on an electric motor for a short time. This starts the pistons moving.
2. As this piston moves down, it sucks in a mixture of petrol and air.
3. As this piston moves up, it squashes the mixture into a small space.
4. An electric spark makes the fuel and air mixture explode, pushing this piston down.
5. This piston moves up and pushes waste gases out to the exhaust pipe.
6. Water, cooled by air blowing on the radiator, is pumped around the engine to keep it cool.
7. Gears link the wheels to the engine. Different gears make the wheels turn at different speeds from the engine.
Cylinder
Spark plug
Piston
Exhaust
Crankshaft
Gearbox

A **diesel engine** is an internal combustion engine that uses diesel fuel. Hot air makes the fuel explode, instead of an electric spark.

The mixture of petrol and air is exploded inside **cylinders**. This is what makes the pistons move up and down.

The **crankshaft** turns the up and down movement into a round and round movement, which turns the wheels.

Most engines are **four-stroke engines**. This means that, at any one time, each cylinder does one of the four jobs shown above.

Things that fly

Hot-air balloons are able to fly because they can float* up in the air. Aeroplanes are too heavy to float in air. They fly because they have wings. Their wings provide a force, called lift, that holds them up.

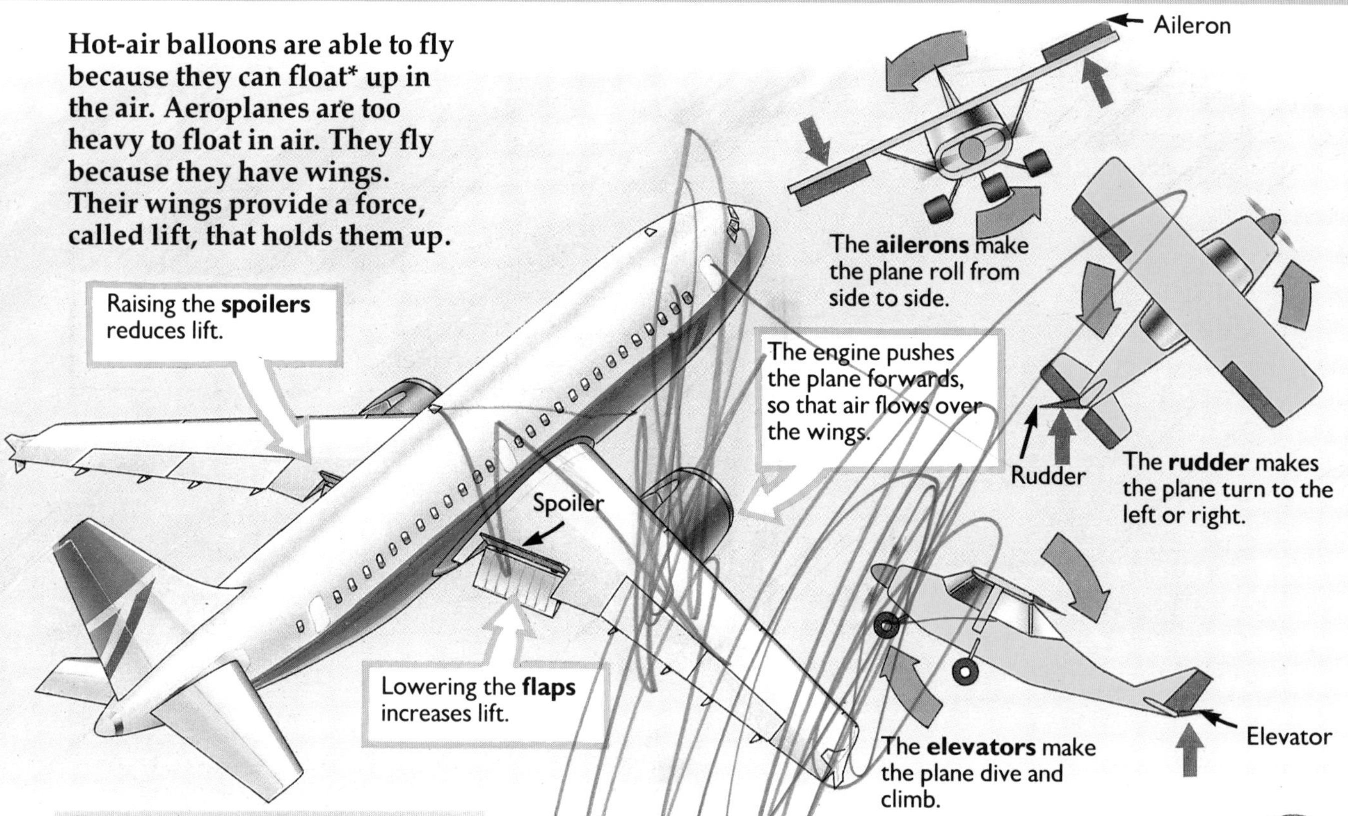

Raising the **spoilers** reduces lift.
Spoiler
Lowering the **flaps** increases lift.
The engine pushes the plane forwards, so that air flows over the wings.
Aileron
The **ailerons** make the plane roll from side to side.
Rudder
The **rudder** makes the plane turn to the left or right.
Elevator
The **elevators** make the plane dive and climb.

How do wings work?

To see how wings work, blow hard over a strip of paper, and watch the paper rise.

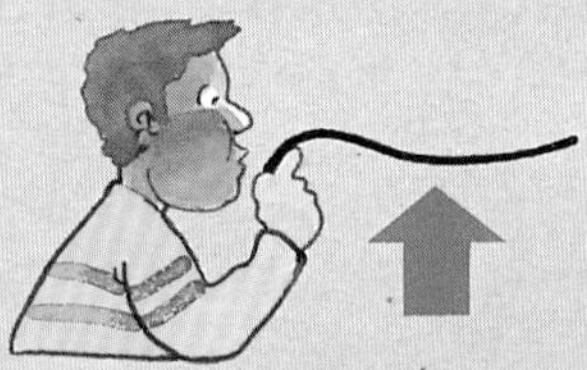

The faster air flows, the lower its pressure*. So as you blow, the pressure under the paper becomes greater than above it. This pushes the paper up.

The force pushing the wing up is called **lift**.

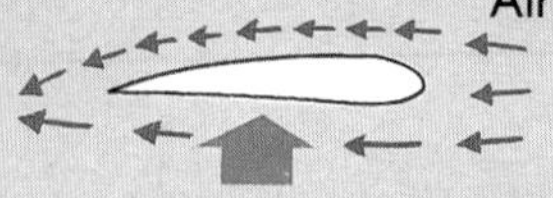

Airflow

The shape of a wing is called an **aerofoil**. It is designed so air flows faster over the top of it. This lifts the plane up.

Jet engines

Most new aeroplanes that are built today have **jet engines**. To see how they work, blow up a balloon and let it go. Air rushing out pushes the balloon forwards.

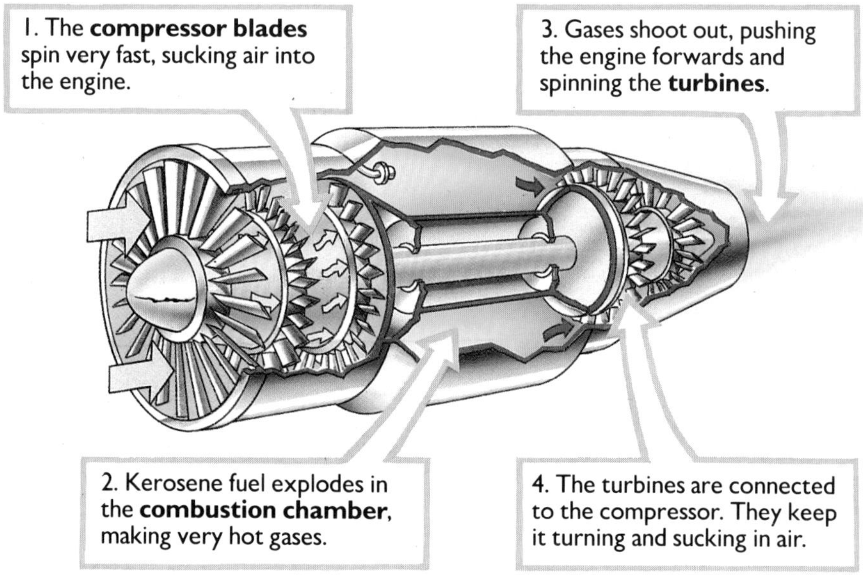

1. The **compressor blades** spin very fast, sucking air into the engine.
2. Kerosene fuel explodes in the **combustion chamber**, making very hot gases.
3. Gases shoot out, pushing the engine forwards and spinning the **turbines**.
4. The turbines are connected to the compressor. They keep it turning and sucking in air.

 Floating, 38; Pressure, 40.

Helicopters

Helicopters have rotor blades instead of wings. The blades are shaped like aerofoils. When the blades spin, the helicopter takes off.

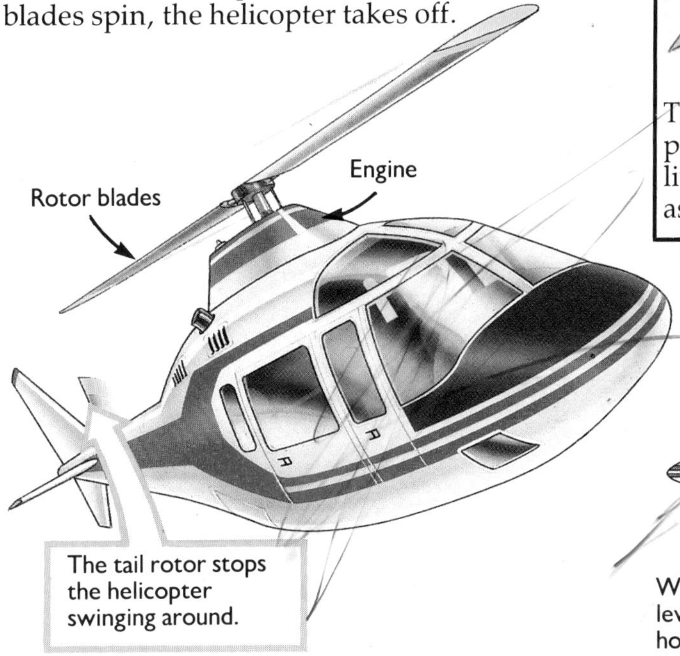
Rotor blades
Engine
The tail rotor stops the helicopter swinging around.

DID YOU KNOW?

The largest flying animal ever was a prehistoric reptile, *Quetsalcoatlus northropi*, that lived 65 million years ago. It had a wingspan as wide as a two-seater plane.

When the rotor blades are level, the helicopter can hover, or fly straight up and down.

Tilting the rotor blades makes the helicopter move backwards, forwards or sideways.

Flying through time

1. The first machine to carry people up in the air was a balloon. It was built by the Montgolfier brothers and first flew in Paris in 1783.

2. Over the next hundred years, people tried to make other kinds of machines fly.

3. In 1903, the first aeroplane flew, for only 12 seconds. It had a propeller fitted to a petrol engine and was made by Orville and Wilbur Wright.

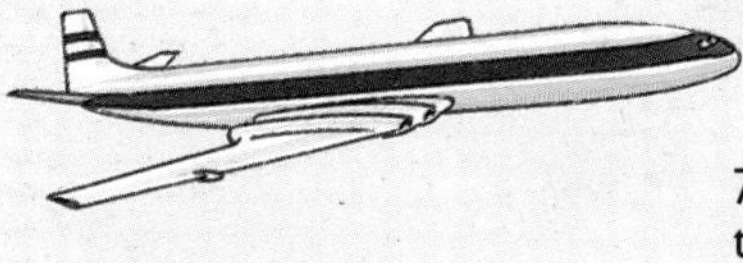

4. In 1919, John Alcock and Arthur Whitten Brown made the first non-stop flight across the Atlantic Ocean.

5. In 1939, Igor Sikorsky designed and made the first helicopter that worked with a single rotor.

6. The De Havilland Comet was the world's first jet airliner. It made its first flight in 1949.

7. In 1969, Concorde was the first passenger plane to fly faster than sound*.

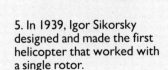

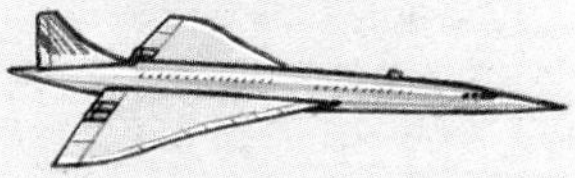

*Sound, 64.

Space

Spacecraft are launched into Space by very powerful rocket engines. A rocket engine is the only kind of engine strong enough to push through Earth's gravity.

Rockets and rocket engines

Rocket engines work in the same sort of way as jet engines*. They move forward by pushing out a powerful stream of gases made by burning fuel.

Nothing burns without oxygen. As there is no oxygen in Space, rockets carry their own supply. They use liquid oxygen or an **oxidant**, which is a chemical containing oxygen, to burn fuel.

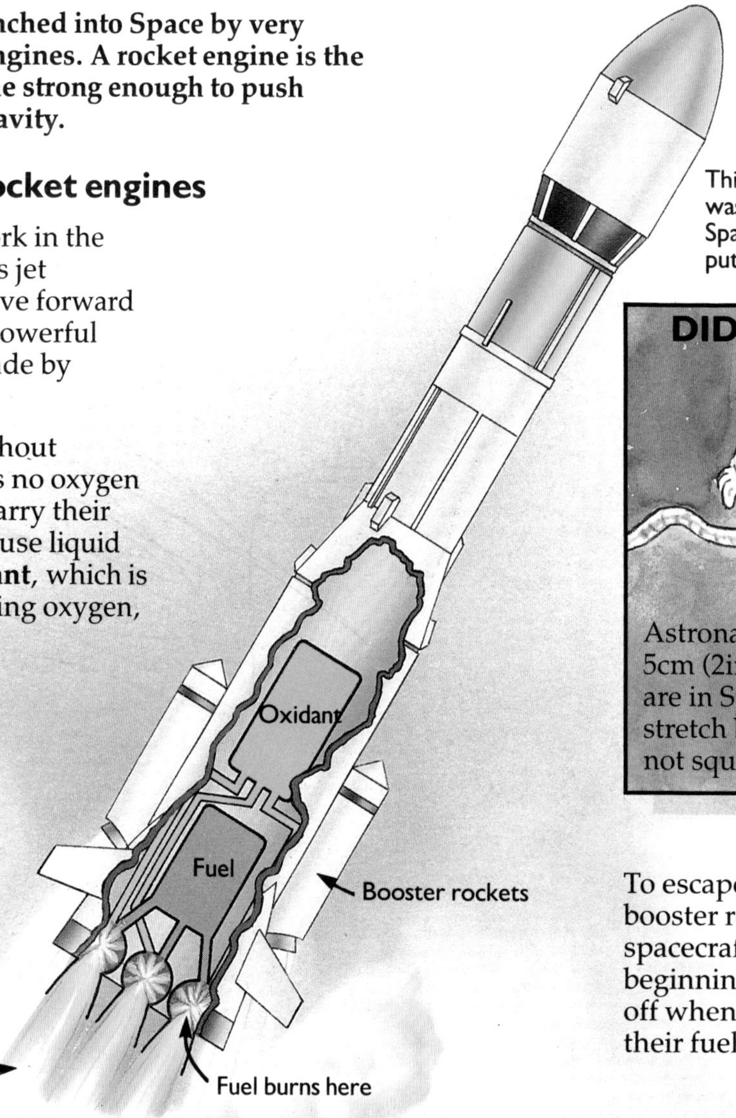
Oxidant
Fuel
Booster rockets
Hot gases rush out, pushing the rocket forwards.
Fuel burns here

This rocket is called Ariane. It was built by the European Space Agency and is used to put satellites into orbit.

DID YOU KNOW?

Astronauts can become about 5cm (2in) taller while they are in Space. Their spines stretch because gravity does not squash them down.

To escape the pull of gravity, booster rocket engines give the spacecraft an extra push at the beginning of a flight. They fall off when they have used up all their fuel.

Space milestones

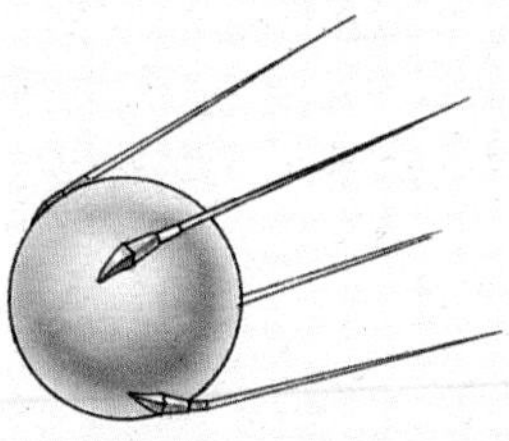

1957. Sputnik 1 (USSR) was the first spacecraft to orbit the Earth. It was a simple satellite. *Sputnik* means "little traveller".

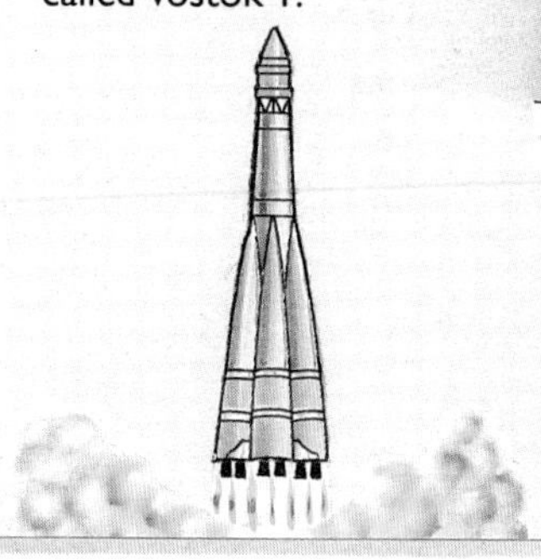

1961. Yuri Gagarin (USSR) was the first man in Space. He orbited the Earth for 108 minutes in a spacecraft called Vostok 1.

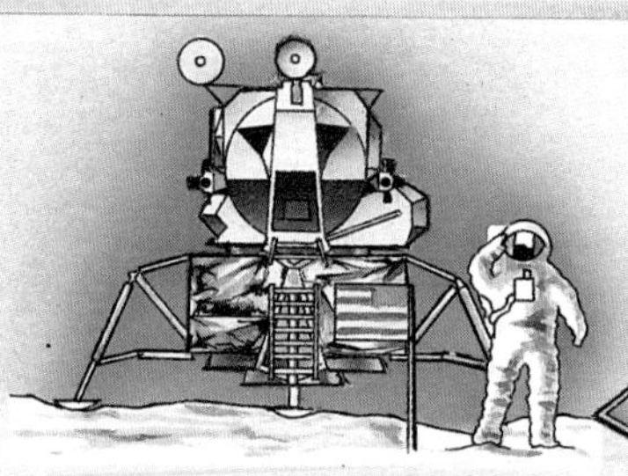

1969. Apollo 11 (USA) landed the first men on the Moon, the astronauts Edwin Aldrin and Neil Armstrong. Their first Moon walk lasted 2½ hours. They collected Moon rock and soil samples to study on Earth.

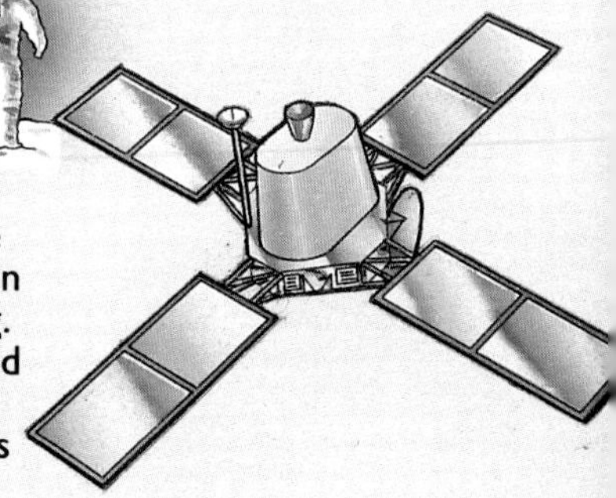

1976. Viking 1 (USA), an unmanned space probe, went to Mars. It tested soil samples and sent pictures back to Earth.

 Jet engines, 46.

What is space like?

People have only travelled as far as our Moon. But unmanned spacecraft, called **probes**, have explored further into Space.

There is no air in Space. Something that is completely empty is called a **vacuum**. On Earth, things may look empty, but they are really full of air.

Spacecraft only need to use their engines to change speed or direction, because in a vacuum there is no air resistance* to slow them down.

A spacesuit protects the astronaut. Liquid pumped through it keeps the temperature steady. The pressure* inside the suit is kept the same as on Earth.

Astronauts carry their own supply of oxygen to breathe.

Sound needs something to travel through. Because Space is a vacuum, astronauts use radios to talk to each other.

Without an atmosphere to absorb temperature changes, it is hotter than an oven when you face the Sun, and colder than a freezer in the shade.

A spacecraft does not use its engines to keep in its orbit. It is kept moving because of Earth's gravity. The Earth's gravity pulls the spacecraft and the astronauts equally. But there is no force pulling the astronauts to the spacecraft, so they float about in it and feel weightless.

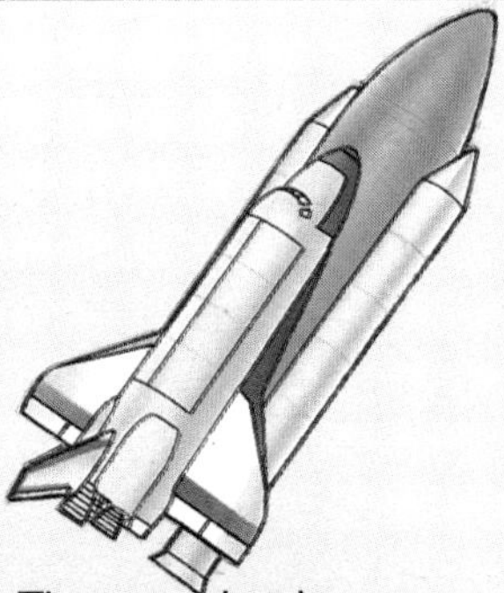

81. The space shuttle ılumbia (USA) was nched. It was the first ıcecraft that could be ed again.

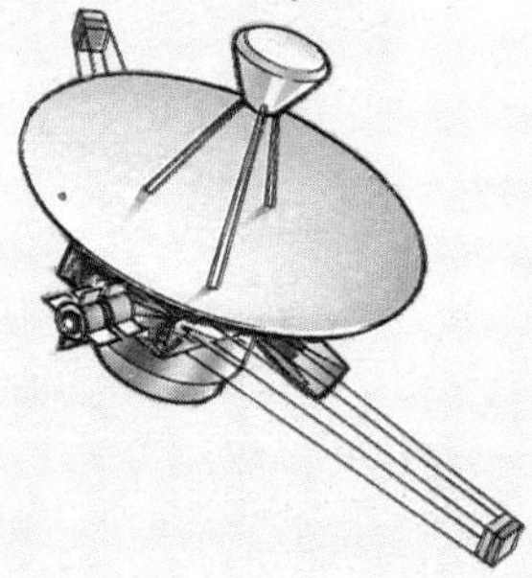

1987. Pioneer 10 (USA) passed Pluto, the furthest planet from the Sun. It is the first man-made object to leave our Solar System.

A light year

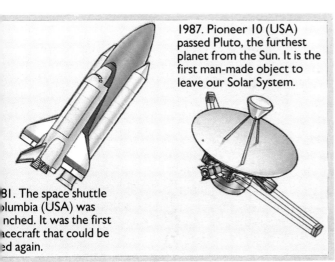

Our nearest star is 4½ light years away. Its light takes 4½ years to reach Earth.

The distances between stars are so large that a unit of length called a **light year** is used. A light year is the distance that light travels in one year, which is about 10 million million km (6 million million miles).

*Air resistance, 31; Pressure, 40.

Light and dark

Light is a form of energy. Things that give out light of their own are called luminous. The Sun, electric light bulbs, candles and televisions are all luminous objects.

Things that do not give out light are lit up by luminous objects. The Earth's biggest source of light is the Sun. All living things on Earth depend on the energy from sunlight.

Light is the fastest thing in the Universe.

Light rays

Light travels in straight lines called **rays**. You can see this when you look at sunlight pouring in through a window or at the beam of a torch.

Light from the Sun takes about eight minutes to travel to the Earth.

Light travels 300,000km (186,500 miles) a second, which is two million times faster than a bullet.

Shadows

Things which light cannot pass through are called **opaque**. Most things are opaque. Shadows are formed on the other side of opaque objects, where light cannot reach.

Things which light can pass through, like glass, are called **transparent**.

Things which only a little light can pass through, like dark glasses, are called **translucent**.

Light and dark shadows

There are different types of shadow. Dark shadow, called **umbra**, is formed where no light reaches. When some light gets through, the shadow looks grey and is called **penumbra**.

Shadows change depending on the size of the light source.

A small source of light casts a very dark shadow with sharp edges.

A large source of light makes a shadow which is dark in the centre, and lighter round the outside.

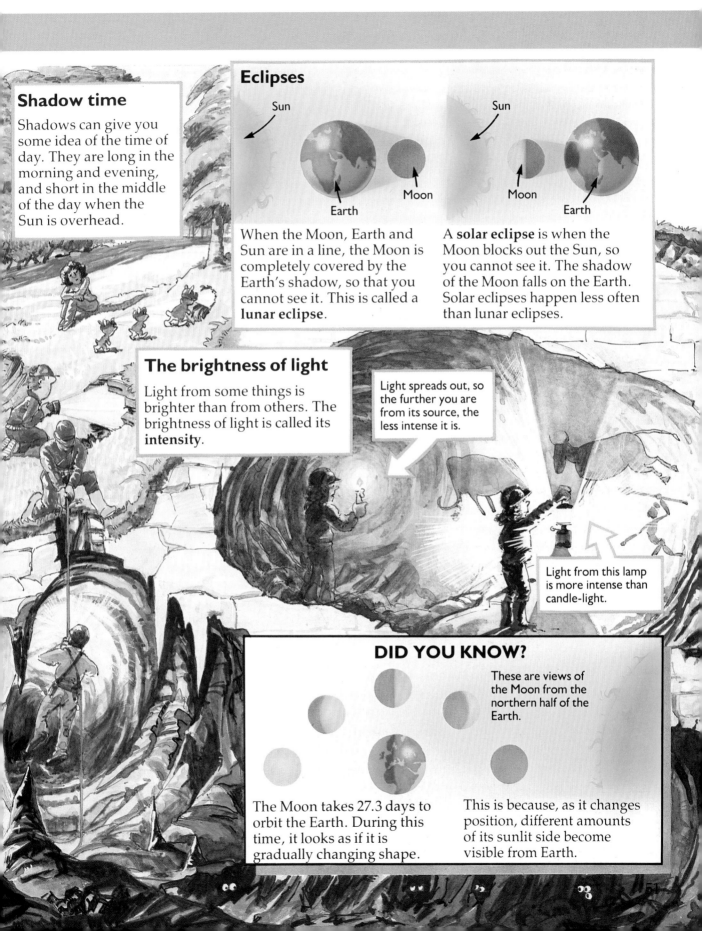

Shadow time

Shadows can give you some idea of the time of day. They are long in the morning and evening, and short in the middle of the day when the Sun is overhead.

Eclipses

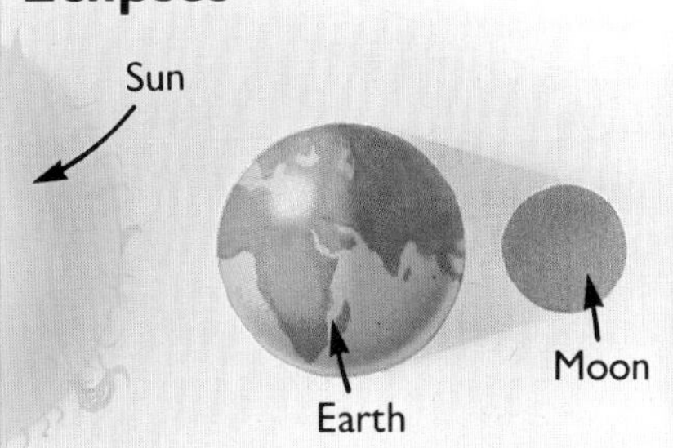
Sun
Earth
Moon

When the Moon, Earth and Sun are in a line, the Moon is completely covered by the Earth's shadow, so that you cannot see it. This is called a **lunar eclipse**.

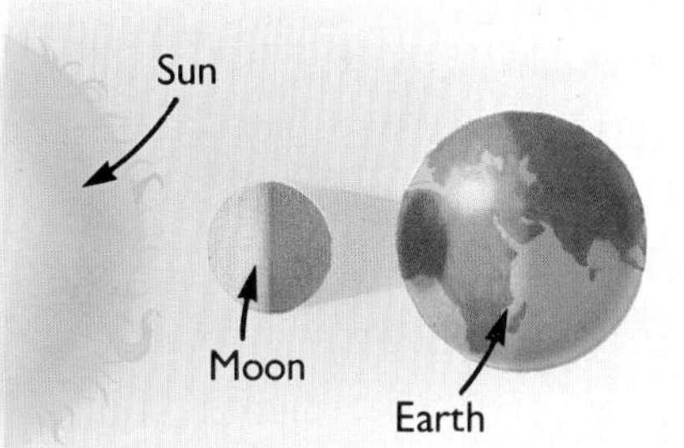
Sun
Moon
Earth

A **solar eclipse** is when the Moon blocks out the Sun, so you cannot see it. The shadow of the Moon falls on the Earth. Solar eclipses happen less often than lunar eclipses.

The brightness of light

Light from some things is brighter than from others. The brightness of light is called its **intensity**.

Light spreads out, so the further you are from its source, the less intense it is.

Light from this lamp is more intense than candle-light.

DID YOU KNOW?

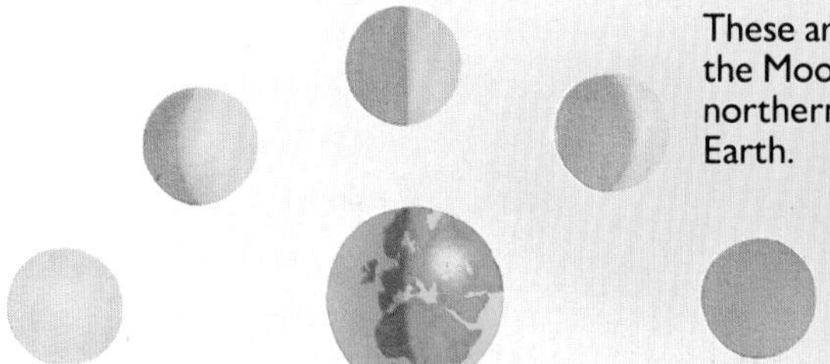

These are views of the Moon from the northern half of the Earth.

The Moon takes 27.3 days to orbit the Earth. During this time, it looks as if it is gradually changing shape.

This is because, as it changes position, different amounts of its sunlit side become visible from Earth.

Bouncing light

A light bulb lights up a whole room because light from it bounces off everything in the room. In the same way, light from the Sun bounces off everything. Days are light because sunlight is bounced in all directions, or scattered, off tiny pieces of dust in the atmosphere. Things that give out light, like the Sun, are called luminous. Most things are not luminous. You only see them because light bounces, or is reflected, off them.

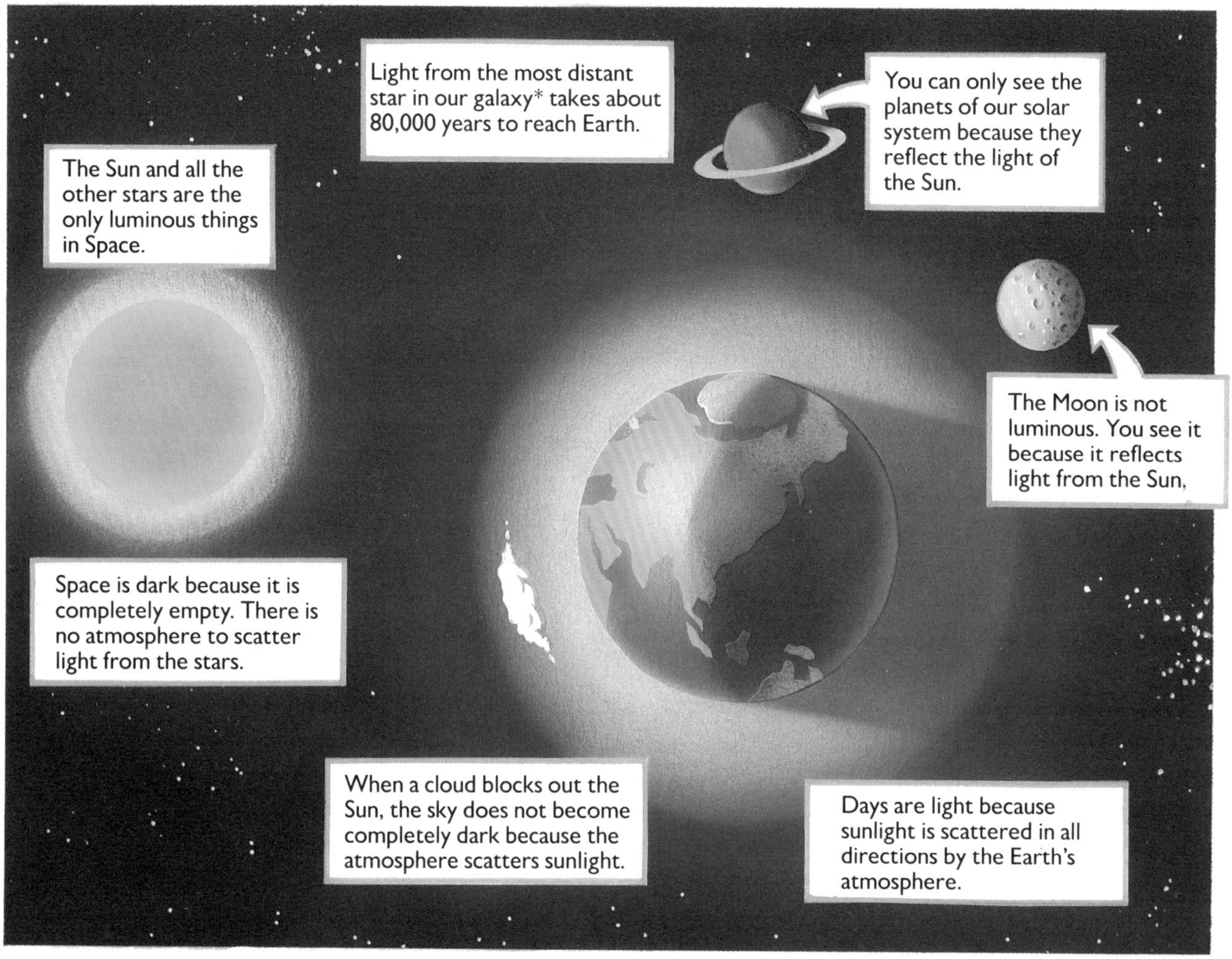
Light from the most distant star in our galaxy* takes about 80,000 years to reach Earth.
You can only see the planets of our solar system because they reflect the light of the Sun.
The Sun and all the other stars are the only luminous things in Space.
The Moon is not luminous. You see it because it reflects light from the Sun.
Space is dark because it is completely empty. There is no atmosphere to scatter light from the stars.
When a cloud blocks out the Sun, the sky does not become completely dark because the atmosphere scatters sunlight.
Days are light because sunlight is scattered in all directions by the Earth's atmosphere.

Scattering light

You can see how the atmosphere scatters light when you are in a cinema. You see the beam from the projector because dust in the air reflects the light.

DID YOU KNOW?

In 1969, the exact distance from the Earth to the Moon was worked out from the time light took to travel there and back. Light from lasers* on Earth was reflected from a mirror that astronauts placed on the Moon.

 **Galaxy, 22; Lasers, 109.*

How light bounces

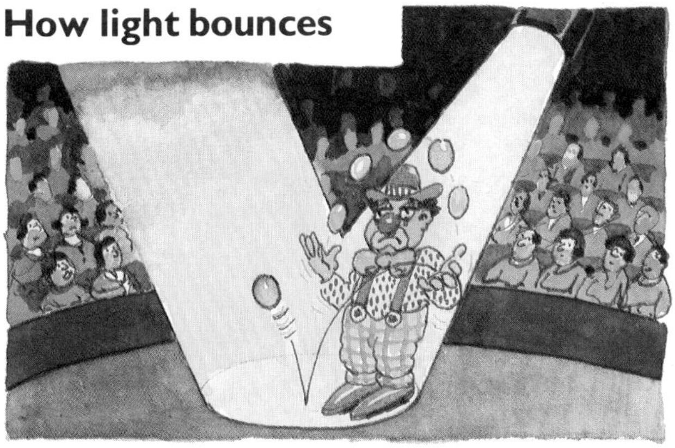

Light bounces just like a ball. When it hits a surface straight on, it bounces straight back. When it hits a surface at an angle, it bounces off at the same angle.

Rough and smooth

When light hits smooth surfaces, it is all reflected in one direction. When light hits rough surfaces, it bounces off in lots of different directions.

White reflects light, so it shows up better than black.

Like heat radiation*, light is reflected off some things better than others. White surfaces reflect more light than they absorb. Black surfaces absorb more light than they reflect.

Mirrors

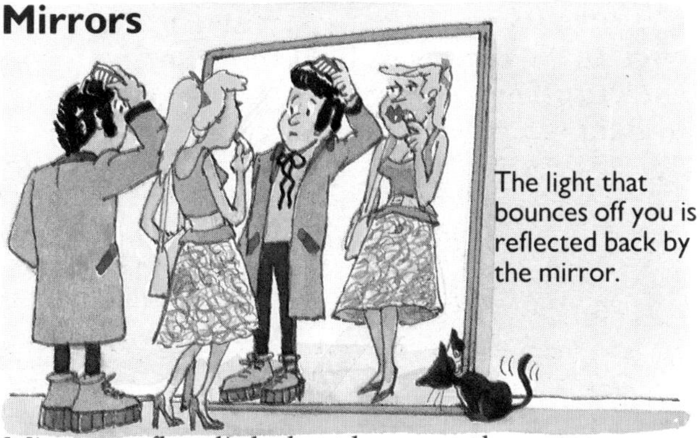

The light that bounces off you is reflected back by the mirror.

Mirrors reflect light best because they are very smooth and shiny. The reflection you see is not the same as you. When you wave your right hand, your reflection waves its left hand. A reflection is the wrong way round.

Mirror writing

Look at writing in a mirror. The mirror turns all the letters the wrong way round so you cannot read them. You can put the mirror writing in this picture back the right way round if you look at it through a mirror.

Seeing with mirrors

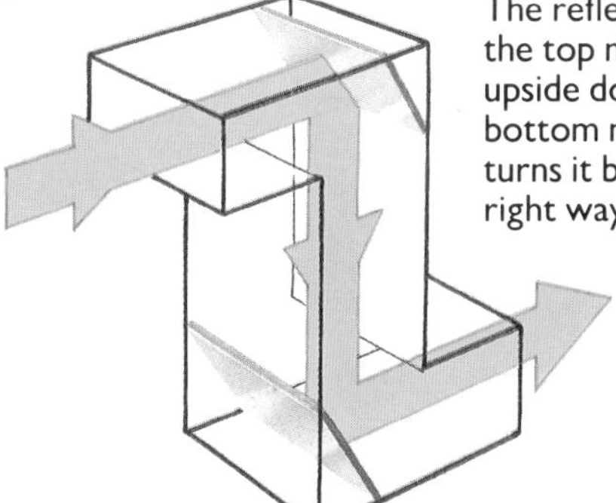

The reflection in the top mirror is upside down. The bottom mirror turns it back the right way up.

The crew of a submarine can look out from under the sea using a **periscope**. This is a long tube with two mirrors, one at each end.

*Heat radiation, 19.

Mirrors and pictures

Mirrors that bulge out

A curved mirror makes things look different. A mirror that bulges outwards is called a **convex mirror**.

Convex mirrors give a wide view. Car door mirrors are convex, to give drivers a wide view of what is behind them.

Mirrors that bulge in

A mirror that bulges inwards is called a **concave mirror**. How you look in one depends on how close you are to it.

From close up, your reflection looks larger, or is **magnified**. Further away, your reflection looks small and is upside down.

Curved mirrors

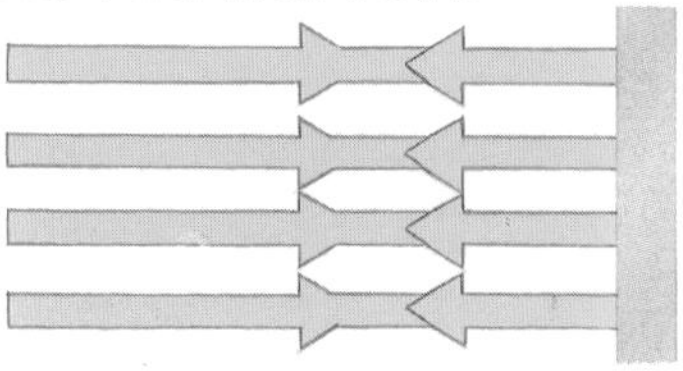

When light hits a flat mirror straight on, it all bounces straight back.

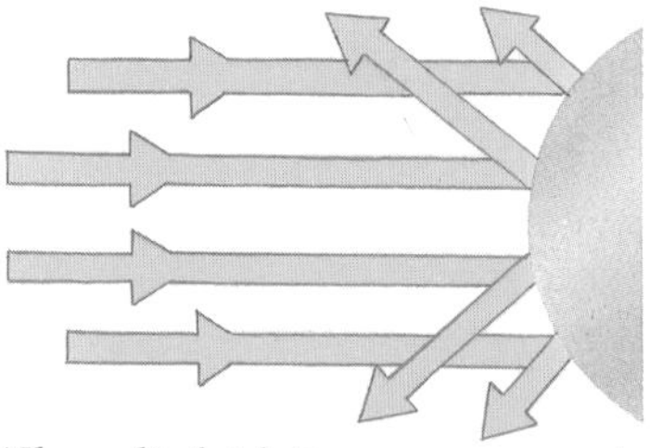

When light hits a convex mirror straight on, it bounces off at a wide angle.

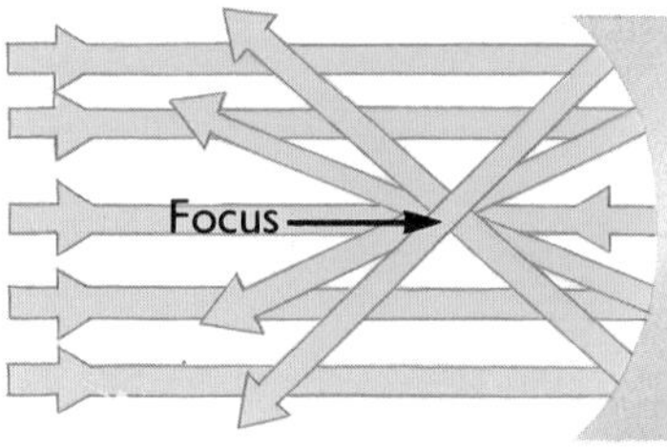

When light hits a concave mirror straight on, it bounces inwards and meets at a point called the **focus**.

Reflector telescopes

Concave mirrors are used in some telescopes. The biggest in the world is on Mount Semirodriki, Russia. Its mirror is 6m (19.7ft) across. You could use this telescope to see candlelight 24,000km (15,000 miles) away.

Heating with mirrors

In Odeillo, France, a huge concave mirror is used to collect the Sun's rays. The rays bounce off and meet at the focus of the mirror, where the temperature is so high that the heat can be used to melt metals.

Seeing far away

If you look down a street, the people in the distance seem much smaller than the people near you. But you know that people do not become smaller as they walk away.

This means you can tell how far away something is by its size. Because things look smaller further away, the road seems to get narrower until it comes to a point in the distance.

Painting what you see

Painted in Egypt, about 3,500 years ago

Painted in Italy, about 650 years ago

The earliest pictures people painted looked flat. Later, people began to paint things as they saw them.

They painted far away things smaller than things that were close by. This feeling of distance is called **perspective**.

Picture trick

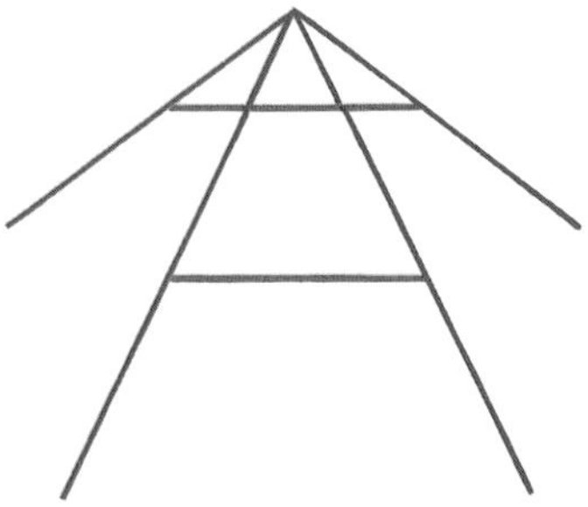

Your eyes can sometimes mislead you. Are both red lines the same length, or is the top one longer? (Answer on page 128.)

Bright lights

Light from a bulb spreads out, so that the light is less bright, or intense, further away. There are concave mirrors inside car headlamps to stop the rays of light spreading out. This keeps the beam of light very bright even a long way off.

DID YOU KNOW?

Mirrors can be used to signal for help in an emergency. On a clear day, a beam of sunlight can be reflected off a mirror and seen up to 40km (25 miles) away.

Bending light

Whenever light passes through one transparent thing into another, it is refracted.

You see things around you because light bounces off them. If you look at something in water, like an oar, it looks bent. This is because light is bent, or refracted, as it passes from water to air.

Make light bend

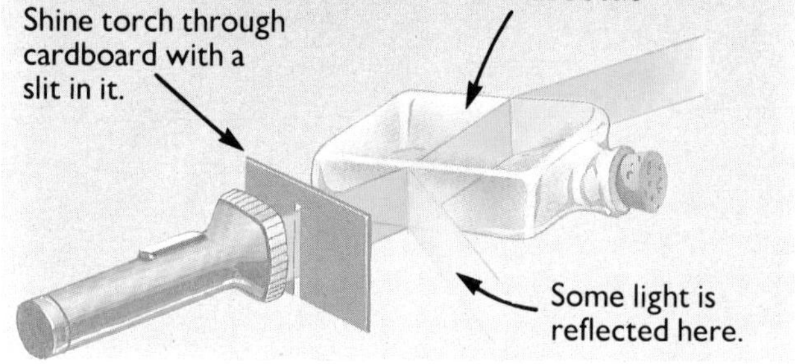

Flat bottle
Shine torch through cardboard with a slit in it.
Some light is reflected here.

Fill a bottle with water and a few drops of milk. In a dark room, shine a thin beam of light through it. The light is refracted by the water. When it passes from water to air on the other side, it bends back the other way.

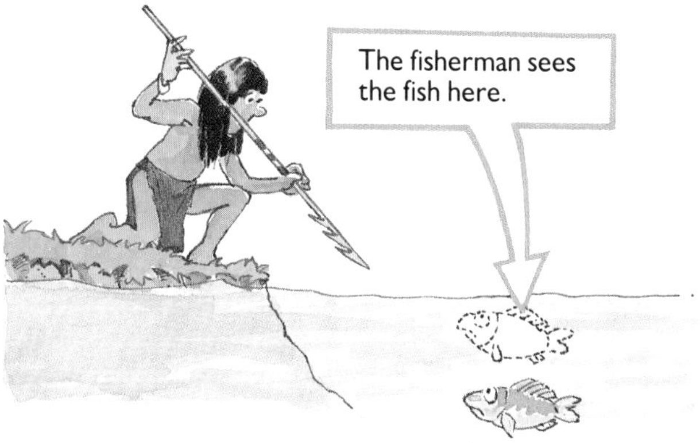

The fisherman sees the fish here.

Because light bends, you see things in water in a different place from where they really are. To catch fish with a spear, people aim below the place where they see the fish.

Refraction also makes water look less deep than it is.

Light bends because it travels at different speeds through different things. It travels faster through air than through water, but faster through water than through glass.

Inner reflections

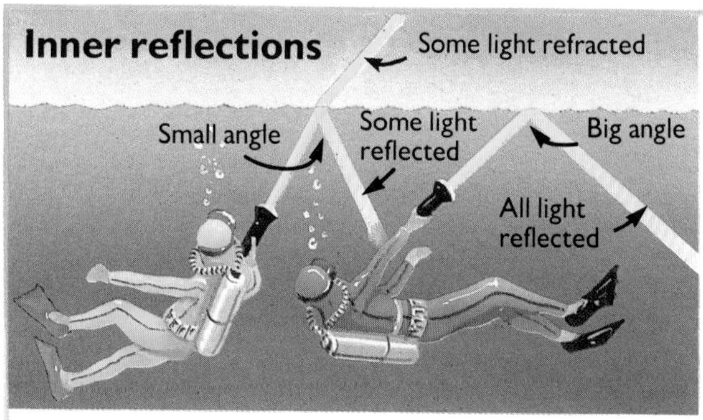

Some light refracted
Small angle
Some light reflected
Big angle
All light reflected

When light passes from water into air, some of it gets through and some is reflected. How much is reflected depends on the angle of the light rays. When all the light is reflected, this is called **total internal reflection**.

Pouring light

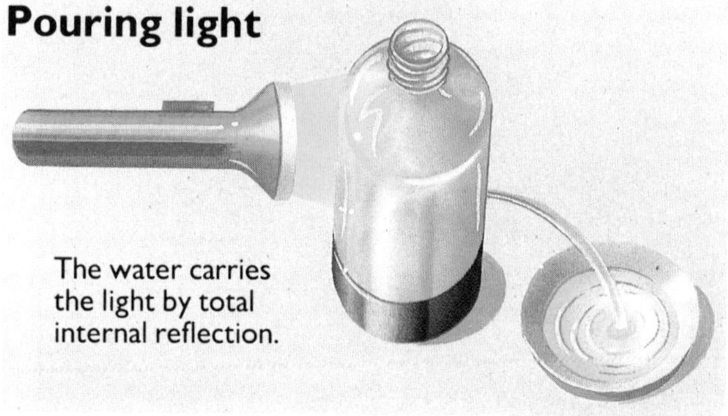

The water carries the light by total internal reflection.

Make a hole in a clear, plastic bottle. Holding your finger over the hole, fill the bottle with water. In a dark room, shine a torch from behind the hole and let the water pour out into a bowl. See how the water carries the light with it.

Lenses

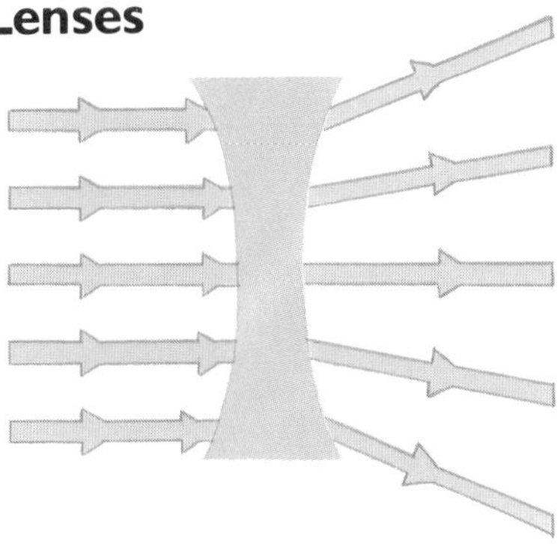

A **concave lens** is shaped to make light rays spread out. When you look through one, things look smaller.

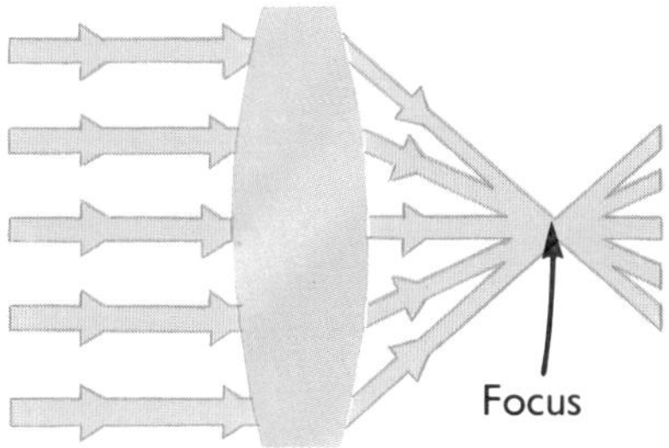
Focus

A **convex lens** is shaped to refract rays of light so they meet. When they hit the lens straight on, all the rays meet at a point called the **focus**.

Making an image

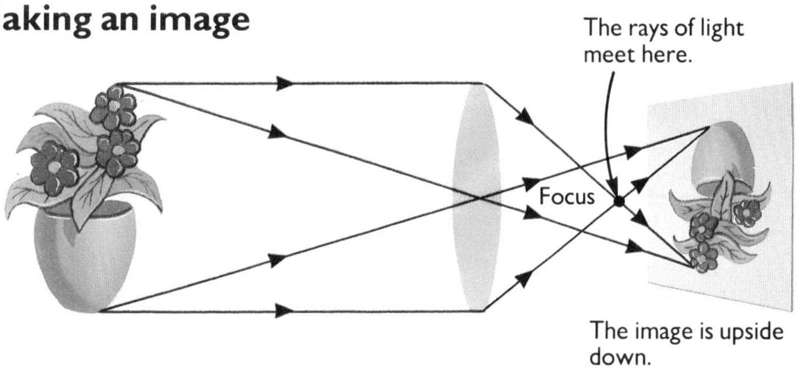
The rays of light meet here.
Focus
The image is upside down.

You can use a convex lens to make an image of something on a screen. The image looks sharp, or in focus, when the screen is at the place where all the rays of light meet. To find where the image is in focus, move the screen around.

Making things look bigger

A magnifying glass is a convex lens. When you hold it close to an object, it makes the object look bigger.

DID YOU KNOW?

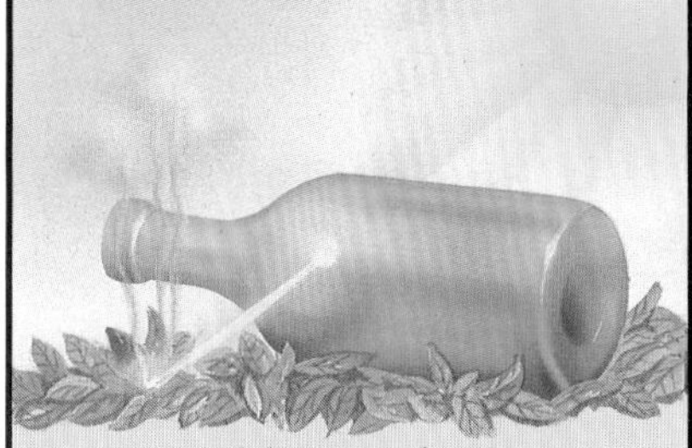

You should never leave bottles lying outside. They can act as lenses, focusing the Sun's rays on the ground, which could start a fire.

Optic fibres

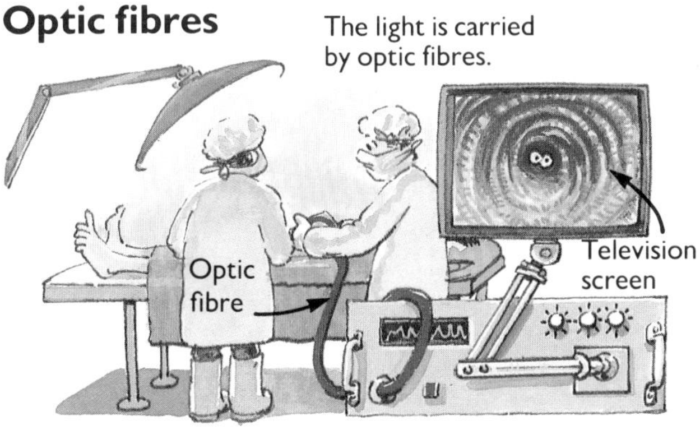
The light is carried by optic fibres.
Television screen
Optic fibre

In the same way as water in the last experiment, thin rods of glass are used to carry light by total internal reflection. These are called **optic fibres**. Doctors use them to look inside people.

Mirages

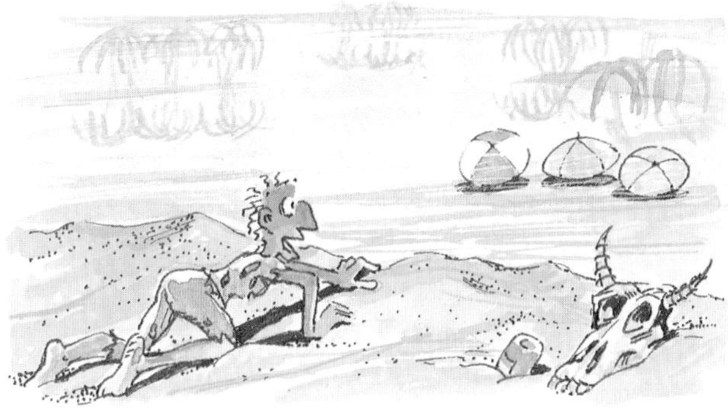

On a hot day, you may think you see water far away. This is a **mirage**. You see a mirage when light from the sky is totally internally reflected off a layer of hot air near the ground.

Seeing pictures

How do your eyes work?

The things around you give out light or reflect light that hits them. You see them when that light enters your eyes.

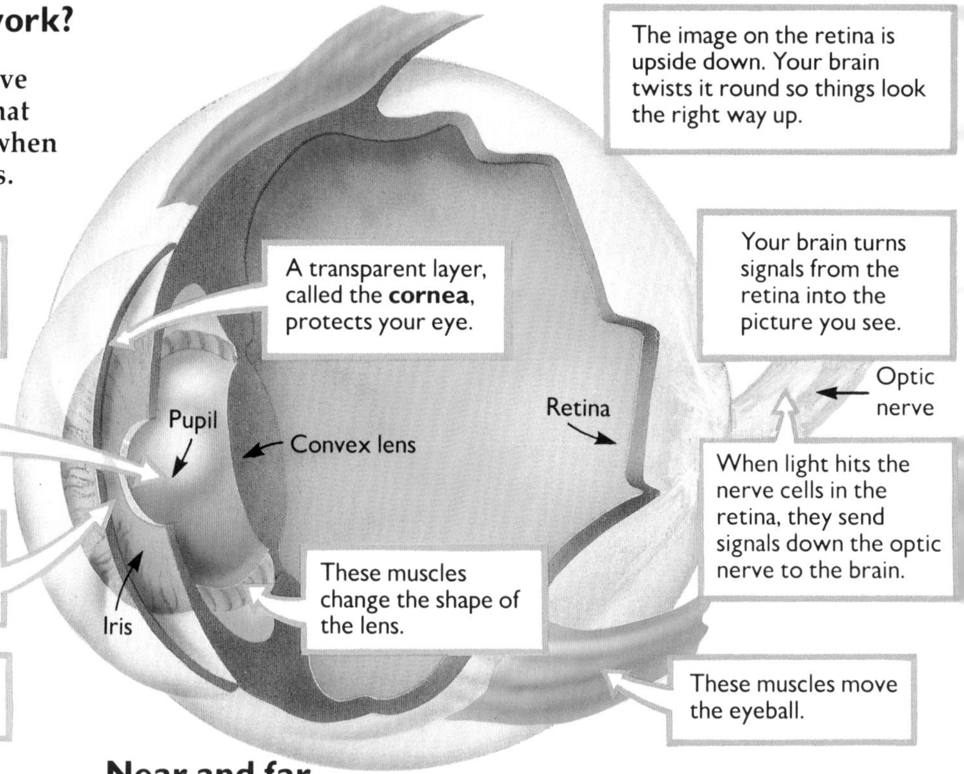

A convex lens in your eye makes an image on the **retina**, at the back of your eye.
A transparent layer, called the **cornea**, protects your eye.
Light enters the eye through a hole called the **pupil**.
The coloured part of your eye is called the **iris**.
The iris controls the size of the pupil.
Pupil
Convex lens
Iris
These muscles change the shape of the lens.
Retina
The image on the retina is upside down. Your brain twists it round so things look the right way up.
Your brain turns signals from the retina into the picture you see.
Optic nerve
When light hits the nerve cells in the retina, they send signals down the optic nerve to the brain.
These muscles move the eyeball.

Light and dark

The iris controls how much light gets into the eye. In the dark, the iris opens. This makes the pupil bigger to let in more light. In bright light, it closes up. Look in a mirror in a dark room and turn on a light. You can see your pupils change size.

Near and far

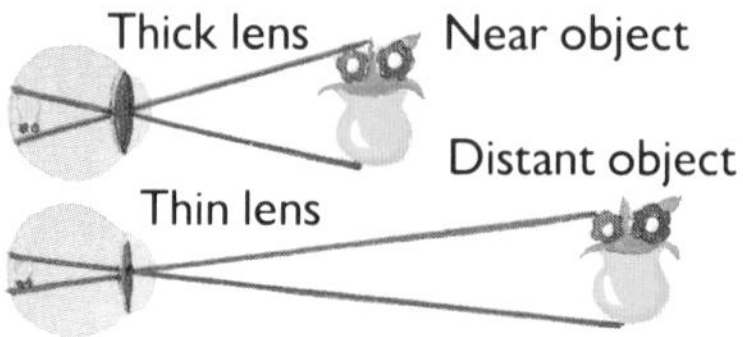

Thick lens
Near object
Distant object
Thin lens

The lenses in your eyes change shape when they focus on things that are near or far away.

Seeing clearly

Long-sighted people cannot focus on near things. Their glasses have convex lenses. Short-sighted people cannot focus on distant things. Their glasses have concave lenses.

Seeing with two eyes

Your eyes are a small distance apart so each sees a different view. This helps you see the shape of things and how far off they are. Most animals that hunt also have eyes facing forwards. They can judge distances well, but have a narrow view. Other animals have eyes facing sideways. They have a wide view to look out for hunters, but cannot judge distances well.

DID YOU KNOW?

An eagle's eyesight is better than any other animal's. Its eyesight is so good that it can see its prey from 3km (2 miles) away.

The camera

A camera works like an eye. Light comes in through a lens. The lens makes an image on film at the back of the camera.

A camera must only let in light when you take a picture.

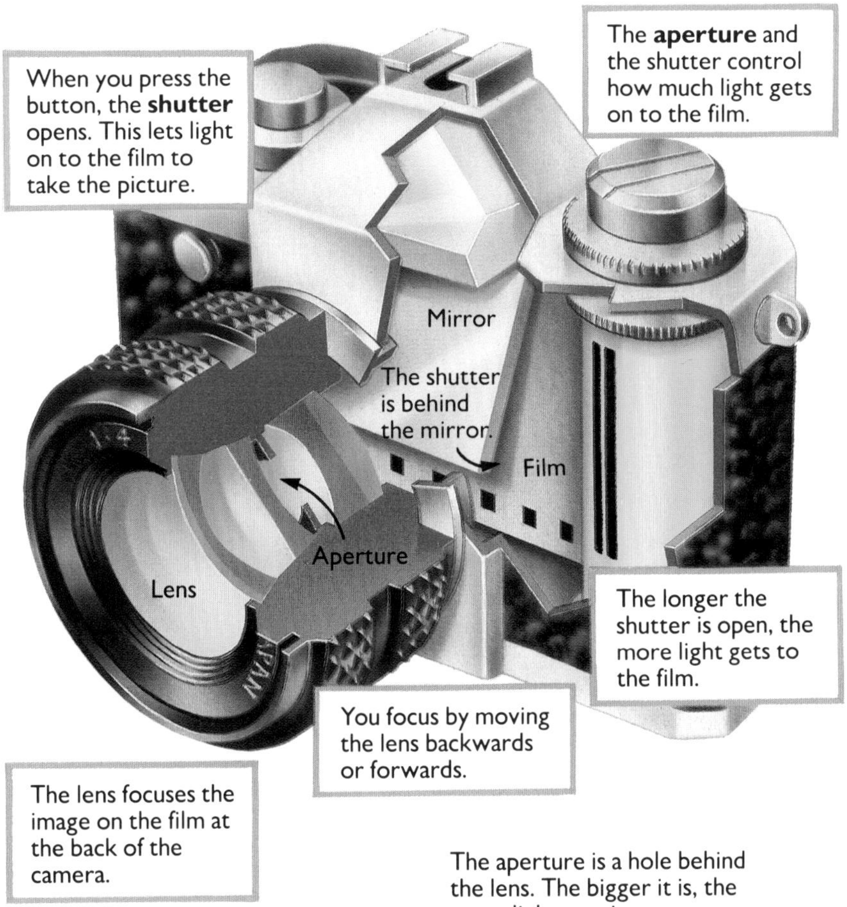

When you press the button, the **shutter** opens. This lets light on to the film to take the picture.
The **aperture** and the shutter control how much light gets on to the film.
Mirror
The shutter is behind the mirror.
Film
Aperture
Lens
The longer the shutter is open, the more light gets to the film.
You focus by moving the lens backwards or forwards.
The lens focuses the image on the film at the back of the camera.

The aperture is a hole behind the lens. The bigger it is, the more light gets in.

Different views

You can change lenses on some cameras. A **wide-angle lens** gives a wide view. A **telephoto lens** gives a close-up view so you can take pictures of something far away.

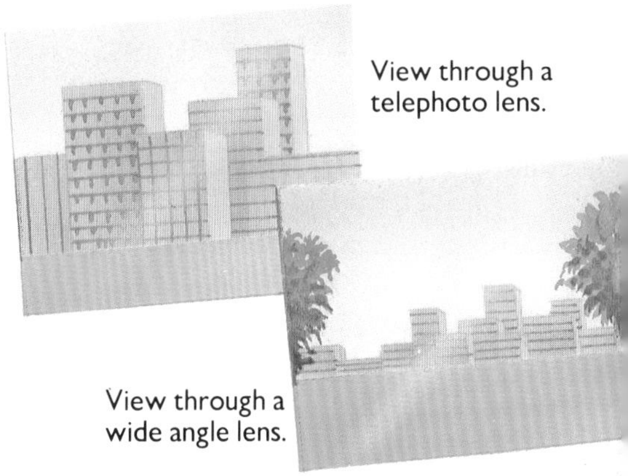

View through a telephoto lens.
View through a wide angle lens.

Moving pictures

Films are made of lots of pictures, or **frames**. The film looks as if it is moving because the frames move so quickly. So you see the next frame before the last one fades in your eye.

How a photograph is made

To take a photograph, you focus the lens of the camera and set the amount of light that goes in it. Automatic cameras are able do this for you.

Chemicals on the film change when light hits them. When you get the film developed, the picture appears on it. This is called a **negative**. On negatives, dark things look light and light things look dark. Light is shone through the negative to make a picture on special paper. This is the print you see.

Coloured light

About 300 years ago, Isaac Newton shone a beam of sunlight through a prism. He discovered that white light is made up of colours. Using a second prism, Newton found he could mix all the colours together to make white light again.

When light goes through a prism, it is bent, or refracted*, because the prism slows it down. White light is a mixture of colours. The colours travel at different speeds through the prism, so they are bent by different amounts.

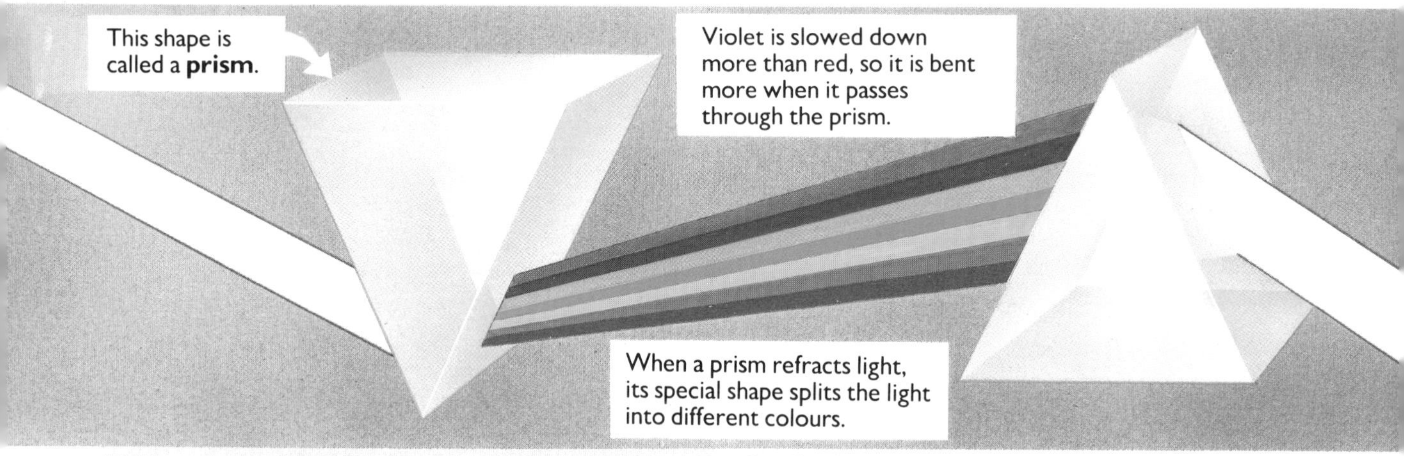
This shape is called a **prism**.
Violet is slowed down more than red, so it is bent more when it passes through the prism.
When a prism refracts light, its special shape splits the light into different colours.

What is a rainbow?

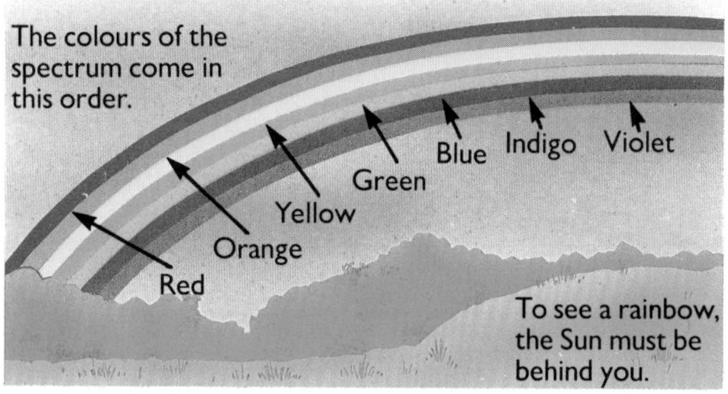
The colours of the spectrum come in this order.
Red
Orange
Yellow
Green
Blue
Indigo
Violet
To see a rainbow, the Sun must be behind you.

When the Sun comes out after a heavy shower, you sometimes see a rainbow. This is because the air is still full of tiny drops of rain. Each drop works like a tiny prism, splitting the light up into all its colours. The colours that make up white light are called the **spectrum**.

Splitting sunlight

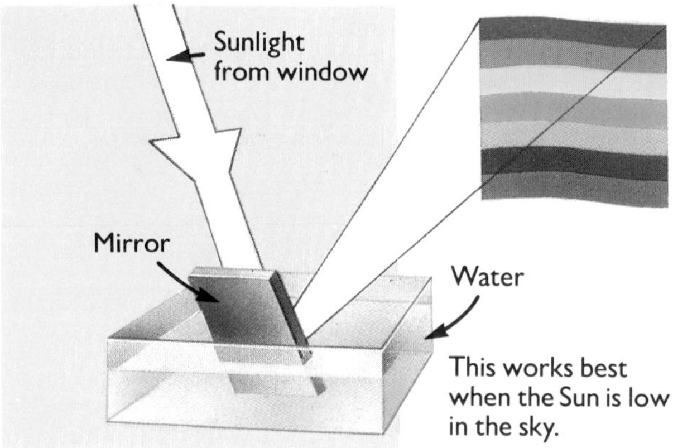
Sunlight from window
Mirror
Water
This works best when the Sun is low in the sky.

Hold a mirror at an angle in water. Bounce sunlight off it on to a wall. Move it around until you see a spectrum. The water works like a prism, splitting the light into its colours.

DID YOU KNOW?

Rattlesnakes can 'see' heat. They can find and catch their prey, even in the dark. They have pits near their eyes full of nerve cells that pick up infra-red radiation*.

Colours from diamonds

You can see the colours of the spectrum in a diamond. It is cut so that it reflects and refracts light, in the same way as a prism does.

Infra-red radiation, 18; Refraction, 56.

What makes colours different from each other?

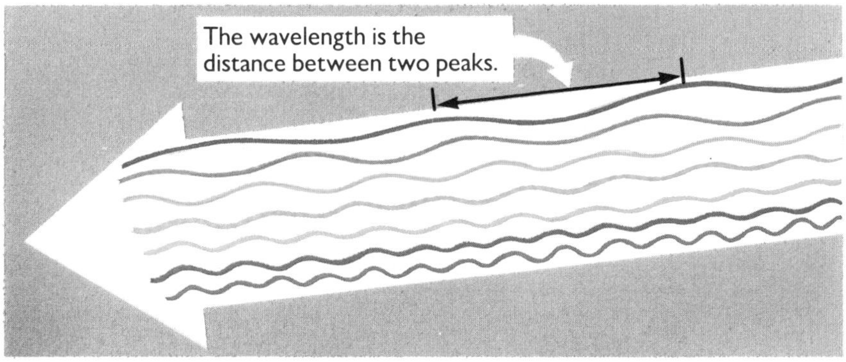
The wavelength is the distance between two peaks.

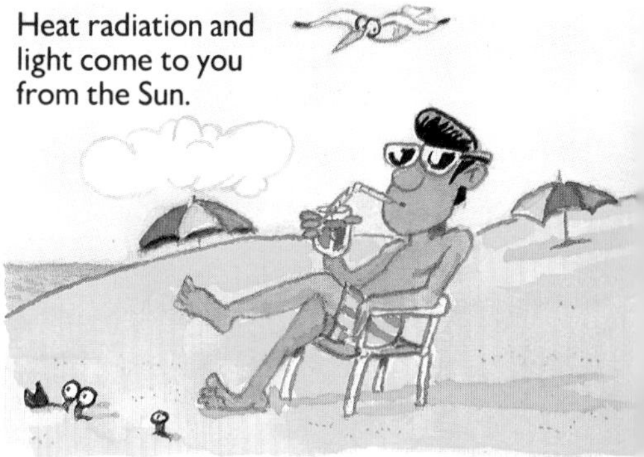
Heat radiation and light come to you from the Sun.

Light rays are made up of tiny waves, much too small to see. The size of the waves is measured by their **wavelength**.

Each colour has a different wavelength. The wavelength of red light is longer than the wavelength of violet light.

Heat radiation* and light are similar. They both travel in waves, but they have different wavelengths.

Why is the sky coloured?

Sun
Scattered red light
Scattered blue light
Earth

Sunlight is scattered by the Earth's atmosphere. Some of the colours in sunlight are scattered more than others. The atmosphere scatters blue light most, so during the day, the sky looks blue.

At sunset, sunlight goes through more atmosphere to get to you. The blue light is then scattered so much that you never see it. The sky looks red because you see the scattered red light.

Seeing colours

There are special nerve cells in your eyes for seeing colour. They only work well in bright light. This is why things look colourless in poor light.

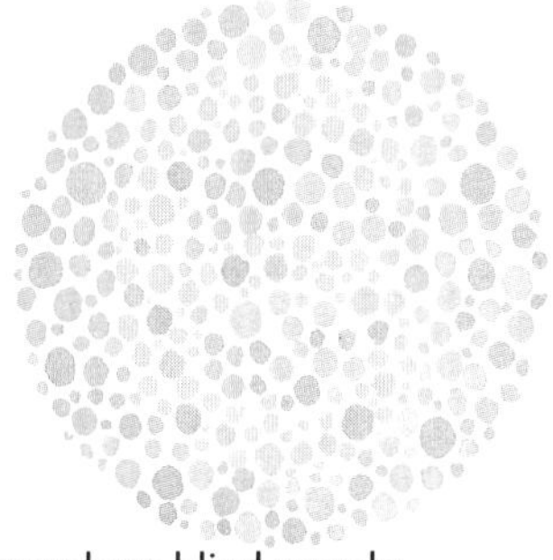

Some colour-blind people cannot see this number.

Colours give you a lot of information. Some people are colour-blind. They cannot tell the difference between certain colours.

How animals see colour

Not all animals see colours in the same way as people. A desert ant sees some colours better than you, but a squid cannot see colours at all.

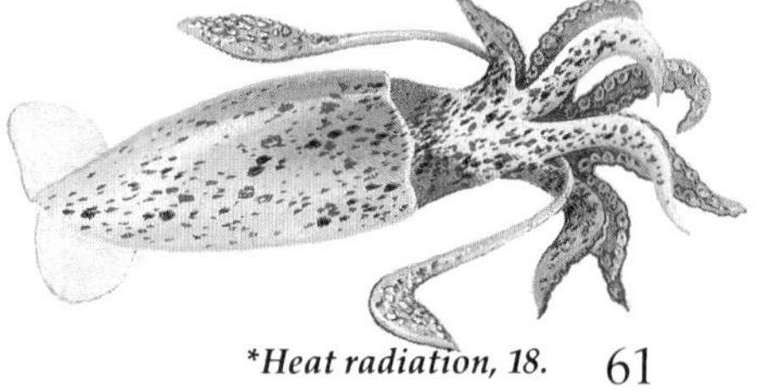

**Heat radiation, 18.*

Mixing colours

A blue filter only lets blue light through.

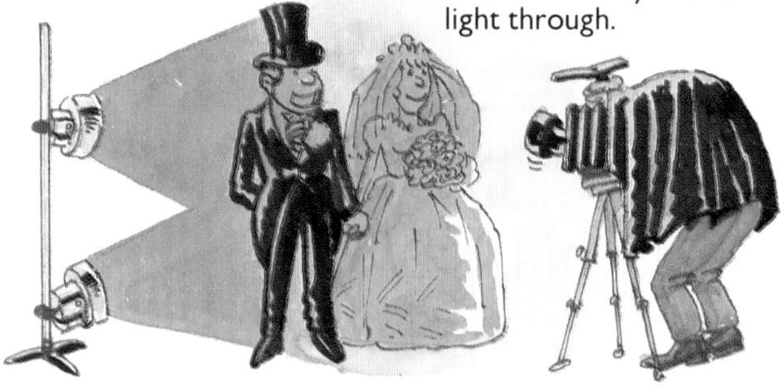

A red filter only lets red light through.

White light is made up of all the colours of the spectrum. You can divide it up into different colours with a colour filter.

A filter is a piece of coloured glass or plastic that makes coloured light. It only lets one colour through, blocking out all the rest.

Primary colours

Red, green and blue are called **primary colours**. They are special, because you can use them to make light of any colour. If you mix any two primary colours, the coloured light they make is called a **secondary colour**.

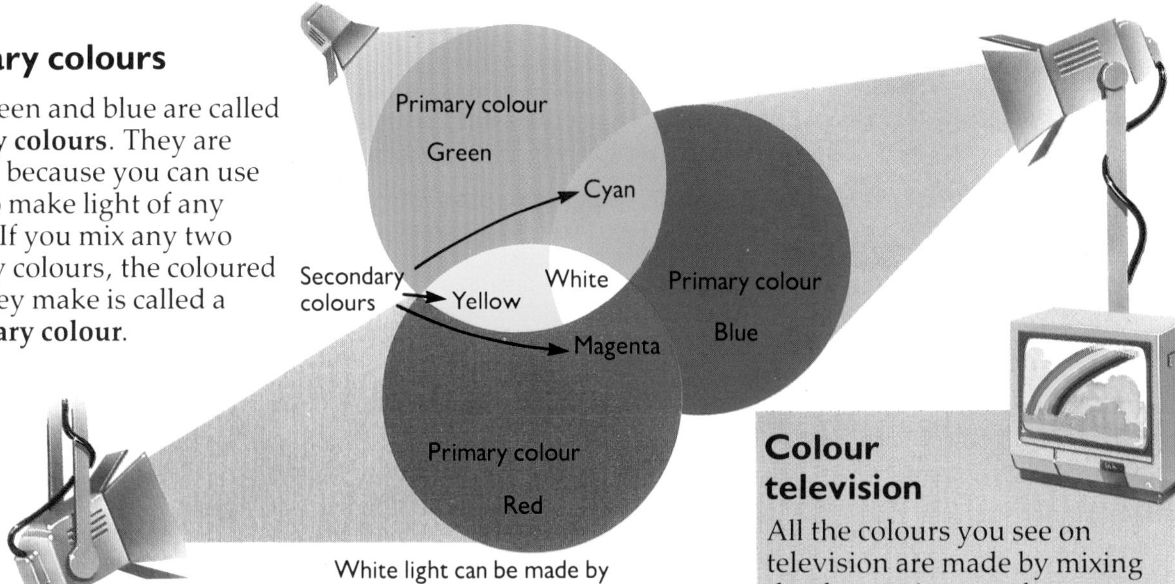

Primary colour
Green
Cyan
Secondary colours
Yellow
White
Magenta
Primary colour
Blue
Primary colour
Red

White light can be made by mixing all the primary colours in the right amounts.

Colour television

All the colours you see on television are made by mixing the three primary colours.

DID YOU KNOW?

Animals often have the same colours as their surroundings. This is called **camouflage**. Polar bears are white because they live in the snow.

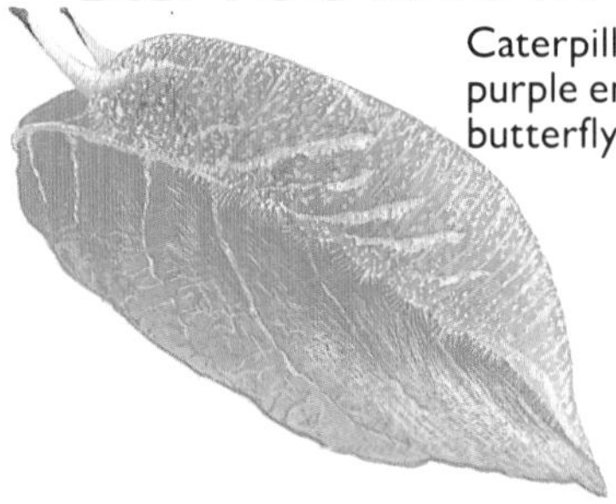

Caterpillar of the purple emperor butterfly.

Some animals change colour. This caterpillar is green in summer while it lives on leaves. But it turns brown in winter as it lives on twigs.

Arrow-poison frog, South America.

Some animals are brightly coloured to scare others away. This frog is one of the most poisonous animals in the world.

Why do things look different colours?

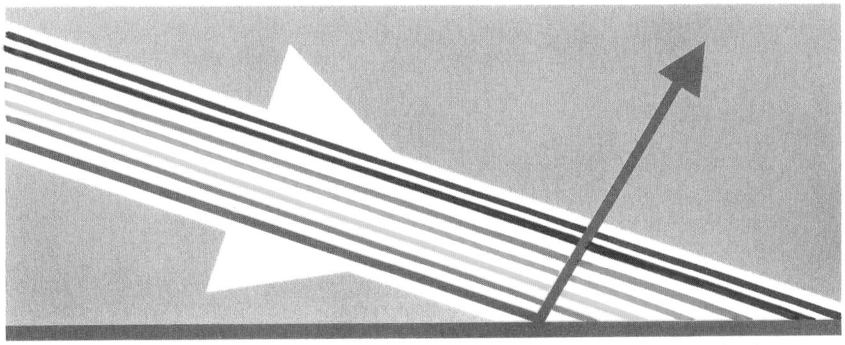

The colour of something depends on the colours of light that it reflects. An object looks red because it reflects red light and absorbs all the other colours. Something looks blue because it reflects blue light and absorbs all the other colours. A white object reflects all the colours of light equally. But a black object reflects no light. It absorbs all colours.

Mixing paints

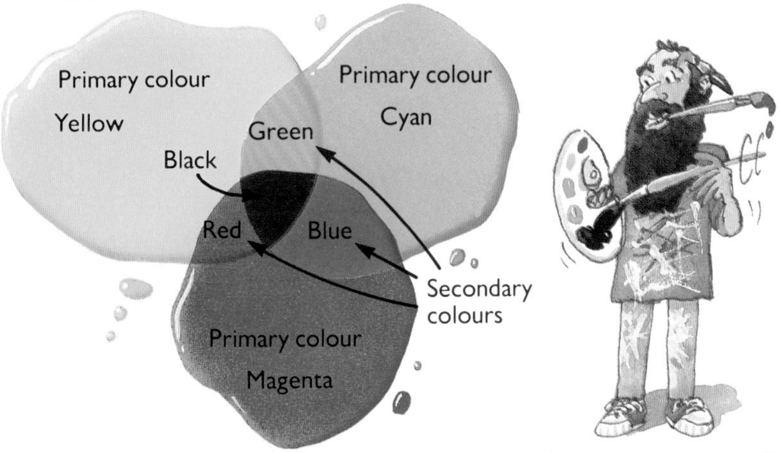

The three primary colours used in painting are magenta, yellow and cyan. They are not the same as the primary colours for light. By mixing them, you can make almost any colour, apart from white. Mixing all three colours together makes black.

Changing colours

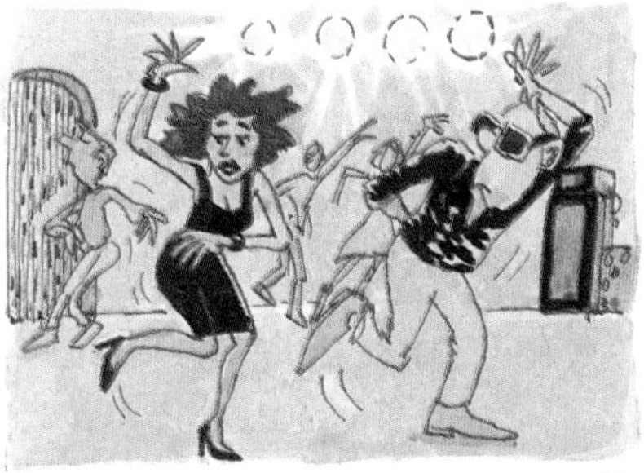

Things can look a different colour when you see them in coloured light. A red dress will look black in blue or green light.

Printing colours

All the colours you see in this book have been printed using only four different coloured inks. They are yellow, cyan, magenta and black.

To print each page, the paper goes through the machine four times, each time with one of the different inks. This is called **four colour printing**.

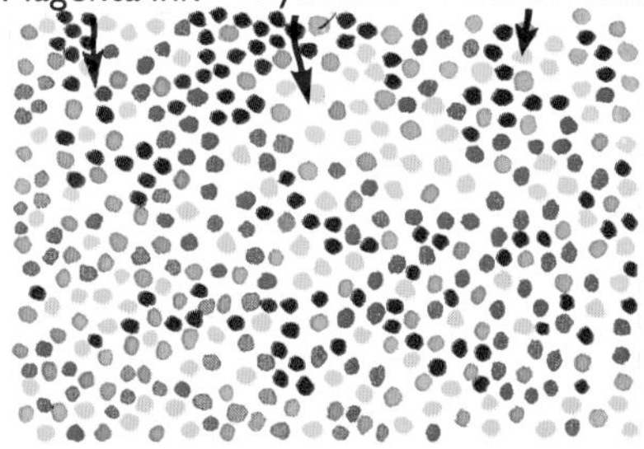
Black ink is used to make the picture darker.
Magenta ink
Cyan ink
Yellow ink

Look at the pictures on this page through a strong magnifying glass. They are made up of thousands of tiny dots of different colours.

Sound

The sounds you hear tell you what is happening around you, even if you cannot see what is making them. You may be able to hear the sound of a telephone ringing, of cars driving by, or of rain falling.

A sound is made when something moves backwards and forwards very quickly. This is called **vibration**. When something vibrates, it makes the air around it vibrate too. The sound you hear is carried by the vibrating air.

Sound is a form of energy, but the energy in most sounds is small. The sound energy of 200 pianos is equal to the electrical energy needed to light just one light bulb.

When you speak, air from your lungs makes vocal cords in your throat vibrate.
The sound from radios and televisions comes from loudspeakers.
The sound of a violin is made by the vibrating strings.
Electrical signals make the loudspeaker vibrate.
You can feel your vocal cords vibrating, if you touch your throat as you speak.
People and animals use sound to communicate with each other.

High and low sounds

The faster something vibrates, the higher the sound it makes. The slower it vibrates, the lower the sound it makes. How high or low a sound is, is called its **pitch**. The number of vibrations per second is called the **frequency** of the sound.

Frequency is measured in **hertz (Hz)**. Bees beat their wings 200 times a second, so the sound you hear has a frequency of 200 hertz. Mosquitoes make a higher pitched sound than bees because they beat their wings faster, about 500 times each second.

The speed of sound

Thunder and lightning happen at the same time, but you see lightning before you hear thunder, because sound travels much slower than light.

You can tell how far away a thunderstorm is. Count the number of seconds between seeing the lightning and hearing the thunder. Then divide the answer by three. This tells you how far away the storm is, in kilometres.

In air, light travels around 880,000 times faster than sound.
Concorde, the fastest passenger aircraft, can fly at twice the speed of sound.
You hear the sound of a crash because the collision makes the cars vibrate.
Sound can travel through liquids.
Sound can travel through solids.

DID YOU KNOW?

Some aeroplanes are **supersonic**. This means that they can travel faster than the speed of sound. Their speed is measured in units called **mach**.

Mach 1 is equal to the speed of sound. The fastest jet in the world is the Lockheed SR-71 (USA) which flies at mach 3.5.

Far away sounds

The further away you are from the source of a sound, the quieter it gets. Because of this, you can sometimes tell how far away something is.

Sound in solids and liquids

As well as travelling through air, sound can travel through liquids and solids. That is why you can hear sounds through walls and through water.

Sound travels

Sound moves

Sound travels in sound waves. They spread through the air like ripples in a pond after you have thrown in a pebble.

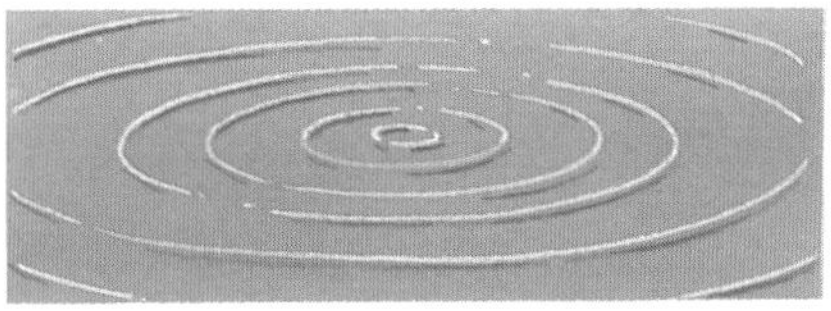

As a bell vibrates, it pushes and pulls the air around it, making layers of different air pressure*. This is a **sound wave**.

Each layer of air bumps into the next layer, carrying the sound to your ears.

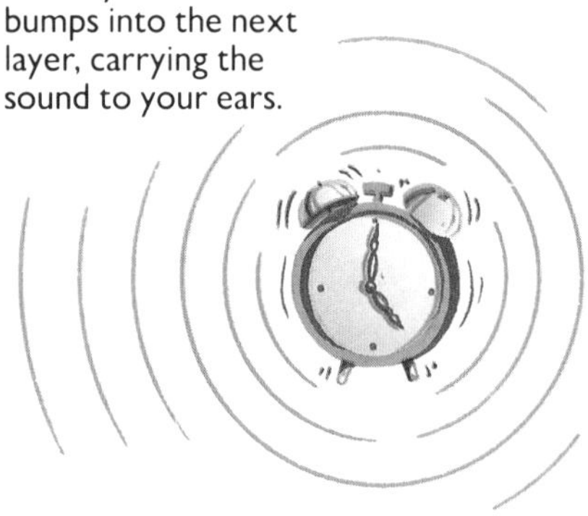

Your ears pick up sound waves. The tiny differences in air pressure make your eardrums* vibrate in time with the sound of the bell.

Light waves* can travel through Space, but sound waves cannot.

Sound waves need something to travel through. Space is completely silent because there is no air to carry the sound.

Sound through gases

Sound waves can travel through gases. Most of the sounds you hear have gone through air to reach you. Through air, sound travels about 340m (1,115ft) each second.

Sound travels slightly faster in hot air and slightly slower in cold air.

Sound through solids

Sound can travel through solids. You can hear something, even if it is very far away, by listening to the ground.

Sound travels best through hard solids. It travels 15 times faster through steel than through air.

Sound through liquids

Sound waves can travel through liquids. You can hear the sound of someone splashing when you are swimming underwater. Sound waves always travel better through liquids than gases.

Sound travels about four times faster through water than through air.

Eardrums, 68; Light waves, 61; Pressure, 40.

Sound spreads out

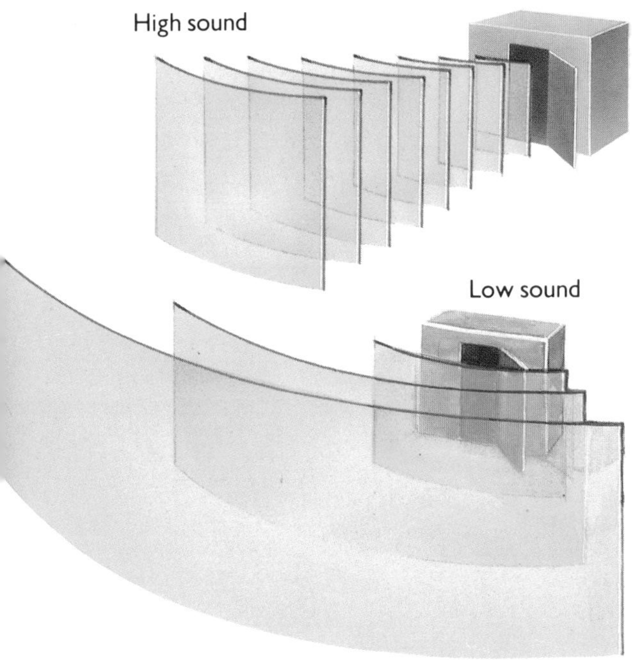

High sound
Low sound

You can hear around corners. This is because sound waves spread out as they go through gaps or around obstacles. This is called **diffraction**. Low sounds spread out, or are diffracted, more than high sounds. So, from far away, you hear the low notes in music better than the high ones.

Echoes

You can only hear sounds separately if they are over 1/10 second apart.

When you hear an echo, you are hearing sound waves reflected back to you from far away. You cannot hear echoes in small rooms because the walls are too close to you. Sound bounces back too quickly for you to hear the echo separately.

DID YOU KNOW?

Sound is reflected very well in the Whispering Gallery of St Paul's Cathedral, London, UK. Standing on one side of the dome, you can hear someone whisper against the opposite wall, 36m (120ft) away.

Sounds from a stage

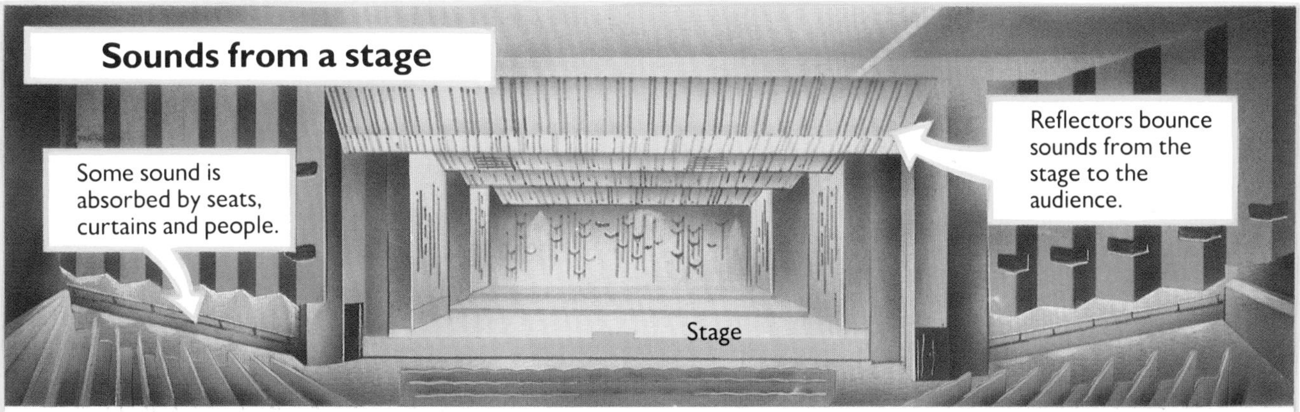

Some sound is absorbed by seats, curtains and people.
Reflectors bounce sounds from the stage to the audience.
Stage

The way sound travels in a room depends on its shape and what is in it. Hard, flat surfaces reflect sound waves well. Soft, bumpy surfaces absorb the sounds that hit them.

When sound waves meet, they can sometimes add up to make a louder sound, or cancel each other out to make a quieter sound. This is called **interference**.

Concert halls are built to avoid interference and echoes, so that sound carries well from the stage to the audience. The way sound travels in a room is called **acoustics**.

Hearing sound

Your ears pick up the vibrations made by sound waves. You hear sounds because nerves in your ears change the vibrations into signals that go to your brain.

As sound waves come into your ear, they make a sheet of skin, called the **ear-drum**, vibrate. The sound waves make the ear-drum vibrate in time with whatever made the sound.

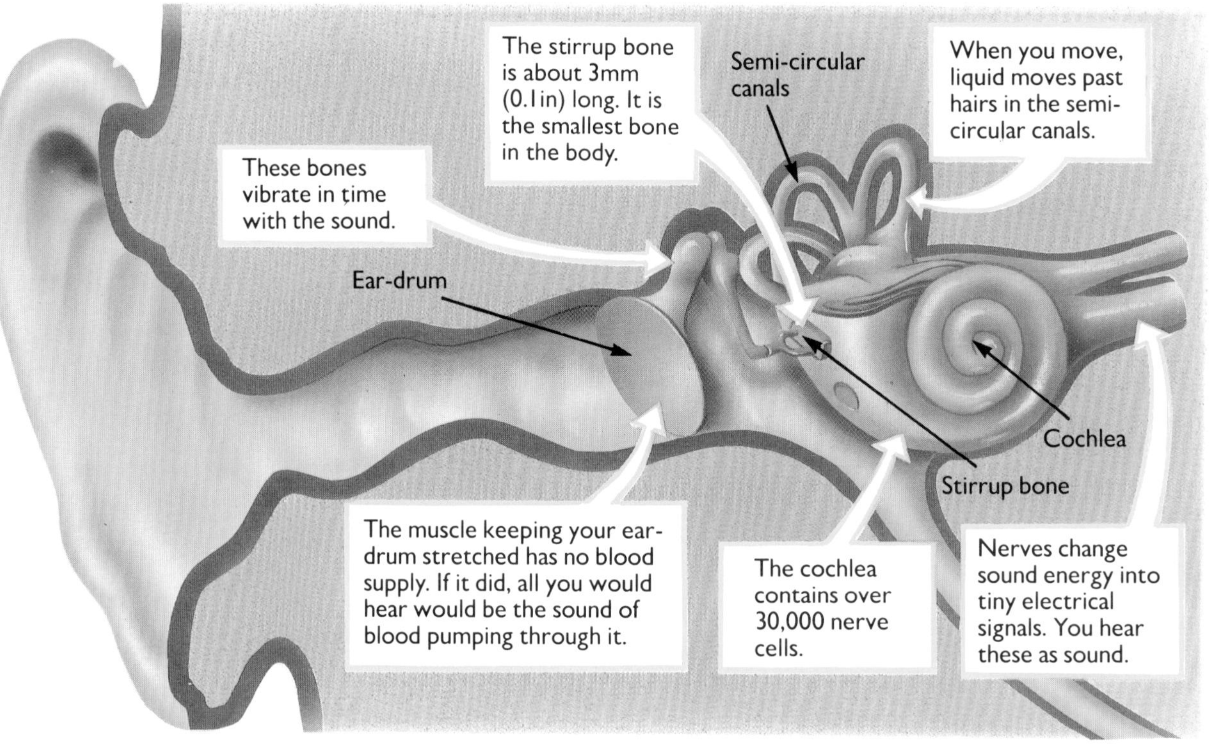

These bones vibrate in time with the sound.
The stirrup bone is about 3mm (0.1in) long. It is the smallest bone in the body.
Semi-circular canals
When you move, liquid moves past hairs in the semi-circular canals.
Ear-drum
Cochlea
Stirrup bone
The muscle keeping your ear-drum stretched has no blood supply. If it did, all you would hear would be the sound of blood pumping through it.
The cochlea contains over 30,000 nerve cells.
Nerves change sound energy into tiny electrical signals. You hear these as sound.

The ear-drum makes three tiny bones vibrate. They work like little levers, increasing the strength of the vibration. They are joined to a tube filled with liquid, called the **cochlea**.

The **stirrup bone** works like a piston, pushing liquid in the cochlea backwards and forwards, in time with the sound. Nerves change the vibration into electrical signals that go to the brain.

Your ears help you balance

The semi-circular canals in your ears help you balance. As you move, liquid inside them pushes on tiny hairs, sending nerve signals to the brain. You feel dizzy after spinning around, because the liquid carries on moving after you have stopped.

Young and old

People can usually hear sounds from about 20Hz, which is a low rumble, to about 18,000Hz, a high-pitched squeak. Children have the best hearing. They can hear very high-pitched sounds, higher than 20,000Hz, that older people cannot hear.

Too much noise

Listening to loud sounds, especially for a long time, damages your ears. People who work near noisy machinery wear ear-muffs to protect their ears.

The direction of sound

You know where a sound comes from because you have two ears. The ear closest to the sound hears it a little louder and slightly before the other one.

DID YOU KNOW?

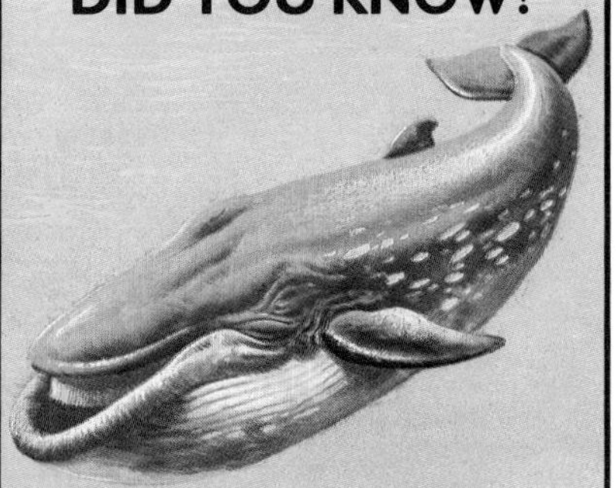

The loudest animal in the world is the blue whale. It can make sounds as loud as 188dB, that can be picked up 850km (530 miles) away.

Loud and soft sounds

Some sounds are louder than others. Because sound spreads out in all directions, the further away you are from the sound, the quieter you hear it.

The loudness, or **intensity**, of a sound is measured in units called **decibels (dB)**. They are named after A.G. Bell who invented the telephone.

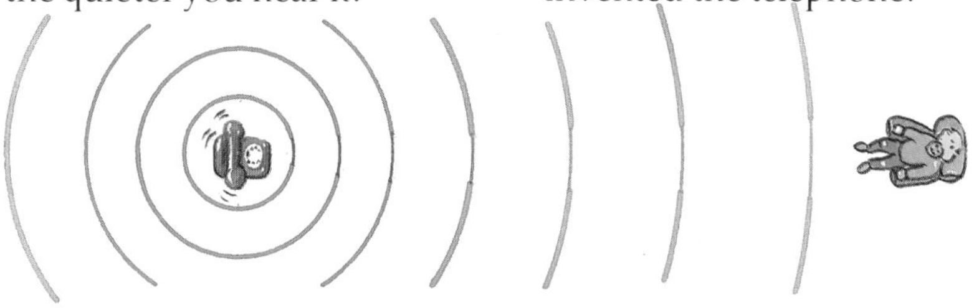

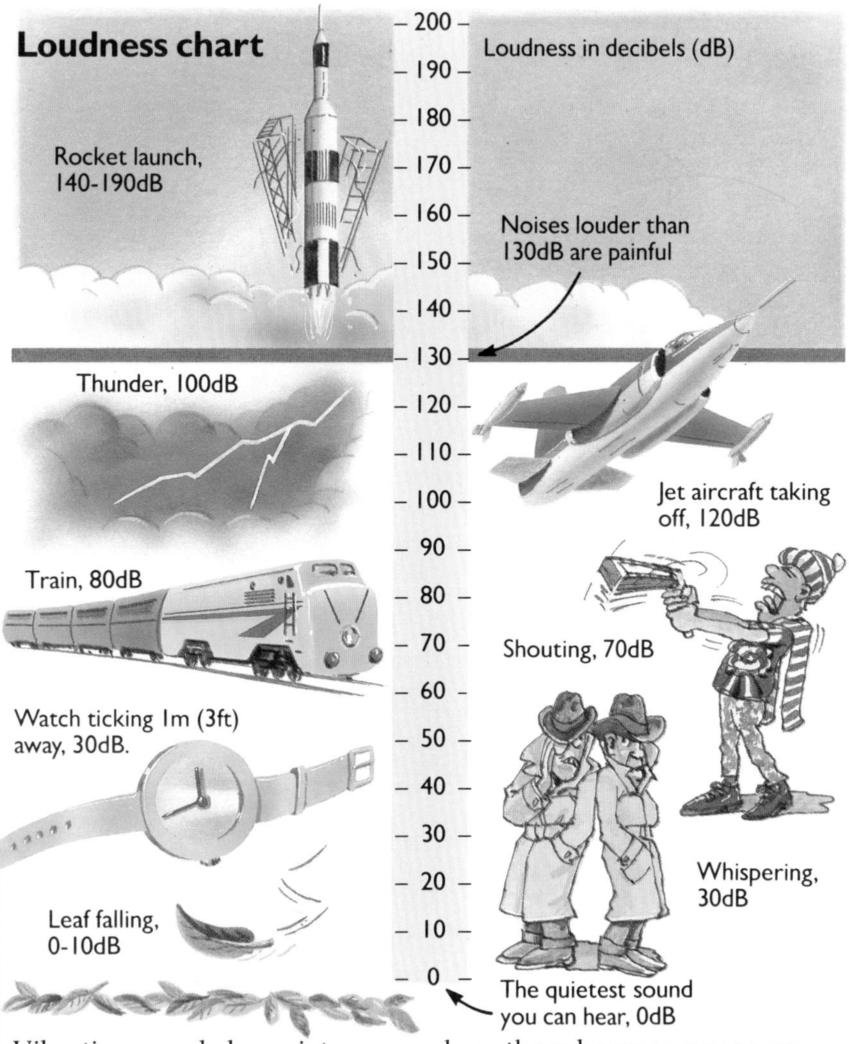
Loudness chart
Loudness in decibels (dB)
200
190
180
170
160
150
140
130
120
110
100
90
80
70
60
50
40
30
20
10
0
Rocket launch, 140-190dB
Noises louder than 130dB are painful
Thunder, 100dB
Jet aircraft taking off, 120dB
Train, 80dB
Shouting, 70dB
Watch ticking 1m (3ft) away, 30dB.
Whispering, 30dB
Leaf falling, 0-10dB
The quietest sound you can hear, 0dB

Vibrations made by quiet sounds make only tiny changes in air pressure. You are able to hear them because your ears are very sensitive, and can pick them up.

Musical sounds

All musical instruments work by making something vibrate. The sounds they make can be high or low, loud or quiet.

High and low

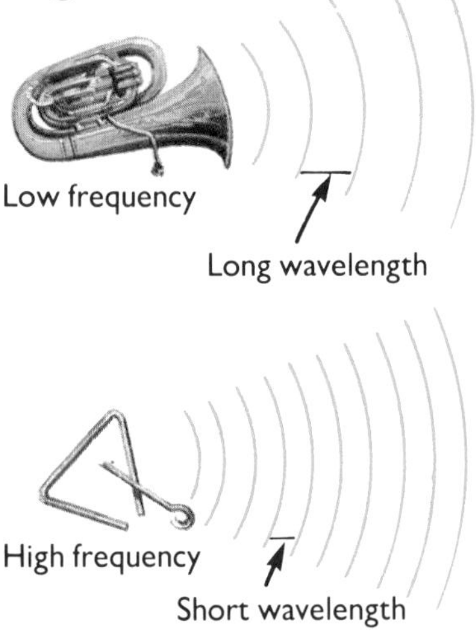

Low frequency
Long wavelength
High frequency
Short wavelength

The higher a sound, the higher its frequency*. This means that more vibrations reach you each second. So the distance between each vibration, called the **wavelength**, is smaller.

Loud and quiet

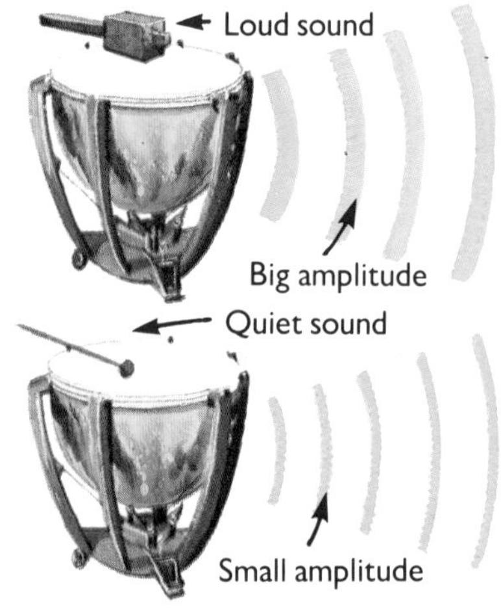

Loud sound
Big amplitude
Quiet sound
Small amplitude

A loud sound makes big vibrations. The size of each vibration is called its **amplitude**. So the louder the sound, the bigger the amplitude.

How musical instruments work

To make a higher sound, the string is shortened by pressing on it.
Pushing on a piano key makes a hammer hit the strings, so that they vibrate. Each note has two or three strings.
The sound of a double bass comes from making the strings vibrate by plucking them or by using a bow.
Blowing into a saxophone makes a thin piece of wood, called a reed, vibrate. This vibrates air in the saxophone.
The keys on a saxophone change the length of the column of air that vibrates inside it. The longer it is, the lower the sound.

Why do musical instruments sound different?

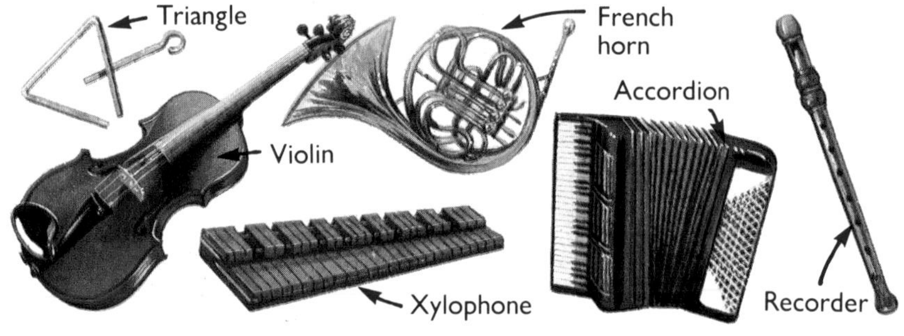

Triangle
French horn
Accordion
Violin
Xylophone
Recorder

Every musical instrument has its own special sound. Any note you hear has other high pitched notes, called **harmonics**, mixed into it. But they are too quiet for you to hear as separate notes. All instruments make different sounds because they have different harmonics from each other.

 **Frequency, 64.*

Hitting drums and cymbals with sticks or wire brushes makes them vibrate.
By making his lips vibrate as he blows, the player makes air in the trumpet vibrate.

Vibrating in time

You can play a piano without touching a key. Hold down the sustain pedal and sing a note. When you stop singing, you will hear the same note coming from the piano. The vibrations from your voice make the piano strings vibrate.

Open piano
Pushing the sustain pedal leaves all the strings in the piano free to vibrate.
The sustain pedal is the one on the right.

When the vibrations of one thing make something else vibrate, it is called **resonance**. Each string in a piano vibrates at one frequency, called its **natural frequency**. Your voice makes the string vibrate at its natural frequency.

Breaking glass

If you tap a glass, the sound you hear is made by the glass vibrating at its natural frequency. By singing loudly at this frequency, some singers can shatter a glass. Only a sound at the natural frequency of the glass can make vibrations big enough for this to happen.

Resonance makes sounds louder

Stringed instruments have a sound-box to make them louder. When the strings vibrate, the air inside the sound-box is made to vibrate by resonance.

Collapsing bridges

Everything has its own natural frequency. In 1940, the Tacoma Bridge, USA, collapsed. This was because wind made it vibrate at its natural frequency, causing huge vibrations. Soldiers do not march in step across bridges, in case their footsteps make the bridge vibrate at its natural frequency.

DID YOU KNOW?

The world's largest and loudest musical instrument is in Atlantic City, USA. It is an organ with 33,112 pipes that can make a sound as loud as 25 brass bands.

Seeing with sound

Night hunters

Some animals use sound to help them 'see'. Bats are able to find their prey at night and fly in the dark without bumping into things. Using sound to find things is called echo-location.

Bats send out lots of very high-pitched squeaks, then listen to the echoes bouncing off things. The shorter the time between the squeak and the echo, the closer they are to the object.

To help them catch moving insects, bats listen to the pitch* of the echo. The pitch changes as the insect moves past the bat. This is called the Doppler effect*.

Some moths can avoid being caught. They can hear the high-pitched sounds that bats make.

Bats can hear higher sounds than any other animal, up to 210,000Hz. The highest sounds people can hear are around 20,000Hz. Sound with a very high frequency is called **ultrasound**.

Sea sounds

Whales and dolphins also use echo-location to find their way through the sea. From the sound of the echo, they are able to tell what type of objects are around them.

Exploring underwater

Ships use ultrasound echoes to search for fish, to measure the depth of water beneath them, and to explore the ocean floor. This is called **sonar**. A computer can be used to build up a picture from the echoes.

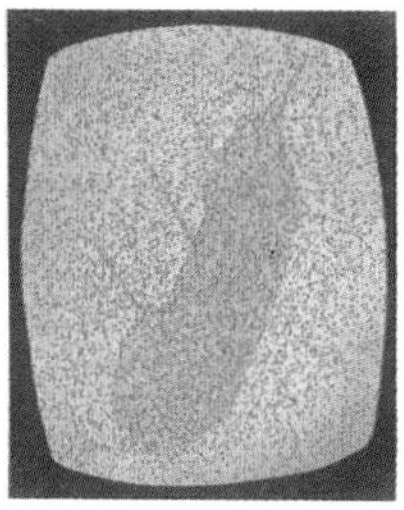

Computer picture

High sounds spread out, or are diffracted*, much less than low sounds. That is why ultrasound is used for echo-location. It is so high that it hardly spreads out, so objects can be located very precisely from the echoes they make.

 ***Diffraction, 67; Doppler effect, 73; Pitch, 64.**

Looking for cracks

Ultrasound is used to test materials. Aircraft are checked this way. Engineers can tell from the echoes whether there are any cracks in the metal.

Ultrasound pictures

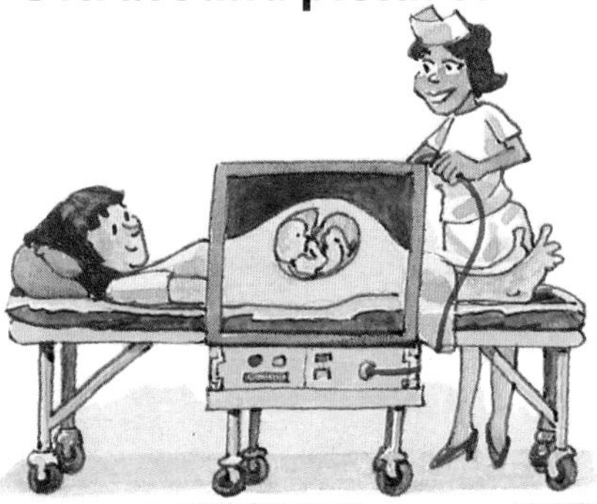

Ultrasound is used to look inside a mother at a growing baby. The echoes are changed into electrical signals and built up into a picture.

DID YOU KNOW?

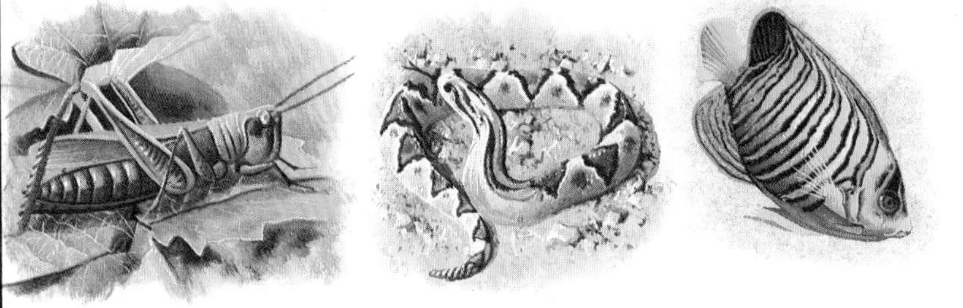

Not all animals hear sounds as you do. Grasshoppers 'hear' with their legs, waving them in the air to tell where a sound is coming from.

Snakes do not have ears so they cannot hear sounds through air. They pick up low sounds from the ground. Fish hear through their bodies.

Exploring underground

Earthquakes or explosions cause huge vibrations through the Earth, called **seismic waves**. They travel at different speeds through different liquids and types of rock.

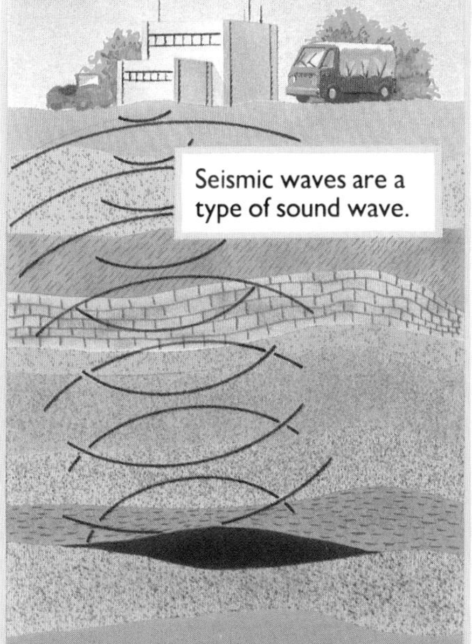
Seismic waves are a type of sound wave.

By measuring their speed, geologists can tell what the inside of the Earth is like. Seismic waves are also used to help people search for oil.

Sounds from moving things

When a racing car passes by, its sound seems to change pitch. As it comes to you, the sound you hear gets higher. As it goes away, the sound gets lower. This is called the **Doppler effect**.

More vibrations reach you each second because the car is moving towards you, making the sound higher. As the car moves away, fewer vibrations reach you each second, making the sound lower.

*Earthquakes, 22.

What are things made of?

Look at all the different kinds of things around you. Everything you see is either a solid, a liquid or a gas. In this picture, you can see some of the differences between them.

You will also find lots of questions about the things around you. The next few pages answer these questions and explain what things are made of and how they change.

Solids keep their shape. They always take up the same amount of space.
Solids cannot be squashed into a smaller space.
Some solids are harder than others.
A solid cannot move unless something pushes or pulls it.
What makes things burn?
Some solids are light for their size, others are heavy for their size.
Some liquids are more difficult to pour than others.
Liquids cannot be squashed into a smaller space.
Some solids, like sand, are divided up into very small pieces.
Liquids do not have their own shape. They take the shape of whatever container they are in.
Liquids can move around and flow.
Both liquids and gases are able to flow. Both are sometimes called **fluids**.

A **vapour** is a gas given off by a liquid. You can smell petrol vapour when you are in a petrol station.
What makes the wind blow?
Where does the rain come from?
Water can be a liquid, a solid or a gas. When water freezes, it turns into a solid, ice. When water boils, it turns into a gas, steam.
Why does sugar dissolve in coffee?
How does a thermometer work?
Why does ice-cream melt when it gets warm?
How do smells reach you?
What makes a drink fizzy?
Gases can be squashed into a smaller space.
Why can you dry yourself with a towel?
Where does a puddle go when it dries up?
Gases can move around and flow. They have no shape of their own. They spread out and fill the container they are in, and take its shape.
Air is a mixture of different gases. Most gases are invisible.

DID YOU KNOW?

Diamond is the hardest thing known in the world. It is so hard that it can even cut through glass. Man-made diamonds are used in many cutting and drilling machines.

Atoms and molecules

Everything around you is made up of tiny pieces, called atoms and molecules, that are much too small to see. Atoms are so small that over 100,000 million would fit in a full-stop.

Imagine you could divide a grain of sand into smaller and smaller pieces. You would eventually get a piece, or **particle**, that could not be divided up any more. This is called a molecule, the smallest possible piece of sand.

Everything in the Universe is made of different atoms and molecules. Molecules are made of two or more atoms joined together. Most molecules contain a few atoms, but others may contain thousands of atoms.

A grain of sand contains 50,000 million million molecules. Each molecule is made up of three atoms.

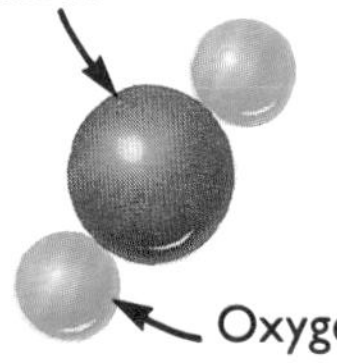
Silicon atom
Oxygen atom

A molecule of hydrogen gas contains two identical atoms.

Hydrogen

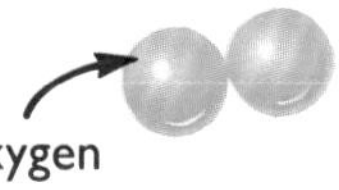
Oxygen

An oxygen molecule contains two identical atoms.

A water molecule contains three atoms, two hydrogen atoms and an oxygen atom.

Oxygen
Hydrogen

What's inside an atom?

There are about 105 different types of atom known. They are all made up of even smaller particles, called **protons**, **neutrons** and **electrons**.

The different atoms contain different numbers of protons, neutrons and electrons. This picture shows what the inside of an atom may look like.

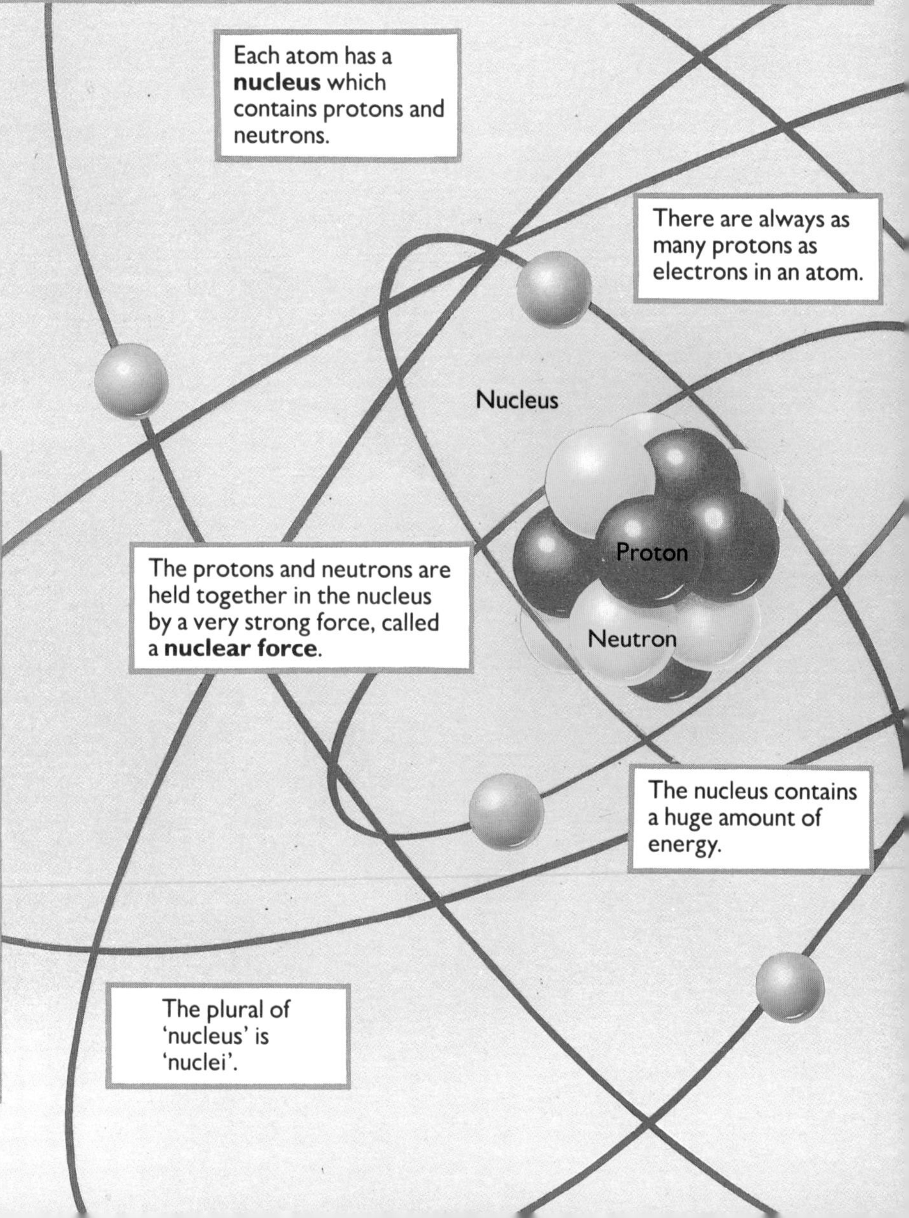
Each atom has a **nucleus** which contains protons and neutrons.
There are always as many protons as electrons in an atom.
Nucleus
Proton
Neutron
The protons and neutrons are held together in the nucleus by a very strong force, called a **nuclear force**.
The nucleus contains a huge amount of energy.
The plural of 'nucleus' is 'nuclei'.

Discovering atoms

The word 'atom' comes from a Greek word that means 'cannot be divided'.

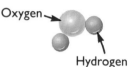

The Greeks thought that things were made of atoms as long as 2,400 years ago. This idea was ignored for the next 2,000 years, until John Dalton did some experiments in 1808 which showed that atoms do exist.

Whizzing electrons

Electrons whiz around the nucleus. They are held in the atom by an electrical force. They have an **electric charge** which means that they carry electricity. There are two types of electric charge, **positive charge** and **negative charge**.

Electrons have a negative charge, protons have a positive charge, neutrons have no charge at all. Because there are the same number of electrons and protons, the positive charges and the negative charges in an atom are balanced equally.

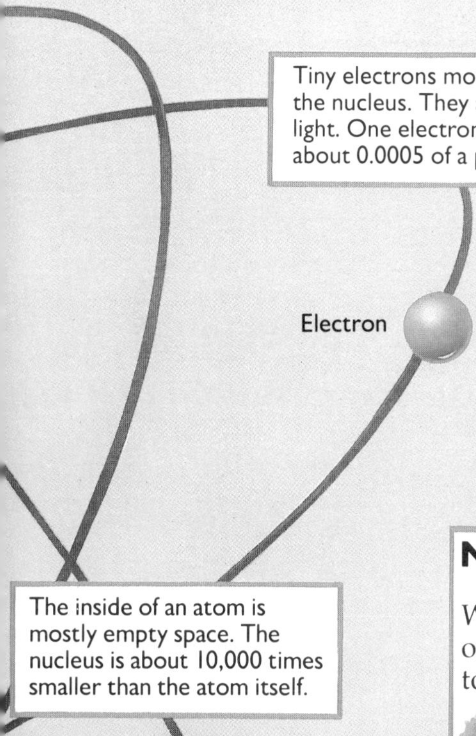

Tiny electrons move around the nucleus. They are very light. One electron weighs about 0.0005 of a proton.

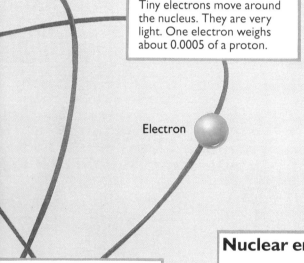

The inside of an atom is mostly empty space. The nucleus is about 10,000 times smaller than the atom itself.

Molecules move

Put a few drops of ink into a glass of water. Eventually, all the ink will spread evenly through the water. This is because the molecules in liquids are always moving around and bumping into each other.

In the same way, molecules in gases are always moving around in all directions. This is why you can smell flowers across a room. Their scent reaches you because their molecules spread through the air.

When molecules spread through liquids and gases, this is called **diffusion**. Gas molecules move much faster than liquid molecules. So it takes longer for ink to spread through water than for smells to spread through air.

Nuclear energy

When a nucleus is split in two or when two nuclei are joined to form a new nucleus, a huge amount of energy, called **nuclear energy**, is given out. Splitting a nucleus is called **fission**, joining up nuclei is called **fusion**.

When nuclear energy is let out slowly, it can be used to produce electricity in nuclear power stations. But if it is let out all at once, it makes an enormous explosion. This is how a nuclear bomb works.

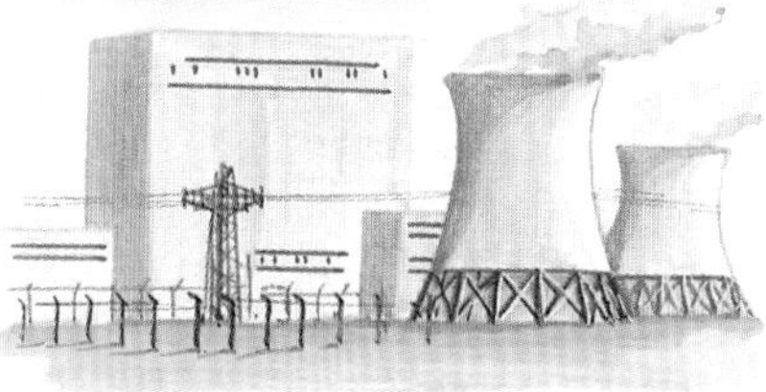

Nuclear power stations use **uranium** fuel. The place where the uranium nuclei are split up is called the **reactor**. It is covered in thick concrete to stop deadly **nuclear radiation** leaking out.

DID YOU KNOW?

Atoms and molecules are so tiny that there are about as many atoms in a grain of sand as there are grains of sand on a beach.

Solids, liquids and gases

Why can you push your finger through jam, but not through steel? Why can you pour water, and not wood? Why does salt mix into water and disappear, but sand stay separate? What makes solids, liquids and gases different from each other?

Solids

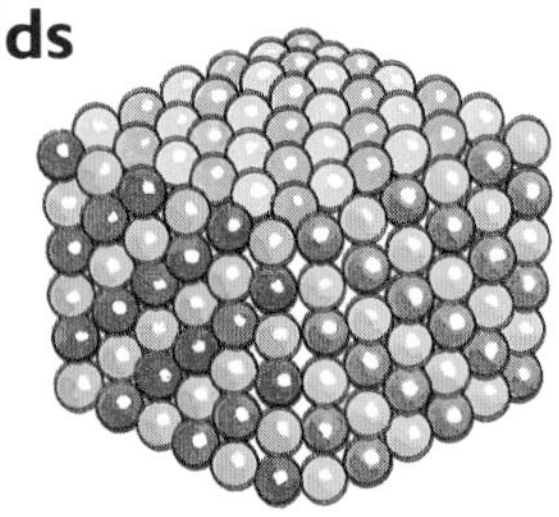

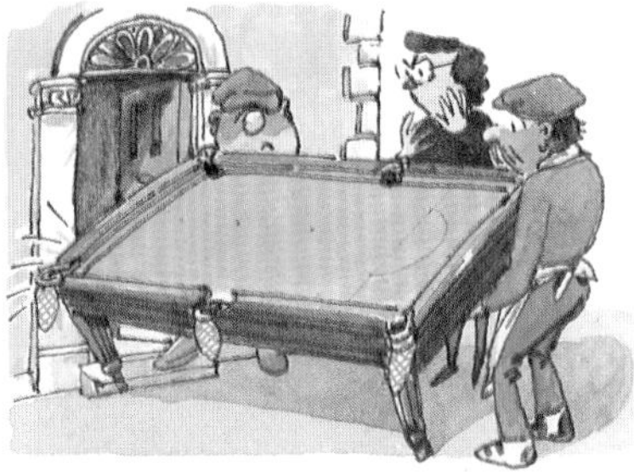

The atoms in solids are held very close together. They vibrate all the time, but, because they are held in rows by very strong forces, they cannot move around each other.

Solids cannot be squashed into a smaller space, as their atoms are already so close together. They keep their shape because their atoms are held together by such strong forces.

Liquids

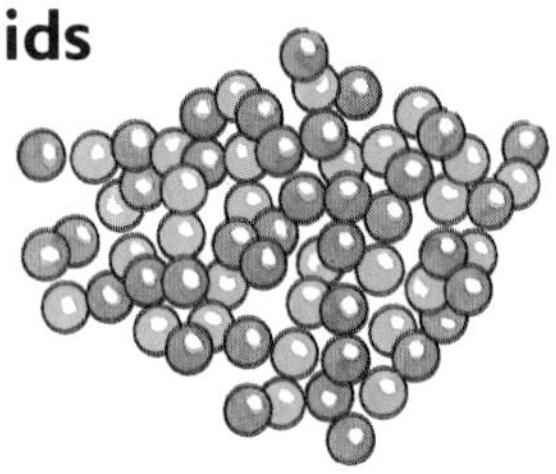

Liquids take the shape of their container.

The molecules in liquids are close to each other, but the forces holding them together are not as strong as in solids. The molecules can move around and change places with each other, so liquids can flow and change shape. Liquids cannot be squashed because their molecules are so close together.

Gases

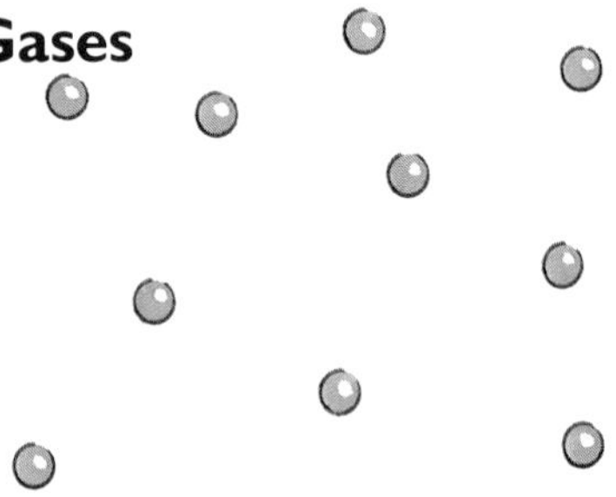

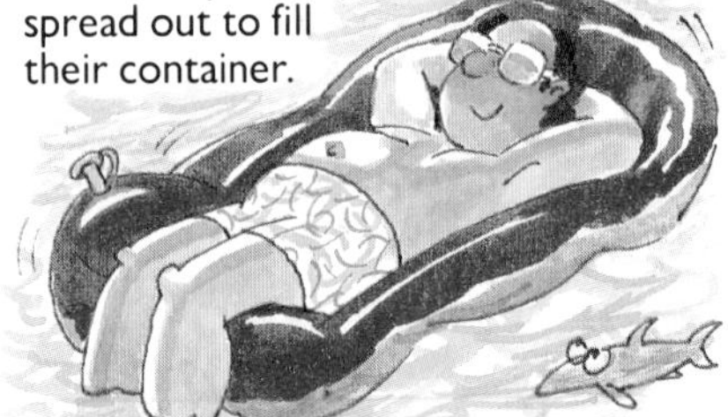
Gases do not have a fixed shape. They spread out to fill their container.

In gases, the molecules are always moving around very quickly in all directions. The forces holding the molecules together are very weak, so gases are able to spread out and flow. Because there are such big gaps between the molecules, gases can be easily squashed into a smaller space.

Liquids hold together

A drop of liquid seems to be held together by an elastic skin. This happens because of surface tension*. Drops form because the liquid molecules are pulled towards each other.

The hairs on a paintbrush cling together when they are wet, but not when they are dry. This is because the water molecules are pulled towards each other.

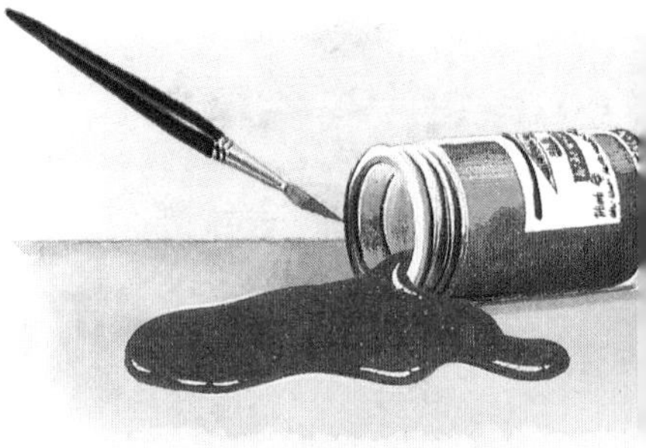

A liquid spreads over a surface if the pull of the molecules from the surface is stronger than the forces holding the liquid molecules together.

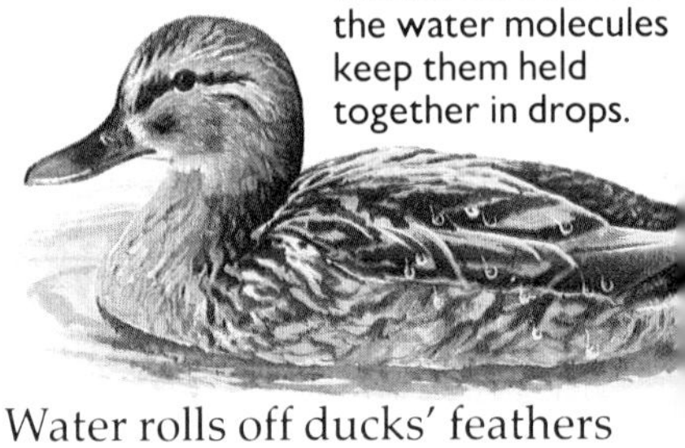
The forces between the water molecules keep them held together in drops.

Water rolls off ducks' feathers because they are covered in a layer of grease which does not pull the water molecules to it.

*Surface tension, 39.

How do things soak up water?

A towel will soak up water. The water is sucked into tiny spaces between the threads of the towel. Sucking liquids up this way is called **capillary action**. Plastic does not soak up liquids because it has no holes in it.

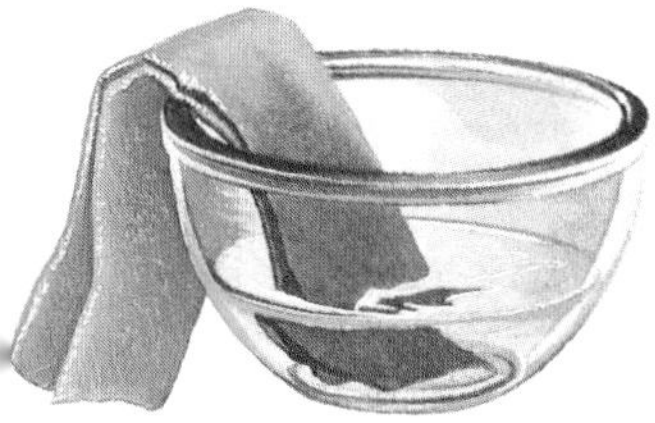

Water creeps up to the leaves of plants from the soil. This is because their roots contain tiny tubes which suck up water by capillary action.

Viscosity

Some liquids, like water, are runny and easy to pour. Others, like honey, are thicker and pour more slowly. How thick a liquid is, is called its **viscosity**.

Try pouring clear honey after leaving it in the fridge for a few hours. Liquids become thicker, or more viscous, the colder they get. As they warm up, they become less viscous.

DID YOU KNOW?

Glass is not a solid, but a liquid. You cannot see it flowing because it is very viscous. Very old windows are thicker at the bottom because the glass has flowed downwards over the years.

Solutions

When you add sugar to coffee, the sugar and coffee mix together and form a **solution**. The sugar **dissolves** in the coffee.

The thing that is dissolved, like salt, is called a **solute**. The thing that does the dissolving, like water, is called a **solvent**.

The sugar molecules spread out evenly through the coffee.
If the coffee is hot, and if you stir it, the sugar dissolves more quickly.
A gas called carbon dioxide is dissolved into drinks to make them fizzy.
Oil
Vinegar
Oil does not dissolve in vinegar. This is why oil and vinegar salad dressing separates into two layers.
The sea is a solution of salt in water.
Salt dissolves in water, but sand does not.

Some things will not dissolve in others. Oil and grease do not dissolve in water. Dry cleaning can get oil stains out of clothes by using another solvent, a chemical called **tetrachloromethane**. It is only used in dry cleaning shops because it gives off poisonous fumes.

Heating and cooling

What happens when things get hot?

As things heat up, they become slightly larger. They occupy more space than when they are cold. This is called thermal expansion. As they cool down again, they shrink back to their normal size. This is called contraction.

Gases expand

Put an open, plastic bottle in a fridge. When it is cold, put a balloon over its top. Then put the bottle in a bowl of hot water. Watch the balloon blow up by itself.

This happens because the air **expands** as it is heated. Put the bottle back in the fridge. The balloon will go down again, because the air shrinks, or **contracts**, as it cools down.

Liquids expand

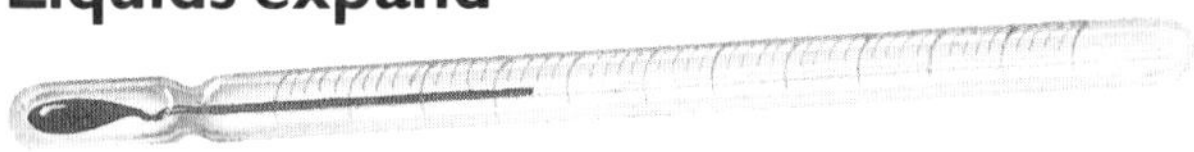

A thermometer works by thermal expansion. It contains liquid in a glass tube. As the thermometer is heated, the liquid rises up the tube. This is because the liquid expands more than the glass. As the thermometer cools, the liquid shrinks back down again.

Solids expand

A 100m (110yd) steel rail may get 4cm (1½in) longer on a hot day.

Solids expand when they heat up. The central part of the Humber Bridge, England is 1,410m (1,540yds) long. In summer, it can be half a metre (half a yard) longer than in winter.

Allowing for expansion

How much something expands depends on its size, what it is made of, and how much it is heated. Small things expand by small amounts. Large things expand by large amounts.

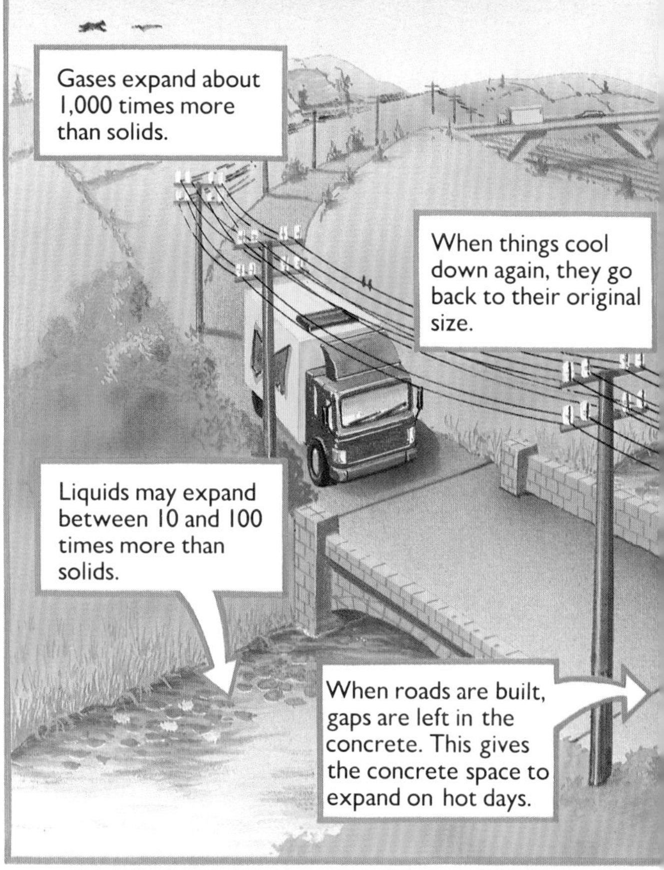
Gases expand about 1,000 times more than solids.
When things cool down again, they go back to their original size.
Liquids may expand between 10 and 100 times more than solids.
When roads are built, gaps are left in the concrete. This gives the concrete space to expand on hot days.

Why things expand when they get hot

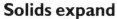

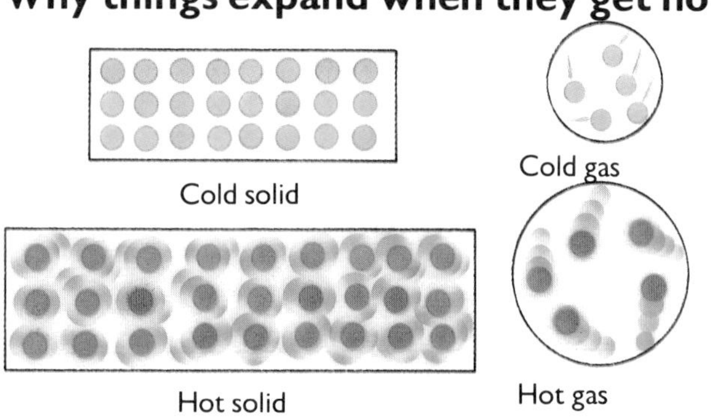
Cold solid
Cold gas
Hot solid
Hot gas

Atoms and molecules are moving and bumping into each other all the time. The hotter they get, the faster they move, and the harder they hit each other. This makes them take up more space.

Gases expand more than liquids and liquids expand more than solids. The bigger the temperature change, the bigger the change in size.

Railway lines are built so they can expand on hot days.
Steel expands more than wood.
Telephone wires are hung slackly. This is so that they do not snap apart when they contract on cold winter days.

Using expansion

If the metal lid on a jar is stuck, hold it under a hot water tap. Because metal expands more than glass, the lid will loosen.

This only works if there is no hole in the ball.

If a ping-pong ball is squashed, put it in warm water. The air inside it expands, pushing the ball back into shape again.

Expansion and density

How heavy something is for its size, its density*, depends on how close its atoms are to each other. When something expands, its atoms move further apart, so it becomes less dense.

Warm air rises. This is because, as it expands and becomes less dense, it floats up through colder air. Heat is carried through liquids and gases this way. This is called convection*.

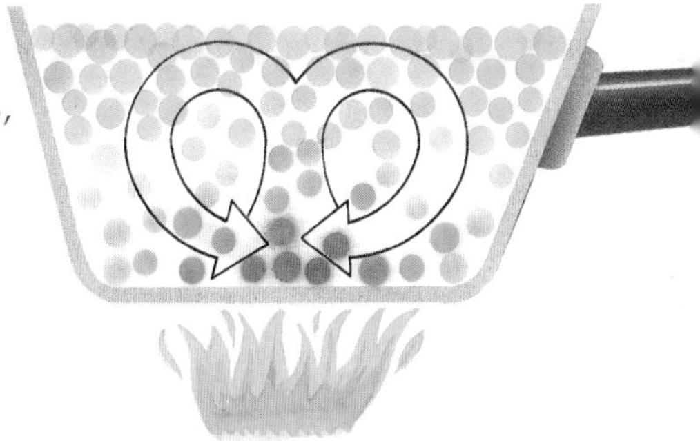

DID YOU KNOW?

Guitars often have to be tuned on stage because the strong lights heat them up. Steel expands more than wood, so the steel strings become slack and out of tune.

Expansion can be dangerous

Never pour boiling water into a glass. Glass conducts heat badly, so the inside gets hot and expands. But the outside stays cold and does not expand. This makes the glass shatter.

You should never let an aerosol heat up or throw it in a fire. This is because there are gases sealed inside aerosols. If heated, the gases would expand, making the can explode.

*Convection, 16; Density, 38.

Boiling and freezing

Things can be solids, liquids or gases, and they can change from one to another. If you freeze water, it turns to ice. If you boil water, it turns to steam. When you melt ice, it changes from a solid back into a liquid, water.

When you boil water, it turns into a gas, steam. To change something from a solid to a liquid and then from a liquid to a gas, you have to heat it. This gives it heat energy. This added energy makes the molecules move around faster.

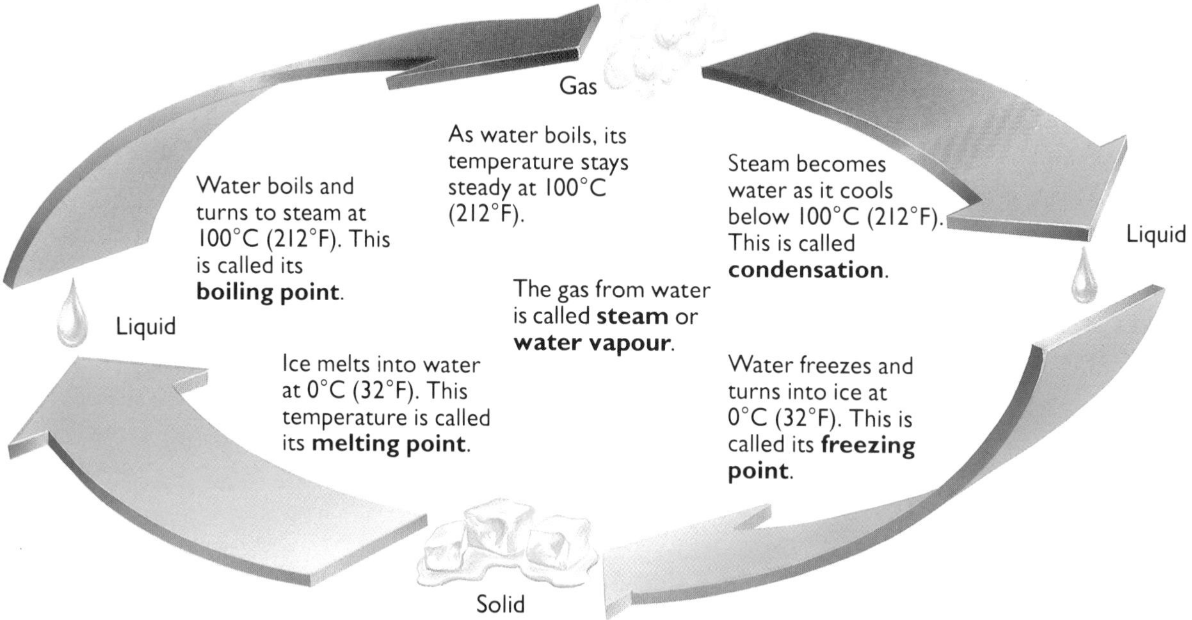

Gas
As water boils, its temperature stays steady at 100°C (212°F).
Water boils and turns to steam at 100°C (212°F). This is called its **boiling point**.
Steam becomes water as it cools below 100°C (212°F). This is called **condensation**.
Liquid
Liquid
The gas from water is called **steam** or **water vapour**.
Ice melts into water at 0°C (32°F). This temperature is called its **melting point**.
Water freezes and turns into ice at 0°C (32°F). This is called its **freezing point**.
Solid

As a solid is heated, the molecules make bigger and bigger vibrations. Eventually, the molecules cannot be held in their fixed positions any more. When this happens, the solid melts and turns into a liquid.

As a liquid is heated, the molecules move around faster and faster until they fly off, forming a gas. When a liquid gets hot enough, it boils. Gas bubbles form in the liquid and rise to the surface.

To change a gas into a liquid, or a liquid into a solid, you have to cool it. This takes out heat energy and slows down the molecules. To turn water into ice, you have to cool it in a fridge to take out the energy.

Why do wet things get dry?

Liquids are evaporating and changing into vapour all the time.
Sweat cools you down as it evaporates from your skin.

Where does the water go when a puddle dries up? The water slowly changes into vapour and spreads out through the air. This is called **evaporation**.

Your skin feels cold when it is wet. This is because water is evaporating from it. The water takes heat energy from your skin as it changes into vapour.

Faster evaporation

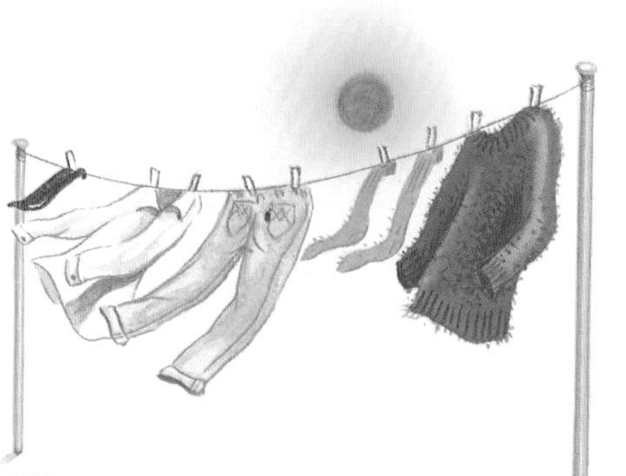

Water evaporates more quickly from wet clothes when it is hot, when the wind is blowing, and if they are spread out so that more air can get to them.

Boiling and freezing temperatures

Different things boil and freeze at different temperatures. Water freezes at 0°C (32°F). Steel melts at 1,400°C (2,550°F). Cooking oil boils at over 200°C (329°F).

Changing melting and boiling points

The melting point and the boiling point of water changes if you mix salt in with it. Salty water freezes at a lower temperature and boils at a higher temperature than pure water.

Mercury freezes at −39°C (−38°F) so it is not suitable for thermometers in cold places.
Pure water freezes at 0°C (32°F), but salt water freezes at −20°C (−4°F).
Putting salt on roads in winter stops water freezing on them so they do not get icy.
Burst pipe
Food cooks faster in salty water, because salty water boils at a higher temperature than pure water.

When most liquids freeze into solids, they take up less space. Water is unusual because, when it freezes into ice, it takes up *more* space. This is why water pipes can burst in winter. The water inside them freezes, splitting the pipe open.

When any liquid changes into gas, the gas takes up much more space. This is what makes a steam engine* work. Water is boiled into steam inside the engine. The steam takes up much more space than the water, pushing the pistons in and out.

Cool drinks

Ice-cubes cool a drink as they melt. Like all solids, ice needs heat energy to melt. It takes this energy from the liquid around it, cooling the drink.

Foggy windows

When water vapour from your breath hits a cold window, it turns into tiny drops of water, making the window fog up. This is called **condensation**.

DID YOU KNOW?

At the top of Mount Everest, where the air pressure is lower, water boils at only 70°C (160°F). The lower the air pressure, the lower the boiling point of a liquid.

**Steam engine, 44.*

The weather

Where does rain come from? What is snow? Why does the weather change? What makes the wind blow? All the world's weather is caused by the Sun, Earth, air and water.

What makes it rain?

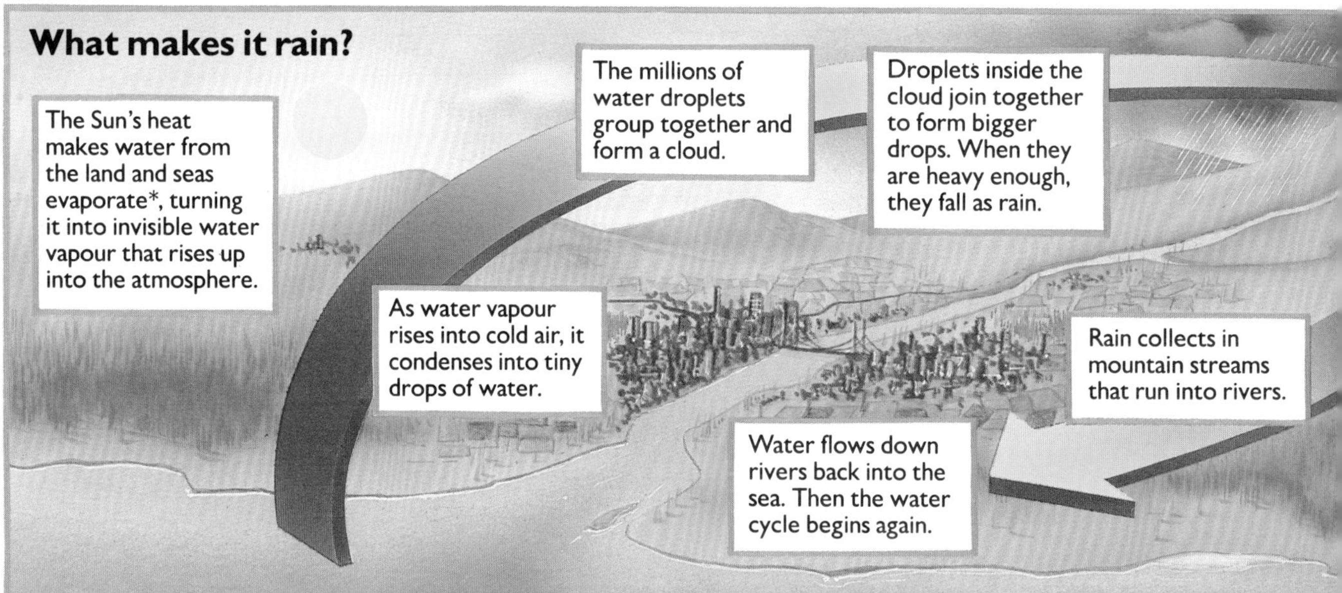

The Sun's heat makes water from the land and seas evaporate*, turning it into invisible water vapour that rises up into the atmosphere.
As water vapour rises into cold air, it condenses into tiny drops of water.
The millions of water droplets group together and form a cloud.
Droplets inside the cloud join together to form bigger drops. When they are heavy enough, they fall as rain.
Rain collects in mountain streams that run into rivers.
Water flows down rivers back into the sea. Then the water cycle begins again.

No new water is ever made. All the water that falls as rain has come from oceans, lakes and moisture on the Earth's surface. The same water has fallen as rain, snow or hail many times before. The water on Earth is used again and again. This is called the **water cycle**.

Where does the wind come from?

Wind is caused by the Sun. The Earth is hotter at the Equator than at the Poles, because the Equator is nearer the Sun.

The air rises over the Equator as it warms up and sinks over the Poles as it cools. This sets up huge convection currents* of moving air around the Earth.

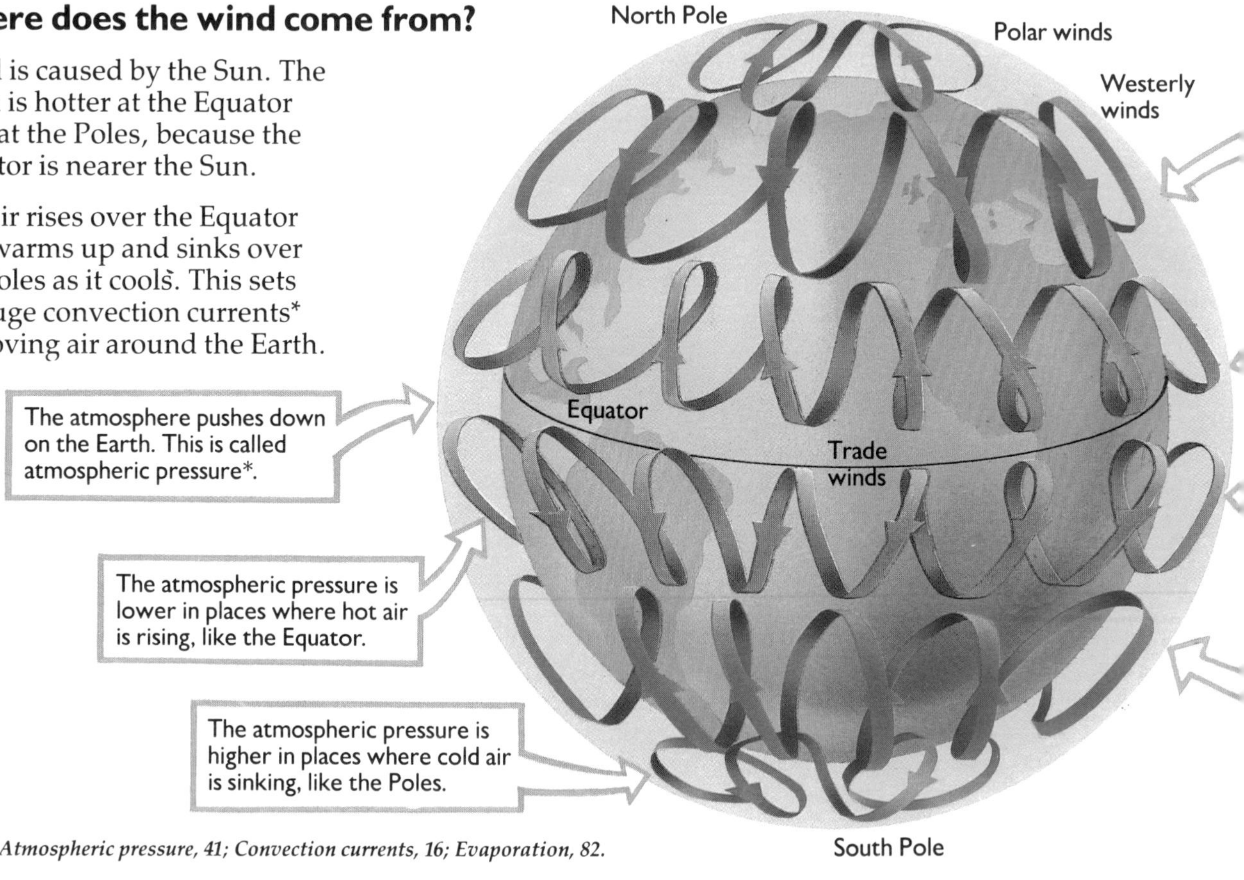

North Pole
Polar winds
Westerly winds
Equator
Trade winds
South Pole
The atmosphere pushes down on the Earth. This is called atmospheric pressure*.
The atmospheric pressure is lower in places where hot air is rising, like the Equator.
The atmospheric pressure is higher in places where cold air is sinking, like the Poles.

Atmospheric pressure, 41; Convection currents, 16; Evaporation, 82.

Not all clouds make rain. If a cloud moves into warmer air, it evaporates.

If a cloud reaches very cold air, the water droplets turn into ice crystals.

If the ice crystals do not melt, they fall as hailstones or snowflakes.

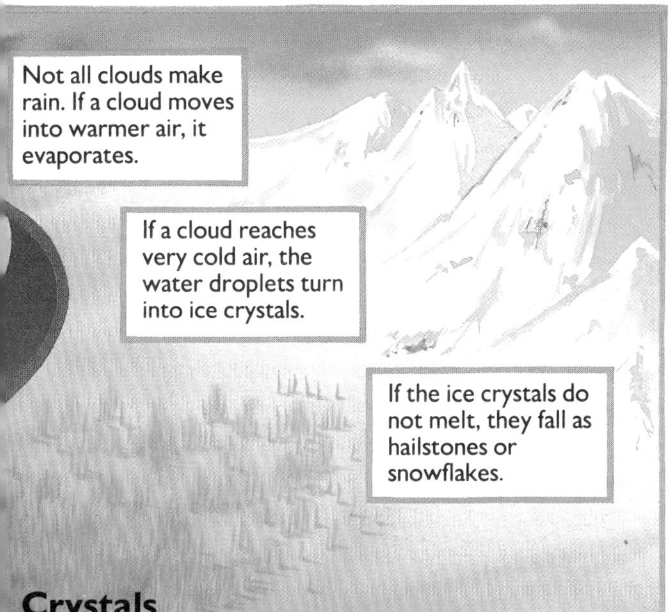

Crystals

Snowflakes are made of tiny, regularly shaped pieces of ice. These are called **crystals**. No two snowflakes are the same. Each one contains ice crystals of different shapes and sizes.

Humidity

The amount of water vapour in the air is called **humidity**. Warm air can carry more water vapour than cold air. When it is very humid, your skin feels sticky because there is so much water in the air already that your sweat cannot evaporate.

Dew and frost

During a cold night, the air cannot hold as much water vapour as hot air, so the vapour condenses into water drops, or **dew**. If the temperature goes below 0°C (32°F), the water vapour freezes and forms **frost.**

As areas of high and low atmospheric pressure move around the world, the weather changes from day to day.

The wind is caused by air flowing from areas of high pressure to areas of low pressure.

The winds are swung sideways as the Earth spins.

Each half of the Earth has three main wind patterns. These are the **trade winds**, the **polar winds** and the **westerlies**.

DID YOU KNOW?

The largest hailstone was found in Kansas, USA. It was 19cm (7½in) wide and as heavy as a melon.

Great storms

Huge storms of whirling wind and rain form over seas near the Equator where the air is warm and damp. They are called **hurricanes**, **typhoons** or **cyclones** depending on where they form.

A **tornado** is a funnel-shaped storm that is around 100m (110yds) across. The hot air at its middle whirls at over 600kmph (370mph), sucking up everything in its path.

Elements and compounds

All the different things in the Universe are made from atoms. There are about 105 different kinds of atom known today. Everything around you is made of these atoms combined in different ways.

Things that are made of one kind of atom are called elements. Because there are 105 kinds of atom, there are 105 different elements. Things that are made of different kinds of atoms joined together are called compounds.

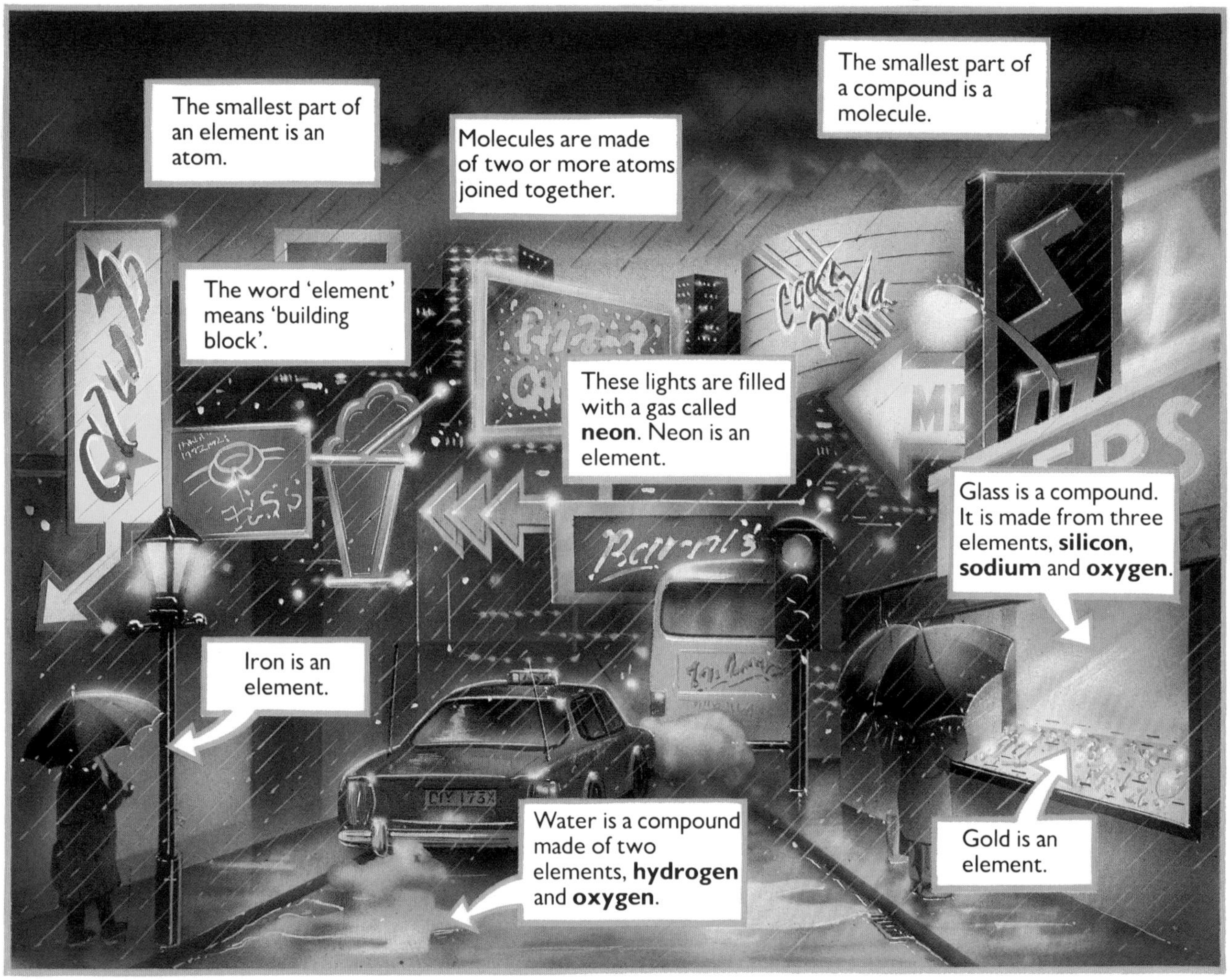

The smallest part of an element is an atom.
Molecules are made of two or more atoms joined together.
The smallest part of a compound is a molecule.
The word 'element' means 'building block'.
These lights are filled with a gas called **neon**. Neon is an element.
Glass is a compound. It is made from three elements, **silicon**, **sodium** and **oxygen**.
Iron is an element.
Water is a compound made of two elements, **hydrogen** and **oxygen**.
Gold is an element.

Naming elements and compounds

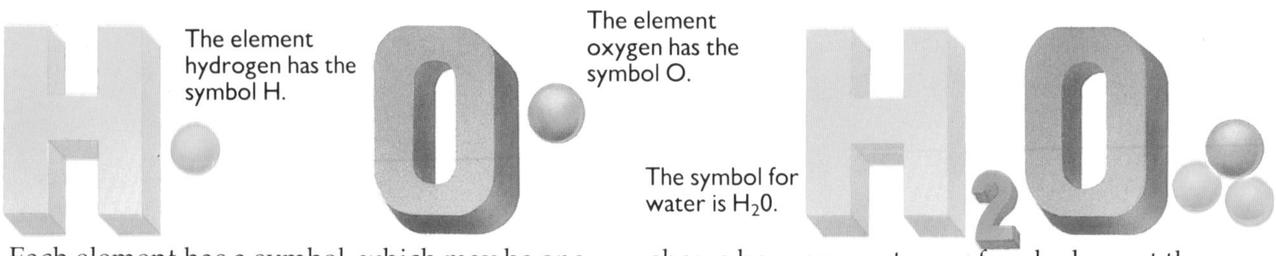

The element hydrogen has the symbol H.
The element oxygen has the symbol O.
The symbol for water is H_2O.

Each element has a symbol, which may be one or two letters. The same symbols are used for compounds. They show which elements the compound contains. A number after the symbol shows how many atoms of each element there are in a molecule. Water is a compound. Each water molecule contains two atoms of hydrogen and one atom of oxygen. Its symbol is H_2O.

Making something new

Salt is a compound called **sodium chloride**.
Salt
Sodium
Chlorine

Compounds are not the same as the elements that they are made up of. The salt that you put on food is a compound of two elements, **sodium** and **chlorine**. Sodium is a shiny metal and chlorine is a green gas. Both these elements are very dangerous on their own.

Chemical reactions

Rust is a compound called **iron oxide**.

Anything made of iron gets rusty if you leave it outside for a long time. Atoms of iron join up with oxygen atoms in air, making a new compound, **rust**. This is called a **chemical reaction**. A compound is made whenever atoms of different elements join, or **react**, together.

Air is a mixture

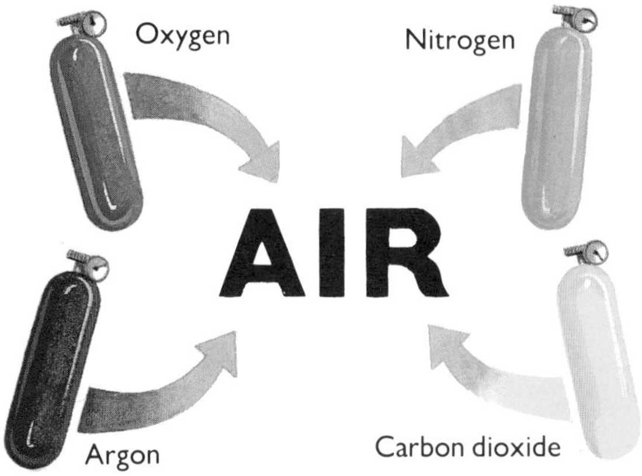
Oxygen
Nitrogen
AIR
Argon
Carbon dioxide

Air contains several gases. The atoms of these gases are mixed up, but not joined together. So air is called a **mixture**, *not* a compound. It contains three elements, **nitrogen**, **oxygen** and **argon**, and one compound, **carbon dioxide**.

Alchemy

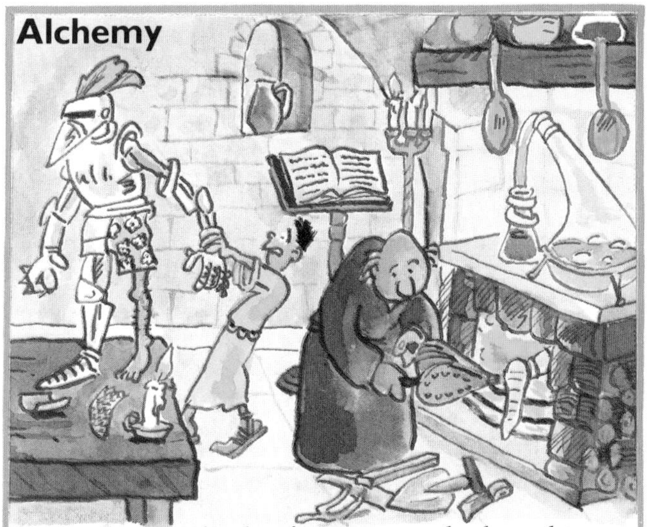

For many hundreds of years, people thought that all things on Earth were made from **air**, **earth**, **fire** and **water**. By mixing them in different amounts, they thought they could turn one thing into another. Some people, called **alchemists**, tried to change ordinary metals into gold.

The Periodic Table*

About 100 years ago, a Russian scientist called Dmitry Mendeleyev listed all the known elements in a chart called the **Periodic Table**. This chart groups elements that are similar and shows which ones will react together to form compounds.

DID YOU KNOW?

Diamond and pencil lead, which is called **graphite**, are made from the same thing. Both of them are forms of the element, **carbon**. They are different because the carbon atoms inside them are held together in different ways.

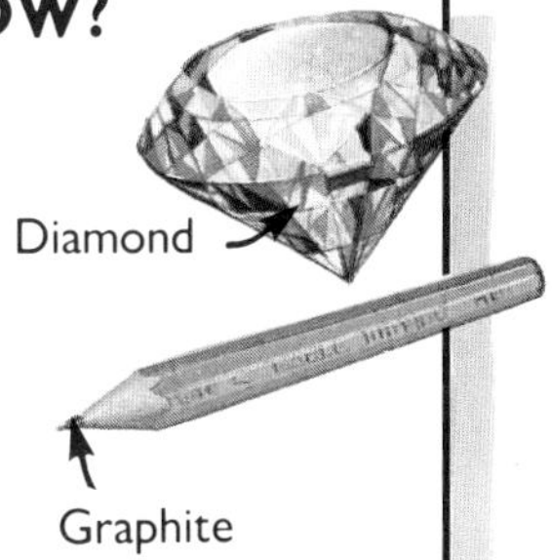
Diamond
Graphite

**Periodic Table, 120*

Fire

If something gets hot enough, it burns. Once it starts burning, it gives out so much heat energy that it carries on burning on its own.

People rely on burning fuels for cooking, heating and for working machines. But when fire gets out of control, it is very dangerous.

What happens when things burn?

Burning is a chemical reaction*. Things burn when they get hot enough to react with the oxygen in the air around them.

As in all chemical reactions, burning produces new compounds. Smoke and ash are a mixture of these compounds.

Fire needs three things: heat, fuel and oxygen. If any one of these things is taken away, the fire goes out.

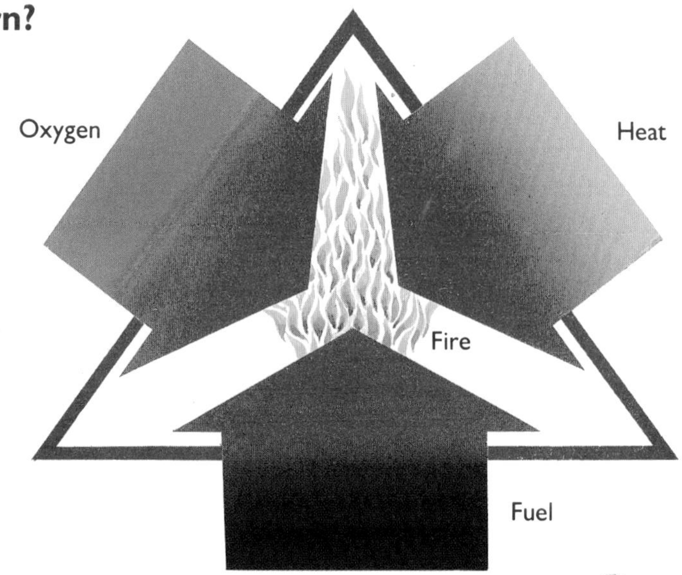

What makes soot?

Soot is a powder made of tiny pieces of the element **carbon**. Many things, like wood and coal, contain carbon. When they burn the carbon reacts with oxygen, producing fumes. But if there is not enough oxygen to react with the carbon, soot is produced.

Dangerous fumes

Fire uses up oxygen in the air and produces fumes that often are as dangerous as the flames. The fumes from plastics, foam rubber and some paints are deadly, even in small amounts. This is why fire-fighters carry air cylinders and wear masks.

How fires spread

Fire can spread by convection*. Convection currents carry heat, smoke and burning materials to other places. Where they land, they can start new fires.

Fire can spread by radiation*. Heat radiation from the flames heats things that are close to the fire. Eventually they get so hot that they burst into flames.

Fire can spread by conduction*. Even though metal does not burn, it can carry the heat from a fire by conduction, setting other things alight.

**Chemical reactions, 87; Conduction of heat, 14; Convection, 16; Heat radiation, 18.*

Putting out fires

If you discover a fire, shout "Fire!" to warn people. Once you are safe, quickly telephone the fire brigade. Never try to tackle a fire on your own.

Taking away either the fuel, heat or oxygen from a fire will put it out. Depending on what is burning, fires have to be put out in different ways.

Shutting doors and windows cuts out the supply of fresh oxygen. This slows down the spread of the fire.

Spraying water on a wood or paper fire takes the heat away. Without heat, the fire goes out.

If someone's clothes are on fire, rolling them on the ground in a rug or curtain cuts out the oxygen.

Putting a lid or a wet towel over a pan of burning fat or oil cuts out the oxygen. *Never* pour water on burning oil. The oil will splash and carry on burning as it floats on the water.

If something electric is on fire, the power should be switched off. Gas or powder fire extinguishers can be used to put the fire out, but *never* use water because it conducts electricity*.

Fire extinguishers

Fire extinguishers are filled with water, foam, powder or a gas. They are used for putting out different kinds of fires.

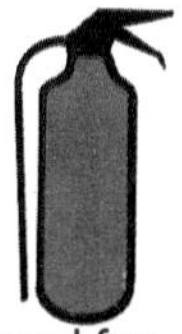

Water is used for most fires *except* burning liquids and electrical fires.

Foam is used for putting out burning liquids. It should *never* be used on electrical fires.

Dry powder is used for putting out burning liquids and electrical fires.

Carbon dioxide is used for putting out burning liquids and electrical fires.

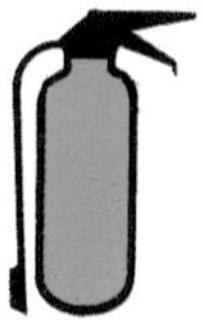

Halon gas is used for putting out burning liquids and electrical fires.

Never breathe in the fumes given out by halon or carbon dioxide extinguishers.

Burning and engines

Burning produces hot gases that take up much more space than the thing that burns. The hot gases from burning fuel make car engines work.

As the gases expand in the engine, they make the pistons* move in and out. Rocket and jet engines are pushed forward as the hot gases rush out behind.

DID YOU KNOW?

The world's most powerful fire engine is the Oshkosh firetruck, used for aircraft fires. In just three minutes, it can spray enough foam to cover a football pitch.

*Electricity, 96; Pistons, 45.

Materials

The things around you are all made out of different materials. Some materials come from plants, animals or things that are dug up from the ground. These are sometimes called natural materials. Others are made in factories. These are called man-made or synthetic materials. Scientists study atoms and molecules so they can design new synthetic materials.

Metals

Many things are made out of metals, or mixtures of different metals, called **alloys**. Metals are found in **ores** that are dug out of the ground. The metals are removed by heating up the ores.

Copper and **bronze** were the first metals that people used. Today, **iron** and **steel** are the most widely used metals. Steel is a mixture of iron and a little carbon.

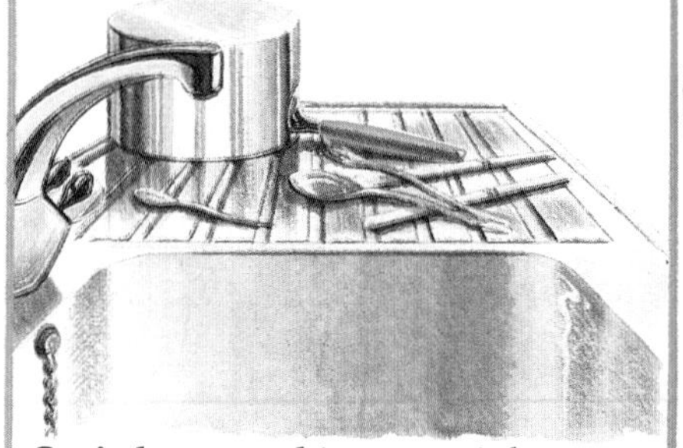

Stainless steel is a special type of steel that does not rust*. **Aluminum** is a very light metal, so is used to make parts for aircraft.

Ceramics

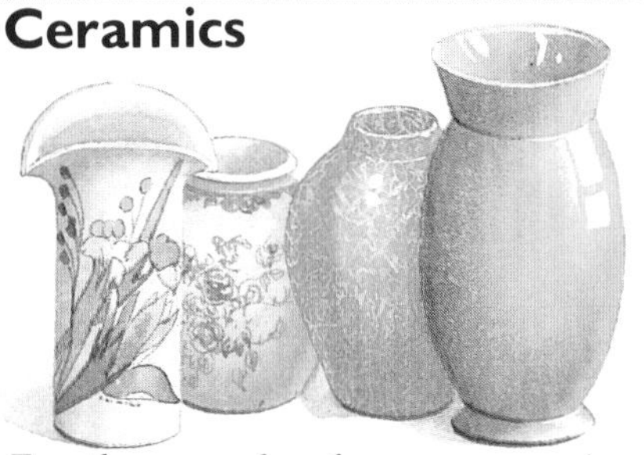

For thousands of years, people have used **clay** to make pots and jugs. The clay is shaped when damp, and then baked in an oven to harden it. Materials like clay are called **ceramics**.

Ceramic materials are used for many things. **Porcelain** is used to make cups and plates. **Bricks** and **tiles** are used for building. Even **glass** is a type of ceramic.

Ceramics can be heated to very high temperatures. New, strong ceramic materials are now being used to make parts for engines.

Fibres

Cloth and fabric are made from thin strands, called **fibres**. Some fibres, like wool, silk and cotton, come from plants and animals. They are called **natural fibres**.

Many fabrics are made from man-made fibres like nylon, rayon and polyester. A special fibre, **kevlar**, is even stronger than steel but very light. It is used in some aircraft and boats.

**Rust, 87.*

Plastics

Most plastics are made from compounds* that are found in crude oil*. There are many different types of plastics that are used for different things.

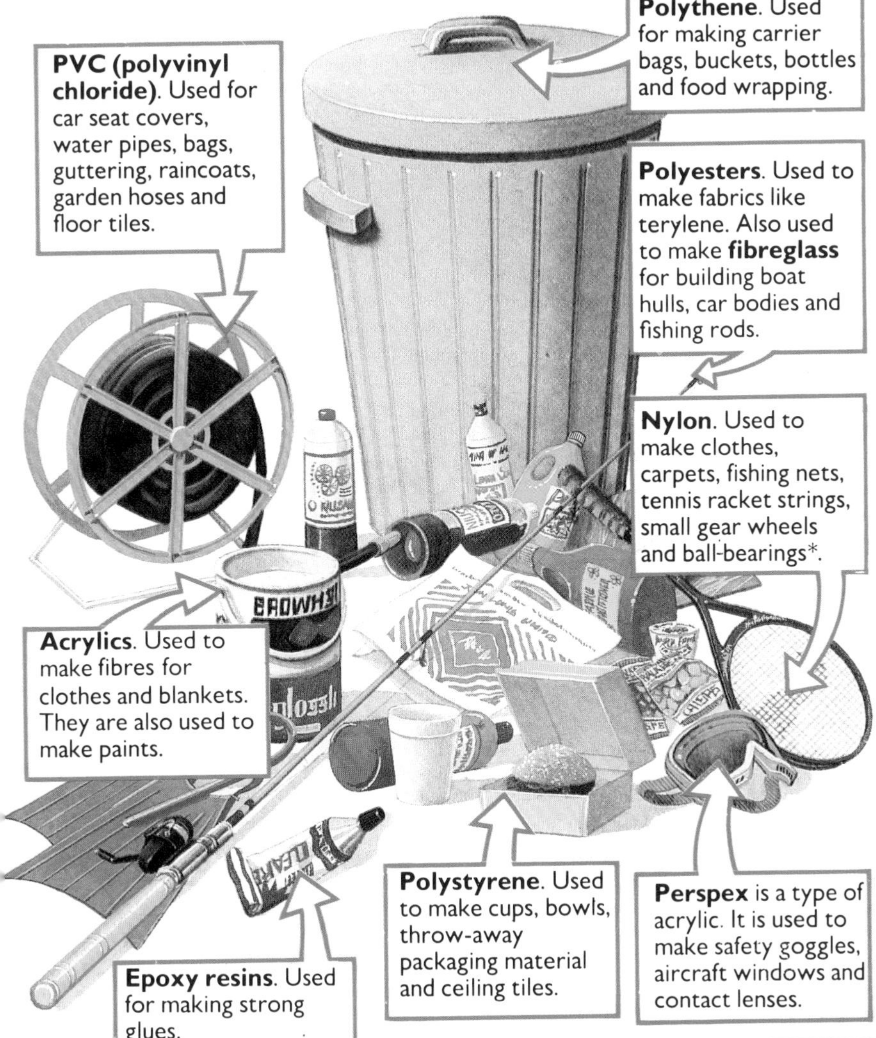

Polythene. Used for making carrier bags, buckets, bottles and food wrapping.

PVC (polyvinyl chloride). Used for car seat covers, water pipes, bags, guttering, raincoats, garden hoses and floor tiles.

Polyesters. Used to make fabrics like terylene. Also used to make **fibreglass** for building boat hulls, car bodies and fishing rods.

Nylon. Used to make clothes, carpets, fishing nets, tennis racket strings, small gear wheels and ball-bearings*.

Acrylics. Used to make fibres for clothes and blankets. They are also used to make paints.

Polystyrene. Used to make cups, bowls, throw-away packaging material and ceiling tiles.

Perspex is a type of acrylic. It is used to make safety goggles, aircraft windows and contact lenses.

Epoxy resins. Used for making strong glues.

Long molecules

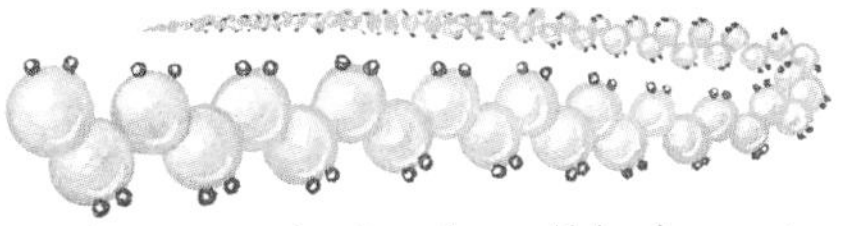

Fibres and plastics all belong to a group of compounds called **polymers**. Polymers are different from other compounds because their molecules are very long. They are made of lots of small molecules joined together.

DID YOU KNOW?

Nylon was first produced in the USA in 1938. It was made by scientists from New York and London, and was named after these cities (NY-Lon).

Using materials with care

Trees are cut down to provide wood, but this destroys whole forests that can never be replaced. These forests are needed to balance gases* and moisture* in the atmosphere.

Natural materials, like wood, are called **biodegradable** because they rot when they are thrown away. Most man-made materials, like plastics, cause pollution because they never rot away.

New plastics are now being made that *are* biodegradable. These materials are not made from crude oil. At the moment, they are more expensive to make, but they do not cause pollution.

**Balancing gases, 21; Ball-bearings, 31; Compounds, 86; Crude oil, 25; Moisture in the air, 84.*

Electricity around you

Think how often you watch television, switch on lights and use telephones. These things, and many others, work using electricity. A world without electricity would be very different.

In this picture, you will find lots of questions about things that work because of electricity. You will find the answers to these questions in the next few pages.

Why does a light bulb light up when you switch it on?
How does a cassette recorder work?
How does a microphone pick up sound?
How is electricity produced in a power station?
How does electricity get from a power station to your home?
What makes the picture on your television?
Why do you need an aerial to make your television work?
How does a radio programme get to your radio?
What makes a compass needle move? What have magnets got to do with electricity?
What makes a robot work?
How does the sound of someone's voice reach you over the telephone?
How does an electric motor work?

Electricity was not invented. It was first discovered by the Greeks, about 2,000 years ago. But people only learned how to produce it and make use of it just over 150 years ago.

Electricity is a form of energy. It can be changed into heat energy, light energy and sound energy. It can also be changed into kinetic energy to make machines work.

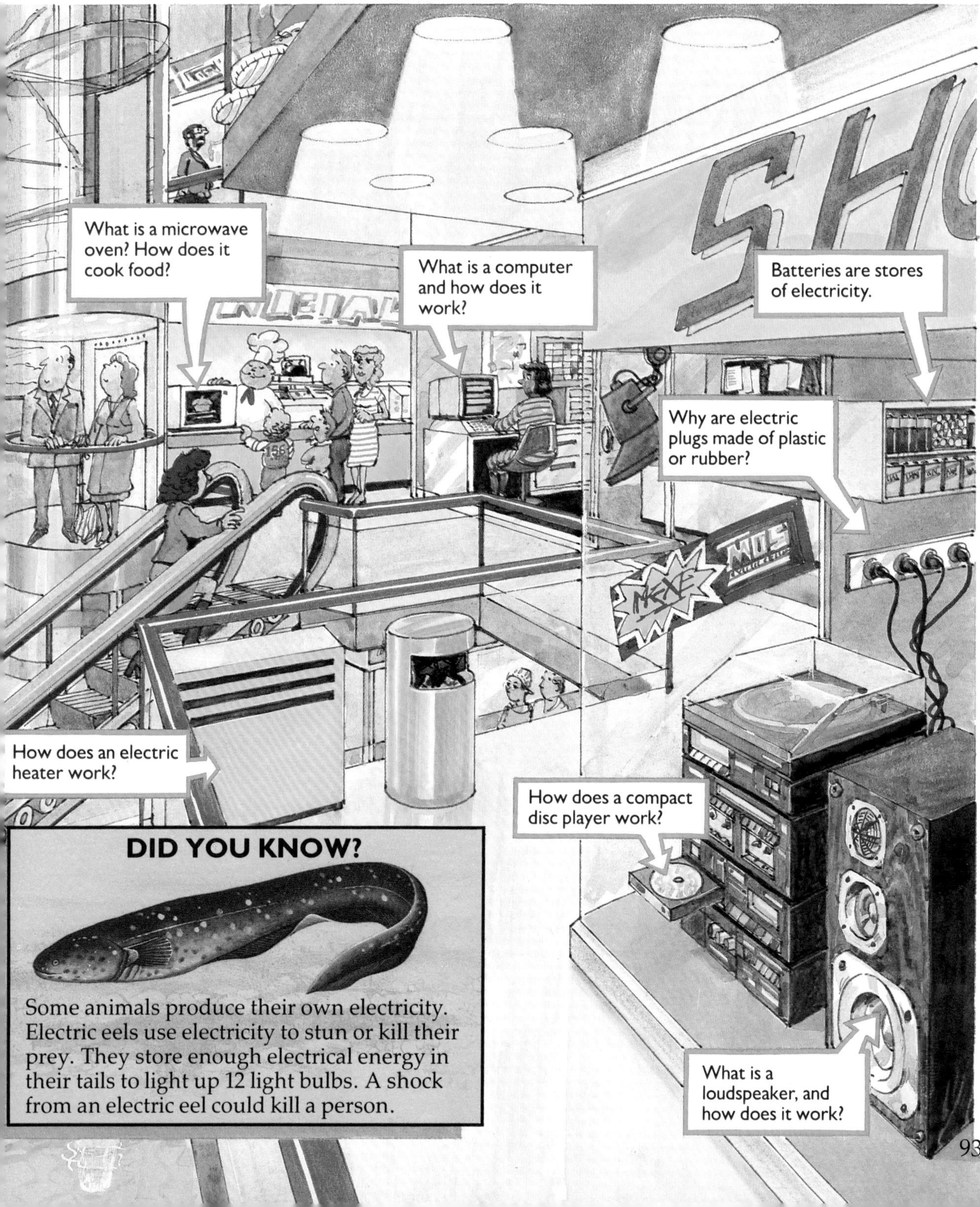
What is a microwave oven? How does it cook food?
What is a computer and how does it work?
Batteries are stores of electricity.
Why are electric plugs made of plastic or rubber?
How does an electric heater work?
How does a compact disc player work?
What is a loudspeaker, and how does it work?

DID YOU KNOW?

Some animals produce their own electricity. Electric eels use electricity to stun or kill their prey. They store enough electrical energy in their tails to light up 12 light bulbs. A shock from an electric eel could kill a person.

Flowing electricity

Many things around you need electricity to make them work. Some things, like torches, use electricity from batteries. Other things, like lamps and televisions, are plugged in. They use mains electricity that is produced in power stations*.

Conductors and insulators

Electricity can flow, or is **conducted**, more easily through some materials than through others. Things through which electricity flows easily are called **conductors**. Things that electricity cannot flow through are called **insulators**.

Glass and other ceramics are insulators.
Air is an insulator.
Wood is an insulator.
Inside this plastic cable there are metal wires that carry electricity.
Rubber is an insulator.
Water conducts electricity.
The prongs on a plug are made of metal to conduct electricity from the socket.
Plugs are made of rubber or plastic because they are insulators.

Metals are good conductors. This is why metals are used to make wires for carrying electricity.

Most plastics are insulators. So metal wires are covered in plastic to stop you getting an electric shock.

What is electricity?

The electrons in atoms carry an electric charge*. When electrons flow together in one direction, they carry electricity with them. Flowing electricity is called **current electricity**.

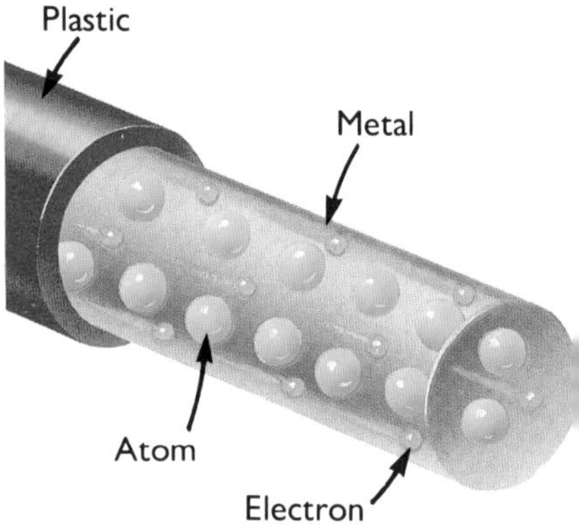

Plastic
Metal
Atom
Electron

Things that conduct electricity, like metals, have electrons* that are free to move. This is because the electrons are not held tightly to their atoms*. The electrons are able to carry electricity from place to place.

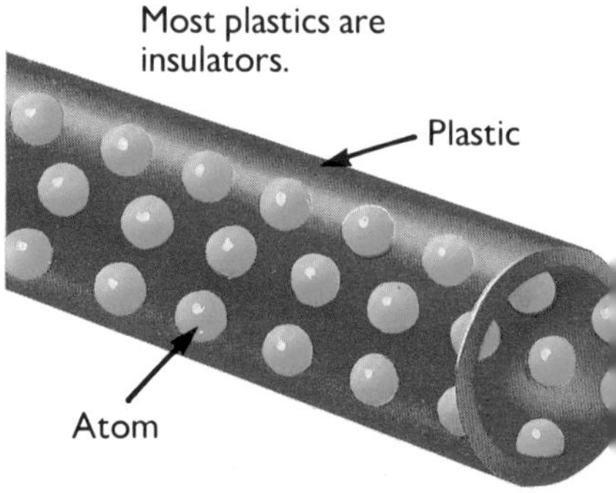

Most plastics are insulators.
Plastic
Atom

The electrons in insulators are held tightly inside their atoms. Because the electrons cannot move, insulators cannot conduct electricity.

The amount of electricity that flows through a wire each second is called an **electric current**. It is measured in **amperes** or **amps (A)**.

**Atoms, 76; Electric charge, 77; Electrons, 77; Power stations, 102.*

Resistance

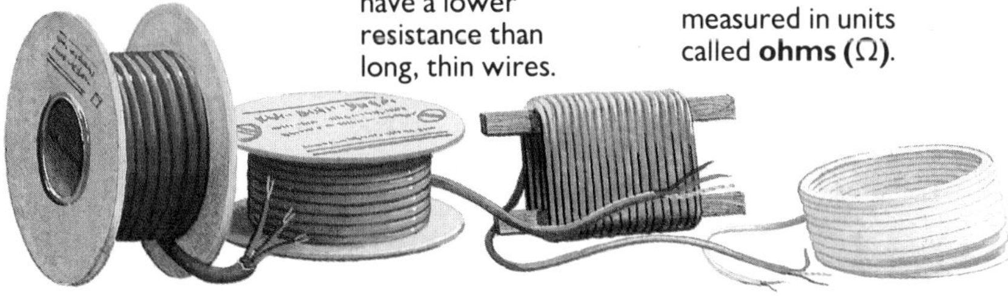

Short, thick wires have a lower resistance than long, thin wires.

Resistance is measured in units called **ohms (Ω)**.

Electricity flows better through some things than others. How well something conducts electricity is measured by its **resistance**. The resistance of a wire depends on what it is made of, its length and its thickness.

The *lower* the resistance of a wire, the *better* it conducts electricity. Copper is used to make wires because it it has a lower resistance than most other metals and therefore conducts electricity better.

Electric circuits

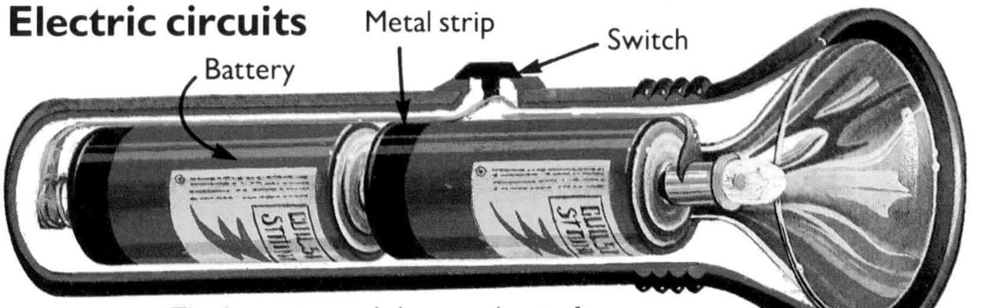

The batteries and the metal strip form an electric circuit.

An electric current will only flow around a continuous wire. This is called a **circuit**. The current stops flowing if there are any breaks in the circuit.

An electric current can be turned on and off with a **switch**. Switching something on joins up the circuit. Switching something off breaks the circuit.

Electricity into heat

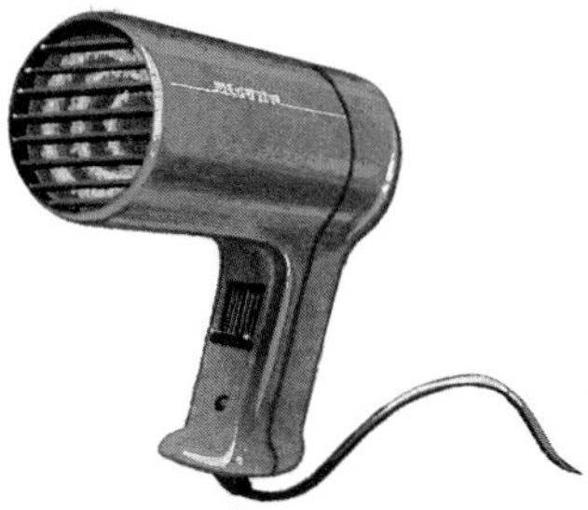

When electricity flows, it makes things heat up. The higher the resistance of a wire, the hotter it gets when electricity flows through it. This is why the coiled up wires inside a hair-drier glow red hot.

Electricity into light

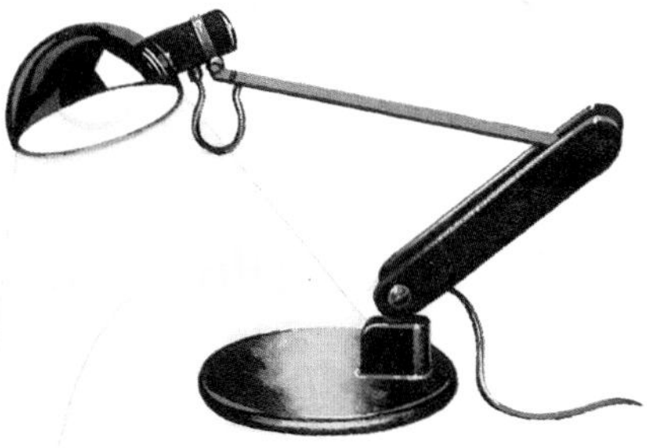

A light bulb contains a thin wire. As electricity flows through the wire, it glows white hot, giving out light. Only 2% of the electrical energy going into a light bulb changes into light. The rest changes into heat.

DID YOU KNOW?

The nerves in your body work by electricity. Electrical signals from your brain make your muscles work. They carry information from your eyes, ears, nose, tongue and skin back to your brain.

Batteries

A battery contains a store of chemical energy. This energy changes into electrical energy when the battery is connected in a circuit.

Batteries provide the electric force that pushes electrons around a circuit. This force is called an **electromotive force** and is measured in **volts (V)**.

Types of electricity

Electricity from power stations is called mains electricity. It is much more powerful than the electricity from batteries.

Circuit breakers and fuses

Things are damaged if too much electric current flows through them. Circuit breakers cut the electricity if the current gets too large. Houses have circuit breakers to protect the wiring.

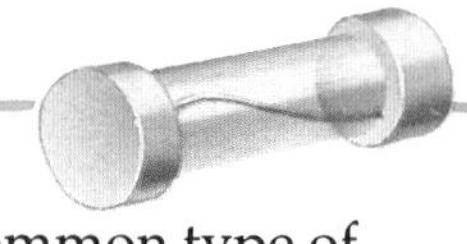

The most common type of circuit breaker is called a **fuse**. It is a piece of special wire that melts if too much current flows through it, breaking the circuit.

When you plug something in and turn it on, mains electricity flows into it from the socket. Each plug has a fuse inside it, to break the circuit if too much current flows through it.

Electric current from batteries flows around circuits in one direction. This is called **direct current**. Mains electricity is different. The current changes direction many times each second. This is called **alternating current**.

Electricity cables contain two wires called **live** and **neutral**. Both carry live electric current. Some cables have a third wire called an **earth** wire. If a circuit is faulty, the earth wire conducts the electricity safely into the ground.

Safe electricity

Mains electricity can be very dangerous. *Never* touch anything with live electricity flowing through it, because you could get a deadly electric shock.

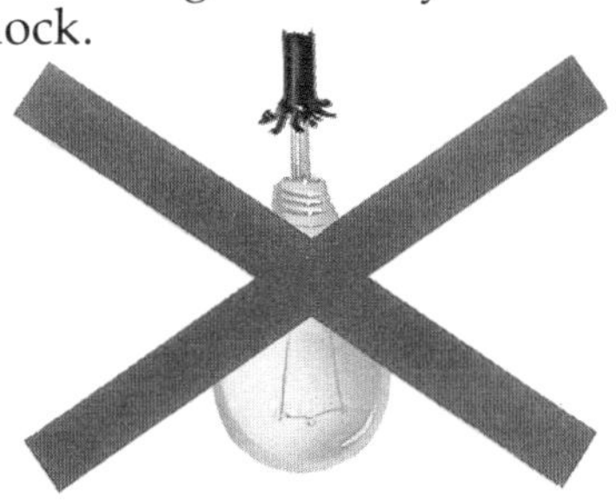

Never use anything with a cable that has the plastic insulation worn through. Touching the cable could give you a shock.

Never plug too many things into one socket. This can make too much current flow through the socket and can cause a fire.

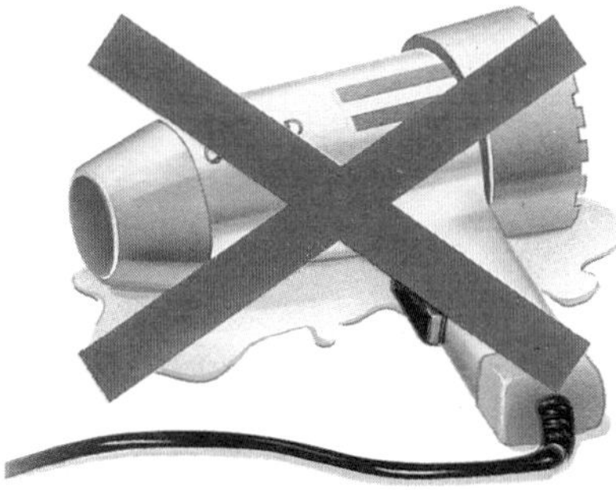

Never use anything that works off mains electricity when you are wet. This is because water conducts electricity very well. This is why water must never be sprayed on an electrical fire*.

*Electrical fires, 89.

Static electricity

Current electricity can flow. But there is another type, called static electricity, that stays in one place.

Rub a balloon on a wool sweater and hold it up to a wall. It will stick there by itself. Now rub two balloons on the sweater and put them beside each other. They will move away from each other without your touching them. These things happen because rubbing the balloons gives them static electricity.

Atoms* contain electrons that carry negative charge and protons that carry positive charge. Normally, there are the same number of protons and electrons in an atom so the positive and negative charges cancel each other out. But when you rub the balloon, it picks up some extra electrons from the wool and becomes electrically charged.

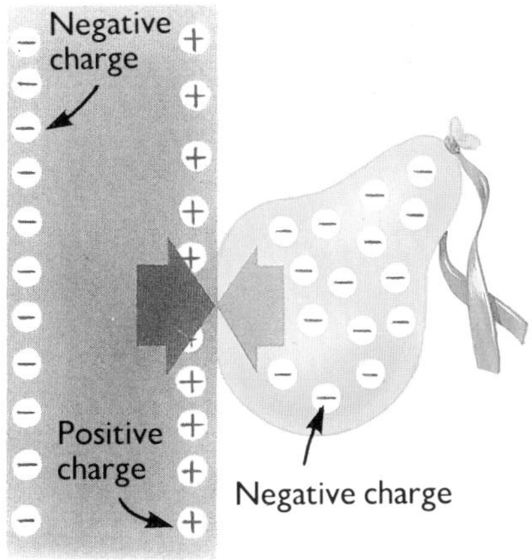
Negative charge
Positive charge
Negative charge

The extra negative charges in the balloon are attracted to the positive charges in the wall, so it sticks there. Negative charges are always attracted to positive charges.

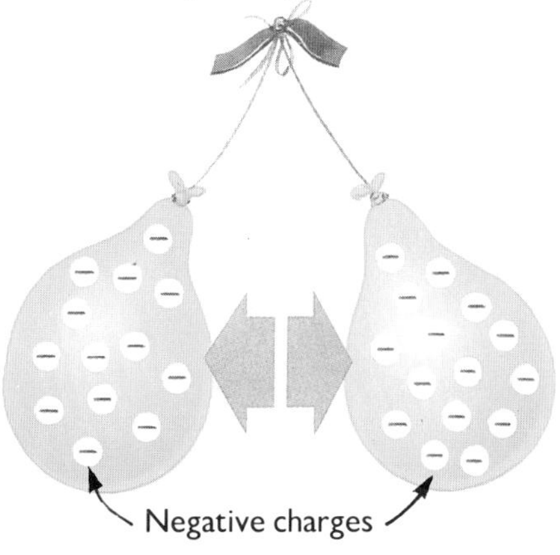
Negative charges

The two balloons push away from each other because both have extra negative charges. Negative charges always repel negative charges and positive charges repel positive charges.

DID YOU KNOW?

Thunder and lightning are caused by static electricity. Clouds become charged as the tiny ice crystals inside them rub against each other.

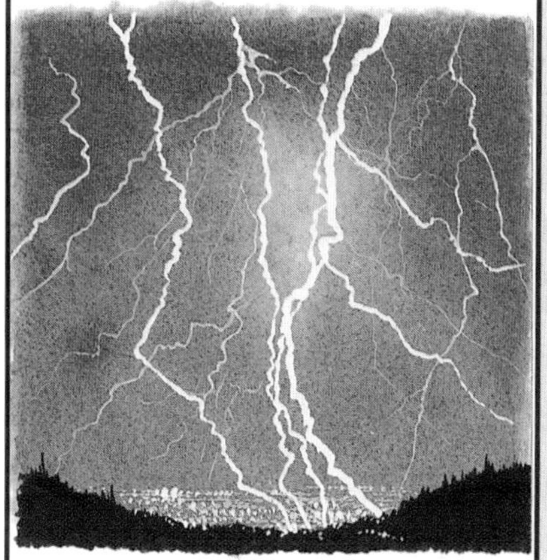

A cloud can get so charged up that electrons jump between it and the ground, or another cloud. This causes a huge spark, which is lightning.

Static around you

Rubbing your shoes on a nylon carpet makes static electricity build up on you. If you touch something metal, you may feel a tiny shock as a spark jumps from you to the metal.

*Atoms, 77.

Magnets and electricity

Magnets can be used for many things. If you spill pins on the floor, a magnet will help you pick them up by pulling the pins to it. A compass, which helps people find their way, has a magnet inside it. Many things that work using electricity have a magnet inside them. Magnets are used to make electric motors spin and to produce electricity in generators.

The magnet picks up steel pins because steel contains iron.

See what you can pick up with a magnet. You cannot pick up anything made of plastic, wood or rubber. But things made of the metals iron, cobalt or nickel are pulled towards it.

Things will be pulled to a magnet if they are inside its magnetic field. They do not need to touch the magnet.

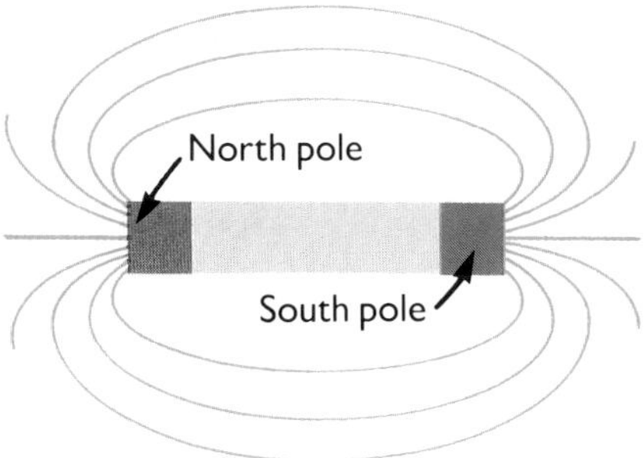
North pole
South pole

Magnets produce a **magnetic force**. The area around a magnet where the force works is called a **magnetic field**. It is strongest at the ends of the magnet, which are called **poles**.

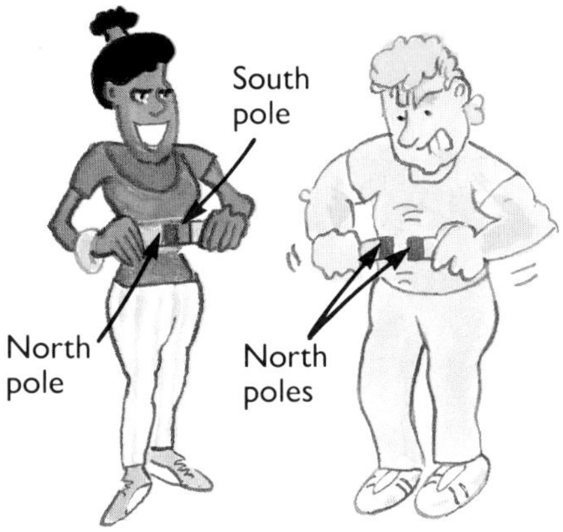
South pole
North pole
North poles

Hold two magnets together. Feel how they pull and push each other as you turn them around. This happens because unlike poles are pulled together, but like poles are pushed apart.

Magnets and compasses

The Greeks used magnets 2,000 years ago. They dug a material out of the ground, called **lodestone**, which is magnetic. They found that if a magnet is able to swing freely, its north pole always points North and its south pole points South. This happens because the Earth has its own magnetic field.

The Earth's magnetic field is strongest at the Poles.

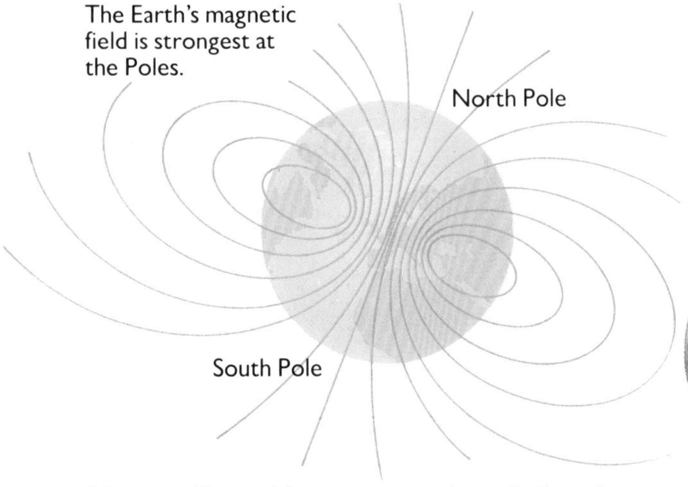
North Pole
South Pole

The needle inside a compass is a magnet. The magnet points North, so you can tell which direction you are facing.

Some materials are naturally magnetic. They can be used to make other magnets.

Sailors have used compasses to help them find their way at sea, or **navigate**, since the 11th century.

DID YOU KNOW?

Birds fly huge distances to escape the winter each year. Arctic terns fly the farthest, from the Arctic to the Antarctic and back, a total of 35,000km (21,750 miles).

Like other birds, they navigate very accurately, but no one is sure how. One idea is that they may be guided by the Earth's magnetic field.

Electromagnetism

Electricity and magnetism together make many things work. This is called **electromagnetism**. Electricity can be used to make a magnetic field and magnetism can be used to produce electricity. Whenever an electric current flows through a wire, it produces a magnetic field around the wire. When the electric current is switched off, the magnetic field disappears.

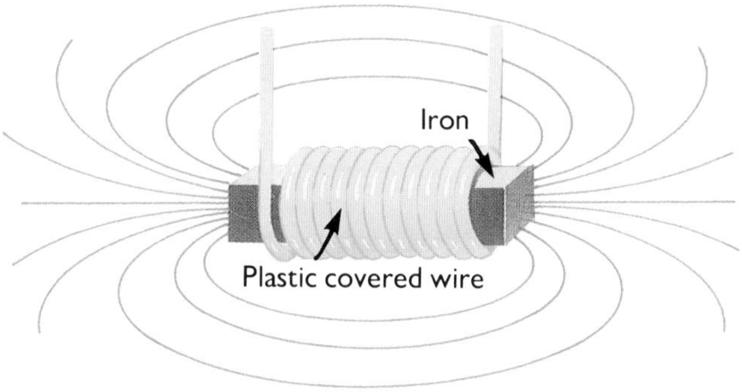
Iron
Plastic covered wire

The bigger the electric current, the stronger the magnetic field around a wire. It can be made even stronger by coiling up the wire many times. A coil of wire that is used to produce a magnetic field is called an **electromagnet**.

Use a battery for this experiment. *Never* connect anything to mains electricity.

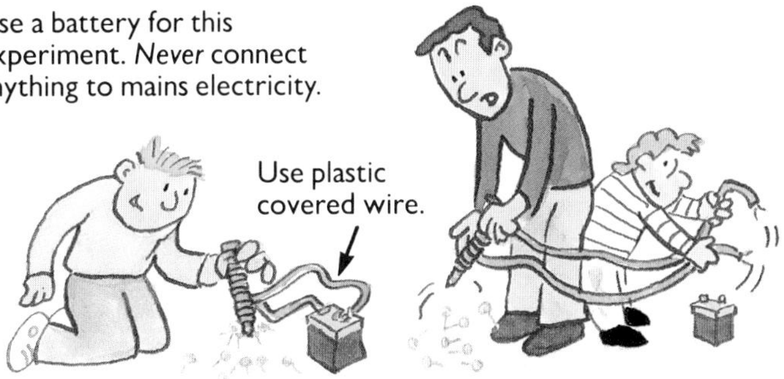
Use plastic covered wire.

Use a wire, a battery and an iron nail to make an electromagnet. Wind the wire around the nail many times. Connect each end of the wire to the battery. Now use the nail to pick up pins. See how they fall off if you disconnect the battery.

Trains that float

Electromagnets are used on some special trains instead of wheels. The magnetic force from electromagnets hold the train a few centimetres above the track, and push it along.

These trains do not touch the track, so there is no friction. They can go very fast.

Electric motors

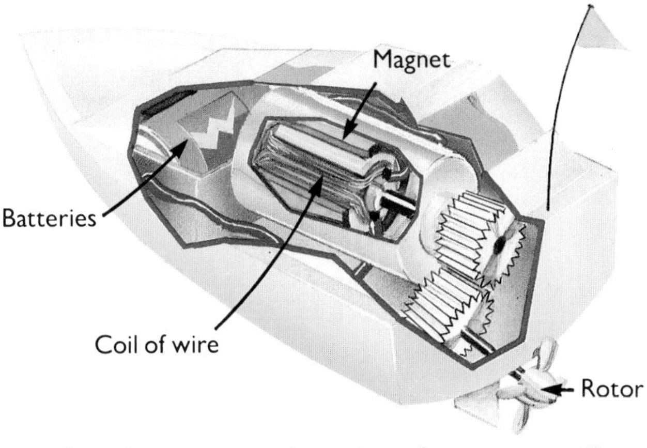
Magnet
Batteries
Coil of wire
Rotor

An **electric motor** works using electromagnetism. It has a coiled up wire inside that sits between the poles of a magnet. When current flows through the coil, a magnetic field is produced. This makes the rotor spin around.

Generating electricity

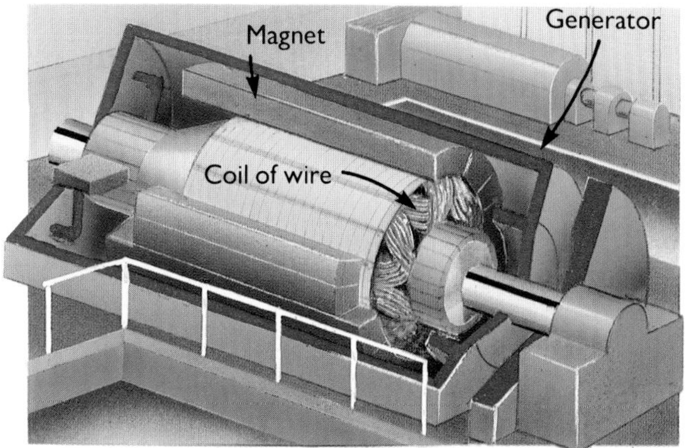
Magnet
Generator
Coil of wire

An electric current is produced inside a wire, if it is moved in a magnetic field. This is how a **generator**, or **dynamo**, produces electricity. An engine spins a coil of wire between the poles of a magnet. This generates electric current.

Records and tapes

What makes a record player work? How is sound recorded on to a tape? How does a loudspeaker work? How does a microphone pick up sound? Electromagnetism makes all these things work. It is used to record sound on to records and tapes and to play back sound through loudspeakers.

Microphones

Microphones change sounds into electrical signals. A thin disc inside a microphone vibrates as sound waves* hit it. This makes a coil of wire vibrate.

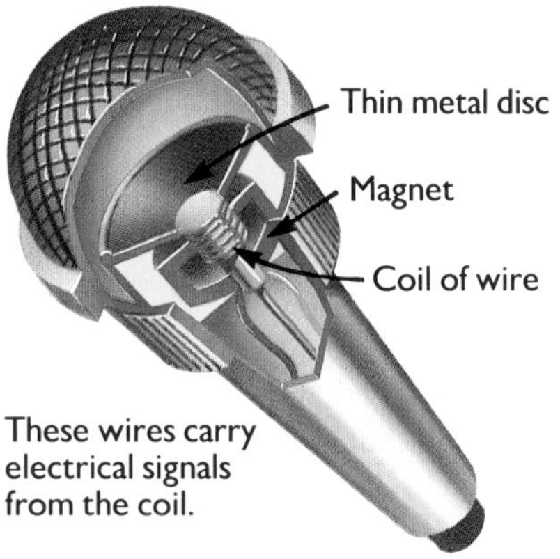

Thin metal disc
Magnet
Coil of wire
These wires carry electrical signals from the coil.

The coil sits between the poles of a magnet*. As the coil moves, it produces an electric current. The current flows backwards and forwards in time with the sound and is carried down a wire to an amplifier*.

How does a loudspeaker work?

A loudspeaker works in the opposite way to a microphone. It changes electrical signals back into sound waves.

The electrical signals from a hi-fi make a thin plastic or paper cone vibrate. This produces the sounds you hear.

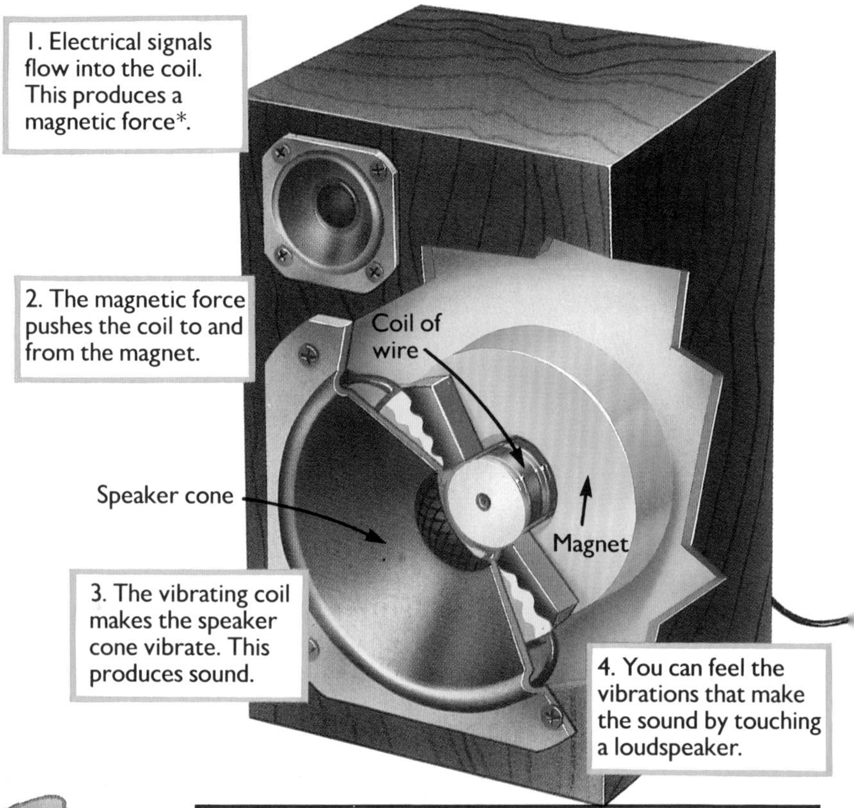

1. Electrical signals flow into the coil. This produces a magnetic force*.
2. The magnetic force pushes the coil to and from the magnet.
Coil of wire
Speaker cone
Magnet
3. The vibrating coil makes the speaker cone vibrate. This produces sound.
4. You can feel the vibrations that make the sound by touching a loudspeaker.

How telephones work

When you make a telephone call, the sound of your voice is changed into electrical signals by a microphone. These signals are carried by cables to a **telephone exchange**. The exchange sends the signals to the person you are calling. A small loudspeaker in their telephone turns the signals back into sound waves.

DID YOU KNOW?

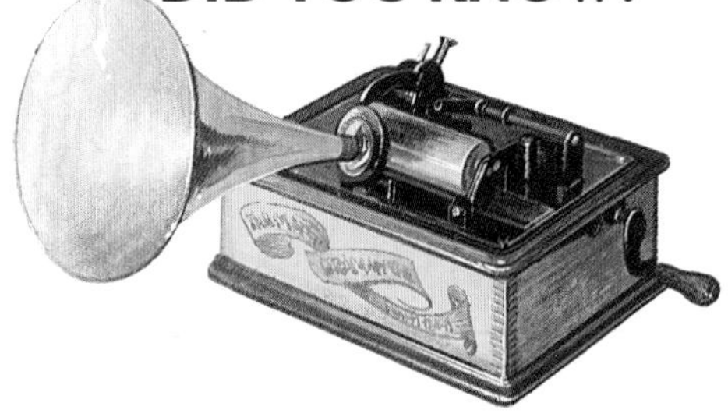

The first machine for recording and playing back sound was called a **phonograph**. It was invented by Thomas Edison in 1878. The sound was recorded on to a drum covered in tin foil.

 **Amplifier, 101; Magnetic force, 98; Poles of magnet, 98; Sound waves, 66.*

Playing records

A record has a thin groove that runs from the outside to the centre. There are millions of tiny bumps in it. When you play a record, a tiny crystal, called a **stylus**, runs along the groove.

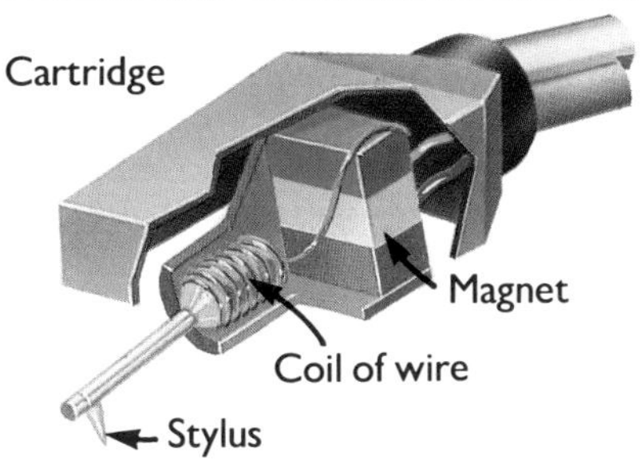

Cartridge
Magnet
Coil of wire
Stylus

The stylus moves up and down over the bumps. This makes a tiny coil vibrate inside the **cartridge**. The coil sits between the poles of a magnet, so it produces electrical signals as it vibrates. The signals go along wires to an amplifier.

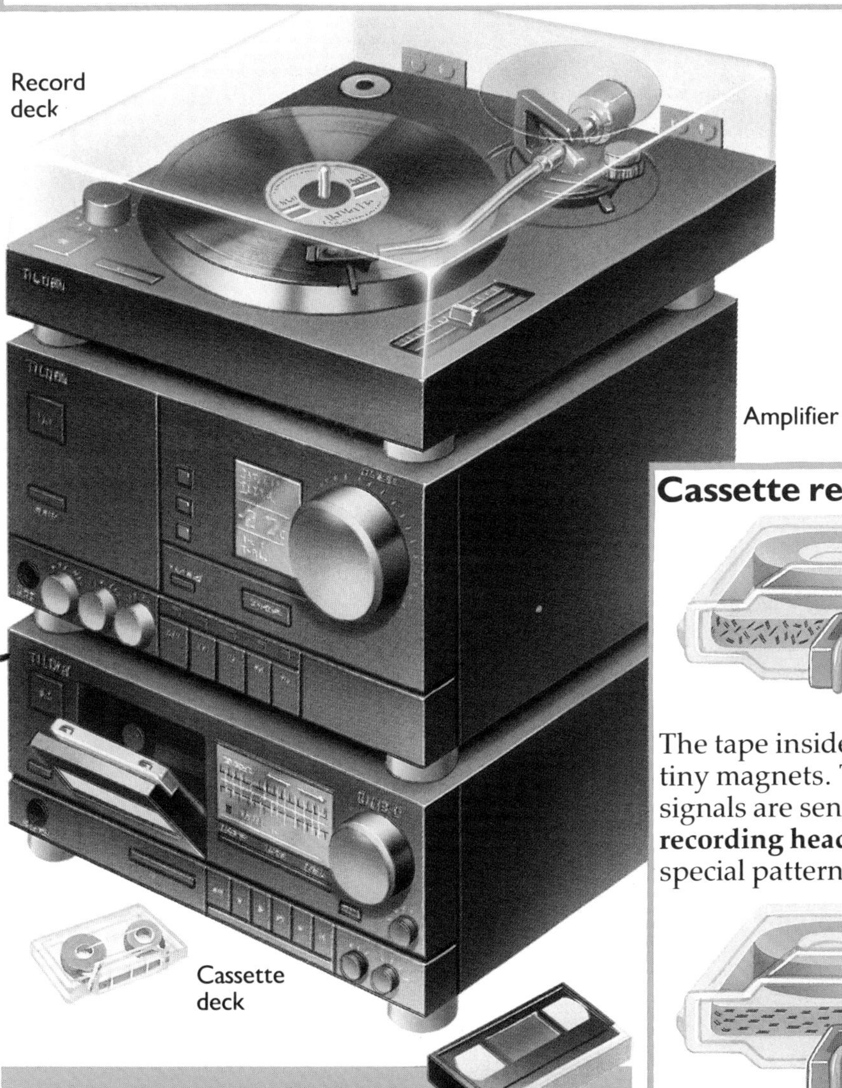

Record deck
Amplifier
Cassette deck

Amplifiers

The electrical signals from record players and cassette decks are too weak to make loudspeakers work on their own. An **amplifier** is used to make the signals stronger. It is connected to the loudspeakers. When you turn the volume control up, the amplifier makes the signals stronger.

Cassette recorders

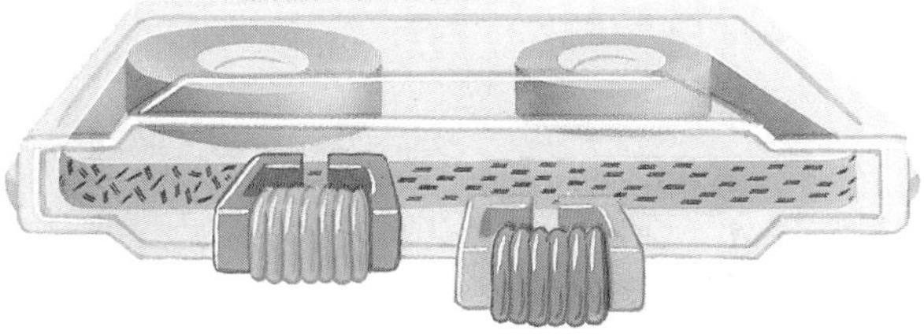

The tape inside a cassette is covered by lots of tiny magnets. To record sound on tape, electrical signals are sent to an electromagnet, called the **recording head**. This arranges the magnets in a special pattern that matches the music.

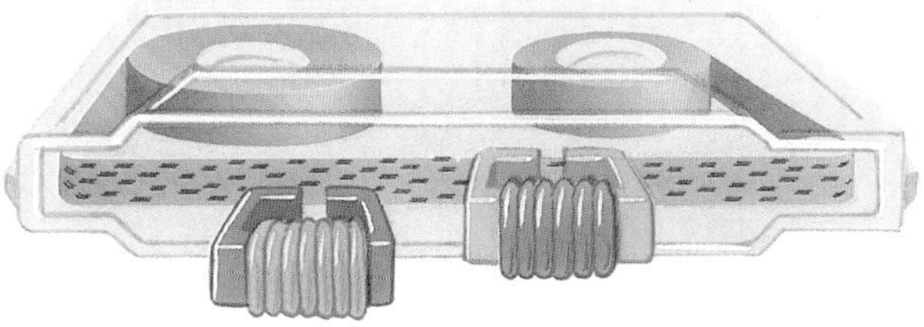

When you play a cassette, the tape moves past the **playback head**. This picks up the pattern on the tape and changes it into electrical signals. The electrical signals go through an amplifier to loudspeakers that change them back into sound.

Video recorders

A video tape recorder works in the same way as a normal cassette recorder. A strip along one edge of the tape is used to record sound, while the picture is recorded along the middle of the tape.

Producing electricity

Many things work using electricity from wall sockets. A light goes on as soon as you press a light switch. Where does the electricity come from and how does it reach your home?

Electricity is produced in power stations. Most of them produce electricity by burning coal, oil or gas. Others use the energy from nuclear power*, moving water or wind*.

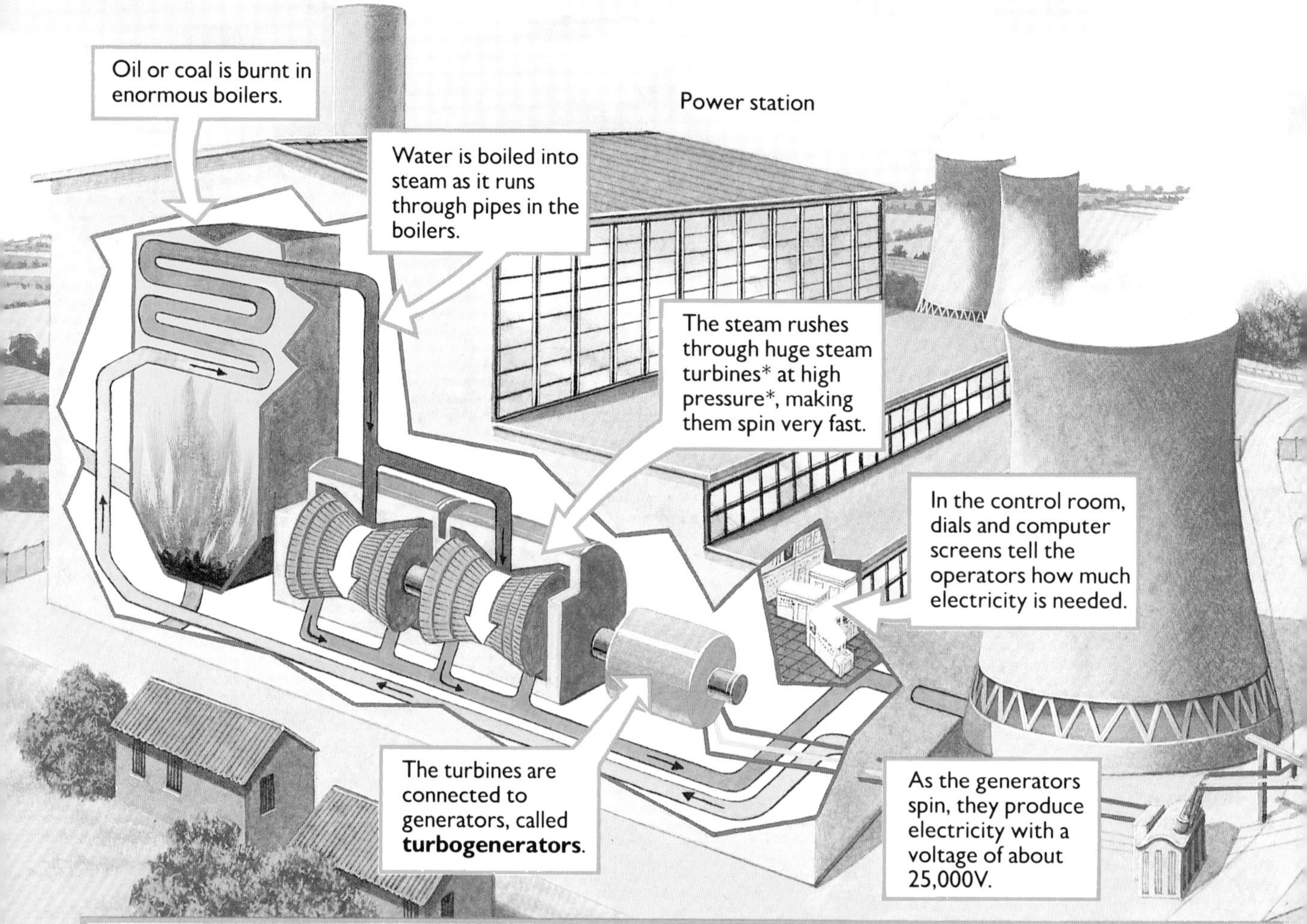

Oil or coal is burnt in enormous boilers.
Power station
Water is boiled into steam as it runs through pipes in the boilers.
The steam rushes through huge steam turbines* at high pressure*, making them spin very fast.
In the control room, dials and computer screens tell the operators how much electricity is needed.
The turbines are connected to generators, called **turbogenerators**.
As the generators spin, they produce electricity with a voltage of about 25,000V.

Solar cells

These panels contain solar cells. They are moved so that they face the Sun.

Light energy from the Sun can be changed into electrical energy in **solar cells**. Satellites and space stations use solar cells to produce their electricity. Solar cells are also used to work some watches and pocket calculators.

Electrical power

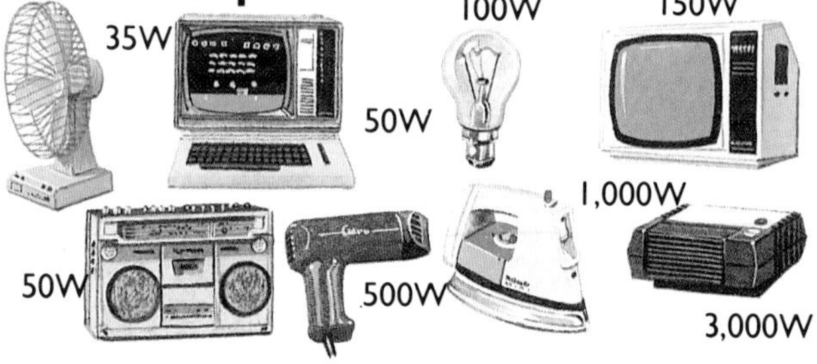

35W
100W
150W
50W
1,000W
50W
500W
3,000W

Some things need more electricity to work than others. The amount of electrical energy something uses in a certain time is called its **power**. Power is measured in **watts (W)**.

 **Nuclear power, 25, 77; Pressure, 40; Steam turbines, 44; Water and wind power, 26.*

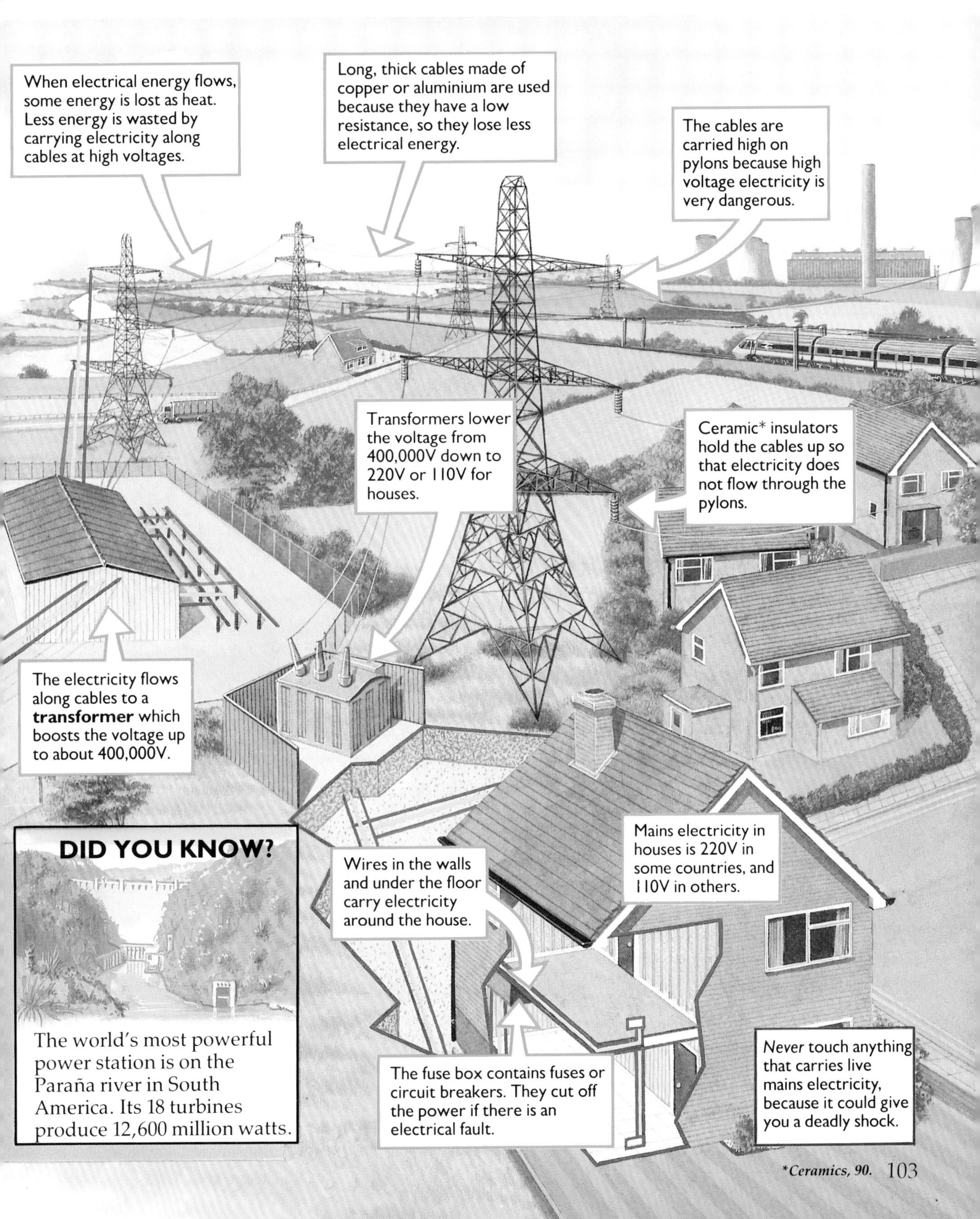
When electrical energy flows, some energy is lost as heat. Less energy is wasted by carrying electricity along cables at high voltages.
Long, thick cables made of copper or aluminium are used because they have a low resistance, so they lose less electrical energy.
The cables are carried high on pylons because high voltage electricity is very dangerous.
Transformers lower the voltage from 400,000V down to 220V or 110V for houses.
Ceramic* insulators hold the cables up so that electricity does not flow through the pylons.
The electricity flows along cables to a **transformer** which boosts the voltage up to about 400,000V.
Mains electricity in houses is 220V in some countries, and 110V in others.
Wires in the walls and under the floor carry electricity around the house.
The fuse box contains fuses or circuit breakers. They cut off the power if there is an electrical fault.
Never touch anything that carries live mains electricity, because it could give you a deadly shock.
DID YOU KNOW?
The world's most powerful power station is on the Paraña river in South America. Its 18 turbines produce 12,600 million watts.

*Ceramics, 90.

The electromagnetic spectrum

Light is made up of waves called electromagnetic waves. Apart from light, there are many other kinds of electromagnetic waves, but they are all invisible. Together they form the electromagnetic spectrum.

All electromagnetic waves travel at 300,000km (186,000 miles) per second and can travel through a vacuum. Electromagnetic waves with different wavelengths and frequencies can be used for different things.

Gamma rays

Gamma rays come from nuclear radiation*. They can travel through many things, even metal. Gamma rays are very dangerous because they kill living cells, but they are used in small amounts to help cure some diseases.

Ultraviolet waves

Ultraviolet (UV) radiation from the Sun gives people a suntan by making their skin produce a brown chemical, called **melanin**.

Too much UV radiation is bad for you. A gas called **ozone** in the atmosphere cuts out some of the Sun's UV radiation. People are worried because pollution is destroying this gas.

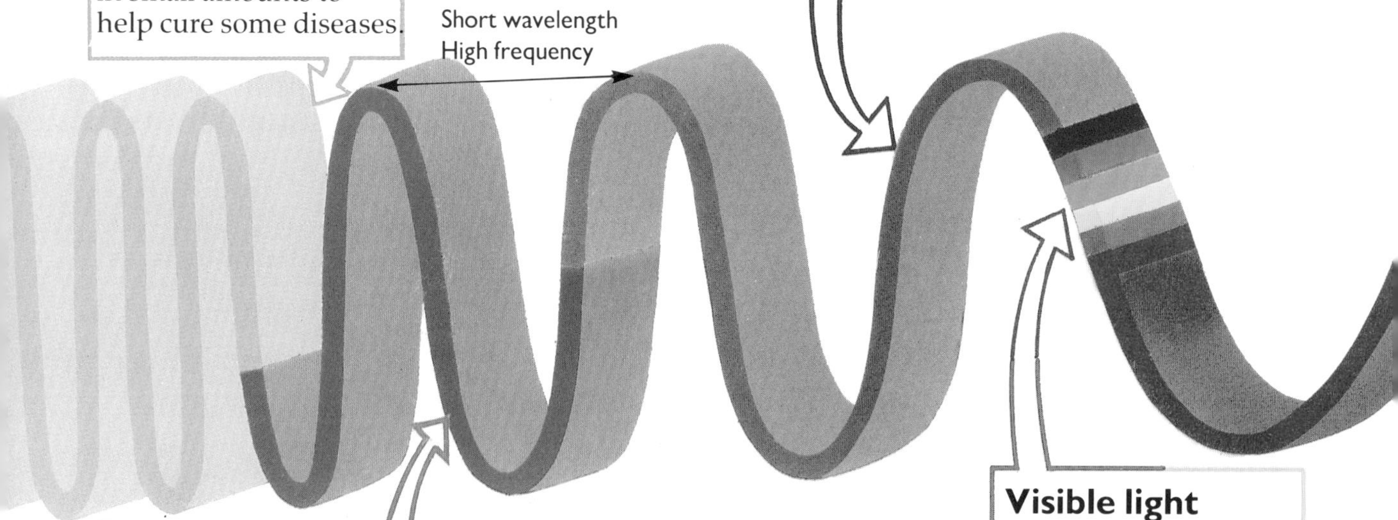

X-rays

X-rays are used to look inside people. They can only travel through soft things, so hard things, like bone, show up as shadows. X-rays are also used in airports to check what may be hidden in people's suitcases.

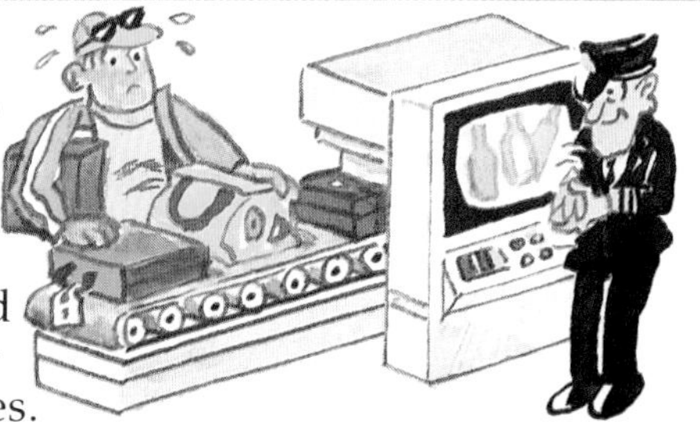

Visible light

The light that you see, called **visible light**, is only a small part of the electromagnetic spectrum. Visible light with different wavelengths produces different colours*.

DID YOU KNOW?

Electromagnetic waves are made of changing electric and magnetic fields*. The first person to understand the link between electricity and magnetism was James Clerk Maxwell, in 1864.

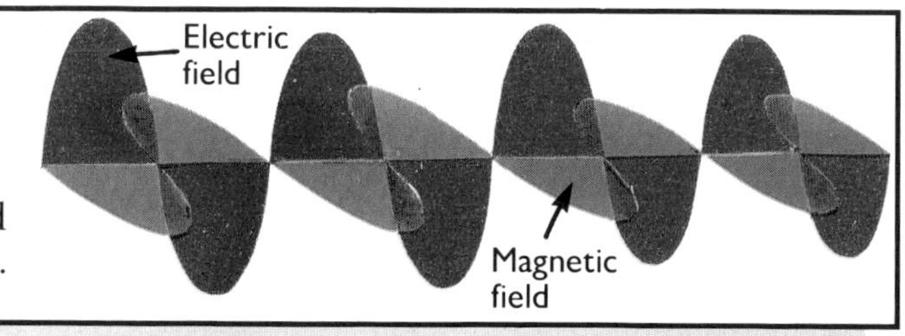

**Coloured light, 61; Electric and magnetic fields, 99; Nuclear radiation, 77.*

Infra-red radiation

Infra-red radiation*, or **heat radiation**, is given out by anything hot.

Infra-red radiation carries heat from a fire to you, and carries the heat of the Sun to Earth.

Radio waves

Radio waves are used to carry signals for televisions, radios and mobile telephones.

You can find out more about the way radio waves are used on the next page.

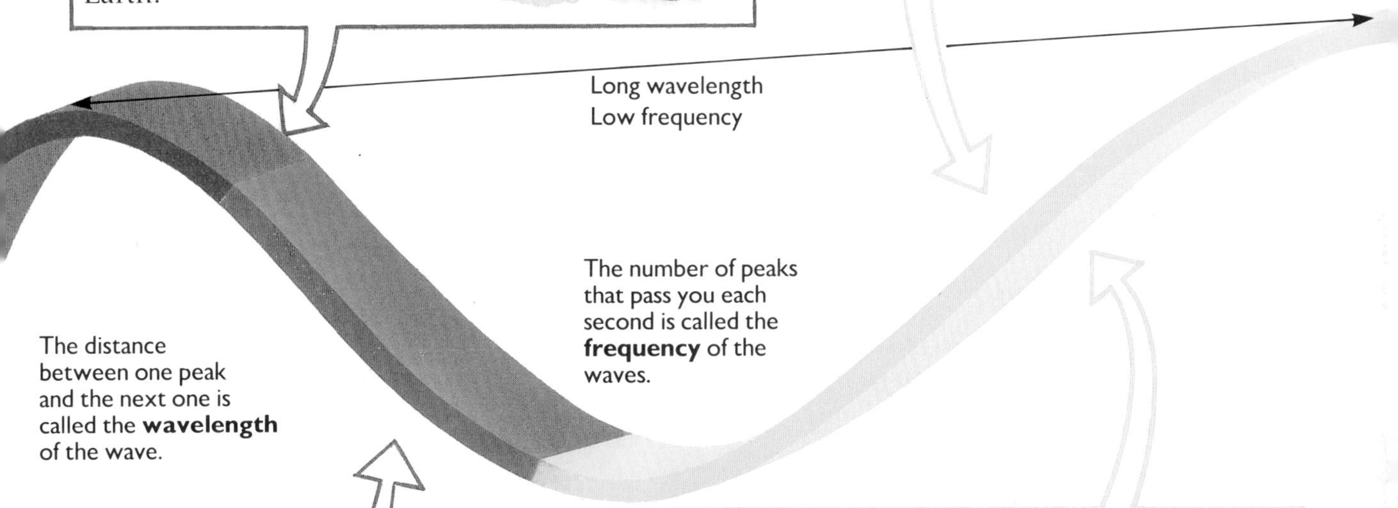

The number of peaks that pass you each second is called the **frequency** of the waves.

The distance between one peak and the next one is called the **wavelength** of the wave.

Microwaves

Microwaves are used to cook food in microwave ovens. They make the molecules in food vibrate very quickly. This makes the food heat up. Microwaves get through into the middle of the food, so they make things cook very quickly.

Microwaves are used for making international telephone calls. Microwave signals are beamed up to satellites and beamed back down to other countries.

Radar

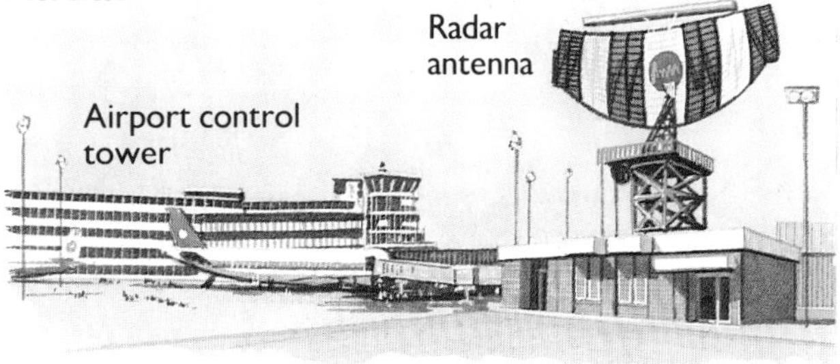

Radar uses radio waves to track aircraft and ships. A **radar transmitter** sends out a beam of radio waves. They bounce off solid objects and are picked up again by the **radar receiver**. A screen shows where things are and how fast they are moving.

Airports use radar to keep track of aircraft in their area. Ships use radar to stop them crashing into other ships and to help them find their way at night.

*Infra-red radiation, 18.

Radio and television

There are radio waves all around you, but you cannot hear or see them. They are picked up by radios that turn them into sound waves and by televisions that turn them into sound waves and light waves.

The sounds you hear on a radio may have gone across huge distances to reach you. Radio waves travel at the speed of light. This is why people living far away from each other can hear the same radio show at the same time.

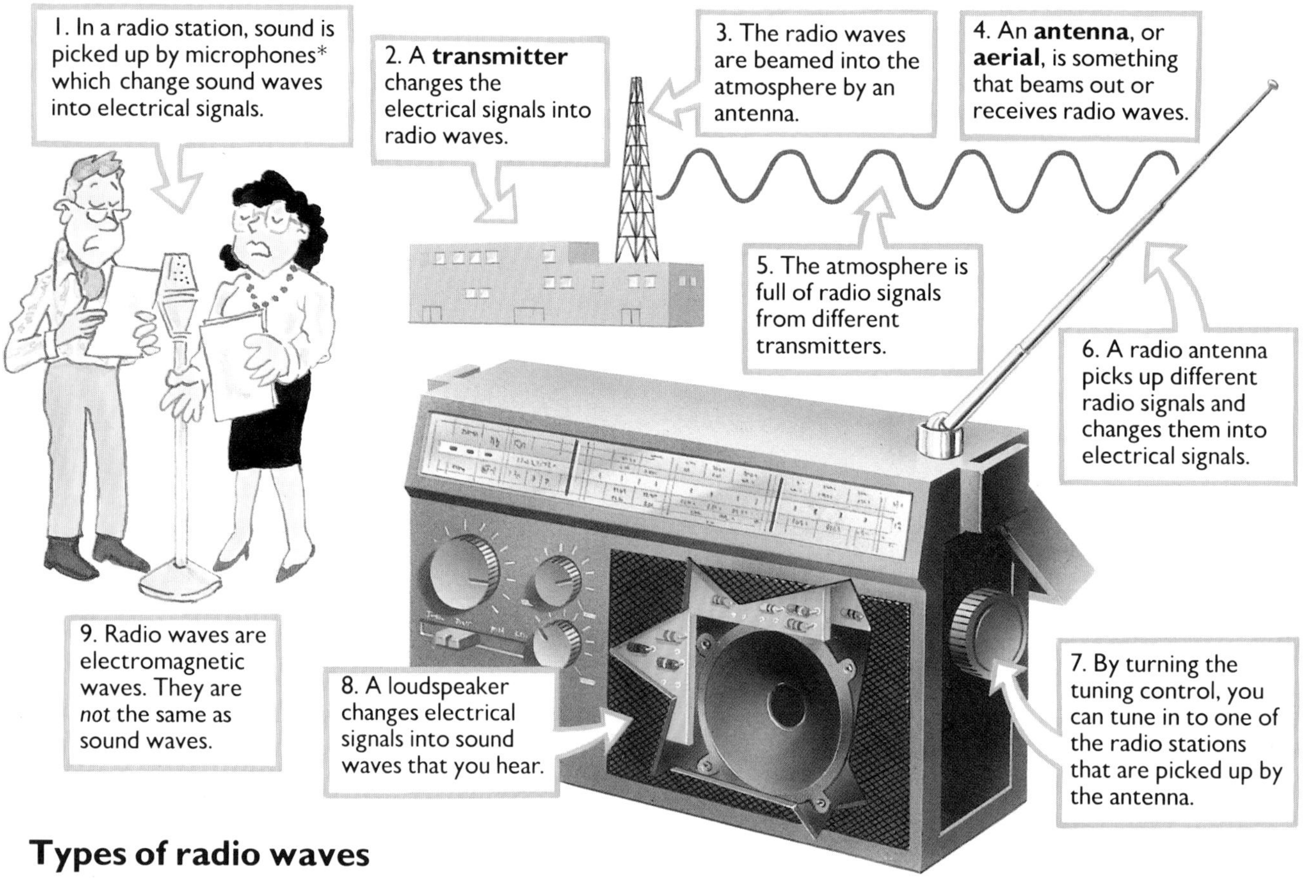
1. In a radio station, sound is picked up by microphones* which change sound waves into electrical signals.
2. A **transmitter** changes the electrical signals into radio waves.
3. The radio waves are beamed into the atmosphere by an antenna.
4. An **antenna**, or **aerial**, is something that beams out or receives radio waves.
5. The atmosphere is full of radio signals from different transmitters.
6. A radio antenna picks up different radio signals and changes them into electrical signals.
7. By turning the tuning control, you can tune in to one of the radio stations that are picked up by the antenna.
8. A loudspeaker changes electrical signals into sound waves that you hear.
9. Radio waves are electromagnetic waves. They are *not* the same as sound waves.

Types of radio waves

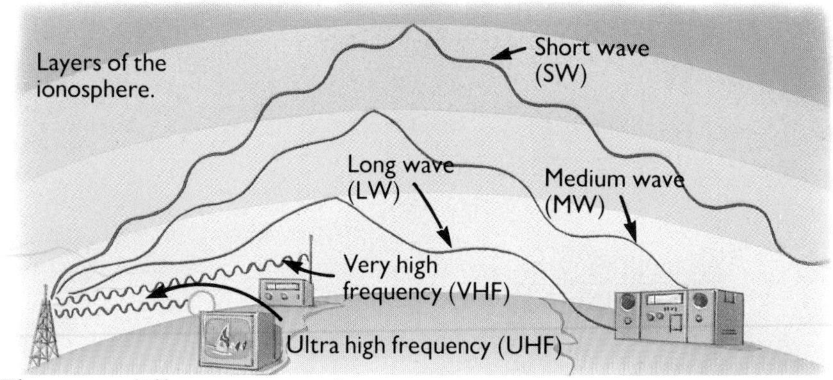
Layers of the ionosphere.
Short wave (SW)
Long wave (LW)
Medium wave (MW)
Very high frequency (VHF)
Ultra high frequency (UHF)

There are different types of radio waves. Long, medium and short waves can travel very far. This is because they bounce off layers in the atmosphere, called the **ionosphere**. VHF radio waves and the UHF waves that carry television signals travel short distances because they cannot bounce off the ionosphere.

Using radio to talk to people

Two-way radios are able to send out and receive radio signals. They are used by many people such as taxi drivers, the police and aircraft pilots.

Some telephones, called **mobile telephones**, use radio waves instead of telephone wires.

**Microphones, 100.*

Radio waves carry sound and pictures to televisions in people's homes. A television set turns the radio waves into light waves and sound waves that you see and hear.

How does television work?

Television cameras pick up light from things in the studio. They divide the light into primary colours* and then change it into electrical signals. The signals are changed into radio waves and sent out by a transmitter.

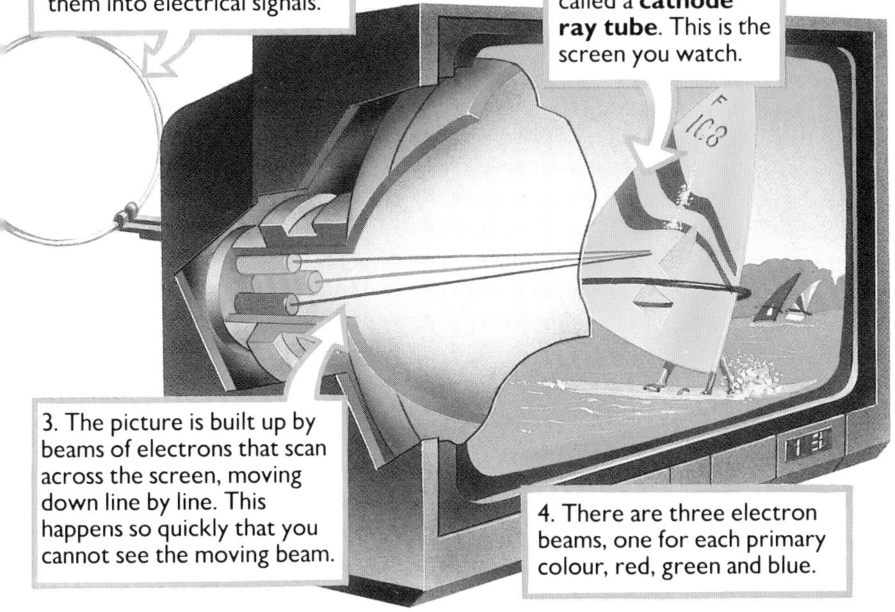

1. The antenna picks up the radio waves and changes them into electrical signals.

2. The main part of a television set is called a **cathode ray tube**. This is the screen you watch.

3. The picture is built up by beams of electrons that scan across the screen, moving down line by line. This happens so quickly that you cannot see the moving beam.

4. There are three electron beams, one for each primary colour, red, green and blue.

5. There are chemicals, called **phosphors**, on the inside of the screen. They glow when the electrons hit them.

6. Three kinds of phosphor glow red, green and blue. All the different colours in the television picture are made by mixing these three colours.

Cable television

Some television channels are transmitted by electrical signals that flow along a special cable to people's homes. This is called **cable television**.

DID YOU KNOW?

The Sun and other stars send out radio waves through Space. They are picked up by huge dish antennas, called **radio telescopes**. Astronomers use them to find out about distant galaxies.

Satellite television

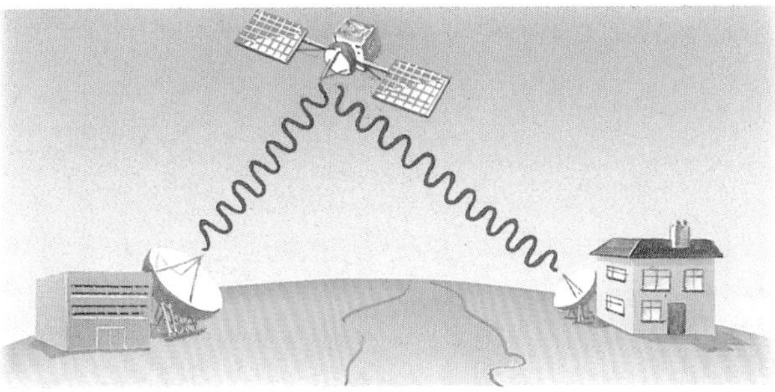

You can watch television programmes from all over the world if you have a satellite receiver. Programmes are sent out, using microwaves*, to an orbiting satellite. The satellite then beams them down to people's houses in other countries.

Microwaves, 105; Primary colours, 62.

Computer technology

Computers can do many different things. They are used to send rockets into Space, to forecast the weather, to make robots work, for typing letters, playing games and making music.

Computers can store huge amounts of information that would fill thousands of pages if it was all written on paper. In only a few seconds, they can find any of the information stored in them.

Computers

In just one second, computers can do millions of calculations that would take people weeks or even years to do. But computers cannot think for themselves.

Computers need to be told what to do. They are given a list of instructions, called a **computer program**. Computer programs are written in special languages, such as **BASIC** or **LOGO**.

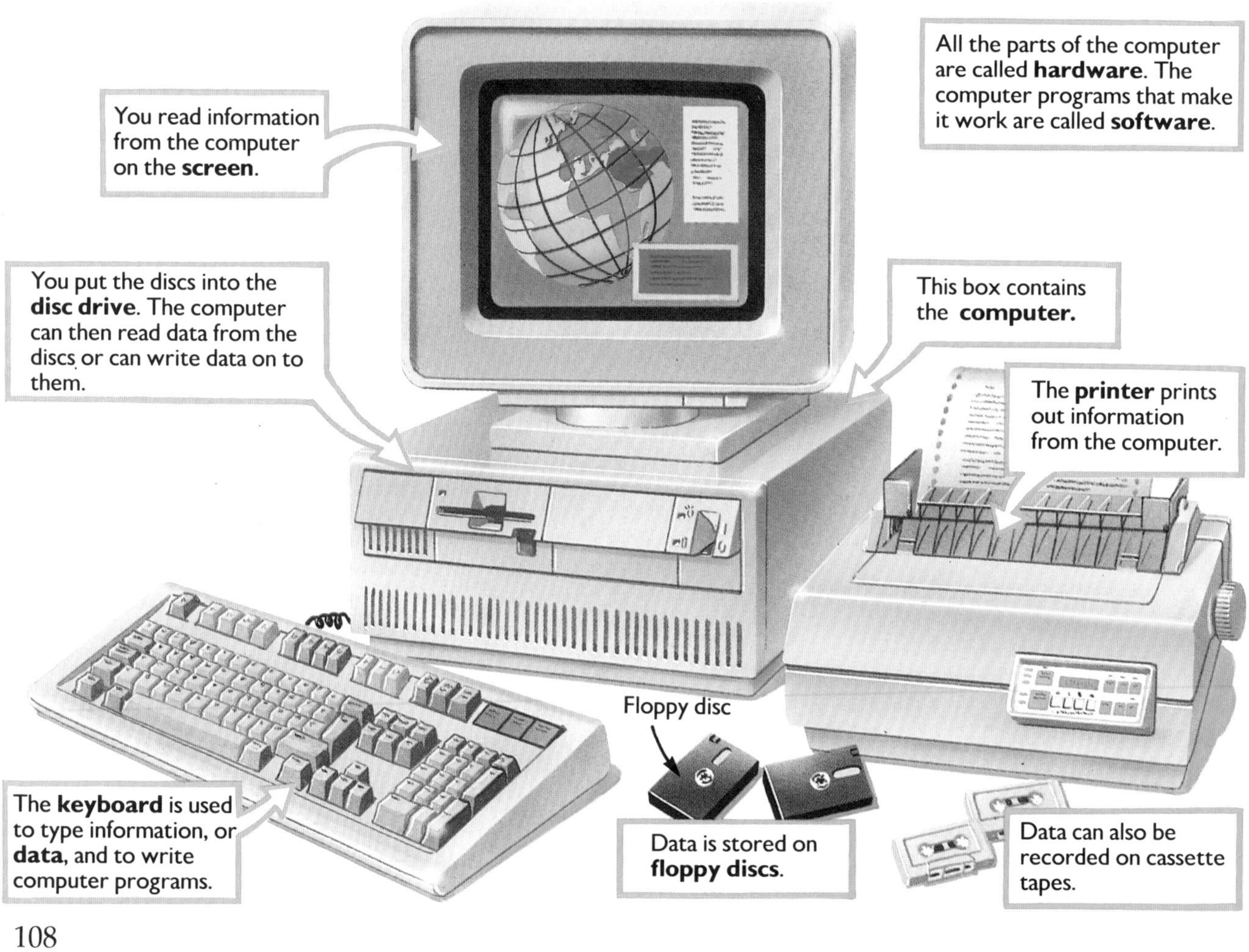
You read information from the computer on the **screen**.
All the parts of the computer are called **hardware**. The computer programs that make it work are called **software**.
You put the discs into the **disc drive**. The computer can then read data from the discs or can write data on to them.
This box contains the **computer.**
The **printer** prints out information from the computer.
Floppy disc
The **keyboard** is used to type information, or **data**, and to write computer programs.
Data is stored on **floppy discs**.
Data can also be recorded on cassette tapes.

How computers work?

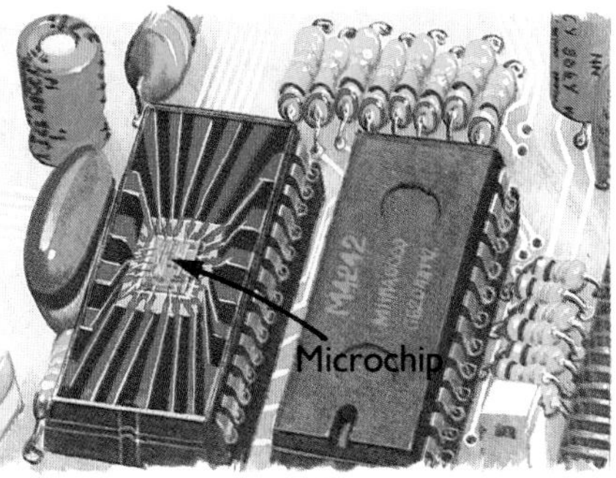

Computers work using **microchips**, which are also called **silicon chips**. The microchips are the 'brains' of the computer. They contain lots of tiny **electronic circuits** that are able to store information and do calculations.

Digital information

Computers store all information in the form of numbers. They use numbers made up of just ones and zeros to make codes that stand for letters, numbers, sounds and pictures. Information that is stored in this way is called **digital information**.

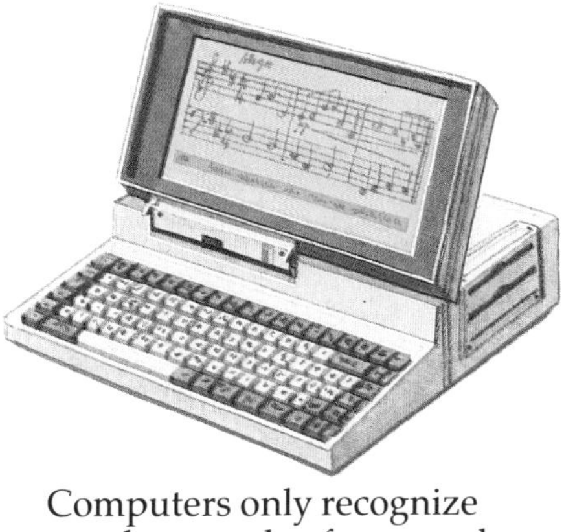

Computers only recognize numbers made of ones and zeros, called binary numbers*. This is because their microchips work using lots of tiny switches. The number 'one' stands for 'switched on' and 'zero' stands for 'switched off'.

Lasers

Lasers produce a fine beam of light that does not spread out like ordinary light. It is the brightest light known, even brighter than sunlight. Laser light has so much energy that it can even cut through metal.

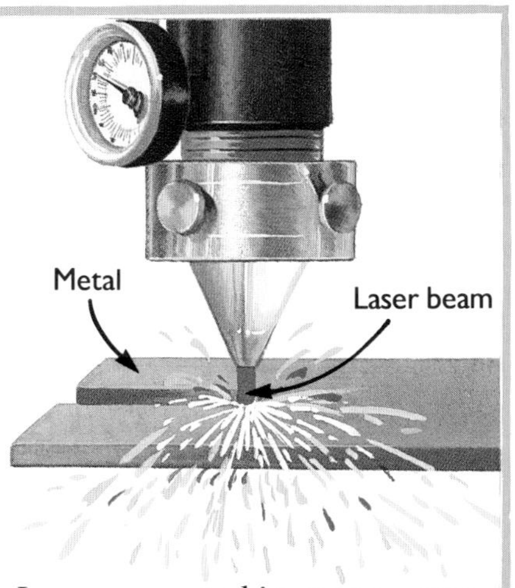

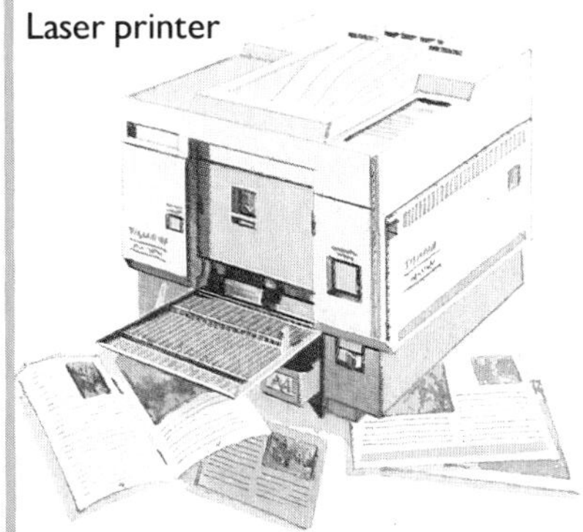

Lasers are used in many ways. They are used to carry computer messages and telephone calls through optic fibres*. They are also used to test people's eyesight, to print newspapers, to measure distances accurately, and by surgeons in operations.

Compact disc players

Sound is recorded on a **compact disc** by changing it into digital information, like computer data. A compact disc player contains a laser. The laser beam reads the digital information from the disc so that it can then be changed back into sound waves.

DID YOU KNOW?

Holograms are special three-dimensional photographs taken with laser beams. The pictures they show look like real objects because you see different views as you walk around them.

Binary numbers, 5; Optic fibres, 57.

Scientists and inventors

Ampère, André 1775-1836
French physicist who first realized that electricity and magnetism are linked. The unit of electric current, the ampere, is named after him.

Archimedes c. 287-212 BC
Greek scientist who first understood how pressure changes with depth in liquids and gases. He developed the theory of pulleys and levers, but is best known for Archimedes' principle, which explains how things float.

Aristotle 384-322 BC
Greek philospher who founded modern scientific thinking. He thought that all things were made of fire, earth, air and water. He believed that the Earth was at the centre of the Universe and that the Universe was a sphere. These ideas were later disproved.

Babbage, Charles 1792-1871
English mathematician who built a mechanical calculating machine, called the analytical engine. His ideas formed the basis for electronic computers.

Baird, John Logie 1888-1946
Scottish inventor who, in 1926, first demonstrated television. He opened the first television studio in 1929.

Becquerel, Antoine 1852-1908
French physicist who discovered nuclear radioactivity in 1896.

Bell, Alexander Graham 1847-1922
Scottish inventor of the telephone. He invented many things, including deaf aids.

Benz, Karl 1844-1929
German engineer who invented the first practical motor car that was powered by an internal combustion engine.

Bohr, Niels 1885-1962
Danish physicist who, in 1913, introduced a new theory which changed people's understanding of the structure of atoms.

Boyle, Robert 1627-1691
Anglo-Irish philosopher who was the first person to suggest that things were made of simple elements. This contradicted Aristotle's ideas. He also made major discoveries about gases.

Braun, Wernher von 1912-1977
German engineer who developed the first long-range rocket, called the V2 missile.

Carothers, Wallace 1896-1937
American chemist who discovered nylon, the first man-made polymer fibre to be widely used.

Cayley, George 1773-1857
English inventor whose ideas led to the invention of the aeroplane. He built the first glider that carried a person.

Chadwick, James 1891-1974
English physicist who discovered the neutron inside atoms.

Cierva, Juan de la 1895-1936
Spanish engineer who invented the autogyro, one of the earliest types of helicopter.

Copernicus, Nicolaus 1473-1543
Polish astronomer who correctly thought that the Earth orbited the Sun. Until then, people had believed that the Sun orbited the Earth.

Curie, Marie 1867-1934 and **Pierre** 1859-1906
French scientists who discovered the radioactive elements, radium and polonium.

Daguerre, Louis 1787-1851
French painter and designer who invented the first practical photographic process.

Daimler, Gottlieb 1834-1900
German engineer who developed the first successful internal combustion engine. It worked using petrol fuel.

Dalton, John 1766-1844
English chemist who established the theory that everything is made of atoms.

Diesel, Rudolf 1858-1913
German engineer who developed a type of internal combustion engine called the diesel engine.

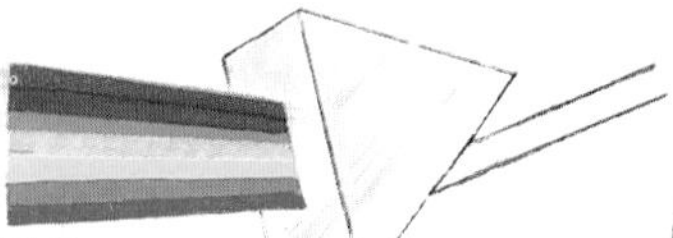
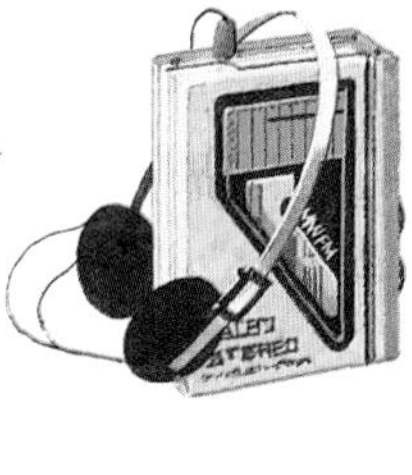
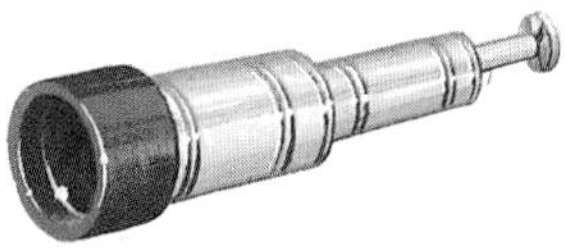

Dunlop, John 1840-1921
Scottish veterinary surgeon who invented the first air-filled, or pneumatic tyre.

Eastman, George 1854-1932
American industrialist who, in 1888, invented the first flexible roll film for use in the first Kodak camera. Until then, photographs were taken on individual glass plates.

Edison, Thomas 1847-1931
American scientist who produced more than 1,000 inventions. He invented the light bulb and the phonograph, which was the first record player.

Einstein, Albert 1879-1955
German physicist who worked out the theories of relativity. They explain what happens when things travel close to the speed of light. He also showed that mass could be changed into energy, which led to the discovery of nuclear energy.

Faraday, Michael 1791-1867
English scientist who invented the electric motor, the dynamo and the transformer. He was the first person to discover many compounds containing carbon and chlorine.

Fermat, Pierre de 1601-1665
French mathematician who founded the modern theory of numbers.

Fermi, Enrico 1901-1954
Italian physicist who designed and built the first nuclear reactor.

Fleming, Alexander 1881-1955
Scottish scientist who discovered penicillin.

Fox Talbot, William 1800-1877
English scientist who invented photographic negatives from which many prints could be made.

Franklin, Benjamin 1706-1790
American scientist and politician. He invented lightning conductors which protect buildings by carrying lightning safely down to the ground.

Gabor, Dennis 1900-1979
Hungarian physicist who invented holograms.

Galilei, Galileo 1564-1642
Italian scientist. He discovered the way pendulums work and showed how gravity affects falling things. He was one of the first people to look at the solar system using a telescope and discovered many things, such as Jupiter's moons. He also invented the thermometer.

Goddard, Robert 1882-1945
American physicist who was one of the pioneers of space rocket design. He launched the first liquid-fuelled rocket in 1926.

Gutenberg, Johannes 1400-1468
German printer who introduced the first printing press into Europe.

Hero of Alexandria
1st century AD
Greek-Egyptian engineer and mathematician who explained how siphons, pumps and fountains work. He also invented the first steam-powered machine, a spinning metal sphere.

Hertz, Heinrich 1857-1894
German physicist who discovered electromagnetic waves and founded the principles of radio transmission. In the late 1880s, he was the first person to show that electromagnetic waves travel at the speed of light. He also showed that they can be reflected and refracted.

Huygens, Christiaan 1629-1695
Dutch physicist, astronomer and mathematician. He built the first pendulum clock, improved the telescope, discovered Saturn's rings, and was the first person to suggest that light was made up of waves.

Joule, James 1818-1889
English scientist who studied heat and energy. He developed the law of conservation of energy with W. Thomson. This law says that you can never get more energy out than you put in. The unit of energy, the joule, is named after him.

Kepler, Johannes 1571-1630
German astronomer who worked out the way that planets move in the solar system. He was the first person to suggest that they moved in oval orbits rather than circles.

Lavoisier, Antoine 1743-1794
French chemist who discovered the role of oxygen in breathing and burning. He also introduced one of the first systems for naming chemicals.

Leclanché, Georges 1839-1882
French inventor of the first kind of dry-cell battery. Dry-cell batteries are used in radios and torches.

Lenoir, Étienne 1822-1900
Belgian engineer who invented the first gas-powered internal combustion engine.

Lilienthal, Otto 1848-1896
German engineer who designed and built gliders. He was one of the pioneers of the basic ideas of manned flight.

Lippershey, Hans c.1570-c.1619
Dutch spectacle maker who invented the telescope.

Lodge, Oliver 1851-1940
English physicist who, at about the same time as Marconi, showed that radio waves could be used for signalling.

Lumière, Auguste 1862-1954 and **Louis** 1864-1948
French inventors who developed the movie camera and colour photography. They were the first people to open a public cinema. The first film was shown in it in 1895.

Mach, Ernst 1838-1916
Czechoslovakian physicist who worked out the 'Mach numbers', the speed of an object compared to the speed of sound in air.

Marconi, Guglielmo 1874-1937
Italian inventor who developed the first radio transmitters and receivers. In 1901, he transmitted the first radio signals across the Atlantic.

Maxwell, James Clerk 1831-1879
Scottish scientist whose theory of electromagnetic radiation predicted the existence of radio waves. He was the first person to realise that light is a type of electromagnetic radiation.

Mendel, Gregor 1822-1884
Austrian monk who founded the science of genetics which explains how the characteristics of parents are handed down to their children.

Mendeleyev, Dmitry 1834-1907
Russian chemist who worked out the Periodic Table of the elements which forms the basis of modern chemistry.

Montgolfier, Joseph 1740-1810 and **Jacques** 1745-1799
French brothers who invented the hot-air balloon. Their balloon carried the first person into the air, in 1783.

Morse, Samuel 1791-1872
American inventor who developed the electric telegraph in the USA and invented Morse code.

Newcomen, Thomas 1663-1729
English inventor of the first practical steam engine, which first began working in 1712.

Newton, Isaac 1642-1727
English scientist who worked out the laws of motion, the theory of gravitation and many new mathematical theories. He discovered that white light is made up of all the colours of the spectrum and invented the reflector telescope. He is recognised as one of the most original thinkers of all time. The unit of force, the newton, is named after him.

Nipkow, Paul 1860-1940
German inventor who was one of the pioneers of television.

Nobel, Alfred 1833-1896
Swedish chemist who invented dynamite. He founded the Nobel Prizes which are given to people who make advances in physics, chemistry, medicine, literature and world peace.

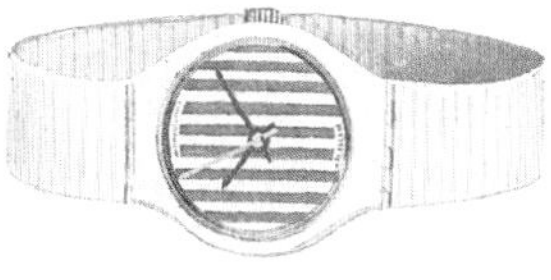

Oersted, Hans 1777-1851
Danish scientist who discovered that an electric current produces magnetism. He was one of the first people to understand electromagnetism.

Otto, Nikolaus 1832-1891
German engineer who built the first four-stroke internal combustion engine.

Pascal, Blaise 1623-1662
French mathematician who invented the mechanical adding machine. He worked out many mathematical theories, including the theory of probability.

Planck, Max 1858-1947
German physicist who worked out quantum theory, which changed people's understanding of energy and led to many new discoveries.

Priestley, Joseph 1733-1804
English scientist who discovered oxygen in 1774. He was also the inventor of the first fizzy drink.

Ptolemy 2nd century AD
Greek scientist and astronomer. He believed that the Sun and planets orbited the Earth in a series of complicated circles. This was only disproved in the 16th century.

Röntgen, Wilhelm 1845-1923
German physicist who discovered X-rays.

Rutherford, Ernest 1871-1937
New Zealand scientist who first suggested that atoms have a nucleus in the centre around which the electrons move.

Sikorsky, Igor 1889-1972
Russian-American engineer who designed the first modern helicopter.

Stephenson, George 1781-1848
English engineer who developed steam locomotives.

Swan, Joseph 1828-1914
English scientist who invented the light bulb at about the same time as Edison.

Tesla, Nikola 1856-1943
Yugoslavian-American scientist. He invented a type of electric motor called an induction motor.

Thomson, Joseph 1856-1940
English physicist who discovered the electron.

Thomson, William (Lord Kelvin) 1824-1907
Irish physicist who developed the science of thermodynamics, which studies the link between heat and other forms of energy.

Torricelli, Evangelista 1608-1647
Italian scientist who invented the barometer.

Vinci, Leonardo da 1452-1519
Italian artist and inventor. Many of the devices he invented were so far ahead of his time that they were not developed till hundreds of years later.

Volta, Alessandro 1745-1827
Italian physicist who invented the first battery.

Watson-Watt, Robert 1892-1973
Scottish scientist who developed radar.

Watt, James 1736-1819
Scottish engineer who developed and improved Newcomen's steam engine. The unit of power, the watt, is named after him.

Whittle, Frank 1907-
English engineer who invented the jet engine.

Wright, Wilbur 1867-1912 and **Orville** 1871-1948
American brothers who built the first successful powered aeroplane. It first flew at Kitty Hawk, USA, in 1903.

Zeppelin, Ferdinand von 1838-1917
German inventor who built the first airship.

Zworykin, Vladimir 1889-1982
Russian-American engineer who was one of the pioneers of television.

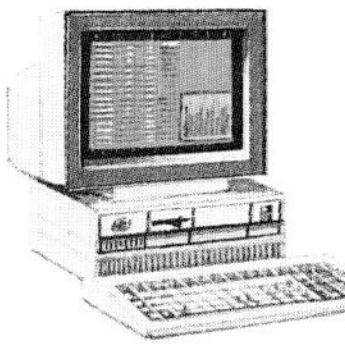
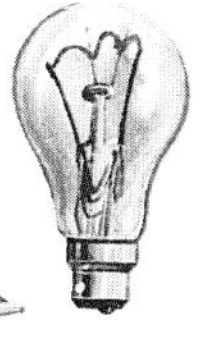
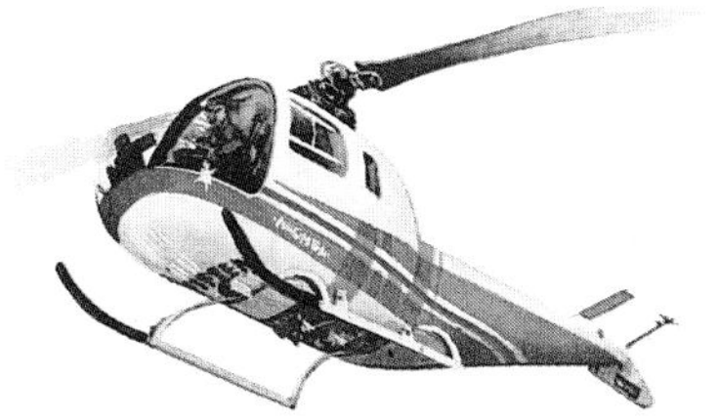

Charts, tables and symbols

The solar system

Planet	Distance from Sun in millions of km (miles)	Diameter in km (miles)	Time taken to orbit Sun	Number of moons
Mercury	58 (36)	4,878 (3,031)	88 days	0
Venus	108 (67)	12,103 (7,521)	225 days	0
Earth	150 (93)	12,756 (7,926)	365.25 days	1
Mars	228 (141)	6,794 (4,221)	687 days	2
Jupiter	778 (483)	143,800 (88,734)	11 years 10 months	16
Saturn	1,427 (887)	120,000 (74,600)	29 years 6 months	18
Uranus	2,870 (1,783)	51,000 (32,600)	84 years	15
Neptune	4,497 (2,794)	49,000 (30,400)	164 years 10 months	8
Pluto	5,900 (3,666)	3,000 (1,900)	247 years 8 months	1

Earth facts

Diameter at Equator	12,756km (7,926 miles)
Diameter at Poles	12,712km (7,881 miles)
Greatest height above sea level (Mt. Everest)	8,848m (29,021ft)
Greatest depth below sea level (Marianas Trench)	11,033m (36,188ft)
Land area	149 million km² (58 million square miles)
Ocean area	361 million km² (141 million square miles)
Amount of Earth covered by sea	71%

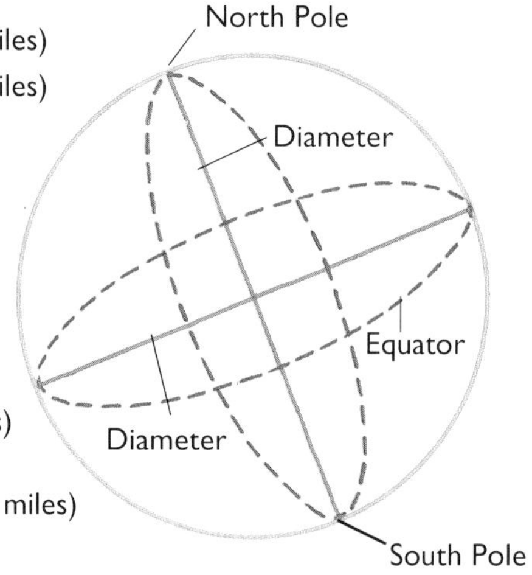
North Pole
Diameter
Equator
Diameter
South Pole

Sun facts

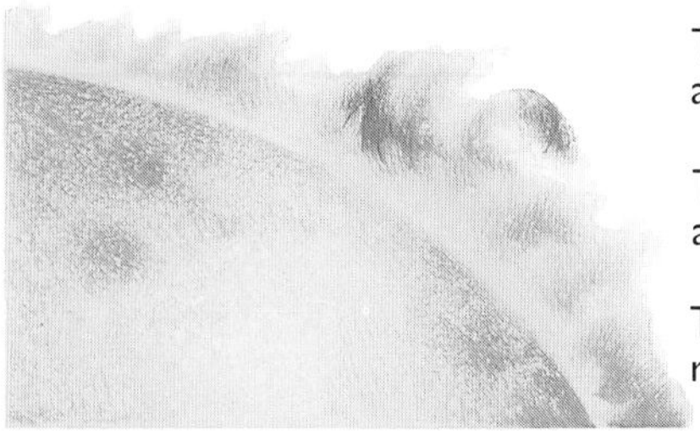

Diameter	1,400,000km (868,000 miles)
Temperature at centre	16 million°C (61 million°F)
Temperature at surface	5,500°C (9,932°F)
Time taken for sunlight to reach Earth	8 minutes, 20 seconds

Temperature chart

Celsius *Fahrenheit*

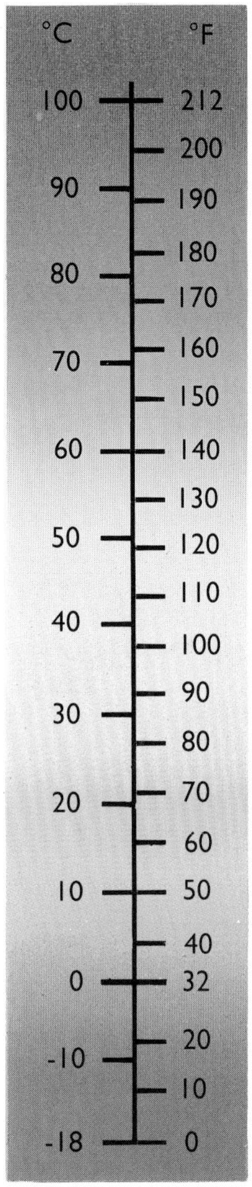
°C
°F
100
212
200
90
190
180
80
170
160
70
150
60
140
130
50
120
110
40
100
90
30
80
20
70
60
10
50
40
0
32
20
-10
10
-18
0

Celsius and Fahrenheit are units for measuring temperature. To change Celsius into Fahrenheit, you multiply the temperature in Celsius by 9, divide by 5, and add 32.

To change Fahrenheit into Celsius, subtract 32 from the temperature in Fahrenheit, multiply by 5, and then divide the answer by 9.

Metric units

Length
1 centimetre (cm) = 10 millimetres (mm)
1 metre (m) = 100 centimetres
1 kilometre (km) = 1,000 metres

Mass
1 kilogram (kg) = 1,000 grams (g)
1 tonne (t) = 1,000 kilograms

Area
100 square millimetres (mm^2) = 1 square centimetre (cm^2)
1 square metre (m^2) = 10,000 square centimetres
1 hectare = 10,000 square metres
1 square kilometre (km^2) = 1 million square metres

Volume
1 cubic centimetre (cc) = 1 millilitre (ml)
1 litre (l) = 1,000 millilitres
1 cubic metre (m^3) = 1000 litres

Imperial units

Length
1 foot (ft) = 12 inches (in)
1 yard (yd) = 3 feet
1 mile = 1,760 yards

Mass
1 pound (lb) = 16 ounces (oz)
1 ton = 2,240 pounds

Area
1 square foot (ft^2) = 144 square inches (in^2)
1 square yard (yd^2) = 9 square feet
1 acre = 4,840 square yards
1 square mile = 640 acres

Volume
1 gallon (UK) = 8 pints
1 cubic foot (ft^3) = 7.48 gallons (UK)
1 gallon (US) = 0.83 gallons (UK)

Metric prefixes

The prefix written before a unit of measurement tells you how much the unit is multiplied by. For example, 1 kilovolt (1kV) equals one thousand volts (1,000V).

Prefix	micro	milli	centi	deci	kilo	mega
Symbol	μ	m	c	d	k	M
Means unit is multiplied by	one millionth (0.000,001)	one thousandth (0.001)	one hundredth (0.01)	one tenth (0.1)	one thousand (1,000)	one million (1,000,000)

Metric units into imperial units

To convert	*into*	*multiply by*
Length		
Centimetres	inches	0.39
Metres	feet	3.28
Kilometres	miles	0.62
Area		
Square metres	square feet	10.76
Hectares	acres	2.47
Square kilometres	square miles	0.39
Volume		
Cubic metres	cubic feet	35.32
Litres	pints	1.76
Litres	gallons	0.22
Mass		
Grams	ounces	0.04
Kilograms	pounds	2.21
Tonnes	tons	0.98

Imperial units into metric units

To convert	*into*	*multiply by*
Length		
Inches	centimetres	2.54
Feet	metres	0.31
Miles	kilometres	1.61
Area		
Square feet	square metres	0.09
Acres	hectares	0.41
Square miles	square kilometres	2.59
Volume		
Cubic feet	cubic metres	0.03
Pints	litres	0.57
Gallons	litres	4.55
Mass		
Ounces	grams	28.35
Pounds	kilograms	0.45
Tons	tonnes	1.02

Physics equations

The study of physics often involves solving equations. The results of some equations can be expressed in two ways. For example, power (the amount of work done, measured in Joules, in a certain time) is expressed as either Joules per second (J/s) or, more conveniently, as Watts (W).

Derived quantity	Abbreviation	Defining equation	Combined unit	Convenient name of combined unit (abbreviation)
Density	d	$\text{density} = \frac{\text{mass}}{\text{volume}}$	kg/m^2	no name
Force	F	force = mass x acceleration	$kg\ m/s^2$	Newton (N)
Work	W	work = force x distance	Nm	Joule (J)
Power	P	$\text{power} = \frac{\text{work done}}{\text{time}}$	J/s	Watt (W)
Velocity	v	$\text{velocity} = \frac{\text{distance moved}}{\text{time}}$	m/s	no name
Momentum	none	moment = mass x velocity	kg m/s	no name
Acceleration	a	$\text{acceleration} = \frac{\text{change in velocity}}{\text{time}}$	m/s^2	no name
Moment	none	moment = force x perpendicular distance	Nm	Newton metre (Nm)
Pressure	P	$\text{pressure} = \frac{\text{force}}{\text{area}}$	N/m^2	Pascal (Pa)
Potential difference	V	$\text{volt} = \frac{\text{energy transferred}}{\text{charge}}$	J/C	Volt (V)
Resistance	R	$\text{resistance} = \frac{\text{potential difference}}{\text{current}}$	V/A	Ohm (Ω)
Charge	Q	Charge = current x time	As	Coulomb (C)

Hazard symbols

Hazard symbols such as the ones shown here are displayed on the containers of dangerous substances, or at entrances to areas where dangerous substances are kept. They are usually displayed with a yellow background. To avoid harming yourself, always pay attention to these labels.

Toxic

Corrosive

Radioactive

Harmful

Infectious

Flammable

Oxidizing

Explosive

Circuit symbols

Electrical appliances contain components which allow electricity to flow around in a circuit. In diagrams, these components can be drawn as symbols, as shown here.

Conductor wire

Carries electricity around the circuit.

Connected wires

Carry electricity from one source in different directions.

Crossed wires, no connections

Unconnected wires that cross each other's paths.

Earth connection

Allows electricity to flow to the ground from an appliance.

Switch

Enables the electrical circuit to be broken.

Power supply terminals

The point where electricity flows into the appliance.

Battery

Provides electricity for appliances that need direct current (d.c.) electricity, such as a flashlight.

Fuse

Fitted in circuits to reduce the possibility of overheating. If the current exceeds the maximum that the fuse will allow, the wire inside the fuse melts and cuts off the electricity supply.

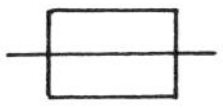

Alternating power source

Provides electricity for appliances that need alternating current (a.c.) electricity. Mains supplies always supply alternating current electricity.

Transistor

Amplifies or reduces electronic signals, allowing an input current to be changed. They have many uses and are the active elements of micro-chips.

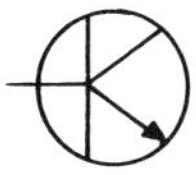

Thermistor

Temperature dependent resistor. Heat lessens its resistance, allowing electricity to flow through it. Used in fire alarm systems.

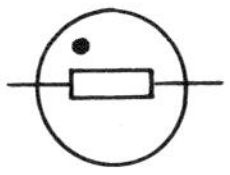

Filament bulb

Ordinary light bulb, containing filaments which glow when electricity flows through them.

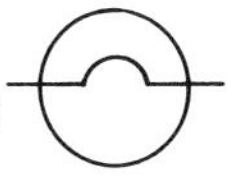

Resistor

Controls the current flowing in a circuit. It limits the current passing through components, reducing the danger of damage caused by overheating.

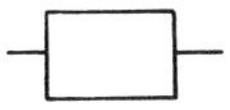

Transformer

Changes the size of a voltage so that appliances that require a different amount of electricity to the supply can be used.

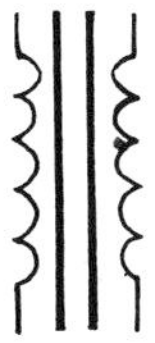

Rheostat

A resistor that can be adjusted, so that the amount of current flowing in a circuit can be altered.

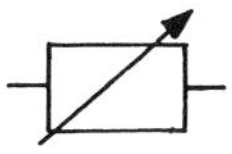

Electrical motor

When electricity flows through the motor, it supplies power to work various moving parts. Washing machines and hair dryers have electrical motors inside them.

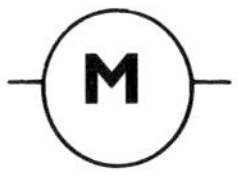

Potential divider

Divides the voltage supplied by a battery, enabling different sized currents to flow through different parts of a circuit.

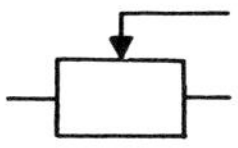

Diode

Allows the flow of current in one direction only.

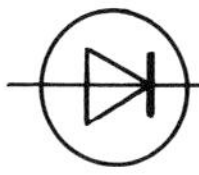

Light emitting diode

Similar to a diode, but glows when an electric current flows through it.

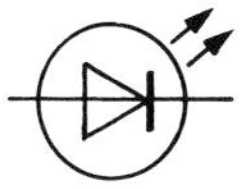

Ammeter

Measures the amount of electrical current flowing through a circuit.

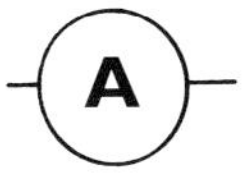

Circuit diagram of a fire detector

A fire detector is triggered by heat. If the temperature gets high the thermistor lets electricity through. The electricity then flows through the transistor, then through the light emitting diode, which lights up.

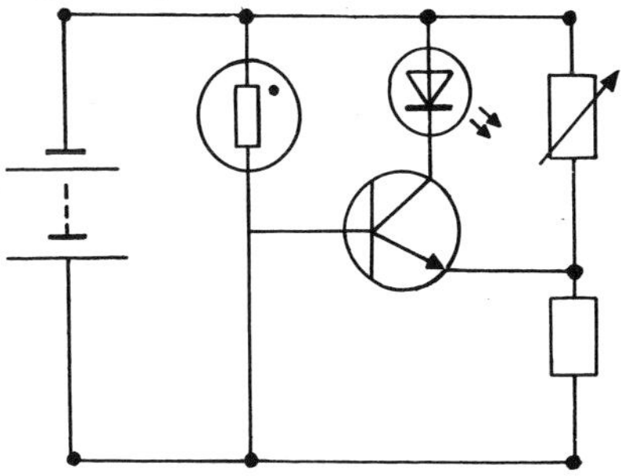

Laboratory apparatus

Equipment that is used in a scientific experiment is called apparatus. In science books, apparatus is usually drawn in a two-dimensional style, as shown in the small boxes on these two pages. You will find this drawing style useful if you want to describe an experiment with the help of a diagram.

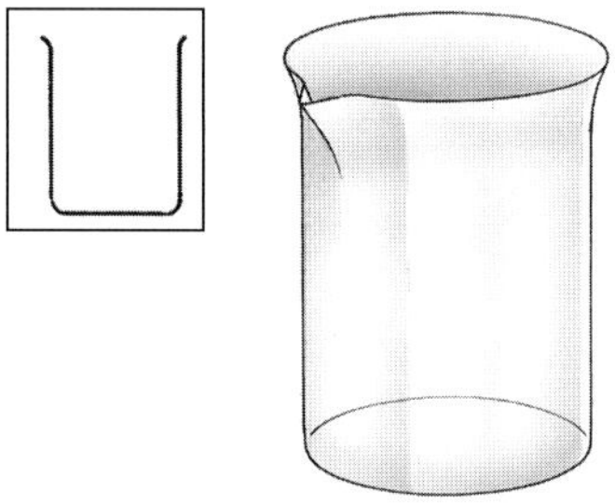

Beaker

Used to hold liquids. It is not suitable for measuring liquids, since it has no calibrated units of measurements marked on the side.

Conical flask

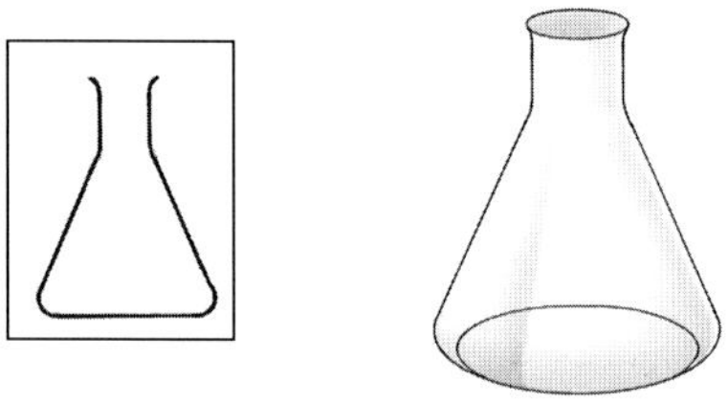

Used to hold liquids. Used in preference to beakers when it is necessary to have a container that can be stoppered.

Buchner flask

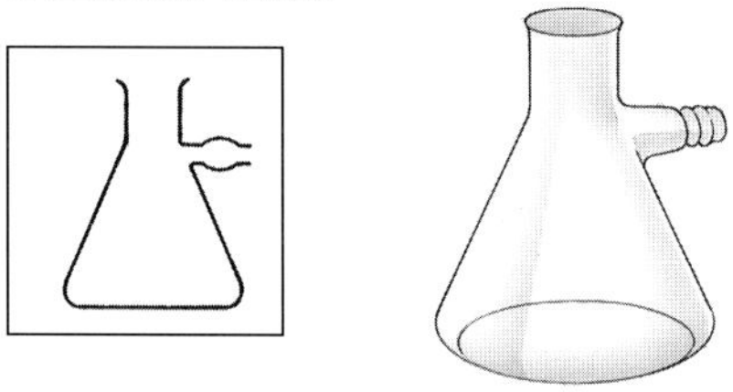

Used when liquids are filtered by suction.

Buchner funnel

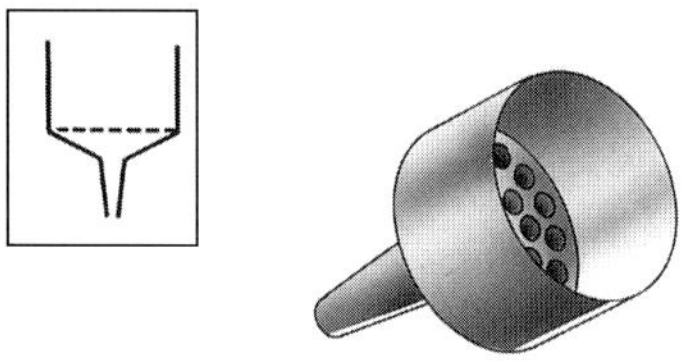

Used with a Buchner flask. It has a flat, perforated plate, on which filter paper is placed.

Liebig condenser

Used to condense gases. Gas passes through the central channel and is cooled by water flowing through the outer pipe.

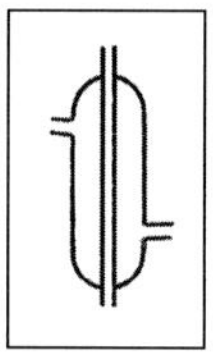

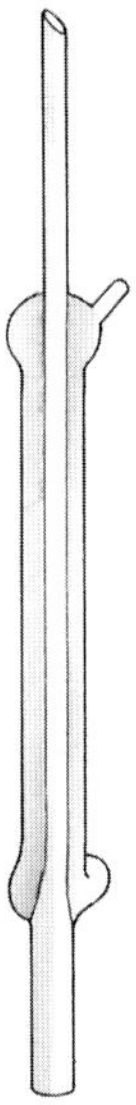

Pipette

Holds a fixed volume of liquid. It is used to dispense an exact amount of liquid during an experiment.

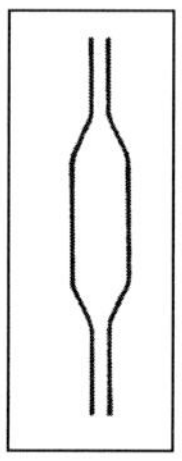

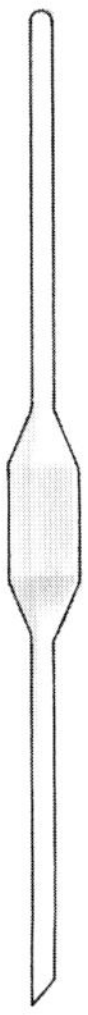

Tap funnel

Used to add a liquid to a reaction mixture, drop by drop.

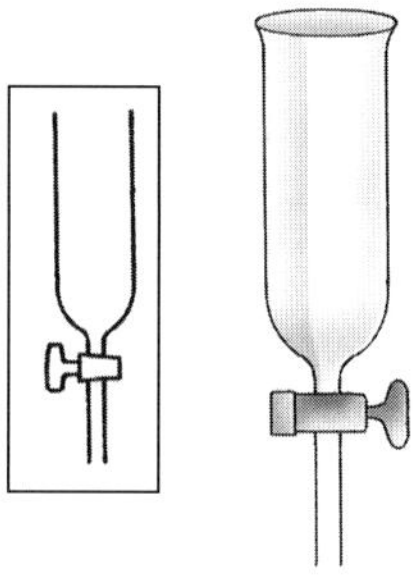

Gas jar

Used when collecting and storing gases. The jar can be sealed, using a glass lid whose rim is coated with a thin layer of grease.

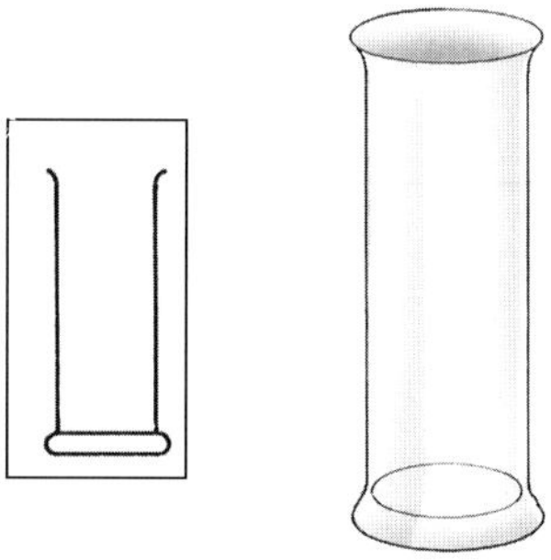

Crystallizing dish

Holds solutions which are being evaporated into crystals.

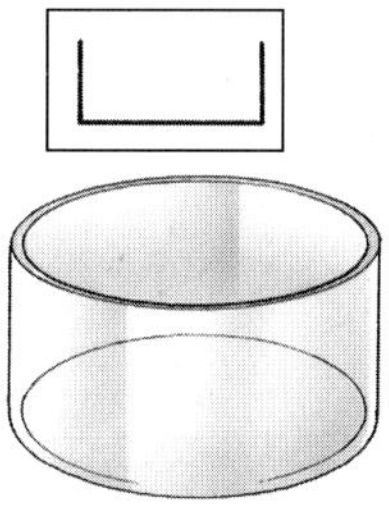

Beehive shelf

Used to support a gas jar, while gas is being collected by the displacement of water.

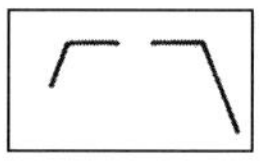

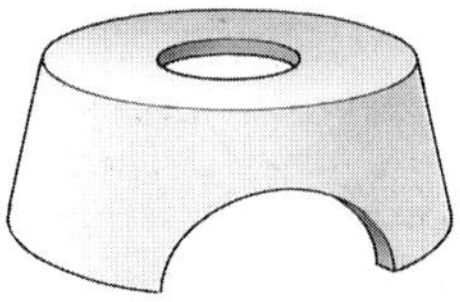

Flat bottomed flask

Used to hold liquids which do not require heating. The flask stands on the work-bench.

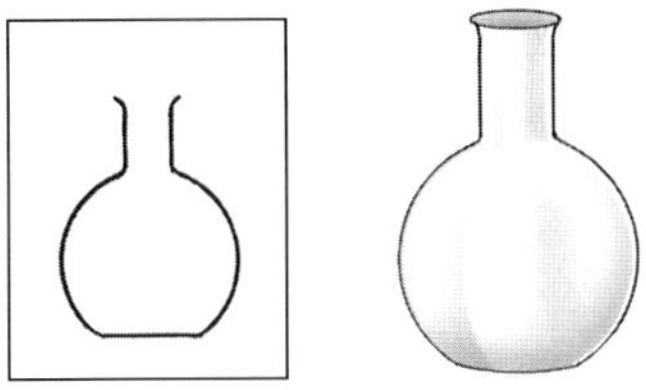

Round bottomed flask

Used to hold liquids, especially when even heating is needed. It is held in position over a flame by a clamp.

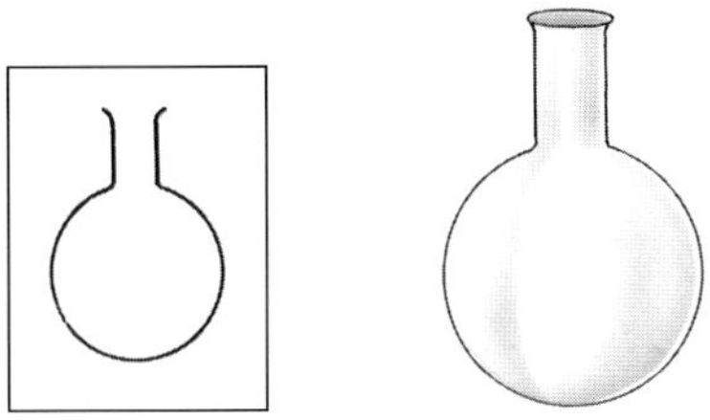

Measuring cylinder

Used to measure approximate volumes of liquids. It is less accurate than a burette.

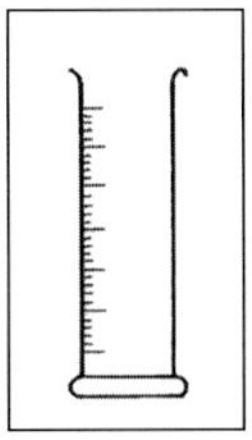

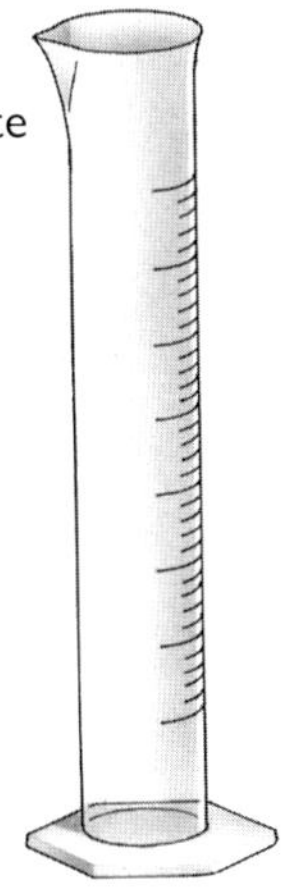

Burette

Used to add accurate volumes of liquid. They are particularly used during experiments to discover the strength of a substance, called titrations.

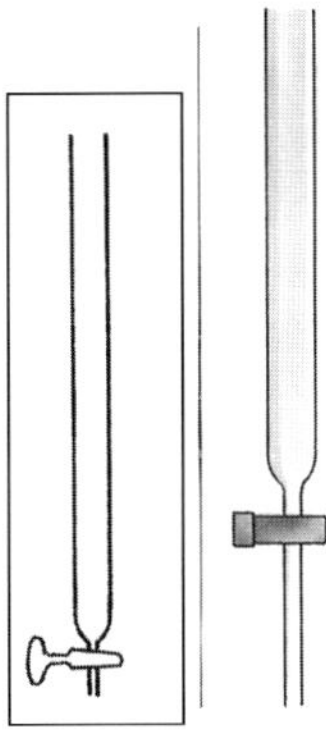

Stopper

A rubber stopper for closing a hole in a container, to prevent substances from escaping. Stoppers often have holes in them, so that pipes can be inserted to draw off or add substances.

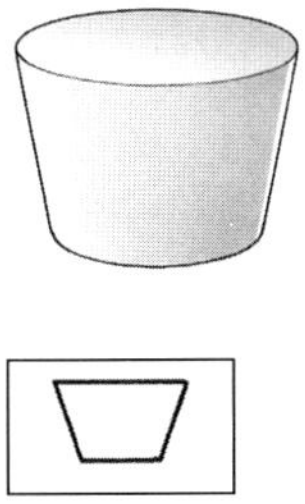

Filter funnel

Used when separating solids from liquids by filtering. Filter paper is put inside the funnel.

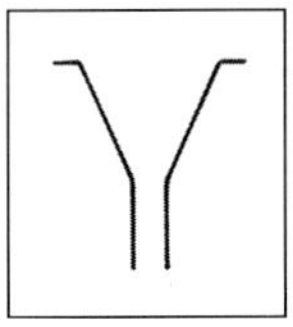

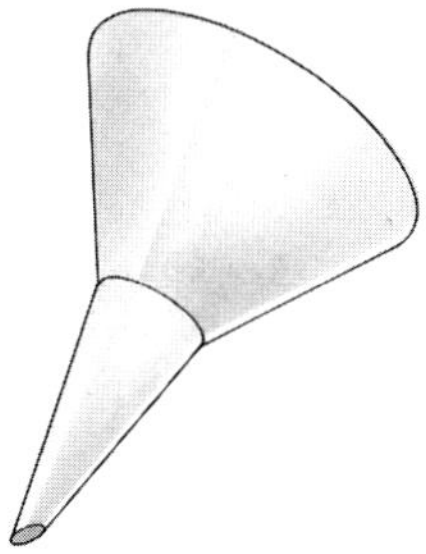

Clamp and stand

Used to hold apparatus, such as round bottomed flasks, in position.

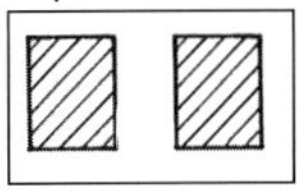

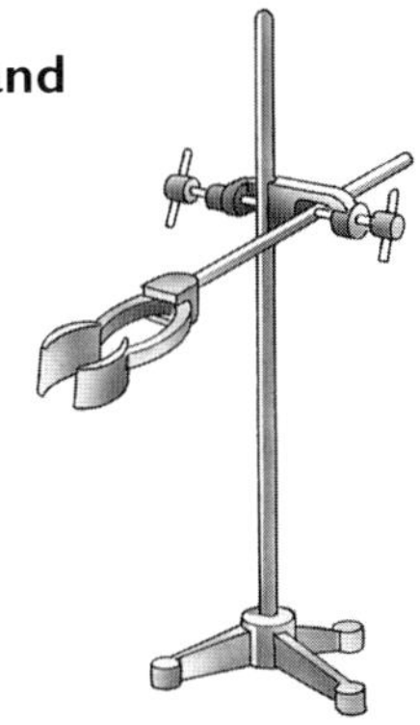

Heating apparatus

The method for supplying heat. This is usually a Bunsen or spirit burner.

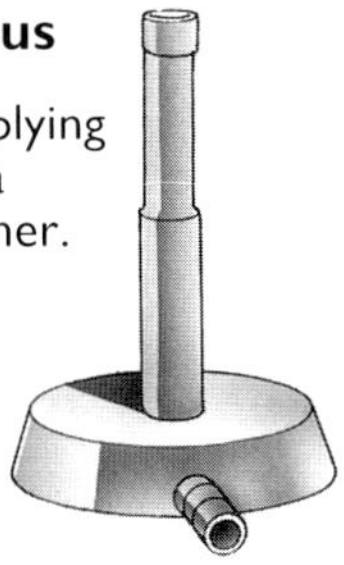

Gauze

Used to spread heat from a flame evenly across the base of an object being heated. Usually, it is held on a tripod.

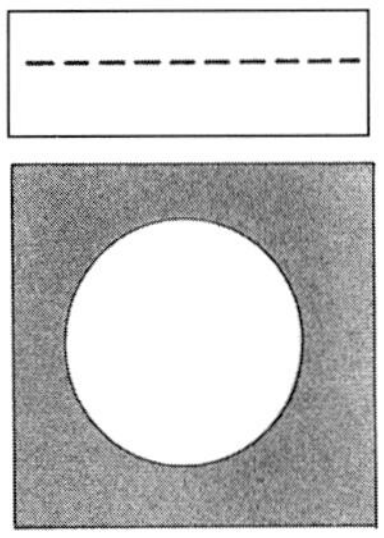

Tripod

Used as a stand for flasks and beakers during heating. It is made of metal.

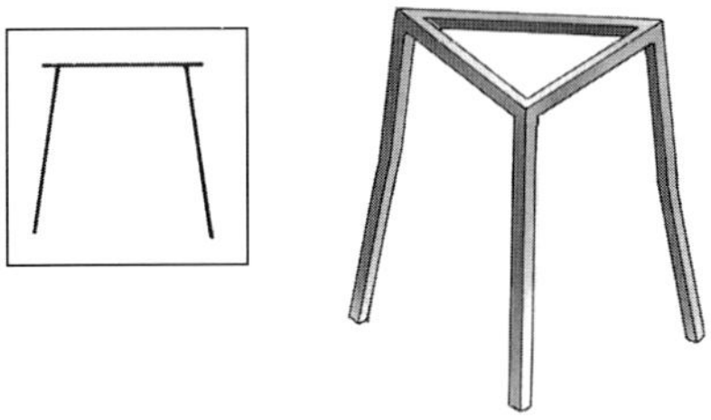

Pipeclay triangle

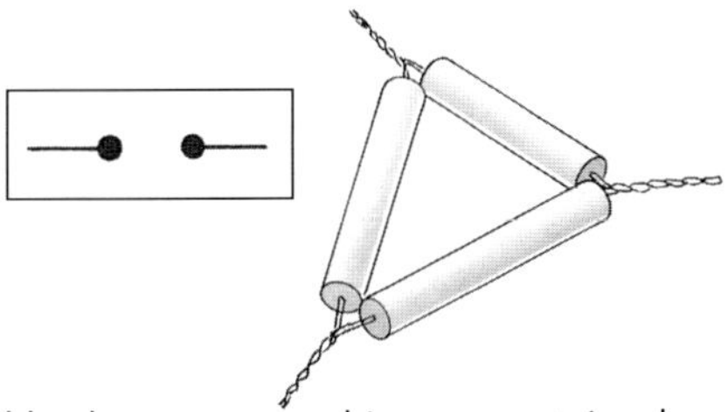

Used to support objects on a tripod when they are heated. It is made of iron or nickel-chromium wire enclosed in pipeclay tubes.

An experiment

This illustration shows a diagram of a typical laboratory experiment.

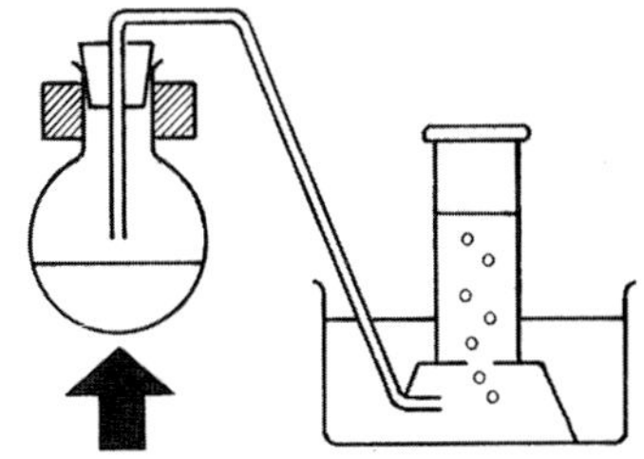

The Periodic Table

The Periodic Table is a structured list of all known elements*, arranged in order of their atomic numbers. The position of an element in the table shows whether it is a metal, non-metal or metalloid. The elements are arranged in rows, called periods. The simplest element is at the top-left of the table. The most complex element is on the right of the bottom row.

This diagram shows the basic structure of an atom.

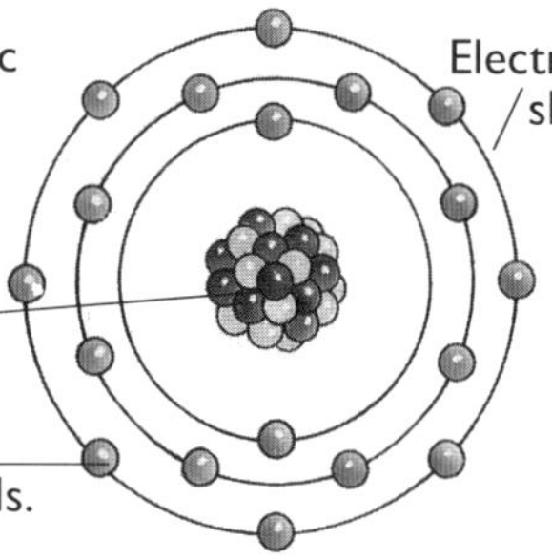

Electron shell
Nucleus, made up of protons and neutrons.
Electrons. These orbit the nucleus within electron shells.

Atomic number. This is the number of protons in the nucleus.

Chemical symbol. (The name of each element is listed below.)

Relative atomic mass. This is the average mass of the atoms found in a sample of the element.

Atomic number	Chemical symbol	Relative atomic mass
1	H	1.008

Key

Metals. All metals are solids, except mercury, which is a liquid. They are also shiny and they have high melting and boiling points.

Transition metals. Mostly, these are hard and tough. Many, such as iron, are used in industry. Others, such as silver and gold, are used in jewellery.

Inner transition metals. These are rare and tend to react easily with other elements, which makes them difficult to use in their natural state.

Non-metals. Mostly, these are solid or gas (bromine is a liquid) and non-shiny. Non-metals melt and boil at low temperatures.

Metalloids. These have a mixture of the properties of metals and non-metals.

	Group I	Group II					
Period 1	1 H 1.008						
Period 2	3 Li 6.941	4 Be 9.012					
Period 3	11 Na 22.990	12 Mg 24.305					
Period 4	19 K 39.098	20 Ca 40.08	21 Sc 44.956				
Period 5	37 Rb 85.468	38 Sr 87.62	39 Y 88.906				
Period 6	55 Cs 132.910	56 Ba 137.34	57 La 138.906	58 Ce 140.12	59 Pr 140.908	60 Nd 144.24	61 Pm 145
Period 7	87 Fr 223	88 Ra 226.025	89 Ac 227	90 Th 232.038	91 Pa 231.036	92 U 238.029	93 Np 237.048

Period 6	62 Sm 150.4	63 Eu 151.96	64 Gd 157.25	65 Tb 158.925	66 Dy 162.50	67 Ho 164.930	68 Er 167.26	69 Tm 168.934
Period 7	94 Pu 244	95 Am 243	96 Cm 247	97 Bk 247	98 Cf 251	99 Es 254	100 Fm 257	101 Md 258

Inner transition metals

Elements and their symbols

actinium	Ac	boron	B	copper	Cu	germanium	Ge	lanthanum	La
aluminium	Al	bromine	Br	curium	Cm	gold	Au	lawrencium	Lr
americium	Am	cadmium	Cd	dysprosium	Dy	hafnium	Hf	lead	Pb
antimony	Sb	caesium	Cs	einsteinium	Es	helium	He	lithium	Li
argon	Ar	calcium	Ca	erbium	Er	holmium	Ho	lutetium	Lu
arsenic	As	californium	Cf	europium	Eu	hydrogen	H	magnesium	Mg
astatine	At	carbon	C	fermium	Fm	indium	In	manganese	Mn
barium	Ba	cerium	Ce	fluorine	F	iodine	I	mendelevium	Md
berkelium	Bk	chlorine	Cl	francium	Fr	iridium	Ir	mercury	Hg
beryllium	Be	chromium	Cr	gadolinium	Gd	iron	Fe	molybdenum	Mo
bismuth	Bi	cobalt	Co	gallium	Ga	krypton	Kr	neodymium	Nd

 * *Atoms, 76-77; Elements, 86-87.*

Periods

There are seven periods. All of the elements in a period have the same number of electron shells around their nuclei. For example, sodium (Na) has the same number of shells as argon (Ar). Each successive element has one more electron in its outer shell of electrons than the element before it.

Alternative names of groups	
Group I	Alkali metals
Group II	Alkaline-earth metals
Group VII	Halogens
Group VIII	Group 0 / Noble gases

Groups

The vertical columns of the periodic table are called groups. All elements in the same group have the same number of electrons in their outermost shell, and so behave in a similar way. All of the groups are numbered (except the transition metal groups) using Roman numerals. Some of them have names, which are given in the table above right.

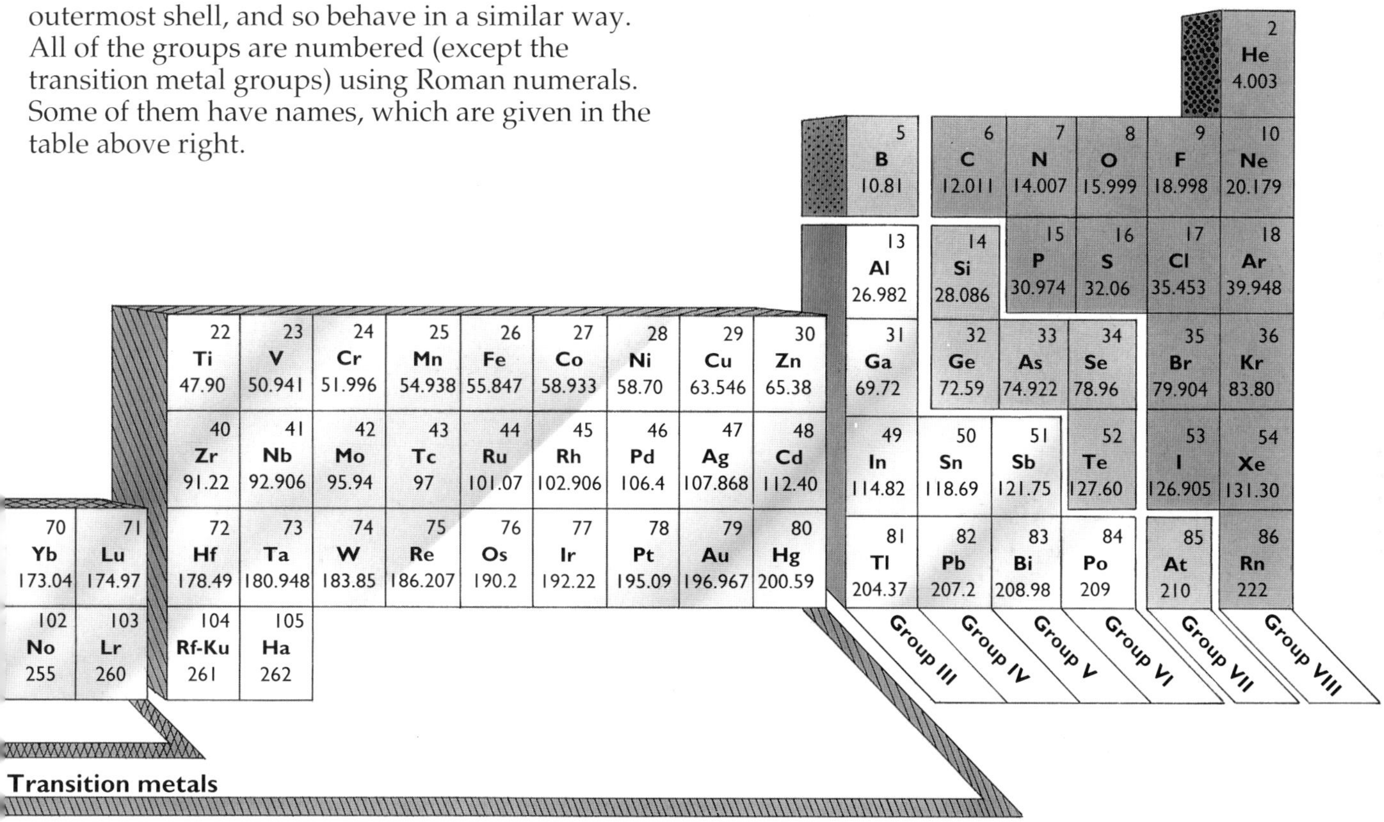

2 He 4.003
5 B 10.81
6 C 12.011
7 N 14.007
8 O 15.999
9 F 18.998
10 Ne 20.179
13 Al 26.982
14 Si 28.086
15 P 30.974
16 S 32.06
17 Cl 35.453
18 Ar 39.948
22 Ti 47.90
23 V 50.941
24 Cr 51.996
25 Mn 54.938
26 Fe 55.847
27 Co 58.933
28 Ni 58.70
29 Cu 63.546
30 Zn 65.38
31 Ga 69.72
32 Ge 72.59
33 As 74.922
34 Se 78.96
35 Br 79.904
36 Kr 83.80
40 Zr 91.22
41 Nb 92.906
42 Mo 95.94
43 Tc 97
44 Ru 101.07
45 Rh 102.906
46 Pd 106.4
47 Ag 107.868
48 Cd 112.40
49 In 114.82
50 Sn 118.69
51 Sb 121.75
52 Te 127.60
53 I 126.905
54 Xe 131.30
70 Yb 173.04
71 Lu 174.97
72 Hf 178.49
73 Ta 180.948
74 W 183.85
75 Re 186.207
76 Os 190.2
77 Ir 192.22
78 Pt 195.09
79 Au 196.967
80 Hg 200.59
81 Tl 204.37
82 Pb 207.2
83 Bi 208.98
84 Po 209
85 At 210
86 Rn 222
102 No 255
103 Lr 260
104 Rf-Ku 261
105 Ha 262
Group III
Group IV
Group V
Group VI
Group VII
Group VIII
Transition metals

neon	Ne	polonium	Po	samarium	Sm	terbium	Tb	xenon	Xe
neptunium	Np	potassium	K	scandium	Sc	thallium	Tl	ytterbium	Yb
nickel	Ni	praseodymium	Pr	selenium	Se	thorium	Th	yttrium	Y
niobium	Nb	promethium	Pm	silicon	Si	thulium	Tm	zinc	Zn
nitrogen	N	protactinium	Pa	silver	Ag	tin	Sn	zirconium	Zr
nobelium	No	radium	Ra	sodium	Na	titanium	Ti		
osmium	Os	radon	Rn	strontium	Sr	tungsten	W		
oxygen	O	rhenium	Re	sulphur	S	unnilpentium	Ha		
palladium	Pd	rhodium	Rh	tantalum	Ta	unnilquadium	Rf-Ku		
phosphorus	P	rubidium	Rb	technetium	Tc	uranium	U		
platinum	Pt	ruthenium	Ru	tellurium	Te	vanadium	V		

Indicators and tests

Identifying gases

Tests to identify gases are called qualitative analyses. The table below shows tests that are used to identify the presence of certain gases.

Some of the tests are dangerous so it is important that you do not attempt them without the help of an adult.

Name	Test
Ammonia	Turns red litmus paper blue.
Bromine	Forms a cream precipitate in silver nitrate solution.
Carbon dioxide	Turns calcium hydroxide solution (limewater) cloudy.
Hydrogen	Burns with a pop, forming water.
Nitrogen monoxide	Forms brown fumes when in air.
Sulphur dioxide	Turns potassium dichromate from orange to green.
Chlorine	Turns blue litmus paper red, then bleaches it.
Ethene	Takes bromine's colour away. Burns to form carbon dioxide and water.
Methane	Burns with a blue flame, forming carbon dioxide and water.
Nitrogen	Puts out a burning splint and does not react with limewater.
Nitrogen dioxide	Forms an acidic and colourless solution when mixed with water.
Oxygen	Relights a glowing splint.

Acids and bases

All substances can be defined as being either **acids** or **bases** or **salts**. Bases that are dissolved in water are called **alkalis**. Strong acids and alkalis can be harmful, so be careful if you use them.

How acid or alkaline a substance is can be tested by using an **indicator**. Indicators change colour when they are brought into contact with another substance.

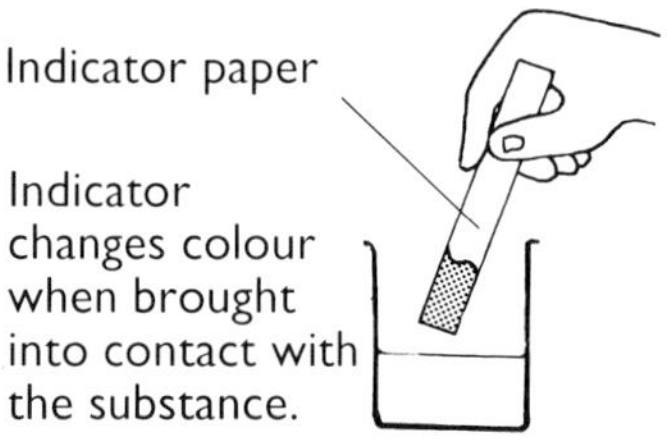
Indicator paper
Indicator changes colour when brought into contact with the substance.

Two types of indicators are commonly used. **Litmus papers** turn red when they come into contact with an acid and turn blue when they come into contact with an alkali. With **universal indicators**, the colour varies according to the strength of the acid or alkali.

The pH scale

A scale, called the **pH scale**, shows how acidic or alkaline a substance is. Values are measured from 0-14. A substance with a pH value below 7 is a base. A substance with a pH value above 7 is an acid. A substance with a pH value of 7 is neutral (called a salt).

The pH scale on the right describes which colours are shown when a universal indicator comes into contact with various strengths of acid and alkali.

1	Red
2	Light red
3	Dark orange
4	Orange
5	Light orange
6	Yellow
7	Light yellow
8	Yellow-green
9	Light green
10	Medium green
11	Dark green
12	Very dark green
13	Dark green-blue
14	Dark blue

Common acids

Below are listed some acids that you may come into contact with every day. They are listed with their pH values, as recorded in the substances in which they are commonly found.

Acid	pH value	Common substance
Ethanoic (acetic)	3	Vinegar
Amino acids	5.5	Proteins
Butyric	3	Perspiration
Carbolic	5.5	Disinfectants
Citric	1	Lemons

Acid	pH value	Common substance
Lactic	2	Sour milk, cheese
Malic	1	Apples
Oxalic	1	Sorrel (a herb)
Sulphuric	1	Batteries
Tartaric	2	Grapes

Common alloys

Metals can be combined by heating them until they are in a liquid state, then mixing them together. This forms a substance called an alloy. This chart shows some common alloys.

Alloy name	Approximate composition	Uses
Brass	Zinc (between 10% and 35%), copper (between 65% and 90%)	Decorative metal work
Common bronze	Zinc 2%, tin 6%, copper 92%	Machinery and decorative metal work
Coinage bronze	Zinc 1%, tin 4%, copper 95%	Coins
Dentist's amalgam	Copper 30%, mercury 70%	Dental fillings
Duralumin	Magnesium 0.5%, copper 4%, manganese 0.5%, aluminium 95%	Aircraft frames
Coinage gold	Copper (between 14% and 28%), silver (between 14% and 28%), gold 58%	Dental fillings
Manganin	Nickel 1.5%, manganese 16%, copper 82.5%	Wire used for fuses and resistors
Nichrome	Chromium 20%, nickel 80%	Wire used for fuses and resistors
Pewter	Lead 20%, tin 80%, antimony (trace)	Utensils and decorative work
Coinage silver	Copper 10%, silver 90%	Old coins
Solder	Tin 50%, lead 50%	Used to join metal objects together, such as wiring.
Stainless steel	Nickel (between 8% and 20%), chromium (between 10% and 20%), iron (between 60% and 80%)	Utensils, sinks
Tool steel	Chromium (between 2% and 4%), molybdenum (between 4% and 7%), iron (between 90% and 94%)	Tools including hammers, chisels and saws.

Glossary

Absorb. To take in. For example, a sponge takes in, or absorbs, water.

Acceleration. The change of velocity caused by changing speed or direction.

Acoustics. The way sound travels in a room. It also means 'the science of sound'.

Aerodynamics. The study of the way air flows around things.

Aerofoil. The special shape of a wing that enables aircraft to lift off the ground.

Aerosol. A pressurized container used to spray liquids, like paint, in a fine mist.

Air resistance. The push of air against moving things that works to slow them down.

Alchemy. An ancient form of chemistry. Alchemists tried to turn things into gold.

Alloy. A metal that is made of a mixture of different metals.

Alternating current. An electric current that changes direction, usually many times each second.

Amplifier. An electronic device that boosts electrical signals.

Antenna. A length of wire that is used to send out or receive radio waves. Also called an aerial.

Astronomy. The scientific study of the objects in Space, such as stars, asteroids and planets.

Atmosphere. The blanket of gases that surrounds the Earth.

Atmospheric pressure. The pressure on the Earth caused by the weight of the gases in the atmosphere.

Atoms. Tiny particles out of which everything is made.

Attract. To make something come closer. A magnet attracts iron.

Barometer. A device for measuring atmospheric pressure.

Biology. The scientific study of all living things.

Boiling point. The temperature at which a liquid boils, changing into a gas.

Botany. The scientific study of plants.

Buoyancy. The ability of something to float.

Calorie. A unit of energy that is often used to measure the energy content of food. One calorie equals 4.18 joules.

Celsius. The temperature scale which sets the melting point of pure water at zero degrees and its boiling point at 100 degrees.

Centigrade scale. A scale that is divided into 100 units.

Chemical reaction. When atoms of different things join up together to make something new.

Chemistry. The scientific study of all substances, and how they react and combine together.

Chlorophyll. The chemical inside leaves that gives green plants their colour and is essential for photosynthesis.

Circuit. A continuous electrical conductor, such as a wire, through which electricity flows.

Combustion. The process of burning.

Compact disc. A disc on which sound or computer data is recorded in digital form.

Compass. A device that uses the Earth's magnetism to show you which direction you are facing.

Compound. A substance made of atoms of different elements chemically joined together.

Compress. To squash up into a smaller space.

Condensation. The way a vapour changes into a liquid as it cools down.

Conductor. A material that allows either electricity or heat to flow through it easily.

Contraction. Shrinking to a smaller size.

Convection. The way heat is carried by a liquid or a gas. A convection current is a flow of liquid or gas carrying heat.

Crude oil. Oil that is extracted from the inside of the Earth, before it has been refined.

Current electricity. The type of electricity that can flow through wires.

Data. Another word for information.

Decelerate. To slow down.

Decibel. A unit for measuring the loudness, or intensity, of sound.

Density. How much something weighs for its size.

Diameter. The straight line between opposite sides of a circle that passes through its centre.

Digital information. Information that is stored in computers as binary numbers.

Diffusion. The way that molecules of one material spread through those of another.

Direct current. Electric current that flows in only one direction around a circuit.

Dynamo. A type of generator that produces direct current.

Earthquake. Vibrations of the Earth's crust caused by the movement of rock beneath its surface.

Echo-location. Navigation using echoes from high-pitched sounds.

Efficiency. The amount of energy you get out compared to how much energy you put in.

Electric charge. Something that has an electric charge carries electricity. There are two types of electric charge, called positive and negative.

Electric field. The space around an electric charge in which its electric force acts.

Electromagnet. A coil of wire that produces a magnetic field when an electric current is passed through it.

Electrons. Tiny particles inside atoms that carry a negative charge.

Electronics. Technology to do with circuits and microchips.

Element. A substance that is made of only one type of atom.

Energy. The ability to do work and provide power. There are many different types of energy including heat energy, light energy, sound energy, chemical energy and nuclear energy.

Evaporation. The way a liquid changes into a gas when it is below its boiling point.

Fahrenheit. The temperature scale which sets the freezing point of pure water at 32 degrees and its boiling point at 212 degrees.

Fission. The splitting up of the nucleus of an atom, producing a huge amount of nuclear energy.

Fluid. Either a liquid or a gas.

Focus. The point where rays of light from a lens or a curved mirror meet.

Force. A push or pull that makes things move, change shape or change direction.

Fossil fuel. Fuel, like coal or oil, that has formed over millions of years and is dug up from the ground.

Freezing point. The temperature at which a liquid freezes, changing into a solid.

Friction. The force that works to stop things moving, or slow them down if they are already moving.

Fusion. The joining up of the nuclei of different atoms, producing a huge amount of nuclear energy.

Generator. A machine that turns the energy of movement, or kinetic energy, into electrical energy.

Geography. The scientific study of the Earth.

Geology. The scientific study of the Earth's rocks and crust.

Graphite. Soft, flaky form of the element carbon, used as a lubricant and in pencil leads.

Heat radiation. The way that heat is carried by infra-red rays.

Hologram. A special three-dimensional photograph that is taken with a laser.

Humidity. The amount of moisture there is in the air.

Hydroelectricity. Electricity that is generated from the energy of moving water.

Ignite. To set on fire.

Inertia. The tendency of things to keep still, or to carry on moving at the same speed in the same straight line, unless they are acted on by a force.

Inflammable. Easily set on fire.

Insulator. A material that does not allow heat or electricity to pass through it easily.

Kerosene. The fuel that is used in jet engines. Also called paraffin.

Laser. A device which produces a very bright beam of light. It can be used for cutting things or carrying information.

Lodestone. Naturally magnetic material. Also called magnetite.

Luminous. A luminous object is something that gives out light.

Lubrication. The use of a thick liquid, called a lubricant, to reduce friction between the moving parts of a machine.

Magnet. A material which produces a magnetic force that attracts the metals iron, cobalt or nickel. If a magnet is held freely, it lines up with the North and South Poles of the Earth.

Magnetic field. The space around a magnet in which its magnetic force works.

Magnify. To make bigger using lenses.

Mass. The amount there is of something.

Mathematics. The science of numbers, quantities and shapes.

Matter. Any physical thing that takes up space.

Melting point. The temperature at which a solid melts, turning into a liquid.

Meteorology. The scientific study of the weather.

Microchip. A tiny piece of silicon that contains thousands of electronic circuits. They are also called silicon chips.

Microscope. A device that uses lenses to magnify small things many times.

Mixture. Two or more elements or compounds that are mixed up together, but are not chemically joined up to each other.

Molecule. A particle that contains two or more atoms joined together.

Neutrons. Particles inside the nuclei of atoms. They carry no electric charge.

Nuclear force. A very strong force which holds protons and neutrons together inside the nucleus of an atom.

Nuclear radiation. Dangerous radiation that is given out by radioactive materials.

Nuclear reactor. The place where the nuclei of atoms are split in order to release energy.

Nucleus. The central part of an atom which contains protons and neutrons. The electrons whiz around the nucleus.

Opaque. An opaque object does not let any light pass through it.

Orbit. The path of a satellite or a planet, often circular or oval in shape.

Optic fibre. A thin piece of glass that can carry light long distances. The light can be used to carry telephone calls and computer data.

Ozone. A layer of gas in the atmosphere that protects the Earth from the Sun's ultraviolet radiation.

Particle. A tiny piece of a material.

Pendulum. A hanging weight that swings backwards and forwards. It is used as a regulator for clocks because each swing lasts the same time.

Periodic Table. A table that shows all the elements arranged in groups. The elements in each group have similar properties.

Perspective. A way of drawing pictures to give a feeling of distance and depth.

Physics. The scientific study of matter and energy.

Pitch. How high or low a sound is.

Planet. A large ball of rock or gas which orbits a star. It reflects the star's light but does not give out light of its own.

Poles. The ends of a magnet, or the places on the Earth, where the magnetic field is strongest.

Pollution. Harmful fumes, waste chemicals and rubbish that dirty the environment.

Polymer. A material that is made up of very long molecules.

Pressure. The force acting on a certain area.

Pressurized container. A container used for holding liquids or gases at high pressure.

Protons. Particles inside the nucleus of an atom that carry a positive charge.

Radar. A device that measures the distance to an object, and the direction it is moving in, by bouncing radio waves off it.

Reaction. The equal and opposite force to any action.

Recycle. To use something again, rather than throwing it away, in order to conserve resources and reduce pollution.

Reflection. The way light or sound bounces.

Refraction. The way light rays bend when they pass through different materials.

Repel. To push something away.

Resistance, electrical. The way a material slows down electric current flowing through it.

Solar cell. A device that changes the energy from sunlight into electrical energy.

Solar system. The Sun and all the objects that orbit it, such as the planets.

Solution. A solid, liquid or a gas which is mixed up, or dissolved, in a liquid. The thing that is dissolved is called the solute, and the thing that does the dissolving is called the solvent.

Sonar. A system that uses the echoes of ultrasound waves to detect things that are underwater.

Spectrum. All the colours which together make up white light.

Speed. How far something goes in a certain time.

Star. An object in Space that gives out light of its own.

Static electricity. Electricity that stays in one place because it builds up on insulators.

Supersonic. Faster than the speed of sound.

Technology. The development of new things as a result of advances in science.

Telescope. A device which uses lenses to magnify distant objects.

Temperature. The measure of how hot or cold something is.

Thermal. Means 'to do with heat'. A thermal is a current of air that rises because it has been heated.

Thermal expansion. The way things get slightly larger when they are heated.

Thermometer. A device for measuring temperature.

Translucent. A translucent object lets some light pass through it.

Transparent. A transparent object lets all light pass through it.

Upthrust. The force pushing on an object that is in a liquid or gas. Things float because the upthrust pushes them up.

Vacuum. A completely empty space, with no solids, liquids or gases inside it.

Velocity. The speed at which an object is moving in a particular direction.

Vibration. A continuous, very fast, backwards and forwards movement.

Viscosity. The measure of how thick a liquid is.

Visible light. All the light and colours that can be seen by human eyes.

Volume. The amount of space that something takes up.

Zoology. The scientific study of animals.

Answers

Page 5
Roman numbers

You may find Roman numerals used in the following places:
- to show the hours on clock faces
- to number the chapters in books
- to show a date on some coins
- to show dates on some monuments
- in the names of some kings and queens, for example, Louis XIV.

Page 7
How tall are you?

Their answers will vary depending on how large they are. People's arms, hands and feet are different sizes, so a unit of measurement based on one person's body is different from a unit of measurement based on someone else's body.

Page 11
Energy quiz

Many things in the picture have kinetic energy:
- the moving cars and lorry
- the moving bicycle
- the ball thrown by the boy
- the sailing boats
- the boy on the swing
- the flying birds
- the falling raindrops

- the hair-drier uses electrical energy
- the lawn-mower uses electrical energy

- the lamp over the door gives out light energy
- the car headlamps give out light energy

- the apples on the tree have potential energy
- the chicks in the nest have potential energy

Page 13
Find the energy changes

The wind's kinetic energy changes into the kinetic energy of the moving sailing boat.

The potential energy of the man on the jetty changes into kinetic energy as he dives into the water.

The chemical energy of fuel in the engine changes into the kinetic energy of the moving motor-boat.

Page 33
Quiz

On Earth, a mass of 1kg (2.2lbs) weighs about 10N. To calculate your weight in newtons, multiply your mass in kilograms by 10 (to work it out using imperial measurements, multiply your mass in pounds by 4.5). For example, if you have a mass of 50kg (110lbs) you will weigh 500N.

On the Moon, a mass of 1kg only weighs 1.6N. To calculate your weight on the Moon, multiply your mass in kilograms by 1.6. If you have a mass of 50kg, you would weigh 80N.

Page 40
Pressure

A sharp knife cuts into things better than a blunt knife because the push of the cutting edge is spread over a smaller area. This means that a sharp knife puts more pressure on an object than a blunt knife.

In the same way, nails have sharp points so that they can be easily hammered into things. The sharper the point of a nail, the higher the pressure, because it pushes on a smaller area.

Page 55
Picture trick

If you check with a ruler, you will find that both lines are exactly the same length.

LIVING WORLD

Leslie Colvin and Emma Speare

Designed by
Steve Page

Illustrated by
Isabel Bowring, Kuo Kang Chen,
Sandra Fernandez, Ian Jackson,
Steve Kirk, Rachel Lockwood
and Chris Shields

Additional designs by
John Russell, Sandy Wegener
and Kathy Ward

Scientific advisors
Steve Pollock and Ruth Taylor

Edited by
Corinne Stockley

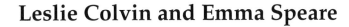

Contents

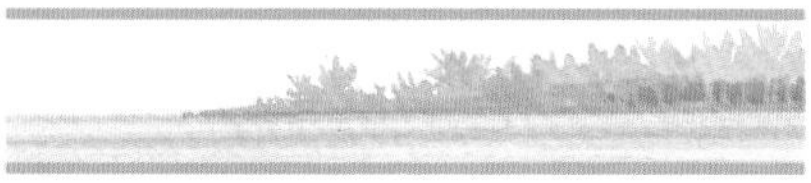

The *Nature* section

There are millions of different kinds of living things on Earth. Some are giant, such as blue whales and redwood trees, but others are very tiny such as insects. All of them need food and shelter, which they get from their natural surroundings, or environment.

The first part of the *Nature* section is about living things and their environments. The rest of this section groups together animals and plants by the environments where they live. For example, squid and seaweed are found in the seas and oceans, so they are in that section.

If you are not sure which section to find an animal or plant in, then look it up in the index at the back of the book.

Some words have an asterisk*. This means they are explained somewhere else in the book. A footnote at the bottom of the page tells you where to look for the explanation. Difficult words are in **bold type** where they are mentioned and explained. There are lots of explanations of words in the glossary (pages 246-248).

This picture shows the Florida Everglades. Many different birds and fish live here as well as alligators and snakes.

The story of the Earth

The Earth is a spinning ball of hot, partly liquid rock, covered with a thin, outer crust. There are large cracks in the crust called plate boundaries, which divide it into separate areas, called plates.

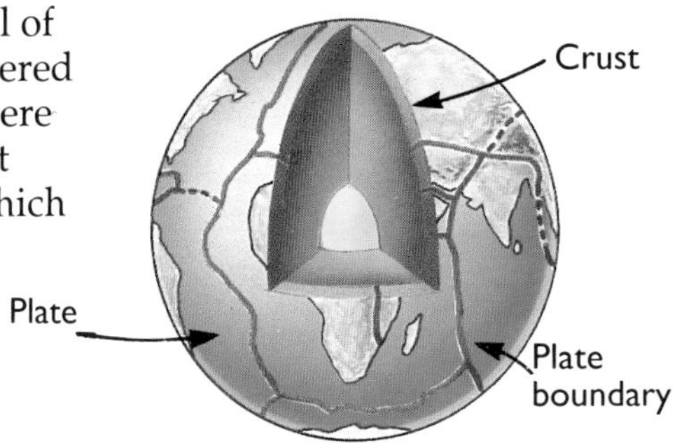

Crust
Plate
Plate boundary

The plates move

The partly liquid rock below the plates moves, making the plates themselves move about two centimetres (one inch) a year. They rub against each other as they move.

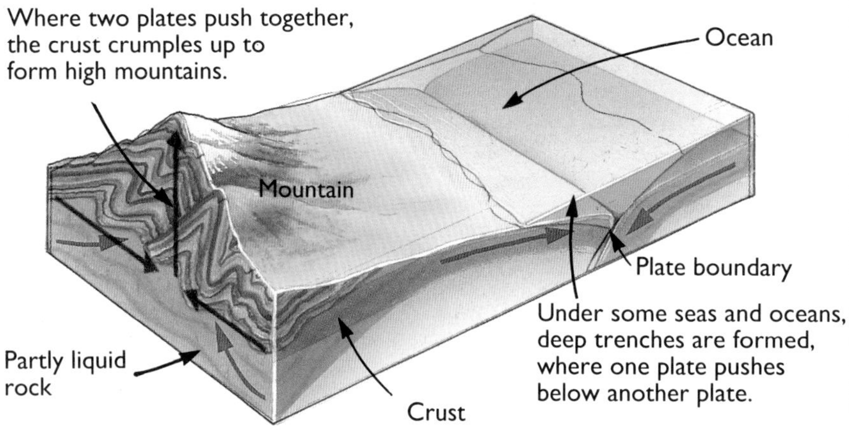

Where two plates push together, the crust crumples up to form high mountains.
Ocean
Mountain
Plate boundary
Under some seas and oceans, deep trenches are formed, where one plate pushes below another plate.
Partly liquid rock
Crust

Fossils

Animals and plants that died a long time ago mostly rotted away. Sometimes their hard parts, such as bones, were preserved in rocks as **fossils**.

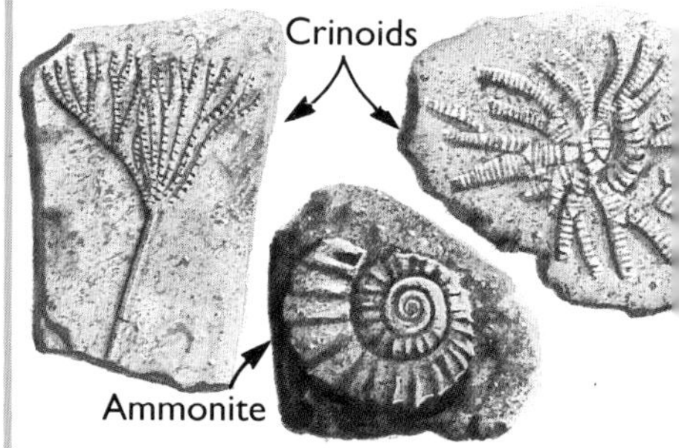

Crinoids
Ammonite

Fossils show us what kinds of plants and animals lived a long time ago. Some, such as corals and crinoids, still live on Earth today, but many more, such as ammonites, died out. When all the members of one kind of living thing have died out, it is extinct. For more about extinctions, see pages 146-147.

Life on Earth

When the Earth formed 4,600 million years ago, it was too hot for rain to fall. It was a very, very long time before the seas and oceans formed.

3,500 million years ago, the first living things were alive in the oceans. They were too small to see, like the germs that make people ill today.

Simple animals, such as jellyfish and corals, and simple plants, such as algae, lived about 700 million years ago.

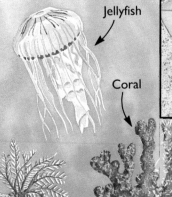

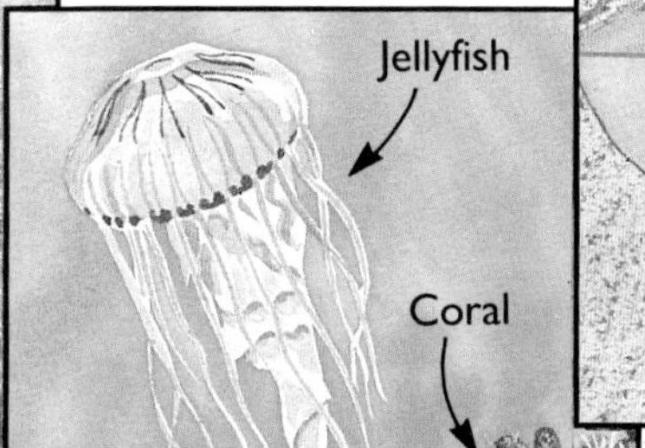

Jellyfish
Coral

400 million years ago, the first land plants grew on Earth. Fish and shelled animals lived in the seas.

This is a family of animals. For more about animal families, see page 244.

Where animals and plants live today

Much of the Earth's land was once joined in one piece. As the plates moved, seas and mountains formed.

This stopped animals from moving over all the land and explains why living things are found in different places today.

Arabian camel
Vicuña
Bactrian camel
Llama

There are lots of camel-like animals around the world. Their ancestors lived when the land was all one piece.

They became cut off from each other when the oceans formed. Over millions of years each group developed differently.

Wombats are burrowing forest animals. They are slightly bigger than badgers.

The duck-billed platypus dives under water to hunt for food.

Tree kangaroos feed on fruit and leaves.

55 million years ago Australia broke away from Antartica. Many animals, such as kangaroos, wombats and platypuses, exist only in Australia.

Some give birth to very tiny babies, which live in the mother's pouch for many weeks. The animals are marsupials*.

340 million years ago, insects and amphibians* lived in the swampy jungles which covered the land.

230 million years ago, dinosaurs were alive on Earth. They were land-living reptiles*. There were also flying reptiles and swimming reptiles.

65 million years ago, the dinosaurs died out (for more about why, see page 146).

Pterodactyl
Triceratops

The first mammals* were small shrew-like animals which lived 225 million years ago.

The first apes lived 35 million years ago.

Apes, such as gorillas, are close relatives of humans. The earliest human fossils were found in Africa. They are two million years old.

Environments

The natural surroundings of an animal or plant are called its environment. There are many different environments around the world. They vary because of such things as temperature, and different amounts of sunshine and rain.

The sections of this book from page 148 to 241 look at the main environments of the world, such as tropical forests, deserts and oceans. All the plants and animals in these areas have become good at living in their particular environment.

Cacti store water in their stems, which helps them live in dry desert areas.

Polar bears have thick fur, which helps them to survive the icy, Arctic winters.

Changing environments

All the environments have regular changes, such as the change between day and night, the changes in the seasons and the movement of the tides on a seashore. Plants and animals are used to living with these changes. Other changes are more gradual, long-term changes (see pages 138-139).

Tidal changes

Animals that live on the seashore are used to living with the regular changes in the tides. There is more about this on pages 158-159.

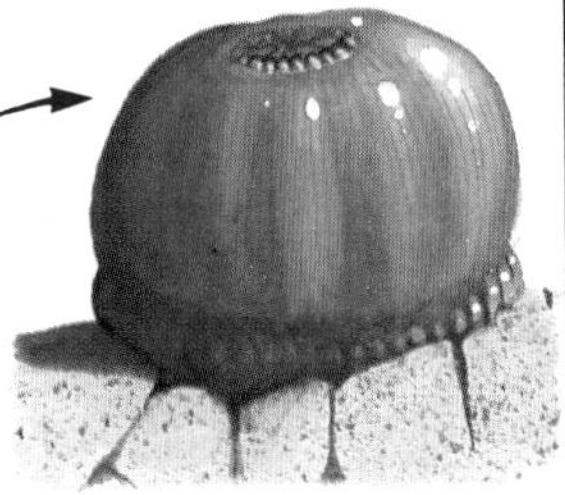

Sea anemones pull their tentacles in when the tide is out, so that they do not dry up.

When the tide comes back up the shore, they unfold and their tentacles wave around in the water.

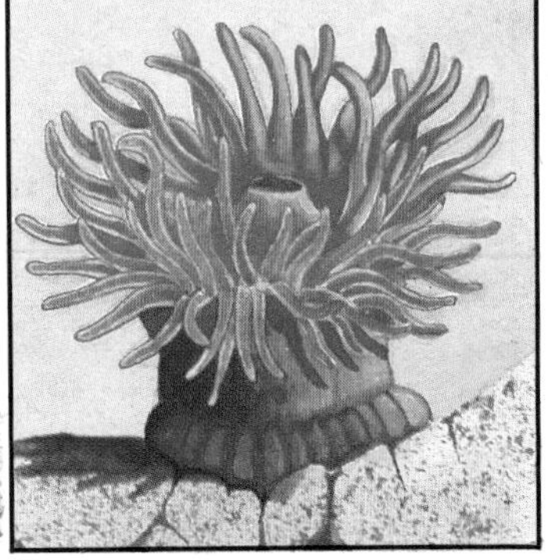

In the daytime

Many animals, from bears to bees, wake up when the sun comes up, live and feed all day, and go to sleep at night. They are active during the day.

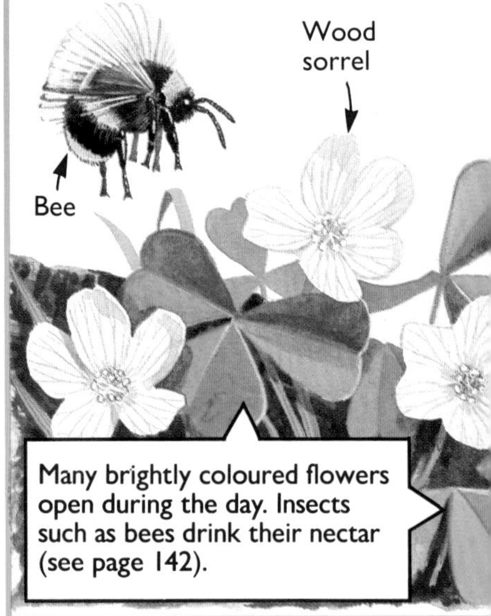

Many brightly coloured flowers open during the day. Insects such as bees drink their nectar (see page 142).

At night

At night, plants cannot make food by photosynthesis, as there is no sunlight. They take in oxygen and give off moisture and carbon dioxide, just like animals do all the time.

The flowers and leaves of some plants close up when night comes.

Green plants make their food in the daytime, because they need sunlight to do it. They use the sun's energy to join water and carbon dioxide (a gas from the air) to make sugar. This is their food. As they do this they make another gas called oxygen, which they let out into the air. The whole process is called **photosynthesis.**

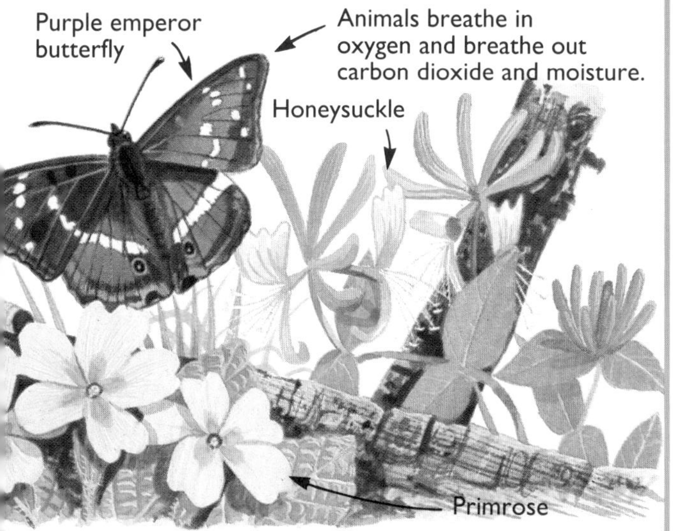
Purple emperor butterfly
Animals breathe in oxygen and breathe out carbon dioxide and moisture.
Honeysuckle
Primrose

Privet hawk moth
Some flowers stay open. Animals can detect their strong, sweet scent. Moths use feathery antennae to find flowers to feed from.
Stag beetle

Finding food at night

Many animals, such as moths, bats and foxes, sleep in the day and are active at night. They are called **nocturnal** animals and often have special things about them that help them to hunt for food at night.

The gecko is a kind of lizard. It feeds on moths and insects at night. Like many nocturnal animals, it has large, sensitive eyes, which help it to see in very dim light.

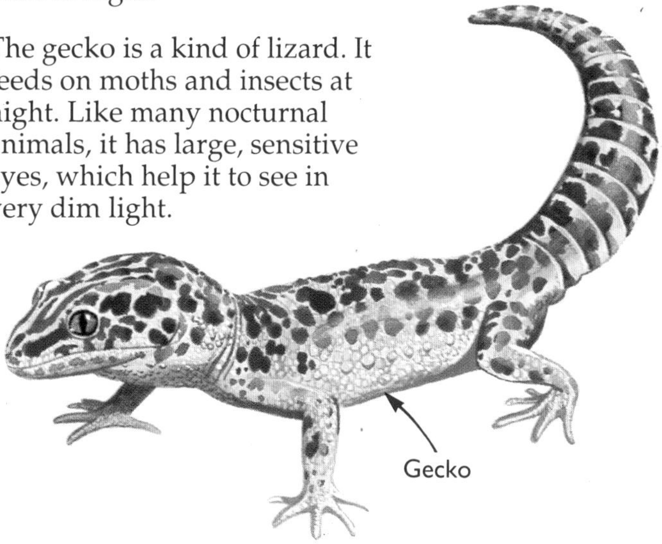
Gecko

Many bats make very high-pitched squeaks to help them find their way at night.

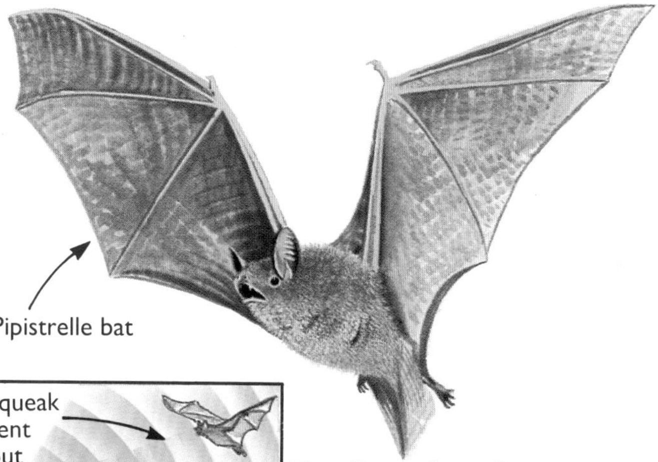
Pipistrelle bat

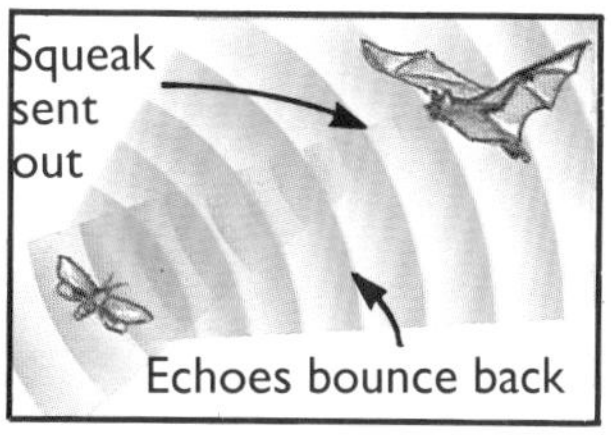
Squeak sent out
Echoes bounce back

Bats listen for echoes as they squeak. Echoes happen when sound bounces off objects.

Bats find their way because they can tell from the echoes where obstacles are. Their large, sensitive ears help them detect different echoes, for example echoes from trees they want to avoid, or from insects they want to catch.

Seasonal changes

Seasons are times of the year with different conditions, such as weather and temperature. They change from one to the next in a yearly cycle. Around the world plants and animals are good at dealing with the changes of seasons.

Seasons around the world

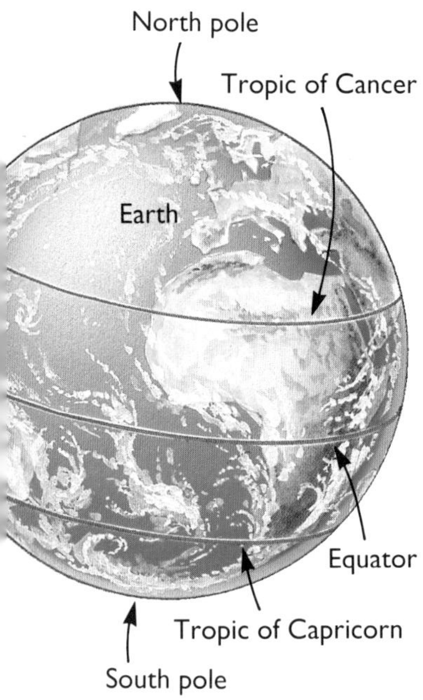
North pole
Tropic of Cancer
Earth
Equator
Tropic of Capricorn
South pole

Most places in the **tropics** (inside the imaginary tropic lines) are never very cold, and have two seasons - a wet, rainy season and a dry one. Near the equator (the middle imaginary line) it is hot and wet all year round.

Temperate areas (outside the tropic lines) have spring, summer, autumn and winter. Generally, the closer a place is to the north or south pole, the cooler its summers are and the colder its winters.

The plant year

Green plants need sunlight and water to make food and grow. They grow most in spring and summer, or the wet season, and have different ways of surviving winter, or the dry season.

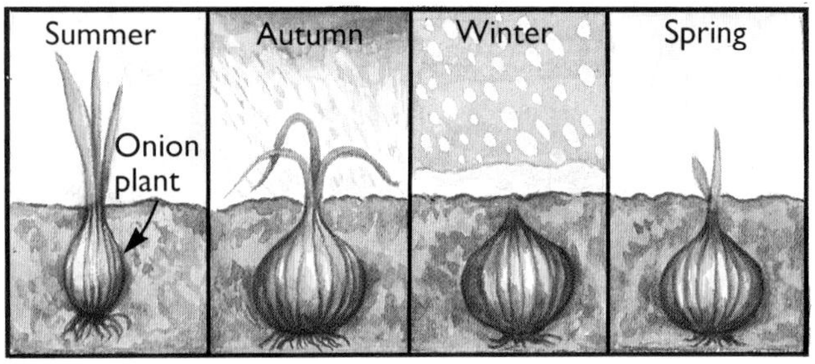
Summer
Autumn
Winter
Spring
Onion plant

Many plants have a resting stage. Some plants store up food in swollen parts of themselves underground. They die away above ground in the winter and rest until spring. Carrots, onions and potatoes are all kinds of plant food stores that people eat.

The animal year

Many animals, such as reptiles*, can survive the cold or dry season by slowing down and becoming less active. When it gets warmer, or wetter, they go back to normal. Other animals cannot do this. They have other ways of surviving harsh seasons.

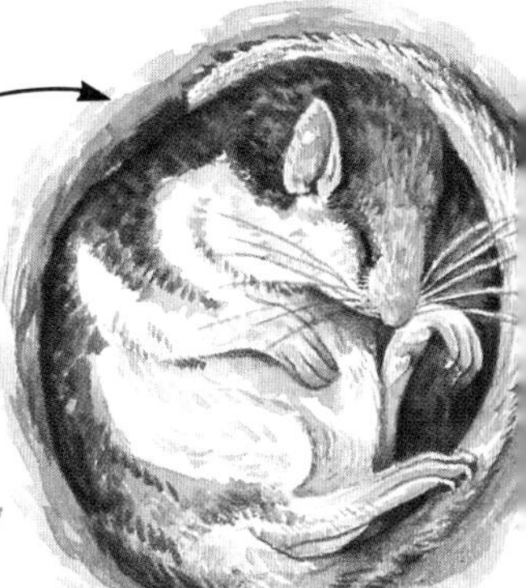

Many animals, such as dormice, sleep all winter. This is called **hibernation**. They feed and get fat all summer so they can sleep a long time without eating.

Most mammals* and birds produce their young in spring when there is more food about, so their young can get older and stronger before winter comes.

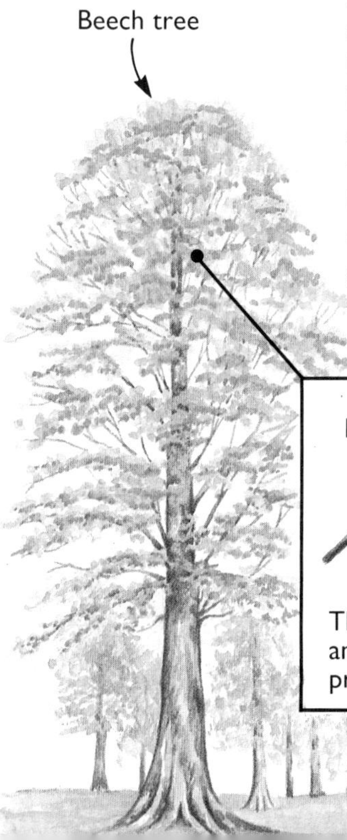
Beech tree

Deciduous trees, such as oak and beech, shed their leaves in autumn, because there is not enough sunshine in the winter for their leaves to make food. They rest over the winter and grow new leaves in spring from buds.

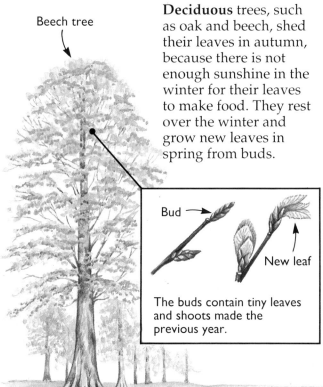

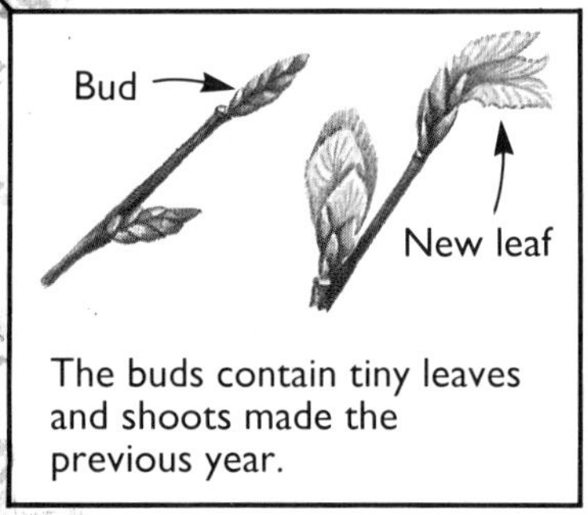
Bud
New leaf

The buds contain tiny leaves and shoots made the previous year.

Mammals, Reptiles, 244.

Many birds and other animals make long journeys each year, called **migrations** (see page 170), to places where there is more food. For example, swallows nest in Europe in the spring. In autumn they fly to Africa. They return in the spring when it is too dry in Africa.

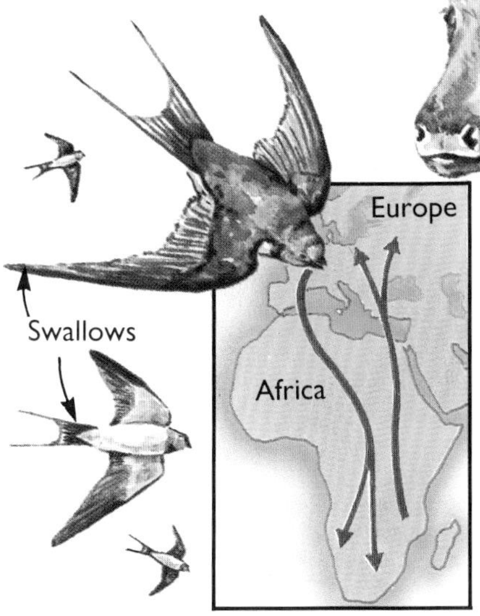

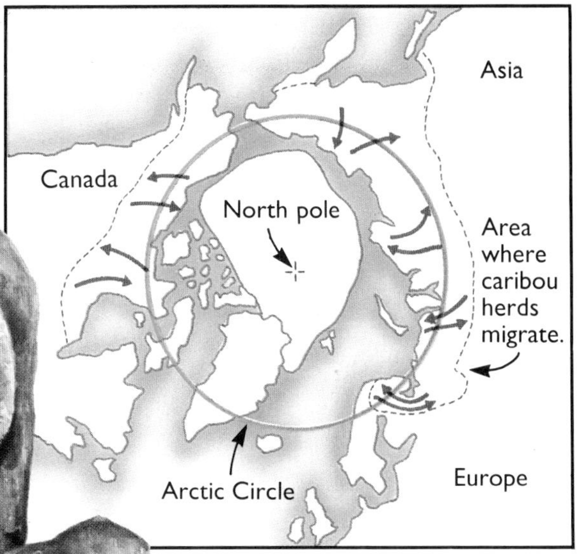

Caribou (called reindeer in Europe and Asia) also migrate. They spend summer in the Arctic north. Huge herds feed on the grass and other small plants which grow quickly when the ice melts. They migrate south in the autumn, to evergreen forests where they feed on small plants, such as lichens, under the snow.

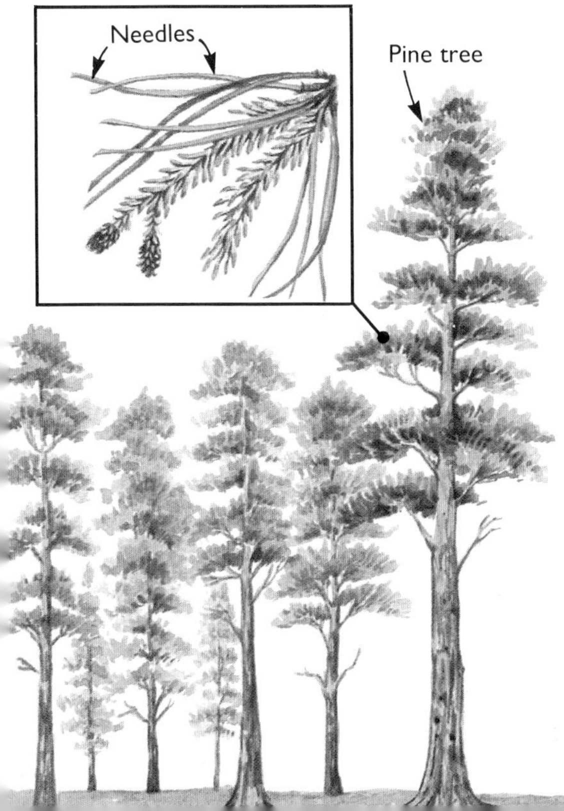

Evergreen trees have leaves that last for several years and fall off gradually. They are never bare. For more about evergreen and deciduous trees, see pages 186-187.

Some evergreen trees, such as pine and fir, have long thin leaves, called needles. Many of them grow quite far north, where summers are short and cool and winters freezing. By keeping their leaves all year, they can start growing fast as soon as spring arrives.

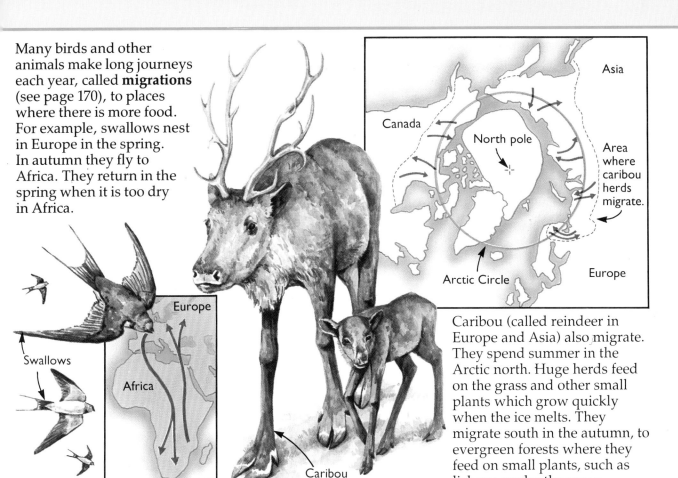

All deserts are very dry. Some years they may have no rain, other years they have a very short rainy season. The seeds of many desert plants only grow into new plants when enough rain falls. Then they flower and produce new seeds very fast. The seeds contain food stores.

Long-term changes

All the animals and plants in one area form a community. From year to year, the community does not change much, but over a long period it can change a great deal.

Food chains and webs

A **food chain** is a series of living things, linked together because each is the food for the next one. Green plants make their own food, so they start food chains. They are called **producers**. Animals cannot make their own food, so they must eat plants or other animals. They are called **consumers**. Animals can be first, second or third level consumers, depending on what kind of food they eat. **Food webs** link together different food chains in a community.

This is a diagram of a North American forest food web

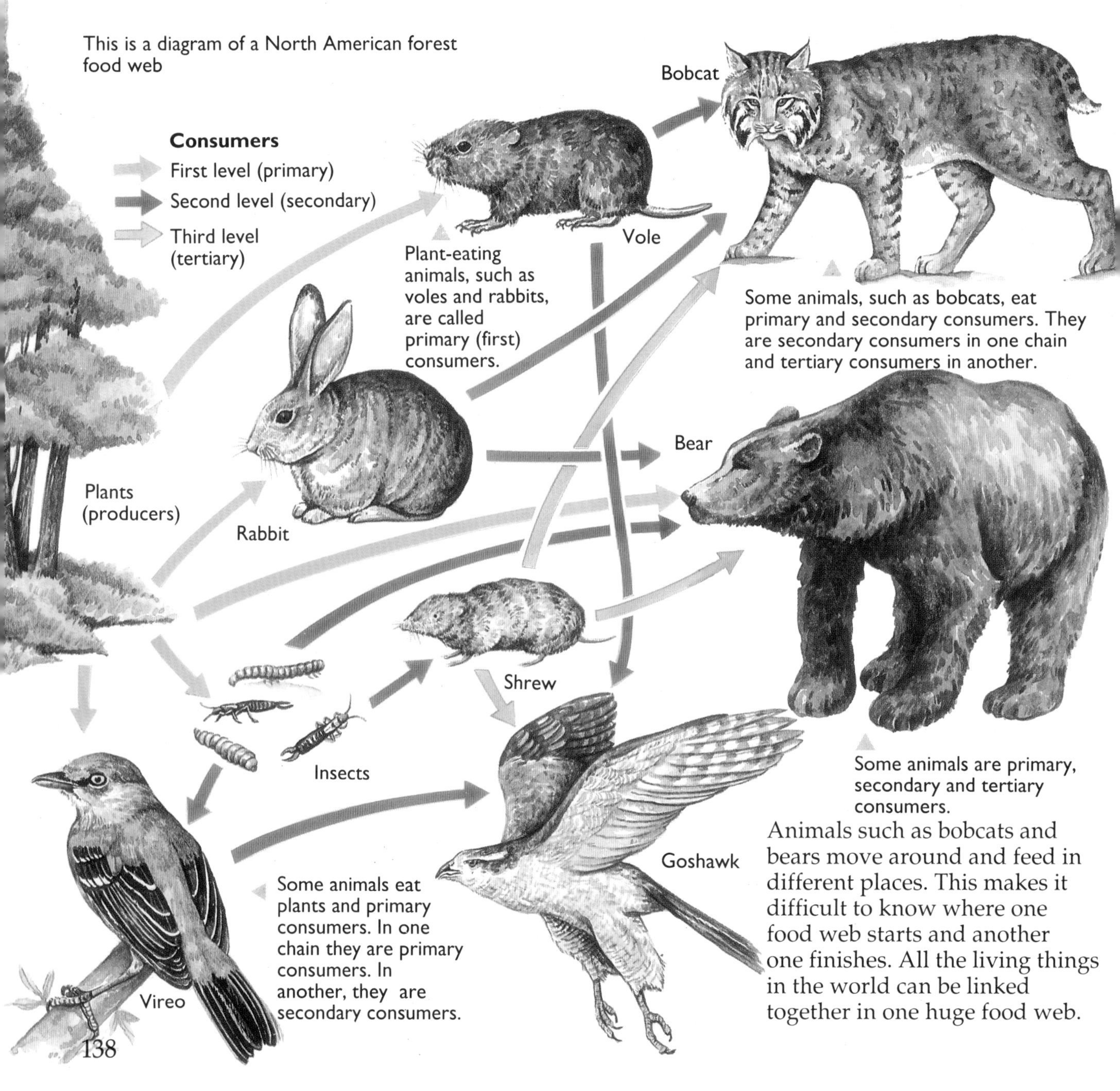

Consumers
First level (primary)
Second level (secondary)
Third level (tertiary)
Bobcat
Vole
Plant-eating animals, such as voles and rabbits, are called primary (first) consumers.
Some animals, such as bobcats, eat primary and secondary consumers. They are secondary consumers in one chain and tertiary consumers in another.
Bear
Plants (producers)
Rabbit
Shrew
Insects
Some animals are primary, secondary and tertiary consumers.
Goshawk
Some animals eat plants and primary consumers. In one chain they are primary consumers. In another, they are secondary consumers.
Vireo

Animals such as bobcats and bears move around and feed in different places. This makes it difficult to know where one food web starts and another one finishes. All the living things in the world can be linked together in one huge food web.

Changing communities

In a natural community the numbers of producers and consumers is balanced. There is enough food and the community does not change. It is stable.

However, the balance is easily upset. For example, if a disease kills all the primary consumers, this affects all the members of the food chain.

Secondary consumers die because there is not enough food.
Primary consumers die.
Plants grow better because they are being eaten less.

Big changes to a community set off a series of long term changes as nature tries to make it stable again.

For instance, after a forest fire the community is destroyed. Plants such as grass and ferns grow fast, covering the ground.

Small bushes grow and kill these plants by blocking their light. As new kinds of plants grow, different animals come to feed.

This type of slow change is called **succession**. After 200 years there may be a new community of forest plants and animals again.

When people clear areas for farming and keep them clear, they stop succession from happening. Natural communities are lost forever.

Regular changes

Natural changes in a community may follow a regular cycle. In the Arctic community, lemming numbers depend on the amount of food (plants) and the number of hunters, such as arctic foxes.

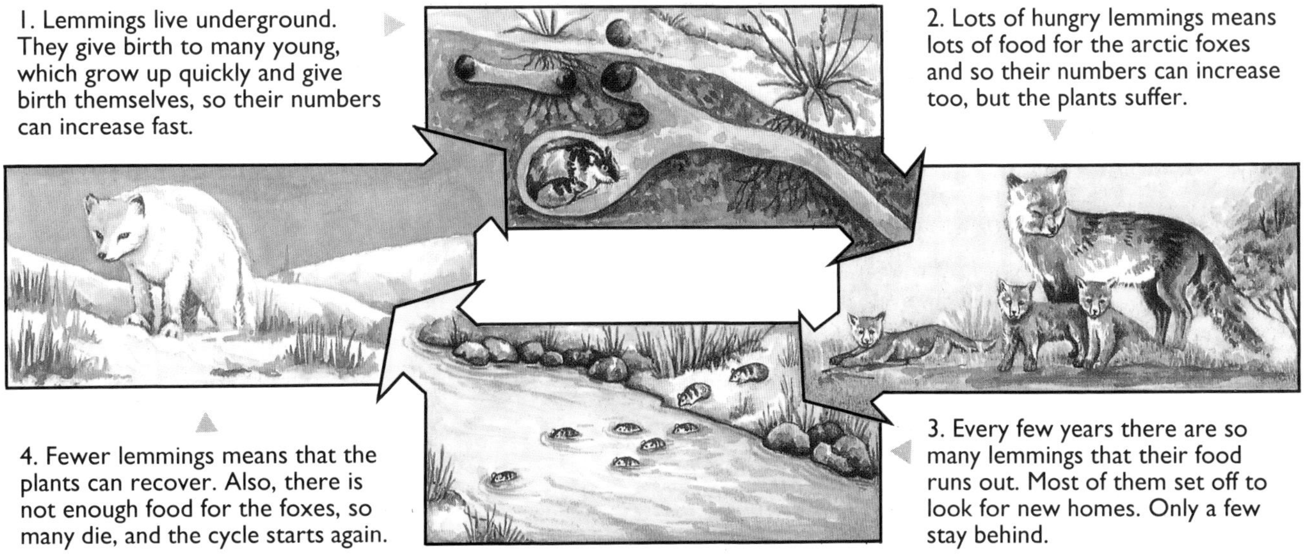

1. Lemmings live underground. They give birth to many young, which grow up quickly and give birth themselves, so their numbers can increase fast.

2. Lots of hungry lemmings means lots of food for the arctic foxes and so their numbers can increase too, but the plants suffer.

3. Every few years there are so many lemmings that their food runs out. Most of them set off to look for new homes. Only a few stay behind.

4. Fewer lemmings means that the plants can recover. Also, there is not enough food for the foxes, so many die, and the cycle starts again.

Cycles in nature

All living things are made up of substances such as water, oxygen, nitrogen and carbon. They take them in from the environment, change them inside their bodies and use them to live and grow. When the living things die, and their bodies rot*, the substances go back to the environment. These substances are recycled, or used again and again, in nature.

The carbon cycle

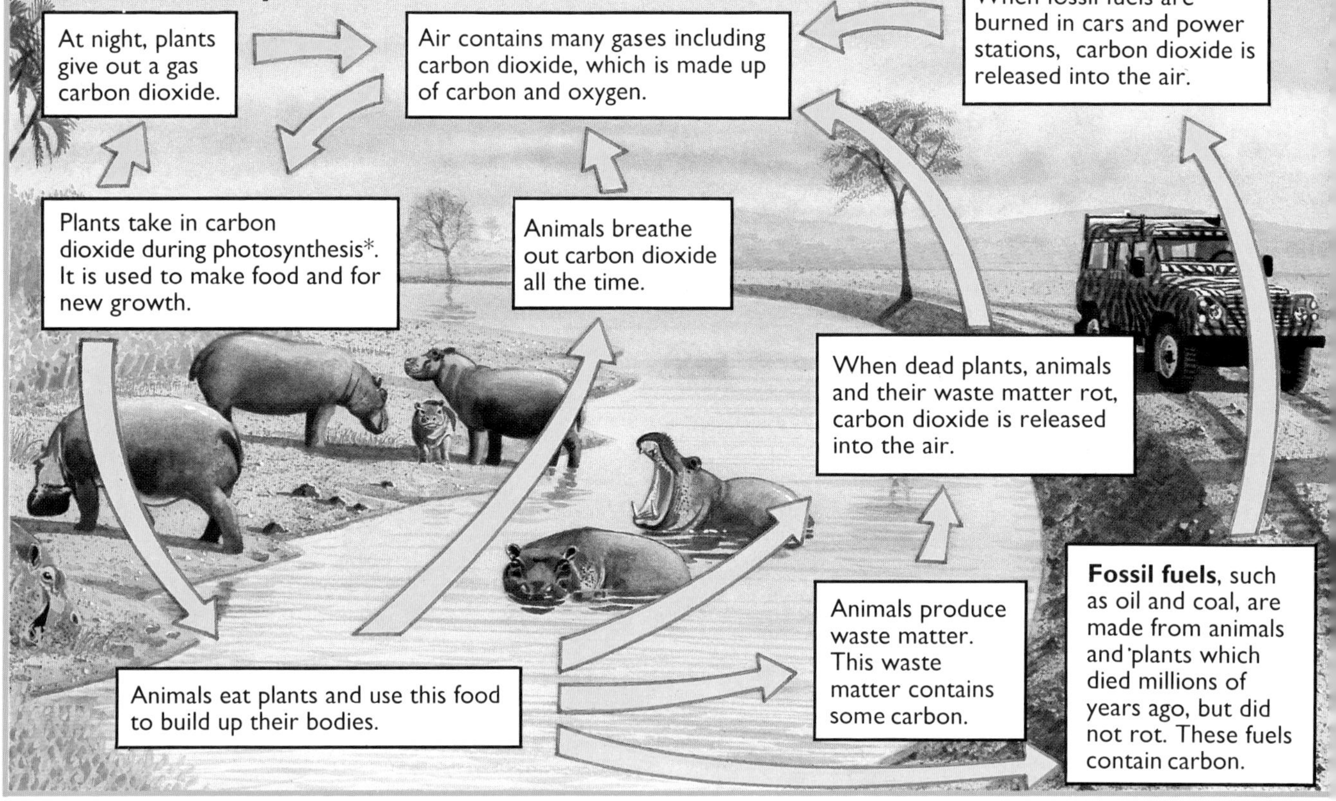
At night, plants give out a gas carbon dioxide.
Air contains many gases including carbon dioxide, which is made up of carbon and oxygen.
When fossil fuels are burned in cars and power stations, carbon dioxide is released into the air.
Plants take in carbon dioxide during photosynthesis*. It is used to make food and for new growth.
Animals breathe out carbon dioxide all the time.
When dead plants, animals and their waste matter rot, carbon dioxide is released into the air.
Animals eat plants and use this food to build up their bodies.
Animals produce waste matter. This waste matter contains some carbon.
Fossil fuels, such as oil and coal, are made from animals and plants which died millions of years ago, but did not rot. These fuels contain carbon.

The greenhouse effect

Carbon dioxide in the air around the Earth keeps it warm, in the same way as glass in a greenhouse keeps everything inside it warm. This is called the **greenhouse effect**.

In a greenhouse, heat from the sun goes through the glass, heating up everything inside.

As it does this, the heat changes so that it cannot get out again through the glass. More and more heat is trapped throughout the day.

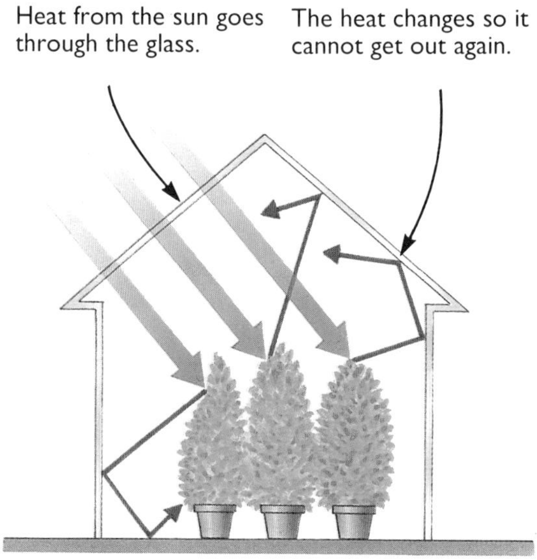
Heat from the sun goes through the glass.
The heat changes so it cannot get out again.

As heat from the sun goes through the carbon dioxide and hits the Earth, it also changes so it cannot get out.

Since people started burning fossil fuels, extra carbon dioxide has been released into the air. It may be building up.

If it does build up, the greenhouse effect may increase and the Earth may get warmer. The warming of the Earth is **global warming**.

 ****Photosynthesis, 135; Rot, 193.***

Nitrogen in nature

Nitrogen is a gas in the air. Tiny living things called bacteria* change it into substances called **nitrates**, which all other living things need. It is then recycled in nature.

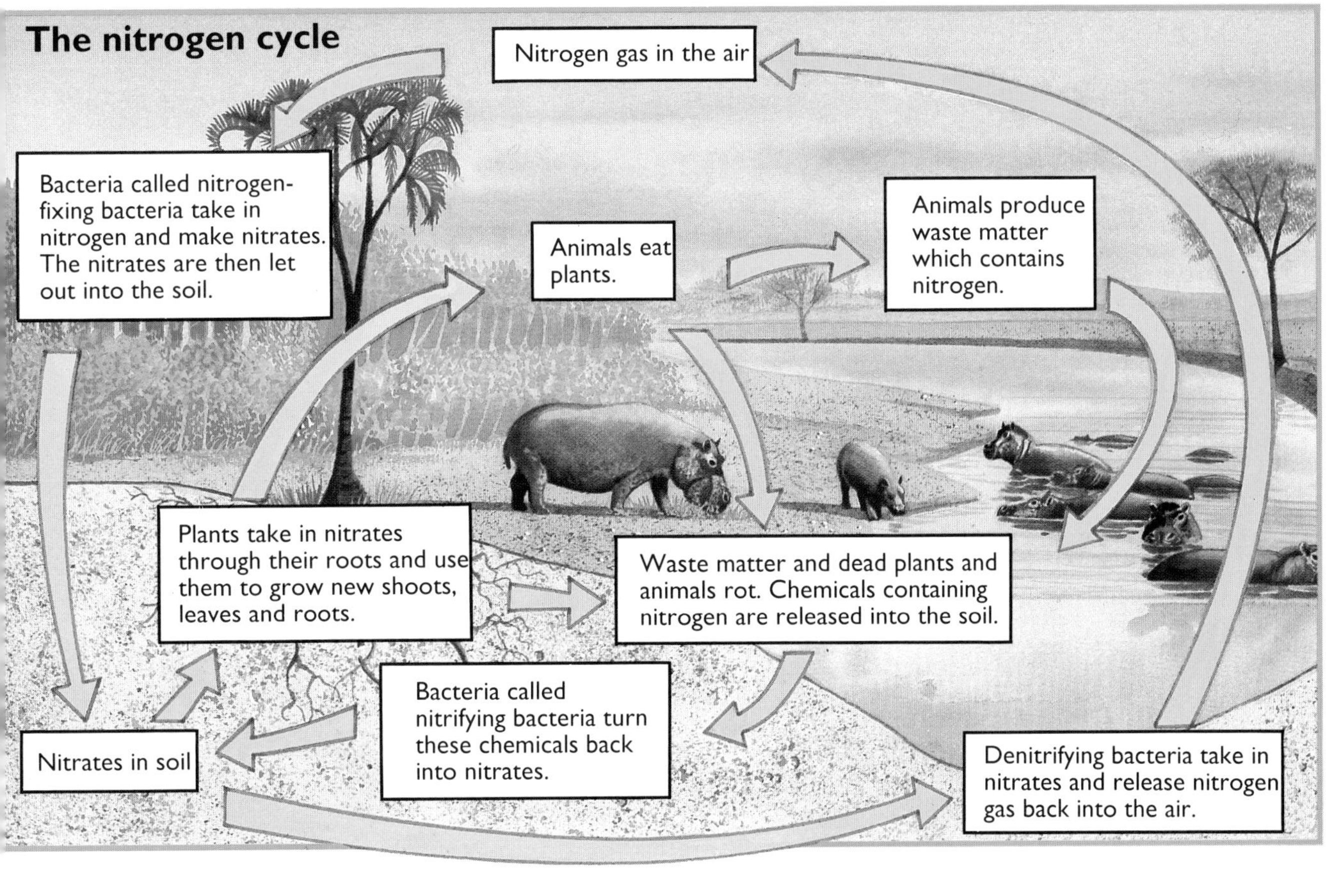
The nitrogen cycle
Nitrogen gas in the air
Bacteria called nitrogen-fixing bacteria take in nitrogen and make nitrates. The nitrates are then let out into the soil.
Animals eat plants.
Animals produce waste matter which contains nitrogen.
Plants take in nitrates through their roots and use them to grow new shoots, leaves and roots.
Waste matter and dead plants and animals rot. Chemicals containing nitrogen are released into the soil.
Bacteria called nitrifying bacteria turn these chemicals back into nitrates.
Nitrates in soil
Denitrifying bacteria take in nitrates and release nitrogen gas back into the air.

Farming

Farming upsets the nitrogen cycle, because crop plants, such as wheat, which take in nitrates from the soil, are cut and taken away to be sold.

Farmers must replace the nitrates, so that they can grow more crop plants in the same field the following year.

Many modern farmers do this by putting chemical fertilizers, which contain nitrates, on their fields.

It is difficult to judge how much fertilizer is needed. If too much is added, the extra nitrates are washed out of the soil, by rain, into rivers.

This pollutes the rivers, lakes and seas, killing many plants, fish and other animals (for more about this, see page 215).

**Bacteria, 241.*

Plant life

All living things produce new life, or reproduce. Most plants do this by growing flowers, which make seeds. (For more about other plants, see pages 244-245.) The seeds then grow into new plants. The changes from seed to plant to flower to seed happen again and again in a natural cycle

From seed to plant

Seeds contain a food store. They need this for energy to grow the first root, shoot and leaves. This first growth is **germination**.

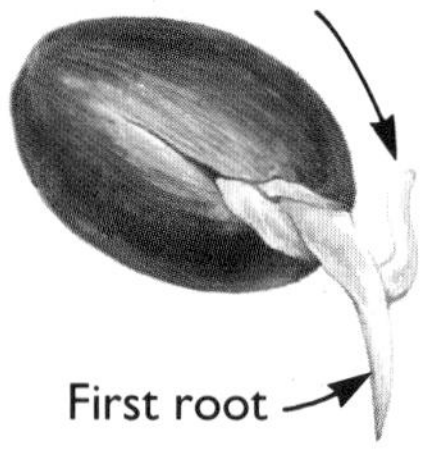
First shoot growing from seed
First root

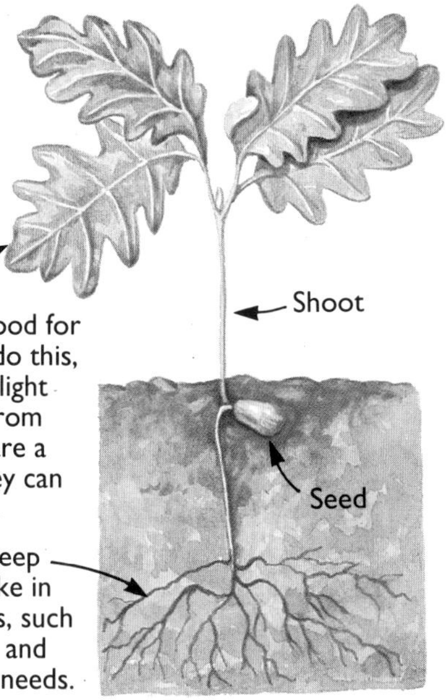
Shoot
Seed

Green leaves make food for the whole plant. To do this, they need water, sunlight and carbon dioxide from the air. Most leaves are a flat, thin shape so they can catch lots of sunlight.

Branching roots go deep into the soil. They take in the simple substances, such as nitrates*, minerals and water, that the plant needs.

Inside the shoots, roots and leaves of land plants there are two kinds of tubes. These carry water and food around the plant. Xylem tubes carry water from the roots up to the leaves. Phloem tubes carry food from the leaves to other parts of the plant.

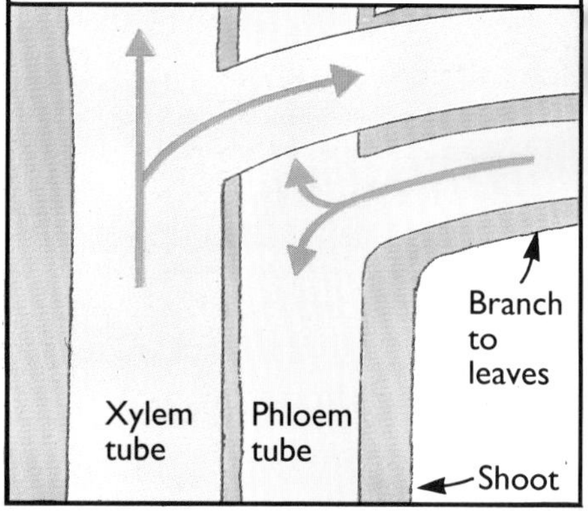
Branch to leaves
Xylem tube
Phloem tube
Shoot

Flowers

Most flowers grow at special times of the year. They make new seeds.

Flowers have male parts and female parts. Some plants have both in the same flower, some have only male parts in one kind of flower and female parts in another kind of flower.

Apple blossom

This flower has been cut in half.

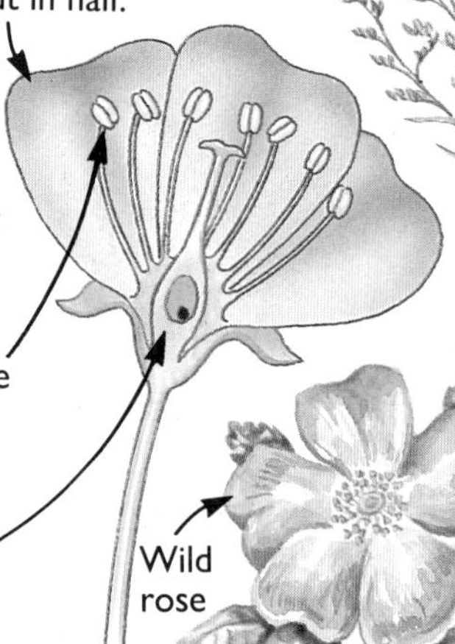

Anthers are the male parts of the flower. They make many tiny pollen grains.

The female part of the flower is the ovary. This makes "eggs" called ovules.

Wild rose

For a flower to make seeds, its ovules need to join up with pollen grains. This is called **pollination**. Plants do this in different ways.

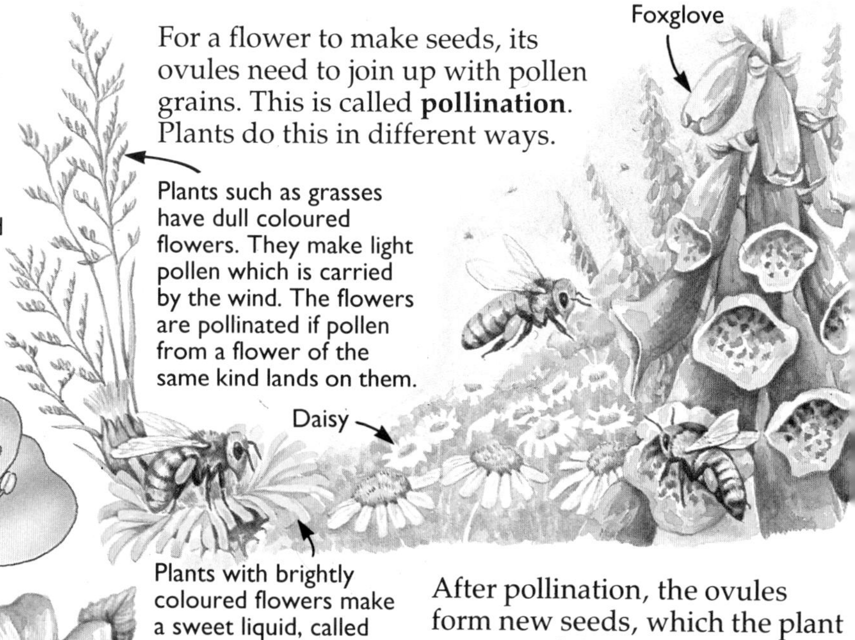
Foxglove
Daisy

Plants such as grasses have dull coloured flowers. They make light pollen which is carried by the wind. The flowers are pollinated if pollen from a flower of the same kind lands on them.

Plants with brightly coloured flowers make a sweet liquid, called nectar. As insects drink this, they touch the anthers and pollen sticks to them. If they carry pollen to another flower of the same kind, it is pollinated.

After pollination, the ovules form new seeds, which the plant scatters. If they land in places where conditions are right, they start to grow and the cycle begins again. Different plants scatter their seeds in different ways (see pages 162-163).

**Nitrates, 141.*

Growth

Plants grow faster at different times. In temperate areas they grow most in spring and summer, in the tropics they grow best whenever there is enough rain.

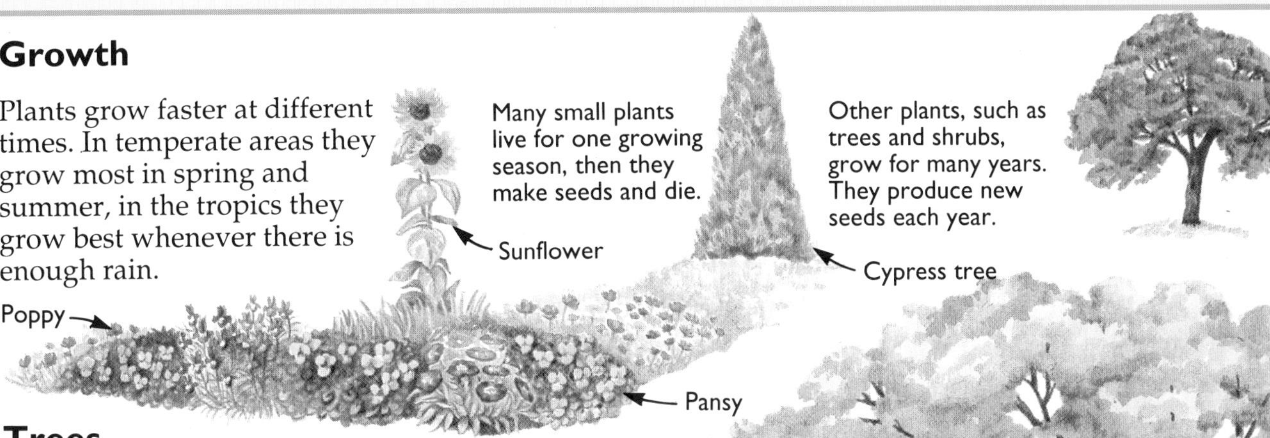
Many small plants live for one growing season, then they make seeds and die.
Other plants, such as trees and shrubs, grow for many years. They produce new seeds each year.
Sunflower
Cypress tree
Poppy
Pansy

Trees

All trees grow new leaves and flowers each year.

A tree's trunk grows thicker and stronger each year as the tree grows larger.

Some trees, such as fruit trees, have large, bright flowers (their pollen is often carried by insects).
Trees such as the oak have small, dull flowers (their pollen is carried by the wind to other oak trees).

Tough bark covers the trunk and branches. It protects the layer of delicate phloem inside.

Inside the phloem, rings of xylem, called **annual rings**, make up the wood. These show the age of the tree because each ring is one year's growth.

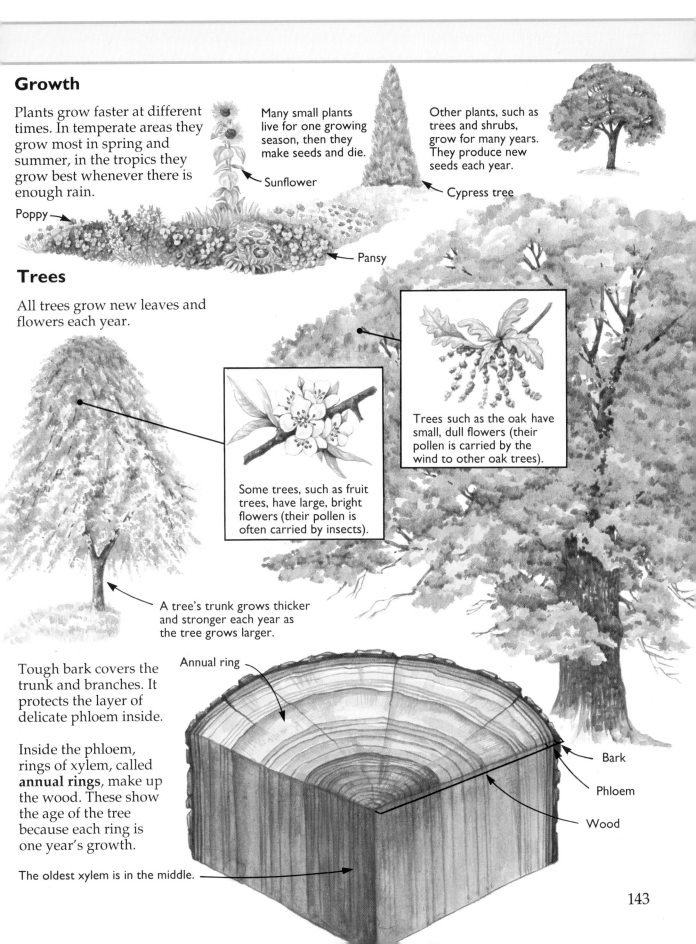

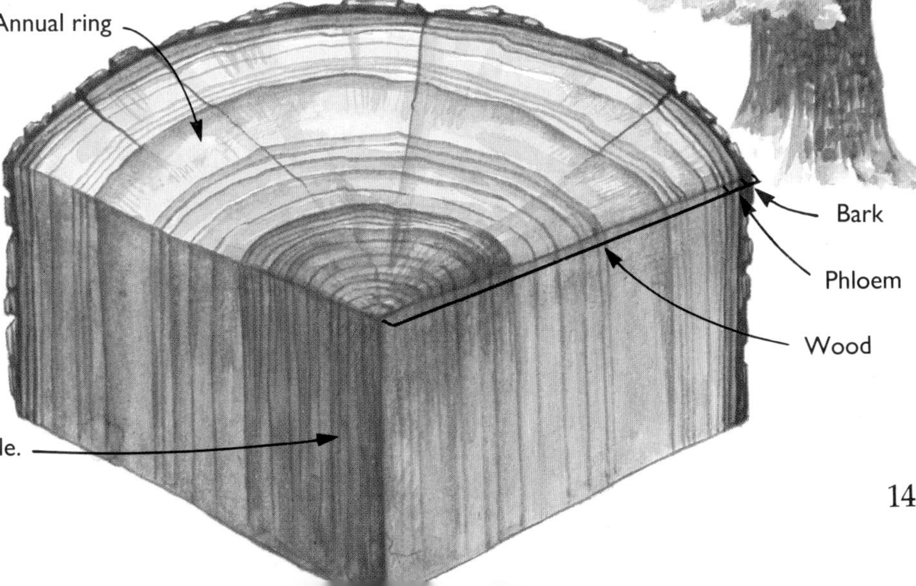
Annual ring
Bark
Phloem
Wood
The oldest xylem is in the middle.

Animal life

Like plants, all animals reproduce (produce new life). Their young grow up and produce new young animals themselves. This happens again and again in a natural cycle. Different animals do this in slightly different ways. Producing young animals is called breeding.

Babies

Most animals lay eggs, and the babies hatch out from them. But one group of animals, called **mammals*** give birth to babies (up to ten at a time). The parents care for their babies until they have grown up and can look after themselves.

Some babies, such as cats, dogs, mice and rats, are born blind and helpless. Their mother makes a nest for them and keeps them warm and clean.

Male deer
Female deer

All mammal babies feed on milk from their mother's body.

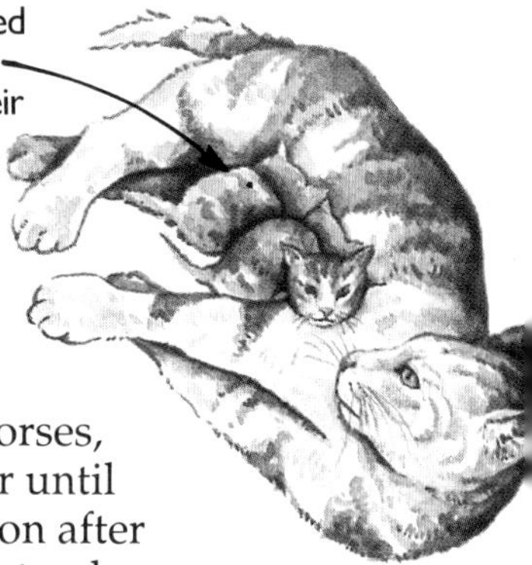

Adult males and females often look different from each other. For example, male deer grow antlers on their head. Female deer never grow antlers.

Some babies, such as horses, stay inside their mother until they are quite large. Soon after they are born they can stand and are on their feet, running with their mother.

There are also differences inside their bodies. These differences allow them to breed, or have babies of their own.

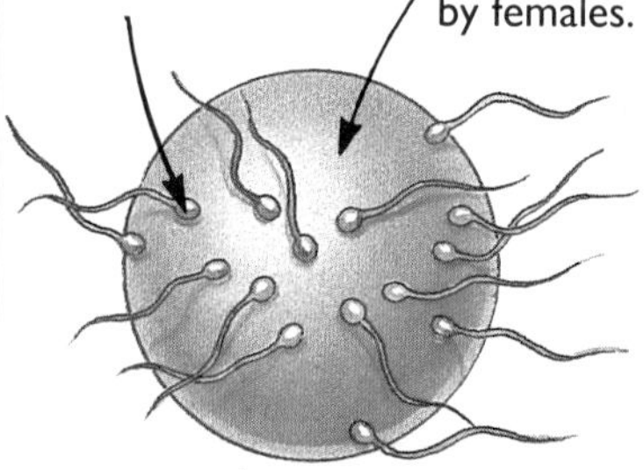
Tiny sperm are produced by males.
Large eggs are produced by females.

For new animal life to be produced, a single sperm must join together with, or **fertilize**, an egg. This happens differently in different animals.

Lions mating

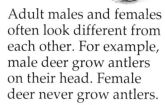

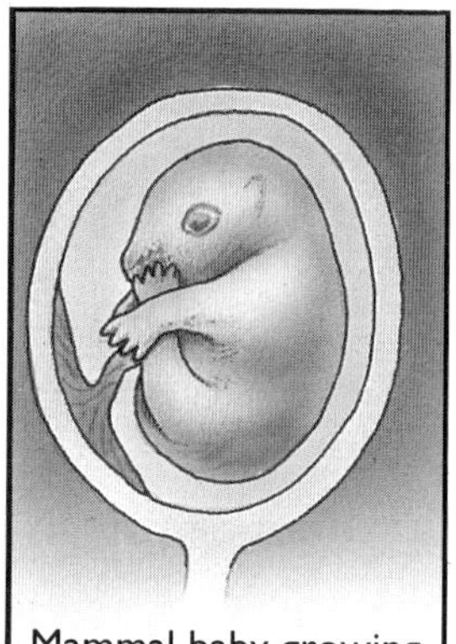

Mammal baby growing inside its mother.

Male mammals, and some other male animals, push their sperm into the female's body. This is called **mating**.

In mammals, the fertilized eggs grow into babies inside the female's body, and then the babies are born.

 **Mammals, 244.*

Egg layers

Most animals, apart from mammals, lay eggs. Some of them mate and lay fertilized eggs. Others shed their sperm and eggs in water and the eggs are fertilized as they mix with the sperm. Babies hatch out of both kinds of eggs.

Female ostriches lay fertilized eggs.

Changes

Many animals' eggs hatch into young that look very different from the adults. The young are called **larvae**. Different larvae change in different ways, until they become adults.

Animals such as frogs live on land, but go to ponds and lakes to lay hundreds of soft eggs in the water.

Frog larvae, called tadpoles, look very different from their parents. They have a tail for swimming.

Most tadpoles are caught and eaten. A few survive long enough to lose their tails slowly and grow legs.

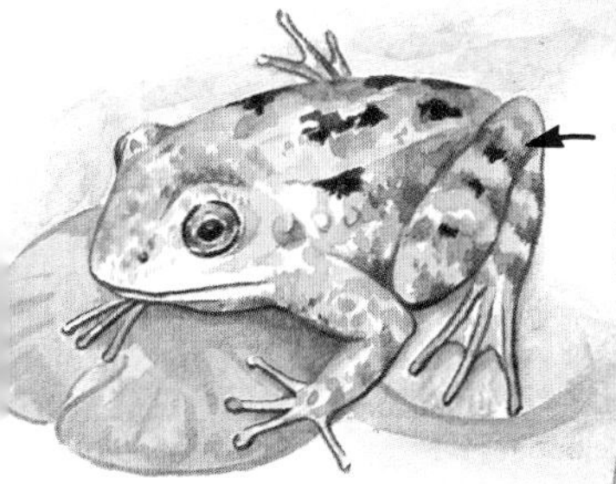

When they are frogs, they leave the water. The next year they come back to lay their own eggs.

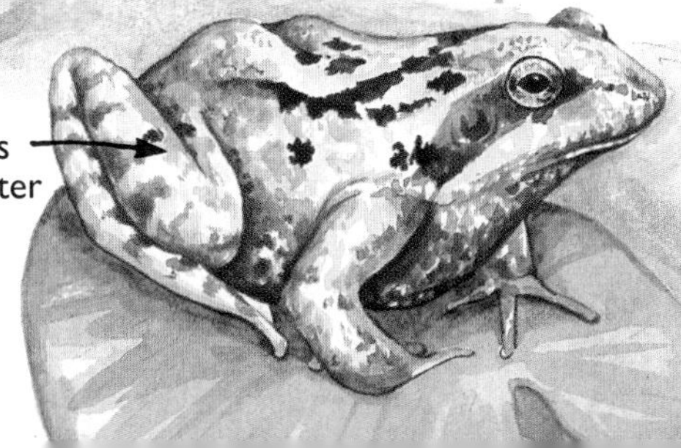

Frogs are threatened by pollution in ponds and rivers because they need clean water for their young to develop.

Fast or slow

Different kinds of animals produce different numbers of young, which take different amounts of time to grow up.

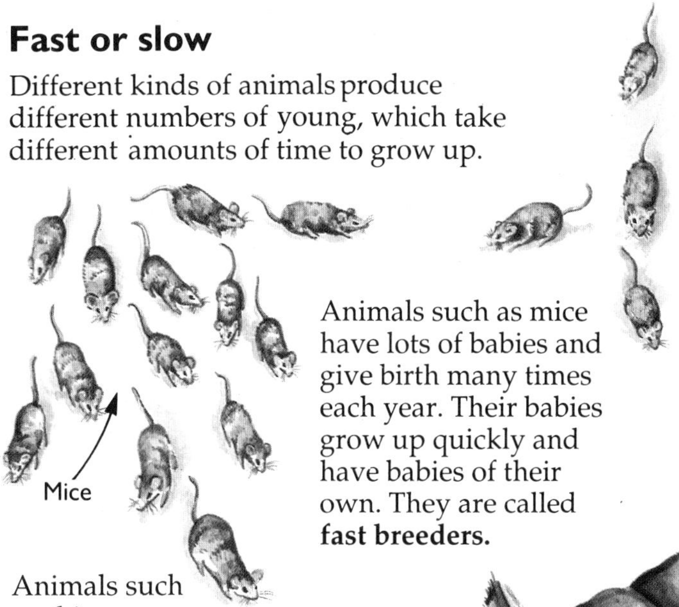

Animals such as mice have lots of babies and give birth many times each year. Their babies grow up quickly and have babies of their own. They are called **fast breeders.**

Animals such as rhinos are **slow breeders.** They have one baby every few years. After several more years it is grown up and can have babies itself.

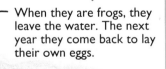

Many endangered species*, such as some tropical butterflies and whales, are slow breeders. This means that if a natural disaster, or too much hunting, kills lots of them they take many years to increase in number again.

**Endangered species, 146.*

Extinctions

A particular kind of plant or animal, such as star cacti or koalas, is called a species. If the last one dies, that species is extinct. There are none left to produce new young ones. Extinctions have happened slowly and naturally throughout the history of life on Earth. But today huge numbers of species are in danger of dying out quickly. They are called endangered species.

In the past

In the past, species died out because of natural changes, such as changes in the Earth's surface or in the weather. New species filled the gaps left by the extinct ones, as nature tried to find a new balance (see page 139).

Dinosaurs

65 million years ago the dinosaurs died out. No one really knows why, but some people think the climate became much colder after a huge rock called a meteor crash landed on Earth.

Woolly mammoth

Mammals* such as woolly mammoths could live in a very cold climate. Over thousands of years new animals such as these filled the gaps left by the extinct dinosaurs.

The people problem

The number of people in the world gets bigger every year. By the year 2050 there may be 14 thousand million. People need food and homes. They clear large areas of wild land to use for farming and building.

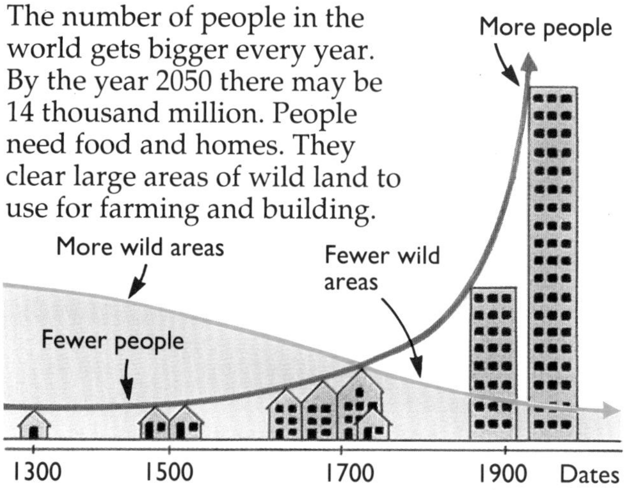
More people
More wild areas
Fewer wild areas
Fewer people
1300
1500
1700
1900
Dates

Why are species endangered?

Endangered species are those whose numbers are now very low. In the case of animals, they are usually slow breeders* and only just produce enough young to replace those that die. Different species of plants and animals are threatened for different reasons.

Many large animals, such as elephants, whales, gorillas, alligators and tigers, are hunted for their tusks, skins and meat.

 Mammals, Reptiles, 244; Slow breeders, 145.

Many plants, such as cacti, and animals, such as butterflies, birds and monkeys, are taken from the wild and sold abroad to collectors. Some animals are sold as pets or to zoos.

Philippine eagle

Spider monkey

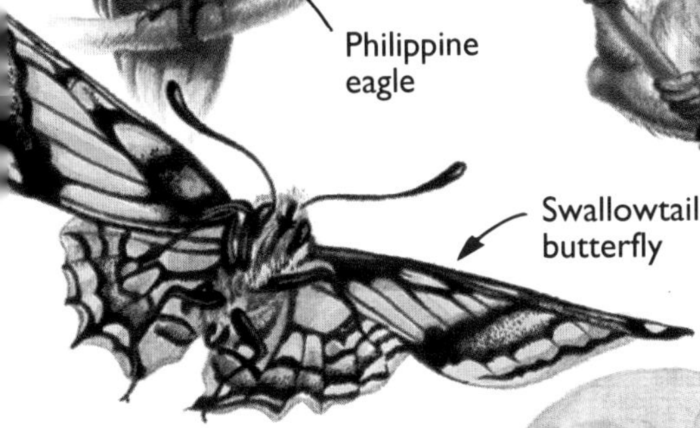

Swallowtail butterfly

Galapagos giant tortoises cannot compete with animals such as rabbits, that eat their food. The rabbits were brought to the islands when people came to live there.

Giant tortoise

Giant pandas are rare animals. In the past many died when the forests where they lived were cleared to make farmland. A disease could make the few that remain die out.

For more about endangered species, see pages 242-243.

Giant panda

Why does it matter?

Not only do we find plants and animals beautiful to look at, but we would also all die without them. Plants and animals are important to people for many different reasons.

Plants and animals recycle all the natural substances needed for life (see pages 140-141).

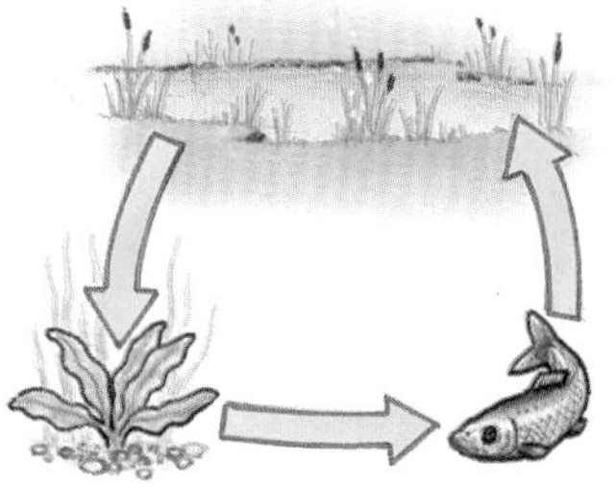

Wood from trees is used for building, making paper and as a fuel.

Drinks such as tea, coffee and cocoa and many herbs, spices, oils and medicines come from plants.

In the past, people tamed wild animals, such as wild cattle, goats and pigs, and kept them for their milk, skins and meat.

Tamed animals are best at surviving in the areas they come from. For example, in Africa, cows from Europe often die of diseases. Today Africans are trying to farm native animals, such as the eland.

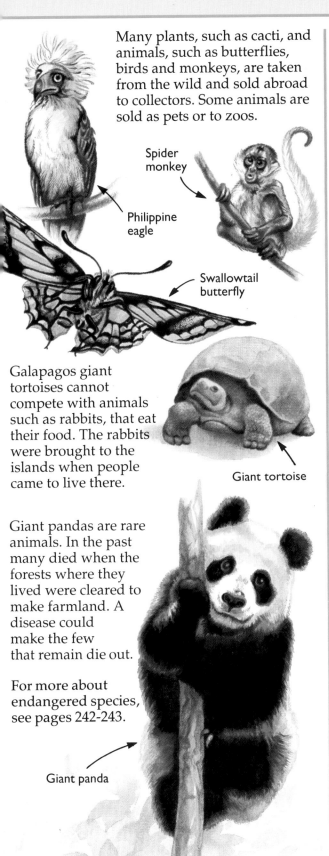

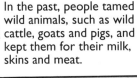

If people manage and protect endangered species today, by preserving the wild areas where they live, then in the future they may help people solve world problems. For example, not long ago people discovered that a tree, called the Moreton Bay chestnut, makes a chemical that may help treat the disease AIDS.

The seas and oceans

Most of the Earth is covered by seas or oceans. There are five great oceans and many smaller seas. The water in them is not like tap water. Instead it is like a salty soup full of millions of very tiny floating plants and animals called plankton (see pages 150-151).

These are views from different sides of the Earth. They show that the Pacific Ocean covers nearly half the Earth.

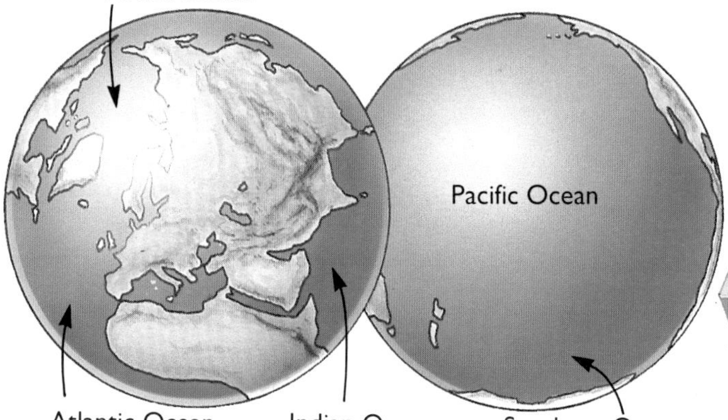
Arctic Ocean
Pacific Ocean
Atlantic Ocean
Indian Ocean
Southern Ocean

The water cycle

All living things need water. The water on Earth is used over and over again.

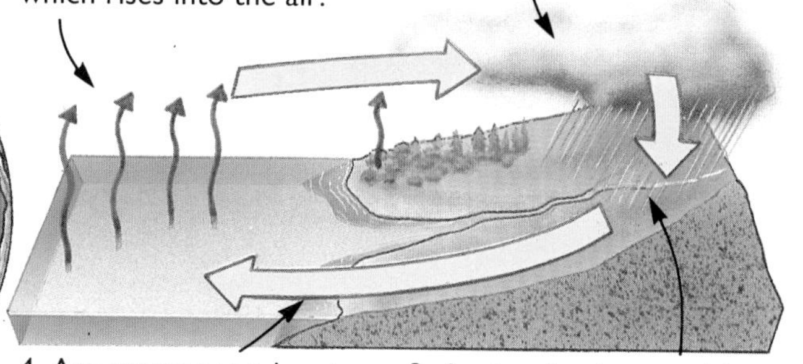
1. The sun heats up the land and the surface of rivers, lakes and the sea. This makes some of this water turn into water vapour, which rises into the air.
2. As water vapour rises, it cools, turning back into water droplets. These form clouds.
3. As the clouds get colder, the droplets get bigger or turn into ice crystals. They then fall as rain, snow or hail.
4. Any water not taken in by plants or the soil joins up with rivers. All the rivers flow back to the sea.

Different parts of the oceans

The temperature of the oceans and the amount and kinds of minerals in them varies in different parts, at different depths and at different times of the year.

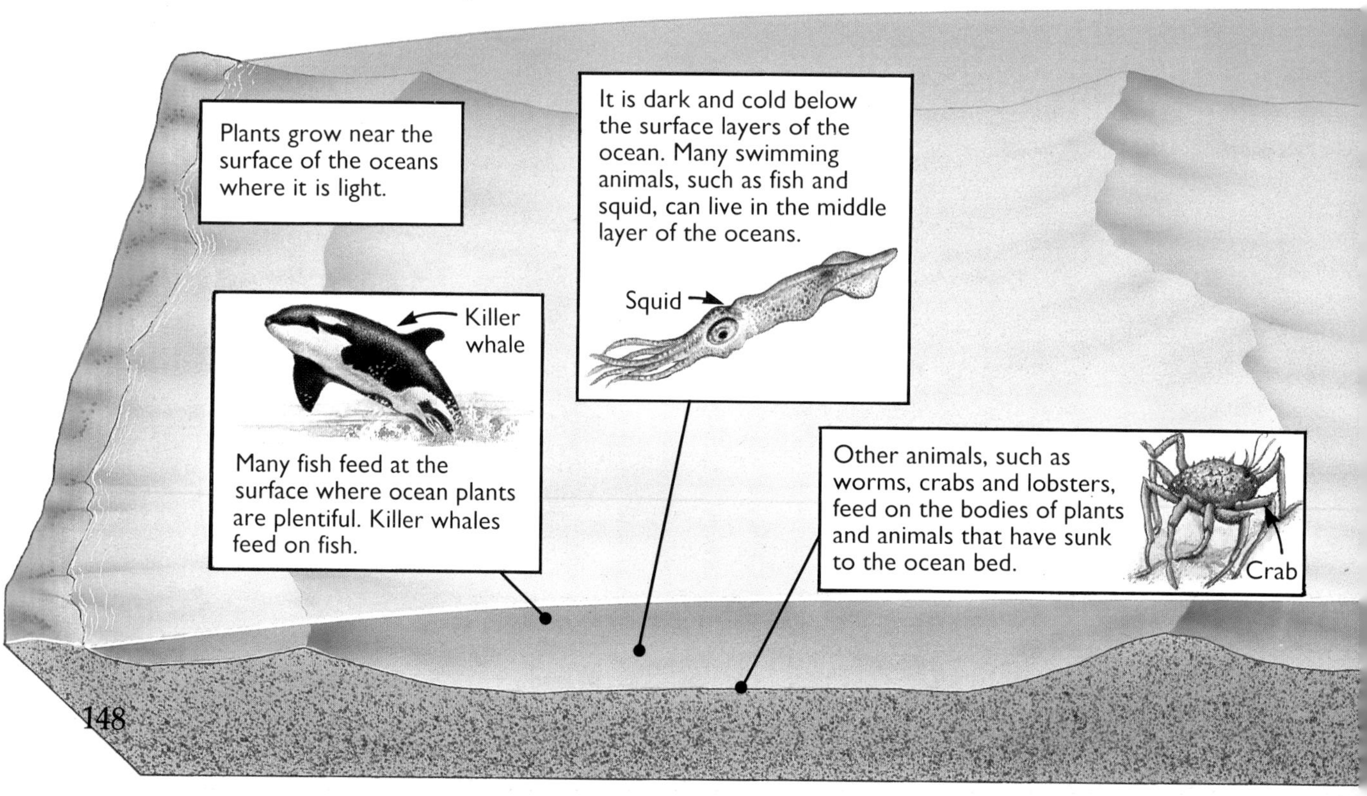
Plants grow near the surface of the oceans where it is light.
Killer whale
Many fish feed at the surface where ocean plants are plentiful. Killer whales feed on fish.
It is dark and cold below the surface layers of the ocean. Many swimming animals, such as fish and squid, can live in the middle layer of the oceans.
Squid
Other animals, such as worms, crabs and lobsters, feed on the bodies of plants and animals that have sunk to the ocean bed.
Crab

Important plants

Ocean plants, including plant plankton, make their own food by photosynthesis* using sunlight. Without these plants there would be no food for fish or other ocean animals.

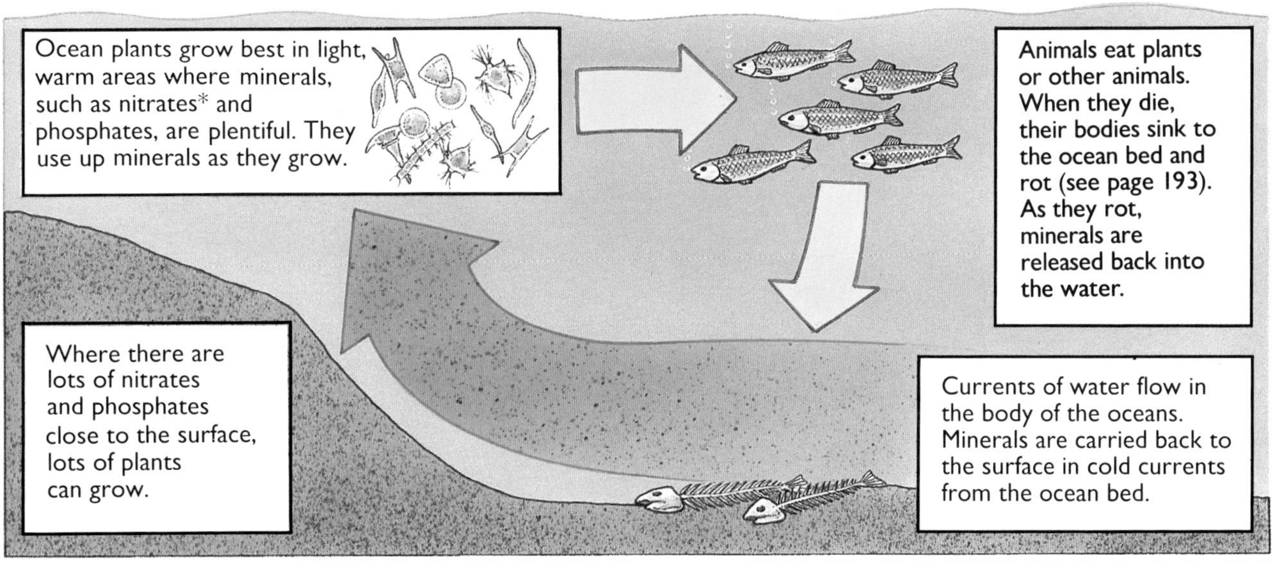
Ocean plants grow best in light, warm areas where minerals, such as nitrates* and phosphates, are plentiful. They use up minerals as they grow.
Animals eat plants or other animals. When they die, their bodies sink to the ocean bed and rot (see page 193). As they rot, minerals are released back into the water.
Where there are lots of nitrates and phosphates close to the surface, lots of plants can grow.
Currents of water flow in the body of the oceans. Minerals are carried back to the surface in cold currents from the ocean bed.

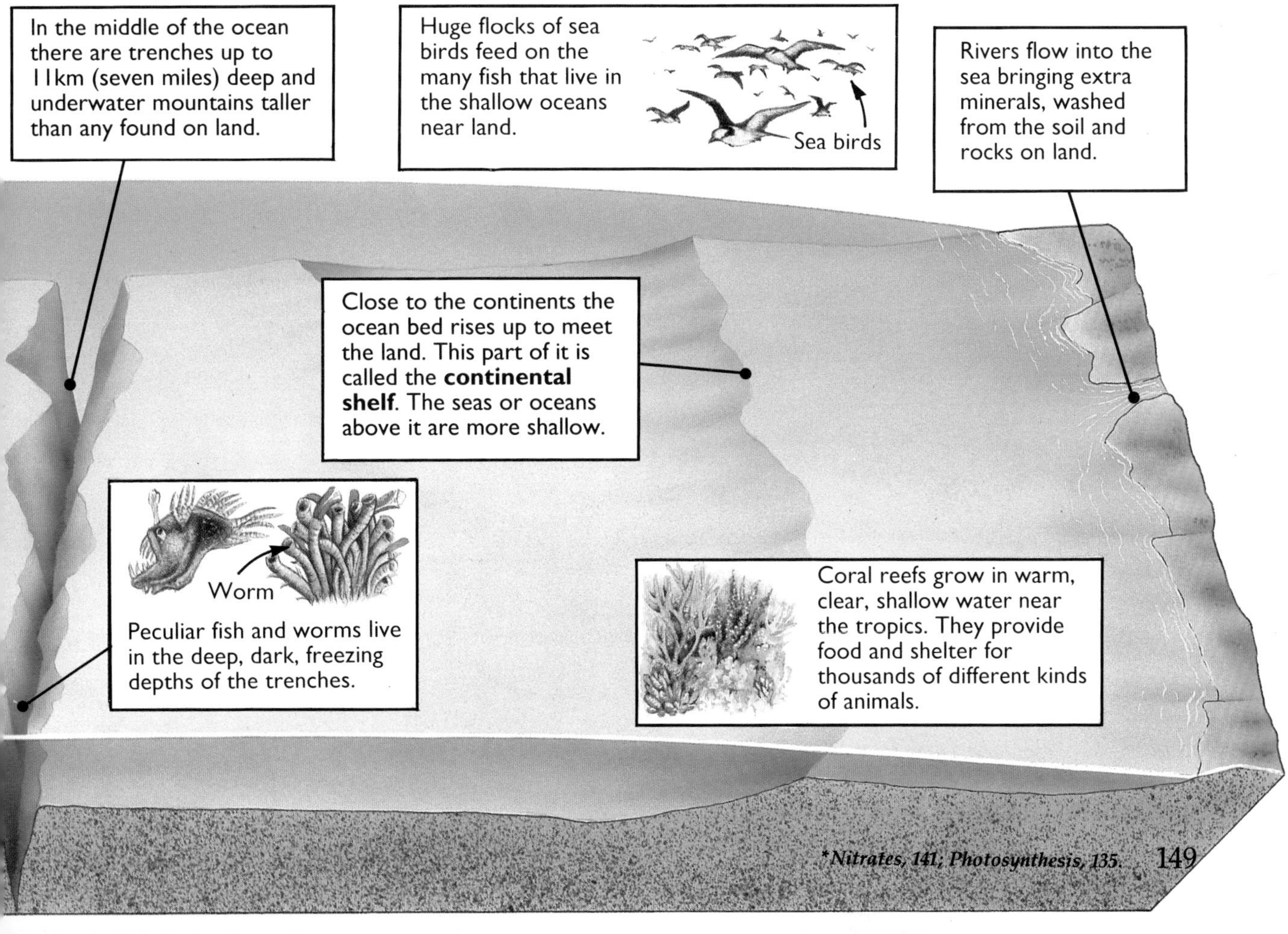
In the middle of the ocean there are trenches up to 11km (seven miles) deep and underwater mountains taller than any found on land.
Huge flocks of sea birds feed on the many fish that live in the shallow oceans near land.
Sea birds
Rivers flow into the sea bringing extra minerals, washed from the soil and rocks on land.
Close to the continents the ocean bed rises up to meet the land. This part of it is called the **continental shelf**. The seas or oceans above it are more shallow.
Worm
Peculiar fish and worms live in the deep, dark, freezing depths of the trenches.
Coral reefs grow in warm, clear, shallow water near the tropics. They provide food and shelter for thousands of different kinds of animals.

*Nitrates, 141; Photosynthesis, 135.

The ocean surface

Sunlight only reaches down about 100m (1,300ft) below the surface of the sea. Plants need the sun's energy to make their food, so this top layer is the only place ocean plants can live. Many animals also live and feed in this top layer.

Plankton

The very tiny plants and animals that float in the top layer of the oceans are called **plankton**. The plants are called **phytoplankton**, the animals **zooplankton**. Phytoplankton are the basis of all life in the oceans. They are food for small animals who in turn are eaten by larger ones.

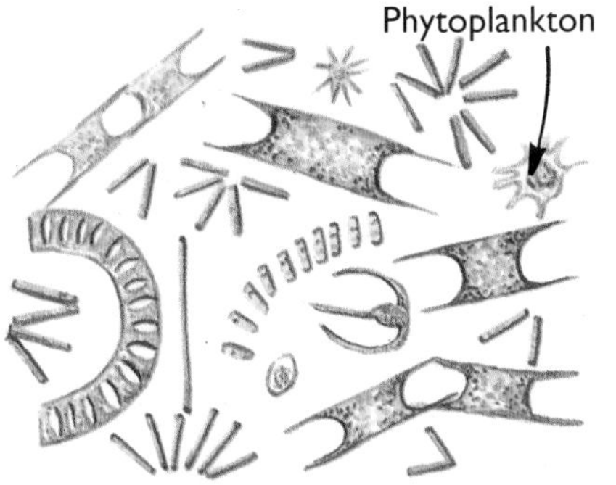
Phytoplankton

Phytoplankton are often amazing shapes. Like all plants, they can make their own food by photosynthesis*. They get substances such as carbon dioxide and minerals from the sea water.

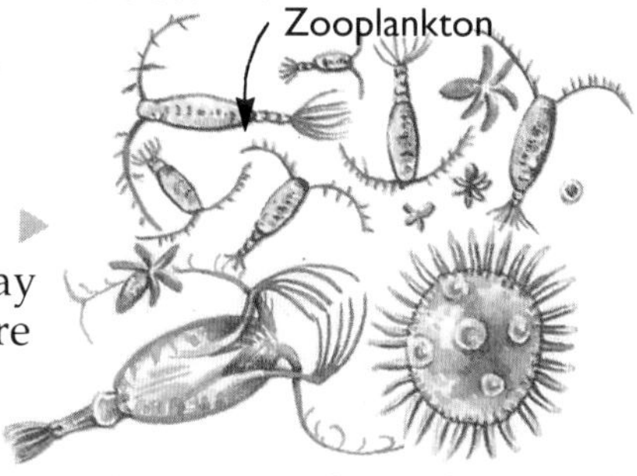
Zooplankton

Zooplankton swim near the surface at night, eating the phytoplankton. During the day they sink deeper to hide where it is darker.

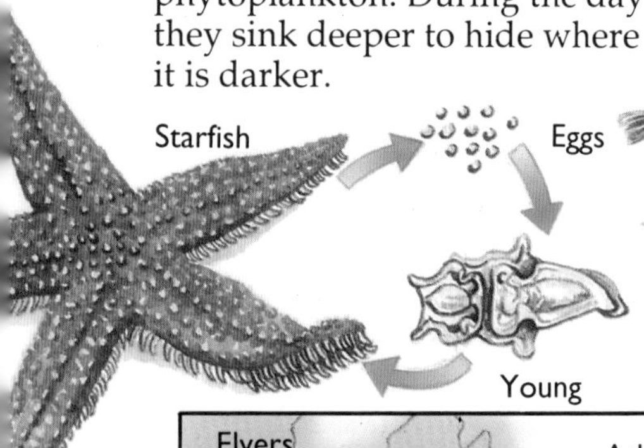
Starfish
Eggs
Young

Many animals, such as starfish, lay thousands of eggs. Their young hatch out, and feed off the plankton. Most of them die before they can lay eggs themselves, but a few survive.

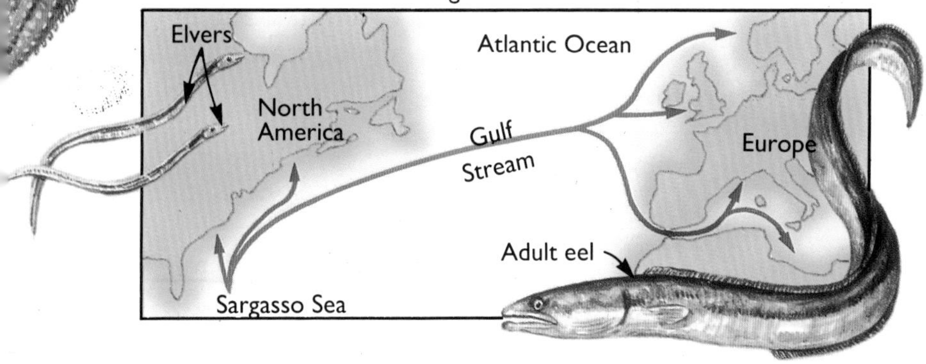
Elvers
Atlantic Ocean
North America
Gulf Stream
Europe
Adult eel
Sargasso Sea

Eels lay eggs in the Sargasso Sea. Their young float to Europe in the Gulf Stream current. Slowly they become elvers (young eels) and swim up rivers. 12 years later they are adults and swim back to the same sea to lay their eggs.

Plankton eaters

Many sea creatures feed on plankton. They sieve it out of the water using special parts of themselves. This is called **filter feeding**.

These creatures spend most of their time near the surface, where the plankton is.

Lots of animals, such as barnacles and other shelled animals, fix themselves in one place. Barnacles often choose a large object such as a ship or a whale.

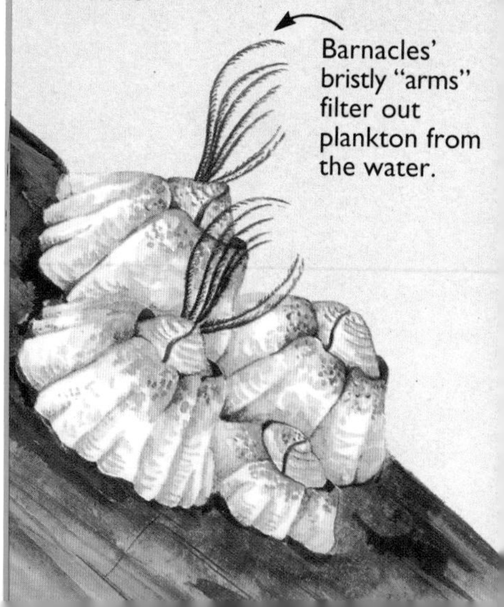
Barnacles' bristly "arms" filter out plankton from the water.

 Photosynthesis, 135.

here are two main kinds of whale. Blue whales elong to the kind called **baleen whales**. The ther kind are toothed whales*. Baleen whales ulp mouthfuls of plankton-rich seawater. As they ush it out again, horny sheets called **baleen lates** filter out tiny animals called krill.

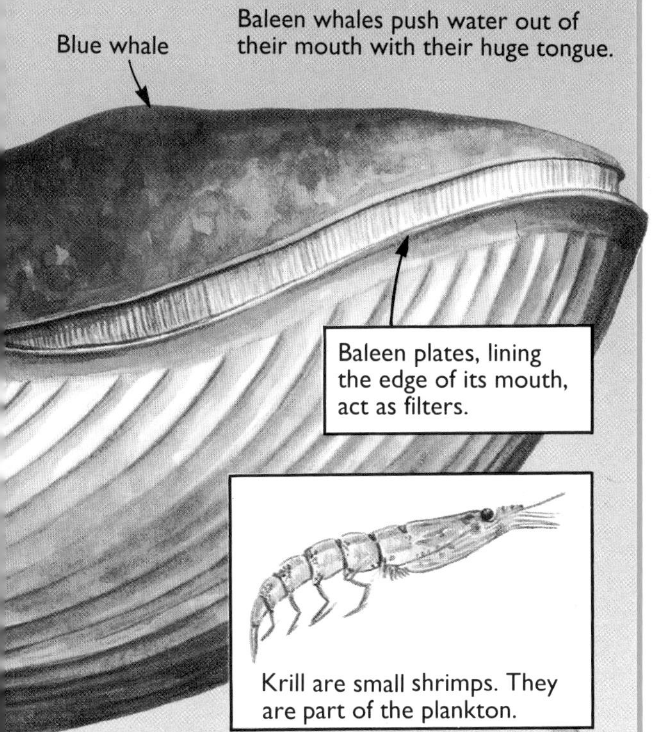
Blue whale
Baleen whales push water out of their mouth with their huge tongue.
Baleen plates, lining the edge of its mouth, act as filters.

Krill are small shrimps. They are part of the plankton.

Many fish of all sizes, from huge whale sharks to tiny anchovies, have fine bones called gill rakers, attached to their gills (their breathing parts). These filter food out of the water as the fishes "breathe" (for more about how gills work, see page 214).

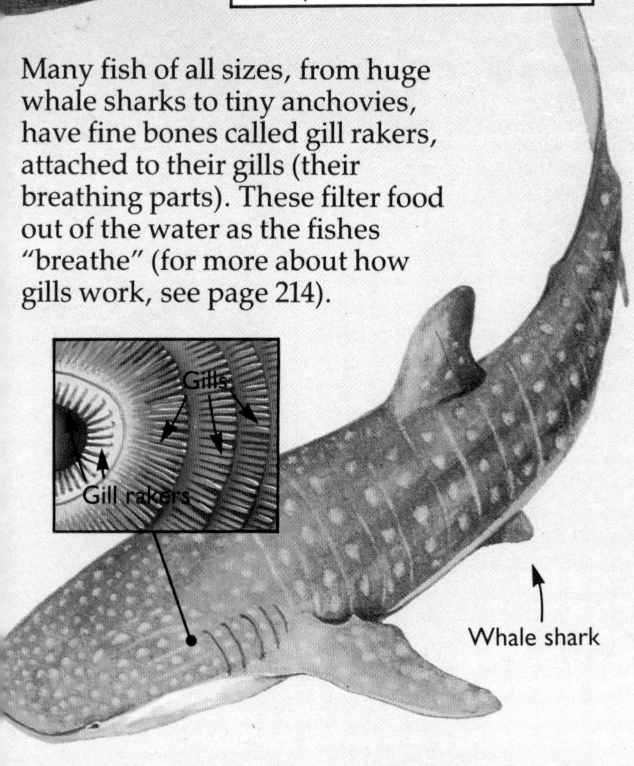
Gills
Gill rakers
Whale shark

Other surface animals

Many other animals spend most of their lives near the ocean surface. They do this for different reasons.

Dolphin

Like all whales, dolphins developed from land-living animals and still breathe air. They swim near the surface, leaping high out of the water.

Sea snake

Sea snakes have the deadliest poison of all snakes. They breathe air (their ancestors were land snakes). They swim by pushing their bodies in and out of an S shape.

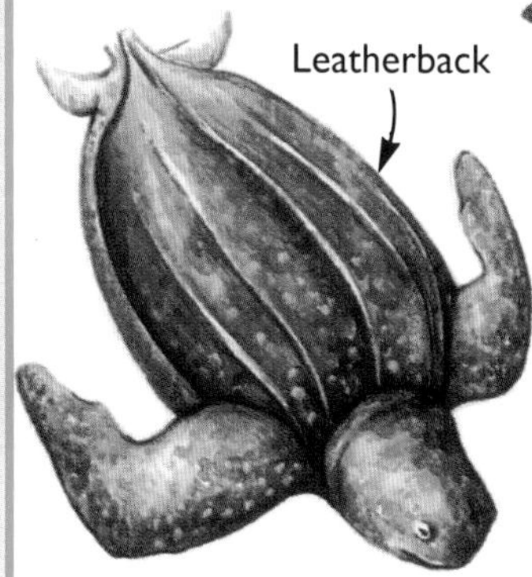
Leatherback

Turtles have flippers and a flat shell to help them swim. They also breathe air. The leatherback is the largest kind. It can grow to be twice as heavy as a polar bear.

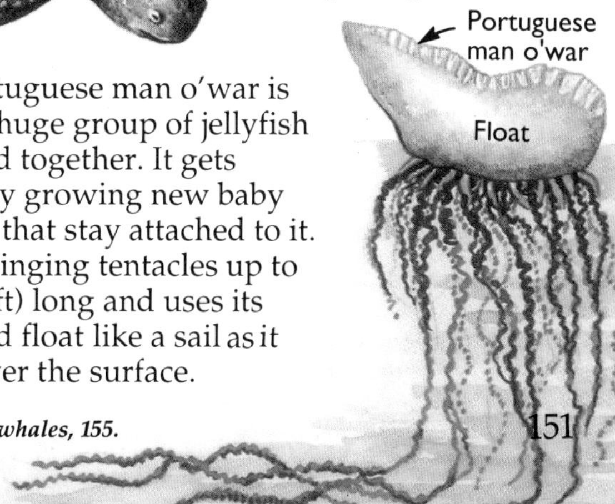
Portuguese man o'war
Float

The Portuguese man o'war is really a huge group of jellyfish all joined together. It gets bigger by growing new baby jellyfish that stay attached to it. It has stinging tentacles up to 20m (66ft) long and uses its gas-filled float like a sail as it drifts over the surface.

***Toothed whales, 155.*

Fish

The first fish lived 400 million years ago. Today, about 20,000 different kinds of fish live in every part of the seas and oceans. They are all superb swimmers.

Swimming

Water is much harder to move through than air. Most fish have bodies that are a smooth shape to help them swim.

Most fish swim by beating their tails from side to side.

Fish turn from side to side using the fins which stick out from the bottom and top of their bodies.

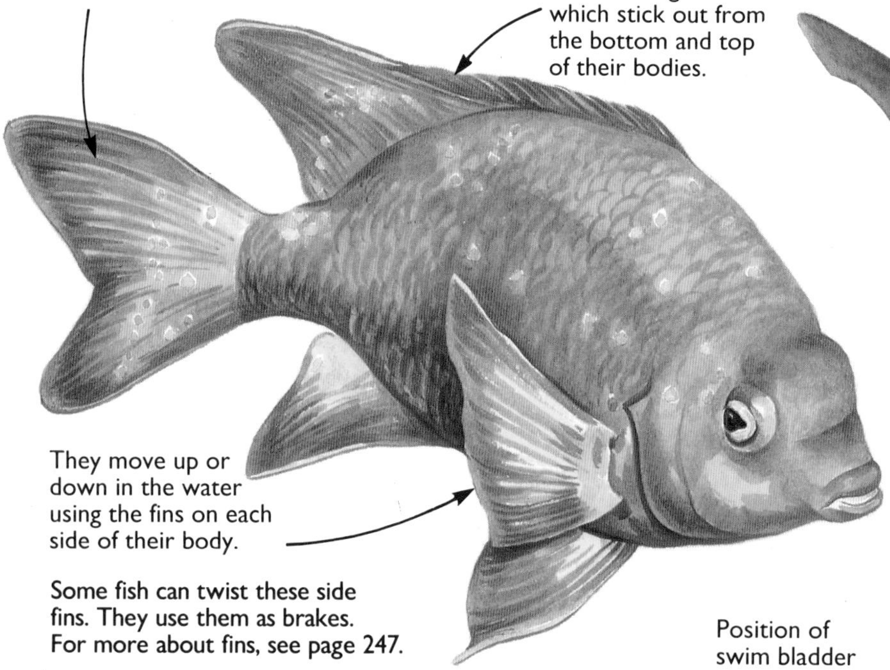

They move up or down in the water using the fins on each side of their body.

Some fish can twist these side fins. They use them as brakes. For more about fins, see page 247.

Position of swim bladder

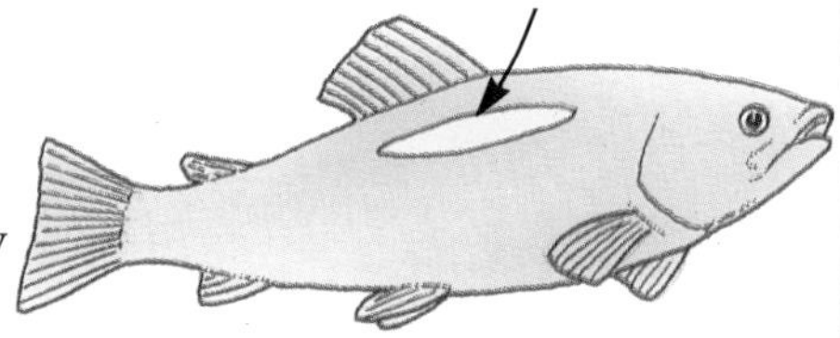

Lots of fish have a "bag" of air, called a **swim bladder**, inside their bodies. This makes them lighter for their size so that they can stop swimming and just float in the water.

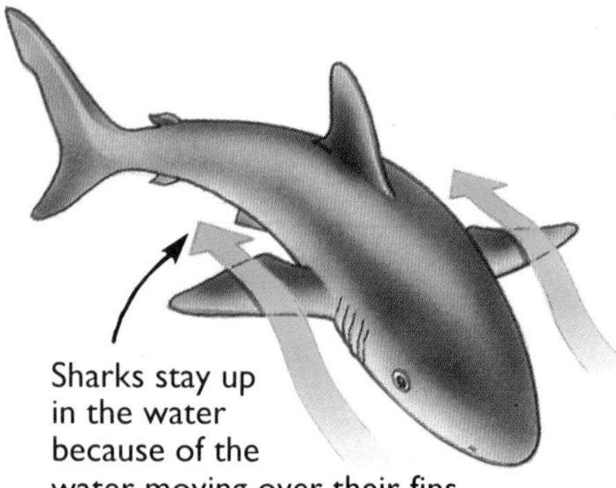

Sharks stay up in the water because of the water moving over their fins.

Other fish have side fins fixed in one position. Water moving over their fins keeps them up in the water, in the same way as air moving over aeroplane wings keeps planes up in the air.

If they stop swimming they sink. Also, they have no "brakes", so they cannot stop quickly.

Body shapes

Different kinds of fish look very different. Some of them are sleek, fast swimming hunters that travel long distances each year. Other flatter or fatter fish spend all their life in one small area of rocky shore, ocean bed or coral reef.

Great white shark

Flying fish are small fast-swimming fish. They do not actually fly. But, to escape attackers, they leap out of the water and glide using their large side fins.

Flying fish

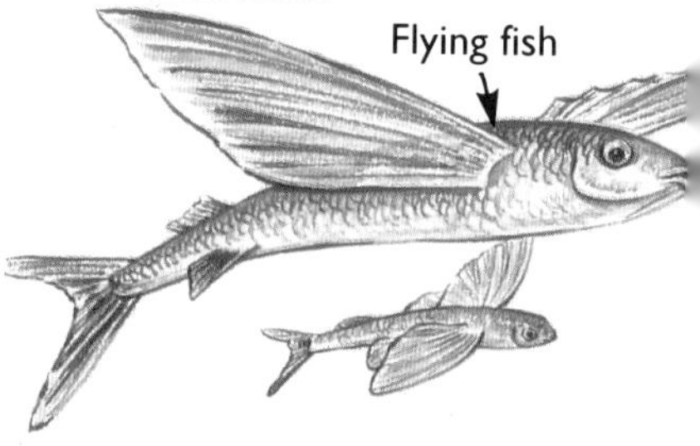

Plaice live close to the sea bed and are flat fish. They can hide by changing colour to blend in with the sea bed. When plaice first hatch they look like normal fish. After a few days one eye has moved over the top of their heads. They swim on their sides.

Plaice

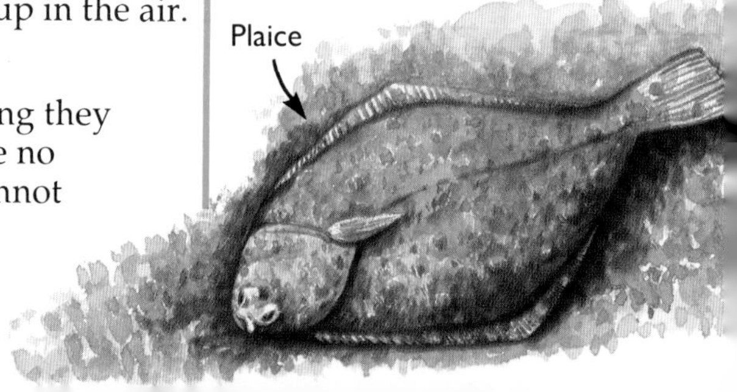

Great white sharks are huge hunting fish. They have an amazing sense of smell which they use to find their food, and many rows of sharp, backward-pointing teeth.

Sail fish are large hunters. Their sleek shape helps them to swim faster than any other fish, at over 100kmph (60mph).

Sail fish

Rays are flat fish. They swim using their huge side fins. The manta ray is the biggest ray in the world, but it only eats plankton*.

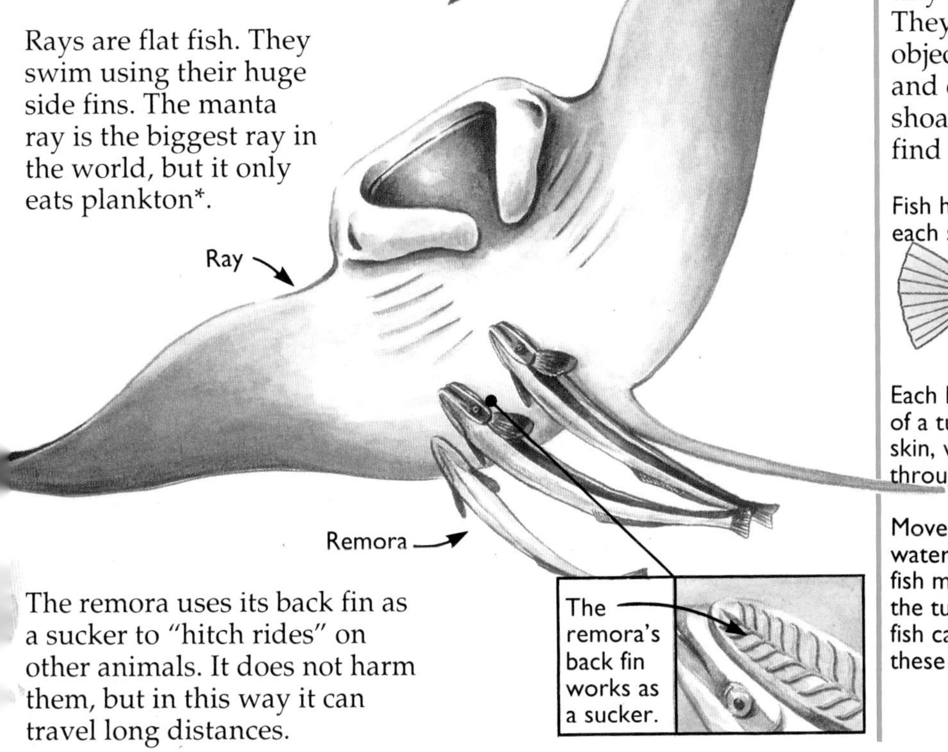
Ray
Remora
The remora's back fin works as a sucker.

The remora uses its back fin as a sucker to "hitch rides" on other animals. It does not harm them, but in this way it can travel long distances.

Living in groups

Many small fish, such as damsel fish, swim in groups called **shoals**. They do this for protection from hunters. One fish on its own is easily caught and eaten, but a group may look like a big animal and confuse an attacker.

Shoal of fish

Most fish have sense organs, called **lateral lines**, that detect tiny movements in the water. They use them to sense other objects, including hunters, food and other members of the shoal. They also use them to find their way around.

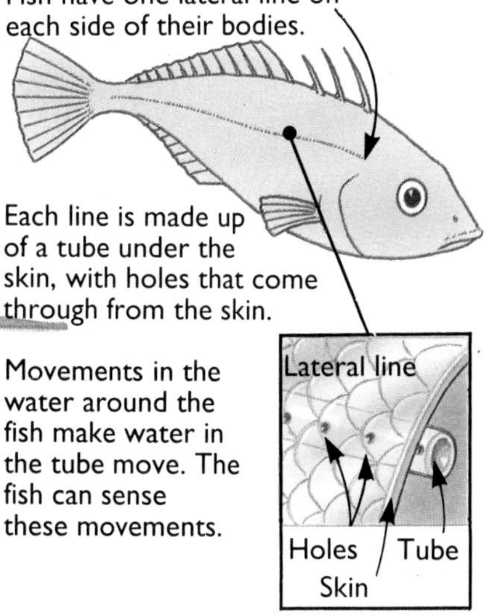
Fish have one lateral line on each side of their bodies.
Each line is made up of a tube under the skin, with holes that come through from the skin.
Movements in the water around the fish make water in the tube move. The fish can sense these movements.
Lateral line
Holes
Skin
Tube

The depths of the ocean

It is cold, dark and still in the depths of the ocean. No plants can grow, so animals eat other animals or dead plants and animals that sink slowly from the surface. Most animals in the ocean depths are small, often less than 30cm (12in) long. They are good at living in their strange world.

Big eaters and strange lights

Many deep sea fishes do not often get a meal, so when they do, they make the most of it.

The gulper eel can open its large mouth very wide and has a stretchy stomach. This means it can eat meals bigger than itself.

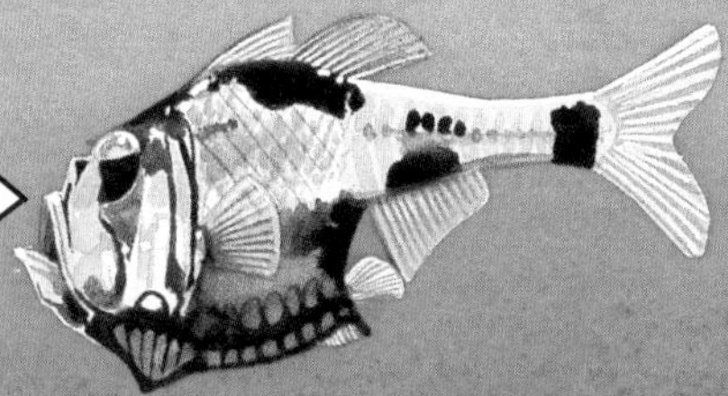

Many creatures of the deep, such as hatchet fish, can produce blue-green light from special parts of their bodies. People say they are **luminous**.

Some deep sea fish, such as viper fish, use their luminous patches to help them find a mate in the pitch darkness.

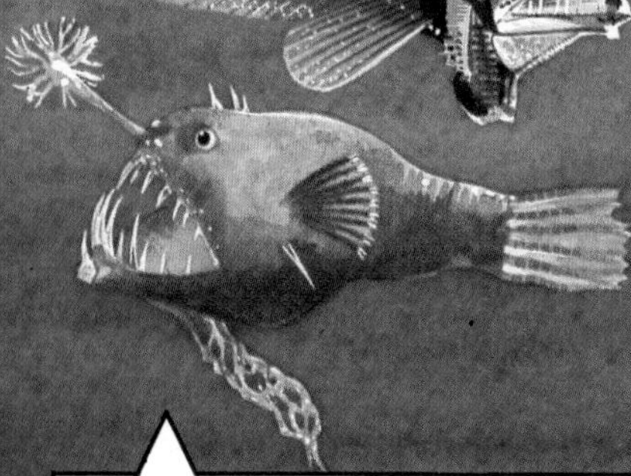

Some angler fish use light to fish for their food (smaller fish). They have one very long fin with a tip which produces light. The fish dangles this over its head and eats any small fish that come too close.

Deep sea hunters

Squid and octopuses are closely related and are both hunting animals, but they live quite different lives.

Squid are fast-swimming animals. They have eight short arms and two long ones, all with claws or suckers on them.

Deep-sea species have luminous patches on their skin. The largest kind, the giant squid, grows up to 14m (46ft) long.

Squid grab their prey with their long arms. They pull it close enough for their short arms to hold it firmly while they eat.

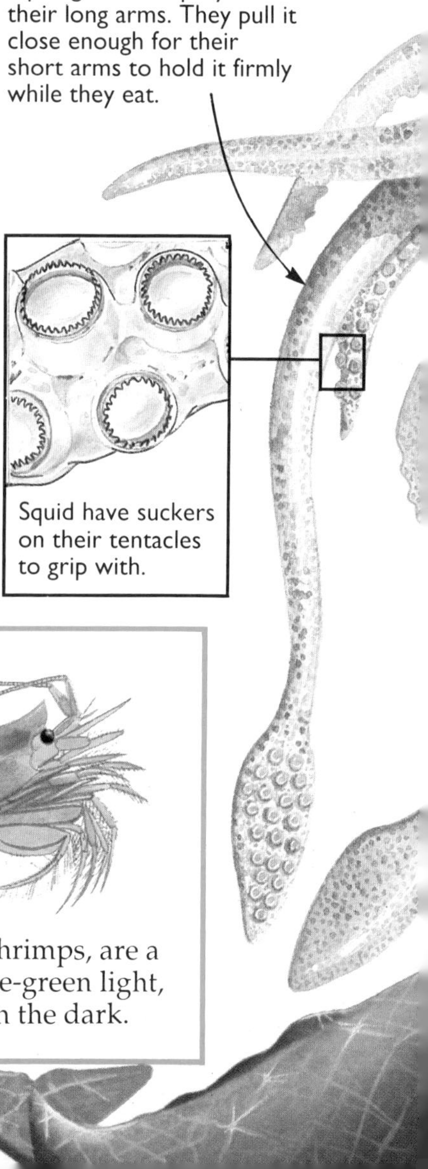

Squid have suckers on their tentacles to grip with.

Hiding in the dark

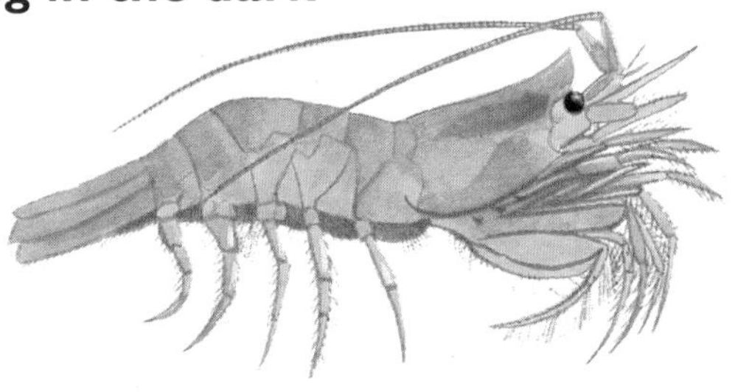

Many deep-sea animals, such as shrimps, are a red colour. This looks black in blue-green light, so they are hidden from hunters in the dark.

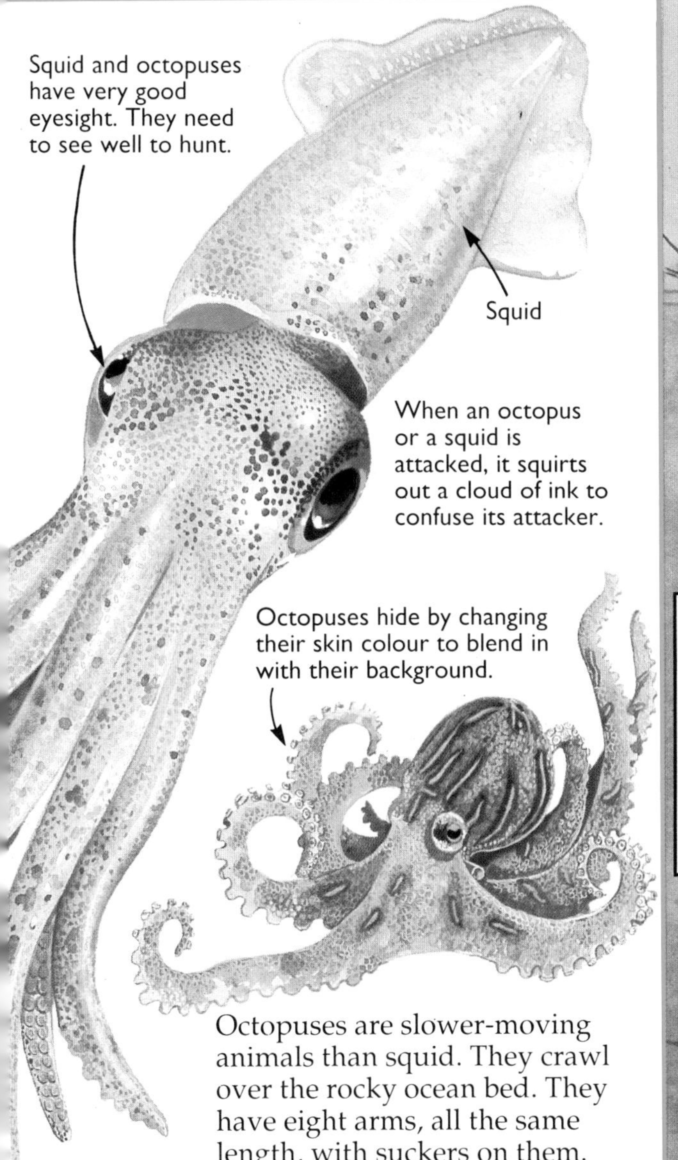

Squid and octopuses have very good eyesight. They need to see well to hunt.
Squid
When an octopus or a squid is attacked, it squirts out a cloud of ink to confuse its attacker.
Octopuses hide by changing their skin colour to blend in with their background.

Octopuses are slower-moving animals than squid. They crawl over the rocky ocean bed. They have eight arms, all the same length, with suckers on them.

Toothed whales, such as sperm whales, have many sharp teeth. Sperm whales hunt squid and some have scars from fighting giant squid. Like all whales, they breathe air and so live near the surface, but they can dive down very deep to find their food.

Sperm whale

The ocean bed

The ocean bed can be over ten kilometres (six miles) below the surface, at the bottom of trenches. It is usually covered in mud, squashed by the weight of water above so that it is firm.

Lobsters are related to crabs. They can swim, but usually walk over the ocean bed, looking for plants and animals to eat. Some lobsters travel very long distances this way.

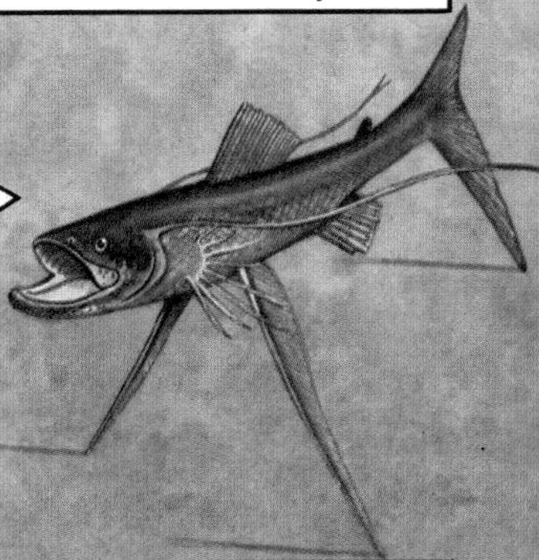

Tripod fish live close to the ocean bed. Three of their fins have an extra long piece on the end, with a sensing tip. They use these to probe the muddy ocean bed for worms to eat.

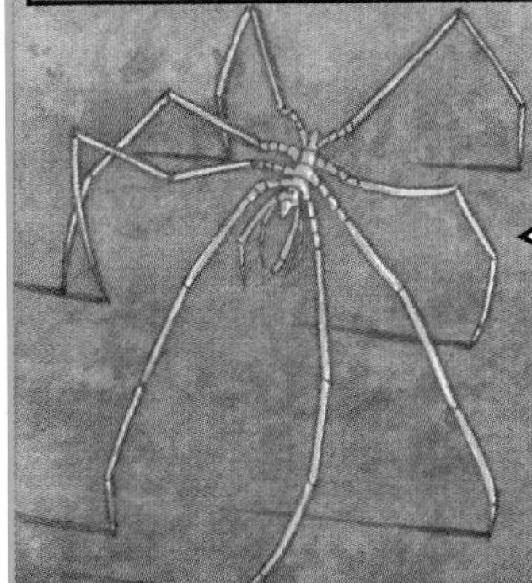

Most sea spiders eat tiny animals, such as sea anemones. The deep-sea species include the largest spider of all, which can be up to about 75cm (30in) across.

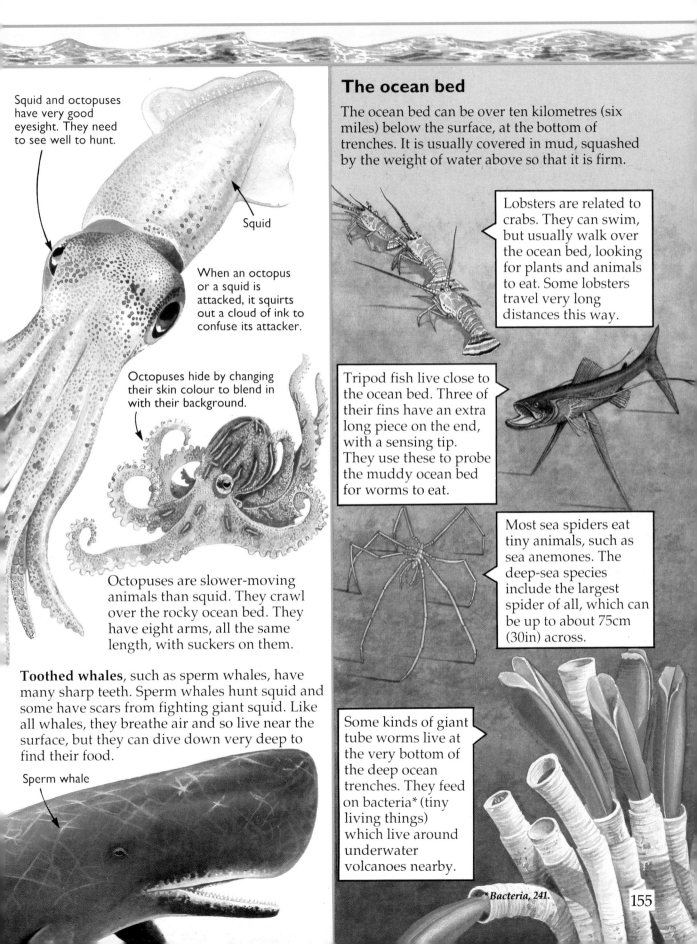

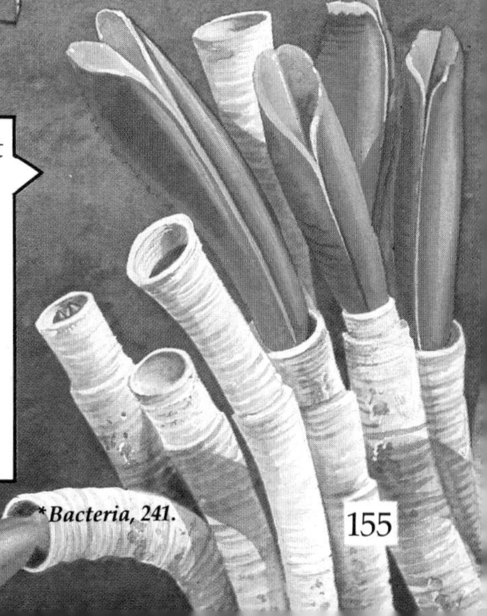

Some kinds of giant tube worms live at the very bottom of the deep ocean trenches. They feed on bacteria* (tiny living things) which live around underwater volcanoes nearby.

*Bacteria, 241.

Coral reefs

Coral reefs are only found in warm, clear, salty water where there is lots of light. They were built by millions of tiny animals, over thousands of years. They are still being built today. Thousands of other animals live in and around them.

Reef builders

The animals that build reefs, called coral polyps, are like tiny sea anemones. Each one grows its own chalky skeleton. The body of the reef is made up of the skeletons of old polyps that have died: only the outermost layer is alive.

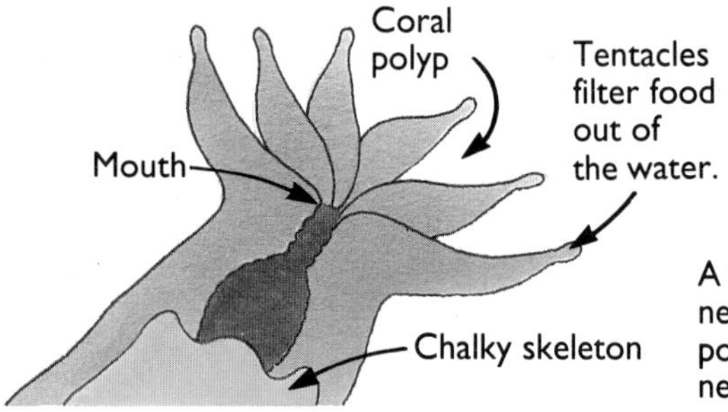

Coral polyp
Tentacles filter food out of the water.
Mouth
Chalky skeleton

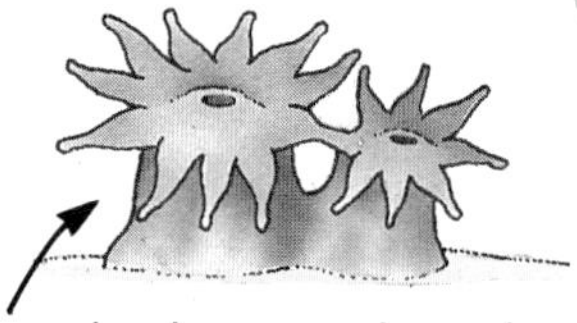

A coral polyp reproduces (produces new life) by growing a new baby polyp, called a **bud**, out of itself. Each new polyp grows its own skeleton.

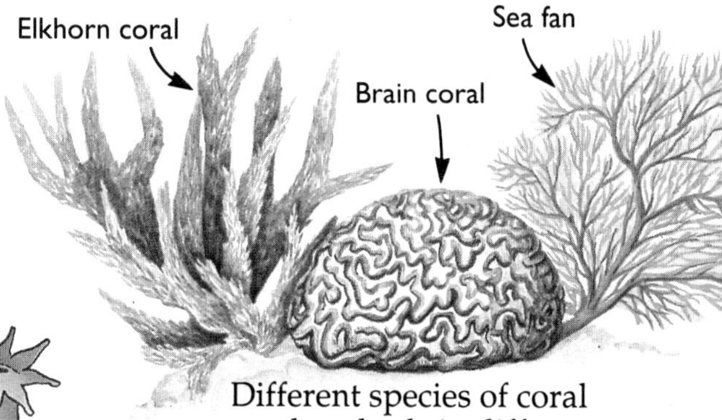

Elkhorn coral
Sea fan
Brain coral

Different species of coral produce buds in different ways. This gives each species its special shape, which builds up slowly. A reef is made of many different species.

Coral-reef animals

Many filter feeding* animals, such as barnacles, clams, fan worms and sponges, shelter in a reef and many fish swim gently around it. Coral reef fish are often special shapes or bright colours.

Sea horses are a type of fish. They swim upright in the water. The male sea horse looks after the eggs after he has fertilized* them. He keeps them in his pouch until they hatch into baby sea horses.

Christmas-tree worms live in holes in the dead coral. They filter food out of the water with tentacles near their mouths.

The crown of thorns starfish eats coral by sucking the polyps out of their shells.

Butterfly fish have stiff, straight snouts which they use to reach the coral polyps they feed on.

Giant clams grow up to one metre (three feet) long and lie buried in the reef, feeding. They sieve bits of food out of the water with the soft part of their bodies.

Sea urchins are hard and spiky. Their spikes are used for defence and moving around. Their mouths are underneath, so they "sit" on their food. Coral-reef species feed on tiny plants growing on the coral.

*Fertilize, 144; Filter feeding 150.

Reefs in danger

Coral reefs grow very slowly. Many of them are destroyed when the coral is sold to tourists. Local people also use bits of coral for building.

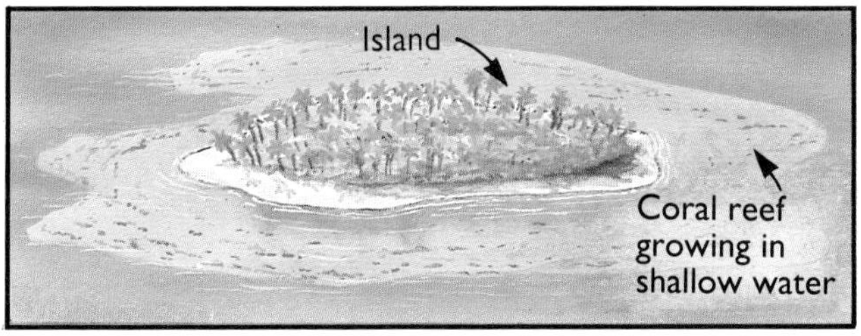
Island
Coral reef growing in shallow water

Reefs are built up by the living polyps on the outermost surface. They need lots of light to do this, and grow very slowly. Damage to the reef in shallow water can be mended if new polyps spread to the damaged parts. But in deep water it is too dark for the polyps, so the reef dies.

Surgeon fish have a sharp bony blade poking out of the skin near their tails. They slash out with their tails when they feel threatened.
When attacked, puffer fish gulp water and swell up like a balloon. Many have spiky scales which stand out like needles when they swell up. One species, called the death puffer, is the most poisonous fish in the world.
Moray eels are hunting fish. They can grow up to three metres (ten feet) long. They have very thin bodies and hide in deep holes in the reef.

Living together

Some animals around coral reefs live with, or on, other animals. By doing this they usually get food more easily or gain protection.

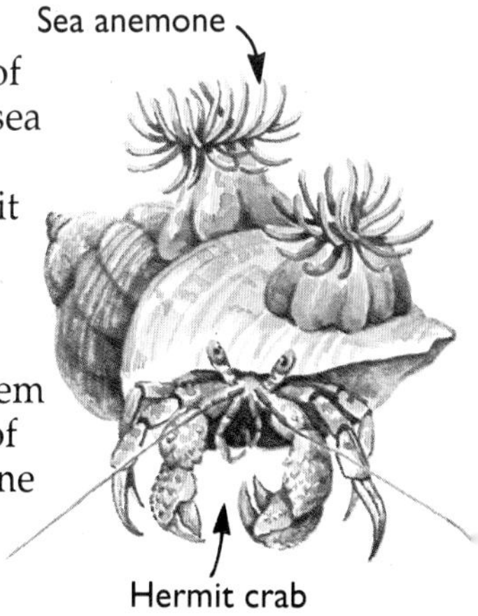
Sea anemone
Hermit crab

The hermit crab has no shell of its own, so it lives inside old sea shells. On coral reefs, sea anemones often share a hermit crab's shell home.

The sea anemone, with its stinging tentacles, protects them both. The crab leaves plenty of food scraps which the anemone can eat.

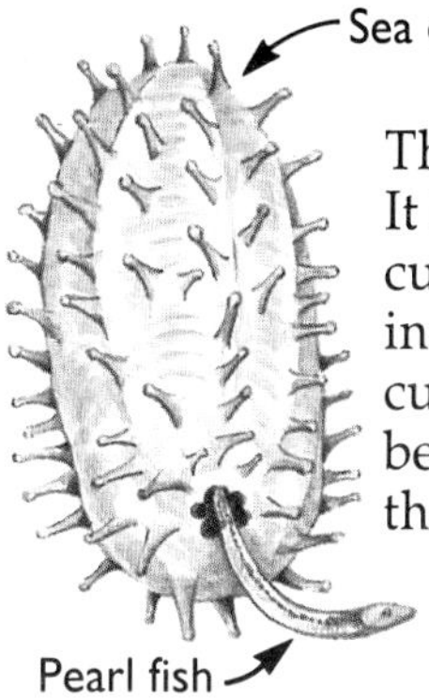
Sea cucumber
Pearl fish

The pearl fish is long and thin. It lives in an animal called a sea cucumber. It feeds on the insides of the cucumber, but the cucumber is not harmed, because it grows back as fast as the pearl fish eats it.

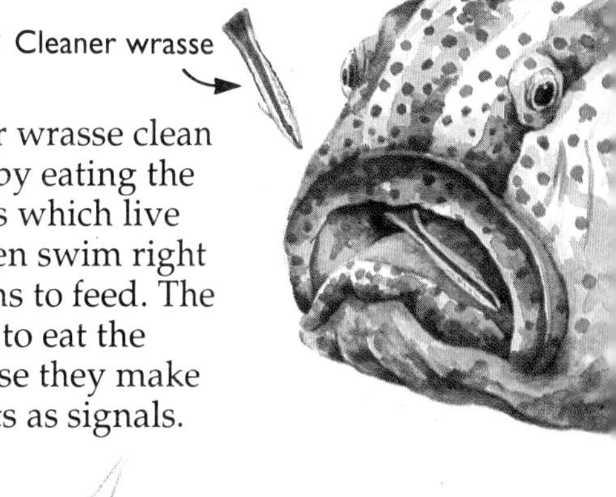
Cleaner wrasse

Fish called cleaner wrasse clean many bigger fish by eating the small animal pests which live on them. They even swim right inside their mouths to feed. The big fish know not to eat the cleaner fish because they make special movements as signals.

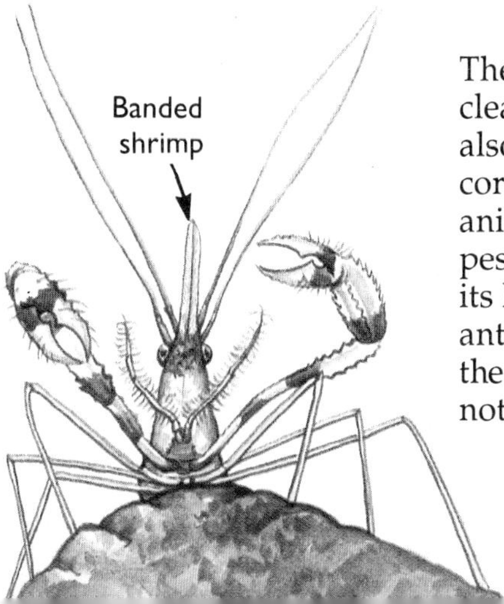
Banded shrimp

The banded, or cleaner, shrimp also cleans other coral reef animals of their pests. It waves its legs and antennae so that the animals know not to eat it.

Shorelines

Shorelines are the areas where the sea meets the land. They can be rocky cliffs, pebble or sandy beaches, mud flats* or a mixture of these. Waves wear away cliffs and move rocks around on beaches. Rocks are slowly worn into smooth pebbles and then into finer sand, which can be carried in sea water and washed up on other shores. Mud flats often form near estuaries*.

The tides

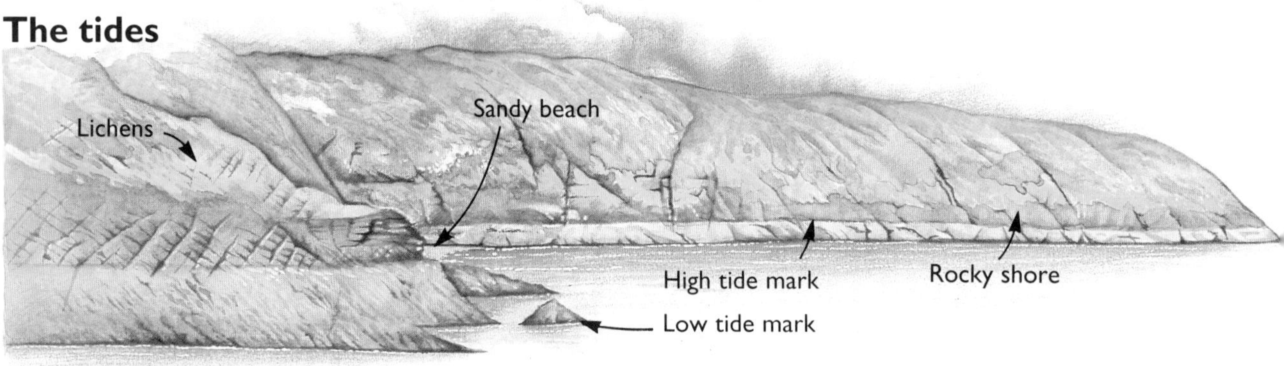
Lichens
Sandy beach
High tide mark
Rocky shore
Low tide mark

Twice a day the sea comes up the shore and then goes back. These sea movements are the **tides**. All sea creatures living on shores are exposed to the sun and the wind at low tide. If they dry out before the high tide covers them, they die.

Many animals live in bands along the shore. Shelled animals can live higher up, where they are uncovered most of the time. Starfish and worms live lower down the shore, where they are uncovered for less of the time.

Living with the tides

Seashore animals can survive even though waves batter the rocks and move the sand and pebbles around. They do this in different ways.

Some animals attach themselves to rocks. Others hide in cracks, or in rock pools which form at low tide. Some burrow under the shifting sand.

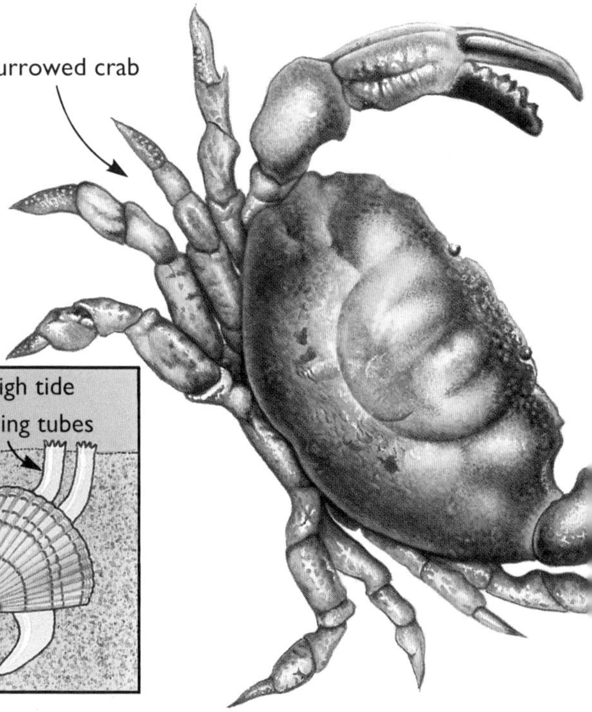
Furrowed crab

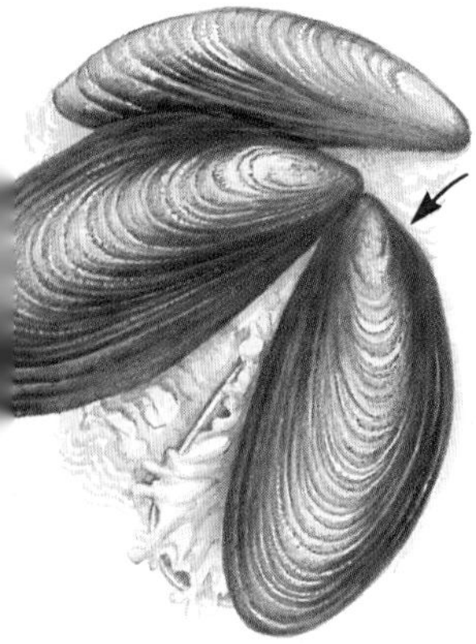

Animals such as mussels clean pollution out of the water. As they feed, they fill up with poisonous chemicals and harmful bacteria*. Other animals that eat them, however, are often poisoned.

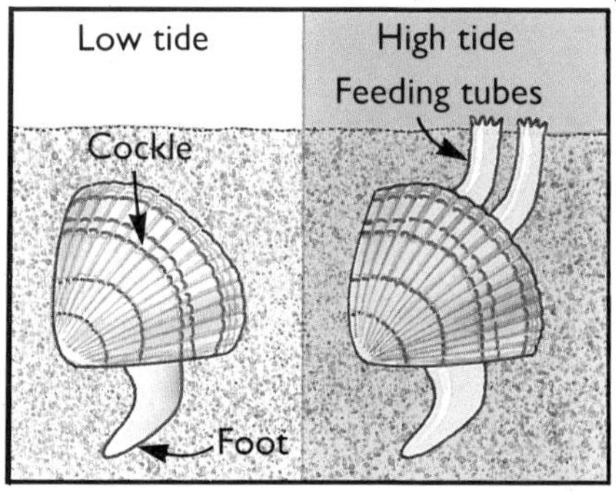
Low tide
High tide
Feeding tubes
Cockle
Foot

Mussels spend all their lives in one place, attached to rocks. When the tide goes out, they clamp their shells shut. This keeps some water inside and stops them from drying out.

Cockles live under the sand or mud, where it is damp. They have a "foot" for burrowing, and two feeding tubes which reach up to the sea. These are pulled in at low tide.

Crabs eat the rotting bodies of dead animals and plants on the seashore. They burrow under the ground at low tide, or live in the sea, so they do not dry out in the air.

 **Bacteria, 241; Estuaries, Mud flats, 160.*

Oil pollution

In many places shorelines are now filthy and poisoned because of oil spilled from tankers, pipelines and oil rigs.

Any small living thing that gets covered in oil will die, and so will animals, such as fish, which eat them. Oil also kills sea birds by destroying the waterproofing layer covering their feathers.

Six per cent of oil pollution in the sea comes from people who pour oil down drains, for example, after they have changed the oil in their car engines.

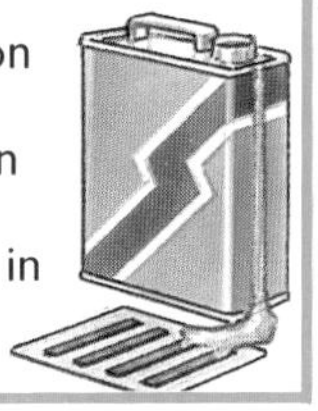

Shore birds

Wading birds, such as curlews, oystercatchers and knots, are common on sandy or muddy shores. Many come to breed at certain times of the year. Others stop for a rest during their migrations*.

Curlews have a long, curved beak with a sensitive tip. They probe in mud or sand, seeking small worms or shelled animals, deep underground.

Knots have a short beak and feed on shallow burrowing animals, such as crabs, shrimps and worms.

Oystercatchers have a long, straight beak. They feed on shelled animals, such as cockles and mussels, by splitting the shells open with their beak.

Dog whelks are hunters. They eat other shelled animals. First the whelk climbs onto the animal and drills a hole in its shell. Then it sucks out the soft parts of the animal.

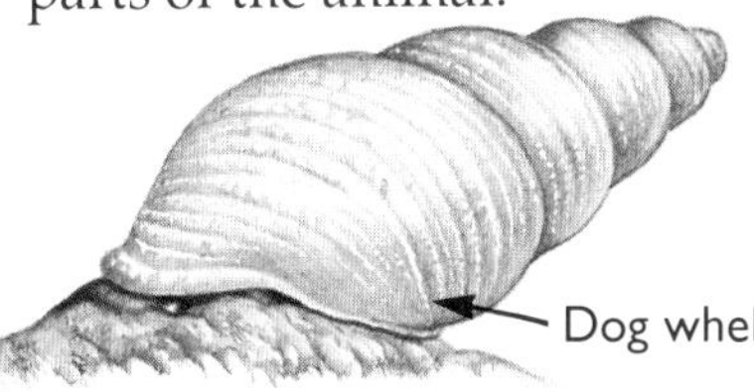

Dog whelk

Starfish have five arms with rows of very powerful suckers on them. They can pull open a tightly shut shell and eat the animal inside.

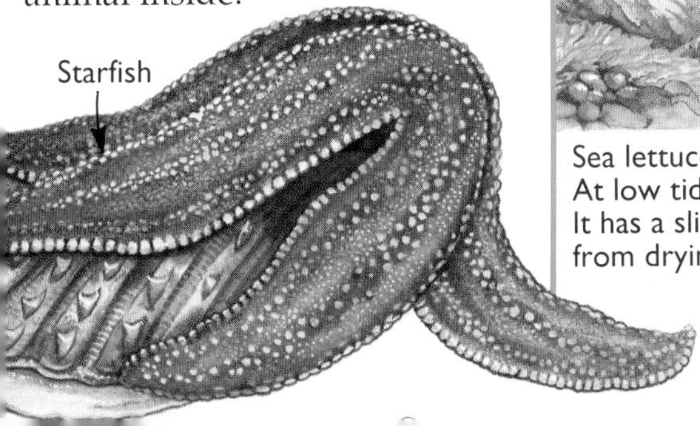

Starfish

Seaweeds

Seaweeds are red, brown or green and feel slimy. They get substances that they need to grow, such as minerals, from the sea. They anchor themselves to rocks near the shore, with a part called a **holdfast** and make food by photosynthesis* in their leaf-like branches, called **fronds.**

Like all plants, seaweeds need light to make their food. They can only grow in shallow areas where sea water holds them up near the ocean surface.

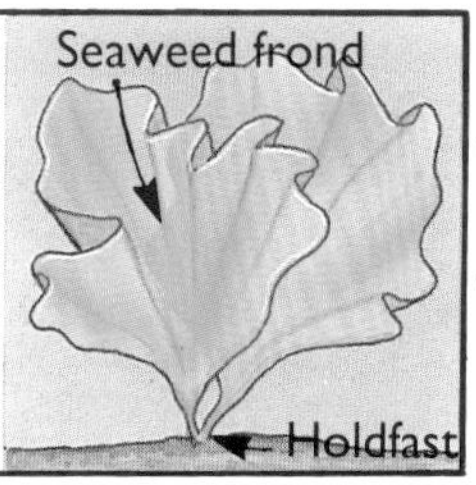

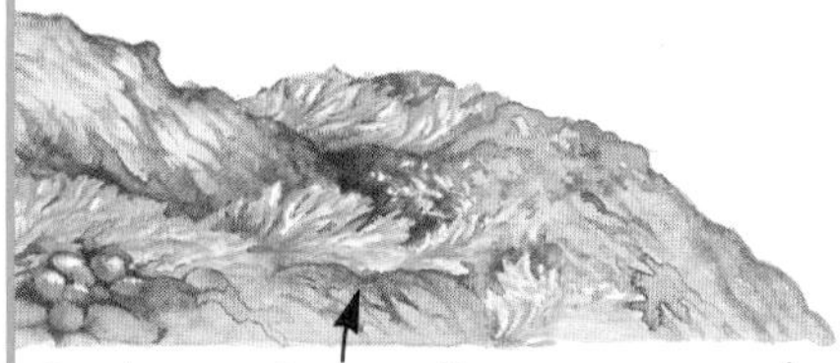

Sea lettuce is a small, green seaweed. At low tide, it lies flat on the rocks. It has a slimy surface which stops it from drying out.

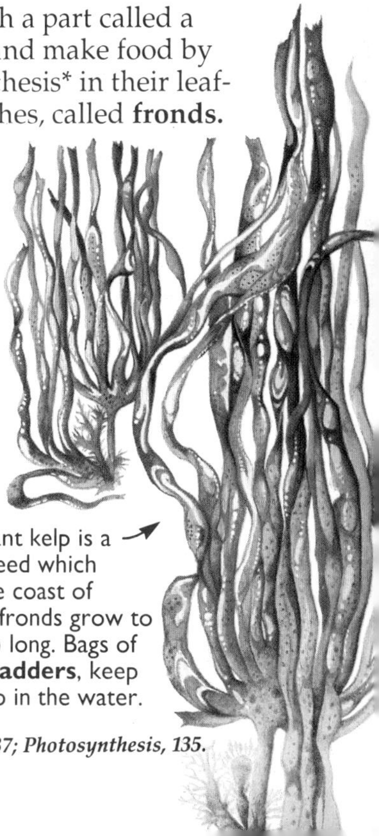

American giant kelp is a brown seaweed which grows off the coast of America. Its fronds grow to 100m (320ft) long. Bags of gas, called **bladders**, keep the fronds up in the water.

**Migrations, 137; Photosynthesis, 135.*

Estuaries

Where a river enters the sea, the tide still comes in and goes out twice a day. When it comes in, it floods the river with salty water. Often the river then overflows and floods the nearby land with a mixture of salt water and fresh river water. The flooded part of the river is the estuary. When the tide goes out, the flood water goes too. The river still flows to the sea.

How estuaries form

Most estuaries are muddy places. Rivers carry **silt** with them. Silt is a mixture of very tiny pieces of rock and plant material. Near the sea, the river flows very slowly, and the silt sinks gently to the bottom.

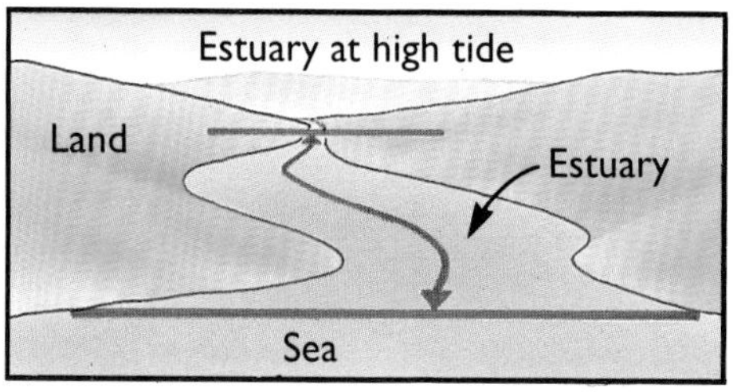

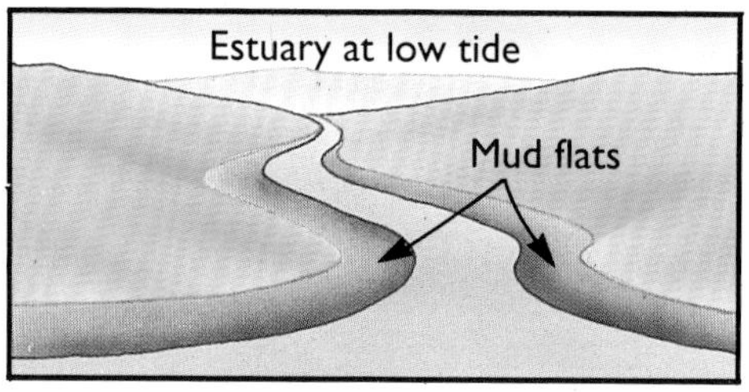

The tide brings in sand and pebbles which mix with the silt, forming mud. When the tide goes out, the mud is left behind in the estuary. Slowly, large muddy areas, called **mud flats**, are built up.

Life in an estuary

Very few living things can survive in both fresh and salt water. But an estuary is home to vast numbers of those that can. They live with big changes in the saltiness of the water.

Plants such as cord grass and eel grass can grow on the mud flats closest to the river, that flood most often. Their roots trap mud and stop it from being moved by the tides.

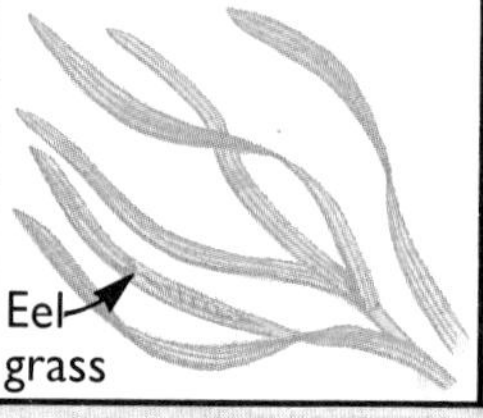

The mud flats further away flood less often. Plants such as thrift and sea aster, which are less good at surviving changes in saltiness, grow here between the grasses.

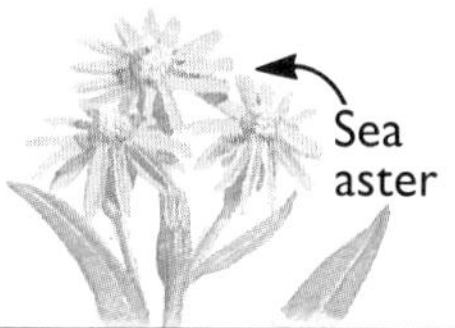

The mud flats furthest from the river are rarely flooded. Many kinds of plants grow on them. The mud below is still quite soft, so these are marshy areas.

Mud flats are made of fine particles with only a few air spaces between them, unlike soil. Roots cannot grow down deep where there is no air, so most mud flat plants are small.

Some fish, such as salmon and eels, can live in both fresh and salt water.

Salmon lay their eggs up near the source (beginning) of rivers. When the young hatch, they swim down river and off into the ocean, where they live and feed for up to six years. Then they return up the same river to lay their own eggs.

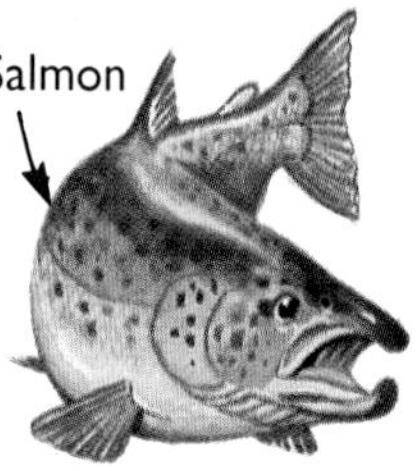

Each river has a special "taste". This is how salmon tell which river they were hatched in.

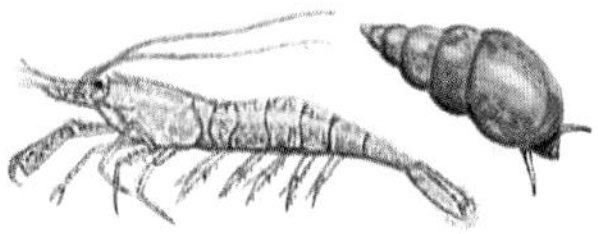

Many tiny shelled animals, such as spire shells and shrimps, live in the mud. 50,000 have been counted in a bucketful of mud.

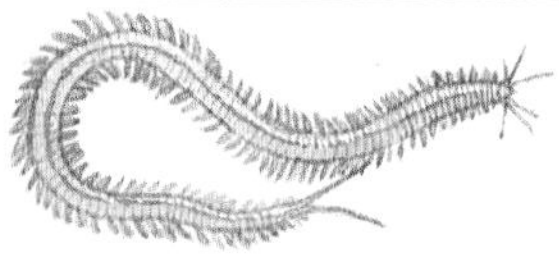

Ragworms are related to earthworms. They live in estuaries and on muddy sea shores. They feed on the tiny animals in the mud.

Mangrove swamps

Sea at high tide
Sea at low tide
Prop roots

The roots growing out and down from the trunk are **prop roots.** They trap silt and support the tree.

Closely-packed mangrove trees often grow on the mud flats in the tropics, forming dense swampy forests. These are called mangrove swamps. Like all estuary plants, mangrove trees cannot grow deep roots, as there is not enough air in the mud. They have roots that grow out and down from the trunk, or loop up out of the mud. This means they are above the water at low tide. The roots have patches on them that can take in the gas oxygen from the air.

Strange animals

Some odd fish live in mangrove swamps. The mudskipper crawls around on its stiff fins. It can leap by flicking itself into the air with its strong tail.

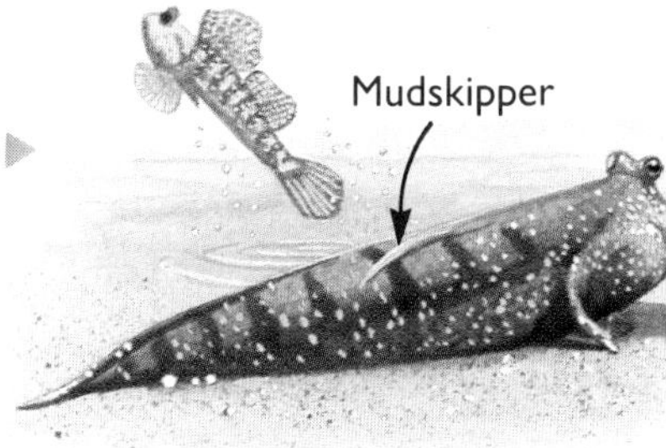
Mudskipper

Archer fish can spit water into the air to knock insects off the underside of leaves.

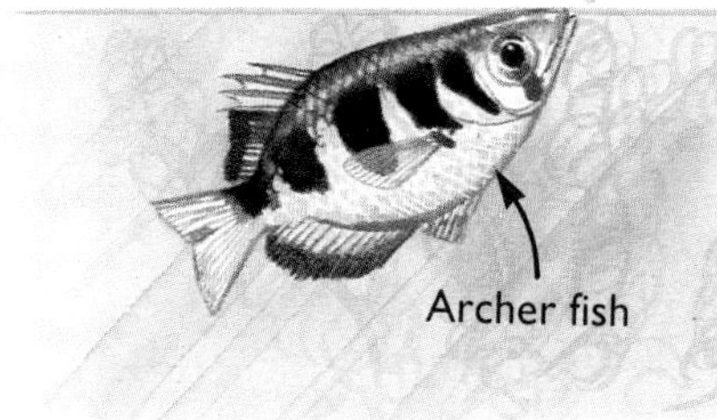
Archer fish

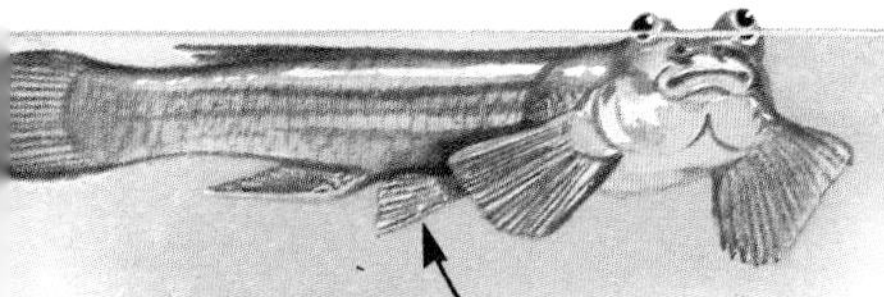
Four-eyed fish

The four-eyed fish only has two eyes, but each is split into two halves. The top parts can see in air, the bottom parts in water, so it can see both above and below water at the same time.

Proboscis monkeys feed on the leaves and shoots of mangrove trees. They spend most of their time in the trees, although they are good swimmers.

Many kinds of crab, such as the fiddler crab, live on the muddy edges of the swamps. The male has one very large claw that it waves in the air to attract females or threaten other males.

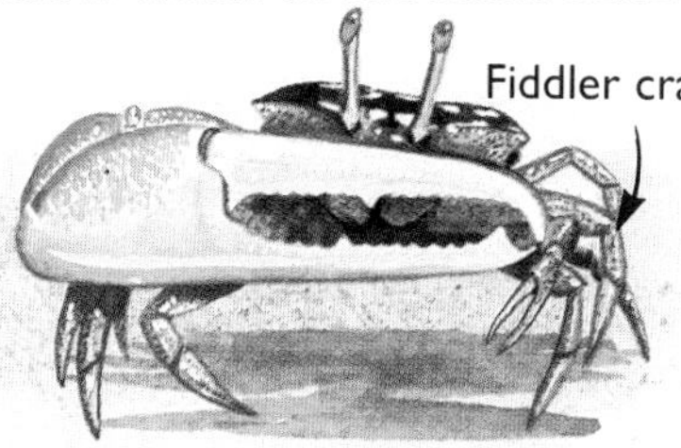
Fiddler crab

Male proboscis monkeys make a honking noise to warm of danger. Their large noses may help them make a loud noise.

There are two types of sea cow, the dugong and the manatee. Both can grow up to four metres (13ft) long. A third kind, Steller's sea cow, lived in the north Pacific but is now extinct.

Manatees have a split top lip that they use to pick up their food (plants).

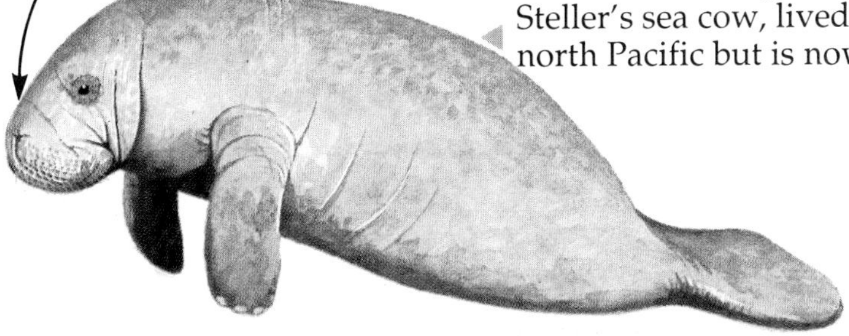

Islands

Islands vary in size from tiny coral islands, with no name, to Australia, a huge continent. Animals and plants on islands are separated by water from those on the mainland. People say island plants and animals are isolated from other plants and animals elsewhere.

How are islands formed?

Islands are formed in two main ways. The first is when land separates from the mainland. For example, Madagascar and New Zealand formed in this way over 20 million years ago. They had plants and animals on them from the start.

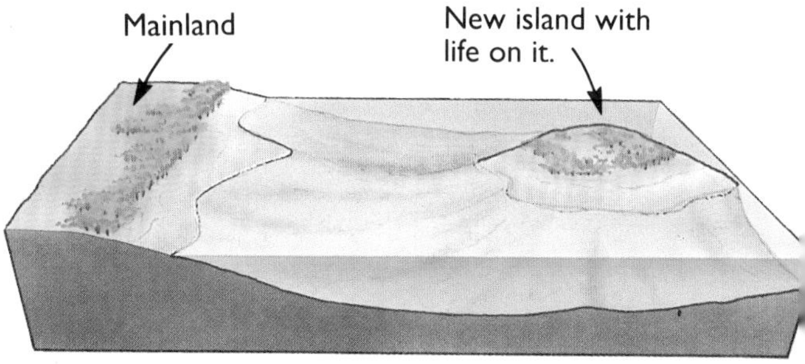
Mainland
New island with life on it.

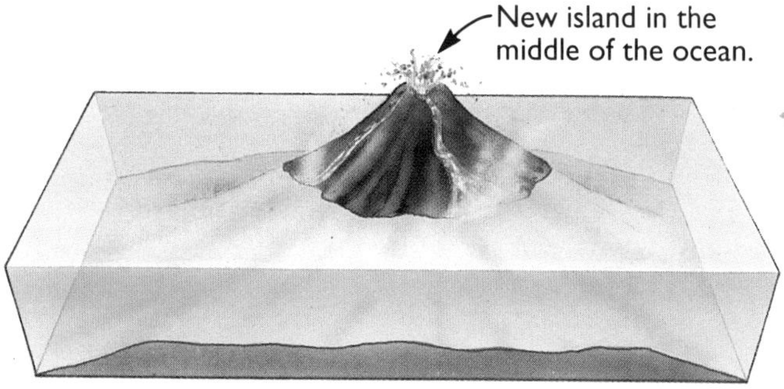
New island in the middle of the ocean.

The other way islands form is when volcanoes on the sea bed push up so much new rock that new land forms in the ocean. This is how the Galapagos and Hawaiian islands were formed, for example. Such volcanic islands have no life on them to start with.

New islands

Most new islands are volcanic islands. Once the volcano has stopped erupting, they are just lumps of bare rock. Gradually soil develops, plants grow and animals come to live on them.

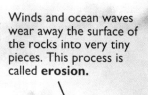

Winds and ocean waves wear away the surface of the rocks into very tiny pieces. This process is called **erosion.**
Animals that feed in the sea, such as sea birds, seals and sea lions, are the first to arrive. They come to breed where there are no predators (hunting animals).
Their droppings rot slowly, mixing with the rock particles to form soil.

New island plants

Once there is soil on a new island, plants can grow. Plants spread by producing seeds. These are carried to islands by wind or water, or by birds and other animals.

Some plants, such as orchids, have seeds that are so light they can be carried by the wind.

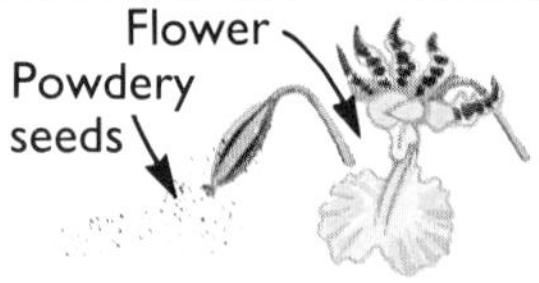
Flower
Powdery seeds

Others, such as thistles, have heavier seeds with feathery parachutes which catch the wind.

Coconuts are the seeds of palm trees. Their shells are waterproof. They float and can be carried by the sea.

Island visitors

Sea birds spend most of their lives at sea, feeding on fish. They come to islands in the middle of the ocean to nest, where there are few predators to threaten their young.

Frigate birds have large wings and small legs. They attack other sea birds to make them vomit their food. Then they dive, catch the food and eat it.

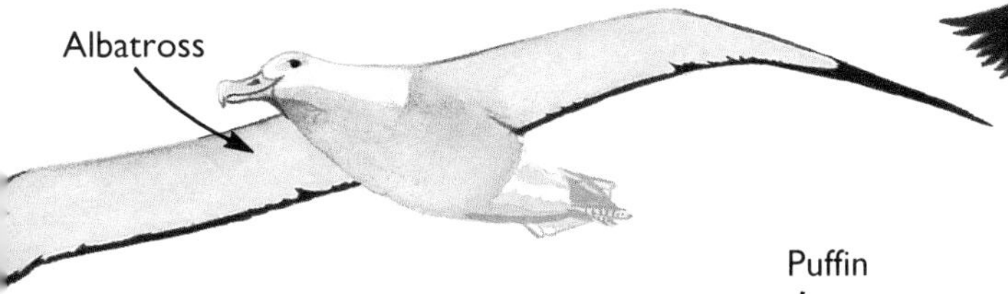

The albatross has the largest wing span of all. One kind, the wandering albatross, spends most of its time in the air. It feeds near Australia but nests on islands in the South Atlantic.

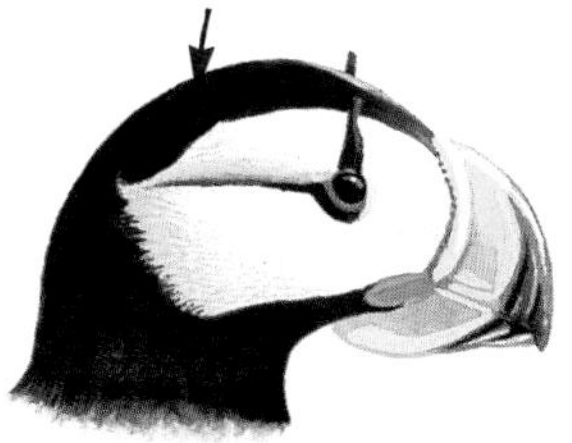

Puffins make a nest by scraping a hole out of the cliffs. The colours on the male's beak only last while he tries to attract a mate.

Blue-footed boobies nest on the ground on islands in the South Pacific. They feed on fish and are good divers.

Some plants, such as burdock, have seeds covered in many tiny hooks. They catch on bird feathers or animal fur and drop off much later.

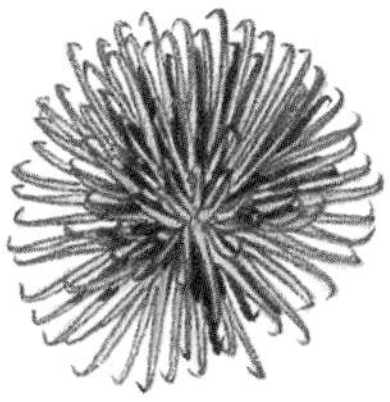

Other plants, such as figs, produce fruit with seeds inside. Animals eat the fruit. The seeds later pass out in the animal droppings.

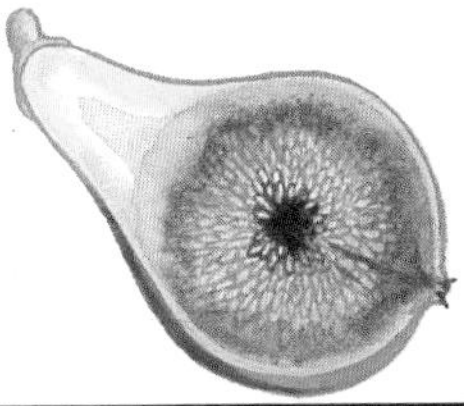

Plant-eating animals can survive if they land on islands where there are plants to eat. They are the next animals to arrive on new islands, after seals and sea birds.

New island animals

For an animal species to survive on a new island, the first animal to arrive must be able to breed* (produce young), so it needs to survive until a mate arrives.

Animals that can fly, such as birds, bats and insects, can cross water. They can easily land on new islands and start breeding.

Land animals, such as squirrels, iguanas and toads, only cross the oceans if they are swept out to sea. This is rare, so they don't arrive very often on new islands. People think a new type of animal only came to Hawaii (an island in the Pacific) once every 12,500 years.

*Breeding, 144.

Island life

Over millions of years, animals and plants on many of the world's islands have developed differently from mainland ones. The older an island is, the more different its plants and animals are. Species that do not live elsewhere in the world are called endemic species.

Ancient plants and animals

Sometimes when a species of animal or plant has died out everywhere else, it may still be living on islands.

The only remaining tuataras live and breed in New Zealand. Fossils* of them have been found around the world. They are the same age as dinosaur fossils.

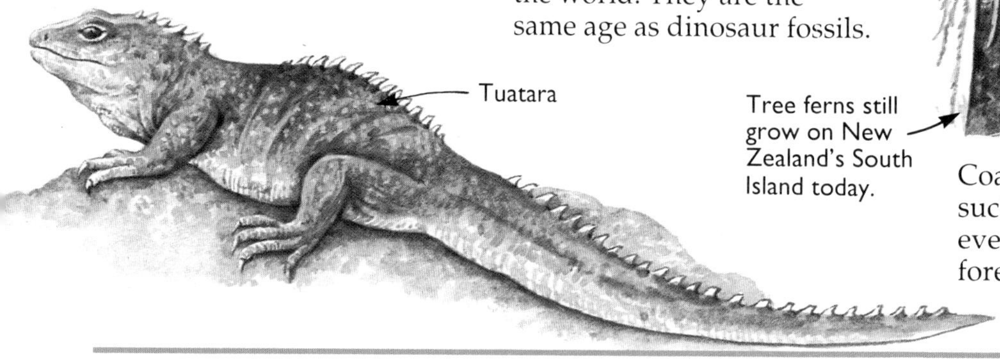

Tuatara

Tree ferns still grow on New Zealand's South Island today.

Coal contains fossils of plants, such as tree ferns, that grew everywhere in huge, swampy forests millions of years ago.

Successful animals

If animals arrive on islands with lots of food and few hunting animals, they survive to have young themselves. This has happened in the past, and over thousands of years of breeding, many island animals have become different from their mainland relatives.

Fossa

The fossa is a cat-like hunter, about the same size as a fox. It hunts small animals and birds. It is only found on one island off the coast of Africa, called Madagascar.

On some islands, a few sea animals have become good at living on land. They first came to the land because there was plenty of food to eat.

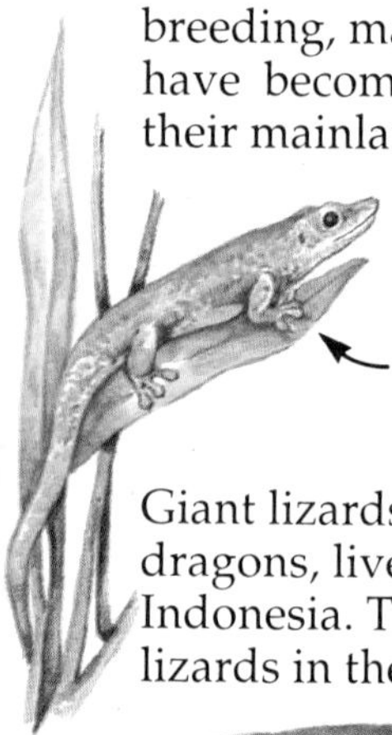

This tiny Seychelles gecko is much smaller than other geckos.

Giant lizards, called komodo dragons, live on two islands in Indonesia. They are the largest lizards in the world.

Komodo dragon

The robber crab's ancestors were sea-living hermit crabs. It eats the insides of coconuts and can climb palm trees.

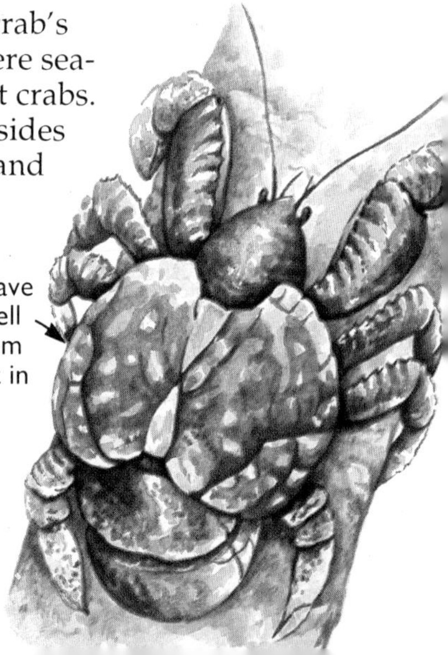

Robber crabs have a very tough shell which stops them from drying out in the air.

*Fossils, 132.

The arrival of people

In the past, people who settled on islands made many animals and plants die out.

They killed them for food, destroyed their homes or brought mainland species with them, which ate the island animals' food.

The New Zealand moa was a giant, flightless bird. It was nearly as tall as a giraffe and fed on leaves at the top of trees. It was hunted to extinction*.

Thylacines used to live in Tasmania. They were fiercely hunted by farmers because they killed the farmers' animals. They may all have died out.

Millions of years ago lemurs lived in forests around the world. Today nearly all of them live on Madagascar, an island off Africa. ▼

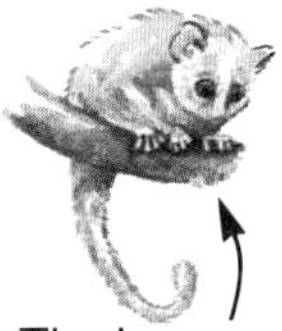

The indri lemur is the largest kind. It grows to one metre (three feet) long.

The lesser mouse lemur is the smallest species. It is only 11cm (four inches) long without its tail.

Now the forests where the lemurs live are being cleared. Three quarters of the forests have disappeared in the last 50 years. Many species of lemur are now in danger of extinction.

On the Galapagos islands there are 14 species of finch. Each one has a beak specially shaped for the food it eats.

The large ground finch is a seed-eater with a short, thick beak for crushing tough seeds.

The vegetarian tree finch eats buds and fruit. It has a hooked beak, like a parrot. Parrots are also vegetarian.

The warbler finch looks very much like a warbler. It eats insects and has a small, pointed beak.

The woodpecker finch uses a cactus spine as a tool to dig out grubs from the bark of trees.

The first pair of finches came to the islands to breed. Soon there were so many finches that they began to run out of food. Some of them had different shaped beaks. They survived because they could eat other foods. Over many years the 14 different species developed.

Flightless birds

Birds that cannot fly are quite common on islands. Scientists think they lose their ability to fly when there is plenty of food near the ground, and also no need to escape because there are no predators (hunting animals). Several birds in New Zealand are flightless.

Kiwis eat worms, snails and other small, ground-living animals. They are the only birds with a good sense of smell (they use whiskers on their beaks).

The kakapo is a giant parrot. It feeds at night on leaves and berries close to the ground.

The takahe is a rare plant-eating bird that cannot fly. It is the size of a chicken and brilliantly coloured.

*Extinction, 146-147.

Grasslands

Natural grasslands are flat, open and windy. The plants are mostly grasses and low bushes, but there are also sometimes a few trees. There are lots of plant-eaters, which in turn attract hunters.

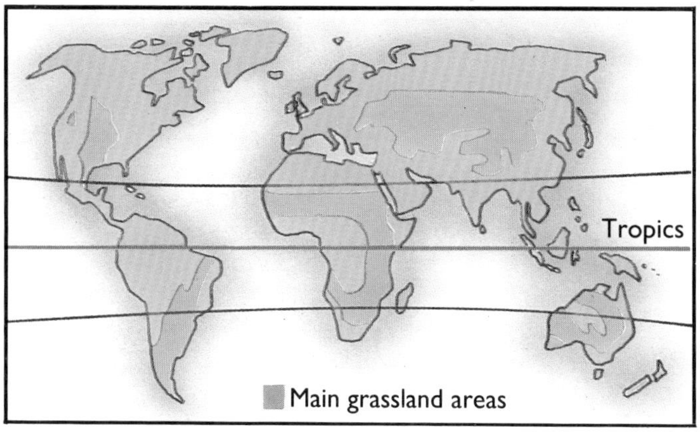

Where are grasslands?

Grasslands cover a quarter of all the land on Earth. Grasses need less water to grow than trees, but most are killed by shade from taller plants. This is why most grasslands grow between forests and deserts.

Grasslands in the tropics have only two seasons, a rainy one and a dry one. It is hot all year round.

Temperate grasslands have the usual four seasons. It is warm in summer, but can be very cold in winter.

The African savannah

The largest remaining natural grasslands are in Africa. They have not been changed by people because of a tiny insect pest, the tse-tse fly, which spreads a disease called sleeping sickness. The disease has stopped people from clearing land and settling down as farmers. So the wild plants and animals are still there. Many of them are protected in huge areas, called **reserves**.

Tall grasses cover the land. After the rainy season they dry out, catching fire easily. When the rain comes again, new leaves grow fast.

Tough, fire-resistant trees, such as acacia and baobab trees, grow in groups wherever there is enough water for them.

There are often lakes and marshy areas after the rainy season. These dry out fast, but larger numbers of trees and plants grow near them.

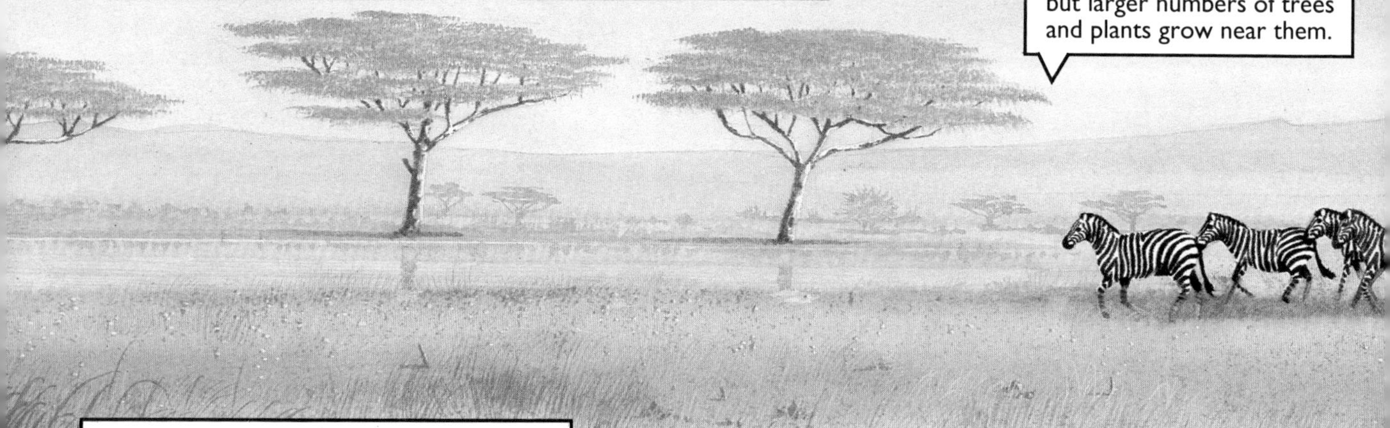

Meerkats stand up on their hind legs, resting on their tails, to see over the tall grass. One watches for danger while the others feed.

Millions of insects, such as grasshoppers, beetles, ants and termites, live among the tall grasses.

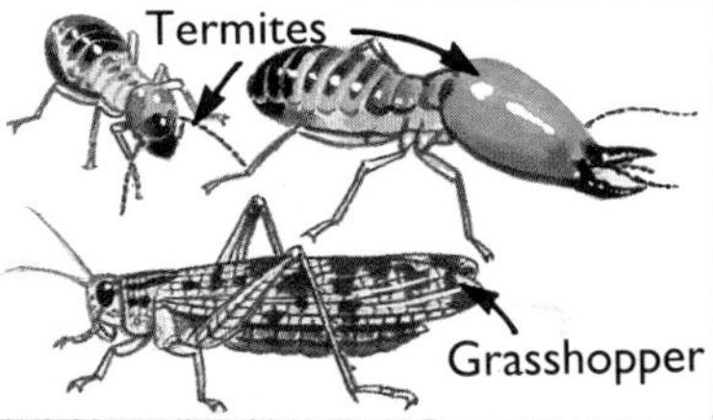

Living together

On the flat, open grasslands, many animals live in groups for their protection. Different kinds of animal groups are organized in different ways.

Huge **herds** (groups) of wildebeest move over the plains, feeding. Together they have more eyes, ears and noses to sense danger. The herd has no leader. New members join and others leave all the time.

Elephants live in herds that are more closely organized. The leader is usually an old female. The other females share tasks, such as caring for the calves. Males leave the group at 12 years old, but the females stay.

Baboons live in family groups called **troops**, which are very closely organized. Each troop is led by an older male. He keeps everyone together and defends them, with the help of younger males, if they are attacked.

Huge herds of large plant-eating animals, such as zebras, wander over the plains, eating the grass.
Vultures, marabou storks and other animals eat the hunter's scraps.
Large hunting animals, such as lions, eat many plant-eating animals.
Many animals, such as servals, have long legs. This helps them see over the long grass.

Grassland plants

The plants which grow in the grasslands are mainly different kinds of grasses. There are about 8,000 different species. All grassland plants have to be able to survive dry periods and having their leaves and shoots eaten. Most trees cannot do this very well.

Land plants and water

Most land plants take up water from the soil through their roots. They need water to make food in their leaves by photosynthesis*.

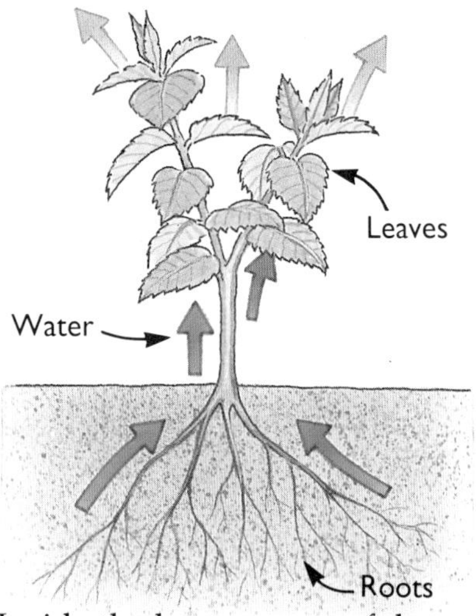
Leaves
Water
Roots

Inside the leaves some of the water turns into a gas called water vapour, which is lost into the air. Water always flows from the soil, through plants and into the air in this way.

If plants run out of water, they wilt at first, then they begin to dry out. If they get no more water, they die.

Coping with dry periods

Most trees are big plants. The bigger plants grow, the more water they need. Even with their long, deep roots, most trees would not be able to find enough water in grassland areas to survive.

Grasses are much smaller than trees, and they also grow many long roots. These help them to find the little water there is on grasslands. They can survive on this water, because they need less than trees.

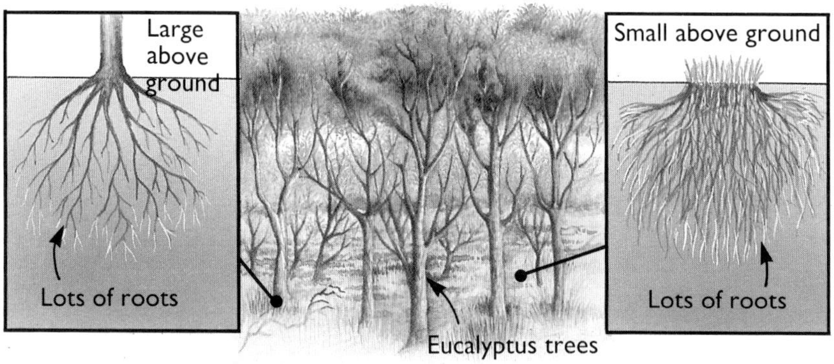
Large above ground
Lots of roots
Small above ground
Lots of roots
Eucalyptus trees

Coping with plant-eaters

Grasses grow long, straight leaves from near the ground which keep getting longer as the plant gets older. When the tips of the leaves are eaten by animals, the leaves continue growing from the bottom. This means that hungry, plant-eating animals are not a real danger to grasses.

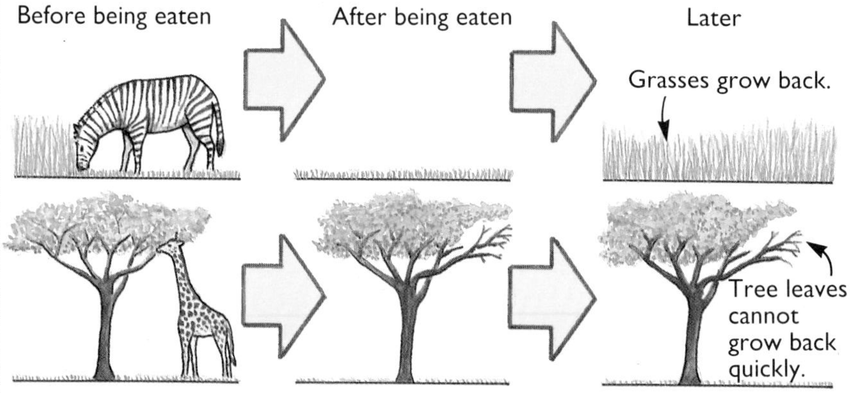
Before being eaten
After being eaten
Later
Grasses grow back.
Tree leaves cannot grow back quickly.

Trees grow new leaves every year. At first their leaves grow quickly, then they stop growing. If they are eaten, the tree cannot grow new ones until next year. The trees need to stop animals from eating their new leaves.

 **Photosynthesis, 135.*

Pampas grass

There are some trees which can survive in areas such as grasslands, where there is little water.

Trees such as acacias, baobabs and eucalyptuses in Africa and Australia grow on grasslands. They all have tough leaves like those on desert plants.

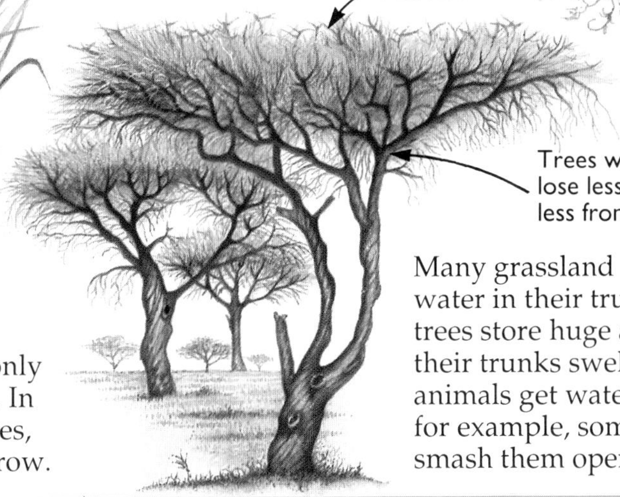
Acacia trees
Trees with tough leaves lose less water and so need less from the ground.

Baobab tree

In very dry areas, only short grasses grow. In slightly wetter places, taller grasses can grow.

Many grassland trees store water in their trunks. Baobab trees store huge amounts and their trunks swell up. Many animals get water from them, for example, some elephants smash them open.

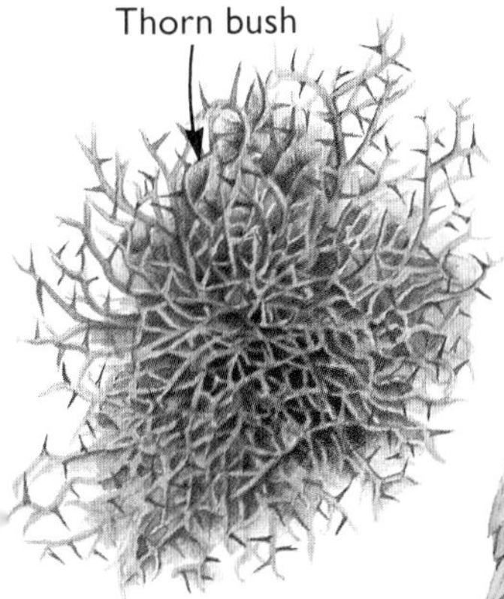
Thorn bush

Some plants, such as thorn bushes, grow sharp spines on their branches. Most animals avoid these prickly plant dinners.

Acacia tree

As well as having thorns, some acacia trees have leaves that make a nasty-tasting chemical when they are eaten. They soon taste so bad that plant-eaters, such as giraffes, go off to find a tastier meal.

Using grasses

Many food plants, such as wheat, oats, barley and rice, are species of grass. Their ancestors were different, wild grass species.

Very early farmers chose seeds from wild plants with the biggest seeds.

They kept these seeds to plant the next year. Over many hundreds of years, modern food plants developed from early wild ones. These crops have many large seeds.

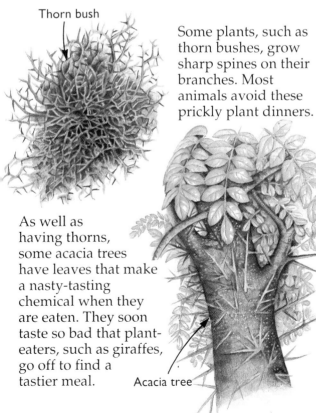

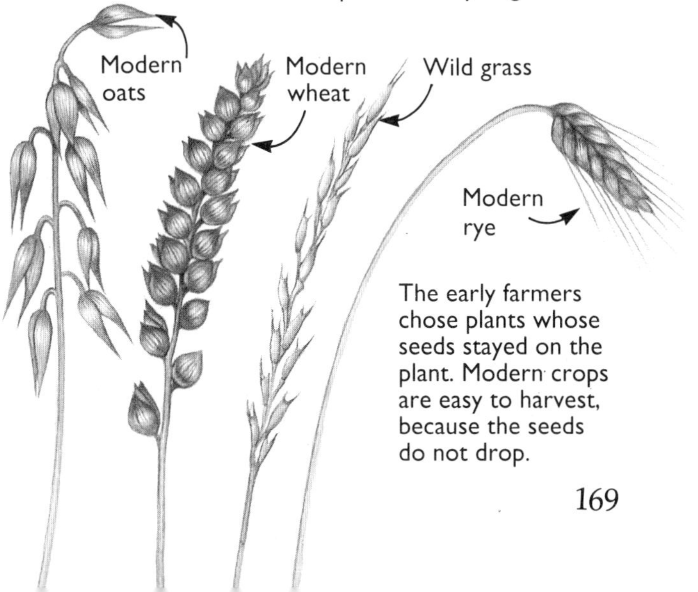
Modern oats
Modern wheat
Wild grass
Modern rye

The early farmers chose plants whose seeds stayed on the plant. Modern crops are easy to harvest, because the seeds do not drop.

Grassland plant-eaters

Large grassland areas provide enough food for lots of herbivores (plant-eating animals). These animals can live together because they all eat slightly different things.

Browsers and grazers

Animals such as giraffes, elephants, black rhinos and some antelopes eat leaves from trees and bushes. They are called **browsers**. Other animals, such as wildebeest, zebras and hippos, eat grass. They are called **grazers**.

Migrations

The best food for grazing animals is the new grass which grows in spring or the rainy season. As the seasons change, many grassland animals make long journeys, called **migrations**, to find this food.

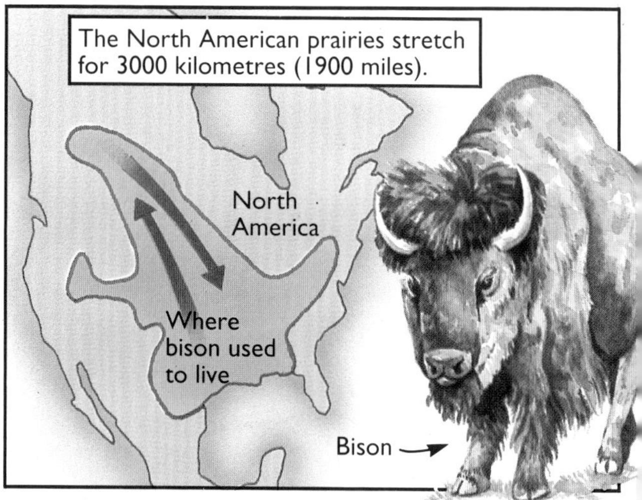
The North American prairies stretch for 3000 kilometres (1900 miles).
North America
Where bison used to live
Bison

Huge herds of bison used to live on the prairies. They spent winter in the south, then followed the spring north to find the best food, returning south in autumn.

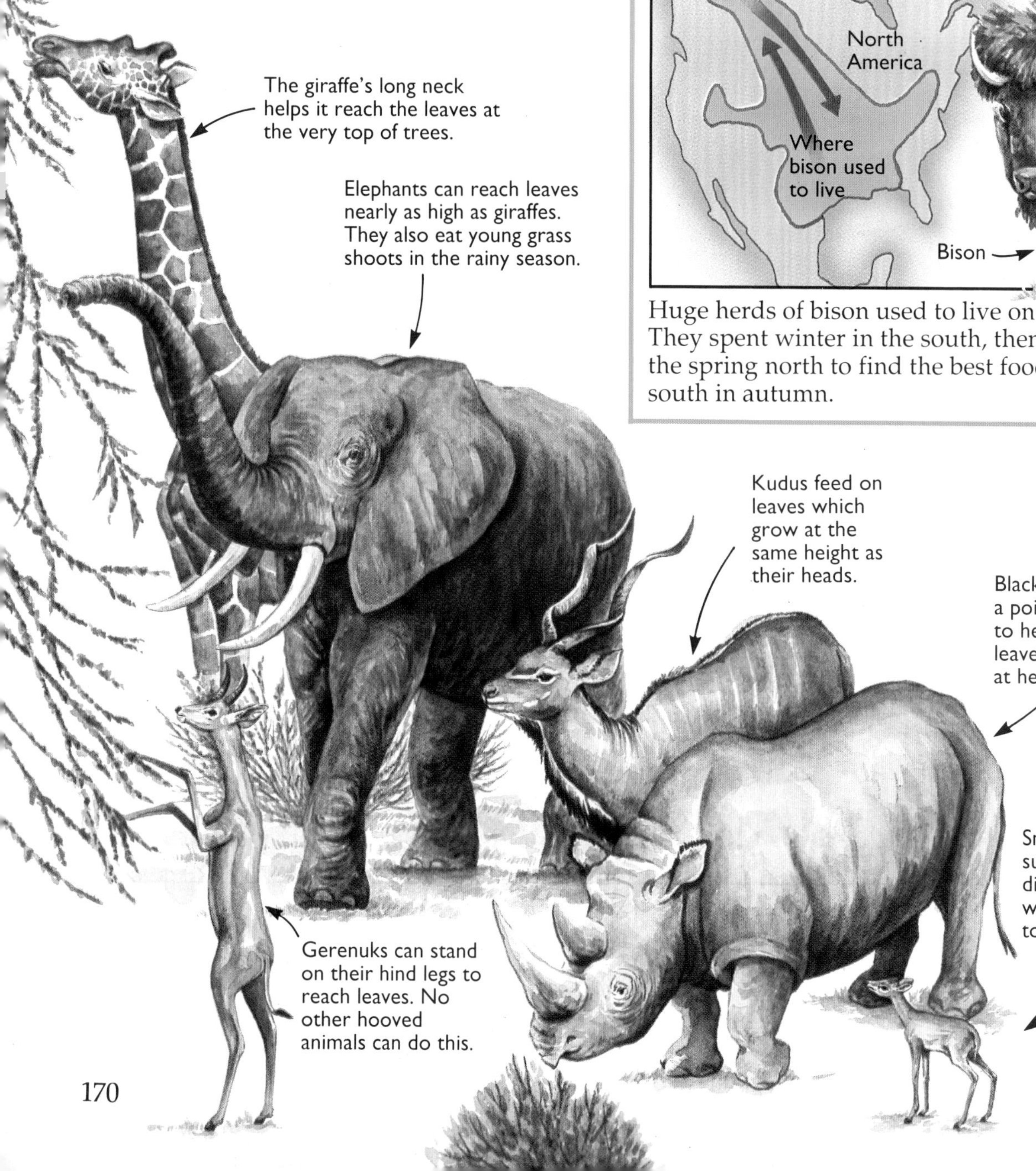
The giraffe's long neck helps it reach the leaves at the very top of trees.
Elephants can reach leaves nearly as high as giraffes. They also eat young grass shoots in the rainy season.
Kudus feed on leaves which grow at the same height as their heads.
Black rhinos have a pointed top lip, to help them pull leaves from bushes at head height.
Small antelopes such as the dik dik eat leaves which grow close to the ground.
Gerenuks can stand on their hind legs to reach leaves. No other hooved animals can do this.

Plants as food

To get energy from their food, animals need to **digest** it (break it up into simple substances inside their bodies). On grasslands, most plant-eaters feed on grass and leaves which are tough and difficult to digest. To survive, they need to eat lots and be good at digesting their food.

Plant-eaters need to chew their food a lot to get it ready to be digested.

Jaw moves sideways

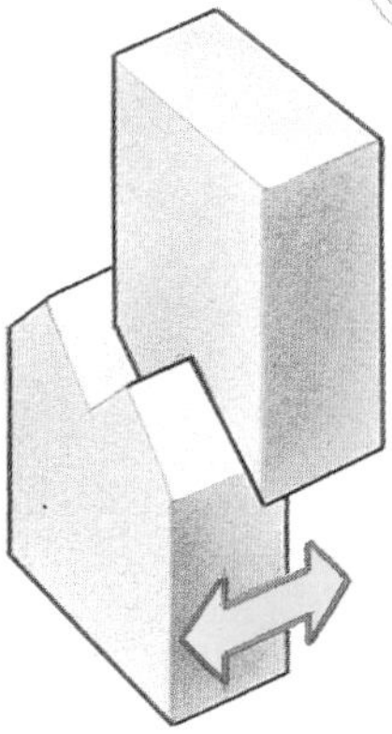

Teeth grind food

They have grinding teeth and jaws that move from side to side.

Some plant-eaters, such as giraffes and bison, have a stomach in two main parts, instead of just one. Their food goes to each part in turn. This means they can digest tough, partly digested food a second time, to get the energy from it.

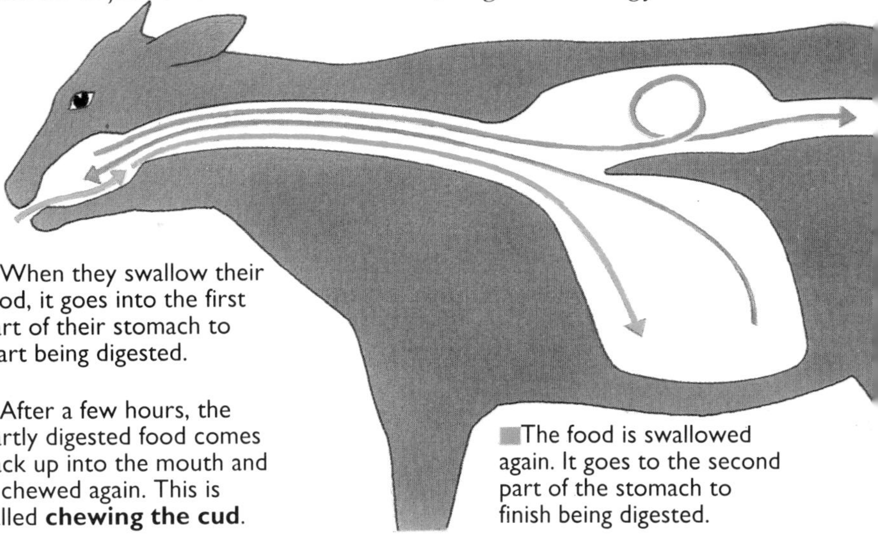

When they swallow their food, it goes into the first part of their stomach to start being digested.

After a few hours, the partly digested food comes back up into the mouth and is chewed again. This is called **chewing the cud**.

The food is swallowed again. It goes to the second part of the stomach to finish being digested.

Zebras like to eat fairly tall grasses. Other grazers prefer eating shorter grasses.

Wildebeest choose shorter grasses to eat than zebras.

White rhinos eat the shoots at ground level. They have a flat top lip.

At night hippos graze on grass on land. As well as normal teeth for munching grass, they have an extra pair of huge, front teeth. They use them to defend their homes and fight for females.

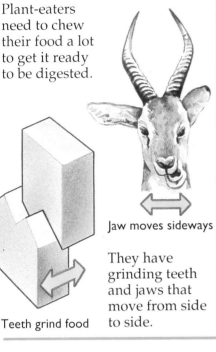

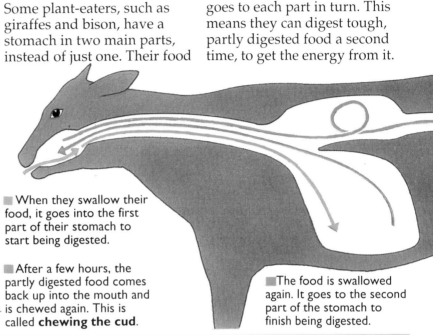

Grassland meat-eaters

Large numbers of herbivores (plant-eaters) on grasslands mean lots of food for carnivores (meat-eaters). Meat is a rich food and much easier to digest* than plants. Carnivores do not need to eat as often as plant-eaters. They spend a lot more time resting or sleeping.

Types of carnivores

Predators are hunting animals. They only eat fresh meat: the animals that they have killed. These animals are their **prey**.

Animals that eat meat they have not killed are **scavengers**. They pick clean the bodies of animals that died naturally and the remains of predators' kills.

All predators have good eyesight. Their eyes are close together in the front of their heads. This helps them judge how far away their prey is, so they can catch it more easily.

Some eagles can spot prey from over eight kilometres (five miles) away.

African savannah predators

African hunting dogs live in groups, called **packs**. The adults hunt together, wearing out large prey, such as wildebeest, by chasing them over very long distances. They share the food.

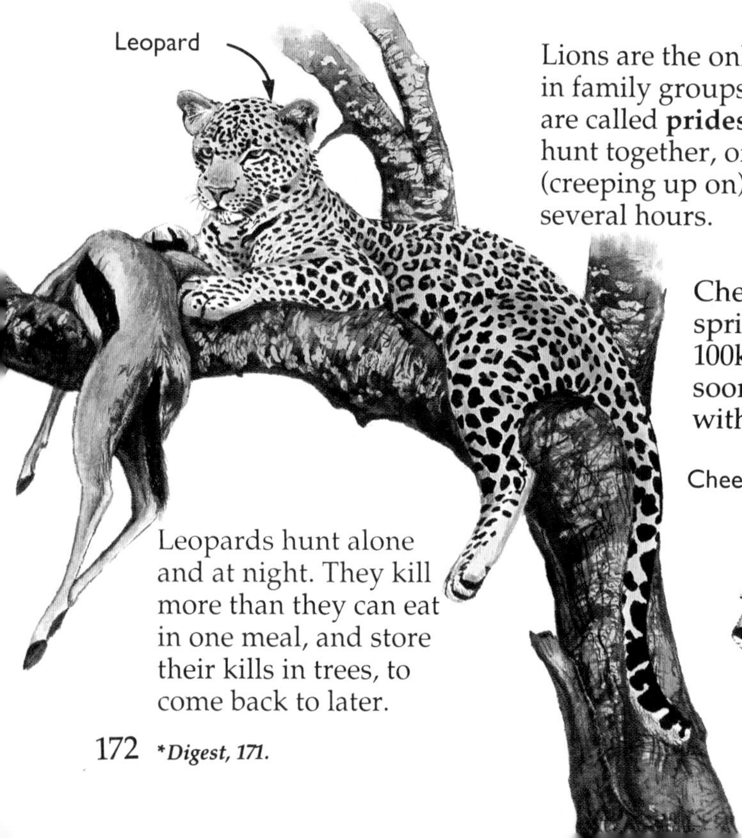

Lions are the only cats that live in family groups. These groups are called **prides**. The females hunt together, often **stalking** (creeping up on) their prey for several hours.

Pride of lions

Cheetahs hunt alone. They sprint after their prey at up to 100kmph (60mph), but they soon get tired. Unless they kill within a minute, they give up.

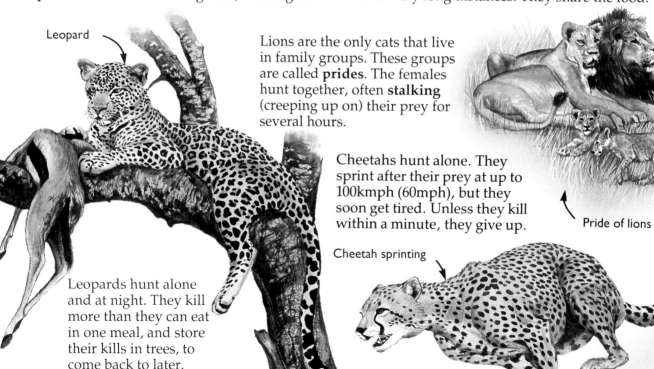

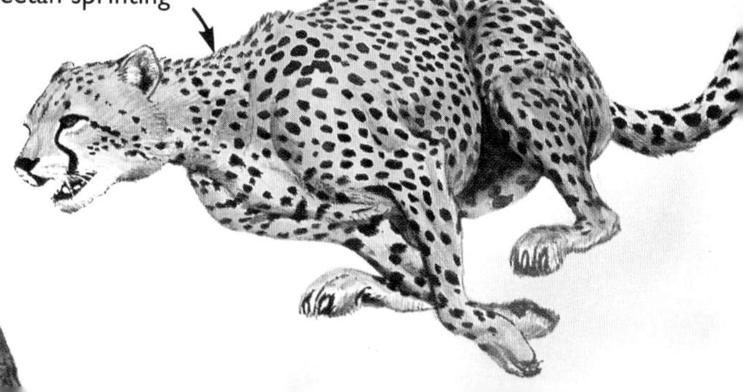

Cheetah sprinting

Leopards hunt alone and at night. They kill more than they can eat in one meal, and store their kills in trees, to come back to later.

 **Digest, 171.*

Snakes

Snakes eat small animals, birds and eggs. Many are too slow to chase their prey, so instead they hide and wait for a meal to pass. Different kinds of snake kill their prey in different ways.

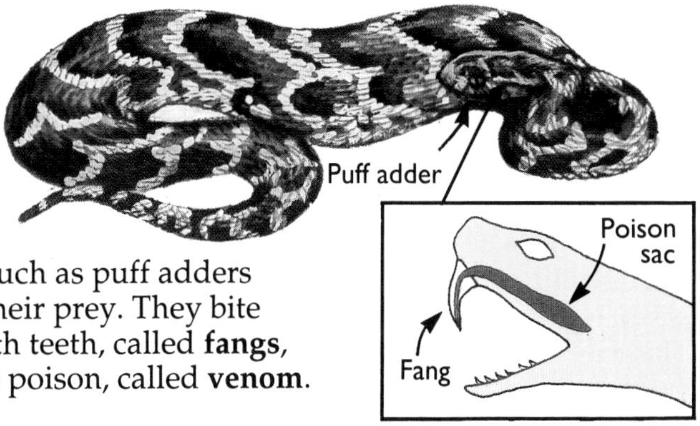

Snakes such as pythons suffocate their prey. They are called **constrictors**. They wrap themselves round their prey and squeeze hard. The prey soon runs out of breath and dies.

Snakes such as puff adders poison their prey. They bite them with teeth, called **fangs**, that drip poison, called **venom**.

Snakes open their jaws very wide and swallow their prey whole. Then they find a quiet place to digest* the meal and only hunt again when they are hungry. A big meal might last a python for several weeks.

Scavengers

Some animals, such as vultures, are always scavengers. Others hunt most of the time but will scavenge when there is less food around.

White-headed vultures can rip open skin to get at the meat inside.

White-backed vultures have a weak beak. They cannot feed until another animal has ripped the skin.

Hyenas have very strong necks and mouths, used for crushing bones. They kill small antelopes but scavenge as well when food is scarce.

Secretary birds hunt and scavenge. They kill and eat small animals, such as snakes.

Survival on the grasslands

There are few hiding places for all the large plant-eating animals on the flat, open grasslands. Some can hide by crouching in the grass or bushes, or burrowing underground, but most are too big. All grassland animals have ways of looking out for predators (hunters). Different animals have different ways of avoiding being caught and eaten.

Looking out for predators

Many grassland animals, such as antelopes, gather in herds for their protection. Together they have more eyes, ears and noses to sense a hunting animal's approach.

Like many herbivores (plant-eaters), saiga antelopes have eyes that are widely spaced on either side of their heads, so they can see all around while grazing.

Saiga antelopes live on the steppes in central Asia.

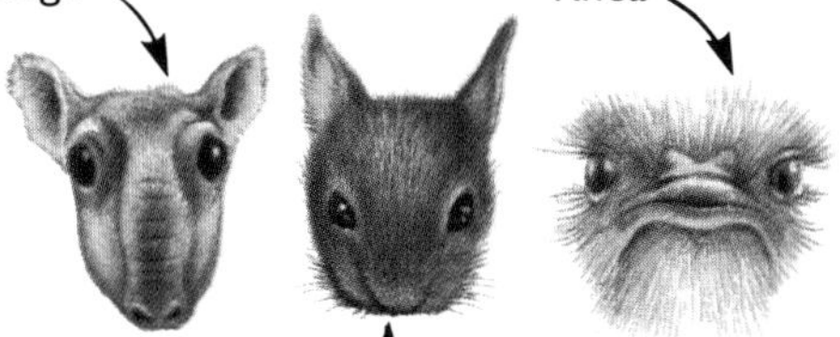
Saiga
Rhea
Rabbit

Getting away

Many animals in different places run away from hunters, but on grasslands it is especially important because there are few hiding places.

Animals such as antelopes need to run faster than their hunters to survive. Hunters such as coyotes need to be fast in order to catch their food.

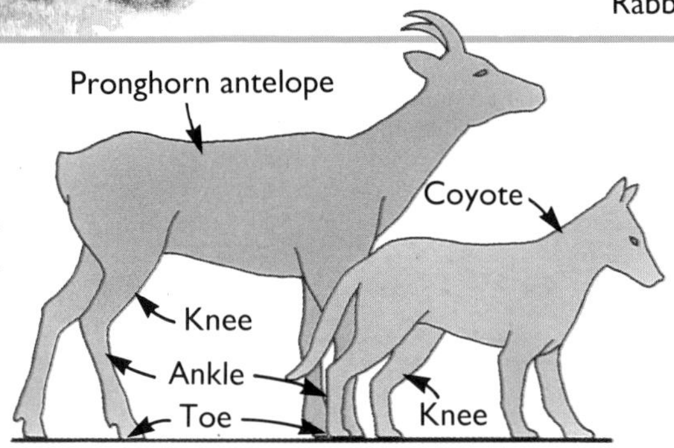
Pronghorn antelope
Coyote
Knee
Ankle
Toe
Knee

All fast runners run on their toes. Their ankle is half-way up their leg and their knee is close to their body.

Hoofs or claws stick into the ground and stop animals from slipping, in the same way that spikes on running shoes help an athlete to run more quickly.

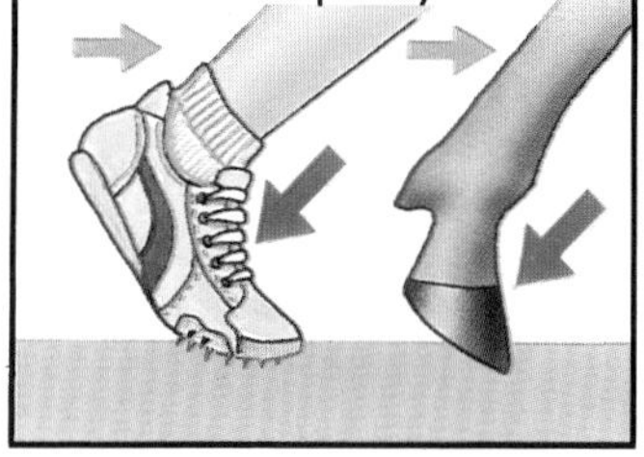

Jumpers

Kangaroos jump instead of run.

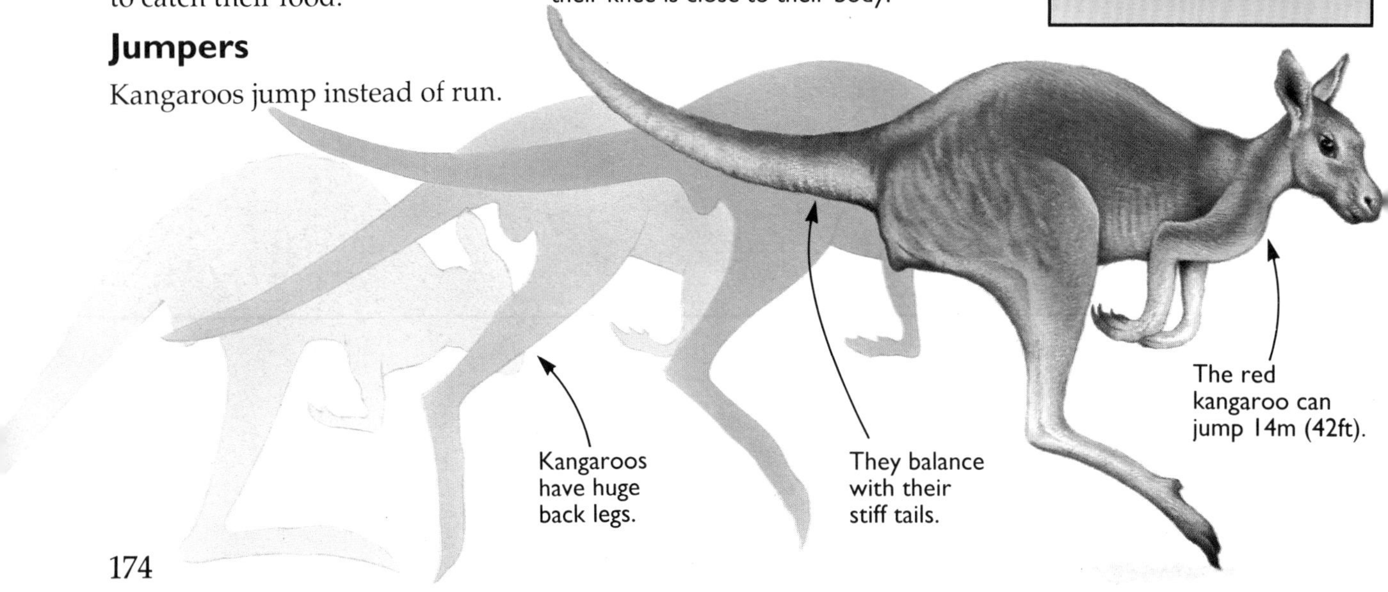
Kangaroos have huge back legs.
They balance with their stiff tails.
The red kangaroo can jump 14m (42ft).

Size and armour

If an animal is big enough or well protected enough, hunters will usually not try to kill it. For example, rhinos and elephants are so big that no other animals hunt them. Only people hunt them for their tusks and horns.

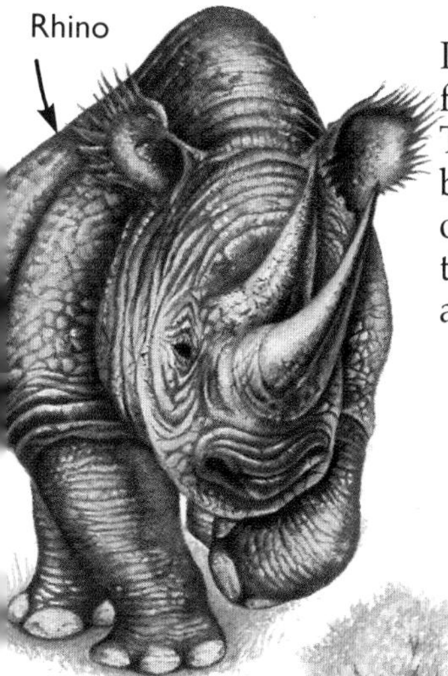

Rhinos have thick skin for extra protection. They are short-sighted, but have a good sense of smell. If they feel threatened by anything, they charge.

Young giraffes are big, but they are sometimes attacked. An adult, though, can kill a lion with one kick.

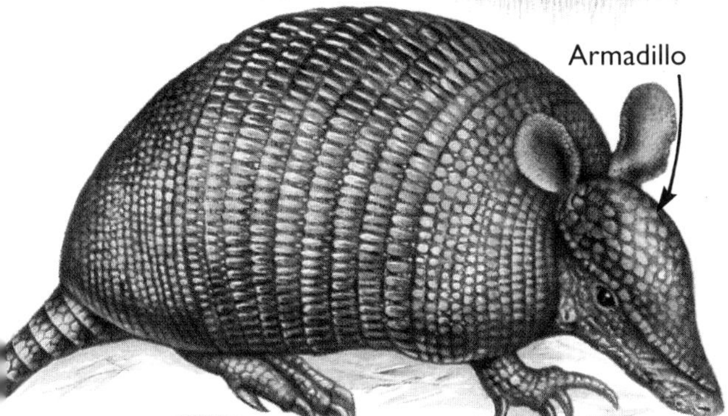

Armadillos eat insects. They have bony plates of armour to protect them. The nine-banded armadillo can roll itself up into a ball.

Blending in with the background

Some animals blend in with their background and so are harder for predators to spot. This is a common way of hiding, known as **camouflage**.

Many grassland antelopes, such as Thompson's gazelles, have sandy coloured backs. This helps them to blend in with their background, making it hard for hunters to spot them.

Many birds, such as the female sage grouse, are dull coloured. A female on her nest on the ground is hard to see, and only flies off if hunters come too close. In spring the males have brightly coloured feathers to attract females, but they shed them later.

Ostriches, rheas and emus are all large flightless birds. They can run very fast to escape the few predators that are large enough to attack them. They are all dull coloured as well, except the black and white male ostrich, which is the largest bird in the world.

Life underground

There is little shelter on grasslands and many different kinds of small animals have solved this by living underground. Some feed on plants or smaller animals above ground and only use their homes for shelter. Others spend all their lives underground.

Burrowing for shelter

Many animals that live underground only use their burrows for shelter. They live in groups and come up to the surface to feed.

Grasslands are home to large numbers of burrowing **rodents**. These are mammals*, such as rats, squirrels and beavers, which have gnawing teeth. They have many young, several times a year, and are food for many animals.

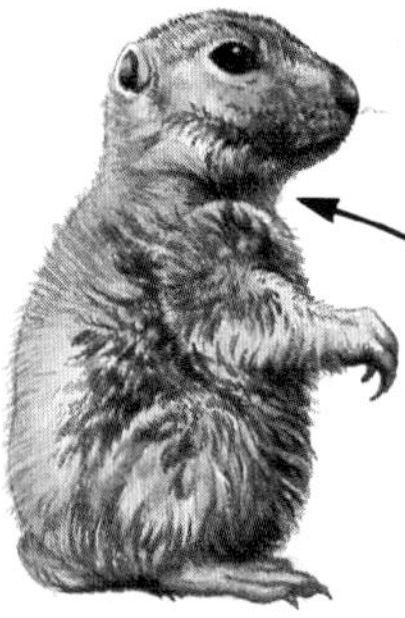

Prairie dogs live in North America. They eat seeds, grasses and roots.

Black-bellied hamsters live on the steppes. They feed on seeds and leaves.

Maras (also called Patagonian hares) are South American. They eat grass.

Prairie rattlesnake

All snakes are deaf, but they can feel tiny movements in the ground. The prairie rattlesnake is poisonous. It shelters in empty burrows and eats small animals, such as prairie dogs.

The rattle at the end of its tail is made of pieces of dead skin. When threatened, it shakes them to make a loud warning sound.

Living in groups

Many burrowing animals, such as prairie dogs, dig burrows with many connecting tunnels, several exits and many different chambers. They live together in groups and share the work.

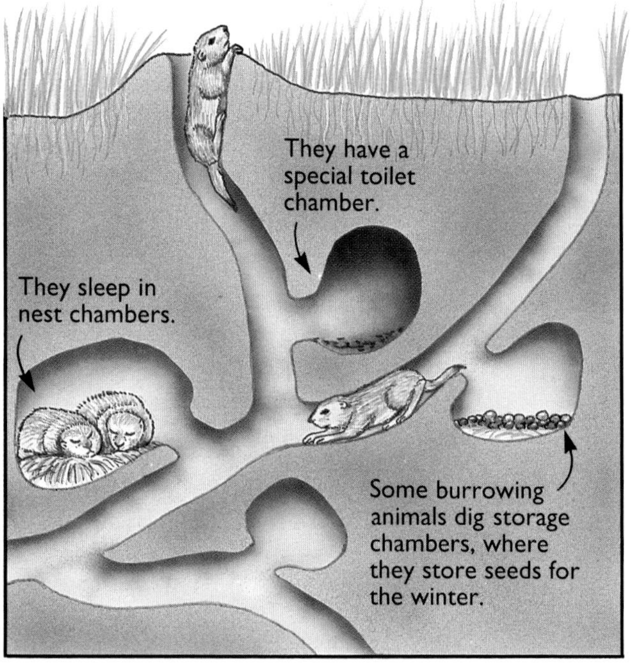
They have a special toilet chamber.
They sleep in nest chambers.
Some burrowing animals dig storage chambers, where they store seeds for the winter.

Burrowing owls

American burrowing owls often nest in old burrows. Their chicks' call sounds like a prairie rattlesnake's rattle. This may deter other hunters.

Meerkats

Meerkats live in family groups. The older ones help to take care of the young ones and take turns to keep a look out, while the others hunt for food or doze.

 **Mammals, 244.*

Insect colonies

Insects such as ants and termites live in huge groups called **colonies**. All the members of the colony hatch from eggs laid by one female, the **queen**. Termite nests have thick walls and the air is warm and damp inside, like a burrow.

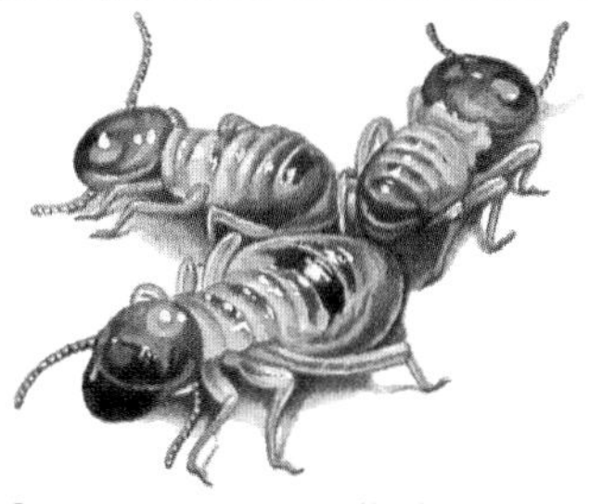

Some termites, called **workers**, build the nest and collect rotting plants to feed the colony.

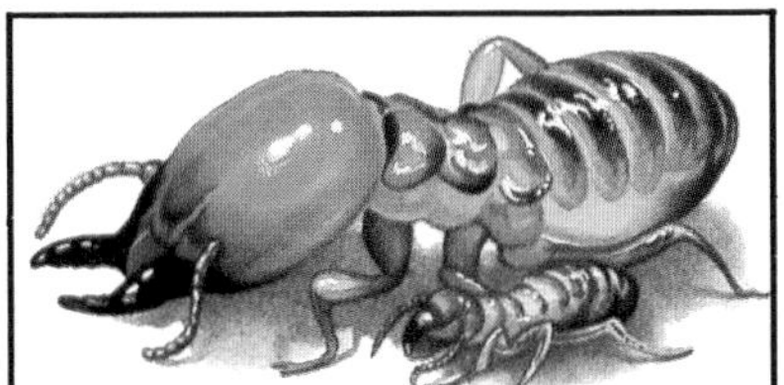

Others are good at fighting, and defend the colony. They have huge heads and are called **soldiers**.

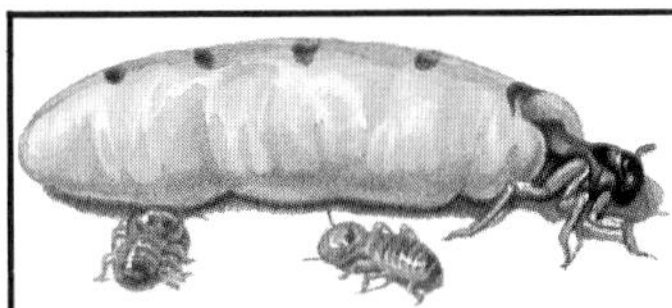

The queen lays up to 30,000 eggs each day. She becomes very big, swollen with so many eggs inside her. She may live for as long as people.

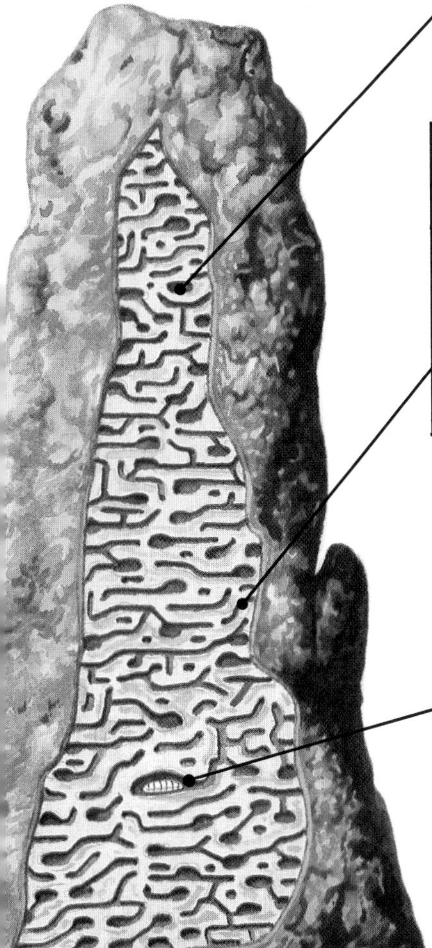

South American anteaters rip open termite nests and use their sticky tongues to catch big mouthfuls of termites.

Naked mole rats

Naked mole rats are one of the few mammal* species that live in colonies with a queen, workers and soldiers, just as insects do.

They are African rodents that spend all their lives under the ground. They are almost blind and feed on swollen plant roots.

Aardwolves are African. They have very weak teeth and feed on insects. They often shelter in old burrows.

The aardvark is African. It is the largest burrowing animal in the world. It can grow up to two metres (six feet) long and uses its sticky tongue to catch termites. It is very shy and only comes out at night.

Deserts

One-seventh of all the land on Earth is desert. Deserts are very dry areas which get less than 25cm (10in) of rain each year. Most deserts, such as the Sahara in Africa, are hot, but there are cold deserts near the poles (see page 200), where the water is frozen for most of the year.

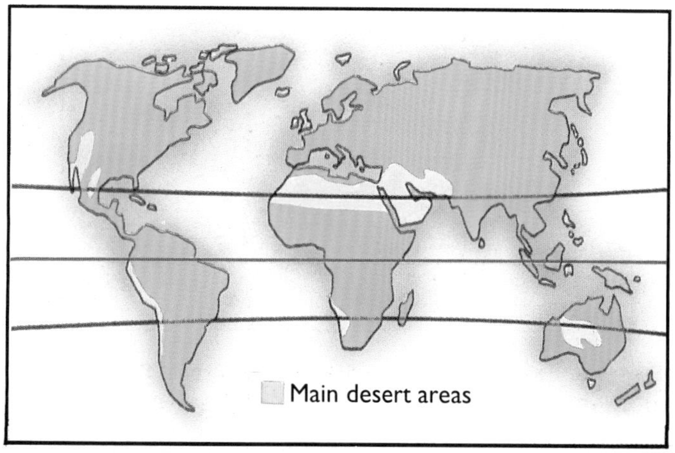
Main desert areas

Day and night

Most hot deserts heat up fast during the day and cool down quickly at night. At midday it can be very hot, but by midnight the temperature may be nearly freezing.

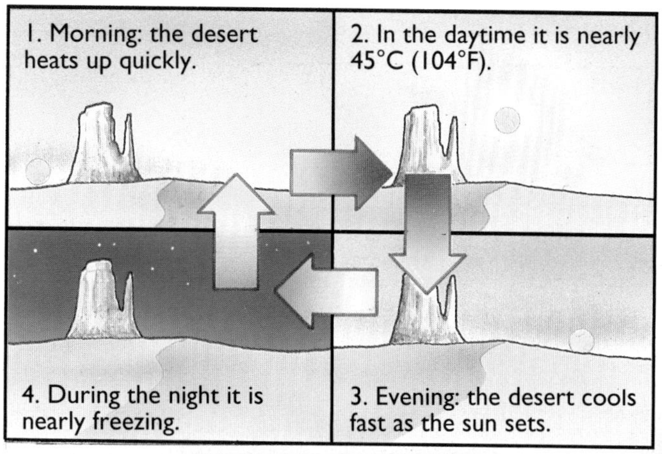
1. Morning: the desert heats up quickly.
2. In the daytime it is nearly 45°C (104°F).
3. Evening: the desert cools fast as the sun sets.
4. During the night it is nearly freezing.

Life in a hot desert

It is often difficult to tell where grasslands finish and deserts begin, because there are areas at the edge of deserts where grasses and bushes grow. In other areas, though, there are large patches of dry earth, rock or sand between plants and in some places no plants can grow at all. Some types of desert animals can survive in even the harshest conditions.

Strong, dry winds wear away rocks into strange shapes and blow sand and soil around. In some places there are large areas of bare rock.
Red-tailed hawk
Hunting birds, such as owls and falcons, can live in deserts. Desert birds' feathers keep them cool in the daytime and warm at night (see page 183).
In some places sand piles up, making sand dunes. Few plants can grow on dunes, because the sand is nearly always moving.
At the edges of deserts a few grasses, bushes and desert plants, such as cacti, grow.

Water in deserts

The little rain that does fall in deserts often comes in short, violent storms. The rain-water soaks into the ground quickly, dries up, or is carried away along old river beds.

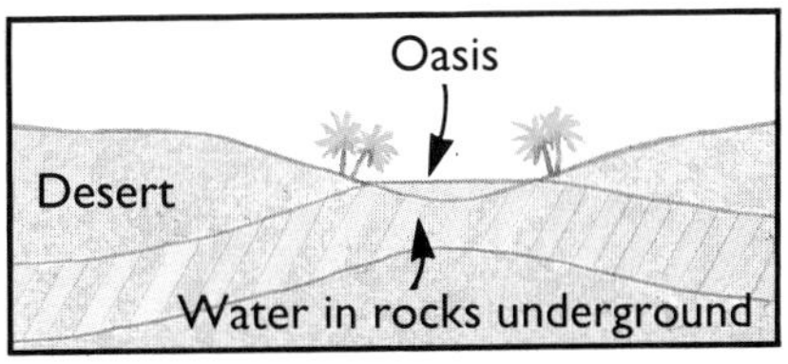

There is water underground almost everywhere, trapped in certain kinds of rock (see page 212). In deserts, this water is usually deep underground, but in a few places, called **oases**, the rocks are at the surface.

Plants such as date palms, that cannot grow elsewhere in deserts, can grow near oases, as their roots can reach the water.

Many desert birds, such as sand grouse, and larger desert animals, such as foxes, visit oases regularly to drink.

Lizards are very good at surviving the heat and dryness in deserts. Many feed on insects.

A few large hunters, such as foxes and cats, can survive in deserts. They feed on many different small animals.

Many insects, such as ants, beetles, moths and locusts, live in deserts. They are food for many animals.

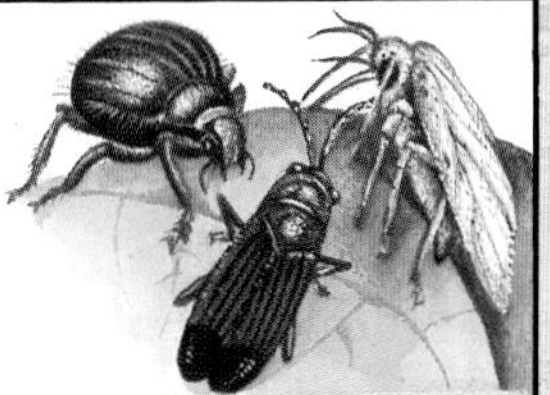

Many desert animals, such as kangaroo rats, avoid the hottest part of the day by getting out of the sun. They burrow underground, and feed at night when it is cooler.

Coping with the dryness

All animals and plants need water to survive and grow, but rain does not always fall every year in deserts.

In the very driest parts, no plants grow and few animals can survive. But in other areas some plants and animals have special ways of coping with the long dry periods.

In the Central Australian Desert rain only falls about once every five or six years.

Desert plants and water

Some desert plants have long roots to find water hidden deep underground. Others make the most of the short rainy periods, storing water inside parts of themselves when there is lots of water around.

Mesquite bushes have roots that grow up to 30m (100ft) long to reach deep underground water.

Most plants in other places lose lots of water through their leaves, but desert plants must save water. Some of them have special "watertight" leaves. Other plants lose their leaves in dry periods.

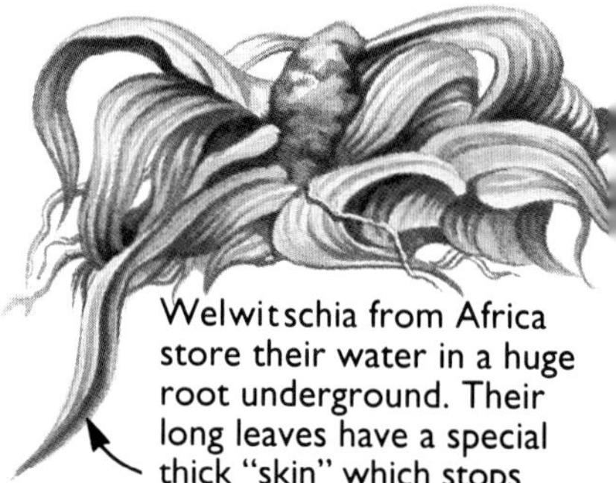

Welwitschia from Africa store their water in a huge root underground. Their long leaves have a special thick "skin" which stops water from getting out.

Water for the animals

All animals get some water from their food, and this is enough for many small desert animals. But most birds and larger animals, such as camels and foxes, also need to visit waterholes to drink. Some of them can last a long time between drinks, and they save as much water as possible.

Many desert birds, such as Australian budgerigars, gather to drink at waterholes in huge flocks every morning.

Most animals lose lots of water in their droppings. Camels have very dry droppings. This helps them save water and last for days between drinks.

When they reach water, camels can drink 123 litres (27 gallons) in ten minutes. This is about two-thirds of a bath-tub full.

Saguaro cacti have a spongy stem which swells up full of water after a rainy period. Most plants make food in their leaves. Cacti do not have leaves. They can make food in their green stems instead.

Cactus spines are dead and hard to stop water from being lost. They also protect the plant from being eaten by animals.
Sometimes dew (drops of water from the air) forms on the cacti. The water runs down to the ground and is taken up by the roots.

The ocotillo cannot store water, but it can make food in its green stem, as well as in its leaves. As soon as the rain-water begins to dry up it drops its leaves to save water.

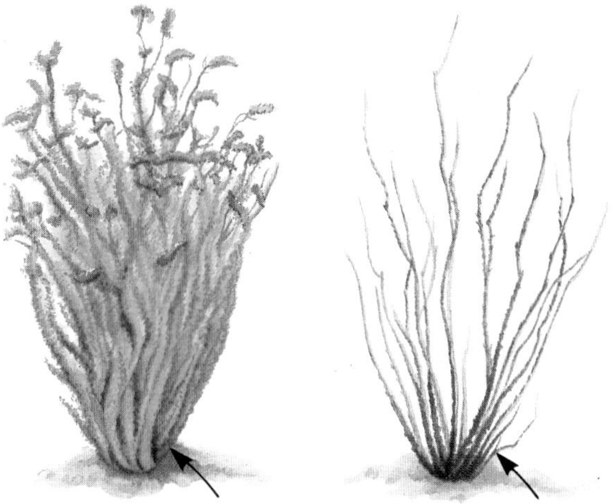
Ocotillo after rain falls
Ocotillo once rain dries up

Many desert rodents*, such as gerbils, never need to drink. They get water from their food and lose only a little water in their very dry droppings.

Gerbil

All reptiles* and insects have a thick skin that stops water from being lost from inside their bodies. This means they need less water. Many of them do not need to drink.

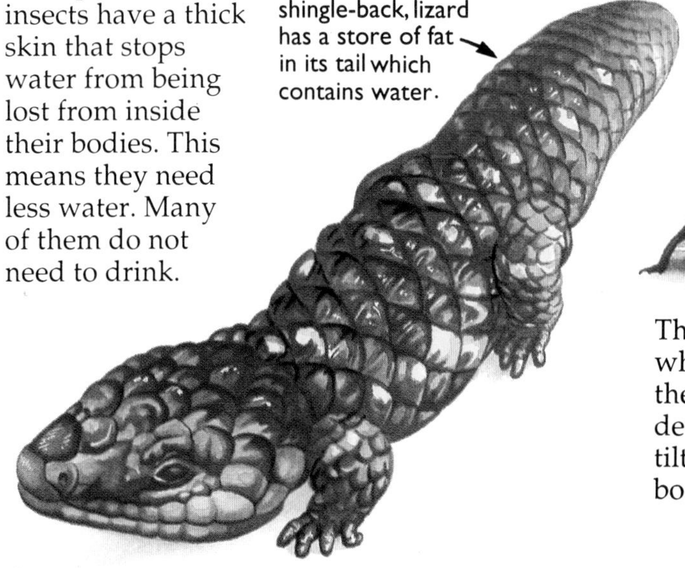
The Australian stumpy-tailed, or shingle-back, lizard has a store of fat in its tail which contains water.

Hunting animals and birds, such as coyotes, roadrunners and shrikes, get some water from the bodies of their prey, but they still have to drink.

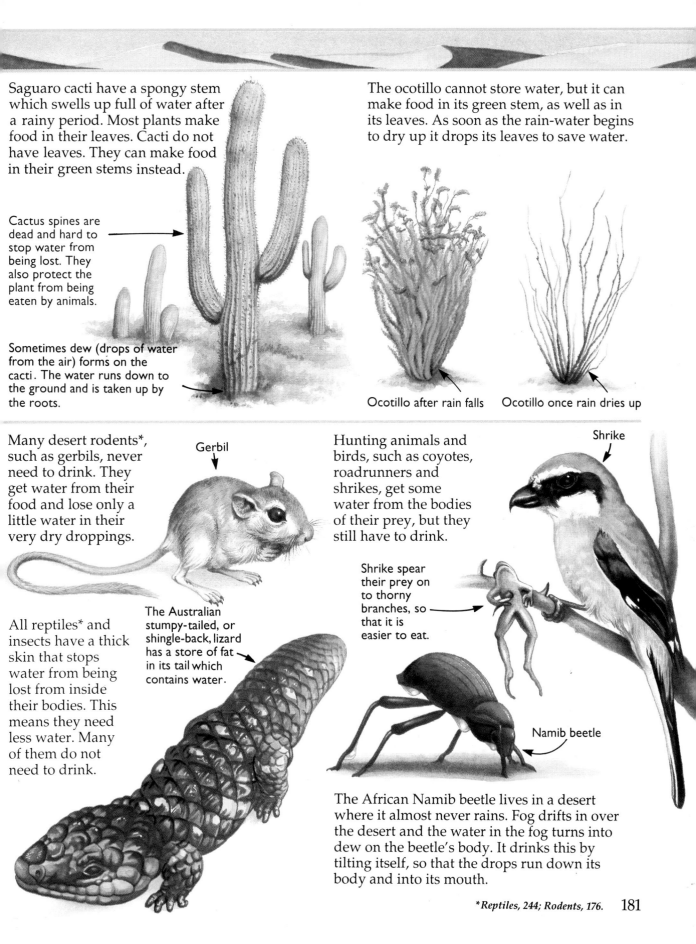

Shrike
Shrike spear their prey on to thorny branches, so that it is easier to eat.

Namib beetle

The African Namib beetle lives in a desert where it almost never rains. Fog drifts in over the desert and the water in the fog turns into dew on the beetle's body. It drinks this by tilting itself, so that the drops run down its body and into its mouth.

Coping with desert temperatures

Desert animals have to be able to cope with the huge changes in temperature each day. Different kinds of animals do this in different ways. Lots of them take shelter during the worst times of day. Some others have special things about their bodies to help them survive.

Body temperature

All animals move around and hunt for food best when their bodies are at a certain temperature. This "best" temperature is different for different kinds of animals.

Desert
Roadrunner

Antarctic

Some animals, such as insects and reptiles*, are called **cold-blooded** animals. Their bodies are always slightly warmer than their surroundings. If it is cold, they are cold. If it is warm, they are warm. When they begin to get too cold they move to a warmer place. When they begin to get too hot they move to a cooler place. They have to do this because if their bodies get too cold or too hot they will die.

Cold-blooded animals, such as lizards, sunbathe in the morning to warm up.

Lizards move into the shade when it gets too hot.

Other animals, such as birds and mammals*, can keep themselves at their "best" temperature all the time. They are called **warm-blooded** animals. They use the energy they get from food to make heat to warm their bodies. They cool down by losing water from their skin, or **sweating**.

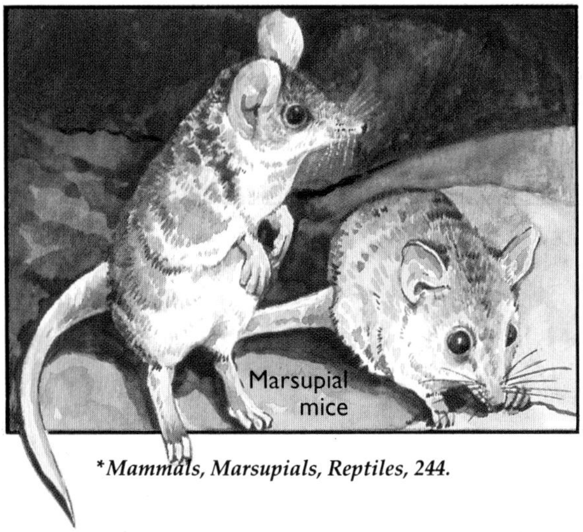
Marsupial mice

Warm-blooded desert animals, such as Australian marsupial* mice, can hunt for food at night even though it is very cold. They can do this because of the heat they make inside themselves.

**Mammals, Marsupials, Reptiles, 244.*

Keeping cool

Warm-blooded animals can control their body temperature, but they cannot afford to lose too much water keeping cool. In the desert in the hottest part of the day, many of them move into the shade, like cold-blooded animals do.

Fennec fox

The African fennec fox spends the hot day resting in burrows. It comes out to hunt for food at night. It can hear very well with its huge ears, and this helps it hunt in the darkness.

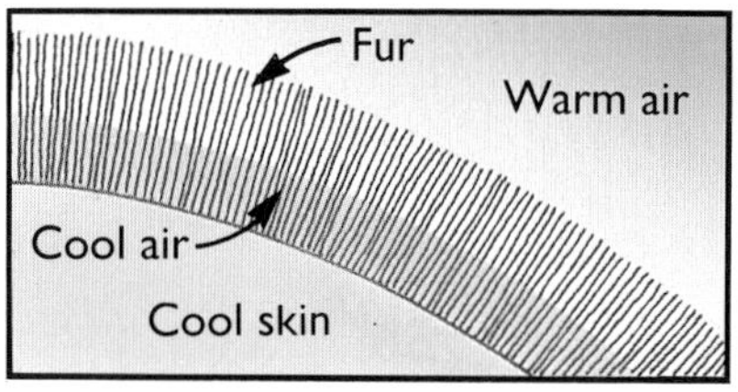
Fur
Warm air
Cool air
Cool skin

As with all furry animals, its fur keeps it warm in the cold, but also helps it keep cool in the heat. The fur traps a layer of air which stops cold air from reaching its warm skin, or hot air from reaching its cool skin.

Some peccaries live in American deserts. They spend the hottest part of the day resting in the shade in order to save water. They also scrape shallow holes in the soil to lie in.

Peccary

Like fennec foxes, American jackrabbits have large ears with lots of blood vessels close to the surface. Animals lose heat into the air from surface blood vessels, so the more there are the more heat can be lost.

Birds have to protect their eggs from getting too hot. Malee fowl bury their eggs under mounds of sand and keep testing how hot it is inside. They scrape away sand or pile more on, to keep their eggs at the right temperature.

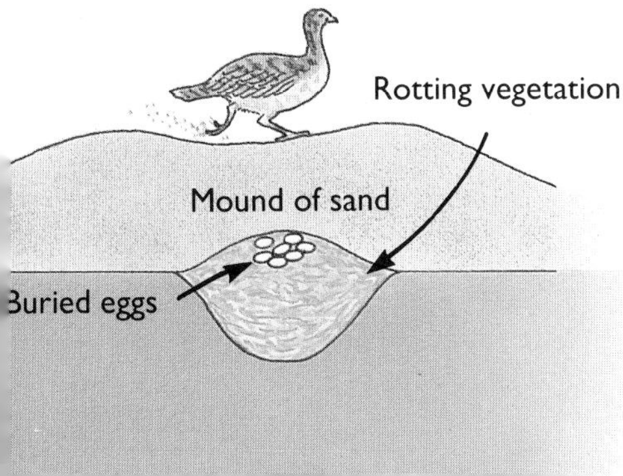
Rotting vegetation
Mound of sand
Buried eggs

Birds' feathers help them to keep cool in the heat as well as warm in the cold, in the same way that fur does for animals.

Malee fowl

Large animals

The few large, warm-blooded animals cannot burrow under the ground to get out of the heat and there isn't enough shade to keep them cool.

Instead they can let their bodies heat up past their "best" temperature during the day, and cool down past it at night. Other smaller animals would suffer if they did this.

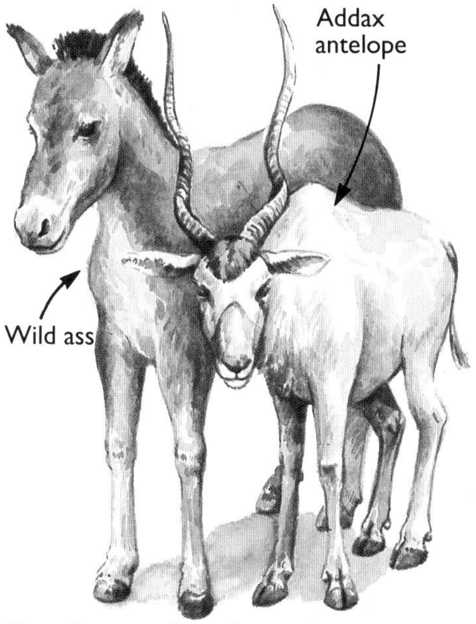
Addax
antelope
Wild ass

They have pale coloured coats because pale colours do not heat up as quickly in bright sunshine as dark ones.

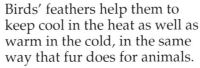

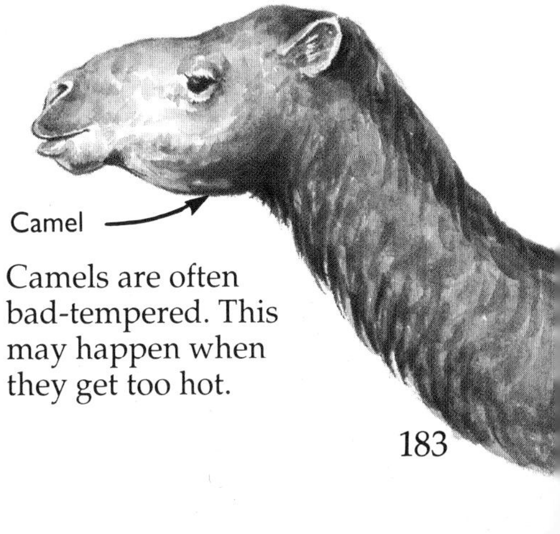
Camel

Camels are often bad-tempered. This may happen when they get too hot.

Rain in the desert

After rain falls in the desert, many plants flower and new plants grow quickly from seeds under the ground. Animals that have hidden underground during the long dry periods come out to feed on the new plants, and to produce their young.

Insects feed on plants and at the same time pollinate* the new flowers, which then make thousands of new seeds. Many of these seeds and new young animals are eaten by other animals, but a few survive.

Desert toads and shrimps

Toads need water to lay their eggs in, and shrimps live in water. Millions of years ago some deserts were covered in water and many toads and shrimps lived there. Over thousands of years the water dried up but a few kinds of toads and shrimps changed so that they could cope with the dryness. There are still desert toads and shrimps today.

The spadefoot toad digs itself underground to survive the dryness. It comes out when it rains, to mate and lay its eggs.

Insect life

All insects lay eggs. In some cases, such as flies and moths, the young that hatch look very different from the adults. For more about these, see pages 190-191. The young of other insects, such as locusts, look similar to the adults, but do not have wings. Many desert animals eat them.

Locusts are desert grasshoppers. They mate and lay their eggs in the soft ground just after it rains.

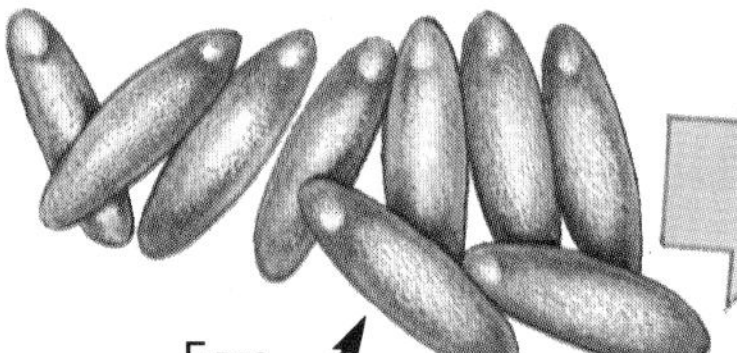
Eggs

The young that hatch soon after the eggs are laid are called **hoppers** (they have no wings). Like all insects, they have hard skins that cannot stretch. As they grow, they have to change their skin for a new, bigger one.

Hopper

They do this by growing a new, soft skin under the hard one. When this new skin is ready, the old one splits and the insect climbs out. The new, stretchy skin hardens in a few hours.

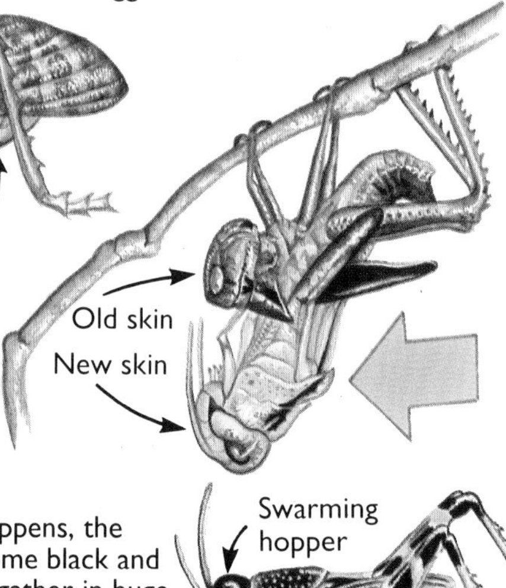
Old skin
New skin

Most locust young feed and live by themselves. Sometimes, though, many hoppers find themselves close to each other and short of food.

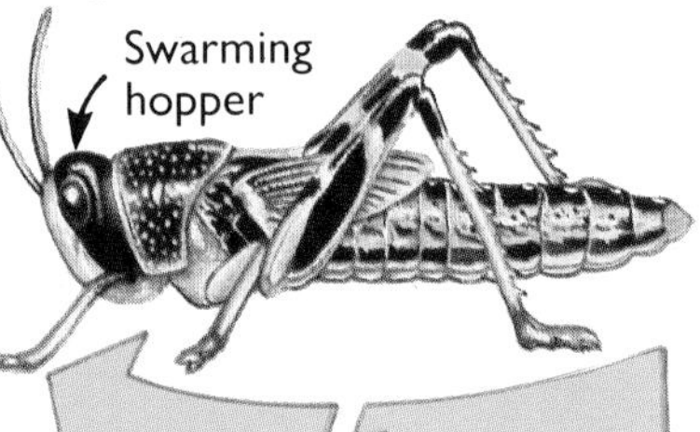
Swarming hopper

When this happens, the hoppers become black and yellow. They gather in huge groups, called **swarms**. Then they march in search of food. They eat any plants they find and do great damage to crops.

Locusts change skins five times as they grow up. The last time, a winged adult climbs out. When it next rains, the cycle starts again.

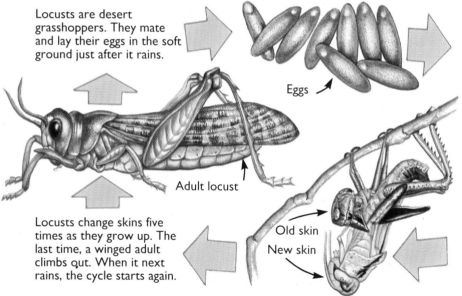

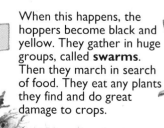

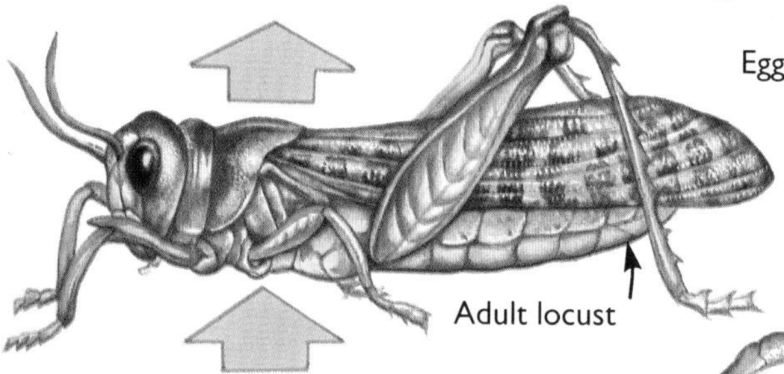
Adult locust

**Pollination, 142.*

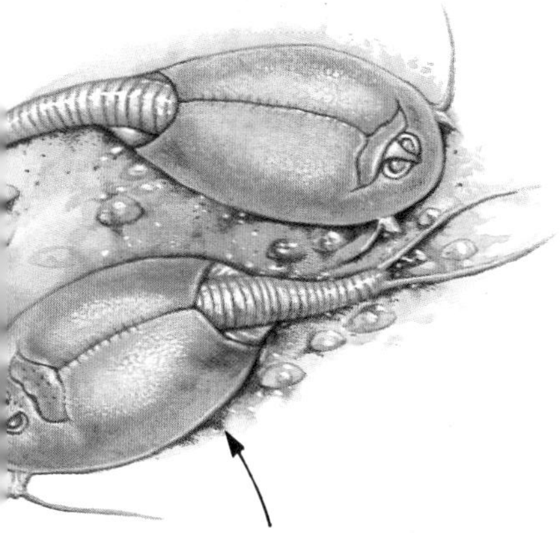

Desert shrimp eggs survive in dried-up mud until it rains. Then the shrimps hatch, grow up fast and lay their eggs in puddles before they die.

Flowers in the desert

Many desert plants produce their flowers after rain. Some plants first grow quickly, from tough seeds that have lain in the ground during the long, dry period. The flowers produce lots of new seeds before the rain-water dries up.

The Australian sungold grows quickly, covering the ground after rain falls.

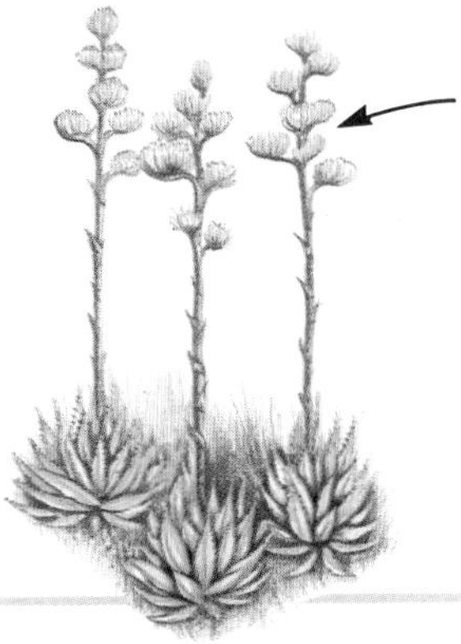

North American century plants grow for about 15 years before flowering. Then when it rains, they flower and produce seeds very fast. New plants grow from the seeds. The old plants die.

Scorpions catch their insect prey with their front pincers and kill it with a sting from their tail.

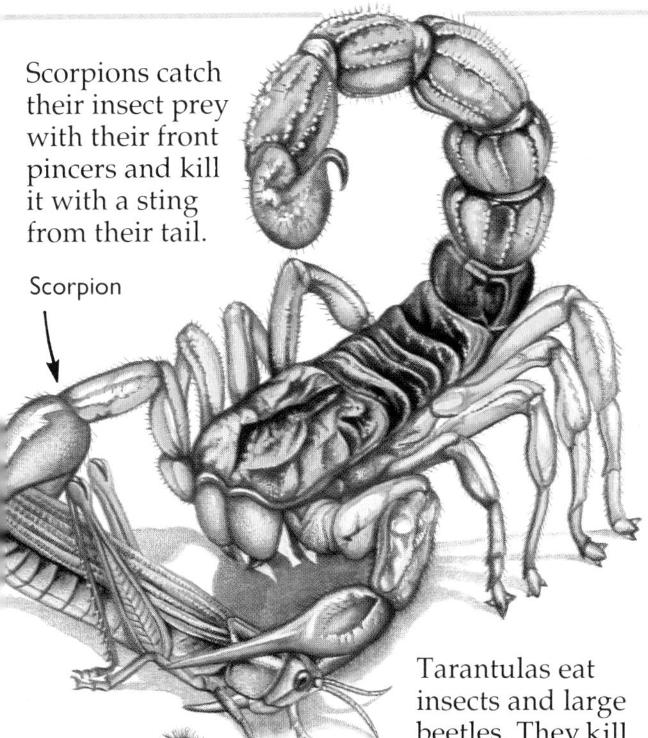

Scorpion

Tarantulas eat insects and large beetles. They kill their prey with a poisonous bite.

Tarantula

Growing deserts

Plants are very important in dry areas. Their roots soak up any rain that falls and trap the soil, stopping it from being blown or washed away.

In the 1920s, large areas of American grassland were cleared for farmland.

Later there were several hot, dry years in a row. The crops died. Farmers kept on ploughing their fields to plant new crops and the soil became very dry.

Strong winds blew away so much of the soil that no new plants could grow, even in the wet years. The area became a "desert", called the dust bowl.

In the last 100 years, the area of "desert" around the world has doubled. Some places have become desert because the weather changed. Others, such as the dust bowl in America, have changed because the plants were cleared and the soil destroyed. If too many people try to farm or graze their animals in very dry areas then even more land may become desert.

Temperate forests

Nearly a third of the land surface on Earth is covered by forests. Forests grow naturally wherever there is enough water for trees to grow, and are home to many other plants and lots of animals. Temperate forests are ones that grow between the tropics and polar regions.

Types of trees

There are two main kinds of trees, deciduous and evergreen trees.

Deciduous trees shed all their leaves at one time, so they are bare for part of the year. They rest during this time. They grow new leaves when there is enough sun and rain for them to grow.

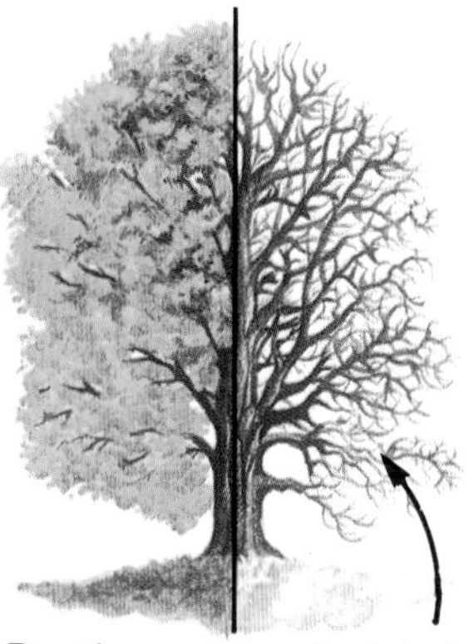

Deciduous trees shed their leaves and rest for part of the year.

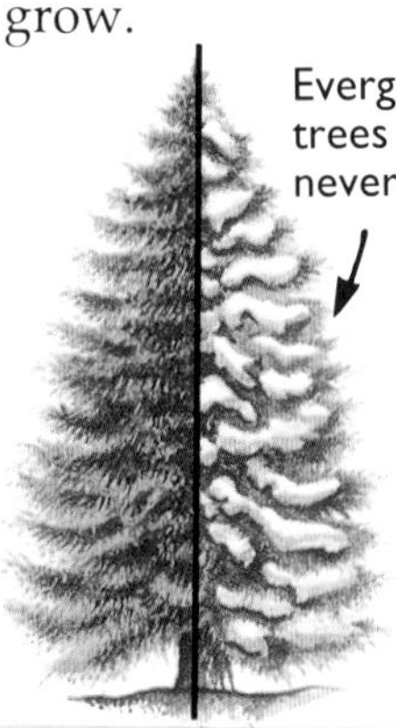

Evergreen trees are never bare.

Evergreen trees keep their leaves for several years and lose them gradually, while growing new ones, so they are never bare.

Which trees grow where?

The biggest, most common species of tree in a forest is called the **dominant species**. Different species can survive different amounts of cold and dryness, so temperate forests have different dominant species in different areas.

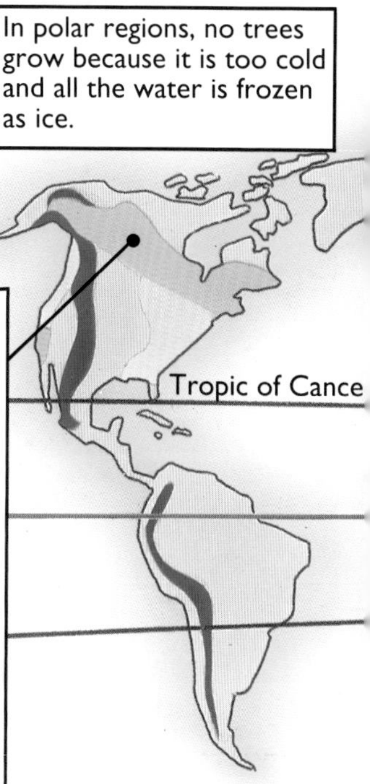
Evergreen forest
Deciduous forest
Mountain forests (see page 207)
In polar regions, no trees grow because it is too cold and all the water is frozen as ice.
Tropic of Cance

Just south of the Arctic Circle there are huge evergreen forests. The dominant species, such as pine, fir and spruce, can survive freezing winters.

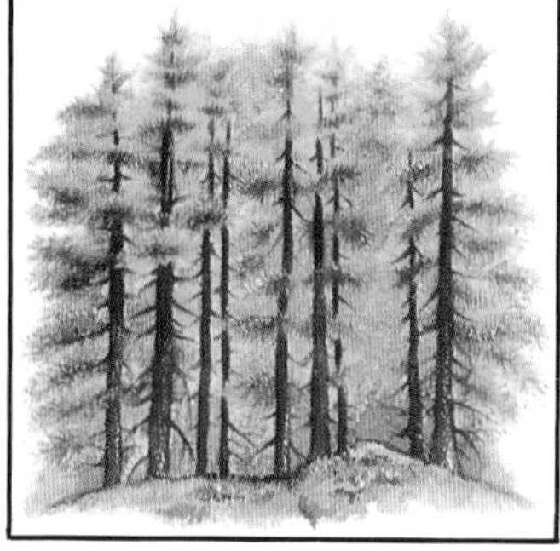

Seasons

All temperate areas have four seasons. The trees and most other forest plants grow in a yearly cycle. They grow new leaves in spring, flowers and new leaf-buds in summer and seeds in the autumn. The lives of forest animals follow a yearly cycle too.

In spring the trees grow new leaves. Many animals produce their young.

In summer many forest plants flower. Insects such as bees and butterflies feed on the nectar. Bees pollinate* the flowers as they feed. Then the plants begin to grow seeds.

*Pollination, 142.

Deciduous trees, such as beech, oak and maple, grow best where summers are warm and winters not too cold. They grow in a broad band across Asia, Europe and North America.

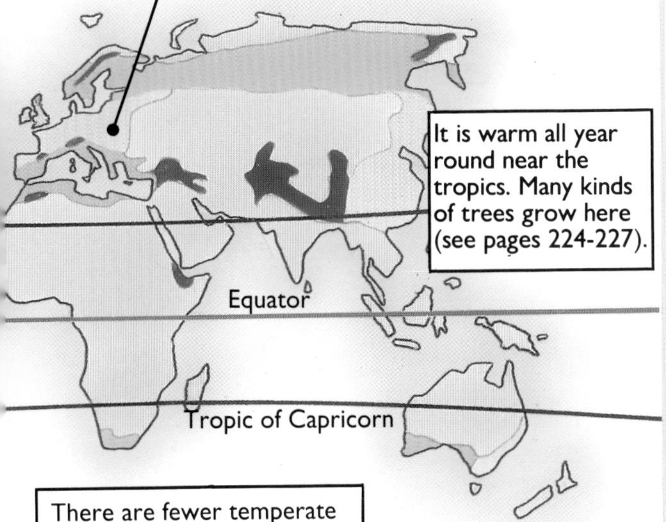

It is warm all year round near the tropics. Many kinds of trees grow here (see pages 224-227).

There are fewer temperate forests south of the tropics because there is a lot less land in the southern half of the Earth.

Caring for forests

Two thousand years ago, forests covered a lot of Europe, America and Asia, but most have now been lost. For instance, less than ten per cent of Britain's forests are left.

As the number of people grew, more and more wanted to live on the land and farm crops, so they cut down the forests.

They still needed wood for building and other uses. They found if they chopped down trees, such as hazel, but left stumps with roots in the ground, the trees grew new stems quickly.

They cut off these stems every few years, though some trees were left to grow naturally. There were trees of many different ages and many animals lived among them.

Today many people farm fast-growing evergreen trees instead. They plant hundreds of new young trees in huge areas. These are not true forests, because all the trees are the same kind. Few animals can live in them.

In autumn many animals, such as European badgers, feast on ripe fruit, berries and seeds. They store up food, which they can use during winter. Deciduous trees shed their leaves.

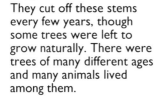

In winter, deciduous trees are bare and there is little food for animals. Many of them migrate (make long journeys) to warmer, winter feeding grounds. Others hibernate (rest) until spring.

Deciduous forests

Most temperate deciduous forests grow in Europe, Asia or North America where summers are long and warm, and winters wet and not too cold. They are home to huge numbers of animals, many of which are tiny insects. One oak tree can house over 4,000 species, including plants, insects and other animals.

Deciduous trees

There are many different kinds of deciduous trees. Most have broad, flat leaves and their seeds grow inside a case. Berries and fruits that people eat, such as plums, apples, figs and oranges, are all cases with seeds inside. Many seeds grow inside other kinds of cases, too.

Most fruits contain seeds.

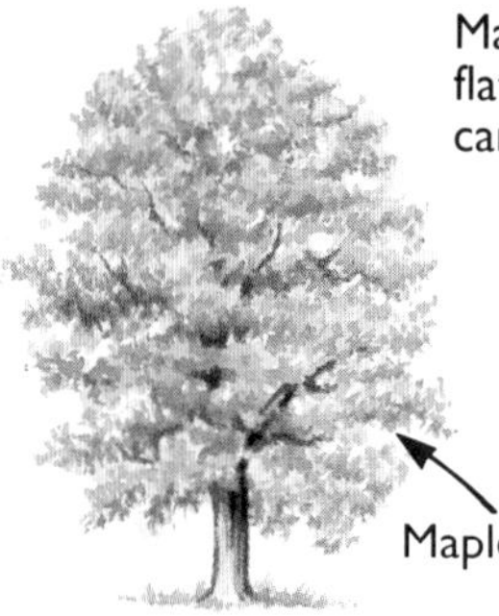
Maple tree

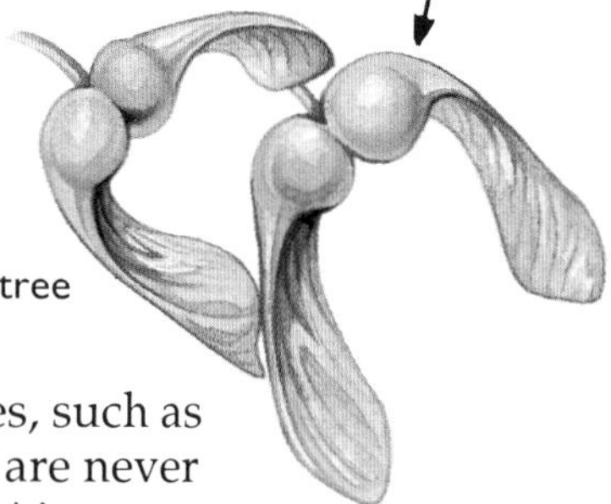
Maple and sycamore seeds have thin, flat cases, which help them to be carried away in the wind.

Many deciduous trees, such as alder and hawthorn, are never the dominant species* in a forest. Instead they grow in scattered places, where conditions are not right for the dominant species to grow.

Alder trees often grow in marshy areas.

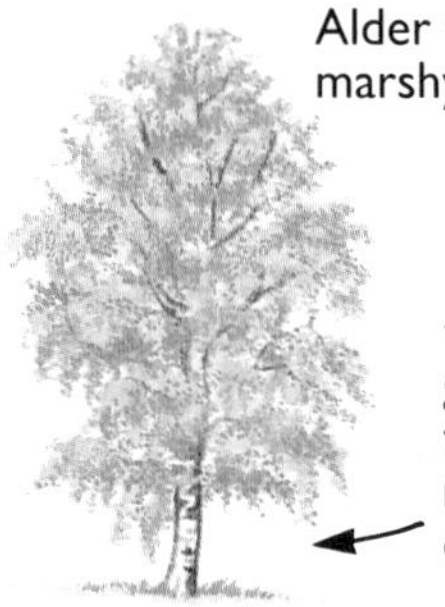
Birch trees are very tough. They can grow a long way further north than most other deciduous trees.

A European oak forest

Oak trees are the dominant species* in oak forests. Their flat, broad, delicate leaves let some light filter through to the forest floor, where many smaller plants grow.

The forest is made up of different layers of plants. Many animals find their food in only one or two layers of the forest; others can move between all the layers.

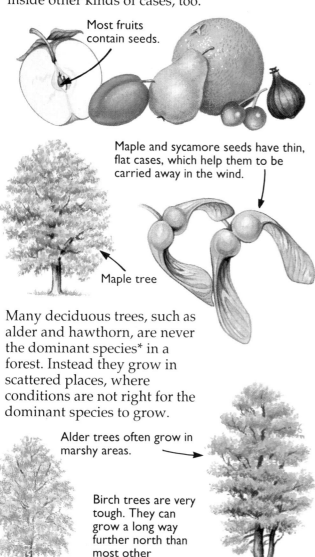

The roof of the forest is made up of the leaves and branches of the tallest trees. This part of the forest is called the **canopy**.
Small trees and bushes grow between the oaks. This is called the **shrub layer**. Some of them, such as holly and rhododendron, are evergreen.
Many small mammals* and birds, such as woodmice, wrens and nightingales, live in the shrub layer. Many male birds sing in spring to attract females.
Woodmouse
Wren
The trees lose their leaves in autumn. Huge amounts of leaf litter (dead plant material) build up on the ground under the trees.

 Dominant species, 186; Mammals, 244.

Many insects live in the canopy, feeding on the wood, leaves and seeds.
Weevil
Butterfly
Many birds, such as jays, build their nests in the canopy, and feed on plant material or insects.
Old dead trees are often used for shelter by birds, such as owls, and other forest animals.
Owl
There are trees of all different ages in a forest. When an old tree dies and falls down, more light gets through into the clearing that is made. Many bushes and new young trees grow quickly to fill the gap.
A few plants, such as ferns, mosses, algae and lichens, grow on the trunks of the oak trees.
Squirrels move between the layers by running up and down tree trunks.
Only adult male deer have antlers. They grow a new pair each summer.
Many young forest animals, such as deer, have spotted coats that blend into the background of light and shade in a forest. This helps them to hide from hunters.
Small streams run through the forest. Different plants, such as willow trees and rushes, grow on the banks where the ground is much wetter.

Up in the canopy

In the spring and summer, the leafy layer of a deciduous forest traps lots of sunshine to make food for the trees. The trees use this food to grow. The canopy fills up with insects. Many of them feed on the new plant material. They are hunted by larger animals, such as birds.

Thousands of insects

Every deciduous tree is home to many different kinds of insects. Many adult insects lay their eggs in spring or early summer. They lay them on or close to the kind of food that their young eat. This means when their young hatch there is lots of food for them.

Ichneumon wasp young are carnivores (they eat meat). The adults lay their eggs in wood-tunnelling grubs. They use a long pointed tube to inject their eggs through the wood.

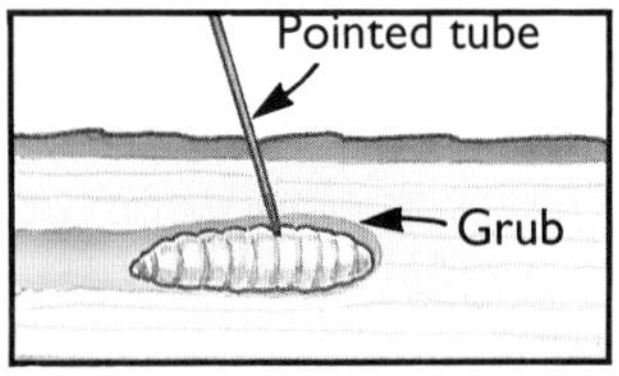
Pointed tube
Grub

When the wasp young hatch they eat the grub's insides. They come out through the grub's skin when they are fully grown. The grub dies.

No one really knows how the adult insects manage to find the wood-tunnelling grubs under the bark.

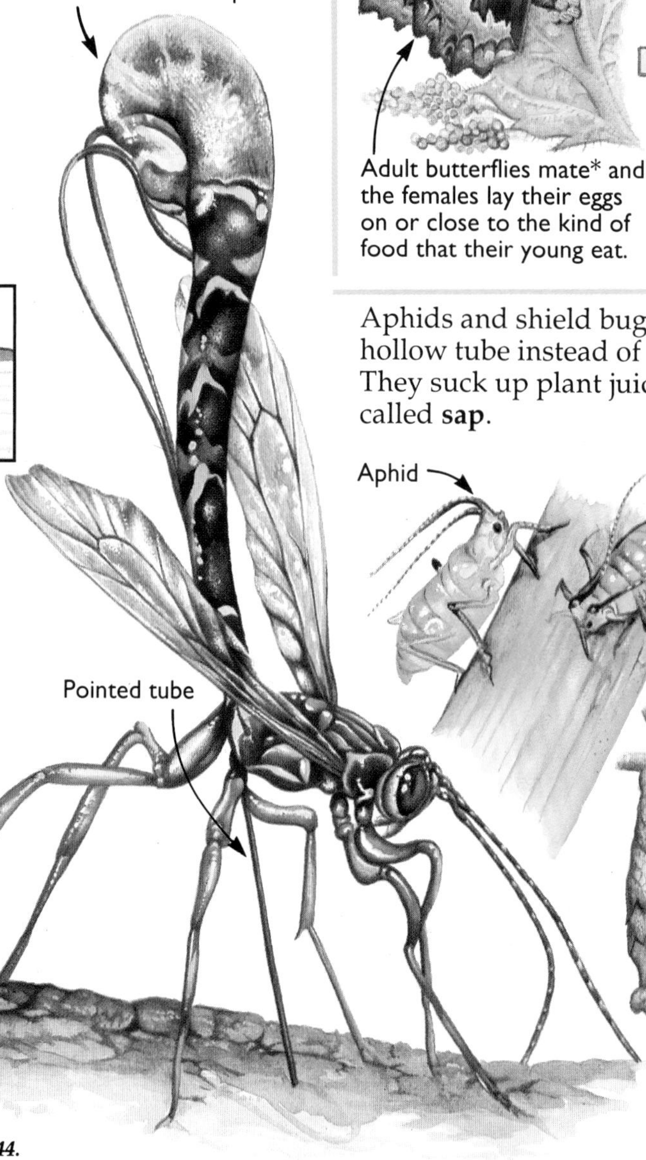
Ichneumon wasp
Pointed tube

Insect life

Some insect young, such as those of locusts and aphids, look similar to their parents. Others, such as grubs and caterpillars, look very different. They are called larvae*.

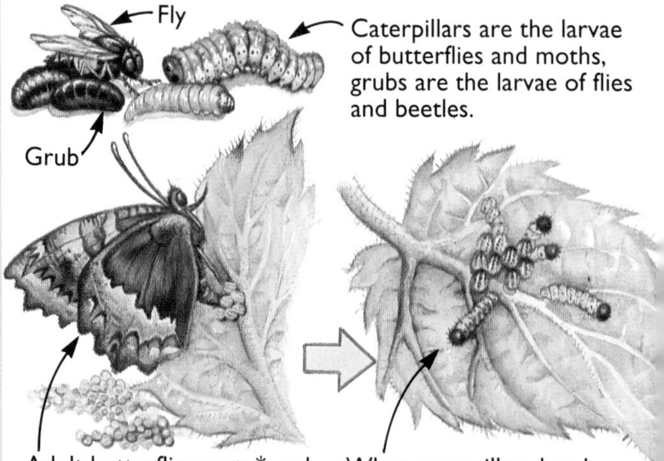
Fly
Grub
Caterpillars are the larvae of butterflies and moths, grubs are the larvae of flies and beetles.
Adult butterflies mate* and the females lay their eggs on or close to the kind of food that their young eat.
When caterpillars hatch, they are tiny. They have strong jaws and start eating leaves right away.

Aphids and shield bugs have a hollow tube instead of a mouth. They suck up plant juices, called **sap**.

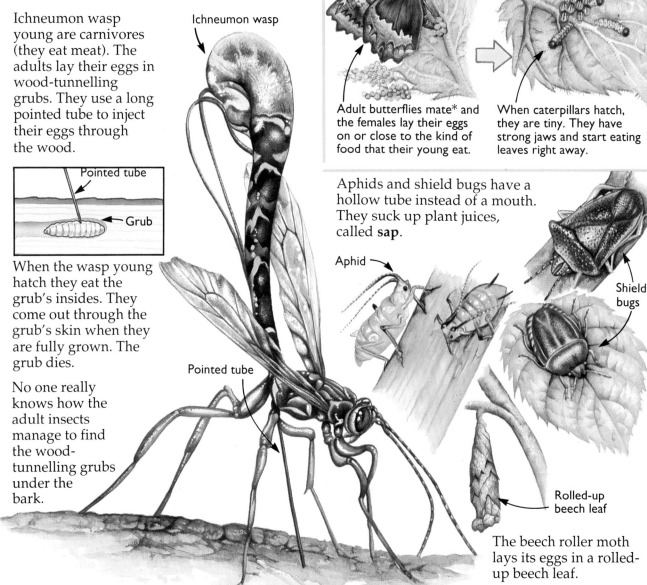

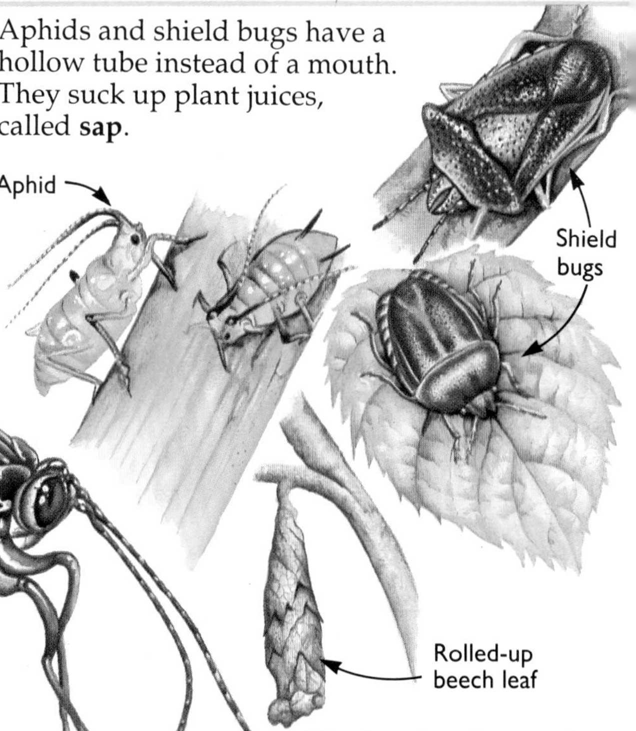
Aphid
Shield bugs
Rolled-up beech leaf

The beech roller moth lays its eggs in a rolled-up beech leaf.

 ****Larvae, 145; Mating, 144.***

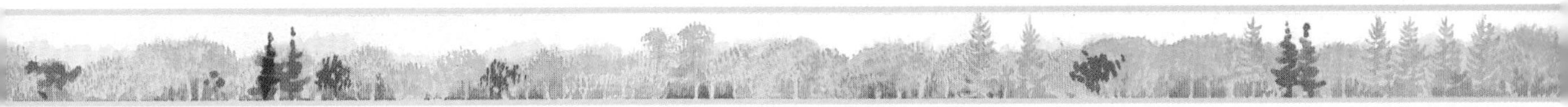

As they eat, they grow. Their skins cannot stretch, so they keep growing new larger ones under the old one, which then splits and falls off.

The last time a caterpillar sheds its skin, the new skin quickly hardens. It is now a pupa. Inside it changes into an adult.

When the hard skin of the pupa splits, the adult butterfly comes out. It rests for a short time, while its soft wings swell up and harden, before flying off.

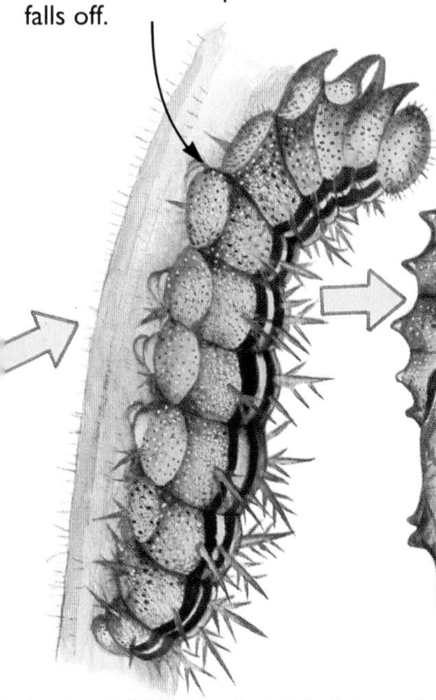

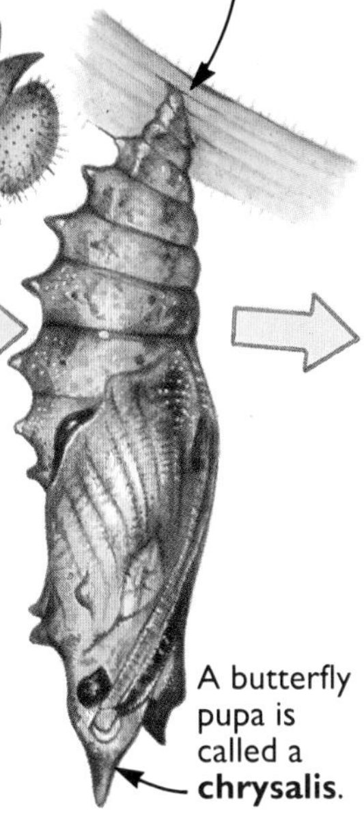

A butterfly pupa is called a **chrysalis**.

The whole process of change is called **metamorphosis**.

In temperate forests, many insects spend winter as a pupa. The adults come out in spring. But insects vary a lot. Some adults live for several years, so there may be larvae, pupae and adults in the canopy at the same time.

Some tiny insects, called leaf miners, lay their eggs into the middle of a leaf.

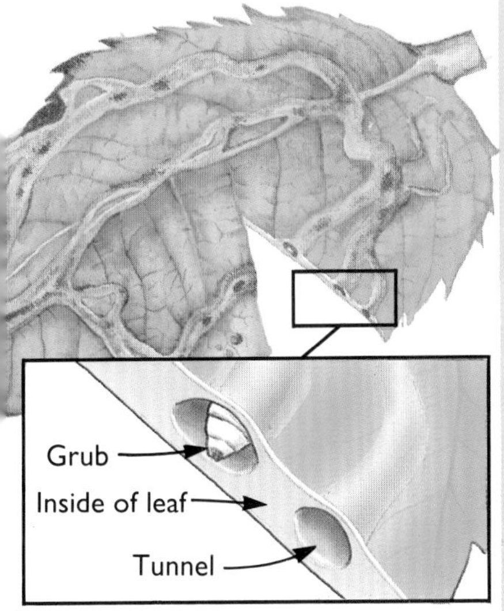

Their tiny young tunnel their way through the inside of the leaf, by eating it. The tunnels show up as winding line patterns on the leaf.

Birds and other animals

Many birds and animals live and feed in the canopy. They have home patches, or **territories**, which they defend from rivals that might compete for food, places to live or mates.

For most of the year, groups of long-tailed tits fly around in a forest looking for food. They keep together by calling to each other.

Long-tailed tits

Woodpecker

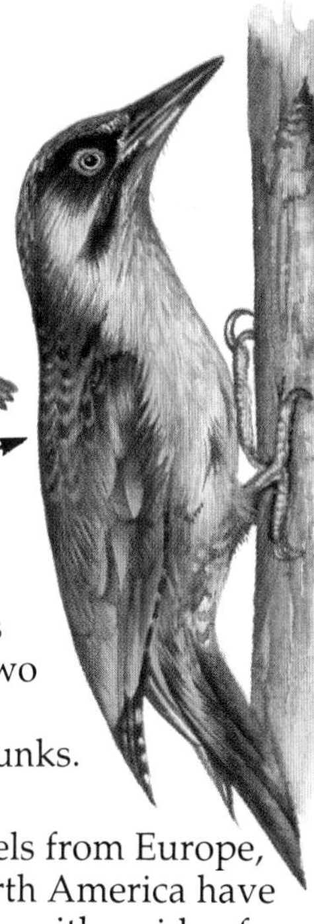

Woodpeckers feed on wood-tunnelling grubs. Their feet have two toes pointing forward and two backwards. This helps them to walk up tree trunks.

Flying squirrel

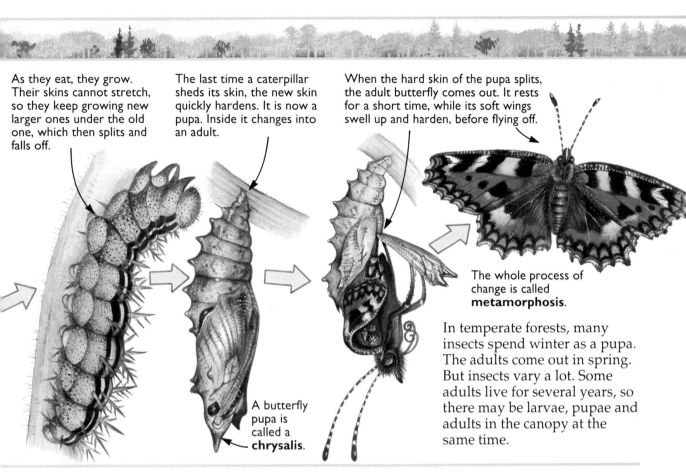

Flying squirrels from Europe, Asia, and North America have flaps of skin on either side of their body. These help them to glide from tree to tree.

The forest floor

In deciduous forests, large amounts of dead leaves and wood fall to the ground every autumn. This forms the leaf litter. By the beginning of spring it has nearly all rotted away and the trees are growing new leaves. Many smaller plants grow between the trees. They make up the undergrowth and provide food and shelter for small and large animals.

Leaf litter animals

Many tiny animals, such as millipedes, beetles, woodlice and slugs, live among the leaf litter. They feed on the dead and rotting leaves and wood.

Slugs and snails scrape at their food with their rough tongues. They usually come out to feed at night.

Many other insects, such as beetles, feed on dead wood.

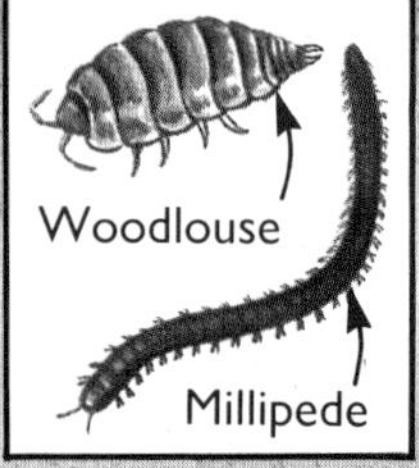

Woodlice and millipedes feed mainly on dead plants. They spend the day under stones in the damp earth.

Earthworms mix up the soil. They tunnel under the ground eating soil as they go.

Hunters on the forest floor

Hunters on the forest floor are all different sizes. Many of the tiny ones, such as spiders, are eaten by larger ones, such as shrews or foxes. Some forest hunters, such as bears, eat both meat and plants. They are **omnivores**.

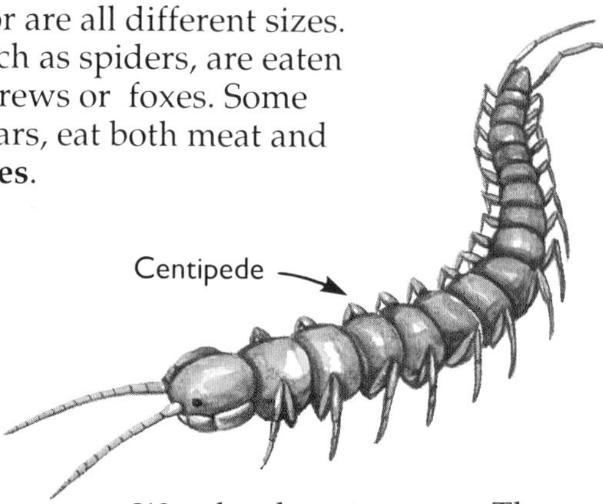

Centipedes have a pair of poison claws. They use them to kill or stun their prey.

Woodcocks eat worms. They rarely fly, but the pattern of their feathers helps them hide among the dead leaves on the ground.

Hedgehogs eat worms, snails and insects. When threatened, they roll their bodies up into a tight ball.

Moles can dig fast with their large front feet. They feed on worms and insect larvae* underground. They have very poor eyesight, but they can hear well.

 **Larvae, 145.*

How things rot

Rotting is when dead plants and animals are turned back into very simple substances by **fungi** and tiny living things called bacteria*. The substances, such as nitrates*, are then used by plants to grow new parts. In this way they are always being recycled (see pages 140-141).

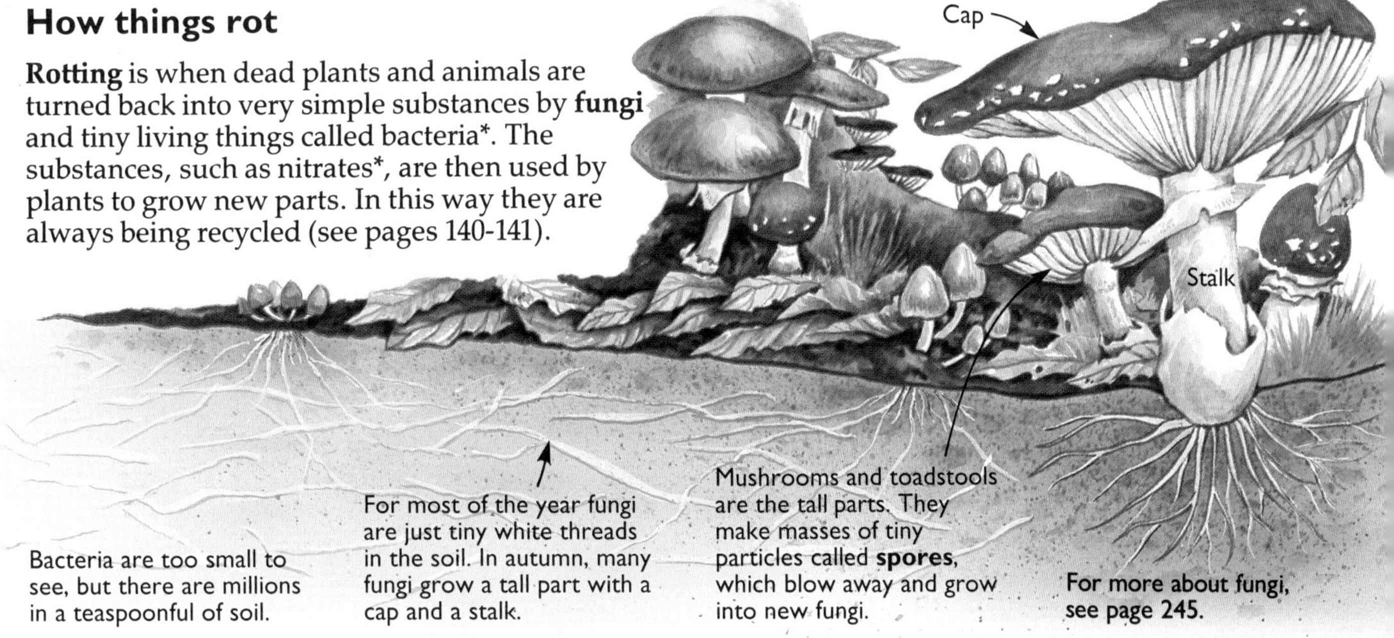

Bacteria are too small to see, but there are millions in a teaspoonful of soil.

For most of the year fungi are just tiny white threads in the soil. In autumn, many fungi grow a tall part with a cap and a stalk.

Mushrooms and toadstools are the tall parts. They make masses of tiny particles called **spores**, which blow away and grow into new fungi.

For more about fungi, see page 245.

Young opossums cling to their mother's fur.

Opossums feed on small forest floor animals, but they can also climb trees. Their tails, like some monkeys' tails, can grip things.

Wild boar use their tusks to scrape for roots, fungi and tiny animals in the leaf litter. Sometimes they kill small animals with their tusks.

Young wild boar have striped coats.

Skunks are related to weasels. They feed on insects, eggs, mice and dead animal remains. If threatened they squirt a nasty smelling liquid at attackers.

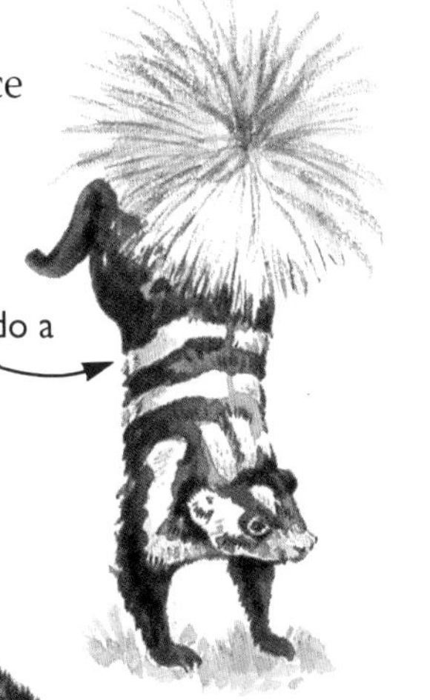

Some kinds of skunks do a handstand just before squirting this liquid.

Raccoon

Raccoons eat berries and nuts from the forest floor. They also fish from forest rivers. They hide and sleep in trees. They are distant relatives of pandas.

Bacteria, 241; Nitrates, 141.

Northern evergreen forests

North of the deciduous forests there are huge forests of evergreen trees, which cover nearly one tenth of the Earth's surface. The trees, such as pine, fir, hemlock and spruce are all types of conifers. In the northernmost parts of these conifer forests, where conditions are harshest, the trees are smallest. Beyond them is the tundra* where no trees can grow.

What are conifers?

Conifers do not produce flowers, but they still produce seeds. They are called conifers because they all grow their seeds inside cones, instead of inside fruit. There is a seed between each scale of the cone.

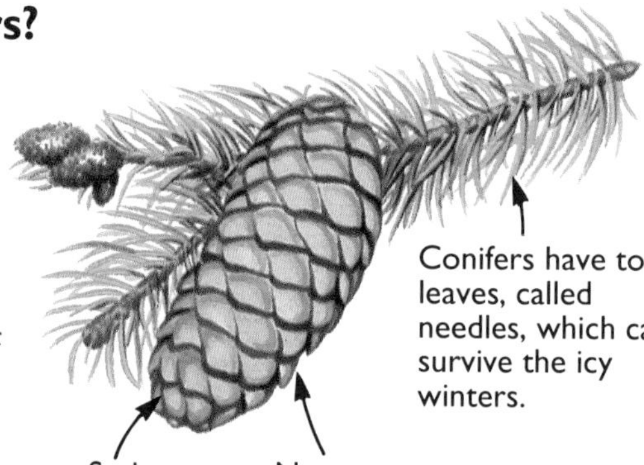

Conifers have tough leaves, called needles, which can survive the icy winters.
Scale
Norway spruce cone

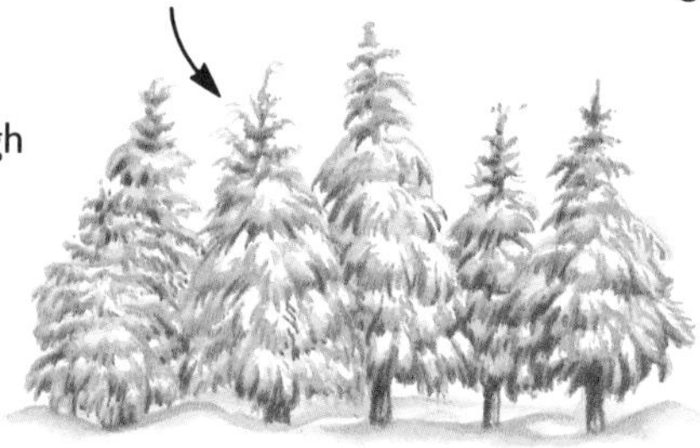

Most northern conifer trees are also shaped like cones. This means that snow slips off them more easily so the branches do not break under its weight.

Inside a conifer forest

Conifer needles rot very slowly and the soil is much poorer than the soil in a deciduous forest. The needles also grow close together on the branches, and little light filters through to the forest floor. These things mean that only a few plants can grow between the trees.

Squirrels eat plants, conifer seeds and even birds' eggs. Most of the birds feed on the insects.

Large areas of northern Canada are covered in almost untouched conifer forest.

Only a few different kinds of insects, such as pine saw flies, live in the canopy, but there are lots of them. Their young feed on the needles.

It is dark inside the forest. Only small plants such as fungi, mosses and lichens grow on the forest floor.

Spruce grouse eat conifer needles.

*Tundra, 201.

Acid rain

Huge areas of conifer forest in Europe and North America are sick and dying. Many people think that pollution from the air is harming the trees.

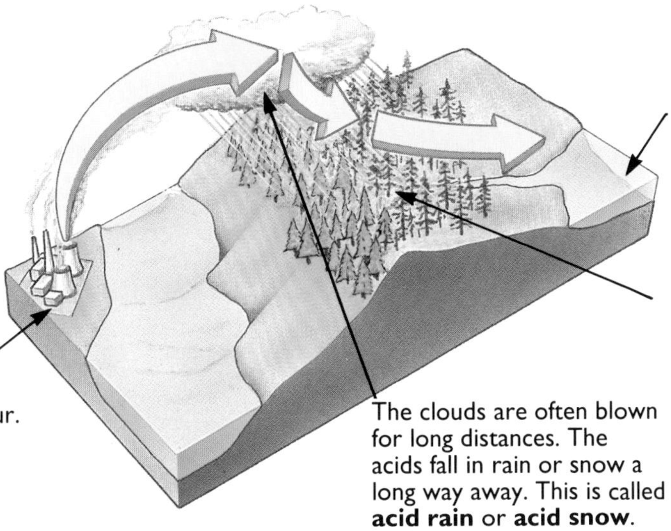

Air pollution from car exhausts, factories and power stations contains chemicals such as sulphur. These turn into substances called **acids** inside clouds.

The clouds are often blown for long distances. The acids fall in rain or snow a long way away. This is called **acid rain** or **acid snow**.

When acids are washed into lakes and rivers they harm the animals living there (for more about how, see page 215).

Acid rain harms the surface of needles, so that the trees can be killed by pests and diseases more easily. It also soaks into the earth and makes the soil poisonous, so trees cannot grow.

Hunting birds and animals of all sizes, from shrews to lynx, live in the forest.
Great grey owl
Beavers chop down trees near rivers to make their homes (for more about them, see page 218). In the process, they flood areas within the forest. The soil is rich in these marshy areas and lots of grasses and flowers grow.
Many plant-eating animals, such as moose (called elk in Europe), hares, lemmings and voles, feed on the juicy plants in and around the lakes.

Winter in the northern forests

Seasons in the northern forests are very like those on the tundra*. Summers are cool, but the days are long, which means plants can grow fast. For most of the rest of the year it is icy and the days are short. Some animals live in the forests all year, but many others come and go.

Finding plants to eat

A few animals can get enough energy to survive by eating conifer needles, bark or seeds. This means they have a year-round food supply. Most animals, though, prefer the juicier plants in clearings and marshy areas. These grow quickly in summer but are covered in snow in winter.

Capercaillies eat conifer needles. They have to spend nearly all day eating, to get enough energy from their poor food.

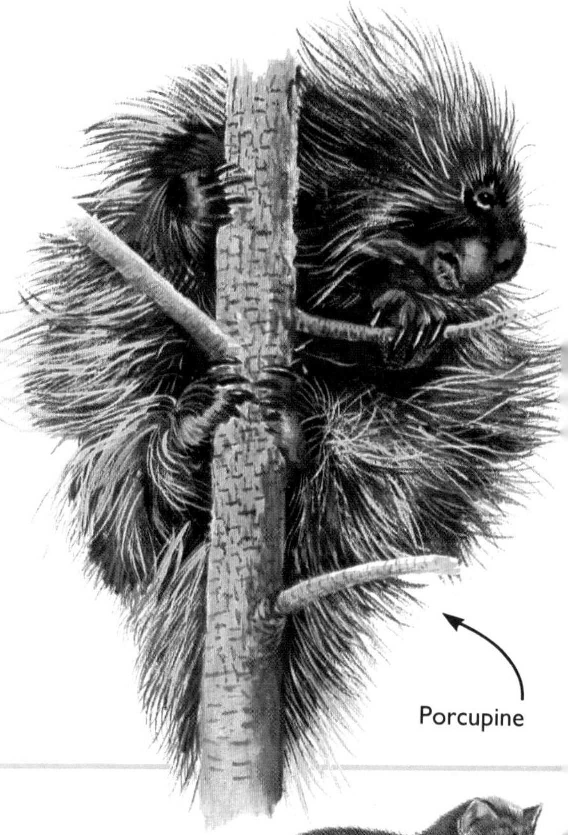

Porcupines eat tree bark. They prefer the soft young bark at the tips of branches and are good climbers.

Hunting animals

Because it is difficult to find food in winter, plant-eaters have to spread out and live alone, or in small groups. So hunters need large territories* to find enough food to survive.

Pine martens are fast and agile enough to hunt squirrels in the tree tops.

Wolverines hunt birds and other small animals, but they are very fierce and will challenge a bear or a wolf for their kill.

Eagles can have wings that are over two metres (six feet) from tip to tip. Golden eagles hunt over clearings and more open parts of the forest.

**Territories, 191; Tundra, 201.*

Chipmunks are related to squirrels. They gather food in cheek pouches. Each pouch can hold up to eight nuts in one go.

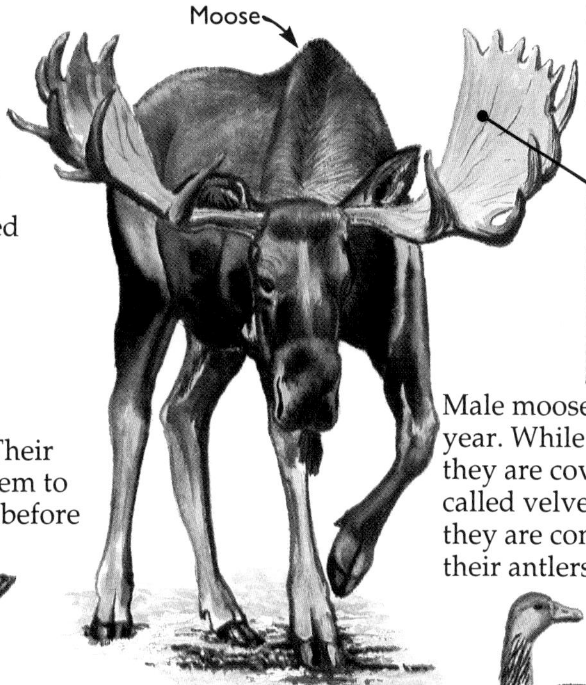

Moose prefer the juicy plants from marshy areas. In winter they have to scrape away the snow to find them.

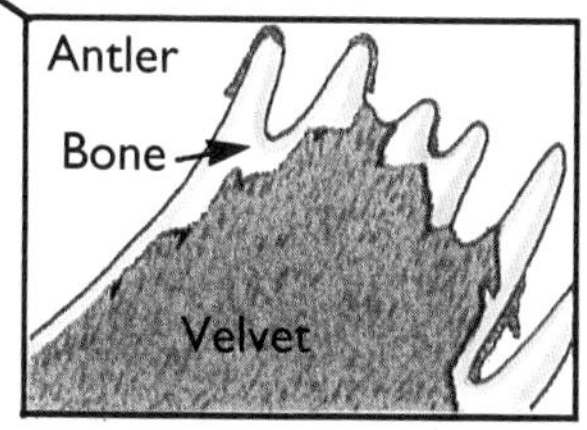

Male moose grow antlers each year. While the antlers grow they are covered in a soft layer, called velvet, which rubs off when they are complete. Males use their antlers to fight for females.

Crossbills eat seeds. Their crossed beaks help them to break open the cones before the seeds are shed.

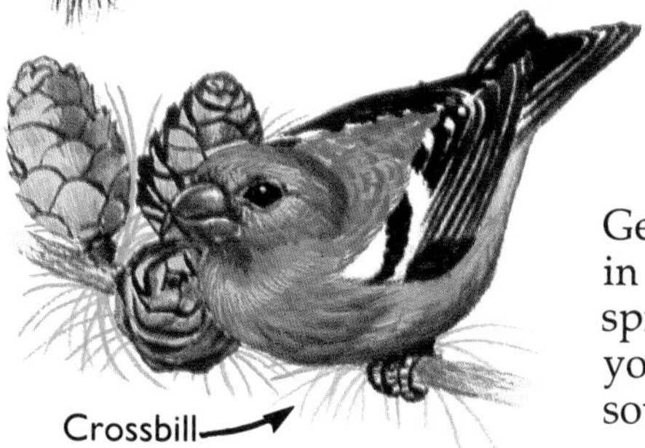

Geese fly north to feed in marshy areas in spring. They rear their young before returning south in winter.

Peregrine falcons hunt other birds in the air above the trees. They swoop on their prey from above, and kill it with a single blow.

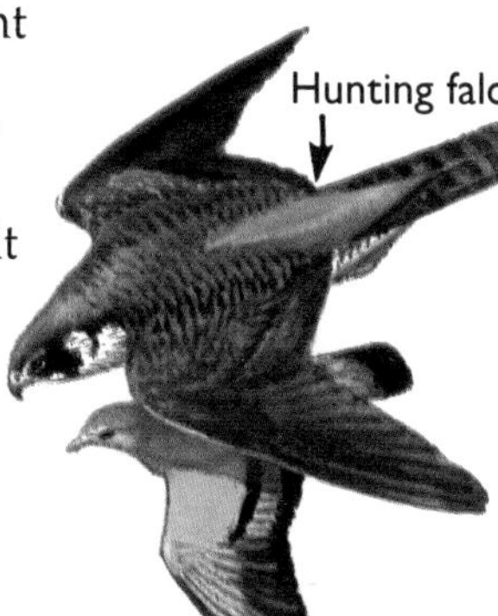

European sparrowhawks have rounded wings, to help them fly between the tree trunks. They can catch smaller birds and animals in the middle of the forest.

Threatened animals

Most conifer forest animals grow thick coats in winter and many of them used to be hunted for their fur. As they became rare, people also began to hunt more common animals, such as muskrat, skunk and fox. Today some animals are farmed and many others protected.

Sable are closely related to stoats. Their fur was used for many things, including paint brushes. Today very few remain in the wild.

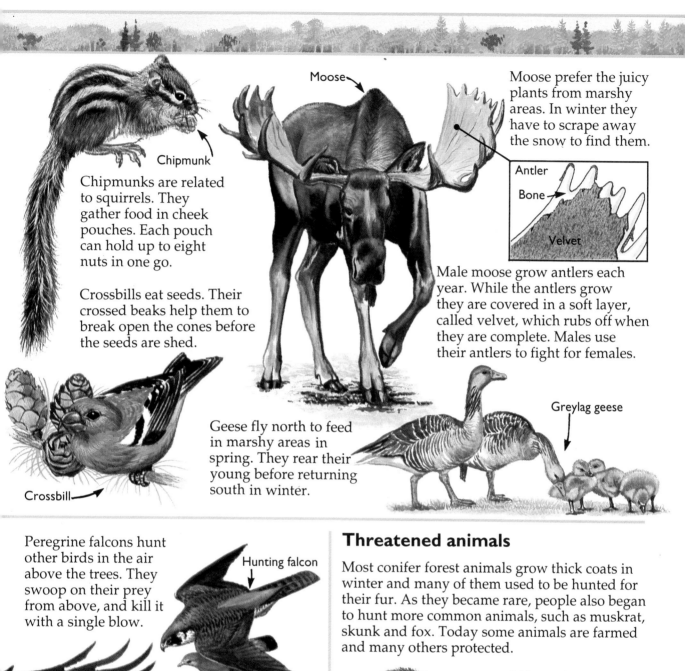

Mink are also related to stoats. In the past, farmed mink escaped to the wild. Today wild mink live close to rivers and marshy areas.

Australia's hot, dry forests

The northern part of Australia is tropical, but the south is temperate. Many Australian plants and animals live nowhere else in the world (for more about why, see page 133). Eucalyptus trees are evergreen trees with long, flat leaves. There are about 500 different species of them in Australia, many growing in forests in the south.

Many of the main forest trees, such as boxes, peppermint, stringy barks, ironbarks, gums and bloodwoods, are used for timber.

The dark line patterns on scribbly gum trunks are made by wood-tunnelling beetles.

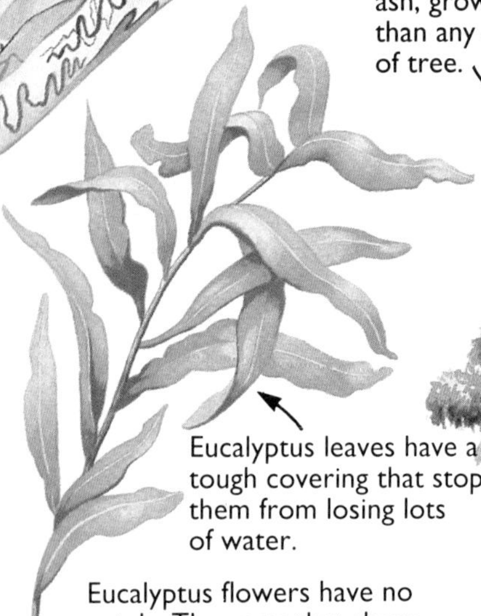

Eucalyptus leaves have a tough covering that stops them from losing lots of water.

One species of eucalyptus tree, the Australian mountain ash, grows taller than any other kind of tree.

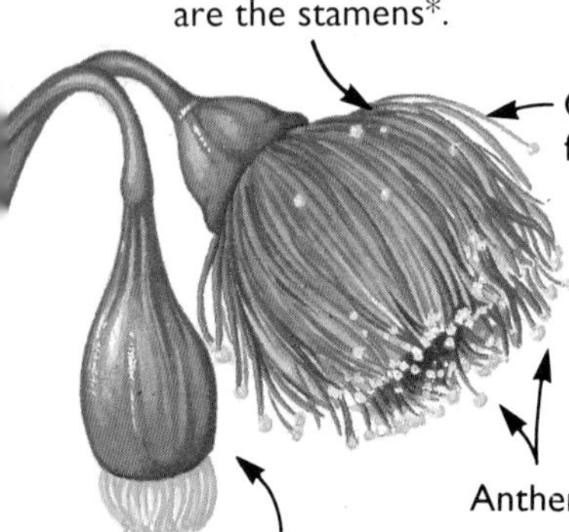

Eucalyptus flowers have no petals. The parts that show are the stamens*.

Life on the ground

Many marsupials* live in the eucalyptus forests. They live the same kind of lives as forest mammals* in other parts of the world, but lots of them look very different. Instead of deer, badgers and bears, there are animals such as wallabies, numbats and tasmanian devils.

Numbats search among the leaf litter for termites to eat.

Life in the canopy

Because eucalyptus forests are evergreen, there are leaves for food and shelter all year round. Several types of animal spend almost all their lives in the canopy. Animals that do this are called **arboreal** animals. There are also lots of birds that live and feed in the canopy.

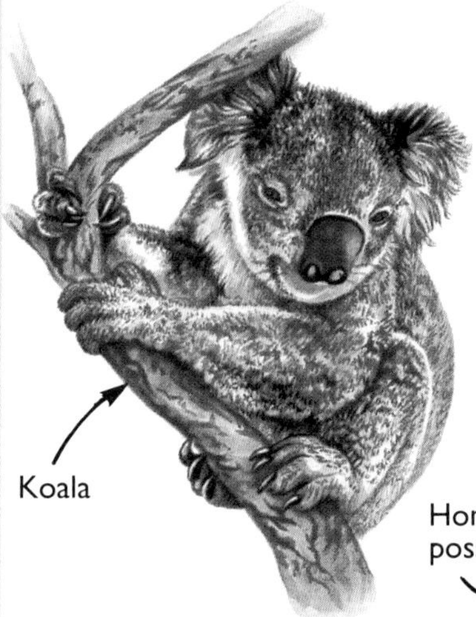

Koalas only eat eucalyptus leaves. They spend most of their lives up trees feeding. Their two thumbs help them grip onto branches.

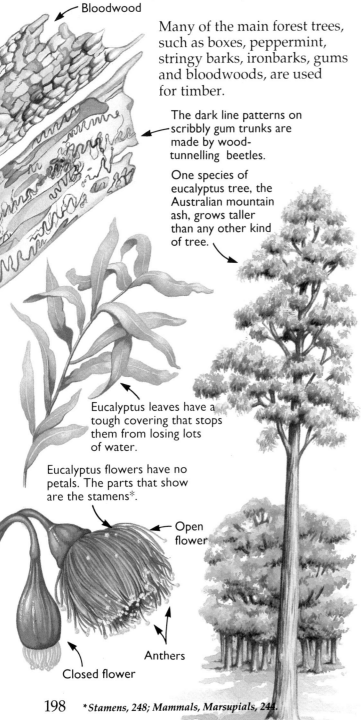

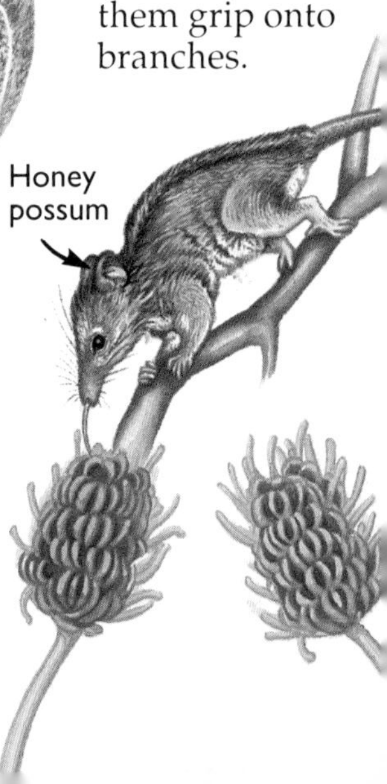

Many kinds of possum live in the canopy. The honey possum has a very long tongue and feeds on nectar in flowers. It can steady itself with its strong gripping tail.

 ***Stamens, 248; Mammals, Marsupials, 244.**

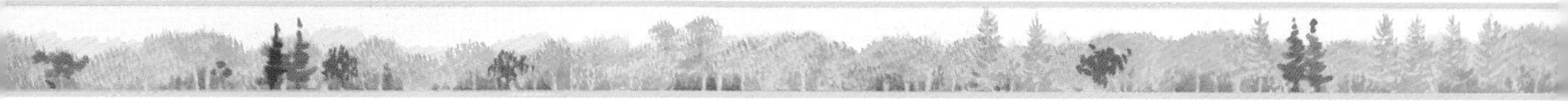

Bandicoots, such as the rabbit bandicoot, dig under the leaf litter to feed on roots, insects and worms.

Wallabies and grey kangaroos eat forest plants.

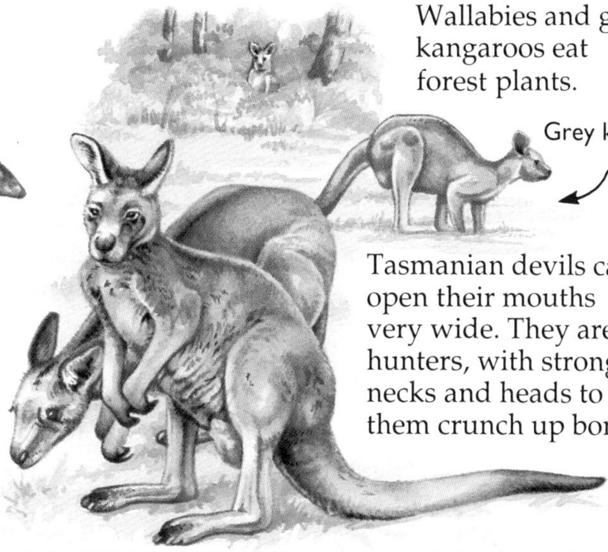

Tasmanian devils can open their mouths very wide. They are hunters, with strong necks and heads to help them crunch up bones.

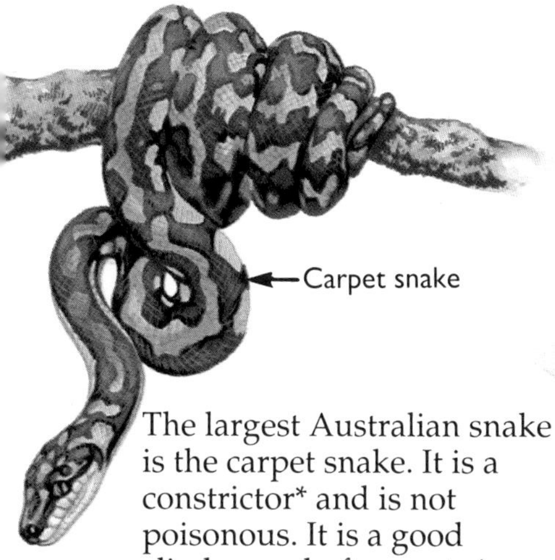

The largest Australian snake is the carpet snake. It is a constrictor* and is not poisonous. It is a good climber and often rests in trees after feeding.

Many different kinds of parrots feed in the canopy. Some eat wood-tunnelling beetles, like woodpeckers do in other forests.

The red-capped parrot has a finely pointed beak, which helps it to get seeds out of the nuts it eats.

The splendid wren is brilliantly coloured. It feeds its young on insects.

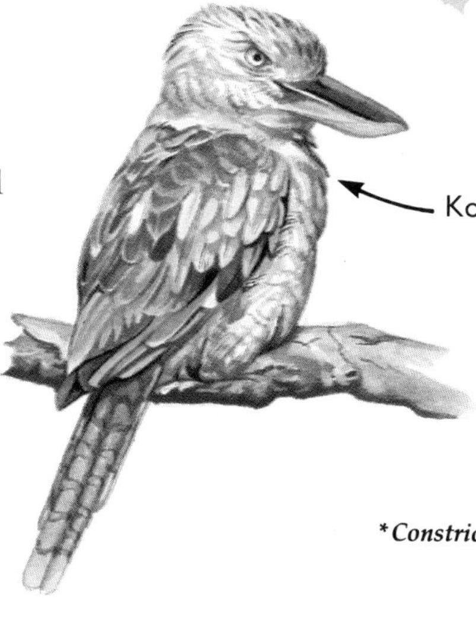

Kookaburras are like kingfishers. They catch reptiles*, fish and other small mammals*.

*Constrictors, 173; Reptiles, 244.

Polar regions

The polar regions are at the far north and south of the Earth. They are the Arctic in the north and the Antarctic in the south. They are freezing cold all year. Near the centre points (or poles) it rarely snows. These areas are called frozen deserts.

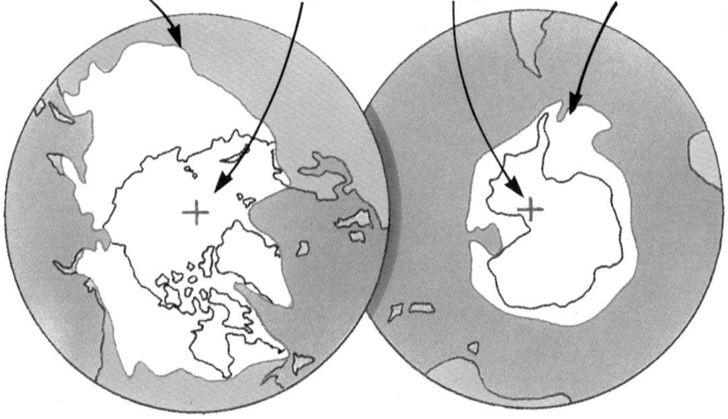
Arctic
North pole
South pole
Antarctic

These are views of the Earth from the top and the bottom.

Polar seasons

Every year the Earth moves gradually around the sun, tilted at an angle. When the northern half of the Earth is tilted towards the sun, it has summer and the south has winter. Because of the Earth's tilt, polar regions have constant daylight in summer and total darkness all winter.

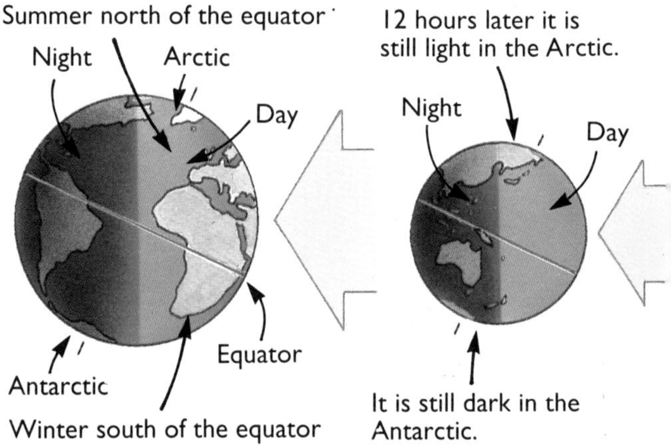
Summer north of the equator
Night
Arctic
Day
Equator
Antarctic
Winter south of the equator
12 hours later it is still light in the Arctic.
Night
Day
It is still dark in the Antarctic.

The Antarctic

The Antarctic is made up of land surrounded by a vast icy ocean. Hardly anything can live on the land, because it is always covered with a thick layer of ice. Almost all the animals find their food in the sea, eating plankton*, or animals that have been eating plankton.

Skua

Because there is constant light in the summer, the plankton can make food all the time and grow quickly, so there is more food for the animals. Penguins and seals produce their young in the summer when there is lots of food.

The ice on the ocean thaws and breaks up into large lumps called **icebergs** in the summer.

Penguins have flipper-like wings and cannot fly. They spend a lot of time on the ice to avoid hunters such as leopard seals.

Birds such as gulls and skuas scavenge* and hunt amongst penguin colonies.

 *Plankton, 150; Scavengers, 172.

Six months later, the southern half is tilted towards the sun, so it has summer. The northern half now has winter.

Six months later, the Arctic has winter and constant darkness.

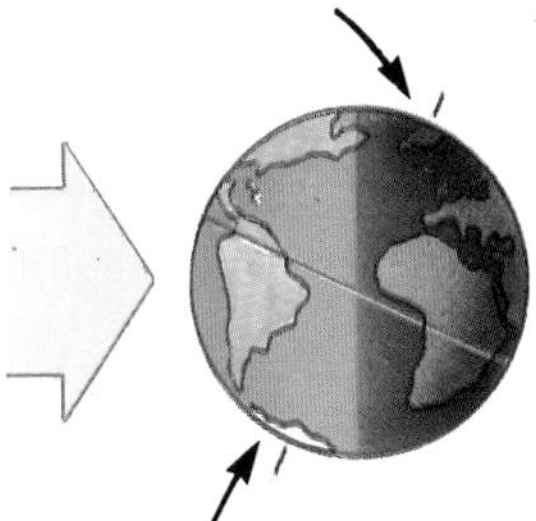

The Antarctic has summer and constant daylight.

Surviving in the cold

Many polar animals are large and rounded, with a thick layer of fat under the skin, to help them keep warm. Whereas desert animals have large ears to lose heat (see page 183), polar animals have small ears to save heat. Hair or feathers trap air around their body which is warmer than the air outside, and keeps the animal warm.

Ptarmigans have feathery legs.

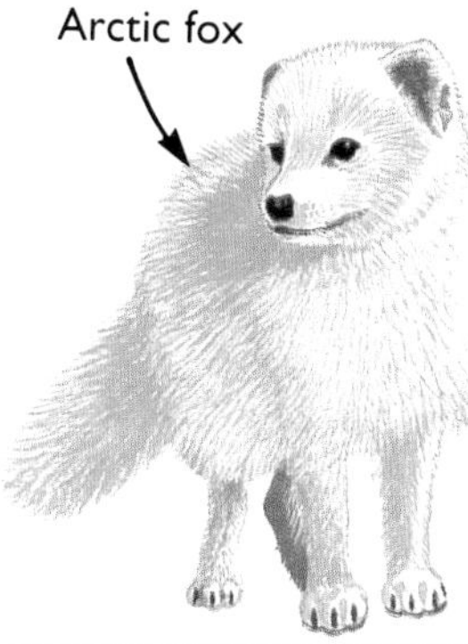

An arctic fox is rounder than a fennec fox (see page 182), with small ears.

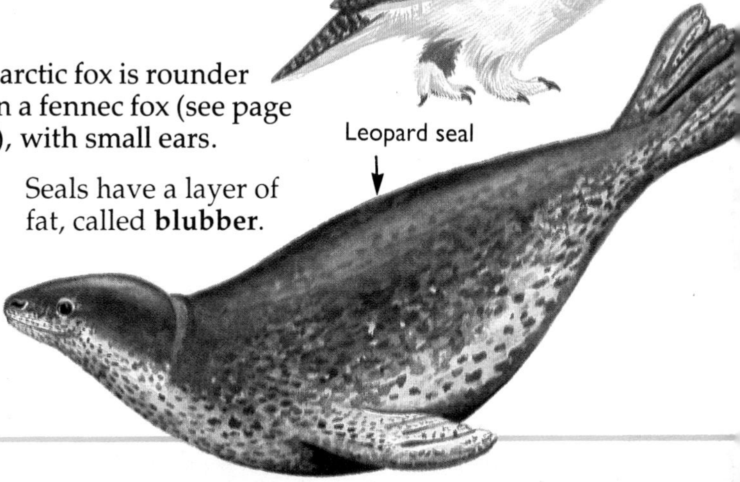

Seals have a layer of fat, called **blubber**.

The Arctic

The Arctic is a huge sea of ice, surrounded by the northern parts of America, Europe and Asia. This land is called the **tundra**. In the tundra, summer and winter are very different.

In the summer the ice on the tundra melts, plants spring up, and animals, such as caribou, arrive from further south to spend the summer (see page 137). Other animals live in the sea all year.

Under the top layer of soil, the ground stays frozen. It is called **permafrost**. This means plants cannot grow long roots. They do not grow very tall because of the strong winds.

Many insects live and feed on the bright tundra flowers.

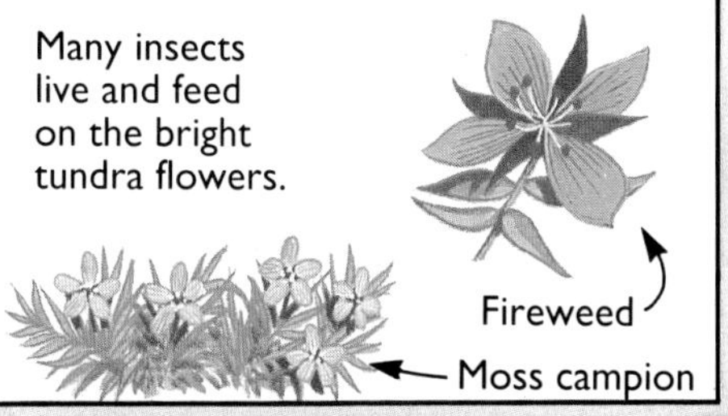

Tundra plant-eaters include insects, lemmings and larger animals, such as caribou. The caribou eat reindeer moss.

Boggy lakes form on the surface, because the melted snow cannot soak into the icy ground. Plovers and other birds feed there.

The Antarctic

Mosses and lichens are the only common land plants in the Antarctic. However the ocean is rich with plankton*, which is the main food for many fish, birds, seals and whales.

Plants

Mosses and lichens are very simple plants. In the Antarctic they live on any bare, wet patches of rock not covered in snow.

Mosses do not need soil to grow. They have tiny root-like things to take in water.

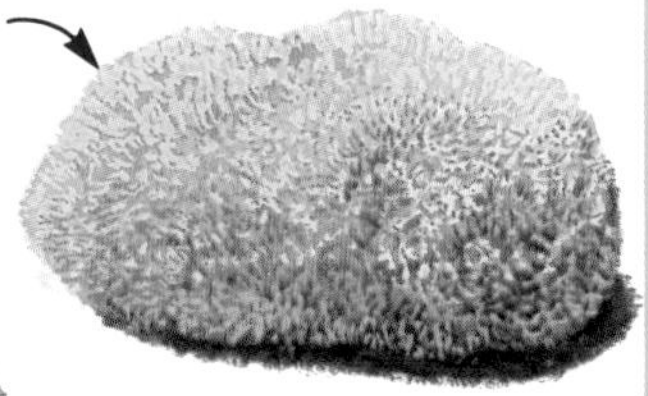

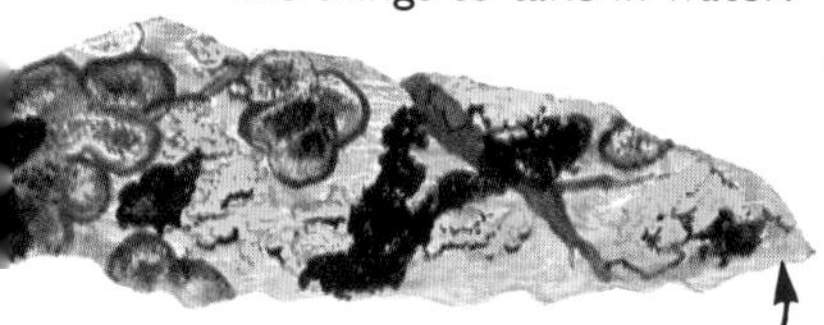

Each lichen is really two plants joined together, a fungus* and an alga. Algae are simple green plants with no roots, stems or leaves. The algae in lichens are very tiny.

Each alga makes its own food, using water which the fungus soaks up, and sunlight. The fungus shares this food as it cannot make its own.

Seals

Seals dive to catch fish and shelled animals, but they have to come up for air. If the ocean is covered in ice they have to scrape a breathing hole in it with their strong front teeth.

Seals have sensitive whiskers to feel objects underwater. Some make high-pitched squeaks, like bats (see page 135), and listen for echoes coming off objects.

Antarctic birds

Lots of different sea birds are found in the Antarctic. The most common birds are petrels and penguins.

Penguins have flippers. They use them like wings, to "fly" through the water. They steer with their feet.

To cope with the cold they have a layer of fat under their skin, and thousands of tiny feathers all over their bodies.

Chinstrap penguin

In an area the size of this box they have 70 feathers.

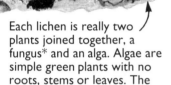

Emperor penguins

The largest penguins, Emperor penguins, live closest to the south pole. It is colder nearer the south pole, and their size helps them to keep warm. They mate* on the ice in winter, in the dark, and lay one egg.

Fungi, 193; Mating, 144; Plankton, 150.

The largest seals, elephant seals, can grow to six metres (19ft) long. In spring each male gathers groups of females on the shore to mate*.

Male elephant seal

If another male arrives he rears up and roars with a short trunk on his nose.

The hole in the ozone layer

A layer of ozone gas stops most of the sun's harmful ultra-violet radiation reaching the Earth. However, gases called CFC's, released from aerosols and fridges, make holes in the ozone layer, letting through extra radiation.

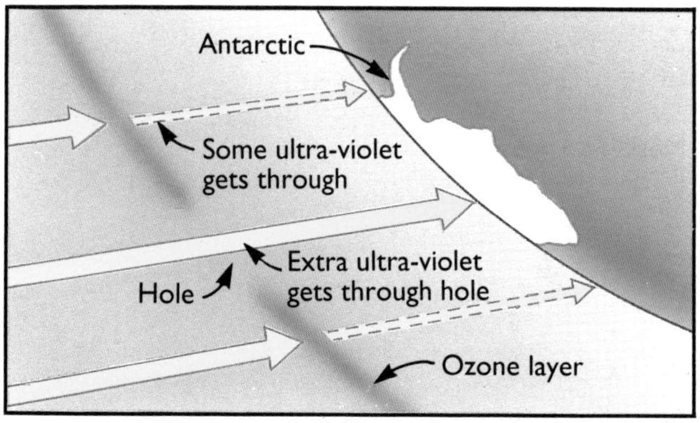
Antarctic
Some ultra-violet gets through
Hole
Extra ultra-violet gets through hole
Ozone layer

There is a huge ozone hole over the Antarctic. The extra ultra-violet radiation may give people skin cancer as far away as Australia. It also kills plankton at the surface of the oceans.

Chick on parent's feet.

Petrel

Petrels rest on the ocean surface, and only go onto land in summer, to lay eggs. If they are attacked, they spit out a jet of stomach oil.

Male emperor penguins carry the egg on their feet under a fold of skin for two months until it is ready to hatch. During this time they do not eat anything, and huddle together in groups of thousands to keep warm.

The mother hunts for squid, and the young chick takes the food from her mouth. The parents know which chick is theirs by its call.

The parents feed their young until the summer comes and there is plenty of food around. Then the young learn to hunt for themselves.
Mother feeding chick

The Arctic

Some animals can live all the year round in the Arctic, both in the sea and on the tundra*. Many others visit during the summer, when the ice melts on the tundra, and breaks up in the sea.

Living in the sea

Seals are found in the Arctic as well as the Antarctic. Walruses are very closely related to seals. They are large and strong, and very few animals attack them. They use two long tusks to attack other walruses and haul themselves onto the ice to rest. They have strong lips and suck clams out of their shells to eat. A walrus can eat 3,000 clams in one day.

Summer in the tundra

The plants which spring up in the summer are the main source of food for many animals. For instance, thousands of insects such as mosquitoes, butterflies and beetles feed on them, and lay eggs which hatch the following spring.

Arctic ringlets have dark colours as this helps them to warm up in the sun.

Many birds, such as swans, divers and waders, travel to the lakes.

Waders have long legs and beaks and poke into the mud for insects and worms.

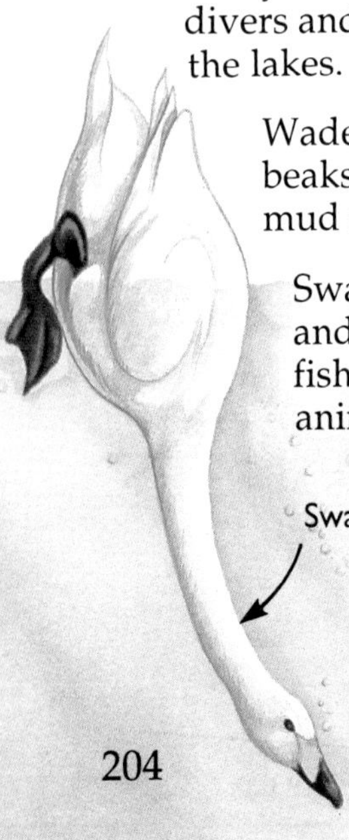

Swans have broad beaks and long necks to find fish, frogs and shelled animals underwater.

Divers plunge underwater to catch food. They can dive for up to 90 seconds.

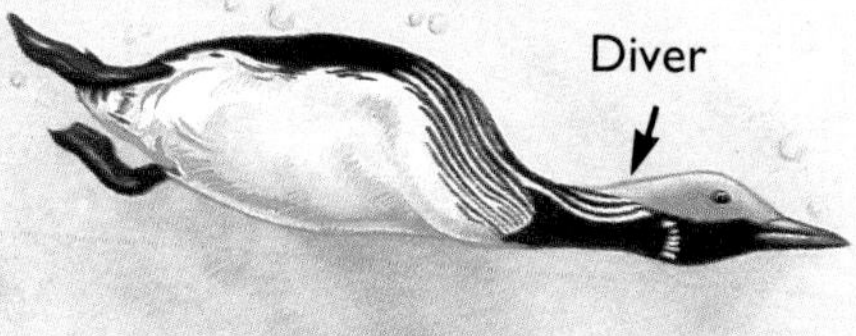

Lots of plant-eating animals means plenty of food for meat-eaters. Wolves hunt in packs (groups). This helps them to wear out stronger musk oxen and faster caribou.

Musk oxen protect their young from wolves inside a ring of adults. They can hook attacking wolves over their shoulders and trample them to death.

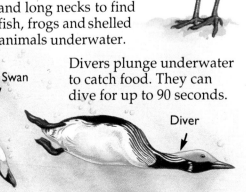

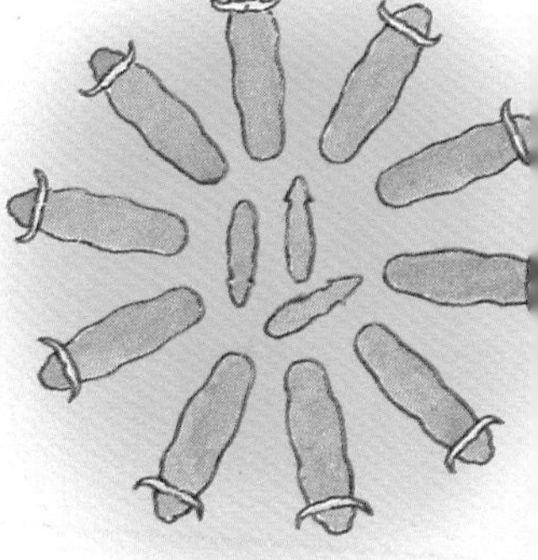

****Tundra, 201.***

Polar bears are the biggest and strongest animals in the Arctic and no other animals attack them. They spend most of the year on the ice of the frozen sea, hunting seals.

Cubs are born in snow dens in the middle of winter. The mother feeds them with her milk, but cannot eat anything herself until it is warm enough to go out hunting.

Polar bears kill seals by grabbing them when they come up for air.

For part of the summer polar bears go onto the land to grow new fur. On land they eat grass, lichen, bilberries and lemmings.

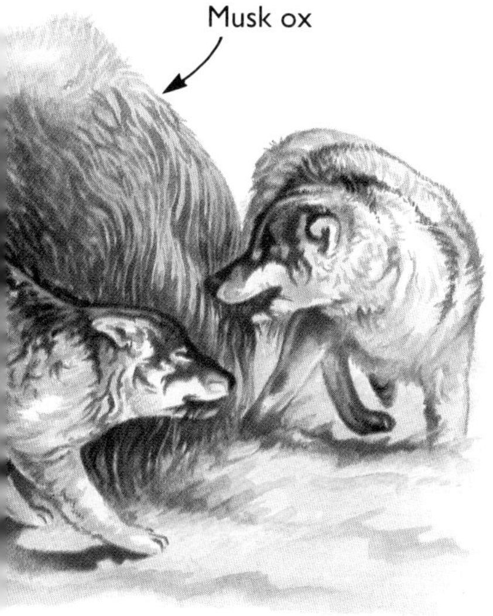

Wolves look for a young or injured animal to attack. Once they have killed and eaten, the wolves will not attack again until they are hungry.

The wolves hold their heads up when they are not hunting.

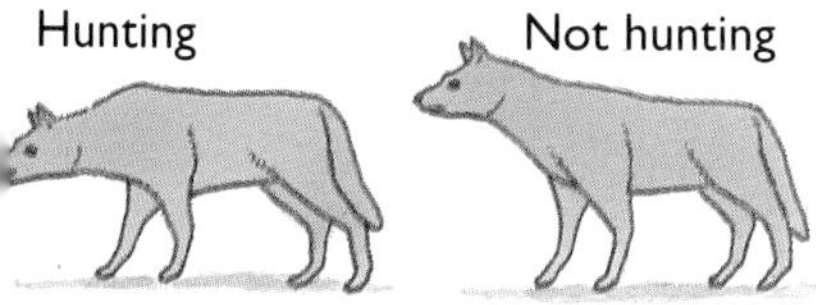

Finding food in winter

In the winter snow, it is hard for plant-eaters to find food. Some, such as caribou, go south, while others, such as lemmings, burrow underground to find plant roots. Other plant-eaters and meat-eaters search for their usual food.

Musk oxen, hares and squirrels look for windy areas where the snow has blown away, and scrape the plants out.

Meat-eaters hunt and scavenge* where they can. Stoats chase lemmings through their burrows, and animals such as foxes scavenge the remains of seals left by polar bears.

Some animals change colour during the year, so that their hunters or their prey cannot spot them easily.

Arctic hares are white in winter to blend in with the snow, but grow brown fur in spring to blend in with the grass.

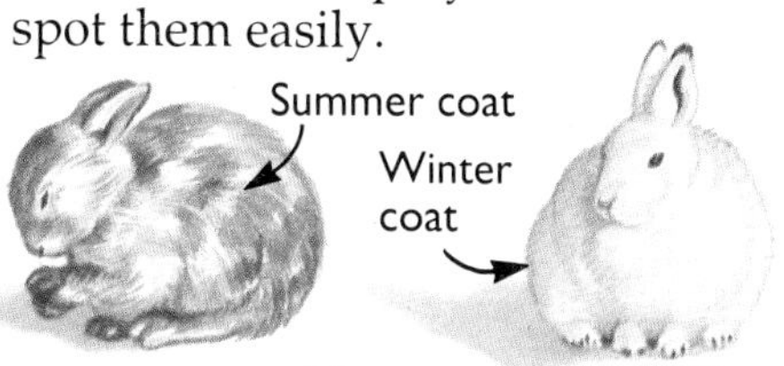

**Scavengers, 172.*

Mountains

Mountains cover five per cent of the land's surface. They were formed over millions of years by movements in the Earth's crust (see page 132). The higher up you go, the colder, drier and windier it gets. There is also less oxygen in the air and the soil is very poor. Few plants and animals can live at the very top of mountains.

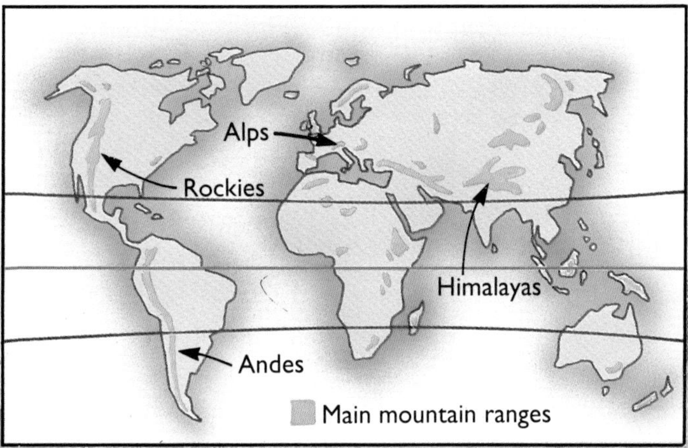
Alps
Rockies
Himalayas
Andes
Main mountain ranges

Mountain bands

As you go down a mountain, there are more and more plants. There are also bands of different types of plant as you go down. This is because the conditions for survival get easier, and more types of plant can survive at each new level.

The Alps are a large range of mountains in Europe.

The top of a mountain is covered in ice and snow, and nothing can grow.

Even though there are no plants, some insects and spiders can live at the very top. This is because they eat pollen, seeds and tiny, dead insects blown up from the valleys by the winds.

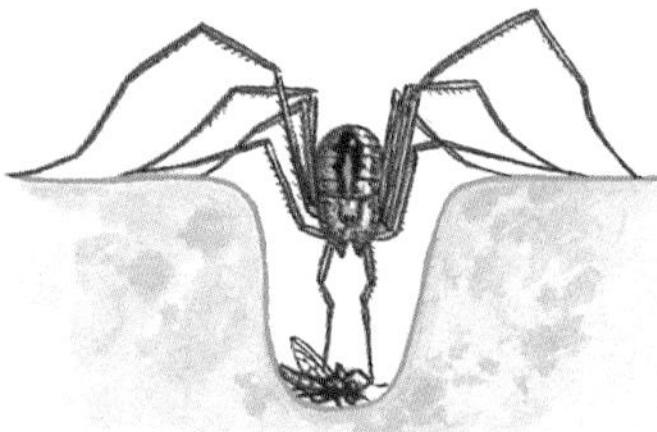

A phalangid spider can lower its body into hollows in the snow to reach dead insects which have sunk down in it.

Below the snow peaks is an area similar to the Arctic tundra*. Only mosses and lichens can grow here, and only a few animals can survive. Lower down, this merges into a band of shrubs and grasses, where more animals can survive.

Golden eagles scavenge and hunt.

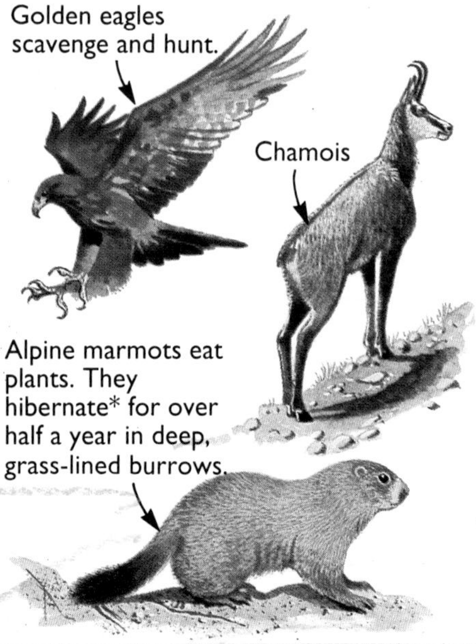

Chamois

Alpine marmots eat plants. They hibernate* for over half a year in deep, grass-lined burrows.

The point at which trees begin to appear is called the **timberline**. Below it, the soil is good enough for them to grow, and the conditions are less cold and harsh. At the timberline itself the trees are shaped by the strong winds into weird, stunted shapes.

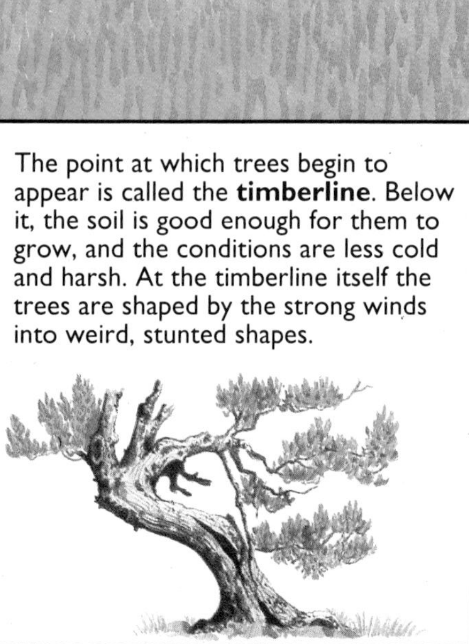

 Hibernation, 136; Tundra, 201.

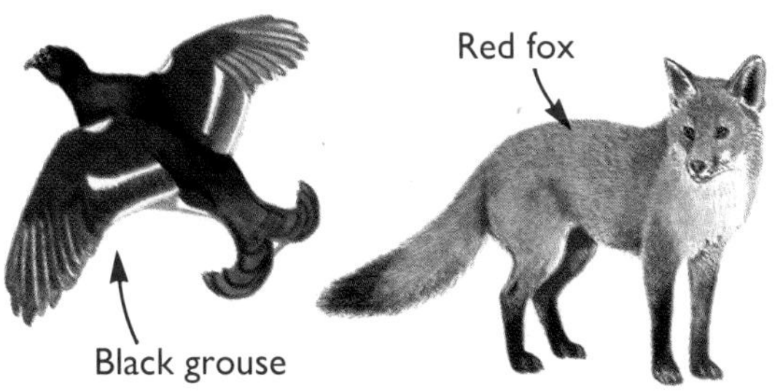

African mountains

The bands of plants and animals found going down a mountain vary in different parts of the world. Mount Kenya in Africa is almost on the equator. Like other tropical mountains, it has different bands of plants on it from those on temperate mountains.

Evergreen* forest grows in a band where the air is cold and dry, and a variety of animals live here. Many birds live in the trees, eating the seeds and the insects living on the trunks.

Pine marten

Crossbill

Few animals live just below the snow peaks, but extraordinary giant plants grow here.

Giant lobelias grow eight metres (26ft) high on African mountains.

Exotic sunbirds feed on the nectar of lobelia flowers.

Malachite sunbird

Leopard

Leopards and wild dogs live in a band of short trees and shrubs.

Many animals such as monkeys, buffalo and forest hogs live in the low bands of warm, wet rain forest.

Elephant

Buffalo

Rhino

Animals such as elephants and rhinos live on the grassland at the bottom.

At the bottom there is a band of deciduous* forest. It is not too cold, and many animals live and feed here throughout the year.

Red fox

Black grouse

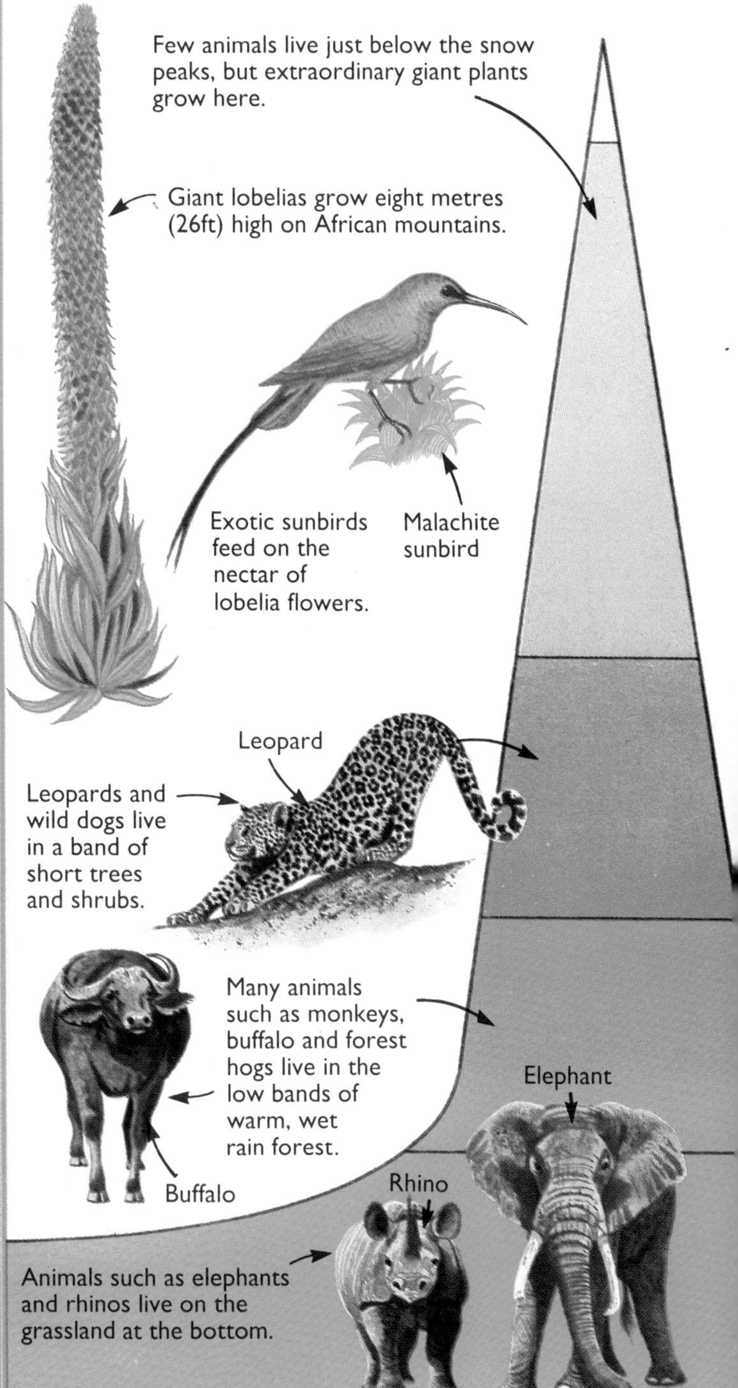

*Deciduous, Evergreen, 186.

Living in a mountain climate

The high mountain climate is very harsh, and plants and animals living there have to cope with the smaller amount of oxygen and the cold, dry, windy conditions.

Using oxygen

Animals need the gas oxygen from their surroundings. They use it in their bodies to get energy from their food. This process produces another gas, carbon dioxide.

Tiny animals can get oxygen from air or water to their whole body through their skin.

Larger animals have a special system, the **blood system**, to carry the oxygen all around their bodies.

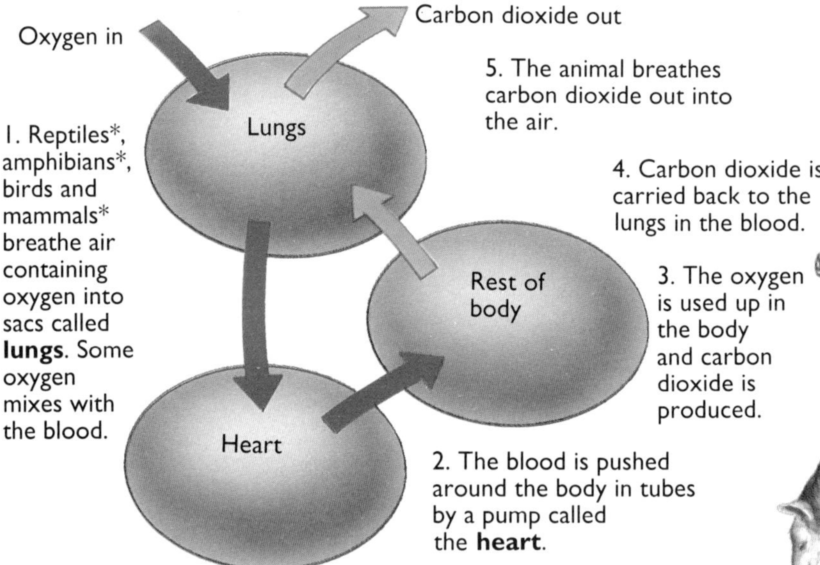
Oxygen in
Carbon dioxide out
Lungs
Rest of body
Heart
1. Reptiles*, amphibians*, birds and mammals* breathe air containing oxygen into sacs called **lungs**. Some oxygen mixes with the blood.
2. The blood is pushed around the body in tubes by a pump called the **heart**.
3. The oxygen is used up in the body and carbon dioxide is produced.
4. Carbon dioxide is carried back to the lungs in the blood.
5. The animal breathes carbon dioxide out into the air.

Coping with the cold

Animals in high mountain regions cope with the cold in similar ways to polar animals (see page 201). They are often large and fat, with thick hair or feathers covering them. Many are less active, and produce young less often than their relatives in other places. High mountain plants tend to grow very slowly.

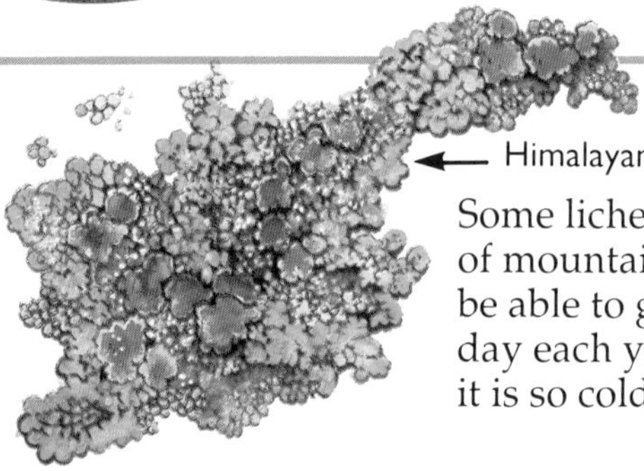

Himalayan lichen

Some lichens at the tops of mountains may only be able to grow for one day each year, because it is so cold.

Some humming birds live high up mountains eating flower nectar. They hover by beating their wings very quickly, using up lots of energy.

Yak

Yaks live in Tibet and China. Their thick coats protect them from freezing temperatures.

Streamertail

To save heat, they often let their body get colder and go into a deep rest called **torpor**.

Amphibians, Mammals, Reptiles, 244.

Because the air around them has less oxygen in it, many mountain animals, such as llamas, have blood which can take in more oxygen with each breath. They breathe more quickly as well.

Mountain grass seeds grow roots and shoots before they are shed from the parent plant, to give them a good start in the poor soil.

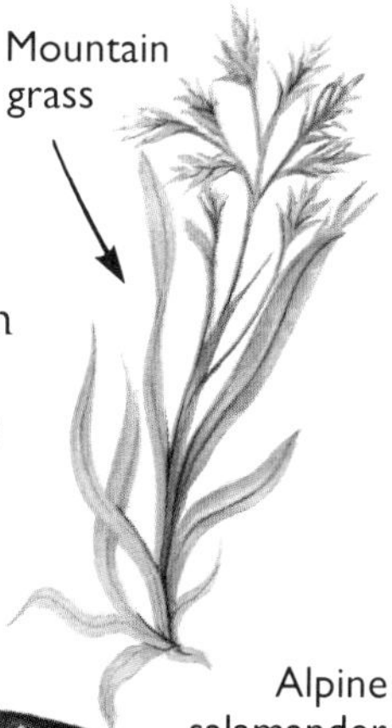

Most salamanders lay eggs. On mountains it is too cold for eggs to hatch, so mountain kinds give birth to live young.

Coping with strong winds

Mountain winds are often very strong. Plants high up often grow in low clumps, so they can avoid being blown away, and have long roots to hold them in the ground. Mountain birds have to be very strong to fly against the wind, so most small birds and insects that live high up never fly.

Plants such as gentian grow in short, round clumps on mountains.

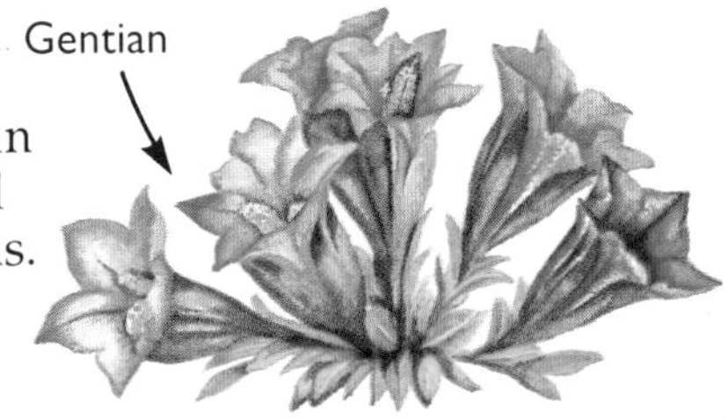

Lammergeiers are strong, fast-flying birds which live high up mountains.

Their talons (huge claws) are strong enough to lift large bones into the air. They drop them from a height to shatter them so they can eat the centre part, or **marrow**.

Eurasian wallcreepers run up and down cliffs with long, sharp claws, using their tail for support. They look for insects in cracks in the rocks.

Springtails use a spring at the back of their body to jump along.

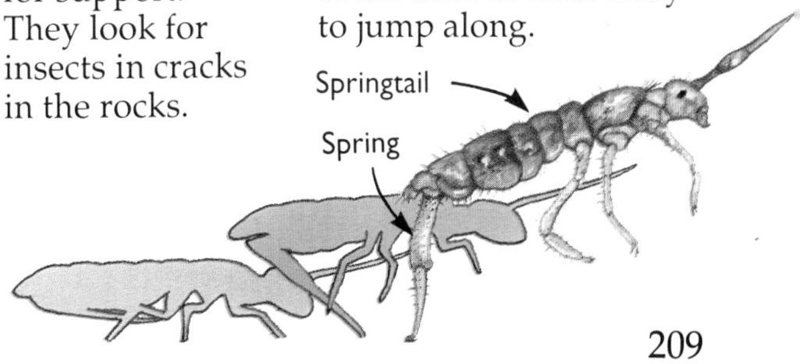

An isolated life

Mountain ranges may be separated from each other by huge distances, but animals which live high up on mountains are often similar because they have to cope with similar problems.

Similar habits

Above the timberline*, winters are harsh. Small plants are covered up by the snow. Around the world, the few plant-eaters which live high up cope with this in similar ways. Many travel down the mountain in winter searching for food. Others collect and store food in advance. The very few meat-eaters which survive high up also have similar ways of life.

Chamois from Europe and Asia are good climbers. They live in herds. One of the herd looks out for danger, and whistles and stamps to warn the others. In winter they feed low down on pine shoots and moss.

Rocky Mountain goats in North America are closely related to chamois. Their small hoofs help them to climb steep rocks to escape hunters.

Ibexes live high up in European, African and Asian mountains, eating grass and lichen. The adults leave their young hidden in holes in the rocks when they have to travel down the mountain to find food. Pads on the back of their feet help them climb steep rocks.

Vicuñas live in groups high up in the Andes. They spit strong smelling liquid and chewed food at attackers. Their hoofs are sharp, with a thick sole and a curved part which grips rock firmly.

***Timberline, 206.**

Rare animals

Many mountain animals can only find their food in one area on a mountain. Because they cannot feed higher up or lower down, they are easily upset by changes to their surroundings. This is why many, such as bears and gorillas, are rare.

Desmans find food in fast-flowing mountain streams in Europe. Building dams there removes this food source.

Spectacled bears live and feed in forests in the Andes. They are rare because many forest areas where they live and find their food have been cut down.

Mountain gorillas that live in the forests low down on African mountains are rare because so much forest has been cut down.

Himalayan snow leopards travel long distances in the day to hunt sheep, small mammals and birds. At night they shelter in dens.

Pumas in American mountains hunt mammals such as sheep by day. They hide extra food to eat later. Most other pumas hunt at night.

Pikas in North America and Asia store dried leaves in hollows for the winter.

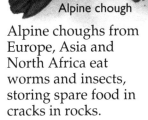

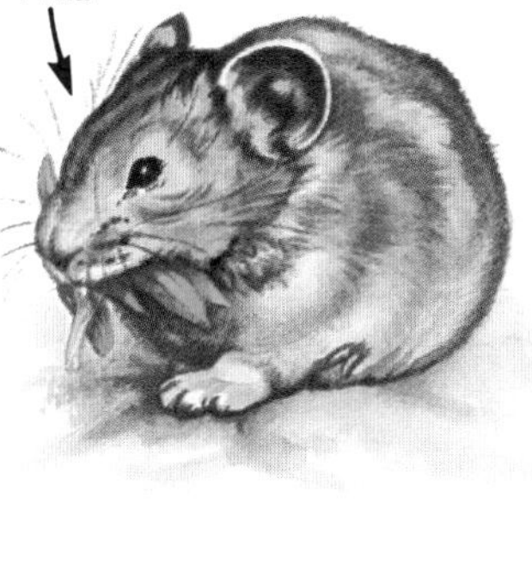

Alpine choughs from Europe, Asia and North Africa eat worms and insects, storing spare food in cracks in rocks.

Rivers and lakes

Water is continually recycled in nature in the water cycle*. Unlike sea water, the rain, snow and hail which falls from clouds has no salt in it. It is called fresh water. When it falls on land some of it soaks in, but most drains off into streams and rivers, which flow to the sea. As they flow, they collect silt (tiny bits of rocks and plants) and the water gets murkier.

How do rivers and lakes form?

Water can soak through some rock, called **permeable rock**, but not other rock, called **impermeable rock**.

Where permeable rock lies at the surface, some water from rain or melted ice soaks down until it reaches impermeable rock, where it stops, and collects in a layer.

The path of a river

Different kinds of plants and animals live in different parts of a river. The river shown here would be found in a temperate area.

In fast-flowing streams, most plants are washed away. Only slim, strong fish such as salmon can live here.

Many more kinds of plants and fish are found lower down the river, in wide bends where the water is shallow and slow-moving.

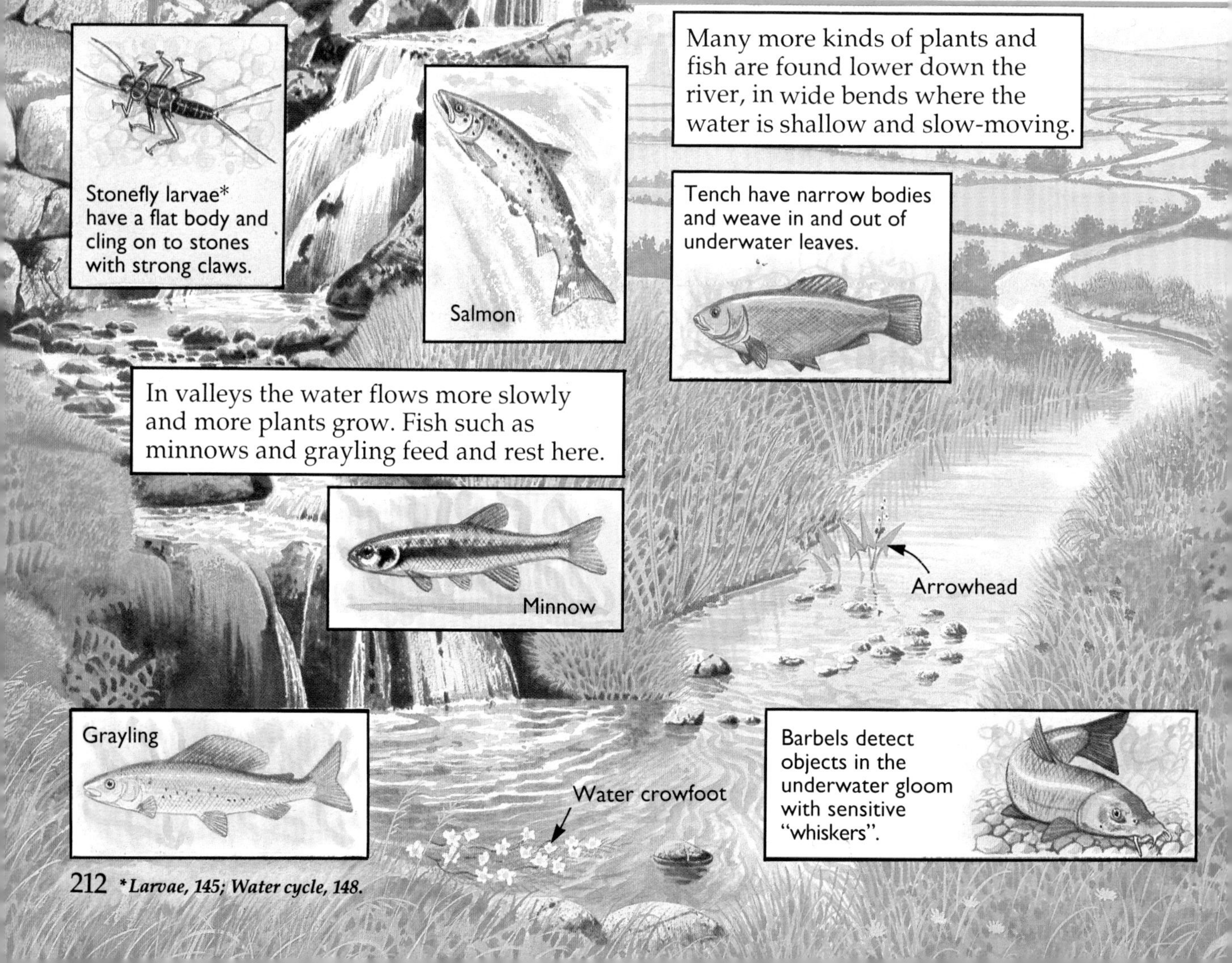

Stonefly larvae* have a flat body and cling on to stones with strong claws.

Salmon

Tench have narrow bodies and weave in and out of underwater leaves.

In valleys the water flows more slowly and more plants grow. Fish such as minnows and grayling feed and rest here.

Minnow

Grayling

Barbels detect objects in the underwater gloom with sensitive "whiskers".

 Larvae, 145; Water cycle, 148.

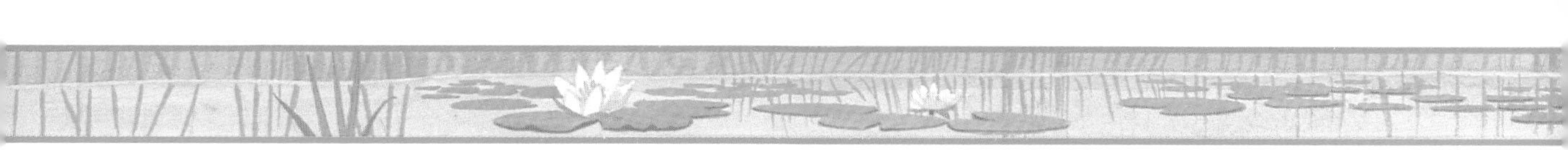

If impermeable rock is on the surface, the water cannot soak away. If the land is sloping, it will flow across the surface, and may form a river.

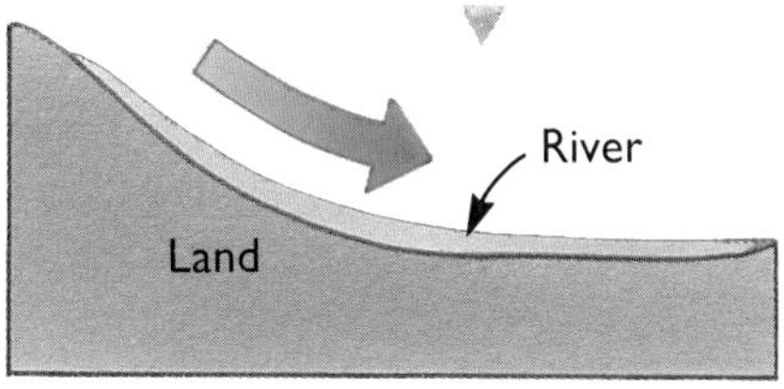

On flatter land, the water may collect in one place and form a lake.

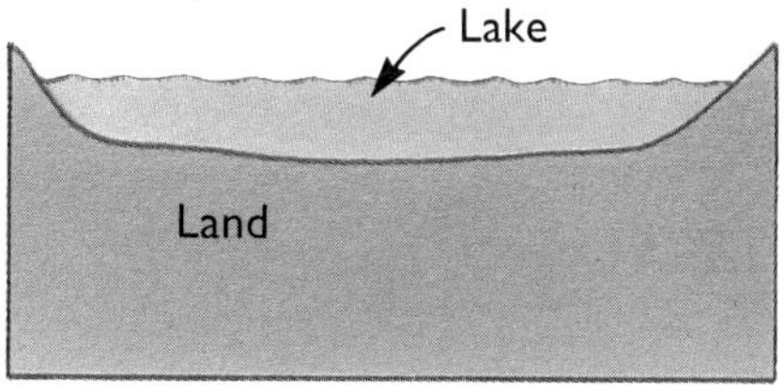

Most rivers start on high, sloping ground. The slope makes most of the water move downwards in a small, fast-flowing stream, even if the rock at the surface is permeable.

As the land flattens out, and other streams join, the river flows more and more slowly. This gives more time for water to soak into permeable rocks. If the rocks get full up, the water cannot soak away, and marshy areas form.

If there is impermeable rock on the surface, a lake may form, because the river "spreads out" over the land. The river flows on through the lake.

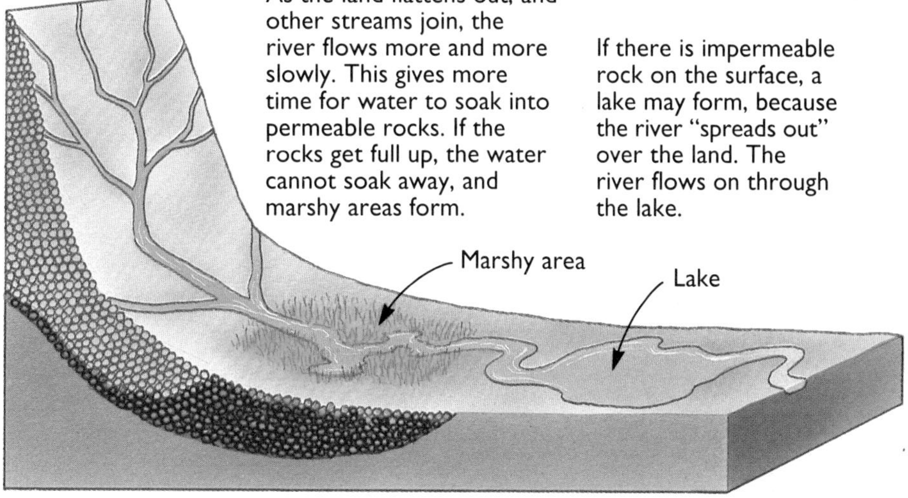

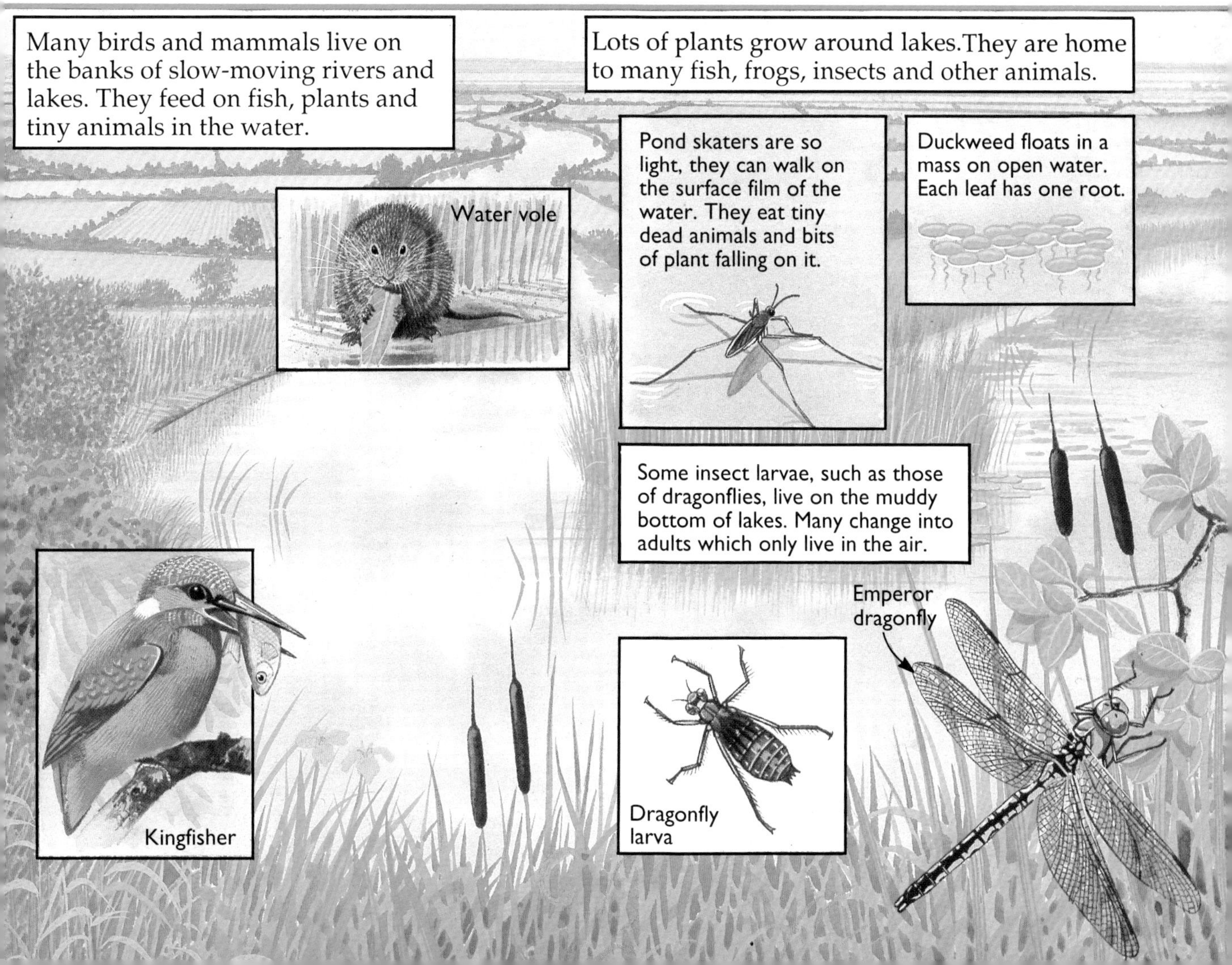

Many birds and mammals live on the banks of slow-moving rivers and lakes. They feed on fish, plants and tiny animals in the water.

Lots of plants grow around lakes. They are home to many fish, frogs, insects and other animals.

Water vole

Pond skaters are so light, they can walk on the surface film of the water. They eat tiny dead animals and bits of plant falling on it.

Duckweed floats in a mass on open water. Each leaf has one root.

Some insect larvae, such as those of dragonflies, live on the muddy bottom of lakes. Many change into adults which only live in the air.

Kingfisher

Dragonfly larva

Emperor dragonfly

Getting oxygen underwater

All animals need oxygen to help them get energy from their food. Most fish and many other water-living animals get their oxygen from the water, instead of from the air. They have special parts called gills which they use to do this.

How gills work

Gills are thin and feathery. Many animals, such as fish, have them inside their bodies, under a flap, or **gill cover**, but others, especially young forms such as tadpoles, have them sticking out from the sides of their heads.

The fish "breathes" in water through its mouth.

Gill
cover

The fish "breathes" out water from behind its gill cover.

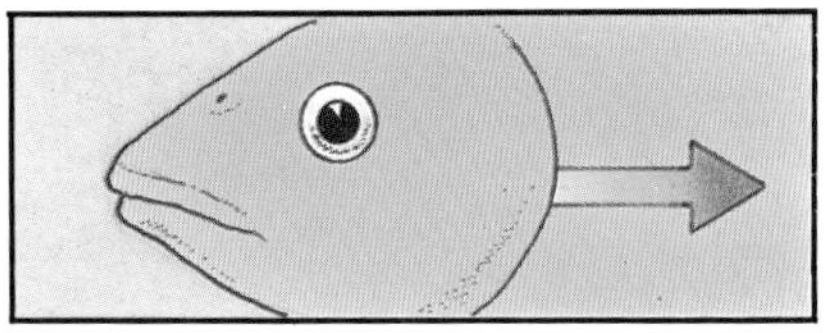

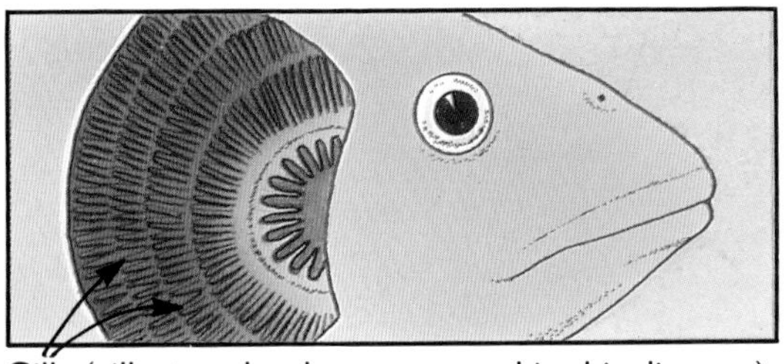

Gills (gill cover has been removed in this diagram)

Oxygen from the water passes into the blood in the gills, and is carried around the body.

Carbon dioxide produced in the body is carried back to the gills in the blood and passes into the water.

Tadpoles have gills growing from their head.
These are called external gills.

Other ways of getting oxygen

Many insects, and larger animals such as frogs and some fish, spend part of their lives on land and part in water. Some of these live on land but feed in water. Others hatch and live in water in their young form, but come onto land as adults. They get oxygen in different ways.

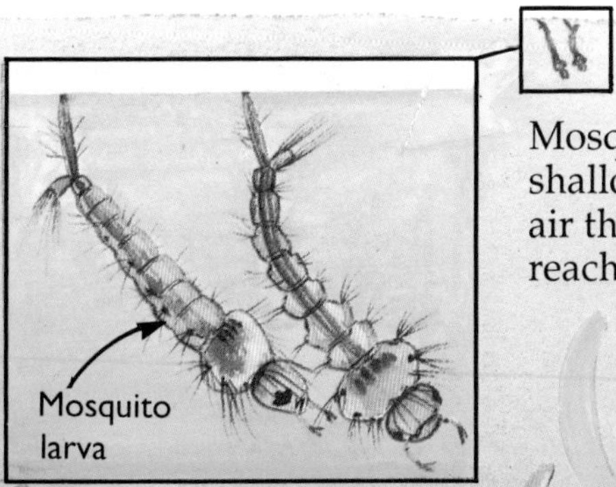

Mosquito
larva

Mosquito larvae* live in shallow ponds. They breathe air through a body tube which reaches to the surface.

Whirligig
beetle

Whirligig beetles carry an air bubble under their wings which they use to breathe under the water for a few minutes. They walk down plant stems to find food.

Water
spider

Water spiders carry bubbles of air under the water and keep them in a net attached to stems. They eat insects and fish in their bubble.

Pollution in rivers and lakes

Acid rain from air pollution (see page 195) makes the water in rivers and lakes acid. Few plants can grow in acid water and animals die because the acid stops oxygen getting into the blood of their gills. Acid lakes and rivers look crystal clear, as hardly anything can live in them.

Dippers used to be common in England, but they are rarer now. The larvae they used to eat have died because of river water turning acid.

Sometimes fertilizers containing nitrates* wash into rivers and lakes from farmland. The nitrates provide lots of food for fresh water algae* so they can grow quickly. However, at night they use up oxygen instead of producing it (see page 134). They get this from the water.

If there are too many algae, the oxygen supply in the water gets used up, so there is not enough for fish and other animals. Many of them die. The water looks green and sludgy with algae.

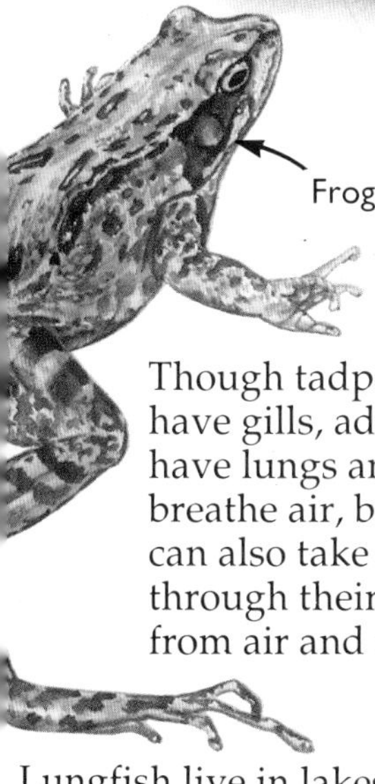

Frog

If their pond dries up, South American armoured catfish can survive for up to four hours by gulping air. They move across wet mud to find water.

Armoured catfish

Though tadpoles have gills, adult frogs have lungs and breathe air, but they can also take oxygen through their skins from air and water.

They have strong spines on two of their fins. They use these to support themselves, and move by wriggling from side to side.

Lungfish live in lakes and rivers which sometimes dry up. They have lungs as well as gills, so they can take oxygen from air as well as from water.

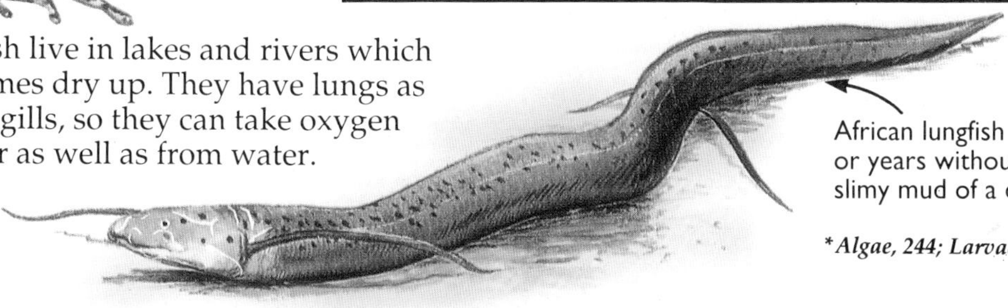

African lungfish can survive for months or years without water, resting in the slimy mud of a dried-up river.

**Algae, 244; Larvae, 145; Nitrates, 141.*

Fresh water plants and animals

Most water plants grow in slow moving or still water, in the later stages of rivers and in lakes. Many animals find their food and lay their eggs among the plants.

Plants

Some plants rooted in a river or lake bed have leaves above water. Others with underwater leaves grow in shallow water where enough sunlight gets through. They all have ways of coping with life in water.

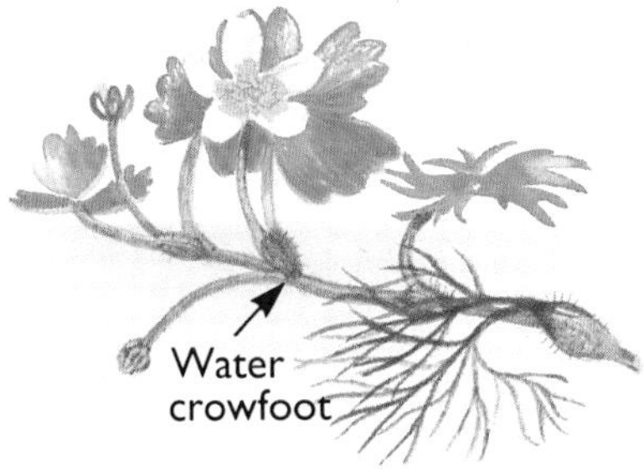

Water crowfoot

Water crowfoot has long, thin leaves under the water. This stops the water currents pulling them off.

Water lily

Water lily leaves and flowers float on the surface. The leaves are waxy so water runs off.

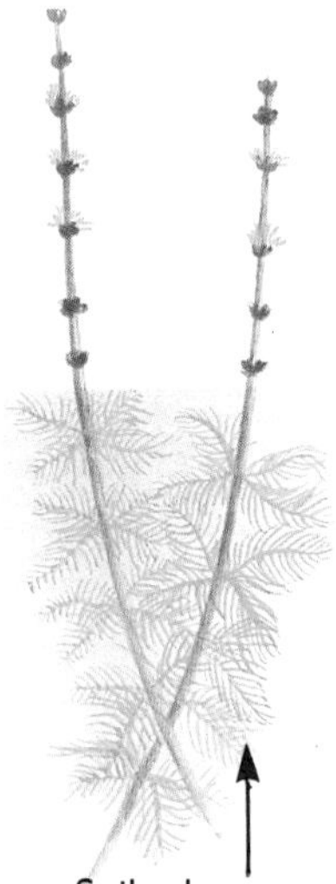

Spiked water milfoil

Spiked water milfoil has all its leaves underwater, but its flowers grow above the surface where they are pollinated*.

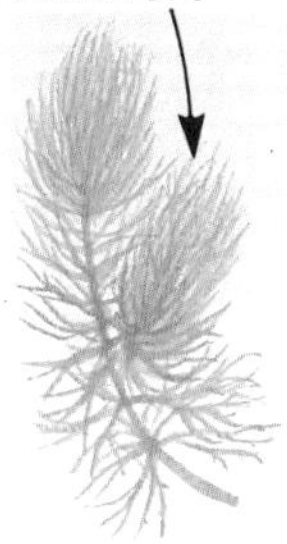

Hornwort

Hornwort grows completely under the water. To pollinate* a female flower, a male flower floats to the surface. Its pollen sinks down, falling on the female part.

Protecting eggs and young

Most female amphibians* and fish lay many eggs in water. The male sheds sperm* over the eggs to fertilize* them, but most drift away before this, or get eaten because they are left unguarded. Only some adults protect their eggs and young.

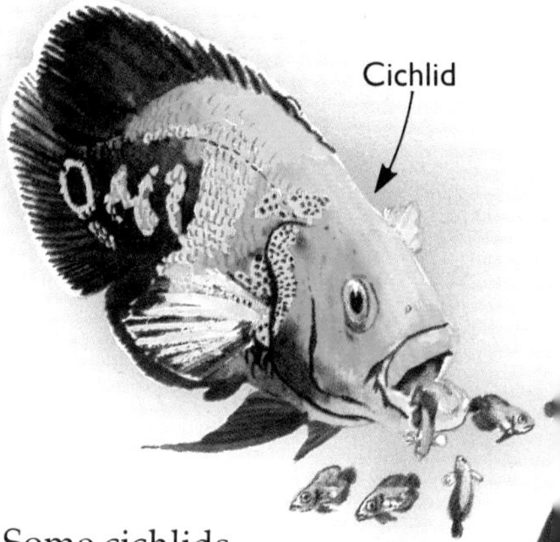

Cichlid

Some cichlids hold their eggs in their mouth. Their young also dart into their mouth, to avoid danger.

Food for fish

There are thousands of different types of fresh water fish in lakes and rivers around the world. Most eat plankton (tiny plants and animals).

Young bream eat plankton, but the adults feed mainly on insect larvae*, worms and shelled animals.

Adult bream

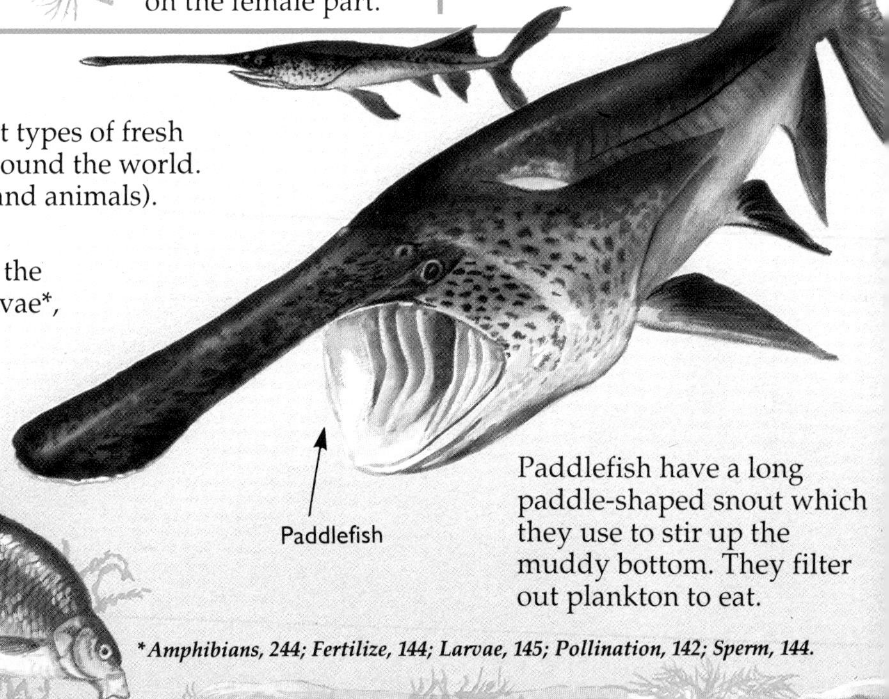

Paddlefish

Paddlefish have a long paddle-shaped snout which they use to stir up the muddy bottom. They filter out plankton to eat.

Amphibians, 244; Fertilize, 144; Larvae, 145; Pollination, 142; Sperm, 144.

Some female newts attach their eggs to underwater plants. They fold leaves over to hide them.

Female newt

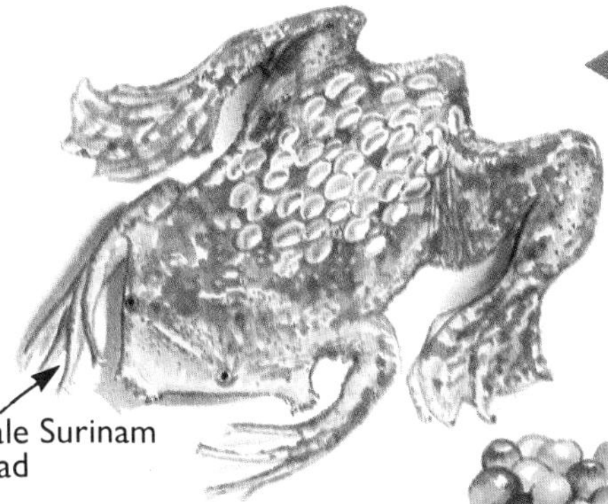
Male Surinam toad

Male Surinam toads push their eggs into the female's back. The skin covers them until they have hatched and grown into frogs.

Male midwife toads carry their eggs safely wound around their legs until they are nearly ready to hatch.

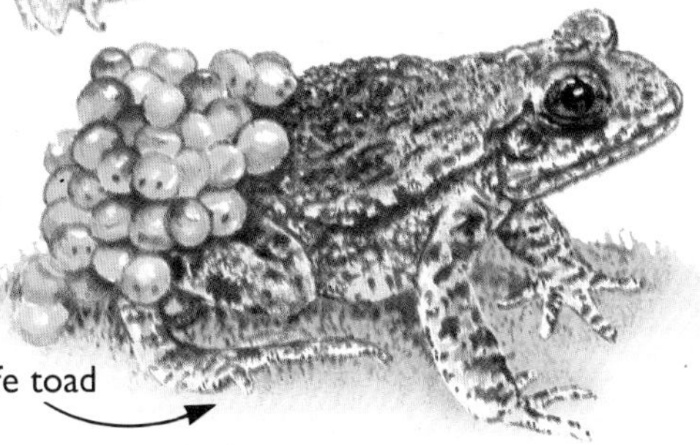
Male midwife toad

Reptiles* lay eggs that are already fertilized. They lay fewer eggs than amphibians and fish. The eggs are laid on land, and have a shell to stop them from drying out. Only a few reptiles guard their eggs, and many eggs get eaten.

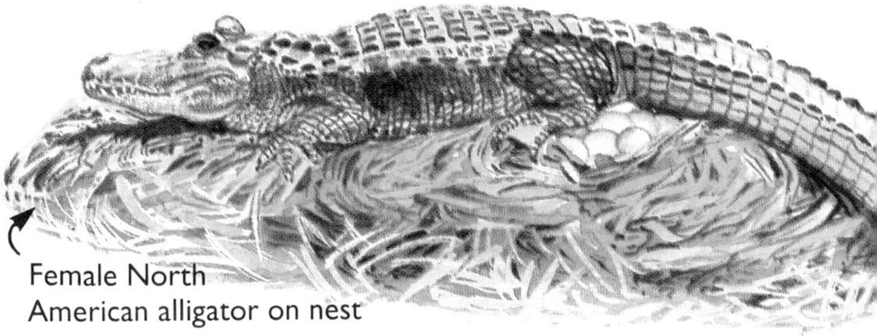
Female North American alligator on nest

Female South American tartarugas gather to lay their eggs in the sand. When the young hatch, they burrow out and run to the river.

Newly-hatched tartarugas

Female North American alligators guard their eggs in nests built out of plants and mud. The young grunt when they hatch, which tells the mother to open the nest. She protects her young for up to three years.

Pike often hide among plants to catch fish and small animals. They are fast-swimming hunters, with slim bodies and sharp, slanting teeth.

Lampreys have a sucker-like mouth, with sharp teeth. They cling to other fish, scrape through their skin and eat their blood and flesh.

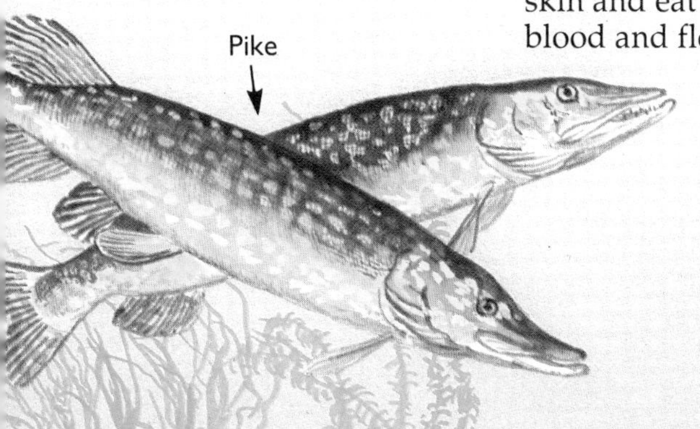
Pike

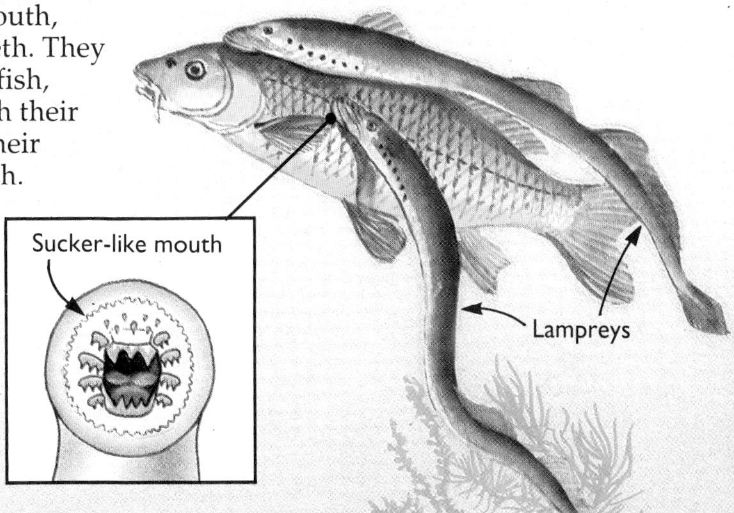
Sucker-like mouth
Lampreys

*Reptiles, 244.

Living by rivers and lakes

As well as amphibians* such as frogs and toads, many mammals* live by rivers and lakes. Some are well shaped for swimming, and hunt underwater. Others dive in to cool down or hide from hunters.

Swimming mammals

Many mammals have flat tails and skin between their toes, making them like paddles. These are called **webbed feet.** They help them to push through the water.

Platypuses are mammals that lay eggs. They swim well and hunt for food such as shrimps under the water.

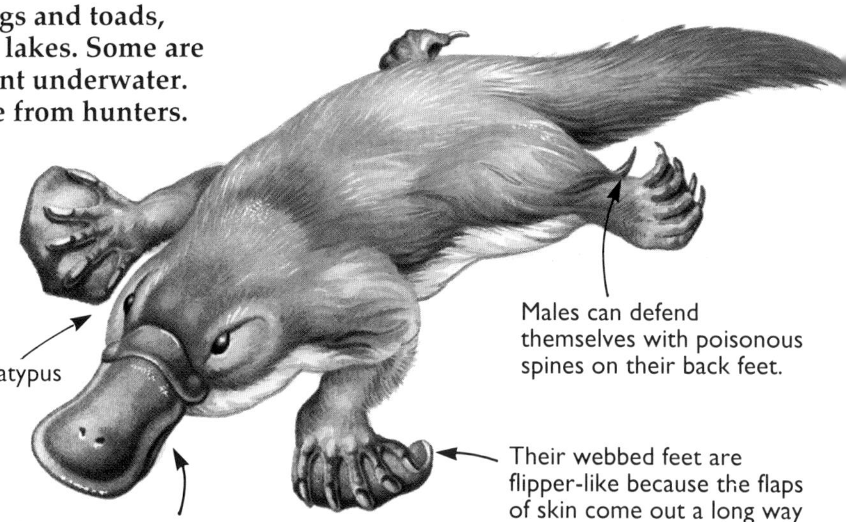
Platypus
Males can defend themselves with poisonous spines on their back feet.
Their webbed feet are flipper-like because the flaps of skin come out a long way past their claws. The skin folds away when they walk on land.
Platypuses have flaps of skin to protect their eyes and ears in water. They use their sensitive snout to detect prey.

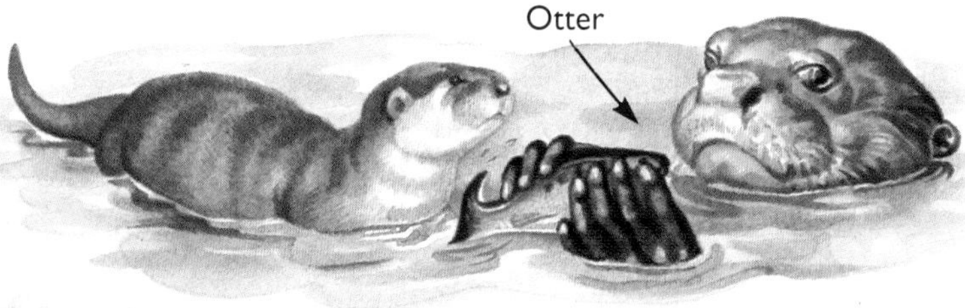
Otter

Otters are energetic, playful animals. Mother otters teach their young to hunt in water by giving them half-dead animals, such as fish, frogs and turtles, so they can practise diving and swooping to catch their prey.

Beavers live in forests in Northern Europe and North America. They build dams out of sticks across small rivers to make lakes. Here they build their homes, called lodges, where they live in family groups of up to 12 beavers.

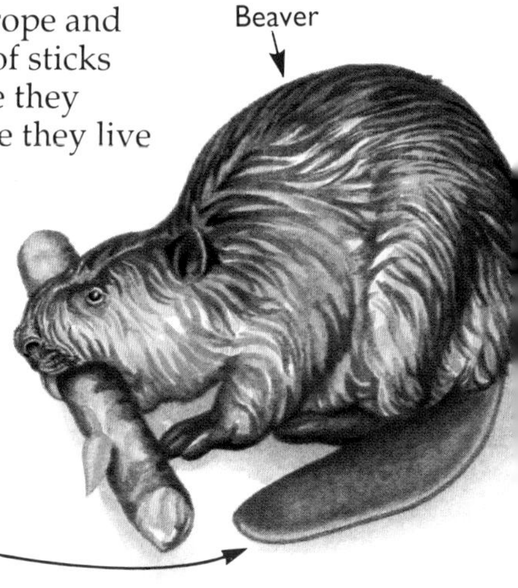
Beaver
Beavers use their huge front teeth to chop down trees. They eat the shoots, and use the sticks for building. They can carry logs in their mouths.
They have webbed back feet and large flat tails to help them move easily in the water.

Amphibians, Mammals, 244.

Water opossums dive to catch fish, frogs and shelled animals. They are marsupials*. The females' pouches close tightly so the young do not drown.

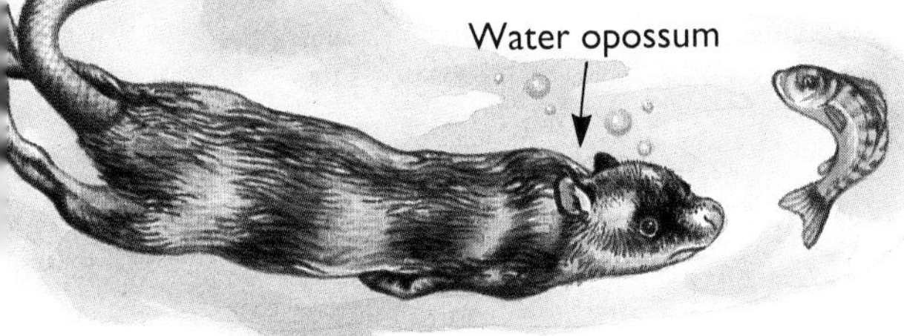

Coypus can stay underwater for five minutes, finding plants and shelled animals to eat.

They have webbed hind feet and produce a special liquid to make their fur waterproof. Females carry their young above the water.

Water shrews chase prey underwater, killing them with a poisonous bite. They have a flat tail and paddle with fringed toes.

Tapirs live near water in dense tropical forests. They have a short, sensitive trunk-like nose to reach out for leaves and shoots.

Malayan tapirs swim expertly to find water plants and escape hunters. The bands of colour on their skin blend in with the shadows so it is hard for hunters to see them.

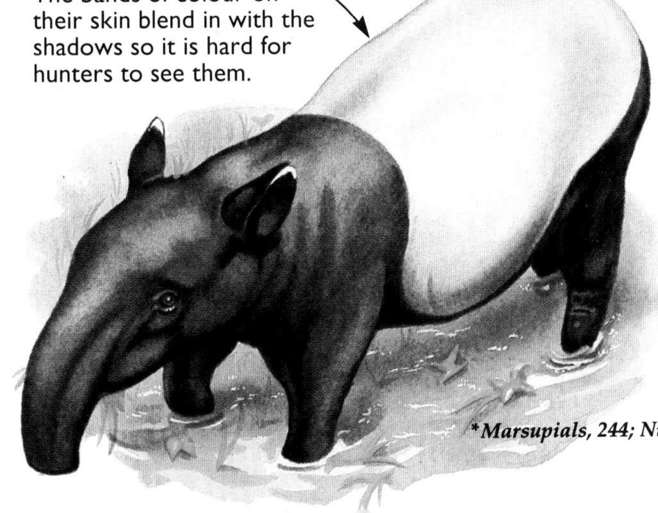

Meat-eating plants

Soil near water is usually rich in nitrates*, but in some marshy areas it is very poor. Few plants can live in these areas, but some special ones can get nitrates from dead, rotting insects. They produce liquids to make them rot faster.

Sundew leaves have tentacles which insects stick to while the leaf rolls over them.

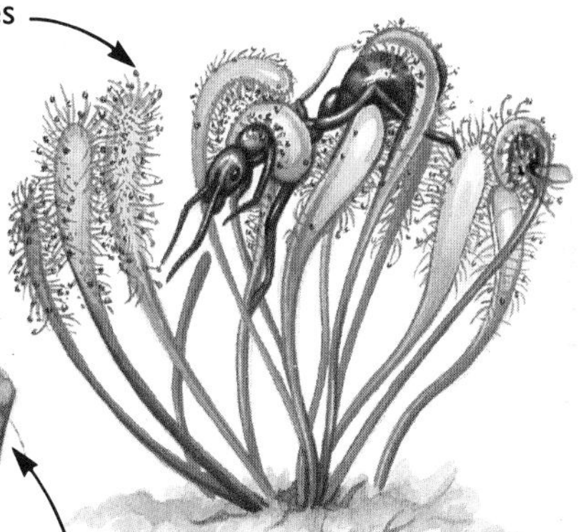

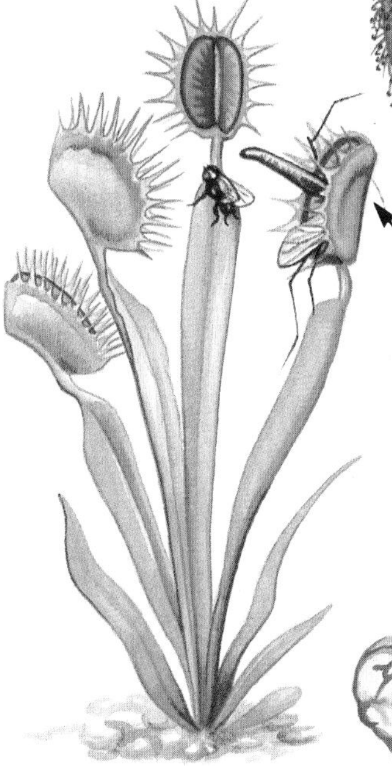

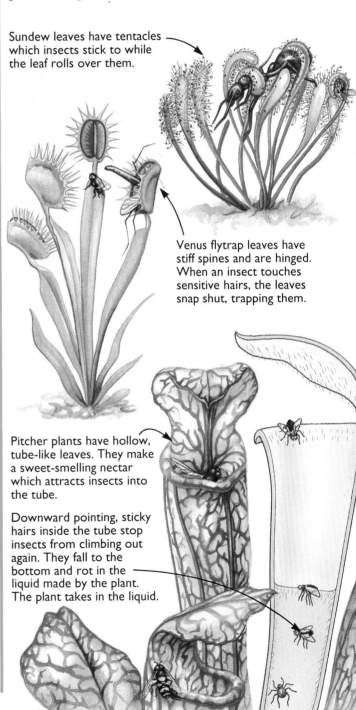

Venus flytrap leaves have stiff spines and are hinged. When an insect touches sensitive hairs, the leaves snap shut, trapping them.

Pitcher plants have hollow, tube-like leaves. They make a sweet-smelling nectar which attracts insects into the tube.

Downward pointing, sticky hairs inside the tube stop insects from climbing out again. They fall to the bottom and rot in the liquid made by the plant. The plant takes in the liquid.

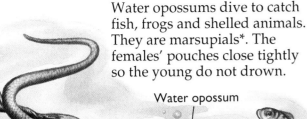

**Marsupials, 244; Nitrates, 141.*

Water birds

Many water birds live around lakes, rivers and wetlands, where there is plenty of food for them. Many dive to find their food. Their feathers are waterproof, and make their body a smooth shape, good for swimming or flying.

Feeding

Many water birds have specially shaped bodies, feet and beaks to help them find food in a particular way.

Kingfishers have a short body with a long beak and strong wings. They dart into the water from a perch to grab a fish.

Feathers

Many adult birds have fluffy **down feathers** on their body which help to keep them warm. These lie under other, stronger feathers which cover them in a smooth, waterproof layer.

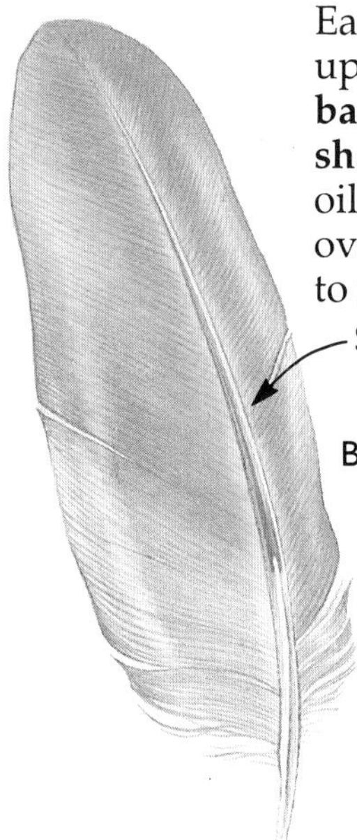

Each covering feather is made up of hundreds of strands, or **barbs**, coming off a central **shaft**. The bird makes a special oil near its tail and spreads this over the feathers with its beak to make water run off.

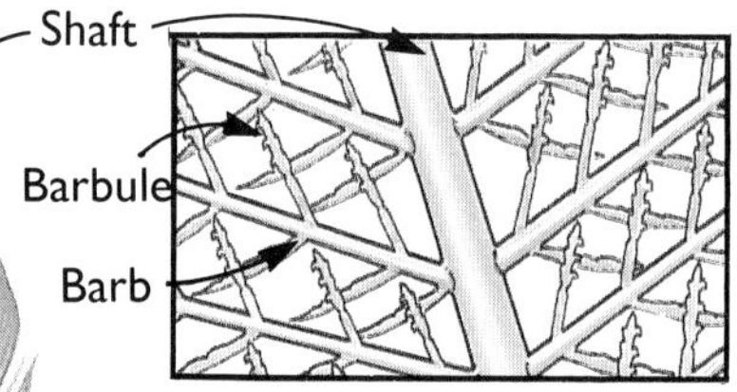

Each barb has lots of **barbules** which hook together to keep the feather in shape. When a bird preens its feathers it is "zipping up" any barbs that are unhooked.

Tropical skimmers fly low over water, skimming fish and shrimps from the surface with long beaks. The lower part of their beaks is longer than the top part.

Jacanas, or lily trotters, have long toes and walk on lily leaves, looking for insects to eat. They step onto the next leaf before the one they are standing on sinks.

Many birds, such as blue herons, have long legs, and stand still or wade in shallow water, waiting to grab fish or frogs.

Birds such as pelicans swim on the surface. The lower part of their beak forms a pouch, which they use to scoop up lots of fish.

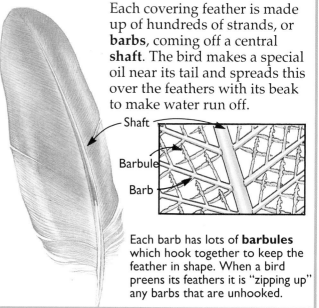

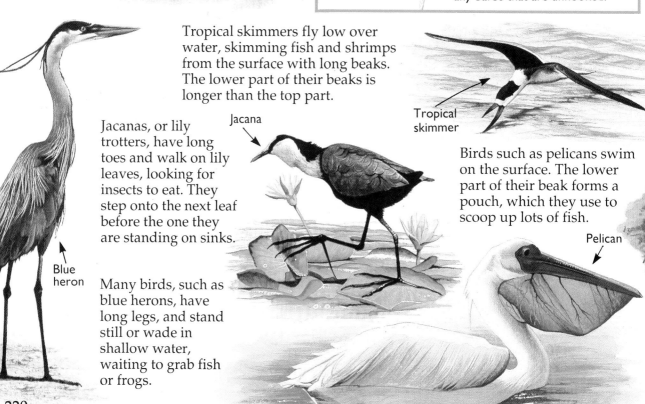

Attracting a mate

All animals try to attract a mate. This is called **courtship**. Different birds have different ways of courting a mate, such as singing, showing off special feathers or moving about in a pattern or dance.

Cranes clatter their beaks and hop up and down in a complicated dance.

When a great crested grebe sees a possible mate, it dives and comes up near it.

The courting grebes swim towards each other, shaking their heads from side to side.

They then dive down and come up breast to breast with weed in their beaks.

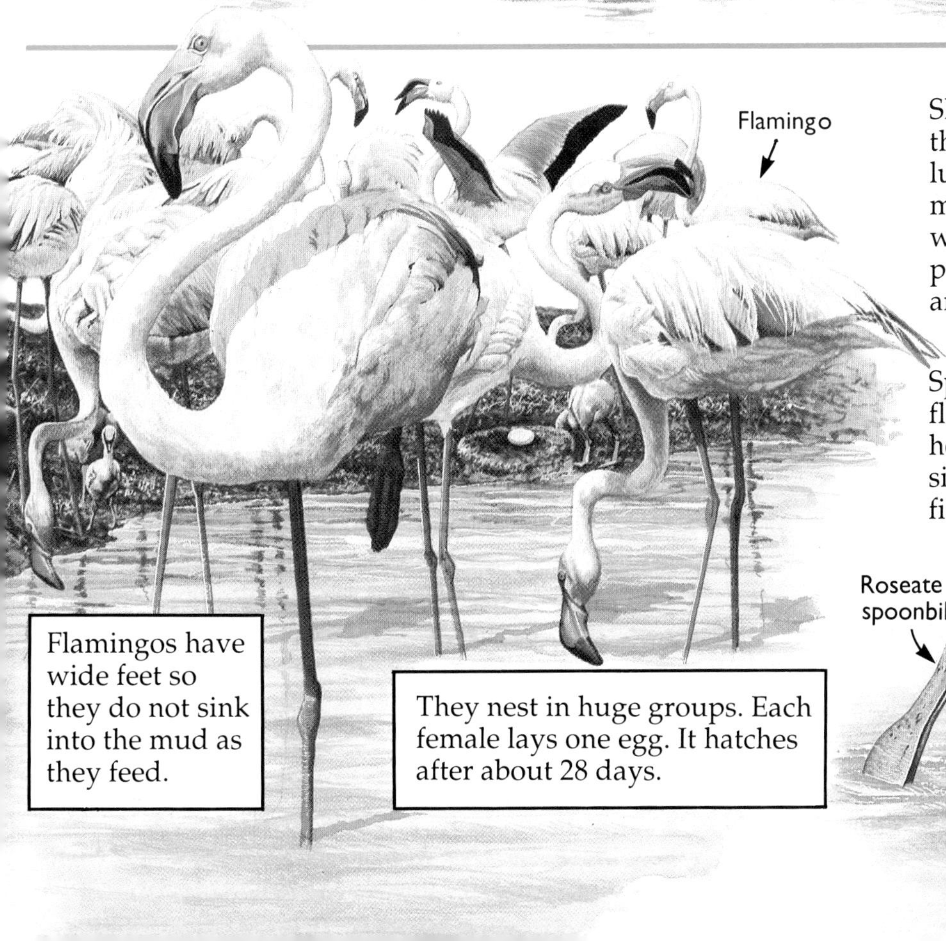

Flamingos have wide feet so they do not sink into the mud as they feed.

They nest in huge groups. Each female lays one egg. It hatches after about 28 days.

Shoebills have a thick beak and dig lungfish out of the mud. They also wait quietly to pounce on fish and frogs.

Spoonbills and flamingos swing their heads from side to side in water or mud, filtering out food.

The Amazon

The Amazon river is a tropical river in South America. It is the largest river in the world, covering thousands of kilometres. By the time it reaches the sea it is very muddy, because it has picked up so much silt*. Because of the hot, wet, tropical conditions, an amazing variety of plants and animals live in and around the Amazon river.

Giants

Because it is hot and there is plenty of water and food, Amazon plants and animals often grow to giant sizes.

Capybaras are the largest rodents* in the world. They are gentle animals, living in family groups and eating water plants.

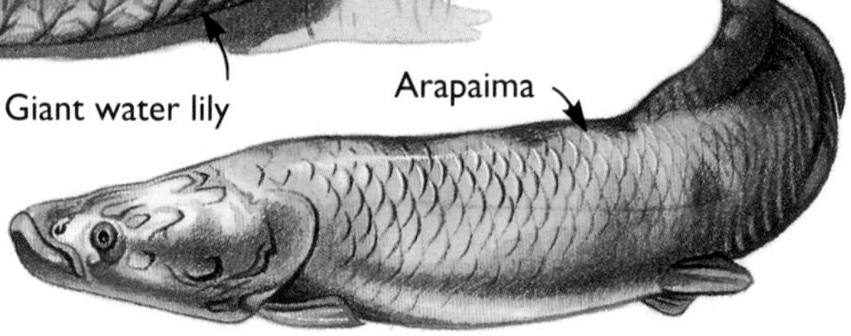

The leaves of an Amazonian giant water lily can be two metres (six feet) across.

Arapaimas are among the largest fresh water fish in the world. They lie very still on the river bottom, eating worms and dead fish.

Moving around underwater

Because the Amazon is so muddy, it is hard for animals to see, and some have special ways to work out where they are and detect their prey.

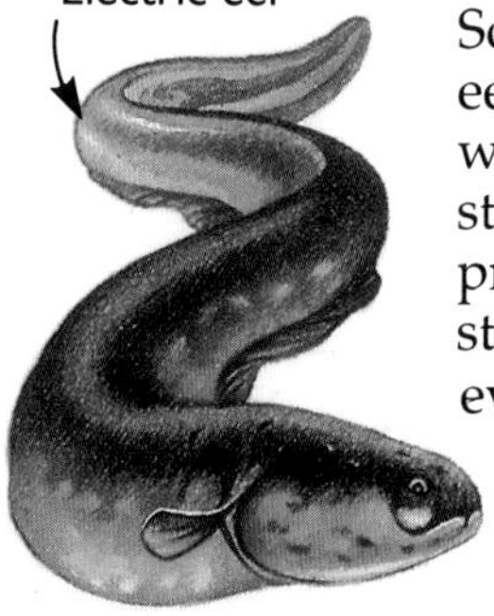

Some fish, such as electric eels, produce electricity which they use to find and stun their prey. They can produce an electric shock strong enough to stun even a horse.

Fresh water river dolphins, like bats (see page 135), make high-pitched sounds and listen for the echoes coming back off objects such as fish and shelled animals (their food).

Matamata turtles lie in wait on the river bottom. When they feel ripples as small fish swim by, they open their jaws and their prey are sucked in.

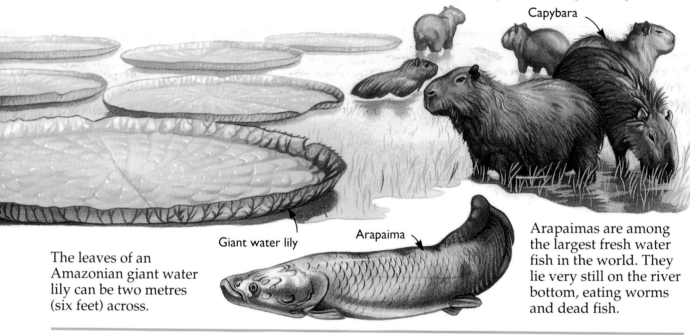

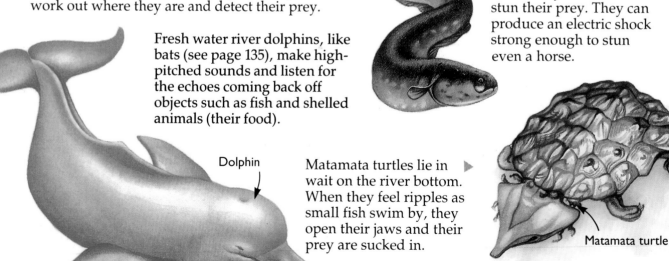

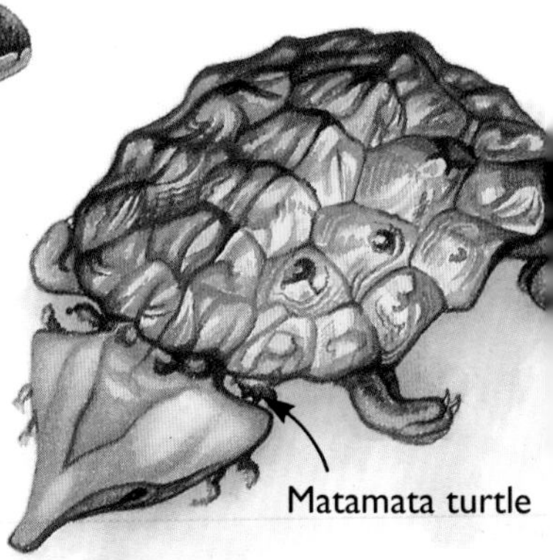

****Rodents, 176; Silt, 160.***

Hunters

Because there is so much animal life, many hunters live in and around the Amazon river, taking advantage of the plentiful supply of food.

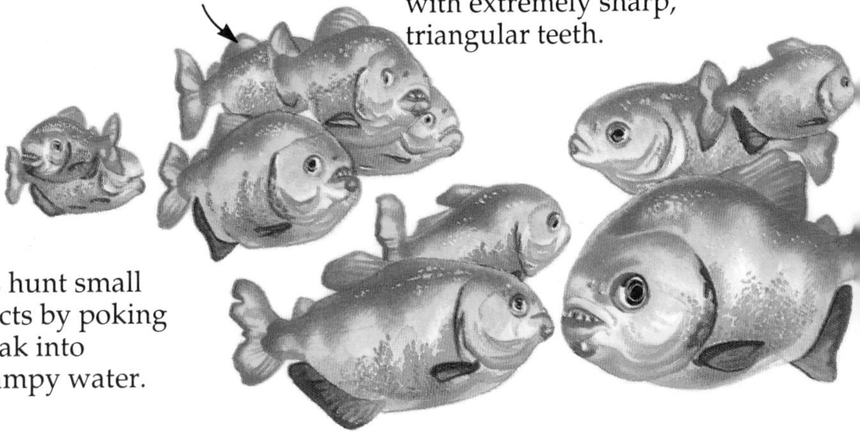

Piranhas have strong jaws, with extremely sharp, triangular teeth.

Scarlet ibises hunt small fish and insects by poking their long beak into shallow, swampy water.

Caimans are related to crocodiles. They hide underwater, breathing air with nostrils on top of their head. They thrash through water with their strong tail catching birds, mammals* and fish.

Anacondas are among the largest snakes in the world. They grow to about eight metres (26ft) long. They attack caimans, mammals and birds, and suffocate them by squeezing them.

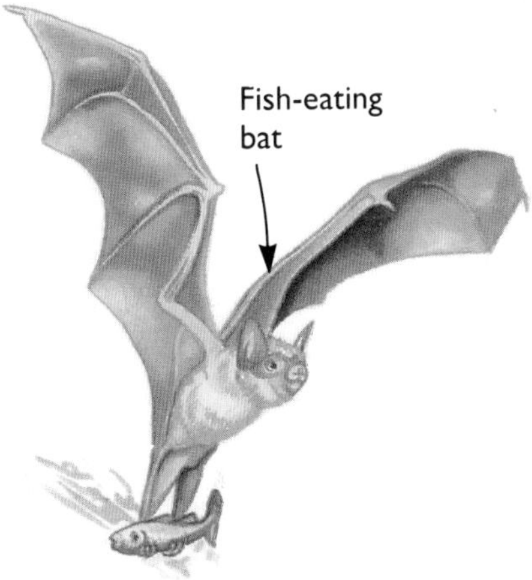

Fish-eating bats look for any fish that ripple the water surface. They swoop and grab their prey with clawed feet.

Poisonous animals

Because there are so many hunters in the Amazon, many animals have special ways to protect themselves. Some of them use poison.

Freshwater stingrays have long tails with poisonous spines that stick into any animal that touches them.

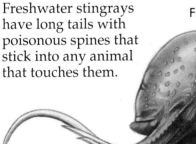

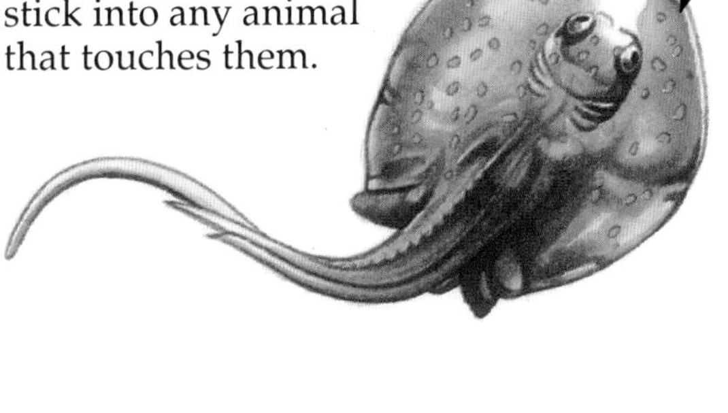

Arrow poison frogs have poison in their skin which kills animals that bite them. Their bright colours warn off predators (see page 237).

*Mammals, 244.

Tropical rain forests

Hot tropical forests grow between the tropic lines (see page 136). In some tropical areas there are wet and dry seasons, and the forest trees rest in the dry season. In other tropical areas, though, it is always wet, with rain every day, and this is where rain forests grow.

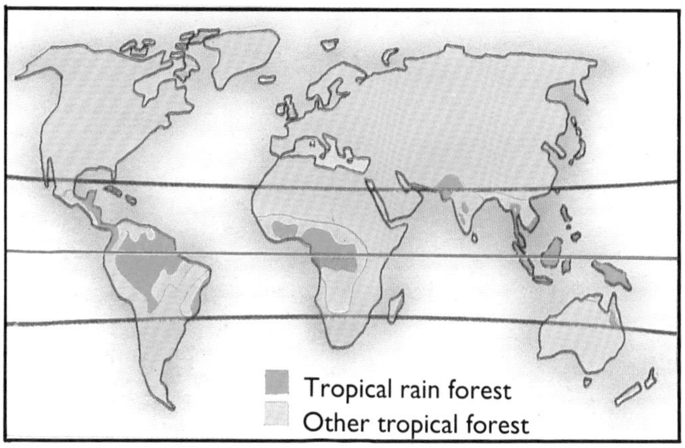
Tropical rain forest
Other tropical forest

Rain forest trees

There are hundreds of different types of trees in rain forests. Many grow up to 45m (150ft) tall. The trees are evergreen* because, since it is always hot and wet, they can keep their leaves and continue growing all year.

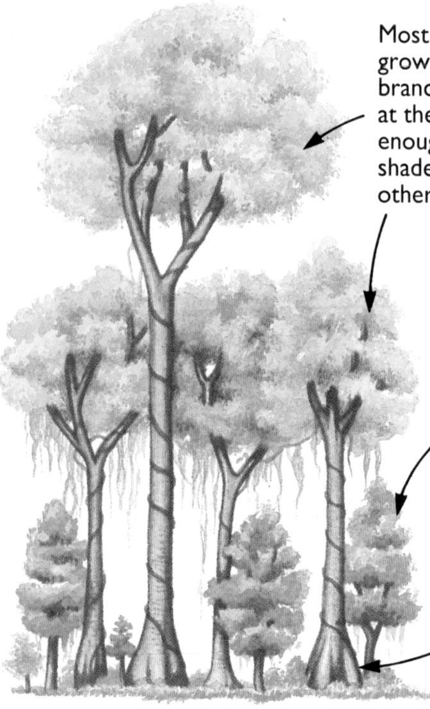

Most of the trees quickly grow very tall, with their branches spread out wide at the top, in a race to get enough light. If they were shaded from the light by other trees they would die.

Some trees cannot grow so tall. They survive if they catch enough light through gaps in the the trees above. Many of these trees are pointed in shape.

Many tall trees have wide roots, called **buttress roots**, above the ground to support their trunks in the thin soil.

Rain forest life

Rain forests are home to an enormous variety of plants and animals. Most animals live in the tree tops (the canopy) among the fruit and flowers.

The rain forest in South East Asia is probably the tallest in the world.

Animals living in the canopy have to be good at climbing. Orang-utans have long toes which help them to grip. They eat fruit and leaves.

To avoid being drenched by heavy rain, many leaves are large and shiny, and end in a point called a drip tip. This lets the water drain off.

Brightly coloured orchids grow in the rain forest.

 *Evergreen, 186.

There is always fruit in the canopy. Some animals hardly eat anything else.

Hornbills have a long, strong beak to push through the leaves and reach fruit.

Fruit bats crush fruit on ridges in their mouth. They drink the juice and spit the rest out.

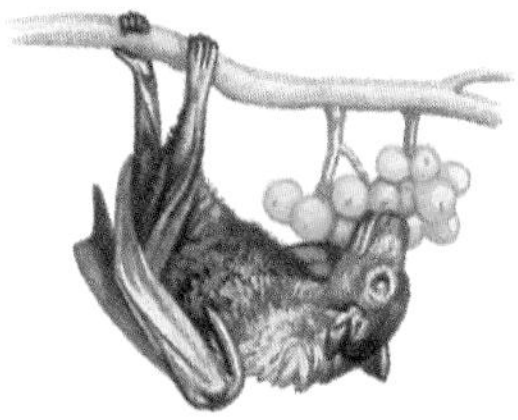

The constant temperature suits cold-blooded* animals. Snakes such as Wagler's pit vipers hang from branches, waiting to strike prey.

Climbing plants such as lianas hang in loops between the tops of trees.

Some big birds, such as the Philippine eagle, fly above the tree tops. There is not room for them to open their wings in the canopy.

Many butterflies and other insects live in the canopy.

Barbirusas eat plants, insect larvae* and dead animals.

To move easily between plants on the ground, animals need to be small, with no parts sticking out. Indian elephants live in rain forests. They have quite small ears.

*Cold-blooded, 182; Larvae, 145.

Rain forest plants

The thick, tangled canopies of the tall rain forest trees form an umbrella which shades the ground. Below the canopy it is still, hot and damp, but many plants grow very well there.

Plants living on plants

Some plants can survive in the shade, but many grow higher up, on the trees, so they get more light.

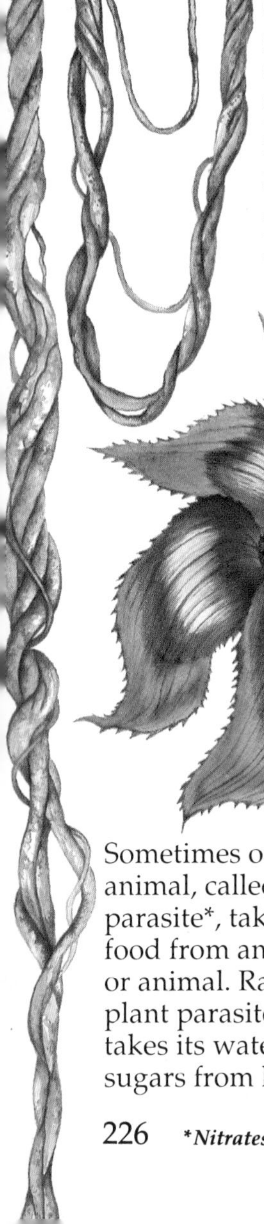

Lianas need light and space to grow. They climb up trees and hang in loops with stems like thick ropes. They do not harm the trees they grow on.

Small plants, such as small palm trees and some grasses, grow in shade.

Many kinds of orchids grow on sunny branches. Their roots do not reach the ground, so they store rain-water in fleshy stems and leaves. They get nitrates* from bits of rotting plant in cracks in the tree.

Some plants that grow on trees, such as bromeliads, have leaves arranged in a cup shape. Water and bits of dead, rotting plant collect in the cup. Insects and tiny frogs live in these "mini pools".

Strangler figs grow when their seeds get stuck between branches of trees. They grow roots which reach down to the soil, twining round the tree.

They grow so big that the tree is shaded out. It dies and rots away, leaving the fig standing.

Sometimes one plant or animal, called a parasite*, takes all its food from another plant or animal. Rafflesia is a plant parasite which takes its water and sugars from liana roots.

 *Nitrates, 141; Parasite, 240.

Flowers and fruit

Many trees grow their flowers and fruit below the flat tangle of branches at the very top. This means they can be reached more easily by insects and other animals which pollinate* the flowers and scatter the fruit seeds as they feed.

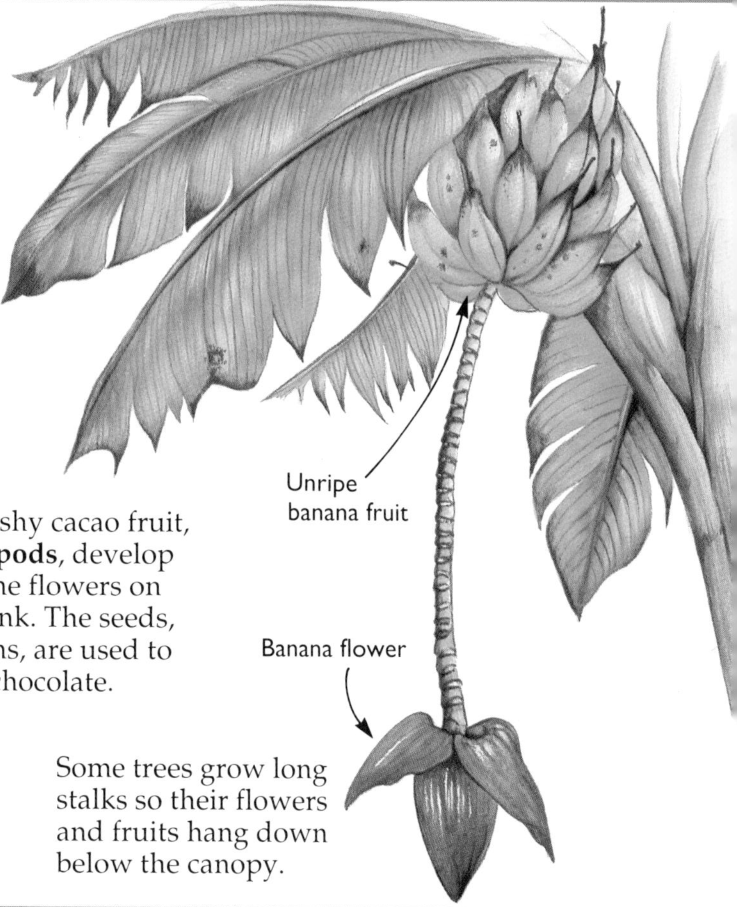

Unripe banana fruit
Banana flower

Some trees, such as cacao trees, grow their flowers straight out of the trunk, not on the tips of branches like other trees.

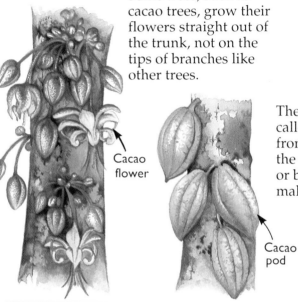

Cacao flower

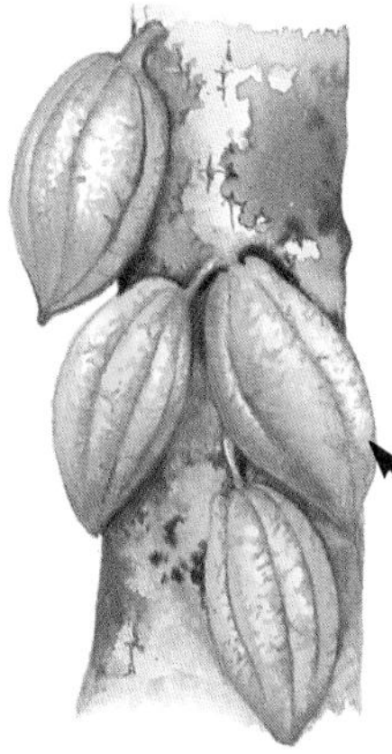

Cacao pod

The fleshy cacao fruit, called **pods**, develop from the flowers on the trunk. The seeds, or beans, are used to make chocolate.

Some trees grow long stalks so their flowers and fruits hang down below the canopy.

Why plants must be saved

Huge areas of rain forest are cut down every day. This destroys the homes of many animals, and makes many rare species of plant extinct*. Many of these plants provide people with food and medicine. Others may also be useful, but are cut down before scientists have time to find out.

Many plants, such as rosy periwinkles, are used to make drugs to treat serious diseases.

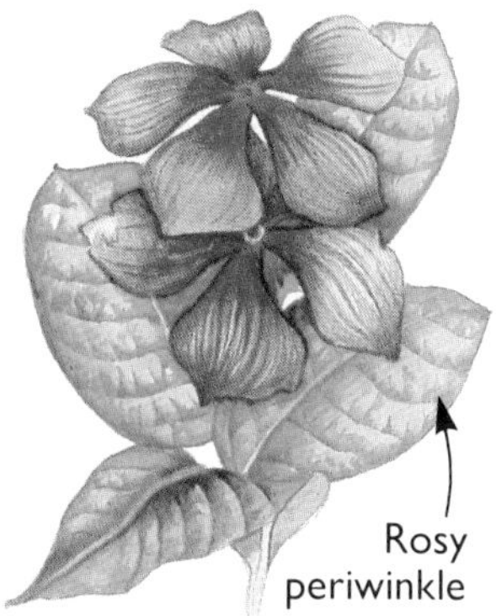

Rosy periwinkle

Many kinds of exotic fruits grow in rain forests.

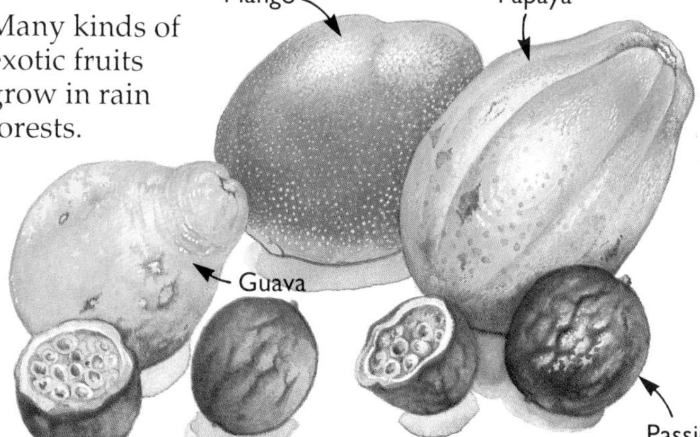

Mango
Papaya
Guava
Passion fruit

Rubber is used to make many things, such as tyres. It comes from rubber trees which grow in rain forests.

Man collecting rubber from rubber tree

****Extinctions, 146; Pollination, 142.***

The rain forest floor

There is always lots of leaf litter (dead leaves and other bits of plants) falling to the rain forest floor, because the trees are always losing some leaves. All these dead bits of plants, and animals too, rot very quickly (for more about rotting, see page 193). The nitrates* which come from rotting are quickly taken out of the soil by all the living plants which need them.

Tiny animals

Huge numbers of insects live on the forest floor, many of which eat up the leaf litter.

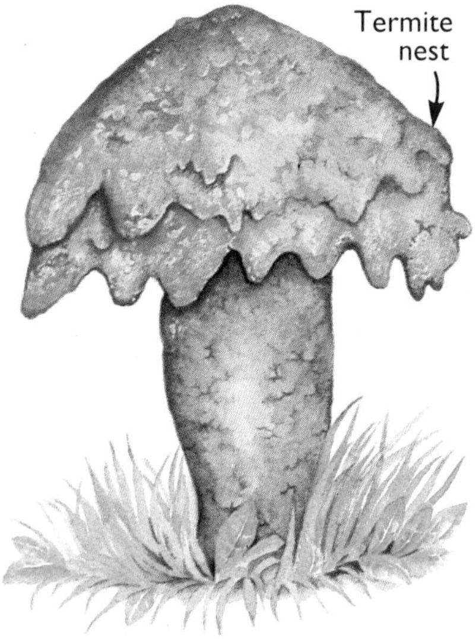

Termites eat dead wood helping it to rot. Some make nests with wide roofs to keep the rain out.

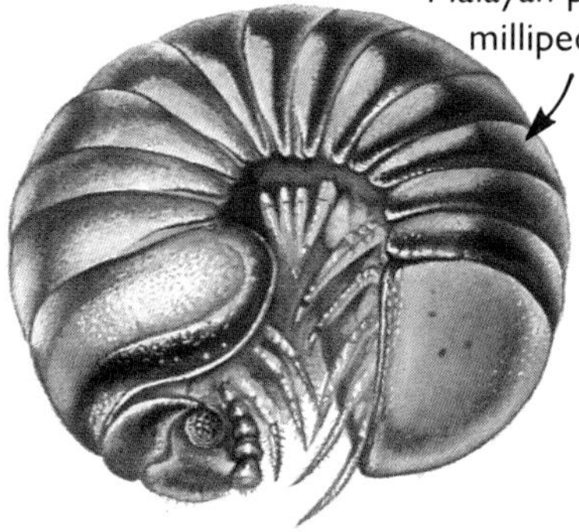

Malayan pill millipedes eat rotting plants. When frightened, they squirt nasty liquids from their body and curl into a ball.

Leaf cutter ants bite leaves from trees and chew them until they are soft and fungus* grows on them. The ants eat the fungus.

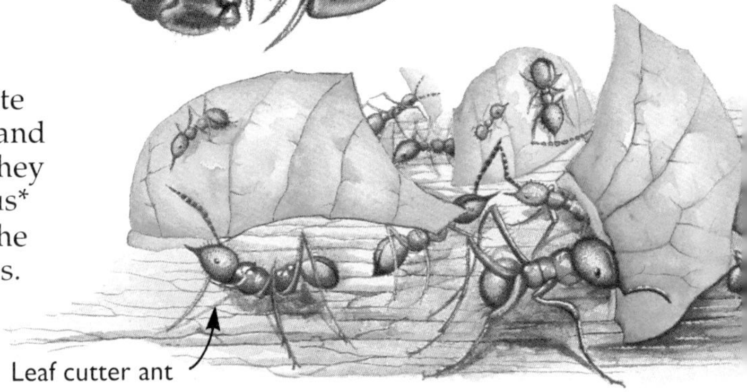

Insect eaters

Because there are so many insects on the forest floor, many other, larger animals feed on them.

Australian spiny anteaters feed on ants and termites, licking them out of their nests with long, sticky tongues. They roll into a prickly ball when scared.

African pangolins eat ants and termites. They are protected by scales when curled up, and can squirt out a nasty liquid.

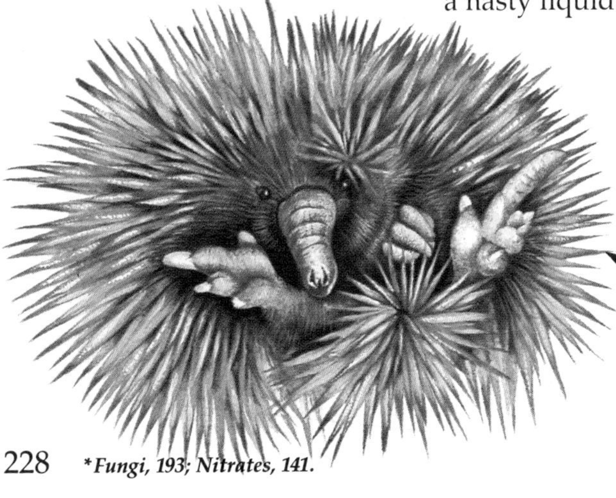

Fungi, 193; Nitrates, 141.

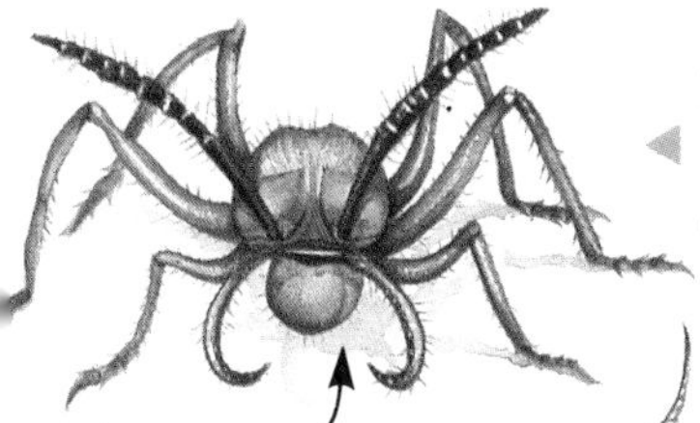
Army ant

Army ants kill any insects or small mammals* they find. They move on when there is no food left in an area.

Giant centipedes can be 30cm (12in) long. They catch and kill their prey with poisonous claws.

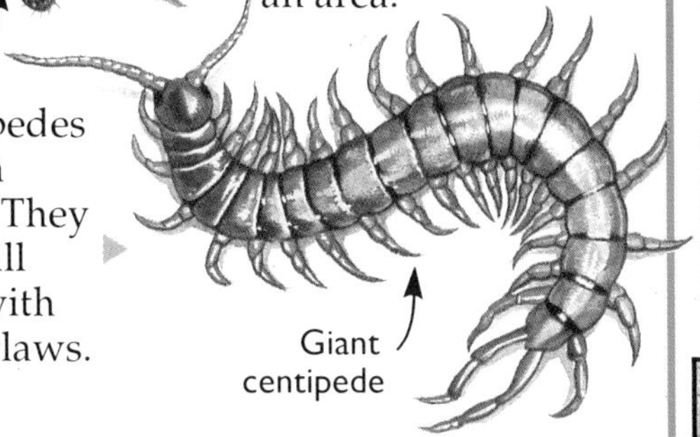
Giant centipede

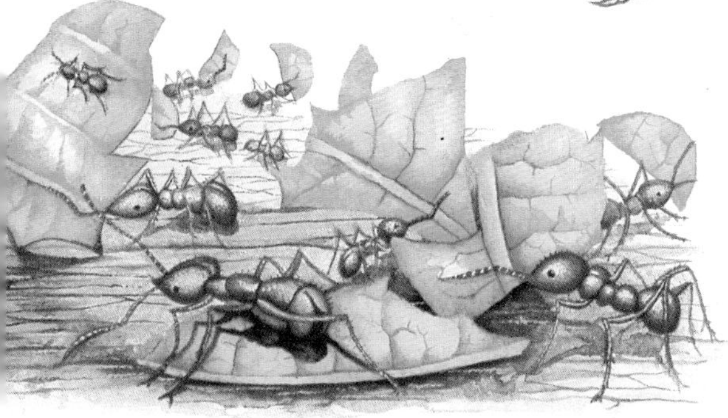

Cutting down rain forests

Most of the nitrates in rain forests are inside the plants and animals, as the plant roots take them from the ground so quickly. This means they are lost if the plants are cut down and removed.

Huge areas of rain forest are cut down every day by people who need land to grow crops. After two or three years the few nitrates in the soil are used up.

No crops will grow, and without roots to bind it the soil gets washed away. The people cannot afford fertilizers, so they move to a new area, cut down the trees and start again.

Today, logging companies are destroying more rain forest to build roads. The roads mean more people can enter the forest and clear more trees for crops.

Mantises have very long, spiny front legs which they can fold up or shoot forward to grab insects.

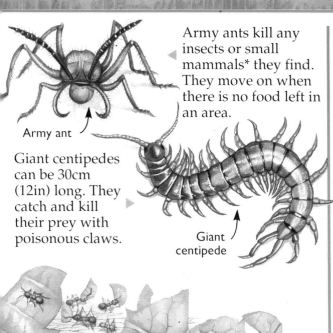

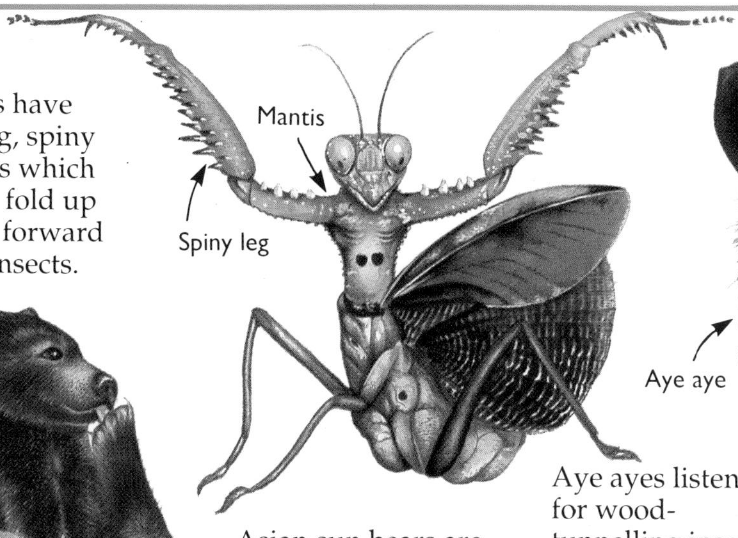
Mantis
Spiny leg

Skinny finger
Aye aye

Sun bear

Asian sun bears are the smallest bears. They eat ants, plants and honey. They put a paw into ants' nests, and lick up the ants.

Aye ayes listen for wood-tunnelling insect larvae* in fallen branches and bite a hole. They use their long, skinny middle finger to scrape them out.

***Larvae, 145; Mammals, 244.**

Climbing and gliding

Because most of the food is up in the canopy, most animals in rain forests can climb trees, and are good at clinging on and jumping about among the branches. This also helps them to escape from hunters. Some are so good at living in the trees that they hardly ever come down.

Clinging on

Many animals have special body parts for climbing, such as strong, clinging tails, called **prehensile tails**, which they use like an extra arm or leg to grip the tree. Some have extra strong fingers and thumbs to help them grip.

Asian tarsiers have "suckers" on their long fingers and toes, to help them grip. They hunt small animals, balancing with their long tails as they leap.

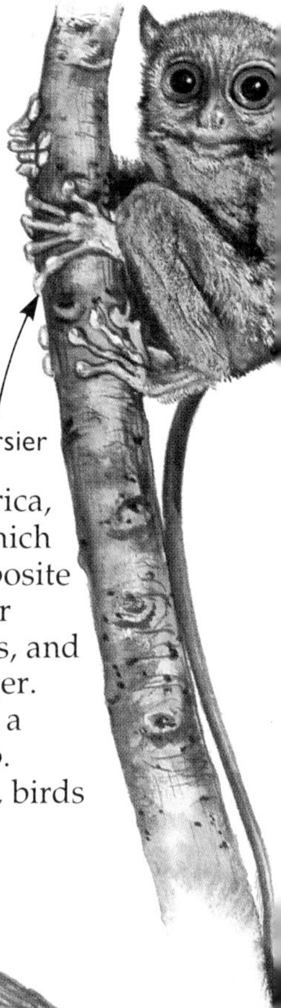

South American kinkajous have a prehensile tail as long as their body. They live in trees, eating plants, honey and small animals.

Pottos, from Africa, have thumbs which move in the opposite direction to their fingers, like ours, and a short first finger. This gives them a very strong grip. They eat insects, birds and fruit.

Sloths spend almost all their lives in trees, and can hardly move on the ground. Some feed only on one kind of tree leaf.

They move very slowly, chewing leaves and fruit, hanging upside down by hook-like claws. Their fur hangs from their belly to their back, so rain runs off.

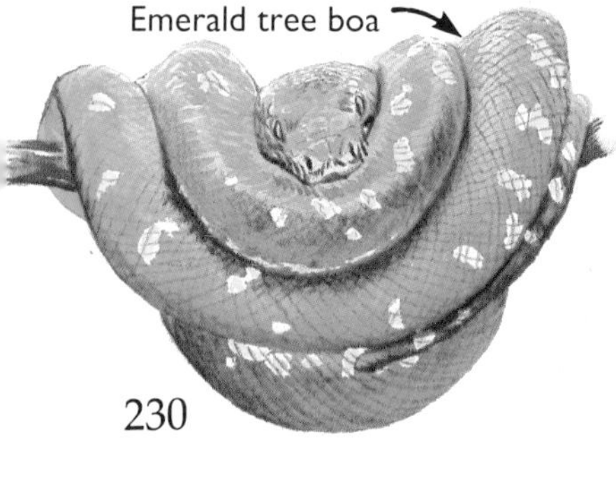

South American emerald tree boas coil over a branch. They uncoil to catch prey and hang on by the last coil.

Gliding

Many tree-living animals jump from tree to tree as they search for food. Some of them have special flaps of skin on their bodies which they use like wings, to help them glide between trees.

Flying frog

Flying frogs glide up to 13m (42ft) on huge webbed feet*.

Flying lizard

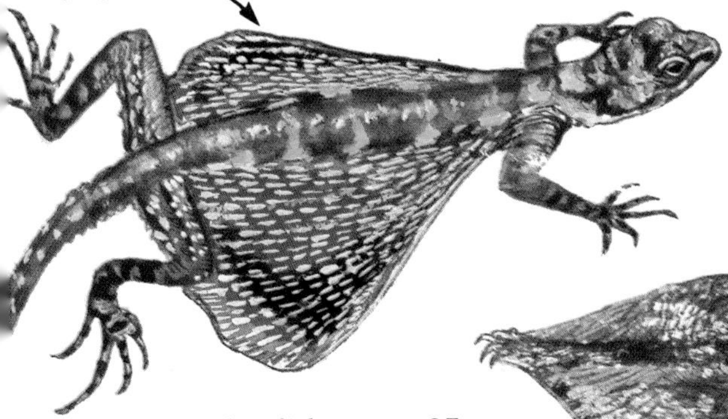

Flying lizards glide up to 25 m (82ft) on flaps of skin on their sides which open out.

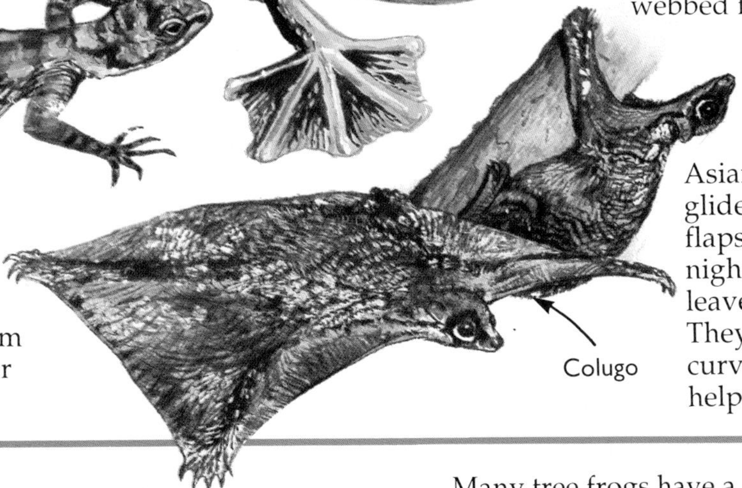

Colugo

Asian colugos glide about on flaps of skin at night, eating leaves and fruit. They have sharp, curved claws to help them climb.

Keeping in touch

Rain forests are very noisy places, because the animals keep in touch by calling and listening out for each other.

Many also have good eyesight to see at night, and to judge distances when they leap.

Tree frog

Many tree frogs have a huge sac on their throat, and call their mate with a special loud croak.

Bushbaby

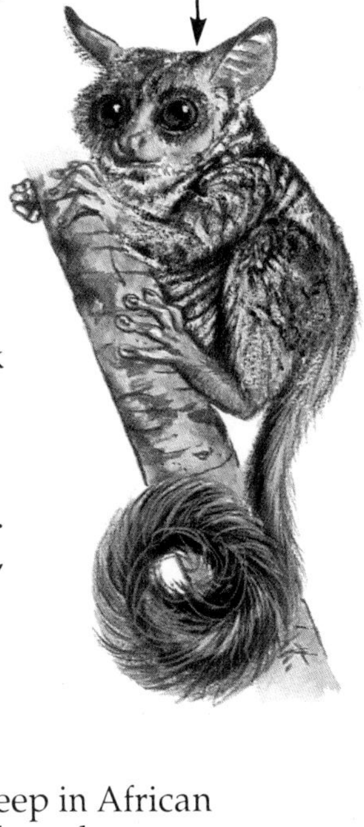

African bush-babies hunt at night, leaping with strong back legs between trees as they search for birds, insects and fruit. They have large, sensitive eyes.

Howler monkey

Howler monkeys have a large, specially shaped throat. They can be heard five kilometres (three miles) away.

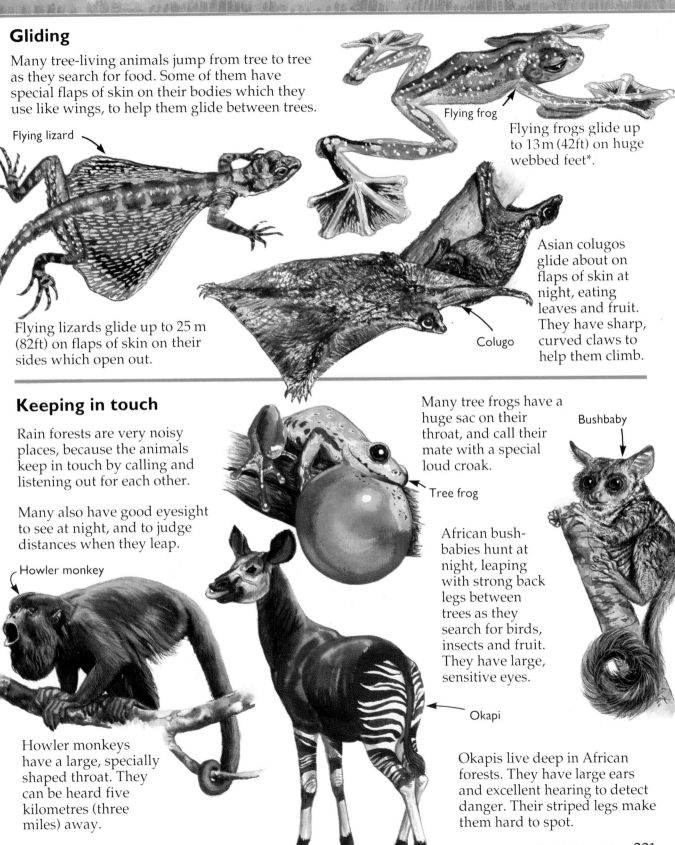

Okapi

Okapis live deep in African forests. They have large ears and excellent hearing to detect danger. Their striped legs make them hard to spot.

**Webbed feet, 218.*

Monkeys and apes

Many monkeys and apes live in rain forests. They are related to people and come from a group of animals called primates. Most primates have grasping, sensitive fingers and thumbs, long arms and legs, good eyesight, and a big brain for the size of their body.

Different kinds of primates

Apes have very long arms. They do not have a tail, and are the closest relatives of people. Monkeys have tails and most climb about high up in the trees. They feed on plant food during the day. Other primates, such as lorises, usually sleep during the day and come out at night, and many of them are insect-eaters.

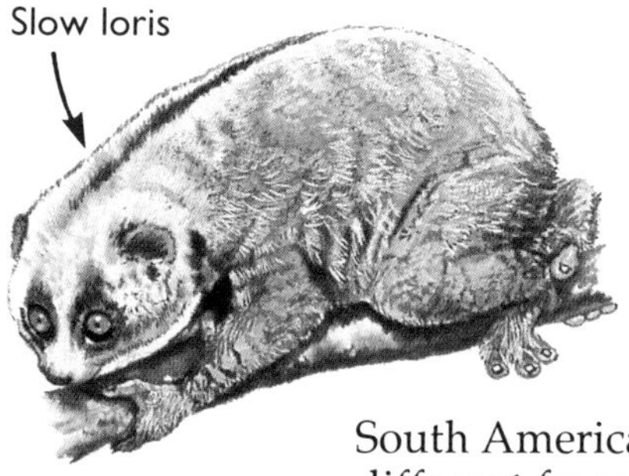

Asian slow lorises quietly climb through the trees at night, eating small animals, fruit and insects.

Gorillas are the biggest apes. They are too big and heavy to climb easily, and they spend most of the time walking on the ground on all fours.

The male leader of a group of gorillas has a silver-grey back. When other groups come near, he hoots, throws branches, beats his chest and hits the ground.

South American monkeys look different from other monkeys. Their nostrils point sideways instead of downwards.

Uakaris are monkeys from South America.

Mandrills are monkeys from Africa.

Moving about in the trees

Most primates are at home in the trees, climbing and jumping about easily, looking for food.

Squirrel monkeys can leap long distances between trees, carrying their young on their backs.

Adult spider monkeys sometimes make a bridge for their young to climb across.

Gibbons are apes. They swing from branch to branch at amazing speed using strong fingers and very long thumbs.

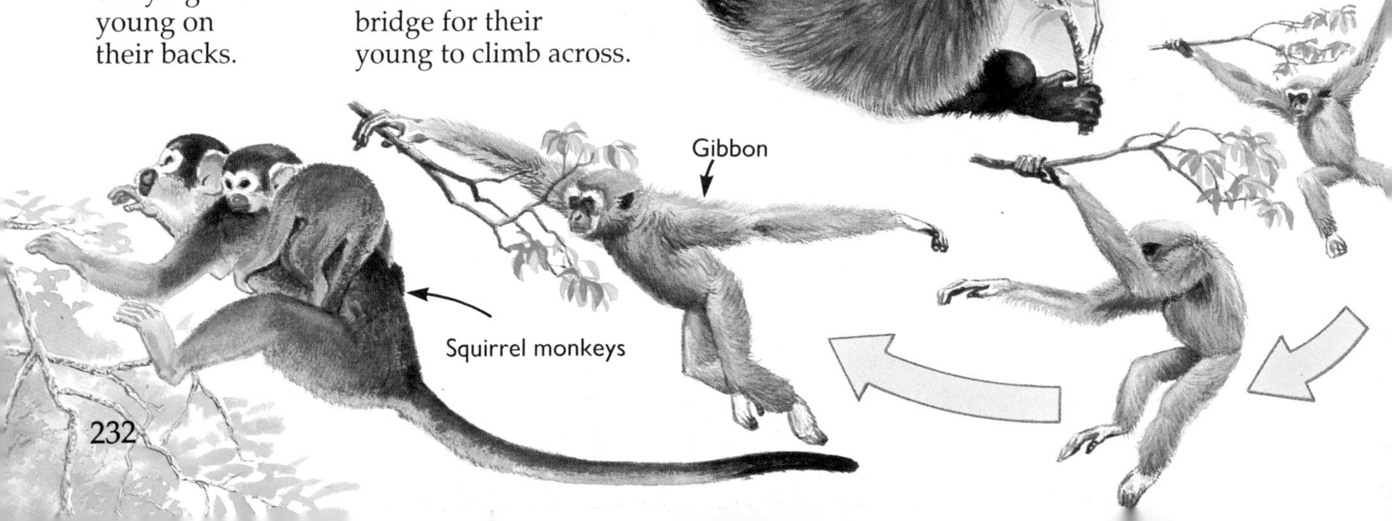

Living together

Most primates live in groups, and defend their home area against other groups.

Black and white colobus monkeys

A male black and white colobus monkey guards a group of 9 to 13 females and young. He stares at other groups, clicks his tongue and shakes branches at them.

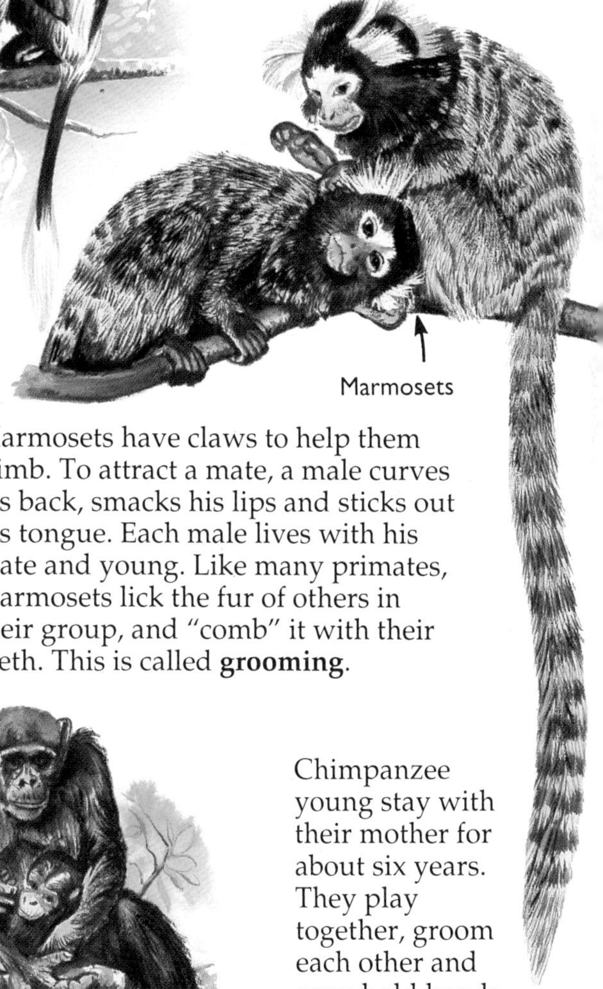

Marmosets

Douroucoulis

Douroucoulis are the only monkeys to come out at night. Their large eyes help them see in the dark. They live in pairs, high up in the trees. The males hit other monkeys which come near them.

Marmosets have claws to help them climb. To attract a mate, a male curves his back, smacks his lips and sticks out his tongue. Each male lives with his mate and young. Like many primates, marmosets lick the fur of others in their group, and "comb" it with their teeth. This is called **grooming**.

Chimpanzees are apes. They climb easily, and run on all fours. They hoot loudly when they gather for a feast, or when the males show off to decide who will be leader.

Chimpanzees make nests in the trees.

Chimpanzee young stay with their mother for about six years. They play together, groom each other and even hold hands.

Chimpanzees hooting

Chimpanzees use sticks and stones as tools. They catch termites on twigs which they prod into termite nests.

Rain forest hunters

The huge number of plant-eating animals in rain forests means there is lots of food for hunters. Most hunt at night, when it is easier for them to surprise their prey and make a kill. They usually have very good eyesight and hearing and a good sense of smell.

Cats

Rain forest cats hunt alone. Big cats, such as tigers, hunt animals bigger than themselves, to last them several meals. Cats are slim, with long tails and strong, sharp claws which fold away when they are walking, to keep them sharp. Their stripes or spots help them to blend in with the patterns of light coming through leaves.

Tiger

Tigers come from Asia. They hunt deer, pigs, buffaloes and smaller animals. They knock prey down from behind, and kill them with a bite in the neck. They cut meat with their teeth and swallow it in lumps.

Young tigers playing

Young tigers and leopards learn to hunt with their mothers, by creeping up on prey and killing it after their mother has caught it. They also learn to hunt by playing.

Leopard

Leopards creep up and jump on their prey. They can run, swim and climb, balancing with their long tails. They kill prey by breaking their necks.

South American jaguars follow groups of animals, such as deer, and attack any that lag behind. They also attack animals that come to drink at rivers.

Ocelots are small South American cats. They hunt small mammals* and birds on the ground and can also climb easily.

Clouded leopards are small cats. They climb trees and catch monkeys, small mammals, birds, reptiles* and also insects.

Other hunters

There are lots of other rain forest hunters. Many of them come out at night.

Tayras can climb easily and run very fast. They hunt at night for birds and small mammals.

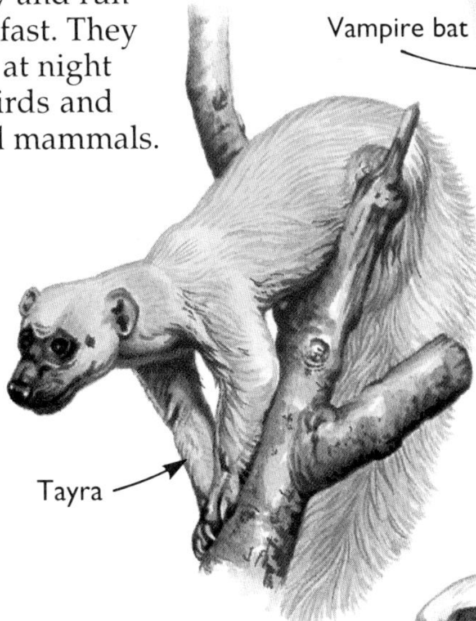

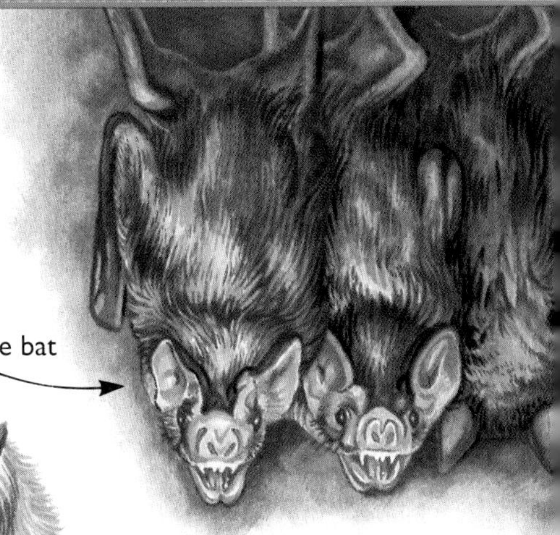

Vampire bats make thin slits with sharp teeth in the flesh of sleeping animals, without waking them. They lick up the blood with their long tongues.

Harpy eagles hunt monkeys, sloths, coatis and small mammals, birds and snakes, killing them with sharp claws. The young practise by grasping dead animals in their claws.

Coatis eat small animals and plants. They search for food on the ground with their long, sensitive noses. At night they sleep in the trees.

Asian bird-eating spiders kill prey with a poisonous bite. They hunt insects, mice and even small birds.

***Mammals, Reptiles, 244.**

Colours in the rain forest

All around the world, animals use their colours to blend into their background. They may also show off especially bright colours when they want to attract a mate, or to show they are frightened or angry. In rain forests, huge numbers of animals are brilliantly coloured.

Bright colours

Many rain forest animals are brightly coloured so they can be seen by other animals of the same kind. Other strikingly coloured animals are able to blend in with the leafy background.

Different kinds of toucan have different bright colours on their beaks. They can easily recognise each other.

Orchid mantises look like orchid flowers, so insects land on them. The mantises eat them.

Rhinoceros vipers from Africa have bright patterns but blend in with the leaves on the floor. Their poisonous bite paralyses their prey.

Day geckos are very bright, but blend in with the leaves.

Attracting a mate

Many of the most dazzling birds in the world live in rain forests. The males are usually more stunning than the females. The males dance or show off special feathers to attract a mate.

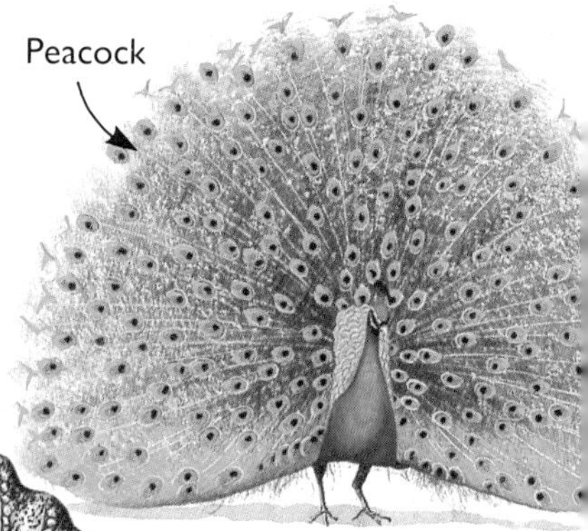

Indian male peacocks have long, brightly coloured tail feathers which they spread out and shake.

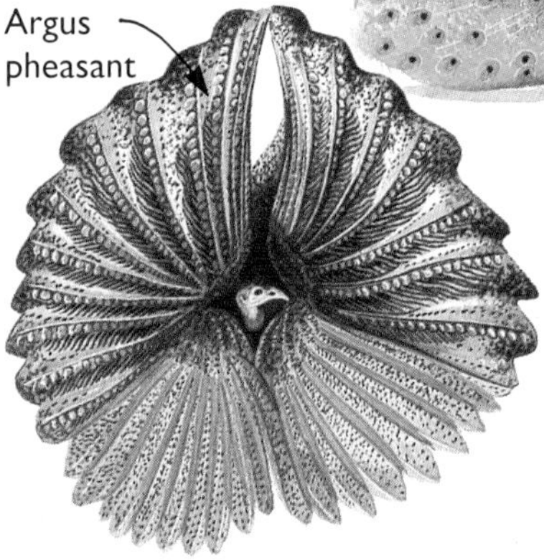

Argus pheasants from Malaya and Borneo clear the ground and dance in a complicated pattern.

Bower birds build a special avenue, column or hut out of sticks. They decorate it with flowers, berries, snake skins, shells and man-made objects such as bottle tops and teaspoons. Sometimes they paint it with charcoal and saliva, using bark as a paintbrush, or plant moss gardens.

Count Raggi's bird of paradise

Birds of paradise from Australia and New Guinea clear leaves off a patch of branches to let light shine onto their brilliant feathers. They bend over, spread out their feathers and clap their wings together.

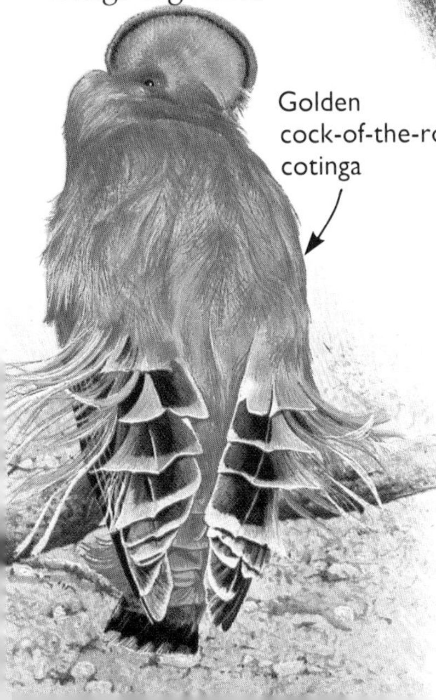
Golden cock-of-the-rock cotinga

South American golden cock-of-the-rock cotingas hide their beak with bright feathers. They make a space on the ground and dance in front of the females.

Colour tricks

Chameleons can change the colour of their skin to blend in with their background, to attract a mate, or when angry or frightened.

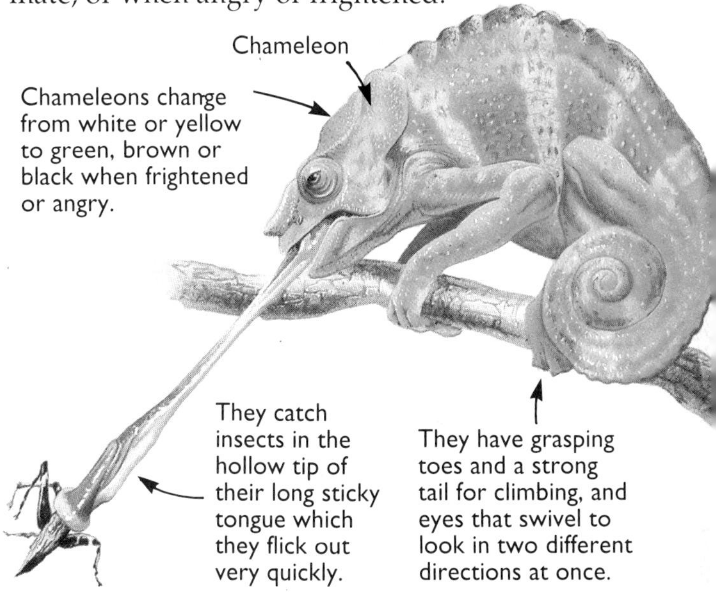
Chameleon
Chameleons change from white or yellow to green, brown or black when frightened or angry.
They catch insects in the hollow tip of their long sticky tongue which they flick out very quickly.
They have grasping toes and a strong tail for climbing, and eyes that swivel to look in two different directions at once.

Warning colours

Many poisonous or nasty-tasting animals are brightly coloured. When predators (hunters) have tasted one, they quickly learn to avoid animals with those bright colours. Other animals, which are not poisonous, are safe if they look like the poisonous ones, because predators avoid them too.

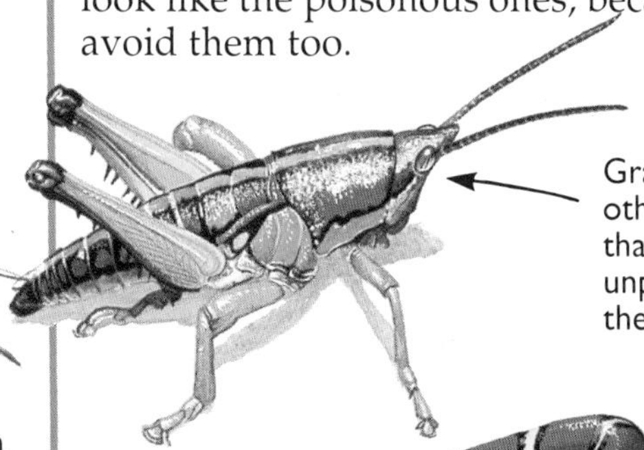
Grasshoppers warn other animals that they taste unpleasant with their bright colours.

Coral snakes are brightly coloured to show that they are poisonous. Some harmless snakes are safe, too, because they look almost the same.

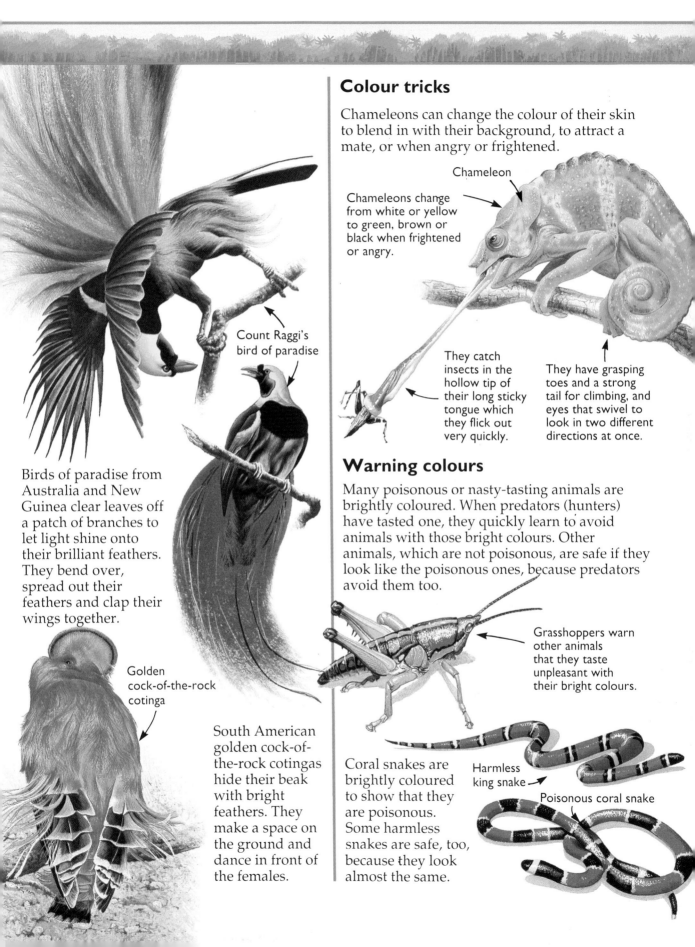

Harmless king snake
Poisonous coral snake

Living with people

As the number of people in the world gets bigger, more and more of the Earth's land surface is covered with towns and cities. This means that natural countryside habitats are lost. However, some plants and animals have learned to cope with life in towns, despite the people and the pollution, and even though there are no large open spaces of land.

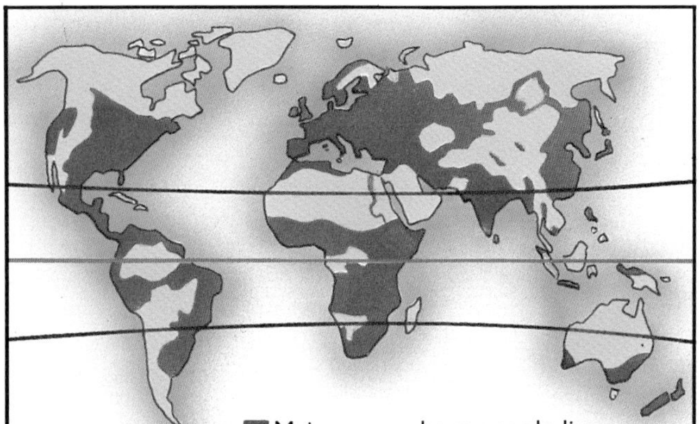

Finding food

Many animals living in towns or cities depend on people for their food.

Red foxes live in many European cities, and raccoons in North American ones. At night they look through rubbish for food to eat.

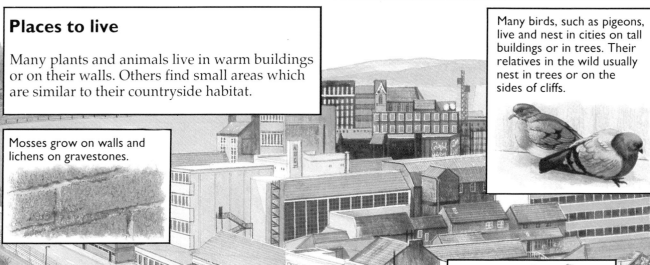

Places to live

Many plants and animals live in warm buildings or on their walls. Others find small areas which are similar to their countryside habitat.

Many birds, such as pigeons, live and nest in cities on tall buildings or in trees. Their relatives in the wild usually nest in trees or on the sides of cliffs.

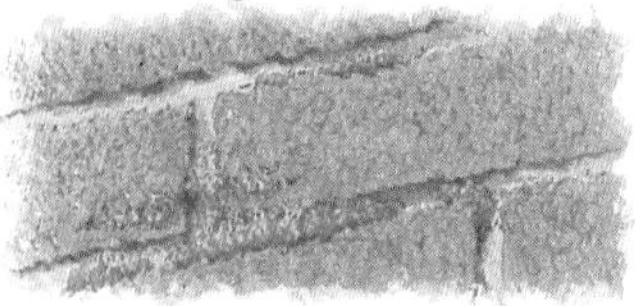

Mosses grow on walls and lichens on gravestones.

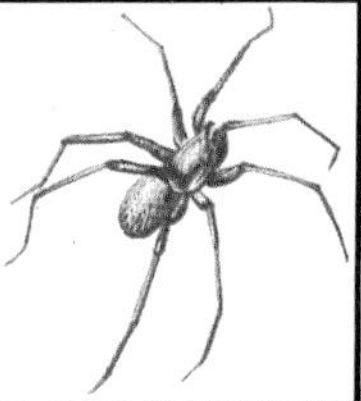

House spiders spin their webs on furniture and walls to catch small insects.

Plants such as dandelions, nettles, groundsel and goosegrass grow between paving stones.

Some plants such as Oxford ragwort first spread into cities along railway lines. They often grow on rubbish dumps and waste land.

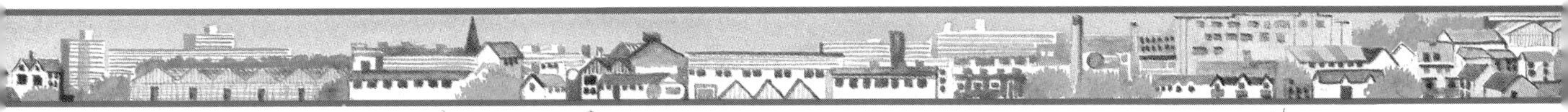

Many gulls find their food on rubbish dumps. They have changed their whole way of life to take advantage of this source of food.

Gull

Mice

Rats and mice live under floorboards and in sewers, coming out to scavenge for food left lying around. Sometimes there are more rats than people living in a city.

In the UK, blue tits have learned how to open milk bottles left outside people's doors, so that they can drink the milk.

Blue tit

Birds at bird table

Many birds survive cold, hard winters, when the plants are covered in snow, because of food left out for them on bird tables.

Bats roost in attics and the tops of tall buildings. They come out at night to hunt insects.

Grassland plants grow in open grassy places such as gardens and playing fields. Many kinds of insects live and feed on them. They are food for many birds and small animals.

Furniture beetles eat dead wood. They are just as at home in wooden furniture as in fallen logs.

House martins in the country build their nests on cliff ledges. In towns, they nest in the sheltered gap between roofs and walls.

Animals such as frogs live near rivers and ponds in parks and gardens.

People and parasites

Parasites are tiny living things that live on or inside other living things, called their hosts, and feed off them. Some kinds of parasites are harmless, but other kinds can cause diseases. Like many animals, people are host to many different kinds of parasites.

Feeding on others

The food that plants make, and animals eat, gives them energy to live and grow. The energy-giving substances travel around inside them in liquids. Plant sap contains these substances, and in animals they are carried in blood and other body liquids. Many parasites feed on these liquids.

Leeches live in swampy jungles. They feed on animal blood, including that of people. They attach themselves with suckers while they feed. When they are full, they drop off. They can survive for weeks on one meal.

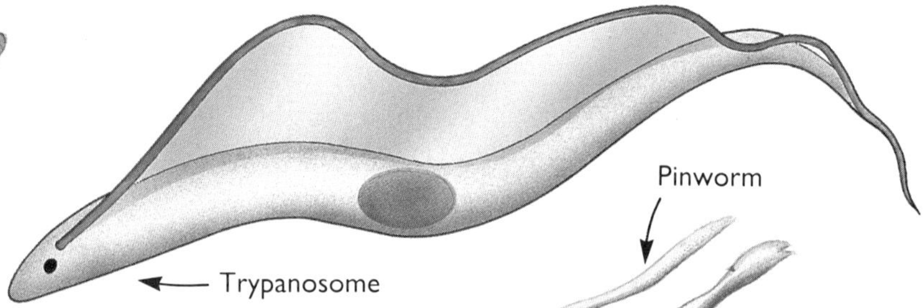

Sleeping sickness (see page 166) is caused by trypanosomes. They swim in people's body liquids and soak up the food they need. People get them from other ill people via blood-sucking insects, such as tse-tse flies.

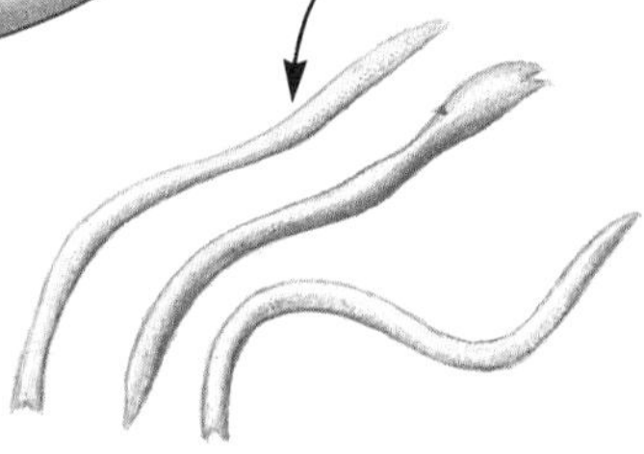

Pinworms are human parasites that live in the gut. They can grow to about 20mm (one inch) long. They eat bits of food.

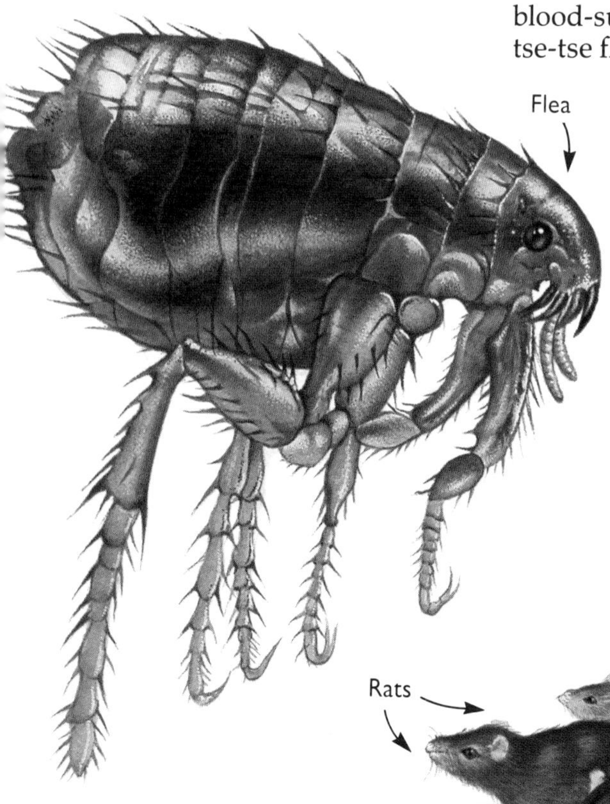

Ticks, lice and fleas are insects that feed on blood. They have sucking mouths and claws to cling onto hairs or fur.

Fleas live on both rats and people. In the 1300's, a bacteria they carried spread to people. It caused a disease, called the Black Death. Millions of people died of the disease.

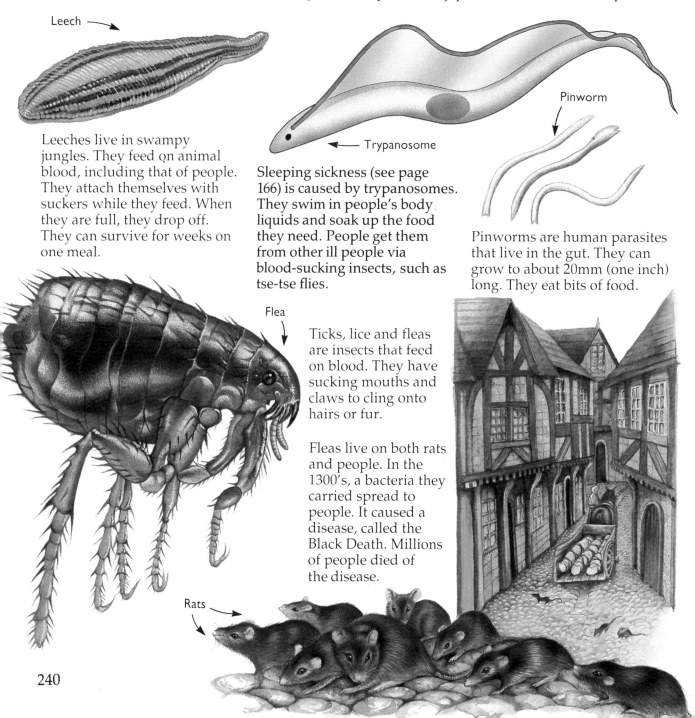

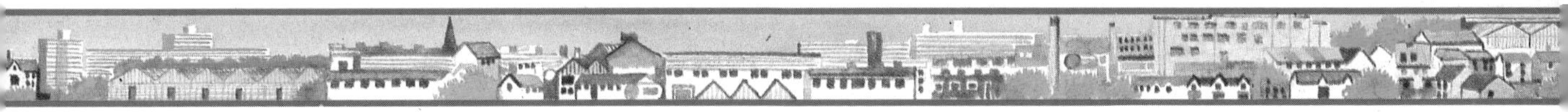

Bacteria and viruses

Bacteria and viruses are very tiny living things. Bacteria are made up of only one very tiny cell*. Some of them live in or on other living things and get all their food from them. Viruses are even smaller than bacteria. Some viruses, such as T4 bacteriophages, live inside bacteria.

Many kinds of harmless bacteria live off people. For example, thousands of tiny bacteria live in our stomachs. The bacteria feed by breaking up plant and animal material into simple substances. This helps us digest* our food.

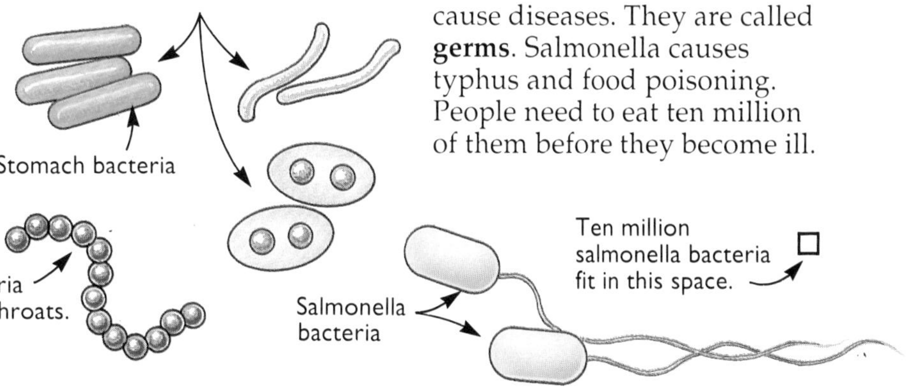

Different kinds of bacteria
Stomach bacteria
These bacteria cause sore throats.
Salmonella bacteria
Ten million salmonella bacteria fit in this space.

Other kinds of bacteria can cause diseases. They are called **germs**. Salmonella causes typhus and food poisoning. People need to eat ten million of them before they become ill.

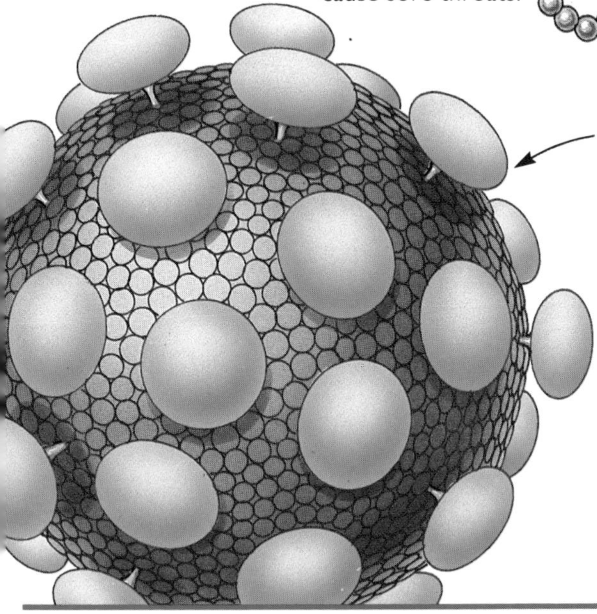

AIDS virus. It is actually 100 times smaller than one of the bacteria in human stomachs.

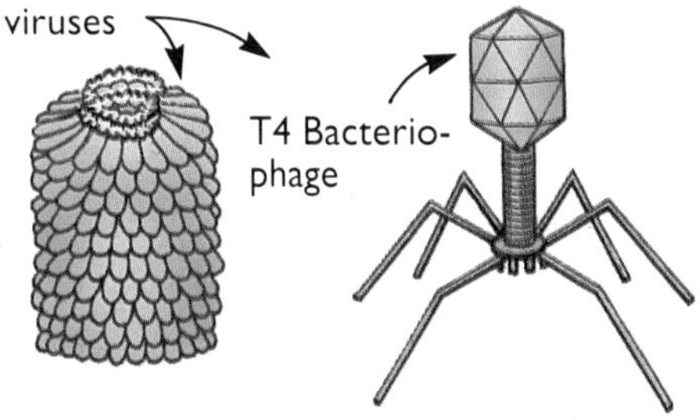

Different kinds of viruses
T4 Bacterio-phage
Tobacco mosaic virus

Viruses live inside plant and animal cells*. They cause diseases, such as colds, AIDS, rabies and chicken pox and are also germs. They attack cells by getting inside and taking over the nucleus (control centre) of the cell. They make the cell make more new viruses.

The war against diseases

Animals, including people, all have defences inside their bodies against diseases. The defences are called the **immune system**.

The immune system is made up of cells* that can tell germs and body cells apart. They fight off diseases by killing the germs that cause them.

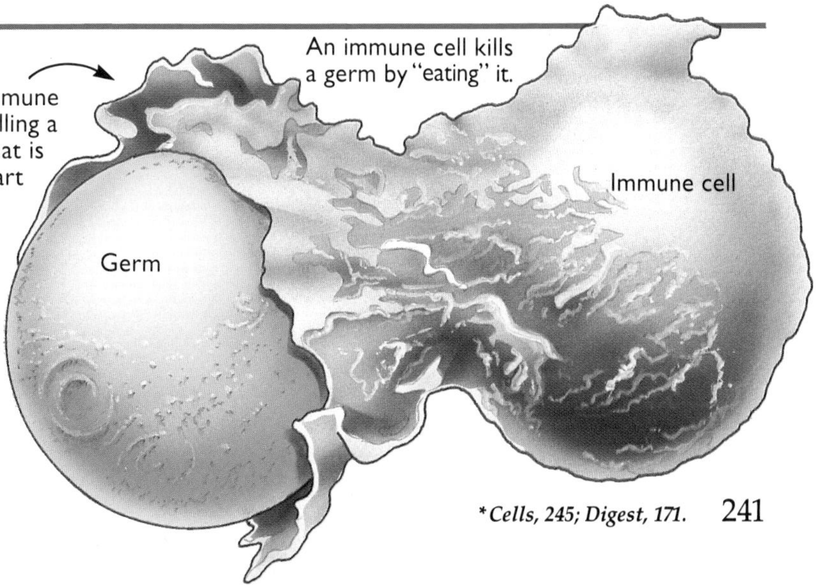

An immune cell killing a cell that is not part of the body.
An immune cell kills a germ by "eating" it.
Immune cell
Germ

Cells, 245; Digest, 171.

Endangered species

Scientists think that a million rare species of plants and animals may die out in the next 10 to 20 years. You can find out some reasons for this on pages 146-147. These species are called endangered species. The biggest threat is the destruction of wild areas when people cut down forests, make new farmland, let deserts spread, build cities, roads and mines, and pollute areas.

Protecting plants

About 60,000 different kinds of plants, about a quarter of the total number of species in the world, are endangered.

Each kind of plant provides food or shelter for many different animals. If the plants become extinct, the animals that depend on them may be threatened.

Many mangrove swamps are destroyed for timber and to make room for farms and towns. The plants die, and the animals lose their homes. In Malaysia, mangrove forests are cut down for timber. To protect them, they are cleared a bit at a time. Each area is then left alone for 40 years. During this time the trees grow again, and new ones are planted. The animals have plenty of forest left to live in.

Mangrove swamp

In places such as Canada, Brazil, Kenya and Australia, people are replanting trees where forests have been chopped down. It will take hundreds of years for the forests to grow back. However, as the new trees grow, many kinds of plants and animals may return that had been lost from these areas.

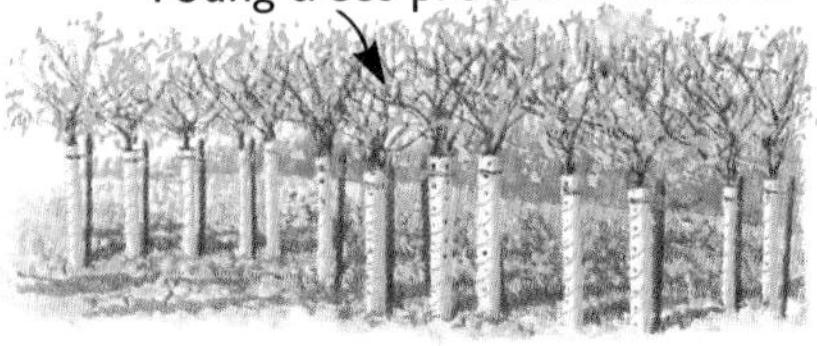
Young trees protected in tubes

Individual species of rare plants become endangered when people collect them. Golden barrel cacti and many kinds of slipper orchids are endangered because they are taken from the wild and sold.

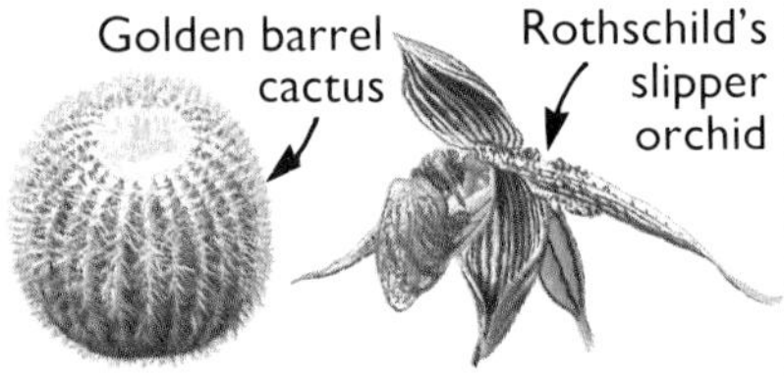
Golden barrel cactus
Rothschild's slipper orchid

African violets are very rare in the wild, but are not likely to die out. This is because they are specially grown for sale, so collectors do not take them from the wild. They are now common as house plants, but will not become common again in the wild unless they are replanted.

African violet

Some rare plants are saved and stored in special botanic gardens, nurseries and reserves. The seeds are stored in seed banks. If the plants die out in the wild, they can be replanted from seeds from the saved plants. For example, in Wales the last two tufted saxifrage plants were saved. New plants were grown from them and replanted in the wild.

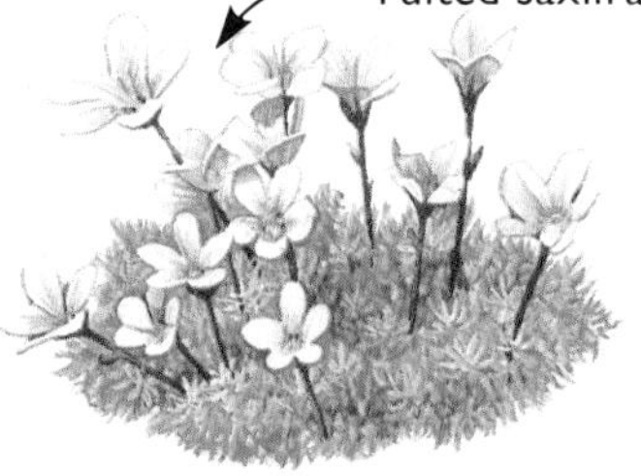
Tufted saxifrage

Protecting animals

Thousands of rare species of animals are endangered because they are hunted, or because the plants that provide their food and homes are destroyed.

Many people now work to save them. There are many different ways that people can help rare animals.

Many animals are hunted for their skins or horns. However, governments have now made it illegal to sell skins of animals such as alligators, vicuñas and koalas, or items such as elephant tusks and turtle shells.

Alligator

Koala

Hawksbill turtle

Rhinoceroses are endangered because people kill them to sell their horns. In parts of Africa, people are protecting rhinoceroses by sawing off their horns, so that hunters leave them alone.

Rhinoceros with horns sawn off

The hunting of tigers was banned in 1970, and since then their numbers have more than doubled.

Polar bears nearly died out because so many were killed for their skins, and for sport. Many were also killed if they came near towns. To save them, many polar bears were moved away from towns, and several countries agreed to protect them and the areas where they live. There are many more in the wild now.

Many butterflies, such as West African orange foresters, are endangered partly because people collect them, but also because so many wild areas where they used to live have been destroyed.

Many wild areas called reserves or national parks are being set aside. Here animals and plants are protected from people, but live in the wild.

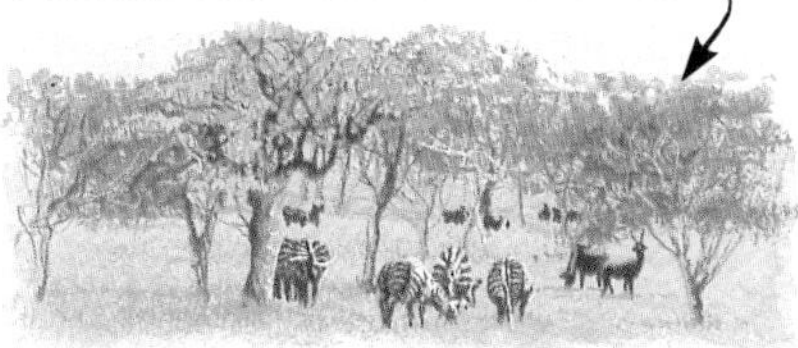

Spanish lynxes were endangered because so much of the forest they lived in had been cut down. However, they are now protected in a reserve in Coto Donana.

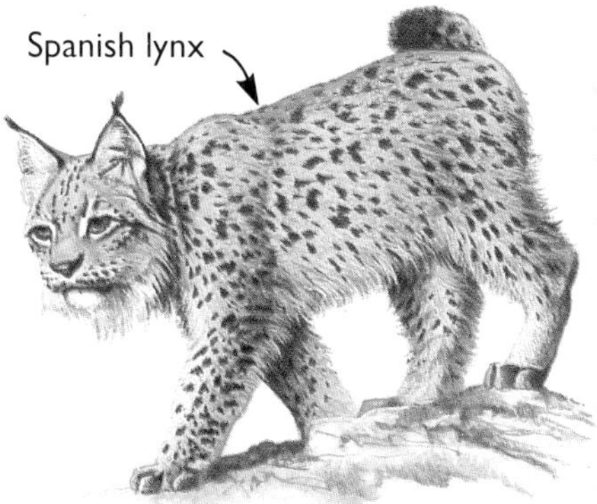

Some reserves are in special areas of the sea. In Florida there are areas where boats are not allowed to go, to protect manatees from being harmed by propellers.

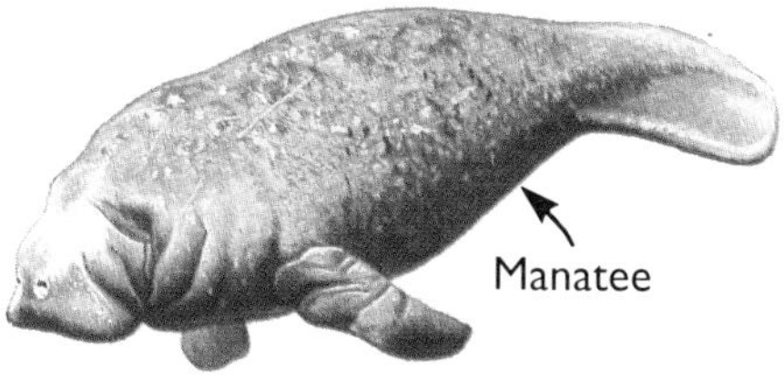

Whales such as humpbacks and blue whales were hunted so much in the past for meat and fat (made into oil), that they nearly died out. Although it is now illegal in most countries to hunt whales, people do still hunt them, or catch them accidentally in fishing nets.

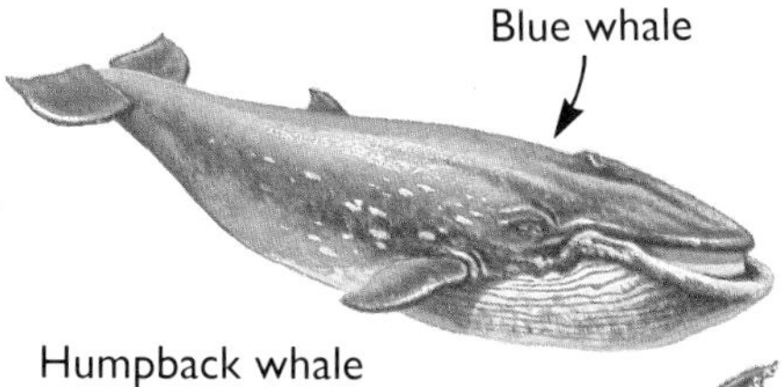

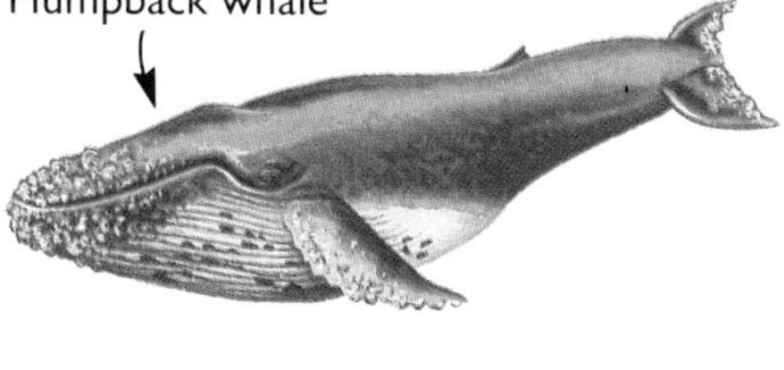

Sometimes when animals have very nearly died out, they are kept in special centres until their numbers have increased. They are put back in protected wild areas when there are enough of them to stand a good chance of surviving.

Californian condors died out in the wild because they are slow breeders*, their food is hard to find and people hunted them. However, before they died out in the wild, some of their eggs were saved and hatched in special centres. The young birds were fed by hand-held puppets of adult condors. When it is safe, they will be let back into the wild.

Many golden lion tamarin monkeys have been bred in zoos, and some have now been put back into a protected area of rain forest in Brazil. At first they live inside big cages in the forest so they learn to survive and find food in the wild while being protected from other animals.

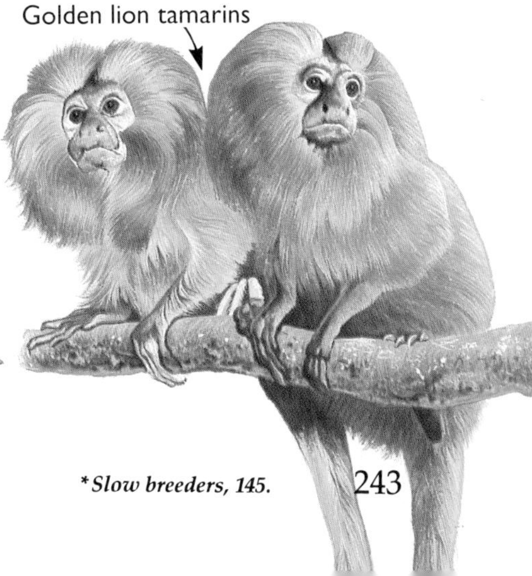

***Slow breeders, 145.**

Describing living things

To help them describe the living world, scientists have grouped together living things that are similar to each other. The biggest groups are called kingdoms. All the animals are in the animal kingdom, and all the plants are in the plant kingdom. Inside these groups there are smaller groups, with even smaller ones inside them. The smallest groups of all are known as species*. The group names tell the scientists about the living things in them.

The plant kingdom

The main difference between plants and animals is that plants make their own food from sunlight, the gas called carbon dioxide and water, and they are called **autotrophs.**

Animals do not make their food, but eat plants or other animals, and are called **heterotrophs**.

Algae are simple plants. They may be tiny, such as phytoplankton*, or much larger, such as seaweed. They are often put with fungi in the group **thallophytes**.

Mosses are in a group called **bryophytes**. They have tiny root-like things (not true roots) which cling to surfaces rather than growing into the ground. They do not have xylem* and phloem* to carry water and food. They produce spores, like the ones produced by fungi (see page 193), in a case on a stalk. When the case opens, the spores blow away, land and grow into new plants.

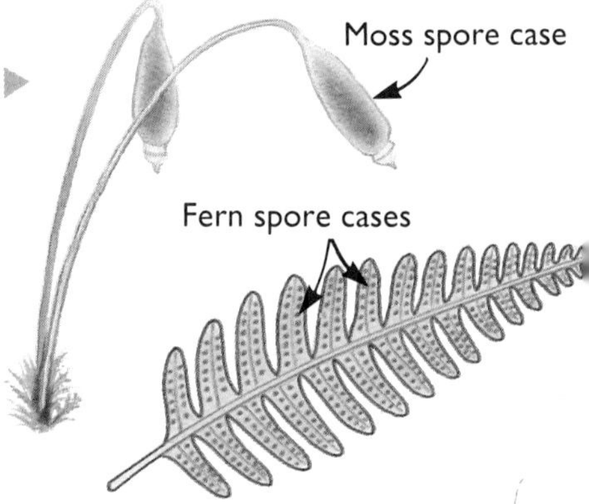
Moss spore case
Fern spore cases

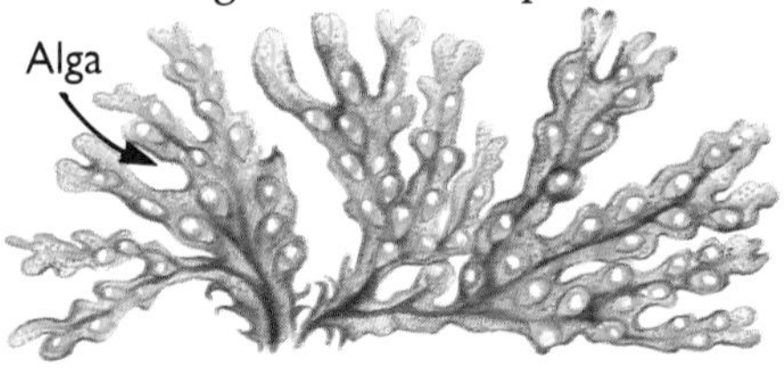
Alga

Ferns also produce spores. The spore cases grow in groups under the leaves. Ferns have xylem and phloem and are in a group known as **pteridophytes**.

The animal kingdom

Scientists call the animals with a backbone in their body **vertebrates** and those without a backbone **invertebrates**. These are the two main groups in the animal kingdom. Both of these big groups contain other, smaller groups.

Vertebrates

There are about 45,000 different kinds of vertebrates living on Earth. They are divided into five main groups: fish, amphibians, reptiles, birds and mammals.

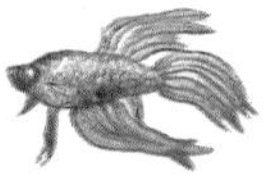

What is a fish?

Fish are cold-blooded* animals which live in water. They breathe using gills*, their bodies are covered with scales and they have fins. They lay many eggs in water.

What is an amphibian?

Newts, salamanders, frogs and toads are all **amphibians**. They are cold-blooded, and spend some time on land, but lay their eggs in water. Their young breathe with gills, but the adults use lungs* on land, and can breathe through their skins in air or water.

What is a reptile?

Turtles and tortoises, lizards, snakes and crocodiles are all **reptiles**. They are cold-blooded animals which live on land. They breathe air using lungs, and have a dry scaly skin. They lay their eggs on land.

What is a bird?

Birds are warm-blooded* animals. They have wings, and their whole bodies are covered with feathers. They breathe air with lungs and produce young by laying eggs. They have beaks but no teeth.

What is a mammal?

Mammals are warm-blooded and have hair. They breathe air with lungs. The females feed their young with milk from their bodies. Two kinds of mammals, spiny anteaters and platypuses, lay eggs and are known as **monotremes**, but the rest produce live young. Some produce tiny live young and nurse them in a pouch. They are **marsupials**, and include kangaroos. All other mammals give birth to larger live young.

 **Cold-blooded, 182; Gills, 214; Lungs, 208; Phloem, 142; Phytoplankton, 150; Species, 146; Warm-blooded, 182; Xylem, 142.*

Plants such as conifers*, called **gymnosperms**, have xylem and phloem. Like flowering plants (see below) they grow new plants from seeds, formed when male **pollen** joins with female **ovules**. However, gymnosperms do not grow flowers, instead the pollen and ovules grow on **cones**. The seeds have no outer cases.

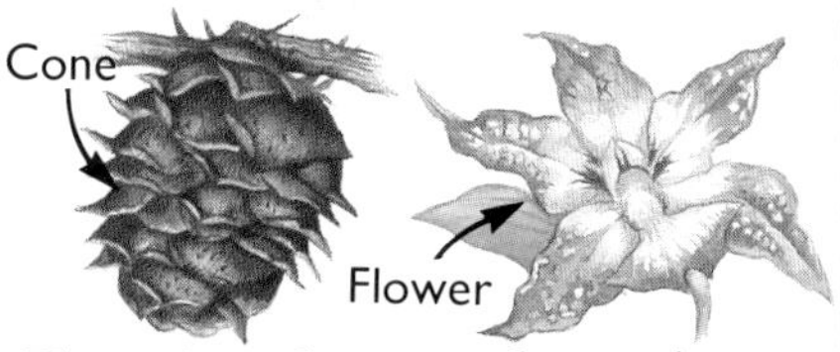
Cone
Flower

Flowering plants, such as palm trees, daffodils and roses, are called **angiosperms**. They have xylem and phloem, and their pollen and ovules are made in flowers (see page 142). The pollen is carried to the ovules by wind, water or animals (see pages 162-163). Cases protect the seeds.

Other kingdoms

Almost all living things are made out of very tiny "building blocks" called **cells**, each of which has a control centre called a **nucleus**. Some of the very tiniest living things have only one cell. They cannot really be called plants or animals, so many scientists put them in separate kingdoms.

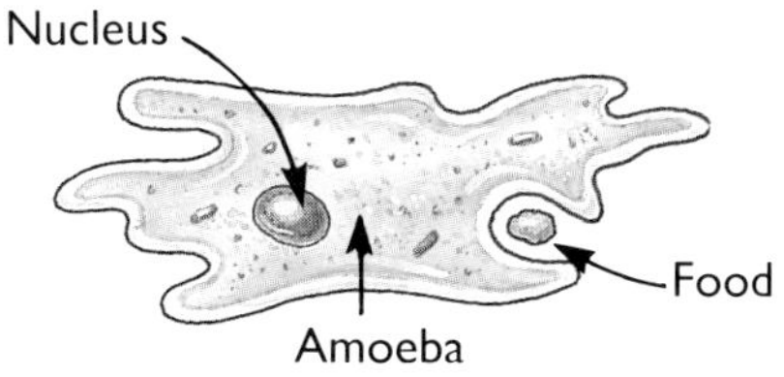
Nucleus
Food
Amoeba

Most tiny living things with one cell are put in a kingdom of their own called **protista**. Some, such as amoeba, take in food. Others make it from sunlight, like plants. Some can do both.

Bacteria* and some very simple algae are often put in a kingdom called **monera**. They are tiny living things with only one cell. They are separated from the protista because the cell does not have a true nucleus.

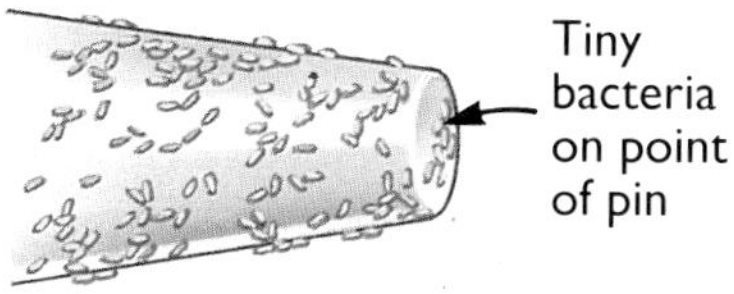
Tiny bacteria on point of pin

Fungi are often put in a separate kingdom, the kingdom **fungi**. They are made up of very thin threads, but these are not made of cells. They get their food by taking in liquids from dead, rotting* plants and animals.

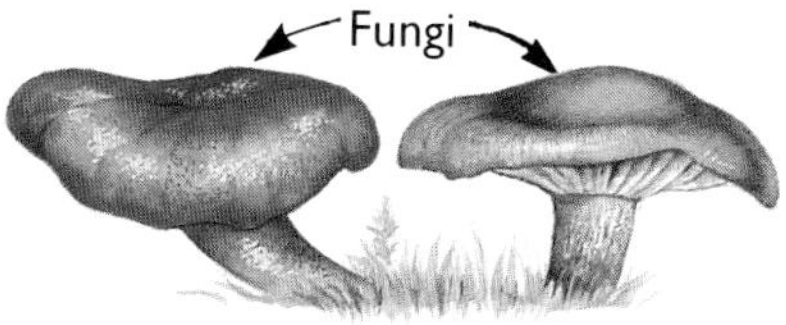
Fungi

Invertebrates

There are far more invertebrates than vertebrates living on Earth, about 950,000 different kinds. Some are so tiny that they can only be seen with a microscope. Others, such as giant squid, grow to 20 metres (65 feet) long. The invertebrates are divided into many different groups.

Jellyfish, sea anemones and corals are put together in one group, called **coelenterates**, because they have soft, jelly-like bodies and catch prey with stinging tentacles.

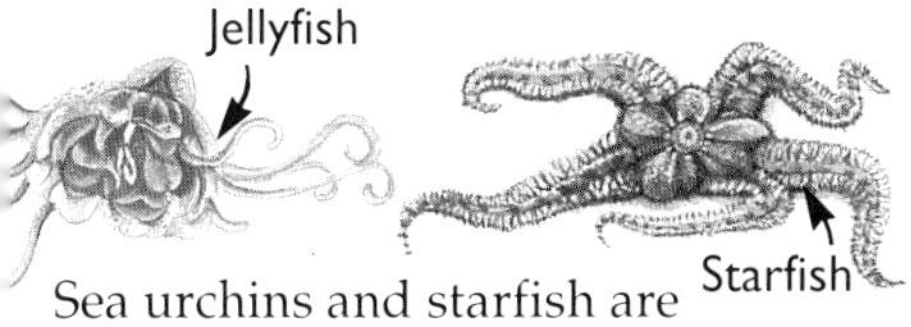
Jellyfish
Starfish

Sea urchins and starfish are both in the same group, called **echinoderms**, because they have tough, spiny skins, and their bodies are made up of five identical parts.

Crabs, spiders, insects and centipedes are in a group called **arthropods**. Their bodies are divided into sections called **segments**, covered with a hard skin or shell. Their legs bend at joints. Spiders have 8 legs, and insects have 6. There are more different kinds of insect in the world than any other animal.

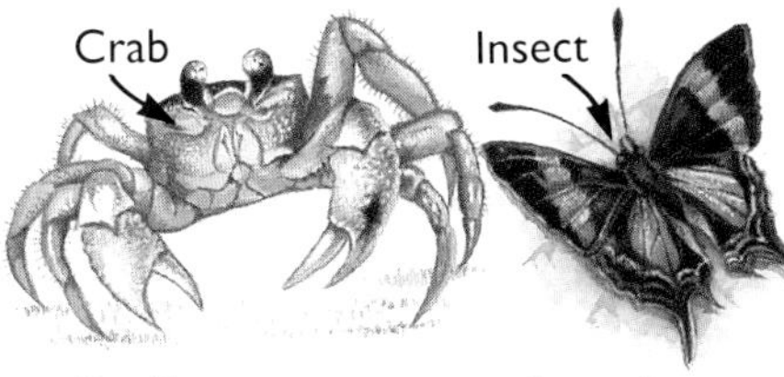
Crab
Insect

Snails, oysters, mussels and octopuses have a soft body, with a hard shell either outside or inside their body. The group they are in is called **molluscs**.

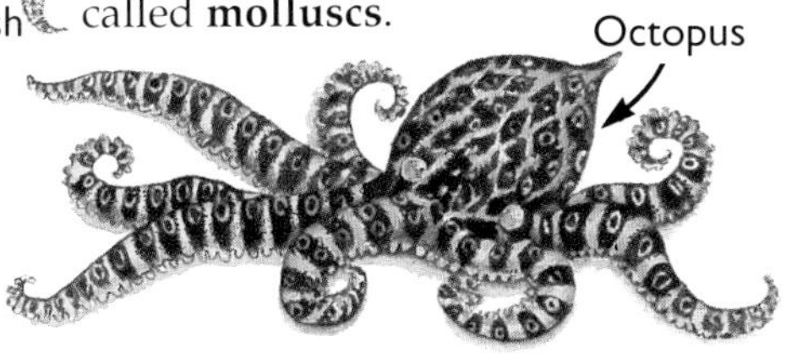
Octopus

Earthworms and ragworms come from a group called **annelids**. Their bodies are made up of sections called **segments**, with an opening at each end.

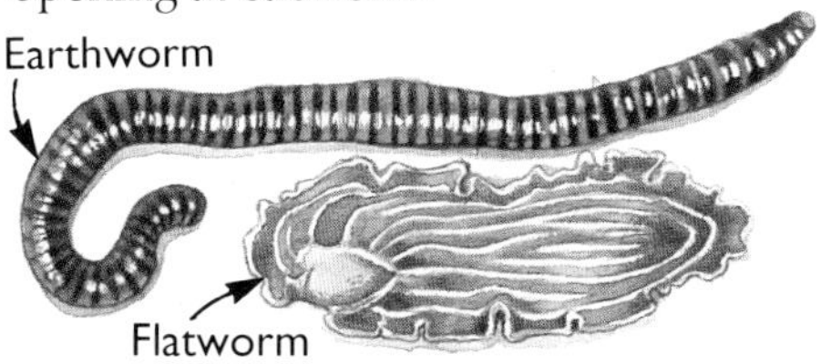
Earthworm
Flatworm

Flatworms, such as tapeworms and liver flukes, are put in a different group from earthworms, called **platyhelminthes**. They have only one opening in their body.

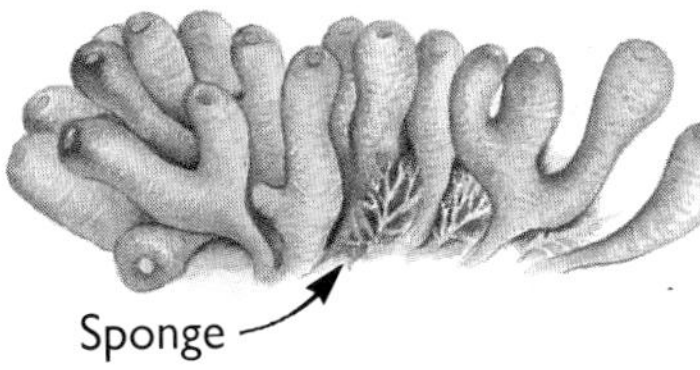
Sponge

Sponges are in a group of creatures called **porifera** which have stiff bodies. They filter feed* by passing water through holes in their bodies.

Bacteria, 241; Conifers, 194-195; Filter feeding, 150; Rotting, 193.

Glossary

Words that are explained in this glossary (pages 246-248) are printed in **bold type**.

Acid. A sour-tasting chemical. Plants and animals contain some harmless weak acids. Some acids, however, are dangerous.

Anthers. The male parts of flowers, where special male **cells** called pollen are made (see **pollination**, **fertilization**).

Aquatic. Living in water.

Arboreal. Living in trees.

Autotrophs. Living things that make their food. Plants make their food from sunlight, carbon dioxide and water, and are autotrophs.

Binary fission. The way that **cells** produce new cells as a plant or animal grows. First the nucleus and then the cell divides into two. This makes two new cells, the same size as the original one, each with a nucleus.

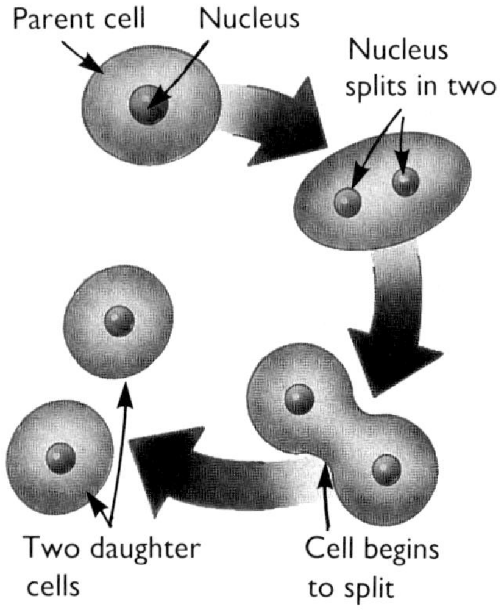

Parent cell
Nucleus
Nucleus splits in two
Two daughter cells
Cell begins to split

Biology. The scientific study of living things.

Blood. A liquid which is pumped around the bodies of animals, carrying oxygen, carbon dioxide and simple sugars and waste.

Blubber. A thick layer of fat under the skin of animals such as whales. It keeps them warm.

Botany. The scientific study of plants.

Bud. Part of a plant that grows into a flower or a leaf. Also part of a cell or simple animal that splits off and grows to be exactly the same. This is called budding. For example, coral polyps produce buds (see page 156).

Camouflage. Skin, fur or feather colours which help an animal to blend in with its background.

Carnivore. A meat-eating animal.

Carpel. The word for the female part of a flower - the **ovary** - together with its outer pieces, called the stigma and style. When **pollination** happens, the pollen first lands on the sticky stigma, and then travels down the style to the ovary.

Cells. Very tiny "building blocks", each with a control centre called a nucleus, from which almost all living things are made.

Chromosomes. Thread-like things in the nucleus of a **cell**, made of a complex chemical called DNA. Each is a chain of **genes**.

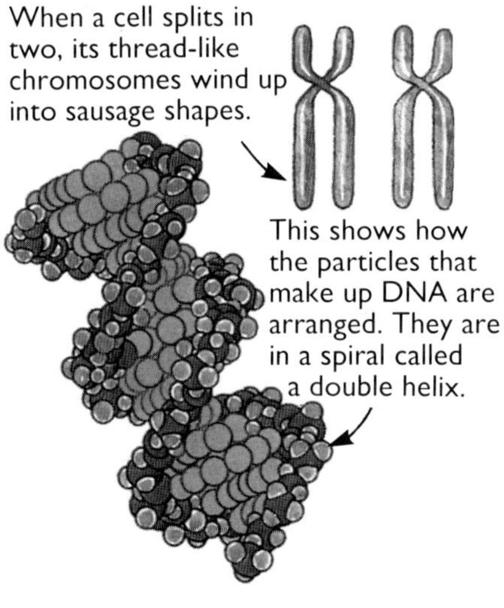

When a cell splits in two, its thread-like chromosomes wind up into sausage shapes.
This shows how the particles that make up DNA are arranged. They are in a spiral called a double helix.

Colony. A group made up of large numbers of one kind of plant or animal, living together. The word is most often used of insects, or sea birds such as gannets.

Community. A group of plants and animals living together in an **environment**, and dependent on each other in a **food web**.

Conservation. Protecting and preserving natural **environments**, so as to protect the plants and animals for the future.

Decomposer. An **organism** which causes dead plants and animals to rot, by breaking them down into simple substances. Bacteria and fungi are decomposers.

Deforestation. The loss of trees from forested areas.

Demersal. Living on the bottom of the sea.

Desertification. The spread of deserts to new areas.

Detritus. Rotting bits of plant or animal material.

Digestion. The breakdown of food inside an animal's body into substances which the body can use to get energy and for growth.

Diurnal. A word describing plants with flowers that open, and animals that are active, during daylight hours.

Dormant. A word describing a plant or animal that is resting for a time without growing, so using up very little energy or food.

Ecology. The study of the relationship between plants and animals and their **environment**.

Ecosystem. A community of plants and animals and their **environment**.

Embryo. A young plant inside a seed, or a young animal inside an egg or its mother's body. It is growing but not yet fully formed.

Endangered species. A species that may die out because of dangers such as a change in the **environment**.

Endemic species. A species found only in a particular area. It is said to be endemic to that area.

Environment. The natural surroundings in which plants and animals live. Environments vary in different parts of the world depending on things such as how much sun and rain there is. Plants and animals living in deserts, tropical forests or polar regions become very good at living in their particular environments.

Epiphyte. A plant which grows on another plant for support, but does not harm it. For example, bromeliads grow on trees (see page 226).

Evolution. The changes which take place in animals and plants over millions of years. One of the ways in which scientists know about these changes is from studying **fossils** and comparing them to species of plants and animals that are alive today.

Extinct. A word describing a plant or animal species that has completely died out.

Fertilization. The joining together of special male and female **cells** to produce a new living thing. The female cells are eggs (see **ovary**) and the male ones are in pollen in flowers (see **pollination**) and **sperm** in animals.

Filter feeding. A way of feeding by sifting very tiny pieces of food out of water.

Fins. Parts which stick out from a fish's body and help it to swim. They are made from spines covered in skin.

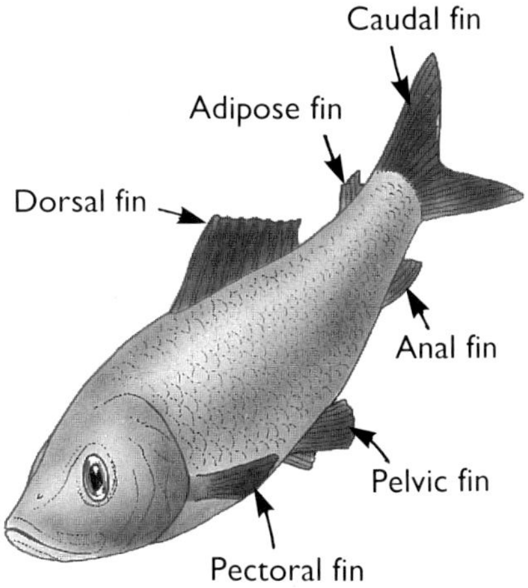
Caudal fin
Adipose fin
Dorsal fin
Anal fin
Pelvic fin
Pectoral fin

Flower. The part of a flowering plant which holds the male and female parts needed to produce seeds (see **anthers**, **ovary**). New young plants grow from the seeds.

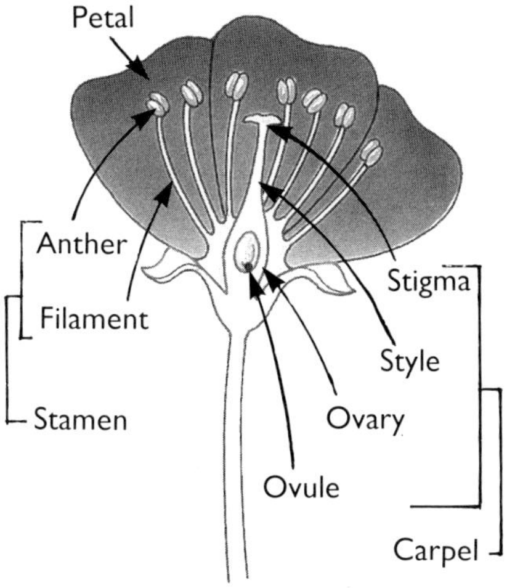
Petal
Anther
Filament
Stamen
Stigma
Style
Ovary
Ovule
Carpel

Food web. A group of living things in a **community**, linked together by what they eat and what they are food for. There is a diagram of a North American forest food web on page 138.

Fossils. The hard parts of plants and animals preserved in rock over millions of years.

Genes. Chemical units that are joined together in chains to form the **chromosomes** of a living thing. Genes are the "codes" which say what a living thing is, and what it looks like. For example one gene may be the code for eye colour, another the code for sex (male or female).

Germination. The early growth of a seed or **spore**.

Herbivore. A plant-eating animal.

Heterotrophs. Living things which depend on plants or other animals to provide their food, and cannot make their own, that is, animals.

Hibernation. A sleep-like resting state which some kinds of animals go into during winter. Their body temperature drops when the conditions are cold and their bodies "slow down". This means they hardly use any energy, so they do not have to eat much.

Incubate. To keep eggs warm until the young hatch out.

Larvae. Young forms that look very different from the adults, but which gradually change to look like them.

Littoral. Living on the sea shore, or near it in shallow water, or living on the bottom of a lake near the shore.

Metamorphosis. The changes a **larva** goes through before it turns into an adult.

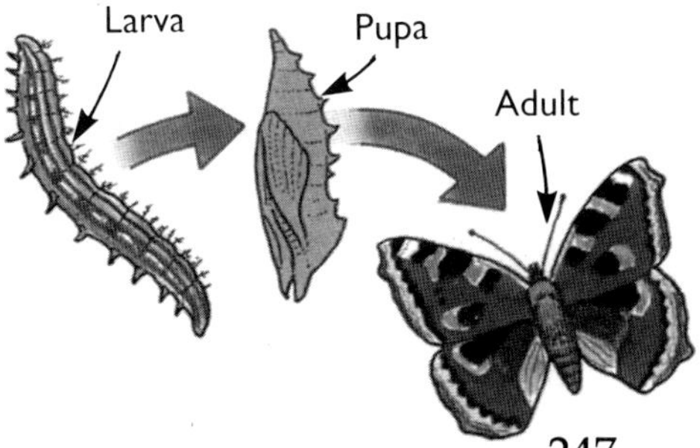
Larva
Pupa
Adult

Microbiology. The study of living things so tiny that they can only be seen through a microscope.

Migration. Regular long journeys made by animals, for example, moving in winter to places where there is more food, and then coming back in the summer.

Mimic. An animal or plant that looks or sounds similar to another. Many gain extra protection from being mimics, because they mimic a poisonous species, and so other animals avoid them.

Minerals. Certain kinds of substances found in the ground, and in the bodies of all living things. Plants take minerals from the ground to help them grow.

Nocturnal. Active at night.

Nutrients. Food substances that plants and animals can break down so they can grow or get energy.

Nymph. A young insect form that looks like the adult, but is smaller and has no wings. Locust hoppers (see page 184) are nymphs.

Omnivore. An animal that eats both plants and other animals.

Organism. A living thing.

Ovary. The female part of a flower, and the part in a female animal, where eggs are made. The eggs are special **cells**, called ovules in flowers and ova in animals (see also **fertilization**).

Parasite. A plant or animal which lives on or in another plant or animal, called its host, and gets all its food from it. The host may or may not be harmed.

Pelagic. Living in the open water of a sea or lake.

Petals. Leaf-like parts of a flower, often colourful to attract insects to **pollinate** the flower.

Pollination. The carrying of male cells called pollen from the **anther** of a flower to an **ovary** (see **fertilization**).

Pollutant. A poisonous substance that harms the **environment**.

Predator. An animal that hunts and kills other animals for food.

Prey. An animal that is hunted by another animal for food. A bird of prey is one that hunts other animals, which are its prey.

Pupa. A stage during the **metamorphosis** of some insect **larvae**. The larva stops moving and feeding and, inside a case, changes into the adult form.

Radiation. A term describing many different kinds of energy. Some kinds are harmless, such as light, heat and sound. Other kinds can be dangerous, such as ultra-violet radiation and radiation from nuclear waste.

Recycling. The return of natural substances to soil, air or water and their re-use by living things.

Reproduction. The production, by adult living things, of new young living things.

Saprophyte. A living thing that feeds on rotting plant or animal material. For example, some fungi are saprophytes.

Scavenger. An animal which does not hunt or kill, but eats dead animals, such as **predator**'s kills.

Scrub. An area of land where most of the plants are small shrubs and bushes, and there are hardly any tall trees.

Soil. A mixture of tiny particles of rock and rotting plant and animal material, with water and air between them.

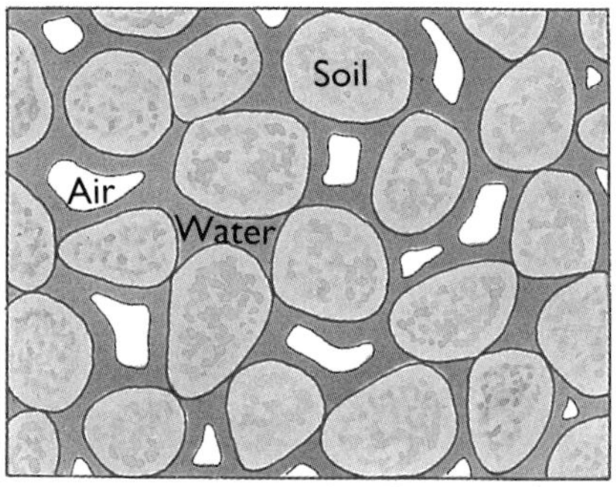

Sperm. The special cells made by a male animal which come together with female cells to produce new life (see **fertilization**).

Spore. Tiny particles produced by some fungi and simple plants. They grow into new plants.

Stamens. The word for a male part of a flower - an **anther** - together with the stalk that supports it, called a filament.

Symbiont. A plant or animals that lives with another plant or animal, each being useful to the other. For example, hermit crabs and sea anemones have a symbiotic relationship (see page 157).

Terrestrial. Living on land.

Territory. An area where an animal or animals live. Animals defend their territory against intruders, especially animals of the same kind.

Zoology. The scientific study of animals.

Classification chart

Organizing living things into different kingdoms* is called classification. Modern classification is based on a system devised in 1735 by a scientist called Linnaeus. The chart below shows how this system works. On the chart, the five kingdoms into which all living things fall are divided into sub-groups. These are split into smaller groups called classes.

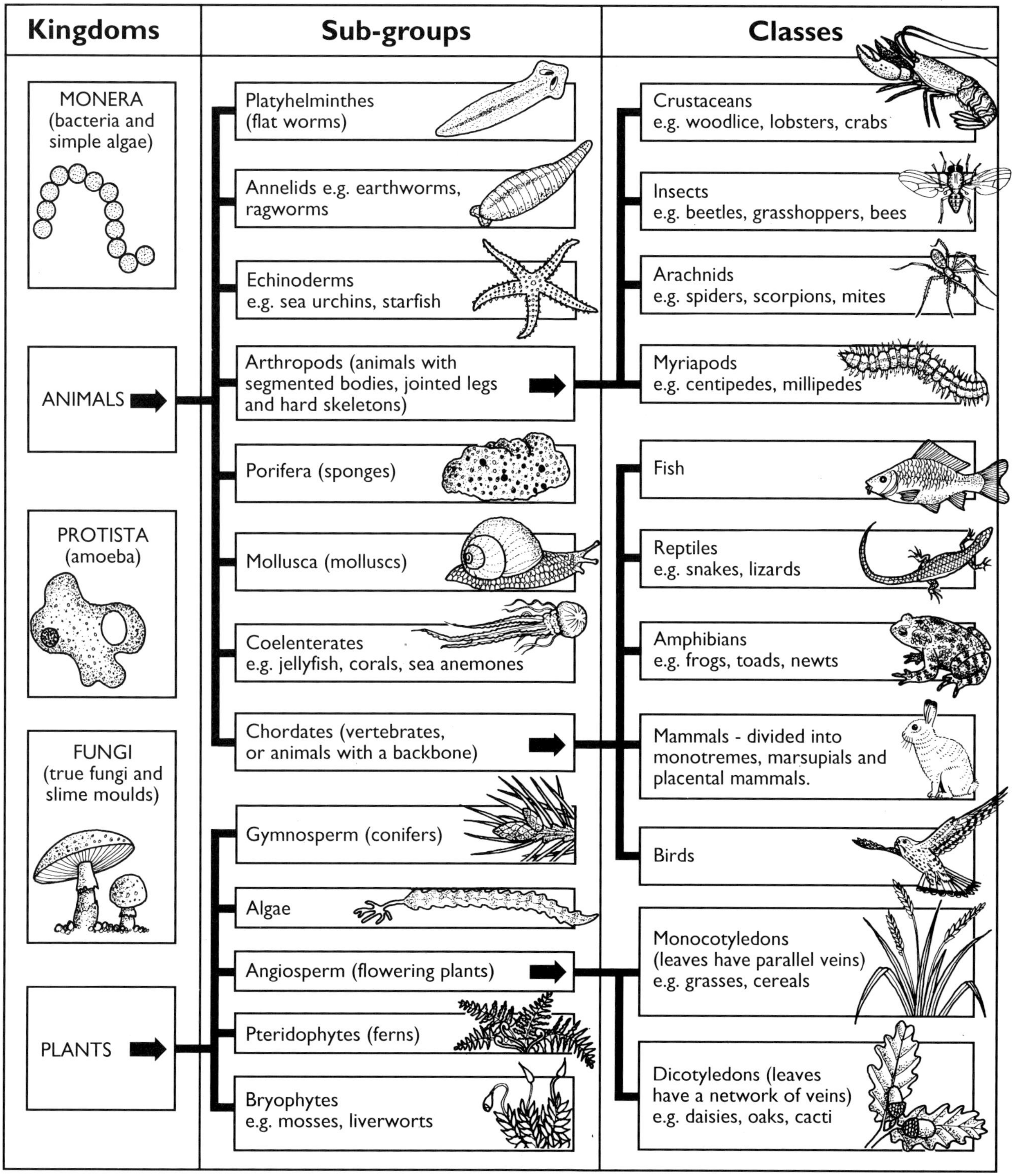
Kingdoms
Sub-groups
Classes
MONERA (bacteria and simple algae)
ANIMALS
PROTISTA (amoeba)
FUNGI (true fungi and slime moulds)
PLANTS
Platyhelminthes (flat worms)
Annelids e.g. earthworms, ragworms
Echinoderms e.g. sea urchins, starfish
Arthropods (animals with segmented bodies, jointed legs and hard skeletons)
Porifera (sponges)
Mollusca (molluscs)
Coelenterates e.g. jellyfish, corals, sea anemones
Chordates (vertebrates, or animals with a backbone)
Gymnosperm (conifers)
Algae
Angiosperm (flowering plants)
Pteridophytes (ferns)
Bryophytes e.g. mosses, liverworts
Crustaceans e.g. woodlice, lobsters, crabs
Insects e.g. beetles, grasshoppers, bees
Arachnids e.g. spiders, scorpions, mites
Myriapods e.g. centipedes, millipedes
Fish
Reptiles e.g. snakes, lizards
Amphibians e.g. frogs, toads, newts
Mammals - divided into monotremes, marsupials and placental mammals.
Birds
Monocotyledons (leaves have parallel veins) e.g. grasses, cereals
Dicotyledons (leaves have a network of veins) e.g. daisies, oaks, cacti

* *Kingdoms, 244.*

Skeletons

All vertebrates (animals with backbones) have a skeleton based on the same plan. The skull, backbone and ribcage form the main base, with shoulders, hips, arms and legs attached. The skeleton acts as a rigid framework and it also protects the internal organs.

Alternative names for bones

Scientific name	Common name	Scientific name	Common name
Cranium	Skull	Phalanges	Finger/toebones
Mandible	Jawbone	Pelvis	Hipbone
Vertebral column	Backbone	Femur	Thighbone
Clavicle	Collarbone	Patella	Kneecap
Scapula	Shoulder blade	Tibia	Shinbone
Sternum	Breastbone	Tarsals	Anklebones
Carpals	Wristbones		

Bird skeleton

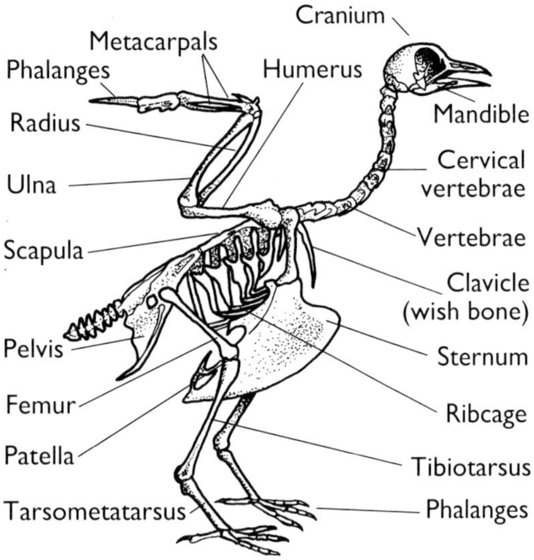

Compared with mammals, birds have light skeletons. They have adapted for flight and have a wide pelvis for laying eggs.

Frog skeleton

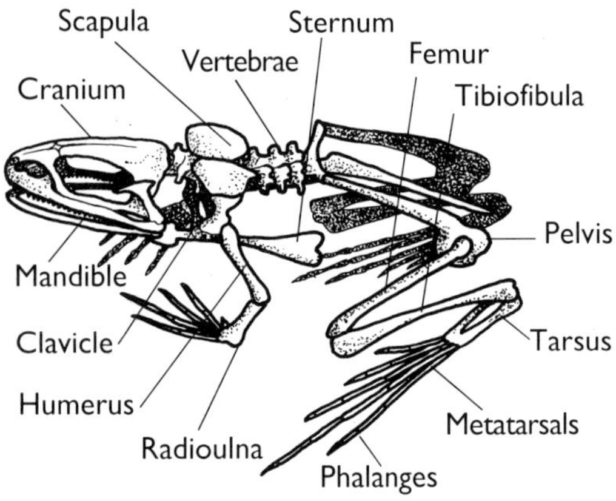

Amphibians have large, bony skeletons. Many, such as frogs (like the one shown here), have no ribs.

Human skeleton

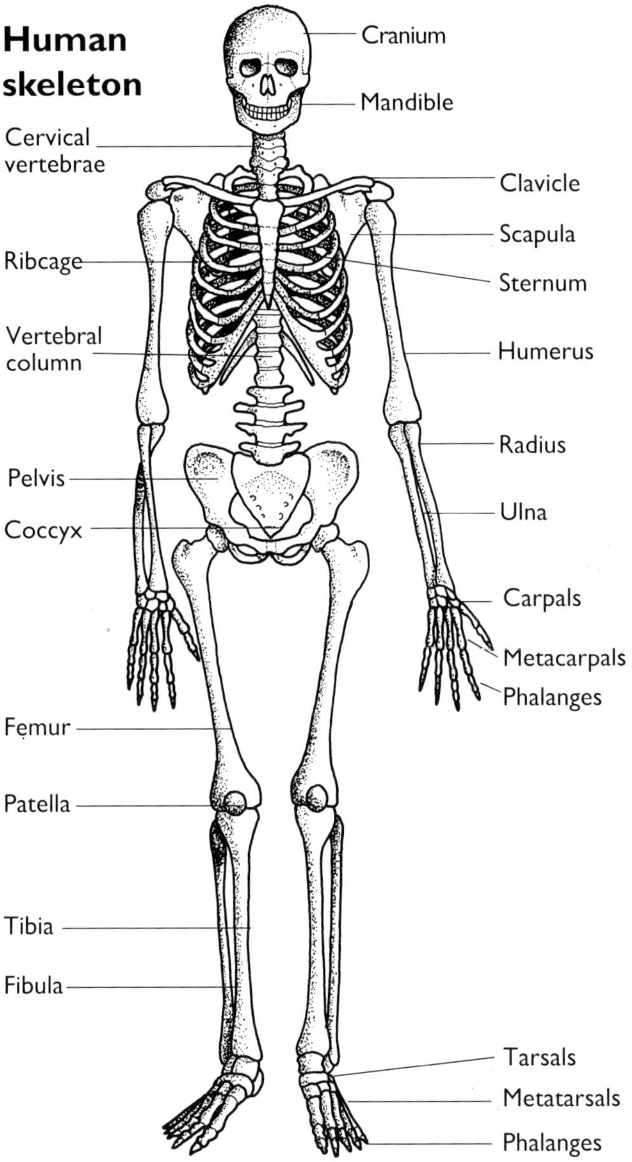

The human skeleton is very flexible and allows a great range of movement. It is made up of 206 bones. Around half of these are in the hands and feet.

Whale skeleton

Whales have adapted for life in the water. Their forelimbs are paddle-like for swimming and the absence of hindlimbs makes them more streamlined.

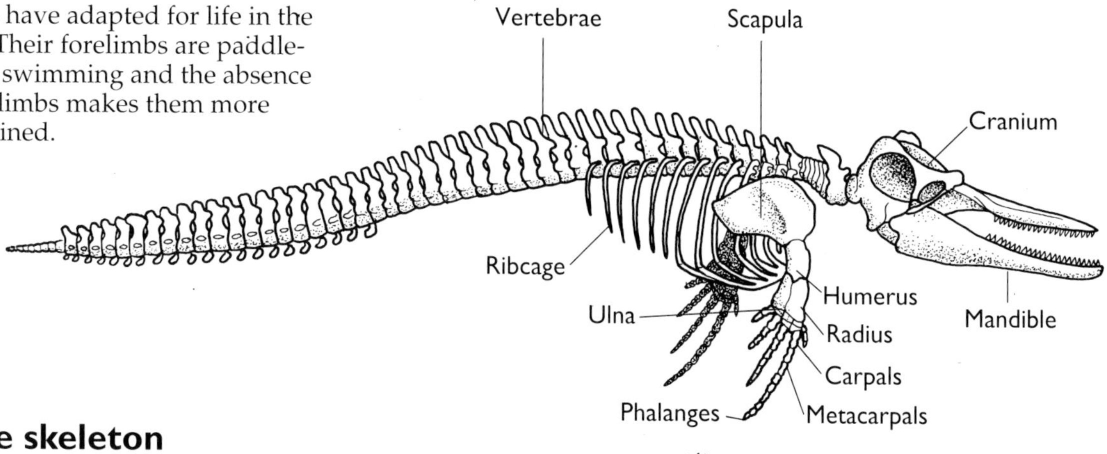
Vertebrae
Scapula
Cranium
Ribcage
Humerus
Mandible
Ulna
Radius
Carpals
Phalanges
Metacarpals

Snake skeleton

Snakes have completely lost their limbs and sternum. They have a huge number of vertebrae and ribs, all of a similar size. The bones of the jaw are loose so the snake can open its mouth very wide and take in prey whole.

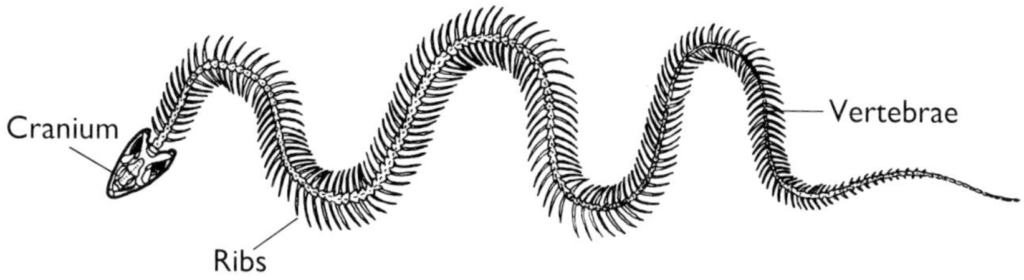
Cranium
Vertebrae
Ribs

Horse skeleton

A horse's skeleton is made up of 205 bones. It is specially adapted for running, with very long limbs and feet. Each limb has just one toe, in the form of a hoof.

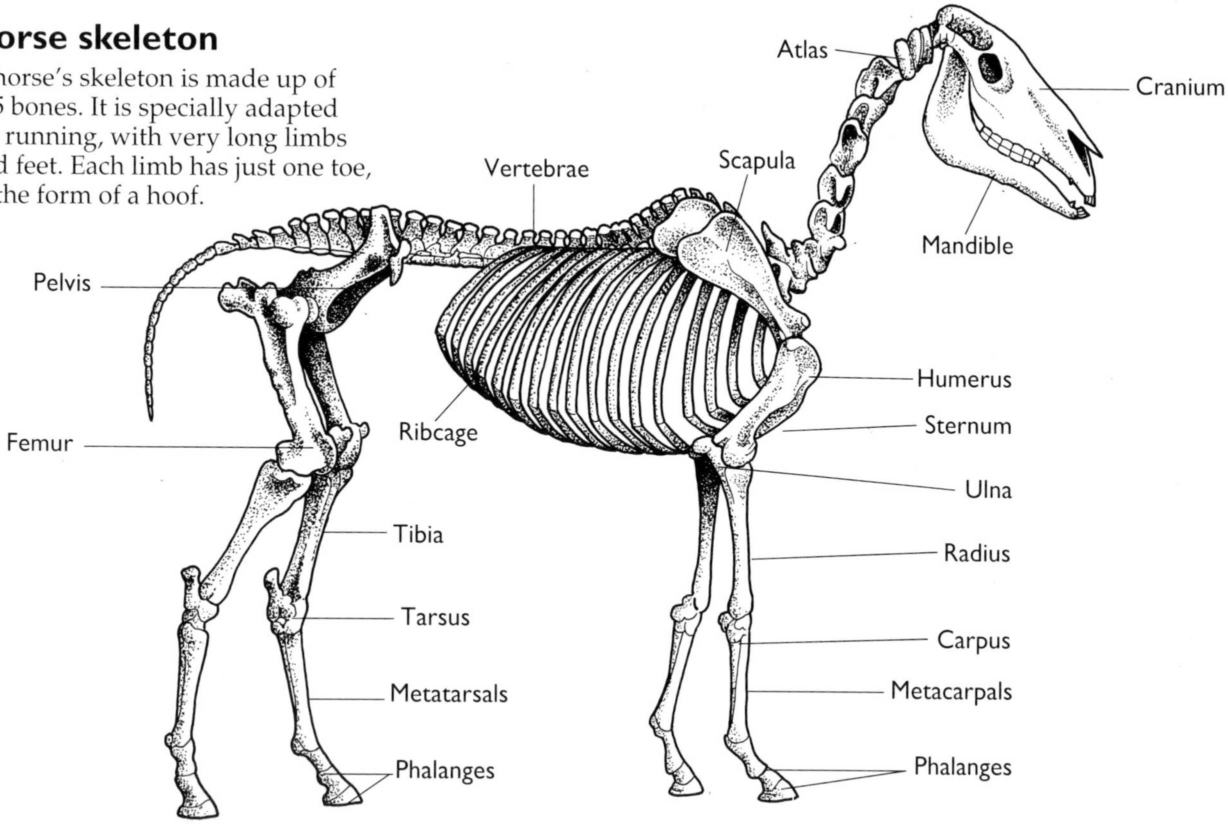
Atlas
Cranium
Vertebrae
Scapula
Mandible
Pelvis
Humerus
Sternum
Femur
Ribcage
Ulna
Tibia
Radius
Tarsus
Carpus
Metatarsals
Metacarpals
Phalanges
Phalanges

Who's who

Below is a list of some of the people throughout history who have made a great contribution to our understanding of life on Earth.

Aristotle (384-322BC)
Greek philosopher and politician. The first naturalist to organize living things into groups or classes and suggest that there was a ladder of nature with man at the top.

Galen (AD130-201)
Greek scientist and doctor who investigated and compared the anatomy of different animals. He applied his discoveries to the human body, which led to many mistakes in medicine.

Harvey, William (1578-1657)
British scientist who made important discoveries about the circulation of the blood and how the heart works. This was a milestone in understanding how the bodies of different species function.

Ray, John (1627-1705)
English clergyman whose work on the classification* of living things helped Linnaeus (see below) to develop his own classification system.

Leeuwenhoek, Anton van (1632-1723)
Dutch shopkeeper who became an expert in grinding and polishing magnifying lenses. With these he constructed microscopes that could magnify up to 400 times. He was the first person to describe red blood cells, sperm, bacteria, pond microbes and other microscopic organisms.

Hooke, Robert (1635-1703)
English inventor of scientific devices who made a microscope powerful enough for him to observe that thin sections of cork were made up of angular spaces which he called "cells".

Linnaeus, Carl (1707-1778)
Swedish naturalist also known as Carl von Linné. He is best known for his system of classifying living organisms, called the binomial system. This classification system is still used today.

Buffon, Georges (1707-1788)
French naturalist who was the first to propose a crude theory of evolution*. He was also the first to suggest that the Earth may be older than it says in the Bible.

Lamarck, Jean-Baptiste de (1744-1829)
French naturalist who realized that the Earth is millions of years old rather than 6,000, as had previously been believed. He was the first person to suggest the idea that species evolve by passing on characteristics from one generation to another.

Cuvier, Baron Georges (1769-1832)
French naturalist who realized from the existence of fossils that many forms of life (such as dinosaurs) had once existed on Earth but had now disappeared. He believed that natural disasters such as great floods had repeatedly destroyed life, which had then begun again with a fresh round of creation.

Schleiden, Jakob (1804-1881)
German botanist and skilled microscopist who observed cells in all plant structures and accurately described many of their properties.

Darwin, Charles (1809-1882)
English naturalist famous for his theory of evolution by natural selection, which is still regarded as the basic mechanism of evolution. His most important works are *On the Origin of Species* (1859) and *The Descent of Man* (1871).

Gosse, Philip Henry (1810-1888)
British naturalist whose important work on marine biology is still valid today. He helped found the world's first public aquarium which opened in London, England, in 1853.

Mendel, Gregor (1822-1884)
Austrian monk who, through his experiments with pea plants, founded the science of genetics, which explains how the characteristics of parents are handed down to their offspring. The importance of his work was not recognized by scientists until the beginning of the 20th century.

Pasteur, Louis (1822-1895)
French chemist who established the strand of science called microbiology. He proposed that disease is caused by tiny living things called micro-organisms. Before this time it was believed that illness was caused by breathing in bad vapours from the air.

Wallace, Alfred Russel (1823-1913)
British naturalist who arrived at the idea of evolution independently of Darwin (see above).

Fabré, Henri (1823-1915)
The first man to make detailed observations of animals in their natural surroundings and record what he saw. He spent 40 years watching insects in his garden in France and astonished the world with evidence of how complex insect behaviour is.

Bates, Henry Walter (1825-1892)
British naturalist who made important studies of how insects mimic one another. He showed how, for example, some butterflies protect themselves by developing markings that mimic other, unpleasant tasting species.

 ***Classification, 249; Evolution, 247.**

Huxley, Thomas Henry (1825-1895)
English zoologist. One of Darwin's greatest contemporary supporters.

Haeckel, Ernst (1834-1919)
German biologist who discovered important evidence to support Darwin's theory of evolution.

Pavlov, Ivan (1849-1936)
Russian psychologist who is best known for his study of conditioned responses in dogs. His findings have allowed other scientists to develop the research into how animals learn.

Morgan, Thomas Hunt (1866-1945)
American biologist who made important discoveries about the way in which characteristics are passed from generation to generation. By studying fruit flies, he realized that particular sets of characteristics are passed on together.

Avery, Oswald T (1877-1955)
American microbiologist who first established that characteristics are passed on from one generation to another via a substance in living cells called DNA.

Frisch, Karl von (1886-1982)
Austrian biologist famous for his studies on how animals obtain information about their environment. He is known particularly for his findings on the dance and language of honeybees.

Lorenz, Konrad (1903-1989)
Austrian zoologist who, through his study of geese and other species, founded a theory that animals are driven by instinct, which triggers certain behaviour.

Skinner, Burrhus Frederic (1904-1990)
American psychologist who studied how animals learn. He perfected a device called the Skinner Box, in which animals were taught how to perform certain tasks by operating levers, and rewarded with food. He believed that these principles of conditioned behaviour could also be applied to humans.

Tinbergen, Nikolaas (1907-1988)
Dutch zoologist who investigated the behaviour of many different species including gulls and sticklebacks. He is particularly known for his discoveries about how animals find their way around their environment.

Crick, Francis (1916-)
English scientist who, with **James Watson (1928-)**, discovered the structure of the DNA molecule in 1953. DNA is the substance that passes on characteristics from one generation to another, enabling species to evolve. This discovery was one of the most important scientific breakthroughs ever achieved.

International organizations

There are many international organizations which work to save and protect endangered species and natural environments. Most have local groups which you can join. If you would like more information about any of the organizations listed below, you can write to the addresses given.

Friends of the Earth (FOE) campaigns on a range of issues including tropical rainforests, the countryside, water and air pollution and energy. It operates at local, national and international levels. The youth section is called Earth Action.

Friends of the Earth International Secretariat
P.O. Box 19199
1000 G.D.
Amsterdam
The Netherlands

Friends of the Earth

Greenpeace uses peaceful but direct action to defend the environment. It campaigns to protect rain forests and marine life, stop global warming and end toxic pollution of air, land and seas. It also opposes nuclear power and weapons.

Greenpeace International
Keizergracht 176
1016 DW Amsterdam
The Netherlands

GREENPEACE

BirdLife International is an organization which works to save endangered birds all over the world.

BirdLife International
Wellbrook Court
Girton Road
Cambridge CB3 0NA
England

BirdLife® INTERNATIONAL

Survival International is a global movement to support tribal peoples and help them protect their lands, environment and way of life.

Survival International
310 Edgware Road
London W2 1DY
England

Survival for tribal peoples

WWF - World Wide Fund For Nature (formerly World Wildlife Fund) is the world's largest private international organization for the conservation of nature and threatened species.

Information Officer
WWF International
Avenue du Mont-Blanc
1196 Gland
Switzerland

WWF®

Directory of mammals

There are over 4,000 species of mammals. Some individual species and groups of species are listed on the following three pages. The measurements given refer to body length.

Monotremes

Echindas. Spiny-coated creatures with long snouts and claws. Found in New Guinea, Australia and Tasmania. Also called spiny anteaters. Measure 30-90cm (12-35in). Eat earthworms, ants, termites.

Platypus. Mammal with duck-like bill, flat tail and webbed feet. Found in Australia and Tasmania. Measures 45-60cm (18-24in). Eats aquatic larvae and invertebrates.

Marsupials

Bandicoots. Rat-like creatures with high reproductive rate. Found in Australia and New Guinea. Measure 15-56cm (6-22in). Eat a wide variety of foods.

Bushtail possum. Common Australian mammal introduced in other Western Pacific islands, including New Zealand. Measures 34-70cm (13-28in). Eats leaves, fruit, bark, eggs, invertebrates.

Kangaroos/wallabies. Plant-eating animals with very powerful hind legs. Found in Australia and New Guinea. Measure up to 1.6m (5ft).

Koala. Australian bear-like animal with thick, grey fur. Once close to extinction. Measures 78cm (31in). Eats eucalyptus leaves.

Marsupial mole. Australian burrowing animal similar to a placental mole. Measures 13-15cm (5-6in). Eats insects and larvae.

Opossums. Mainly tree-living creatures which pretend to be dead when frightened. Found in South and Central America and much of the USA. Measure 7-55cm (3-22in). Eat earthworms, fruit, insects, fish, frogs, reptiles.

Rat kangaroos. Small versions of kangaroo, found in Australia and New Guinea. Measure 20-30cm (8-12in). Eat grasses and plants.

Wombats. Burrowing, plant-eating animals with poor eyesight but keen sense of smell and hearing. Found in southern Australia and Tasmania. Measure 87-115cm (34-45in).

Placental mammals

Aardvark. African animal with long, tubular snout. Measures up to 2m (7ft). Eats ants and termites.

Anteaters. Long-snouted mammals found in Central and South America. Measure 16-120cm (6-47in). Eat ants and termites.

Armadillos. Insect-eating mammals, covered in tough, protective plates. Found in Central and South America. Measure 13-100cm (5-39in).

Baboons/mandrils. African monkeys which live mainly on the ground. Measure 56-80cm (22-31in). Eat fruit, plants, insects, small mammals.

Badgers. Nocturnal mammals found in Europe, Asia and North America. European species have black and white markings. Measure 50-100cm (20-39in). Eat small animals, fruit, roots, earthworms.

Bats. The only mammals that can fly. Found all over the world except for polar regions. Wingspans measure 15-100cm (6-39in). Eat insects, small animals, fish.

Bear, grizzly (brown). Large bear found in North America, northern Europe and Asia. Measures 2-2.8m (7-9ft). Eats a wide range of foods.

Bear, North American black. Smaller than grizzly (brown) bear, measuring 1.3-1.8m (4-6ft). Found in North America. Eats a wide variety of foods.

Beaver. Broad-tailed rodent that builds dams in ponds and streams. Measures 80-120cm (31-47in). Found in North America, Asia and Europe. Eats tree bark.

Bison. North American and European ox, once widespread on the grasslands, now only found in parks. Measures up to 3.8m (12ft). Eats grasses.

Boar, wild. Wild pig, found in Europe, northern Africa and southern Asia. Measures up to 2.1m (7ft). Eats plants, larvae, frogs, mice, earthworms.

Bush-babies. African tree-living mammals. Measure 12-32cm (5-13in). Eat insects, fruit, tree gum.

Camel, Bactrian. Plant-eating mammal with two humps for storing fat. Widely used as a domestic animal in central Asia. Measures up to 2.3m (8ft).

Capybara. The largest rodent, measuring 1-1.3m (3-4ft). Found in South America. Eats grass.

Cattle. Farm animals found all over the world. May be long or short-horned. Measure up to 2m (7ft).

Chamois. Agile goat which lives on snowy mountains in Europe and Asia. Measures about 1.3m (4ft). Eats grass, leaves, lichen.

Cheetah. African cat with spotted coat. Fastest land animal, reaching speeds of 96kmph (60mph). Measures 1-1.4m (3-5ft). Eats hoofed animals.

Chimpanzee. Second most sophisticated mammal after man in its use of tools. Found in central and western Africa. Measures 70-85cm (28-33in). Eats fruit, leaves, seeds, insects, small mammals.

Civets. Cat-like animals found in Africa and Asia. Their oil is used in perfume. Measure 33-84cm (13-33in). Eat fruit, small mammals, birds, insects.

Deer. Hoofed grazing mammals found in North and South America, Europe and Asia. Males have antlers. Measure 41-250cm (16-98in). Eat grass, shoots, leaves, flowers, fruits.

Dingo. Type of dog, descended from the domestic dog. Found in Australia. Measures 1.5m (5ft). Eats rabbits, lizards, grasshoppers, wild pigs, kangaroos.

Dolphins. Intelligent sea mammals found all over the world. Measure up to 4m (13ft). Eat fish and squid.

Dormouse. Small mouse-like rodent with a long, hairy tail. Found in Europe, Africa, Asia and Japan. Measures 6-19cm (2-7in). Eats plant food.

Eland. African antelope with twisted horns. Measures 2.5-3.5m (8-11ft). Eats grasses.

Elephant, African. Largest living land mammal, measuring 6-7.5m (20-25ft). Found in Africa. Eats grass, plants, leaves, twigs, flowers, fruit.

Elephant shrews. Large-eyed creatures with long pointed noses. Live in Africa. Measure 10-29cm (4-11in). Eat invertebrates, plants, fruit, seeds.

Fox. Member of the dog family notorious for its cunning. Found in North and South America, Europe, Asia and Africa. Measures 24-100cm (9-39in). Eats rodents, birds, fruit, fish, rabbits, earthworms.

Gazelles. Graceful African and Arabian antelopes. Measure 1.2-1.7m (4-6ft). Eat leaves, grass, fruit.

Gerbil. Mouse-like desert rodent with long hind legs. Found in Africa and Asia. Measures 6-7cm (about 3in). Eats seeds, fruit, leaves, stems, roots, bulbs, insects, snails.

Giraffe. Tallest living animal, having a long neck for reaching foliage. Measures 3.8-4.7cm (12-15ft). Found in Africa. Eats leaves, shoots, flowers, fruit.

Gnu. African antelope with huge head, mane and beard. Also known as wildebeest. Measures about 2m (7ft). Eats grasses.

Goat, Rocky Mountain. Hardy, hoofed mammal, excellent at rock climbing. Found in North America. Measures up to 1.7m (6ft). Eats grasses.

Gopher. North American burrowing animal. Measures 12-23cm (5-9in). Eats plant materials.

Gorilla. Large, intelligent mammal. Found in central and western Africa. Measures 1.5-1.7m (5-6ft). Eats leaves and stems.

Guinea pig. South American tailless rodent. Measures approximately 28cm (11in). Eats herbs and grasses.

Hamsters. Rodents with large cheek pouches for storing food. Popular as pets. Found in Europe, the Middle East, northern Asia and China. Measure 5-15cm (2-6in). Eat seeds, shoots, root vegetables.

Hares. Large rabbit-like animals able to run very fast. Found in North America, Africa, Europe, Asia and the Arctic. Measure 40-76cm (16-30in). Eat grass, herbs, plants, bark, twigs.

Hartebeest. African antelope with a long face and sloping back. Measures about 2m (7ft). Eats grass and vegetation.

Hedgehog. Spiny-coated, nocturnal mammal. Found in Europe, Asia and Africa. Measures 10-15cm (4-6in). Eats earthworms, slugs, insects.

Hippopotamuses. Large, thick-skinned African mammals that wallow in water. Measure 1.5-3.5m (5-11ft). Eat vegetation.

Horse. Hoofed mammal widely used for riding and to carry or pull loads. Wild horses are found in Asia, North and South America and Australia. Measure about 2m (7ft). Eat grass and leaves.

Hyenas. Scavengers and hunters resembling dogs but with hindlimbs shorter than forelimbs. Found in Africa and Asia. Measure 85-140cm (33-55in). Eat dead animals, insects, eggs, fruit, vegetables.

Ibex. Large, horned wild goat found in mountainous areas of central Europe, Asia and Africa. Measures 85-143cm (33-56in). Eats grasses.

Impala. Graceful African antelope. Measures about 1.4m (5ft). Eats grass, leaves, flowers, fruit.

Jackal. Wild dog-like mammal found in Africa, Europe and Asia. Measures 65-106cm (26-42in). Eats fruit, reptiles, birds, small mammals, dead animals.

Jaguar. Large, spotted cat found in Central and South America. Measures 1.1-1.8m (4-6ft). Eats deer, monkeys, birds, turtles, frogs, fish, small rodents.

Jerboas. Desert rodents with long hind legs and the ability to jump like a kangaroo. Found in north Africa, Turkey, the Middle East and central Asia. Measure 5-10cm (2-4in). Eat seeds and vegetation.

Lemmings. Rodents similar to voles. Found in North America, northern Europe and Asia. Measure 10-11cm (4in). Eat plants, bulbs, roots, mosses.

Lemurs. Nocturnal, forest-living, monkey-like animals found in Madagascar. Measure 12-70cm (5-28in). Eat flowers, leaves, bamboo shoots.

Leopard. Large, spotted cat found in Africa and Asia. Hunts at night. Good at climbing trees. Measures 1-1.9m (3-6ft). Eats mammals and birds.

Lion. Large African cat that lives in groups called prides. Measures 2.6-3.3m (9-11ft). Eats mainly antelopes and zebra.

Llama. South American woolly mammal. Member of the camel family. Measures 2.3-4m (8-13ft). Eats grasses and other vegetation.

Lynx. Member of the cat family with spotted fur, short tail and tufted ear-tips. Found in Europe and North America. Measures 67-110cm (26-43in). Eats rabbits, hares, rodents.

Marmosets. Small, squirrel-like monkeys with long bushy tails. Found in South America. Measure 17-40cm (7-16in). Eat fruit, flowers, tree gum, frogs, snails, lizards, spiders, insects.

Martens. Weasel-like animals found in North America, Europe and Asia. Measure 30-75cm (12-30in). Eat mice, squirrels, rabbits, grouse, fruit, nuts.

Mole. Small burrowing animal with very small eyes. Found in Europe, Asia and North America. Measures 8-18cm (3-7in). Eats earthworms, larvae and slugs.

Mongooses. Small mammals that often stand up on their hind legs. Found in Africa, southern Asia and southern Europe. Measure 24-58cm (9-23in). Eat vertebrates, fruit, insects, snakes.

Narwhal. White whale with one large tusk. Found in Arctic regions. Measures 4-5m (13-16ft). Eats fish, squid and shellfish.

Otters. The only members of the weasel family to live in water. Found in North and South America, Europe, Asia and Africa. Measure 40-123cm (16-48in). Eat frogs, crabs, fish, birds.

Panda, giant. Very rare mammal with distinctive black and white markings. Found in China and Tibet. Measures up to 1.8m (6ft). Eats bamboo.

Polar bear. Large, white bear found around the North Pole. Measures 2.5-3m (8-10ft). Eats seals and carcasses of large sea animals.

Porcupines. Large rodents with spiny bodies. Found in North and South America, Africa and Asia. Measure 30-86cm (12-34in). Eat bark, roots, bulbs, berries, fruit, seeds.

Porpoise. Short-snouted relative of the dolphin family. Found in coastal waters. Measures 1.2-1.5m (4-5ft). Eats fish.

Puma (cougar). Large red-brown cat found in North and South America. Measures 1-2m (3-7ft). Eats deer and rodents.

Rabbit, European. Social, burrowing creature that lives in a system of burrows called a warren. Native to southern Europe and north Africa. Introduced into northern Europe, Australia, and New Zealand. Measures 38-45cm (15-18in). Eats plant materials.

Racoons. Greyish brown nocturnal animals with black masked faces and black and white ringed tails. Found in North, South and Central America. Measure up to 55cm (22in). Eat frogs, fish, birds, eggs, fruit, nuts, insects.

Rat, brown. Rodent originally from Asia but now found all over the world as a pest to man. Measures up to 20cm (8in). Eats virtually anything.

Rhinoceros. Thick-skinned creature found in Africa and tropical Asia. Hunted for its horn. Measures 2.5-4m (8-13ft). Eats leaves.

Seals. Graceful sea mammals with flippers and webbed feet. Found in seas around the Poles and temperate regions. Measure 1.2-4.9m (4-16ft). Eat fish, squid, crustaceans.

Sheep. Horned animals with long woolly coats. Species include American bighorn, barbary, and blue sheep. Domestic sheep are farmed all over the world for their wool and meat. Measure up to 2m (7ft). Eat grass.

Shrews. Mouse-like animals with poor eyesight. Found in Europe, Asia, North America and Africa. Measure 4-10cm (2-4in). Eat insects and earthworms.

Skunks. Black and white striped or spotted animals that spray foul-smelling fluid to defend themselves from attackers. Found in North and South America. Measure 40-68cm (16-27in). Eat insects, small mammals, eggs, fruit.

Sloths. Tree-living, nocturnal animals that move very slowly. Found in South America. Measure 56-70cm (22-28in). Eat leaves.

Springbok. South African gazelle which runs with high, springing leaps. Measures 96-115cm (38-45in). Eats grasses.

Squirrels. Tree-living rodents with long, bushy tails. Related to marmots, prairie dogs and chipmunks, which have short, smooth tails and live on or in the ground. Found in North and South America, Europe, Africa and Asia. Measure 10-40cm (4-16in). Eat nuts, seeds, plants, insects.

Tiger. Large, striped cat which hunts alone. Found in India, China and Indonesia. Measures 2.2-3.1m (7-10ft). Eats mainly wild pig and deer.

Voles. Mouse-like rodents found in North America, Europe, Asia and the Arctic. Measure 5-11cm (2-4in). Eat grasses, seeds, plants, insects.

Walrus. Sea-living mammal with tusks and thick folds of skin. Found in Arctic seas. Measures 2.5-3.2m (8-10ft). Eats shellfish.

Waterbuck. African antelope with long, shaggy coat. Measures 1.8-2.3m (6-8ft). Eats grasses, reeds, rushes, aquatic plants.

Weasels. Small, slender mammals related to mink, ermine, ferrets, polecats and wolverines. Found in the Arctic, North and South America, Europe, Asia and Africa. Measure 15-22cm (6-9in). Eat rodents, rabbits, birds, insects, lizards, frogs.

Whales, beaked. Marine mammals with dolphin-like beaks. Found all over the world. Measure 4-13m (13-43ft). Eat squid.

Whale, blue. Largest mammal that has ever lived, measuring up to 30m (98ft). Found in Arctic and sub-tropical seas. Eats krill.

Whale, humpback. Acrobatic whale, found all over the world. Measures 16m (52ft). Eats fish and krill.

Whale, killer. Has distinctive black and white markings. Found all over the world in cool, coastal waters. Measures 9-10m (30-33ft). Eats fish, squid, birds, marine mammals.

Whale, sperm. Largest toothed whale. Found in temperate and tropical waters. Measures up to 21m (69ft). Eats mainly squid.

Wolf, grey. Wild dog that hunts in packs. Found in North America, Europe, Asia and the Middle East. Measures 1-1.5m (3-5ft). Eats moose, deer, caribou.

Zebra. Black and white striped relation to the horse. Found in Africa. Measures about 2.5m (8ft). Eats grass and leaves.

GEOGRAPHY

Carol Varley and Lisa Miles

Designed by
Fiona Brown, Nigel Reece
and Ruth Russell

Illustated by
Guy Smith, Peter Dennis,
Chris Lyon, Peter Bull,
Kuo Kang Chen,
Wigwam Publishing Services
and Chris Shields

Computer cartography by
EUROMAP Ltd

Additional illustration by
Mick Gillah and Derek Brazell

Geography consultants
Rex Walford, Bill Chambers
and Margaret Smeaton

Contents

The *Geography* section

Geography is the study of the Earth's surface and the people who live on it. This part of the book introduces you to the world of geography. It is divided into thirteen sections of information.

Each section has a different coloured band along the tops of the pages. You can see what these sections are, and the colours used for them, in the Contents list opposite.

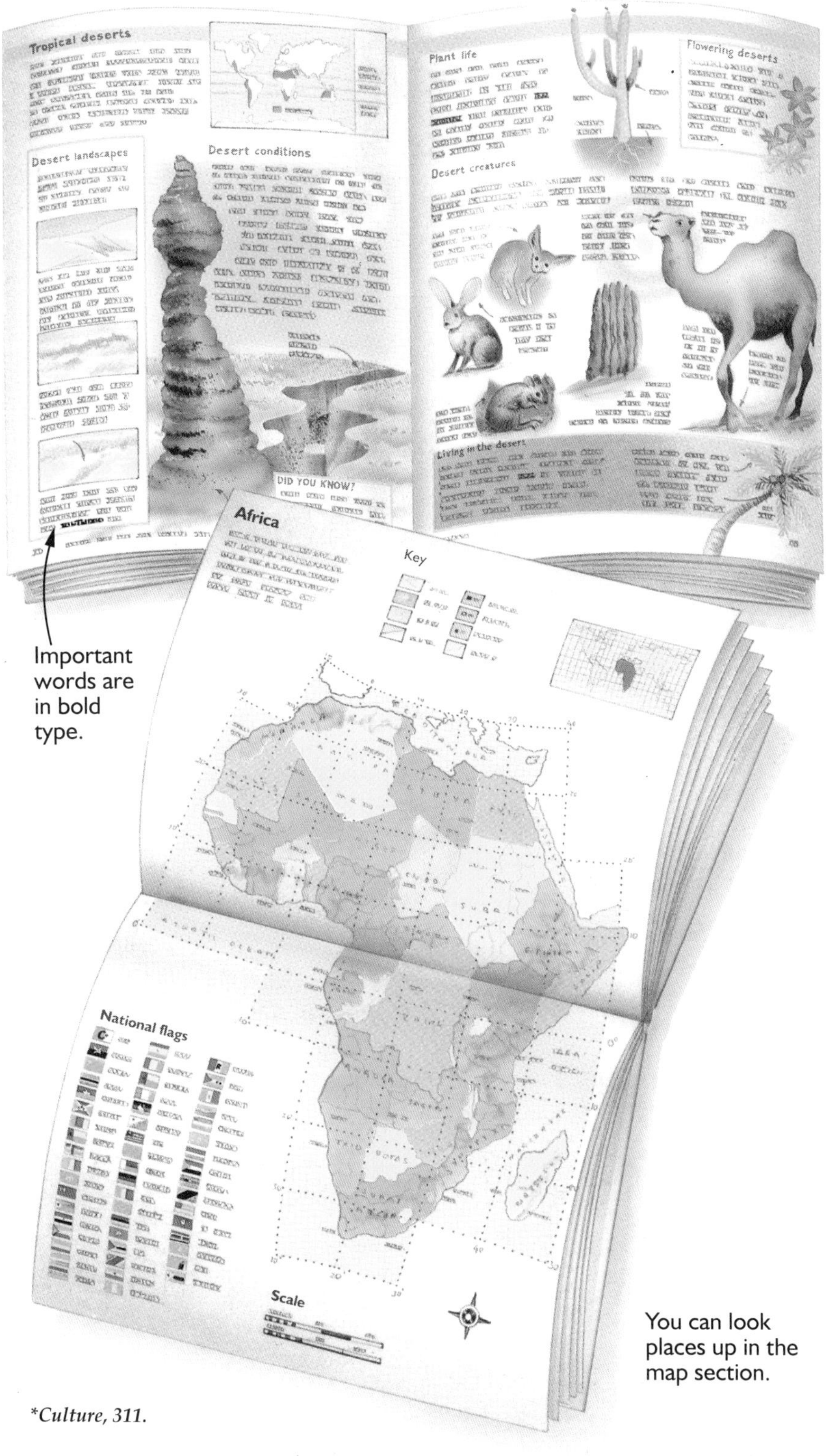

Important words are in bold type.

You can look places up in the map section.

Important words

Some words are printed in bold type. These are important words which are explained at that point.

Some words have an asterisk after them, like this – culture*. It means that this word is explained somewhere else. The footnote at the bottom of the page tells you where you can find the explanation.

Using the maps

There is also a map section, called Maps of the world. Each map in this section shows a different area of the world, its countries, major towns and cities, and its main features, such as mountains and rivers. These pages also show the national flags of each country.

The atlas maps have their own index, starting on page 374. When you come across place names, you can look them up on the maps and find out exactly where they are in the world.

Looking up facts

There is a reference section on pages 366-384. You can use the reference section to look up lots of facts about the Earth and its countries.

It includes a glossary, where important words to do with geography are explained. There is also an index at the back of the book, so that you can find information easily.

**Culture, 311.*

What is geography?

The word geography originally comes from the Greek word *geographia*, which means "writing about the Earth". It is a living subject about people and places and the relationship between people and the Earth.

The Earth and its inhabitants are always changing, so geography is also about how things change.

Geography may be split into two areas: physical geography, about the Earth and places; and human geography, about people and how they live. Together, they make a very broad subject. This book covers many aspects of geography, some of which are introduced on these two pages.

The planet Earth

Geography is about how the Earth moves in space, creating the days, nights and seasons. It is about how energy comes from the Sun so that animals and plants can live.

Weather patterns

Geographers study weather and climate change. They record and predict weather patterns and look at how the climate affects the way that people, animals and plants live.

Water and rocks

Water is essential to life on Earth. It forms part of the air around us and it covers part of the Earth's surface. Oceans shape the rocks on the coasts and rivers carve out features in the land.

Studying the oceans and the landscape helps people to understand how the Earth developed, how it may change in the future and how we can make better use of our surroundings.

People

Geographers study the people who live in the world, their lifestyles and their differences and similarities. Geography is about how the populations of different places change and how different societies work.

Settlements

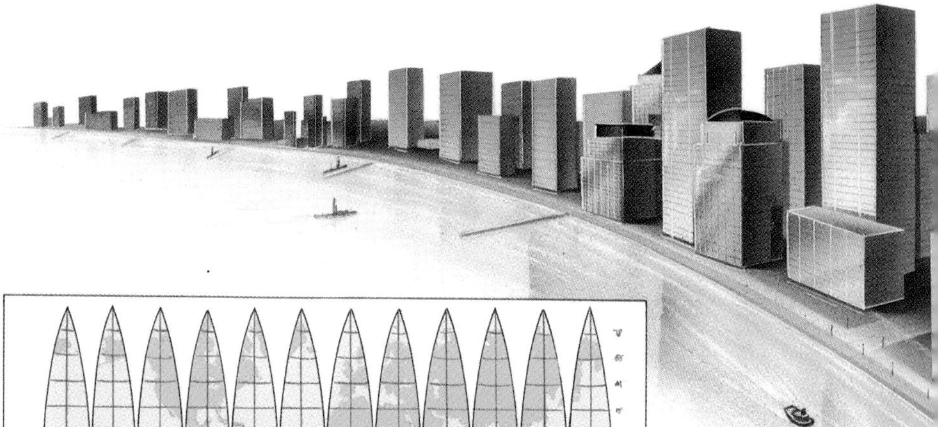

Geography is about the places where people live and why they live there. It is about how communities grow and how villages, towns and cities have an impact on the environment around them.

Maps

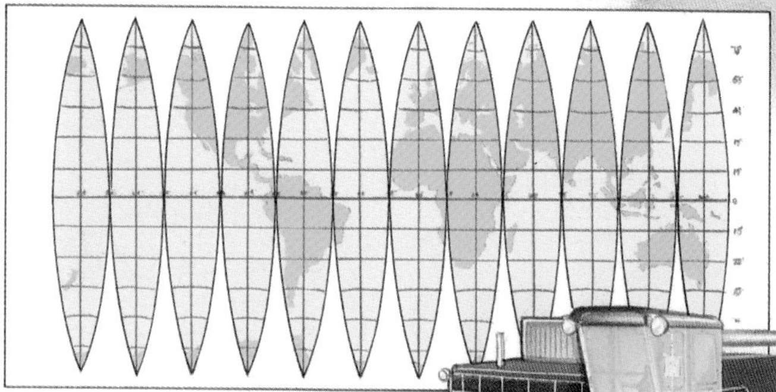

Maps are an important part of geography. They show us where places are and what they are like. They help us to compare different places and understand our surroundings.

Using our surroundings

Geography shows how people use their surroundings for food, water and resources. It is about what jobs people do and how they change the world around them.

Communication

Geography is about how places around the world are linked together and how people communicate. It is about how transport systems and the landscape affect each other.

The environment

Geography is about how the environment is changed by everything that people do. It is about how fragile the Earth is and how we can conserve and protect our resources.

Why is geography important?

The population on Earth is growing and our way of life is changing faster than ever. Pollution levels are high and people are changing the Earth so much that its resources are in danger.

Geography is important because it helps us to understand why the landscape looks as it is does and why we live as we do. It explains the world we live in and shows us how we can use it effectively and protect it for the future.

The Earth, our planet

Our planet, Earth, is a large ball of rock and metal covered with water and soil. It belongs to a group of nine planets which travel around a star called the Sun. Together, the Sun and everything that travels around it is called the **Solar System**.

The planets of the Solar System travel along almost circular paths, called **orbits**. They also spin. The four planets nearest to the Sun are called the inner planets. Beyond them are the outer planets.

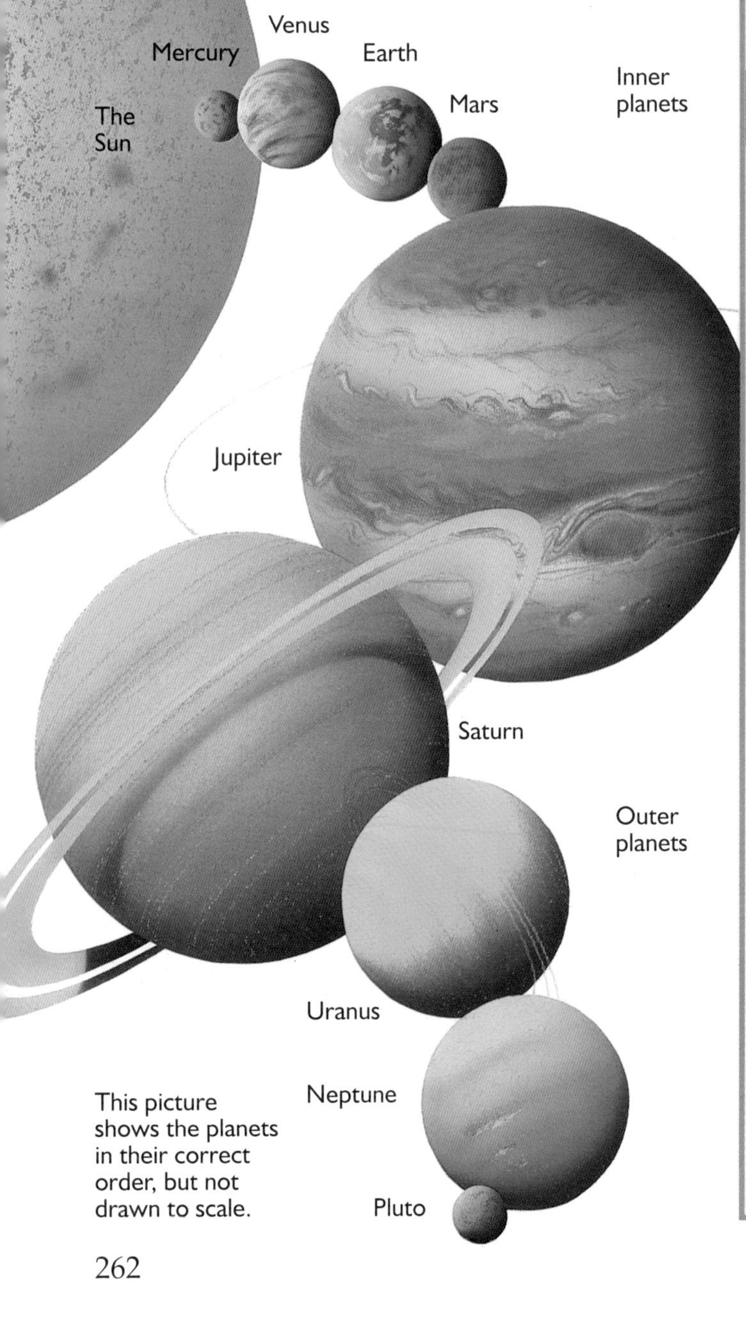

This picture shows the planets in their correct order, but not drawn to scale.

About the Earth

The Earth travels along its orbit at a speed of 107,200kmph (66,000mph). It also spins on its **axis**, an imaginary rod through the very north and south of the Earth, which leans at an angle of 23½°. The ends of the axis are called the **North Pole** and **South Pole**.

Around the Earth's middle, halfway between the Poles, is an imaginary line called the **Equator**. It divides the Earth into the **northern** and **southern hemispheres**.

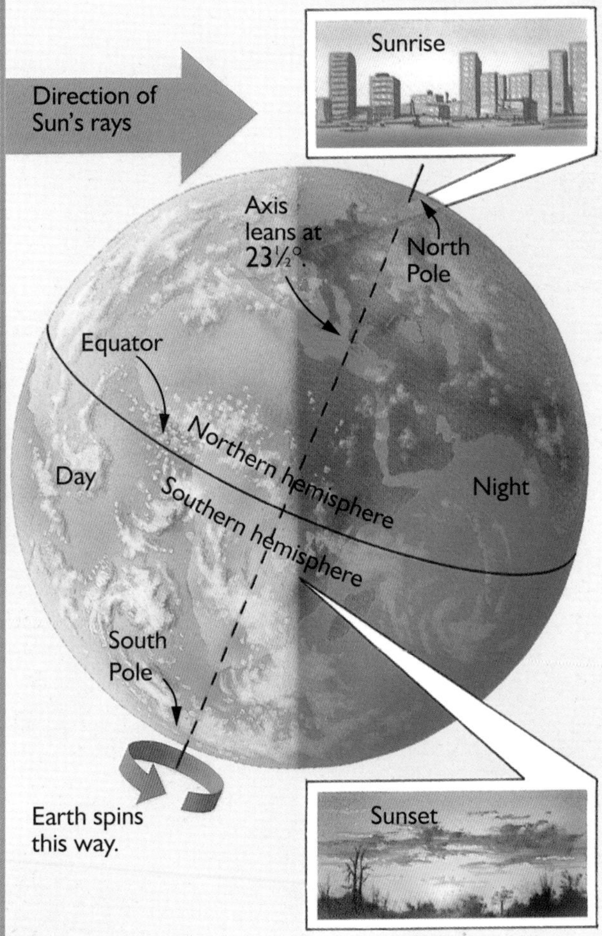

It takes 24 hours (one day) for the Earth to spin once. As it spins, its surface passes through the Sun's rays (daylight) then turns towards the darkness of space (night).

Sunrise is when your part of the Earth turns towards the Sun. At sunset, the Sun seems to sink below the horizon as your part of the Earth turns away from its rays.

The year and seasons

It takes one year (365¼ days) for the Earth to orbit the Sun. Because the Earth is on a tilt, the northern hemisphere is tilted towards the Sun in June and the southern hemisphere is tilted towards the Sun in December. The hemisphere that is towards the Sun is in summer. The one tilted away is in winter.

Imaginary lines called the **Tropic of Cancer** and **Tropic of Capricorn**, north and south of the Equator, mark where the Sun's rays are most direct in June and December. In the picture below, the Tropics are shown by dotted lines. In spring and autumn (March and September), the Sun's rays are most direct at the Equator.

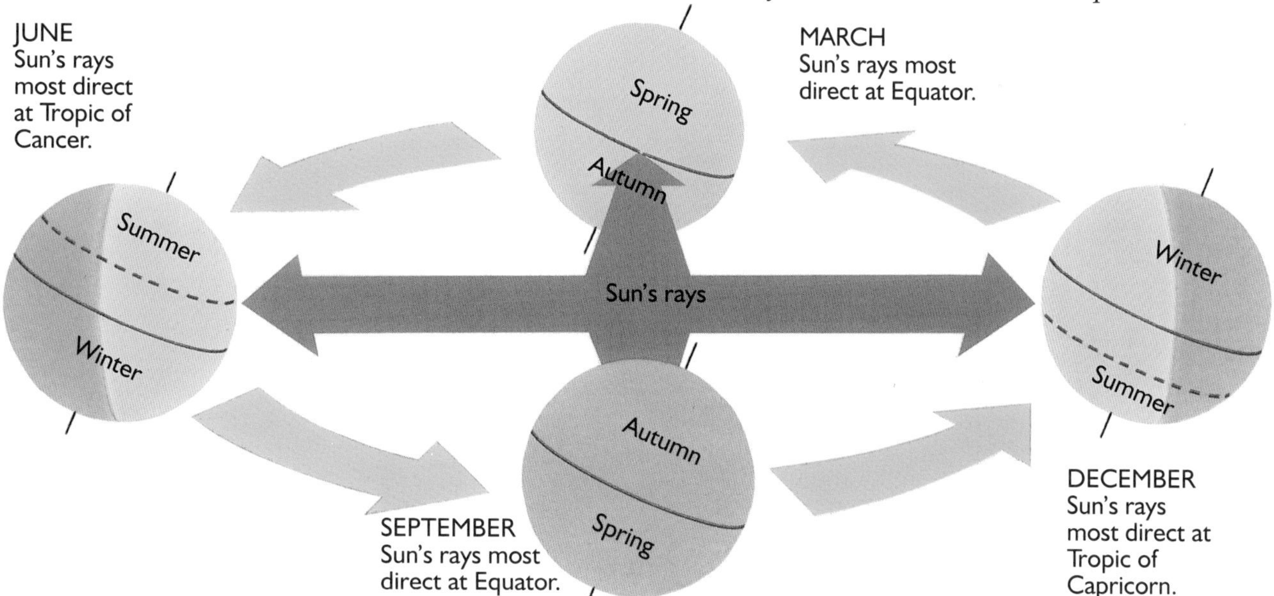
JUNE
Sun's rays most direct at Tropic of Cancer.
Summer
Winter
MARCH
Sun's rays most direct at Equator.
Spring
Autumn
Sun's rays
Winter
Summer
DECEMBER
Sun's rays most direct at Tropic of Capricorn.
Autumn
Spring
SEPTEMBER
Sun's rays most direct at Equator.

DID YOU KNOW?

Our Solar System is just a tiny part of an enormous group of stars and planets called a **galaxy**. There are billions of galaxies in the Universe. Ours is called the Milky Way.

The Solar System is a tiny part of the Milky Way.

Long and short days

The length of day and night varies depending on which season it is and where you are on the Earth. Only places on the Equator have equal lengths of day and night all year around. In every other part of the world, the days are longer in summer than in winter. The length of day and night varies most at the Poles, which have 24 hours of daylight in summer and 24 hours of darkness in winter.

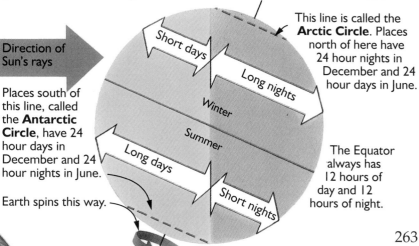

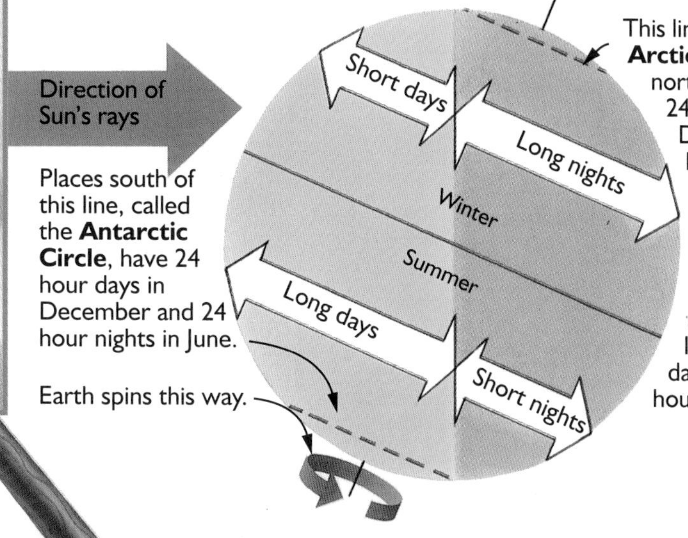
Direction of Sun's rays
Short days
Long nights
Winter
Summer
Long days
Short nights
This line is called the **Arctic Circle**. Places north of here have 24 hour nights in December and 24 hour days in June.
Places south of this line, called the **Antarctic Circle**, have 24 hour days in December and 24 hour nights in June.
The Equator always has 12 hours of day and 12 hours of night.
Earth spins this way.

Mapping the Earth

To discover where places are on the Earth you need either a globe or a map. A globe is a model of the Earth, whereas maps show the Earth's surface as a flat sheet.

Lines around the globe

Lines drawn on a globe, called **lines of latitude** and **longitude**, help you to find where places are. You may see these lines on maps too.

Lines of longitude, or **meridians**, divide the Earth into segments like an orange. All lines of longitude meet at the Poles. Longitude is measured in degrees (°). The line through Greenwich, England is 0°. It is called the **Prime Meridian**. Lines to either side are measured in degrees east or west of the Prime Meridian.

Lines of latitude, or **parallels**, tell you how far north or south a place is. The Equator, around the Earth's middle, is 0° latitude. Lines of latitude north of the Equator are measured in degrees north (°N). Lines south of the Equator are measured in degrees south (°S). The Poles are 90° north and south of the Equator.

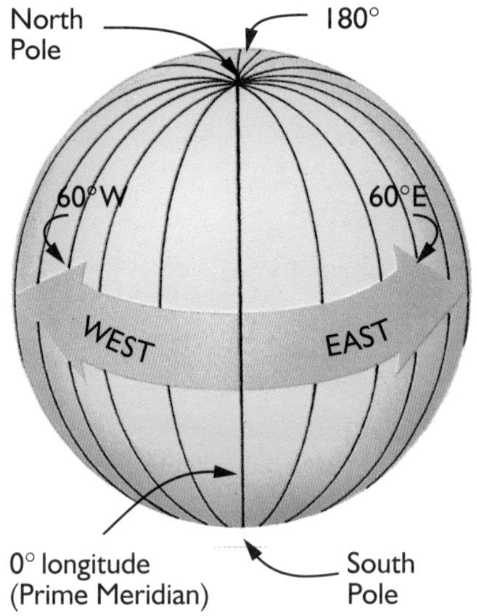

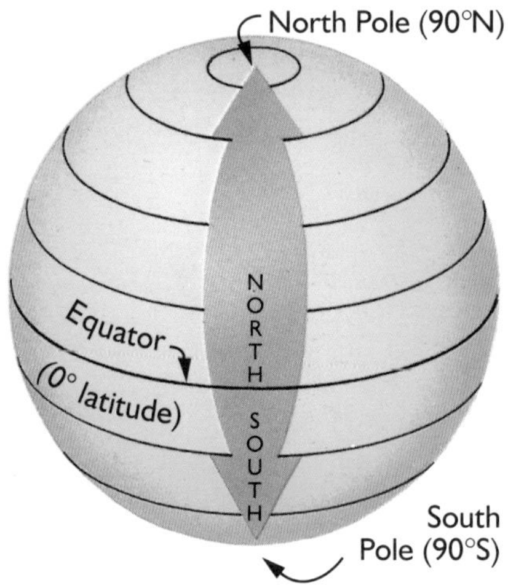

Flattening the Earth

Making a flat map of the Earth is like trying to flatten out an orange peel. For it to lie flat some parts would have to be stretched. Different areas of the Earth can be stretched to make it lie flat, so two world maps can look quite different from each other.

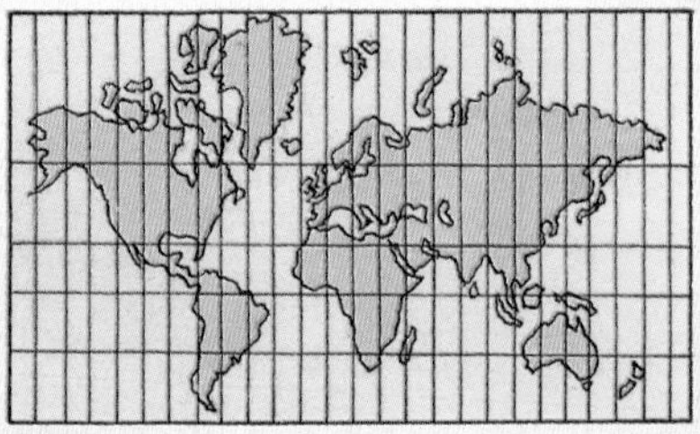

On this map, countries furthest from the Equator are stretched and this makes them look much bigger than they really are.

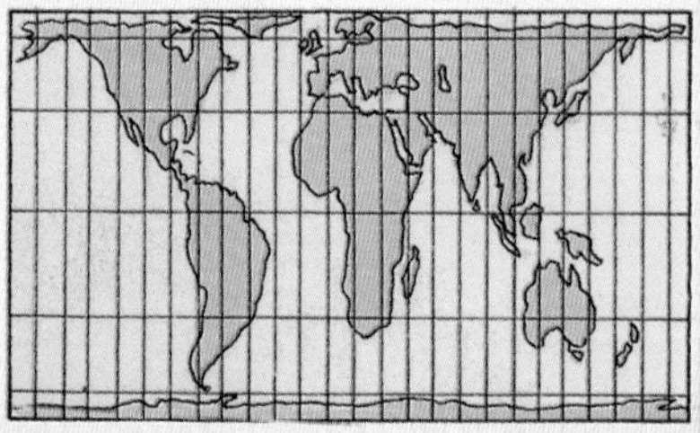

This map makes places near the Equator look much longer than they really are. Places near the Poles are squashed.

Where are you on the globe?

If you want to find a place on the globe, you will need to look up its latitude and longitude in the index of an atlas. For example, Madrid, in Spain, is 40°N, 3°W. This means it is 40° north of the Equator and 3° west of the Prime Meridian. Now follow the lines of latitude and longitude on a globe until they cross.

To be more precise, an atlas may give positions in degrees and minutes (′). A minute is one sixtieth of a degree. Madrid's exact position is 40°25′N, 3°43′W.

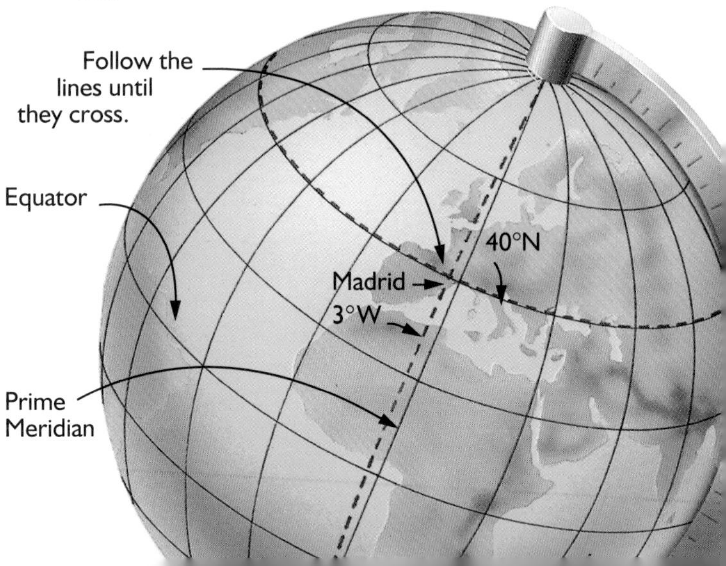

The story of maps

Early maps were carved into clay tablets.

People have been making maps since the early ages. The earliest maps anyone knows of were made by Babylonians and Egyptians over four thousand years ago. They were based on travellers' descriptions of places they had seen.

Scholars in Ancient Greece worked out that the Earth is a sphere. The Greek geographer, Ptolemy, worked out distances between places by studying the positions of the stars and collecting information from travellers.

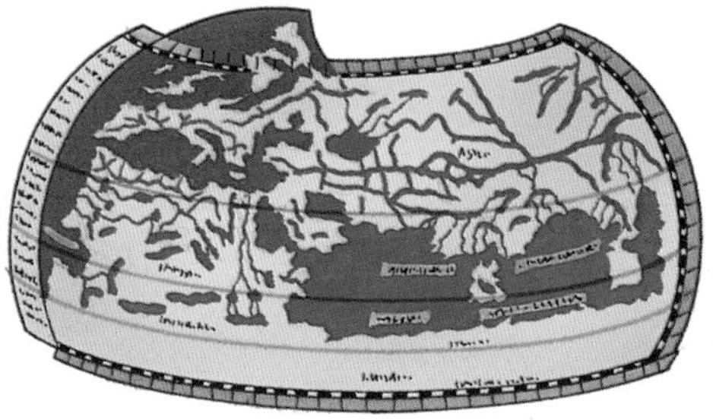

When Ptolemy created this map of the world, he thought Europe, Asia and Africa were the only continents.

Over the past thousand years, many explorers have set out by land and sea to discover the world. In 1787 the theodolite was invented. This is a telescope with a device for measuring angles. It makes map-making easier.

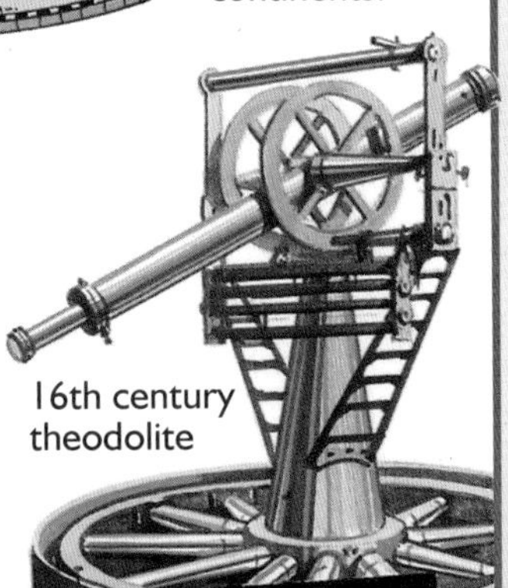

16th century theodolite

Satellite maps such as this can show every part of the Earth's surface.

Now, the whole Earth has been mapped. Many maps are drawn from photographs taken from the air. Satellites orbit the Earth and send back data about places no one has ever visited and computers turn this information into maps.

24 hour globe

The Earth has been divided into 24 time zones. Without them no one would know what time it is anywhere else in the world. The zones roughly follow lines of longitude.

In each time zone, people set their clocks and watches to their own standard time. The picture below shows how standard time varies around the world. For example, when the standard time at A is 3.00 in the morning, the standard time at B is 3.00 in the afternoon.

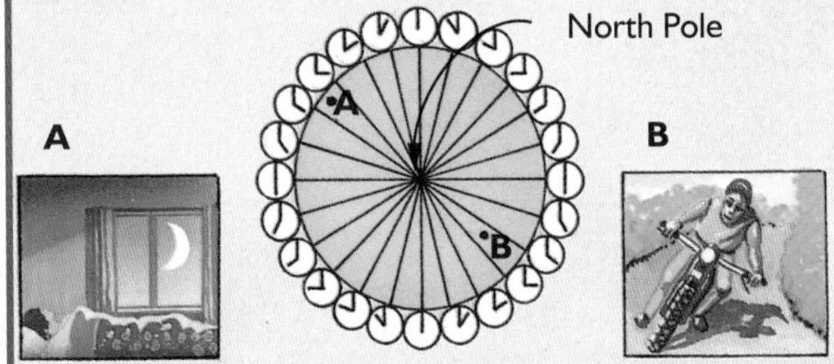
North Pole
A
B
A
B

If you travel east or west into a different time zone you have to alter the time on your watch to the standard time in the new zone. If you cross a time zone travelling east, put your watch forward. If you cross a time zone travelling west, put your watch back.

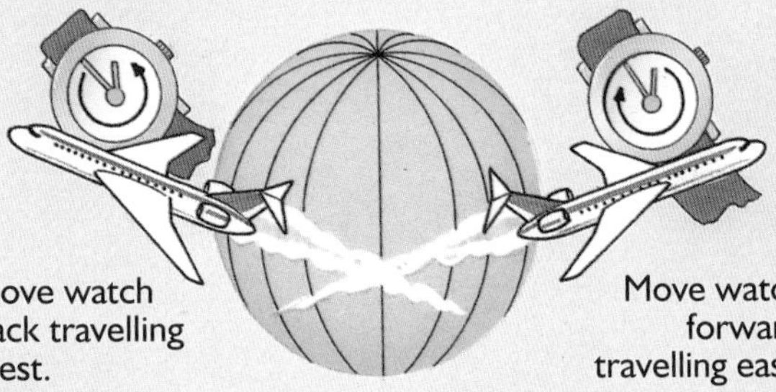
Move watch back travelling west.
Move watch forward travelling east.

The 180° line of longitude is called the **International Date Line**. Places just west of this line are 24 hours ahead of places just to the east. If you cross it, the time stays the same but you gain or lose a whole day.

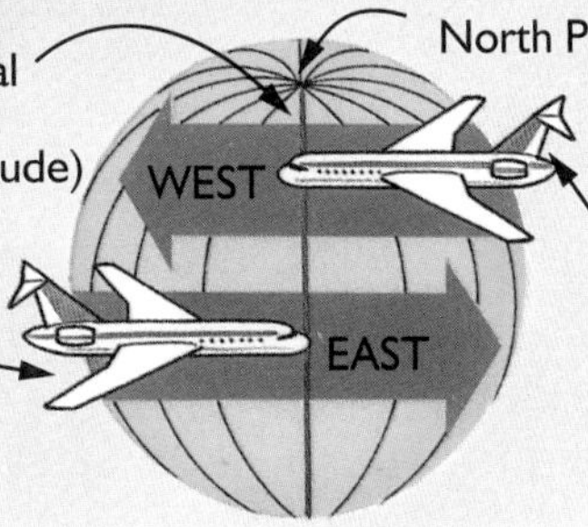
International Date Line (180° longitude)
North Pole
WEST
EAST
Go back a day travelling east.
Go forward a day travelling west.

Looking at maps

To show even a tiny part of the Earth's surface on a map, it usually has to be drawn much smaller than it really is. Drawing something smaller or larger than it is and keeping it all in proportion is called **drawing to scale**. The smaller something is drawn, the smaller the scale.

This park has been drawn 500 times smaller than it really is. The scale of the map is described as one in five hundred, written 1:500.

Scale 1:100,000

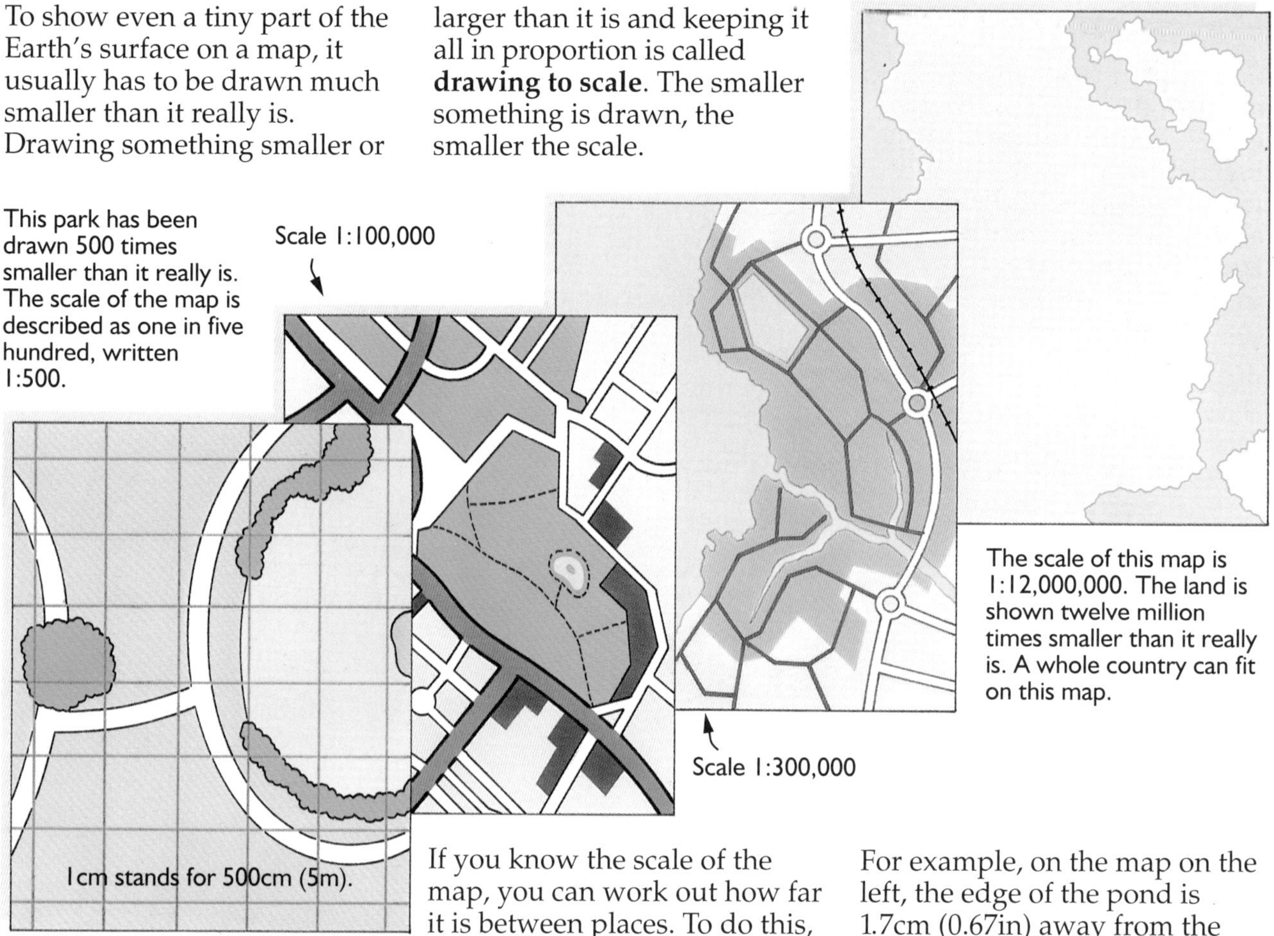

The scale of this map is 1:12,000,000. The land is shown twelve million times smaller than it really is. A whole country can fit on this map.

Scale 1:300,000

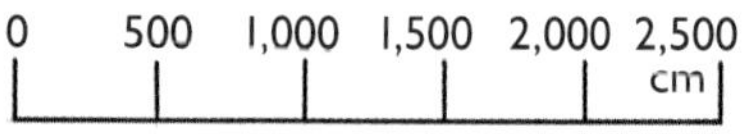

A scale bar helps you to measure distances on a map.

If you know the scale of the map, you can work out how far it is between places. To do this, you need to measure the distance on the map then multiply this distance by the scale of the map.

For example, on the map on the left, the edge of the pond is 1.7cm (0.67in) away from the edge of the tree. The map scale is 1:500 so the real distance is 1.7cm x 500 = 850cm, or 8.5m (9.3yd).

Sign language

A small scale map is like a view from high above the Earth. If everything was drawn as it really looked, most things in the landscape would be far too small for you to see.

So that you can see features more clearly, map-makers (cartographers) show them as symbols. These are called conventional signs. A **key** to the map tells you what the symbols mean.

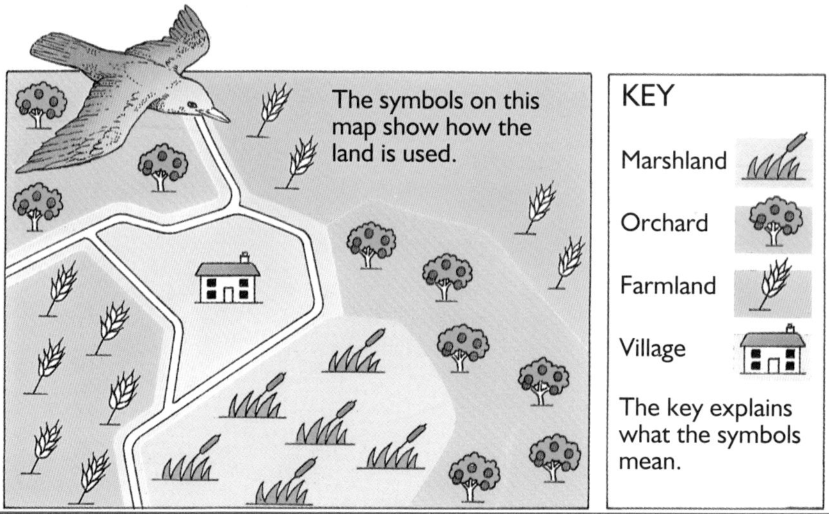

How hilly is it?

Surveyors, who study the shape of the land, have equipment to measure how high it is. They work out how far it rises above sea-level. The easiest way to show how the land rises is with a side-on drawing called a **cross-section**.

When cartographers draw maps, they have to show the shape of the land from above. One way to do this is with lines called **contours**. Contours join up all the places on the map that are the same height above sea-level. Small numbers on or next to the contours tell you what height they stand for.

On some maps, spaces between contours are coloured in different shades. This is called **layer tinting**. A key tells you what heights the colours stand for. Layer tinting makes it easier to see where the land is highest.

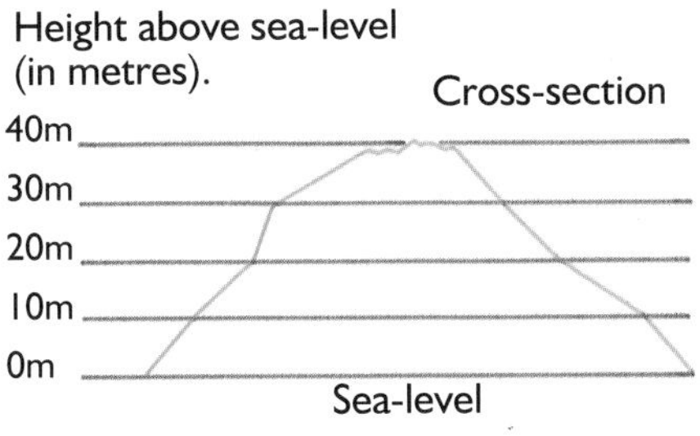
Height above sea-level (in metres).
Cross-section
40m
30m
20m
10m
0m
Sea-level

Contours join up places of same height.

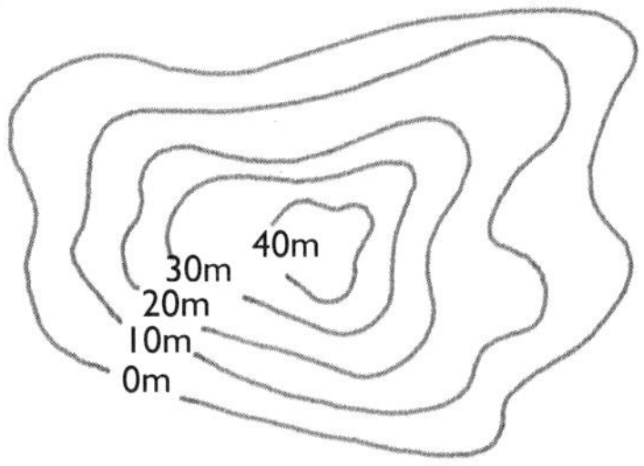

Key shows what height the colours stand for.

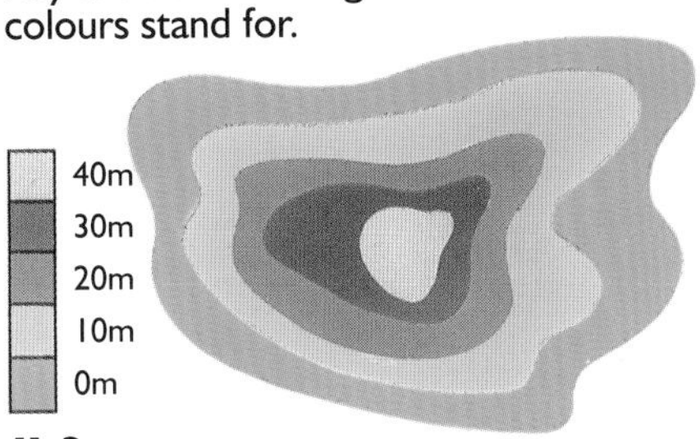

Types of slope

Here are some slopes you might find in a landscape and the patterns they make when they are shown as contours on a map.

Steady slope

Steady slopes have evenly spaced contours.

Concave slope

A **concave** slope is gentle at the bottom but becomes much steeper higher up. The contours are closer together where the land is steeper.

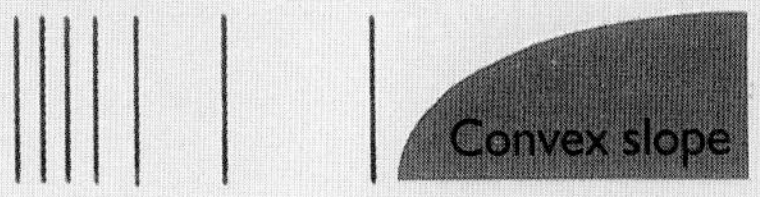
Convex slope

A **convex** slope rises very steeply but becomes more gentle higher up.

How long will it take to walk?

If you are planning a walk, you will probably need a map to help you decide the route. Using the scale and contours, you can work out how long the walk will take.

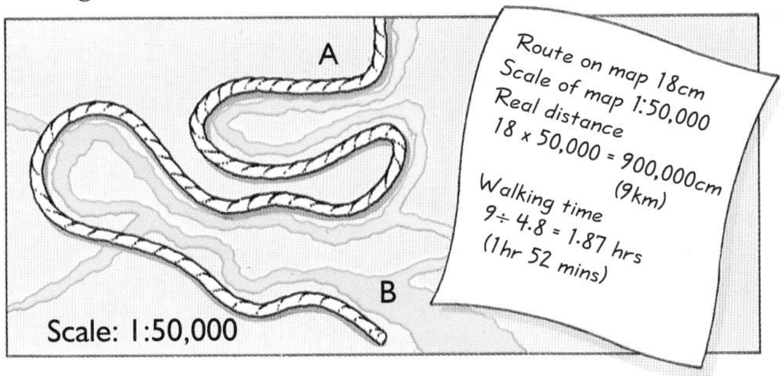
A
B
Scale: 1:50,000
Route on map 18cm
Scale of map 1:50,000
Real distance
18 x 50,000 = 900,000cm
(9km)
Walking time
9 ÷ 4.8 = 1.87 hrs
(1hr 52 mins)

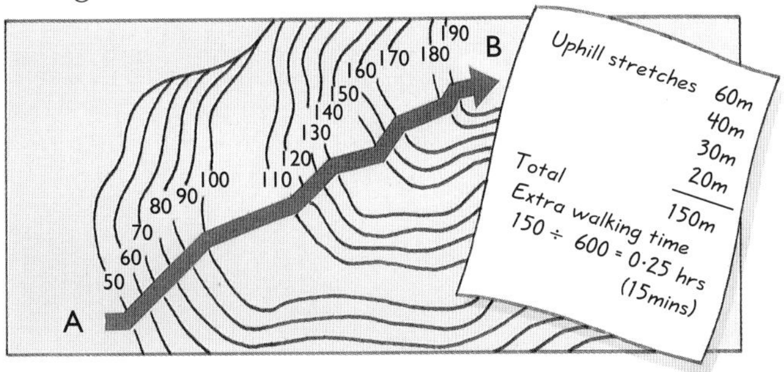

If the walk is across flat ground, measure the route on the map. To do this you could lay a piece of string along the route. Now use the method described on the opposite page to calculate the real distance. Most people walk at a speed of 4.8km (3 miles) per hour, so divide the walking distance by this figure to work out how long the walk will take.

A hilly walk will take longer than a flat one. To calculate how much longer, you need to work out how far you will climb. Follow your route on a map. Each time you cross a contour line going uphill, note how much the land rises. Add up the figures and, for every 600m (2,000ft) you climb, add one hour to your journey. Downhill stretches count as flat.

Using maps

When reading a map, you can find out which direction is which by using a compass. The compass needle is turned by the Earth's magnetic force* so that it always points towards north. The eight main points of a compass, called the **cardinal points**, are marked around the edge of the compass dial. The dial is also split up into 360 degrees (°). If you turn the dial so that the N for north lines up with the compass needle, you can work out the direction of things around you.

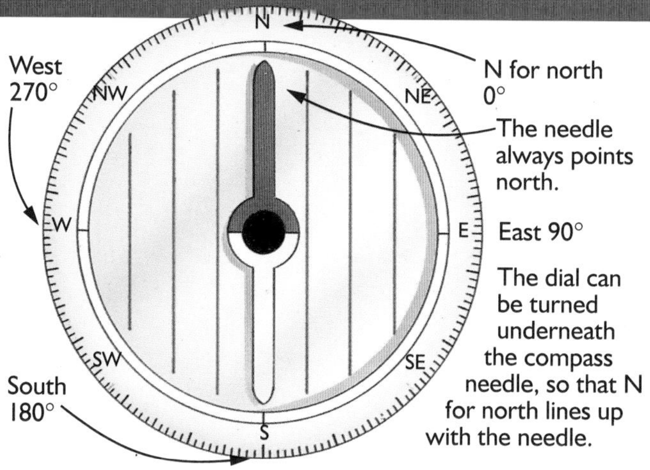

West
270°
N
NW
NE
N for north
0°
The needle always points north.
W
E
East 90°
The dial can be turned underneath the compass needle, so that N for north lines up with the needle.
SW
SE
S
South
180°

Finding your way

To find your way to a place (point X), which you cannot yet see in the distance, you can work out in which direction to go by taking a **compass bearing**. This is the angle, measured in degrees on a map, between north, the point where you are standing and the place where you want to get to (point X). To take a compass bearing follow the instructions below.

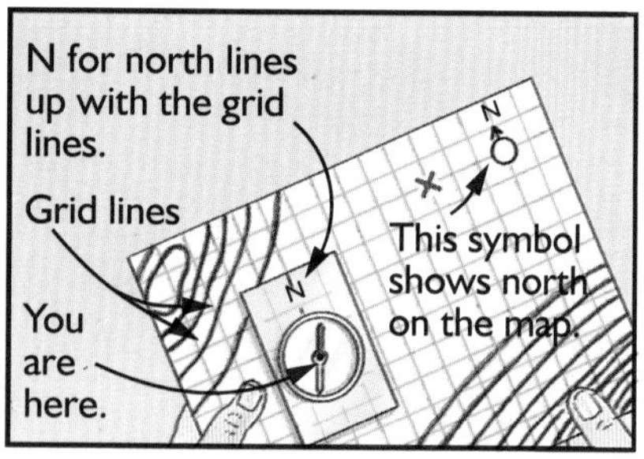

N for north lines up with the grid lines.
Grid lines
You are here.
This symbol shows north on the map.
N

1. Look at the map to find out where you are, and place the compass on that point. Turn the dial of the compass around so that N for north lines up with the vertical grid lines. These run from north to south on the map.

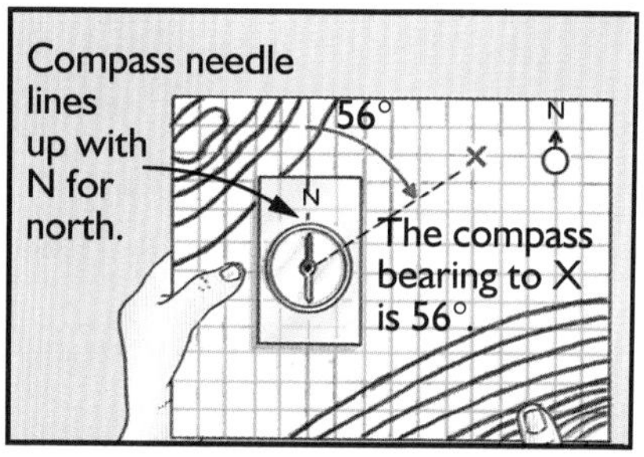

Compass needle lines up with N for north.
56°
N
The compass bearing to X is 56°.

2. Turn your body and the map around until the needle lines up with N for north. Imagine a line between X and the middle of the compass. The place at which this line crosses the dial shows the direction or compass bearing to follow.

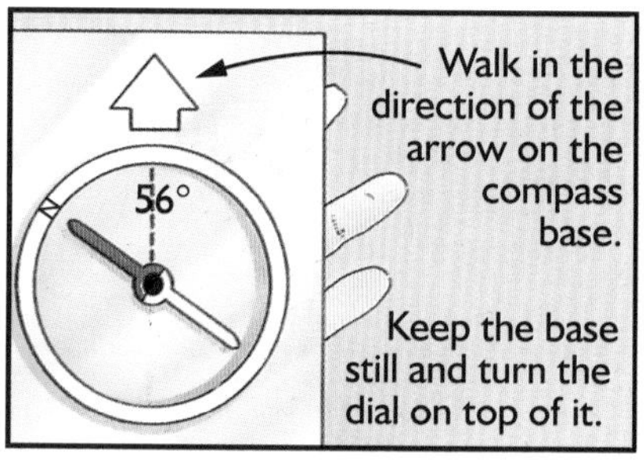

Walk in the direction of the arrow on the compass base.
56°
N
Keep the base still and turn the dial on top of it.

3. Turn the dial so that the compass bearing lines up with the arrow on the compass base. Turn around until the needle lines up with N for north. Walk forward, making sure that the needle stays level with N for north.

Grid references

The grid squares on a map are given numbers or letters. You can find places by knowing the number or the letter of the square where they are found. This is called the **grid reference**. On the map on the right, Newtown is in the square next to the vertical line 02 and the horizontal line 13. Giving the vertical line first, Newtown's grid reference is 0213.

For accuracy, the space between the grid lines may be split into ten. Newtown station is at point 026132, because it is 6 spaces along and 2 spaces up in square 0213.

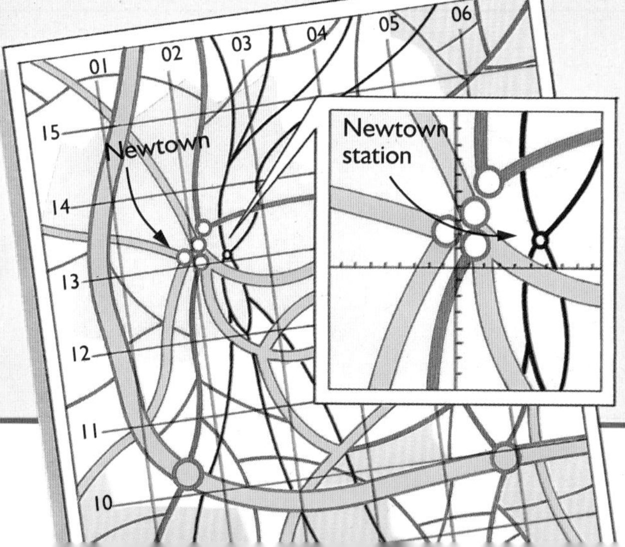

 *Earth's magnetic force, 271.

How to make a map

Anyone can make a map. You could start by making a map of a room or a garden. Here are some simple steps to follow.

First, you need to measure the area by pacing along each side. Choose a scale* for the map, for example 1cm (½in) for each pace. Draw the edges of the area on paper. Use a pencil in case you need to erase any mistakes.

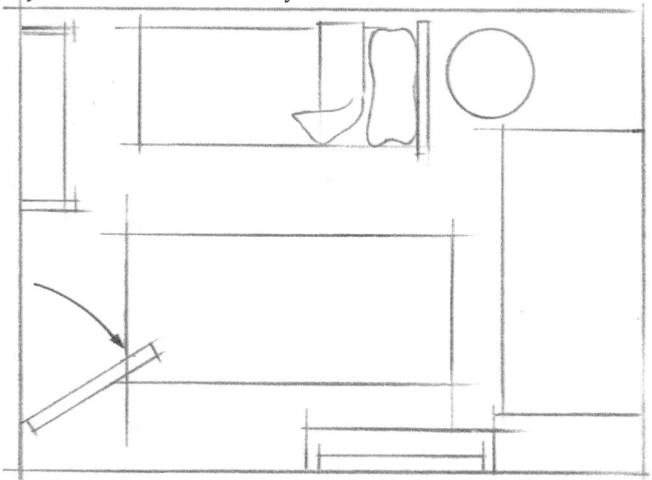

Now work out the sizes and positions of the main features and draw them in. For example, if you are mapping a room, draw the doors, windows and large pieces of furniture. Draw them as if you are looking down from above.

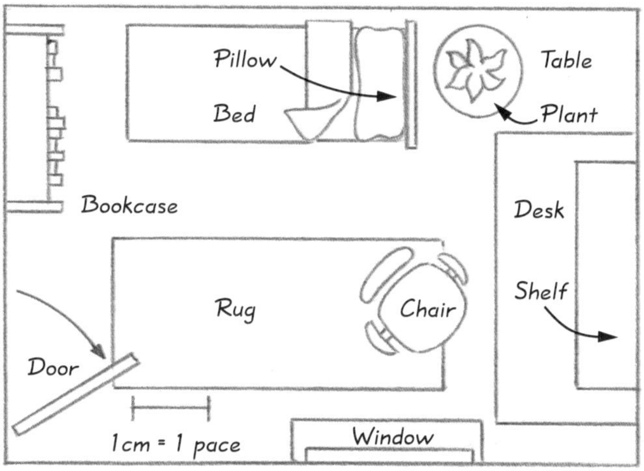

Next, fill in the smaller features between the main ones. For example, add in things such as a bedside table or a plant.

Last, label everything on the map. Also write the scale that you have used on the map.

Types of maps

Different types of maps have different uses. Tourist maps, for instance, have symbols to show places of interest in a certain area.

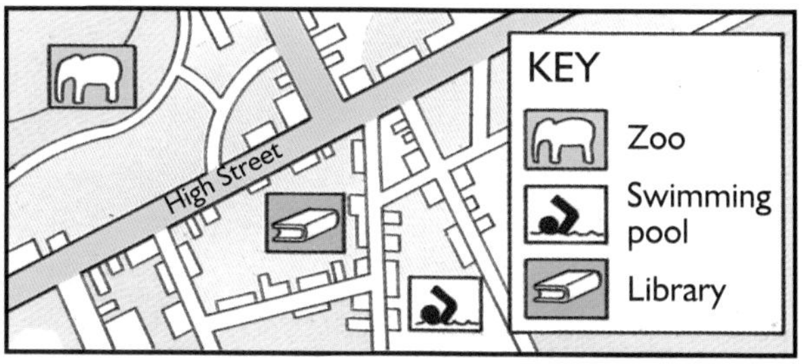

Road maps show large areas so that people can plan long journeys. The different types of roads are shown in different colours.

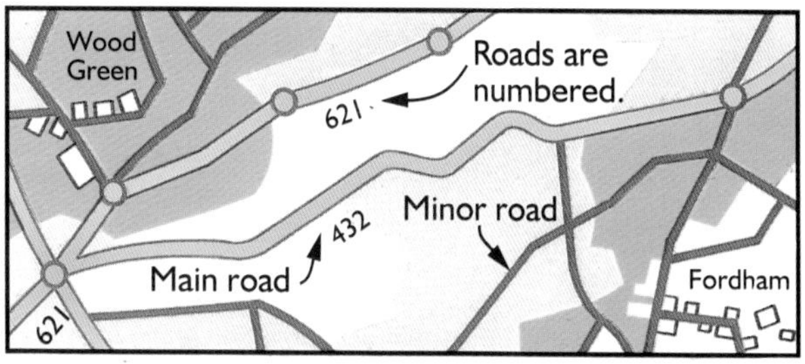

Distribution maps use colours or symbols to show facts about a particular area, for example where different languages are spoken.

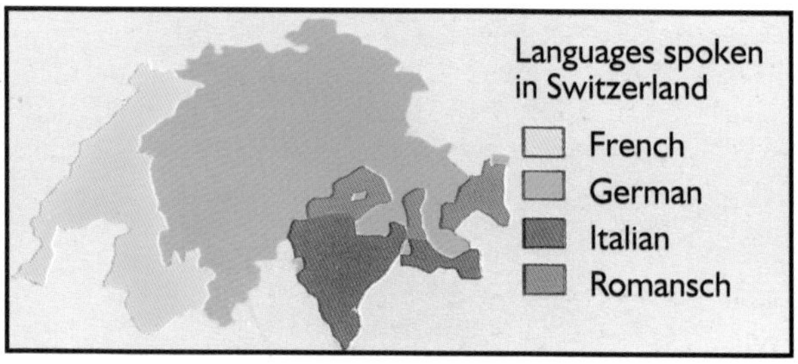

Some maps, such as maps of railway systems, show each part of the route as a straight line. The detail is left out, which makes them easy to read.

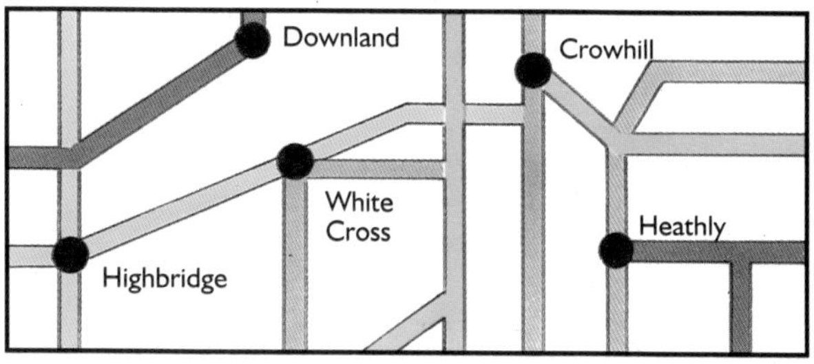

**Scale, 266.*

What the Earth is made of

The Earth began 4,500 million years ago as a ball of gases. Gradually, heavy metals sank to the centre and solidified. Lighter rocks and minerals* floated to the surface, cooled and hardened.

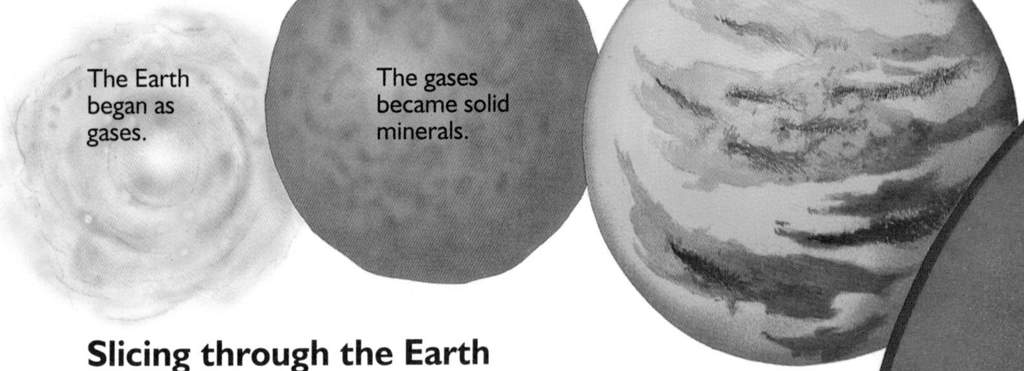
Heavy metals such as iron and nickel sank to the Earth's centre.
Earth 4,500 million years ago.
The Earth began as gases.
The gases became solid minerals.

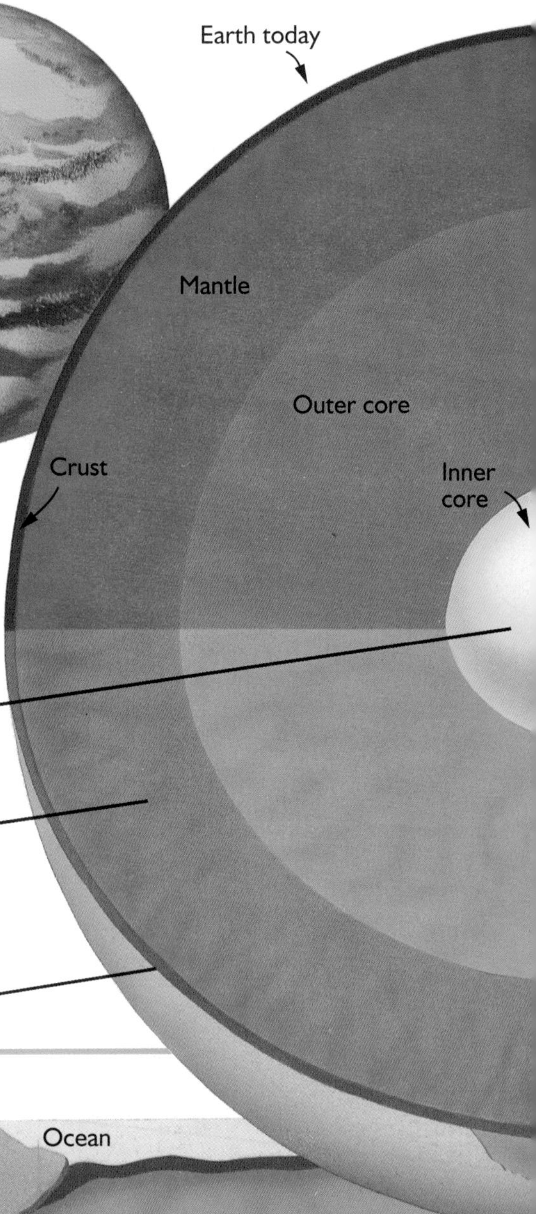
Earth today
Mantle
Outer core
Crust
Inner core

Slicing through the Earth

If you sliced through the Earth you would see three layers: the **core** in the middle, the **mantle** surrounding the core, and a hard outer shell called the **crust**.

The core has two layers. The inner core is made of solid iron and nickel and the outer core of liquid (molten) iron and nickel.

The mantle is made of rock. The upper part is semi-molten rock, called **magma**.

The crust is the thinnest of the three layers. If you imagine the Earth as a tennis ball, the crust would be thinner than a postage stamp attached to its surface.

A close-up of the crust

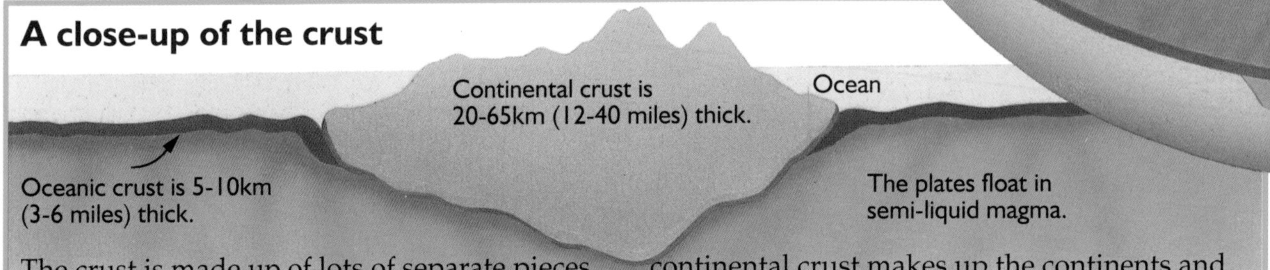
Continental crust is 20-65km (12-40 miles) thick.
Ocean
Oceanic crust is 5-10km (3-6 miles) thick.
The plates float in semi-liquid magma.

The crust is made up of lots of separate pieces, called **plates**, which fit together rather like an enormous jigsaw puzzle. The plates float in the semi-molten upper mantle.

There are two different types of crust; thick continental crust makes up the continents and much thinner oceanic crust makes up the ocean floors. Continental crust is made of granite, which is a light rock. Oceanic crust is made of dense basalt rock.

 *Minerals, 276.

Investigating the Earth

It is not easy finding out about the inside of the Earth. Geologists, who study rocks, have tried drilling holes in the crust to collect rock samples but there is no drill big enough to go more than a short distance below the Earth's surface. To find out what is deeper down, geologists study records of earthquakes*, called seismographs. During an earthquake, vibrations called seismic waves travel through the Earth, and as they pass through different types of rock, the waves change speed and direction (see picture below). By studying seismographs, it is possible to work out what the rocks are like at different depths.

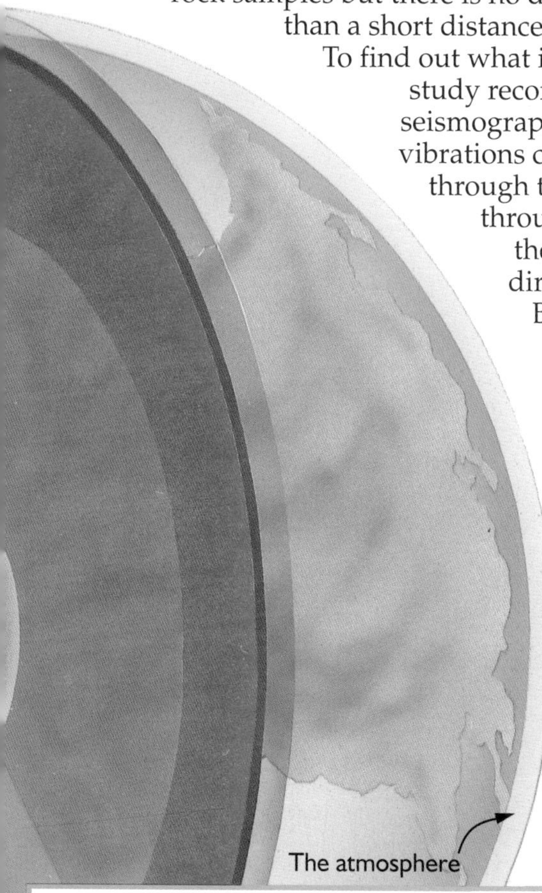
The atmosphere

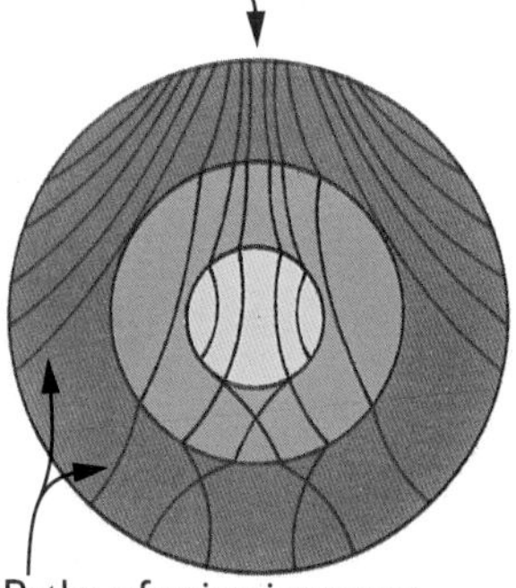
Earthquake
Paths of seismic waves

The Earth's blanket

As the Earth formed, gases escaped and settled in layers around its surface. These gases are the **atmosphere**.

Without the atmosphere, nothing could live on Earth. It contains a thin layer of gas, called the **ozone layer**, which filters out harmful rays from the Sun. It also contains the gases we need to breathe. It has other uses too. For example, radio waves can be bounced off layers of dust in the atmosphere to different parts of the world.

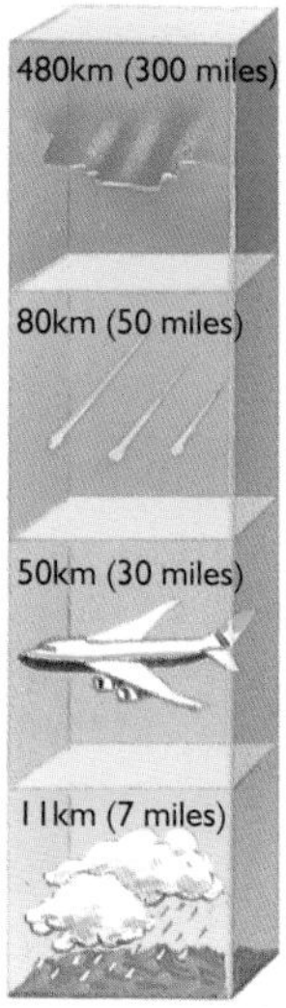
480km (300 miles)
80km (50 miles)
50km (30 miles)
11km (7 miles)

Thermosphere: electrically charged particles in this layer sometimes cause lights in the night sky, called the aurora.

Mesosphere: rocks that enter the atmosphere (meteorites), burn up in this layer.

Stratosphere: jets fly in this layer because it is very still.

Troposphere: weather happens in this layer.

Magnetic Earth

The Earth is magnetic. It is as though a giant magnetic rod runs through its core. The ends of the magnet are called the **magnetic poles**.

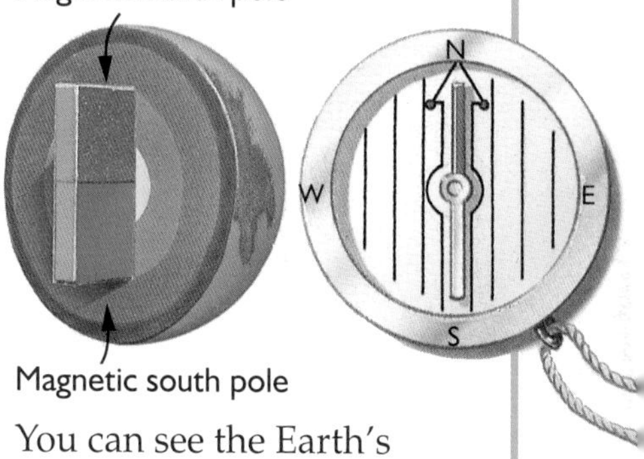
Magnetic north pole
N
W
E
S
Magnetic south pole

You can see the Earth's magnetic force at work if you use a compass. The compass needle, which is also magnetic, is pulled by the Earth's magnetic force so it always points to the Earth's magnetic north pole.

The Earth's pull

Gravity is a force that pulls objects towards each other. It holds you and everything around you on the Earth's surface.

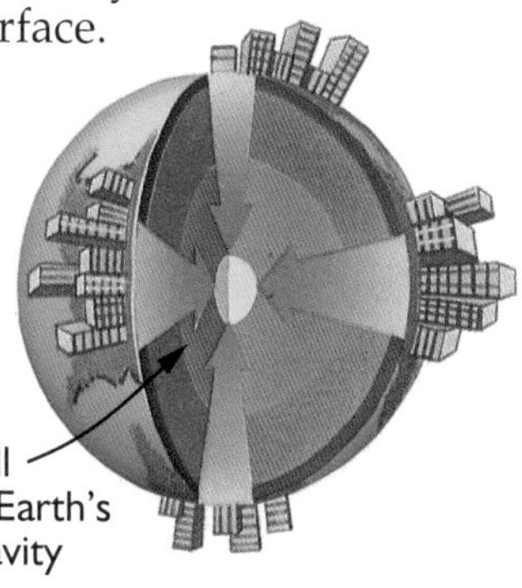
Pull of Earth's gravity

Gravity is strongest at the centre of the Earth. The further something is from the Earth's centre, the weaker the pull. Gravity is weaker at the top of a mountain than the bottom, for example.

**Earthquakes, 274.*

The restless Earth

The plates of the Earth's crust* are always moving – gradually pushing together, pulling apart or sliding past each other. These plate movements are caused by currents of magma* (molten rock) beneath the crust. Heat from the Earth's core* warms the magma and makes it rise. It pushes against the plates and drags them along.

Where two plates are pulled apart, hot magma oozes up to fill the gap. As it cools, it sets to form new rock. These areas, where new rock is being made, are called **constructive plate boundaries**. The new rock may form a **ridge** along the plate boundary. For example, the Mid-Atlantic Ridge, which runs beneath the Atlantic Ocean* (see map below) has formed in this way.

As plates move apart in one area, they push together in another. One plate slides over the other and the lower one disappears into the magma, where it eventually melts. The groove where the plates meet is called a **trench**. These boundaries are called **destructive plate boundaries**.

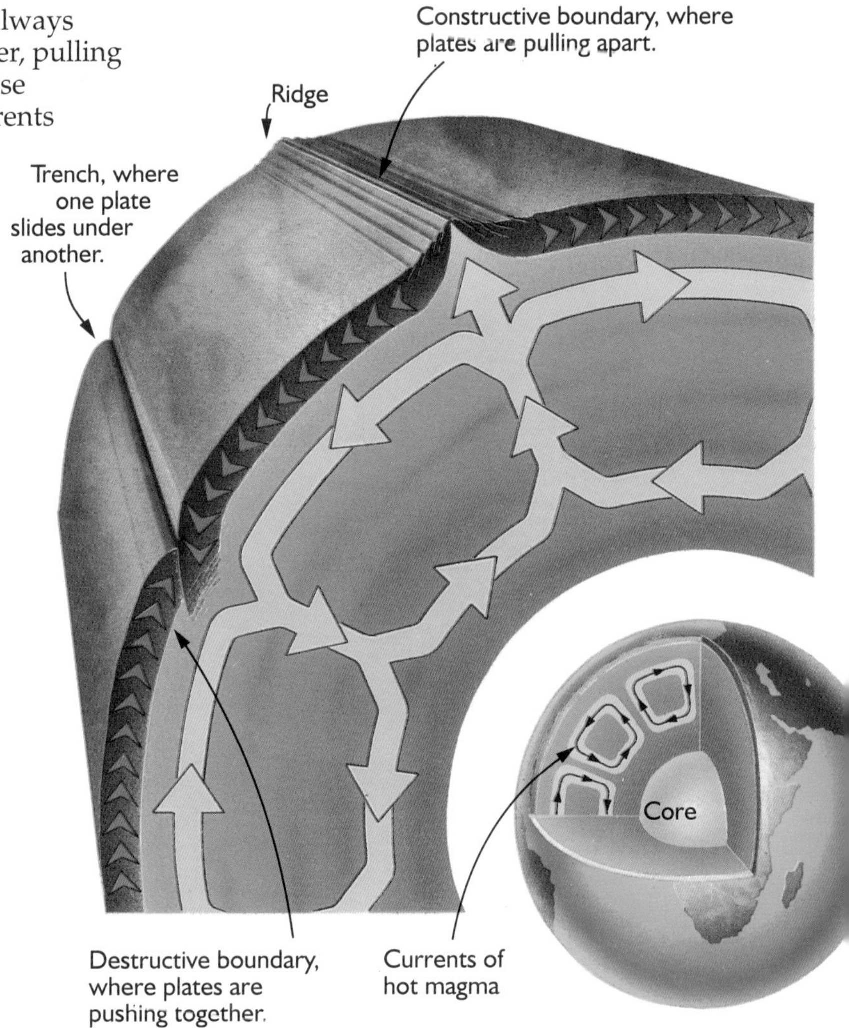
Constructive boundary, where plates are pulling apart.
Ridge
Trench, where one plate slides under another.
Core
Destructive boundary, where plates are pushing together.
Currents of hot magma

Where are the boundaries?

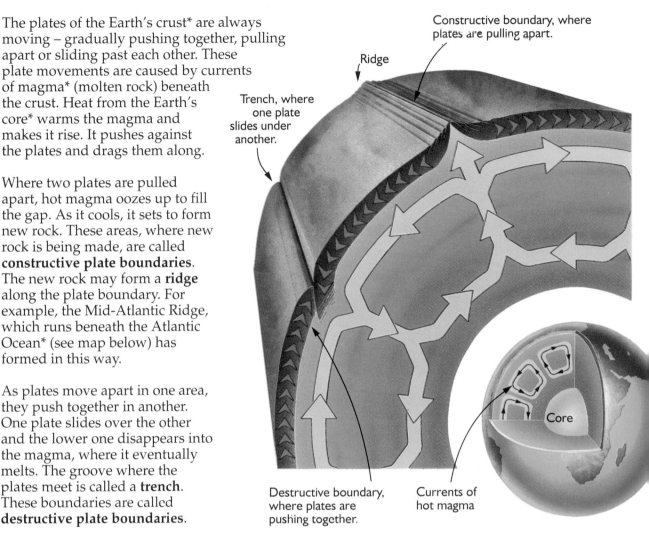

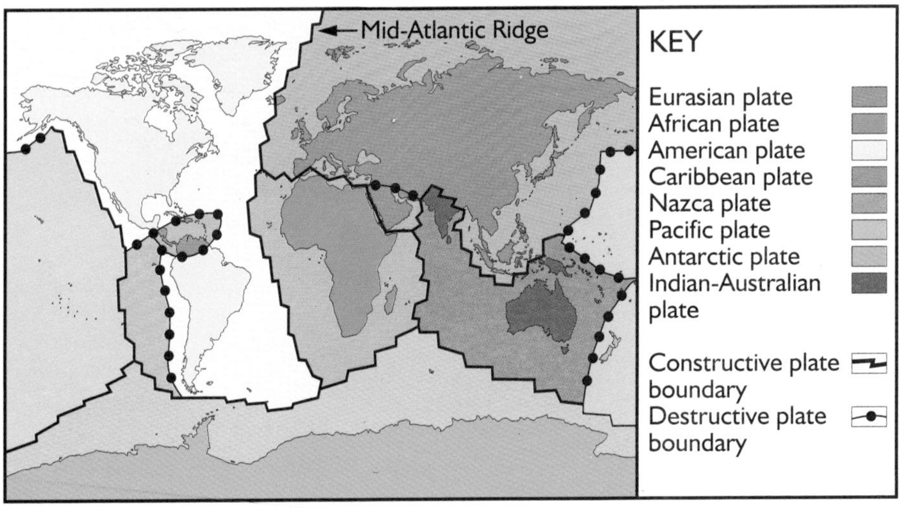
Mid-Atlantic Ridge
KEY
Eurasian plate
African plate
American plate
Caribbean plate
Nazca plate
Pacific plate
Antarctic plate
Indian-Australian plate
Constructive plate boundary
Destructive plate boundary

The map on the left shows the positions of the world's constructive and destructive plate boundaries. The movement of the plates in these areas has caused many of the world's mountain ranges to form there. The Earth's crust is weaker along the plate boundaries, so most of the world's volcanoes and earthquakes occur in these areas too. You can find out about these over the page.

 *Core, Crust, Magma, 270; Oceans, 280.

Drifting continents

The plates move very slowly – only about a hand's width a year. Over millions of years, however, this is enough to make continents drift huge distances, as these maps show.

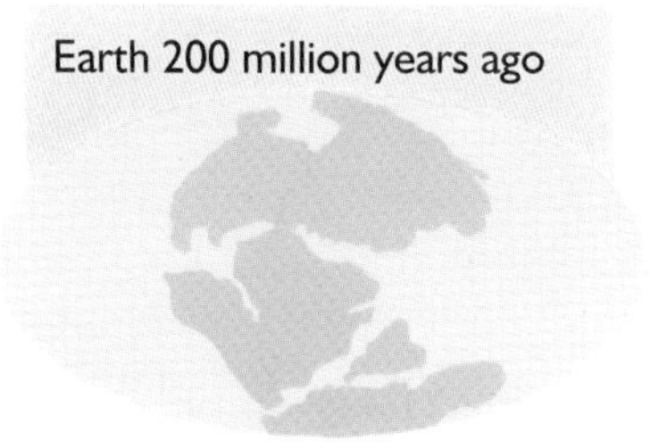
Earth 200 million years ago

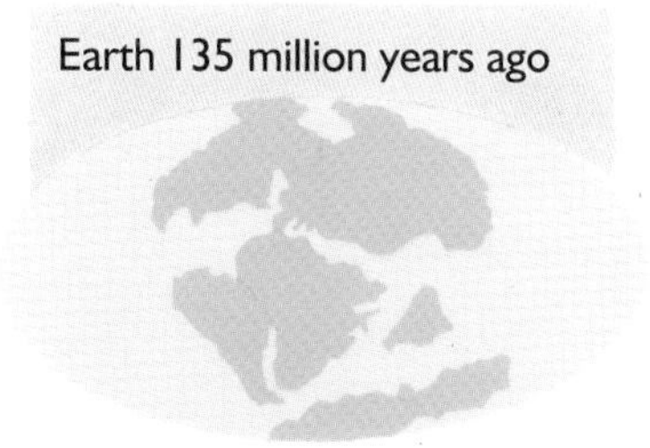
Earth 135 million years ago

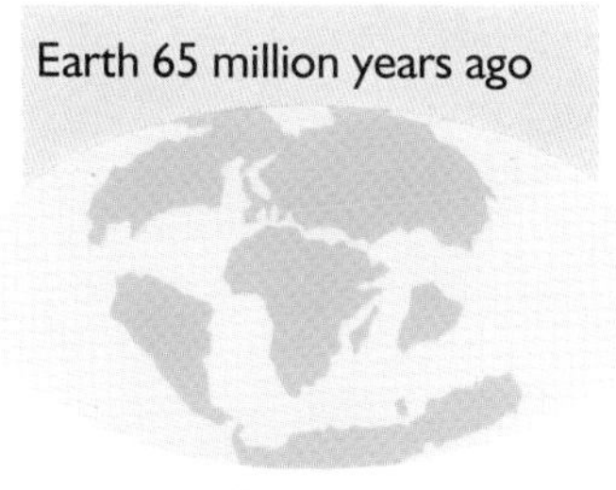
Earth 65 million years ago

Earth today

The continents are still drifting. Every year the Pacific Ocean is 9cm (3.5in) wider. In 50 million years, the shapes and positions of the continents will be quite different from today.

Fold mountains

Many of the world's highest mountain ranges are **fold mountains**. They began to form millions of years ago when plates pushed together under the oceans.

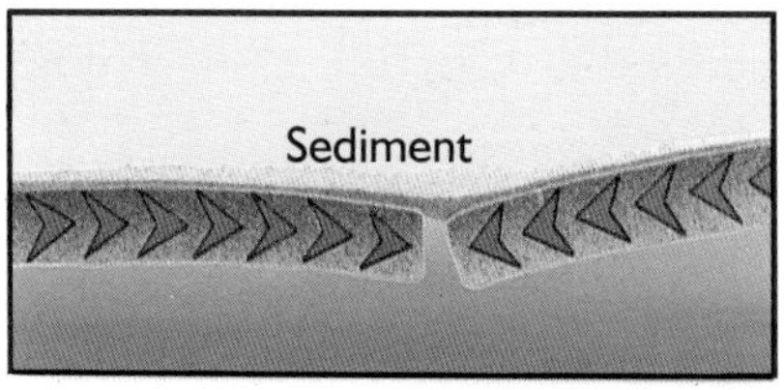
Sediment

As one plate slid beneath the other, particles of rock (sediment) on the seabed piled up. Heat and pressure gradually turned the sediment to solid sedimentary rock*.

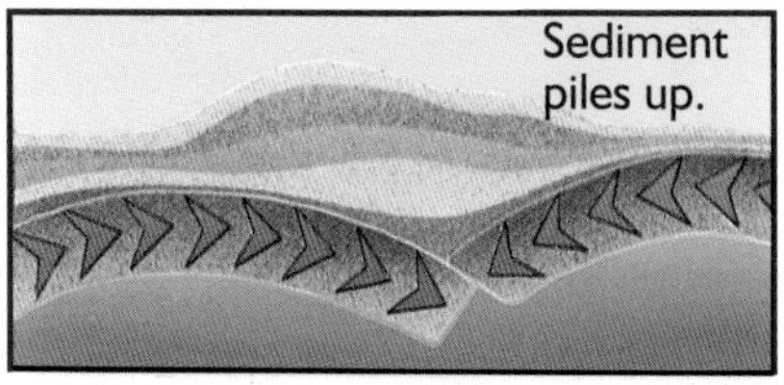
Sediment piles up.

The Himalayas, Andes and Alps are all chains of fold mountains. Some mountains, such as Mount Everest in the Himalayas, are still growing in this way.

The Himalayas

Crust under pressure

If pressure builds up under the Earth's surface, brittle rocks in the crust may crack. Cracks in rocks are called **faults**.

If two faults occur close together, the chunk of crust between them may be pushed up or slip down below the surrounding rock. Chunks that are pushed up are called **block mountains** or **horsts**. A low area between two horsts is called a **rift valley**.

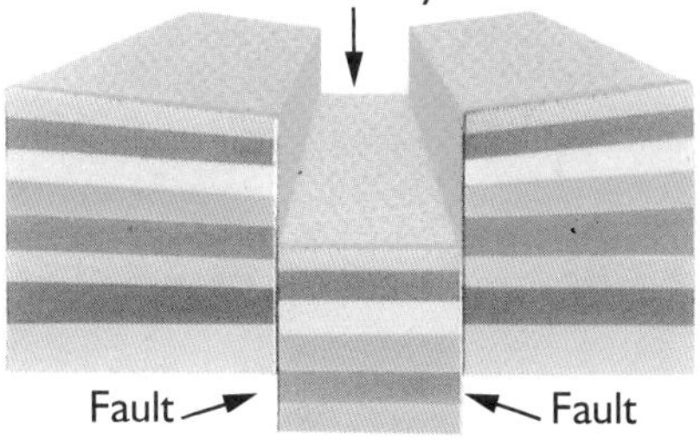
Horst
Rift valley
Horst
Fault
Fault

The most famous rift valley is the Rift Valley in East Africa. The Rhine Valley in Germany and Death Valley in the USA are also rift valleys.

In some areas, currents of magma under the crust flow together from opposite directions. The pressure may squeeze the crust and make it buckle and form **folds** such as those shown here.

Simple folds

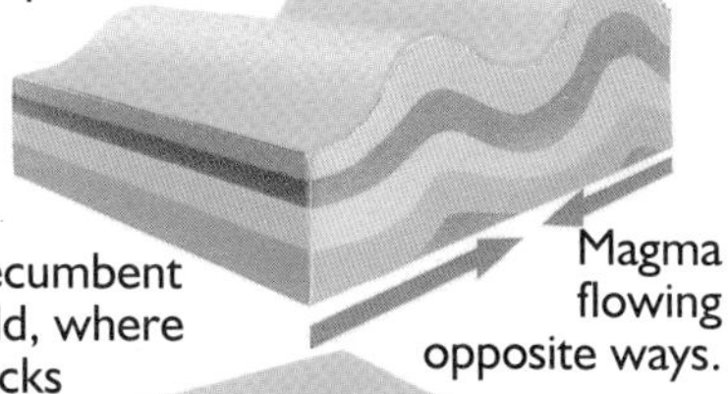
Magma flowing opposite ways.

Recumbent fold, where rocks form a pleat.

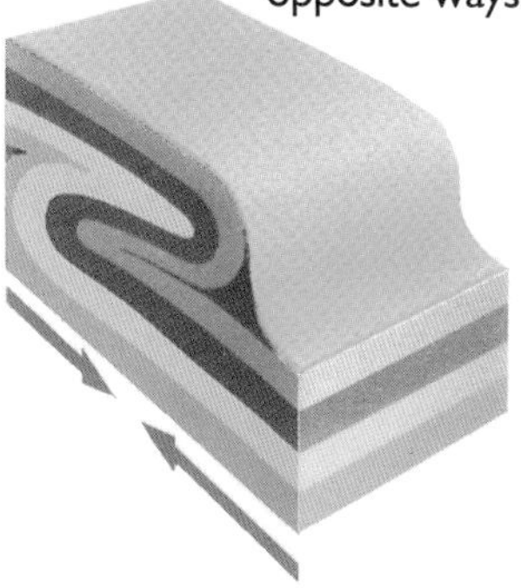

Overfold, where rocks lean over gently.

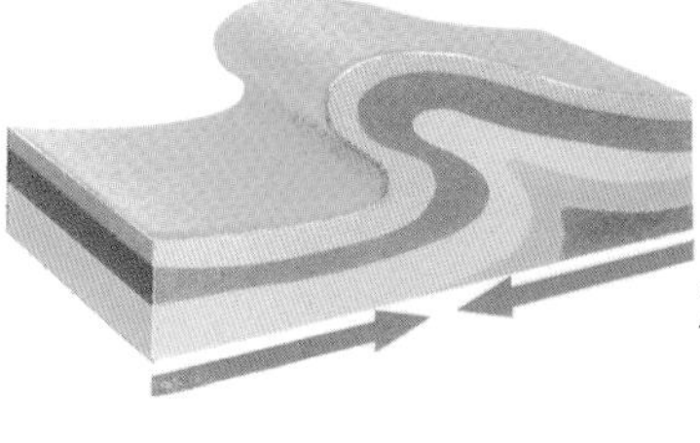

Sedimentary rocks, 276.

Earthquakes and volcanoes

Activity along the Earth's plate boundaries* is usually very slow but sometimes pressure builds up underground and causes dramatic earthquakes and volcanic eruptions.

Earthquakes occur where two plates slide past each other and their jagged edges jam. Strain builds up until one plate finally gives way and there is a sudden movement, which makes the earth shudder or quake.

The actual point where the rocks move is usually about 5-15km (3-10 miles) underground. It is called the **focus** of the earthquake. The point on the Earth's surface directly above the focus is called the **epicentre**.

The vibrations of an earthquake are called **seismic waves**. They are strongest at the focus and become weaker as they spread out.

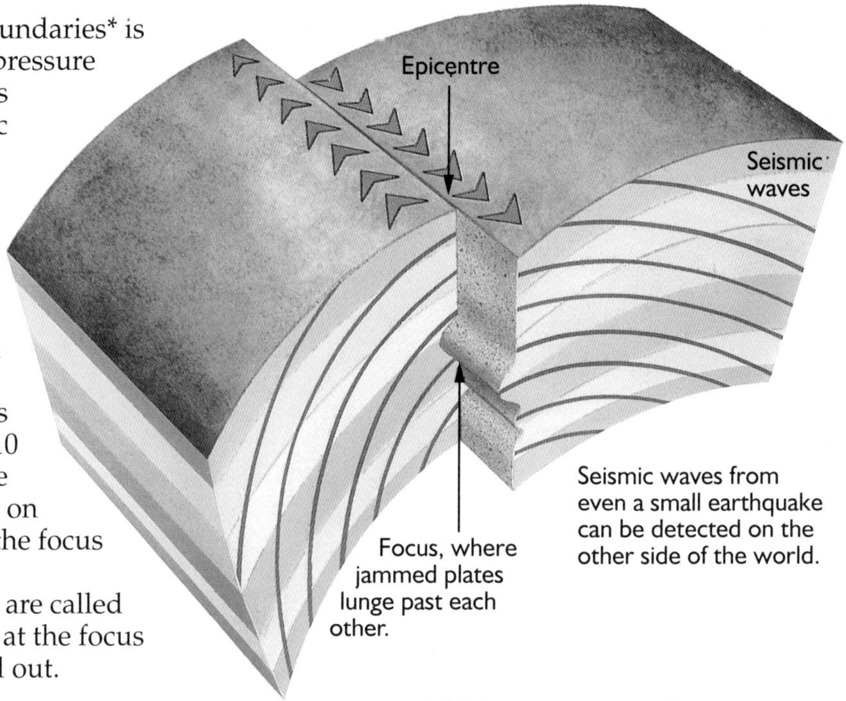
Epicentre
Seismic waves
Focus, where jammed plates lunge past each other.
Seismic waves from even a small earthquake can be detected on the other side of the world.

Making records

People who study earthquakes are called seismologists. The instrument they use to measure seismic waves is called a seismometer. It has a revolving drum and a suspended pen fixed to a weight. During an earthquake the drum shakes and the pen draws a chart called a seismograph.

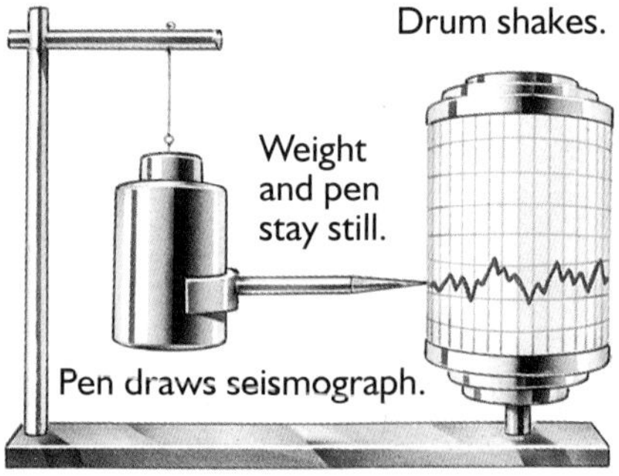
Drum shakes.
Weight and pen stay still.
Pen draws seismograph.

Taking precautions

Seismologists try to predict where and when earthquakes may happen so that people can be prepared. An earthquake can sometimes be prevented by injecting water into the rocks to release the jammed plates. Also, a small explosion can make the plates move before too much stress builds up.

Measuring earthquakes

There are two scales for measuring earthquakes. The **Richter Scale** measures the power of the seismic waves. The **Mercalli Scale**, described on the right, measures the effects of the earthquake on people and buildings.

A weak earthquake may be more serious than a very powerful one if it happens in a city where there are a lot of buildings and people.

Mercalli Scale

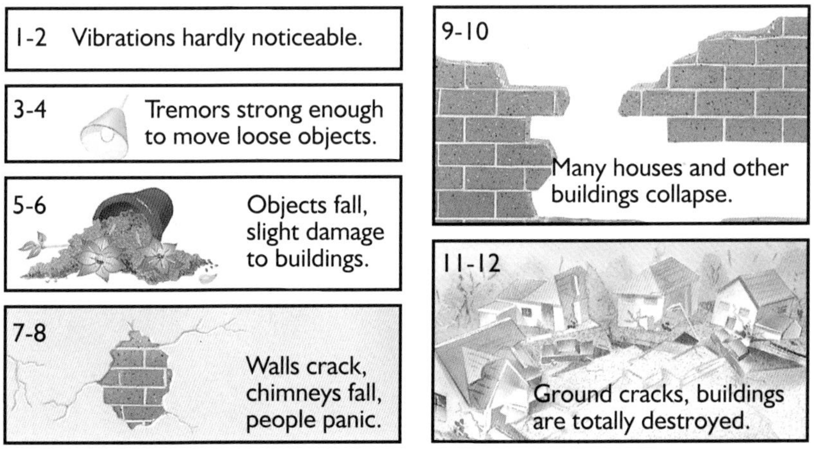
1-2 Vibrations hardly noticeable.
3-4 Tremors strong enough to move loose objects.
5-6 Objects fall, slight damage to buildings.
7-8 Walls crack, chimneys fall, people panic.
9-10 Many houses and other buildings collapse.
11-12 Ground cracks, buildings are totally destroyed.

 *Plate boundaries, 272.

What is a volcano?

There are about 600 volcanoes in the world. Most are found at weak points along plate boundaries, where red-hot magma* rises up from within the Earth and reaches the surface.

A typical volcano is a mound with a pipe, or **vent**, down the middle and a **magma chamber** below. Channels called **sills** and **dykes** may also lead from the magma chamber. When pressure builds up in the magma chamber, a mixture of magma and solid rock, called **lava**, pushes up the vent and the volcano erupts. If the lava is very thick it may set inside the vent and form a plug. Great pressure builds up and finally explodes the plug, hurling chunks of rock called volcanic bombs high into the air. If lava is thin, it erupts much more gently.

Each time a volcano erupts, the lava sets as a solid layer. As the layers build up, the volcano grows. Thick lava flows only a short way before setting so it forms steep-sided **cone volcanoes**. Thin lava flows further before it sets, so it forms volcanoes with gently sloping sides. These are called **shield volcanoes**.

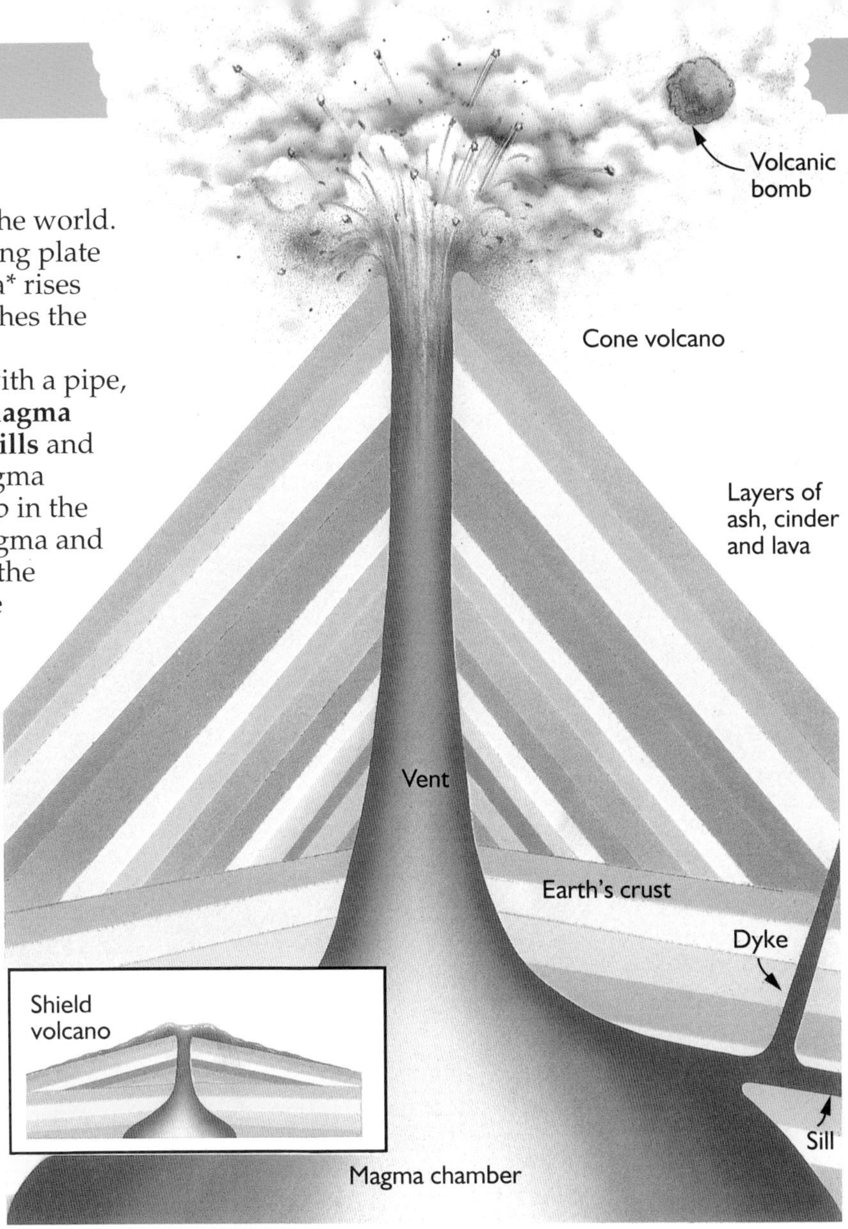
Volcanic bomb
Cone volcano
Layers of ash, cinder and lava
Vent
Earth's crust
Dyke
Shield volcano
Sill
Magma chamber

Hot water

If underground water is close to magma, it becomes extremely hot and may rise up and erupt. It may spurt out of the ground as a jet of super-heated water called a **geyser** or as a jet of steam called a **fumarole**. Mud pools form if steam bubbles through volcanic ash.

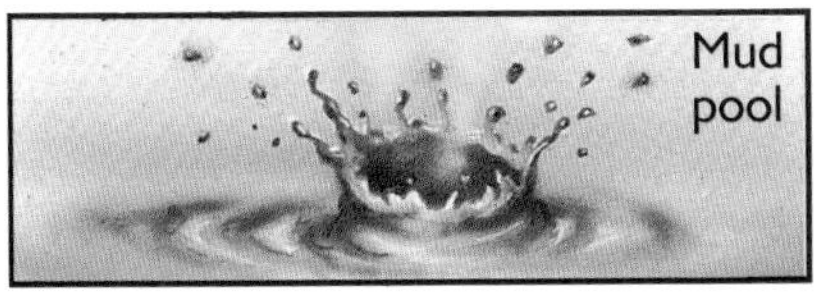
Mud pool

Alive, asleep or dead?

Volcanoes that erupt regularly are called active volcanoes. Volcanoes that will never erupt again are extinct. It may be difficult to tell if a volcano is extinct or whether it is sleeping (dormant). In 1973, for example, the volcano on the island of Heimaey, near Iceland, erupted and destroyed 300 buildings. Everyone thought it was extinct because it had not erupted for over 5,000 years .

Undersea volcanoes

Many volcanoes are under the sea. Some grow so big that they emerge above sea-level as new islands. Iceland is a volcanic island. It is still growing with each eruption.

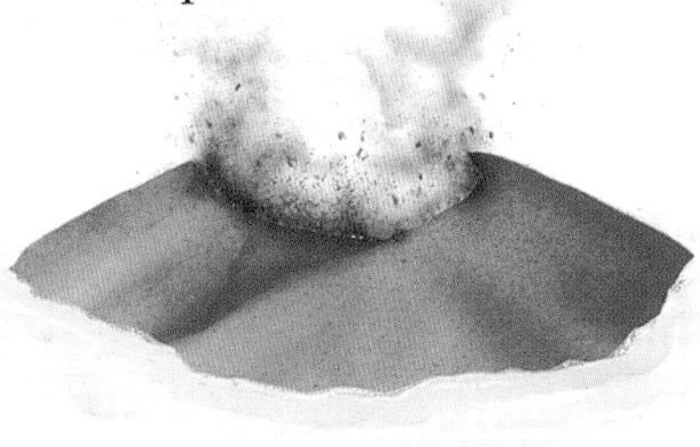

**Magma, 270.*

Rocks and minerals

The Earth's crust* is made up of rocks. Many are millions of years old but new rocks are being created all the time. There are three categories of rocks: sedimentary rocks, metamorphic rocks and igneous rocks.

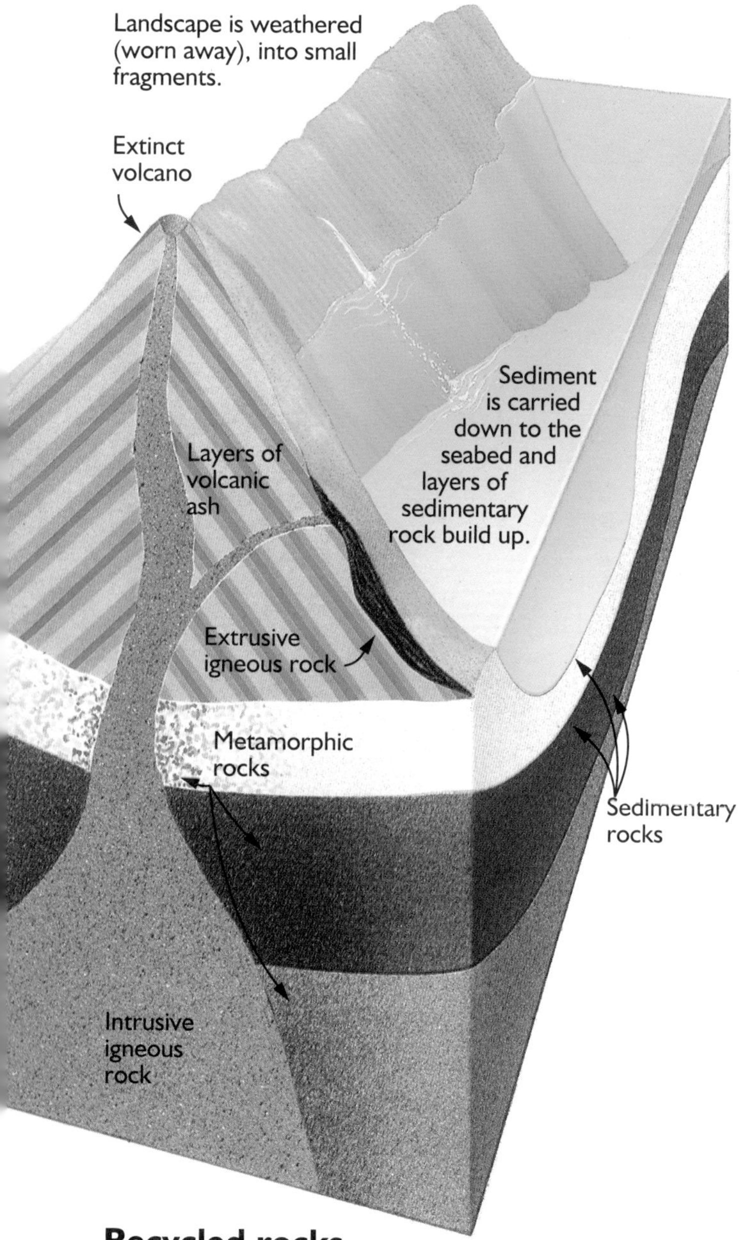
Landscape is weathered (worn away), into small fragments.
Extinct volcano
Sediment is carried down to the seabed and layers of sedimentary rock build up.
Layers of volcanic ash
Extrusive igneous rock
Metamorphic rocks
Sedimentary rocks
Intrusive igneous rock

Chalk is made from shells of tiny sea creatures.

Shale is solidified mud or clay.

Sandstone is made of fragments of rock.

Sedimentary rocks form from fragments of rock, plants and animals that are washed or blown from the landscape. The fragments (sediment) settle, usually on the seabed. As layers build up, deeper sediment is squeezed tightly and eventually turns into solid rock.

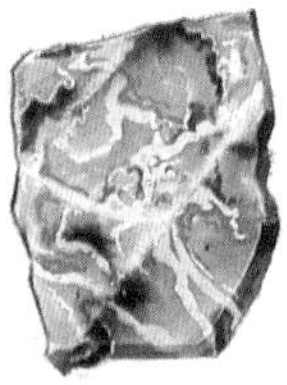

Marble is a hard metamorphic rock formed from chalk.

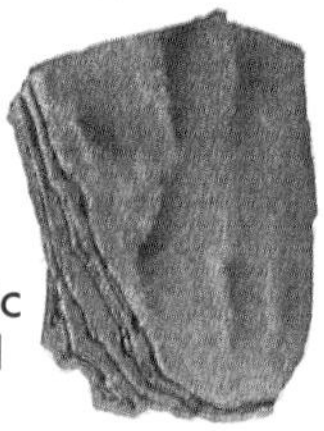

Slate is a layered metamorphic rock formed from shale.

Metamorphic rocks are rocks that have been changed by heat or pressure. They may have been baked by heat from a nearby magma chamber* or forced together by movement within the crust. Some rocks become very hard, others are rearranged into fine layers.

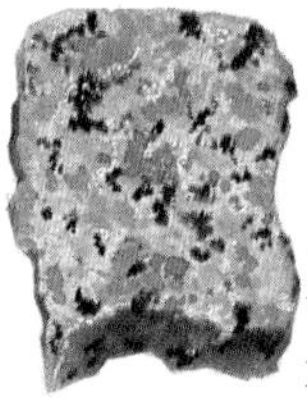

Granite is the most common intrusive igneous rock.

Basalt is an extrusive igneous rock.

Igneous rocks form when magma from inside the Earth cools and sets. If it sets underground, the rocks are called **intrusive igneous rocks**. If magma spills out through volcanoes* or gaps in the crust and sets on the surface, it forms **extrusive igneous rock**.

Recycled rocks

As ancient rocks in the landscape wear down, their sediment helps to make new rocks, so rocks are always being renewed. The new sedimentary rocks may be buried for many millions of years. During this time they may be baked or squashed to form metamorphic rocks, or melted then cooled to form igneous rocks. Sooner or later, movements in the crust will heave the rocks back up to the surface and the process will begin again.

**Crust, 270; Magma chamber, Volcanoes, 275.*

Mineral ingredients

Rocks are made of basic ingredients called **minerals**. Some rocks are made of just one mineral but most rocks are made of two or more minerals. Granite, for example, is made of quartz, mica and felspar. If you look at a piece of rock under a magnifying glass, you may be able to see the different minerals that it is made of.

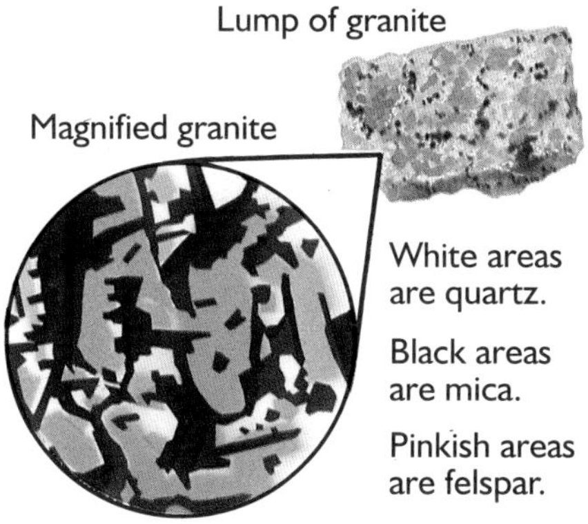
Lump of granite
Magnified granite
White areas are quartz.
Black areas are mica.
Pinkish areas are felspar.

Buried treasure

Valuable, pure minerals may be found within rocks. Many form as shapeless lumps, some collect within cracks and form veins. If there is plenty of space, some minerals form beautiful, angular crystals. Different minerals form different shaped crystals.

Quartz crystal

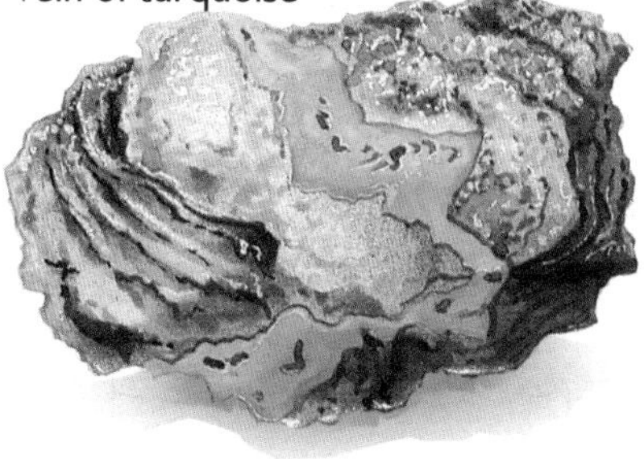
Vein of turquoise

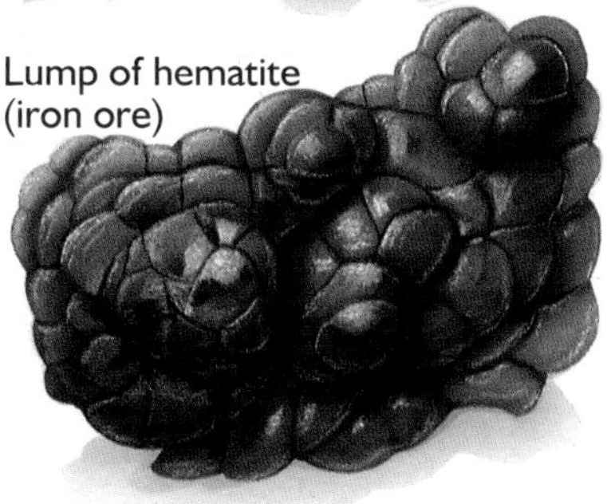
Lump of hematite (iron ore)

What are fossils?

Fossils are found inside certain rocks. They are the preserved shapes of things that were once alive.

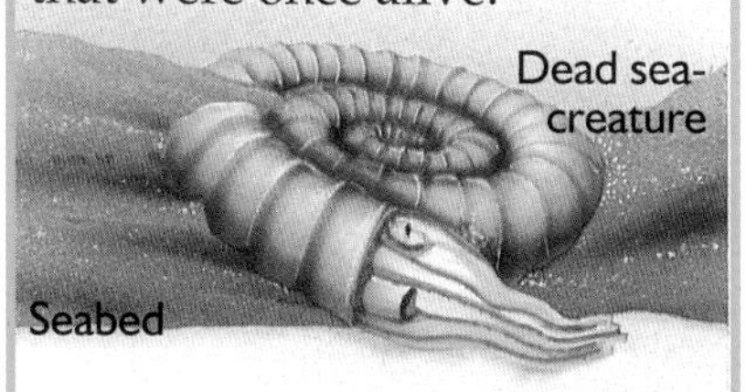
Dead sea-creature
Seabed

Fossils form when sediment settles on top of dead plants and animals and turns to rock around them.

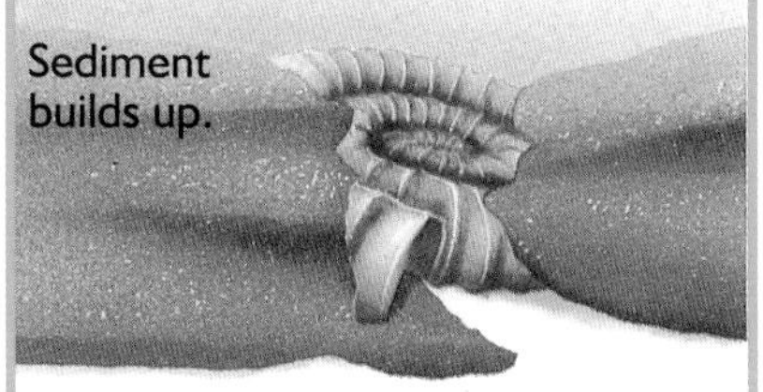
Sediment builds up.

The plant or animal may be preserved whole within the rock but usually it decays and the space it leaves is filled with minerals.

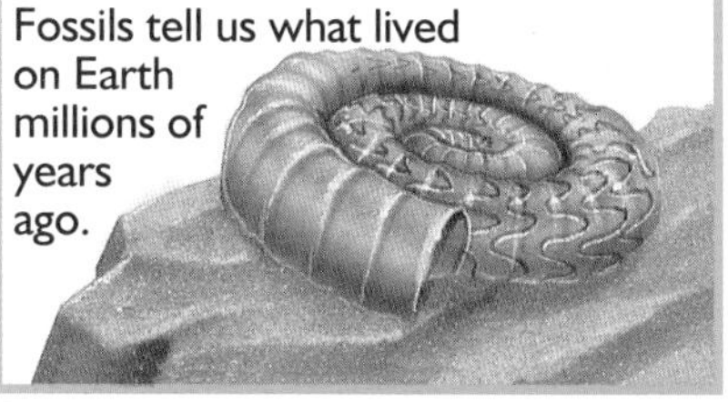
Fossils tell us what lived on Earth millions of years ago.

Minerals around you

Minerals are mined and used to make many everyday things. Here are some examples.

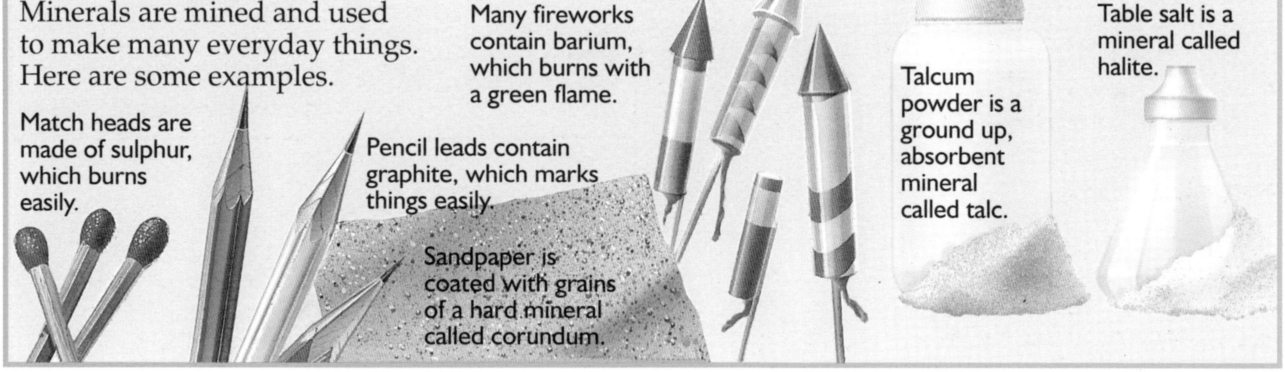
Match heads are made of sulphur, which burns easily.
Pencil leads contain graphite, which marks things easily.
Sandpaper is coated with grains of a hard mineral called corundum.
Many fireworks contain barium, which burns with a green flame.
Talcum powder is a ground up, absorbent mineral called talc.
Table salt is a mineral called halite.

Weathering

The rocks in the landscape are constantly being worn down by rain and temperature changes. This is called **weathering**.

There are two types of weathering. One type, called **mechanical weathering**, happens when water in rock crevices freezes. When water freezes, it expands (swells) and gradually breaks the rock apart.

Mechanical weathering happens fastest in areas where the temperature often rises and falls above and below freezing point, such as the Poles, mountain tops and deserts*.

Water in cracks expands when it freezes, breaking off chunks of rock.

Sharp pieces of weathered rocks, called **scree**, may collect at the base of a slope.

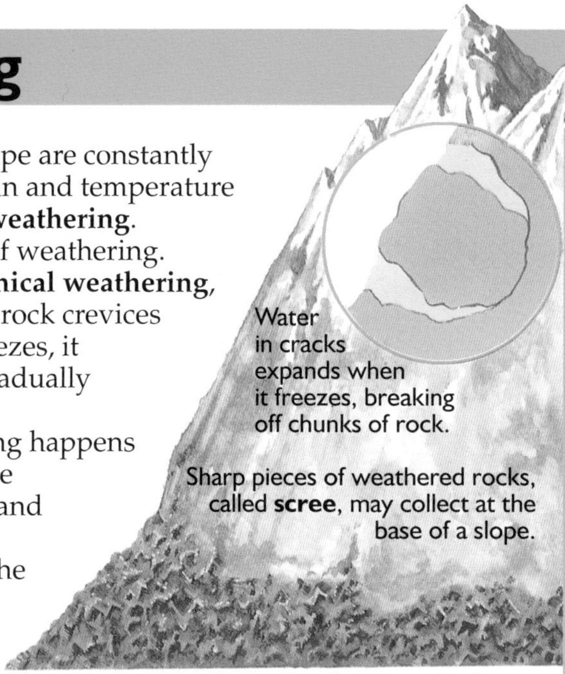

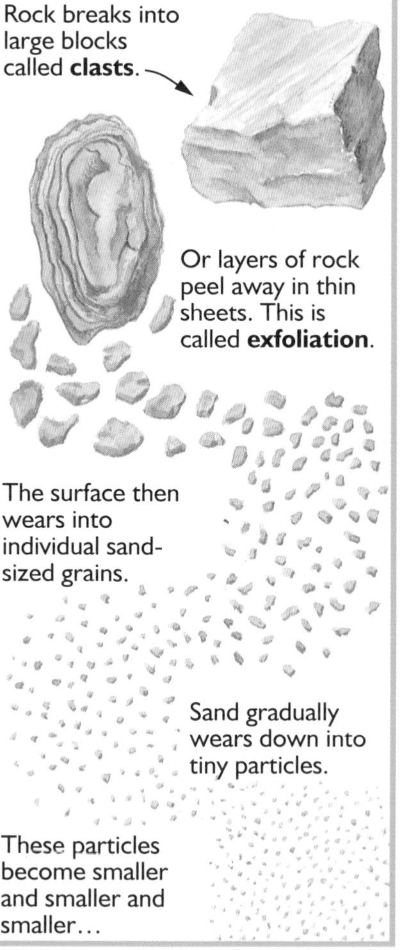

The other type of weathering is called **chemical weathering**. This is caused by rain-water or water in the soil, which are weak acids. The rock surface dissolves as the water trickles over it.

Some types of rock dissolve much more easily than others. It depends which minerals* the rock is made of. Also, rocks with lots of cracks weather fast because there are plenty of places for water and frost to work their way in.

Water trickles between cracks and dissolves the rock.

Products of weathering

When rocks are weathered, they break into smaller and smaller pieces.

Rock breaks into large blocks called **clasts**.

Or layers of rock peel away in thin sheets. This is called **exfoliation**.

The surface then wears into individual sand-sized grains.

Sand gradually wears down into tiny particles.

These particles become smaller and smaller and smaller…

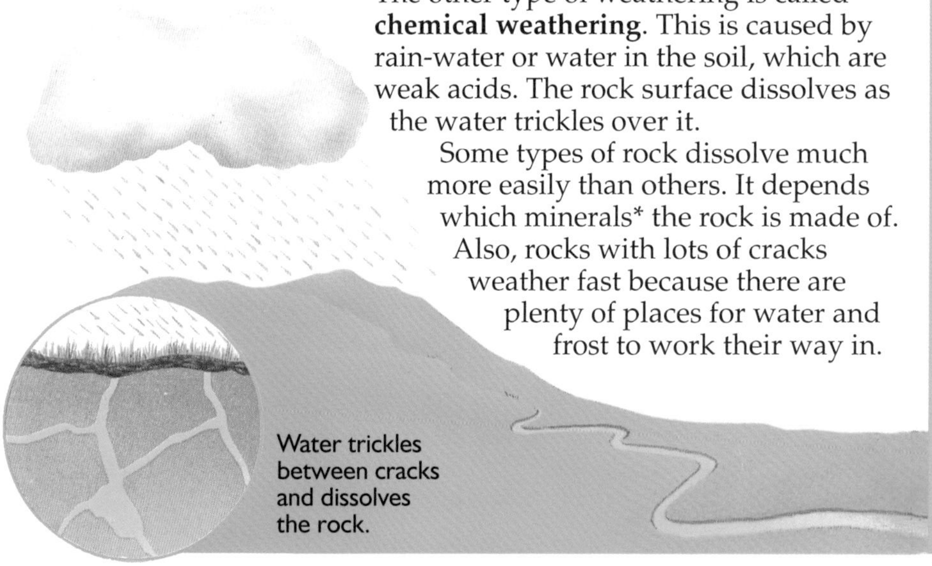

Weathering and soil

Soil contains particles from the weathered rock below, such as clay, sand and minerals such as calcium and magnesium. These are mixed with decaying plant and animal matter, air and water. If you dug down through the ground to the rock you would see that soil has several layers, or **horizons**.

Surface layer of plant and animal remains, called **leaf litter**.

Top soil where leaf litter has decayed and mixed with minerals from the rock.

Sub-soil, mainly made up of weathered rock and a small amount of plant matter.

Unweathered rock, called **parent material**.

278 *Deserts, 302; Minerals, 277.

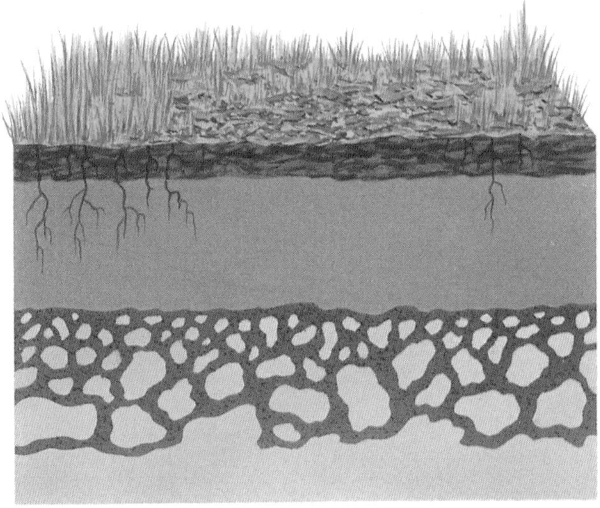

Landscape detective

Different types of rock weather at different rates. It is sometimes possible to identify rocks in the landscape by studying the way they have worn down and the features that are left.

Igneous rocks* such as granite are very tough and weather slowly. Weaker surrounding rocks wear down more quickly. At the sites of ancient volcanoes*, solidified magma chambers* called **batholiths** may be exposed and stand as huge mounds. Sills* and dykes* may stick out as ridges, and piles of granite boulders, called **tors**, may be left standing on hilltops.

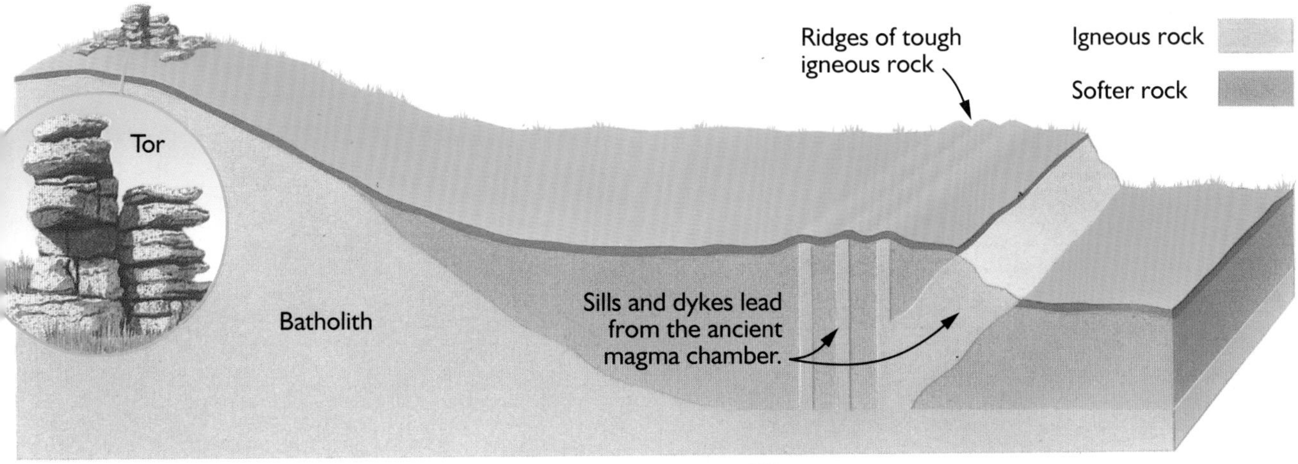
Ridges of tough igneous rock
Igneous rock
Softer rock
Tor
Batholith
Sills and dykes lead from the ancient magma chamber.

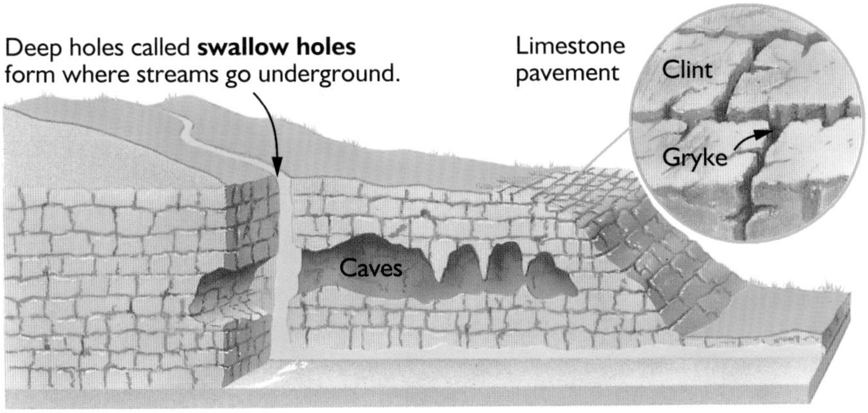
Deep holes called **swallow holes** form where streams go underground.
Limestone pavement
Clint
Gryke
Caves

Rocks such as limestone, that contain the mineral calcite, dissolve easily. Rain, soil-water and streams seep down through the limestone and may carve out underground caves. Cracks in the rock surface are worn into wide gaps called **grykes**. The solid blocks that are left, called **clints**, form a series of stepping stones called a **limestone pavement**.

Weathering around town

Weathering does not only affect the landscape – stone buildings and statues wear away too.

One way to study the effects of weathering is to compare tombstones of different ages. The dates on the stones make it easy to work out how long the rain and frost have been wearing them away.

This statue of Queen Victoria in London, England, was so badly weathered that the nose crumbled away and had to be replaced.

Weathered tombstones

Dykes, 275; Igneous rock, 276; Magma chamber, Sills, Volcanoes, 275.

Oceans

Water covers almost three quarters of the Earth's surface. Over 97% of all this water is stored in the Earth's four huge oceans: the Pacific, Atlantic, Indian and Arctic Oceans.

Exploring the seabed

The shallowest parts of the oceans are the **continental shelves**, where land slopes gently down into the water. There is then a steep slope, called the **continental slope**, leading to the ocean floor, or **abyssal plain**.

Some of the Earth's most spectacular land formations are found on the ocean floor. Deep trenches* and huge ridges* run across it. Some stretch for over 60,000km (37,300 miles).

How the oceans formed

The Earth has not always had oceans. Millions of years ago it was just a ball of hot rock. Its surface was covered with erupting volcanoes*, which released huge amounts of gas, including a gas made up of water particles, called **water vapour**.

Eventually the Earth cooled, causing the water vapour to turn back into liquid water and fall from the skies as torrential rain. The rain lasted for thousands and thousands of years and gradually filled all the hollows around the Earth's surface, forming the oceans and seas.

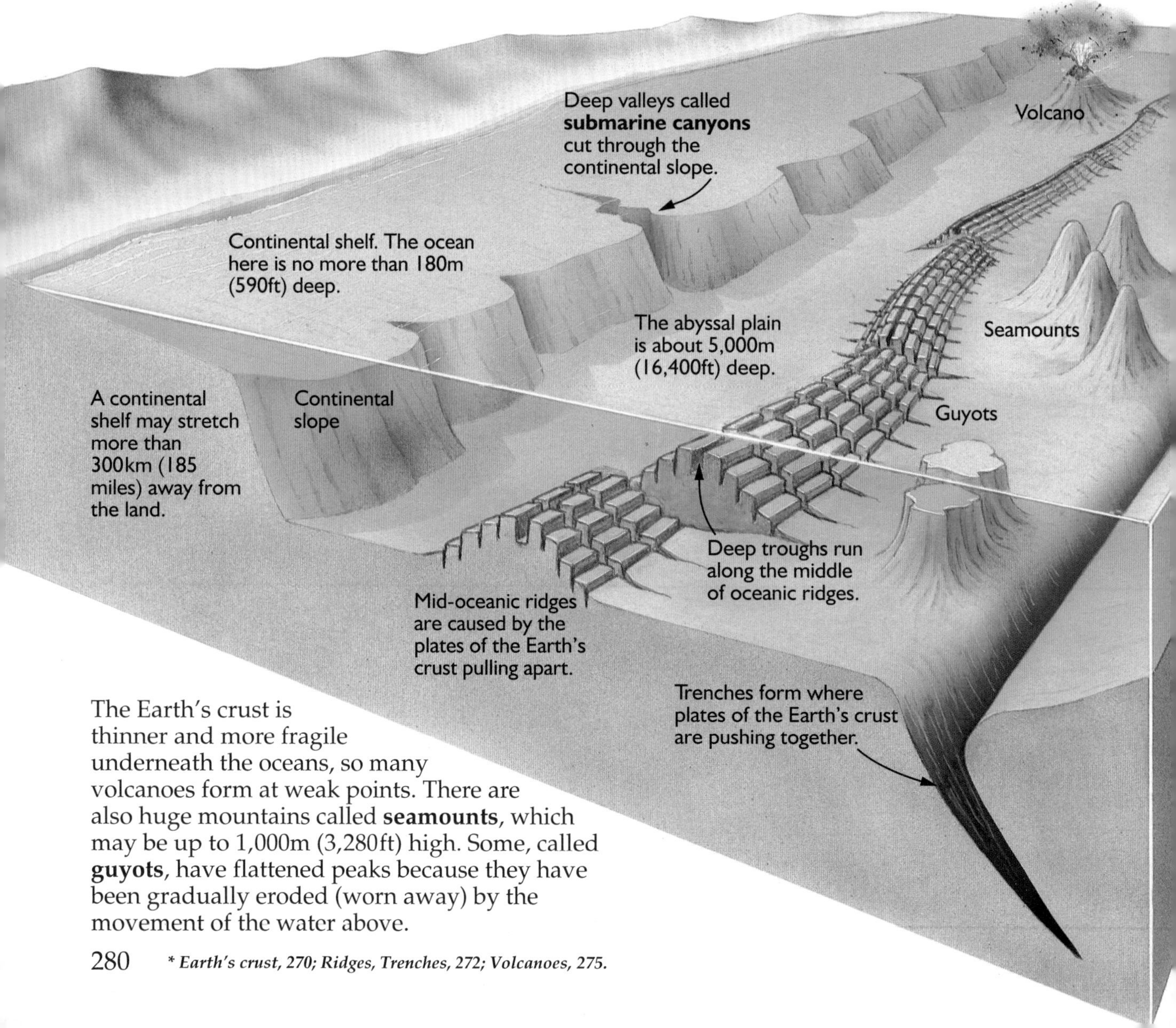

Deep valleys called **submarine canyons** cut through the continental slope.
Volcano
Continental shelf. The ocean here is no more than 180m (590ft) deep.
The abyssal plain is about 5,000m (16,400ft) deep.
Seamounts
A continental shelf may stretch more than 300km (185 miles) away from the land.
Continental slope
Guyots
Deep troughs run along the middle of oceanic ridges.
Mid-oceanic ridges are caused by the plates of the Earth's crust pulling apart.
Trenches form where plates of the Earth's crust are pushing together.

The Earth's crust is thinner and more fragile underneath the oceans, so many volcanoes form at weak points. There are also huge mountains called **seamounts**, which may be up to 1,000m (3,280ft) high. Some, called **guyots**, have flattened peaks because they have been gradually eroded (worn away) by the movement of the water above.

** Earth's crust, 270; Ridges, Trenches, 272; Volcanoes, 275.*

Restless water

The water in the oceans is constantly moving in currents, waves and tides. **Currents** are wide bands of water that flow around the oceans in huge circles. They are caused by global winds*, which gradually drag the water along with them. The Earth's spin makes currents swing to the side.

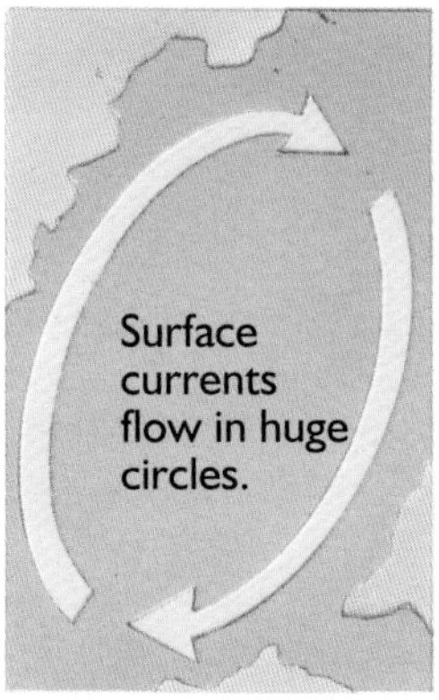
Surface currents flow in huge circles.

Waves are caused by the wind blowing across the surface of the water. The water does not move along with the waves, though – it is blown up into a crest, then falls down and back again in a circle. This is why an object floating in the waves bobs up and down but does not move along.

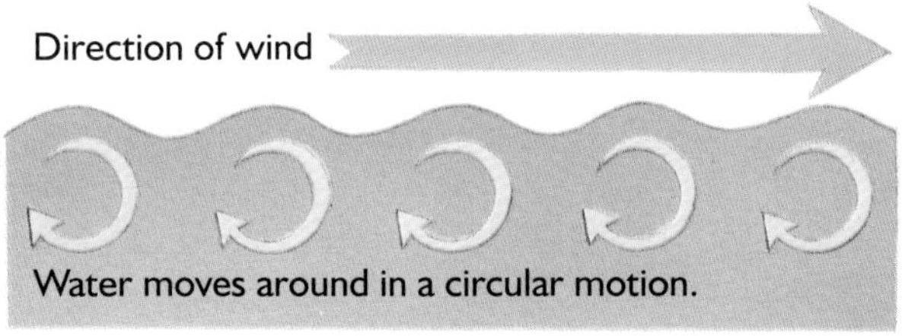
Direction of wind
Water moves around in a circular motion.

Tides are the rise and fall of the sea-level. High tide is when the water comes way up the shore. Low tide is when the sea is a long way out. Tides are caused by the Sun and Moon's gravity* pulling on the Earth's oceans.

When the Sun and Moon are in line with each other, their gravity pulls together on the oceans so there is a big difference between high and low tide. This is called a **spring tide**. Spring tides occur every 14 days.

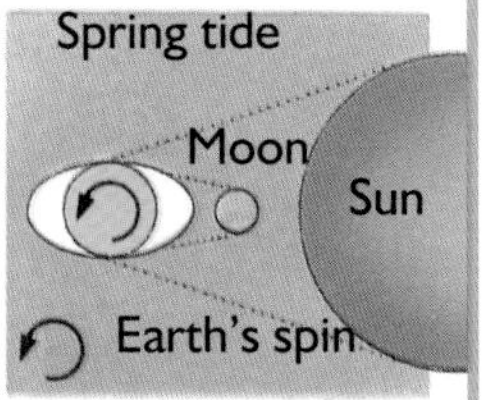
Spring tide
Moon
Sun
Earth's spin

When the Sun and Moon are at right angles to each other, the pull of one almost cancels out the pull of the other, so there is less difference between high and low tide. This is called a **neap tide**. Neap tides occur halfway between spring tides.

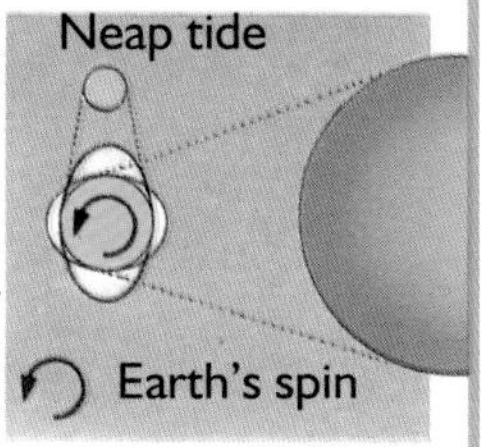
Neap tide
Earth's spin

Ocean layers

The temperature of the oceans changes with depth. The surface is the warmest layer because it is heated by the Sun's rays. This is called the **sunlight zone**.

As the water moves around in waves and surface currents, warm water mixes with cooler water below so the warmth spreads downwards into the next layer, called the **twilight zone**. Below this is a cold, dark layer, where the water is very still.

In the deepest parts of the ocean – the trenches – the water is icy-cold and there is no light at all.

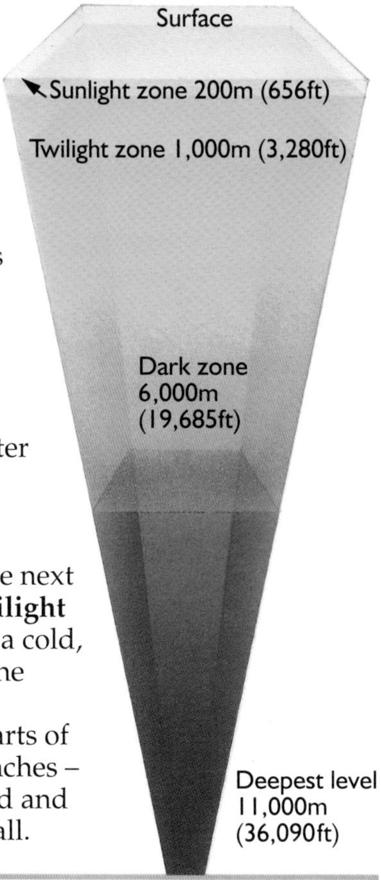
Surface
Sunlight zone 200m (656ft)
Twilight zone 1,000m (3,280ft)
Dark zone 6,000m (19,685ft)
Deepest level 11,000m (36,090ft)

DID YOU KNOW?

The deepest part of the ocean is the Mariana Trench in the Pacific Ocean. It is 11,034m (36,200ft) deep. Mount Everest could fit inside without its peak poking out.

Giant waves

Earthquakes, landslides and volcanic eruptions under the ocean can create giant waves, called **tsunami**. These waves (sometimes wrongly called tidal waves) can be over 60m (200ft) high and travel at speeds of up to 800kmph (500mph).

Tsunami are most common in Japan where they come in from the Pacific Ocean.

*Global winds, 290; Gravity, 271.

Water on the land

Water can be a liquid, a solid (ice) or a gas (water vapour). Because it can change form, it moves from the sea to the air to the land and back again in a circular journey called the **water cycle**. The water cycle is driven by the Sun's heat, which turns liquid water into water vapour. This process is called **evaporation**. When water in the air cools, it turns back into liquid water. This process is called **condensation**. The water then falls from the air as rain or snow.

Salty or fresh?

Sea-water contains large amounts of salts, or minerals*. These are left behind when sea-water evaporates, so water that falls as rain or snow is fresh (non-salty). Land-living plants and animals cannot live on salt water so it is important that there is fresh water on the land.

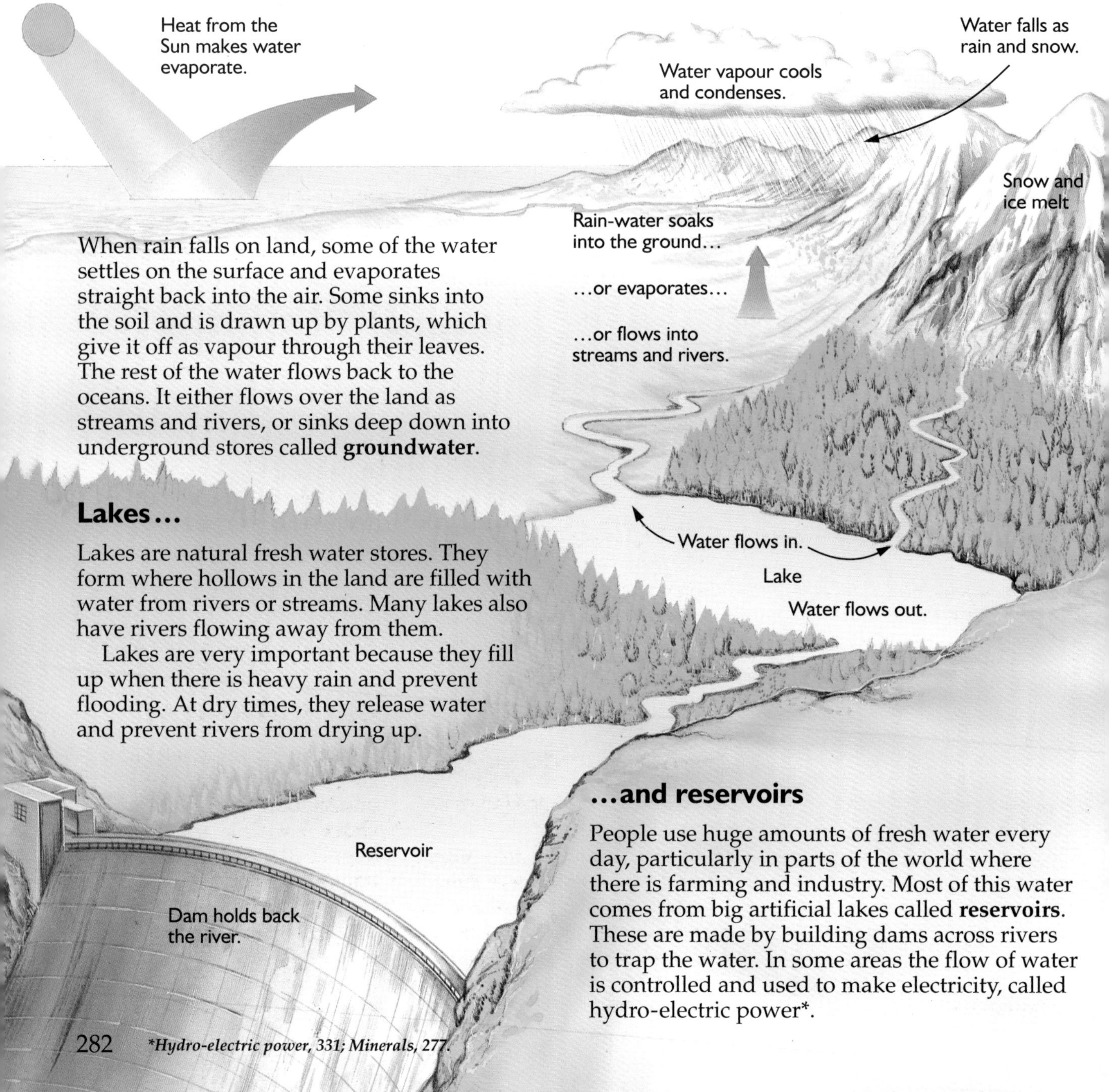
Heat from the Sun makes water evaporate.
Water vapour cools and condenses.
Water falls as rain and snow.
Snow and ice melt
Rain-water soaks into the ground...
...or evaporates...
...or flows into streams and rivers.
Water flows in.
Lake
Water flows out.
Reservoir
Dam holds back the river.

When rain falls on land, some of the water settles on the surface and evaporates straight back into the air. Some sinks into the soil and is drawn up by plants, which give it off as vapour through their leaves. The rest of the water flows back to the oceans. It either flows over the land as streams and rivers, or sinks deep down into underground stores called **groundwater**.

Lakes...

Lakes are natural fresh water stores. They form where hollows in the land are filled with water from rivers or streams. Many lakes also have rivers flowing away from them.

Lakes are very important because they fill up when there is heavy rain and prevent flooding. At dry times, they release water and prevent rivers from drying up.

...and reservoirs

People use huge amounts of fresh water every day, particularly in parts of the world where there is farming and industry. Most of this water comes from big artificial lakes called **reservoirs**. These are made by building dams across rivers to trap the water. In some areas the flow of water is controlled and used to make electricity, called hydro-electric power*.

 **Hydro-electric power*, 331; *Minerals*, 277.

Water-level

The level of the groundwater is called the **water-table**. In areas with plenty of rain, the water-table may be just a short distance below the ground. In some parts of the world, people dig wells to reach this water.

If the level of the land dips down below the water-table, water appears at the surface as streams. During long periods of dry weather, the water-table may fall and wells and streams may dry up.

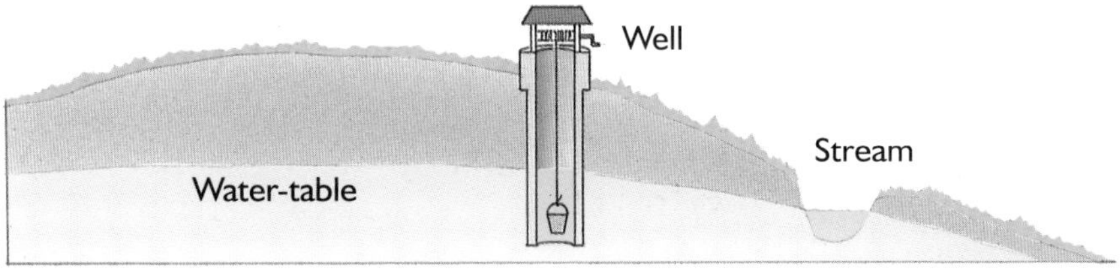

Well
Stream
Water-table

Upsetting the balance

When people change the natural landscape, they can upset the water balance and cause the ground to dry out or become flooded. Building towns and cities, for example, covers the land with a waterproof layer of asphalt and concrete. Instead of slowly soaking into the ground, rain flows into the drains and is carried straight into the rivers. Because of this, the level of the groundwater may fall and rivers may flood if there is heavy rain.

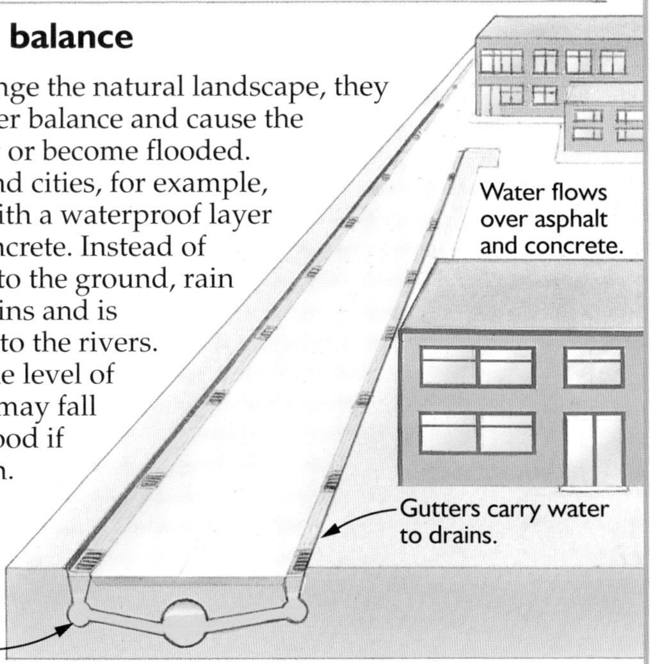

Water flows over asphalt and concrete.
Gutters carry water to drains.
Drains carry water to the sewers and then to rivers.

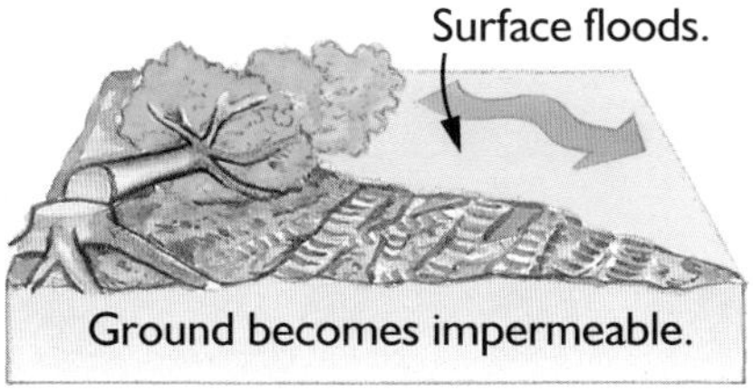

Surface floods.
Ground becomes impermeable.

Clearing forest for farming can cause problems too. The pounding of raindrops and pressure of tractor tyres may make the ground impermeable. Water flows over the surface and washes away the soil.

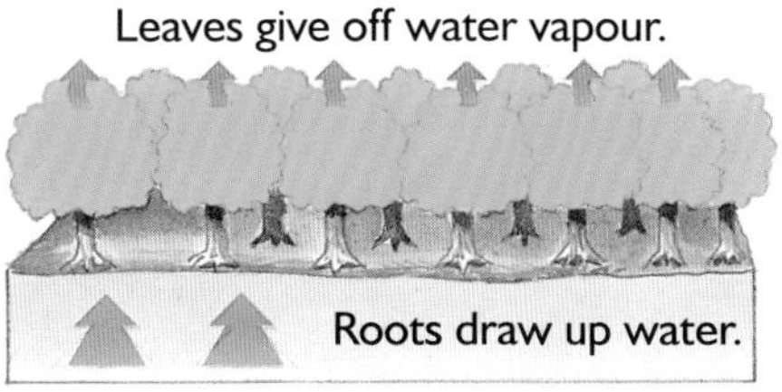

Leaves give off water vapour.
Roots draw up water.

The water balance is also upset if forest is planted where there was none before. The foliage cuts down the amount of rain that reaches the ground. Also, water in the soil is drawn up by the tree roots.

Passing through rocks

Some rocks are **pervious**, which means they have cracks which water can flow through. **Porous rocks** have tiny spaces (pores) that can fill with water. Rocks that allow water to pass through them are called **permeable rocks**. Rocks that do not let water pass through are called **impermeable rocks**.

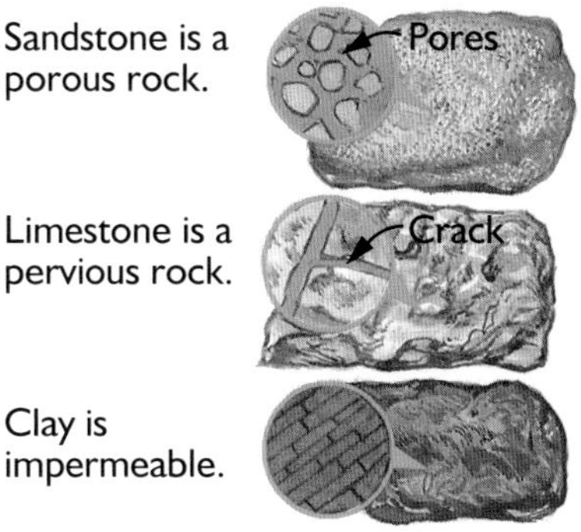

Sandstone is a porous rock.
Pores
Limestone is a pervious rock.
Crack
Clay is impermeable.

If a layer of permeable rock is above a layer of impermeable rock, water can only seep down until it meets the impermeable layer. Water may flow out of the ground as springs where the two layers meet.

Springs
Permeable rock
Impermeable rock

DID YOU KNOW?

If people pump up a large amount of water from underground, the land above may sink. This happened in Pisa, Italy, in the 1960s, causing its famous leaning tower to lean at an even steeper angle.

Rivers

As rivers flow over the land they do several important things. They wear away, or **erode**, the rock, creating channels. They then carry the rock particles (their load) to the oceans. This is called **transportation**.

For a river to erode its channel and transport rock particles, or sediment, it needs energy. The faster a river flows, the more energy it has. Rivers flow fastest down steep, narrow, smooth channels. If the channel levels out, widens, or the river-bed becomes coarse, the river slows down and loses energy. The river can no longer transport all its load so it leaves sediment on the river-bed. This process is called **deposition**.

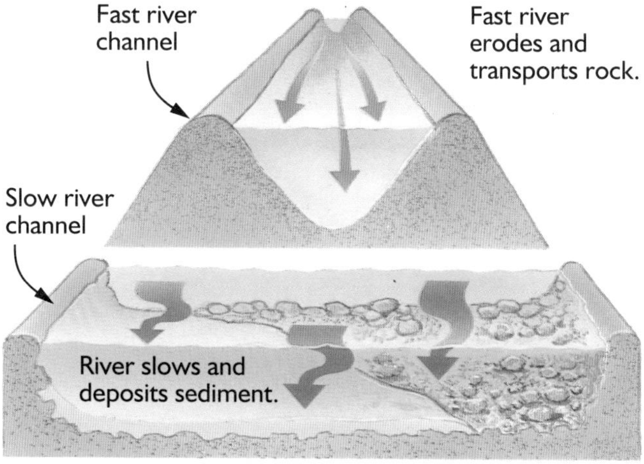

Fast river channel
Fast river erodes and transports rock.
Slow river channel
River slows and deposits sediment.

How does erosion happen?

Rivers erode their channels in several ways. The pressure of water forces into cracks, or joints, in the rock, breaking pieces away. As these are swept along, they chip away more rock. The loose rocks also collide with, and erode, each other. Some rocks dissolve in the water too.

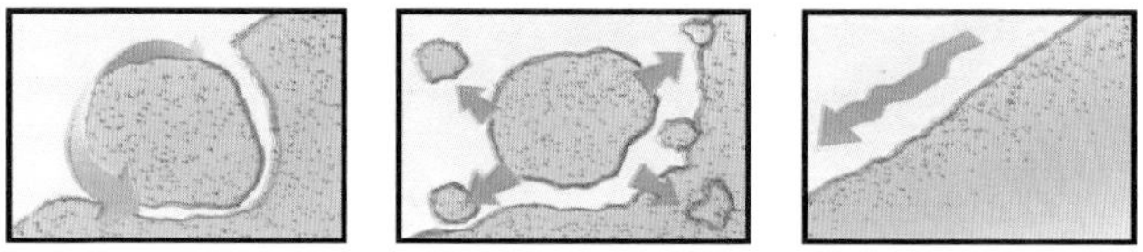

Pressure forces air into joints.
Rocks chip away the channel.
Water dissolves some rocks.

Following a river

Rivers begin high up in hills and mountains and flow down until they eventually meet the oceans. The upper part is steep and the river cuts a deep V-shaped channel. Further towards the sea, the slope is more gentle and the river has a wider channel.

In the lower areas, the river forms bends called **meanders**. Water on the outer edge of the bend has further to travel than water flowing on the inside so it speeds up and has more energy for erosion and transportation. Water flowing on the inside of the bend slows down so deposition happens here.

Over time, the meanders extend further and further, creating a wide, flat valley called a **flood plain**. Where meanders loop back on each other very tightly, the neck separating two loops may be completely eroded and the river may create a new, straight channel. The old loop that is left alongside is called an **ox-bow lake**.

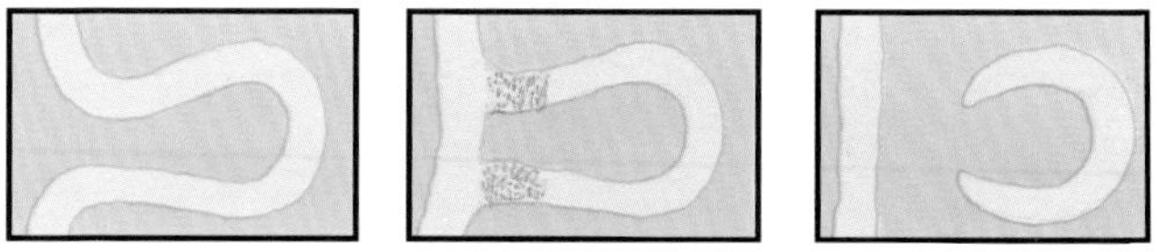

River loops back very tightly.
Narrow neck of land is eroded.
Sediment seals off ox-bow lake.

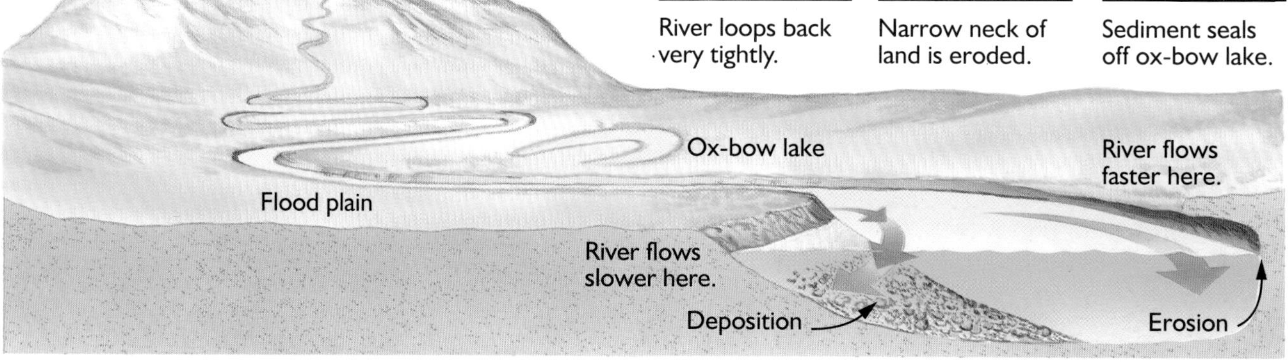

Ox-bow lake
Flood plain
River flows faster here.
River flows slower here.
Deposition
Erosion

Waterfalls and rapids

Waterfalls form where a river-bed crosses from hard rock to softer rock. The river wears down the softer rock and creates a step. The falling water erodes a hollow at the base, called a **plunge pool**.

Spray from the waterfall may under-cut the step and eventually cause it to collapse. Over time, the waterfall may cut back into the hard rock, leaving a steep valley called a **gorge**. Niagara Falls on the Canada/USA border, for example, is cutting into the rock at a rate of 1m (3.3ft) a year and has cut a gorge 11km (6.8 miles) long.

If a river-bed has alternate bands of hard and soft rock, the river may erode it into a series of ledges. This makes the river flow irregularly. Stretches of river where this has happened are called **rapids** or **cataracts**.

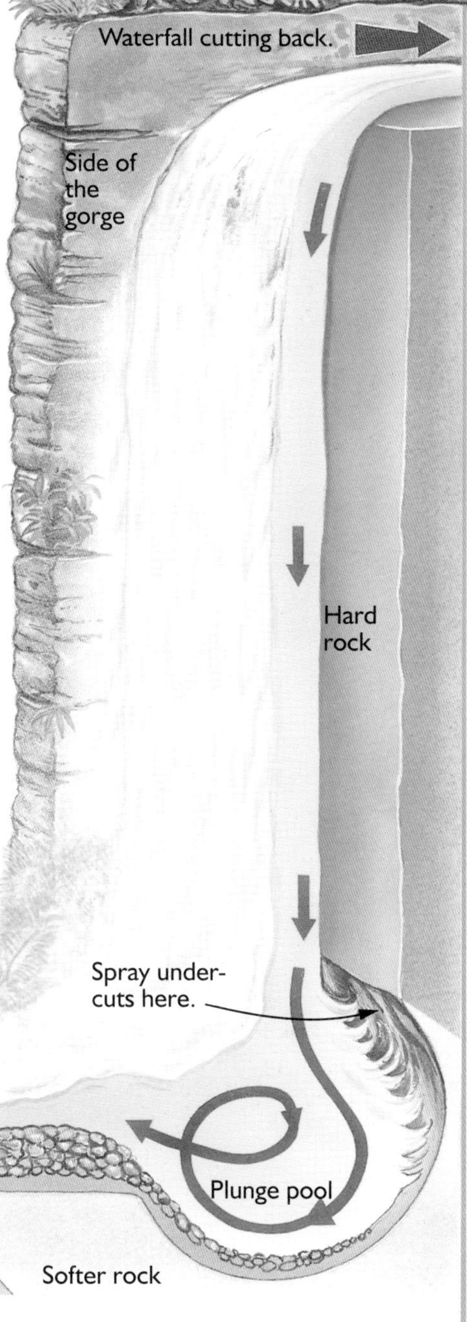
Waterfall cutting back.
Side of the gorge
Hard rock
Spray under-cuts here.
Rapids
Plunge pool
Layers of hard rock
Softer rock

River basins

Rivers are fed by a network of streams called **tributaries**. The area of land that they drain is called a **drainage basin**. Seen from above, river networks make recognizable patterns.

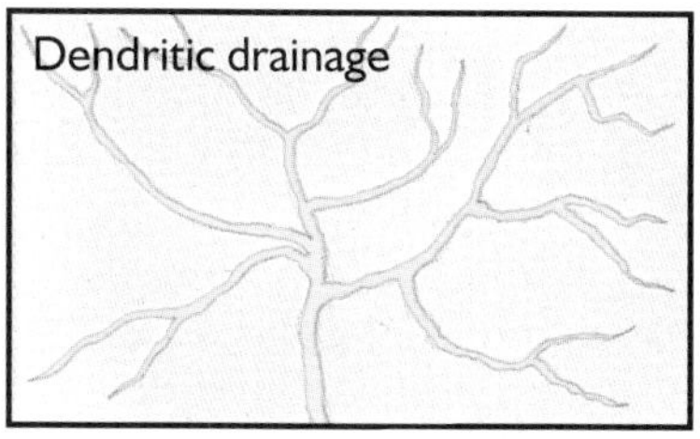
Dendritic drainage

Dendritic patterns, where the river is like a tree trunk with branches, form where the landscape is made up of only one type of rock.

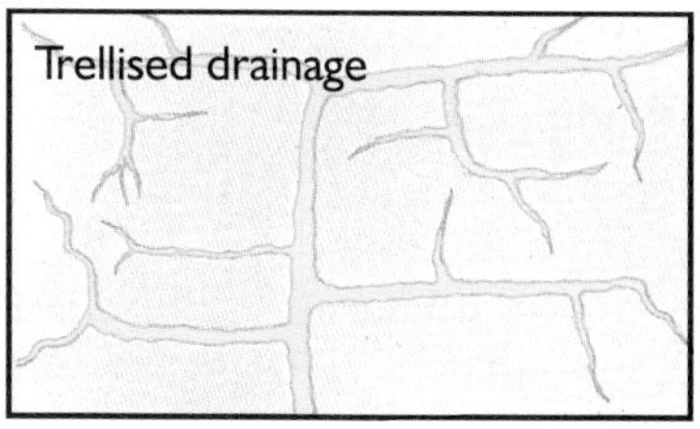
Trellised drainage

Trellised patterns, where the tributaries flow in a rectangular network, form if there are strips of different types of rock. Streams flow along the weak areas where the rocks join.

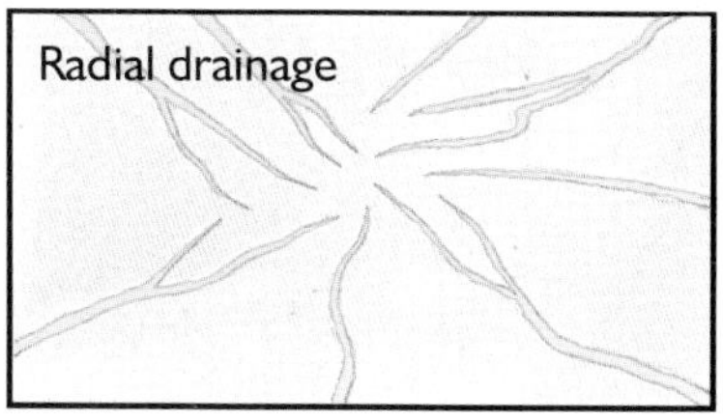
Radial drainage

Radial drainage, where the streams flow away from a central point, happens where rocks have been lifted up into a dome.

Deltas

Deposition often happens where a river channel enters the still water of a lake or the sea. If sediment is deposited faster than it is carried away, it builds up and forms a raised area called a **delta**. As the river flows across the delta, it splits into lots of channels. The most famous deltas are the Nile delta in Egypt and the Mississippi delta in the USA.

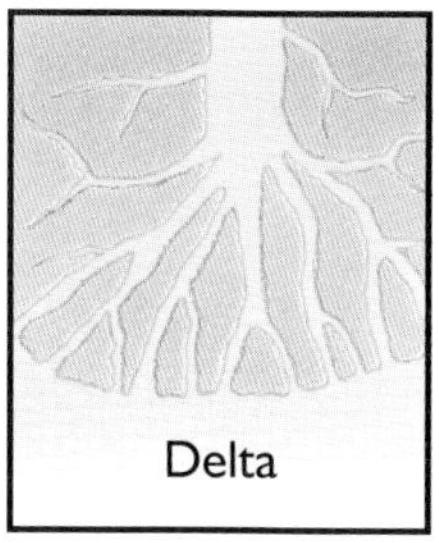
Delta

Coasts

The coast, where the land meets the sea, is constantly being shaped by the in and out motion of the waves. Over many years, the action of the waves can produce some spectacular features.

There are two types of waves. **Destructive waves** erode the coast. They are tall and frequent and form in stormy weather. They crash against the shore and carry sand, pebbles and other beach material out to sea.

Constructive waves build up the coast. They have a gentle lapping motion and form in calm weather. They carry beach material on to the shore and leave deposits of sand and pebbles behind.

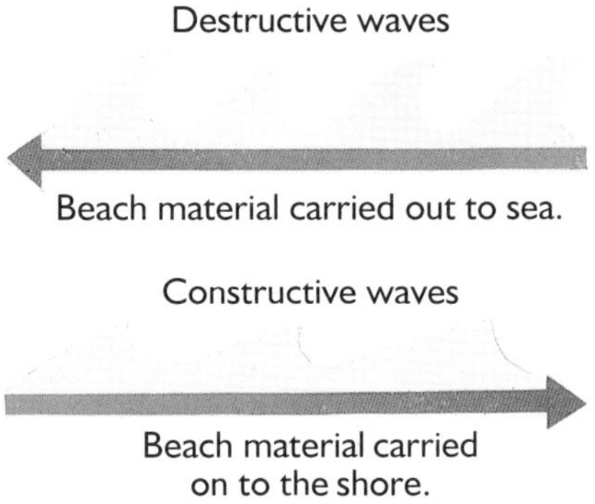

Destructive waves
Beach material carried out to sea.
Constructive waves
Beach material carried on to the shore.

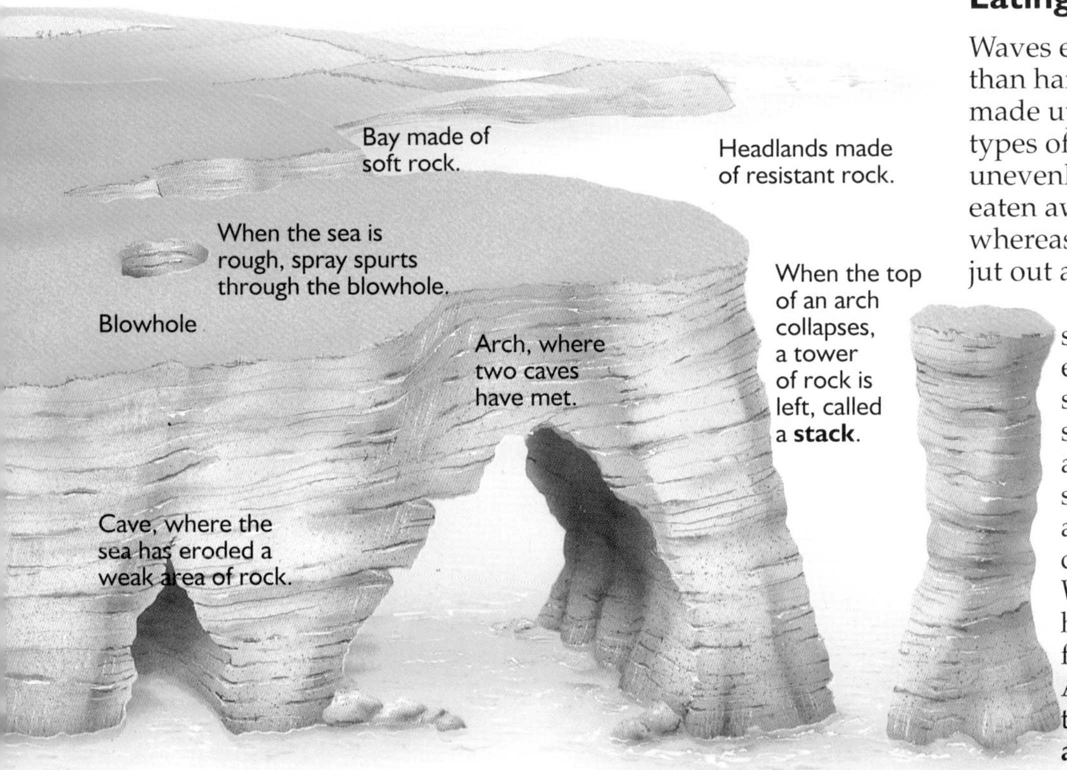

Bay made of soft rock.
Headlands made of resistant rock.
When the sea is rough, spray spurts through the blowhole.
Blowhole
Arch, where two caves have met.
When the top of an arch collapses, a tower of rock is left, called a **stack**.
Cave, where the sea has eroded a weak area of rock.

Eating away the coast

Waves erode soft rocks faster than hard ones so a coastline made up of various different types of rock wears away unevenly. The softer rocks are eaten away into curved bays, whereas more resistant rocks jut out as cliffs and headlands.

Weak points in cliffs, such as joints or cracks, erode faster than the surrounding rock. The sea carves out these areas into caves. Sea-spray may eat out a hole at the top of the cave, called a **blowhole**. Where waves attack a headland, caves may form on both sides. After many years, the two caves meet and an **arch** forms.

Crumbling cliffs

Cliffs erode fastest at the base because this area is constantly attacked by the sea. Waves attack the cliff base by hurling rocks at it, chipping away the rock. The surging water also forces air into joints and breaks the rock apart. The sea dissolves some rocks too, such as chalk and limestone.

Collapsing cliff-face
Notch eroded by the sea.

Over time, the waves erode a notch at the foot of the cliff and eventually the cliff-face crumbles and collapses.

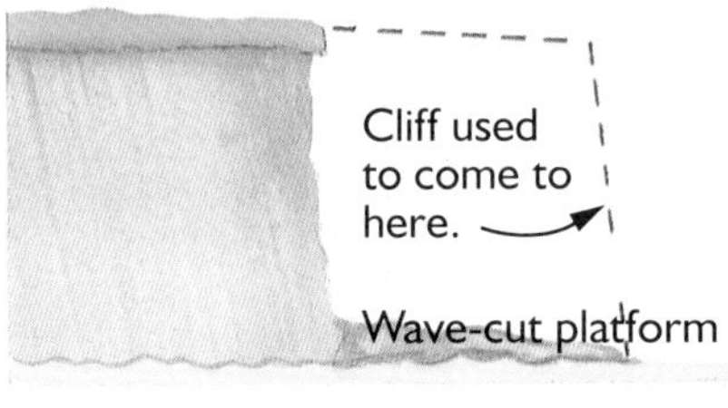

Cliff used to come to here.
Wave-cut platform

The cliff gradually crumbles back and back. A flat area of rock is left at the base, called a **wave-cut platform**.

Drifting sands

Waves can move beach material along the shore. They do this by a process called **longshore drift**. Longshore drift happens in places where the wind blows waves in at an angle to the shore. The water does not run back the way it came but flows away straight down the beach, so the waves go in and out in a zig-zag pattern. Sand and pebbles picked up by the waves zig-zag their way along the shore too.

In places where the wind blows from the same direction most of the time, beach material may be carried huge distances by longshore drift. Waves continue to carry sand and pebbles along the shore until the angle of the coast changes, at a bay or the mouth of a river, for example. At this point, the sea deepens and this makes the waves move more slowly. They have less energy for carrying beach material, so they let it fall on to the seabed. The beach material may eventually pile so high that it rises above the level of the sea to form some of the features shown in the picture below.

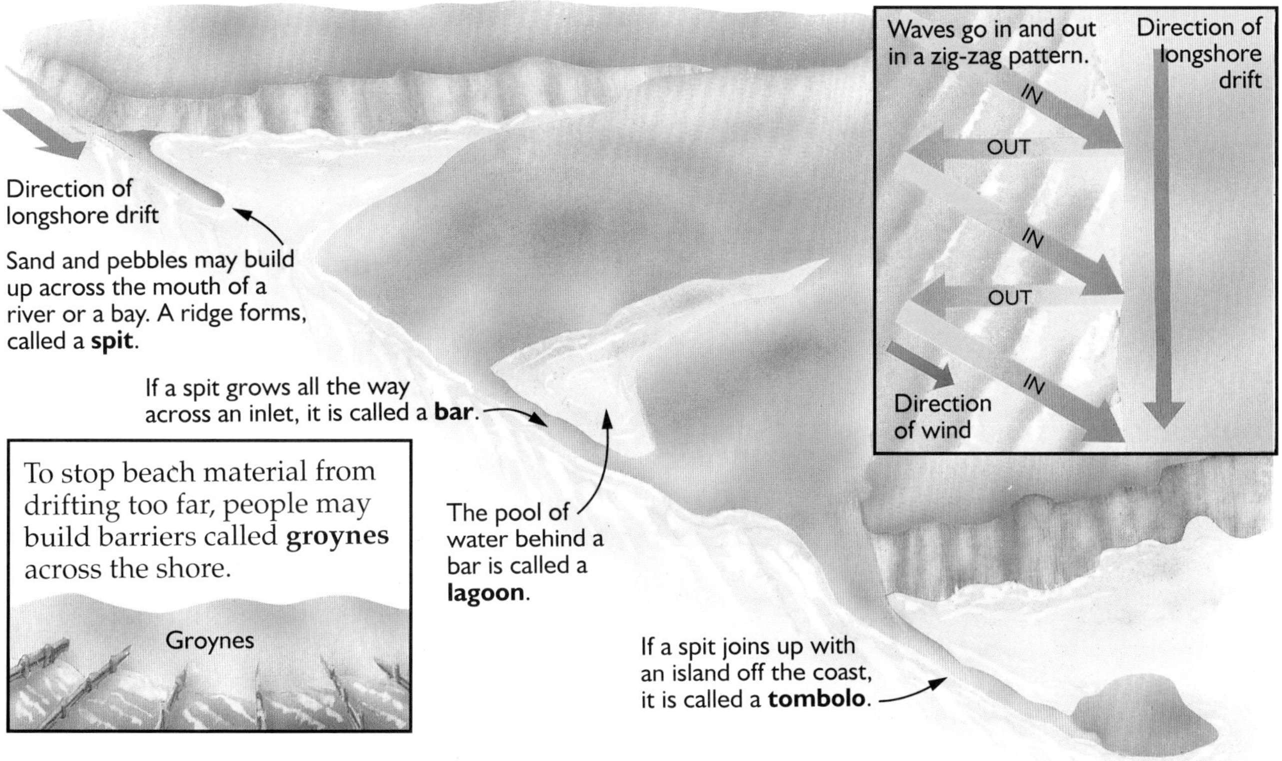

Direction of longshore drift
Sand and pebbles may build up across the mouth of a river or a bay. A ridge forms, called a **spit**.
If a spit grows all the way across an inlet, it is called a **bar**.
The pool of water behind a bar is called a **lagoon**.
If a spit joins up with an island off the coast, it is called a **tombolo**.
Waves go in and out in a zig-zag pattern.
Direction of longshore drift
IN
OUT
IN
OUT
IN
Direction of wind
Groynes

To stop beach material from drifting too far, people may build barriers called **groynes** across the shore.

Beaches

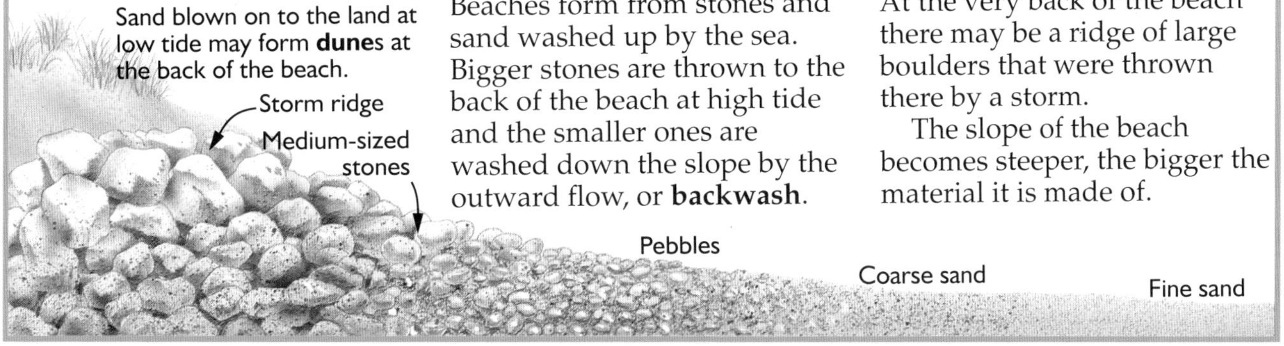

Sand blown on to the land at low tide may form **dunes** at the back of the beach.
Storm ridge
Medium-sized stones
Pebbles
Coarse sand
Fine sand

Beaches form from stones and sand washed up by the sea. Bigger stones are thrown to the back of the beach at high tide and the smaller ones are washed down the slope by the outward flow, or **backwash**.

At the very back of the beach there may be a ridge of large boulders that were thrown there by a storm.

The slope of the beach becomes steeper, the bigger the material it is made of.

Glaciers

Ice covers 10% of the Earth's land surface. Nearly all of it is found in Greenland and Antarctica, near the North and South Poles. The rest is in small areas on high mountains.

In the history of the Earth, there have been long periods of time, called **ice ages**, when the climate was so cold that much more of the land was covered in ice sheets. The last ice age began 2 million years ago and ended only 10,000 years ago, though there were times in between when the ice in some areas melted. One day, there may be another ice age. This map shows where ice covered the Earth during the last ice age and where ice can be found today.

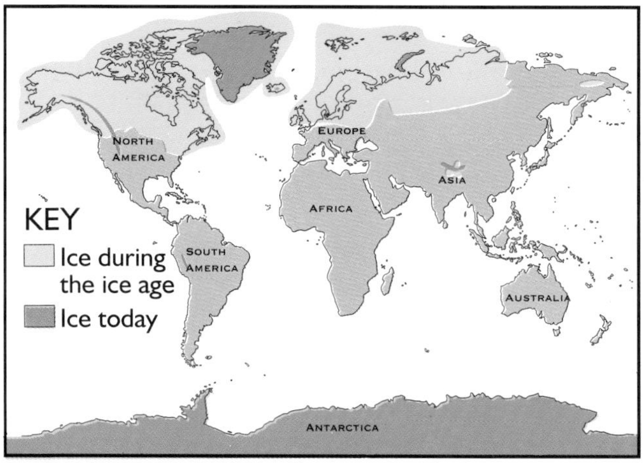

North America
Europe
Asia
Africa
South America
Australia
Antarctica
KEY
Ice during the ice age
Ice today

Flowing ice

In places where it is always cold and shaded from sunshine, layers of snow become packed into hard, strong ice. If this ice is under pressure or if gravity* pulls it, it slowly flows over the land. Flowing ice is called a **glacier**.

The higher part of a glacier is called the **accumulation zone**. This is where new layers of snow fall and become glacial ice. At the lower end of the glacier is the **ablation zone**, where the ice melts into water, called **meltwater**. As a glacier flows downhill, the ice may stretch and crack into deep openings called **crevasses**.

Most glaciers are less than 2km (1.2 miles) long. However, some are much longer. The Vatnajokul ice cap in Iceland is over 100km (62 miles) long.

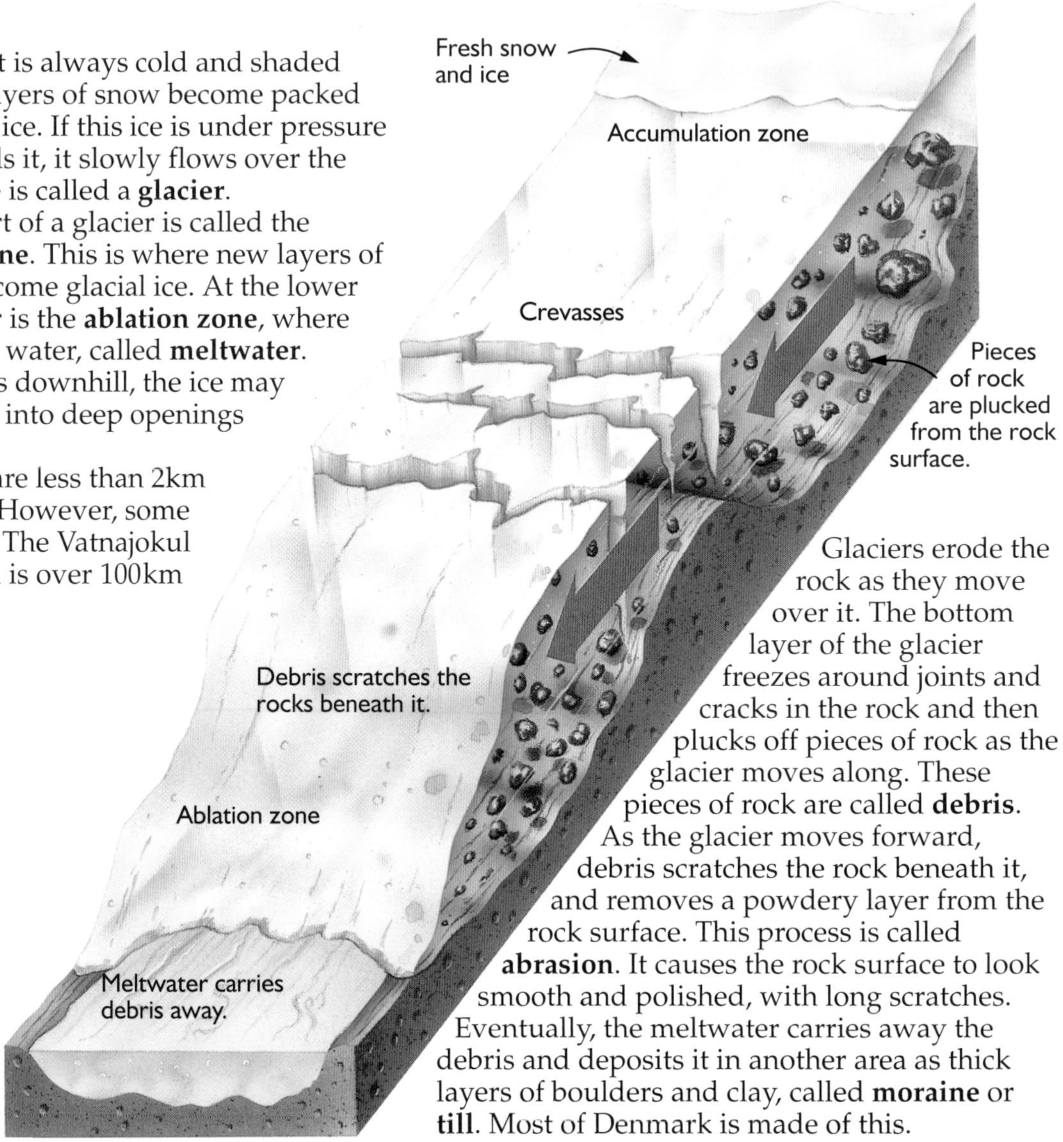

Fresh snow and ice
Accumulation zone
Crevasses
Pieces of rock are plucked from the rock surface.
Debris scratches the rocks beneath it.
Ablation zone
Meltwater carries debris away.

Glaciers erode the rock as they move over it. The bottom layer of the glacier freezes around joints and cracks in the rock and then plucks off pieces of rock as the glacier moves along. These pieces of rock are called **debris**. As the glacier moves forward, debris scratches the rock beneath it, and removes a powdery layer from the rock surface. This process is called **abrasion**. It causes the rock surface to look smooth and polished, with long scratches. Eventually, the meltwater carries away the debris and deposits it in another area as thick layers of boulders and clay, called **moraine** or **till**. Most of Denmark is made of this.

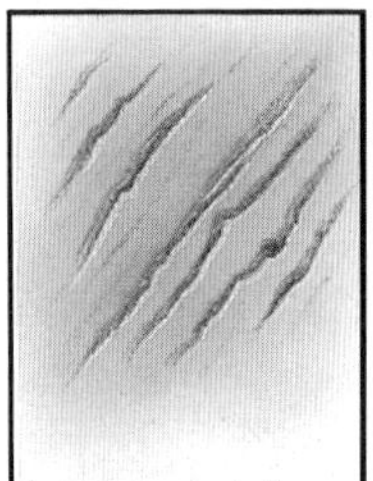

Long scratches show that rock has been eroded by a glacier.

*Gravity, 271.

Looking at the landscape

Over many centuries, glaciers carve easily-recognized shapes in the land. For example, when ice collects in a mountain hollow, it may eventually erode the rock and form a deep basin, called a **cirque**, **corrie** or **cwm**. If a mountain has several cirques, a sharp pyramid-shaped peak is formed, like that of the Matterhorn in Switzerland.

Ice from several cirques may flow into a nearby valley, forming a valley glacier. It erodes the sides and bottom into a **U-shaped valley**. Smaller valleys, called **hanging valleys**, which were not cut by a glacier, may be left high above the main valley.

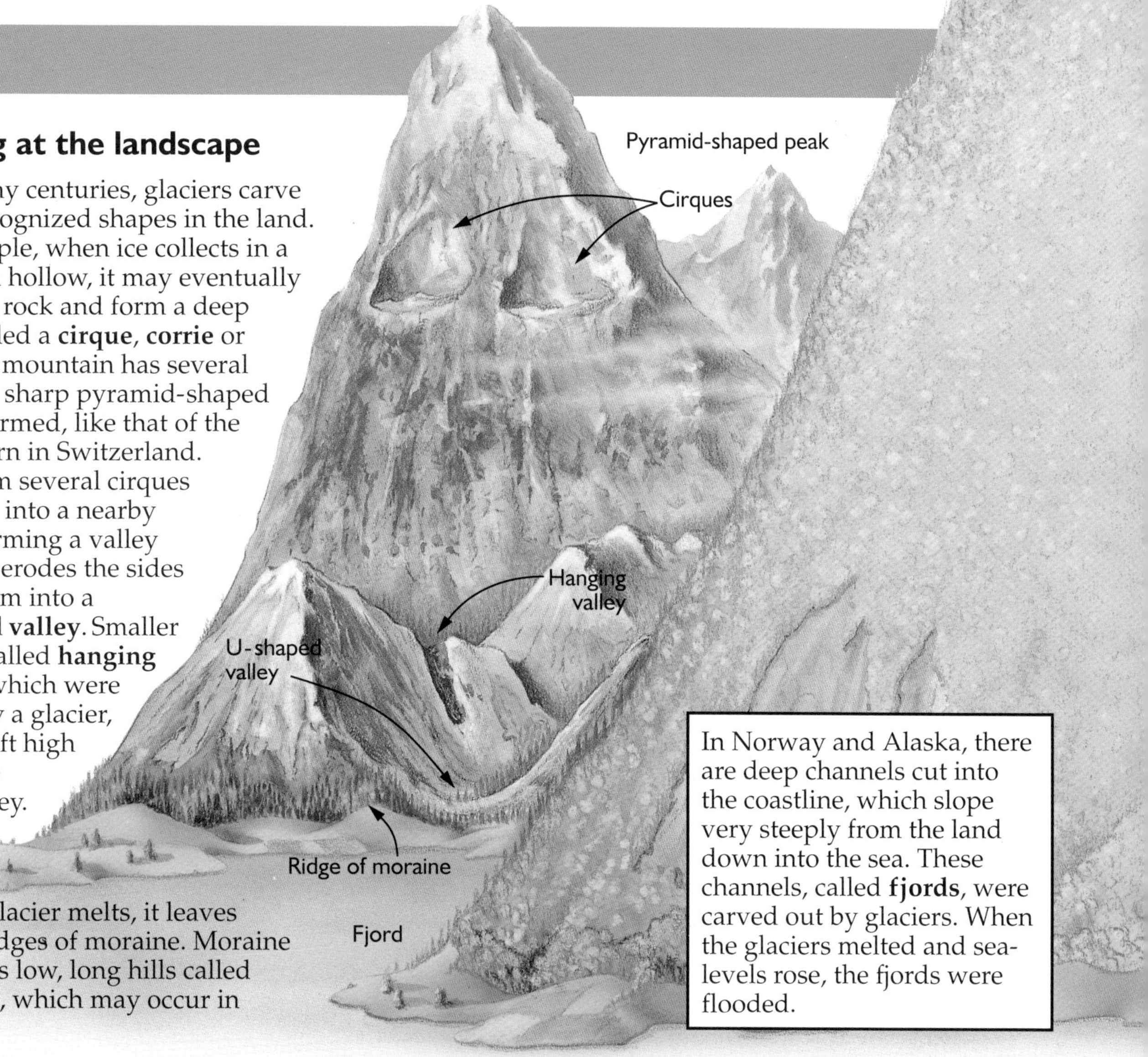

When a glacier melts, it leaves behind ridges of moraine. Moraine also forms low, long hills called **drumlins**, which may occur in groups.

In Norway and Alaska, there are deep channels cut into the coastline, which slope very steeply from the land down into the sea. These channels, called **fjords**, were carved out by glaciers. When the glaciers melted and sea-levels rose, the fjords were flooded.

Ice hazards

Ice and snow may cause problems for people who live nearby. If a glacier blocks a valley, water may build up. Eventually it breaks through the ice and pours downhill, flooding any villages below.

Most glaciers move only very slowly. However, a glacier may suddenly surge forward very quickly and swallow everything in its path. Earth tremors can cause surges to happen.

In some areas, vibrations from traffic, skiers or earth tremors can make ice and snow fall in an avalanche from the mountains. People plant trees or build fences above the villages to catch the snow.

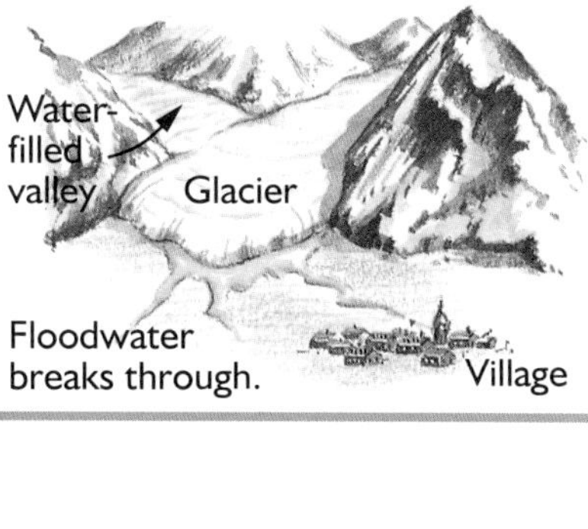

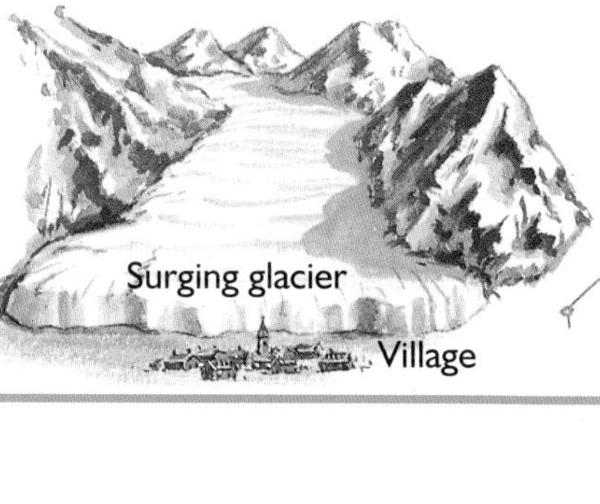

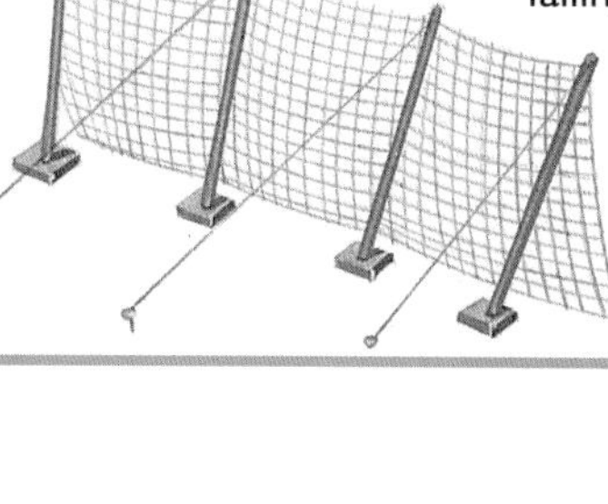

Snow nets protect villages by catching falling snow.

What makes weather happen?

The atmosphere is constantly moving. As it circulates around the surface of the Earth, movements and changes in the lower layer (the troposphere*) cause different types of weather.

Air moves because of changes in **atmospheric pressure**. This is the push of the atmosphere against the Earth's surface. It is caused by gravity*, which exerts a pull on every particle of air. When air is warmed, it rises, causing low pressure (the particles are further apart). When air is cooled, it sinks, causing high pressure (the particles are closer together). The temperature of the Earth's surface varies a great deal – between the land and sea*, for example – so the air is warmed in some areas and cooled in others.

The atmosphere is always trying to be the same pressure all the way around the Earth, so if pressure is low in one area, air blows in from where the pressure is higher. This air movement is the wind.

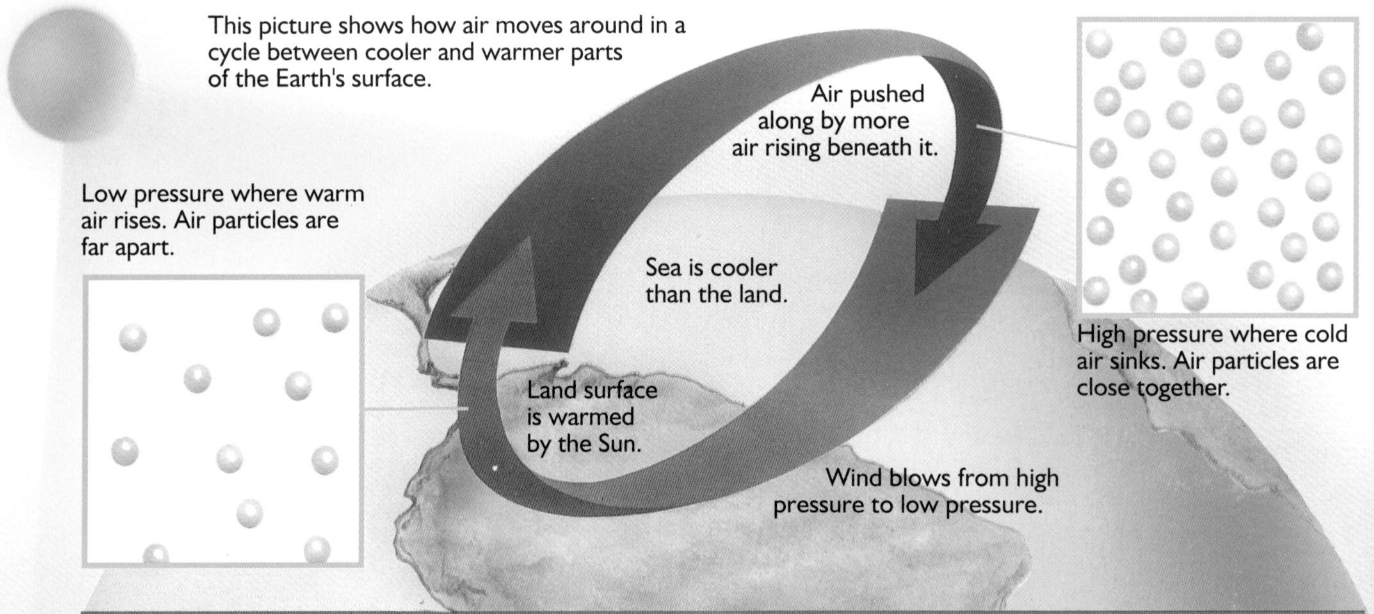
This picture shows how air moves around in a cycle between cooler and warmer parts of the Earth's surface.
Air pushed along by more air rising beneath it.
Low pressure where warm air rises. Air particles are far apart.
Sea is cooler than the land.
High pressure where cold air sinks. Air particles are close together.
Land surface is warmed by the Sun.
Wind blows from high pressure to low pressure.

Global winds

At certain latitudes* on the Earth, there are belts of high pressure and low pressure. Atmospheric pressure is low around the Equator, for example, because the Earth's surface is very hot there.

Strong global winds called **Westerlies** and **Trade Winds** blow from the high pressure belts to the low pressure belts. They do not blow directly north-south between the pressure belts, however. This is because the Earth's spin causes global winds to swing to the side.

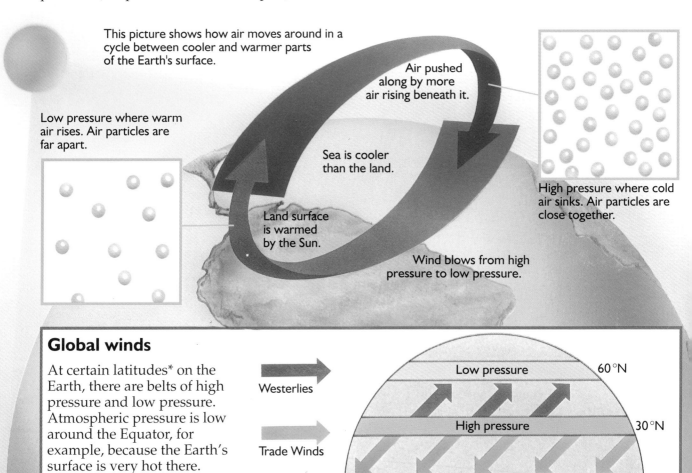

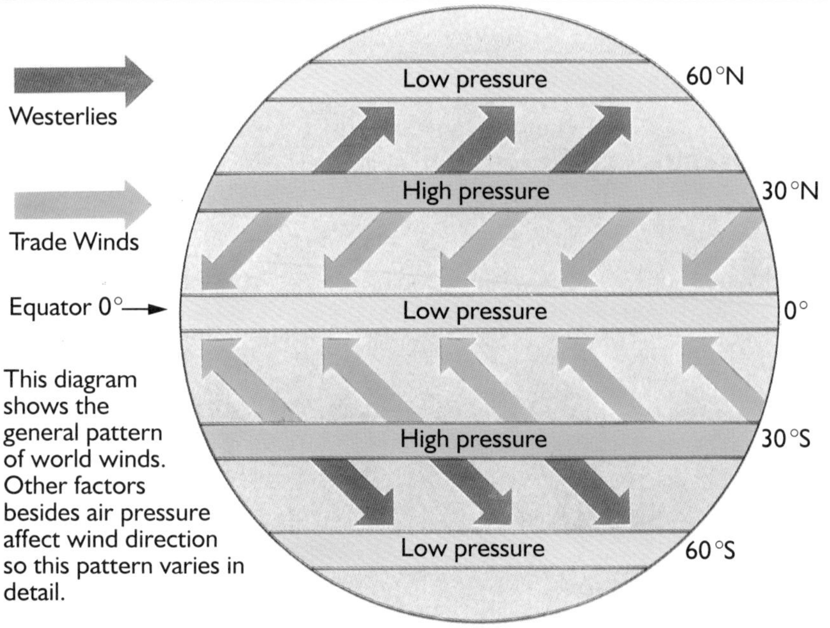
Westerlies
Trade Winds
Equator 0°
Low pressure
60 °N
High pressure
30 °N
Low pressure
0°
High pressure
30 °S
Low pressure
60 °S

This diagram shows the general pattern of world winds. Other factors besides air pressure affect wind direction so this pattern varies in detail.

Gravity, 271; Land and sea temperatures, 295; Latitude, 264; Troposphere, 271.

What makes it rain?

The atmosphere contains water vapour*. When air rises into the higher, colder atmosphere, the water vapour cools and condenses* into tiny droplets of liquid water. You can see these droplets as clouds. The height where the temperature of the atmosphere is low enough to turn water vapour into droplets of liquid water is called the **dew point**.

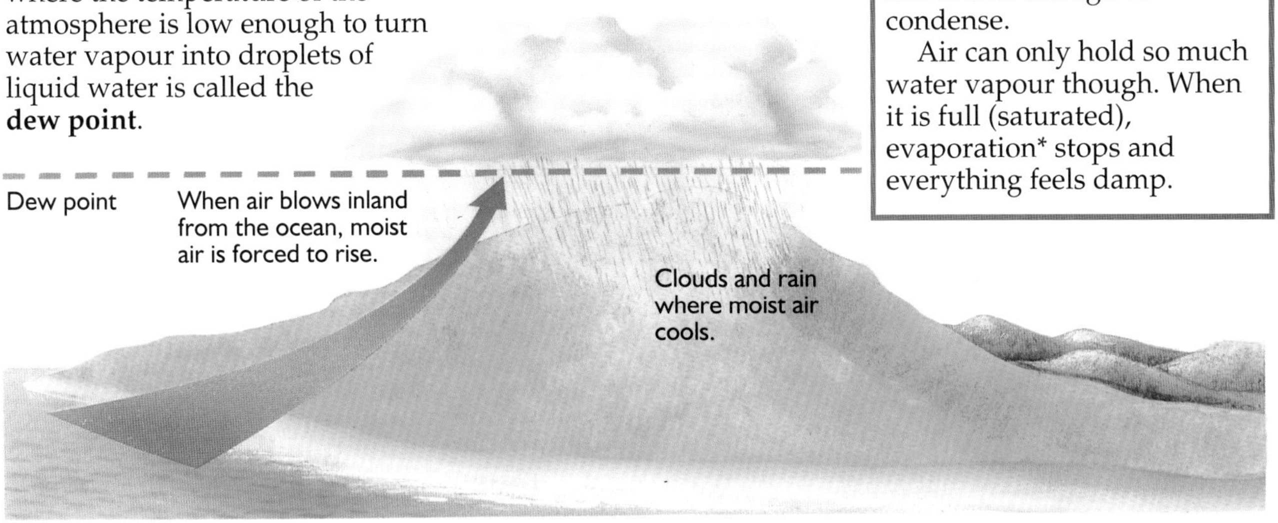
As it rises, water vapour cools and condenses. Clouds are made of tiny droplets of water.
Dew point
When air blows inland from the ocean, moist air is forced to rise.
Clouds and rain where moist air cools.

Wet air

The amount of water vapour in the air is called **humidity**. In some hot countries, humidity is very high because the water vapour is not cooled enough to condense.

Air can only hold so much water vapour though. When it is full (saturated), evaporation* stops and everything feels damp.

As more water vapour cools and condenses, droplets in the clouds grow bigger. The droplets become heavy and eventually fall to earth as rain. When water falls from the air as a liquid such as rain or dew, or as a solid such as snow or hail, it is called **precipitation**.

There is often rain in hilly, coastal areas where the wind blows inland from the ocean. This is because ocean wind contains lots of water vapour. When it reaches the land, the air is forced to rise. It cools and the water vapour condenses and falls as rain.

Types of precipitation

When the temperature is very low, water vapour turns into tiny ice crystals and forms snowflakes.

Snow may melt and turn to rain as it falls to earth. Sleet is a mixture of partly melted snow and rain.

Raindrops may freeze within clouds and form hailstones. Hailstones are made up of lots of layers of ice.

Dew settles when warm, moist air passes over cold land and the water vapour condenses around the land surface.

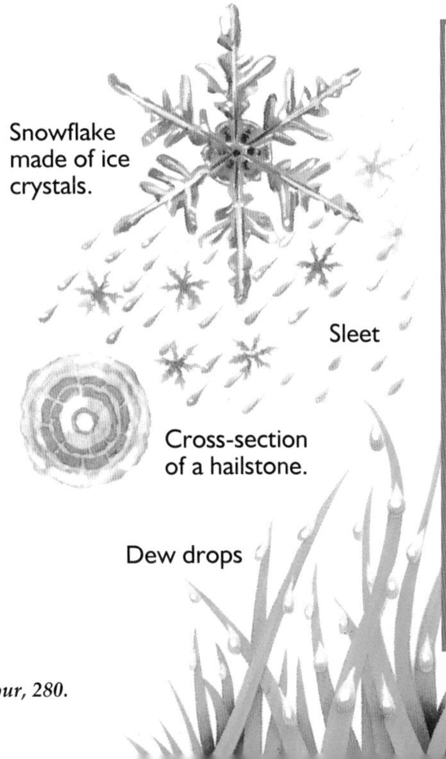
Snowflake made of ice crystals.
Sleet
Cross-section of a hailstone.
Dew drops

DID YOU KNOW?

Sailors out at sea have always been able to tell if land is on the horizon because of the tell-tale clouds that form along the coastline.

Condensation, Evaporation, 282; Water vapour, 280.

Weather watching

In many parts of the world the weather changes from day to day. People called meteorologists study weather so they can work out what it might do next. To record weather, they need instruments that measure heat, moisture and atmospheric pressure* because weather is a mixture of all these things.

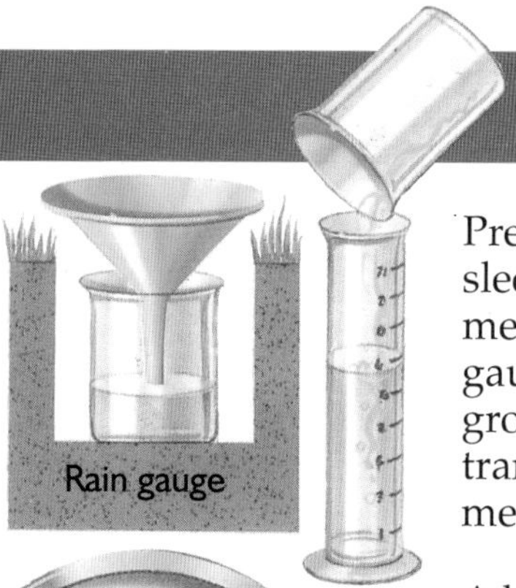
Rain gauge

Precipitation* (rain, sleet, snow or hail) is measured with a rain gauge. It is collected at ground level and transferred to a measuring cylinder.

A thermometer is a device used to measure heat. It contains mercury or alcohol, which expands and moves up the tube when it is warmed. The liquid rises further up the tube, the hotter it becomes.

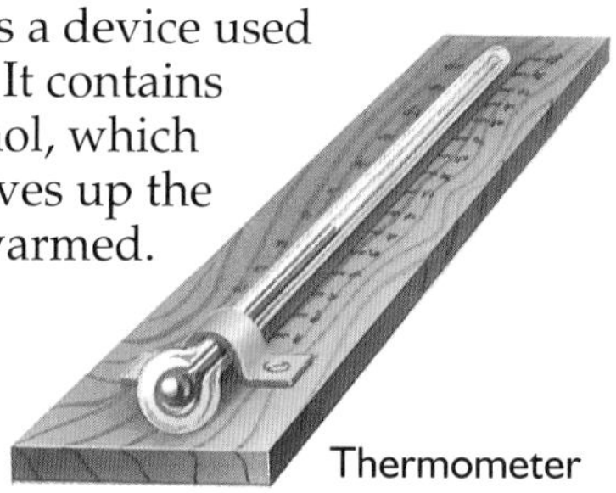
Thermometer

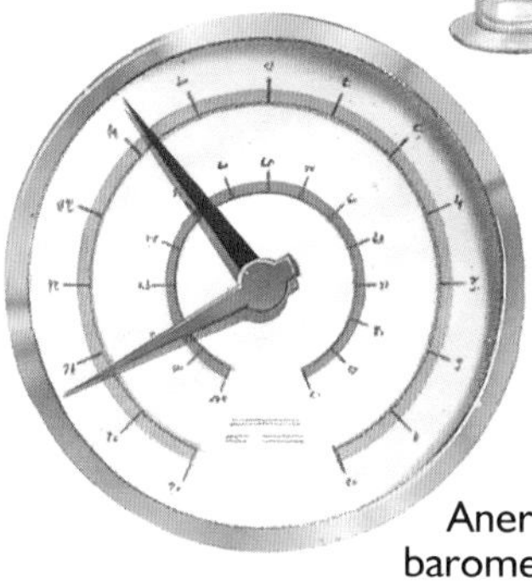
Aneroid barometer

A barometer measures air pressure. One type, called an aneroid barometer, has a dial and a needle, which moves around when the air pressure changes. It measures air pressure in hectopascals (hPa) or in millibars (mb).

Humidity* is measured by wet and dry bulb thermometers. Wet muslin covers one bulb. When there is not much moisture in the air, water evaporates* from the muslin. Evaporation cools the bulb so the temperature falls below that of the dry bulb thermometer. The temperature difference shows how humid it is.

Wet and dry bulb thermometer

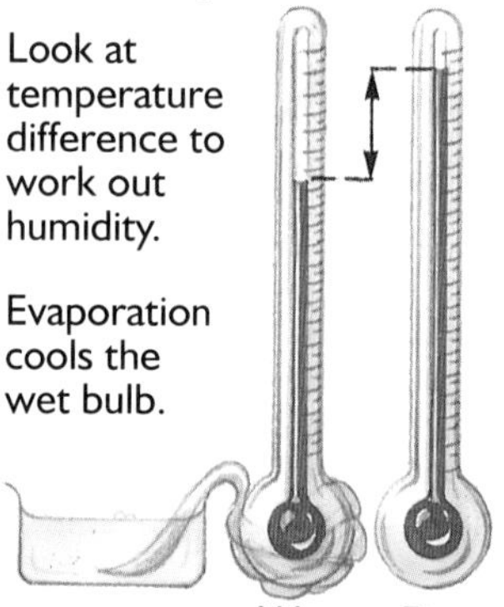
Look at temperature difference to work out humidity.
Evaporation cools the wet bulb.
Wet bulb
Dry bulb

A weather vane shows wind direction. An arrow points towards where the wind is coming from.

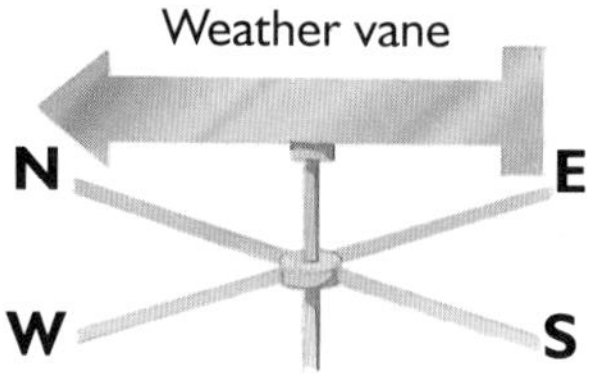

Weather vane

An anemometer measures how fast the wind is blowing. Cups catch the wind and are pushed around. A meter records how quickly they spin.

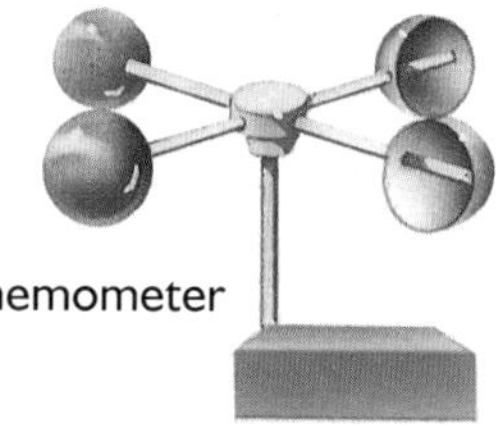
Anemometer

Weather charts

Meteorologists work at weather stations. They collect data about the weather and plot it on charts. On the charts, lines called **isobars** join up places with the same atmospheric pressure. Arrows show which way the wind is blowing. Lines, or feathers, on the end show wind speed in knots. Half a feather stands for five knots, a whole feather stands for ten knots. Symbols on the charts show how much cloud cover there is.

KEY

Air pressure

Isobars ——
High pressure (H)
Low pressure (L)

Wind speed

15 knots
20 knots
25 knots
Calm ◎

Cloud cover

Sky clear ○
Partly cloudy ◐
Overcast ●

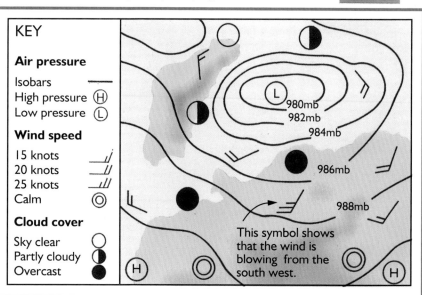

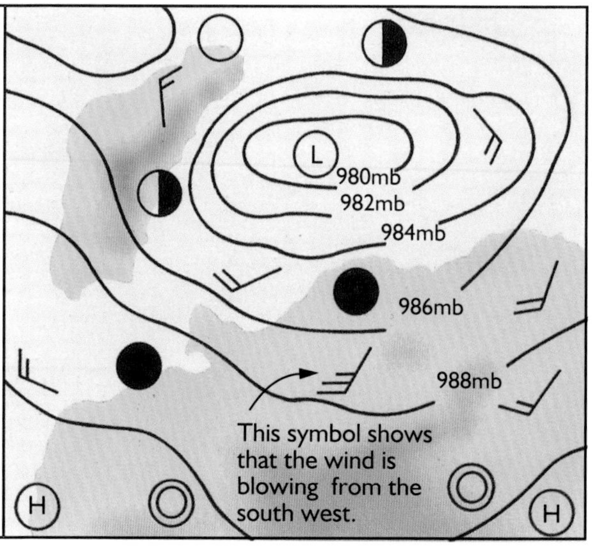
L
980mb
982mb
984mb
986mb
988mb
H
H
This symbol shows that the wind is blowing from the south west.

 **Atmospheric pressure, 290; Evaporation, 282; Humidity, Precipitation, 291.*

Fronts and depressions

A **front** is where an area of cold air and an area of warm air meet. A **warm front** is where warm air is moving in to replace cold air. A **cold front** is where cold air is replacing warm air. On weather charts, fronts are shown by lines marking their leading edge. Warm fronts have rounded nobbles along them. Cold fronts have triangles.

If an area of warm air is wedged in an expanse of colder air it is called a **depression**. The cold air pushes underneath the warm air and eventually the warm and cold fronts meet. When this happens it is called an **occluded front**.

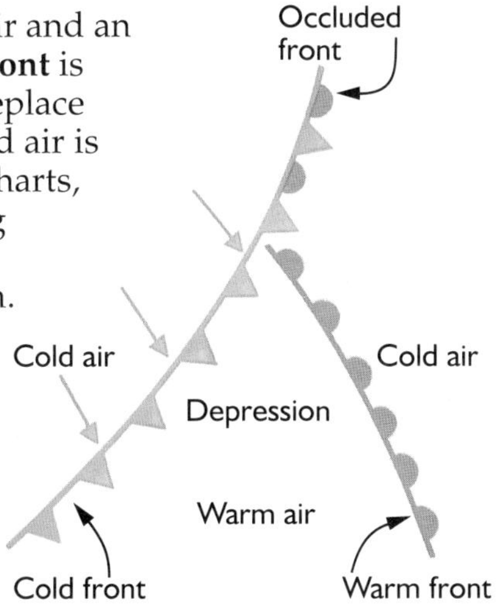

Occluded front
Cold air
Cold air
Depression
Warm air
Cold front
Warm front

Satellite pictures

Satellites out in space take pictures of the Earth. From these, meteorologists can see the pattern and movement of clouds around the world. This helps them to understand how the weather works.

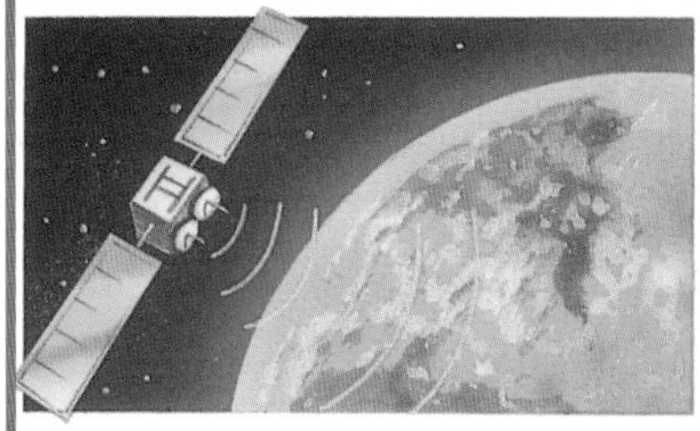

Cloud spotting

It is often possible to work out what the weather will do next by studying the height, shape and colour of the clouds. Clouds form along fronts, so they often signal that a depression is on its way – and this usually means unsettled weather.

There are three main categories of cloud. **Cirrus** clouds are high and wispy, **cumulus** clouds are lower and look like heaps of cotton wool, and **stratus** clouds form in layers. Many clouds are a combination of two types, as shown below.

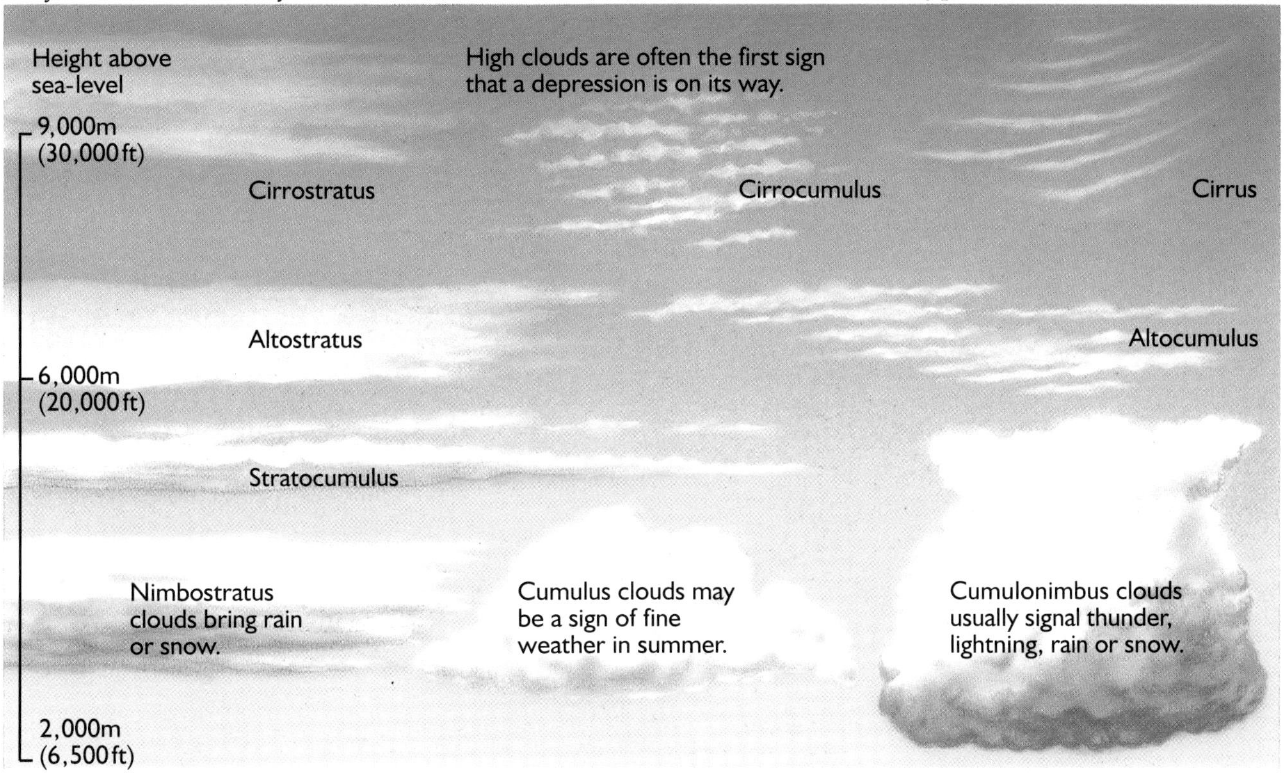

Height above sea-level
High clouds are often the first sign that a depression is on its way.
9,000m (30,000ft)
Cirrostratus
Cirrocumulus
Cirrus
Altostratus
Altocumulus
6,000m (20,000ft)
Stratocumulus
Nimbostratus clouds bring rain or snow.
Cumulus clouds may be a sign of fine weather in summer.
Cumulonimbus clouds usually signal thunder, lightning, rain or snow.
2,000m (6,500ft)

Hot and cold places

In some areas of the world, the average weather, or **climate**, is much hotter than in other areas. The main reason for this is to do with the area's latitude*. Areas near the Equator (low latitudes) have a hot climate because the Sun rises high overhead and its rays strike the Earth almost at right angles. The land and sea become very warm and pass on heat to the air. Passing on heat like this is called **radiation**.

Areas near the Poles (high latitudes) are cold because the Sun stays low in the sky and its rays spread out over a much wider area. The land and sea are hardly warmed so they have very little heat to radiate.

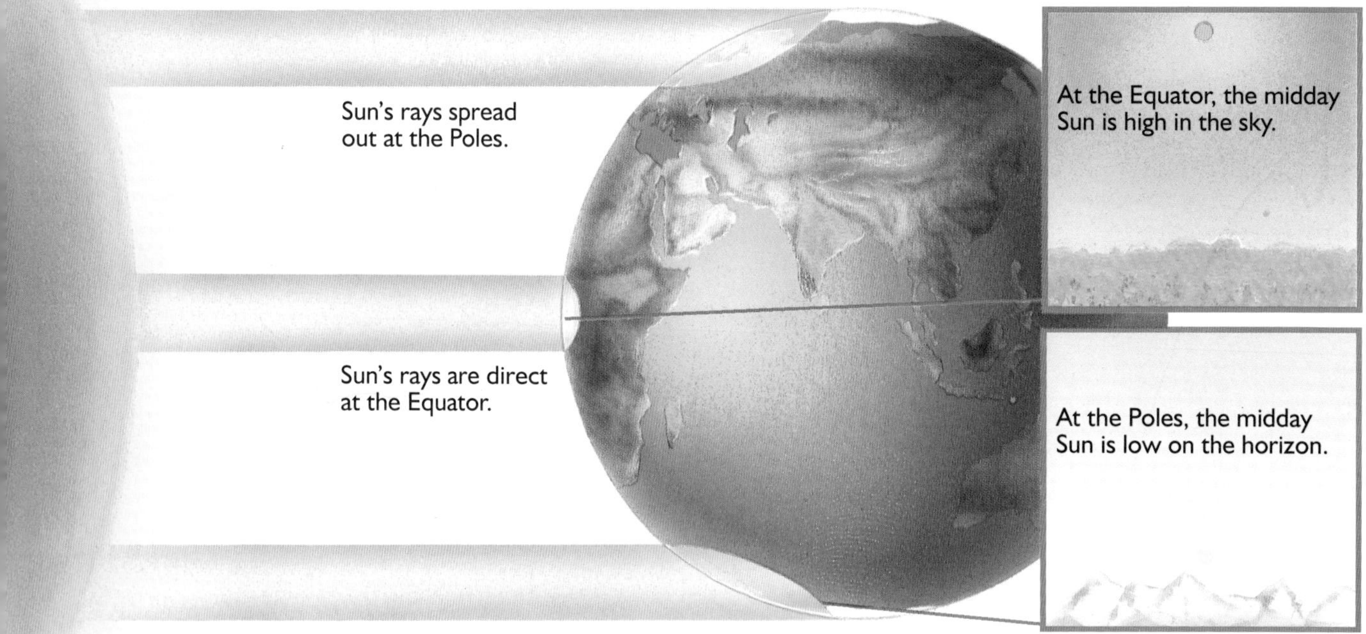
Sun's rays spread out at the Poles.
Sun's rays are direct at the Equator.
At the Equator, the midday Sun is high in the sky.
At the Poles, the midday Sun is low on the horizon.

Daylight hours

In every part of the world except the Equator, the length of day and night varies depending on the time of year. When days are long* the land and sea have a long time to warm up so they have more heat to radiate. This makes the climate warmer. At night, the Earth's surface is turned away from the Sun's rays so it cools down. Therefore, when the nights are long, the climate becomes colder.

High places

The temperature of the air around you depends partly on the atmospheric pressure*. If atmospheric pressure is low, there are fewer particles of air close to the Earth's surface to trap heat, so the air stays cold.

Atmospheric pressure is low in high, mountainous areas, where gravity* is weaker. This is why mountainous areas are cold and snowy – even those close to the Equator.

DID YOU KNOW?

The hottest place on Earth is Dalol in Ethiopia. The average temperature there is 34°C (94°F). The coldest place on Earth is Polus Nedostupnosti in Antarctica, where the average temperature is -58°C (-72°F).

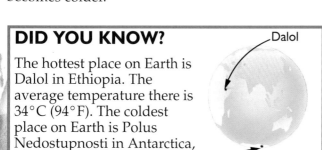

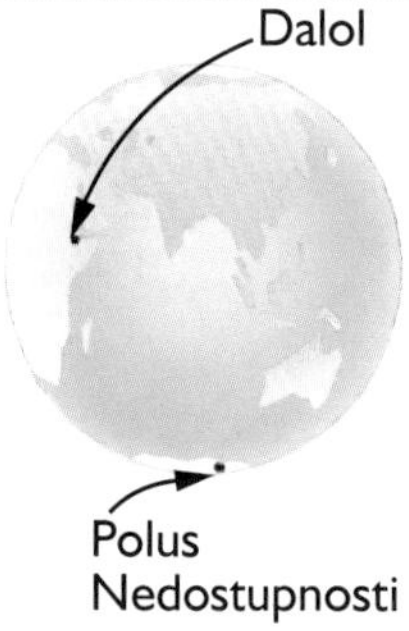
Dalol
Polus Nedostupnosti

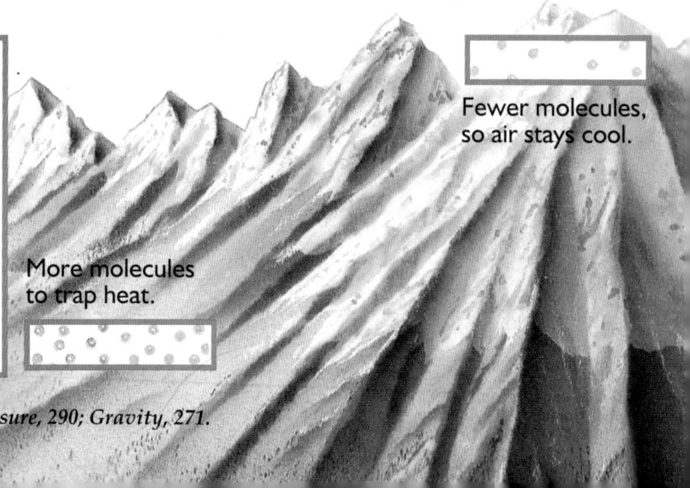
Fewer molecules, so air stays cool.
More molecules to trap heat.

 Latitude, 264; Long and short days, 263; Atmospheric pressure, 290; Gravity, 271.

Land and sea temperatures

Places close to the sea have a milder climate than places a long way inland. Oceans heat up more slowly than land because their shiny surface reflects the Sun's rays, but they stay warm longer. Places near the coast are cooled by the sea in summer and warmed by the sea in winter. The central parts of continents have much hotter summers and colder winters.

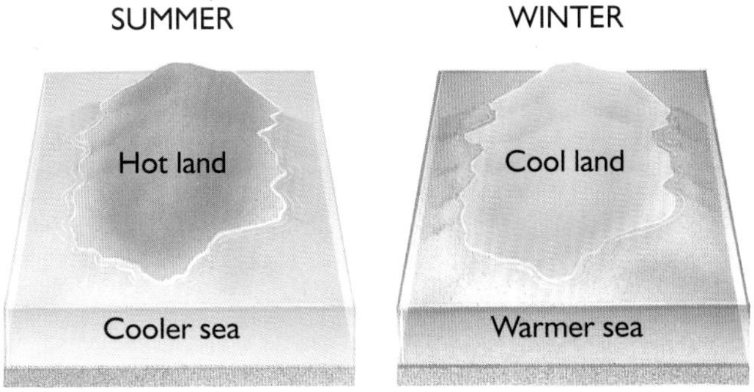

Winds and ocean currents*

Warm and cold winds blowing around the world also influence climate. The temperature of the wind depends on where it has blown from. Winds blowing from the Tropics to higher latitudes are warm because they drag currents of warm tropical water with them. The ocean's heat makes the wind warm too. Winds blowing from the Poles are very cold because they are chilled by the cold ocean currents beneath them. This map shows the main ocean currents.

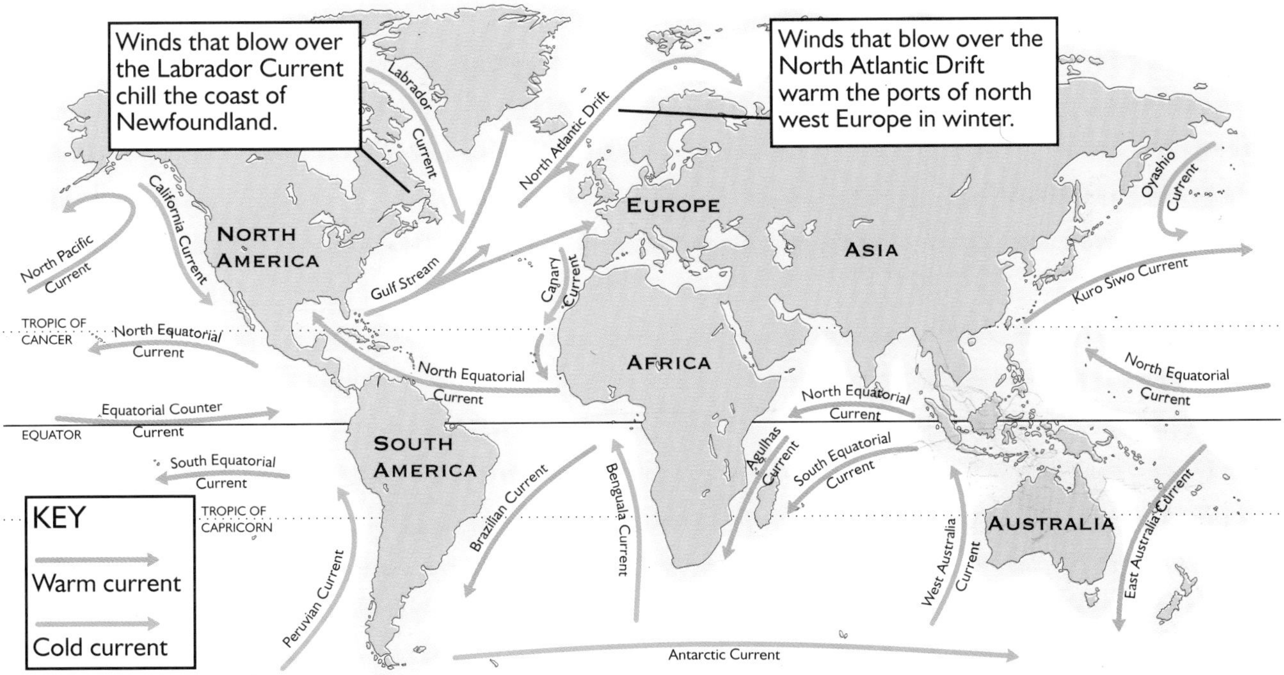

Cloud cover

Clouds make places cooler during the day because they block some of the Sun's rays. At night they trap in heat and keep the air warm. Blocking out or trapping in heat is called **insulation**. Some areas, such as equatorial regions*, are always cloudy. Days would be much hotter and nights much colder there if the sky was clear.

*Currents, 281; Equatorial regions, 298.

Extreme weather

Sometimes weather can behave in such extreme or violent ways that it makes news headlines. Violent weather can cause a lot of damage to land and buildings, and even kill people.

Thunderstorms

Thunderstorms are also called **electrical storms**. They happen when raindrops and hailstones crash into each other and create an electrical charge in a cloud. The electricity jumps through the air to land, or to other clouds nearby. The air becomes very hot and expands quickly, which causes a bang like an explosion (thunder) and a flash (lightning).

Light travels faster than sound so you see the lightning before you hear the thunder. To work out how far away the centre of a storm is, count the seconds between when you see the lightning and when you hear the thunder. Divide the number of seconds by three to work out how far away the storm is in kilometres or divide the number by five to work it out in miles.

You see sheet lightning if cloud blocks your view.
You see forked lightning if the path of the electricity is visible.

Revolving storms

Hurricanes, **typhoons** and **cyclones** are all names for tropical revolving storms. These develop when air rises over the warm, tropical seas and starts spinning. No one is sure what sets it off. Most revolving storms develop in the Pacific Ocean and blow over the Philippines, Hong Kong, China and Japan. They also affect northern Australia and the southern USA.

Revolving storms are usually about 500km (310 miles) across and travel at about 15kmph (9mph). The centre of the storm, called the **eye**, is calm but fast winds circle around it. At the edge of the storm, the wind may blow at speeds of over 120kmph (75mph) and can blow down buildings. There is also torrential rain, which may cause flooding.

Satellites out in space can detect the spiral cloud pattern of a revolving storm before it reaches land. Forecasters are able to send out warnings so that people can be prepared.

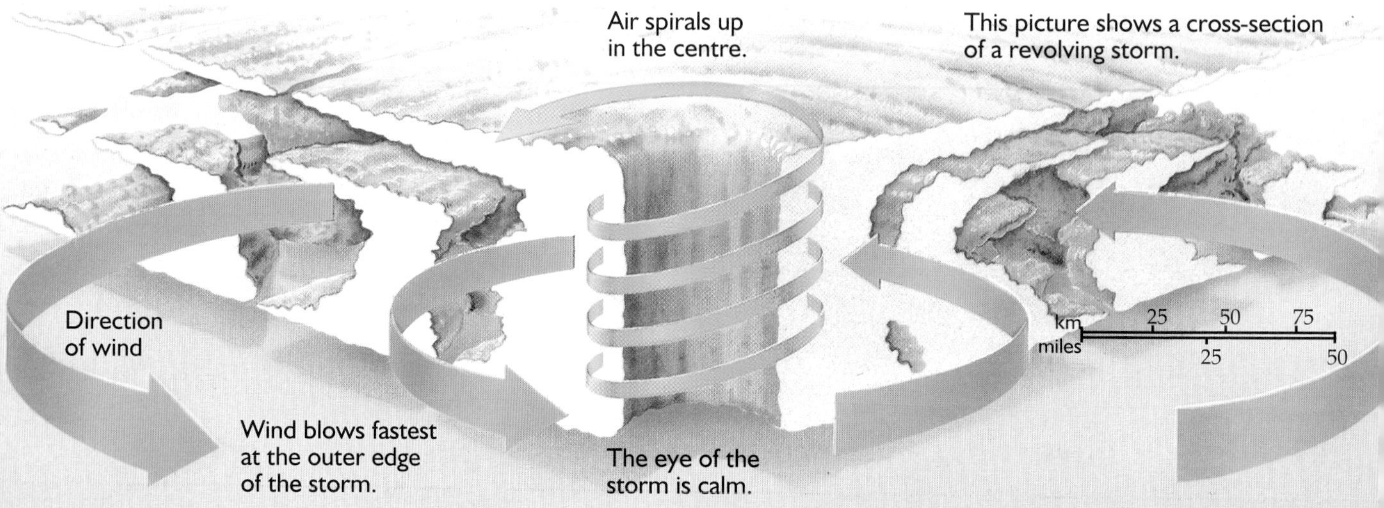

Air spirals up in the centre.
This picture shows a cross-section of a revolving storm.
Direction of wind
km 25 50 75
miles 25 50
Wind blows fastest at the outer edge of the storm.
The eye of the storm is calm.

Tornadoes and water-spouts

A **tornado** is a spinning column of air, usually about 0.5km (0.3 miles) wide. There is very low atmospheric pressure* at its centre and this causes the tornado to suck things up off the ground as it passes.

Tornadoes travel at speeds of around 400kmph (248mph). They usually die out after about 20km (12.5 miles).

Tornadoes are most common in Australia and the USA, where they are sometimes called twisters. They form during summer storms.

Water-spouts are similar to tornadoes but they form over the sea. The centre of the storm sucks up sea water and spray, so a long funnel of mist and cloud forms between the sea and the sky.

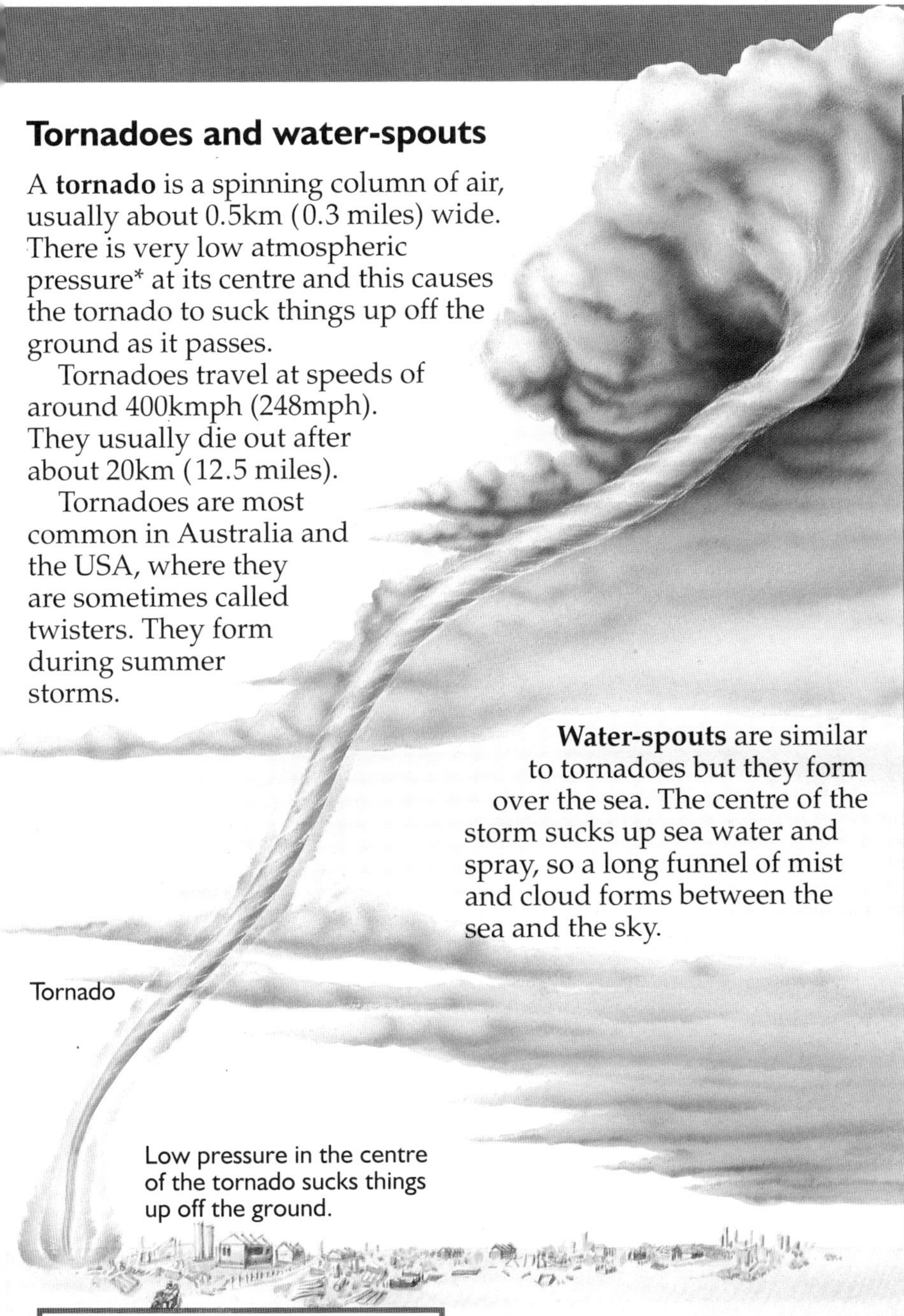
Tornado
Low pressure in the centre of the tornado sucks things up off the ground.

High winds

When wind blows at more than 63kmph (40mph) it is called a **gale**. Gales may develop when winds blow across oceans or large flat areas of land. In coastal areas, gales can whip up the waves and cause floods. The salt water can make land near the coast impossible to farm for several years.

Strong winds can cause giant waves.

Wind can also reach gale force if it is channelled through a valley or between tall buildings. This is called the **funnel effect**.

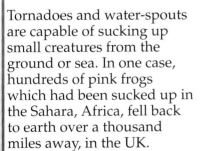

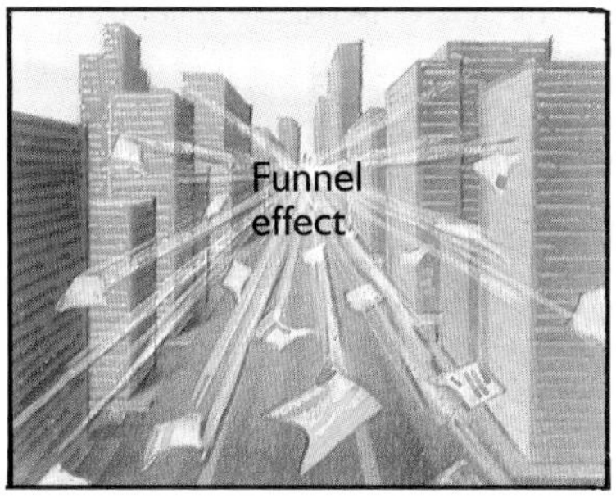
Funnel effect

DID YOU KNOW?

Tornadoes and water-spouts are capable of sucking up small creatures from the ground or sea. In one case, hundreds of pink frogs which had been sucked up in the Sahara, Africa, fell back to earth over a thousand miles away, in the UK.

Too little rain

In most parts of the world, it is possible to forecast how much rain there will be each month. If there is a lot less rain than expected, the conditions are classed as **drought**.

In countries where there is usually plenty of rain, drought does not affect people very much. They just have to use less water in their homes and gardens until it is over.

Drought can be disastrous, though, in areas of the world where rainfall is unreliable, such as India, parts of Africa and central Australia. If there is no rain, crops do not grow and there is no pasture for sheep and cattle.

**Atmospheric pressure, 290.*

Mountainous areas have a cooler climate.
Equatorial regions

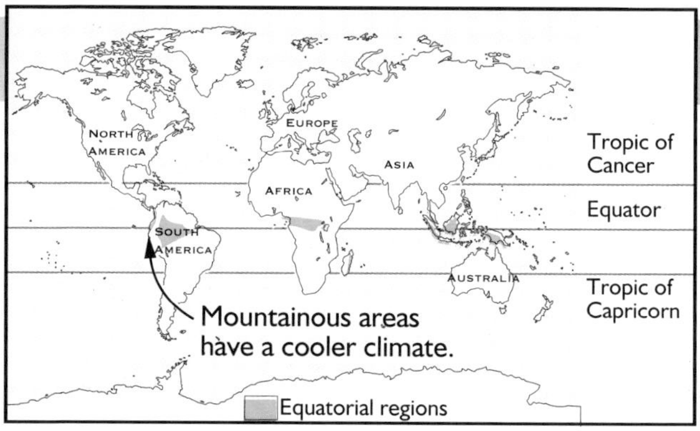

Most places near to the Equator have an equatorial climate. The Sun's rays are very direct there so the climate is hot. It is also very rainy because the Sun's heat makes lots of water evaporate*. Warm, humid air rises and cools to form huge storm clouds.

The equatorial regions are the only areas of the world where the seasons* do not change.

The rainforests

Most of the equatorial region is covered in thick forest, called **equatorial rainforest**. Hundreds of types of hardwood trees grow there, such as mahogany, rosewood and ebony.

The rainforest is so dense that the trees have to fight for sunlight. They grow very tall and spread out their upper branches to catch more light. Their tops form a thick layer of foliage called a **canopy**, which cuts out sunlight to the forest floor. Some giant trees, called **emergent trees**, tower above the canopy.

Beneath the canopy the rainforest is damp and gloomy. Plants that grow on the forest floor have broad, flat leaves to catch as much sunlight as possible. The leaves have a waxy surface and a point at the tip, called a **drip tip**, to let rain run off more easily.

At ground level there is a mass of rotting vegetation and fungus. In clearings, where trees have fallen, new trees shoot up in a race to claim a share of the sunlight. The one that grows fastest will replace the tree that has fallen. Climbing plants called **lianas** attach themselves to the young trees and grow with them up to the sunlight.

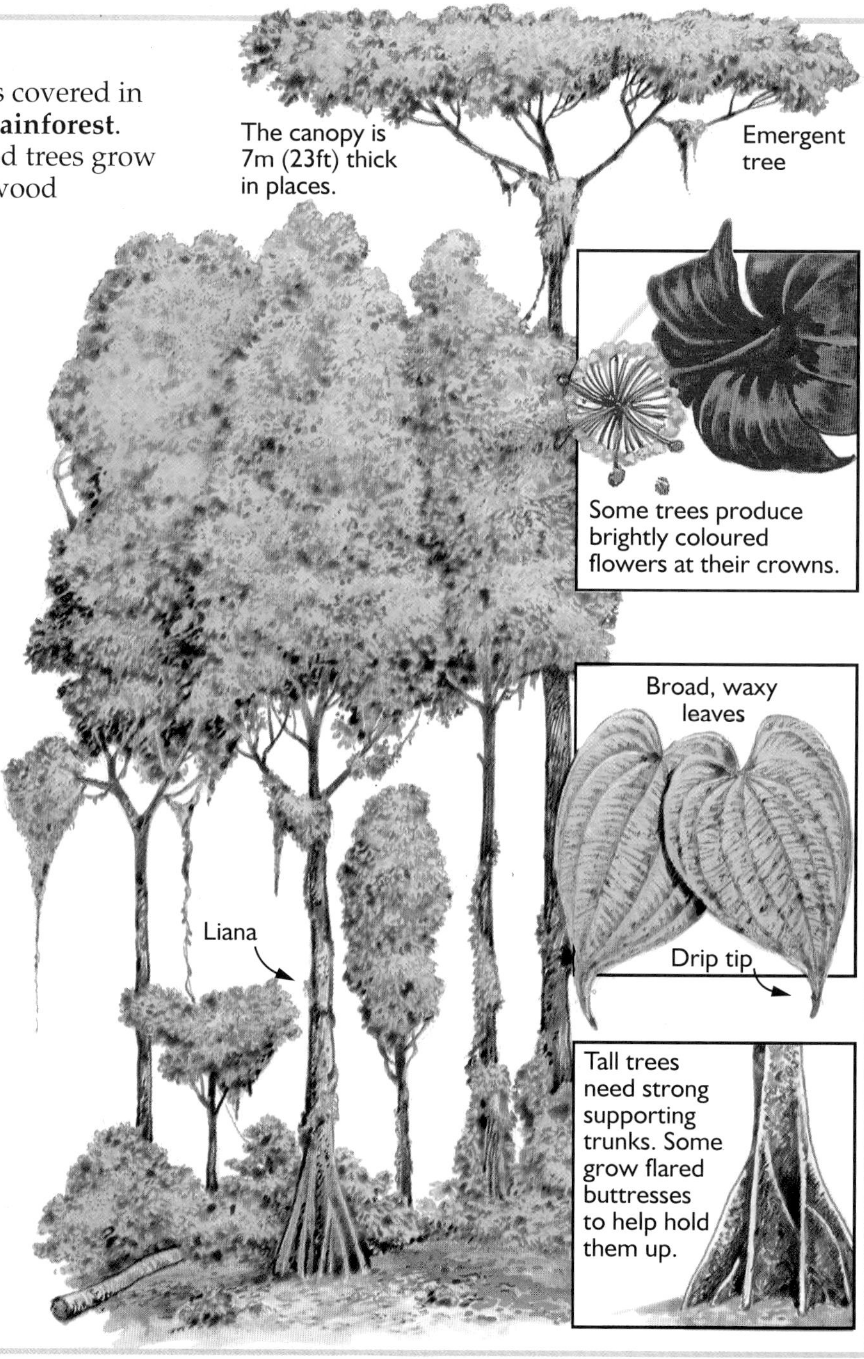

The canopy is 7m (23ft) thick in places.
Emergent tree
Some trees produce brightly coloured flowers at their crowns.
Broad, waxy leaves
Drip tip
Liana
Tall trees need strong supporting trunks. Some grow flared buttresses to help hold them up.

 **Evaporation, 282; Seasons, 263.*

Forest creatures

Millions of different types of creatures live in the equatorial rainforests as there is plenty of food, water and warmth.

Birds of prey live in the emergent trees. From there they have a clear view over their hunting ground.

Creatures that live in the canopy, such as those below, feed on fruit, nuts, flowers, leaves and bark.

Animals that live among the branches need to be able to move easily from tree to tree.

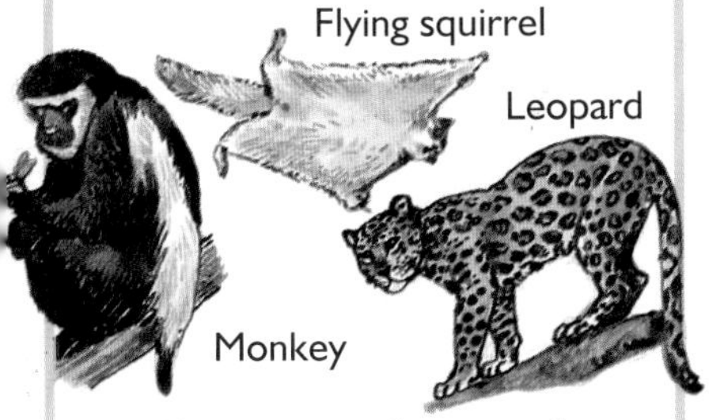

Small creatures live on the forest floor. The tangled vegetation makes it hard for large animals to move about.

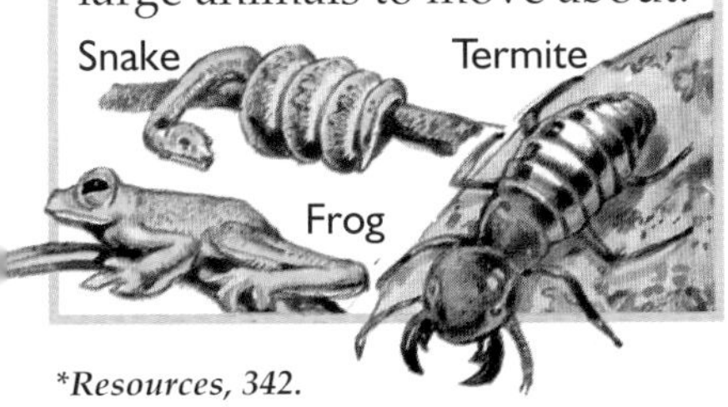

People of the rainforests

Various tribes live in the rainforests, such as the Pygmies of Zaire, Africa, and the Amazonian Indians of South America. They are **nomads**, which means they move from place to place. Some are **hunter-gatherers**, which means they live on whatever they find or catch in the forest.

Some rainforest people make small clearings to grow some of their own food. They burn the chopped down trees and spread the ashes, which make the soil fertile for a while. When the fertility has been used up, the people move to a new patch. This way of farming is called **slash and burn**.

Rainforest people are small – usually no more than 140cm (4½ft) tall. They can move through the forest easily.

Forest dwellers make clothing from materials around them. This Pygmy is wearing a loincloth of softened bark.

Hunter-gatherers hunt animals and gather other food such as nuts, fruit and honey.

Shelters are covered with waxy leaves to keep out the rain.

Smoke from fires drives away insects.

Shrinking forests

Huge areas of rainforest are cleared each year. A lot of the land is used for farming commercial crops such as palm oil, coffee, cocoa and rubber. Forest is also cleared to build roads and cities, and to mine minerals such as copper, zinc and diamonds. Some wood is sold abroad for furniture-making and building. Some goes to industries to be made into charcoal for fuel. Many people worry that clearing large areas of rainforest will destroy important resources*.

**Resources, 342.*

Savanna regions

Areas a few degrees north and south of the Equator have a climate which is usually very dry. At certain times of the year, though, they become very hot and have torrential rain. These areas of the world are called the savanna regions. They are named after the Savanna in Africa, which is the largest region with this type of climate.

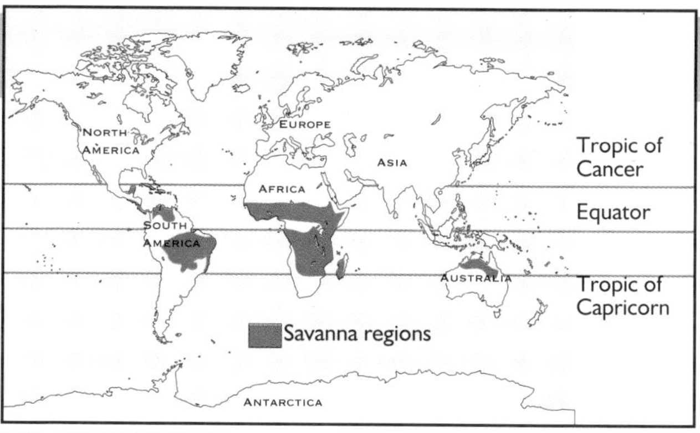

When the rain comes

The savanna regions are within the Tropics, where the Sun is directly overhead twice each year. It is hotter at these times of the year so more water evaporates* and this causes heavy rain. In areas of savanna closest to the Equator, the Sun is directly overhead at opposite times of the year (around March and September) so the rainy seasons are several months apart. In areas of savanna furthest from the Equator, both rainy seasons are so close together that they merge into one.

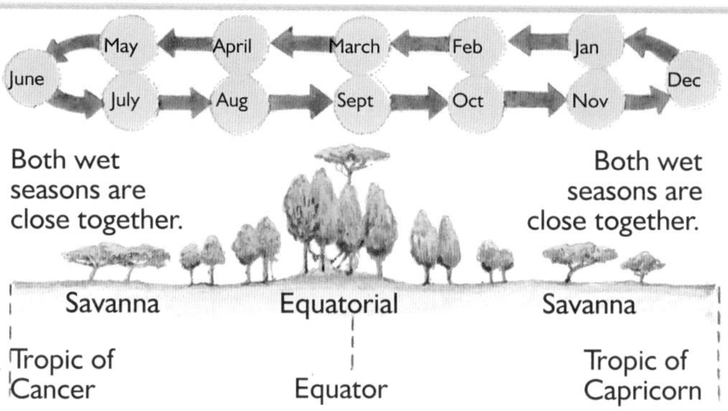

This picture shows where the Sun is most direct, month by month.

What grows in the savanna?

Conditions in the savanna are harsh. The soil contains few nutrients, dries out during the dry season and becomes boggy during the wet season. Also, there are often fires at the end of the dry season.

Grasses are very tough and can grow easily in savanna conditions. Thousands of different types grow there. For trees to survive, though, they need certain features to protect them against drought and fire.

One type of tree, called the baobab tree, has developed a thick, fireproof trunk, which stores water like a sponge. Its long roots draw water from deep underground. Other trees, such as acacia trees, have broad, flat crowns to shade the lower leaves and prevent them from drying out.

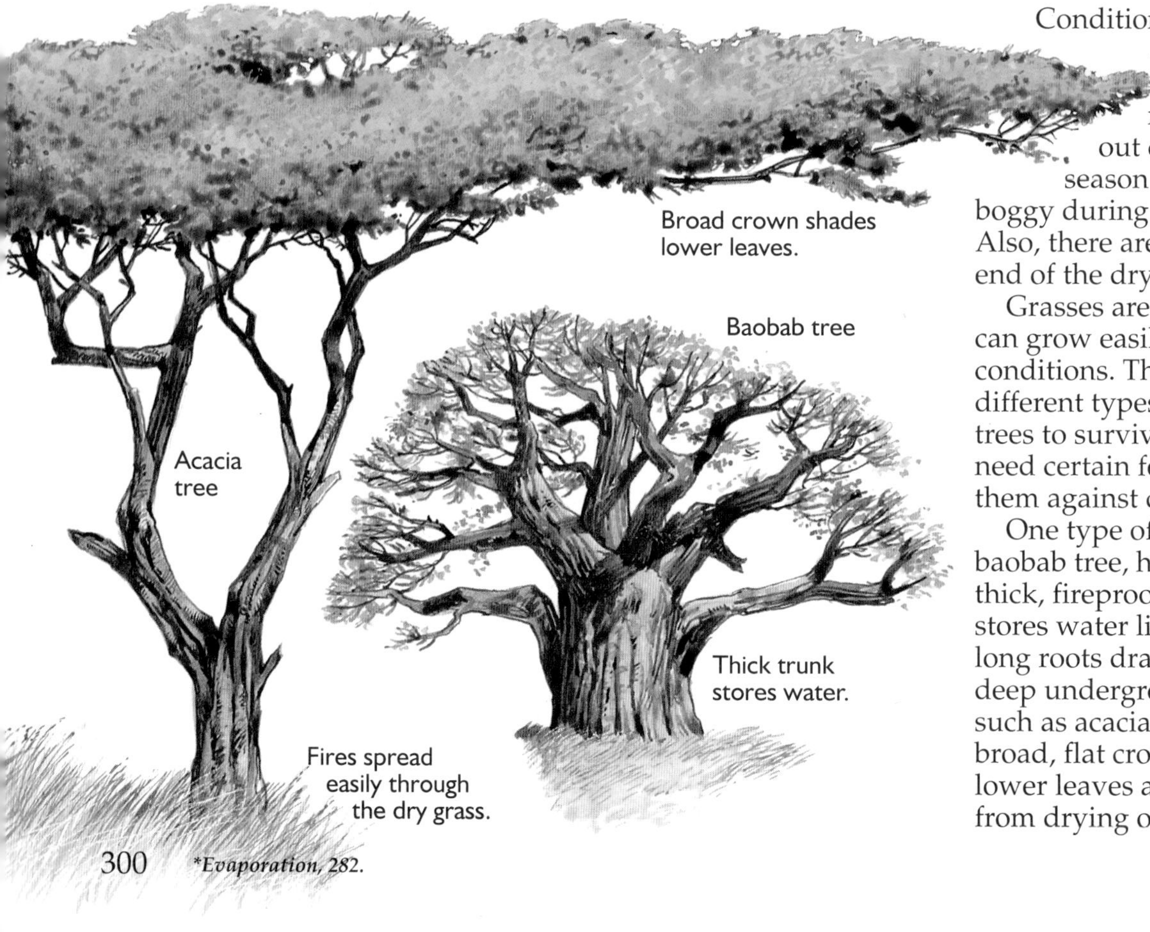

 *Evaporation, 282.

Savanna wildlife

Many savanna areas have been used for farming cattle and the natural wildlife has gone. In the African Savanna, though, there are huge national parks where wild animals still live.

Savanna animals have to be able to survive the drought. Large plant-eaters (herbivores) such as giraffes, zebras, wildebeest, elephants and rhinos can travel huge distances so, when one area becomes too dry, they wander to where there is rain and vegetation. Meat-eaters (carnivores), such as lions, cheetahs and hyenas prey on the roaming herds. Animals too small to travel to water may sleep through the dry season. This is called aestivation. Many small creatures live underground and only come out after sunset when it is cooler.

Herds of wildebeest may travel huge distances in search of water and vegetation.

Savanna people

Many tribes live in the African Savanna. The Fulani tribe, for example, are nomads*. They keep cattle, sheep and goats and travel the land in search of water and fresh pasture.

The Fulani live mainly on milk from their herds. They also sell leather and milk to buy cereals. In the rainy season they make shelters from branches and leather. In the dry season they sleep in the open air.

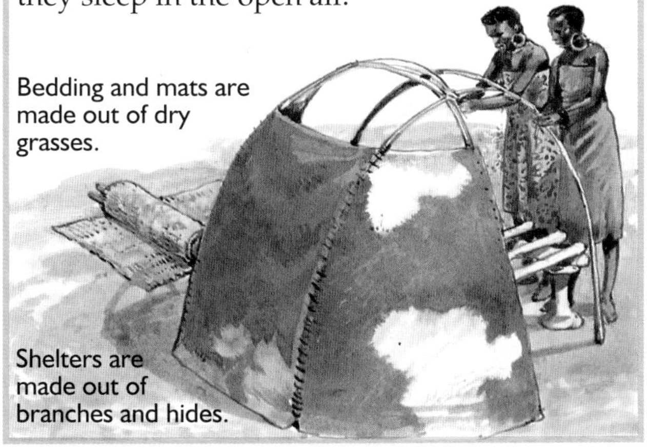

Bedding and mats are made out of dry grasses.

Shelters are made out of branches and hides.

Commercial farming

Higher areas of the African Savanna are cooler than the lower regions so they have more rain. The soil has more moisture and fertility so commercial crops such as tea and coffee may be grown on the hillsides there.

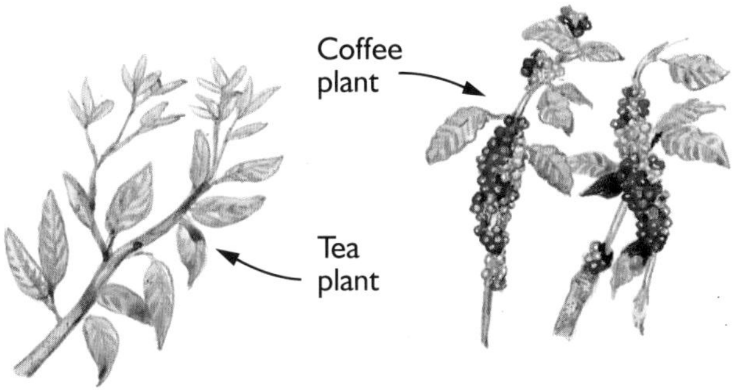

The Brazilian and Australian savanna regions also have fairly regular rain. This makes them ideal for cattle farming. Over the past century, European settlers have made large areas into cattle ranches. Much of the beef reared there is sold to European countries.

**Nomads, 299.*

Tropical deserts

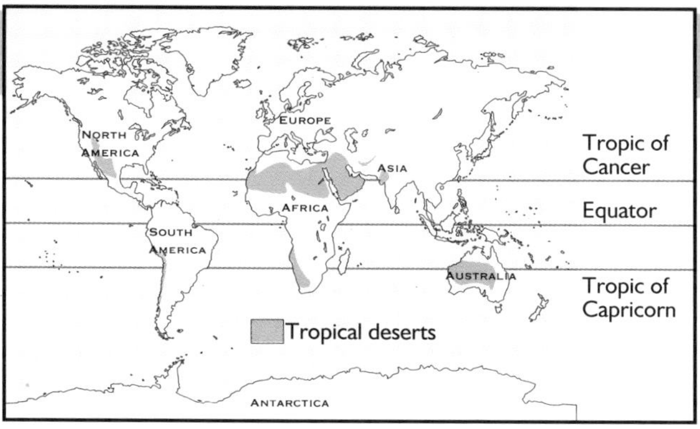

The world's tropical deserts are between about 15° and 30° north and south of the Equator. Air that rose at the Equator sinks here, causing high atmospheric pressure*. The air becomes warm as it nears the Earth's surface, so it can hold lots of water vapour without it condensing*. Because of this, clouds hardly ever form within these regions and rain is very rare.

Desert landscapes

All desert landscapes are very dry. The landscape usually has little vegetation because of lack of rain.

Sand desert

About 25% of the world's deserts are made up of sand, which has been blown from rock faces. It forms hills called **dunes**. The Sahara in Africa is a sandy desert.

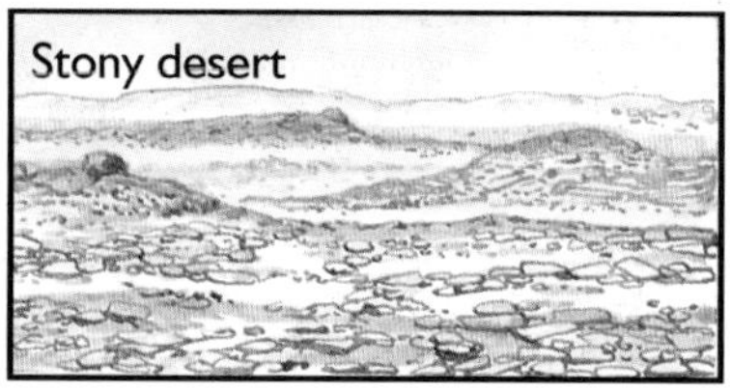

Stony desert

Some deserts are made up of bare stone. There is stony desert in Algeria and Libya, for example.

Salt crystals

In some places, such as Salt Lake City in the USA, large lakes have dried up, leaving a layer of salt crystals.

Desert conditions

The tropical deserts are the hottest places on Earth. With no clouds to block the Sun's rays, the ground becomes baking hot. Nights can be very cold, though, and even frosty in winter, because cloudless skies let heat escape.

Strong Trade Winds* blow across the deserts. In sandy deserts, the wind sweeps up fine sand and causes dust storms. As sand is blown along, it erodes rocks in its path. Over many years the rocks may be sand-blasted into weird, sculptural shapes.

Although desert rain is rare, it is usually heavy. Wide rivers form, which carry lots of rock particles (sediment). This erodes rocks and eats out deep canyons. The rivers soon dry up, leaving dry courses called **wadis**.

Deep canyon eroded by floodwater
Rock eroded by the desert wind

DID YOU KNOW?

Some parts of the Atacama Desert in South America, have had no rain for several hundred years.

**Atmospheric pressure, 290; Condensation, 282; Trade Winds, 290.*

Plant life

Desert plants have to survive with very little rain. Some, such as cacti, store water in their stems, leaves or roots. These are called **succulent plants**. Many plants have spines instead of leaves because spines allow less moisture to escape. Many desert plants have long roots for finding water.

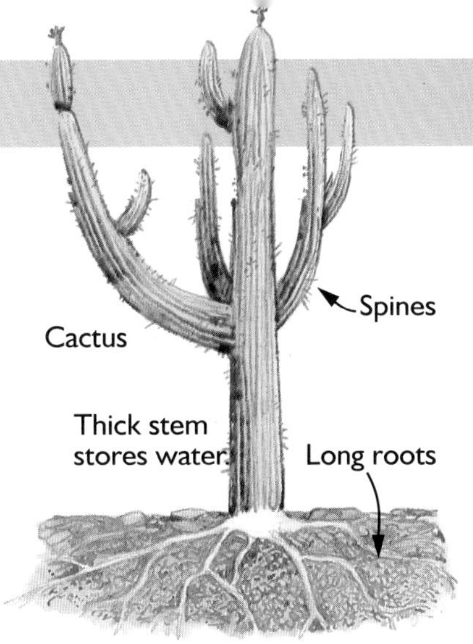
Cactus
Spines
Thick stem stores water
Long roots

Flowering deserts

Some desert plants only grow when it rains. Their seeds may lie in the ground for years, just waiting. When rain comes, they grow, flower and die within a few days.

Desert creatures

Desert creatures need to keep their bodies as cool and moist as possible. Small animals cope by staying in the shade. Some desert creatures have developed particular features and types of behaviour that help them to live more easily in the hot, dry desert conditions.

Carnivores such as this desert fox take in moisture from the blood of their prey.

Many desert animals have long ears, which lose heat easily.

Desert rats stay in moist underground burrows.

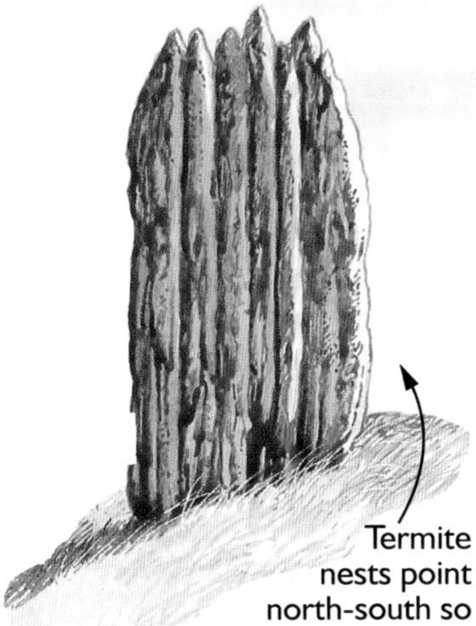
Termite nests point north-south so only a small area faces the general direction of the Sun.

Camels can close their nostrils partly during dust storms to stop them from breathing in sand.
Long eyelashes protect a camel's eyes from dust storms.
A camel has no fat under its skin so it stays cooler. Instead, fat is stored in its hump.
Wide, padded feet stop camels from sinking into the sand.

Living in the desert

Only 5% of the world's people live in desert areas. Many are nomads*, others live in small fertile areas called **oases**. Oases form around springs or wells where people can settle permanently. In the Sahara and Arabian desert, the date palm is a major oasis crop.

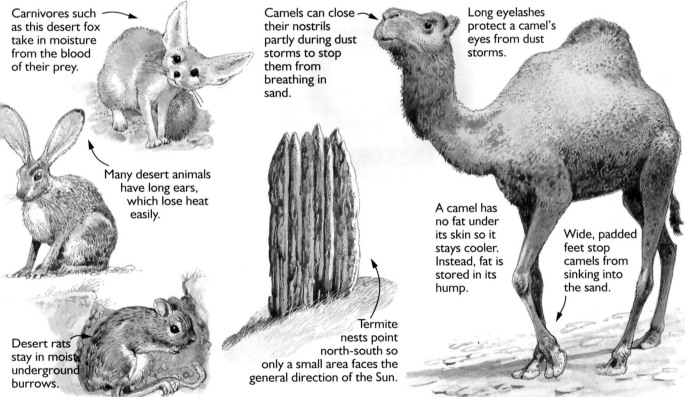

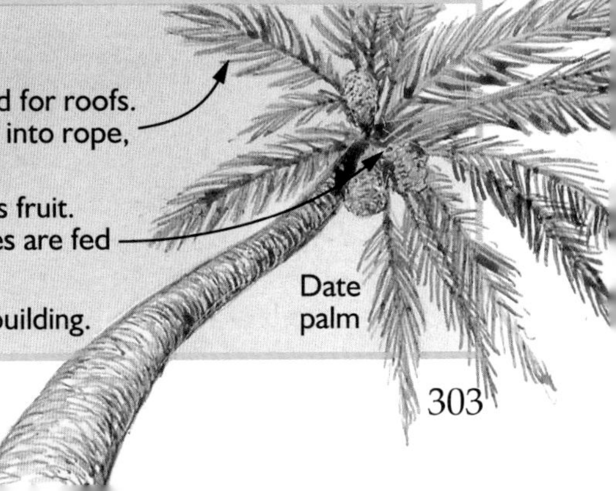
Broad leaves are used for roofs. They are also woven into rope, and used as fuel.
Dates are a nutritious fruit. The ground-up stones are fed to camels.
Trunks are used for building.
Date palm

**Nomads, 299.*

Monsoon regions

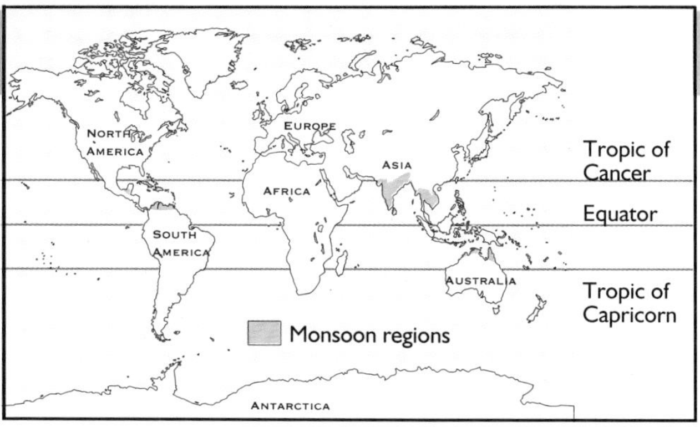

Monsoons are very heavy rainstorms that blow in from the oceans and affect large land masses in the Tropics. About a quarter of the world's population lives in monsoon areas.

Monsoons only occur during a particular part of the year. In the northern hemisphere, they arrive in June. In the monsoon regions of Australia, they arrive in December.

Monsoon seasons

Monsoon areas have three seasons. Before the rains arrive, there is a hot, humid season as the air becomes more moist. The land is dry and bare from months without rain.

During the rainy season (the monsoon), the sky is grey for several weeks. There are thunderstorms almost every day and there is often flooding.

After the monsoon, there is a long, cool, dry season. The sky clears and the floodwater settles. There may be no more rain until the following year.

Rain in the wind

For most of the year, monsoon areas are fairly dry. This is because the atmospheric pressure* is higher over the land than the sea. Wind blows from high pressure to low so dry winds blow from inland towards the sea.

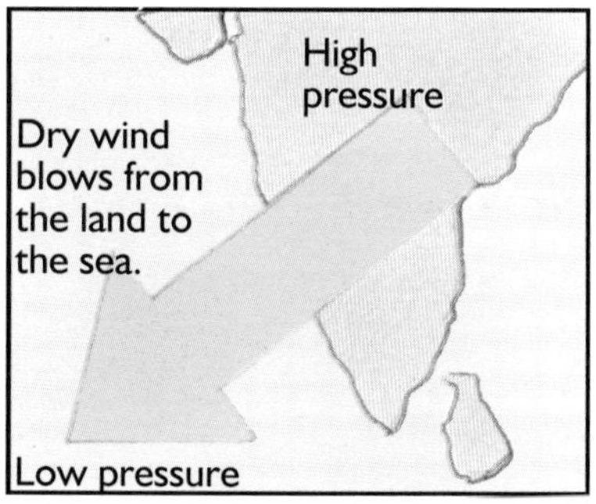

High pressure
Dry wind blows from the land to the sea.
Low pressure

During the hottest months of the year, the air pressure over the land is lower than over the sea so the wind changes direction and blows inland.

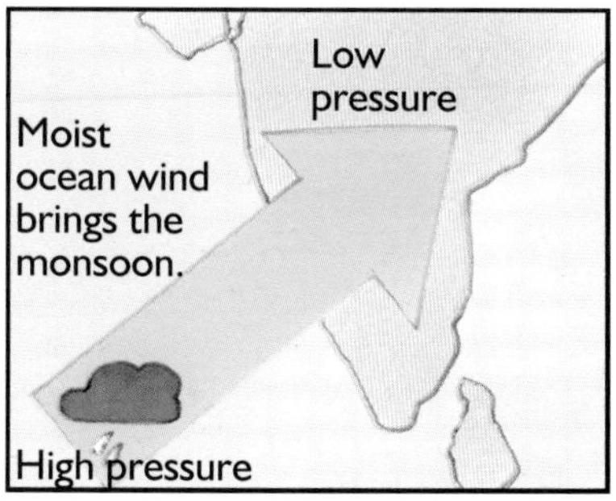

Low pressure
Moist ocean wind brings the monsoon.
High pressure

The ocean wind has travelled over large areas of warm sea and holds lots of moisture. This falls over the land as torrential, monsoon rain.

**Atmospheric pressure, 290.*

Farming

Most monsoon areas have a very dense population, which relies on farming for food. Many areas of natural forest have been chopped down so that the land can be used to grow rice, wheat and millet.

Rice needs lots of water so the seedlings are planted during the monsoon in flooded fields called **paddy fields**. Floodwater is stored in wells and reservoirs to irrigate* crops during drier months.

Tea is also grown in monsoon areas, particularly India and Sri Lanka, which are the world's main tea producers.

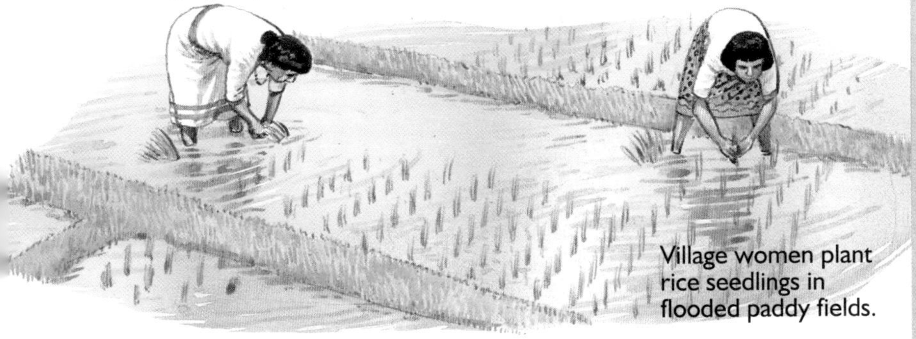

Village women plant rice seedlings in flooded paddy fields.

Animal life

Many of Asia's wild animals have almost died out as the natural vegetation has disappeared. They include tigers, leopards, Indian elephants and wild boars. In the wet season, many areas are infested by insects, snakes, frogs and toads.

In northern Australia's monsoon areas, crocodiles live in the river estuaries.

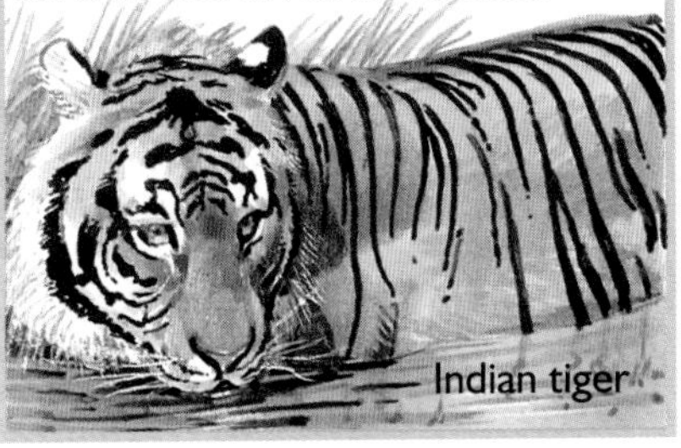

Indian tiger

Too much or too little

It is usually possible to predict when the monsoon will arrive but no one knows how much rain there will be. Some years there is too much and towns and cities are flooded. If there is too little rain, however, crops cannot grow, the cattle die of thirst and the people may starve.

Because people rely on the monsoon rain for their existence, there is great relief and excitement when it arrives. The weeks beforehand are hot and uncomfortable so the rain is refreshing. In some areas, people celebrate the arrival of the monsoon with parties or parades.

Floods can damage people's homes but too little rain may lead to starvation.

Water diseases

Serious diseases such as cholera and typhoid are common in monsoon areas. The bacteria that cause them breed in water, so during the monsoon floods it is easy for the diseases to spread. Mosquitoes that carry the disease, malaria, also breed in the pools of stale water.

Malarial mosquito

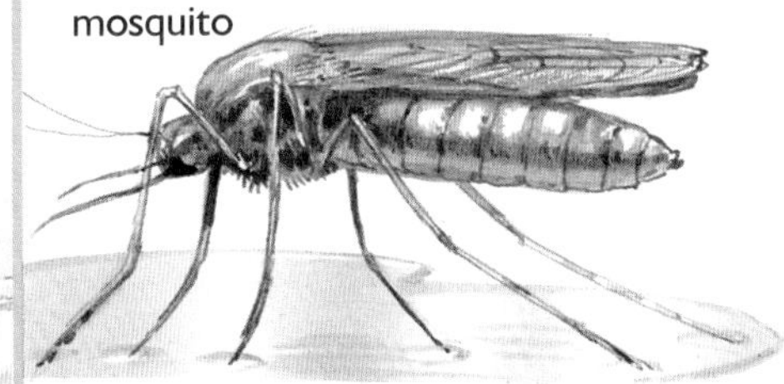

DID YOU KNOW?

At the height of the monsoon season, Cherrapunji in India is the wettest place on Earth. It has an average rainfall of almost 1m (over 3ft) each day.

Irrigation, 325.

Temperate regions

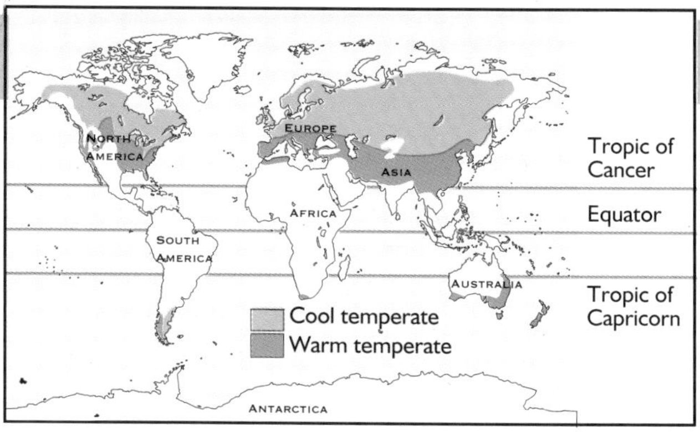

Most places that are between the cold polar regions and the hot Tropics have a temperate climate, which is neither extremely hot nor extremely cold. There are two types of temperate climate. Areas that are further towards the Tropics have a warm temperate climate and areas further towards the Poles have a cool temperate climate.

Temperate seasons

Temperate regions have four seasons: spring, summer, autumn and winter. Cool temperate regions may have frosty winters but summers are mild. Warm temperate regions are closer to the Equator so all the seasons are several degrees hotter. The average temperature in these parts of the world is 27°C (80°F), so the climate is comfortable to live in. Most temperate areas have some rain most months. In winter, cool temperate regions may have snow.

Living in temperate lands

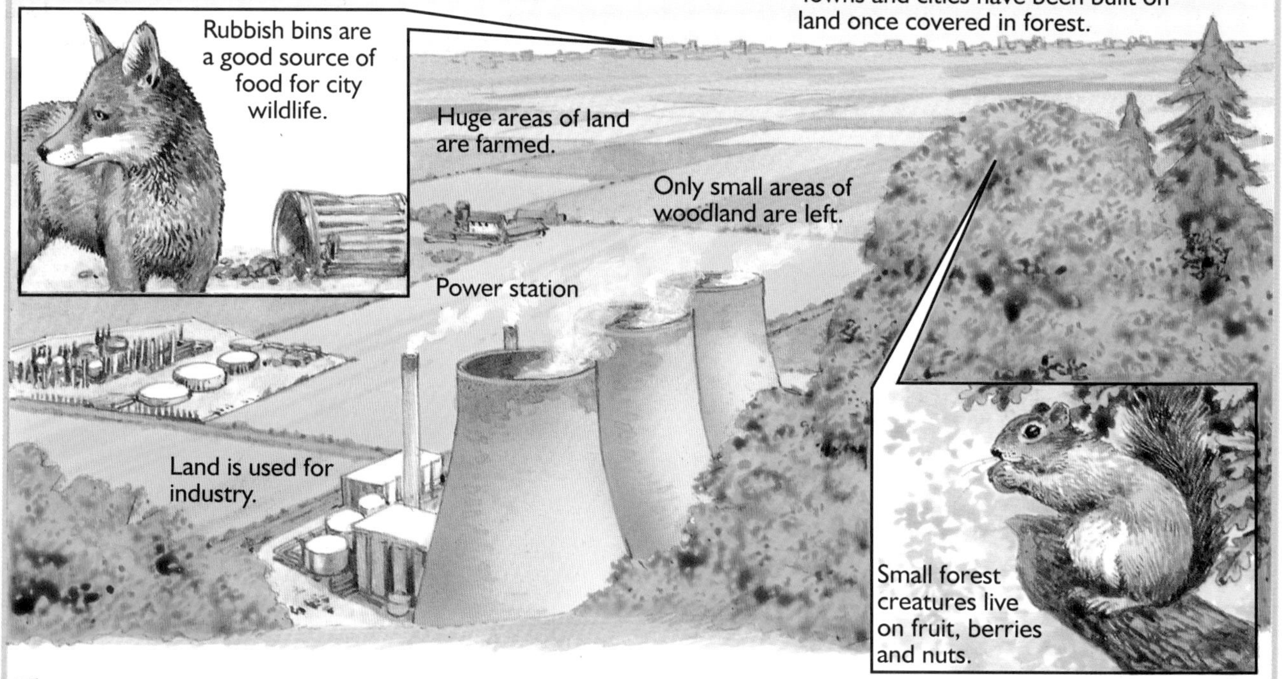
Rubbish bins are a good source of food for city wildlife.
Towns and cities have been built on land once covered in forest.
Huge areas of land are farmed.
Only small areas of woodland are left.
Power station
Land is used for industry.
Small forest creatures live on fruit, berries and nuts.

The temperate climate is ideal for agriculture because the weather is not too hot or too cold and there is regular rain. Huge areas are farmed, such as the Steppes in Russia and Asia and the Prairies in North America, where most of the world's cereals are grown.

Farming has produced wealth, so industries have grown too. As areas have become more developed, natural vegetation such as forests and grasslands have been cleared so that more land can be used for towns and factories.

As land has been farmed or built on, many wild animals have disappeared. For example, herds of bison once grazed on the grasslands and huge numbers of deer and wolves lived in the forests. Now, mainly birds and small rodents such as squirrels are left in the patches of forest that are still standing.

Some temperate creatures have adapted to living in the towns and cities. For example, foxes, many rodents, birds and insects now make their homes among buildings.

Temperate winds

The temperate climate varies between the east and west of a land mass. This is because it is affected by global winds.

Cool temperate regions have Westerly Winds*. The west has more rain than the east because the wind reaches the west coast first, after crossing the ocean. Western areas also have milder winters and cooler summers because the wind is cooled by the ocean in summer and warmed in winter. Inland, the ground becomes very hot in summer and very cold in winter and it heats or cools the wind as it blows to the east.

Warm temperate regions only have Westerly Winds during the winter. In summer, they are affected by Trade Winds*, which blow from east to west. In summer, therefore, these regions have most rain in the east.

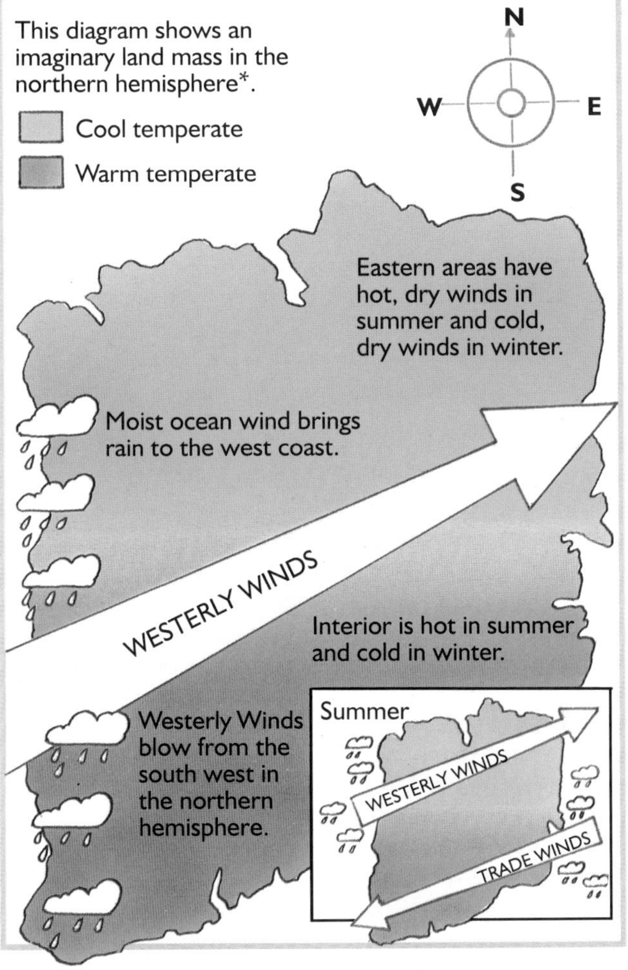
This diagram shows an imaginary land mass in the northern hemisphere*.
Cool temperate
Warm temperate
N
W
E
S
Eastern areas have hot, dry winds in summer and cold, dry winds in winter.
Moist ocean wind brings rain to the west coast.
WESTERLY WINDS
Interior is hot in summer and cold in winter.
Westerly Winds blow from the south west in the northern hemisphere.
Summer
WESTERLY WINDS
TRADE WINDS

Temperate vegetation

Just as the climate varies across the temperate regions, so does the vegetation. Some typical vegetation is shown in the pictures below. The maps, which are of an imaginary land mass in the northern hemisphere, show where each type of vegetation would be found.

In the coldest areas, trees have needle-like leaves because narrow leaves save moisture in winter when water freezes. These trees are called **conifers**. Coniferous forests still exist in Canada, Siberia and Scandinavia.

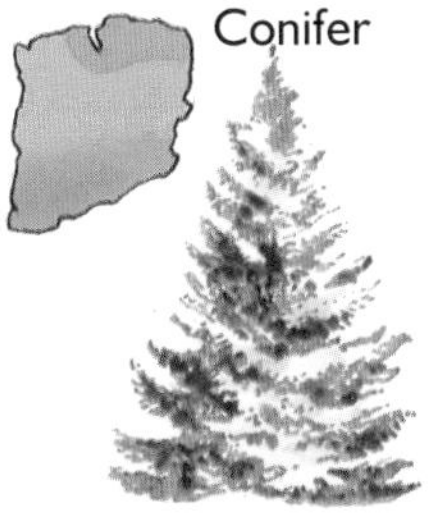
Conifer

Most of the trees that grow in temperate regions lose their leaves in winter when there is not very much sunlight. Trees that lose their leaves are called **deciduous trees**. Oak, beech, chestnut and maple are examples of deciduous trees.

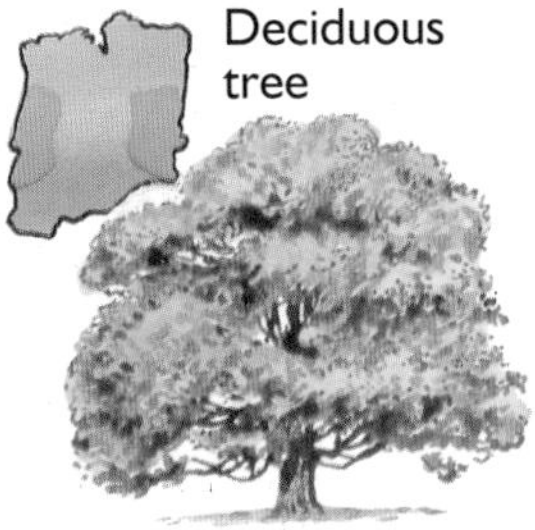
Deciduous tree

In warm temperate regions, the west normally has more vegetation than the east. This is because the west has rain in winter when it is cool so the moisture stays in the soil. Evergreen oak, cypress and cedar trees grow there.

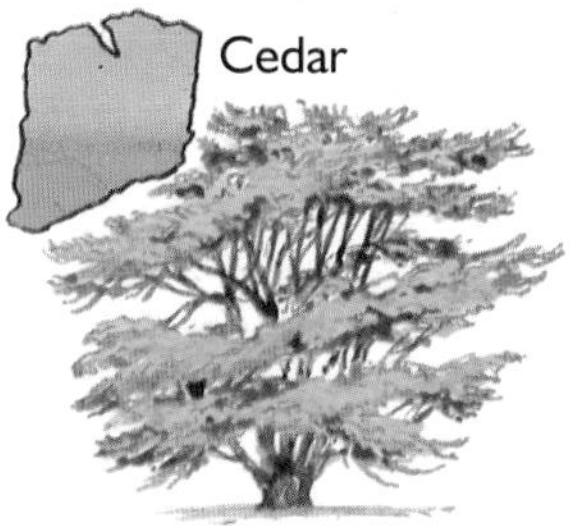
Cedar

The eastern parts of warm temperate regions have most rain in the summer. The heat causes moisture to evaporate* quickly so the soil is dry. Few trees can grow in the dry soil but shrubs can grow easily.

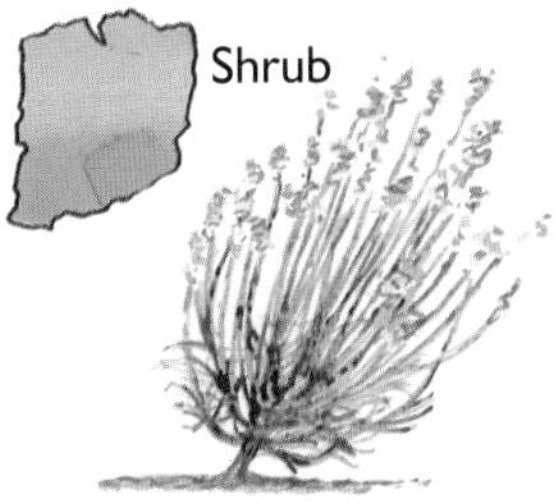
Shrub

In central areas, the climate is too harsh for trees but ideal for grasses. The temperate grasslands are as follows: the Prairies (USA); the Steppes (Russia and Asia); the Veld (South Africa); the Downs (Australia) and the Pampas (South America).

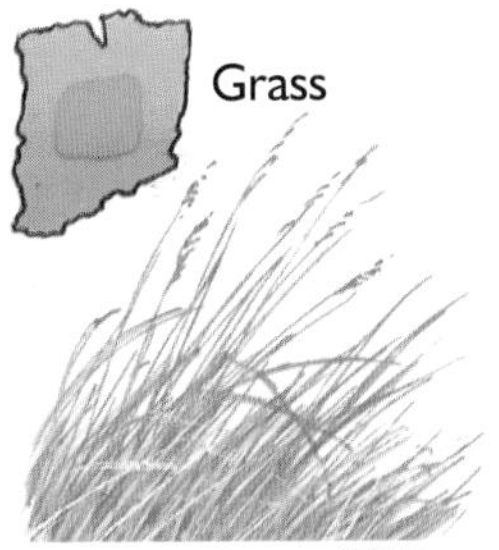
Grass

**Evaporation, 282; Northern hemisphere, 262; Trade Winds, Westerly Winds, 290.*

Polar regions

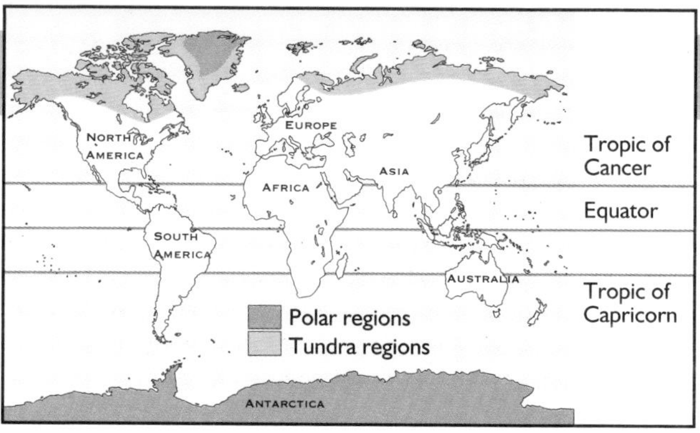

The Sun's rays are weakest at the Poles so they are the coldest parts of the Earth. The region around the North Pole, called the Arctic, is an expanse of frozen ocean. The Antarctic in the south is ice-covered land. These frozen areas are called the **polar ice caps**. The areas of land around the edges of the northern ice cap are called **tundra regions**.

Powerful, icy-cold polar winds blow across Arctic and Antarctic regions throughout the year. Often the wind sweeps up powdery snow from the ground and swirls it around, causing blizzards. Very little new snow or rain falls as it is too cold for moisture to evaporate*.

DID YOU KNOW?

The Antarctic ice cap is 3.7km (2.3 miles) thick in places. If it all melted, the oceans would rise by 55m (180ft).

Life on Antarctica

Very few plants grow on the icy continent of Antarctica so there is no food inland for animals to live on. Therefore, Antarctic animals live in or near the sea. There are many seabirds, such as petrels, albatross, gulls, and terns. Penguins also live on Antarctica.

Penguins are well protected against the cold. Deep feathers trap warmth close to their bodies. Thick skin and a layer of fat give extra insulation. In fact, penguins are so snug that they may over-heat. If they do, they stick out their wings to cool down.

Penguins' feathers grow very close together. The tip of each feather curls inwards to trap heat.

Soft, tufty underfeathers trap warmth close to the penguin's body. Wind and water cannot get through.

Antarctic laboratory

No one lives permanently in Antarctica so it has not been spoilt. Scientists do tests on the atmosphere there because it is so pure.

Antarctic sea life

The sea around Antarctica is home to dolphins, porpoises, whales, seals and other sea creatures. They have a thick layer of oily fat called blubber to keep them warm.

Blubber protects sea creatures from the icy-cold water.

*Evaporation, 282.

The tundra regions

The tundra lands around the northern ice cap stay frozen for nine months of the year. In the summer months (May, June, July), only the surface thaws. Deeper ground stays frozen. This frozen layer is called **permafrost**. Melted snow cannot seep through the permafrost so, in summer, the surface of the tundra lands becomes boggy.

When ice crystals in the land melt, the ground shrinks. When the land freezes again, it expands. Thawing and freezing over and over again cause the surface of the tundra to form angular patterns called **polygons**.

Tundra vegetation such as moss, shrubs, and spreading plants called lichens grow close to the ground to avoid the strong winds.

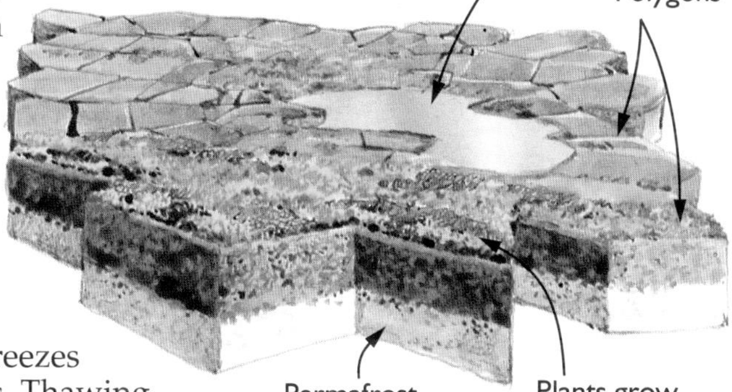
Tundra is boggy in summer.
Polygons
Permafrost
Plants grow close to the ground.

Tundra people

Only a few thousand people live in the tundra regions. The Inuit live in northern Canada, Greenland and Alaska. The Lapps herd reindeer in northern Scandinavia.

Traditionally, the Inuit were hunters and fishermen. They travelled by sledge and built temporary ice shelters called igloos during hunting trips. For warmth, the Inuit wore a double layer of fur clothing. They wore the inner layer with the furry side towards their skin to trap body heat.

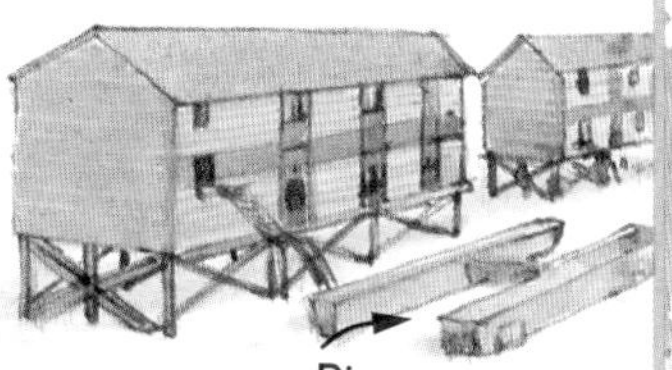
Houses built on stilts.
Pipes

Inuit hunter wearing traditional furs.
Snowmobile

Today, hunters may still wear traditional furs but many Inuit dress in modern clothes. Some have motor-powered snowmobiles and homes made of modern materials. Some homes have electricity and telephones. Heated houses have to be built on stilts so that the permafrost does not thaw. If it did, the ground would give way. Water pipes are insulated and run above ground to stop them from freezing.

Arctic animals

Over thousands of years, land animals have spread north and adapted to living in the Arctic.

Polar bears live on the frozen ocean. Long, waterproof fur covers the soles of their paws to help grip the ice.

Musk oxen

Musk oxen have a fine layer of wool under a thick outer coat. They crowd together so water vapour in their breath forms a cloud to trap heat.

Lemming

Small rodents such as lemmings live in snow-tunnels.

Caribou

Reindeer, also called caribou, travel south in winter. Their huge hoofs do not sink into the boggy ground or soft snow.

Many polar creatures have white fur for camouflage. Some tundra animals, such as ermine, go darker in the summer.

Winter coat
Ermine's summer coat

People of the world

Most experts believe that humans probably evolved (developed gradually) in Africa around two or three million years ago. As time went by, they spread out into other parts of Africa and into Asia and Europe. Their physical features slowly adapted to their surroundings and three main groups developed – **Negros**, **Mongolians** and **Caucasians**. Eventually, people arrived in America and Australasia, where the American Indians and the Australasian Aborigines and Maoris developed.

Though it is still possible to recognize the features of the different groups in modern people, pure types no longer exist. Physical features are mixed together as people migrate around the world and inter-marry.

This map shows how humans spread out all over the world.

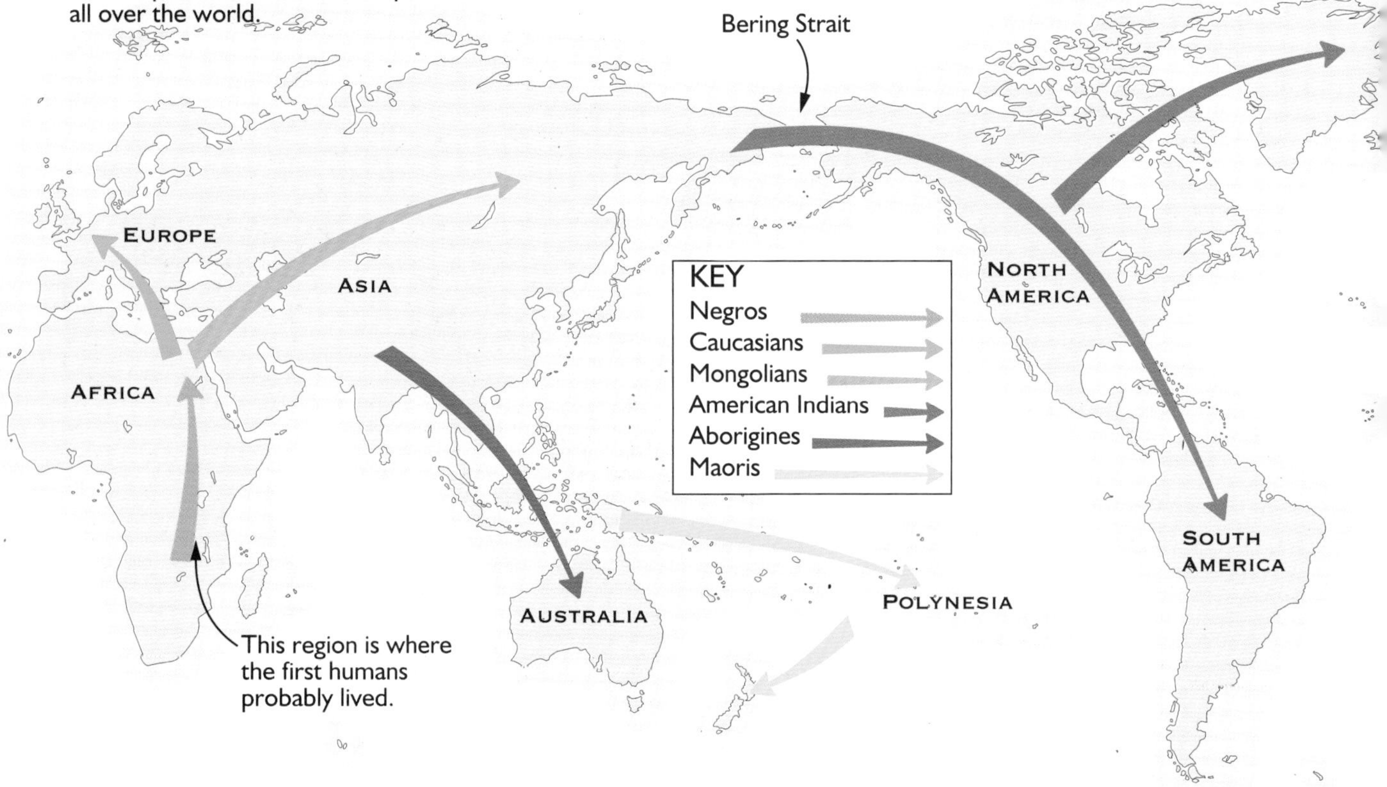
Bering Strait
EUROPE
ASIA
AFRICA
NORTH AMERICA
SOUTH AMERICA
AUSTRALIA
POLYNESIA
KEY
Negros
Caucasians
Mongolians
American Indians
Aborigines
Maoris
This region is where the first humans probably lived.

Negros

Pure Negros evolved in Africa, where it is very hot. Their dark skin and eyes had a lot of pigment for protection against the hot sun. Tightly-curled hair protected their heads from heat. The people of the Sudan, west and central Africa, and the Bantu people are descended from them.

Negro from central Africa

Mongolians

Pure Mongolians came from Asia, where it can be very cold. Their round faces were padded with fat for warmth. Narrow eyes with an extra fold of skin on the eyelids protected them from snow glare and biting winds. The Japanese, Chinese and people of central Asia are their descendants.

Mongolian from China

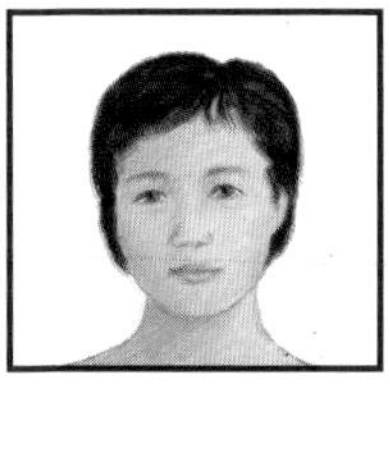

Caucasians

Caucasian people came from Europe, northern Africa, the Middle East and the Indian sub-continent, where the climate is not as hot as places nearer the Equator. Caucasians had pale skin and eyes because they did not need so much pigment to protect them as those people living in hotter places.

Caucasian from Scandinavia

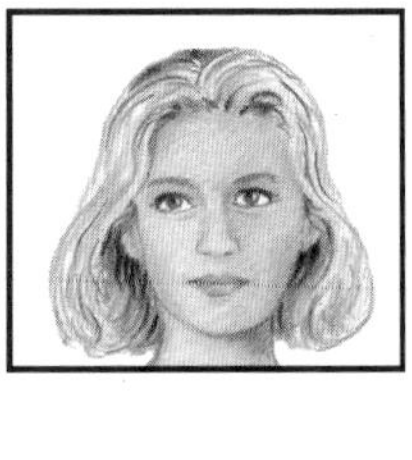

People in America

The first people to live in America were the ancestors of the American Indians. Around 35,000 years ago, they walked from Asia across the Bering Strait, which was then land, forming a bridge between Asia and America. Gradually, people spread out from the north into South America. American Indians are descended from Asian people, so they have Mongolian features.

North American Indian

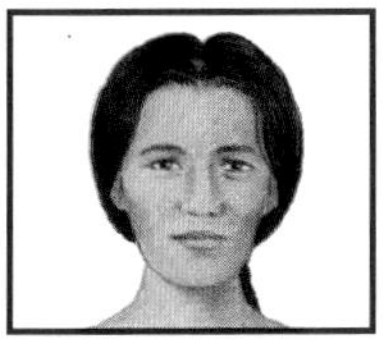

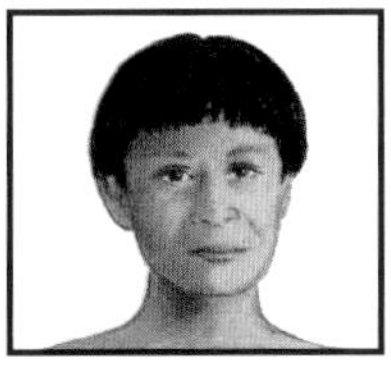

South American Indian

People in Australasia

No one lived in Australia until around 38,000 years ago, when Caucasian people arrived there. They either sailed in canoes or walked from Malaysia, which may then have been a bridge of land between Asia and Australia. These people were the ancestors of the Australian Aborigines. In New Zealand, the Maoris descended from Polynesians, who arrived 1,200 years ago.

Aborigine

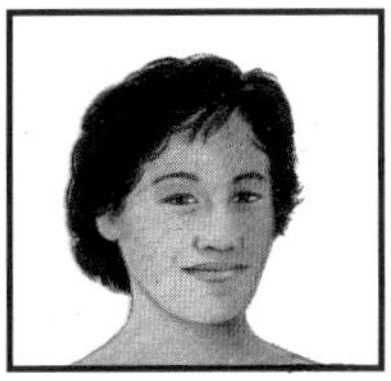

Maori

Merging cultures

People around the world are different from one another partly because of their looks, but also because of their religion, language, food, music and customs. All of these things put together make up a people's **culture**.

People have always travelled in search of new places in which to settle. Today, many countries have different groups of people living in them. Cultures merge as new people bring customs with them from their old country, but also adopt the culture of their new country.

You can try food from different cultures in the restaurants of most cities.

Endangered peoples

When people settle in new areas, they may disrupt the native way of life. Natives may lose the land off which they live, and then have to adopt the new people's culture. The Inuit, the North and South American Indians and the Aborigines have all suffered in this way. Many of those who have lost their homelands now live in smaller, protected areas called **reservations**.

Rich world, poor world

Over many years, a country gradually develops as its industry improves and its people raise their standard of living.

The countries of the world are at different stages of **development** and there is a great difference between the most and the least developed. Poorer countries are known as **less developed countries** and richer countries are known as **more developed countries**.

In recent years, some countries which were less developed countries have set up modern industries and have become richer. These countries are called **newly industrialized countries**.

This map shows how much of the world is poor. On the map, the areas of the continents are accurate in relation to each other.

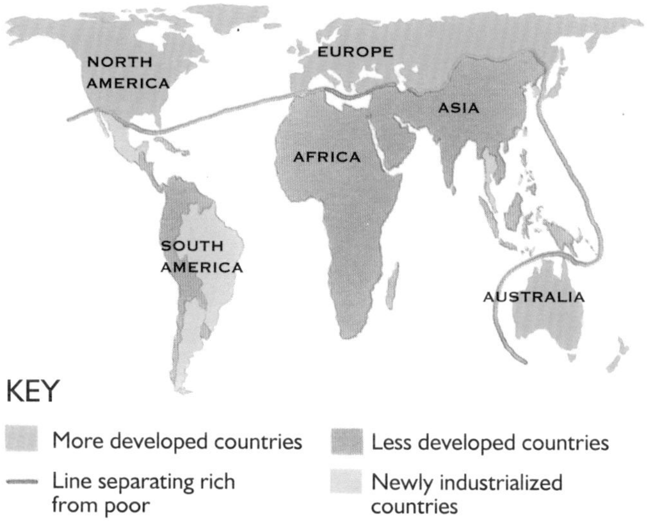

How is development measured?

People's daily lives are affected by how much money their country has to spend. So, looking at facts about a country and its people shows how developed it has become.

The bar chart on the right compares some facts about more developed countries and less developed countries. It shows that, although less developed countries have a greater share of the world's population, they produce less food, do less trade, use less energy, and manufacture fewer goods. They also spend far less on schools and hospitals.

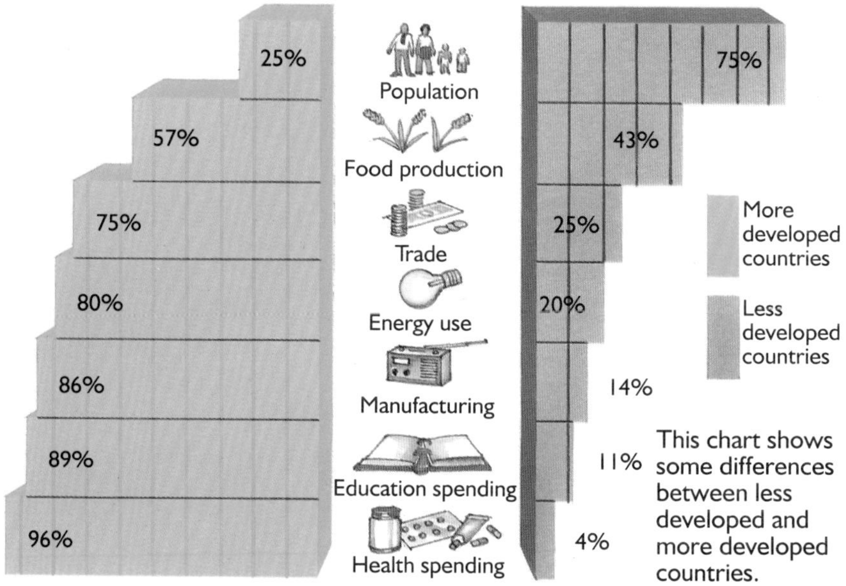
25%
Population
75%
57%
Food production
43%
75%
Trade
25%
80%
Energy use
20%
86%
Manufacturing
14%
89%
Education spending
11%
96%
Health spending
4%
More developed countries
Less developed countries

This chart shows some differences between less developed and more developed countries.

Life in a poor country

Life in poor countries is often hard. Children spend less time at school and so people are less able to read and write. They may spend much time looking for basic items, such as fuel and water. Water may be polluted and there may not be enough food, which causes malnutrition. There may be few hospitals and high death rates.

The flow chart on the right shows how people in poor countries may easily become trapped in a cycle of poverty and disease.

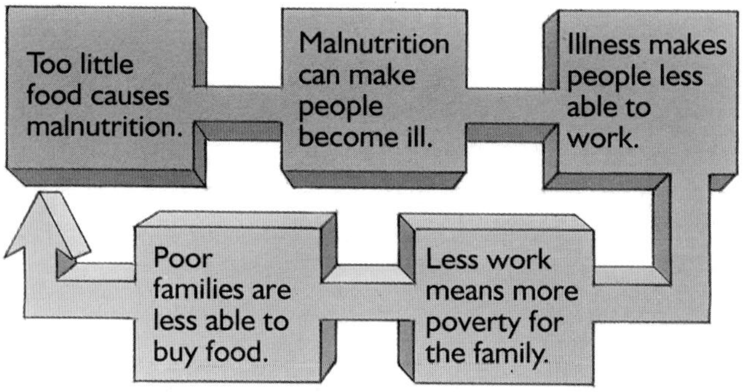
Too little food causes malnutrition.
Malnutrition can make people become ill.
Illness makes people less able to work.
Less work means more poverty for the family.
Poor families are less able to buy food.

Why are some countries poor?

Countries are poor for different reasons. Some have few resources such as minerals and crops. In others, there may be mountains, deserts or jungles, or the area may be affected by pests such as locusts, and hazards such as floods. Elsewhere, the climate may be too cold, too hot or too dry. All these things make farming, industry and transport difficult and slow development down.

There are other reasons to do with politics and trade why some countries are poor. Until the mid 1900s, European countries governed over regions, called colonies, around the world. The colonies were used to make Europe rich by providing minerals for industry and food for Europe's growing population. However, the colonies gained little profit. Even today, many industries in poor countries are owned by people from rich countries, who take the profits away from the industry.

This picture shows an example of trade between rich and poorer nations and how the rich ones may make a bigger profit.

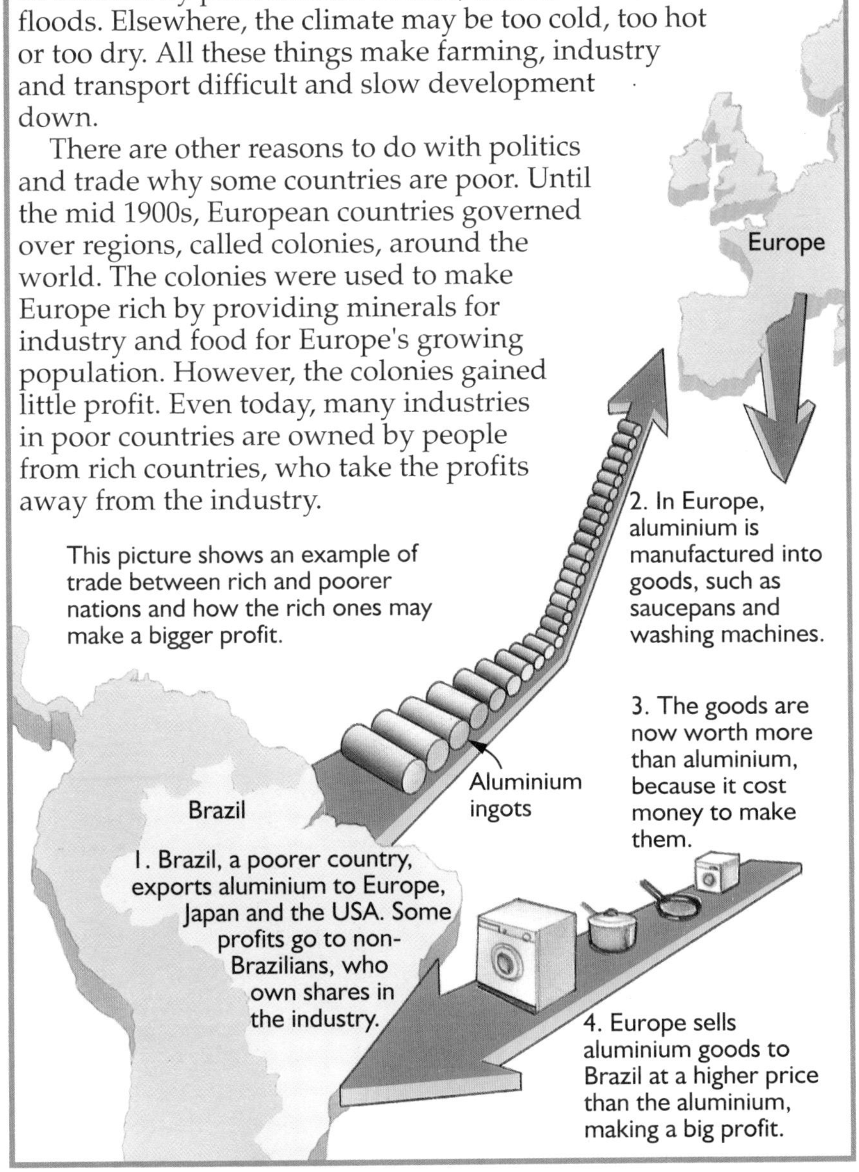

Europe
2. In Europe, aluminium is manufactured into goods, such as saucepans and washing machines.
3. The goods are now worth more than aluminium, because it cost money to make them.
Aluminium ingots
Brazil
1. Brazil, a poorer country, exports aluminium to Europe, Japan and the USA. Some profits go to non-Brazilians, who own shares in the industry.
4. Europe sells aluminium goods to Brazil at a higher price than the aluminium, making a big profit.

Aid from the rich

Rich countries give aid to help poor countries develop. Aid comes from governments, banks and aid agencies. They give or loan money for big projects, such as building a new dam.

Food and supplies are given to people after disasters, such as floods. This is called **short-term aid** because it helps people who are in immediate need.

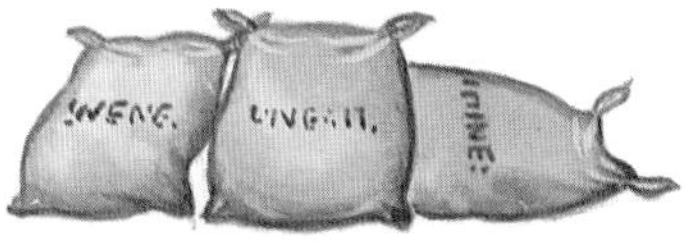

Technology is provided by foreign engineers and teachers who work with local people. This is **long-term aid** because people benefit in the future.

Not all aid is good. People may give the wrong aid, such as machines with no spare parts. Or, aid may not be shared out and may not reach those who need it. Some governments lend aid rather than give it, and then only if poor nations promise to buy goods from them.

DID YOU KNOW?

Millions of people around the world become poor because they have to leave their homes and live in a strange city or even another country. These people are called **refugees**. Some become refugees because they cannot find work and others lose their homes in disasters or wars. Many people become refugees because they disagree with their government and are forced to leave their country and seek a new life elsewhere.

Population

A population is the number of people who live in a particular place. The population of the world is about 5 billion (5,000 million). By the year 2025, it will have risen to around 8.5 billion. This means that the world will have to support the needs of over one and a half times as many people as there are today.

The speed at which a population grows is called the **growth rate**. In the past, the world's population grew steadily but slowly. People have estimated that in the 17th century the world's population was about 500 million. Since then, the growth rate has gone up rapidly. The graph shows how the population is changing and how the change will continue.

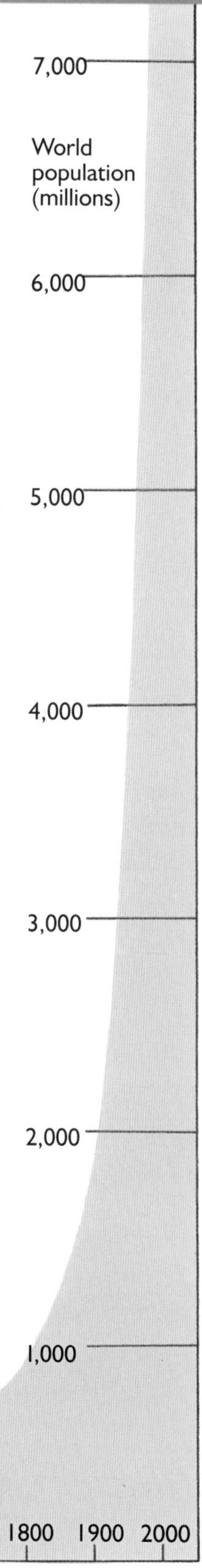

World population (millions)
7,000
6,000
5,000
4,000
3,000
2,000
1,000
Date (year)
1200
1300
1400
1500
1600
1700
1800
1900
2000

Population study

Many countries carry out a census once every ten years or so, when everyone fills in a questionnaire about themselves. This helps the government find out how many people live in the country and what their needs will be in the future. People who study population are called **demographers**.

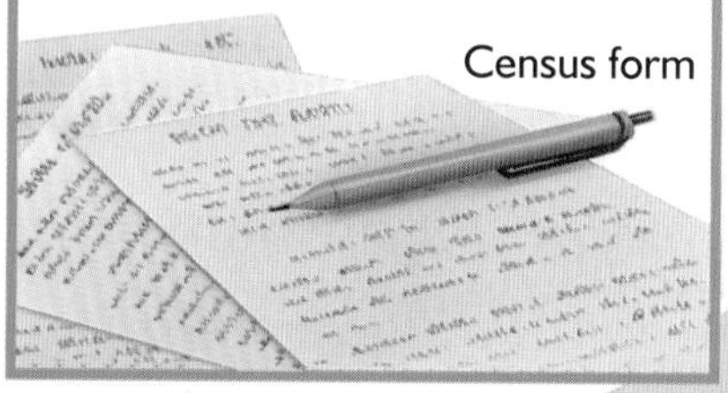

Census form

Population change

The population changes depending on how many people are born and how many die each year. In Australia, around 15 people are born and 7 people die for every thousand people in the population, so its population is growing. These are called the **birth** and **death rates**.

A country's birth and death rates are affected by its standard of health care. If doctors and drugs are available, more babies survive and adults live longer.

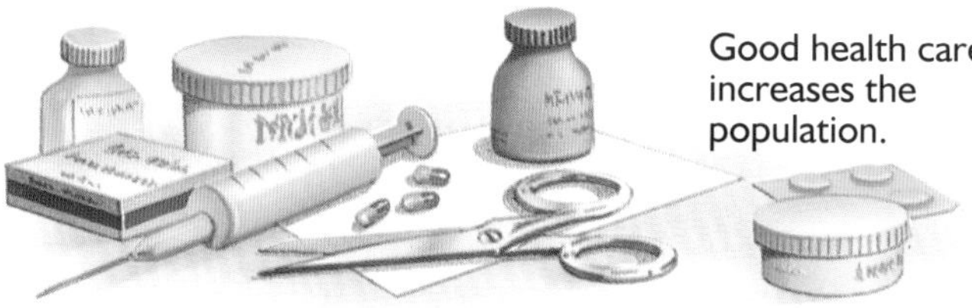

Good health care increases the population.

Family planning also affects the population of a country because it allows couples to choose when to have children and also how many children to have.

Family planning controls the population.

Population can be drastically affected if there is a war or a natural disaster. Many people may die during war, famine, an earthquake, a volcanic eruption or a flood.

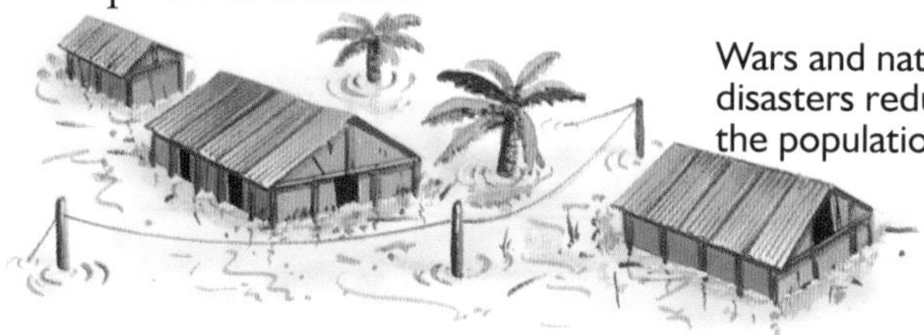

Wars and natural disasters reduce the population.

People leaving a country are called **emigrants**. Those settling in a new country are called **immigrants**. Population changes according to how many immigrants and emigrants there are.

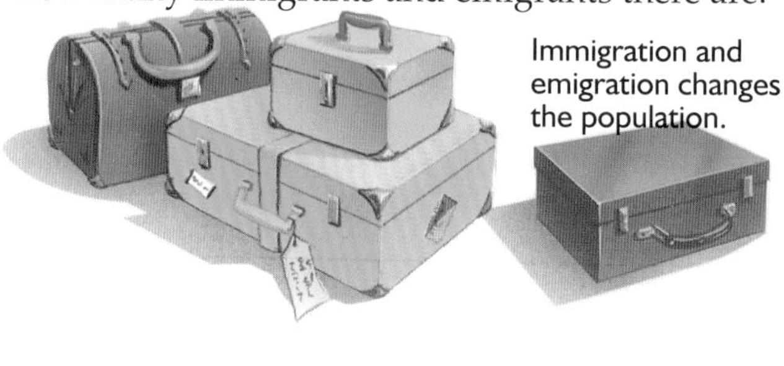

Immigration and emigration changes the population.

The growing world

The populations of different countries change at different rates. In more developed countries*, such as Japan or the USA, the growth rate is very low. Families are not very large and people live longer because they have good health care.

However, in less developed countries*, the population is growing much faster. It is in these countries that over 90% of the world's population growth is happening. In some of these countries, there is not enough money and food to care for millions of extra people.

In the past, people in poorer countries needed large families to help earn a living, and as some children were expected to die, couples did not want to limit the number of babies they had.

In recent years, health care has improved in these countries, so more people are living longer and more babies are surviving. However, many people are still having large families, so the population is rising fast. These days, couples are encouraged to have fewer children so the population growth will slow down.

This map shows how the population is changing in different areas around the world.

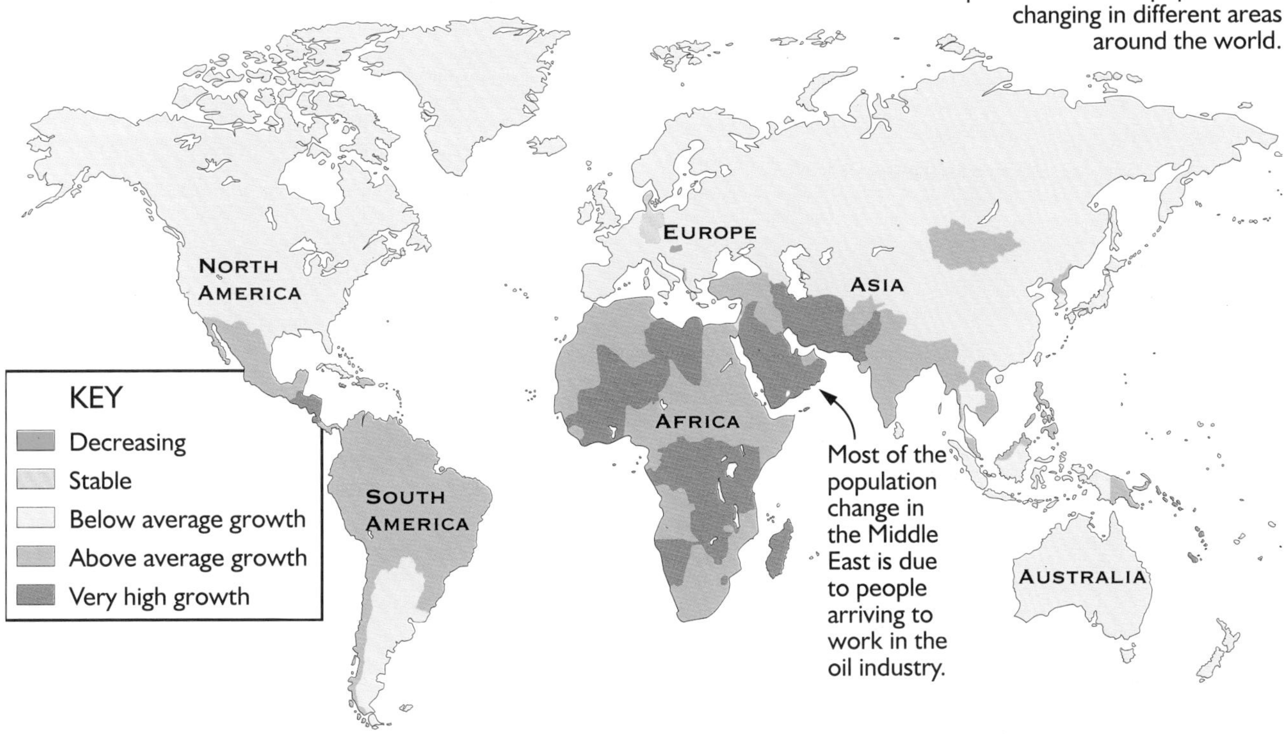

North America
Europe
Asia
Africa
South America
Australia
KEY
Decreasing
Stable
Below average growth
Above average growth
Very high growth
Most of the population change in the Middle East is due to people arriving to work in the oil industry.

DID YOU KNOW?

Each year, the world population grows by over 90 million. This means that it increases by almost three people every second. In the time that it takes you to read this paragraph, there will be enough extra people in the world to make at least two soccer teams.

One-child families

There are 1.2 billion people in China, which is more than in any other country. To help control the population growth, the government introduced a law to make couples have no more than one child. If this law succeeds, brothers, sisters, uncles, aunts and cousins may become rare in China in the future. This Chinese government poster reminds people that they should have only one child.

*Less developed and more developed countries, 312.

Where we live

There are many reasons why people live where they do today and why people settled in those places originally. When people first looked for permanent places to settle long ago, they had to think about what they needed, such as food, water, warmth and shelter. They also had to be able to defend themselves. These maps show how settlers may have chosen a place to build their homes.

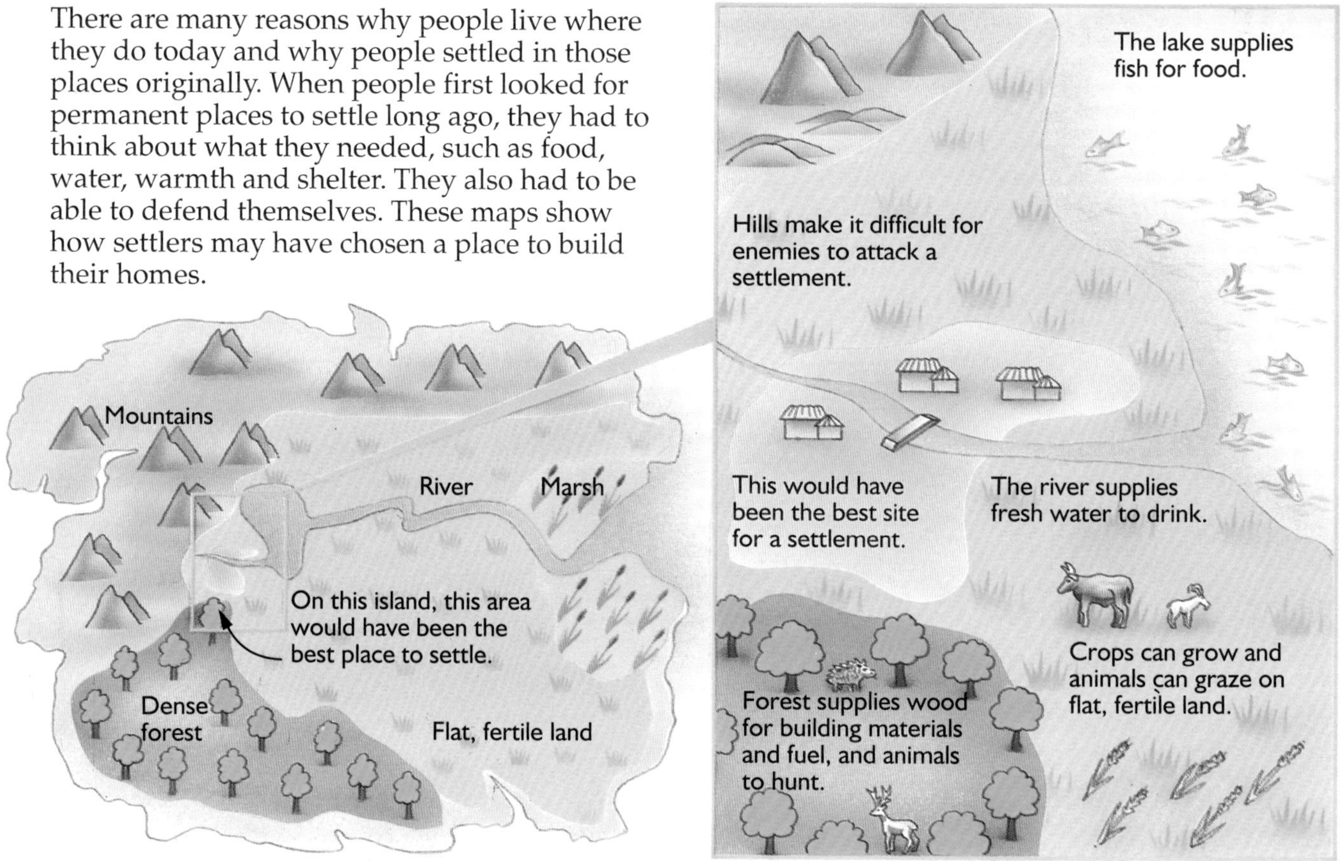

Mountains
River
Marsh
On this island, this area would have been the best place to settle.
Dense forest
Flat, fertile land
The lake supplies fish for food.
Hills make it difficult for enemies to attack a settlement.
This would have been the best site for a settlement.
The river supplies fresh water to drink.
Crops can grow and animals can graze on flat, fertile land.
Forest supplies wood for building materials and fuel, and animals to hunt.

First, settlers had to look around to make sure that the area could provide food, water and materials for building and clothes. Early settlements were usually near rivers or springs, and on land where people could raise animals and grow crops.

After deciding on a good area, people had to choose the exact site for their settlement very carefully. They preferred to live in places that were easy to defend, such as hillsides. They also chose places that were protected from floods or bad weather.

Temporary settlements

The first settlements were probably just campsites. People chose a spot near food and water and then built temporary shelters out of materials found close by, such as leaves, branches and animal skins. When food ran out, they moved on to a new spot, leaving their shelters behind. Some groups of people, such as the Maasai of East Africa, still live in temporary settlements.

In the dry season, the Maasai move their cattle on to new grazing land, leaving villages empty.
The Maasai and their cattle come back to their villages in the rainy season.

Hamlets to megacities

Today, people live in all kinds of areas and in settlements of different sizes. They also travel around a lot more. This is because they can obtain food, water and materials wherever they live, due to modern technology. Where people live now depends on where they work, how they travel there and what services* they need nearby.

Hamlet
Minor road
Farms
Houses

Hamlets are the smallest kind of settlement. They may be just a collection of buildings, perhaps centred around a few farms. There may not even be a shop there.

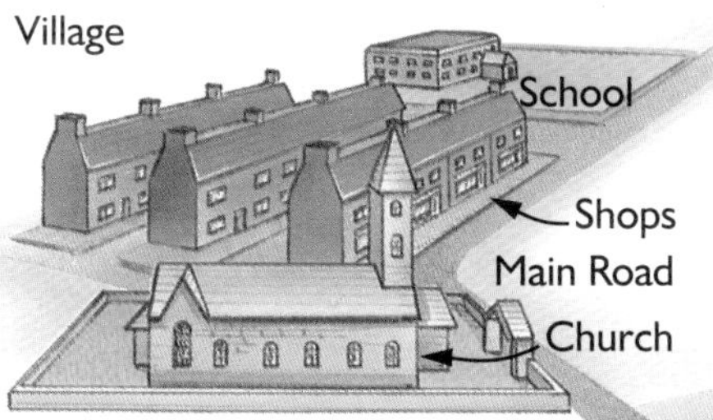

Village
School
Shops
Main Road
Church

Villages may centre around farms, with several hundred people living there. They may have a few shops and a place of worship. Large villages may have a school.

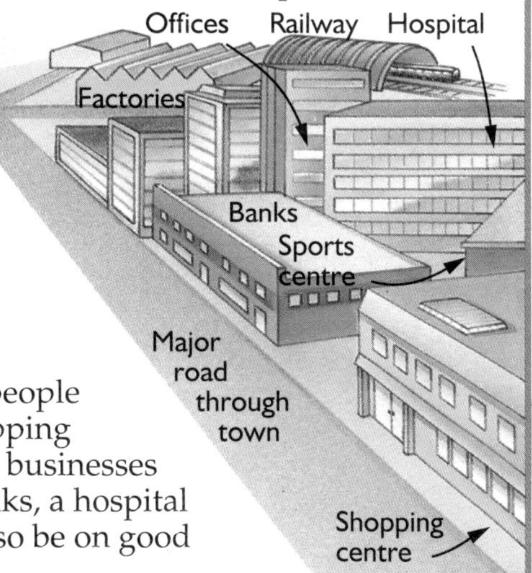

Offices
Railway
Hospital
Factories
Banks
Sports centre
Major road through town
Shopping centre

Towns may have thousands of people living in them. They have a shopping centre or market, and also many businesses and special services, such as banks, a hospital and a sports centre. They will also be on good transport routes.

Cities are the centre of local government, business, culture* and religion. Each city has different zones (areas), such as residential areas with houses, industrial areas with factories and commercial areas with shops and banks. Cities with populations of over a million are called **megacities**. Mexico City is the largest, with nearly 20 million people.

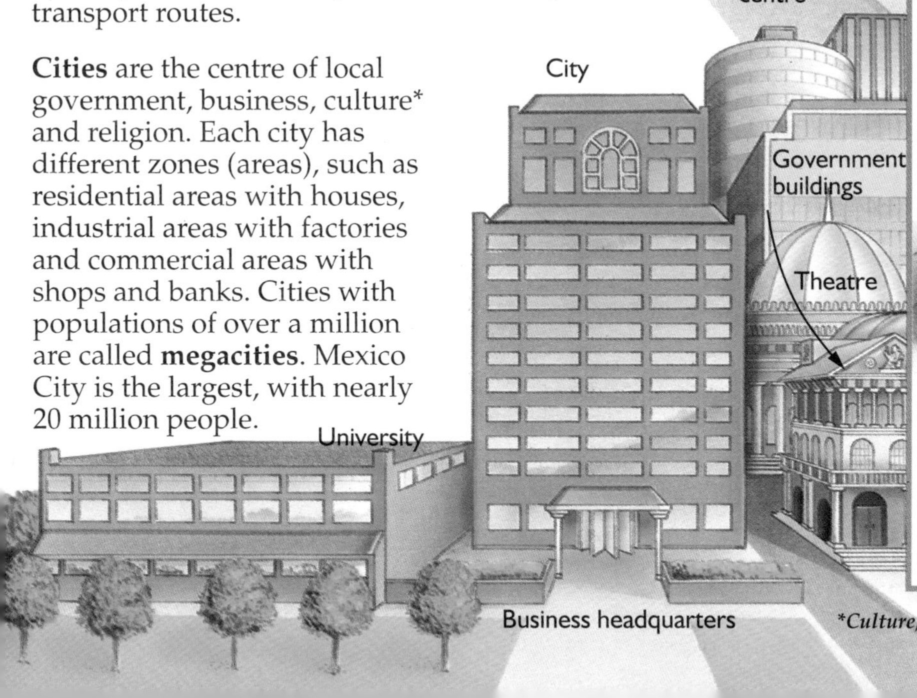

City
Government buildings
Theatre
University
Business headquarters

Traditional homes

Wherever people settled in the world, they had to use local materials to build shelters. They had to design their homes to suit their environment and climate. Here are some examples of traditional homes which developed in certain areas.

Igloo

The Inuit, who live in the Arctic, needed shelter from the cold, but had few materials to build with. So they built igloos from blocks of ice.

Log cabin

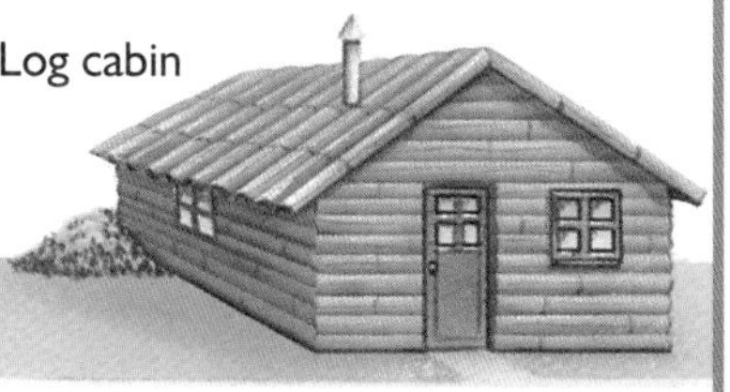

In northern Europe, people were surrounded by plenty of wood, so they built log cabins. The roofs were steep so that heavy snow would slide off in winter.

Tent

In hot desert regions, people had to move around to find water and food. Nomads* made tents to shelter under, which could be packed away and moved.

*Culture, 311; Nomads, 299; Services, 334.

Villages and towns

Just over half of the world's population lives in villages in **rural** areas (the countryside). Most of these people live in less developed countries* in Africa and Asia and earn their living by farming. However, many people are leaving the traditional villages and going to work in **urban** areas (towns). This map shows where most people live in rural areas and where most people live in urban areas. Areas with a mostly urban population are not always crowded with people. The towns in those areas may be quite spread out.

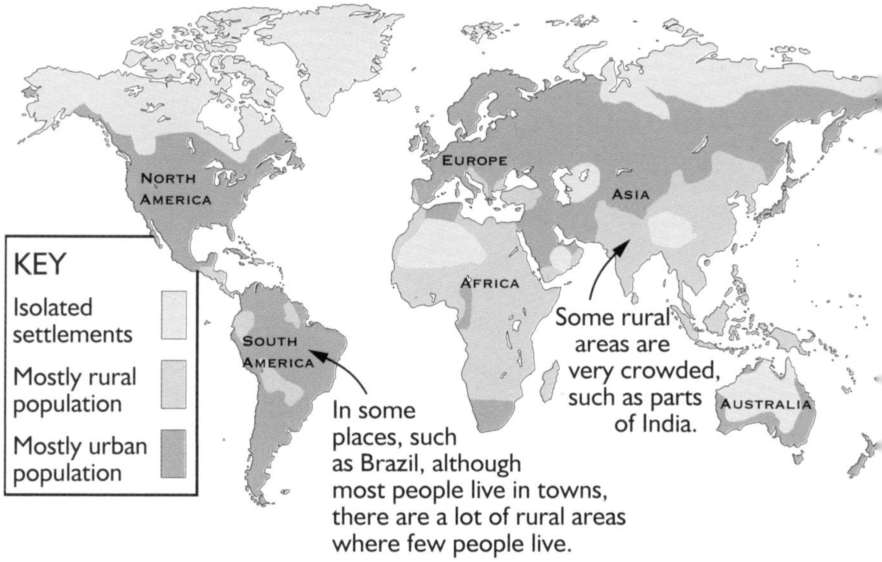
NORTH AMERICA
EUROPE
ASIA
AFRICA
SOUTH AMERICA
AUSTRALIA
KEY
Isolated settlements
Mostly rural population
Mostly urban population
Some rural areas are very crowded, such as parts of India.
In some places, such as Brazil, although most people live in towns, there are a lot of rural areas where few people live.

How towns grow

Originally, people built their homes close together in villages for companionship and safety. Living close together meant that they could also share services*. Over a long period of time, many villages grow into towns. There is usually a good reason why this growth happens. This picture shows some examples.

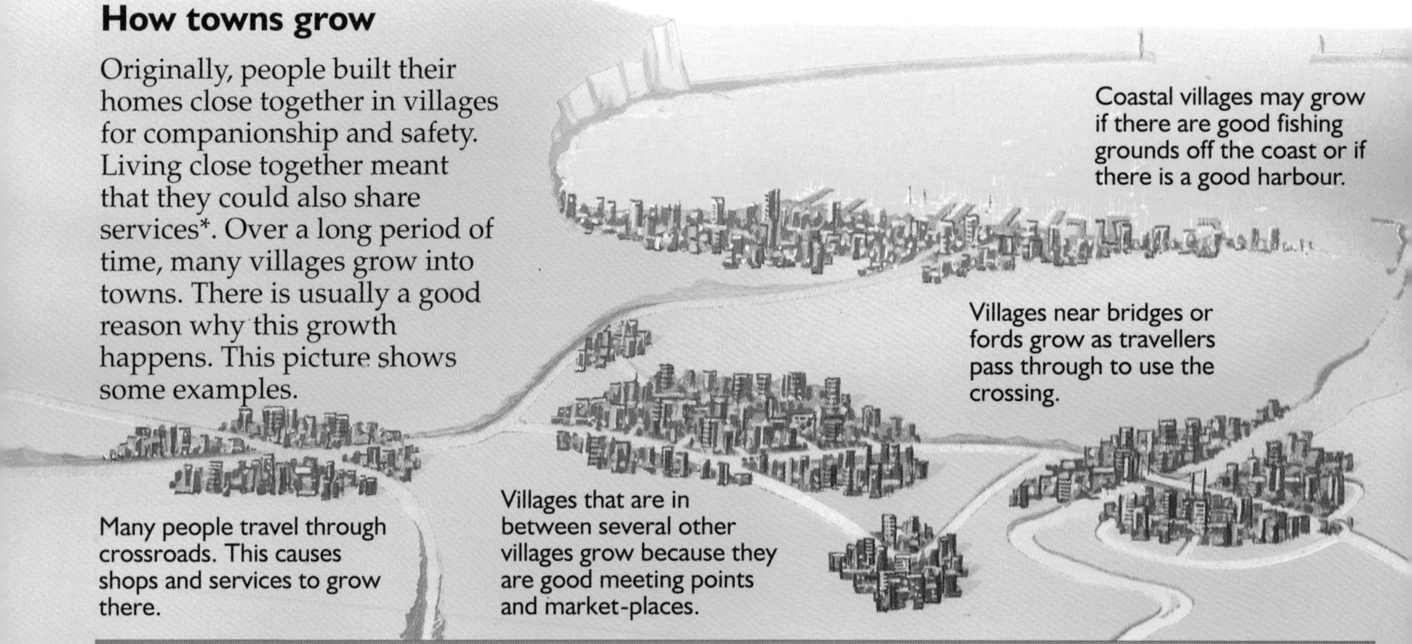
Coastal villages may grow if there are good fishing grounds off the coast or if there is a good harbour.
Villages near bridges or fords grow as travellers pass through to use the crossing.
Many people travel through crossroads. This causes shops and services to grow there.
Villages that are in between several other villages grow because they are good meeting points and market-places.

Village patterns

In different parts of the world, village houses and other buildings are clustered together in different patterns.

In parts of Africa, houses are arranged around a circular space called a kraal. Cattle are kept inside the kraal at night.

Kraal

Village on high strip of land

In lowland areas, like some parts of Europe, houses may be built on the higher strips of land, which are safe from floods. The low-lying land is then used for farming.

Closely-packed village

In places that have little good farmland available, like Japan, village buildings may be packed closely together. This saves more space for farming.

Less developed countries, 312; Services, 334.

Town planning

Old towns may become too cramped for modern traffic and for the amount of people who live and work in them. To keep towns up-to-date, people called **town planners** decide what changes need to be made.

Every town has its own needs, which town planners have to consider. For example, a holiday resort needs hotels where people can stay. A university town needs cheap housing for students to rent.

Towns may be surrounded by an area of countryside, called a **green belt**. Planners make sure that the town does not expand into the green belt. They also make sure that valuable, old buildings are preserved.

If there is no room for a town to expand, and space is needed for new industries and homes, governments may build brand-new towns. These are called **satellite towns** because they are built in the surroundings of old cities.

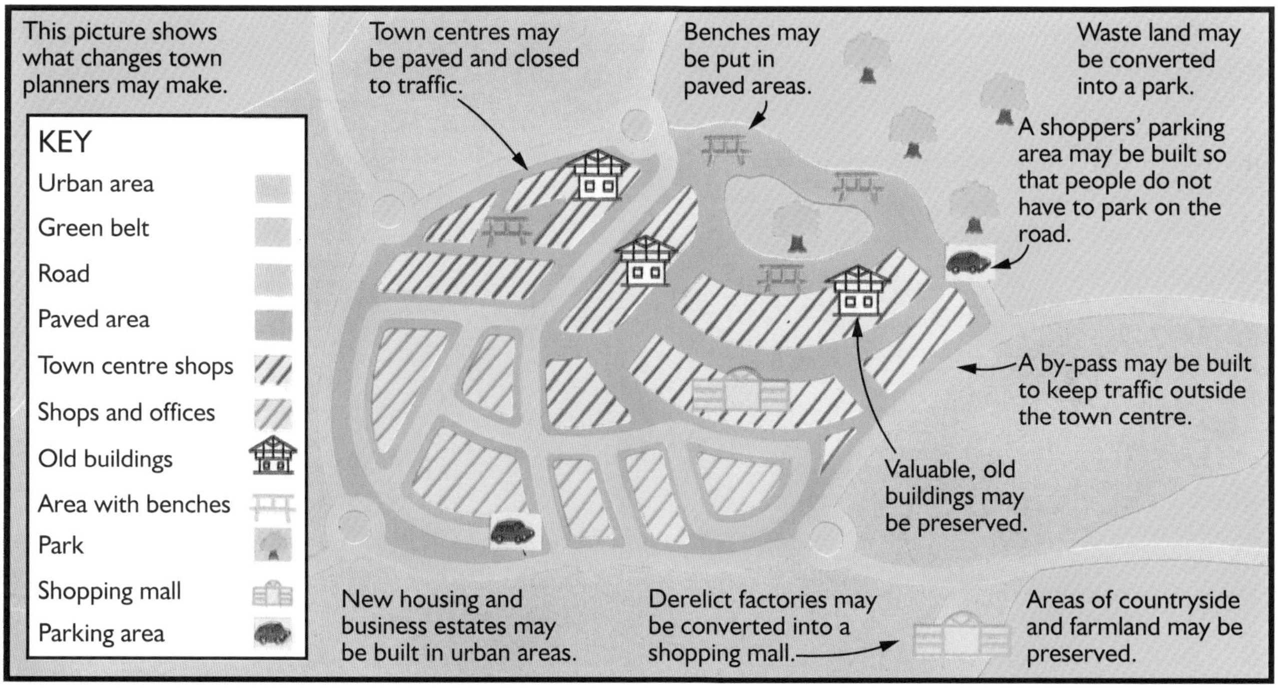
This picture shows what changes town planners may make.
KEY
Urban area
Green belt
Road
Paved area
Town centre shops
Shops and offices
Old buildings
Area with benches
Park
Shopping mall
Parking area
Town centres may be paved and closed to traffic.
Benches may be put in paved areas.
Waste land may be converted into a park.
A shoppers' parking area may be built so that people do not have to park on the road.
A by-pass may be built to keep traffic outside the town centre.
Valuable, old buildings may be preserved.
New housing and business estates may be built in urban areas.
Derelict factories may be converted into a shopping mall.
Areas of countryside and farmland may be preserved.

Boom towns and ghost towns

If a town becomes rich fast, it is called a **boom town**. Many new people and industries may arrive suddenly. If an area becomes poor, towns which were busy can become deserted. These are called **ghost towns**.

For example, when gold was discovered in the USA in 1848, towns grew up all over California. When the mines ran out of gold, trade stopped. Many of the once prosperous towns were abandoned.

Boom town
Ghost town

DID YOU KNOW?

Some towns do not have a good geographical reason for growing. Clermont-Ferrand in France became a wealthy tyre-producing town, even though it is a long way from other manufacturing areas and it is inland, away from its sources of raw materials*. However, Mr Michelin, who founded the tyre-producing business, chose Clermont-Ferrand because he happened to live there.

**Raw materials, 332.*

Cities

In Greek and Roman times, the population of a city was only a few thousand. Cities did not become much bigger until the Industrial Revolution in the 1800s, when transport and industry suddenly expanded. Now, many cities have over a million people living in them.

A city develops when it becomes a focus for its region and outgrows other towns. Many cities grow on major transport routes, where people meet to trade. The city then becomes a centre of business and government. Chicago, in the USA, grew in the mid 1800s because it became the centre of transport, services* and industry between the new farms on the prairies and the old eastern cities, such as Boston, New York and Washington.

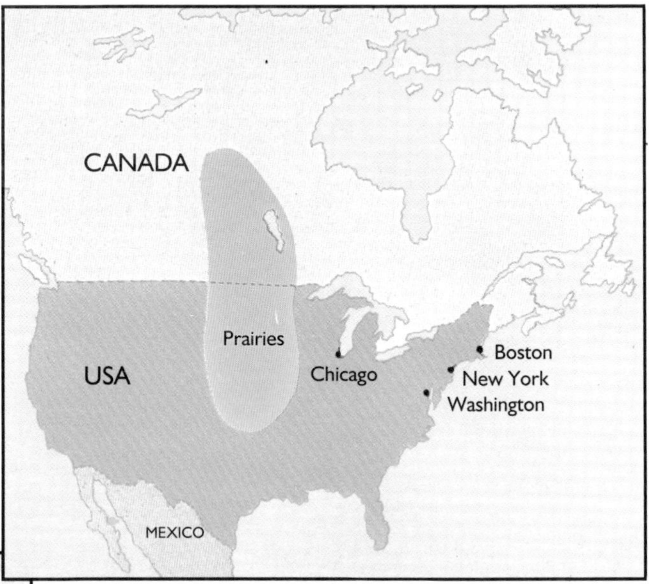

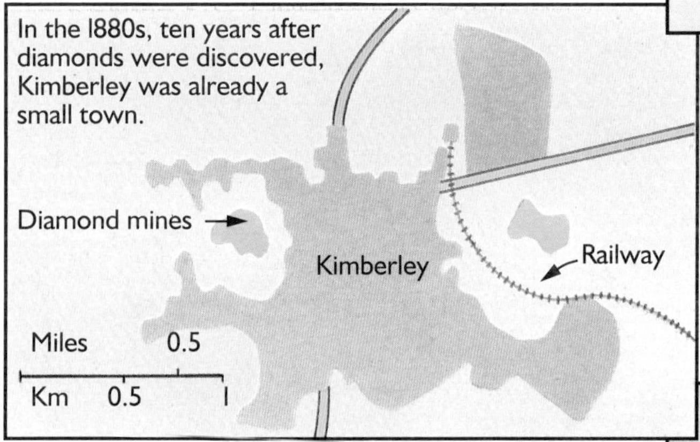
Diamond mines
Kimberley
Railway
Miles 0.5
Km 0.5 1

In the 1880s, ten years after diamonds were discovered, Kimberley was already a small town.

Other cities grow because they are educational or religious centres, or because they have important resources and industry there. These things bring people into an area to work or to visit. In South Africa, the town of Kimberley was built after diamonds were discovered there. There was no settlement at all beforehand, but the diamond industry has made it a busy city.

Transport improvements help cities spread out. If a new transport route is built, more people can live outside the city centre and travel in to work. New residential areas, called **suburbs**, are then built around the city. London, in the UK, spread out along transport routes in the early 1900s.

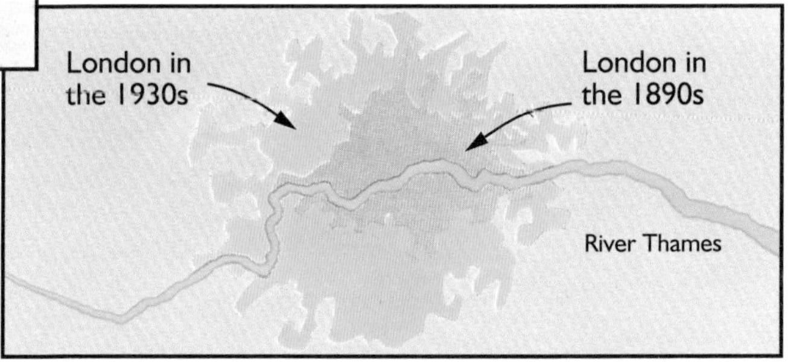
London in the 1930s
London in the 1890s
River Thames

Capital cities

Every nation has a capital city, which is an important city for that country. It is the place of government and may also be the focus of the country's culture*.

Some countries have replaced their old capitals by building new, modern cities. They are designed to be practical and spacious. Canberra in Australia, Islamabad in Pakistan and Brasilia in Brazil are all new capitals.

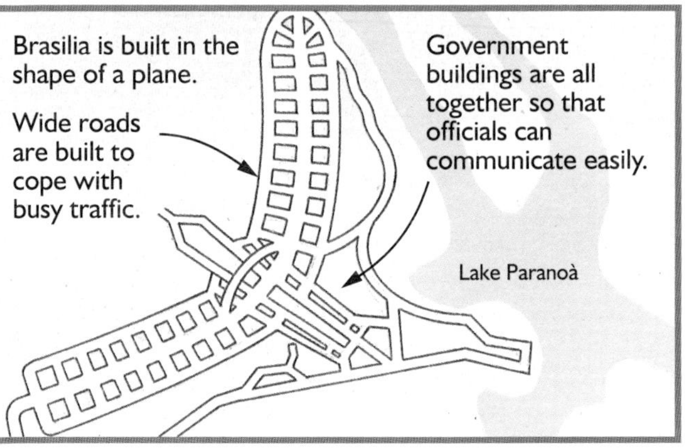
Brasilia is built in the shape of a plane.
Wide roads are built to cope with busy traffic.
Government buildings are all together so that officials can communicate easily.
Lake Paranoà

 *Culture, 311; Services, 334.

City zones

Cities can be divided into different areas or zones. Each zone has its own particular purpose. For example, it may be mostly residential, with houses, or it may be mostly industrial, with factories. Here are some main areas which you can see in most cities.

The middle of the city is where most shops, banks and offices are. This area is called the **central business district (CBD)**. Most of the trade and financial business goes on there. People travel into the CBD to work.

Around the CBD, there may be industrial zones of older industries. Circled around these may be residential areas. The older areas near the middle may decay and become redeveloped into houses, shops or offices.

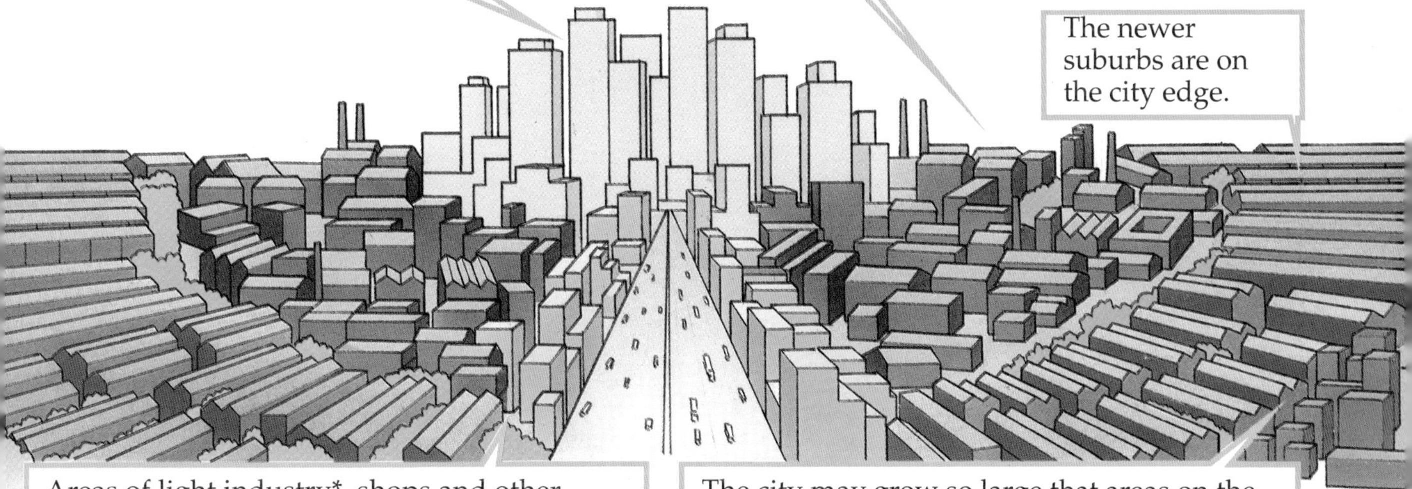
The newer suburbs are on the city edge.

Areas of light industry*, shops and other businesses may line the major roads leading out of the city.

The city may grow so large that areas on the edge become centres too, with their own zone patterns.

Giant cities

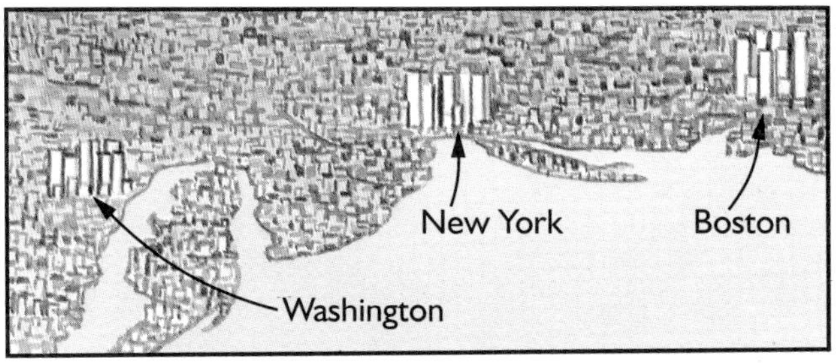
New York
Boston
Washington

As cities grow, they spread out into the countryside. Eventually, towns and cities may merge and become one huge urban area, called a **conurbation**. The biggest urban area in the world is in the USA. The towns almost join for 625km (390 miles) from Boston, through New York, to Washington. Some people call this area Bosnywash, from the first letters in each name.

Poverty in the city

All around the world, people move to cities to find work. However, they may have nowhere to live when they arrive. Some of these newcomers build makeshift homes. In less developed countries*, many cities are surrounded by areas of makeshift homes called **shanty towns**. These are very crowded and may have no clean water or power supply.

In shanty towns, people make homes from whatever they can find, such as scrap metal and cardboard.

Less developed countries, 312; Light industry, 332.

Farming around the world

Most of the food we eat, and some of the things we use, come from farms. Different types of goods come from different places around the world, because each area has its own particular environment where certain plants and animals like to live.

Farmers need to grow crops and raise animals that are suited to their land. They need to think about what the climate is like, what type of soil there is and how hilly the land is. In the picture are some of the questions they need to ask themselves.

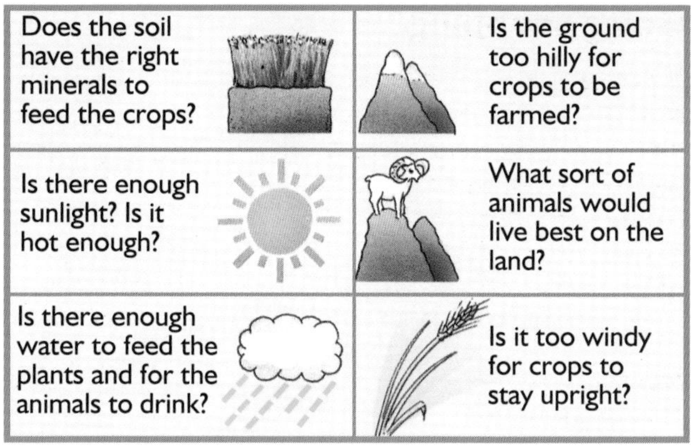
Does the soil have the right minerals to feed the crops?
Is the ground too hilly for crops to be farmed?
Is there enough sunlight? Is it hot enough?
What sort of animals would live best on the land?
Is there enough water to feed the plants and for the animals to drink?
Is it too windy for crops to stay upright?

Types of farm

People who only grow crops are **arable farmers**. Those who only keep animals are **livestock farmers**. Some do both and are called **mixed farmers**. The size of farms around the world varies too. The map shows what type of farm is most common in each area of the world.

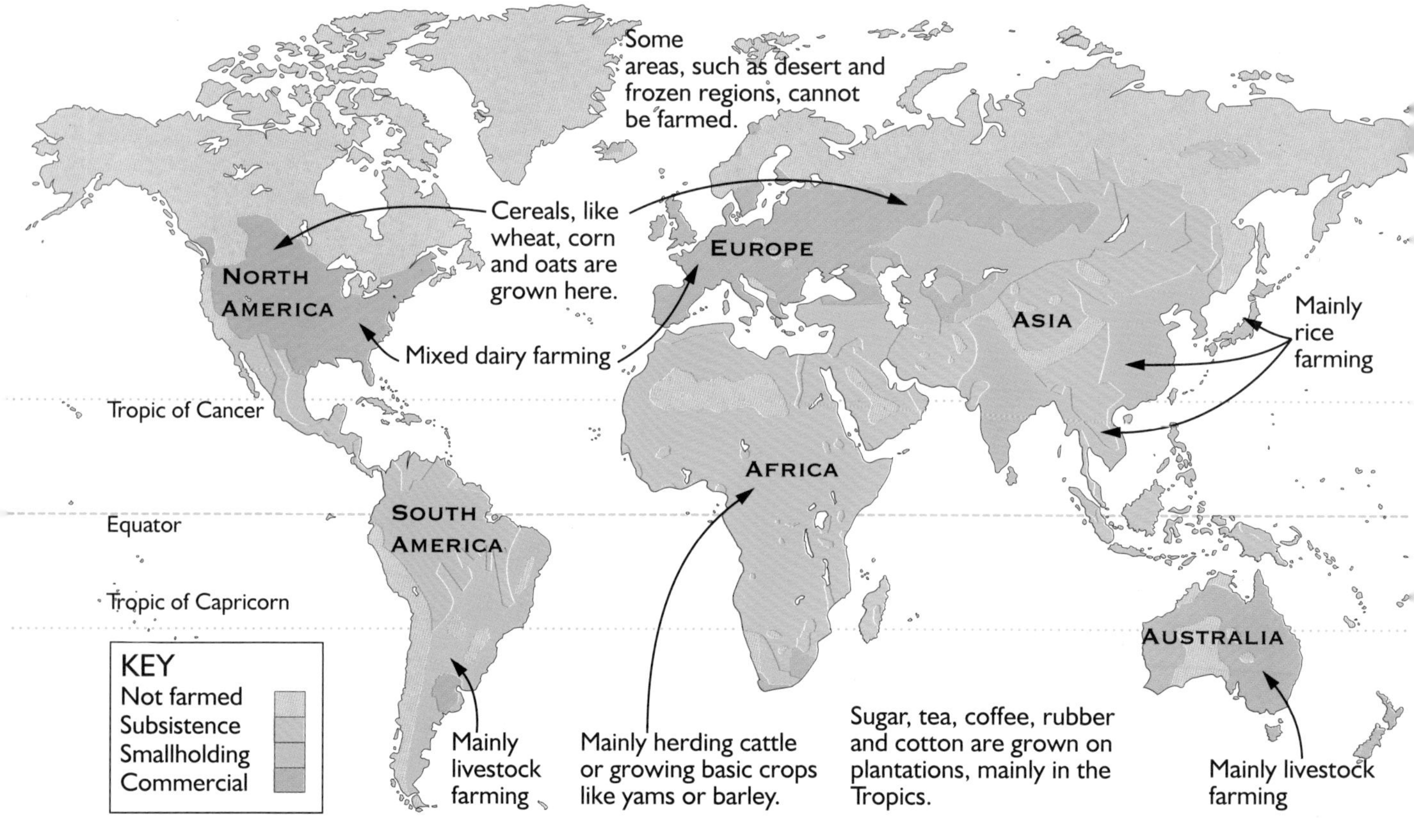
Some areas, such as desert and frozen regions, cannot be farmed.
Cereals, like wheat, corn and oats are grown here.
NORTH AMERICA
EUROPE
ASIA
Mainly rice farming
Mixed dairy farming
Tropic of Cancer
AFRICA
SOUTH AMERICA
Equator
Tropic of Capricorn
AUSTRALIA
KEY
Not farmed
Subsistence
Smallholding
Commercial
Mainly livestock farming
Mainly herding cattle or growing basic crops like yams or barley.
Sugar, tea, coffee, rubber and cotton are grown on plantations, mainly in the Tropics.
Mainly livestock farming

Subsistence farmers produce enough to feed their families but have nothing left to sell. Some subsistence farmers move from place to place. This is called **shifting cultivation**.

Smallholdings are small areas of land farmed by a family or a small company. They sell food to local people or to bigger firms which transport goods to shops further away.

Commercial farms produce very large amounts of food to sell to supermarkets and food manufacturers. **Plantations** are huge commercial farms that grow just one crop.

Going shopping

If you go into a supermarket, you will find many different kinds of goods that have come from all over the world. Countries buy food from each other so that people have a bigger choice of things to eat and drink.

Tea is grown on plantations in hot places like India and Sri Lanka.

North America produces flour from its wheat fields.

Lamb comes from places with mild weather and good grass, like England or New Zealand.

Some food is from a variety of countries, like the fruit in cans of mixed fruit.

The Netherlands has many dairy farms which make cheese.

Oranges and lemons are grown in warm places, like Spain and Portugal.

Bananas may grow on smallholdings in hot places like the West Indies.

Coffee grows on plantations in hot places, like Brazil and Kenya.

Farming in the past

The first humans hunted wild animals and gathered the stems, leaves and berries of wild plants.

Early plough

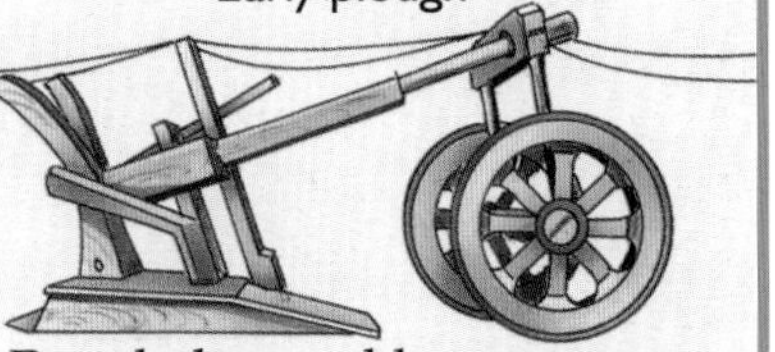

People learned how to tame animals and plant crops. They invented machinery to help them, like the plough. Ploughs turn soil over and leave a furrow so that seeds can be put in the ground.

To keep food fresh, refrigerated trucks may be used to transport it.

Communities traded with each other by taking food to local markets. Today, people transport food across great distances.

A banana's journey

Bananas are picked...
...washed and packed...
...and shipped abroad...
...where they are sold.

Many bananas are grown in the West Indies. When it is time for the bananas to be cut down, almost everyone from the local village helps, even the children.

They take the bananas to a local boxing plant, where they are washed and packed. Big firms buy the best bananas to sell abroad at a profit.

The bananas are transported inside huge refrigerators on ships and trucks. This keeps them fresh on their long journey to the shops.

More about farming

Farmers try to produce as much as they can from their land. To do this, they adapt and improve the natural environment so that they get a bigger harvest. They may even be able to produce crops which would not normally grow well in their particular region.

In cooler countries, farmers can bring extra heat to their plants by keeping them in a glass or plastic greenhouse. Greenhouses trap warmth so it is possible to grow things in them that would normally need a warmer season or climate to survive.

Fruit and salad vegetables may be grown in greenhouses.

Fertilizer spreader

Manure spreader

Tractors pull machinery over the fields.

Chemical sprayer

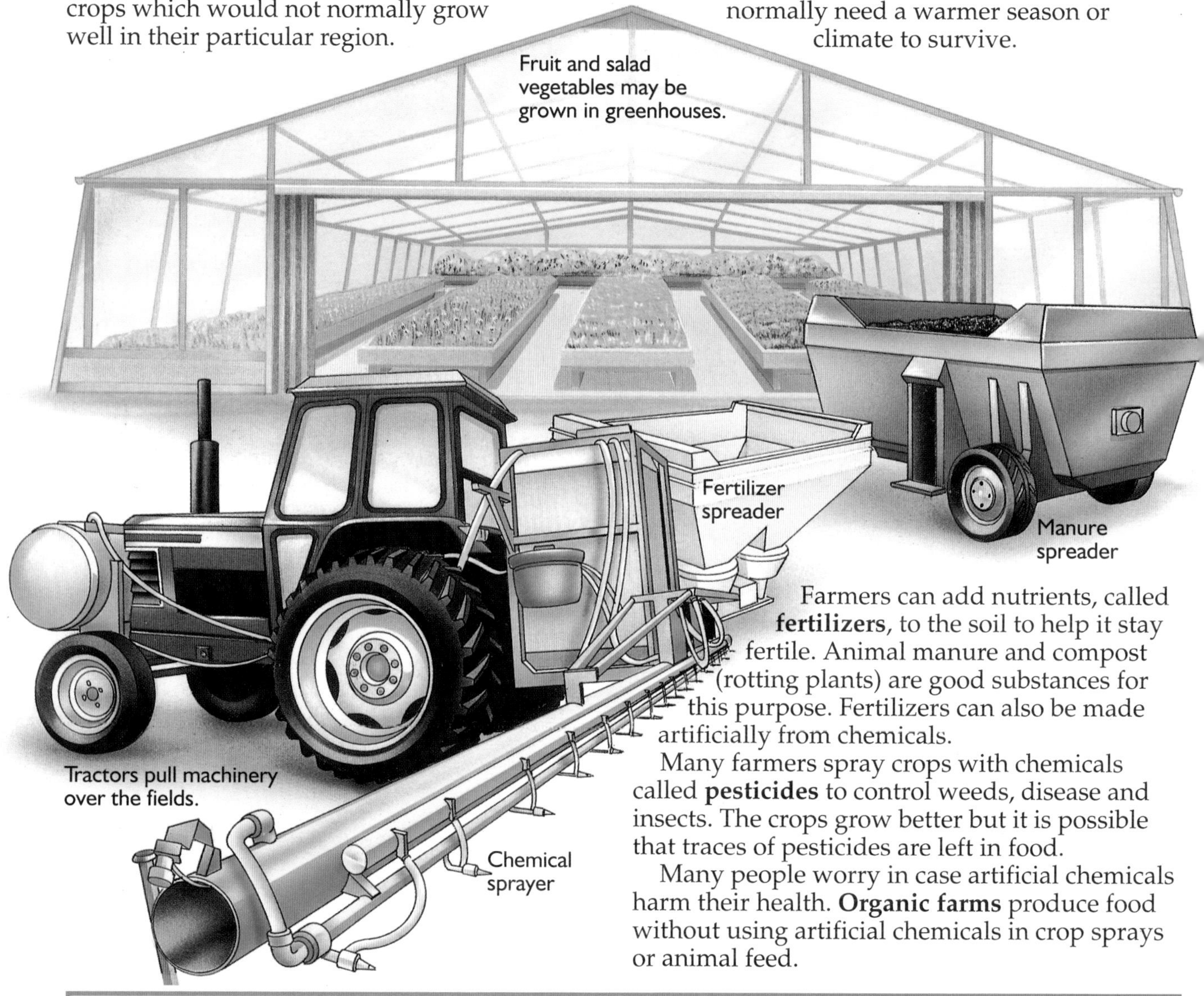

Farmers can add nutrients, called **fertilizers**, to the soil to help it stay fertile. Animal manure and compost (rotting plants) are good substances for this purpose. Fertilizers can also be made artificially from chemicals.

Many farmers spray crops with chemicals called **pesticides** to control weeds, disease and insects. The crops grow better but it is possible that traces of pesticides are left in food.

Many people worry in case artificial chemicals harm their health. **Organic farms** produce food without using artificial chemicals in crop sprays or animal feed.

Caring for the soil

Fertile soil is rich in nutrients. Different plants, like wheat and sugar-beet, use up different kinds of nutrients. So, to keep the soil fertile, farmers change the crops grown in each field every year. This is called **crop rotation**. Some crops, like clover, are good at putting nutrients back into the soil. This plan shows how crop rotation works.

KEY			Field A	Field B	Field C
Wheat		Year 1	wheat	sugar-beet	clover
Sugar-beet		Year 2	clover	wheat	sugar-beet
Clover		Year 3	sugar-beet	clover	wheat

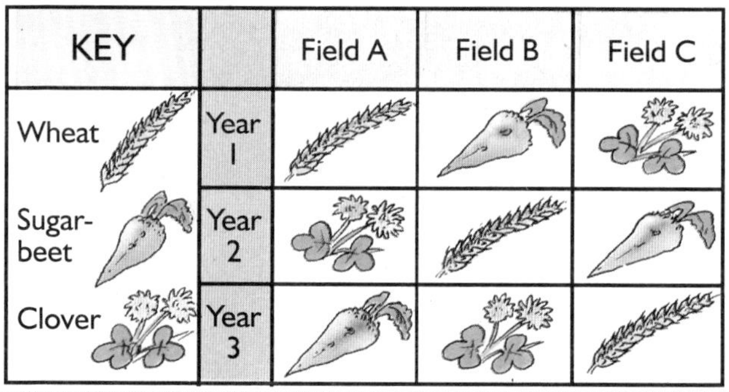

Watering the plants

Plants need water to grow. When there is not enough water in the soil, farmers bring it to the crops by artificial means. This is called **irrigation**.

The Ancient Egyptians were the first to use irrigation. They invented ways to transport water from the River Nile to the fields. Some of their methods, such as the Archimedean Screw, are still in use today.

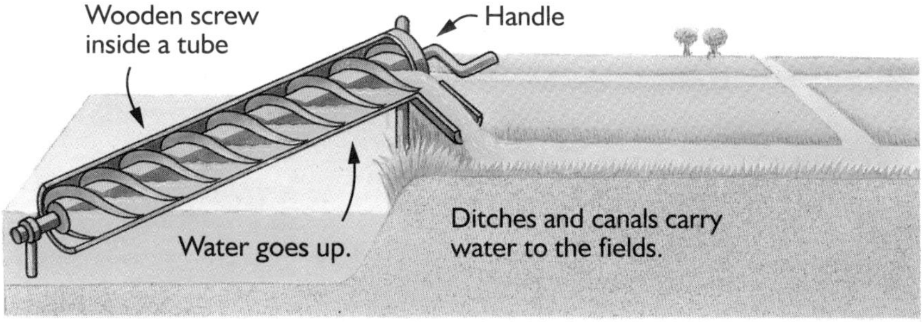

Wooden screw inside a tube
Handle
Water goes up.
Ditches and canals carry water to the fields.

The Archimedean Screw is a big, wooden screw inside a tube, which has one end lying in a river. Someone turns the handle of the screw. This forces water up the tube, through a pipe and into a ditch leading to the fields.

Extensive farming

In places like Australia and North America where there is lots of inexpensive land, farmers run big farms which produce huge amounts of food. These farms need few workers because big machines do much of the work and the farmers grow crops and raise animals which do not need close care. This is called **extensive farming**.

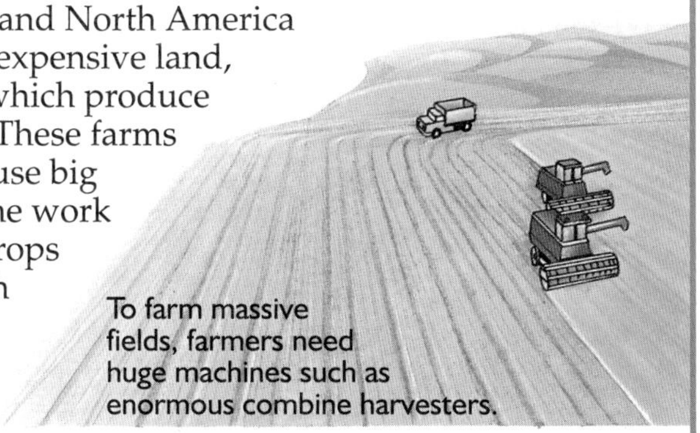

To farm massive fields, farmers need huge machines such as enormous combine harvesters.

Intensive farming

Intensively reared chickens are kept in cages, where food is brought to them.

In places like Europe, where there is less land available, farms may be smaller. Huge machines are not suitable on small farms. Instead, farmers may use more workers and grow more crops or animals per unit of land. They farm the land all year and produce goods that sell at high prices. This is called **intensive farming**.

Steps in the land

Terraces are steps cut in a hillside. They make work easier on hilly land and make more land usable. Terracing is used, for example, in the rice fields of South East Asia.

Farming technology

Scientists have found a way to grow plants by choosing which features they will inherit. This process, called **genetic engineering**, helps them grow lots of high quality plants.

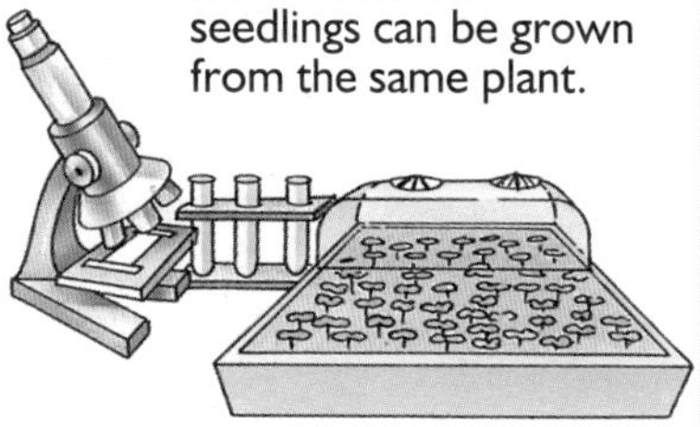

Lots of identical seedlings can be grown from the same plant.

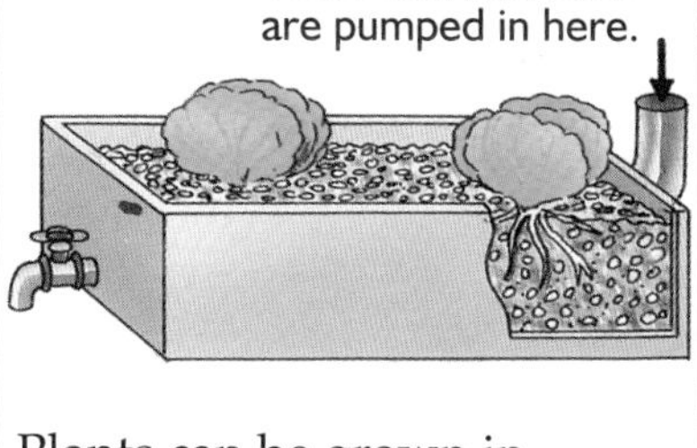

Water and nutrients are pumped in here.

Plants can be grown in polythene or gravel instead of soil. Nutrients and water are pumped past their roots, so they grow well. This is called **hydroponics**.

Forestry and fishing

People have always used wood and fished the oceans. Today, forestry and fishing are huge industries which employ lots of people and provide many useful things.

Centuries ago, much of the land was covered in forest. Over the years, people have cut trees down for fuel, building materials and to make room for farming. Forests have become smaller and some have even disappeared altogether.

Many forests are still being destroyed because they are not managed properly. To look after forests, people must limit how many trees are felled and also plant new trees to replace them.

This picture shows the cycle of how forests are managed.

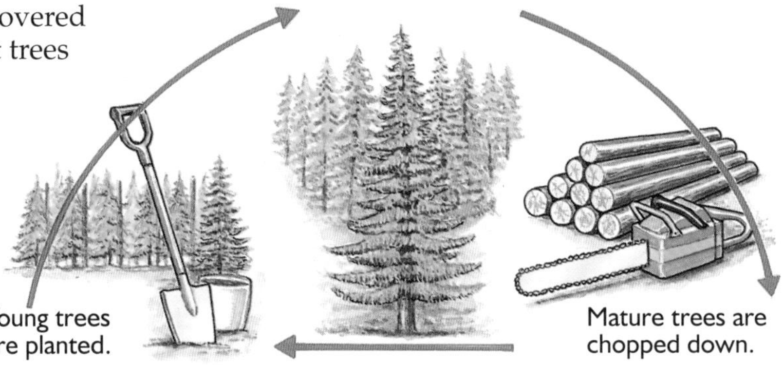

Young trees grow into mature trees.
Mature trees are chopped down.
Young trees are planted.

Why we need trees

Trees are not just needed for wood. They do many important things, such as releasing oxygen for living things to breathe.

Many birds and other wild animals make their homes in trees.
Trees stop wind from blowing dry soil away.
Leaves give out oxygen.
Trees are a barrier against heavy rain damaging the soil.
Roots soak up water so that top-soil is not washed away.

Trees protect soil from wind and rain. Roots help to bind soil together. Also, rubber, some waxes, resins, gums and many medicines come from trees.

The world's forests

Different forests grow in different climates. In cool areas, forests of conifers grow, called **boreal forests**. **Temperate forest** grows in mild regions and can be made of conifers, deciduous trees or a mixture of both. Rainforest* (tropical and equatorial forest) grows in hot, rainy places. Thousands of different types of trees grow in rainforests.

Conifers have needle-like leaves.

Deciduous trees have broad, flat leaves.

Rainforest has many types of trees.

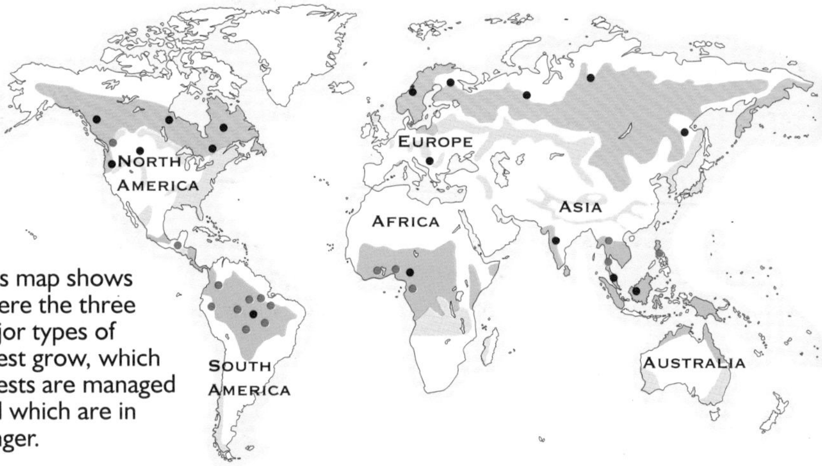

This map shows where the three major types of forest grow, which forests are managed and which are in danger.

KEY
- Boreal forest
- Temperate forest
- Rainforest
- Managed forest
- Forest in danger

*Rainforest, 298.

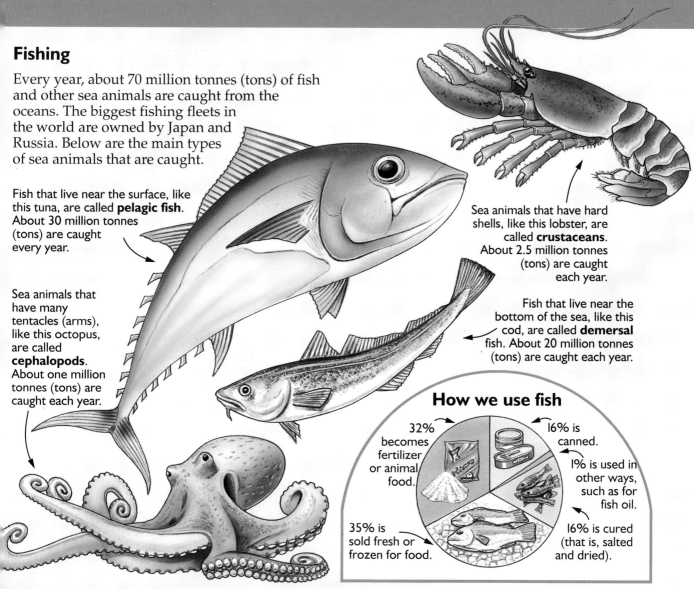

Fishing

Every year, about 70 million tonnes (tons) of fish and other sea animals are caught from the oceans. The biggest fishing fleets in the world are owned by Japan and Russia. Below are the main types of sea animals that are caught.

Sea animals that have hard shells, like this lobster, are called **crustaceans**. About 2.5 million tonnes (tons) are caught each year.

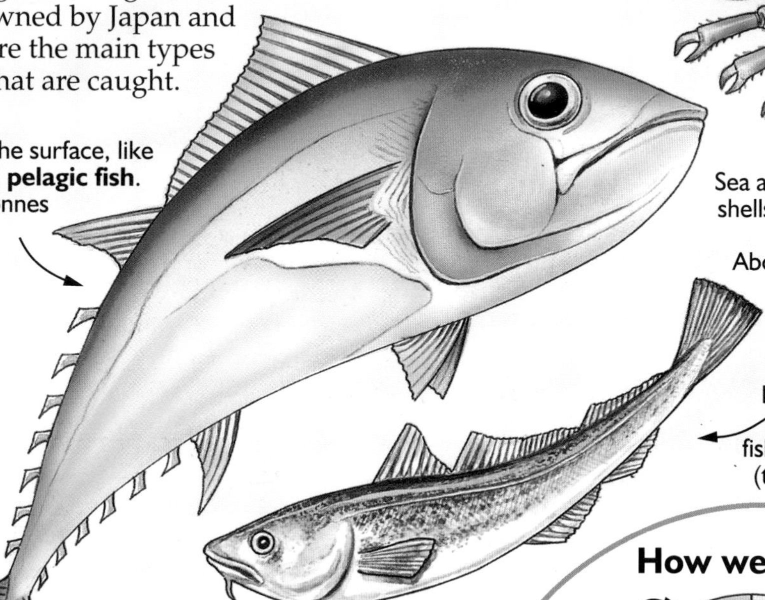
Fish that live near the surface, like this tuna, are called **pelagic fish**. About 30 million tonnes (tons) are caught every year.
Fish that live near the bottom of the sea, like this cod, are called **demersal** fish. About 20 million tonnes (tons) are caught each year.

Sea animals that have many tentacles (arms), like this octopus, are called **cephalopods**. About one million tonnes (tons) are caught each year.

How we use fish

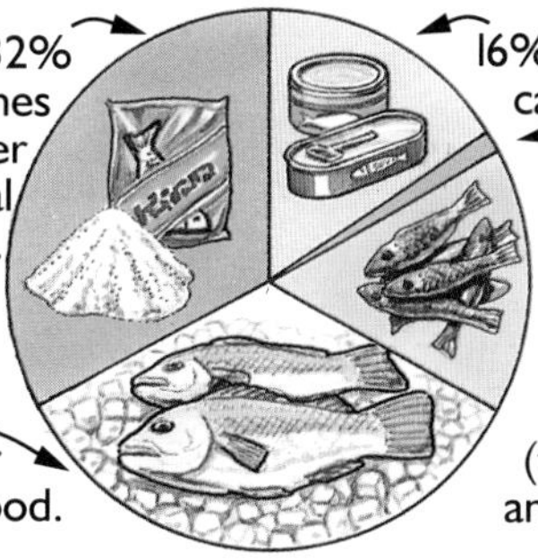
32% becomes fertilizer or animal food.
16% is canned.
1% is used in other ways, such as for fish oil.
16% is cured (that is, salted and dried).
35% is sold fresh or frozen for food.

Fishing efficiency

Large fishing fleets may have a factory ship which cleans and freezes the fish. This means the fleet can stay out at sea longer and catch more. Modern ships use echo-sounding to trace fish shoals (groups). A beam of sound is sent down into the water and then echoes back off the fish. A computer detects where the echo comes from.

Factory ship
A screen image shows where the fish are.

Fish for the future

If fishermen catch too many fish, there will not be enough left in the seas for the future. This is called overfishing. To avoid it, they use nets with large holes so that young fish can escape and breed.

Instead of taking fish from the sea, people can also breed them in fish farms. This is cheaper and safer than sea-fishing and it means that stocks of fish can be controlled and not run down too low. Fish such as salmon, trout and lobster can be bred in coastal waters, rivers and lakes.

Mining the Earth

Mining the Earth's crust* produces the rocks and minerals* that industries use for making goods. They are some of our most valuable raw materials*. There are many kinds of rocks and minerals beneath the Earth's surface, which are useful in a variety of ways.

Some rocks and minerals provide energy. Coal, oil and natural gas are fossil fuels*. Uranium is a nuclear fuel.

Gemstones are found inside rocks. Many are rare and valuable. They are cut and polished before use.

Uranium ore

Limestone

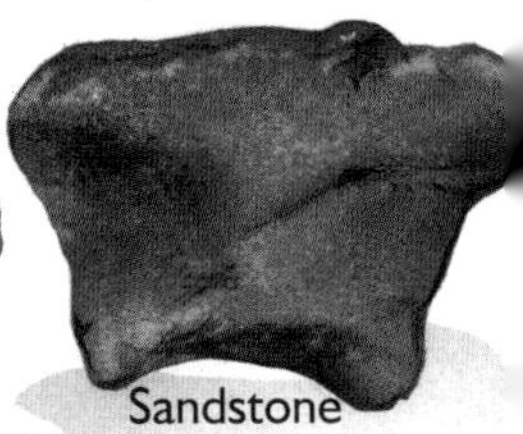
Sandstone

Chalk

Gold may be found in a pure state.

Iron is found as an ore.

Corundum rock which contains ruby

Cut ruby

Cut diamond

Many rocks are mined for building. Some, such as sandstone, are cut up and used as they are. Others are mixed to make new building materials, such as limestone and chalk, which are used in cement.

Metals are often found as **ores**, mixed with other rock materials, rather than in a pure state. Metal is separated from ore by heating in a furnace. This is called **smelting**.

Types of mining

In the 1800s, miners dug shallow, sloping tunnels into the hillside to reach rocks and minerals, such as gold. They are called **drift**, or **adit**, **mines**. Some are still used today.

Minerals that are just beneath the surface, such as copper, are mined by digging huge, wide holes in the ground. These are called **open-cast mines**, or **quarries**.

Some materials, such as coal, are found deep underground. To reach them, miners dig **shaft mines**. From these shafts, tunnels stretch for great distances.

Many reservoirs of oil and gas are trapped between rocks under the seabed. To mine oil and gas, which are important energy resources, engineers build rigs in the sea to drill the seabed. Pipes carry the oil and gas to refineries on land where they are processed.

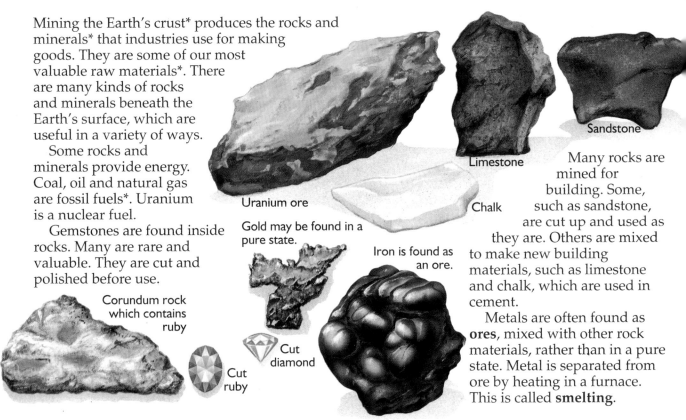

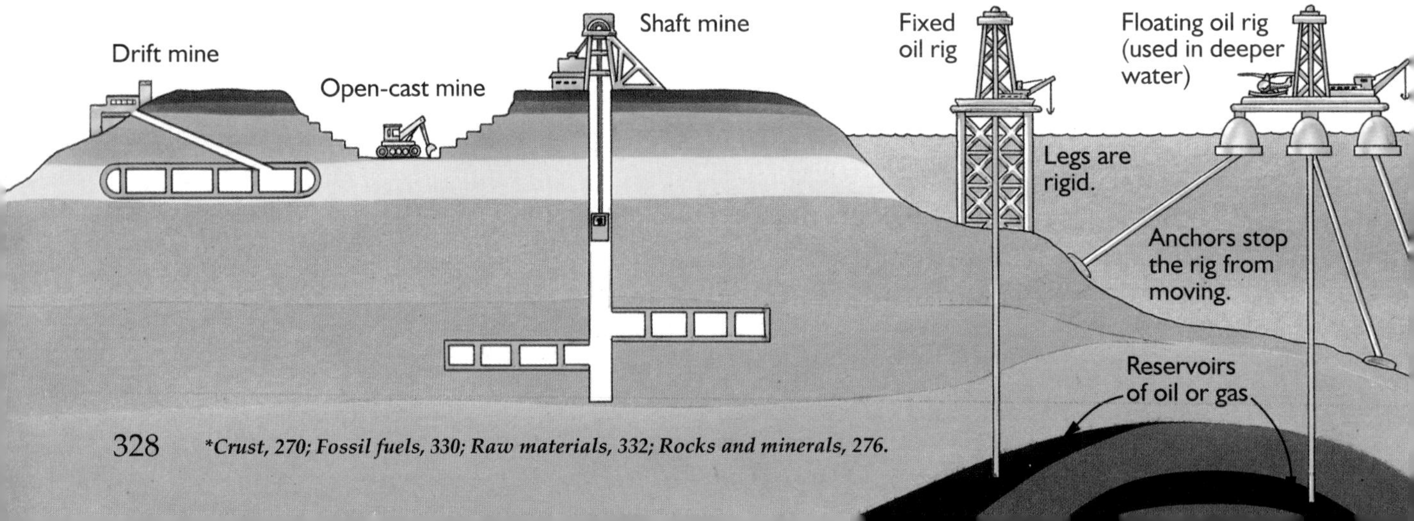
Drift mine
Open-cast mine
Shaft mine
Fixed oil rig
Floating oil rig (used in deeper water)
Legs are rigid.
Anchors stop the rig from moving.
Reservoirs of oil or gas

**Crust, 270; Fossil fuels, 330; Raw materials, 332; Rocks and minerals, 276.*

DID YOU KNOW?

Diamonds are very hard stones. Some are used as a cutting edge on tools. For example, a dentist's drill is covered with diamond grit.

Where things are mined

Different areas of the world are rich in different types of rocks and minerals. The map below shows which places produce the largest amounts of some well-known materials.

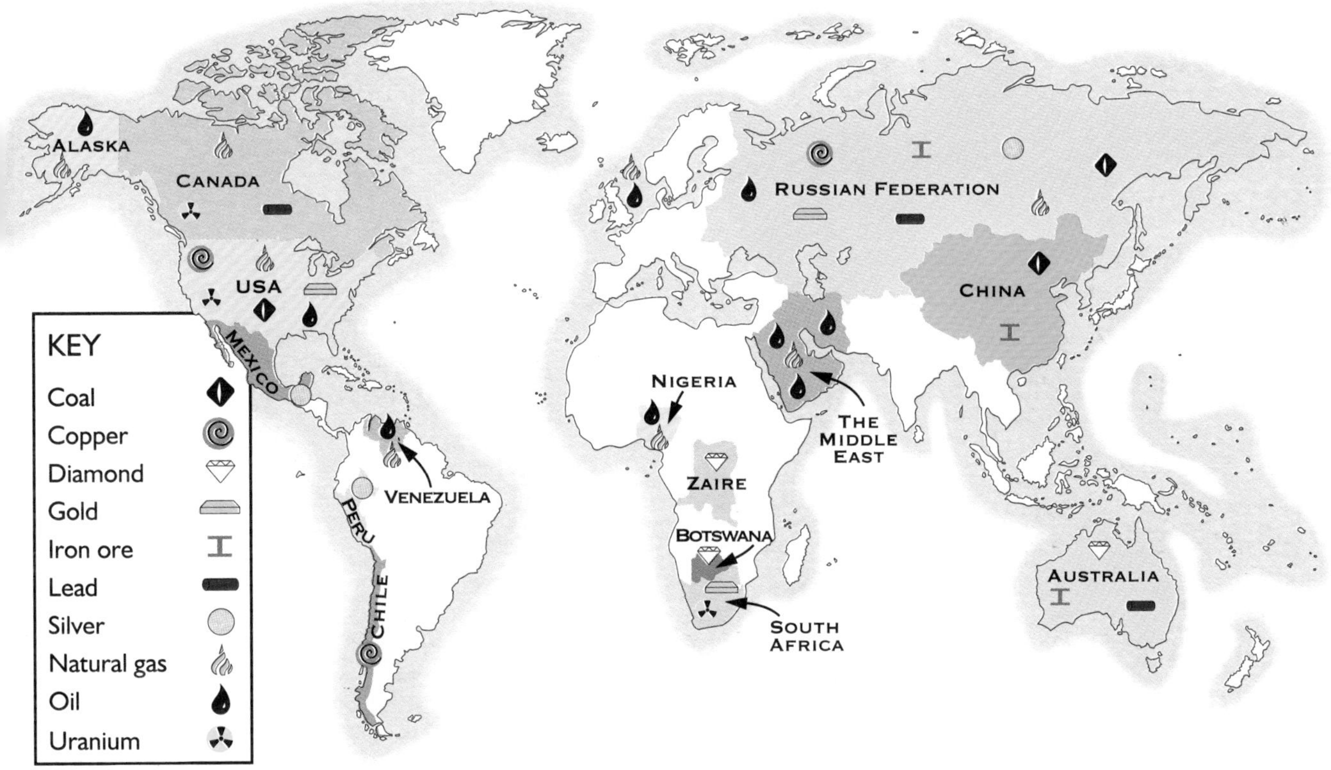

Raw materials running low

This picture shows in which year geologists think our present materials may run out, if they continue to be used at today's rate.

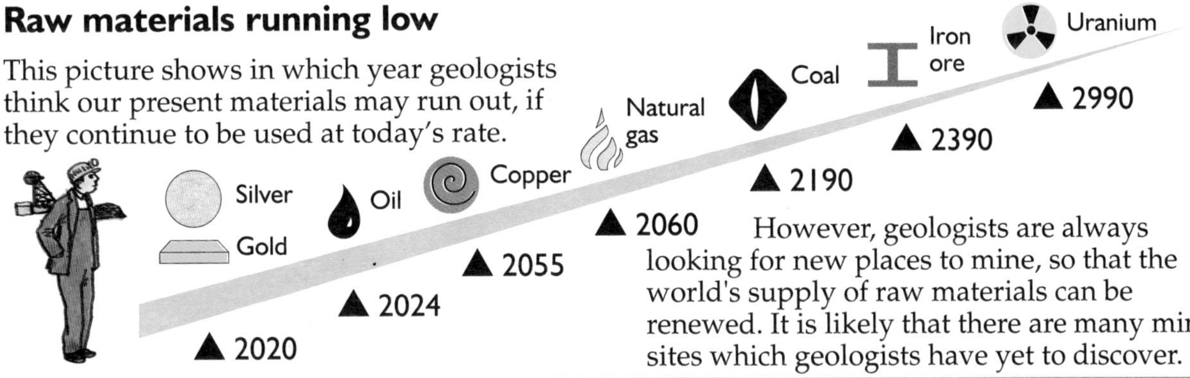

However, geologists are always looking for new places to mine, so that the world's supply of raw materials can be renewed. It is likely that there are many mining sites which geologists have yet to discover.

Energy

Most of the world's energy comes from coal, oil and natural gas, which are called **fossil fuels**. This type of energy is called **non-renewable energy** because once used, it cannot be reused. For example, once a piece of coal has been burned, it can no longer produce any energy. Fossil fuels cause pollution*, but people still use them because world energy needs are so great.

Unlike fossil fuels, **renewable energy**, such as wind, water, the Sun and heat from inside the Earth, can be reused. For example, water can be used over again to drive a water wheel. The pie chart below shows the percentages of different types of energy used by homes and industry.

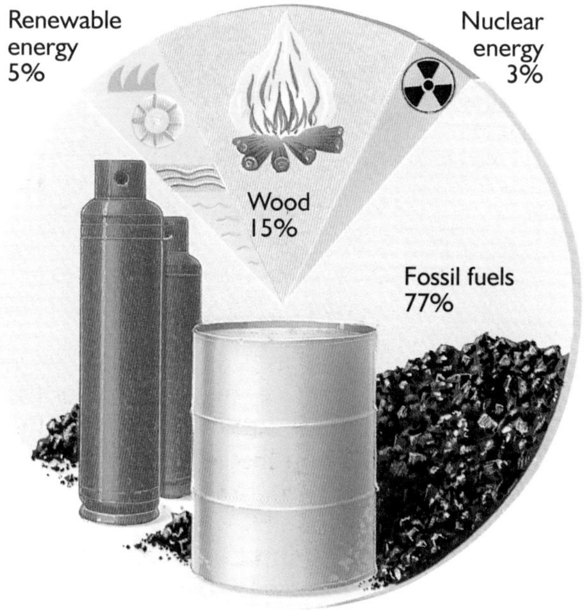
Renewable energy 5%
Nuclear energy 3%
Wood 15%
Fossil fuels 77%

Energy from wood 15%

Trees use energy from the Sun to grow. When wood is burned, energy is released as heat. In many poor areas, such as Ethiopia and Nepal, nearly 90% of energy comes from wood.

Fossil fuels 77%

Coal, oil and natural gas are non-renewable fossil fuels. They were formed over millions of years from fossilized* animals and plants. Like wood, fossil fuels release heat energy when burned. Both fossil fuels and wood release gases which can harm the atmosphere.

Nuclear energy 3%

Nuclear energy is produced when atoms (tiny particles) of a nuclear fuel, such as uranium, are split apart. This releases huge amounts of heat from tiny amounts of fuel. However, nuclear energy can be dangerous because the fuel gives off radioactive particles which damage living things.

Renewable energy – see next page 5%

Hydro-electric power 3% Others 2%

Power stations

Most electricity is produced in power stations. Both fossil fuel and nuclear power stations use fuels to make heat. The picture shows how this heat makes electricity.

Power stations are usually built close to their fuel source, or near good transport links, such as a main railway line or a port. They use a great deal of water for cooling, so they also need to be near large rivers or the sea.

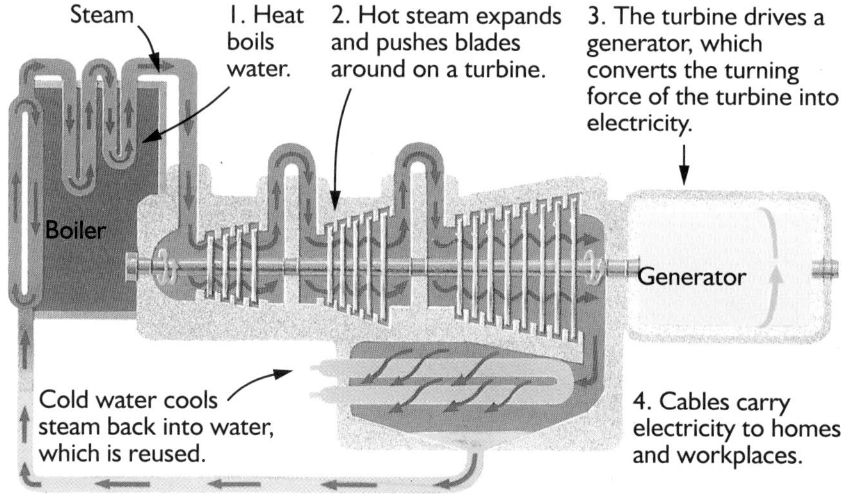
Steam
1. Heat boils water.
2. Hot steam expands and pushes blades around on a turbine.
3. The turbine drives a generator, which converts the turning force of the turbine into electricity.
Boiler
Generator
Cold water cools steam back into water, which is reused.
4. Cables carry electricity to homes and workplaces.

 Fossils, 277; Pollution, 344.

Renewable energy

Renewable energy makes less pollution than non-renewable energy, but at the moment not enough is turned into power to meet all the world's needs. This kind of energy is also called **alternative energy** because, although it is not greatly used now, it may be a good source of energy for the future. The main forms of renewable energy are shown below.

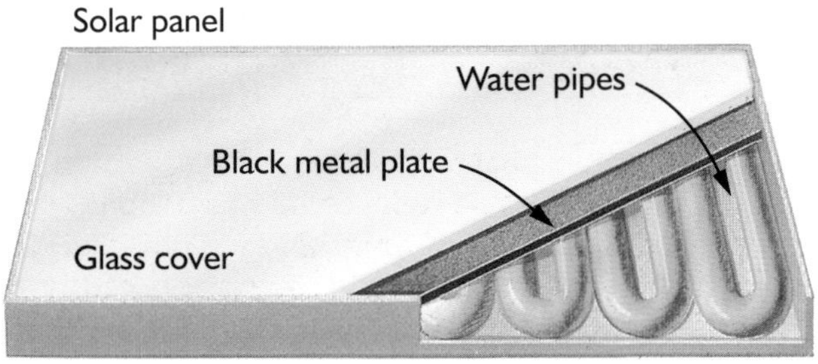

Solar panel
Water pipes
Black metal plate
Glass cover

Solar energy

Solar panels are built on some buildings to absorb and use the Sun's heat. The heat warms black metal plates, which then heat the water pipes behind. Glass covers keep the heat in.

Solar cells power some machines, such as calculators and satellites, by turning the Sun's energy directly into electricity.

Hydro-electric power

In mountain areas of places such as Canada, where there are fast streams, dams can be built to control the water flow. When the water is released, it can generate electricity by turning the blades on a turbine, as shown on the right. This is called **hydro-electric power**, or **HEP**.

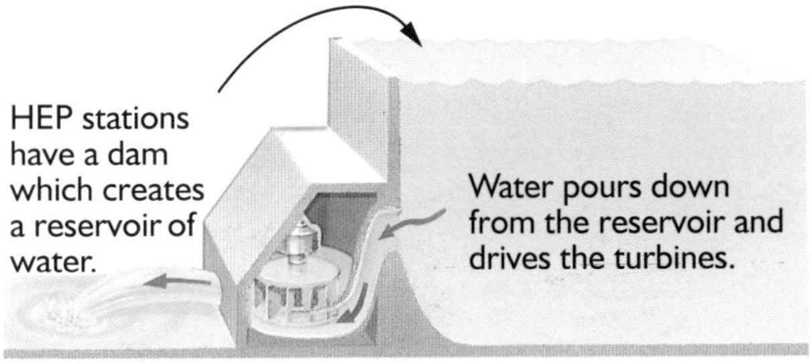

HEP stations have a dam which creates a reservoir of water.
Water pours down from the reservoir and drives the turbines.

Energy from underground

Heat from hot rocks in the Earth's crust* can generate electricity, as shown on the right. Cold water is pumped down through boreholes in the rock and steam comes back up, which drives a turbine. This is called **geothermal power**. It is used in places such as New Zealand and Iceland.

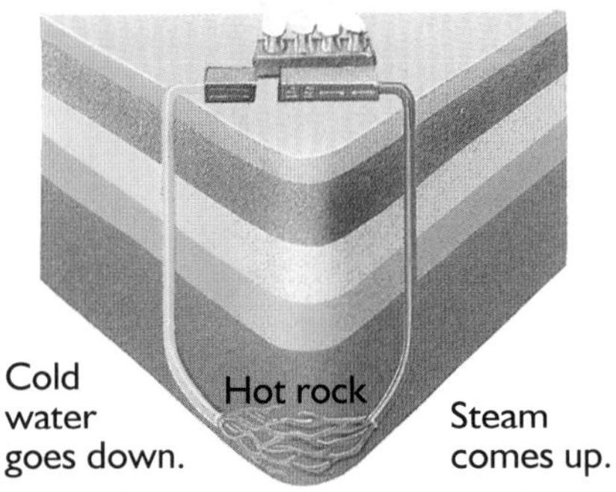

Cold water goes down.
Hot rock
Steam comes up.

Wind power

The wind can produce electricity by turning blades on big wind turbines like the one on the right. They work best where wind is very strong. However, it takes thousands of wind turbines to make as much energy as a fossil fuel power station.

Wind turbine

Turbines at sea

The sea can also provide power. The up and down motion of the waves can work machines which drive a turbine. The machine shown on the right is called a nodding duck.

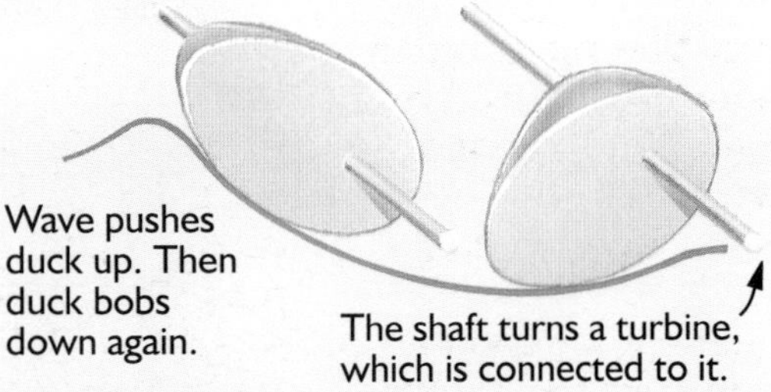

Wave pushes duck up. Then duck bobs down again.
The shaft turns a turbine, which is connected to it.

Tide going in.
Tide going out.

The in and out motion of the tides can also drive a turbine, as shown on the left. Tidal power is used in the La Rance Estuary in France, where there is a big difference between high and low tide.

*Crust, 270.

Manufacturing

Making new products is called **manufacturing**. The materials that are used in making new products are called **raw materials**.

In the past, people manufactured things in their own homes. Then, in the 1700s, a steam engine which could power big machines was developed. The new machinery made products more quickly and cheaply than human-powered machines. Employers built factories for the machines and paid people to work in them.

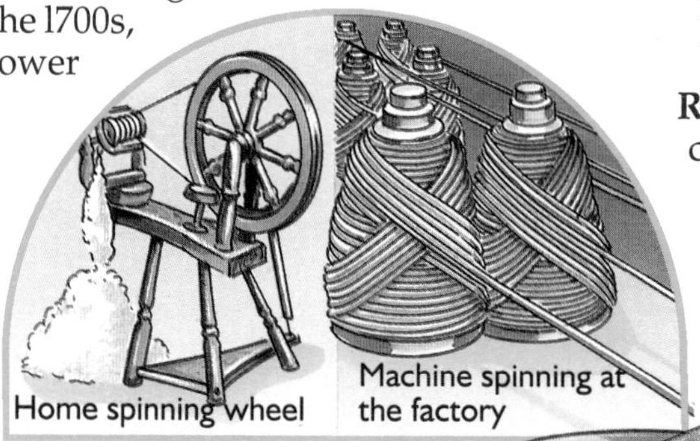
Home spinning wheel
Machine spinning at the factory

The first factories were in the UK, because the machines were invented there. After the arrival of these machines, fewer people worked at home because they could not make a profit. This time of change is known as the **Industrial Revolution**. These days, most countries manufacture goods in factories. However, some people still manufacture goods at home, especially in parts of the world where human labour is far cheaper than machine power.

Heavy or light?

Manufacturing industries are divided into two types. **Heavy industries**, such as ship-building, use large machines and heavy raw materials.

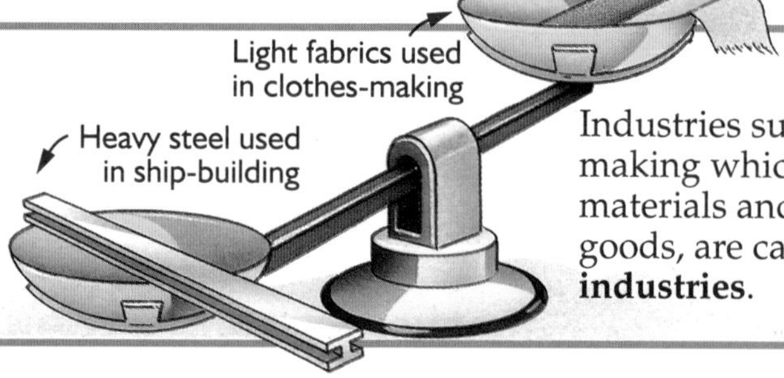
Light fabrics used in clothes-making
Heavy steel used in ship-building

Industries such as clothes-making which use light raw materials and produce light goods, are called **light industries**.

Choosing a location

When a company builds a new factory, it has to choose the area carefully. Where will the workers, customers and raw materials come from? Is there a power supply and good road and rail links? Is there an airport or seaport nearby to import and export goods (bring goods in and out of the country)? This map shows where different kinds of factories may be found.

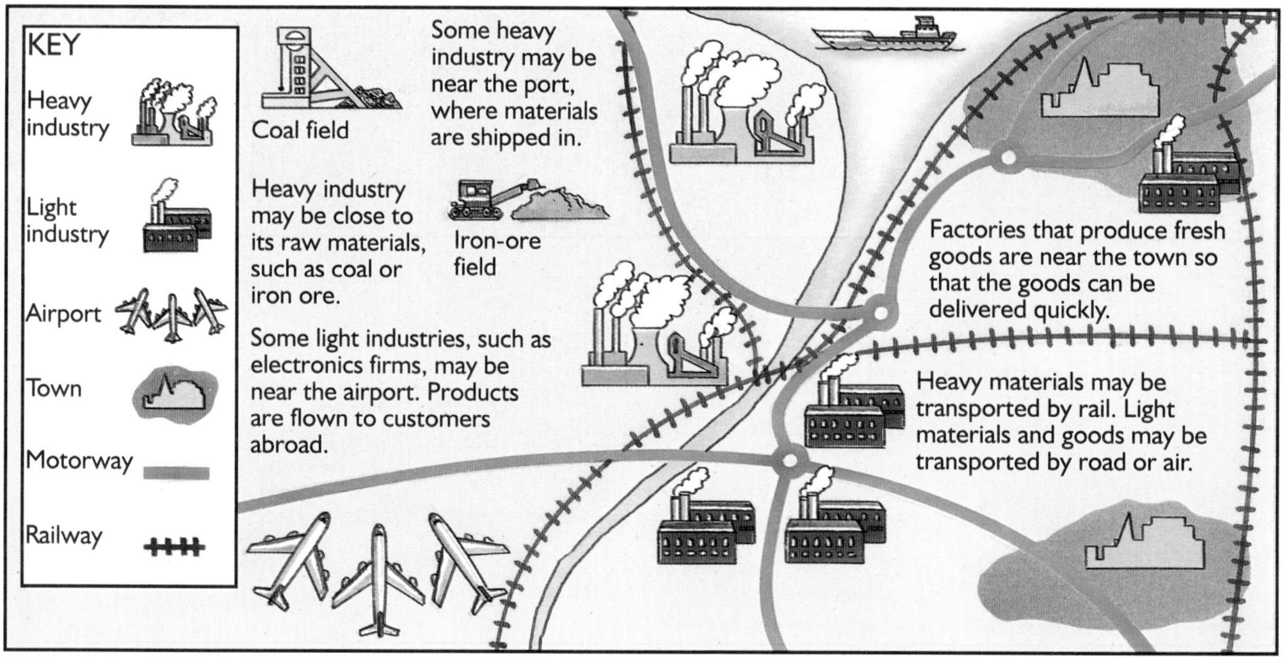
KEY
Heavy industry
Light industry
Airport
Town
Motorway
Railway
Coal field
Some heavy industry may be near the port, where materials are shipped in.
Heavy industry may be close to its raw materials, such as coal or iron ore.
Iron-ore field
Some light industries, such as electronics firms, may be near the airport. Products are flown to customers abroad.
Factories that produce fresh goods are near the town so that the goods can be delivered quickly.
Heavy materials may be transported by rail. Light materials and goods may be transported by road or air.

International companies

A company with factories in different countries is called a **multinational**. Many motor companies are multinationals, with factories in different places making different parts of cars. These are then put together at an assembly plant. The picture shows how parts may come from many places.

Multinationals have some advantages over companies that are based in one country. More workers and customers are available to them and they can sell goods more easily in countries where they own a factory. They can also make each part of their product where it is cheapest to do so.

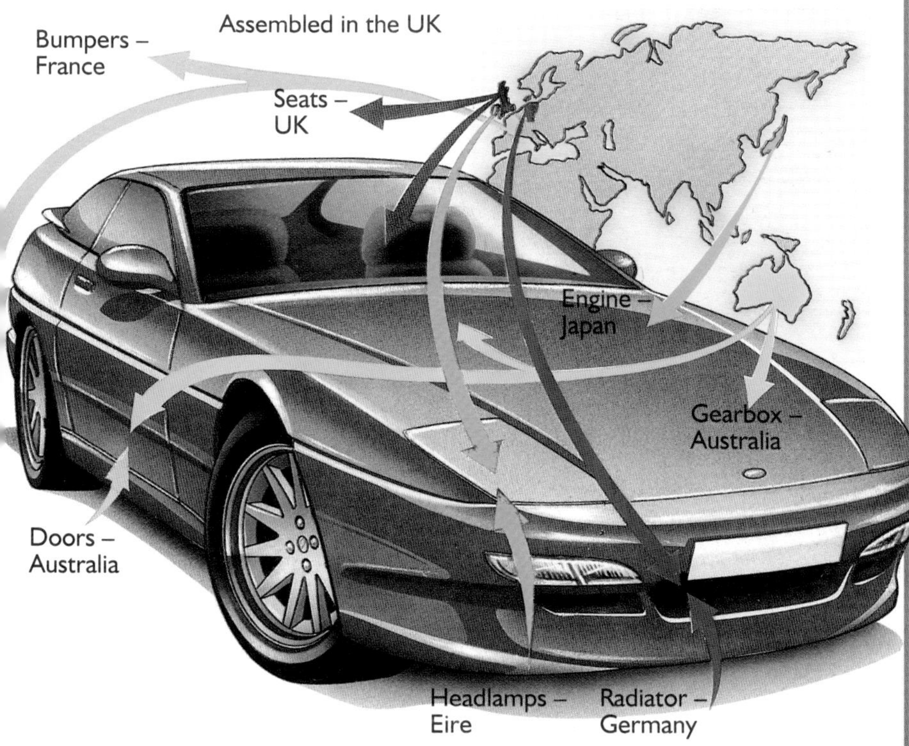
Assembled in the UK
Bumpers – France
Seats – UK
Engine – Japan
Gearbox – Australia
Doors – Australia
Headlamps – Eire
Radiator – Germany

Government control

Companies build models to show what their new factory may look like.

Governments sometimes study plans for new factories before they are built. They may encourage new factories in an area which needs more jobs. They may also help foreign companies to bring their business into the country. If a factory will spoil an area by polluting it or by making it look ugly, governments can stop it from being built.

High technology

Manufacturers of products like electronic equipment and computers are called **high technology industries**. They use the latest ideas and skills for their work.

High technology products

Most technology firms are light industries. They employ fewer, but higher-skilled, workers than the heavy industry of the past.

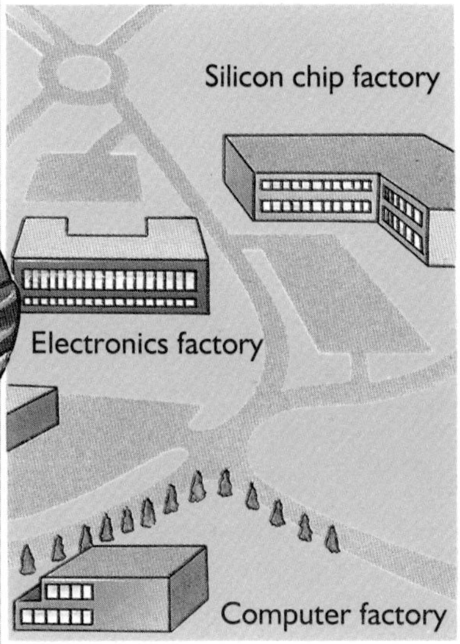
Silicon chip factory
Electronics factory
Computer factory

High technology firms use few raw materials and make products that are easy to transport. They do not need to be in any one kind of area, so they are called **footloose industries**. They may be grouped together on science parks where they can provide materials and services* for each other. Universities may be nearby to help think up new ideas.

**Services*, 334.*

Services

Anyone who has a job doing or supplying something for other people is providing a **service**. In some countries, plenty of services are available and many people are employed doing them. In other countries, people do most things for themselves.

What services are there?

This picture shows some of the people who supply services around the town and what sort of services are supplied.

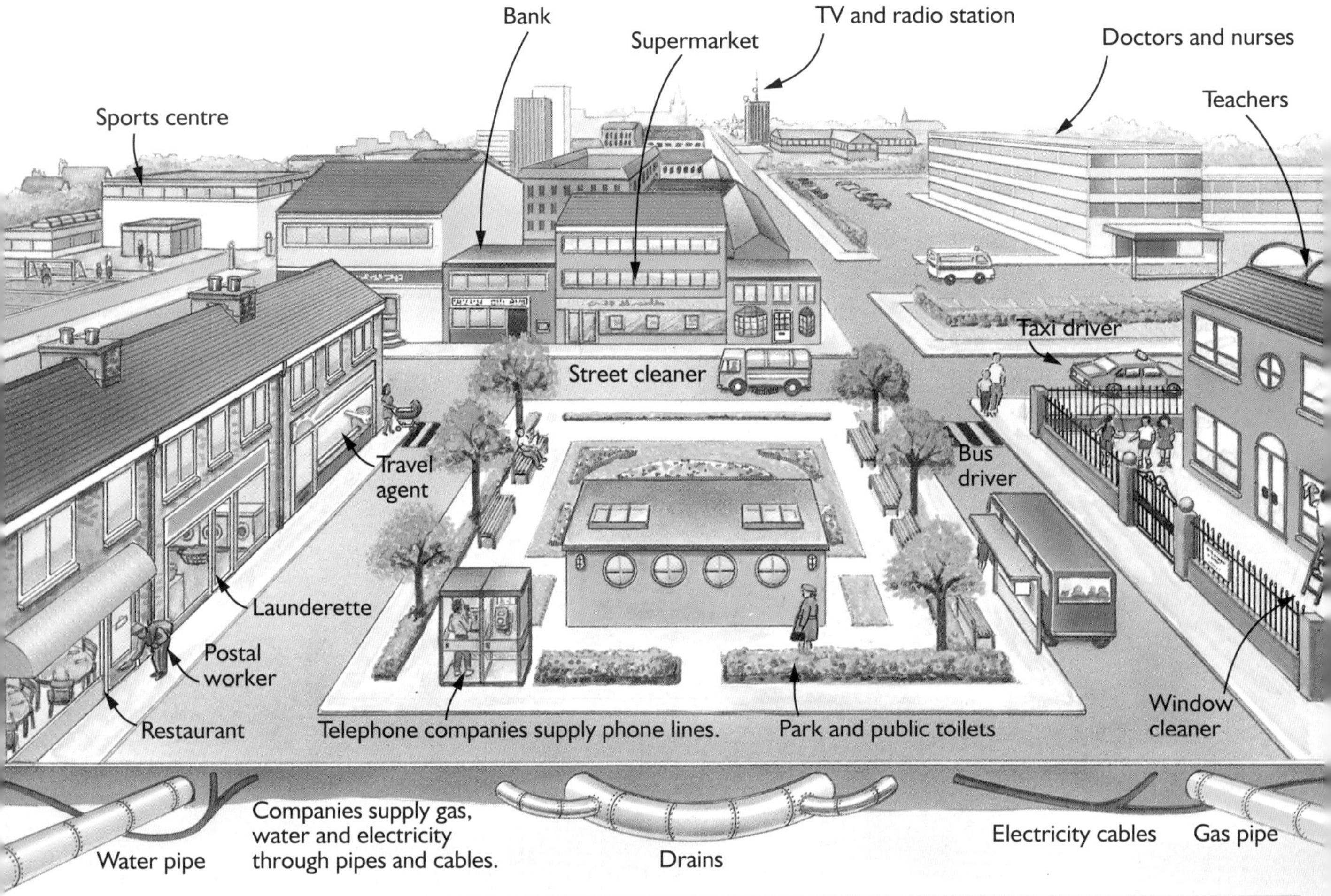

City services

Cities are organized for providing lots of different services. Some services may be grouped together in areas which are known for providing that type of service. For example, a city may have an entertainment district, a retail area with shops, and a financial sector with banks and finance companies.

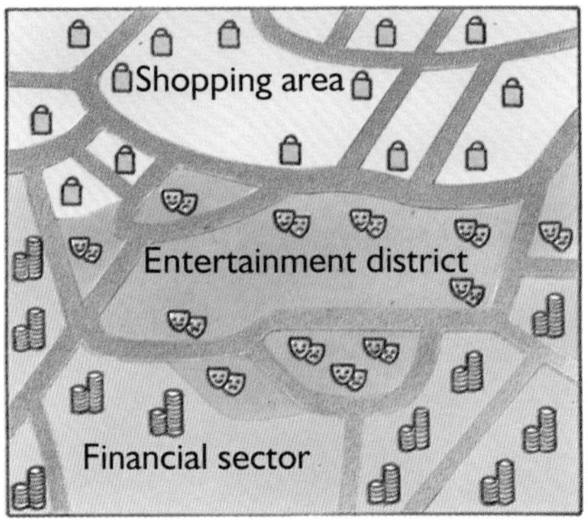

Out-of-town shopping

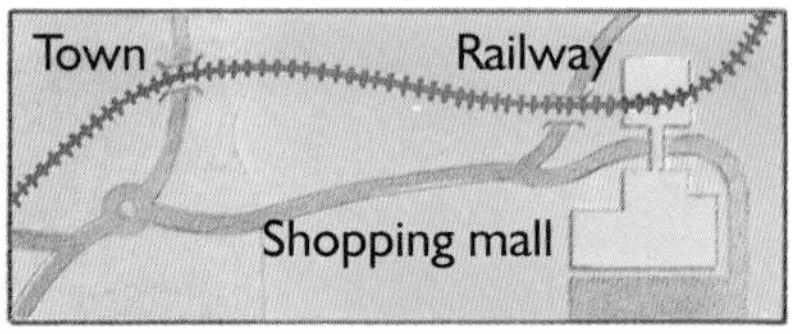

If space runs out in a town, people may build out-of-town shopping areas. Many services are together in one place and there is plenty of parking space for cars.

Richer or poorer?

In richer countries, there are usually more workers employed in service jobs than in poorer countries. This is because the people there have more leisure time and can afford to pay for things like hobbies and travel, which create service jobs. This picture shows the percentage of workers who do service jobs in some different countries.

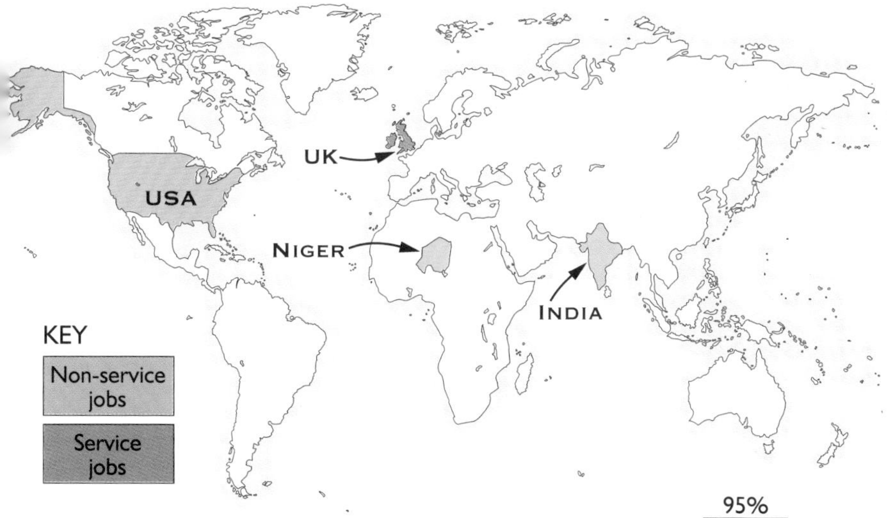

UK
USA
NIGER
INDIA
KEY
Non-service jobs
Service jobs

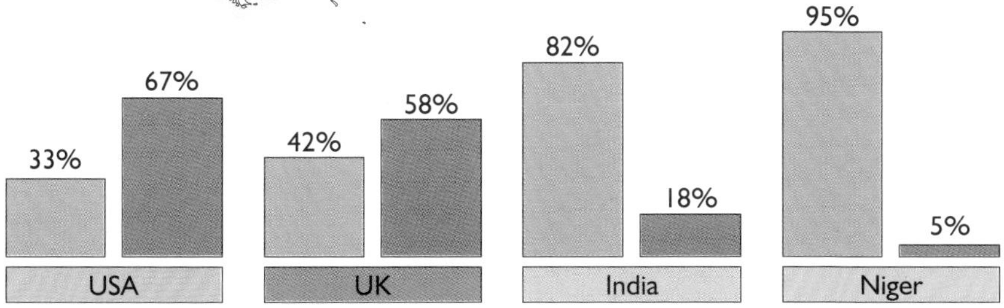

Doing things yourself

In poorer countries, some villages may have only a few basic services available. People have to do most things for themselves and have no spare time or money.

There may be no electricity, so people use wood for heating and cooking. People get their water for cooking and washing from a well.

A doctor may come only once a year and if there is no local transport, children may walk a long way to get to their school.

In poorer countries, women may spend hours finding fuel, food and water.

Computerized services

Today, many service jobs are done with the help of computers. Computers speed things up and make people's jobs easier. For example, people can withdraw money from a bank's computerized cash machine instead of being served by a bank clerk.

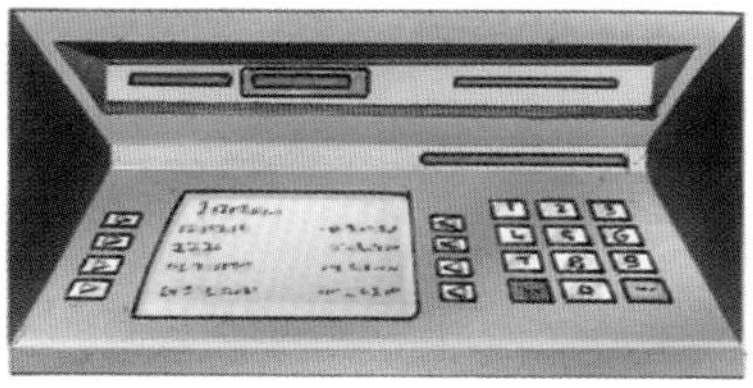

In many stores, scanners at the check-out register the prices of goods by reading computer codes. Assistants no longer have to key in the prices.

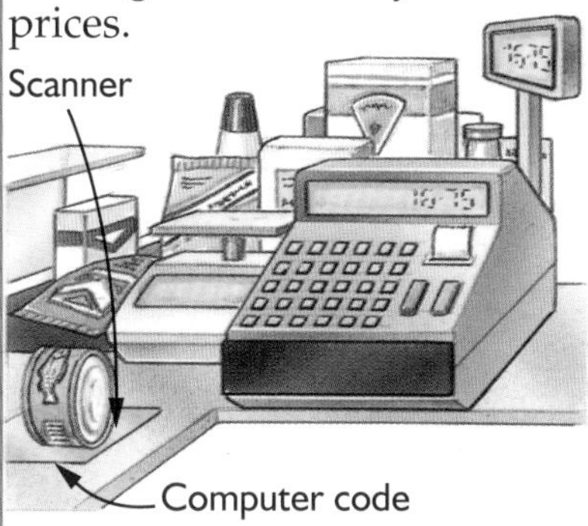

Scanner
Computer code

Cash registers record how much is sold, so that no one has to count the stock.

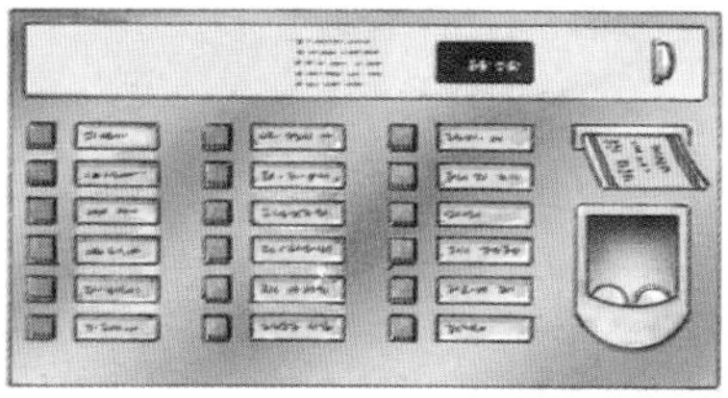

Bus and train tickets may be sold and collected by computerized machines instead of by transport workers.

Transport

Centuries ago, much of the land was covered in forest. The easiest way to move around was to travel along the rivers, so canoes were probably the first vehicles to be built. Today they are still the best way to travel through areas of thick jungle.

On land, animals used to provide the only form of transport. In countries where there are few motor vehicles, people still ride on animals and use them to pull carts. For example, oxen are used in places such as India and Thailand.

Oxen can pull heavy loads.

As steam engines developed in the early 1800s, machines began to replace animals as the best form of transport. Roads became better too with the invention of new materials such as tarmac. Transport then improved quickly as people began to want to move goods around and travel more.

Today, many people rely on modern transport. If there were no cars, ships, trains and planes, people would have much less choice in where to live, work and spend their leisure time.

Travelling across sky...

Air travel began with hot air balloons. In the late 1800s, powered airships were invented.

Airship

The first plane flight was made in 1903. Planes then improved quickly when they were needed in World War I (1914-18).

World War I plane

Today, the passenger jet *Concorde* can fly at twice the speed of sound.

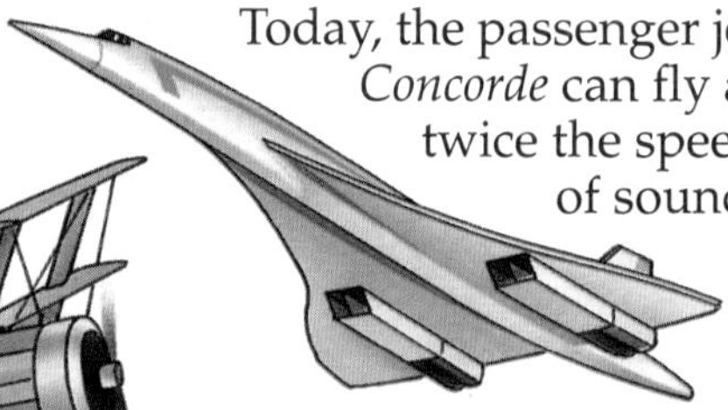

Concorde

...sea...

Paddle-steamer

In the late 1700s, paddle-steamers travelled on rivers in France and the USA.

From the 1840s, ocean liners were built. By the 1930s, they were crossing the Atlantic in about four days.

Ocean liner

Today, people seldom travel by ocean liner. For short journeys, they use car ferries or hydrofoils.

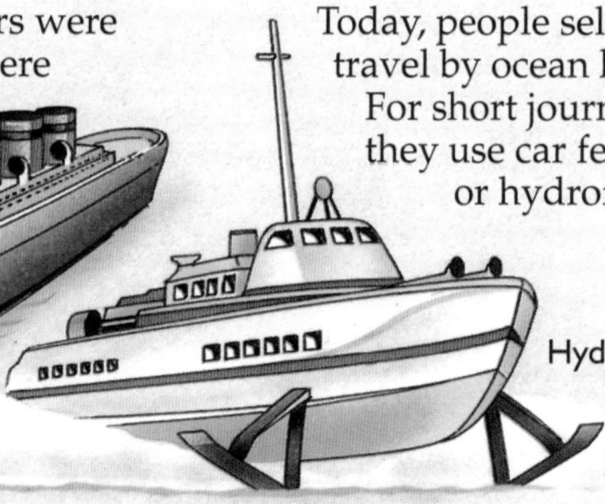

Hydrofoil

...and land

The first trains, in the early 1800s, carried goods. They travelled at less than 16kmph (10mph).

The *Rocket* – one of the first trains

The first car was built by Karl Benz in 1885. It could travel no faster than 16kmph (10mph).

Benz's car

Modern cars and trains can travel a long way at high speed. They are comfortable and reliable.

Modern sports car

Passenger travel

Many people travel short distances to nearby places every day. They need cheap and reliable transport, so they use cars, trains, buses or trams which stop locally.

City-centre tram

Fast train

For longer distances, people sometimes need faster transport. Trains, coaches and also planes travel directly between cities, with few stops.

Passenger jet

When people need to travel great distances in a short time, the best way to go is by plane, though it may be expensive. Planes may fly over continents without stopping.

Carrying goods

Planes only carry a certain weight, so heavy goods are transported around the world by ship, truck or train. These take longer to reach their destination, but they are much cheaper to use.

Cargo truck

Owning a car

Motor vehicles give people freedom over where and when they travel. In rich countries, many adults own vehicles. In poor ones, more people walk, use cheap mopeds or local transport. The graph below shows approximately what percentage of people own cars in some different countries.

% of people who own a car

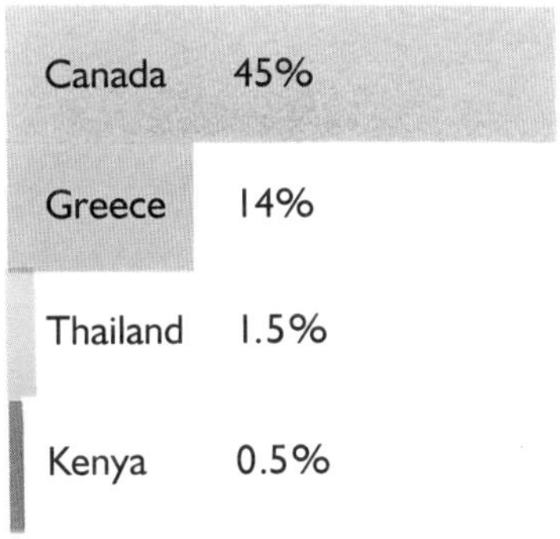

Canada 45%
Greece 14%
Thailand 1.5%
Kenya 0.5%

Traffic jams

In many places, the roads are clogged up with traffic. In some cities, such as Athens and Los Angeles, traffic is causing serious pollution*. This causes damage to health and to the environment. To help solve these problems, people could walk or cycle more often. Governments could also encourage people to use public transport rather than cars.

Exhaust gases eat away at brick and stone.

*Pollution, 344.

Routes

A network of roads and other routes connects places around the world. Some routes have been used for hundreds of years and are still in use today. Others have been built especially for today's modern transport.

The quickest way to get from one place to another is to travel along a straight, level route. However, obstacles in the landscape, such as hills, rivers, forests and towns, make it impossible to travel always in a straight line. These two pages show some ways to take routes around obstacles.

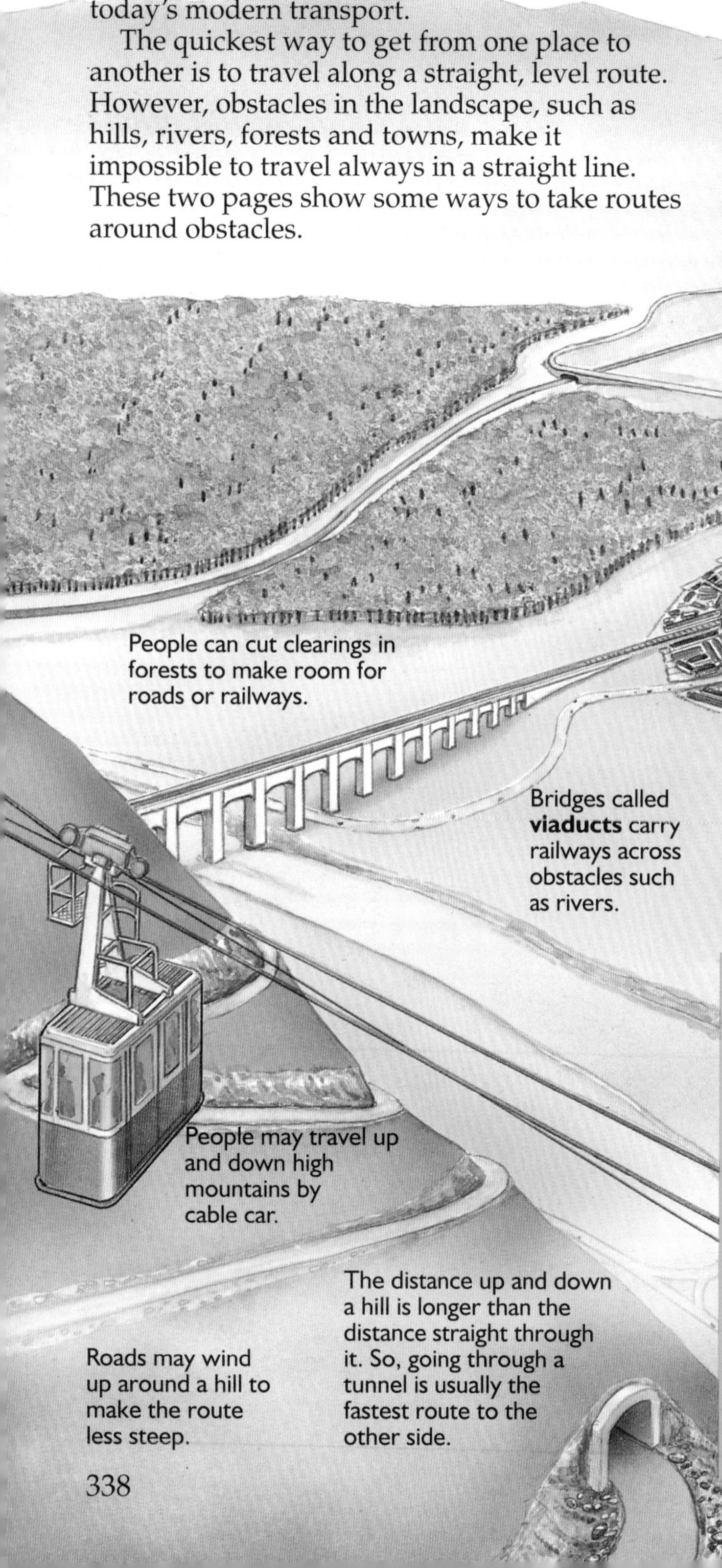

It may be possible to dig part of a hill away to make a cutting for a road, canal or railway.
Travelling through a busy town slows traffic down. By going around a ring-road or a by-pass, traffic avoids the town.
People can cut clearings in forests to make room for roads or railways.
Bridges called **viaducts** carry railways across obstacles such as rivers.
People may travel up and down high mountains by cable car.
The distance up and down a hill is longer than the distance straight through it. So, going through a tunnel is usually the fastest route to the other side.
Roads may wind up around a hill to make the route less steep.

Roads and railways

Cities and towns are linked by roads and railways. Roads take people from door to door, while trains only stop at certain places. Railway journeys, though, are fast because the track is as straight and flat as possible.

Roman roads

The Romans were expert road builders. They built roads as straight as possible. Many modern roads run along old Roman ones, such as Watling Street and Fosse Way in Britain.

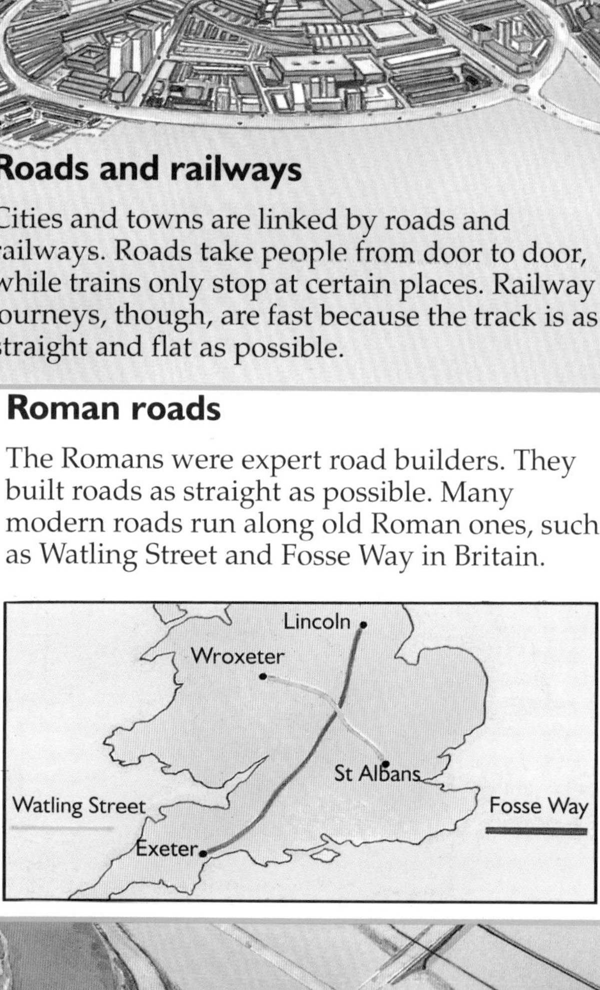

Lincoln
Wroxeter
St Albans
Watling Street
Fosse Way
Exeter

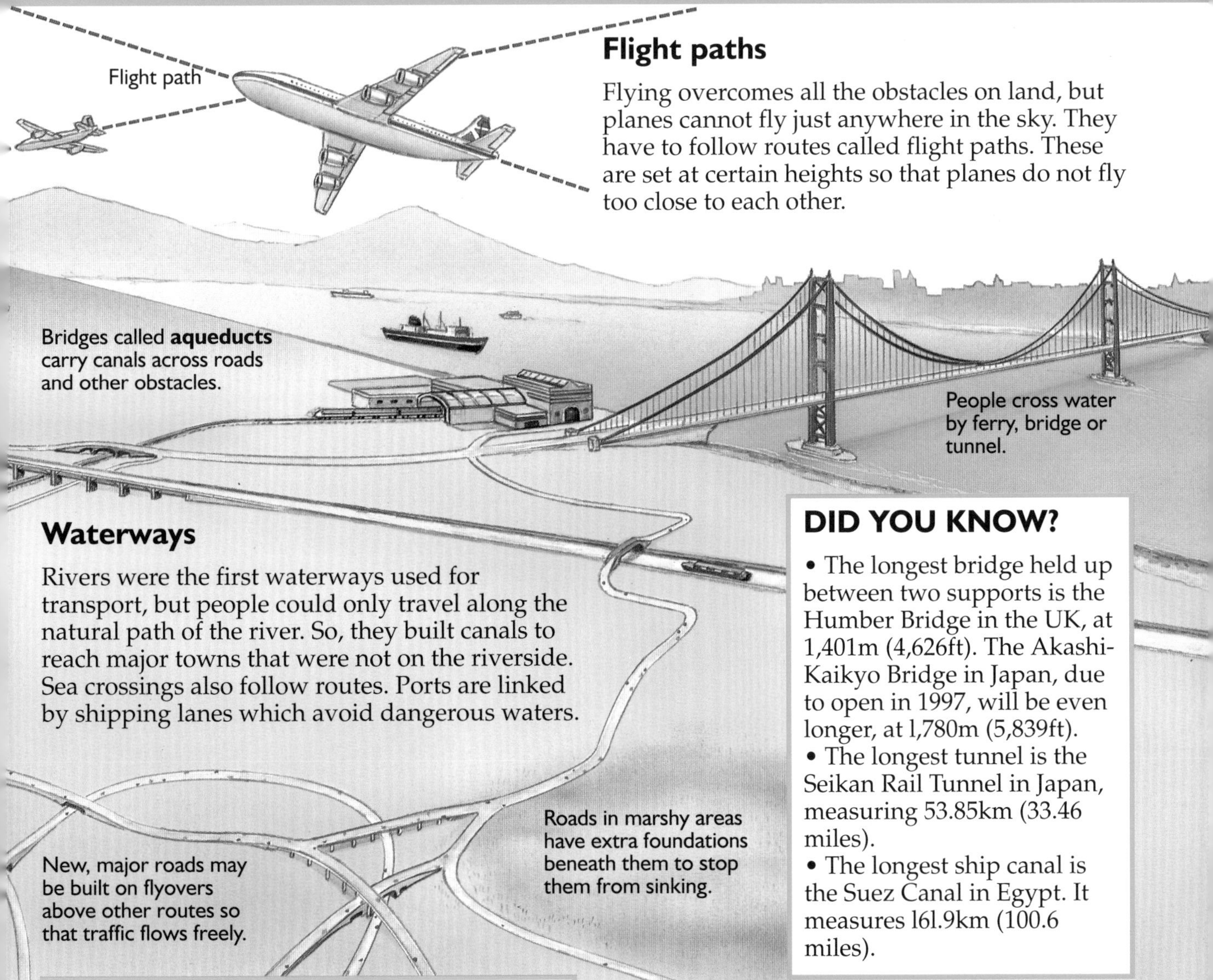
Flight path
Bridges called **aqueducts** carry canals across roads and other obstacles.
People cross water by ferry, bridge or tunnel.
Roads in marshy areas have extra foundations beneath them to stop them from sinking.
New, major roads may be built on flyovers above other routes so that traffic flows freely.

Flight paths

Flying overcomes all the obstacles on land, but planes cannot fly just anywhere in the sky. They have to follow routes called flight paths. These are set at certain heights so that planes do not fly too close to each other.

Waterways

Rivers were the first waterways used for transport, but people could only travel along the natural path of the river. So, they built canals to reach major towns that were not on the riverside. Sea crossings also follow routes. Ports are linked by shipping lanes which avoid dangerous waters.

DID YOU KNOW?

- The longest bridge held up between two supports is the Humber Bridge in the UK, at 1,401m (4,626ft). The Akashi-Kaikyo Bridge in Japan, due to open in 1997, will be even longer, at 1,780m (5,839ft).
- The longest tunnel is the Seikan Rail Tunnel in Japan, measuring 53.85km (33.46 miles).
- The longest ship canal is the Suez Canal in Egypt. It measures 161.9km (100.6 miles).

Route through America

The Panama Canal saves ships a long journey around South America. It cuts through Central America, making a direct route between the Pacific and the Atlantic Oceans.

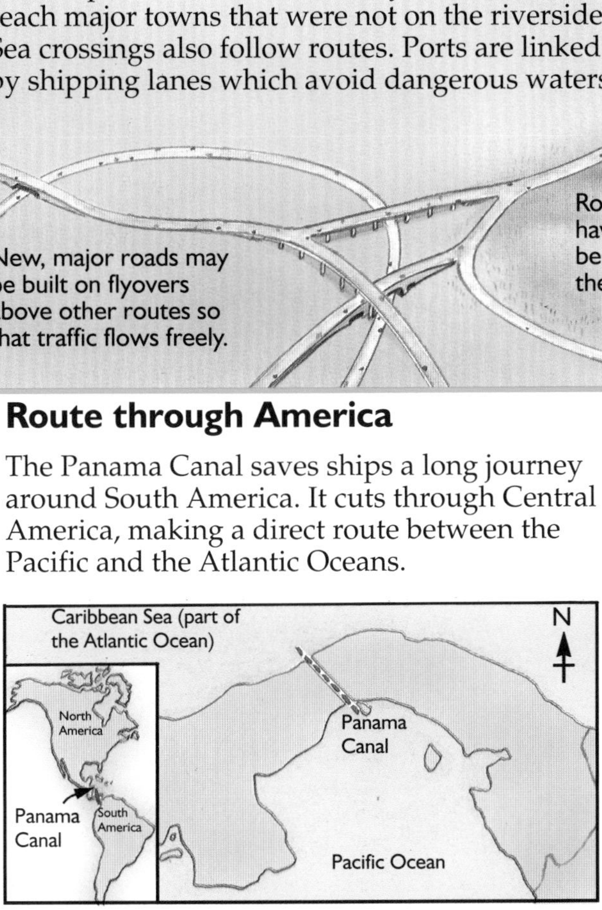
Caribbean Sea (part of the Atlantic Ocean)
N
North America
South America
Panama Canal
Panama Canal
Pacific Ocean

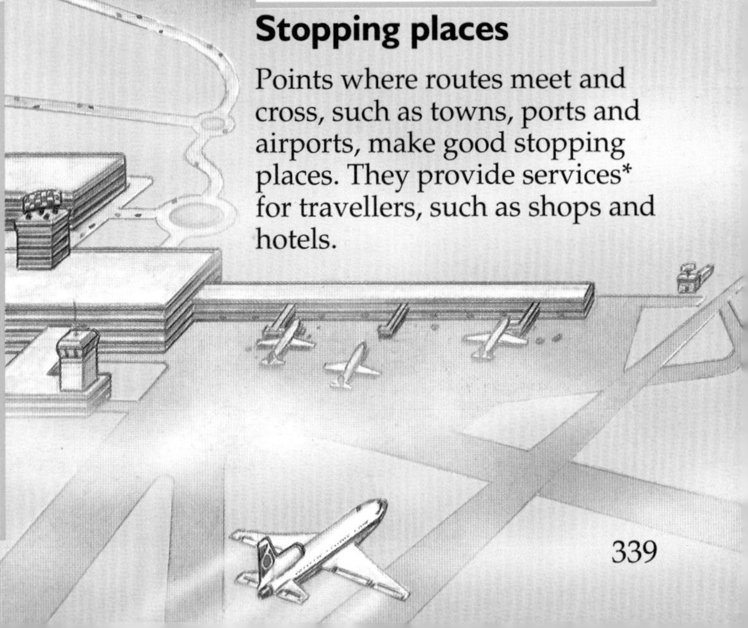

Stopping places

Points where routes meet and cross, such as towns, ports and airports, make good stopping places. They provide services* for travellers, such as shops and hotels.

**Services*, 334.

Communication

In the 20th century, the speed of communication has increased enormously. Some people say that the world is shrinking because, as communication improves, it takes less and less time to get a message to the other side of the world. Quick communication makes it easier for people in different countries to organize business, sport, politics and many other events together.

These days, messages in the form of pictures, writing and sound can be sent electrically. Telephones, televisions, radios, fax machines and computers all work in this way. Electrical signals travel instantly along cables and through radio waves in the air, so people can receive messages as soon as they are sent. These two pages show some ways in which signals can be transmitted.

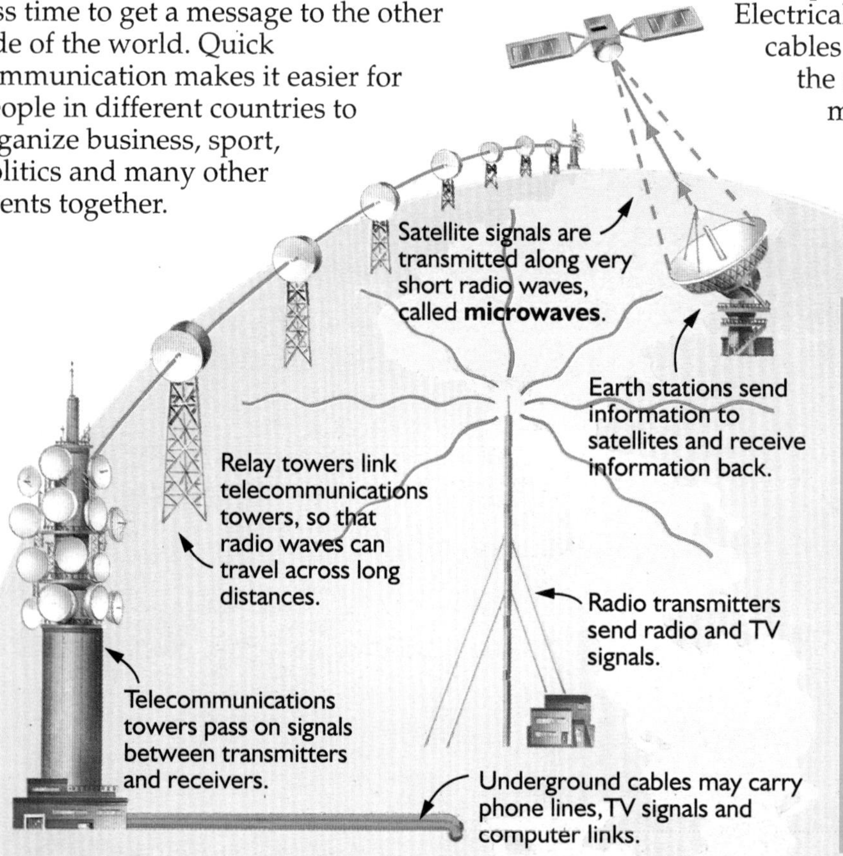

Satellite signals are transmitted along very short radio waves, called **microwaves**.
Earth stations send information to satellites and receive information back.
Relay towers link telecommunications towers, so that radio waves can travel across long distances.
Radio transmitters send radio and TV signals.
Telecommunications towers pass on signals between transmitters and receivers.
Underground cables may carry phone lines, TV signals and computer links.

DID YOU KNOW?

In 1912, an ocean liner, called the *Titanic*, sank in the Atlantic. The nearest ship had its radio switched off and did not hear the distress call, so many people died. After this disaster, it became law for all ships to carry radios and always listen for emergency calls.

The *Titanic*

Communication satellites

There are many satellites orbiting the Earth. Communication satellites carry TV programmes and phone calls. They travel at the same speed as the Earth, so they are always above the same patch of land. They are called **geostationary satellites.**

Big events, such as sports matches or rock concerts, are broadcast live by geostationary satellite, so that people around the world can watch them instantly as they happen. This picture shows how a live event is broadcast from one side of the world to the other.

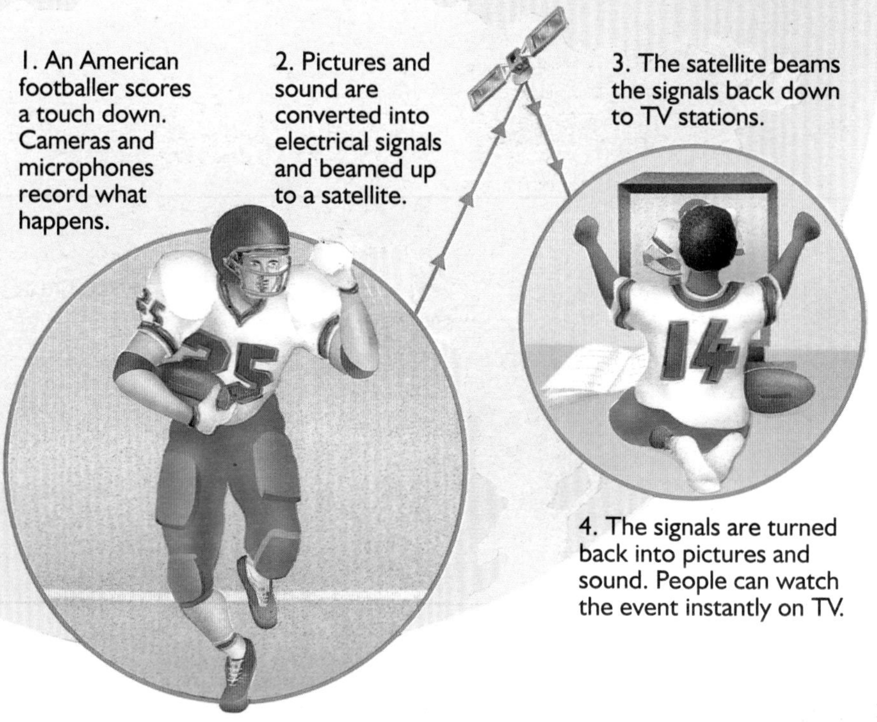

1. An American footballer scores a touch down. Cameras and microphones record what happens.
2. Pictures and sound are converted into electrical signals and beamed up to a satellite.
3. The satellite beams the signals back down to TV stations.
4. The signals are turned back into pictures and sound. People can watch the event instantly on TV.

Satellites watching Earth

Some satellites help scientists to know what is happening on Earth, by sending back information. These are called **observation satellites** and they orbit the Earth on different paths and at different speeds.

These satellites, such as the American LANDSAT, send back data, which can be turned into multi-coloured images of the Earth's surface. Some gather information about the weather, some look for changes on land and at sea, and others monitor changes in climate.

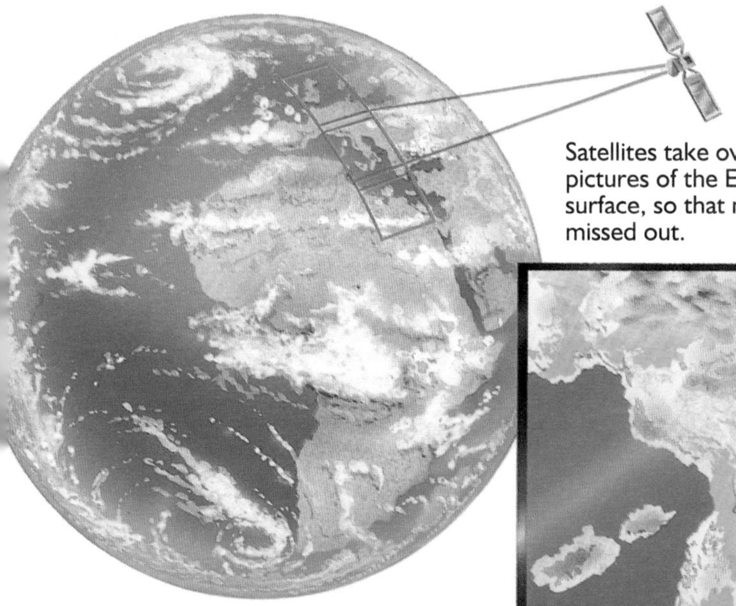

Satellites take overlapping pictures of the Earth's surface, so that nothing is missed out.

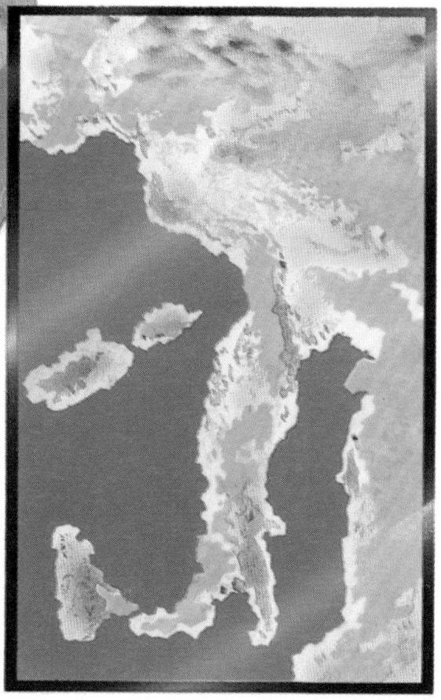

The satellite image on the right shows the temperature in Italy. The orange areas show where it is warmest and the yellow and green areas show where it is cooler.

Owning a phone

Although communication equipment is very advanced, there are still many places in the world where it is not easily available to ordinary people. For example, two thirds of the world's population do not have a phone in their house. The graph on the right shows the percentage of people who own a phone in some different countries.

% of people who own a phone
France 60%
Hungary 9%
Niger 0.15%

The history of signals

The earliest way to send a message, without taking it by hand, was to display a sign that could be seen from far away, such as smoke or fire, or by waving flags.

Morse's telegraph

The operator tapped words in code into the machine.

In the 1830s, Samuel Morse invented the **telegraph**, which sent electrical signals along a wire. People sent messages with a code of short and long bleeps, called **Morse Code**.

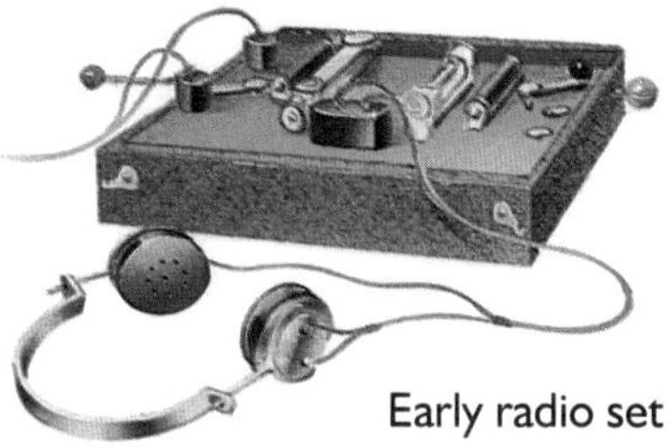

Early radio set

In 1901, the first radio message was sent across the Atlantic by a man called Marconi. He proved that radio waves can carry electrical signals.

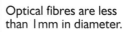

Optical fibres are less than 1mm in diameter.

Today, information can be turned into light pulses as well as electrical signals. Tiny glass tubes called **optical fibres** carry light pulses. Each pair of optical fibres can carry 2,000 phone calls at any one time.

Resources

A **resource** is anything that people find useful. Almost everything in the natural world can be a resource, such as wind, water, rocks, metals, or even the countryside. Many of our natural resources are the raw materials* that are used in manufacturing.

However, materials only become a resource when people find a use for them. For example, rubber trees existed long before their sap, called latex, was used in manufacturing tyres or raincoats. Also, resources can only be used if reaching them does not cost more money than they are worth. People use tin much less than before because it has become too expensive to mine and aluminium can now be used instead.

Today, a bigger range of resources is being used because new technology helps the development of resources and new uses for them are discovered. However, it is possible that some resources may run out if they are overused.

Using resources

There are many different kinds of resources. Our most important ones are soil, wind, water and heat and light from the Sun. People use them to generate energy and grow food.

Minerals* are some of our most valuable raw materials. They are split into two groups: metals, including copper, zinc and lead; and non-metals, including oil, sand and silicon. Minerals are used in the building and chemical industries and some, such as fossil fuels*, are used to generate energy.

Forests are also valuable resources. Around two billion people use wood for heating and cooking. There is such demand for wood that many forests in developing countries* are being destroyed. Wood is also needed for building and manufacturing, for which there are two types of wood. Softwood is produced by quick-growing conifers* and hardwood is produced by slow-growing deciduous trees*.

Wood is not the only forest resource. Forests are the source of many raw materials, such as those used to make drugs. There may be thousands more plants and animals that will benefit people, which are still undiscovered in the world's forests.

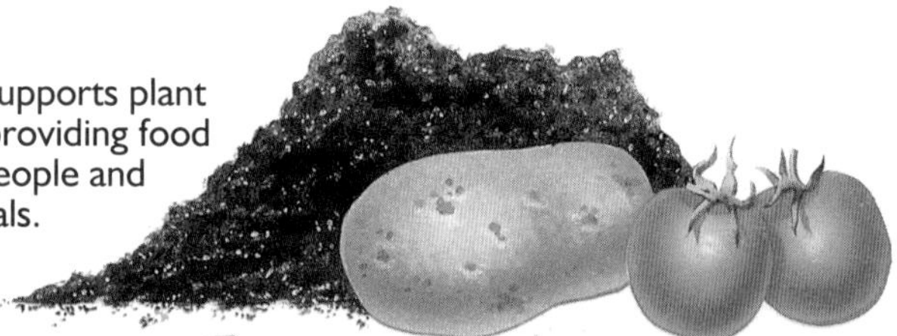
Soil supports plant life, providing food for people and animals.

Copper is manufactured into items such as pipes and copper wire.

Sand is used in glass-making and building.

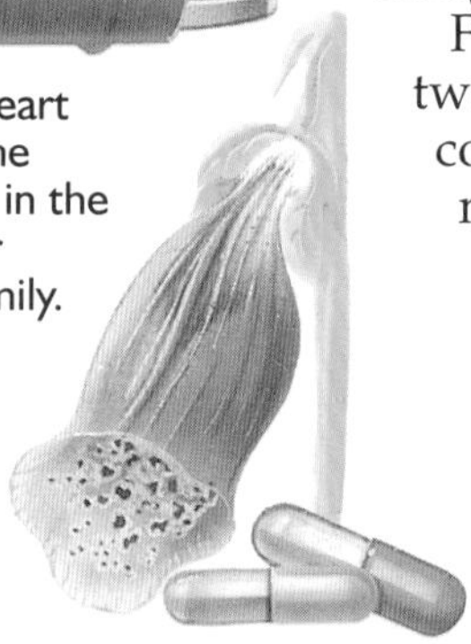
Drugs for heart disease come from plants in the foxglove, or *Digitalis*, family.

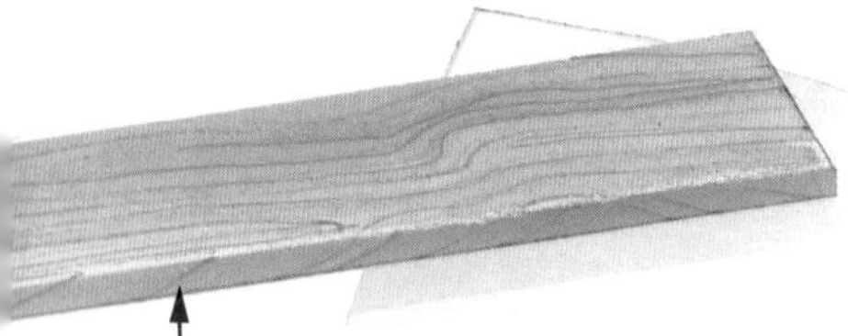
Softwood is used in paper-making and for light building materials.

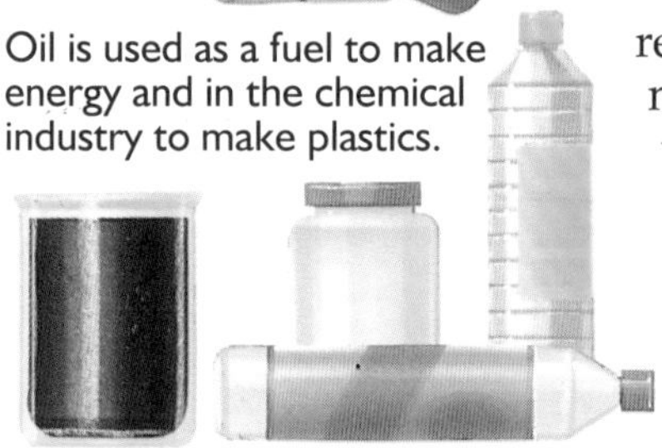
Oil is used as a fuel to make energy and in the chemical industry to make plastics.

Latex for rubber manufacturing comes from tropical rubber trees.

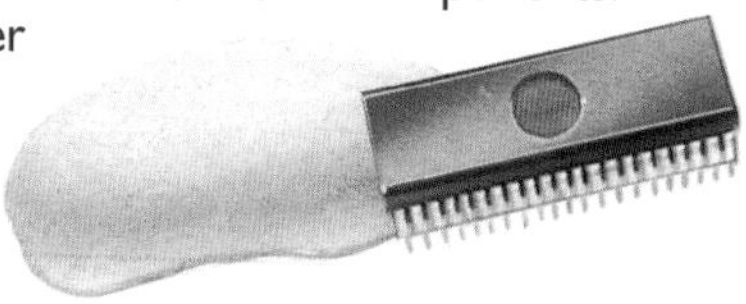
Silicon comes from quartz rock. It is used to make electronic components.

Hardwood is used for furniture-making and strong building materials.

 Conifers, 307; Deciduous trees, 307; Development, 312; Fossil fuels, 330; Minerals, 276; Raw materials, 332.

Tourists and the environment

As towns and cities grow faster than ever, scenery and wide-open spaces are becoming more and more valuable as a resource. Many people have more leisure time and often prefer to spend it in the countryside.

However, the countryside is threatened by the growth of tourism, as well as the growth of cities. Thousands of visitors can cause great damage to the environment and destroy wildlife habitats.

On the Mediterranean coast, vast areas have been taken up by hotels.

In Britain, many footpaths have been eroded by walkers.

In the Alps and the Rocky Mountains, skiers have worn away mountain plants and caused landslides.

In the Philippines and on the Great Barrier Reef, coral has been destroyed by divers touching and treading on it.

Keeping the environment safe

Using resources changes the environment. Activities such as tourism, mining and road-building must be well planned. Planners make a study called an environmental assessment to show the possible effects of their project. If the project will be too damaging, then it has to change. For example, world banks no longer lend money to projects developing the Amazon Basin, due to environmental damage there.

Conservation and recycling

Many of our resources are non-renewable*, and will eventually run out. To make them last longer, people need to conserve (save) materials and recycle them as much as possible. Industries can play a major part in doing this. The picture below shows how one of them, the aluminium can manufacturing industry, has managed to increase its efficiency so that it saves both energy and materials.

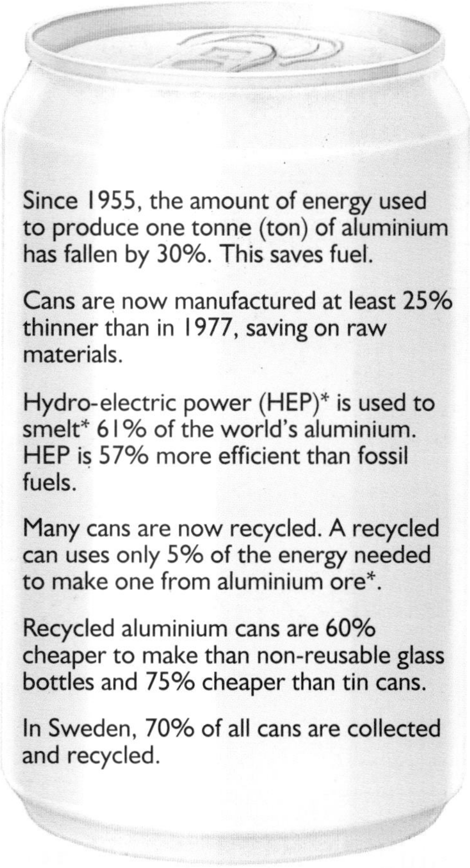

Since 1955, the amount of energy used to produce one tonne (ton) of aluminium has fallen by 30%. This saves fuel.

Cans are now manufactured at least 25% thinner than in 1977, saving on raw materials.

Hydro-electric power (HEP)* is used to smelt* 61% of the world's aluminium. HEP is 57% more efficient than fossil fuels.

Many cans are now recycled. A recycled can uses only 5% of the energy needed to make one from aluminium ore*.

Recycled aluminium cans are 60% cheaper to make than non-reusable glass bottles and 75% cheaper than tin cans.

In Sweden, 70% of all cans are collected and recycled.

Individuals can also conserve and recycle materials. Always switching off appliances when they are not in use, using cars less and insulating the house better are all easy ways to save energy. Reusing materials, such as bottles and plastic bags saves resources and also cuts down on the amount of waste. Aluminium cans, paper, glass, and some plastics can all be recycled, which saves on fuels and materials.

*Hydro-electric power, 331; Non-renewable energy, 330; Ore, 328; Smelting, 328.

Pollution

Pollution can damage the health of living things. Some kinds of pollution occur naturally, such as smoke from forest fires and volcanoes, or pollen from flowers. However, industries, farms, power stations, traffic and day-to-day living make a great deal more pollution by creating harmful substances, waste and noise.

Pollution on land and at sea

The landscape is polluted by waste. Large areas of land are taken up by ugly waste dumps, which are created by the massive amounts of refuse people throw away every day. Some people even dump litter in rivers or on the street.

Industrial waste, such as slag from coal mining, is also disposed of in huge dumps. Some waste is poisonous and may be buried beneath the ground to get rid of it. However, this is not always safe, as the poisons can leak out through underground streams. If water becomes polluted, it can easily affect a wide area, because rivers carry the pollution downstream. When it reaches the sea, currents spread it even further.

Chemicals from industry, and pesticides* and fertilizers* from farming are washed into rivers, where bacteria live off them. Bacteria use up the oxygen in water, so fish and water animals suffocate. In some places, untreated sewage is released into rivers and seas, causing disease in both animals and people.

Many animals are trapped and injured by litter, such as plastic can rings.

Fish are poisoned by metals in waste from industry. Animals that feed on fish are poisoned too.

Oil spilled from tanker ships sticks to birds and poisons them if they swallow it. Feathers covered in oil no longer keep birds warm, so they can die of cold.

Sewage and industrial waste may flow into rivers and the sea, where people sail and swim.

Cleaning up

So much pollution is being made that it is difficult to get rid of it safely. To keep the environment clean, governments can make laws to stop people from creating pollution. For example, it is illegal for oil tankers to pump out oil at sea. If they do, their captains may be fined.

Some famous cases of pollution have been caused by oil tankers, such as the *Exxon Valdez*, which crashed off the coast of Alaska in 1989. Oil from the ship affected beaches, fishing-grounds and sea life. After an oil spill, experts must act quickly to rescue animals and clean up the sea and beaches.

There are several ways to clean up oil at sea. Peat or straw, which absorb oil, can be spread on it and scraped up. Or, floating barriers called booms can stop oil from spreading, so that it can then be sucked up by a tanker.

 Fertilizers, Pesticides, 324.

Air pollution

Industrial processes and motor vehicles all release substances into the air, such as lead, which can damage health. Some cities, for example Mexico City, are smothered by polluted air, called **smog**, which is bad to breathe. Loud noise is another kind of air pollution. It can cause deafness and other illnesses.

Acid rain

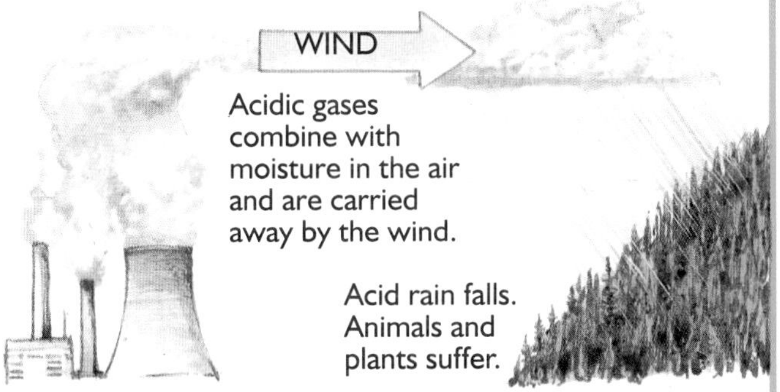

WIND
Acidic gases combine with moisture in the air and are carried away by the wind.
Acid rain falls. Animals and plants suffer.

Acid rain is a major form of air pollution. It is caused by acidic gases, such as nitrogen oxides and sulphur dioxide, which are released into the air by factory chimneys and vehicle exhaust pipes. These gases make moisture in the air up to a thousand times more acidic than usual.

Wind carries the moisture away, until it falls as acid rain, often in a nearby country. In Norway, 80% of rivers and streams either have, or soon will have, no life left in them. Ancient buildings, such as the Parthenon in Athens, are being worn away and forests in Europe and North America are dying.

The ozone layer

The ozone layer* is part of the atmosphere and protects us from the Sun's harmful rays. Chemicals called **CFCs** (chlorofluorocarbons), used in insulation material, aerosols and refrigerators attack ozone if they escape into the air. Holes are forming in the ozone layer and it will only return to its natural state if people stop using CFCs.

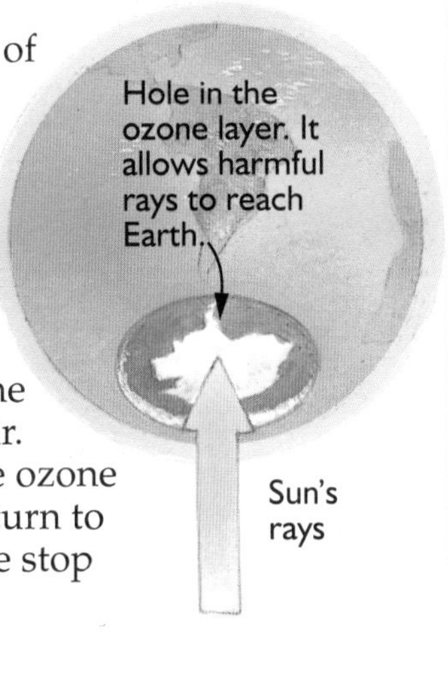

Hole in the ozone layer. It allows harmful rays to reach Earth.
Sun's rays

Ozone layer, 271.

The Greenhouse Effect

The Earth is kept warm by the atmosphere which holds heat in. This process, called the **Greenhouse Effect**, happens naturally. However, many scientists agree that the Earth is getting warmer.

This warming is caused by an increase in certain gases, called **greenhouse gases**, in the air. These include carbon dioxide, CFCs and methane. They increase the atmosphere's ability to keep heat in. This diagram shows how the Greenhouse Effect works.

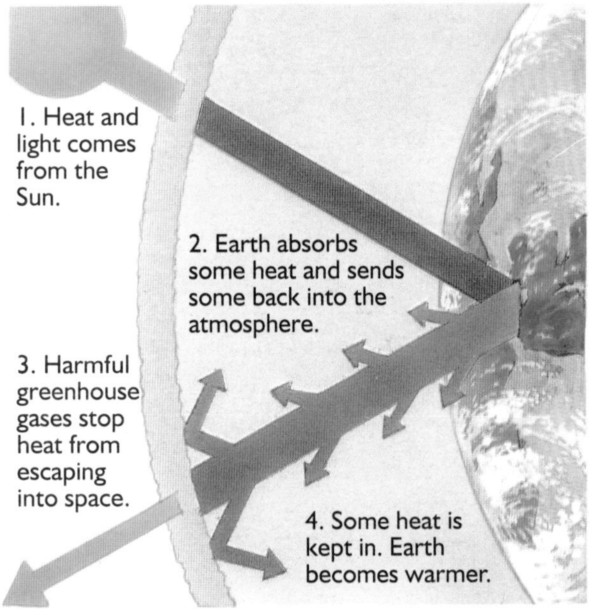

1. Heat and light comes from the Sun.
2. Earth absorbs some heat and sends some back into the atmosphere.
3. Harmful greenhouse gases stop heat from escaping into space.
4. Some heat is kept in. Earth becomes warmer.

If the temperature on Earth increases too much, the weather and climate will change, harming animal and plant life. Ice at the Poles will melt, causing sea-levels to rise and land to be flooded.

What makes greenhouse gases?

Most greenhouse gases occur naturally, but now there is too much of them in the air. Carbon dioxide is produced by burning fuels and in industrial waste. Plants absorb carbon dioxide, but many trees are being cut down, so much less of it is used up. Methane is produced by some kinds of farming, such as cattle-raising and rice-growing, and from rotting waste. CFCs are not natural gases and are produced by the manufacturing industries.

Tomorrow's world

The world is changing faster than ever. It used to take years for new technology to be put into practice, but now it may take only months. The future is difficult to predict exactly, but many things which now seem strange may soon be part of everyday life.

Cities in the future

Cities in the future may be very different from today's cities. In order to create a warm environment where the weather is always pleasant, people may build cities in a see-through bubble, like the one in the picture. In Europe, there are already leisure parks enclosed in bubbles, so that visitors always get good weather. As land to build on becomes more scarce, people may even build cities under the sea or perhaps in space.

Each year, roads become busier and the air becomes more polluted* by petrol-driven vehicles. Future forms of transportation should be less harmful to the environment.

For some journeys, people may fly personal, one-seater aircraft or drive silent, electric cars. However, for regular journeys into and around the city, most people may travel on underground or overground light railways or monorails which run overhead.

Passenger aircraft for use on longer journeys may be able to take off and land vertically. This would save space on land, as these types of planes need only short runways. For very long journeys, people may even travel in low-level spacecraft.

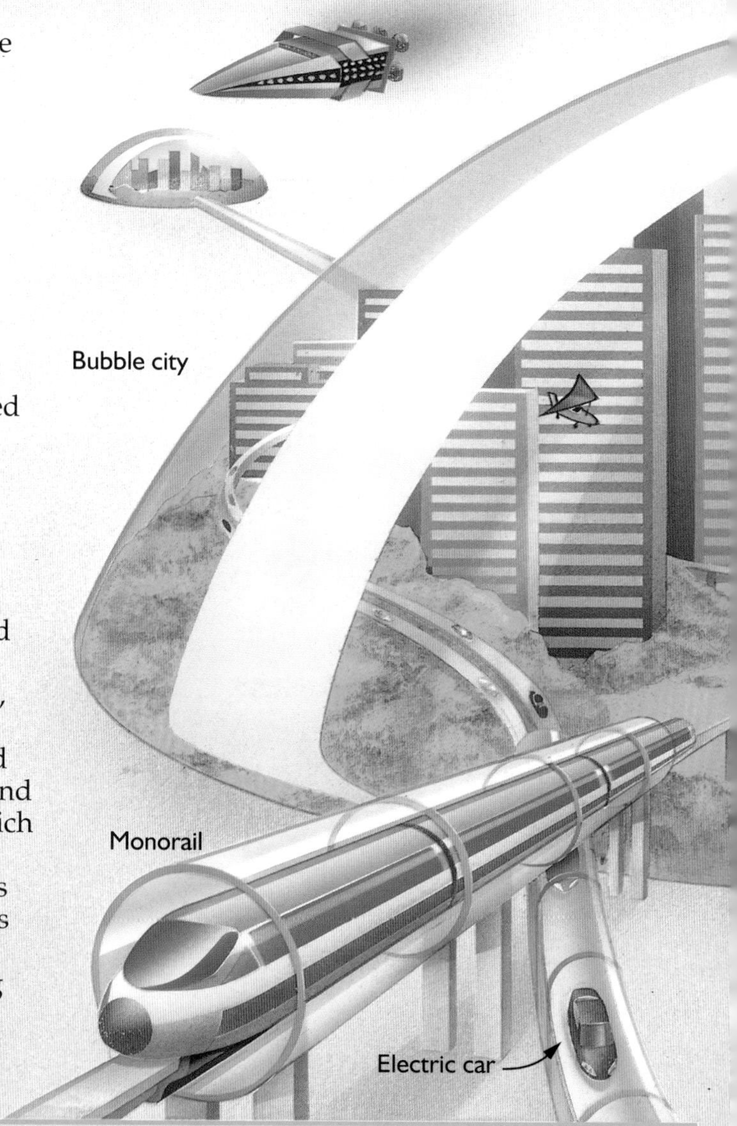
Low-level spacecraft
Bubble city
Monorail
Electric car

The environment

The world population is expanding, so people will need more food, and more fresh water for drinking, farming and industry. It is now possible to have some control over the weather and the environment, and this may help to provide food and water for the future.

In low areas, such as the Netherlands, the sea has been drained away from coastal areas to make more land for building and farming. In dry areas, such as parts of Israel, it is possible to sprinkle the clouds with chemicals to make it rain on the crops. In the Middle East, factories take salt out of sea-water, to make it safe to drink. These methods may all be used more in the future, though people must be careful that they do not harm the environment.

Planes can sprinkle chemicals on clouds to make them rain.

*Pollution, 344.

City in space
Personal aircraft
Airport with short runways, for planes that take off vertically.

DID YOU KNOW?

Scientists say that in the future, meals of vegetables and meat may be replaced by a diet of vitamin and mineral pills. However, people would probably not want to give up real food.

Communication

In the future, people will invent new ways of communication. People may own phones, called view-phones, which will have TV screens so that people can see, as well as hear, each other. It would be possible to have a view-phone meeting with people who were all in different places. Everyone would appear on the screen at once and be able to communicate with anyone else.

One day, we may even be able to invent machines that send tastes and smells, as we now send messages of sound and pictures.

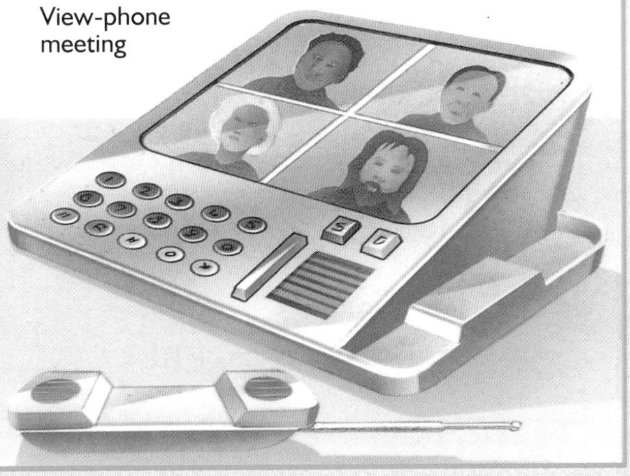
View-phone meeting

Energy

In the future, as fossil fuels* run out, we are likely to need new sources of energy. Scientists are working on many new ideas, such as **nuclear fusion**. This is the process of joining parts of atoms together to release massive amounts of energy.

Scientists are also developing a method of making power called **Ocean Thermal Energy Conversion (OTEC)**. This uses the difference in temperature between layers of tropical sea-water to boil a liquid into gas, which then drives a turbine and generates electricity.

A new lifestyle

As technology improves, our everyday lives may change. Many more jobs may be done by computers or robots. There will still be a need for workers, but jobs may be shared by more people. This means that people may have shorter working hours and more leisure time.

People also need to change their way of life so that they look after the Earth and waste less of its natural resources. If people want to preserve the Earth and its resources for future generations, they must use materials efficiently and reuse as much as possible.

**Fossil fuels, 330.*

The world

Over 70% of the Earth's surface is covered by water. Most of it is contained in the four oceans: the Arctic, the Atlantic, the Indian and the Pacific. The total land area is around 150,000,000km^2 (58,000,000 square miles). It is divided into seven continents — Asia, North America, South America, Africa, Europe, Antarctica and Australia.

The world is split up into different countries. There are currently 185 countries, but this number is always changing as some countries join together and others split up to form separate states.

Key

- ■ London — Population over 1,000,000
- • Oslo — Population under 1,000,000
- Country border
- State border
- River
- Lake
- Canal
- Mountainous area

Scale

Km: 0 500

Miles: 0 500 1000

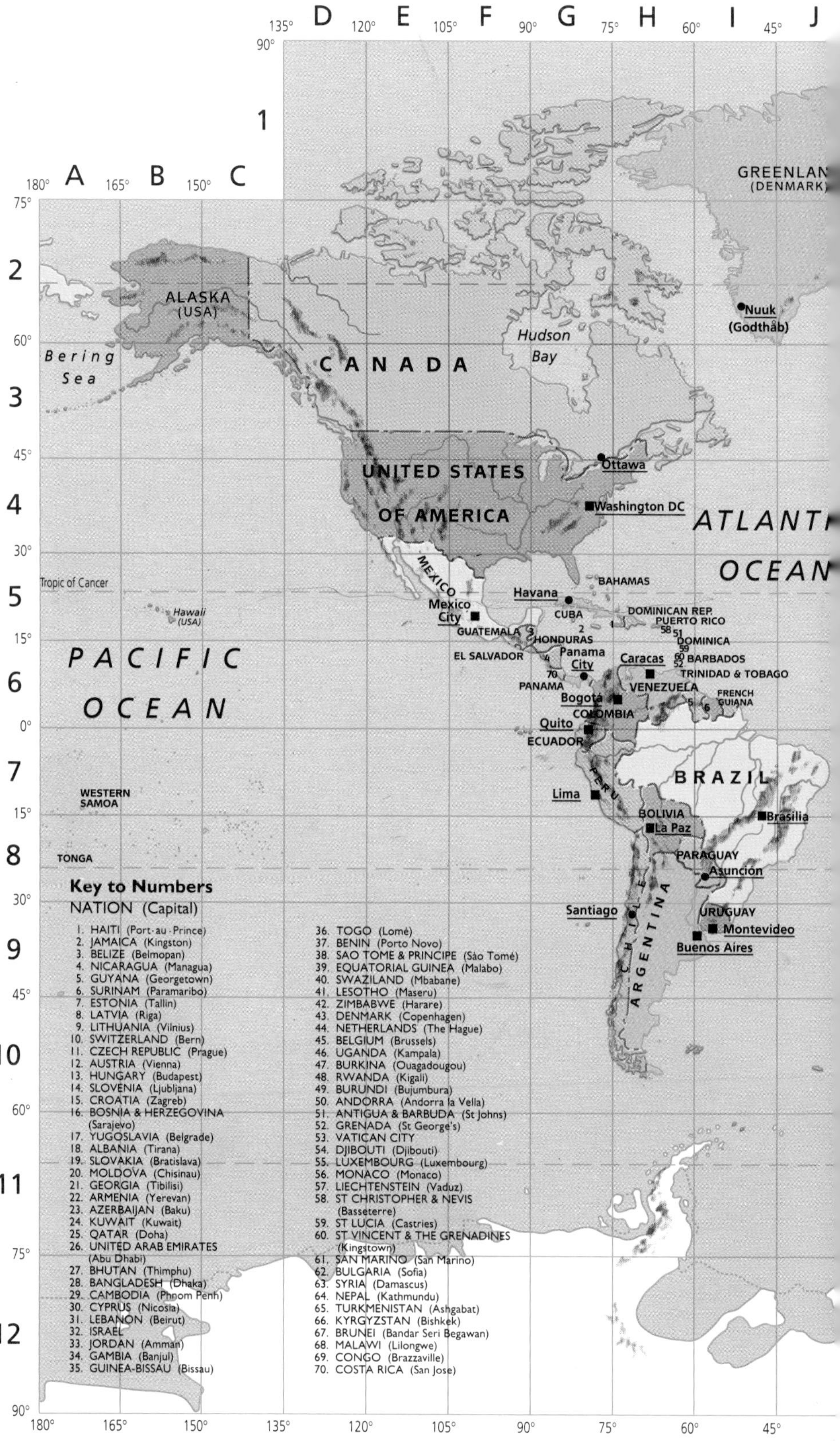

East of Greenwich
L M N O P Q R S T U V W X Y
0° 15° 30° 45° 60° 75° 90° 105° 120° 135° 150° 165° 180° 165°
90° 75° 60° 45° 30° 15° 0° 15° 30° 45° 60° 75° 90°
ARCTIC OCEAN
Barents Sea
Arctic Circle
RUSSIAN FEDERATION
FINLAND
SWEDEN
NORWAY
Helsinki
Oslo
Stockholm
UNITED KINGDOM
Dublin
London
Paris
FRANCE
GERMANY
Berlin
Warsaw
POLAND
BELARUS
Moscow
UKRAINE
Kiev
ROMANIA
Bucharest
ITALY
Rome
SPAIN
Madrid
Tunis
Algiers
Rabat
MOROCCO
ALGERIA
TUNISIA
MALTA
Tripoli
LIBYA
Black Sea
GREECE
Athens
TURKEY
Ankara
Tehran
IRAN
IRAQ
Baghdad
Cairo
EGYPT
SAUDI ARABIA
Riyadh
BAHRAIN
OMAN
Muscat
KAZAKHSTAN
Alma-Ata
UZBEKISTAN
Tashkent
TAJIKISTAN
Dushanbe
AFGHANISTAN
Kabul
JAMMU & KASHMIR
Islamabad
PAKISTAN
New Delhi
INDIA
Ulan Bator
MONGOLIA
CHINA
Beijing
N KOREA
P'yongyang
Seoul
S KOREA
JAPAN
Tōkyō
PACIFIC OCEAN
Tai-Pei
TAIWAN
Tropic of Cancer
MYANMAR (BURMA)
Rangoon
LAOS
THAILAND
Bangkok
VIETNAM
Hanoi
Manila
PHILIPPINES
Arabian Sea
SRI LANKA
Colombo
MALDIVES
Kuala Lumpur
MALAYSIA
MALI
MAURITANIA
Bamako
NIGER
Niamey
CHAD
N'Djamena
SUDAN
Khartoum
San'a
REP. OF YEMEN
NIGERIA
Abuja
GUINEA
IVORY COAST
GHANA
LIBERIA
Accra
Yamoussoukro
CAMEROON
Yaoundé
CENTRAL AFRICAN REPUBLIC
Bangui
ETHIOPIA
Addis Ababa
SOMALIA
Mogadishu
KENYA
Nairobi
GABON
Libreville
ZAÏRE
Kinshasa
Luanda
ANGOLA
TANZANIA
Dodoma
SEYCHELLES
ZAMBIA
Lusaka
COMOROS
MOZAMBIQUE
MADAGASCAR
Antananarivo
Port Louis
MAURITIUS
NAMIBIA
Walvis Bay (S.A.)
Windhoek
BOTSWANA
Gaborone
Pretoria
Maputo
SOUTH AFRICA
INDIAN OCEAN
Equator
Jakarta
INDONESIA
PAPUA NEW GUINEA
Port Moresby
NAURU
SOLOMON ISLANDS
Honiara
TUVALU
KIRIBATI
VANUATU
Suva
FIJI
Tropic of Capricorn
AUSTRALIA
Canberra
TASMANIA
NEW ZEALAND
Wellington
Antarctic Circle
ANTARCTICA
N
S
E
W

North America

America is made up of three main areas, North, Central and South America. North America, shown here, covers 19,343,000km^2 (7,468,000 square miles). There are only two countries in North America — the United States of America and Canada. Canada is the largest country in the world. Central and South America are shown on pages 352-355.

Key

Ottawa	Capital city		River
■Phoenix	Population over 1,000,000		Lake
●Billings	Population 100,000 - 1,000,000		Canal
⊙Fairbanks	Population under 100,000		Mountainous area
	Country border	McKinley ▲ 6194 (20316)	Mountain Peak - height in metres (feet)
	State border		

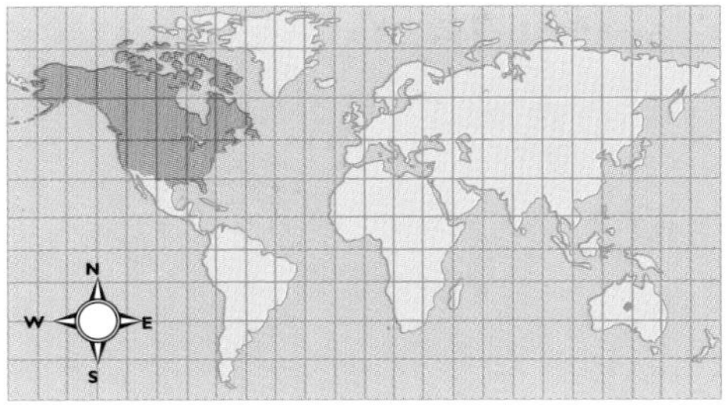

National flags

Canada

United States of America

Key to numbers

1. MASSACHUSETTS
2. CONNECTICUT

Scale

Km: 0 500 1000

Miles: 0 500 1000

Central and South America

Together, Central and South America cover an area of 23,617,000km^2 (9,119,000 square miles). The Amazon forest, which is the biggest area of rainforest in the world, is in South America. This area is also the largest river basin in the world.

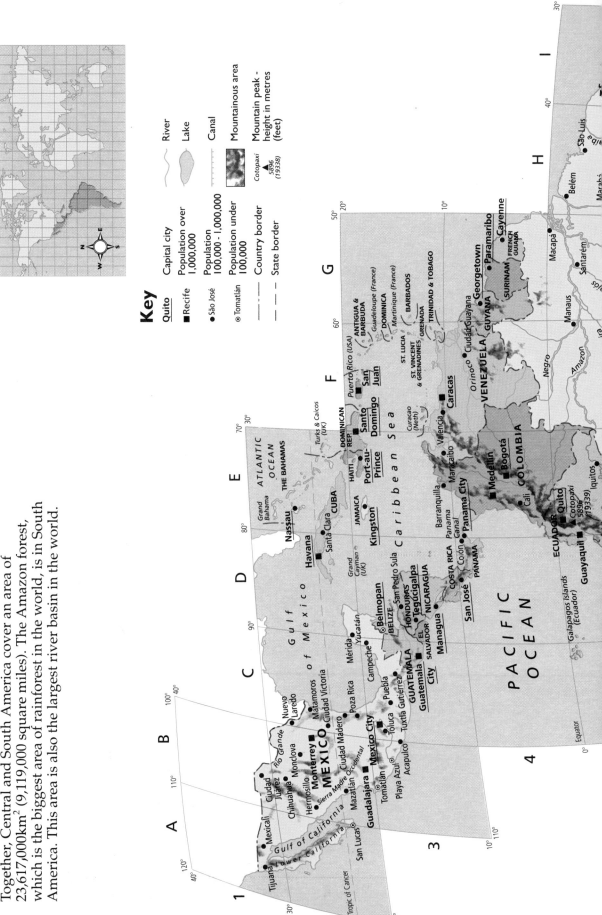

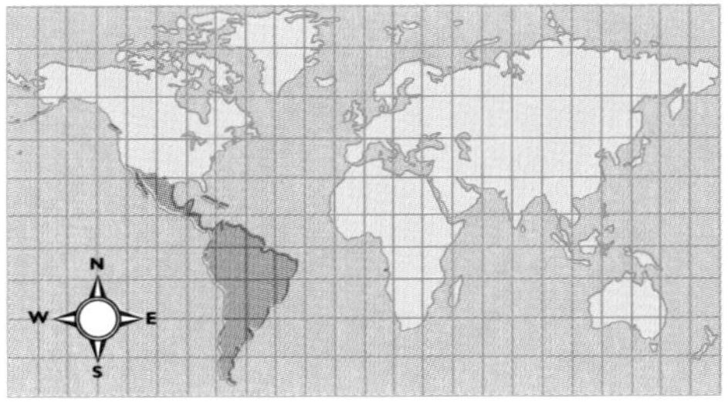

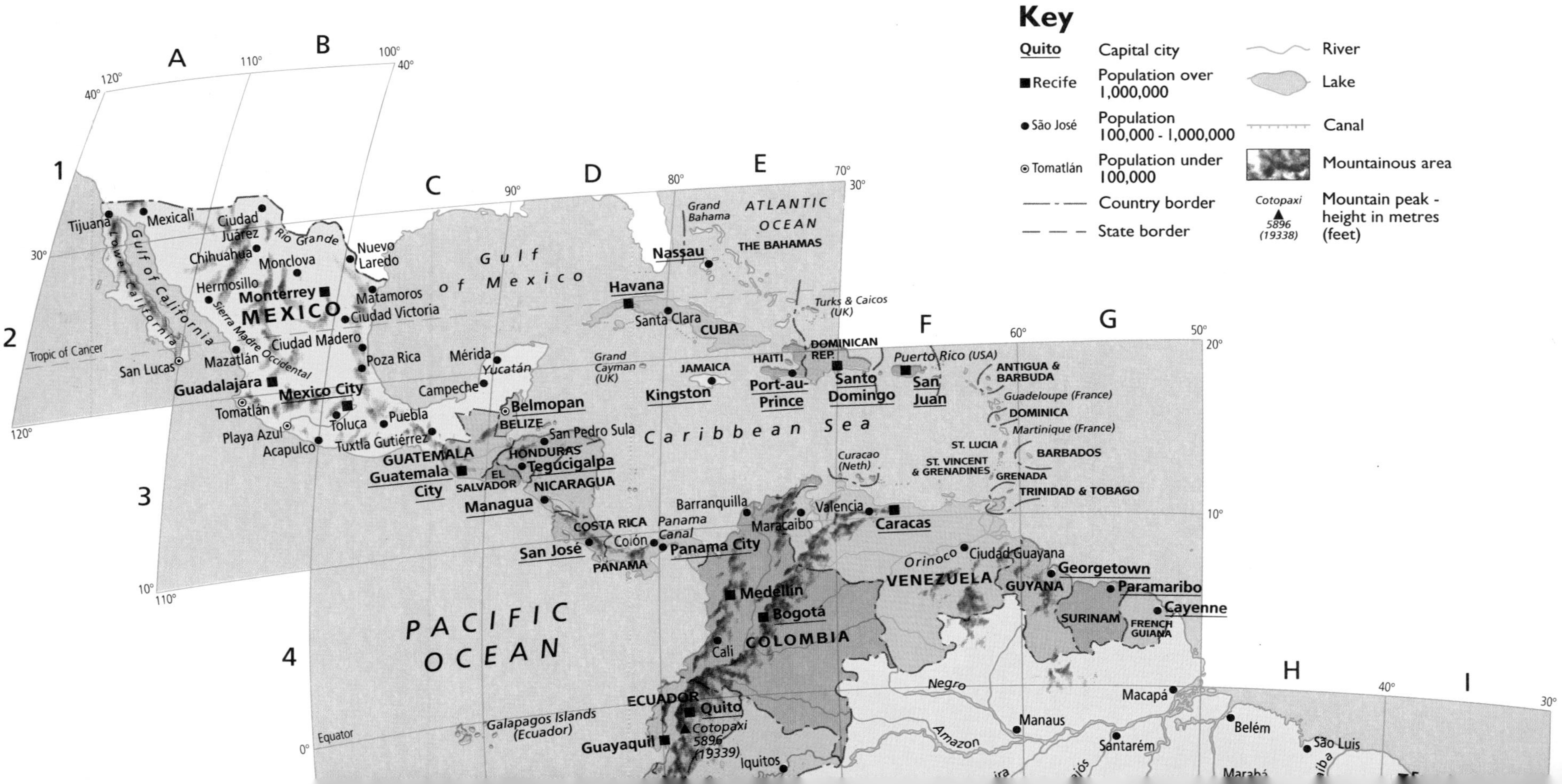

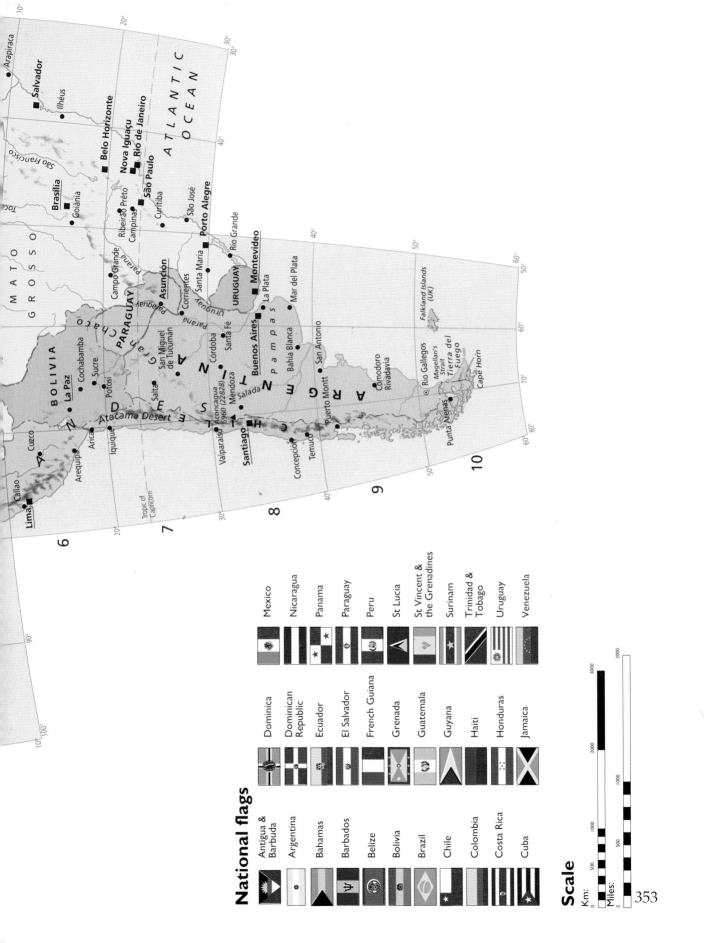

National flags

Antigua & Barbuda	Dominica	Mexico
Argentina	Dominican Republic	Nicaragua
Bahamas	Ecuador	Panama
Barbados	El Salvador	Paraguay
Belize	French Guiana	Peru
Bolivia	Grenada	St Lucia
Brazil	Guatemala	St Vincent & the Grenadines
Chile	Guyana	Surinam
Colombia	Haiti	Trinidad & Tobago
Costa Rica	Honduras	Uruguay
Cuba	Jamaica	Venezuela

Scale

Km: 0 500 1000 2000 3000

Miles: 0 500 1000 2000

Africa

Africa is the second biggest continent, covering 30,335,000km² (11,712,000 square miles). The Nile, which is the longest river in the world, runs through Africa. The Sahara, which is the biggest desert in the world, is also in Africa.

Key

Nairobi	Capital city
■ Abidjan	Population over 1,000,000
● Suez	Population 100,000 - 1,000,000
⊙ Kayes	Population under 100,000
—·—	Country border
— —	State border
(line)	River
(shape)	Lake
(line)	Canal
(shading)	Mountainous area
Kilimanjaro ▲ 5895 (19335)	Mountain peak - height in metres (feet)

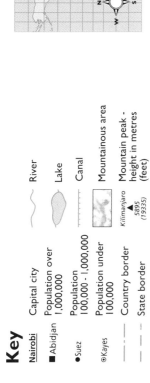

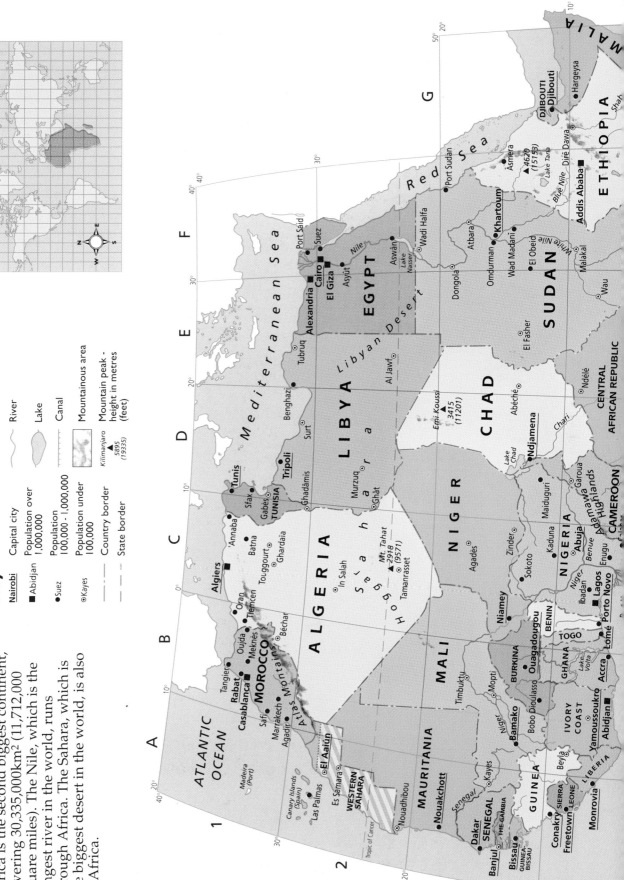

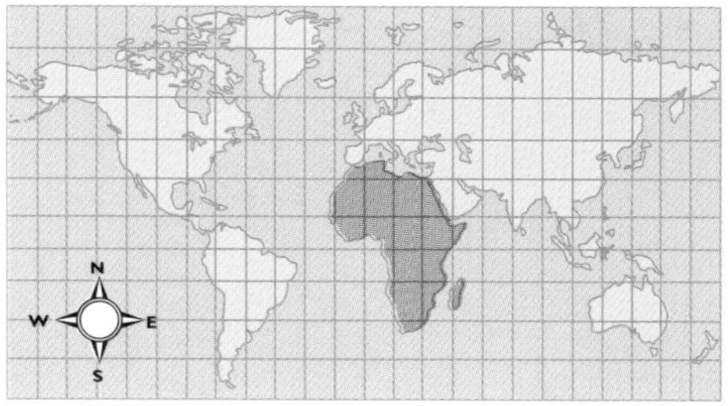

National flags

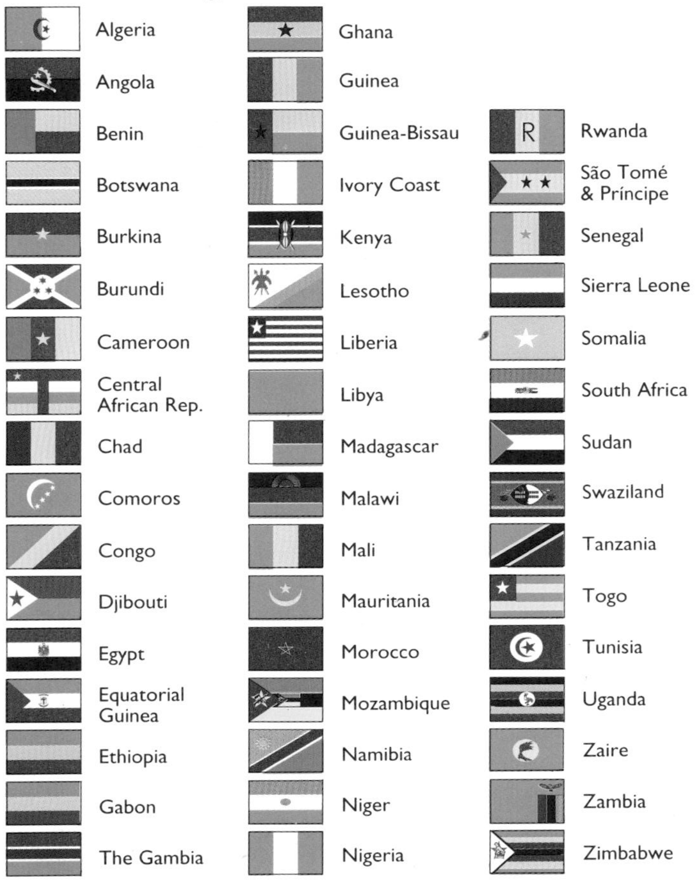

Scale

Km: 0 500 1000

Miles: 0 500 1000

Europe

Europe is the region that stretches from Britain in the west to the Ural Mountains of Russia in the east. It is the second smallest continent, covering 10,498,000km^2 (4,052,000 square miles). It is the most densely populated continent, where the towns and cities are crowded together more than anywhere else.

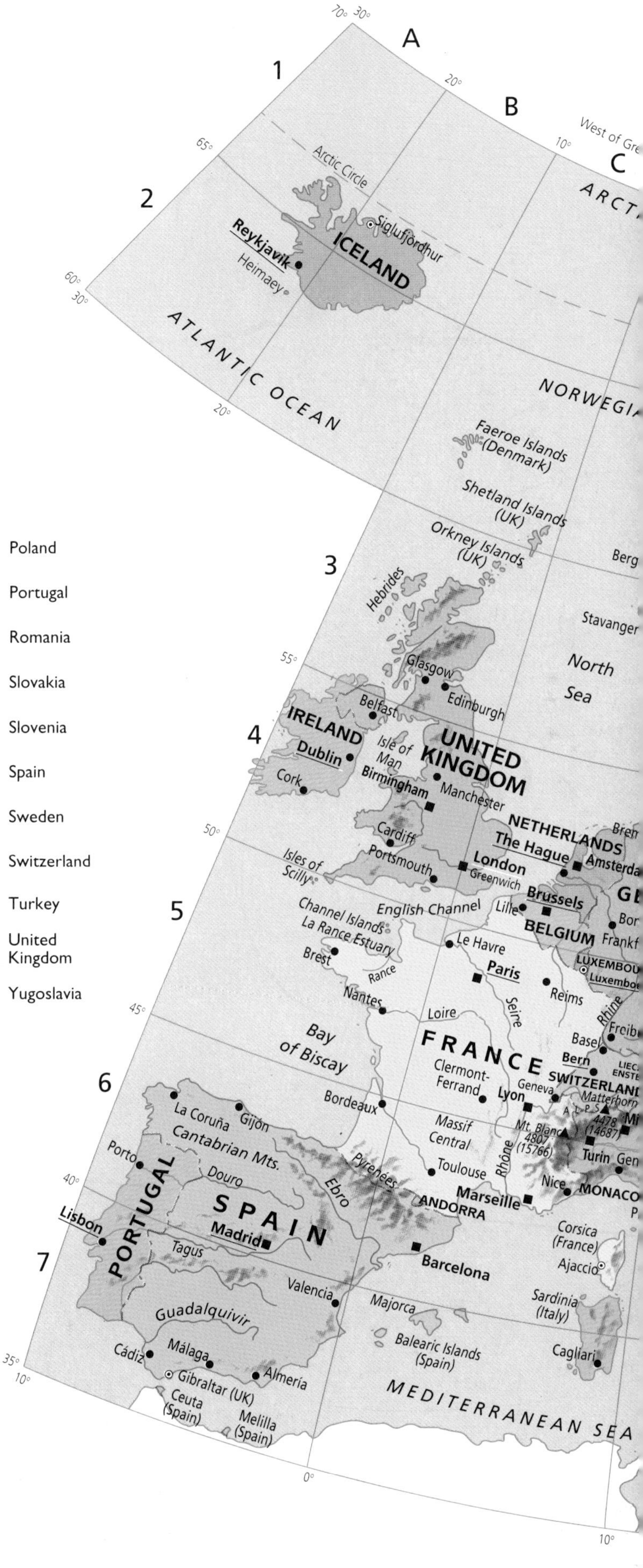

National flags

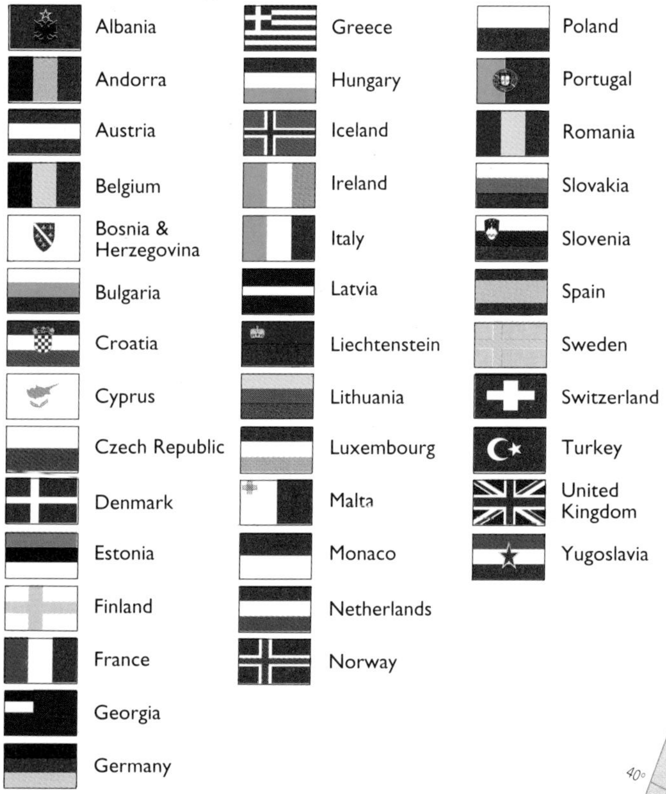

Albania
Andorra
Austria
Belgium
Bosnia & Herzegovina
Bulgaria
Croatia
Cyprus
Czech Republic
Denmark
Estonia
Finland
France
Georgia
Germany
Greece
Hungary
Iceland
Ireland
Italy
Latvia
Liechtenstein
Lithuania
Luxembourg
Malta
Monaco
Netherlands
Norway
Poland
Portugal
Romania
Slovakia
Slovenia
Spain
Sweden
Switzerland
Turkey
United Kingdom
Yugoslavia

Scale

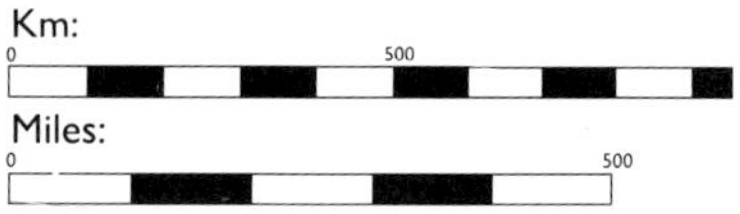

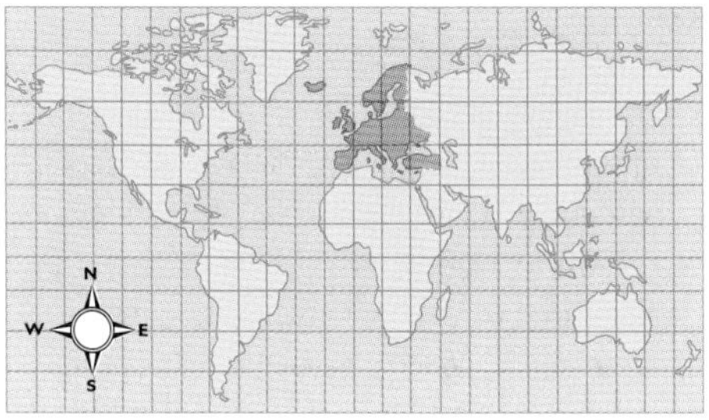

t of Greenwich
D
E
F
G
H
10°
20°
30°
40°
70°
65°
60°
55°
50°
45°
40°
35°
50°
EAN
Hammerfest
Tromsø
Narvik
Luleå
Kemi
Oulu
Umeå
Vaasa
Trondheim
SWEDEN
FINLAND
RWAY
Glåma
Gulf of Bothnia
Varkaus
Tampere
Turku
Helsinki
Åland Is. (Finland)
Gulf of Finland
Oslo
Västerås
Lake Vänern
Stockholm
Lake Vättern
Tallinn
ESTONIA
enburg
lborg
Jönköping
Gotland
Baltic Sea
Riga
LATVIA
MARK
penhagen
Daugavpils
Klaipeda
LITHUANIA
jerg
Malmö
Bornholm (Denmark)
PART OF RUSSIAN FEDERATION
Vilnius
Hamburg
Gdańsk
Elbe
POLAND
Berlin
Poznań
Oder
Vistula
Warsaw
ANY
Łódź
Dresden
Wrocław
Kraków
Prague
CZECH REPUBLIC
SLOVAKIA
Carpathians
unich
Brno
Vienna
Bratislava
Košice
Budapest
Prut
AUSTRIA
Danube
Cluj-Napoca
Graz
HUNGARY
Ljubljana
SLOVENIA
Zagreb
ROMANIA
CROATIA
Sava
Drava
enice
BOSNIA & HERZEGOVINA
Belgrade
Craiova
Bucharest
rence
Split
Sarajevo
YUGOSLAVIA (Serbia & Montenegro)
Danube
BULGARIA
Adriatic Sea
Sofia
Balkan Mts.
ennines
ITALY
ome
Podgorica
Skopje
Tirana
ALBANIA
Naples
Thessaloniki
İstanbul
İzmit
Bursa
rrhenian Sea
GREECE
Aegean Sea
Ionian Sea
İzmir
Palermo
Reggio di Calabria
Sicily
Pátrai
Athens
Valletta
MALTA
Crete (Greece)
Rhodes (Greece)
CYPRUS
Black Sea
Caucasus Mts.
GEORGIA
Tbilisi
Samsun
Mt. Ararat 5123 (16803)
Ankara
TURKEY
Van Gölü
Elâziğ
Kayseri
Fırat
Konya
Sanliurfa
Mersin
Antalya

Key

- **London** — Capital city
- ■ **Munich** — Population over 1,000,000
- ● Bremen — Population 100,000 - 1,000,000
- ⊙ Esbjerg — Population under 100,000
- Country border
- State border
- River
- Lake
- Canal
- Mountainous area
- *Mt. Blanc* ▲ *4807 (15766)* — Mountain peak - height in metres (feet)

Russia and surrounding countries

Russia and its surrounding countries cover northern Asia and part of eastern Europe. They used to be a part of the former Soviet Union. The Russian Federation is the largest of these countries and is the second largest country in the world.

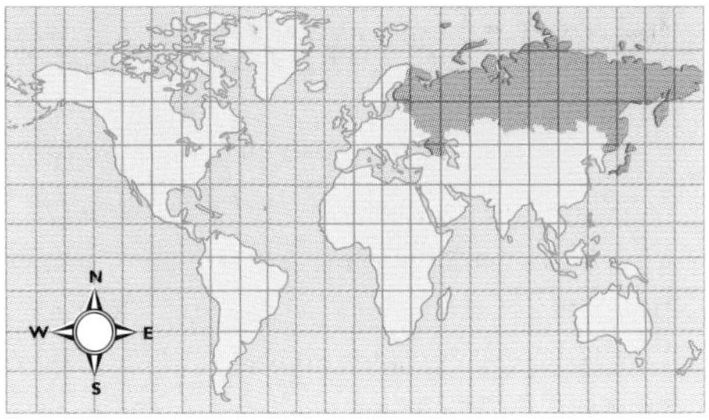

Scale

Km:
0 500 1000

Miles:
0 500 1000

National flags

Armenia

Azerbaijan

Belarus

Kazakhstan

Kyrgyzstan

Moldova

Russian Federation

Tajikistan

Turkmenistan

Ukraine

Uzbekistan

Asia and the Middle East

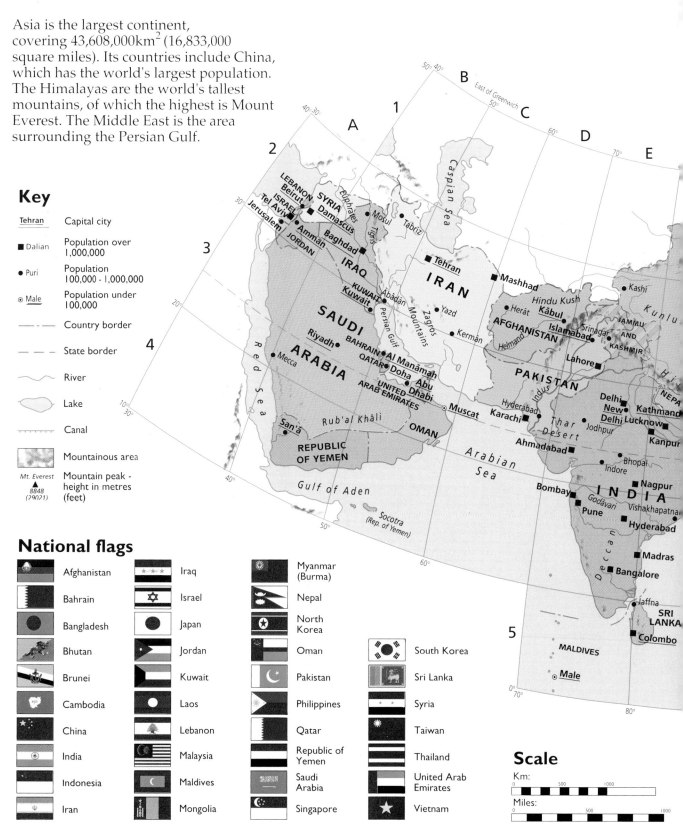

Asia is the largest continent, covering 43,608,000km^2 (16,833,000 square miles). Its countries include China, which has the world's largest population. The Himalayas are the world's tallest mountains, of which the highest is Mount Everest. The Middle East is the area surrounding the Persian Gulf.

Key

- Tehran — Capital city
- ■ Dalian — Population over 1,000,000
- ● Puri — Population 100,000 - 1,000,000
- ⊙ Male — Population under 100,000
- Country border
- State border
- River
- Lake
- Canal
- Mountainous area
- Mt. Everest ▲ 8848 (29021) — Mountain peak - height in metres (feet)

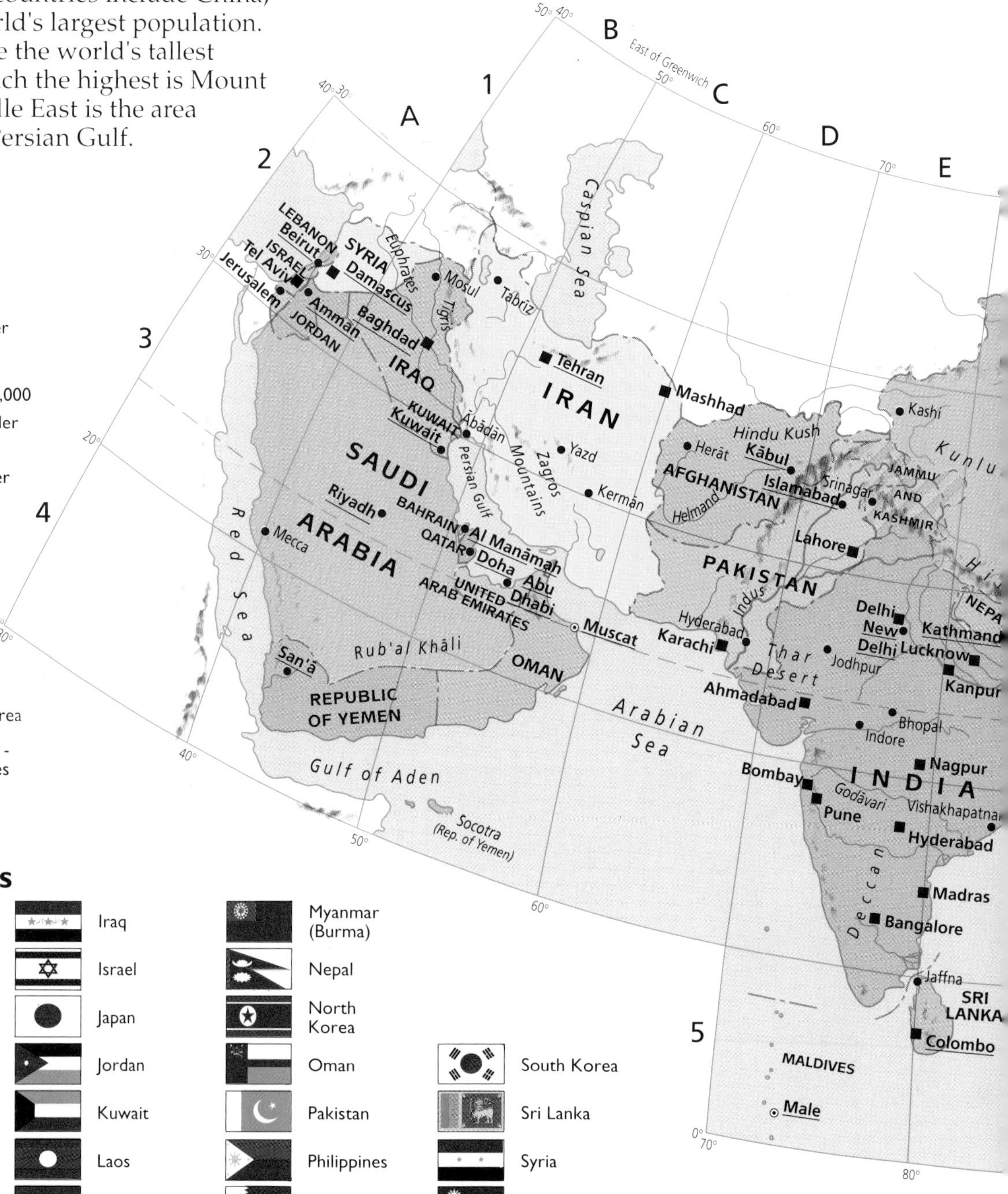

National flags

- Afghanistan
- Bahrain
- Bangladesh
- Bhutan
- Brunei
- Cambodia
- China
- India
- Indonesia
- Iran
- Iraq
- Israel
- Japan
- Jordan
- Kuwait
- Laos
- Lebanon
- Malaysia
- Maldives
- Mongolia
- Myanmar (Burma)
- Nepal
- North Korea
- Oman
- Pakistan
- Philippines
- Qatar
- Republic of Yemen
- Saudi Arabia
- Singapore
- South Korea
- Sri Lanka
- Syria
- Taiwan
- Thailand
- United Arab Emirates
- Vietnam

Scale

Km: 0 500 1000

Miles: 0 500 1000

F
G
H
I
J
K
L
MONGOLIA
Ulan Bator
Gobi Desert
Nan Shan
Ürümqi
CHINA
Plateau of Tibet
Lhasa
Himalayas
Everest 8848 (29021)
Thimphu
BHUTAN
Cherrapunji
Brahmaputra
Ganges
BANGLADESH
Dhaka
Chittagong
Calcutta
MYANMAR (BURMA)
Irrawaddy
Rangoon
Bay of Bengal
Andaman Is.
Nicobar Is. (India)
INDIAN OCEAN
Harbin
Amur
Fushun
Tangshan
Peking (Beijing)
Tianjin
Dalian
Taiyuan
Huang He
Lanzhou
Zhengzhou
Qingdao
Xi'an
Shanghai
Wuhan
Yangtze
Chengdu
Chongqing
Changsha
Nanchang
Hangzhou
Fuzhou
Guiyang
Kunming
Guangzhou
Wuzhou
Xi Jiang
Macau (Portugal)
Hong Kong (UK)
Hanoi
LAOS
Vientiane
Mekong
VIETNAM
Da Nang
THAILAND
Bangkok
CAMBODIA
Phnom Penh
Ho Chi Minh City
Gulf of Thailand
NORTH KOREA
P'yŏngyang
Seoul
SOUTH KOREA
Pusan
Sea of Japan
JAPAN
Sapporo
Hokkaido
Honshū
Tōkyō
Yokohama
Kyōto
Osaka
Fukuoka
Kyūshū
Ryuku Islands
East China Sea
Taipei
TAIWAN
Tropic of Cancer
PACIFIC OCEAN
Luzon
Quezon City
Manila
PHILIPPINES
Cebu
Mindanao
Davao
South China Sea
Spratly Islands
Sulu Sea
Celebes Sea
MALAYSIA
BRUNEI
Bandar Seri Begawan
George Town
Kuala Lumpur
SINGAPORE
Medan
Sumatra
Padang
Kuching
Borneo
Balikpapan
Palu
Sulawesi
Ujung Pandang
Maluku
Seram
Jayapura
New Guinea
Equator
INDONESIA
Arafura Sea
Jakarta
Semarang
Java
Surabaya
Bali
Flores
Sumba
Timor
6
7
N
S
E
W

Australasia and Oceania

Australasia is the area south-east of Asia, which includes Australia, New Zealand, Papua New Guinea and their surrounding islands. Oceania is the name given to all the other islands in the Pacific Ocean. Australia itself is the smallest continent in the world, covering 7,682,300km^2 (2,966,150 square miles).

Key

<u>Canberra</u>	Capital city
■ Brisbane	Population over 1,000,000
• Perth	Population 100,000 - 1,000,000
⊙ Albany	Population under 100,000
—·—	Country border
— — —	State border
(line)	River
(shape)	Lake
(line)	Canal
(shading)	Mountainous area
Ayers Rock ▲ 867 (2843)	Mountain peak - height in metres (feet)

National flags

Australia

Fiji

Kiribati

Nauru

New Zealand

Papua New Guinea

Solomon Islands

Tonga

Tuvalu

Vanuatu

Western Samoa

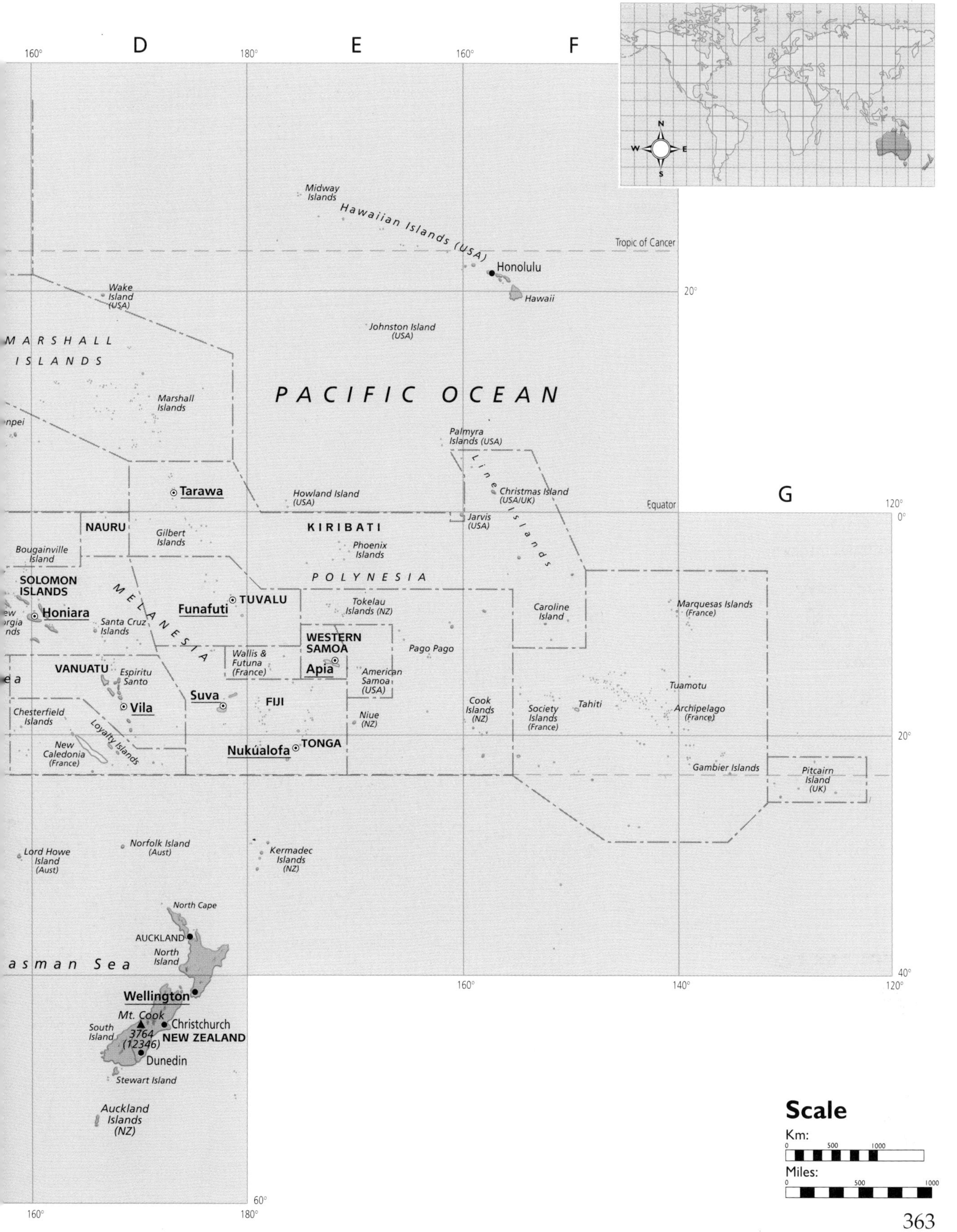
D
E
F
G
160°
180°
Tropic of Cancer
Equator
20°
0°
40°
60°
140°
120°
Midway Islands
Hawaiian Islands (USA)
Honolulu
Hawaii
Wake Island (USA)
Johnston Island (USA)
MARSHALL ISLANDS
Marshall Islands
PACIFIC OCEAN
Palmyra Islands (USA)
Line Islands
Christmas Island (USA/UK)
Tarawa
Howland Island (USA)
Jarvis (USA)
NAURU
KIRIBATI
Gilbert Islands
Phoenix Islands
Bougainville Island
POLYNESIA
SOLOMON ISLANDS
MELANESIA
Honiara
TUVALU
Funafuti
Tokelau Islands (NZ)
Caroline Island
Marquesas Islands (France)
Santa Cruz Islands
WESTERN SAMOA
Apia
Pago Pago
Wallis & Futuna (France)
American Samoa (USA)
VANUATU
Espiritu Santo
Vila
Suva
FIJI
Niue (NZ)
Cook Islands (NZ)
Society Islands (France)
Tahiti
Tuamotu Archipelago (France)
Chesterfield Islands
Loyalty Islands
New Caledonia (France)
Nukúalofa
TONGA
Gambier Islands
Pitcairn Island (UK)
Lord Howe Island (Aust)
Norfolk Island (Aust)
Kermadec Islands (NZ)
North Cape
AUCKLAND
North Island
Tasman Sea
Wellington
Mt. Cook 3764 (12346)
Christchurch
NEW ZEALAND
South Island
Dunedin
Stewart Island
Auckland Islands (NZ)
N
S
E
W
Scale
Km:
0 500 1000
Miles:
0 500 1000

The polar world

The Arctic (around the North Pole) and Antarctica (around the South Pole) are both covered in ice. Antarctica is the third smallest continent, covering 13,340,000km^2 (5,150,000 square miles). Many different countries claim parts of its land. In the Arctic, there is no land beneath the ice, only sea.

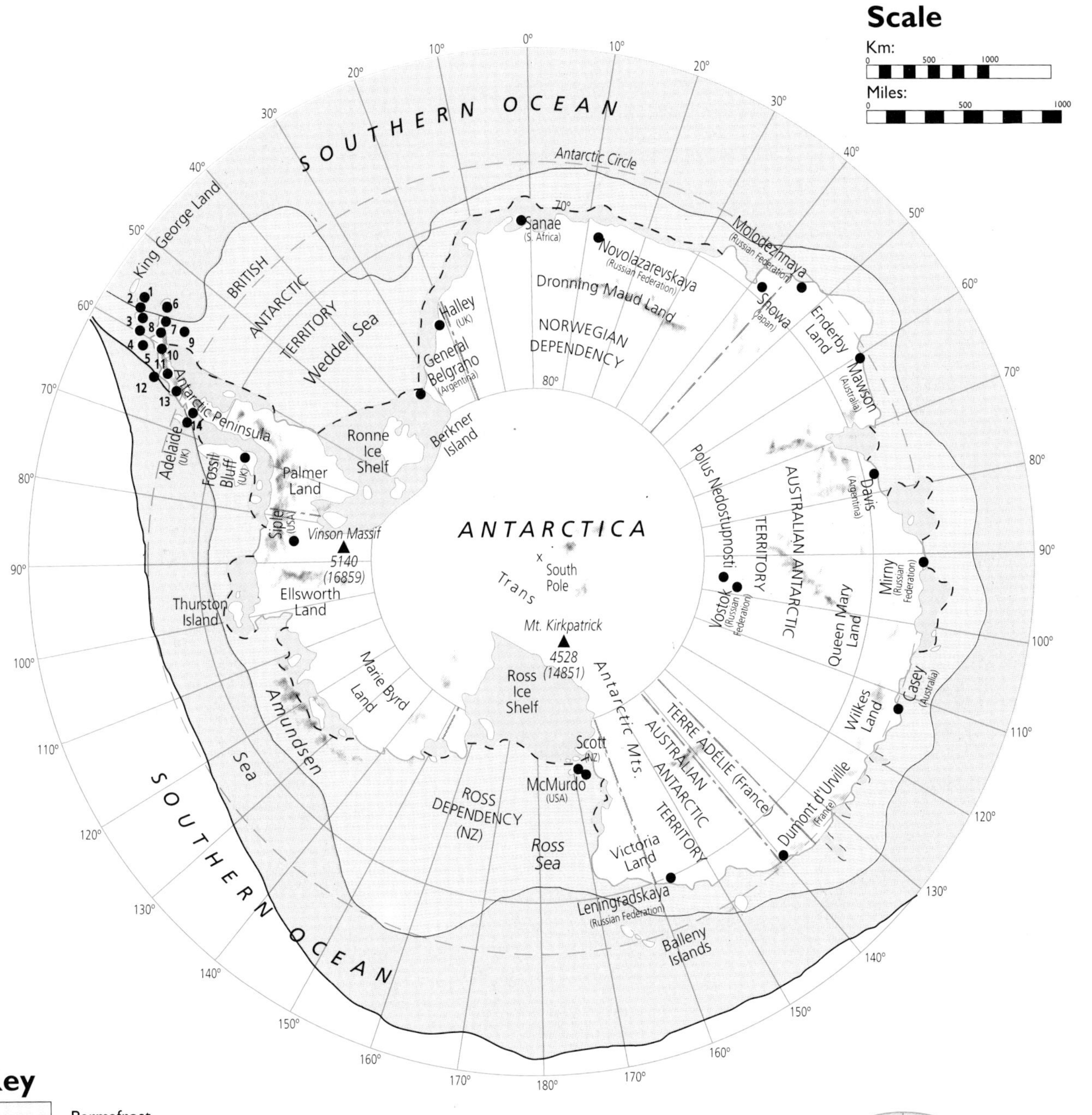

Scale
Km:
0 500 1000
Miles:
0 500 1000
SOUTHERN OCEAN
Antarctic Circle
King George Land
BRITISH ANTARCTIC TERRITORY
Weddell Sea
Sanae (S. Africa)
Novolazarevskaya (Russian Federation)
Dronning Maud Land
NORWEGIAN DEPENDENCY
Molodezhnaya (Russian Federation)
Showa (Japan)
Enderby Land
Mawson (Australia)
Halley (UK)
General Belgrano (Argentina)
Ronne Ice Shelf
Berkner Island
Antarctic Peninsula
Adelaide (UK)
Fossil Bluff (UK)
Palmer Land
Siple (USA)
Vinson Massif
5140 (16859)
ANTARCTICA
South Pole
Trans
Ellsworth Land
Thurston Island
Polus Nedostupnosti
AUSTRALIAN ANTARCTIC TERRITORY
Davis (Argentina)
Mirny (Russian Federation)
Vostok (Russian Federation)
Queen Mary Land
Mt. Kirkpatrick
4528 (14851)
Marie Byrd Land
Ross Ice Shelf
Antarctic Mts.
TERRE ADÉLIE (France)
AUSTRALIAN ANTARCTIC TERRITORY
Wilkes Land
Casey (Australia)
Amundsen Sea
Scott (NZ)
McMurdo (USA)
ROSS DEPENDENCY (NZ)
Ross Sea
Victoria Land
Dumont d'Urville (France)
Leningradskaya (Russian Federation)
Balleny Islands
SOUTHERN OCEAN

Key

- Permafrost
- Drift ice
- Ice shelf
- Pack ice
- Land covered by ice
- ⊙ Esbjerg — Population under 100,000
- *Mt. Kirkpatrick* ▲ *4528 (14851)* — Mountain peak - height in metre (feet)

● Antarctic Stations

1. Arctowski, Poland
2. Bellinghausen, Russian Federation
3. Presidente Frei, Chile
4. Arturo Prat, Chile
5. Deception, Argentina
6. Petrel, Argentina
7. Esperanza, Argentina
8. General Bernardo O'Higgins, Chile
9. Vicecomodoro Marambio, Argentina
10. Matienzo, Argentina
11. Almirante Brown, Argentina
12. Palmer, USA
13. Faraday, UK
14. San Martin, Argentina

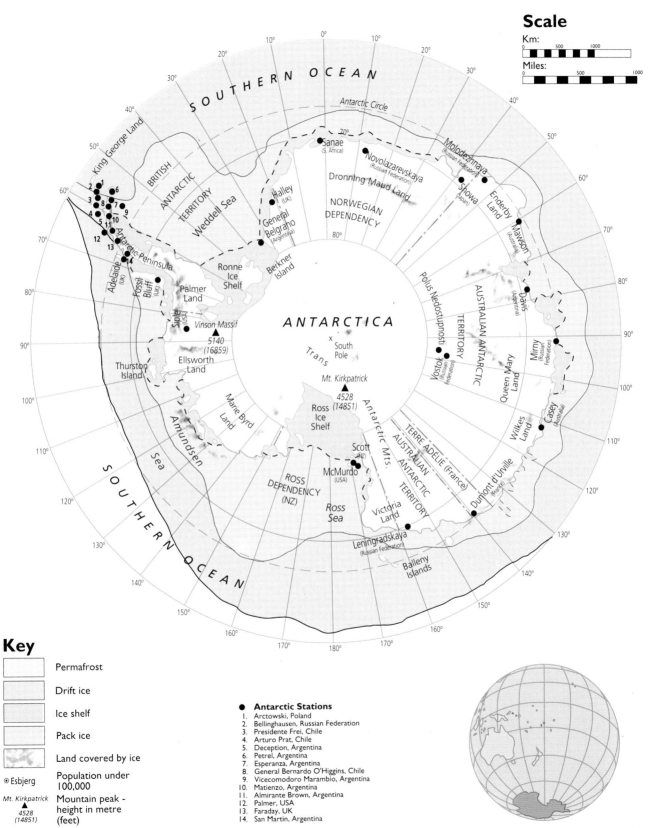

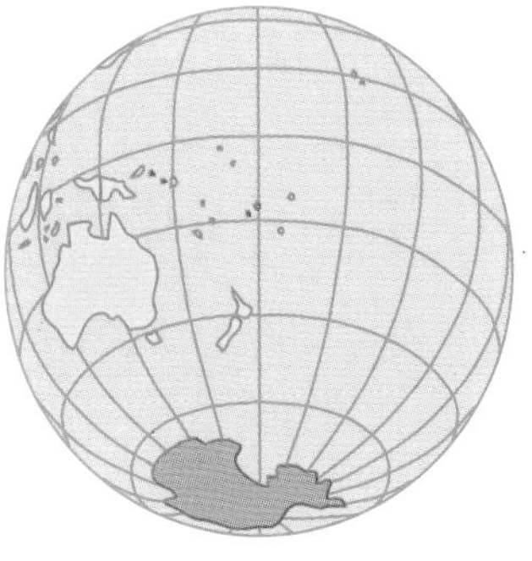

World facts

Our Solar System

Planet	Diameter in km (miles)	Distance from Sun in millions of km (miles)	Number of moons
Mercury	4,878 (3,031)	58 (36)	0
Venus	12,103 (7,521)	108 (67)	0
Earth	12,756 (7,926)	150 (93)	1
Mars	6,794 (4,221)	228 (141)	2
Jupiter	142,800 (88,700)	778 (483)	16
Saturn	120,000 (74,600)	1,427 (887)	18
Uranus	51,000 (31,700)	2,870 (1,783)	15
Neptune	49,000 (30,400)	4,497 (2,794)	8
Pluto	3,000 (1,900)	5,900 (3,666)	1

Phases of the Moon

As the Moon moves around the Earth, different parts of it are lit up by the Sun, so that it looks as if the Moon is changing shape. It seems to wax and wane (grow and shrink), depending on its position, or **phase**. This diagram shows the phases of the Moon and what the Moon looks like from Earth.

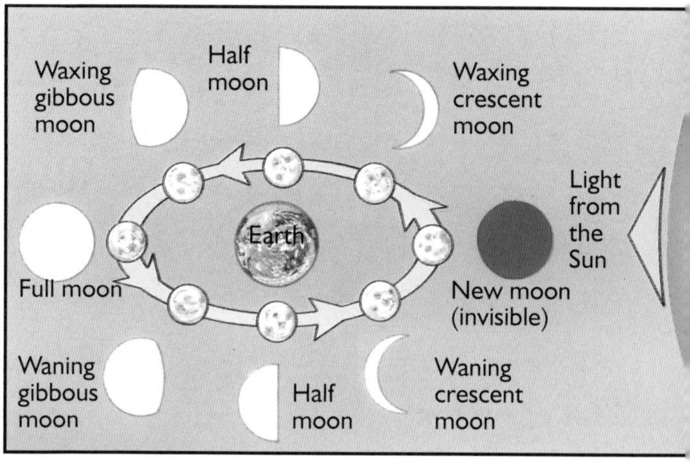

How big are the oceans?

165,384,000km^2 (63,838,000 square miles)

82,217,000km^2 (31,736,000 square miles)

73,481,000km^2 (28,364,000 square miles)

14,056,000km^2 (5,426,000 square miles)

Longest rivers

Nile, Africa	6,695km (4,160 miles)
Amazon, South America	6,516km (4,050 miles)
Yangtze (Chang Jiang), Asia	6,380km (3,965 miles)
Mississippi-Missouri, North America	6,019km (3,740 miles)
Ob-Irtysh, Asia	5,570km (3,460 miles)
Yenisey-Angara, Asia	5,550km (3,450 miles)
Huang He (Yellow River), Asia	5,464km (3,395 miles)
Zaire (Congo), Africa	4,667km (2,900 miles)
Paranà, South America	4,500km (2,800 miles)
Mekong, Asia	4,425km (2,750 miles)

Highest mountains

The world's highest mountains are all in the Himalayas in Asia. This diagram shows the highest mountain in each continent.

Mount Everest, Asia	8,848m (29,021ft)
Aconcagua, South America	6,960m (22,828ft)
McKinley, North America	6,194m (20,316ft)
Mount Kilimanjaro, Africa	5,895m (19,335ft)
Elbrus, Europe	5,633m (18,476ft)
Vinson Massif, Antarctica	5,140m (16,859ft)
Mount Wilhelm, Australasia	4,508m (14,786ft)

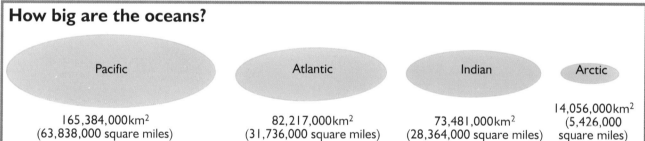

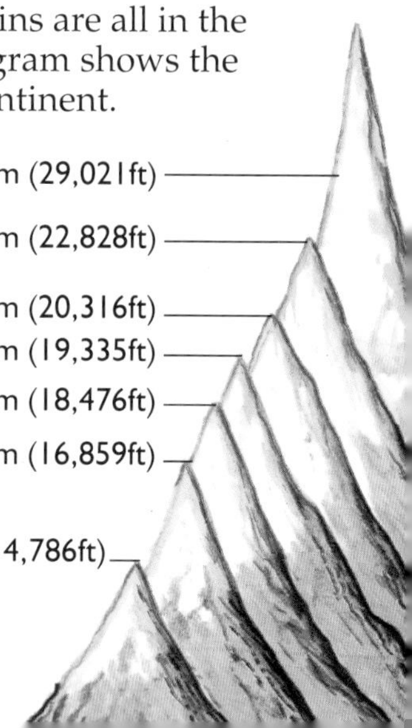

The world's biggest cities

City	Population
Mexico City, Mexico	18,748,000
New York, USA	16,121,000
Tokyo/Yokohama, Japan	14,804,000
Los Angeles, USA	11,498,000
São Paulo, Brazil	10,099,000
Buenos Aires, Argentina	9,968,000
Seoul, South Korea	9,639,000
Calcutta, India	9,194,000
Moscow, Russia	8,967,000
Paris, France	8,707,000

Famous earthquakes

There are two different scales for measuring earthquakes – the Richter Scale and the Mercalli Scale. You can find out about these on page 18. Below are six famous earthquakes that have happened within the last century.

Date	Earthquake	Richter Scale	Mercalli Scale
1906	San Francisco, USA	8.3	10
1960	Agadir, Morocco	5.8	8
1963	Skopje, Yugoslavia	6.0	8
1964	Anchorage, Alaska, USA	7.5	9
1976	Tangshan, China	8.5	11
1985	Mexico City, Mexico	8.1	10

The climates

These graphs show what the climate is like in different areas of the world. The top lines of the coloured areas give an example of the average temperature (shown on the left-hand scale), in each month of the year. The bar charts give the average rainfall (shown on the right-hand scale).

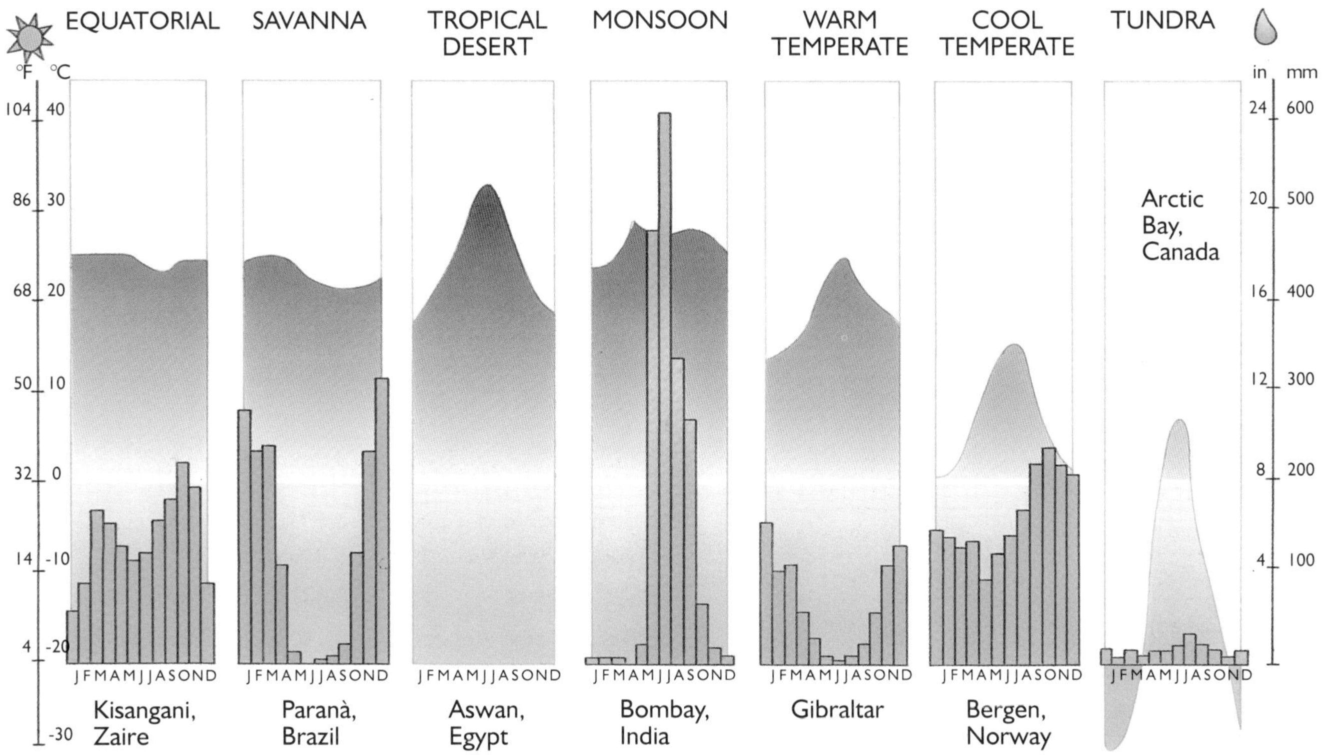

Nation facts

Nation	Area km²	(sq miles)	Population	Main languages	Main religions	Currency
Afghanistan	652,225	(251,773)	16,600,000	Pushto/Dari	Islam	Afghani
Albania	28,748	(11,100)	3,300,000	Albanian	Islam/Orthodox	Lek
Algeria	2,381,741	(919,595)	26,000,000	Arabic/French/Berber	Islam	Dinar
Andorra	467	(180)	50,000	Catalan/French/Spanish	Roman Catholic	Franc/Peseta
Angola	1,246,700	(481,354)	8,500,000	Portuguese	Roman Catholic/Animist	Kwanza
Antigua and Barbuda	442	(171)	100,000	English	Anglican	Dollar
Argentina	2,766,889	(1,068,302)	32,700,000	Spanish	Roman Catholic	Austral
Armenia	30,000	(11,500)	3,300,000	Armenian	Armenian Christian	Rouble
Australia	7,682,300	(2,966,150)	17,500,000	English	Anglican/Roman Catholic	Dollar
Austria	83,855	(32,367)	7,700,000	German	Roman Catholic	Schilling
Azerbaijan	87,000	(33,500)	7,000,000	Turkic	Islam	Rouble
Bahamas	13,939	(5,382)	300,000	English	Baptist/Anglican/Roman Catholic	Dollar
Bahrain	691	(267)	500,000	Arabic	Islam	Dinar
Bangladesh	143,998	(55,598)	116,600,000	Bengali	Islam	Taka
Barbados	430	(166)	300,000	English	Anglican	Dollar
Belarus	207,500	(80,000)	10,000,000	Byelorussian/Russian	Roman Catholic	Rouble
Belgium	30,519	(11,783)	9,900,000	Flemish/French	Roman Catholic	Franc
Belize	22,965	(8,867)	200,000	English/Creole/Spanish	Roman Catholic	Dollar
Benin	112,622	(43,484)	4,800,000	French/Fon	Aminist/Islam	Franc
Bhutan	46,500	(17,954)	700,000	Dzongkha	Buddhism	Ngultrum
Bolivia	1,098,581	(424,164)	7,500,000	Spanish/Quéchua	Roman Catholic	Boliviano
Bosnia & Herzegovina	51,113	(19,735)	4,360,000	Serbo-Croat	Orthodox/Islam	Dinar
Botswana	582,000	(224,711)	1,300,000	English/Setswana	Animist/Anglican	Pula
Brazil	8,511,965	(3,286,488)	153,300,000	Portuguese	Roman Catholic	Cruzeiro
Brunei	5,765	(2,226)	300,000	Malay/Chinese/English	Islam	Dollar
Bulgaria	110,912	(42,823)	9,000,000	Bulgarian	Orthodox	Lev
Burkina	274,200	(105,869)	9,400,000	French/Mossi	Animist/Islam	Franc
Burundi	27,834	(10,747)	5,800,000	Kirundi/French/Kiswahili	Roman Catholic	Franc
Cambodia	181,035	(69,898)	7,100,000	Khmer/French	Buddhism	Riel
Cameroon	475,442	(183,569)	11,400,000	French/English	Animist/Islam/Roman Catholic	Franc
Canada	9,970,610	(3,849,674)	26,800,000	English/French	Roman Catholic	Dollar
Cape Verde	4,033	(1,557)	400,000	Portuguese/Crioulu	Roman Catholic	Escudo
Central African Republic	622,984	(240,535)	3,000,000	French/Sangho	Animist/Roman Catholic	Franc
Chad	1,284,000	(495,790)	5,100,000	French/Arabic	Islam/Animist	Franc
Chile	756,945	(292,258)	13,400,000	Spanish	Roman Catholic	Peso
China	9,571,300	(3,695,500)	1,151,300,000	Chinese	Buddhism/Islam/Confucianism	Yuan
Colombia	1,141,748	(40,831)	33,600,000	Spanish	Roman Catholic	Peso
Comoros	1,862	(719)	500,000	French/Arabic	Islam	Franc
Congo	342,000	(132,047)	2,300,000	French/Lingala	Roman Catholic	Franc
Costa Rica	51,100	(19,730)	3,100,000	Spanish	Roman Catholic	Colón
Croatia	56,526	(21,825)	4,660,000	Serbo-Croat	Roman Catholic	Dinar
Cuba	110,860	(42,803)	10,700,000	Spanish	Roman Catholic	Peso
Cyprus	9,251	(3,572)	700,000	Greek/Turkish	Orthodox/Islam	Pound
Czech Republic	78,864	(30,449)	10,400,000	Czech	Roman Catholic/Protestant	Koruna
Denmark	43,092	(16,638)	5,100,000	Danish	Lutheran	Krone
Djibouti	23,200	(8,950)	400,000	Arabic/French	Islam	Franc
Dominica	751	(290)	100,000	English/French patois	Roman Catholic	Dollar

Nation	Area km² (sq miles)		Population	Main languages	Main religions	Currency
Dominican Republic	48,422	(18,696)	7,300,000	Spanish	Roman Catholic	Peso
Ecuador	270,670	(104,506)	10,800,000	Spanish	Roman Catholic	Sucre
Egypt	997,739	(385,229)	54,500,000	Arabic	Islam	Pound
El Salvador	21,393	(8,260)	5,400,000	Spanish	Roman Catholic	Colón
Equatorial Guinea	28,051	(10,831)	400,000	Spanish/Fang/Bubi	Roman Catholic	Franc
Estonia	45,091	(17,410)	1,573,000	Estonian	Lutheran	Kroon
Ethiopia	1,223,600	(472,435)	53,200,000	Amharic/Arabic	Islam/Ethiopian Orthodox	Birr
Fiji	18,376	(7,095)	700,000	English/Fijian/Hindi	Methodist/Hindu	Dollar
Finland	338,145	(130,557)	5,000,000	Finnish	Lutheran	Markka
France	543,965	(210,026)	56,700,000	French	Roman Catholic	Franc
Gabon	267,667	(103,347)	1,200,000	French	Animist/Roman Catholic	Franc
Gambia	11,295	(4,361)	900,000	English	Islam	Dalasi
Germany	357,050	(137,857)	79,500,000	German	Lutheran	Deutschmark
Georgia	2,716,588	(1,048,880)	5,500,000	Georgian	Georgian Church	Rouble
Ghana	238,537	(92,099)	15,500,000	English/Asante/Ewe	Animist/Protestant	Cedi
Greece	131,957	(50,949)	10,100,000	Greek	Orthodox	Drachma
Grenada	344	(133)	100,000	English	Roman Catholic/Anglican	Dollar
Guatemala	108,889	(42,042)	9,500,000	Spanish	Roman Catholic	Quetzal
Guinea	245,857	(94,926)	7,500,000	French/Soussou/Manika	Islam	Franc
Guinea-Bissau	36,125	(13,948)	100,000,000	Portuguese/Crioulo	Animist/Islam	Peso
Guyana	214,969	(83,000)	800,000	English/Hindi/Urdu	Hindu	Dollar
Haiti	27,750	(10,714)	6,300,000	Creole/French	Voodoo/Roman Catholic	Gourde
Honduras	112,088	(43,277)	5,300,000	Spanish	Roman Catholic	Lempira
Hungary	93,036	(35,921)	10,400,000	Magyar	Roman Catholic	Forint
Iceland	103,001	(39,769)	300,000	Icelandic	Lutheran	Króna
India	3,287,263	(1,269,212)	859,200,000	Hindi/English	Hindu/Islam	Rupee
Indonesia	1,919,443	(741,101)	181,400,000	Bahasa Indonesia	Islam	Rupiah
Iran	1,648,000	(636,296)	58,600,000	Farsi/Azerbaijani	Islam	Rial
Iraq	441,839	(170,595)	17,100,000	Arabic/Kurdish	Islam	Dinar
Ireland	70,282	(27,136)	3,500,000	Irish/English	Roman Catholic	Pound
Israel	21,946	(8,473)	6,600,000	Hebrew/Arabic	Judaism/Islam	Shekel
Italy	301,277	(116,324)	57,700,000	Italian	Roman Catholic	Lira
Ivory Coast	322,462	(124,503)	12,500,000	French/Dioula/Baoulé	Animist/Islam/Roman Catholic	Franc
Jamaica	10,991	(4,244)	2,500,000	English	Protestant	Dollar
Japan	377,815	(145,874)	123,800,000	Japanese	Shintoism/Buddhism	Yen
Jordan	89,206	(34,443)	3,400,000	Arabic	Islam	Dinar
Kazakhstan	2,717,500	(1,049,000)	16,691,000	Russian/Kazakh	Islam	Rouble
Kenya	580,367	(224,081)	25,200,000	Swahili/English	Animist/Roman Catholic	Shilling
Kiribati	717	(277)	69,600	English/I-Kiribati	Roman Catholic/Protestant	Dollar
Korea, North	120,538	(46,540)	21,800,000	Korean	Buddhism/Confucianism/ Daoism	Won
Korea, South	99,143	(38,279)	43,200,000	Korean	Buddhism/Christianity	Won
Kuwait	17,818	(6,880)	1,400,000	Arabic	Islam	Dinar
Kyrgyzstan	76,500	(29,500)	4,400,000	Kyrgyz	Islam	Rouble
Laos	236,800	(91,400)	4,100,000	Lao	Buddhism	Kip
Latvia	63,687	(24,590)	2,681,000	Latvian	Lutheran/Roman Catholic	Lat
Lebanon	10,452	(4,036)	3,400,000	Arabic	Islam/Christianity	Pound
Lesotho	30,355	(11,720)	1,800,000	Sesotho/English	Roman Catholic	Loti
Liberia	111,369	(43,000)	2,700,000	English	Animist	Dollar

Nation	Area km²	(sq miles)	Population	Main languages	Main religions	Currency
Libya	1,759,540	(679,363)	4,400,000	Arabic	Islam	Dinar
Liechtenstein	160	(62)	30,000	German	Roman Catholic	Franc
Lithuania	65,177	(25,165)	3,690,000	Lithuanian	Roman Catholic	Litas
Luxembourg	2,586	(999)	400,000	Letzeburgish/French	Roman Catholic	Franc
Madagascar	587,041	(226,658)	12,400,000	Malagasy/French	Animist/Christianity	Franc
Malawi	118,484	(45,747)	9,400,000	English/Chichewa	Animist/Roman Catholic	Kwacha
Malaysia	329,758	(127,320)	18,300,000	Malay/English/Chinese	Islam	Dollar
Maldives	298	(115)	200,000	Dhivehi	Islam	Rufiyaa
Mali	1,240,192	(478,841)	8,300,000	French/Bambara	Islam/Animist	Franc
Malta	316	(122)	400,000	Maltese/English	Roman Catholic	Lira
Mauritania	1,030,700	(397,950)	2,100,000	Arabic/French	Islam	Ouguiya
Mauritius	2,040	(788)	1,100,000	English/Creole/Hindi	Hindu/Roman Catholic/Islam	Rupee
Mexico	1,958,201	(756,066)	85,700,000	Spanish	Roman Catholic	Peso
Moldova	33,700	(13,000)	4,400,000	Moldavian	Russian Orthodox	Rouble
Monaco	2.21	(0.85)	29,000	French/Monegasque	Roman Catholic	Franc
Mongolia	1,565,000	(604,250)	2,200,000	Khalkh Mongolian/Kazakh	Officially no religion	Tugrik
Morocco	710,850	(274,461)	26,400,000	Arabic/Berber/French	Islam	Dirham
Mozambique	799,380	(308,641)	16,100,000	Portuguese	Animist	Metical
Myanmar (Burma)	676,552	(261,218)	42,100,000	Burmese	Buddhism	Kyat
Namibia	823,168	(317,827)	1,500,000	Afrikaans/English	Lutheran/Roman Catholic	Rand
Nauru	21	(8)	8,100	Nauruan/English	Protestant/Roman Catholic	Dollar
Nepal	147,181	(56,827)	19,600,000	Nepali/Maithir	Hindu/Buddhism	Rupee
Netherlands	41,785	(33,937)	15,000,000	Dutch	Roman Catholic/Protestant	Guilder
New Zealand	269,057	(103,883)	3,500,000	English/Maori	Protestant/Roman Catholic	Dollar
Nicaragua	120,254	(46,430)	3,900,000	Spanish/Miskito	Roman Catholic	Córdoba
Niger	1,267,000	(489,191)	8,000,000	French/Hausa	Islam	Franc
Nigeria	923,768	(356,669)	122,500,000	English	Islam/Christianity	Naira
Norway	323,878	(125,050)	4,300,000	Norwegian	Lutheran	Krone
Oman	300,000	(120,000)	1,600,000	Arabic/Baluchi	Islam	Rial
Pakistan	803,943	(310,403)	117,500,000	Urdu/Punjabi/Sindhi	Islam	Rupee
Panama	77,082	(29,762)	2,500,000	Spanish	Roman Catholic	Balboa
Papua New Guinea	462,840	(178,704)	3,900,000	English/Pidgin English	Roman Catholic/Protestant	Kina
Paraguay	406,752	(157,048)	4,400,000	Spanish/Guaraní	Roman Catholic	Guaraní
Peru	1,258,216	(496,225)	22,000,000	Spanish/Quechua/Aymara	Roman Catholic	Inti
Philippines	300,000	(120,000)	62,300,000	Pilipino/English	Roman Catholic	Peso
Poland	312,683	(120,727)	38,200,000	Polish	Roman Catholic	Zloty
Portugal	92,072	(33,549)	10,400,000	Portuguese	Roman Catholic	Esucdo
Qatar	11,437	(4,416)	500,000	Arabic	Islam	Riyal
Romania	237,500	(91,699)	23,400,000	Romanian	Orthodox	Leu
Russian Federation	17,075,500	(6,591,000)	148,500,000	Russian	Russian Orthodox	Rouble
Rwanda	26,338	(10,169)	7,500,000	French/Kinyarwanda	Animist/Roman Catholic	Franc
St Christopher and Nevis	262	(101)	40,000	English	Anglican	Dollar
St Lucia	616	(238)	200,000	English/French patois	Roman Catholic	Dollar
St Vincent and the Grenadines	389	(150)	100,000	English	Anglican/Methodist/Roman Catholic	Dollar
San Marino	61	(23)	23,000	Italian	Roman Catholic	Lira
São Tomé and Príncipe	964	(372)	100,000	Portuguese	Roman Catholic	Dobra
Saudi Arabia	2,240,000	(864,869)	15,500,000	Arabic	Islam	Riyal

Nation	Area km²	(sq miles)	Population	Main languages	Main religions	Currency
Senegal	196,722	(75,954)	7,500,000	French	Islam	Franc
Seychelles	454	(173)	100,000	Creole/English/French	Roman Catholic	Rupee
Sierra Leone	71,740	(27,699)	4,300,000	English/Krio/Mende	Animist	Leone
Singapore	623	(240)	2,800,000	Malay/Chinese/English/Tamil	Buddhism	Dollar
Slovakia	49,035	(18,932)	5,400,000	Slovak	Roman Catholic/Protestant	Koruna
Slovenia	20,240	(7,815)	1,930,000	Slovene	Roman Catholic	Dinar
Solomon Islands	27,556	(10,639)	300,000	English/Pidgin English	Protestant/Roman Catholic	Dollar
Somalia	637,657	(246,201)	7,700,000	Somali/Arabic	Islam	Shilling
South Africa	2,347,661	(906,437)	40,600,000	English/Afrikaans	Christianity/Hindu/Islam	Rand
Spain	504,782	(194,897)	39,000,000	Spanish/Catalan	Roman Catholic	Peseta
Sri Lanka	65,610	(25,332)	17,400,000	Sinhala/Tamil/English	Buddhism/Hindu	Rupee
Sudan	2,505,813	(967,500)	25,900,000	Arabic	Islam	Pound
Surinam	163,265	(63,037)	400,000	Dutch/Sranang Togo	Hindu/Roman Catholic/Islam	Guilder
Swaziland	17,363	(6,704)	800,000	SiSwati/English	Christianity	Lilangeni
Sweden	449,964	(173,732)	8,600,000	Swedish	Lutheran	Krona
Switzerland	41,293	(15,943)	6,800,000	German/French/Italian/Romansch	Roman Catholic/Protestant	Franc
Syria	185,180	(71,498)	12,800,000	Arabic	Islam	Pound
Taiwan	38,981	(13,893)	20,500,000	Chinese	Buddhism/Daoism	Dollar
Tajikistan	143,000	(55,000)	5,000,000	Tajik	Islam	Rouble
Tanzania	945,087	(364,900)	26,900,000	English/Swahili	Islam/Roman Catholic	Shiling
Thailand	513,115	(198,115)	58,800,000	Thai	Buddhism/Islam	Baht
Togo	56,785	(21,925)	3,800,000	French/Ewe/Kabiye	Animist/Roman Catholic/Islam	Franc
Tonga	748	(289)	95,900	Tongan/English	Methodist/Roman Catholic	Dollar
Trinidad and Tobago	5,130	(1,981)	1,300,000	English/Hindi	Roman Catholic/Hindu	Dollar
Tunisia	163,610	(63,170)	8,400,000	Arabic	Islam	Dinar
Turkey	779,452	(300,948)	58,500,000	Turkish	Islam	Lira
Turkmenistan	488,000	(188,500)	3,600,000	West Turkic	Islam	Rouble
Tuvalu	26	(10)	9,000	Tuvaluan/English	Protestant	Dollar
Uganda	241,139	(93,104)	18,700,000	English/Swahili	Roman Catholic/Protestant	Shiling
Ukraine	604,000	(233,000)	51,700,000	Ukrainian	Ukrainian Orthodox/Catholic	Hryvna
United Arab Emirates	77,700	(30,000)	2,400,000	Arabic/English	Islam	Dirham
United Kingdom	244,103	(94,249)	57,500,000	English	Anglican/Roman Catholic	Pound
United States of America	9,372,614	(3,618,770)	252,800,000	English	Roman Catholic/Baptist	Dollar
Uruguay	176,215	(68,037)	3,100,000	Spanish	Roman Catholic	Peso
Uzbekistan	447,500	(172,500)	20,000,000	Uzbek	Islam	Rouble
Vanuatu	12,189	(4,706)	200,000	English/French	Protestant	Vatu
Vatican City	0.44	(0.17)	850	Italian/Latin	Roman Catholic	Lira
Venezuela	912,050	(352,144)	20,100,000	Spanish	Roman Catholic	Bolívar
Vietnam	329,566	(127,246)	67,600,000	Vietnamese	Buddhism	Dông
Western Samoa	2,831	(1,093)	200,000	English/Samoan	Protestant	Tala
Yemen	531,869	(205,356)	10,100,000	Arabic	Islam	Riyal
Yugoslavia	127,841	(49,360)	12,320,000	Serbo-Croat	Orthodox/Roman Catholic	Dinar
Zaire	2,344,885	(905,365)	37,800,000	French	Roman Catholic	Zaïre
Zambia	752,614	(290,586)	8,400,000	English	Christianity/Animist	Kwacha
Zimbabwe	390,759	(150,873)	10,000,000	English/Chishona/Sindebele	Anglican/Roman Catholic	Dollar

Glossary

Words that are explained in this glossary are printed in **bold type**.

Alternative energy. Energy from natural sources, such as the wind and the Sun.

Antarctic Circle. An imaginary line 66½° south of the **Equator**, bordering the sea and frozen land around the **South Pole**.

Arctic Circle. An imaginary line 66½° north of the **Equator**, bordering the area of frozen sea and land around the **North Pole**.

Atmosphere. The gases which surround the Earth.

Atmospheric pressure. The weight of the **atmosphere** pressing down on the Earth's surface.

Boreal forests. Forests of **conifers** which grow in the northern **hemisphere**.

Cardinal points. The eight main directions on a compass: north, north-east, east, south-east, south, south-west, west, and north-west.

Cartography. The practice of mapmaking.

CFCs (Chlorofluorocarbons). Gases made by the chemical industry for use in refrigerators, aerosols and packaging material. They attack the **ozone layer**.

Climate. The variations in weather pattern, including temperature, rainfall and wind, of a particular area, measured over many years.

Condensation. The changing of a gas into a liquid as it cools down, for example when water vapour changes to water.

Conifer. An evergreen tree with needle-like leaves which does not lose its leaves in winter.

Conservation. Protecting the **environment** around us and the animals and plants which live in it.

Continent. One of the Earth's six main land masses, which are Africa, America, Antarctica, Asia, Australia and Europe.

Continental drift. The slow movement of the **plates** which make up the Earth's **crust**.

Contours. Lines drawn on maps which join places that are the same height above sea-level.

Conurbation. An area where several large towns or cities have merged together to make one big city.

Core. The middle of the Earth, which is made up of a solid metal centre, called the inner core, and a hot, liquid metal outer core.

Crust. The solid outer layer of the Earth, which makes up the Earth's land surface.

Deciduous tree. A broad-leaved tree which loses its leaves in winter.

Demography. The study of population and how it changes.

Depression. An area of low **atmospheric pressure**, where an area of warm air is surrounded by cooler air.

Desert. An area of land that has little or no rain and where only a few plants and animals live.

Development. The improvement of a country's industry, wealth and standard of living.

Environment. The natural world around us and the features of our surroundings that have been built and changed by people.

Equator. The imaginary line around the middle of the Earth, at latitude 0°.

Equatorial. Anything relating to the **Equator**.

Erosion. Wearing away of the Earth's surface or buildings by wind, water, or ice, for example.

Evaporation. The changing of a liquid into gas when it warms up, for example when water turns into water vapour.

Fault. A weak line in the Earth's **crust**, which causes breaks in the surface.

Fossil fuels. Coal, oil and natural gas, which were made by **fossilization**, and which can be burned to produce energy.

Fossilization. The way in which the hard parts of animals and plants are preserved within layers of **rock** over millions of years.

Front. A narrow layer of air between two large masses of air that are different in temperature and **humidity**.

Fuel. A material which can be used to produce heat.

Geology. The study of **rocks** and **minerals**.

Gravity. The force that attracts objects toward each other. Gravity attracts everything on and around the Earth to its centre.

Greenhouse Effect. The ability of the Earth's **atmosphere** to keep heat in, which many scientists say is becoming greater.

Heavy industry. The type of industry that needs large machines and uses heavy **raw materials**, such as steel-making.

Hemisphere. One half of the globe, either side of the **Equator** or either side of the **Prime Meridian**, for example.

Humidity. The amount of water vapour (water in the form of a gas) in the **atmosphere**.

Indian subcontinent. The area covered by India, Pakistan, Bangladesh, Nepal, Bhutan and Sri Lanka.

Industrial Revolution. A period of change when a country's industry and transport improve greatly, the population expands, and towns and cities grow quickly. The first Industrial Revolution was in Britain, between 1750 and 1850.

Irrigation. How farmers bring water to their plants, along channels or by using machines.

Latitude. Distance north or south of the **Equator**, measured in degrees.

Light industry. The type of industry that uses few **raw materials** and produces light, easily transportable goods.

Longitude. Distance east or west of the **Prime Meridian**, measured in degrees.

Magma. Hot, molten rock beneath the Earth's **crust**.

Meteorology. The study of weather and **climate** patterns.

Mineral. A natural substance that is not an animal or a plant.

Non-renewable resource. A **resource** that cannot be reused, or that is being used up faster than it is being reproduced, such as coal.

North Pole. One end of the Earth's axis, at **latitude** 90°N.

Ocean. One of the four large masses of salt-water which cover the Earth's surface: the Arctic, the Atlantic, the Indian and the Pacific Oceans.

Ore. A **rock** which contains metal.

Ozone layer. A layer of the Earth's **atmosphere** that contains the gas ozone, which is a form of oxygen. The ozone layer filters out the Sun's harmful rays.

Plates. The separate pieces of the Earth's **crust**.

Polar. Anything relating to the area around either the **North** or the **South Pole**.

Pollute. To make something dirty or unpleasant, especially the **environment**.

Precipitation. Water that falls from the **atmosphere** to the Earth's surface, in the form of rain, snow, sleet or hail.

Prime Meridian. An imaginary line from the **North Pole** to the **South Pole**, following the 0° line of **longitude**.

Rainforest. Evergreen, deciduous forest that grows in the **Tropics**.

Raw materials. Basic natural materials, such as wood, crops or oil, which are used in manufacturing.

Renewable resource. A **resource** that can be reused over and over again, such as water or wind.

Resource. Anything in the world that can be used by people.

Rock. A natural substance which is made up of one or more **minerals**.

Rural. Anything relating to the countryside, rather than the city.

Satellite. Something that travels around a central object, for example the Moon, which travels around the Earth.

Sea. An area of **ocean**, usually enclosed by or near to land, for example the Mediterranean Sea.

Sediment. Particles of **rock**, plant or animal matter that have been washed or blown from the landscape.

South Pole. One end of the Earth's axis, at **latitude** 90°S.

Spring. A place where water naturally comes out of the ground.

Stalactite. An icicle-shaped mass of **minerals** which hangs from a cave roof, formed by water evaporating as it drips through limestone. A **stalagmite** is the same, except it sits on the floor and points up to the ceiling.

Suburb. An area of usually newer buildings surrounding a town or city.

Temperate forests. Forests made up of **conifers** and **deciduous trees**, which grow between the **polar** areas and the tropical areas.

Tropics. The area between the Tropic of Cancer and the Tropic of Capricorn. These are imaginary lines which circle the globe. The Tropic of Cancer is 23½° north of the **Equator** and the Tropic of Capricorn is 23½° south of the **Equator**.

Tundra. Frozen land, bordering the Arctic, where no trees grow.

Urban. Anything relating to towns or cities, rather than countryside.

Water cycle. The circular journey of the Earth's water from the **sea** to the air to the land and back again.

Map index

This index helps you to find places on the maps. For each place name, it gives the page number of the map, the grid reference and the longitude and latitude. You can find out about longitude and latitude and how to read grid references on pages 264-269.

Some abbreviations have been used in the index to show what each entry refers to. These are as follows:

mt.	mountain	mts.	mountains
r.	river	st.	state or province
i.	island	is.	islands

A

Abādān Iran **360 B2** 30°21'N 48°15'E
Abéché Chad **354 E3** 13°49'N 20°49'E
Abidjan Ivory Coast **354 B4** 5°19'N 4°01'W
Abu Dhabi United Arab Emirates **360 C3** 24°27'N 54°23'E
Abuja Nigeria **354 C4** 9°12'N 7°11'E
Acapulco Mexico **352 B3** 16°51'N 99°56'W
Accra Ghana **354 B4** 5°33'N 0°15'W
Aconcagua mt. Argentina **353 F8** 32°39'S 70°00'W
Adamawa Highlands mts. Cameroon/Nigeria **354 D4** 7°05'N 12°00'E
Addis Ababa Ethiopia **354 F4** 9°03'N 38°42'N
Adelaide Australia **362 B4** 34°56'S 138°36'E
Aden, Gulf of Indian Ocean **360 B4-C4**
Adriatic Sea Europe **356-357 E6**
Aegean Sea Europe **357 F7**
Afghanistan Asia **360 D2**
Agadès Niger **354 C3** 17°00'N 7°56'E
Agadir Morocco **354 B1** 30°26'N 9°36'W
Ahmadabad India **360 E3** 23°02'N 72°37'E
Ajaccio France **356 D6** 41°55'N 8°44'E
Aktau Kazakhstan **358 E4** 43°37'N 51°11'E
Aktyubinsk Kazakhstan **358 E3** 50°16'N 57°13'E
Alabama st. USA **351 J5**
Åland Is. Finland **357 E2**
Alaska st. USA **350 C2**
Alaska, Gulf of USA **350 D3**
Albania Europe **357 F6**
Albany Australia **362 A4** 34°57'S 117°54'E
Albert, Lake Uganda/Zaire **355 F4** 1°45'N 31°00'E
Alberta st. Canada **350 G3**
Ålborg Denmark **356 D3** 57°03'N 9°56'E
Aldan Russian Federation **359 L3** 58°44'N 125°22'E
Aleutian Is. Alaska **350 B3**
Alexander Bay South Africa **355 D7** 28°36'S 16°26'E
Alexandria Egypt **354 E1** 31°13'N 29°55'E
Algeria Africa **354 B2-C2**
Algiers Algeria **354 C1** 36°50'N 3°00'E
Alice Springs Australia **362 B4** 23°42'S 133°52'E
Al Jawf Libya **354 E2** 24°12'N 28°18'E
Alma-Ata Kazakhstan **358 G4** 43°19'N 76°55'E
Al Manāmah Bahrain **360 C3** 26°12'N 50°36'E
Almería Spain **356 C7** 36°50'N 2°27'W
Amazon r. Brazil **352 F5**
Amderma Russian Federation **358 F2** 69°44'N 61°35'E
American Samoa is. Pacific Ocean **363 E3**
Amman Jordan **360 A2** 31°57'N 35°56'E
Amsterdam Netherlands **356 D4** 52°22'N 4°54'E
Amudar'ya r. Turkmensitan/Uzbekistan **358 F5**
Amundsen Sea Antarctica **365**
Amur r. Asia **359 L3-M3**
Anadyr' Russian Federation **359 Q2** 64°40'N 177°32'E
Anadyr' r. Russian Federation **359 Q2**
Anchorage Alaska **350 D2** 61°10'N 150°00'W
Andaman Is. Indian Ocean **361 G4**
Andes mts. Peru/Chile **353 E6-E7**
Andorra Europe **356 D6**
Angara r. Russian Federation **358** I3
Angola Africa **355 D6**
Ankara Turkey **357 G7** 39°55'N 32°50'E
Annaba Algeria **354 C1** 36°55'N 7°47'E
Antalya Turkey **357 G7** 36°53'N 30°42'E
Antananarivo Madagascar **355 G6** 18°55'S 47°31'E
Antarctic Circle 365
Antarctic Peninsula Antarctica **365**
Antigua and Barbuda Central America **352 F3**
Apia Western Samoa **363 E3** 13°48'S 171°45'W
Appenines mts. Italy **356 E6**
Arabian Sea Asia **360 D3-D4**
Arafura Sea Australasia **362 B3**
Aral Sea Kazakhstan **358 F4**
Arapiraca Brazil **353 I5** 9°45'S 36°40'W
Ararat, Mt. Turkey **357 H7** 39°45'N 44°15'E
Archipelago Pacific Ocean **363 G3-G4**
Arctic Bay North West Territories Canada **351 J1** 73°05'N 85°20'W
Arctic Circle 364
Arctic Ocean 349 N1
Arequipa Peru **353 E6** 16°25'S 71°32'W
Argentina South America **353 F7**
Arica Chile **353 E6** 18°29'S 70°20'W
Arkansas st. USA **351 I5**
Arkhangel'sk Russian Federation **358 D2** 64°32'N 41°10'E
Arizona st. USA **350 G5**
Armenia Asia **358 D4**
Ashgabat Turkmenistan **358 E5** 37°58'N 58°24'E
Asmera Ethiopia **355 F3** 15°20'N 38°58'E
Astrakhan Russian Federation **358 D4** 46°22'N 48°00'E
Asunción Paraguay **353 G7** 25°15'S 57°40'W
Aswân Egypt **354 F2** 24°05'N 32°56'E
Asyût Egypt **354 F2** 27°14'N 31°07'E
Atacama Desert South America **353 F6-F7**
Atbara Sudan **355 F3** 17°42'N 33°59'E
Athabasca, Lake Alberta Canada **350 H3** 59°07'N 110°00'W
Athens Greece **357 F7** 38°00'N 23°44'E
Atlanta Georgia USA **351 J5** 33°45'N 84°23'W
Atlantic Ocean 348 I5-J5
Atlas Mts. Morocco **354 B1**
Auckland New Zealand **363 D4** 36°55'S 174°45'E
Auckland Is. Pacific Ocean **363 D5**
Australia 362 B4
Australian Antarctic Territory Antarctica **365**
Austria Europe **356-357 E5**
Ayers Rock Australia mt. **362 B4** 25°18'S 131°18'E
Azerbaijan Asia **358 D4**
Azov, Sea of Ukraine/Russian Federation **358 C4**

B

Baffin Bay Greenland/Canada **351 M1**
Baffin I. North West Territories Canada **351 K1** 68°50'N 70°00'W
Baghdad Iraq **360 B2** 33°20'N 44°26'E
Bahamas Central America **352 E2**
Bahía Blanca Argentina **353 F8** 38°45'S 62°15'W
Bahrain Asia **360 C3**
Baikal Lake Russian Federation **359 K3**
Baku Azerbaijan **358 E4** 40°22'N 49°53'E
Balearic Is. Spain **356 D7**
Bali i. Indonesia **361 I6** 8°20'S 115°07'E
Balikpapan Indonesia **361 I6** 1°15'S 116°50'E
Balkan Mts. Bulgaria **357 F6**
Balkhash, Lake Kazakhstan **358 G4**
Balleny Is. Antarctica **365**
Baltic Sea Europe **357 E3**
Bamako Mali **354 B3** 12°40'N 7°59'W
Bandar Seri Begawan Brunei **361 I5** 4°56'N 114°58'E
Bangalore India **360 E4** 12°58'N 77°35'E
Bangassou Central African Republic **354 E4** 4°50'N 23°07'E
Bangkok Thailand **361 H4** 13°44'N 100°30'E
Bangladesh Asia **361 G3**
Bangui Central African Republic **354 D4** 4°23'N 18°37'E
Banjul The Gambia **354 A3** 13°28'N 16°39'W
Banks I. North West Territories Canada **350 F1** 73°00'N 122°00'W
Barbados Central America **352 G3**
Barcelona Spain **356 D6** 41°23'N 2°11'E
Barents Sea Arctic Ocean **349 O1-O2**
Barnaul Russian Federation **358 H3** 53°21'N 83°15'E
Barranquilla Colombia **352 E3** 11°10'N 74°50'W
Basel Switzerland **356 D5** 47°33'N 7°35'E
Bass Strait Australia **362 C4**
Batna Algeria **354 C1** 33°35'N 6°11'E
Beaufort Sea Arctic Ocean **364**
Béchar Algeria **354 B1** 31°37'N 2°13'W
Beira Mozambique **355 F6** 19°49'S 34°52'E
Beirut Lebanon **360 A2** 33°52'N 35°30'E
Belarus Europe **358 B3**
Belém Brazil **352 H5** 1°27'S 48°29'W
Belfast UK **356 C4** 54°36'N 5°57'W
Belgium Europe **356 D4**
Belgorod Russian Federation **358 C3** 50°38'N 36°36'E
Belgrade Yugoslavia **357 F6** 44°49'N 20°28'E
Belize Central America **352 D3**
Belmopan Belize **352 D3** 17°25'N 88°46'W
Belo Horizonte Brazil **353 H6** 19°45'S 43°54'W
Bengal, Bay of Indian Ocean **361 F4-G4**
Benghazi Libya **354 E1** 32°07'N 20°05'E
Benin Africa **354 C3-C4**
Benue r. Nigeria **354 C4**
Bergen Norway **356 D2** 60°23'N 5°20'E
Bering Sea 348 A3
Bering Strait Arctic Ocean **350 B2**
Berkner I. Antarctica **365** 79°30'S 50°00'W
Berlin Germany **356 E4** 52°31'N 13°24'E
Bern Switzerland **356 D5** 46°57'N 7°26'E
Betroka Madagascar **355 G7** 23°16'S 46°06'E
Beyla Guinea **354 B4** 8°42'N 8°39'W
Bhopal India **361 E3** 23°16'N 77°24'E
Bhutan Asia **361 F3-G3**
Billings Montana USA **350 H4** 45°47'N 108°27'W
Birmingham UK **356 C4** 52°30'N 1°55'W
Birmingham Alabama USA **351 J5** 33°30'N 86°55'W
Biscay, Bay of France **356 C5**
Bishkek Kyrgyzstan **358 G4** 42°53'N 74°46'E
Bissau Guinea-Bissau **354 A3** 11°52'N 15°39'W
Black Sea Europe **357 G6**
Blagoveshchensk Russian Federation **359 L3** 50°19'N 127°30'E
Blanc, Mont mt. France **356 D5** 45°50'N 6°52'E
Blantyre Malawi **355 F6** 15°46'S 35°00'E
Bloemfontein South Africa **355 E7** 29°07'S 26°14'E
Blue Nile r. Sudan **354 F3**
Bobo Dioulasso Burkina **354 B3** 11°11'N 4°18'W
Bogotá Colombia **352 E4** 4°38'N 74°05'W
Boise Idaho USA **350 G4** 43°37'N 116°13'W
Bolivia South America **353 F6**
Bombay India **360 E4** 18°58'N 72°50'E
Bonn Germany **356 D4** 50°44'N 7°05'E
Bordeaux France **356 C6** 44°50'N 0°34'W
Borneo i. Asia **361 I6** 1°00'N 114°00'E
Bornholm i. Denmark **357 E3** 55°10'N 15°00'E
Bosnia & Herzegovina Europe **357 E6**
Boston Massachusetts USA **351 K4** 42°21'N 71°04'W
Bothnia, Gulf of Europe **357 E2**
Botswana Africa **355 E7**
Bougainville I. Pacific Ocean **363 C3** 6°00'S 155°00'E
Brahmaputra r. Asia **361 G3**
Brasília Brazil **353 H6** 15°45'W 47°57'W
Bratislava Slovakia **357 E5** 48°10'N 17°10'E
Bratsk Russian Federation **359 J3** 56°20'N 101°15'E
Brazil South America **353 G5**
Brazzaville Congo **355 D5** 4°14'S 15°10'E
Bremen Germany **356 D4** 53°05'N 8°49'E
Brest France **356 C5** 48°24'N 4°29'W
Brisbane Australia **362 C4** 27°30'S 153°00'E
British Antarctic Territory Antarctica **365**
British Columbia st. Canada **350 F3**
Brno Czech Republic **357 E5** 49°11'N 16°39'E
Brownsville Texas USA **351 I6** 25°54'N 97°30'W
Brunei Asia **361 I5**
Brussels Belgium **356 D4** 50°50'N 4°23'E
Bryansk Russian Federation **358 C3** 53°15'N 34°09'E
Bucharest Romania **357 F6** 44°25'N 26°06'E
Budapest Hungary **357 E5** 47°30'N 19°03'E
Buenos Aires Argentina **353 G8** 34°40'S 58°25'W
Bujumbura Burundi **355 E5** 3°22'S 29°21'E
Bulawayo Zimbabwe **355 E7** 20°10'S 28°43'E
Bulgaria Europe **357 F6**
Burkina Africa **354 B3**
Burma see Myanmar
Burundi Africa **355 F5**
Buta Zaire **355 E4** 2°50'N 24°50'E

C

Cabinda Angola **355 D5** 5°34'S 12°12'E
Cádiz Spain **356 C7** 36°32'N 6°18'W
Cagliari Italy **356 D7** 39°13'N 9°06'E
Cairns Australia **362 C3** 16°51'S 145°43'E
Cairo Egypt **354 F2** 30°03'N 31°15'E
Calabar Nigeria **354 C4** 4°56'N 8°22'E
Calcutta India **361 F3** 22°32'N 88°22'E
Calgary Alberta Canada **350 G3** 51°00'N 114°10'W
Cali Colombia **352 E4** 3°24'N 76°30'W
California st. USA **350 G5**

California, Gulf of Mexico **352 A2**
Callao Peru **353 E6** 12°05'S 77°08'W
Cambodia Asia **361 H4**
Cameroon Africa **354 D4**
Campeche Mexico **352 C3** 19°50'N 90°30'W
Campinas Brazil **353 H7** 22°54'S 47°06'W
Campo Grande Brazil **353 G7** 20°24'S 54°35'W
Canada North America **350-351**
Canary Is. Africa **354 A2**
Canberra Australia **362 C4** 35°18'S 149°08'E
Cantabrian Mts. Spain **356 C6**
Cape Town South Africa **355 D8** 33°55'S 18°27'E
Cape Verde Atlantic Ocean **348 K5**
Cape York Australia **362 C3** 12°40'S 142°20'E
Caracas Venezuela **352 F3** 10°35'N 66°56'W
Cardiff UK **356 C4** 51°28'N 3°11'W
Caribbean Sea Central America **352 E3-F3**
Carnarvon Australia **362 A4** 24°53'S 113°40'E
Caroline I. Kiribati **363 F3** 10°00'S 150°30'W
Caroline Is. Pacific Ocean **362 C2** 7°50'N 145°00'E
Carpathians mts. Europe **357 F5** 48°45'N 23°45'E
Casablanca Morocco **354 B1** 33°39'N 7°35'W
Caspian Sea Asia **358 E4**
Caucasus Mts. Russian Federation **358 D4**
Cebu Philippines **361 J4** 10°17'N 123°56'E
Celebes Sea Asia **361 J5**
Central African Republic Africa **354 D4-E4**
Central Siberian Plateau Russian Federation **359**
Ceuta Spain **356 C7** 35°53'N 5°19'W
Chad Africa **354 D3-E3**
Chad, Lake Chad **354 D3** 13°30'N 14°00'E
Changsha China **361 I3** 28°09'N 112°59'E
Channel Is. UK **356 C5** 49°28'N 2°13'W
Chari r. Cameroon/Chad **354 D3**
Charleston South Carolina USA **351 J5** 32°48'N 79°58'W
Charlotte North Carolina USA **351 J5** 35°03'N 80°50'W
Chelyabinsk Russian Federation **358 F3** 55°12'N 61°25'E
Chengdu China **361 H2** 30°41'N 104°05'E
Cherrapunji India **361 G3** 25°18'N 91°42'E
Cherskly Range mts. Russian Federation **359 N2**
Chesterfield Is. Pacific Ocean **363 C3**
Chicago Illinois USA **351 J4** 41°50'N 87°45'W
Chihuahua Mexico **352 B2** 28°38'N 106°05'W
Chile South America **353 E7-E8**
China Asia **361**
Chinde Mozambique **355 F6** 18°27'S 36°24'E
Chisinau Moldova **358 B4** 47°00'N 28°50'E
Chita Russian Federation **359 K3** 52°03'N 113°35'E
Chittagong Bangladesh **361 G3** 22°20'N 91°50'E
Chongqing China **361 H3** 29°31'N 106°35'E
Christchurch New Zealand **363 D5** 43°33'S 172°40'E
Christmas I. Kiribati **363 E2** 1°52'N 157°20'W
Churchill r. Manitoba Canada **350 H3**
Ciudad Guayana Venezuela **352 F4** 8°22'N 62°40'W
Ciudad Juárez Mexico **352 B1** 31°44'N 106°29'W
Ciudad Madero Mexico **352 C2** 22°19'N 97°50'W
Ciudad Victoria Mexico **352 C2** 23°43'N 99°10'W
Clermont-Ferrand France **356 D5** 45°47'N 3°05'E
Cleveland Ohio USA **351 J4** 41°30'N 81°41'W
Cluj-Napoca Romania **357 F5** 46°47'N 23°37'E
Cochabamba Bolivia **353 F6** 17°24'S 66°09'W
Colombia South America **352 E4**
Colombo Sri Lanka **360 F5** 6°55'N 79°52'E
Colón Panama **352 D4** 9°21'N 79°54'W
Colorado r. USA **350 G5**
Colorado st. USA **350 H5**
Columbia r. Canada/USA **350 F4**
Communism Peak mt. Tajikistan **358 G5** 38°59'N 72°01'E
Comodoro Rivadavia Argentina **353 F9** 45°50'S 67°30'W
Comoros Africa **355 G6**
Conakry Guinea **354 A4** 9°30'N 13°43'W
Concepción Chile **353 E8** 36°50'S 73°03'W
Congo Africa **355 D5**
Cook, Mt. New Zealand **363 D5** 43°45'S 170°12'E
Cook Is. Pacific Ocean **363 F3**
Cooper Creek r. Australia **362 B4**
Copenhagen Denmark **356 E3** 55°40'N 12°35'E
Coppermine North West Territories Canada **350 G2** 67°49'N 115°12'W
Connecticut st. USA **351 K4**
Coral Sea Pacific Ocean **362 C3**
Córdoba Argentina **353 F8** 31°25'S 64°10'W
Cork Ireland **356 C4** 51°54'N 8°28'W
Corrientes Argentina **353 G7** 27°30'S 58°48'W
Corsica i. France **356 D6** 40°00'N 9°10'E
Costa Rica Central America **352 D3**
Cotopaxi mt. Ecuador **352 E5** 0°40'S 78°28'W
Craiova Romania **357 F7** 44°18'N 23°46'E
Crete i. Greece **357 F6** 35°29'N 24°42'E
Croatia Europe **357 E5**
Cuba Central America **352 E2**
Curacao i. South America **352 F3** 12°15'N 69°00'W
Curitiba Brazil **353 H7** 25°24'S 49°16'W
Cuzco Peru **353 E6** 13°32'S 71°57'W
Cyprus Europe **357 G7**
Czech Republic Europe **356-357 E5**

D

Dakar Senegal **354 A3** 14°38'N 17°27'W
Dalian China **361 J2** 38°53'N 121°37'E
Dallas Texas USA **351 I5** 32°47'N 96°48'W
Dalol Ethiopia **354 G3** 14°15'N 40°18'E
Damascus Syria **360 A2** 33°30'N 36°19'E
Da Nang Vietnam **361 H4** 16°04'N 108°13'E
Danube r. Europe **356-357 E5**
Dar es Salaam Tanzania **355 F5** 6°51'S 39°18'E
Darling r. Australia **362 C4**
Darwin Australia **362 B3** 12°23'S 130°44'E
Daugavpils Latvia **357 F3** 55°52'N 26°31'E
Davao Philippines **361 J5** 7°05'N 125°38'E
Davis Strait Greenland/Canada **351 M2**
De Aar South Africa **355 E8** 30°39'S 24°01'E
Deccan India **361 E4**
Delaware st. USA **351 K5**
Delhi India **360 E3** 28°40'N 77°13'E
Denmark Europe **356 D3**
Denver Colorado USA **350 H5** 39°43'N 105°01'W
Derby Australia **362 B3** 17°19'S 123°38'E
Detroit Michigan USA **351 J4** 42°20'N 83°03'W
Devon I. North West Territories Canada **351 J1** 75°00'N 86°00'W
Dhaka Bangladesh **361 G3** 23°43'N 90°25'E
Dirē Dawa Ethiopia **354 G4** 9°35'N 41°50'E
Djibouti Africa **354 G3**
Djibouti Djibouti **354 G3** 11°35'N 43°11'E
Dnepr r. Belarus/Ukraine **358 C4**
Dnipropetrovs'k Ukraine **358 C4** 48°29'N 35°00'E
Dodoma Tanzania **355 F5** 6°10'S 35°40'E
Doha Qatar **360 C3** 25°15'N 51°34'E
Dominica Central America **352 F3**
Dominican Republic Central America **352 E3**
Don r. Russian Federation **358 D4**
Donets'k Ukraine **358 C4** 48°00'N 37°50'E
Dongola Sudan **354 F3** 19°10'N 30°27'E
Douala Cameroon **354 D4** 4°05'N 9°43'E
Douro r. Portugal **356 C6**
Drakensberg Mts. South Africa/Lesotho **355 E8**
Drava r. Yugoslavia (Serbia & Montenegro) **357 E5**
Dresden Germany **356 E4** 51°03'N 13°44'E
Dronning Maud Land Antarctica **365**
Dublin Ireland **356 C4** 53°21'N 6°18'W
Dunedin New Zealand **363 D5** 45°52'S 170°30'E
Durban South Africa **355 F7** 29°50'S 30°59'E
Dushanbe Tajikistan **358 F5** 38°38'N 68°51'E

E

East China Sea Asia **361 J2-J3**
East London South Africa **355 E8** 33°00'S 27°54'E
East Siberian Sea Arctic Ocean **359 O1-R1**
Ebro r. Spain **356 C6**
Ecuador South America **352 E4-E5**
Edinburgh UK **356 C3** 55°57'N 3°13'W
Edmonton Alberta Canada **350 G3** 53°30'N 113°30'W
Egypt Africa **354 E2**
El Aaiún Western Sahara **354 A2** 27°09'13°12'W
Elâzig Turkey **357 G7** 38°41'N 39°14'E
Elbe r. Germany **356 E4**
Elbert, Mt. Colorado USA **351 H5** 39°07'N 106°27'W
Elbrus mt. Europe (Russian Federation) **357 H6** 43°21'N 42°29'E
El Fasher Sudan **354 E3** 13°37'N 25°22'E
El Gîza Egypt **354 F2** 30°01'N 31°12'E
Ellesmere I. North West Territories Canada **351 J1** 78°00'N 82°00'W
Ellsworth Land Antarctica **365**
El Obeid Sudan **354 F3** 13°11'N 30°10'E
El Paso Texas USA **350 H5** 31°45'N 106°29'W
El Salvador Central America **352 D3**
Emi Koussi mt. Chad **354 D3** 19°58'N 18°30'E
Enderby Land Antarctica **365**
English Channel Europe **356 C4-D4**
Entebbe Uganda **355 F4** 0°08'N 32°29'E
Enugu Nigeria **354 C4** 6°20'N 7°29'E
Equatorial Guinea Africa **355 D4**
Esbjerg Denmark **356 D3** 55°28'N 8°27'E
Esperance Australia **362 B4** 33°49'S 121°52'E
Espiritu Santo i. Vanuatu **363 D3** 15°50'S 166°50'E
Es Samara Western Sahara **354 A2** 26°44'N 14°41'W
Estonia Europe **357 F3**
Ethiopia Africa **354 F4-G4**
Euphrates r. Asia **360 A2-B2**
Everest, Mt. China/Nepal **361 F3** 27°59'N 86°56'E
Eyre, Lake Australia **362 B4** 28°30'S 137°25'E

F

Faeroe Is. Denmark **356 C2**
Fairbanks Alaska USA **350 D2** 64°50'N 147°50'W
Falkland Is. Atlantic Ocean **353 G10**
Farewell, Cape Greenland **351 N2** 60°00'N 44°20'W
Fiji Pacific Ocean **363 E3**
Finland Europe **357 F2**
Finland, Gulf of Europe **357 F3**
Firat r. Turkey **357 G7**
Florence Italy **356 E6** 43°46'N 11°15'E
Flores i. Indonesia **361 J6** 8°40'S 121°20'E
Florida st. USA **351 J6**
Fortaleza Brazil **352 I5** 3°45'S 38°35'W
Fort Rupert Québec Canada **351 K3** 51°29'N 78°45'W
France Europe **356 D5**
Frankfurt Germany **356 D4** 50°07'N 8°40'E
Franz Josef Land is. Russian Federation **364**
Fraser r. British Columbia Canada **350 F3**
Freetown Sierra Leone **354 A4** 8°30'N 13°17'W
Freiburg Germany **356 D5** 47°59'N 7°51'E
Fremantle Australia **362 A4** 32°07'S 115°44'E
French Guiana South America **352 G4**
Frobisher Bay North West Territories Canada **351 L2** 63°45'N 68°30'W
Fukuoka Japan **361 J2** 33°39'N 130°21'E
Funafuti Tuvalu **363 D3** 8°31'S 179°13'E
Fushun China **361 J1** 41°50'N 123°55'E
Fuzhou China **361 I3** 26°09'N 119°21'E

G

Gabès Tunisia **354 D1** 33°53'N 10°07'E
Gabon Africa **355 D5**
Galapagos Is. Ecuador **352 C5**
Gambia, The Africa **354 A3**
Gambier Is. Pacific Ocean **363 G4** 23°10'S 135°00'W
Ganges r. India **361 F3**
Garoua Cameroon **354 D4** 9°17'N 13°22'E
Gdańsk Poland **357 E4** 54°22'N 18°38'E
Geneva Switzerland **356 D5** 46°12'N 6°09'E
Genoa Italy **356 D6** 44°25'N 8°57'E
Georgetown Guyana **352 G4** 6°46'N 58°10'W
George Town Malaysia **361 H5** 5°30'N 100°16'E
Georgia Europe **357 H6**
Georgia st. USA **351 J5**
Ghadāmis Libya **354 C1** 30°08'N 9°30'E
Ghana Africa **354 B4**
Ghardaïa Algeria **354 C1** 32°29'N 3°40'E
Ghāt Libya **354 D2** 24°58'N 10°11'E
Gibraltar Europe **356 C7** 36°09'N 5°21'W
Gijón Spain **356 C6** 43°32'N 5°40'W
Gilbert Is. Kiribati **363 D3**
Glåma r. Norway **356 E2**
Glasgow UK **356 C3** 55°52'N 4°15'W
Gobi Desert Asia **361 G1-H1**
Godāvari r. India **360 E4**
Godhavn Greenland **351 M2** 69°20'N 53°30'W
Godthåb see Nuuk
Goiânia Brazil **353 H6** 16°43'S 49°18'W
Good Hope, Cape of Africa **355 D8** 34°21'S 18°28'E
Goose Bay Newfoundland Canada **351 L3** 53°19'N 60°24'W
Gora Pobeda mt. Russian Federation **359 N2** 65°10'N 146°00'E
Gothenburg Sweden **356 E3** 57°43'N 11°58'E
Gotland i. Sweden **357 E3** 57°30'N 18°33'E
Gran Chaco South America **353 F7**
Grand Bahama i. Bahamas **352 E2** 26°40'N 78°20'W
Grand Cayman i. Central America **352 D3** 19°20'N 81°30'W
Graz Austria **356 E5** 47°05'N 15°27'E
Great Australian Bight Australia **362 B4**
Great Barrier Reef Australia **362 C3**

Luzon i. Philippines **361 J4** 17°50'N 121°00'E
L'viv Ukraine **358 B4** 49°50'N 24°00'E

M

Macapá Brazil **352 G5** 0°04'N 51°04'W
Macau Asia **361 I3** 22°11'N 113°33'E
MacKenzie r. Canada **350 F2**
Madagascar Africa **355 G7**
Madang Papua New Guinea **362 C3** 5°14'S 145°45'E
Madeira i. Africa **354 A1** 32°45'N 17°00'W
Madeira r. Brazil **352 F5**
Madras India **360 E4** 13°05'N 80°18'E
Madrid Spain **356 C6** 40°24'N 3°41'W
Magadan Russian Federation **359 O3** 59°38'N 150°50'E
Magellan's Strait Chile **353 F10**
Mahajanga Madagascar **355 G6** 15°43'S 46°19'E
Maiduguri Nigeria **354 D3** 11°53'N 13°16'E
Maine st. USA **351 L4**
Majorca i. Spain **356 D7** 39°30'N 3°00'E
Malabo Equatorial Guinea **354 C4** 3°45'N 8°48'E
Malaga Spain **356 C7** 36°43'N 4°25'W
Malakal Sudan **355 F4** 9°31'N 31°39'E
Malanje Angola **355 D5** 9°36'S 16°21'E
Malawi Africa **355 F6**
Malaysia Asia **361 H5**
Maldives Indian Ocean **360 E5**
Male Maldives **360 E5** 4°00'N 73°28'E
Mali Africa **354 B3**
Malmö Sweden **356 E3** 55°36'N 13°00'E
Malta Europe **356 E7**
Maluku is. Indonesia **361 J5** 4°00'S 129°00'E
Man, Isle of UK **356 C4** 54°15'N 4°30'W
Managua Nicaragua **352 D3** 12°06'N 81°18'W
Manaus Brazil **352 F5** 3°06'S 60°00'W
Manchester UK **356 C4** 53°30'N 2°15'W
Manila Philippines **361 J4** 14°36'N 120°59'E
Manitoba st. Canada **351 I3**
Maputo Mozambique **355 F7** 25°58'S 32°35'E
Marabá Brazil **352 H5** 5°23'S 49°10'W
Maracaibo Venezuela **352 E3** 10°44'N 71°37'W
Mar del Plata Argentina **353 G8** 38°00'S 57°32'W
Marie Byrd Land Antarctica **365**
Marka Somalia **355 G4** 1°42'N 44°47'E
Marquesas Is. Pacific Ocean **363 G3**
Marrakech Morocco **354 B1** 31°49'N 8°00'W
Marshall Is. Pacific Ocean **363 D2**
Marseille France **356 D6** 43°18'N 5°24'E
Martinique i. Central America **352 F3** 14°40'N 61°00'W
Maryland st. USA **351 K5**
Maseru Lesotho **355 E7** 29°18'S 27°28'E
Mashhad Iran **360 C2** 36°16'N 59°34'E
Massachusetts st. USA **351 K4**
Massif Central mts. France **356 D6**
Matamoros Mexico **352 C2** 25°32'N 103°15'W
Mato Grosso Brazil **353 G6**
Matterhorn mt. Switzerland/Italy **356 D5** 45°59'N 7°43'E
Mauritania Africa **354 A3**
Mauritius Indian Ocean **349 P8**
Mayotte i. Comoros **355 G6** 12°50'S 45°10'E
Mazatlán Mexico **352 B2** 23°13'N 106°25'W
Mbabane Swaziland **355 F7** 26°19'S 31°08'E
Mbala Zambia **355 F5** 8°50'S 31°24'E
Mbuji-Mayi Zaire **355 E5** 6°08'S 23°39'E
McKinley, Mt. Alaska USA **350 C2** 63°00'N 151°00'W
Mecca Saudi Arabia **360 B3** 21°26'N 39°49'E
Medan Indonesia **361 G5** 3°35'N 98°39'E
Medellin Colombia **352 E4** 6°15'N 75°36'W
Mediterranean Sea Europe/Africa **356 D7**
Meknès Morocco **354 B1** 33°53'N 5°37'W
Mekong r. Asia **361 H4**
Melanesia is. Pacific Ocean **362 D3**
Melbourne Australia **362 C4** 37°45'S 144°58'E
Melilla Spain **356 C7** 35°17'N 2°57'W
Melville I. Canada **350 G1** 75°30'N 110°00'W
Memphis Tennessee USA **351 J5** 35°08'N 90°03'W
Mendoza Argentina **353 F8** 32°54'S 68°50'W
Menongue Angola **355 D6** 14°40'S 17°41'E
Mérida Mexico **352 D2** 20°59'N 89°39'W
Mersin Turkey **357 G7** 36°47'N 34°37'E
Mexicali Mexico **352 A1** 32°40'N 115°29'W
Mexico Central America **352 B2**
Mexico, Gulf of North America **351 I6-J6**
Mexico City Mexico **352 C3** 19°25'S 99°10'W
Mezen Russian Federation **358 D2** 65°50'N 44°20'E
Miami Florida USA **351 J6** 25°45'N 80°15'W
Michigan st. USA **351 J4**
Michigan, Lake USA **351 J4** 44°00'N 87°00'W
Micronesia is. Pacific Ocean **362 C2**
Midway Is. Hawaiian Is. **363 E1**
Milan Italy **356 D5** 45°28'N 9°12'E
Milwaukee Wisconsin USA **351 J4** 43°02'N 87°55'W
Mindanao i. Philippines **361 J5** 7°30'N 125°00'E
Minneapolis Minnesota USA **351 I4** 44°59'N 93°13'W
Minnesota st. USA **351 I4**
Minsk Belarus **358 B3** 53°51'N 27°30'E
Mississippi r. USA **351 I4-I5**
Mississippi st. USA **351 J5**
Missouri r. Nebraska USA **351 I4**
Missouri st. USA **351 I5**
Moçambique Mozambique **355 G6** 15°00'S 40°47'E
Mogadishu Somalia **355 G4** 2°02'N 45°21'E
Moldova Europe **358 B4**
Monaco Europe **356 D6**
Monclova Mexico **352 B2** 26°54'N 101°25'W
Mongolia Asia **361 G1-H1**
Monrovia Liberia **354 A4** 6°20'N 10°46'W
Montana st. USA **350 H4**
Monterrey Mexico **352 B2** 25°40'N 100°19'W
Montevideo Uruguay **353 G8** 34°53'S 56°11'W
Montréal Québec Canada **351 K4** 45°31'N 73°34'W
Mopti Mali **354 B3** 14°29'N 4°10'W
Morocco Africa **354 B1**
Moroni Comoros **355 G6** 11°40'S 43°19'E
Moscow Russian Federation **358 C3** 55°45'N 37°42'E
Mosul Iraq **360 B2** 36°21'N 43°08'E
Mount Gambier Australia **362 C4** 37°51'S 140°50'E
Mozambique Africa **355 F6**
Mozambique Channel Indian Ocean **355 G6**
Mtwara Tanzania **355 G6** 10°17'S 40°11'E
Munich Germany **356 E5** 48°08'N 11°34'E
Murmansk Russian Federation **358 C2** 68°59'N 33°08'E
Murray r. Australia **362 C4**
Murzuq Libya **354 D2** 22°55'N 13°55'E
Muscat Oman **360 C3** 23°36'N 58°37'E
Mwanza Kenya **355 F5** 7°51'S 26°43'E
Mwaya Tanzania **355 F5** 9°33'S 33°56'E
Myanmar (Burma) Asia **361 G3**

N

Nagpur India **360 E3** 21°09'N 79°06'E
Nairobi Kenya **355 F5** 1°17'S 36°50'E
Namibe Angola **355 D6** 15°10'S 12°09'E
Namibia Africa **355 D7**
Nampula Mozambique **355 F6** 15°09'S 39°14'E
Nanchang China **361 I3** 28°37'N 115°57'E
Nan Shan mts. China **361 G2**
Nantes France **356 C5** 47°13'N 1°33'W
Naples Italy **356 E6** 40°51'N 14°17'E
Narvik Norway **357 E1** 68°26'N 17°25'E
Nassau Bahamas **352 E2** 25°05'N 77°21'W
Nasser, Lake Egypt **354 F2** 22°40'N 32°00'E
Natal Brazil **352 I5** 5°46'S 35°15'W
Nauru Pacific Ocean **363 D3**
Ndélé Central African Republic **354 E4** 8°24'N 20°39'E
N'Djamena Chad **354 D3** 12°10'N 14°59'E
Ndola Zambia **355 E6** 12°58'S 28°39'E
Nebraska st. USA **351 I4**
Negro r. Brazil **352 F5**
Nelson r. Manitoba Canada **351 I3**
Nepal Asia **361 F3**
Netherlands Europe **356 D4**
Nevada st. USA **350 G5**
New Brunswick st. Canada **351 L4**
New Caledonia is. Pacific Ocean **363 D3**
Newcastle Australia **362 C4** 32°55'S 151°46'E
New Delhi India **361 E3** 28°36'N 77°12'E
New Georgia Is. Solomon Is. **363 C3**
New Guinea i. Australasia **362 B3** 5°00'S 140°00'E
Newfoundland st. Canada **351 M3**
New Hampshire st. USA **351 K4**
New Jersey st. USA **351 K4**
New Mexico st. USA **351 H5**
New Orleans Louisiana USA **351 I6** 29°58'N 90°07'W
New Siberian Is. Russian Federation **359 M1-N1**
New South Wales st. Australia **362 C4**
New York st. USA **351 K4**
New York New York USA **351 K4** 40°43'N 74°01'W
New Zealand Australasia **363 D5**
Niamey Niger **354 C3** 13°32'N 2°05'E
Nicaragua Central America **352 D3**
Nice France **356 D6** 43°42'N 7°16'E
Nicobar Is. Indian Ocean **361 G5**
Nicosia Cyprus **357 G7** 35°11'N 33°23'E
Niger Africa **354 C3-D3**
Niger r. Africa **354 C4**
Nigeria Africa **354 C4**
Nile Egypt **354 F2**
Niue i. Cook Is. **363 E3** 19°02'S 169°52'W
Nizhneangarsk Russian Federation **359 K3** 55°48'N 109°35'E
Nizhnevartovsk Russian Federation **358 G2** 60°57'N 76°40'E
Nizhniy Novgorod Russian Federation **358 D3** 56°20'N 44°00'E
Nordvik Russian Federation **359 K1** 73°40'N 110°50'E
Norfolk Virginia USA **351 K5** 36°54'N 76°18'W
Norfolk I. Pacific Ocean **363 D4** 29°02'S 167°57'E
Noril'sk Russian Federation **358 H2** 69°21'N 88°02'E
Normanton Australia **362 C3** 17°40'S 141°05'E
North Cape New Zealand **363 D4** 34°23'S 173°04'E
North Carolina st. USA **351 K5**
North Dakota st. USA **351 I4**
North Dvina r. Russian Federation **358 D2**
Northern Marianas is. Pacific Ocean **362 C1-C2**
Northern Territory st. Australia **362 B3**
North I. New Zealand **363 D4** 39°00'S 175°00'E
North Magnetic Pole (1985) Arctic Ocean **364**
North Pole Arctic Ocean **364** 90°00'N
North Sea Europe **356 D3**
North West Territories st. Canada **350-351 G2-I2**
Norway Europe **356 D2**
Norwegian Dependency Antarctica **365**
Norwegian Sea Europe **356 D2**
Nouadhibou Mauritania **354 A2** 20°54'N 17°01'W
Nouakchott Mauritania **354 A3** 18°09'N 15°58'W
Nova Iguaçu Brazil **353 H7** 22°45'S 43°27'W
Nova Scotia st. Canada **351 L4**
Novaya Zemlya i. Russian Federation **358 E1** 74°00'N 56°00'E
Novgorod Russian Federation **358 C3** 58°30'N 31°20'E
Novosibirsk Russian Federation **358 H3** 55°05'N 83°05'E
Nuevo Laredo Mexico **352 C2** 27°30'N 99°31'W
Nukualofa Tonga **363 E3** 21°07'S 175°12'W
Nuuk Greenland **351 M2** 64°10'N 51°40'W
Nyasa, Lake Malawi **355 F6** 12°00'S 34°30'E

O

Ob r. Russian Federation **358 H3**
Ob, Gulf of Russian Federation **358 G2**
Oder r. Poland **357 E4**
Odessa Ukraine **358 C4** 46°30'N 30°46'E
Ohio r. USA **351 J5**
Ohio st. USA **351 J5**
Okhotsk, Sea of Russian Federation **358 N3-O3**
Oklahoma st. USA **351 I5**
Oklahoma City Oklahoma USA **351 I5** 35°28'N 97°32'W
Olekminsk Russian Federation **359 L2** 60°25'N 120°00'E
Olenëk Russian Federation **359 L2** 68°38'N 112°15'E
Omaha Nebraska USA **351 I4** 41°16'N 95°57'W
Oman Asia **360 C3**
Omdurman Sudan **354 F3** 15°37'N 32°59'E
Omsk Russian Federation **358 G3** 55°00'N 73°22'E
Onega, Lake Russian Federation **358 C2** 62°00'N 35°30'E
Ontario st. Canada **351 J3**
Oran Algeria **354 B1** 35°42'N 0°38'W
Orange r. South Africa **355 D7**
Oregon st. USA **350 F4**
Orenburg Russian Federation **358 E3** 51°50'N 55°00'E
Orinoco r. Venezuela **352 F4**
Orkney Is. UK **356 C3**
Osaka Japan **361 K2** 34°40'N 135°30'E
Oslo Norway **356 E3** 59°55'N 10°45'E
Ottawa Ontario Canada **351 K4** 45°25'N 75°42'W
Ouagadougou Burkina **354 B3** 12°20'N 1°40'W
Oudtshoorn South Africa **355 E8** 33°35'S 22°11'E
Oujda Morocco **354 B1** 34°41'N 1°45'W
Oulu Finland **357 F1** 65°01'N 25°28'E

P

Pacific Ocean **348 B7**
Padang Indonesia **361 H6** 0°55'S 100°21'E
Pago Pago i. Pacific Ocean **363 E3** 14°16'S 170°42'W
Pakistan Asia **360 D3**
Palau Is. Pacific Ocean **362 B2**
Palermo Italy **356 E7** 38°07'N 13°21'E

Palmer Land Antarctica **365**
Palmyra I. Line Is. **363 E2** 5°52'N 162°05'W
Palu Indonesia **361 I6** 0°54'S 119°52'E
Pampas Argentina **353 F8**
Panama Central America **352 D4**
Panama City Panama **352 E4** 8°57'N 79°30'W
Papua New Guinea Australasia **362 C3**
Paraguay South America **353 F7-G7**
Paraguay r. Paraguay **353 G7**
Paramaribo Surinam **352 G4** 5°52'N 55°14'W
Paraná r. Brazil **353 G7**
Paris France **356 D5** 48°52'N 2°20'E
Parnaíba r. Brazil **352 H5**
Pátrai Greece **357 F7** 38°15'N 21°44'E
Peace r. Alberta Canada **350 G3**
Pechora r. Russian Federation **358 E2**
Peking (Beijing) China **361 I1** 39°55'N 116°25'E
Pemba I. Tanzania **355 F5** 5°10'S 39°45'E
Pennsylvania st. USA **351 K4**
Penza Russian Federation **358 D3** 53°11'N 45°00'E
Perm Russian Federation **358 E3** 58°01'N 56°10'E
Perth Australia **362 A4** 31°58'S 115°49'E
Peru South America **353 E5**
Petropavlovsk-Kamchatskiy Russian Federation **359 O3** 53°03'N 158°43'E
Philadelphia Pennsylvania USA **351 K4** 39°57'N 75°07'W
Philippines Asia **361 J4-J5**
Philippine Sea Pacific Ocean **362 B2**
Phnom Penh Cambodia **361 H4** 11°35'N 104°55'E
Phoenix Arizona USA **350 G5** 33°27'N 112°05'W
Phoenix Is. Kiribati **363 E3**
Pietersburg South Africa **355 E7** 23°54'S 29°27'E
Pisa Italy **356 E6** 43°43'N 10°23'E
Pitcairn I. Pacific Ocean **363 G4** 25°04'S 130°06'W
Pittsburgh Pennsylvania USA **351 K4** 40°26'N 80°00'W
Piura Peru **352 D5** 5°15'S 80°38'W
Platte r. USA **351 H5**
Playa Azul Mexico **352 B3** 18°00'N 102°24'W
Podgorica Yugoslavia **357 E6** 42°26'N 19°14'E
Pohnpei i. Pacific Ocean **362 C2** 6°30'N 155°30'E
Pointe Noire Congo **355 D5** 4°46'S 11°53'E
Poland Europe **357 E4**
Polus Nedostupnosti Antarctica **365** 78°00'S 96°00'E
Polynesia Pacific Ocean **363 E3**
Port Augusta Australia **362 B4** 32°30'S 137°46'E
Port-au-Prince Haiti **352 E3** 18°33'N 72°20'W
Port Elizabeth South Africa **355 E8** 33°57'S 25°34'E
Port Gentil Gabon **355 C5** 0°40'S 8°46'E
Port Harcourt Nigeria **354 C4** 4°43'N 7°05'E
Port Hedland Australia **362 A4** 20°24'S 118°36'E
Portland Oregon USA **350 F4** 45°33'N 122°36'W
Port Moresby Papua New Guinea **362 C3** 9°30'S 147°07'E
Porto Portugal **356 C6** 41°11'N 8°36'W
Porto Alegre Brazil **353 G7** 30°03'S 51°10'W
Porto Novo Benin **354 C4** 6°30'N 2°47'E
Pôrto Velho Brazil **353 F5** 8°45'S 63°54'W
Port Said Egypt **354 F1** 31°17'N 32°18'E
Port Sudan Sudan **354 F3** 19°39'N 37°01'E
Portugal Europe **356 C6-C7**
Potosí Bolivia **353 F6** 19°35'S 65°45'W
Poza Rica Mexico **352 C2** 20°34'N 97°26'W
Poznań Poland **357 E4** 52°25'N 16°53'E
Prague Czech Republic **356 E5** 50°05'N 14°26'E
Pretoria South Africa **355 E7** 25°43'S 28°11'E
Pripyat r. Belarus **358 B3**
Prince Edward I. st. Canada **351 L4**
Prudhoe Bay Alaska USA **350 D1** 70°20'N 148°25'W
Prut r. Moldova/Romania/Ukraine **357 F5**
Puebla Mexico **352 C3** 19°03'N 98°10'W
Puerto Montt Chile **353 E9** 41°28'S 73°00'W
Puerto Rico i. Central America **352 F3** 18°20'N 66°30'W
Pune India **360 E4** 18°34'N 73°58'E
Punta Arenas Chile **353 E10** 53°10'S 70°56'W
Puri India **361 F3** 19°48'N 85°51'E
Pusan South Korea **361 J2** 35°05'N 129°02'E
P'yongyang North Korea **361 J2** 39°00'N 125°47'E
Pyrenées mts. France/Spain **356 C6**

Q

Qatar Asia **360 C3**
Qingdao China **361 J1** 36°02'N 120°25'E
Québec st. Canada **351 K3**
Québec Québec Canada **351 K4** 46°50'N 71°20'W
Queen Charlotte Is. British Columbia Canada **350 E3**
Queen Elizabeth Is. North West Territories Canada **351 H1**
Queen Mary Land Antarctica **365**
Queensland st. Australia **362 C4**
Quezon City Philippines **361 J4** 14°39'N 121°01'E
Quito Ecuador **352 E5** 0°14'S 78°30'W

R

Rabat Morocco **354 B1** 34°02'N 6°51'W
Rance r. France **356 C5**
Rangoon Myanmar **361 G4** 16°47'N 96°10'E
Recife Brazil **353 I5** 8°06'S 34°53'W
Red r. USA **351 I5**
Red Sea Asia **360 A3-A4**
Reggio di Calabria Italy **356 E7** 38°07'N 15°39'E
Regina Saskatchewan Canada **350 H3** 50°25'N 104°39'W
Reims France **356 D5** 49°15'N 4°02'E
Reykjavik Iceland **356 A2** 64°09'N 21°58'W
Rhine r. Europe **356 D5**
Rhodes i. Greece **357 F7** 36°10'N 28°00'E
Rhône r. France **356 D6**
Ribeirão Prêto Brazil **353 H7** 21°09'S 47°48'W
Riga Latvia **357 F3** 56°53'N 24°08'E
Rio Branco Brazil **353 F5** 9°59'S 67°49'W
Rio de Janeiro Brazil **353 H7** 22°53'S 43°17'W
Rio Gallegos Argentina **353 F10** 51°37'S 69°10'W
Rio Grande Brazil **353 G8** 32°02'S 52°08'W
Rio Grande r. Mexico/USA **351 I6**
Riyadh Saudi Arabia **360 B3** 24°39'N 46°44'E
Rocky Mts. North America **350 G3-H5**
Romania Europe **357 F5**
Rome Italy **356 E6** 41°54'N 12°29'E
Ronne Ice Shelf Antarctica **365**
Rostov Russian Federation **358 C4** 57°11'N 39°23'E
Ross Dependency Antarctica **365**
Ross Ice Shelf Antarctica **365**
Ross Sea Antarctica **365**
Rub'al Khāli Saudi Arabia **360 B4-C4**
Russian Federation Europe/Asia **358-359**
Rwanda Africa **355 E5**
Ryuku Is. Pacific Ocean **361 J3-K3**

S

Sable I. Atlantic Ocean **351 M4** 43°55'N 59°50'W
Sacramento Nevada USA **350 F5** 38°35'N 121°30'W
Safi Morocco **354 B1** 32°30'N 9°17'W
Sahara Africa **354 C2-D2**
St. Christopher and Nevis Central America **348 H5**
St. John's Newfoundland Canada **351 M4** 47°34'N 52°43'W
St. Lawrence r. Canada/USA **351 L4**
St. Louis Missouri USA **351 I5** 38°38'N 90°11'W
St. Lucia Central America **352 F3**
St. Paul Minnesota USA **351 I4** 45°00'N 93°10'W
St. Petersburg Russian Federation **358 C3** 59°55'N 30°25'E
St. Vincent and the Grenadines Central America **352 F3**
Saipan i. Northern Marianas **362 C2** 15°12'N 145°43'E
Sakhalin i. Russian Federation **359 N3** 50°00'N 143°00'E
Salada r. Argentina **353 F8**
Salekhard Russian Federation **358 F2** 66°33'N 66°35'E
Salta Argentina **353 F7** 24°47'S 65°24'W
Salt Lake City Utah USA **350 G4** 40°46'N 111°53'W
Salvador Brazil **353 I6** 12°58'S 38°29'W
Samara Russian Federation **358 E3** 53°10'N 50°10'E
Samarkand Uzbekistan **358 F5** 39°40'N 66°57'E
Samsun Turkey **357 G6** 41°17'N 36°22'E
San'a Yemen **360 B4** 15°23'N 44°14'E
San Antonio Argentina **353 F9** 40°46'S 64°45'W
San Antonio Texas USA **351 I6** 29°28'N 98°31'W
San Diego California USA **350 G5** 32°43'N 117°09'W
San Francisco California USA **350 F5** 37°48'N 122°24'W
San José Costa Rica **352 D4** 9°59'N 84°04'W
San Juan Puerto Rico **352 F3** 18°29'N 66°08'W
Sanliurfa Turkey **357 G7** 37°08'N 38°45'E
San Lucas Mexico **352 B2** 23°00'N 110°00'W
San Marino Europe **349 M4**
San Miguel de Tucumán Argentina **353 F7** 26°49'S 65°13'W
San Pedro Sula Honduras **352 D3** 15°26'N 88°01'W
Santa Clara Cuba **352 E2** 22°25'N 79°58'W
Santa Cruz Is. Solomon Is. **363 D3**
Santa Fé Argentina **353 F8** 31°40'S 60°40'W
Santa Maria Brazil **353 G7** 29°40'S 53°47'W
Santarém Brazil **352 G5** 2°26'S 54°41'W
Santiago Chile **353 E8** 33°27'S 70°40'W
Santo Domingo Dominican Republic **352 F3** 18°30'N 69°57'W
São Francisco r. Brazil **353 H6**
São José Brazil **353 H7** 27°35'S 48°40'W
São Luis Brazil **352 H5** 2°34'S 44°16'W
São Paulo Brazil **353 H7** 23°33'S 46°39'W
São Tomé and Príncipe Africa **355 C4**
Sapporo Japan **361 L1** 43°05'N 141°21'E
Sarajevo Bosnia & Herzegovina **357 E6** 43°52'N 18°26'E
Saransk Russian Federation **358 D3** 54°12'N 45°10'E
Saratov Russian Federation **358 D3** 51°30'N 45°55'E
Sardinia i. Italy **356 D6** 40°00'N 9°00'E
Saskatchewan st. Canada **350 H3**
Saskatoon Saskatchewan Canada **350 H3** 52°07'N 106°38'W
Saudi Arabia Asia **360 B3**
Sava r. Croatia/Yugoslavia (Serbia & Montenegro) **357 E5**
Scilly, Isles of UK **356 C5**
Seattle Oregon USA **350 F4** 47°36'N 122°20'W
Seychelles Indian Ocean **349 P7**
Seine r. France **356 D5**
Selvas Brazil **352 F5**
Semarang Indonesia **361 I6** 6°58'S 110°29'E
Semipalatinsk Kazakhstan **358 G3** 50°26'N 80°16'E
Senegal Africa **354 A3**
Senegal r. Senegal **354 A3**
Seoul South Korea **361 J2** 37°30'N 127°00'E
Seram i. Indonesia **361 J6** 3°10'S 129°30'E
Serowe Botswana **355 E7** 22°22'S 26°42'E
Sevastopol Ukraine **358 C4** 44°36'N 33°31'E
Severnaya Zemlya is. Russian Federation **358-359 I1-J1**
Sfax Tunisia **354 D1** 34°45'N 10°43'E
Shabeelle r. Somalia **354 G4**
Shanghai China **361 J2** 31°18'N 121°50'E
Shetland Is. UK **356 C2**
Sicily i. Italy **356 E7** 37°30'N 14°00'E
Sierra Leone Africa **354 A4**
Sierra Madre Occidental mts. Mexico **352 B2**
Sierra Nevada mts. USA **350 F4**
Siglufjördhur Iceland **356 B1** 66°12'N 18°55'W
Singapore Asia **361 H5** 1°20'N 103°45'E
Sioux Falls South Dakota USA **351 I4** 43°32'N 96°44'W
Skopje Yugoslavia **357 F6** 42°01'N 21°32'E
Slovakia Europe **357 E5**
Slovenia Europe **356 E5**
Society Is. Pacific Ocean **363 F3**
Socotra i. Yemen **360 C4** 12°30'N 54°00'E
Sofia Bulgaria **357 F6** 42°41'N 23°19'E
Sokoto Nigeria **354 C3** 13°02'N 5°15'E
Solomon Is. Pacific Ocean **363 C3-D3**
Somalia Africa **354-355 G4**
Søndre Strømfjord Greenland **351 M2** 66°30'N 50°52'W
Songea Tanzania **355 F6** 10°42'S 35°39'E
South Africa Africa **355 E7-E8**
Southampton I. Canada **351 J2** 64°30'N 84°00'W
South Carolina st. USA **351 J5**
South China Sea Asia **361 I4**
South Dakota st. USA **351 I4**
Southern Ocean 365
South I. New Zealand **363 D5** 43°00'S 171°00'E
South Pole Antarctica **365**
Spain Europe **356 C6-C7**
Spence Bay North West Territories **351 I2** 69°30'N 93°20'W
Spitsbergen i. Europe **364** 78°00'N 17°00'E
Split Croatia **357 E6** 43°31'N 16°27'E
Spratly Is. South China Sea **361 I5**
Sri Lanka Asia **360 F5**
Srinagar Jammu and Kashmir **361 E2** 34°05'N 74°49'E
Stavanger Norway **356 D3** 58°58'N 5°45'E
Stavropol Russian Federation **358 D4** 45°03'N 41°59'E
Stavropol'-na-Volge Russian Federation **358 E3** 53°32'N 49°24'E
Stewart I. New Zealand **363 D5** 47°00'S 168°00'E
Stockholm Sweden **357 E3** 59°20'N 18°03'E
Sucre Bolivia **353 F6** 19°02'S 65°17'W
Sudan Africa **354 E3**
Sudbury Ontario Canada **351 J4** 46°30'N 81°00'W
Suez Egypt **354 F2** 29°59'N 32°33'E
Suez Canal Egypt **354 F1** 30°40'N 32°20'E
Sulawesi i. Indonesia **361 I6-J6** 2°00'S 120°30'N
Sulu Sea Asia **361 J5**
Sumatra i. Indonesia **361 H5-H6** 2°00'S 102°00'E
Sumba i. Indonesia **361 J6** 9°30'S 119°55'E

Suntar Russian Federation **359 K2** 62°10'N 117°35'E
Superior, Lake Canada/USA **351 J4** 48°00'N 88°00'W
Surabaya Indonesia **361 I6** 7°14'S 112°45'E
Surgut Russian Federation **358 G2** 61°13'N 73°20'E
Surinam South America **352 G4**
Surt Libya **354 D1** 31°13'N 16°35'E
Suva Fiji **363 D3** 18°08'S 178°25'E
Swaziland Africa **355 F7**
Sweden Europe **356-357 E2**
Switzerland Europe **356 D5**
Sydney Australia **362 C4** 33°55'S 151°10'E
Syktyvkar Russian Federation **358 E2** 61°42'N 50°45'E
Syria Asia **360 A2**
Syr Darya r. Kazakhstan **358 F4**

T

Tabrīz Iran **360 B2** 38°05'N 46°18'E
Tagus r. Portugal **356 C7**
Tahat, Mt. Algeria **354 C2** 23°18'N 5°32'E
Tahiti i. Society Is. **363 F3** 17°37'S 149°27'W
Taipei Taiwan **361 J3** 25°05'N 121°30'E
Taiwan Asia **361 J3**
Taiyuan China **361 I2** 37°48'N 112°33'E
Tajikistan Asia **358 G5**
Tallinn Estonia **357 F3** 59°22'N 24°48'E
Tamanrasset Algeria **354 C2** 22°47'N 5°31'E
Tampa Florida USA **351 J6** 27°58'N 82°38'W
Tampere Finland **357 F2** 61°30'N 23°45'E
Tana, Lake Ethiopia **354 F3** 12°00'N 37°20'E
Tanganyika, Lake Tanzania **355 F5** 6°00'S 29°30'E
Tangier Morocco **354 B1** 35°48'N 5°45'W
Tangshan China **361 I1** 39°32'N 118°08'E
Tanzania Africa **355 F5**
Tapajós r. Brazil **352 G5**
Tarawa i. Kiribati **363 D2** 1°25'N 173°00'E
Tashkent Uzbekistan **358 F4** 41°16'N 69°13'E
Tasmania st. Australia **362 C5**
Tasman Sea Pacific Ocean **363 D4**
Taymyr Peninsula Russian Federation **358-359 I1-J1**
Tbilisi Georgia **357 H6** 41°43'N 44°48'E
Tegucigalpa Honduras **352 D3** 14°05'N 87°14'W
Tehran Iran **360 C2** 35°40'N 51°26'E
Tel Aviv Israel **360 A2** 32°05'N 34°46'E
Temuco Chile **353 E8** 38°44'S 72°36'W
Tennessee st. USA **351 J5**
Terre Adélie Antarctica **365**
Texas st. USA **351 I5**
Thailand Asia **361 H4**
Thailand, Gulf of Asia **361 H4-H5**
Thar Desert India/Pakistan **361 E3**
Thessaloniki Greece **357 F6** 40°38'N 22°56'E
Thimphu Bhutan **361 G3** 27°32'N 89°43'E
Thunder Bay Ontario Canada **351 J4** 48°25'N 89°14'W
Thurston I. Antarctica **365**
Tianjin China **361 I2** 39°07'N 117°08'E
Tian Shan mts. Asia **358 G4**
Tibet, Plateau of China **361 F2-G2**
Tierra del Fuego i. Argentina/Chile **353 F10** 54°00'S 69°00'W
Tigris r. Iraq **360 B2**
Tijuana Mexico **352 A1** 32°32'N 117°01'W
Tiksi Russian Federation **359 L1** 71°40'N 128°45'E
Timbuktu Mali **354 B3** 16°49'N 2°59'W
Timor i. Indonesia **361 J6** 9°30'S 125°00'E
Tirana Albania **357 E6** 41°20'N 19°50'E
Tlemcen Algeria **354 B1** 34°52'N 1°19'W
Tocantins r. Brazil **353 H5**
Togo Africa **354 C4**
Tokelau Is. Pacific Ocean **363 E3**
Tokyo Japan **361 K2** 35°42'N 139°46'E
Tôlañaro Madagascar **355 G7** 25°01'S 47°00'E
Toliara Madagascar **355 G7** 23°21'S 43°40'E
Toluca Mexico **352 C3** 19°02'N 99°40'W
Tomatlán Mexico **352 B3** 19°54'N 105°18'W
Tomsk Russian Federation **358 H3** 56°30'N 85°05'E
Tonga Pacific Ocean **363 E3**
Toronto Ontario Canada **351 K4** 43°39'N 79°23'W
Touggourt Algeria **354 C1** 33°06'N 6°04'E
Toulouse France **356 D6** 43°36'N 1°26'E
Townsville Australia **362 C3** 19°13'S 146°48'E
Trans Antarctic Mts. Antarctica **365**
Trinidad and Tobago Central America **352 F3**
Tripoli Libya **354 D1** 32°58'N 13°12'E
Tromsø Norway **357 E1** 69°42'N 19°00'E
Trondheim Norway **356 E2** 63°36'N 10°23'E
Trujillo Peru **353 E5** 8°06'S 79°00'W
Truk I. Caroline Is. **362 C2** 8°00'N 152°00'E
Tsumeb Namibia **355 D6** 19°12'S 17°43'E
Tuamotu i. Pacific Ocean **363 F3** 17°00'S 142°00'W
Tubruq Libya **354 E1** 32°06'N 23°58'E
Tula Russian Federation **358 C3** 54°11'N 37°38'E
Tunis Tunisia **354 D1** 36°48'N 10°11'E
Tunisia Africa **354 C1**
Turin Italy **356 D5** 45°03'N 7°40'E
Turkana, Lake Kenya **355 F4** 4°00'N 36°00'E
Turkey Europe **357 G7**
Turkmenistan Asia **358 E5-F5**
Turks and Caicos Is. Central America **352 E2**
Turku Finland **357 F2** 60°27'N 22°17'E
Turukhansk Russian Federation **358 H2** 65°21'N 88°05'E
Tuvalu Pacific Ocean **363 D3**
Tuxtla Gutiérrez Mexico **352 C3** 16°45'N 93°09'W
Tyrrhenian Sea Europe **356 E7**

U

Ubangi r. Zaire **355 D4**
Ufa Russian Federation **358 E3** 54°45'N 55°58'E
Uganda Africa **355 F4**
Ujung Pandang Indonesia **361 I6** 5°09'S 119°28'E
Ukraine Europe **358 B4**
Ulan Bator Mongolia **361 H1** 47°54'N 106°52'E
Ulan-Ude Russian Federation **359 J3** 51°55'N 107°40'E
Umeå Sweden **357 E2** 63°45'N 20°20'E
Umtata South Africa **355 E8** 31°35'S 28°47'E
United Arab Emirates Asia **360 C3**
United Kingdom Europe **356 C4**
United States of America North America **350-351**
Ural r. Russian Federation **358 E3**
Ural Mts. Russian Federation **358 E3**
Urengoy Russian Federation **358 G2** 65°59'N 78°30'E
Uruguay South America **353 G8**
Uruguay r. Uruguay **353 G7-G8**
Ürümqi China **361 F1** 43°43'N 87°38'E
Utah st. USA **350 G5**
Uzbekistan Asia **358 F4**

V

Vaal r. South Africa **355 E7**
Vaasa Finland **357 F2** 63°06'N 21°36'E
Valencia Spain **356 C7** 39°28'N 0°22'W
Valencia Venezuela **352 F3** 10°14'N 67°59'W
Valletta Malta **356 E7** 35°53'N 14°31'E
Valparaíso Chile **353 E8** 33°02'S 71°38'W
Vancouver British Columbia Canada **350 F4** 49°20'N 123°10'W
Vancouver I. British Columbia Canada **350 F4** 49°45'N 126°00'W
Vänern, Lake Sweden **357 E3** 58°55'N 13°30'E
Van Gölü, Lake Turkey **357 H7** 38°35'N 42°52'E
Vanuatu Pacific Ocean **363 D3**
Varkaus Finland **357 F2** 62°20'N 27°50'E
Västerås Sweden **357 E3** 59°37'N 16°33'E
Vatican City Europe **349 M4**
Vättern, Lake Sweden **357 E3** 58°24'N 14°36'E
Venezuela South America **352 F4**
Venice Italy **356 E6** 45°26'N 12°20'E
Verkhoyansk Range mts. Russian Federation **359 M2**
Vermont st. USA **351 K4**
Victoria st. Australia **362 C4**
Victoria British Columbia Canada **350 F4** 48°30'N 123°25'W
Victoria I. North West Territories Canada **350 H1** 71°00'N 110°00'W
Victoria, Lake Africa **355 F5** 1°00'S 33°00'E
Victoria Land Antarctica **365**
Vienna Austria **357 E5** 48°13'N 16°22'E
Vientiane Laos **361 H4** 17°59'N 102°38'E
Vietnam Asia **361 H4**
Vila Vanuatu **363 D3** 17°44'S 168°19'E
Vilnius Lithuania **357 F4** 54°40'N 25°19'E
Vilyuy r. Asia **359 K2**
Vinson Massif mt. Antarctica **365** 78°00'S 85°00'W
Virginia st. USA **351 K5**
Vishakhapatnam India **360 F4** 17°42'N 83°24'E
Vistula r. Poland **357 E4**
Vitim Russian Federation **359 K3** 59°28'N 112°35'E
Vitsyebsk Belarus **358 B3** 55°10'N 30°14'E
Vladivostok Russian Federation **359 M4** 43°09'N 131°53'E
Volga r. Russian Federation **358 D3**
Volgograd Russian Federation **358 D4** 48°45'N 44°30'E
Volta, Lake Ghana **354 B4** 7°00'N 0°00'E
Vorkuta Russian Federation **358 F2** 67°27'N 64°00'E
Voronezh Russian Federation **358 C3** 51°40'N 39°13'E

W

Wadi Halfa Sudan **355 F2** 21°56'N 31°20'E
Wad Madanī Sudan **354 F3** 14°24'N 33°32'E
Wake I. Pacific Ocean **363 D2** 19°17'N 166°36'E
Wallis and Futuna is. Pacific Ocean **363 E3**
Walvis Bay South Africa **355 D7** 22°57'S 14°30'E
Warsaw Poland **357 F4** 52°15'N 21°00'E
Washington st. USA **350 F4**
Washington District of Columbia USA **351 K5** 38°55'N 77°00'W
Wau Sudan **354 E4** 7°40'N 28°04'E
Weddell Sea Antarctica **365**
Wellington New Zealand **363 D5** 41°17'S 174°47'E
Weser r. Germany **356 E4**
Western Australia st. Australia **362 B4**
Western Sahara Africa **354 A2**
Western Samoa Pacific Ocean **363 E3**
Western Sayan Russian Federation **358 H3**
West Siberian Lowlands Asia **358 G2-G3**
West Virginia st. USA **351 J5**
Whitehorse Yukon Territory Canada **350 E2** 60°43'N 135°03'W
White Nile r. Sudan **354 F3**
White Sea Russian Federation **358 C2**
Whitney, Mt. California USA **350 G5** 36°35'N 118°18'W
Wilhelm, Mt. Papua New Guinea **362 C3** 6°00'S 144°55'E
Wilkes Land Antarctica **365**
Windhoek Namibia **355 D7** 22°34'S 17°06'E
Winnipeg Manitoba Canada **351 I4** 49°53'N 97°09'W
Winnipeg, Lake Manitoba Canada **351 I3** 52°00'N 97°00'W
Wisconsin st. USA **351 I4**
Wrangel I. Russian Federation **359 Q1-R1** 71°00'N 180°00'E
Wroclaw Poland **357 E4** 51°05'N 17°00'E
Wuhan China **361 I2** 30°37'N 114°19'E
Wuzhou China **361 I3** 23°28'N 111°21'E
Wyoming st. USA **350 H4**

X

Xi'an China **361 H2** 34°11'N 108°55'E
Xi Jiang r. China **361 H3**

Y

Yakutsk Russian Federation **359 L2** 62°10'N 129°20'E
Yamal Peninsula Russian Federation **358 F1-G1**
Yamoussoukro Ivory Coast **354 B4** 6°51'N 5°18'W
Yangtze r. China **361 G2-H2-H3**
Yaoundé Cameroon **354 D4** 3°51'N 11°31'E
Yap i. Caroline Is. **362 B2** 9°30'N 138°09'E
Yaroslavl Russian Federation **358 C3** 57°34'N 39°52'E
Yazd Iran **360 C2** 31°54'N 54°22'E
Yekaterinburg Russian Federation **358 F3** 56°52'N 60°35'E
Yellowknife North West Territories Canada **350 G2** 62°27'N 114°21'W
Yellowstone r. Montana USA **350 H4**
Yemen Asia **360 B4**
Yenisey r. Russian Federation **358 H2-I3**
Yerevan Armenia **358 D4** 40°10'N 44°31'E
Yokohama Japan **361 K2** 35°27'N 139°39'E
Yucatán Mexico **352 D2**
Yugoslavia (Serbia & Montenegro) Europe **357 F6**
Yukon r. Yukon Territory Canada **350 C2**
Yukon Territory st. Canada **350 E2**
Yuzhno-Sakhalinsk Russian Federation **359 N4** 46°58'N 142°45'E

Z

Zagros Mts. Iran **360 C2-C3**
Zaire Africa **355 E5**
Zaire (Congo) r. Zaire/Congo **355 D4-E4**
Zagreb Croatia **357 E5** 45°48'N 15°58'E
Zambezi Zambia **355 E6** 13°30'S 23°12'E
Zambezi r. Zambia **355 E6**
Zambia Africa **355 E6**
Zanzibar Tanzania **355 F5** 6°10'S 39°16'E
Zhengzhou China **361 I2** 34°40'N 113°38'E
Zhigansk Russian Federation **359 L2** 66°48'N 123°27'E
Zimbabwe Africa **355 E6-F6**
Zinder Niger **354 C3** 13°46'N 8°58'E

Index

Where a page number is in **bold type**, this means it is a main entry for this word. If you want to look up places in the map section, turn to the map index on pages 374-379.

N

O

P